FICTIONS

FOURTH EDITION

FICTIONS

FOURTH EDITION

JOSEPH F. TRIMMER
BALL STATE UNIVERSITY

C. WADE JENNINGS
BALL STATE UNIVERSITY

HARCOURT BRACE COLLEGE PUBLISHERS

Fort Worth Philadelphia San Diego New York Orlando Austin San Antonio
Toronto Montreal London Sydney Tokyo

PUBLISHER	Christopher C. Klein
EXECUTIVE EDITOR	Michael Rosenberg
ACQUISITIONS EDITOR	John Meyers
DEVELOPMENTAL EDITOR	Helen Triller
PROJECT EDITOR	John Haakenson
PRODUCTION MANAGER	Serena Manning
ART DIRECTOR	Candice Johnson Clifford
PICTURE AND RIGHTS EDITOR	Beverly Wyatt
PERMISSIONS EDITOR	Carol L. Trimmer

Cover image, table of contents, spine and part openers: Childe Hassam, *The Room of Flowers.* Oil on canvas, 34" × 34". Courtesy of The Mannogian Collection.

Copyright © 1998, 1994, 1989, 1985 by Harcourt Brace & Company

All rights reserved. No part of this publication may be reproduced or transmitted in any form or by any means, electronic or mechanical, including photocopy, recording or any information storage and retrieval system, without permission in writing from the publisher.

Requests for permission to make copies of any part of the work should be mailed to: Permissions Department, Harcourt Brace & Company, 6277 Sea Harbor Drive, Orlando, Florida 32887-6777.

Address for Editorial Correspondence: Harcourt Brace College Publishers, 301 Commerce Street, Suite 3700, Fort Worth, TX 76102.

Address for Orders: Harcourt Brace & Company, 6277 Sea Harbor Drive, Orlando, FL 32887-6777. 1-800-782-4479 (in Florida).

(Copyright Acknowledgements begin on page 1223, which constitutes a continuation of this copyright page.)

Harcourt Brace College Publishers may provide complimentary instructional aids and supplements of supplement packages to those adopters qualified under our adoption policy. Please contact your sales representative for more information. If as an adopter or potential user you receive supplements you do not need, please return them to your sales representative or send them to:

Attn: Returns Department
Troy Warehouse
465 South Lincoln Drive
Troy, MO 63379

Printed in the United States of America

ISBN: 0-15-503967-9

Library of Congress Catalog Card Number: 96-79899

8   9   0   1   2   3   4   5   6   066   9   8   7   6   5   4

PREFACE

Fictions is an anthology of short fiction designed for college courses in which the short story and the novella are the principal subjects for discussion and writing. This collection of one hundred stories includes some of the most memorable work of the world's classic and contemporary writers. Many of the selections are masterpieces that have fascinated students of literature for generations. Others, while less well known, possess similar virtues and may thus achieve a comparable position within our literary tradition.

Most of the stories appear in the anthology section, where they are arranged alphabetically by author. A thematic table of contents is included for those who wish to analyze stories according to thematic grouping. The collection includes many stories by new voices. Rudolfo A. Anaya, Fiona Barr, Mary Hood, and Pamela Zoline, for example, appear in the book for the first time with this edition. Other authors, including Alice Adams, Ernest Gaines, and W. D. Wetherell, reappear at the request of instructors who used earlier editions of the book. Ten writers—William Faulkner, Ellen Gilchrist, Nathaniel Hawthorne, James Joyce, D. H. Lawrence, Joyce Carol Oates, Flannery O'Connor, John Updike, Alice Walker, and Eudora Welty—are represented by two stories each to allow students to compare the way an individual writer varies theme and technique. The collection also includes four novellas *(Heart of Darkness, Big Two-Hearted River, The Dead,* and *The Death of Ivan Ilych)* to enable students to experience works of greater length and complexity.

The introduction, "Reading and Writing about Short Stories," begins by defining the five basic elements of fiction—plot, characterization, setting, point of view, and theme. Each element is discussed clearly and simply and is illustrated concretely with examples from stories in the text. The introduction then provides a set of guidelines or practical strategies for reading, analyzing, and interpreting a story. Kate Chopin's minor classic, "The Story of an Hour," is reprinted in its entirety, along with a headnote and study questions, so that students can apply their knowledge of literary terminology and test their ability to use recommended reading strategies on one very short example.

The second part of this chapter introduces students to the process of writing an essay about a short story. This section illustrates how the various steps in the process—keeping a journal, brainstorming, restricting a topic, planning your essay and developing an outline, writing the first draft, and revising the first draft—lead to a successful paper.

Most of the rest of the apparatus, with the several exceptions noted below, is minimal by design. A brief headnote provides essential information about the author of each selection and includes a reference to the story's source and date. Five study questions follow the story, one for each of the five elements of fiction discussed in the introduction. These questions are not meant to be exhaustive; they are intended merely to open up the story for discussion and to suggest possible writing assignments. A glossary of critical terms concludes the text.

Features New to This Edition

- Instruction on how to use sources to write a critical analysis of a story is now included. Advice is provided for all aspects of the research process—finding sources (including electronic sources), evaluating sources, documenting sources, and citing sources.

- A student research paper, "Fact, Fiction, and Film: A Comparison of *The Joy That Kills* and Kate Chopin's 'The Story of an Hour,'" concludes the critical analysis section.

- "Paired Stories," a short anthology section, is organized to enable students to compare how two writers develop one of the major fictional elements in their story. Although each pairing is designed to emphasize one of the five elements, the "Questions for Discussion and Writing" call attention to the way this one element interacts with the other elements to create a carefully crafted story.

- "Stories for Comparison," an entry that follows each story, suggests two other stories in the collection that instructors and students might read in tandem for purposes of class discussion or writing assignments.

- An entirely new instructor's manual by Mary Brown of Indiana Wesleyan University provides information in the following categories for each story: analysis of major critical readings, discussion of common student questions, possible answers to the text's questions, selected writing assignments, and a list of resources.

Acknowledgments

We are pleased to acknowledge the many people who have helped prepare this edition of *Fictions*. For their assistance in helping us read and formulate useful questions about the stories, we thank our students. Special thanks go to Kathy Conrow, who allowed us to reprint her writing in the book's introduction. For their assistance in researching and preparing the manuscript, we thank Terry Rillera and Karen Taylor. At Harcourt Brace, we thank John Meyers, Helen Triller, Candice Clifford, Serena Manning, and John Haakenson. Carol Trimmer acquired the literary permissions for the book. And for their thoughtful responses to our *Fictions* questionnaire, we thank the following individuals: Michael L. Storey and Norice Sullivan, College of Notre Dame of Maryland; Guyanne D. Baker, Jane Hawkins, Mary Kaiser, David Matchen, and Christinia K. Woods, Jefferson State Community College; Cedric Jerome Burden, Lawson State Community College; Dorothy Bankston, Charlotte Chaney, Anthony J. Fonseca, Carol A. Moore, Deborah B. Normand, June Pulliam, Jean M. Rohloff, and Barbara B. Sims, Louisiana State University, Baton Rouge; Monette DePew and Linda Kay Hunt, Pratt Community College and Area Vocational School; Gary Harrington, Salisbury State University; William P. Campbell, Carol S. Chadwick, Stephen D. Chennault, Esperanza M. Cintrón, Ella Davis, Ruth E. Goldman-Sarcus, Edward L. Truskey, and Louvert Weldon, Wayne County Community College.

CONTENTS

....

INTRODUCTION

PAIRED STORIES

A COLLECTION OF STORIES

THEMATIC TABLE OF CONTENTS

INITIATION AND MATURATION

PARENTS AND CHILDREN

MEN AND WOMEN

THE INDIVIDUAL AND SOCIETY

THE ORDEAL OF NATURE

THE EXTRAORDINARY AND THE FANTASTIC

INTRODUCTION

READING AND WRITING ABOUT SHORT STORIES

One of the most enduring pleasures in life is a well-told story. From childhood on, we crave accounts of people, experiences, ways of living that lie beyond our own immediate lives, probably because we are insatiably curious about the possibilities of human existence. Whatever the reason, we spend a significant amount of our time and money in order to live imaginatively in created worlds.

Our bargain with storytellers is a simple one: we give them our time, our attention, and our cooperation in the imagining process; they give us the pleasure of a story that interests and involves us—that intensifies our experience with life as we already know it or gives us a taste of life as we have not experienced it. Our first response is basic: either we like the story—a reaction usually implying that it has stirred our imaginations, thoughts, and feelings—or it bores us, unpleasantly confuses us, or introduces us to worlds and people we don't want to know.

Although it may be strong, this first response is often entirely private. We may not feel any need to explain or justify our reaction to anyone else. If we are asked for an opinion, our reply may be terse: "It was all right." "Not worth the time." "A lot of fun." "Interesting." Often, such a reply is all anybody really wants to know. On other occasions, we may want to say more about a story, either because we want to understand our own reaction more clearly or because something in the story has affected us so strongly that we want the pleasure of discussing it with others. And finally, of course, students in literature classes are often required to talk or write about their experiences with a story.

Whatever the reason, when we move from our strong but unexpressed *private* reaction to some sort of developed response addressed to other people—our *public* reaction—we need to have the language that allows us to say directly and precisely what we mean. We need not only clarify what our response was, but also explain *why* we responded as we did. This introduction will explain the basic terminology used to discuss short fiction and will then illustrate various strategies that can be used to write about it.

DISCUSSING SHORT STORIES: The Basic Elements

One of the most difficult terms to explain is the basic one: what is a *short story?* Arbitrary definitions are convenient but not very accurate. We can say that a short story is a work of prose fiction that is less than 40,000 words in length. Obviously, however, a story of 41,000 words is not magically transformed into some wholly different kind of creation. Nor would we care to term such things as biblical parables or Aesop's fables short stories, even though they are short works of prose fiction.

We need to add to our definition. Traditionally, the short story has been defined as a work of fiction that is unified by a structured *plot* in which a chain of circumstances and events is separated from the rest of human experience and treated as a coherent whole. We expect the *characters* in such a story to be developed enough for us to understand both what they do and why. We usually expect that the people and their actions in the story will lead to some understanding on our part of why these things matter—a sense of meaning or *theme.* We also expect the writer to give us a clear sense of the *setting* of the story—the place, time, and social circumstances within which the narrative unfolds. Finally, we have to know from whose perspective we are seeing the events and the characters—the *point of view* in the story. These five elements—plot, characters, theme, setting, and point of view—almost always work together to achieve the short story's purpose, direction, and movement, so we call them the *basic elements* of the traditional short story.

Any full consideration of short stories will probably touch on all five elements, though individually they vary in importance from story to story. In a well-crafted short story there is no separation of these elements: we expect what happens in the plot to be at least in part a result of what characters choose, we understand that setting may influence profoundly the development of a character, and we see that our understanding of theme in a story is often dependent on the point of view from which we have seen the situation. For the sake of clarity, however, we may often choose to consider each of these elements in turn, both as an end in itself and as a means of deepening our overall understanding of the story. When we divide a story into its elements for the sake of such examination, we have begun the process of *critical analysis.* Since the basic elements are important to our reading, discussing, and writing about the short stories in this collection, we will begin with a brief discussion of each.

Plot

In the events of a traditional short story, unlike the events of life, we expect to find a clear-cut pattern, an order. The *plot* often provides the essential structure in the story by arranging its action in a unified order from the beginning through the middle to the end. The writer must begin by showing us where and when the story takes place, who the characters are, and what the initial situation in the story is. This introductory material is termed *exposition.* In some instances it may be brief, since the writer expects us to understand immediately most things about the setting and circumstances. In "A & P," for example, John Updike does not need to spend much time showing his readers what a supermarket is like, what a cashier does, or how adolescent boys respond to attractive girls. On the other hand, in "Heart of Darkness," Joseph Conrad has to provide a lengthy exposition to prepare his readers for the significance of a mysterious trip up the Congo River.

After the writer has established the original situation in the story, we expect complications to arise. These complications are almost always the result of *conflicts*—among characters, between a character and his or her environment, or among the thoughts, needs, and emotions of a single character. In some cases, all three kinds of conflicts may occur together. In "A & P" the central character has a disagreement with his manager, he runs afoul of the rules of the supermarket, and he cannot decide in his own mind whether he is acting the fool or the hero.

In a traditional story, the conflicts develop to a moment of crisis—often a moment in which a choice must be made, an action performed, or a recognition achieved that will in some way focus and then resolve the conflict. This moment of crisis, the *climax* of the story, usually marks an end of the development of the major action of the story. In whatever remains of the plot, we expect the writer to show us the consequences of the action that occurred in the climax. This final section of the plot is the *denouement,* a French word meaning the untangling of a knot. The denouement may add a surprising twist or turn to the plot, but often it does not add any significant new action or conflict.

Our sense of a plot's integrity, its coherence as a story, may also depend on *structuring devices,* the return at key points in the story to particular images, events, or even particular words or phrases. In Leslie Marmon Silko's "Storyteller," for example, we find the color red serving such a purpose. It is associated with the horror in the protagonist's childhood, but it also represents her home and the saving power of a fixed point in a world in which other boundaries have been lost. Each return to red in the story not only adds a level of meaning but also reinforces our sense of the unity of the plot. The allusions to chrysanthemums serve much the same function in D. H. Lawrence's "Odour of Chrysanthemums." Observant readers often find that their keenest insights into a story arise from a consideration of such devices and the purposes that they serve.

In addition to these essential elements of plot, writers may add suspense or richness to their plots by using such techniques as *foreshadowing* and *flashback.* In the first technique, writers provide hints or clues early in the story of events that will occur later. In the second, they interrupt the forward flow of the story to introduce a scene or episode from the past that explains or comments on the present situation. Writers may also add to our pleasure in the story by building *situational irony* into the plot, letting us believe that events will move in one direction when in fact they will take a surprising and contradictory turn. Overall, however, a traditional plot should satisfy us by being coherent, unified, and meaningful—by making a pattern. But some modern fiction writers are seriously challenging this premise by experimenting with new forms of structure, as in the stories in this collection by writers such as Jorge Luis Borges.

Characterization

Many readers believe that plot is the most crucial element to their enjoyment of a story, but most of us soon recognize that no matter how exciting, eventful, or surprising the plot of a short story may be, we care most about finding convincing portrayals of human nature in action. We have to care about the *characters,* the people in the stories, before we can care about what happens to them. The method by which writers create, reveal, and develop characters is called *characterization.*

In short fiction, writers usually focus on a single character and show us the complexities, contradictions, and difficulties in that person's life and personality. Sometimes this central character, the *protagonist,* undergoes little change in the story: he or she is simply revealed more fully. More often, however, this character is changed in some ways by experience. Characters who remain relatively unchanged are called *static.* Those who go through some development are called *dynamic.*

The central characters in most short stories are *round:* they have fully developed, complex personalities that may defy simple analysis or description. Less significant characters in the story are likely to be *flat:* we see only the surface, so for us they have no real depth or complexity. At times a writer may employ a type of flat character known as a *stereotype.* This stock type—the shrewish wife, the town drunk, the Don Juan—we already know from earlier experiences as readers or viewers.

Writers develop their characters in a number of ways. When concerned primarily with the *external reality* of their characters, writers describe their physical appearance, dramatize their actions or conversations, and summarize their previous histories for us. In portraying the external reality, writers give us what other characters in the story see, hear, and know about the character. However, in most short fiction, writers also penetrate the minds and hearts of some characters, particularly the protagonist, to show their *inner reality*—the thoughts and feelings of which others in the story may be unaware. This portrayal of inner reality is often more complex and more central to the major concern in the story than external reality. In fact, there may be a large difference between the two, a discrepancy between what the character appears to be and what we finally know him or her to be. Our perception of this difference results from *dramatic irony,* in which writers allow us to know more about their characters than the characters themselves know. In John Cheever's "The Swimmer," for example, we suspect early in the story that Neddy Merrill's cross-country swim is a symptom of some unacknowledged personal crisis.

Not all short stories focus exclusively on one protagonist, of course. In some stories the emphasis may instead be on relationships in a group or on particular roles that people play in society. When the fiction writer is primarily interested in *why* characters choose and respond as they do—their *motivation*—we as readers must respond by seeking an explanation for their behavior. On the other hand, if the writer's main intent is to explore relationships among characters as they interact in groups or in socially defined roles, our emphasis as readers must be to understand that outer reality. Of course, many stories approach characters from both these directions.

Finally, some characters in fiction lend themselves to neither kind of analysis. Instead, they may represent abstractions or ideas rather than complex human beings in action. Particularly in *allegories,* stories in which all the elements have symbolic meanings, characters may also be *symbols,* and our chief concern will be with those ideas or qualities they represent. In "The Greatest Man in the World," for instance, James Thurber represents Pal Smurch as the anti-hero, a character who in every way is the opposite of such popular heroes as Charles Lindbergh. Smurch is useful and delightful as a character precisely because he is pure abstraction, not a credible human being.

Setting

In simple terms, *setting* is the time, place, and social reality within which a story takes place. Setting seems to be an insignificant element in some stories; they could take place just as well in any time or place. In other stories—most, in fact—setting is much more important. We have to understand where the characters are—in which period of time, in which society, and at which level in that society—if we are to interpret correctly the other elements in the story.

In stories in which *place* is an important element of setting, the writer usually provides specific, sometimes extended descriptions of that place, focusing especially on those particular details that are most important to our understanding of the story. In Alice Walker's "Everyday Use," we have two visions of the house in which the mother and sister live. The mother describes the hard clay yard as clean and comfortable, and she loves the house even though it has a tin roof and no real windows. But we also see the place from the point of view of the city daughter, who as a child had wanted to tear down the place and later finds it a quaint curiosity worth photographing. As readers, we need to have a clear sense of the place because that perception is central to our interpretation of characters, conflicts, and meaning. On the other hand, place is sometimes of no real consequence in a story: For example, Nathaniel Hawthorne provides almost no description of Young Goodman Brown's house since that part of the setting is irrelevant to his main purpose. We understand, therefore, that in well-crafted short stories, descriptions of place matter and should be noted as carefully as any other part of the story.

In other stories, the *time period* is more significant than place. Again, in the Hawthorne story we have to know that we are in New England in the time of the Puritans if we are to understand the events in the story, the outlook and motivation of the central character, and the story's theme. In some stories, however, we find universal human situations that seem largely independent of any particular cultural moment. In "The Death of Ivan Ilych," Leo Tolstoy depicts an agony and enlightenment that death may bring to any individual in any time or place.

Just as important as place and time, sometimes even more important, is the *social context* in the story, often a product of time and place. We must understand enough about the society—its customs, values, and possibilities—to know what constraints the characters face, what they are free to choose, and what they may not do. American readers unfamiliar with Japanese society will be disturbed and confused by the action in Yukio Mishima's "Patriotism" until they understand the tradition of ritualized suicide at times when dishonor is the only alternative.

Setting is also an important element in establishing the *tone* in a work of fiction, the writer's attitude toward the situations and characters in a story. In describing the law offices in "Bartleby the Scrivener," for instance, Herman Melville sets a tone of tame, even boring, ordinariness. The extraordinary events that unfold in this world have greater intensity for us because they contrast so markedly with the matter-of-fact tone that the opening description has established.

Like other elements in a story, setting may, of course, be used occasionally for symbolic purposes. The dark wood in "Young Goodman Brown" has demonic connotations for Puritans. Therefore, we understand that by walking in the woods at night, Brown is courting evil consequences. Likewise, the jungle in Joseph Conrad's "Heart of Darkness" comes to represent the impenetrable mystery of Africa and the human heart.

Point of View

When we read a successful work of fiction, its *point of view*—the perspective from which readers will view events—often seems inevitable, as though no other is possible. For example, it is almost inconceivable that Ernest Gaines's "The Sky Is Gray" could be told from anyone else's point of view than that of eight-year-old James. We often forget that selecting this perspective is one of the most important decisions writers make. Each potential point of view offers significant advantages and corresponding limitations. In fact, when writers choose their point of view, they often choose their theme and even their protagonist as well.

A writer must first decide whether the story will be told by a narrator who is outside the story or by one of the characters within the world created in the story. An outside point of view provides greater flexibility and suggests a greater sense of objectivity. An inside point of view provides a more intimate, often more engrossing narration. Since the character narrating is within the story, he or she may be incorrectly informed or may have some motive for misrepresenting events; therefore, we cannot always trust his or her account as we generally can that of an outside narrator.

Perhaps because it gives them greater scope, writers often choose the third-person *omniscient* point of view. In such cases the all-knowing narrator is usually assumed to be the writer, so he or she can move at will from time to time and place to place within the story's world, telling us not only of the external events in the story but also of the inner reality of any or all of the characters—their very thoughts and feelings. The advantages of such a point of view are clear: we can know anything that the writer wants us to know; we are not limited by the experience or understanding of any of the characters. The disadvantages may be less obvious: we usually don't have the opportunity to grow gradually in understanding along with the characters through sharing their experience. Therefore, the omniscience we share with the writer provides the pleasure of absolute knowledge but takes away the pleasure of learning and of interpreting experience as we do in life.

If writers wish to maintain some objectivity while permitting readers a gradual understanding, they may give up omniscience and choose the third-person *limited omniscient* point of view, which is restricted to the external experiences and internal thoughts of one character. We remain with that character throughout the entire story, seeing what he or she sees, knowing what he or she knows, though the narrator remains separate from that character. This point of view may at times be frustrating because we cannot know fully what is happening outside a character's experience. For that very reason, however, we—like the character—must interpret others' motives and assimilate information to reach conclusions about what others have done. A detective story is especially well suited to this point of view, of course, since there would be no suspense—no "mystery"—if we were to know more than the detective about the facts of the case.

In some instances, writers choose the *objective* point of view—that is, they limit themselves exclusively to exterior reality, to those things a video camera might record if it was placed in the scene. Like a camera, the story records without comment and interpretation. All that we understand we must gather from observation and inference. The detachment provided by this point of view removes us from direct confrontation with the characters' emotions except as we interpret them.

Mary Wilkins Freeman in "The Revolt of 'Mother'" dramatizes the conflict between husband and wife almost exclusively in their words and actions, giving us the pleasure and responsibility of interpretation. In such stories we do not have the security of the authorial explanation, but we have the delight of seeing for ourselves.

If writers choose to have one of their characters tell us the story, thus employing the *first-person* point of view, they then have other decisions to make. They may have the protagonists tell their own stories or have a secondary character do so. First-person narrators may even be bystanders, or they may recount stories they have heard from others. In all of these cases, however, we as readers have some questions to answer: how reliable is our narrator? Does he or she mean to tell the truth? Is he or she clever enough to know what matters in the story? Does he or she have personal prejudices or emotional biases that make for unreliability? These are all vital questions if we are to understand stories that use the first-person point of view. To answer them, we must learn to know our narrators, perhaps better than they know themselves. In a first-person narrative, we must pay attention to small things as well as to those the narrator emphasizes. We must differentiate between the narrator's interpretation and our own. The process is a complex one, but it is one we are familiar with already since we do the same thing in our daily lives when responding to what others tell us.

The first-person point of view often works especially well in stories where the writer intends to emphasize the difference between a character's view of a situation and the reader's view of the same matters. In Updike's "A & P," for example, the nineteen-year-old cashier who tells us his story has only fleeting glimpses of himself as he really is. He obviously thinks of himself as hard-nosed, realistic, knowledgeable in the ways of the world. But beneath his pose we see a tender-hearted, callow, and highly romantic boy—we see the difference between what he means to be and what he is, a distinction that is emphasized by the point of view.

In some instances, we do not find a fixed point of view in the story, but a shifting one. With little or no explanation, the writer may shift from one perspective to another, leaving it to the reader to see the connections—or perhaps insisting that the illusion of connectedness itself must be dropped. In Pamela Zoline's "The Heat Death of the Universe," some of the paragraphs recount the protagonist's story from a limited third-person point of view, providing an intense portrait of a woman struggling to maintain her grasp on things. However, interspersed irregularly through that narration are other paragraphs in which scientific fact is reported coldly and objectively. In such cases the shift in point of view requires the reader to become part of the creative process and to come to an independent, unified vision of the story as a whole.

No matter what the point of view in the story, we usually find that we come to recognize the narrator's *voice* and style—the way he or she uses words, the things he or she chooses to include or omit from the account. Whether we believe the voice to be that of the writer, as in Stephen Crane's "The Open Boat," or that of a created character, as in Updike's story, our response to that personality, that voice, may do as much as anything else in the story to color our intellectual and emotional response to it. Therefore, a good reader tries to recognize and interpret voice as an important part of the reading experience.

Theme

By *theme,* we mean the central and unifying idea about human experience that grows out of all the other elements in the story. Since a good short story is likely to raise a number of related issues and pose a number of complex questions for perceptive readers, we may find it difficult to decide which is the most important theme, which potential statement of theme best integrates all our perceptions and insights about the story. Because the question of theme is often the most difficult as well as one of the most important ones to consider, we may differ more as readers and writers in our consideration of this element than of any of the others. However, these differences may be instructive if they send us back to the story itself to reexamine our thinking about its central idea.

Some particular techniques may help us discover and state theme. For example, we should look closely at the generalizations about human experience that the author makes in the story, either directly or through one of the characters. Occasionally, we will find that the writer has already provided a statement of theme that we find entirely satisfactory. In "The Open Boat," for instance, Stephen Crane writes of an experience in which men battle nature—the sea—for their lives. The correspondent, the character we come to know the best, is irresolute during much of the story. He is unsure whether nature is either basically friendly, in which case the men must be saved, or basically cruel, in which case they will be destroyed. He finally comes to the following recognition, one that might serve as a statement of theme in the story: "She [nature] did not seem cruel to him then, nor beneficent, nor treacherous, nor wise. But she was indifferent, flatly indifferent."

If we find no such authorial statement of theme, we may have to ask ourselves what the central characters have learned from their experiences since the story's beginning, or what *we* have learned that the characters did not perceive as a result of this experience. In "Young Goodman Brown," the protagonist concludes that all human beings are hopelessly corrupt, totally damned, and must therefore be rejected. As readers, however, we may arrive at a different conclusion, one that might serve as a statement of theme: since no human being is without sin, we must learn to accept and love one another because of our shared weakness and mutual need.

We may also gain an insight into theme by the ways in which writers use literary devices that compress a good deal of meaning into a small space. For example, a *symbol* is a thing, a person, or an action that has both a literal significance and an additional abstract meaning. An elaborate and comprehensive symbol is sometimes the thematic core of a piece of short fiction, particularly in the recent kind of fiction termed *postmodern.* This type of symbol is often based on esoteric information such as complex scientific principles with which most readers are unacquainted, so the writer may have to educate readers by explaining the symbol before its implications will be evident. Both Thomas Pynchon's "Entropy" and Pamela Zoline's "The Heat Death of the Universe" use individual situations to illustrate the notion in physics called *entropy,* and, in turn, their discussion of entropy provides a way of understanding the human crisis in the stories. The use of such symbols suggests a fundamental shift in the traditional reader–writer relationship where symbols—such as crosses, devils, and trials of initiation—were based on a sense of mutually shared knowledge and understanding.

An *allusion,* or reference, is another device that often suggests a thematic connection between something in the story and something similar in literature, history, or myth. In "Babylon Revisited," F. Scott Fitzgerald compares the Paris that Charlie knew in the twenties to the biblical Babylon, a place of ungodliness, temptation, and threatened spiritual destruction. By means of the allusion in his title, Fitzgerald suggests that the story deals with a spiritual crisis. Recognizing this idea will sharpen our consideration of theme in that story.

Another equally fundamental change occurs in that kind of storytelling that we now term *reflexive fiction.* In such stories, writers drop the pretense that they are reporting reality and instead insist upon readers recognizing that they are engaged in a creative process in which arbitrary choices are constantly being made. The writers of reflexive fiction may share with their readers some of their thinking about the directions they are choosing in the process of creation, or they may even address readers directly, asking them to cooperate in the creation of the illusion that is fiction. *Verisimilitude,* the traditional notion that fiction ought to resemble credible reality as much as possible, is revealed as a trick, an absurdity that neither writer nor reader can take seriously.

Borges's "The Garden of Forking Paths" provides a good example of reflexive fiction. The narrator in the story discovers that the novel written by an illustrious ancestor and the maze created by that same man are in fact the same creation—the work of fiction *is* the intricate maze. The rest of the short story illustrates this point in various ways. The narrator takes us into a world of apparent contradictions, unexplained conflicts and motivations, and uncertain resolutions. We have no clear sense of traditional character, plot, or theme. As the image in the title suggests, we eventually understand that Borges is choosing among a vast number of paths that his story might follow, and he allows us to contemplate that creative process while the story is forming. Therefore, the process of choosing becomes more important than any of the particular paths chosen. The thematic connection between the process of fiction making and the process of living is, of course, obvious and important in such stories.

Our view of theme finally must be broad enough to include the whole story and all its implications. We may in fact discover that a discussion of theme will necessarily involve a consideration of all the other basic elements of the short story.

As convenient and useful as it may be for us to separate these basic elements so that we can consider them individually, it is important to recognize that they interact with one another in rich and diverse ways to produce works that are greater than the sum of their parts. After the process of separation and discovery, the critical analysis best ends with an attempt to reintegrate the story in our own minds, to find all the reinforcing connections that exist among the elements of the story, and—very important—to understand and respond to the whole experience with appropriate emotions.

GUIDELINES FOR READING SHORT STORIES

Although you have already discovered ways of reading that no doubt work for you, the following section will provide some practical advice that may help you as you read the stories in this book.

Preview the Story

It is possible to learn several important things about a story before you read even the first sentence.

1. Begin with a close consideration of the title. Since it provides our first impression of the world we are about to enter, the title gives important clues about what to expect. For instance, García Márquez's title "A Very Old Man with Enormous Wings" should prepare us for a story that will challenge our usual sense of reality, whereas Updike's "A & P" suggests a familiar world about which we may learn more. Cather's title "Paul's Case" tells us which character most matters in her story, whereas John Cheever's impersonal title "The Swimmer" may suggest more focus on the role the character plays in his world than on his individual nature. You should, of course, reconsider the significance of the title after you read the story to see how accurate your first impression may have been.

2. Ask what you know about the author of the story. If you recognize the name because you have read other things by that same writer, you may already have some expectations about the story. Or if you know the writer by reputation, your initial insight may again prove valuable. For example, readers who know that William Faulkner wrote almost exclusively about the South may enter into his world more quickly than those who have yet to discover that fact.

3. Read the headnote carefully. The biography of the writer in the headnote may amplify what you already know or tell you significant facts about that person. In addition to helping you understand the writer, each headnote concludes with a statement that will help you focus on the central situation or theme in the story that follows.

Read the Story Actively

There is a difference between passively absorbing words on a page and seriously engaging the situation and ideas that those words convey. If you find that you are not always an active reader, the following techniques will help you.

1. Always read with a pen or pencil in your hand. Underline the things in a story that seem to you important: clues to a character's motivation, for instance, or a generalization that may serve as a statement of theme; a description of setting that helps to establish a particular tone, or a choice of words that gives us a sense of the narrator's voice. You will find that even after brief practice you will become adept at spotting many such significant details in a story and that your reading will improve because you have paid attention. When you underline, it is a good practice also to make a marginal notation that will help you understand later why

you thought the marked material significant. Many experienced readers work out a private code that allows them to make brief but meaningful marginal notations, but at first you may have to jot down phrases that connect the underlined passages to such things as the basic elements in the story: *character* as a marginal note in "The Sky Is Gray," for instance, helps you remember why the passage mattered, but *James's character* may be a more useful notation. You may also note questions, ambiguities, your own reactions. Anything that you mark or write that reflects your active reading of the story is likely to be useful later. At the very least, the process of annotating keeps you alert.

2. Keep asking questions as you read. Sometimes you may want to write them in the margins. Other times you may simply pause in the reading to ask them of yourself. You should wonder as you read, for example, how a sequence of events is likely to turn out, whether a character has made a wise decision, whether the narrator is to be trusted in this instance. All such questions indicate that you are reading actively, that you are cooperating imaginatively in the creative process with the writer. Your reading will inevitably be more pleasurable and more illuminating as a consequence.

Respond Promptly to the Story

1. Write out, preferably in complete sentences, a few initial responses as soon as you finish the story. The responses may take the form of questions or statements or both, but they should reflect your strongest immediate impressions, including your basic attitude toward the story. Did you like it or not? Even more important, why did you like it or not? You will be writing about yourself as well as the story, but also try to consider all five of the basic elements as part of these initial written responses.

    You may find it useful to keep an informal journal in which you record such first impressions as well as later, more considered responses. Such a journal provides much useful raw material when you move from your private response to the public response of discussing or writing about the story.

2. Consult the questions at the end of the story to see how other active readers have responded. Your editors are, like you, readers who have tried to understand what has happened in a story and why it matters. Their questions, like yours, represent an attempt to open their response to your consideration and to stimulate further private response on your part. You may find that you have already answered some of the questions in your own reading and preliminary response. However, other questions may send you back to the story to look more closely at parts you may not have examined fully in your first reading. You may find it helpful on occasion to write out responses to certain questions in order to clarify your own understanding.

    Now test the advice we have given you by reading the following story, including the headnote. Then answer the questions that follow the story.

I

KATE CHOPIN

The Story of an Hour

KATE CHOPIN (1851–1904) was born in St. Louis, the daughter of an
Irish immigrant father who was killed in a train wreck when she was four.
She was raised by her mother's French-speaking Creole family and educated at the local Academy of the Sacred Heart. At the age of eighteen, she
traveled to New Orleans, where she met and two years later married Oscar
Chopin, a cotton trader. After her husband's death by swamp fever in 1882,
Chopin and her six children returned to St. Louis, where she began to write
about her experiences in the South. These local-color stories appeared in
magazines such as *Century* and *Harper's,* and some of them were collected
in *Bayou Folk* (1894) and *A Night in Acadie* (1897). Chopin's work was
well received until the publication of *The Awakening* (1899). This novel, a
classic study of a woman's struggle for personal freedom, was condemned
by contemporary reviewers for its realistic treatment of adultery. Shocked
by this critical reaction, Chopin published little in the remaining years of
her life. "The Story of an Hour," first published in *Vogue* magazine in 1894,
is a brief portrait of a woman's reaction to the inevitability of death and the
possibility of freedom.

K nowing that Mrs. Mallard was afflicted with a heart trouble, great care was
taken to break to her as gently as possible the news of her husband's death.

It was her sister Josephine who told her, in broken sentences; veiled hints
that revealed in half concealing. Her husband's friend Richards was there, too,
near her. It was he who had been in the newspaper office when intelligence of
the railroad disaster was received, with Brently Mallard's name leading the list
of "killed." He had only taken the time to assure himself of its truth by a second telegram, and had hastened to forestall any less careful, less tender friend
in bearing the sad message.

She did not hear the story as many women have heard the same, with a paralyzed inability to accept its significance. She wept at once, with sudden, wild abandonment, in her sister's arms. When the storm of grief had spent itself she went away
to her room alone. She would have no one follow her.

There stood, facing the open window, a comfortable, roomy armchair. Into this she sank, pressed down by a physical exhaustion that haunted her body and seemed to reach into her soul.

She could see in the open square before her house the tops of trees that were all aquiver with the new spring life. The delicious breath of rain was in the air. In the street below a peddler was crying his wares. The notes of a distant song which some one was singing reached her faintly, and countless sparrows were twittering in the eaves.

There were patches of blue sky showing here and there through the clouds that had met and piled one above the other in the west facing her window.

She sat with her head thrown back upon the cushion of the chair, quite motion-less, except when a sob came up into her throat and shook her, as a child who has cried itself to sleep continues to sob in its dreams.

She was young, with a fair, calm face, whose lines bespoke repression and even a certain strength. But now there was a dull stare in her eyes, whose gaze was fixed away off yonder on one of those patches of blue sky. It was not a glance of reflec-tion, but rather indicated a suspension of intelligent thought.

There was something coming to her and she was waiting for it, fearfully. What was it? She did not know; it was too subtle and elusive to name. But she felt it, creep-ing out of the sky, reaching toward her through the sounds, the scents, the color that filled the air.

Now her bosom rose and fell tumultuously. She was beginning to recognize this thing that was approaching to possess her, and she was striving to beat it back with her will—as powerless as her two white slender hands would have been.

When she abandoned herself a little whispered word escaped her slightly parted lips. She said it over and over under her breath: "free, free, free!" The vacant stare and the look of terror that had followed it went from her eyes. They stayed keen and bright. Her pulses beat fast, and the coursing blood warmed and relaxed every inch of her body.

She did not stop to ask if it were or were not a monstrous joy that held her. A clear and exalted perception enabled her to dismiss the suggestion as trivial.

She knew that she would weep again when she saw the kind, tender hands folded in death; the face that had never looked save with love upon her, fixed and gray and dead. But she saw beyond that bitter moment a long procession of years to come that would belong to her absolutely. And she opened and spread her arms out to them in welcome.

There would be no one to live for her during those coming years; she would live for herself. There would be no powerful will bending hers in that blind persistence with which men and women believe they have a right to impose a private will upon a fellow-creature. A kind intention or a cruel intention made the act seem no less a crime as she looked upon it in that brief moment of illumination.

And yet she had loved him—sometimes. Often she had not. What did it matter! What could love, the unsolved mystery, count for in face of this possession of self-assertion which she suddenly recognized as the strongest impulse of her being!

"Free! Body and soul free!" she kept whispering.

Josephine was kneeling before the closed door with her lips to the keyhole, im-ploring for admission. "Louise, open the door! I beg; open the door—you will make yourself ill. What are you doing, Louise? For heaven's sake open the door."

"Go away. I am not making myself ill." No; she was drinking in a very elixir of life through that open window.

Her fancy was running riot along those days ahead of her. Spring days, and summer days, and all sorts of days that would be her own. She breathed a quick prayer that life might be long. It was only yesterday she had thought with a shudder that life might be long.

20   She arose at length and opened the door to her sister's importunities. There was a feverish triumph in her eyes, and she carried herself unwittingly like a goddess of Victory. She clasped her sister's waist, and together they descended the stairs. Richards stood waiting for them at the bottom.

Some one was opening the front door with a latchkey. It was Brently Mallard who entered, a little travel-stained, composedly carrying his gripsack and umbrella. He had been far from the scene of accident, and did not even know there had been one. He stood amazed at Josephine's piercing cry; at Richards' quick motion to screen him from the view of his wife.

But Richards was too late.

When the doctors came they said she had died of heart disease—of joy that kills.

QUESTIONS FOR DISCUSSION AND WRITING

1. The major divisions of the story are marked by movements from downstairs to upstairs to downstairs again. What is the difference between the kind of action that takes place in the two locations?

2. What important things do we learn about Mrs. Mallard from the very brief description of her face? How does this description help us understand what she has been and what she might be?

3. Why does Chopin contrast Mrs. Mallard's profound grief with the details of the scene she sees through the bedroom window?

4. What attitudes distinguish the points of view of Mrs. Mallard and those who are concerned with her welfare?

5. What do we discover about the connection between freedom and death during the "hour" of the story?

STORIES FOR COMPARISON

Charlotte Perkins Gilman's "The Yellow Wallpaper (pages 117–128); Gail Godwin's "Dream Children" (pages 583–593).

TWO SAMPLE STUDENT RESPONSES

What was your initial response to "The Story of an Hour"? How did you respond to it intellectually and emotionally? What ambiguous feelings did it arouse in you? Was there anything you are not sure you understood? Can you analyze this story by submitting it to the critical process we outlined earlier and looking at its basic elements individually? Compare your own basic response to the story with the two journal entries that follow, in which two student readers responded privately to the story in entirely different ways. Since they knew these entries were to be read by a teacher, their responses are perhaps a little more formal than yours may be. However, both entries accomplish their major purpose: they show active readers responding intellectually and emotionally to the story.

STUDENT A

My first reaction to the story is one of amazement. I cannot imagine anyone being so elated about his or her spouse dying. Even if she really had not loved him there was a bond that had kept her there. This woman must have been a very selfish person. If she had wanted her husband out of her life so she could be free, she should have left him or divorced the poor man, instead of being joyous at the news of his death.

When she is in her room alone, it seems as if for the first time in her life she can hear things she had never heard before and see things she had never paid much attention to before. I can relate to this in some sense. My father died from cancer when I was eleven. The night he died I couldn't bear to stay in the house so I went outside and sat by myself. Now, when I look back I never remember a night that was so dark or so quiet, yet I could hear the birds chirping in the trees so distinctly. I never liked birds before, but my father adored them. That night I felt as if a part of my father were coming out in me.

As you can tell, I have experienced the loss of someone very close and I cannot understand why anyone would be delighted over someone's death. If the person has been suffering with a terminal illness, I can understand that the family and friends would be relieved because he is not suffering any more, but to be overjoyed by the death, I think not.

I didn't particularly like the woman in the story so I think it was ironic that she died from the shock that her husband was not dead. If her life with him had been miserable, his life with her probably was too, so maybe he was grateful that she died.

If I were to write a formal essay on the story I would write on her feelings when she was alone.

STUDENT B

Kate Chopin's "The Story of an Hour" is realistic in both situation and character. The situation, a woman's husband thought to be dead from a tragic accident, can and continues to happen even today. Her emotions are experienced by everyone. Though not willing to admit it, women who break up relationships often rationalize their feelings like the woman in the story. The thoughts "I can live without him" and "I'm free" are the two common feelings shared by both the audience and the writer. These two elements combined add to the meaning of the story.

I think the writer's purpose here was to put down on paper what no one would admit to feeling. I think she is also asking us, "How many times do you really feel the way others want you to feel?"

My overall response to this story is enjoyment. I liked the truthfulness, the non-typical response from the widow, and especially the ending. I thrive on surprise endings.

The first of these responses is somewhat ambiguous. The writer is "amazed" by what he perceives to be the central character's callous indifference to the death of her husband. On the other hand, he knows from his own experience that the death of a loved one may indeed sharpen one's awareness of the world. His observation that Mrs. Mallard should have left or divorced her husband if she was not happy in the marriage reveals a misunderstanding of the social values of the nineteenth-century setting, a misunderstanding that somewhat distorts his understanding of the character and the theme of the story.

The second response is more emphatic: this reader believes that Chopin has touched a truth in this story which is commonly felt but rarely expressed—that many people feel trapped in relationships that look happy to others. This writer also reveals an interesting fact about her own taste in plots when she tells us she "thrives" on surprise endings.

Obviously, these two readers would have a great deal to discuss with each other about this story. No doubt they would be stimulated to reconsider their own views and perhaps return to the story to find the evidence that led them to these responses.

Equally important, both of these writers have done a good deal to move from private to public responses. Both have offered not only initial responses but also some explanation of those responses. If they were asked to write an essay-length public response to the story as the next step in the process of discovery, both would find that they had already made a number of observations worth further exploration. For example, both are obviously interested in the contradictions in the characterization of the protagonist. Both see that she is responding in a surprising way to the death of a spouse, and both understand something of the difference between the reality of that response and others' views of it. While the first reader concludes that Mrs. Mallard is "very selfish," he also acknowledges the credibility of her heightened awareness at a time of crisis. The second reader sees Mrs. Mallard as a much more sympathetic and understandable character, one whose reaction is in fact usual rather than amazing, though no one speaks of such feelings.

Which of these two views of character is more valid? We would have to return to the story to test them—the first step in any theorizing we do about short fiction. Perhaps this time, Student A would notice the time period indicated in the headnote and realize that Mrs. Mallard was trapped by social realities in a marriage that she couldn't simply leave at will. Given such facts, this reader would have to reconsider his amazement at the character's thoughts and feelings, though he might still conclude that Chopin has given us a limited, selfish woman in Mrs. Mallard.

Student B would have to find further evidence to support her contention that the protagonist's reaction was as normal as she suggests. She would have to show what details Chopin provides that allow a careful reader to form such a conclusion.

In short, both these readers have begun an exploration of characterization in the story, one that they might choose to pursue in further writing assignments. Both also touch on theme, raising other issues worth consideration. For example, Student A writes of the intensification of life in the face of death, certainly one of the story's surprising points. Student B sees clearly the point that all of us lead buried lives, experiencing feelings that we are not permitted to express. This recognition of emotional alienation is another theme that she might choose to pursue at length in a subsequent essay.

If you are asked to write an essay about the Chopin story or one of the other stories in this book, your private response can be an extremely useful beginning point, whether you choose the topic of the essay or whether it is assigned by your teacher. The following section presents some practical suggestions for approaching and developing both types of topics. Again, we'll use the Chopin story as an example.

WRITING AN ESSAY ON A TOPIC OF YOUR OWN CHOICE

If you have followed the guidelines in the previous section, you have already performed the crucial first step in selecting and developing a topic. You know well the story you are going to write about, you have thought about its implications from several perspectives, and you have considered the ways in which it achieves its purpose. Now you can begin exploring several potential topics.

Brainstorm About the Story

It is often a mistake to choose a topic too quickly, since your first choice may not be the best. One way to see how many options you have is to *brainstorm* about the story; that is, in a limited amount of time—fifteen to twenty minutes—list as many points as occur to you about the story you have just read. You may discover that you have many more perceptions and possibilities than you supposed, and in addition to finding a variety of potential topics in this way, you will also generate a number of sub-points that may well be useful to you in developing the topic you finally select.

Once you have exhausted your first reactions, go back and look at the list your brainstorming has produced. Ask yourself how you might group your responses into logical units. For example, you may wish to use the five basic elements to cluster and arrange your perceptions. You may discover that some points overlap: some you can group under characterization and setting; others involve both plot and theme. Experiment with arranging the points in several ways. Consider the following brainstorming list that one reader generated after her initial reading of the Chopin headnote, story, and questions.

Louise Mallard

Cries like a child

Gazes out at nature

Young, fair, calm face

Setting

    1800's–no divorce laws, I think. Check this.

    The house–two stories. Seems like a comfortable place. Why?

    Nature–spring outside, storm breaking up

Theme

    The big question: why does she feel "monstrous joy"?

    What about love for husband?

    She knows grief and will again, but feels freedom.

    Others don't know the truth about why she dies.

Plot

    Question points out movement from downstairs to upstairs,

    back again: why is that significant?

    Stages in the plot?

    Foreshadowing about "heart trouble" in opening.

    Stages of her response: shock, grief, joy, grief again, death?

    (Is this characterization, or plot?)

    Climax? When she accepts what she feels or when she finds

    out husband is not dead?

Point of View

    Third-person, limited omniscient. Why?

    Difference in her point of view about events and those of others

    in the story (character point?)

    Why not first-person? Objectivity, advantages of seeing her in

    part from outside.

As you see, this reader has grouped even these first responses into categories suggested by the basic elements. However, she recognizes that these categories are not hard and fast, that some of her observations seem to connect in one way or another to several elements. She wisely notes those overlappings in her first list, and may discover other points as she reconsiders and rearranges her list. Since the brain-storming session is only a preliminary step, however, it is a good idea to cut it short after a limited amount of time and go on to the selection stage.

Restrict Your Topic

The first and most important step in moving from loosely grouped ideas to an organized essay is to express a significant point about the story drawn from those observations—a *thesis sentence* that will give direction, shape, and purpose to the entire essay.

The thesis is a one-sentence statement of the central idea in your essay. A clear, unified, and specific thesis sentence focuses the topic so that both you and your readers know just exactly how you intend to interpret the story. It guides you in your selection of material to include and in your choices of what to exclude from consideration. It may even suggest the rhetorical method by which your topic will be developed.

A good thesis sentence has a clearly stated subject and a strong verb. It is expressed in concrete, specific words, and it commits the writer to a particular task in the paper. A weak thesis sentence is vague in diction and meaning and leaves so many options open that the writer must *still* make hard decisions about what to include or omit. Consider the two pairs of thesis statements below. Which ones would be really useful to a writer planning an essay? Which ones would provide little focus?

1a. Mrs. Mallard is a woman facing a unique situation.

1b. We see Mrs. Mallard from contrasting perspectives—the exterior view that others have of her and the interior view that we gain through Chopin's revelation of her thoughts.

2a. The description of the spring day outside is pleasant and happy.

2b. The description of the spring day outside Mrs. Mallard's window suggests the theme of the story, that even in the face of death life renews itself in a strong, joyous manner.

Sentence **1a** obviously provides no significant focus. Words like *unique, interesting,* and *nice* are empty, conveying little meaning. They should be avoided in thesis statements.

Sentence **1b** offers a much more specific and focused point: we can see the writer's intention to contrast the view that other characters have of Mrs. Mallard and our final understanding of her. In this case, we understand not only the point of the essay to follow, but also the method by which it will be developed.

Sentence **2a** states a bland, pointless fact. It leads nowhere.

Sentence **2b,** however, suggests a connection between that observation and the theme of the story. The writer means to show us not only *what* Chopin has described, an obvious point, but also *why* she has described it, a matter that requires interpretation.

Since the thesis statement is so crucial to the success of the paper, you will need to spend time and thought working it out, but don't stop with the first one you compose. Consider other possibilities that you discovered during brainstorming. Try to transform each promising item on the list into a solid thesis statement. If, after you have made the effort, you find that you really cannot express a thesis idea that seems worth developing, discard the topic, but don't give up too quickly or easily. Sometimes the thesis statements that have cost you the most effort to compose turn out to be the best.

Plan Your Essay

As soon as you have several promising thesis statements, you should test them by projecting plans for the essays that arrange and develop these ideas. At this stage you should again go back to the story, your notes, your initial private response, your answers to the editors' questions, and your brainstorming. The essential question you must answer for your readers is how you arrived at the conclusion you have stated in the thesis sentence. What evidence in the story made that conclusion logical, even inevitable? After all, you mean to convince your readers of the validity of your analysis by sharing with them the evidence that led to your interpretation.

Begin by breaking the thesis idea into its logical parts. Like other essays you write, this essay will have an introductory paragraph that will state or imply the thesis point, followed by a number of paragraphs in which you will present evidence to clarify, develop, and illustrate that point. Each of those paragraphs will have a topic idea that will be a logical subdivision of the thesis idea. Like the thesis sentence itself, the topic sentence of a paragraph should be clear, specific, and unified: you should know exactly what you mean to accomplish in the paragraph. As part of your plan, then, work out topic sentences for each of your paragraphs. Since you must be certain that you will have a focused, clear point for each paragraph in the final paper, it's a good idea to write out these topic ideas as complete sentences. You will find that you are less likely to fool yourself about what you mean to do in the paragraph if you have stated its purpose explicitly and fully at the beginning. Also check carefully to see that the topic sentence is indeed a logical subdivision of the thesis idea.

Consider the thesis statement below. Is it clear and focused? Do the sample topic sentences seem to be logical subdivisions of the thesis point? Do they express specific ideas that are suitable for development in single paragraphs? Or will they require several paragraphs to develop in sufficient detail?

Thesis: Although Mrs. Mallard's friends and relatives see her as the victim of life and of her own emotions, the reader knows that she has experienced an internal victory.

Topic Sentence 1. Those around Mrs. Mallard see her as a victim of circumstances.

Topic Sentence 2. The reader sees her as strong enough to face the truth about herself and to triumph over circumstances.

Develop Your Paragraphs

Once you have a thesis and topic sentences that meet the criteria we have discussed, you are ready to move to the next stage in the writing process—gathering the specific details and illustrations that best develop the topic ideas. This step also involves selection and arrangement. You will want the most relevant details and the strongest illustrations, of course, and you will want to arrange them in a coherent, logical manner. If you were searching for evidence to develop the first topic sentence above, you would find the following details to develop your point about the exterior view of Mrs. Mallard: she has a heart condition; the family friend is so worried about her that he means to deliver the news himself so that it can be broken gently to her; her sister is very concerned about her while she is alone in her room; her sister supports her physically when she comes back downstairs; the doctor assumes that her own emotion of joy has killed her when she sees her husband. Since these details are drawn from the story in the order in which they occurred, chronological order might well be the method in which you choose to develop the paragraph. On the other hand, you might also consider alternative methods. For instance, you might choose climactic order, in which you first discuss the most objective view—that of the doctor and the medical profession; then the closer, warmer point of view of the family friend; and finally the most intimate and sympathetic of the exterior points of view, that of her sister. Whichever method of organization you choose, you will have ample evidence to develop your topic idea in the paragraph. Your plan for that paragraph might now look like this:

1. Those around Mrs. Mallard see her as a victim of circumstances and her own weakness.

   a. The doctor sees her as a frail patient with a weak heart.

   b. Her friend sees her as an emotionally and physically fragile woman who must be protected from shock.

   c. Her sister sees her as a pitiful creature who must be watched over and supported at all times.

The plan here guarantees that you have both a point worth developing and a means of developing it in an organized, coherent paragraph. Having made those decisions, you will be able to concentrate on such other things as precise diction and clear syntax when you actually write the paragraph.

You will discover with only a little practice that you can go through all the stages from brainstorming to complete plan in a reasonably brief time. You can even make two or three plans for the development of thesis ideas you like so that you can finally select the one that seems most interesting, insightful, and useful.

When you write the first draft of your paper, however, you may find other points more worthy of making than the ones included in your plan. View the early draft as an experiment, a way of discovering more about the story, rather than as a finished product slavishly based on a plan. Be prepared to rethink, replan, and rewrite.

Notice how the following student writer critically responds to her own first draft and then rewrites it, avoiding weaknesses and developing strengths.

SAMPLE ROUGH DRAFT

Two Views of Mrs. Mallard

"The Story of an Hour" was written by Kate Chopin. Mrs. Mallard, its central character, was really two different people. She was the woman other people saw. This is her external character. She was also what the reader saw. This is her internal character. The two were very different. The others think of her as kind of weak, not able to take care of herself. Upstairs by herself, she is much stronger. She develops that after she finds out about the death of her husband in a train accident. She finds that inside she is happy and strong. The other characters do not know this, however, because she dies before she can tell them. That is the irony in the story. The irony is not humorous--it's more tragic. No one ever really gets to know her. But the important thing is that Chopin gives us the two different pictures of Mrs. Mallard.

The others think of her as weak. The doctor thinks she is so frail that she might die of shock. The author tells us at the very beginning of the story that she has a heart condition. This is foreshadowing. That's why the friend comes to the house to tell her about the accident. Her husband has been killed and he wants to keep the news from her--or to have somebody tell her gently, I guess. I believe that this shows how weak he thinks she is. Her sister does too. She even listens at her keyhole. This is after she goes upstairs. The sister isn't snooping. She's genuinely concerned about her sister. She thinks she is too weak to bear it.

At the end the doctor says she died of joy. This shows the exterior view one more time.

Up in her room, Mrs. Mallard goes through a big change. She first feels grief. That's understandable. Any wife who has lost a husband is likely to feel really bad about it at first. Mrs. Mallard does. She also feels something creeping up on her and that makes her uncomfortable. I think what she is seeing at first is that she will also be free because her husband is dead. She thinks she will be "free, free, free." This thought surprises her, but I think it's believable. After all, she is living in a time when wives weren't very free, so it's natural for her to like it. When she goes back downstairs like a "goddess of Victory," she has obviously changed a lot. This is what I see about her interior character.

I think Chopin did a good job of contrasting the two Mrs. Mallards. I like the ending because I think it shows how different a person may be from what that person seems to be. Not even close friends or relatives may see what's really there. In a way, other people keep them from being themselves. It's joy that kills Mrs. Mallard all right. But it's not the kind the doctor thinks. It's joy that comes from finding strength and freedom.

Although the writer may recognize that her essay does not express her thoughts clearly and well, she may not know how to improve it. At this point the response of other readers may help her. Following her teacher's directions, she exchanged essays with another student in her class so that they could clarify problems and suggest solutions by giving one another objective comments.

The student critic made three major observations about the essay: it sounded rough, didn't read smoothly and naturally; it rambled and didn't seem to come to a clear point; and the writer was probably wrong about Mrs. Mallard's having felt relief at her husband's death.

The writer agreed with the first two observations and knew that these were problems that had to be resolved in the next draft. However, she disagreed with her critic's point about the character; she understood the other point of view but felt that the story justified her interpretation. The writer has therefore benefited from criticism, but she has not blindly accepted every suggestion for revision. She understands that finally it is her view of the story that must be expressed.

The writer next talked with her teacher about the ways in which she might effectively revise. Her teacher pointed out that the most significant problem is focus: the essay does not clearly establish the unifying purpose of the details that the writer has used. The reader may wind up thinking "So what?" The teacher simply asked at this point, "What is the most important thing you have discovered about why Chopin thought this story worth telling?" Such simple but basic questions at this stage in the writing process often take the writer back to a consideration of the central thesis.

The teacher also made some suggestions about improving style and coherence, especially by using more dependent clauses for the less significant points and more transitions as she moves from point to point. After a little practice with material drawn from the rough draft, the writer felt confident that she could make such revisions easily.

However valuable the writer finds the criticism of others, she must not lose sight of the fact that the essay is ultimately hers—her ideas, style, and purpose. Therefore, the next step is for her to go through the essay, incorporating suggestions but asking her own questions and devising her own strategy for revision. In the following notes, the student comments on problems in the first draft that she can resolve in the next version.

SAMPLE REVISION STRATEGY

Title: Meaning is not clear here. It should say more about the thesis point.

Introduction: There are too many short sentences, and I get off the subject. The big problem is that I don't really have a clear thesis point here.

Second paragraph: This is a mess. Too many short sentences again, and it doesn't really go anywhere. I need to give more specific information to illustrate what others think about her. I need a clear topic sentence that relates back to the thesis idea.

Third paragraph: This one is a little better than the second one because there's a little more detail in it, but I need more. I should prove that she is strong and that she has found joy in her freedom. Combine some of the short sentences so it will read better and be easier to understand.

Conclusion: I say more here than in the introduction about what I really see happening in the story. The point is that the writer shows two views of the character to illustrate that grief can lead to joy and that we don't really know each other well. No, those are two ideas. Which one is worth developing? Can I combine them? Anyway, that's where I'll get my thesis point from.

The writer is correct in noting that her most important discovery is the connection between the characterization of the protagonist and the theme of the story, a point that she doesn't fully recognize until she expresses it in the conclusion. In trying to express that thesis idea, she came up with the following statements. Which is the richest and clearest thesis sentence?

1. Mrs. Mallard has been living a false life because others have not recognized her joy and strength.

Obviously, this statement is still not entirely clear. What is a "false life"? Is the problem that others haven't recognized her strength? This statement still suggests that the exterior view is correct, that she is a victim of others.

2. Mrs. Mallard finds in her response to grief that she has the strength to embrace the freedom that her life has earlier lacked.

This statement provides a clear statement of the change that takes place in the character, but it doesn't connect clearly to the exterior and interior views of character that the writer began with and wants to keep as part of the thesis statement.

3. Although Mrs. Mallard and those around her believe that she is a weak and help-less victim of circumstances, she discovers in herself the strength to embrace life and freedom joyfully.

This thesis statement is comprehensive enough to include almost all the points that the writer has made in her draft of the essay. It requires that the writer first show the limited view that everyone had of the character, then show the change that takes place within the character's mind and heart, and finally show the implicit thematic point of this change.

Having revised her thesis sentence to her satisfaction, the writer can now re-construct her plan. She does not have to change the basic structure, but she will de-vise new topic sentences that will reflect the change in the thesis idea. As she rewrites the essay, she will also make changes based on her earlier criticism of the first draft. The following essay is the product of this restructuring and revising process.

SAMPLE REVISED ESSAY

The Significance of the Two Mrs. Mallards

In her short story "The Story of an Hour," Kate Chopin gives contrasting views of Mrs. Mallard, her central character, in order to develop the theme that a person can find a renewed sense of life and joy if he or she has the strength to face the truth. The others in the story feel that Mrs. Mallard is a frail victim of circumstances, but the reader sees that she has found the strength in herself to admit that in her loss and grief she has found freedom and joy.

The view that others have of Mrs. Mallard is clearly presented in the first few paragraphs. The doctor sees her only as a woman with a heart condition. A friend of the family who hears of her husband's death in the train accident brings the news to the house himself, probably to avoid the risk of giving her a shock that might kill her. Finally, her sister assists her up the stairs and later checks on her by speaking to her through the keyhole. All of these people, from the impersonal doctor to the sister who seems to love her very much, seem to agree that Mrs. Mallard is a physically and emotionally frail woman who will have great difficulty accepting the reality of her life. When she dies of a heart attack at the end of the story, they feel their view of her is confirmed.

The reader has no reason to doubt this interpretation of Mrs. Mallard until the scene when she is alone in her room. The description Chopin provides at this point suggests that the earlier view is not entirely correct: "She was young, with a fair, calm face, whose lines bespoke repression and even a certain strength." We see that strength emerge after she has given in to her grief for a while. Then she has to face a new thought that seems to be coming against her will, something "too subtle and elusive to name." Mrs. Mallard doesn't want to face this perception, whatever it is, and if she was really as weak as the others think she is, she would probably hide from it or call in others to distract her from it. Instead, she has the strength to face it and is surprised to discover that what she feels is "free, free, free!" Recognizing that she is free "body and soul" gives her joy finally, even though such a reaction is contrary to everything conventional women are supposed to feel, particularly in Chopin's time. She therefore has the strength not only to face the truth but to accept what others would find shocking.

Chopin's portrayal of Mrs. Mallard from the exterior and interior points of view helps to develop her major theme, that human beings should not be bound by the view of others since freedom and joy come only to those strong enough to face and accept the truth. The fact that Mrs. Mallard is physically frail and ironically dies "of joy" at the end of the story does not change the fact that in a single hour she has found herself and her own kind of victory.

Although the writer will want to reread, edit, and again revise this draft, she has already greatly improved the focus, coherence, and development in her essay.

WRITING AN ESSAY WITH SOURCES

In many literature courses, you will be asked to write an essay based on research. This sort of writing has three primary purposes. First, it teaches you how to conduct literary research—how to find, evaluate, document, and cite literary sources. Second, it encourages you to examine the research that has been published about ways to interpret a specific literary text. And third, it invites you to become a researcher by composing your own interpretation of a text, citing and countering other interpretations to create your argument.

FINDING SOURCES

The best way to find literary sources is to use the author's name to sort through the holdings of your library [A = Chopin, Kate]. You can also narrow your sources by restricting your search to the title of a literary text [T = "The Story of an Hour"] or broaden your search by investigating the larger and related contexts for your text [K = film adaptation].

Begin your search by checking your library's computerized catalogue for books and periodicals. Next, examine specialized bibliographies such as the listing of critical interpretations of literary texts found in the *MLA International Bibliography.* Finally, browse through the World Wide Web (WWW), using a "search engine" such as Yahoo, Alta-Vista, Infoseek, or Magellan to see if there are any "sites" or "bulletin boards" devoted to your author or story.

EVALUATING SOURCES

After you have found your sources, evaluate their potential usefulness for your essay by determining if they are *relevant, current,* and *reliable.* Such evaluation is tricky because you may not know what you want to write about until after you have read several sources. A source that might initially seem irrelevant to your paper may suddenly become crucial to its development once you have restricted or revised your topic. A source that may seem out-of-date may prove useful to your argument if you decide to place your story in a historical context. And a source's reliability may not be easy to establish until you trace its chain of references. That is, you may want to determine whether its author has acknowledged and assessed the work of previous researchers.

DOCUMENTING SOURCES

Because the status of a particular source may change as you become more knowledgeable about your topic, document all the sources you find by preparing a preliminary "works cited" list. You may not cite all these sources in the first draft of your paper, but if you prepare a list using the format represented in the following examples, you will have the information you need if you decide to cite a source.

A Book by a Single Author

Ewell, Barbara C. Kate Chopin. New York: Ungar, 1986.

A Signed Article in a Reference Book

Inge, Tonette Bond. "Kate Chopin." Dictionary of Literary Biography. 1989 ed.

A Signed Article from a Daily Newspaper

Chopin, Kate. "On Certain Brisk, Bright Days." St. Louis Post-Dispatch 26 Nov. 1899, sec. 4: 1.

An Unsigned Article from a Daily Newspaper

"The Killing Pace." St. Louis Post-Dispatch 23 Jan. 1898: 4.

Online Database

"Kate Chopin: The Story of an Hour (1894)." Reading About the World, 2. Online. Netscape. 3 Apr. 1996.

Film

The Joy That Kills. Dir. Tina Rathborne. Cypress, 1984.

For comprehensive suggestions about how to document sources, consult *MLA
Handbook for Writers of Research Papers,* 4th Edition. New York: Modern Language Association, 1995.

CITING SOURCES

Once you have compiled your preliminary list of "works cited," you can cite relevant
passages in your paper to support and advance your argument. Remember, you are
the *author* of your paper. You are not a scrapbook maker, someone who assembles a
paper by pasting together citations from other researchers. Your purpose is to compose your own essay, citing other experts at appropriate places to enhance the credibility of your research.

The two basic ways to cite the research of others in your research paper is to
paraphrase and to *quote*. A *paraphrase* restates the content of a particular passage
in your *own words*. A *quotation* cites the author's original passage *word for word*.
Both citations must be documented and refer the reader to the complete information
on the source found in your Works Cited. For example, here is an original citation
from Linda Seger's *The Art of Adaptation: Turning Fact and Fiction into Film*. New
York: Holt, 1992.

Original Passage

The work of adapting a short story demands adding rather than subtracting. Usually
a short story has fewer characters than a novel, and they are in a simple situation,
sometimes without a beginning, middle, and end.

Passage in Paraphrase

Adapting a short story into a film often requires a filmmaker to

add characters and complicate the plot (Seger 3).

Works Cited

Seger, Linda. *The Art of Adaptation: Turning Fact and Fiction into Film*. New
York: Holt, 1992.

Passage in Quotation

As Linda Seger explains in *The Art of Adaptation,* "The work of adapting a short story demands adding rather than subtracting" information (3).

Works Cited

Seger, Linda. *The Art of Adaptation: Turning Fact and Fiction into Film.* New York: Holt, 1992.

For further advice about how to paraphrase and quote passages to develop your essay, consult a standard rhetoric or the *MLA Handbook for Writers of Research Papers,* 4th Edition.

SAMPLE RESEARCH PAPER

In the student research paper that follows, Kathy Conrow cites and documents a variety of sources to suggest how Kate Chopin's "The Story of an Hour" was adapted into a film.

Conrow 1

Kathy Conrow

Mr. Myers

English 104, Section 4

18 April 1996

Fact, Fiction, and Film:
A Comparison of <u>The Joy That Kills</u>
and Kate Chopin's "The Story of an Hour"

When a film is said to be based on a work of literature, it usually means one of two things: either the film is an almost exact reproduction of the story, remaining completely faithful to its model, or it is an adaptation of the text, in which original material is reorganized or deleted, and new material is created and added where necessary. The film <u>The Joy That Kills</u> is an example of an adaptation, and it is based on Kate Chopin's short story titled "The Story of an Hour."

As Linda Seger explains in <u>The Art of Adaptation</u>, "The work of adapting a short story demands adding rather than subtracting" information (3). New scenes and situations are created to round out and develop the story line (4). In <u>The Joy That Kills</u>, quite a few scenes, as well as several characters, are added to the original three-page story to extend it into a film. These additions are used to illustrate the events of the day and night that lead up to the one hour described by Kate Chopin.

When developing a film adaptation the goal is always to find the "balance between preserving the spirit of the original and creating a new form" (Seger 9). In <u>The Joy That Kills</u>, the spirit of Kate Chopin's story and of her own life are preserved in the details of the film's additions and changes. Looking closely at the differences between the film and text versions, particularly in settings, characters, and conflicts, illustrates how <u>The Joy That Kills</u> tells a story of more than one hour, while also remaining true to the work and times of the original author, Kate Chopin.

The first of these differences is presented as the film opens. Over the hazy image of a two-story white house are printed the words "New Orleans, 1877." This clearly places the setting of the film, and it also provides the first link to the real life of Kate Chopin. Two-thirds of the stories she wrote grew out of the people, places, and customs she experienced in New Orleans (Bell 241). So even though the original "Story of an Hour" gives little information about the Mallards' home or the surrounding area, New Orleans is a logical choice for the film's setting.

Also justifying this choice is the fact that Chopin herself lived in Louisiana for nearly twelve years, nine of those in New Orleans. She moved there from St. Louis with her husband, Oscar, shortly after they were married. This, however, was not Kate's first encounter with the city. That came two years earlier when she was eighteen and traveling with her family. She recorded her first impressions of her future home in her journal, writing very favorably, "N. Orleans I liked immensely; it is so clean--so white and green . . . we had profusions of flowers--strawberries and even blackberries" (Ewell 10).

A similar description could also be given by Louise Mallard, as she arranges the plants on her balcony and listens to the vendor below calling out the names of fresh berries for sale. For Mrs. Mallard, these street sights and sounds can only be experienced from her balcony, where they float up to her and provide her few connections with life outside of her home and husband. For Kate Chopin, however, these elements of New Orleans were to provide the backdrop for much of her married life, as well as the inspiration and setting for many of her most memorable stories.

In the nine years that the Chopins lived in New Orleans, Kate came to know the people of Louisiana nearly as well as the place: "She was aware of and receptive to Creole, Cajun, black, and Indian cultures, and when she later came to write fiction, she would incorporate people from these cultures in her work" ("Kate Chopin" Online). There is no evidence of this in her brief "Story of an Hour," but the film version does introduce a character similar to one of those Chopin may have created. In fact, the character of Maggie in <u>The Joy That Kills</u> may also be much like someone Kate Chopin knew in her own life.

In a journal entry written on the occasion of her son's birth, Kate gave an accurate description of Maggie, "the quadroon nurse with her high bandanna tignon, her hoop-earrings and placid smile" (Ewell 13). This is the exact image of Louise Mallard's companion and servant in the film. Maggie acts as a mother-figure to Louise, and she is also Louise's only close friend. Despite this connection, though, Maggie actually contributes to Louise's restriction through her over-protective actions. Her intentions in sheltering Louise are not deliberately cruel or selfish, like Brently's, but as Chopin originally wrote, "a kind intention or a cruel intention [makes] the act seem no less a crime" ("Story" 4).

Two other characters added to the film version do seem to be genuinely kind to Louise and are also understanding of her situation. Dr. Lebrun and his wife, Eugenie, are encouraging and insightful characters who are partially responsible for sparking Louise's desire for freedom. Dr. Lebrun (possibly named for Robert Lebrun of Chopin's novel <u>The Awakening</u>) gives Louise great hope in the first scene of the film by telling her that her heart is stronger than ever. He even encourages her to travel if she likes, something Brently had always forbidden, except through the cards of the stereoscope.

Kate Chopin received similar encouragement from a doctor in her life--Dr. Frederick Kolbenheyer. He was Kate's family physician and also a good friend, especially after the death of her husband. According to Per Seyersted, Dr. Kolbenheyer was "the only one who seems to have been able to help her in her grief" (48). Part of his helping included reading Kate letters that she had sent him from Louisiana and urging her to use them as a starting point for writing fiction. By encouraging her to write, Dr. Kolbenheyer hoped to "give her some relief from the emptiness and deep despair" she was experiencing (Seyersted 49). Dr. Lebrun's encouraging report to Louise works in much the same way, giving her a feeling of relief and freedom, if only for a short while.

Eugenie Lebrun has a more subtle part in spurring Louise's thoughts of freedom, and in foreshadowing her reaction to Brently's "death." In the dinner party scene, Eugenie and her husband discuss the story of a woman who wanted to kill herself when her husband was terminally ill, but who, after his death, was walking happily with a bunch of violets tucked in her belt. Louise acts somewhat shocked at the widow's behavior, but Eugenie quietly adds, "Sometimes one's reaction to calamity is just the opposite of what one expects" (Joy).

Eugenie's words not only give a clue to the future events of the story, but the description given of the other woman who lost her husband provides another link to Kate Chopin. She also was not as subdued as widows were often expected to be (Toth, "Kate Chopin Remembered" 22). "One of Kate's 'ways' was to take long solitary walks," which Emily Toth described as "a declaration of independence" (Kate Chopin 125). And Chopin herself revealed in the <u>St. Louis Post-Dispatch</u> that after a few such experiments, she began to feel that she had the "walking habit" ("On Certain Days" 1). The importance Kate placed on her walking habit and the strange freedom it symbolizes for Louise in <u>The Joy That Kills</u> are illustrated in a passage from Chopin's novel <u>The Awakening</u>. She described women who don't like to walk or, in Louise's case, are not allowed to take walks, by saying, "they miss so much--so many rare little glimpses of life; and we women learn so little of life on the whole" (278). These words could also be the thoughts of Louise Mallard in the film, as she quietly sits at Brently's side and listens to Eugenie and Dr. Lebrun.

Through their encouraging words and subtle hints the Lebruns spark some of Louise's future thoughts and feelings, but another added character makes up her remembrances of the past. He is Louise's father, and he appears in several flashbacks of her childhood. The purpose of these scenes is to show that even as a child Louise had little freedom. She was her widowed father's "pet" but was always left behind when he went away, left peering through the gates or sitting on the stairs, just as she is years later when Brently says she must stay home.

Chopin's father also went off each day, leaving young Kate standing on the steps watching him go and wondering about his destinations. When she finally asked him about this mystery, though, he took her with him for the day and showed her sights that Louise only imagines in the film, like the levee, the steamboats, and the river.

There is also a sadder similarity between the fathers of Louise and Kate. Both men died when their daughters were still quite young. This is a small connection, but it leads to another more intriguing link between Kate's life and the story. When his daughter was five years old, Thomas O'Flaherty was killed in a train accident. It was a horrifying wreck, in which two men were mistakenly reported dead. One, a Mr. Moore, had only been injured, but the other, Mr. Bryan, had not been on the train at all and was "far from the scene of accident" ("Story" 5). Based on this information, Emily Toth suggests that "through 'The Story of an Hour' Kate Chopin rewrote a childhood grief" (Kate Chopin 33).

Chopin mourned the tragic death of her father for a long time, as did Louise in the film, but when another father figure in Chopin's life died, other feelings were raised--feelings similar to the true emotions Louise experiences at Brently's "death." Kate Chopin's father-in-law, Dr. Jean Baptiste Chopin, could in fact have been the model for the Brently Mallard of The Joy That Kills. Unlike the Mr. Mallard of the text, whose treatment of his wife is only alluded to, the Mr. Mallard of the film is a fully developed character who is shown to treat Louise with selfish cruelty. He deliberately limits Louise so he can keep her isolated in his world, and only lets her experience places outside that world through the scenes printed on the stereoscope cards. Dr. J. B. Chopin treated his wife, Julie Benoist, in much the same way. According to Toth, "Dr. Chopin isolated his young wife from all her friends and family," not even letting her visit her own mother and locking her in her room when she tried (Kate Chopin 123).

In The Joy That Kills, Brently does not literally lock Louise in her room, but he does forbid her to leave the house, reproaching her if she even too vividly imagines going out. Through his selfishness, Brently "spoil[s] even her solitary enjoyments," just as Dr. Chopin did with his wife (Toth, Kate Chopin 123). Both Louise Mallard and Julie Benoist Chopin fell into what one of Kate's friends called "the degrading life of most married ladies" (Inge 90). And both escaped this life in much the same way. Like Louise, Julie Benoist Chopin was thought of as "a fragile person" by those who knew her, and, like Louise, she died very suddenly, most likely from an oppression that kills (Toth, Kate Chopin 124).

This oppression, which Louise Mallard experiences in the film, is much more tangible and threatening than that described in the original text. It is extended to include strict physical confinement, and as a result the conflict of the story is deepened. It is not just Louise versus the stifling expectations of married life, but also includes Louise's struggles against perceptions about her health, against her physical confinement, and against Brently, the enforcer of these restraints.

In Brently's character the limitations created by the society of Kate Chopin's time can also be seen. Two articles written for the St. Louis Post-Dispatch in 1898 give a basis for the arguments Brently uses to isolate Louise. The first, from January 23, explains the importance of carefully guarding women from any hardships ("Killing Pace"). The second, printed a month later, supports that assertion by stating that "the strain [of society] is too great for a person of nervous and excitable disposition" and "women it must be admitted are particularly susceptible to the effects of excitement. Many of them need a balance wheel" (Griffith 12).

In The Joy That Kills, Brently claims he is only trying to provide this balance and protection for Louise by keeping her always at home. He explains this to Maggie by saying, "Inside the walls of this building we can protect her. We can't control what happens if she goes out the front door" (Joy). It is this need of Brently's to control his wife, more than his desire to protect her health, that keeps Louise isolated and trapped. No matter how she struggles to explain her improving condition, he will not let her venture out of the caged world in which he has placed her.

Though this literal confinement is not evidenced in the original "The Story of an Hour," the images of cages, houses, gates, and doors are seen repeatedly in other pieces of Kate Chopin's work. In much of her writing, the house is shown as an asylum or a prison (Clatworthy 2059A). The same is true of Louise's home in The Joy That Kills. At the beginning of the film, she says, "I was born in this house, and I rarely leave it" (Joy). And she is shown several times, both as an adult and as a child, peering through the green cage-like bars of the gates and railings.

The world in which Louise is confined in the film is comparable to the world of a captive animal that appears in one of Chopin's earliest stories, "Emancipation: A Life Fable." In it she wrote, "He saw above and about him confining walls, and before him were bars of iron through which came air and light from without" (Complete Works 37). Louise endures the same situation as she peers through the gates of her home and stares at the small pieces of the outside life she is not permitted to experience.

The cage, which became one of Chopin's "prominent symbols for spiritual and physical captivity," is used in the same way in The Joy That Kills (Podlasli 57). The Mallards' cage-like home represents all of the confining forces in Louise's life and reinforces Brently's power over her. When Brently's death is reported, however, the house is no longer a prison. Louise walks through one of the large windows onto the balcony and stands in sunlight. And when she does reenter the house, it is not the ironwork screen on the door that she notices, but how the light shines through it. When the animal in Chopin's "Emancipation" finds his freedom, he also notices the light. He watches "the canopy of the sky grow broader . . . seeing each time more light" (Complete Works 37). In this story and in the film, the "light assumes significance only when experienced in freedom" (Podlasli 59).

For the animal this light and freedom continue, but for Louise they are short-lived. This point of the story does not change from the text to the film. Brently returns, opening the door and blocking out the light that Louise just discovered. With his imposing figure comes "the realization that her epiphany must forever be forgotten" (Dyer 78).

This final scene, ending with the death of Louise, remains completely true to Chopin's original work. The scenes leading up to it, though altered and extended, also remain true to Kate Chopin and her writing. The people she knew, experiences she collected, and places she called home are subtly woven into the film's developed characters, deepened conflicts, and detailed setting. <u>The Joy That Kills</u> is not only based on "The Story of an Hour"; it is also based on pieces of a life- -the real life of the author Kate Chopin.

Works Cited

Bell, Pearl K. "Kate Chopin and Sarah Orne Jewett." <u>Partisan Review</u> Spring 1988: 238-54.

Chopin, Kate. <u>The Awakening</u>. New York: Capricorn Books, 1964.

—. <u>The Complete Works of Kate Chopin</u>. Ed. Per Seyersted. Baton Rouge: Louisiana State UP, 1969.

—. "On Certain Brisk, Bright Days." <u>St. Louis Post-Dispatch</u> 26 Nov. 1899, sec. 4: 1.

—. "The Story of an Hour." <u>Women and Fiction: Short Stories by and About Women</u>. Ed. Susan Cahill. New York: New American Library, 1975. 3-5.

Clatworthy, Joan Mayerson. "Kate Chopin: The Inward Life Which Questions." <u>DAI</u> 40 (1979): 2059A. State University of New York at Buffalo.

Dyer, Joyce Coyne. "Epiphanies Through Nature in the Stories of Kate Chopin." <u>University of Dayton Review</u> Winter 1983-84: 75-81.

Ewell, Barbara C. <u>Kate Chopin</u>. New York: Ungar, 1986.

Griffith, Martha Davis. "Has Society Struck the Pace That Kills?" St. Louis Post-Dispatch 6 Feb. 1898: 2.

Inge, Tonette Bond. "Kate Chopin." Dictionary of Literary Biography 1989 ed.

The Joy That Kills. Dir. Tina Rathborne. Cypress Films, 1984.

"Kate Chopin: The Story of an Hour (1894)." Reading About the World, Volume 2. Online. Netscape. 3 April 1996.

"The Killing Pace." St. Louis Post-Dispatch 23 Jan. 1898: 4.

Podlasli, Heidi M. Freedom and Existentialist Choice in the Fiction of Kate Chopin. Diss. Ball State University, 1991.

Seger, Linda. The Art of Adaptation: Turning Fact and Fiction into Film. New York: Holt, 1992.

Seyersted, Per. Kate Chopin: A Critical Biography Baton Rouge: Louisiana State UP, 1969.

Toth, Emily. Kate Chopin. New York: Morrow, 1990.

—. "Kate Chopin Remembered." The Kate Chopin Newsletter Winter 1975-76: 21-27.

A FINAL WORD

Writing about short stories is as much a process of discovery as it is reporting what has been discovered. We hope that our suggestions will be helpful to you, particularly if you have not had much experience in writing about literature. However, you will find that with practice you will develop your own methods of discovering, organizing, and developing your ideas. Remember that all critics have a single purpose: to lend their minds to their readers, to give others a way of seeing more clearly or with more pleasure matters of mutual interest. Your manner of writing must finally be shaped by the unique point of view that you alone can offer your readers.

PAIRED STORIES

PAIRED STORIES

O ne of the best ways to understand how fiction works is to compare the ways in which two or more skillful writers develop the major elements in their stories. In the following section, we have paired stories that offer rich possibilities for such comparisons. In two of the cases, a contemporary writer almost insists that such comparison be made by using as his or her title a slight modification of the title of an earlier classic piece of short fiction. In the other three instances, similarities in certain key elements of the stories suggest that comparison might be illuminating.

You will find many points in each pair that you may wish to compare, but we will emphasize one of the elements in each pair for the purposes of this discussion, focusing in the first instance on plot, in the second on character, in the third on setting, in the fourth on point of view, and in the final section on theme. As we have already discussed, however, it is the interaction of all the elements that creates good fiction. For that reason, the questions following each pair of stories will ask you to consider the relationship between one element and the others in the stories.

P L O T

Anton Chekhov's "The Lady with the Dog"
Joyce Carol Oates's
"The Lady with the Pet Dog"

Like all artists, fiction writers find inspiration in the work of previous masters. In the title of her story "The Lady with the Pet Dog," Joyce Carol Oates acknowledges her debt to one of the great masters of short fiction, Anton Chekhov. As we compare her story to Chekhov's "The Lady with the Dog," we quickly see that she has borrowed much of his central plot as well. Without question, Oates is inviting a comparison of her story to the master's. A century apart in time and growing out of two vastly different cultures, these parallel stories of adulterous affairs suggest that the contradictions and ambiguities of human passion are independent of time, place, and perhaps even gender.

The major events in the two stories are quite similar: an early middle-aged man and woman of comfortable means meet at a fashionable seaside resort. Though both are married, they are also bored and lonely and quickly begin an affair that neither intends to take seriously. Despite the pleasure and passion of their relationship, both are wary and somewhat relieved when their time together is over and they seem to part for good. Later, they meet at a theater in the city where she lives with her husband, discover that their passion is more intense than ever, and resume their affair in clandestine meetings that leave them to face the surprising fact that in spite of their fears and uncertainties, they have come to need each other as they face lives in which their own mortality and emotional confusion increasingly haunt them. Neither version of the story offers any final resolution of the conflicts that have developed. The "most complicated and difficult part" of their story lies in an unknowable future beyond the bounds of the story. There is no conventional climax and certainly no resolving denouement.

The major differences between the two stories are equally important, though perhaps less striking. Chekhov's plot is structured traditionally, beginning with the lovers' first meeting and following events in chronological order through the rest of the story. Oates, on the other hand, begins near the end of the sequence of events with the meeting in the theater and then, in a series of flashbacks, moves us from present to past and back again in a cycle so that only gradually does the whole pattern of events emerge as a coherent whole. The difference in the structures of the two plots is fundamentally important. Chekhov's linear structure implies a world in which human motivation and its consequences develop in strong, comprehensible cause-and-effect patterns, while Oates's cyclic structure suggests a far more complex and less explicable interaction of past action and present consequence. We have to return to the past repeatedly to comprehend the present, and our memory of the past is a powerful part of any present moment. The century between Chekhov and Oates has revised our basic notions of such things as time and human consciousness, a fact clearly reflected in these stories.

The shift in point of view in the two versions shows how directly such elements as plot, character, and point of view interact so that a change in one necessarily changes all the others. In Chekhov's story the protagonist is the male lover, and we know only what he knows, have access only to his inner reality. Oates makes the female lover her protagonist, and again she limits our knowledge of inner and outer reality to that of the woman. The basic nature of the plot therefore changes; in Chekhov's story we see, for example, a domestic moment such as the protagonist walking his daughter to school, whereas in Oates's story we have instead a scene in which her protagonist watches her exhausted husband asleep at the dinner table. But in both stories, the basic conflict is between the emotionally stable if somewhat dull life of the protagonist before the affair and the difficult, unpredictable situation that arises from the passion generated by the affair.

Because Oates is obviously writing in full awareness of Chekhov's story, we can assume that her story is in part a response to his work. Both the similarities and the differences in plot are therefore especially intriguing and lead to basic questions of purpose and meaning in the two versions of the story. After you have read the stories and developed your own comparison, respond to the questions that follow to see if they amplify or challenge your first impressions.

2

ANTON CHEKHOV

The Lady with the Dog

TRANSLATED BY CONSTANCE GARNETT

ANTON CHEKHOV (1860–1904) was born in Taganrog, Russia, and studied to be a doctor at the University of Moscow. In 1884, Chekhov completed his medical training and published his first collection of short stories. For a few years he worked as an assistant to a doctor in a small provincial town, but he soon decided to pursue an active literary career. By 1887, Chekhov had written more than six hundred stories and humorous sketches. Although Chekhov dismissed this early work as "thoughtless and frivolous," it won him wide acclaim and enabled him to purchase a small estate near Moscow. During the next decade, Chekhov's work focused on the difficulties of social injustice. It was during this period that Chekhov also began to write for the stage, producing such classic dramas as *The Seagull* (1896), *Uncle Vanya* (1897), and *The Cherry Orchard* (1904). Chekhov's disillusionment, perhaps caused in part by his failing health, permeated his later work. "The Lady with the Dog," the title story of a collection translated into English in 1917, describes the love affair between a cynical older man and an innocent young woman.

It was said that a new person had appeared on the sea-front: a lady with a little dog. Dmitri Dmitritch Gurov, who had by then been a fortnight at Yalta, and so was fairly at home there, had begun to take an interest in new arrivals. Sitting in Verney's pavilion, he saw, walking on the sea-front, a fair-haired young lady of medium height, wearing a *béret;* a white Pomeranian dog was running behind her.

And afterwards he met her in the public gardens and in the square several times a day. She was walking alone, always wearing the same *béret,* and always with the same white dog; no one knew who she was, and every one called her simply "the lady with the dog."

"If she is here alone without a husband or friends, it wouldn't be amiss to make her acquaintance," Gurov reflected.

He was under forty, but he had a daughter already twelve years old, and two sons at school. He had been married young, when he was a student in his second year, and by now his wife seemed half as old again as he. She was a tall, erect woman with dark eyebrows, staid and dignified, and, as she said of herself, intellectual. She read a great deal, used phonetic spelling, called her husband, not Dmitri, but Dimitri, and he secretly considered her unintelligent, narrow, inelegant, was afraid of her, and did not like to be at home. He had begun being unfaithful to her long ago—had been unfaithful to her often, and, probably on that account, almost always spoke ill of women, and when they were talked about in his presence, used to call them "the lower race."

5   It seemed to him that he had been so schooled by bitter experience that he might call them what he liked, and yet he could not get on for two days together without "the lower race." In the society of men he was bored and not himself, with them he was cold and uncommunicative; but when he was in the company of women he felt free, and knew what to say to them and how to behave; and he was at ease with them even when he was silent. In his appearance, in his character, in his whole nature, there was something attractive and elusive which allured women and disposed them in his favour; he knew that, and some force seemed to draw him, too, to them.

Experience often repeated, truly bitter experience, had taught him long ago that with decent people, especially Moscow people—always slow to move and irresolute—every intimacy, which at first so agreeably diversifies life and appears a light and charming adventure, inevitably grows into a regular problem of extreme intricacy, and in the long run the situation becomes unbearable. But at every fresh meeting with an interesting woman this experience seemed to slip out of his memory, and he was eager for life, and everything seemed simple and amusing.

One evening he was dining in the gardens, and the lady in the *béret* came up slowly to take the next table. Her expression, her gait, her dress, and the way she did her hair told him that she was a lady, that she was married, that she was in Yalta for the first time and alone, and that she was dull there. . . . The stories told of the immorality in such places as Yalta are to a great extent untrue; he despised them, and knew that such stories were for the most part made up by persons who would themselves have been glad to sin if they had been able; but when the lady sat down at the next table three paces from him, he remembered these tales of easy conquests, of trips to the mountains, and the tempting thought of a swift, fleeting love affair, a romance with an unknown woman, whose name he did not know, suddenly took possession of him.

He beckoned coaxingly to the Pomeranian, and when the dog came up to him he shook his finger at it. The Pomeranian growled: Gurov shook his finger at it again.

The lady looked at him and at once dropped her eyes.

10   "He doesn't bite," she said, and blushed.

"May I give him a bone?" he asked; and when she nodded he asked courteously, "Have you been long in Yalta?"

"Five days."

"And I have already dragged out a fortnight here."

There was a brief silence.

15   "Time goes fast, and yet it is so dull here!" she said, not looking at him.

"That's only the fashion to say it is dull here. A provincial will live in Belyov or Zhidra and not be dull, and when he comes here it's 'Oh, the dullness! Oh, the dust!' One would think he came from Granada."

She laughed. Then both continued eating in silence, like strangers, but after dinner they walked side by side; and there sprang up between them the light jesting conversation of people who are free and satisfied, to whom it does not matter where they go or what they talk about. They walked and talked of the strange light on the sea: the water was of a soft warm lilac hue, and there was a golden streak from the moon upon it. They talked of how sultry it was after a hot day. Gurov told her that he came from Moscow, that he had taken his degree in Arts, but had a post in a bank; that he had trained as an opera-singer, but had given it up, that he owned two houses in Moscow. . . . And from her he learnt that she had grown up in Petersburg, but had lived in S——— since her marriage two years before, that she was staying another month in Yalta, and that her husband, who needed a holiday too, might perhaps come and fetch her. She was not sure whether her husband had a post in a Crown Department or under the Provincial Council—and was amused by her own ignorance. And Gurov learnt, too, that she was called Anna Sergeyevna.

Afterwards he thought about her in his room at the hotel—thought she would certainly meet him next day; it would be sure to happen. As he got into bed he thought how lately she had been a girl at school, doing lessons like his own daughter; he recalled the diffidence, the angularity, that was still manifest in her laugh and her manner of talking with a stranger. This must have been the first time in her life she had been alone in surroundings in which she was followed, looked at, and spoken to merely from a secret motive which she could hardly fail to guess. He recalled her slender, delicate neck, her lovely grey eyes.

"There's something pathetic about her, anyway," he thought, and fell asleep.

2

A week had passed since they had made acquaintance. It was a holiday. It was sultry indoors, while in the street the wind whirled the dust round and round, and blew people's hats off. It was a thirsty day, and Gurov often went into the pavilion, and pressed Anna Sergeyevna to have syrup and water or an ice. One did not know what to do with oneself.

In the evening when the wind had dropped a little, they went out on the groyne to see the steamer come in. There were a great many people walking about the harbour; they had gathered to welcome some one, bringing bouquets. And two peculiarities of a well-dressed Yalta crowd were very conspicuous: the elderly ladies were dressed like young ones, and there were great numbers of generals.

Owing to the roughness of the sea, the steamer arrived late, after the sun had set, and it was a long time turning about before it reached the groyne. Anna Sergeyevna looked through her lorgnette at the steamer and the passengers as though looking for acquaintances, and when she turned to Gurov her eyes were shining. She talked a great deal and asked disconnected questions, forgetting next moment what she had asked; then she dropped her lorgnette in the crush.

The festive crowd began to disperse; it was too dark to see people's faces. The wind had completely dropped, but Gurov and Anna Sergeyevna still stood as though waiting to see some one else come from the steamer. Anna Sergeyevna was silent now, and sniffed the flowers without looking at Gurov.

"The weather is better this evening," he said. "Where shall we go now? Shall we drive somewhere?"

25   She made no answer.

Then he looked at her intently, and all at once put his arm round her and kissed her on the lips, and breathed in the moisture and the fragrance of the flowers; and he immediately looked round him, anxiously wondering whether any one had seen them.

"Let us go to your hotel," he said softly. And both walked quickly.

The room was close and smelt of the scent she had bought at the Japanese shop. Gurov looked at her and thought: "What different people one meets in the world!" From the past he preserved memories of careless, good-natured women, who loved cheerfully and were grateful to him for the happiness he gave them, however brief it might be; and of women like his wife who loved without any genuine feeling, with superfluous phrases, affectedly, hysterically, with an expression that suggested that it was not love nor passion, but something more significant; and of two or three others, very beautiful, cold women, on whose faces he had caught a glimpse of a rapacious expression—an obstinate desire to snatch from life more than it could give, and these were capricious, unreflecting, domineering, unintelligent women not in their first youth, and when Gurov grew cold to them their beauty excited his hatred, and the lace on their linen seemed to him like scales.

But in this case there was still the diffidence, the angularity of inexperienced youth, an awkward feeling; and there was a sense of consternation as though some one had suddenly knocked at the door. The attitude of Anna Sergeyevna—"the lady with the dog"—to what had happened was somehow peculiar, very grave, as though it were her fall—so it seemed, and it was strange and inappropriate. Her face dropped and faded, and on both sides of it her long hair hung down mournfully; she mused in a dejected attitude like "the woman who was a sinner" in an old-fashioned picture.

30   "It's wrong," she said. "You will be the first to despise me now."

There was a water-melon on the table. Gurov cut himself a slice and began eating it without haste. There followed at least half an hour of silence.

Anna Sergeyevna was touching; there was about her the purity of a good, simple woman who had seen little of life. The solitary candle burning on the table threw a faint light on her face, yet it was clear that she was very unhappy.

"How could I despise you?" asked Gurov. "You don't know what you are saying."

"God forgive me," she said, and her eyes filled with tears. "It's awful."

35   "You seem to feel you need to be forgiven."

"Forgiven? No. I am a bad, low woman; I despise myself and I don't attempt to justify myself. It's not my husband but myself I have deceived. And not only just now; I have been deceiving myself for a long time. My husband may be a good, honest man, but he is a flunkey! I don't know what he does there, what his work is, but I know he is a flunkey! I was twenty when I was married to him. I have been tormented by curiosity; I wanted something better. 'There must be a different sort of life,' I said to myself. I wanted to live! To live, to live! . . . I was fired by curiosity . . . you don't understand it, but, I swear to God, I could not control myself; something happened to me: I could not be restrained. I told my husband I was ill, and came here. . . . And here I have been walking about as though I were dazed, like a mad creature; . . . and now I have become a vulgar, contemptible woman whom any one may despise."

Gurov felt bored already, listening to her. He was irritated by the naïve tone, by this remorse, so unexpected and inopportune; but for the tears in her eyes, he might have thought she was jesting or playing a part.

"I don't understand," he said softly. "What is it you want?"

She hid her face on his breast and pressed close to him.

"Believe me, believe me, I beseech you . . ." she said. "I love a pure, honest life,   40 and sin is loathsome to me. I don't know what I am doing. Simple people say: 'The Evil One has beguiled me.' And I may say of myself now that the Evil One has beguiled me."

"Hush, hush! . . ." he muttered.

He looked at her fixed, scared eyes, kissed her, talked softly and affectionately, and by degrees she was comforted, and her gaiety returned; they both began laughing.

Afterwards when they went out there was not a soul on the sea-front. The town with its cypresses had quite a deathlike air, but the sea still broke noisily on the shore; a single barge was rocking on the waves, and a lantern was blinking sleepily on it.

They found a cab and drove to Oreanda.

"I found out your surname in the hall just now: it was written on the board—   45 Von Diderits," said Gurov. "Is your husband a German?"

"No, I believe his grandfather was a German, but he is an Orthodox Russian himself."

At Oreanda they sat on a seat not far from the church, looked down at the sea, and were silent. Yalta was hardly visible through the morning mist; white clouds stood motionless on the mountain-tops. The leaves did not stir on the trees, grasshoppers chirruped, and the monotonous hollow sound of the sea rising up from below, spoke of the peace, of the eternal sleep awaiting us. So it must have sounded when there was no Yalta, no Oreanda here; so it sounds now, and it will sound as indifferently and monotonously when we are all no more. And in this constancy, in this complete indifference to the life and death of each of us, there lies hid, perhaps, a pledge of our eternal salvation, of the unceasing movement of life upon earth, of unceasing progress towards perfection. Sitting beside a young woman who in the dawn seemed so lovely, soothed and spellbound in these magical surroundings—the sea, mountains, clouds, the open sky—Gurov thought how in reality everything is beautiful in this world when one reflects: everything except what we think or do ourselves when we forget our human dignity and the higher aims of our existence.

A man walked up to them—probably a keeper—looked at them and walked away. And this detail seemed mysterious and beautiful, too. They saw a steamer come from Theodosia, with its lights out in the glow of dawn.

"There is dew on the grass," said Anna Sergeyevna, after a silence.

50   "Yes. It's time to go home."

They went back to the town.

Then they met every day at twelve o'clock on the sea-front, lunched and dined together, went for walks, admired the sea. She complained that she slept badly, that her heart throbbed violently; asked the same questions, troubled now by jealousy and now by the fear that he did not respect her sufficiently. And often in the square or gardens, when there was no one near them, he suddenly drew her to him and kissed her passionately. Complete idleness, these kisses in broad daylight while he looked round in dread of some one's seeing them, the heat, the smell of the sea, and the continual passing to and fro before him of idle, well-dressed, well-fed people, made a new man of him; he told Anna Sergeyevna how beautiful she was, how fascinating. He was impatiently passionate, he would not move a step away from her, while she was often pensive and continually urged him to confess that he did not respect her, did not love her in the least, and thought of her as nothing but a common woman. Rather late almost every evening they drove somewhere out of town, to Oreanda or to the waterfall; and the expedition was always a success, the scenery invariably impressed them as grand and beautiful.

They were expecting her husband to come, but a letter came from him, saying that there was something wrong with his eyes, and he entreated his wife to come home as quickly as possible. Anna Sergeyevna made haste to go.

"It's a good thing I am going away," she said to Gurov. "It's the finger of destiny!"

55   She went by coach and he went with her. They were driving the whole day. When she had got into a compartment of the express, and when the second bell had rung, she said:

"Let me look at you once more . . . look at you once again. That's right."

She did not shed tears, but was so sad that she seemed ill, and her face was quivering.

"I shall remember you . . . think of you," she said. "God be with you; be happy. Don't remember evil against me. We are parting forever—it must be so, for we ought never to have met. Well, God be with you."

The train moved off rapidly, its lights soon vanished from sight, and a minute later there was no sound of it, as though everything had conspired together to end as quickly as possible that sweet delirium, that madness. Left alone on the platform, and gazing into the dark distance, Gurov listened to the chirrup of the grasshoppers and the hum of the telegraph wires, feeling as though he had only just waked up. And he thought, musing, that there had been another episode or adventure in his life, and it, too, was at an end, and nothing was left of it but a memory. . . . He was moved, sad, and conscious of a slight remorse. This young woman whom he would never meet again had not been happy with him; he was genuinely warm and affectionate with her, but yet in his manner, his tone, and his caresses there had been a shade of light irony, the coarse condescension of a happy man who was, besides, almost twice her age. All the time she had called him kind, exceptional, lofty; obviously he had seemed to her different from what he really was, so he had unintentionally deceived her. . . .

Here at the station was already a scent of autumn; it was a cold evening.   60

"It's time for me to go north," thought Gurov as he left the platform. "High time!"

3

At home in Moscow everything was in its winter routine; the stoves were heated, and in the morning it was still dark when the children were having breakfast and getting ready for school, and the nurse would light the lamp for a short time. The frosts had begun already. When the first snow has fallen, on the first day of sledge-driving it is pleasant to see the white earth, the white roofs, to draw soft, delicious breath, and the season brings back the days of one's youth. The old limes and birches, white with hoar-frost, have a good-natured expression; they are nearer to one's heart than cypresses and palms, and near them one doesn't want to be thinking of the sea and the mountains.

Gurov was Moscow born; he arrived in Moscow on a fine frosty day, and when he put on his fur coat and warm gloves, and walked along Petrovka, and when on Saturday evening he heard the ringing of the bells, his recent trip and the places he had seen lost all charm for him. Little by little he became absorbed in Moscow life, greedily read three newspapers a day, and declared he did not read the Moscow papers on principle! He already felt a longing to go to restaurants, clubs, dinner-parties, anniversary celebrations and he felt flattered at entertaining distinguished lawyers and artists, and at playing cards with a professor at the doctors' club. He could already eat a whole plateful of salt fish and cabbage. . . .

In another month, he fancied, the image of Anna Sergeyevna would be shrouded in a mist in his memory, and only from time to time would visit him in his dreams with a touching smile as others did. But more than a month passed, real winter had come, and everything was still clear in his memory as though he had parted with Anna Sergeyevna only the day before. And his memories glowed more and more vividly. When in the evening stillness he heard from his study the voices of his children, preparing their lessons, or when he listened to a song or the organ at the restaurant, or the storm howled in the chimney, suddenly everything would rise up in his memory: what had happened on the groyne, and the early morning with the mist on the mountains, and the steamer coming from Theodosia and the kisses. He would pace a long time about his room, remembering it all and smiling; then his memories passed into dreams, and in his fancy the past was mingled with what was to come. Anna Sergeyevna did not visit him in dreams, but followed him about everywhere like a shadow and haunted him. When he shut his eyes he saw her as though she were living before him, and she seemed to him lovelier, younger, tenderer than she was; and he imagined himself finer than he had been in Yalta. In the evenings she peeped out at him from the bookcase, from the fireplace, from the corner—he heard her breathing, the caressing rustle of her dress. In the street he watched the women, looking for some one like her.

He was tormented by an intense desire to confide his memories to some one. But   65
in his home it was impossible to talk of his love, and he had no one outside; he could

not talk to his tenants nor to any one at the bank. And what had he to talk to? Had he been in love, then? Had there been anything beautiful, poetical, or edifying or simply interesting in his relations with Anna Sergeyevna? And there was nothing for him but to talk vaguely of love, of woman, and no one guessed what it meant; only his wife twitched her black eyebrows, and said: "The part of a lady-killer does not suit you at all, Dimitri."

One evening, coming out of the doctors' club with an official with whom he had been playing cards, he could not resist saying:

"If only you knew what a fascinating woman I made the acquaintance of in Yalta!"

The official got into his sledge and was driving away, but turned suddenly and shouted:

"Dmitri Dmitritch!"

70   "What?"

"You were right this evening: the sturgeon was a bit too strong!"

These words, so ordinary, for some reason moved Gurov to indignation, and struck him as degrading and unclean. What savage manners, what people! What senseless nights, what uninteresting, uneventful days! The rage for card-playing, the gluttony, the drunkenness, the continual talk always about the same thing. Useless pursuits and conversations always about the same things absorb the better part of one's time, the better part of one's strength, and in the end there is left a life grovelling and curtailed, worthless and trivial, and there is no escaping or getting away from it—just as though one were in a madhouse or a prison.

Gurov did not sleep all night, and was filled with indignation. And he had a headache all next day. And the next night he slept badly; he sat up in bed, thinking, or paced up and down his room. He was sick of his children, sick of the bank; he had no desire to go anywhere or to talk of anything.

In the holidays in December he prepared for a journey, and told his wife he was going to Petersburg to do something in the interests of a young friend—and he set off for S———. What for? He did not very well know himself. He wanted to see Anna Sergeyevna and to talk with her—to arrange a meeting, if possible.

75   He reached S——— in the morning, and took the best room at the hotel, in which the floor was covered with grey army cloth, and on the table was an inkstand, grey with dust and adorned with a figure on horseback, with its hat and its hand and its head broken off. The hotel porter gave him the necessary information; Von Diderits lived in a house of his own on Old Gontcharny Street—it was not far from the hotel: he was rich and lived in good style, and had his own horses; every one in the town knew him. The porter pronounced the name "Dridirits."

Gurov went without haste to Old Gontcharny Street and found the house. Just opposite the house stretched a long grey fence adorned with nails.

"One would run away from a fence like that," thought Gurov, looking from the fence to the windows of the house and back again.

He considered: to-day was a holiday, and the husband would probably be at home. And in any case it would be tactless to go into the house and upset her. If he were to send her a note it might fall into her husband's hands, and then it might ruin everything. The best thing was to trust to chance. And he kept walking up and down the street by the fence, waiting for the chance. He saw a beggar go in at the gate and dogs fly at him; then an hour later he heard a piano, and the sounds were faint and indistinct. Probably it was Anna Sergeyevna playing. The front door suddenly opened, and an old woman came out, followed by the familiar white Pomeranian. Gurov was on the point of calling to the dog, but his heart began beating violently, and in his excitement he could not remember the dog's name.

He walked up and down, and loathed the grey fence more and more, and by now he thought irritably that Anna Sergeyevna had forgotten him, and was perhaps already amusing herself with some one else, and that that was very natural in a young woman who had nothing to look at from morning till night but that confounded fence. He went back to his hotel room and sat for a long while on the sofa, not knowing what to do, then he had dinner and a long nap.

"How stupid and worrying it is!" he thought when he woke and looked at the 80 dark windows: it was already evening. "Here I've had a good sleep for some reason. What shall I do in the night?"

He sat on the bed, which was covered by a cheap grey blanket, such as one sees in hospitals, and he taunted himself in his vexation:

"So much for the lady with the dog . . . so much for the adventure. . . . You're in a nice fix. . . ."

That morning at the station a poster in large letters had caught his eye. "The Geisha" was to be performed for the first time. He thought of this and went to the theatre.

"It's quite possible she may go to the first performance," he thought.

The theatre was full. As in all provincial theatres, there was a fog above the 85 chandelier, the gallery was noisy and restless; in the front row the local dandies were standing up before the beginning of the performance, with their hands behind them; in the Governor's box the Governor's daughter, wearing a boa, was sitting in the front seat, while the Governor himself lurked modestly behind the curtain with only his hands visible; the orchestra was a long time tuning up; the stage curtain swayed. All the time the audience were coming in and taking their seats Gurov looked at them eagerly.

Anna Sergeyevna, too, came in. She sat down in the third row, and when Gurov looked at her his heart contracted, and he understood clearly that for him there was in the whole world no creature so near, so precious, and so important to him; she, this little woman, in no way remarkable, lost in a provincial crowd, with a vulgar lorgnette in her hand, filled his whole life now, was his sorrow and his joy, the one happiness that he now desired for himself, and to the sounds of the inferior orchestra, of the wretched provincial violins, he thought how lovely she was. He thought and dreamed.

A young man with small side-whiskers, tall and stooping, came in with Anna Sergeyevna, and sat down beside her; he bent his head at every step and seemed to be continually bowing. Most likely this was the husband whom at Yalta, in a rush of bitter feeling, she had called a flunkey. And there really was in his long figure, his side-whiskers, and the small bald patch on his head, something of the flunkey's obsequiousness; his smile was sugary, and in his buttonhole there was some badge of distinction like the number on a waiter.

During the first interval the husband went away to smoke; she remained alone in her stall. Gurov, who was sitting in the stalls, too, went up to her and said in a trembling voice, with a forced smile:

"Good-evening."

90 She glanced at him and turned pale, then glanced again with horror, unable to believe her eyes, and tightly gripped her fan and the lorgnette in her hands, evidently struggling with herself not to faint. Both were silent. She was sitting, he was standing, frightened by her confusion and not venturing to sit down beside her. The violins and the flute began tuning up. He felt suddenly frightened; it seemed as though all the people in the boxes were looking at them. She got up and went quickly to the door; he followed her, and both walked senselessly along passages, and up and down stairs, and figures in legal, scholastic, and civil service uniforms, all wearing badges, flitted before their eyes. They caught glimpses of ladies, of fur coats hanging on pegs; the draughts blew on them, bringing a smell of stale tobacco. And Gurov, whose heart was beating violently, thought:

"Oh, heavens! Why are these people here and this orchestra! . . ."

And at that instant he recalled how when he had seen Anna Sergeyevna off at the station he had thought that everything was over and they would never meet again. But how far they were still from the end!

On the narrow, gloomy staircase over which was written "To the Amphitheatre," she stopped.

"How you have frightened me!" she said, breathing hard, still pale and overwhelmed. "Oh, how you have frightened me! I am half dead. Why have you come? Why?"

95 "But do understand, Anna, do understand . . ." he said hastily in a low voice. "I entreat you to understand. . . ."

She looked at him with dread, with entreaty, with love; she looked at him intently, to keep his features more distinctly in her memory.

"I am so unhappy," she went on, not heeding him. "I have thought of nothing but you all the time; I live only in the thought of you. And I wanted to forget, to forget you; but why, oh, why, have you come?"

On the landing above them two schoolboys were smoking and looking down, but that was nothing to Gurov; he drew Anna Sergeyevna to him, and began kissing her face, her cheeks, and her hands.

"What are you doing, what are you doing!" she cried in horror, pushing him away. "We are mad. Go away to-day; go away at once. . . . I beseech you by all that is sacred, I implore you. . . . There are people coming this way!"

100 Some one was coming up the stairs.

"You must go away," Anna Sergeyevna went on in a whisper. "Do you hear, Dmitri Dmitritch? I will come and see you in Moscow. I have never been happy; I am miserable now, and I never, never shall be happy, never! Don't make me suffer still more! I swear I'll come to Moscow. But now let us part. My precious, good, dear one, we must part!"

She pressed his hand and began rapidly going downstairs, looking round at him, and from her eyes he could see that she really was unhappy. Gurov stood for a little while, listened, then, when all sound had died away, he found his coat and left the theatre.

4

And Anna Sergeyevna began coming to see him in Moscow. Once in two or three months she left S———, telling her husband that she was going to consult a doctor about an internal complaint—and her husband believed her, and did not believe her. In Moscow she stayed at the Slaviansky Bazaar hotel, and at once sent a man in a red cap to Gurov. Gurov went to see her, and no one in Moscow knew of it.

Once he was going to see her in this way on a winter morning (the messenger had come the evening before when he was out). With him walked his daughter, whom he wanted to take to school: it was on the way. Snow was falling in big wet flakes.

"It's three degrees above freezing-point, and yet it is snowing," said Gurov to 105 his daughter. "The thaw is only on the surface of the earth; there is quite a different temperature at a greater height in the atmosphere."

"And why are there no thunderstorms in the winter, father?"

He explained that, too. He talked, thinking all the while that he was going to see *her,* and no living soul knew of it, and probably never would know. He had two lives: one, open, seen and known by all who care to know, full of relative truth and of relative falsehood, exactly like the lives of his friends and acquaintances; and another life running its course in secret. And through some strange, perhaps accidental, conjunction of circumstances, everything that was essential, of interest and of value to him, everything in which he was sincere and did not deceive himself, everything that made the kernel of his life, was hidden from other people; and all that was false in him, the sheath in which he hid himself to conceal the truth—such, for instance, as his work in the bank, his discussions at the club, his "lower race," his presence with his wife at anniversary festivities—all that was open. And he judged of others by himself, not believing in what he saw, and always believing that every man had his real, most interesting life under the cover of secrecy and under the cover of night. All personal life rested on secrecy, and possibly it was partly on that account that civilised man was so nervously anxious that personal privacy should be respected.

After leaving his daughter at school, Gurov went on to the Slaviansky Bazaar. He took off his fur coat below, went upstairs, and softly knocked at the door. Anna Sergeyevna, wearing his favourite grey dress, exhausted by the journey and the suspense, had been expecting him since the evening before. She was pale; she looked at him, and did not smile, and he had hardly come in when she fell on his breast. Their kiss was slow and prolonged, as though they had not met for two years.

"Well, how are you getting on there?" he asked. "What news?"

"Wait; I'll tell you directly. . . . I can't talk." 110

She could not speak; she was crying. She turned away from him, and pressed her handkerchief to her eyes.

"Let her have her cry out. I'll sit down and wait," he thought, and he sat down in an arm-chair.

Then he rang and asked for tea to be brought him, and while he drank his tea she remained standing at the window with her back to him. She was crying from emotion, from the miserable consciousness that their life was so hard for them; they could only meet in secret, hiding themselves from people, like thieves! Was not their life shattered?

"Come, do stop!" he said.

115   It was evident to him that this love of theirs would not soon be over, that he could not see the end of it. Anna Sergeyevna grew more and more attached to him. She adored him, and it was unthinkable to say to her that it was bound to have an end some day; besides, she would not have believed it!

He went up to her and took her by the shoulders to say something affectionate and cheering, and at that moment he saw himself in the looking-glass.

His hair was already beginning to turn grey. And it seemed strange to him that he had grown so much older, so much plainer during the last few years. The shoulders on which his hands rested were warm and quivering. He felt compassion for this life, still so warm and lovely, but probably already not far from beginning to fade and wither like his own. Why did she love him so much? He always seemed to women different from what he was, and they loved in him not himself, but the man created by their imagination, whom they had been eagerly seeking all their lives; and afterwards, when they noticed their mistake, they loved him all the same. And not one of them had been happy with him. Time passed, he had made their acquaintance, got on with them, parted, but he had never once loved; it was anything you like, but not love.

And only now when his head was grey he had fallen properly, really in love—for the first time in his life.

Anna Sergeyevna and he loved each other like people very close and akin, like husband and wife, like tender friends; it seemed to them that fate itself had meant them for one another, and they could not understand why he had a wife and she a husband; and it was as though they were a pair of birds of passage, caught and forced to live in different cages. They forgave each other for what they were ashamed of in their past, they forgave everything in the present, and felt that this love of theirs had changed them both.

120   In moments of depression in the past he had comforted himself with any arguments that came into his mind, but now he no longer cared for arguments; he felt profound compassion, he wanted to be sincere and tender. . . .

"Don't cry, my darling," he said. "You've had your cry; that's enough. . . . Let us talk now, let us think of some plan."

Then they spent a long while taking counsel together, talked of how to avoid the necessity for secrecy, for deception, for living in different towns and not seeing each other for long at a time. How could they be free from this intolerable bondage?

"How? How?" he asked, clutching his head. "How?"

And it seemed as though in a little while the solution would be found, and then a new and splendid life would begin; and it was clear to both of them that they had still a long, long road before them, and that the most complicated and difficult part of it was only just beginning.

3

JOYCE CAROL OATES

The Lady with the Pet Dog

JOYCE CAROL OATES was born in 1938 in Lockport, New York, and educated at Syracuse University and the University of Wisconsin. Even as an undergraduate, Oates was a prolific writer, winning the 1959 *Mademoiselle* college fiction award for her short story "In the Old World." While she was a graduate student, Oates published stories in magazines such as *Cosmopolitan, Prairie Schooner,* and *The Literary Review.* She accepted her first teaching assignment at the University of Detroit and then moved to the University of Windsor in Ontario, where she taught and wrote for twelve years. Since 1978, she has been a member of the faculty at Princeton University. By any standards, Oates's literary productivity has been astonishing: she has published almost forty books, including more than a dozen novels and about one hundred short stories. She has also written several volumes of literary criticism, such as *New Haven, New Earth: The Visionary Experience in Literature* (1974). Oates's best-known novels include *A Garden of Earthly Delights* (1967), *Them* (1969), which won the National Book Award, *Wonderland* (1971), *Do with Me What You Will* (1973), *Childwold* (1976), *Angel of Light* (1981), *A Bloodsmoor Romance* (1982), *You Must Remember This* (1987), and *Black Water* (1992). Her short stories have been published in a wide range of magazines and collected in volumes such as *By the North Gate* (1963), *The Wheel of Love* (1970), *Marriages and Infidelities* (1972), *Nightside* (1977), *A Sentimental Education* (1980), *Last Days* (1984), and *Will You Always Love Me* (1996). "The Lady with the Pet Dog," reprinted from *Marriages and Infidelities,* describes a woman's attempt to redefine herself in a romantic affair.

I

Strangers parted as if to make way for him.

There he stood. He was there in the aisle, a few yards away, watching her.

She leaned forward at once in her seat, her hand jerked up to her face as if to ward off a blow—but then the crowd in the aisle hid him, he was gone. She pressed both hands against her cheeks. He was not there, she had imagined him.

"My God," she whispered.

5   She was alone. Her husband had gone out to the foyer to make a telephone call; it was intermission at the concert, a Thursday evening.

Now she saw him again, clearly. He was standing there. He was staring at her. Her blood rocked in her body, draining out of her head . . . she was going to faint. . . . They stared at each other. They gave no sign of recognition. Only when he took a step forward did she shake her head *no—no—keep away.* It was not possible.

When her husband returned, she was staring at the place in the aisle where her lover had been standing. Her husband leaned forward to interrupt that stare.

"What's wrong?" he said. "Are you sick?"

Panic rose in her in long shuddering waves. She tried to get to her feet, panicked at the thought of fainting here, and her husband took hold of her. She stood like an aged woman, clutching the seat before her.

10   At home he helped her up the stairs and she lay down. Her head was like a large piece of crockery that had to be held still, it was so heavy. She was still panicked. She felt it in the shallows of her face, behind her knees, in the pit of her stomach. It sickened her, it made her think of mucus, of something thick and gray congested inside her, stuck to her, that was herself and yet not herself—a poison.

She lay with her knees drawn up toward her chest, her eyes hotly open, while her husband spoke to her. She imagined that other man saying, *Why did you run away from me?* Her husband was saying other words. She tried to listen to them. He was going to call the doctor, he said, and she tried to sit up. "No, I'm all right now," she said quickly. The panic was like lead inside her, so thickly congested. How slow love was to drain out of her, how fluid and sticky it was inside her head!

Her husband believed her. No doctor. No threat. Grateful, she drew her husband down to her. They embraced, not comfortably. For years now they had not been comfortable together, in their intimacy and at a distance, and now they struggled gently as if the paces of this dance were too rigorous for them. It was something they might have known once, but had now outgrown. The panic in her thickened at this double betrayal: she drew her husband to her, she caressed him wildly, she shut her eyes to think about that other man.

A crowd of men and women parting, unexpectedly, and there he stood—there he stood—she kept seeing him, and yet her vision blotched at the memory. It had been finished between them, six months before, but he had come out here . . . and she had escaped him, now she was lying in her husband's arms, in his embrace, her face pressed against his. It was a kind of sleep, this love-making. She felt herself falling asleep, her body falling from her. Her eyes shut.

"I love you," her husband said fiercely, angrily.

15   She shut her eyes and thought of that other man, as if betraying him would give her life a center.

"Did I hurt you? Are you—?" her husband whispered.

Always this hot flashing of shame between them, the shame of her husband's near failure, the clumsiness of his love—

"You didn't hurt me," she said.

2

They had said good-by six months before. He drove her from Nantucket, where they had met, to Albany, New York, where she visited her sister. The hours of intimacy in the car had sealed something between them, a vow of silence and impersonality: she recalled the movement of the highways, the passing of other cars, the natural rhythms of the day hypnotizing her toward sleep while he drove. She trusted him, she could sleep in his presence. Yet she could not really fall asleep in spite of her exhaustion, and she kept jerking awake, frightened, to discover that nothing had changed—still the stranger who was driving her to Albany, still the highway, the sky, the antiseptic odor of the rented car, the sense of a rhythm behind the rhythm of the air that might unleash itself at any second. Everywhere on this highway, at this moment, there were men and women driving together, bonded together—what did that mean, to be together? What did it mean to enter into a bond with another person?

No, she did not really trust him; she did not really trust men. He would glance   20 at her with his small cautious smile and she felt a declaration of shame between them.

Shame.

In her head she rehearsed conversations. She said bitterly, "You'll be relieved when we get to Albany. Relieved to get rid of me." They had spent so many days talking, confessing too much, driven to a pitch of childish excitement, laughing together on the beach, breaking into that pose of laughter that seems to eradicate the soul, so many days of this that the silence of the trip was like the silence of a hospital—all these surface noises, these rattles and hums, but an interior silence, a befuddlement. She said to him in her imagination, "One of us should die." Then she leaned over to touch him. She caressed the back of his neck. She said, aloud, "Would you like me to drive for a while?"

They stopped at a picnic area where other cars were stopped—couples, families— and walked together, smiling at their good luck. He put his arm around her shoulders and she sensed how they were in a posture together, a man and a woman forming a posture, a figure, that someone might sketch and show to them. She said slowly, "I don't want to go back. . . ."

Silence. She looked up at him. His face was heavy with her words, as if she had pulled at his skin with her fingers. Children ran nearby and distracted him—yes, he was a father too, his children ran like that, they tugged at his skin with their light, busy fingers.

"Are you so unhappy?" he said.   25

"I'm not unhappy, back there. I'm nothing. There's nothing to me," she said.

They stared at each other. The sensation between them was intense, exhausting. She thought that this man was her savior, that he had come to her at a time in her life when her life demanded completion, an end, a permanent fixing of all that was troubled and shifting and deadly. And yet it was absurd to think this. No person could save another. So she drew back from him and released him.

A few hours later they stopped at a gas station in a small city. She went to the women's rest room, having to ask the attendant for a key, and when she came back her eye jumped nervously onto the rented car—why? did she think he might have driven off without her?—onto the man, her friend, standing in conversation with the young attendant. Her friend was as old as her husband, over forty, with lanky, sloping shoulders, a full body, his hair thick, a dark, burnished brown, a festive color that made her eye twitch a little—and his hands were always moving, always those rapid conversational circles, going nowhere, gestures that were at once a little aggressive and apologetic.

She put her hand on his arm, a claim. He turned to her and smiled and she felt that she loved him, that everything in her life had forced her to this moment and that she had no choice about it.

30   They sat in the car for two hours, in Albany, in the parking lot of a Howard Johnson's restaurant, talking, trying to figure out their past. There was no future. They concentrated on the past, the several days behind them, lit up with a hot, dazzling August sun, like explosions that already belonged to other people, to strangers. Her face was faintly reflected in the green-tinted curve of the windshield, but she could not have recognized that face. She began to cry; she told herself: *I am not here, this will pass, this is nothing.* Still, she could not stop crying. The muscles of her face were springy, like a child's, unpredictable muscles. He stroked her arms, her shoulders, trying to comfort her. "This is so hard . . . this is impossible . . ." he said. She felt panic for the world outside this car, all that was not herself and this man, and at the same time she understood that she was free of him, as people are free of other people, she would leave him soon, safely, and within a few days he would have fallen into the past, the impersonal past. . . .

"I'm so ashamed of myself!" she said finally.

She returned to her husband and saw that another woman, a shadow-woman, had taken her place—noiseless and convincing, like a dancer performing certain difficult steps. Her husband folded her in his arms and talked to her of his own loneliness, his worries about his business, his health, his mother, kept tranquilized and mute in a nursing home, and her spirit detached itself from her and drifted about the rooms of the large house she lived in with her husband, a shadow-woman delicate and imprecise. There was no boundary to her, no edge. Alone, she took hot baths and sat exhausted in the steaming water, wondering at her perpetual exhaustion. All that winter she noticed the limp, languid weight of her arms, her veins bulging slightly with the pressure of her extreme weariness. *This is fate,* she thought, to be here and not there, to be one person and not another, a certain man's wife and not the wife of another man. The long, slow pain of this certainty rose in her, but it never became clear, it was baffling and imprecise. She could not be serious about it; she kept congratulating herself on her own good luck, to have escaped so easily, to have freed herself. So much love had gone into the first several years of her marriage that there wasn't much left, now, for another man. . . . She was certain of that. But the bath water made her dizzy, all that perpetual heat, and one day in January she drew a razor blade lightly across the inside of her arm, near the elbow, to see what would happen.

Afterward she wrapped a small towel around it, to stop the bleeding. The towel soaked through. She wrapped a bath towel around that and walked through the empty rooms of her home, lightheaded, hardly aware of the stubborn seeping of blood. There was no boundary to her in this house, no precise limit. She could flow out like her own blood and come to no end.

She sat for a while on a blue love seat, her mind empty. Her husband telephoned her when he would be staying late at the plant. He talked to her always about his plans, his problems, his business friends, his future. It was obvious that he had a future. As he spoke she nodded to encourage him, and her heartbeat quickened with the memory of her own, personal shame, the shame of this man's particular, private wife. One evening at dinner he leaned forward and put his head in his arms and fell asleep, like a child. She sat at the table with him for a while, watching him. His hair had gone gray, almost white, at the temples—no one would guess that he was so quick, so careful a man, still fairly young about the eyes. She put her hand on his head, lightly, as if to prove to herself that he was real. He slept, exhausted.

One evening they went to a concert and she looked up to see her lover there, in 35 the crowded aisle, in this city, watching her. He was standing there, with his over-coat on, watching her. She went cold. That morning the telephone had rung while her husband was still home, and she had heard him answer it, heard him hang up—it must have been a wrong number—and when the telephone rang again, at 9:30, she had been afraid to answer it. She had left home to be out of the range of that ring-ing, but now, in this public place, in this busy auditorium, she found herself staring at that man, unable to make any sign to him, any gesture of recognition. . . .

He would have come to her but she shook her head. *No. Stay away.*

Her husband helped her out of the row of seats, saying, "Excuse us, please. Ex-cuse us," so that strangers got to their feet, quickly, alarmed, to let them pass. Was that woman about to faint? What was wrong?

At home she felt the blood drain slowly back into her head. Her husband em-braced her hips, pressing his face against her, in that silence that belonged to the ear-liest days of their marriage. She thought, *He will drive it out of me.* He made love to her and she was back in the auditorium again, sitting alone, now that the concert was over. The stage was empty; the heavy velvet curtains had not been drawn; the musi-cians' chairs were empty, everything was silent and expectant; in the aisle her lover stood and smiled at her—her husband was impatient. He was apart from her, work-ing on her, operating on her; and then, stricken, he whispered, "Did I hurt you?"

The telephone rang the next morning. Dully, sluggishly, she answered it. She rec-ognized his voice at once—that "Anna?" with its lifting of the second syllable, ques-tioning and apologetic and making its claim—"Yes, what do you want?" she said.

"Just to see you. Please—"   40

"I can't."

"Anna, I'm sorry, I didn't mean to upset you—"

"I can't see you."

"Just for a few minutes—I have to talk to you—"

"But why, why now? Why now?" she said.   45

She heard her voice rising, but she could not stop it. He began to talk again, drowning her out. She remembered his rapid conversation. She remembered his ges-tures, the witty energetic circling of his hands.

"Please don't hang up!" he cried.

"I can't—I don't want to go through it again—"

"I'm not going to hurt you. Just tell me how you are."

50   "Everything is the same."

"Everything is the same with me."

She looked up at the ceiling, shyly. "Your wife? Your children?"

"The same."

"Your son?"

55   "He's fine—"

"I'm glad to hear that. I—"

"Is it still the same with you, your marriage? Tell me what you feel. What are you thinking?"

"I don't know. . . ."

She remembered his intense, eager words, the movement of his hands, that impatient precise fixing of the air by his hands, the jabbing of his fingers.

60   "Do you love me?" he said.

She could not answer.

"I'll come over to see you," he said.

"No," she said.

What will come next, what will happen?

65   Flesh hardening on his body, aging. Shrinking. He will grow old, but not soft like her husband. They are two different types: he is nervous, lean, energetic, wise. She will grow thinner, as the tension radiates out from her backbone, wearing down her flesh. Her collarbones will jut out of her skin. Her husband, caressing her in their bed, will discover that she is another woman—she is not there with him—instead she is rising in an elevator in a downtown hotel, carrying a book as a prop, or walking quickly away from that hotel, her head bent and filled with secrets. Love, what to do with it? . . . Useless as moths' wings, as moths' fluttering. . . . She feels the flutterings of silky, crazy wings in her chest.

He flew out to visit her every several weeks, staying at a different hotel each time. He telephoned her, and she drove down to park in an underground garage at the very center of the city.

She lay in his arms while her husband talked to her, miles away, one body fading into another. He will grow old, his body will change, she thought, pressing her cheek against the back of one of these men. If it was her lover, they were in a hotel room: always the propped-up little booklet describing the hotel's many services, with color photographs of its cocktail lounge and dining room and coffee shop. Grow old, leave me, die, go back to your neurotic wife and your sad, ordinary children, she thought, but still her eyes closed gratefully against his skin and she felt how complete their silence was, how they had come to rest in each other.

"Tell me about your life here. The people who love you," he said, as he always did.

One afternoon they lay together for four hours. It was her birthday and she was intoxicated with her good fortune, this prize of the afternoon, this man in her arms! She was a little giddy, she talked too much. She told him about her parents, about her husband. . . . "They were all people I believed in, but it turned out wrong. Now, I believe in you. . . ." He laughed as if shocked by her words. She did not understand. Then she understood. "But I believe truly in you. I can't think of myself without you," she said. . . . He spoke of his wife, her ambitions, her intelligence, her use of the children against him, her use of his younger son's blindness, all of his words gentle and hypnotic and convincing in the late afternoon peace of this hotel room . . . and she felt the terror of laughter, threatening laughter. Their words, like their bodies, were aging.

She dressed quickly in the bathroom, drawing her long hair up around the back 70 of her head, fixing it as always, anxious that everything be the same. Her face was slightly raw, from his face. The rubbing of his skin. Her eyes were too bright, wearily bright. Her hair was blond but not so blond as it had been that summer in the white Nantucket air.

She ran water and splashed it on her face. She blinked at the water. Blind. Drowning. She thought with satisfaction that soon, soon, he would be back home, in that house on Long Island she had never seen, with that woman she had never seen, sitting on the edge of another bed, putting on his shoes. She wanted nothing except to be free of him. Why not be free? *Oh,* she thought suddenly, *I will follow you back and kill you. You and her and the little boy. What is there to stop me?*

She left him. Everyone on the street pitied her, that look of absolute zero.

3

A man and a child, approaching her. The sharp acrid smell of fish. The crashing of waves. Anna pretended not to notice the father with his son—there was something strange about them. That frank, silent intimacy, too gentle, the man's bare feet in the water and the boy a few feet away, leaning away from his father. He was about nine years old and still his father held his hand.

A small yipping dog, a golden dog, bounded near them.

Anna turned shyly back to her reading; she did not want to have to speak to 75 these neighbors. She saw the man's shadow falling over her legs, then over the pages of her book, and she had the idea that he wanted to see what she was reading. The dog nuzzled her; the man called him away.

She watched them walk down the beach. She was relieved that the man had not spoken to her.

She saw them in town later that day, the two of them brown-haired and patient, now wearing sandals, walking with that same look of care. The man's white shorts were soiled and a little baggy. His pullover shirt was a faded green. His face was broad, the cheekbones wide, spaced widely apart, the eyes stark in their sockets, as if they fastened onto objects for no reason, ponderous and edgy. The little boy's face was pale and sharp; his lips were perpetually parted.

Anna realized that the child was blind.

The next morning, early, she caught sight of them again. For some reason she went to the back door of her cottage. She faced the sea breeze eagerly. Her heart hammered. . . . She had been here, in her family's old house, for three days, alone, bitterly satisfied at being alone, and now it was a puzzle to her how her soul strained to fly outward, to meet with another person. She watched the man with his son, his cautious, rather stooped shoulders above the child's small shoulders.

The man was carrying something, it looked like a notebook. He sat on the sand, 80 not far from Anna's spot of the day before, and the dog rushed up to them. The child

approached the edge of the ocean, timidly. He moved in short jerky steps, his legs
stiff. The dog ran around him. Anna heard the child crying out a word that sounded
like "Ty"—it must have been the dog's name—and then the man joined in, his voice
heavy and firm.

"Ty—"

Anna tied her hair back with a yellow scarf and went down to the beach.

The man glanced around at her. He smiled. She stared past him at the waves. To
talk to him or not to talk—she had the freedom of that choice. For a moment she felt
that she had made a mistake, that the child and the dog would not protect her, that
behind this man's ordinary, friendly face there was a certain arrogant maleness—
then she relented, she smiled shyly.

"A nice house you've got there," the man said.

85   She nodded her thanks.

The man pushed his sunglasses up on his forehead. Yes, she recognized the eyes
of the day before—intelligent and nervous, the sockets pale, untanned.

"Is that your telephone ringing?" he said.

She did not bother to listen. "It's a wrong number," she said.

Her husband calling: she had left home for a few days, to be alone.

90   But the man, settling himself on the sand, seemed to misinterpret this. He smiled
in surprise, one corner of his mouth higher than the other. He said nothing. Anna
wondered: *What is he thinking?* The dog was leaping about her, panting against her
legs, and she laughed in embarrassment. She bent to pet it, grateful for its busyness.
"Don't let him jump up on you," the man said. "He's a nuisance."

The dog was a small golden retriever, a young dog. The blind child, standing
now in the water, turned to call the dog to him. His voice was shrill and impatient.

"Our house is the third one down—the white one," the man said.

She turned, startled. "Oh, did you buy it from Dr. Patrick? Did he die?"

"Yes, finally. . . ."

95   Her eyes wandered nervously over the child and the dog. She felt the nervous
beat of her heart out to the very tips of her fingers, the fleshy tips of her fingers: little hearts were there, pulsing. *What is he thinking?* The man had opened his notebook. He had a piece of charcoal and he began to sketch something.

Anna looked down at him. She saw the top of his head, his thick brown hair, the
freckles on his shoulders, the quick, deft movement of his hand. Upside down, Anna
herself being drawn. She smiled in surprise.

"Let me draw you. Sit down," he said.

She knelt awkwardly a few yards away. He turned the page of the sketch pad.
The dog ran to her and she sat, straightening out her skirt beneath her, flinching from
the dog's tongue. "Ty!" cried the child. Anna sat, and slowly the pleasure of the moment began to glow in her; her skin flushed with gratitude.

She sat there for nearly an hour. The man did not talk much. Back and forth the
dog bounded, shaking itself. The child came to sit near them, in silence. Anna felt
that she was drifting into a kind of trance while the man sketched her, half a dozen
rapid sketches, the surface of her face given up to him. "Where are you from?" the
man asked.

"Ohio. My husband lives in Ohio."

She wore no wedding band.

"Your wife—" Anna began.

"Yes?"

"Is she here?"

"Not right now."

She was silent, ashamed. She had asked an improper question. But the man did not seem to notice. He continued drawing her, bent over the sketch pad. When Anna said she had to go, he showed her the drawings—one after another of her, Anna, recognizably Anna, a woman in her early thirties, her hair smooth and flat across the top of her head, tied behind by a scarf. "Take the one you like best," he said, and she picked one of her with the dog in her lap, sitting very straight, her brows and eyes clearly defined, her lips girlishly pursed, the dog and her dress suggested by a few quick irregular lines.

"Lady with pet dog," the man said.

She spent the rest of that day reading, nearer her cottage. It was not really a cottage—it was a two-story house, large and ungainly and weathered. It was mixed up in her mind with her family, her own childhood, and she glanced up from her book, perplexed, as if waiting for one of her parents or her sister to come up to her. Then she thought of that man, the man with the blind child, the man with the dog, and she could not concentrate on her reading. Someone—probably her father—had marked a passage that must be important, but she kept reading and rereading it: *We try to discover in things, endeared to us on that account, the spiritual glamour which we ourselves have cast upon them; we are disillusioned, and learn that they are in themselves barren and devoid of the charm that they owed, in our minds, to the association of certain ideas. . . .*

She thought again of the man on the beach. She lay the book aside and thought of him: his eyes, his aloneness, his drawings of her.

They began seeing each other after that. He came to her front door in the   evening, without the child; he drove her into town for dinner. She was shy and extremely pleased. The darkness of the expensive restaurant released her; she heard herself chatter; she leaned forward and seemed to be offering her face up to him, listening to him. He talked about his work on a Long Island newspaper and she seemed to be listening to him, as she stared at his face, arranging her own face into the expression she had seen in that charcoal drawing. Did he see her like that, then?—girlish and withdrawn and patrician? She felt the weight of his interest in her, a force that fell upon her like a blow. A repeated blow. Of course he was married, he had children—of course she was married, permanently married. This flight from her husband was not important. She had left him before, to be alone, it was not important. Everything in her was slender and delicate and not important.

They walked for hours after dinner, looking at the other strollers, the weekend visitors, the tourists, the couples like themselves. Surely they were mistaken for a couple, a married couple. *This is the hour in which everything is decided,* Anna thought. They had both had several drinks and they talked a great deal. Anna found herself saying too much, stopping and starting giddily. She put her hand to her forehead, feeling faint.

"It's from the sun—you've had too much sun—" he said.

At the door to her cottage, on the front porch, she heard herself asking him if he would like to come in. She allowed him to lead her inside, to close the door. *This is not important,* she thought clearly, *he doesn't mean it, he doesn't love me, nothing will come of it.* She was frightened, yet it seemed to her necessary to give in; she had to leave Nantucket with that act completed, an act of adultery, an accomplishment she would take back to Ohio and to her marriage.

Later, incredibly, she heard herself asking: "Do you . . . do you love me?"

115   "You're so beautiful!" he said, amazed.

She felt this beauty, shy and glowing and centered in her eyes. He stared at her. In this large, drafty house, alone together, they were like accomplices, conspirators. She could not think: how old was she? which year was this? They had done something unforgivable together, and the knowledge of it was tugging at their faces. A cloud seemed to pass over her. She felt herself smiling shrilly.

Afterward, a peculiar raspiness, a dryness of breath. He was silent. She felt a strange, idle fear, a sense of the danger outside this room and this old, comfortable bed—a danger that would not recognize her as the lady in that drawing, the lady with the pet dog. There was nothing to say to this man, this stranger. She felt the beauty draining out of her face, her eyes fading.

"I've got to be alone," she told him.

He left, and she understood that she would not see him again. She stood by the window of the room, watching the ocean. A sense of shame overpowered her: it was smeared everywhere on her body, the smell of it, the richness of it. She tried to recall him, and his face was confused in her memory: she would have to shout to him across a jumbled space, she would have to wave her arms wildly. *You love me! You must love me!* But she knew he did not love her, and she did not love him; he was a man who drew everything up into himself, like all men, walking away, free to walk away, free to have his own thoughts, free to envision her body, all the secrets of her body. . . . And she lay down again in the bed, feeling how heavy this body had become, her insides heavy with shame, the very backs of her eyelids coated with shame.

120   "This is the end of one part of my life," she thought.

But in the morning the telephone rang. She answered it. It was her lover: they talked brightly and happily. She could hear the eagerness in his voice, the love in his voice, that same still, sad amazement—she understood how simple life was, there were no problems.

They spent most of their time on the beach, with the child and the dog. He joked and was serious at the same time. He said, once, "You have defined my soul for me," and she laughed to hide her alarm. In a few days it was time for her to leave. He got a sitter for the boy and took the ferry with her to the mainland, then rented a car to drive her up to Albany. She kept thinking: *Now something will happen. It will come to an end.* But most of the drive was silent and hypnotic. She wanted him to joke with her, to say again that she had defined his soul for him, but he drove fast, he was serious, she distrusted the hawkish look of his profile—she did not know him at all. At a gas station she splashed her face with cold water. Alone in the grubby little rest room, shaky and very much alone. In such places are women totally alone with their bodies. The body grows heavier, more evil, in such silence. . . . On the beach everything had been noisy with sunlight and gulls and waves; here, as if run to earth, everything was cramped and silent and dead.

She went outside, squinting. There he was, talking with the station attendant. She could not think as she returned to him whether she wanted to live or not.

She stayed in Albany for a few days, then flew home to her husband. He met her at the airport, near the luggage counter, where her three pieces of pale-brown luggage were brought to him on a conveyer belt, to be claimed by him. He kissed her on the cheek. They shook hands, a little embarrassed. She had come home again.

"How will I live out the rest of my life?" she wondered.   125

In January her lover spied on her: she glanced up and saw him, in a public place, in the DeRoy Symphony Hall. She was paralyzed with fear. She nearly fainted. In this faint she felt her husband's body, loving her, working its love upon her, and she shut her eyes harder to keep out the certainty of his love—sometimes he failed at loving her, sometimes he succeeded, it had nothing to do with her or her pity or her ten years of love for him, it had nothing to do with a woman at all. It was a private act accomplished by a man, a husband or a lover, in communion with his own soul, his manhood.

Her husband was forty-two years old now, growing slowly into middle age, getting heavier, softer. Her lover was about the same age, narrower in the shoulders, with a full, solid chest, yet lean, nervous. She thought, in her paralysis, of men and how they love freely and eagerly so long as their bodies are capable of love, love for a woman; and then, as love fades in their bodies, it fades from their souls and they become immune and immortal and ready to die.

Her husband was a little rough with her, as if impatient with himself. "I love you," he said fiercely, angrily. And then, ashamed, he said, "Did I hurt you? . . ."

"You didn't hurt me," she said.

Her voice was too shrill for their embrace.   130

While he was in the bathroom she went to her closet and took out that drawing of the summer before. There she was, on the beach at Nantucket, a lady with a pet dog, her eyes large and defined, the dog in her lap hardly more than a few snarls, a few coarse soft lines of charcoal . . . her dress smeared, her arms oddly limp . . . her hands not well drawn at all. . . . She tried to think: did she love the man who had drawn this? did he love her? The fever in her husband's body had touched her and driven her temperature up, and now she stared at the drawing with a kind of lust, fearful of seeing an ugly soul in that woman's face, fearful of seeing the face suddenly through her lover's eyes. She breathed quickly and harshly, staring at the drawing.

And so, the next day, she went to him at his hotel. She wept, pressing against him, demanding of him, "What do you want? Why are you here? Why don't you let me alone?" He told her that he wanted nothing. He expected nothing. He would not cause trouble.

"I want to talk about last August," he said.

"Don't—" she said.

135 She was hypnotized by his gesturing hands, his nervousness, his obvious agitation. He kept saying, "I understand. I'm making no claims upon you."

They became lovers again.

He called room service for something to drink and they sat side by side on his bed, looking through a copy of *The New Yorker,* laughing at the cartoons. It was so peaceful in this room, so complete. They were on a holiday. It was a secret holiday. Four-thirty in the afternoon, on a Friday, an ordinary Friday: a secret holiday.

"I won't bother you again," he said.

He flew back to see her again in March, and in late April. He telephoned her from his hotel—a different hotel each time—and she came down to him at once. She rose to him in various elevators, she knocked on the doors of various rooms, she stepped into his embrace, breathless and guilty and already angry with him, pleading with him. One morning in May, when he telephoned, she pressed her forehead against the doorframe and could not speak. He kept saying, "What's wrong? Can't you talk? Aren't you alone?" She felt that she was going insane. Her head would burst. Why, why did he love her, why did he pursue her? Why did he want her to die?

140 She went to him in the hotel room. A familiar room: had they been here before? "Everything is repeating itself. Everything is stuck," she said. He framed her face in his hands and said that she looked thinner—was she sick?—what was wrong? She shook herself free. He, her lover, looked about the same. There was a small, angry pimple on his neck. He stared at her, eagerly and suspiciously. Did she bring bad news?

"So you love me? You love me?" she asked.

"Why are you so angry?"

"I want to be free of you. The two of us free of each other."

"That isn't true—you don't want that—"

145 He embraced her. She was wild with that old, familiar passion for him, her body clinging to his, her arms not strong enough to hold him. Ah, what despair!—what bitter hatred she felt!—she needed this man for her salvation, he was all she had to live for, and yet she could not believe in him. He embraced her thighs, her hips, kissing her, pressing his warm face against her, and yet she could not believe in him, not really. She needed him in order to live, but he was not worth her love, he was not worth her dying. . . . She promised herself this: when she got back home, when she was alone, she would draw the razor more deeply across her arm.

The telephone rang and he answered it: a wrong number.

"Jesus," he said.

They lay together, still. She imagined their posture like this, the two of them one figure, one substance; and outside this room and this bed there was a universe of disjointed, separate things, blank things, that had nothing to do with them. She would not be Anna out there, the lady in the drawing. He would not be her lover.

"I love you so much . . ." she whispered.

150 "Please don't cry! We have only a few hours, please. . . ."

It was absurd, their clinging together like this. She saw them as a single figure in a drawing, their arms and legs entwined, their heads pressing mutely together.

Helpless substance, so heavy and warm and doomed. It was absurd that any human being should be so important to another human being. She wanted to laugh: a laugh might free them both.

She could not laugh.

Sometime later he said, as if they had been arguing, "Look. It's you. You're the one who doesn't want to get married. You lie to me—"

"Lie to you?"

"You love me but you won't marry me, because you want something left over— something not finished—all your life you can attribute your misery to me, to our not being married—you are using me—"

"Stop it! You'll make me hate you!" she cried.

"You can say to yourself that you're miserable because of *me*. We will never be married, you will never be happy, neither one of us will ever be happy—"

"I don't want to hear this!" she said.

She pressed her hands flatly against her face.

She went to the bathroom to get dressed. She washed her face and part of her body, quickly. The fever was in her, in the pit of her belly. She would rush home and strike a razor across the inside of her arm and free that pressure, that fever.

The impatient bulging of the veins: an ordeal over.

The demand of the telephone's ringing: that ordeal over.

The nuisance of getting the car and driving home in all that five o'clock traffic: an ordeal too much for a woman.

The movement of this stranger's body in hers: over, finished.

Now, dressed, a little calmer, they held hands and talked. They had to talk swiftly, to get all their news in: he did not trust the people who worked for him, he had faith in no one, his wife had moved to a textbook publishing company and was doing well, she had inherited a Ben Shahn painting from her father and wanted to "touch it up a little"—she was crazy!—his blind son was at another school, doing fairly well, in fact his children were all doing fairly well in spite of the stupid mistake of their parents' marriage—and what about her? what about her life? She told him in a rush the one thing he wanted to hear: that she lived with her husband lovelessly, the two of them polite strangers, sharing a bed, lying side by side in the night in that bed, bodies out of which souls had fled. There was no longer even any shame between them.

"And what about me? Do you feel shame with me still?" he asked.

She did not answer. She moved away from him and prepared to leave.

Then, a minute later, she happened to catch sight of his reflection in the bureau mirror—he was glancing down at himself, checking himself mechanically, impersonally, preparing also to leave. He too would leave this room: he too was headed somewhere else.

She stared at him. It seemed to her that in this instant he was breaking from her, the image of her lover fell free of her, breaking from her . . . and she realized that he existed in a dimension quite apart from her, a mysterious being. And suddenly, joyfully, she felt a miraculous calm. This man was her husband, truly—they were truly married, here in this room—they had been married haphazardly and accidentally for a long time. In another part of the city she had another husband, a "husband," but she had not betrayed that man, not really. This man, whom she loved above any other person in the world, above even her own self-pitying sorrow and her own life, was her truest lover, her destiny. And she did not hate him, she did not hate herself any longer; she did not wish to die; she was flooded with a strange certainty, a sense of gratitude, of pure selfless energy. It was obvious to her that she had, all along, been behaving correctly; out of instinct.

170   What triumph, to love like this in any room, anywhere, risking even the craziest of accidents!

"Why are you so happy? What's wrong?" he asked, startled. He stared at her. She felt the abrupt concentration in him, the focusing of his vision on her, almost a bitterness in his face, as if he feared her. What, was it beginning all over again? Their love beginning again, in spite of them? "How can you look so happy?" he asked. "We don't have any right to it. Is it because . . . ?"

"Yes," she said.

QUESTIONS FOR DISCUSSION AND WRITING

1. **Plot**   What are the advantages of Chekhov's linear plot structure? What are the advantages of Oates's cyclical plot structure? How do the conclusions of the two stories resolve the conflicts?

2. **Character**   How does Chekhov arrange exterior events to depict his protagonist? How does Oates juxtapose exterior events to develop her protagonist? How do Chekhov and Oates reveal the internal conflicts of their protagonists?

3. **Setting**   How are the plots of the two stories influenced by their initial setting in romantic seaside resorts? How do the attitudes toward marriage and divorce in nineteenth-century Russia and twentieth-century America affect the plot of the stories?

4. **Point of View**   How does the change from male protagonist (Chekhov) to female protagonist (Oates) affect the development of the conflict in the two stories? In what ways does the sex of the protagonist control the pace and point of view in each story?

5. **Theme**   How does the sentence "they still had a long, long road before them" comment on the plot and theme in Chekhov's story? How does the phrase "it was beginning all over again" comment on the plot and theme of Oates's story? Why are the differences implied by these statements important to understanding these two stories?

CHARACTER

Willa Cather's "Paul's Case"
Ellen Gilchrist's "Among the Mourners"

The characterization in these two stories illustrates the immense range of techniques available to writers of short fiction as they create their characters, especially their protagonists.

In the first few pages of her widely read story, Willa Cather creates Paul, her adolescent protagonist, using most of the established techniques of the traditional short story. Every aspect of Paul's exterior and inner reality is portrayed and analyzed. We have a complete description of his appearance and manner, his clothing, and his deportment. At the same time, Cather dramatizes Paul's personality, showing him in an emotionally charged conflict with others, letting us see him as they see him. That unfavorable impression is immediately challenged by a metaphorical comparison of Paul to a helpless cat being attacked by vicious dogs, developing our sympathy for Paul as victim.

However, Cather's most powerful technique for developing Paul as a character is direct exposition—a revelation of everything about Paul's motivation that the other characters in the story, including Paul himself, have no way of knowing, but that the authoritative narrator presents to the reader in thorough detail. We see both the poignant yearning after beauty that is an inherent part of Paul's nature and the disengagement from reality that will inevitably lead to his destruction. Paul has no choice because he cannot imagine having the freedom to choose.

The tone of the story grows directly out of the depiction of the protagonist. Although Cather is obviously sympathetic to this misunderstood and finally self-destructive boy, she does not allow that sympathy to mitigate the scrupulous objectivity with which she draws the fully rounded portrait. In every sense, we have comprehended Paul as his creator intends. We have his complete case laid out for us.

In Ellen Gilchrist's story, on the other hand, the characterization of the protagonist is almost completely indirect. We have no physical description of her, no authoritative outside exposition of motivation, no objective dramatization of the character in action. The first-person narrator in this story, an adolescent girl, is obviously so immature in her understanding of herself and others that we have to reinterpret everything she tells us in order to understand her and her experience. In other words, we finally see a very different character than the one the narrator thinks she is presenting.

We delight in the ironic, often comic discrepancy between the naive interpretation of self, others, and events that Aurora offers and our presumably mature response to that information. Her irritation with her parents, her jealousy of her little sister, and her tentative explorations of sexual intimacy seem to us temporary problems natural to her time in life. We are likely to believe that time will solve them. On the other hand, we cannot be certain of that—or indeed of anything about Aurora. Her choices are limitless. Her story is still unfolding; her character still forming. It is impossible to think in terms of Aurora's "case."

The characterizations of the protagonists in these two stories illustrate very different but equally rich pleasures that short fiction may produce. Cather's story gives us what life never provides: a certainty that we understand another human being completely, that we see the inevitability with which the fate of that person emerges from his revealed character. However, Gilchrist offers a character whom we must interpret. That interpretation grows out of our own experiences with life and is therefore less certain, more open to widely differing views. We have the pleasure of exploration rather than the comfort of knowing.

4

WILLA   CATHER

Paul's Case

WILLA CATHER (1873–1947) was born in Gore, Virginia, but grew up in Red Cloud, Nebraska, the setting for some of her best-known fiction. After graduating from the University of Nebraska, Cather moved to Pittsburgh, Pennsylvania, working first as a journalist and then as a high-school teacher of English and Latin. During this period she was able to publish some of her poetry and stories in magazines, especially *McClure's*. In 1906 Cather joined the editorial staff of *McClure's*, eventually becoming managing editor. With the successful publication of her first novel, *Alexander's Bridge* (1912), Cather resigned from her job to devote full time to her writing. Her next three novels, *O Pioneers!* (1913), *The Song of the Lark* (1915), and *My Antonia* (1918), concern her experiences on the Nebraska frontier. In her later novels, Cather abandoned her autobiographical experiences to write about historical material such as the struggles of early Roman Catholic missionaries during the Mexican War in *Death Comes for the Archbishop* (1927) and the lives of settlers in eighteenth-century Quebec in *Shadows on the Rock* (1931). Cather's short stories have been collected in several volumes. "Paul's Case," reprinted from *Youth and the Bright Medusa* (1932), describes a young boy's doomed attempts to fulfill his romantic fantasies.

It was Paul's afternoon to appear before the faculty of the Pittsburgh High School to account for his various misdemeanors. He had been suspended a week ago, and his father had called at the Principal's office and confessed his perplexity about his son. Paul entered the faculty room suave and smiling. His clothes were a trifle out-grown, and the tan velvet on the collar of his open overcoat was frayed and worn; but for all that there was something of a dandy about him, and he wore an opal pin in his neatly knotted black four-in-hand, and a red carnation in his buttonhole. This latter adornment the faculty somehow felt was not properly significant of the con-trite spirit befitting a boy under the ban of suspension.

Paul was tall for his age and very thin, with high, cramped shoulders and a nar-row chest. His eyes were remarkable for a certain hysterical brilliancy, and he con-tinually used them in a conscious, theatrical sort of way, peculiarly offensive in a boy. The pupils were abnormally large, as though he were addicted to belladonna, but there was a glassy glitter about them which that drug does not produce.

When questioned by the Principal as to why he was there, Paul stated, politely enough, that he wanted to come back to school. This was a lie, but Paul was quite accustomed to lying; found it, indeed, indispensable for overcoming friction. His teachers were asked to state their respective charges against him, which they did with such a rancor and aggrievedness as evinced that this was not a usual case. Disorder and impertinence were among the offenses named, yet each of his instructors felt that it was scarcely possible to put into words the real cause of the trouble, which lay in a sort of hysterically defiant manner of the boy's; in the contempt which they all knew he felt for them, and which he seemingly made not the least effort to conceal. Once, when he had been making a synopsis of a paragraph at the blackboard, his English teacher had stepped to his side and attempted to guide his hand. Paul had started back with a shudder and thrust his hands violently behind him. The aston-ished woman could scarcely have been more hurt and embarrassed had he struck at her. The insult was so involuntary and definitely personal as to be unforgettable. In one way and another, he had made all his teachers, men and women alike, conscious of the same feeling of physical aversion. In one class he habitually sat with his hand shading his eyes; in another he always looked out of the window during the recita-tion; in another had made a running commentary on the lecture, with humorous intent.

His teachers felt this afternoon that his whole attitude was symbolized by his shrug and his flippantly red carnation flower, and they fell upon him without mercy, his English teacher leading the pack. He stood through it smiling, his pale lips parted over his white teeth. (His lips were continually twitching, and he had a habit of rais-ing his eyebrows that was contemptuous and irritating to the last degree.) Older boys than Paul had broken down and shed tears under that ordeal, but his set smile did not once desert him, and his only sign of discomfort was the nervous trembling of the fingers that toyed with the buttons of his overcoat, and an occasional jerking of the other hand which held his hat. Paul was always smiling, always glancing about him, seeming to feel that people might be watching him and trying to detect some-thing. This conscious expression, since it was as far as possible from boyish mirth-fulness, was usually attributed to insolence or "smartness."

5   As the inquisition proceeded, one of his instructors repeated an impertinent re-mark of the boy's, and the Principal asked him whether he thought that a courteous speech to make to a woman. Paul shrugged his shoulders slightly and his eyebrows twitched.

"I don't know," he replied. "I didn't mean to be polite or impolite, either. I guess it's a sort of way I have, of saying things regardless."

The Principal asked him whether he didn't think that a way it would be well to get rid of. Paul grinned and said he guessed so. When he was told that he could go, he bowed gracefully and went out. His bow was like a repetition of the scandalous red carnation.

10   His teachers were in despair, and his drawing master voiced the feeling of them all when he declared there was something about the boy which none of them under-stood. He added: "I don't really believe that smile of his comes altogether from in-solence; there's something sort of haunted about it. The boy is not strong for one thing. There is something wrong about the fellow."

The drawing master had come to realize that, in looking at Paul, one saw only his white teeth and the forced animation of his eyes. One warm afternoon the boy had gone to sleep at his drawing-board, and his master had noted with amazement what a white, blue-veined face it was; drawn and wrinkled like an old man's about the eyes, the lips twitching even in his sleep.

His teachers left the building dissatisfied and unhappy; humiliated to have felt so vindictive toward a mere boy, to have uttered this feeling in cutting terms, and to have set each other on, as it were, in the gruesome game of intemperate reproach. One of them remembered having seen a miserable street cat set at bay by a ring of tormentors.

As for Paul, he ran down the hill whistling the Soldiers' Chorus from *Faust,* looking behind him now and then to see whether some of his teachers were not there to witness his light-heartedness. As it was now late in the afternoon and Paul was on duty that evening as usher at Carnegie Hall, he decided that he would not go home to supper. When he reached the concert hall, the doors were not yet open. It was chilly outside, and he decided to go up into the picture gallery—always deserted at this hour—where there were some of Raffelli's gay studies of Paris streets and an airy blue Venetian scene or two that always exhilarated him. He was delighted to find no one in the gallery but the old guard, who sat in the corner, a newspaper on his knee, a black patch over one eye and the other closed. Paul possessed himself of the place and walked confidently up and down, whistling under his breath. After a while he sat down before a blue Rico and lost himself. When he bethought him to look at his watch, it was after seven o'clock, and he rose with a start and ran downstairs, making a face at Augustus Caesar, peering out from the cast-room, and an evil ges-ture at the Venus of Milo as he passed her on the stairway.

When Paul reached the ushers' dressing-room, half a dozen boys were there al-ready, and he began excitedly to tumble into his uniform. It was one of the few that at all approached fitting, and Paul thought it very becoming—though he knew the tight, straight coat accentuated his narrow chest, about which he was exceedingly sensitive. He was always excited while he dressed, twanging all over to the tuning of the strings and the preliminary flourishes of the horns in the music-room; but tonight he seemed quite beside himself, and he teased and plagued the boys until, telling him that he was crazy, they put him down on the floor and sat on him.

Somewhat calmed by his suppression, Paul dashed out to the front of the house to seat the early comers. He was a model usher. Gracious and smiling he ran up and down the aisles. Nothing was too much trouble for him; he carried messages and brought programs as though it were his greatest pleasure in life, and all the people in his section thought him a charming boy, feeling that he remembered and admired them. As the house filled, he grew more and more vivacious and animated, and the color came to his cheeks and lips. It was very much as though this were a great reception and Paul were the host. Just as the musicians came out to take their places, his English teacher arrived with checks for the seats which a prominent manufacturer had taken for the season. She betrayed some embarrassment when she handed Paul the tickets, and a *hauteur* which subsequently made her feel very foolish. Paul was startled for a moment, and had the feeling of wanting to put her out; what business had she here among all these fine people and gay colors? He looked her over and decided that she was not appropriately dressed and must be a fool to sit downstairs in such togs. The tickets had probably been sent to her out of kindness, he reflected, as he put down a seat for her, and she had about as much right to sit there as he had.

When the symphony began, Paul sank into one of the rear seats with a long sigh of relief, and lost himself as he had done before the Rico. It was not that symphonies, as such, meant anything in particular to Paul, but the first sight of the instruments seemed to free some hilarious spirit within him; something that struggled there like the Genius in the bottle found by the Arab fisherman. He felt a sudden zest of life; the lights danced before his eyes and the concert hall blazed into unimaginable splendor. When the soprano soloist came on, Paul forgot even the nastiness of his teacher's being there, and gave himself up to the peculiar intoxication such personages always had for him. The soloist chanced to be a German woman, by no means in her first youth, and the mother of many children; but she wore a satin gown and a tiara, and she had that indefinable air of achievement, that world-shine upon her, which always blinded Paul to any possible defects.

After a concert was over, Paul was often irritable and wretched until he got to   15
sleep—and tonight he was even more than usually restless. He had the feeling of not being able to let down; of its being impossible to give up his delicious excitement which was the only thing that could be called living at all. During the last number he withdrew and, after hastily changing his clothes in the dressing-room, slipped out to the side door where the singer's carriage stood. Here he began pacing rapidly up and down the walk, waiting to see her come out.

Over yonder the Schenley, in its vacant stretch, loomed big and square through the fine rain, the windows of its twelve stories glowing like those of a lighted cardboard house under a Christmas tree. All the actors and singers of any importance stayed there when they were in Pittsburgh, and a number of the big manufacturers of the place lived there in the winter. Paul had often hung about the hotel, watching the people go in and out, longing to enter and leave schoolmasters and dull care behind him forever.

At last the singer came out, accompanied by the conductor, who helped her into her carriage and closed the door with a cordial *auf wiedersehen*—which set Paul to wondering whether she were not an old sweetheart of his. Paul followed the carriage over to the hotel, walking so rapidly as not to be far from the entrance when the singer alighted and disappeared behind the swinging glass doors which were opened by a Negro in a tall hat and a long coat. In the moment that the door was ajar, it seemed to Paul that he, too, entered. He seemed to feel himself go after her up the steps, into the warm, lighted building, into an exotic, a tropical world of shiny, glistening surfaces and basking ease. He reflected upon the mysterious dishes that were brought into the dining-room, the green bottles in buckets of ice, as he had seen them in the supper-party pictures of the Sunday supplement. A quick gust of wind brought the rain down with sudden vehemence, and Paul was startled to find that he was still outside in the slush of the gravel driveway; that his boots were letting in the water and his scanty overcoat was clinging wet about him; that the lights in front of the concert hall were out, and that the rain was driving in sheets between him and the orange glow of the windows above him. There it was, what he wanted—tangibly before him, like the fairy world of a Christmas pantomime; as the rain beat in his face, Paul wondered whether he were destined always to shiver in the black night outside, looking up at it.

He turned and walked reluctantly toward the car tracks. The end had to come sometime; his father in his night-clothes at the top of the stairs, explanations that did not explain, hastily improvised fictions that were forever tripping him up, his upstairs room and its horrible yellow wallpaper, the creaking bureau with the greasy plush collar-box, and over his painted wooden bed the pictures of George Washington and John Calvin, and the framed motto, 'Feed my Lambs,' which had been worked in red worsted by his mother, whom Paul could not remember.

Half an hour later, Paul alighted from the Negley Avenue car and went slowly down one of the side streets off the main thoroughfare. It was a highly respectable street, where all the houses were exactly alike, and where business men of moderate means begot and reared large families of children, all of whom went to Sabbath School and learned the shorter catechism, and were interested in arithmetic; all of whom were as exactly alike as their homes, and of a piece of the monotony in which they lived. Paul never went up Cordelia Street without a shudder of loathing. His home was next to the house of the Cumberland minister. He approached it tonight with the nerveless sense of defeat, the hopeless feeling of sinking back forever into ugliness and commonness that he had always had when he came home. The moment he turned into Cordelia Street he felt the waters close above his head. After each of these orgies of living, he experienced all the physical depression which follows a debauch; the loathing of respectable beds, of common food, of a house permeated by kitchen odors; a shuddering repulsion for the flavorless, colorless mass of every-day existence; a morbid desire for cool things and soft lights and fresh flowers.

20   The nearer he approached the house, the more absolutely unequal Paul felt to the sight of it all: his ugly sleeping chamber; the old bathroom with the grimy zinc tub, the cracked mirror, the dripping spigots; his father, at the top of the stairs, his hairy legs sticking out from his nightshirt, his feet thrust into carpet slippers. He was

so much later than usual that there would certainly be enquiries and reproaches. Paul stopped short before the door. He felt that he could not be accosted by his father tonight; that he could not toss again on that miserable bed. He would not go in. He would tell his father that he had no carfare, and it was raining so hard he had gone home with one of the boys and stayed all night.

Meanwhile, he was wet and cold. He went around to the back of the house and tried one of the basement windows, found it open, and raised it cautiously, and scrambled down the cellar wall to the floor. There he stood, holding his breath, terrified by the noise he had made; but the floor above him was silent, and there was no creak on the stairs. He found a soap-box, and carried it over to the soft ring of light that streamed from the furnace door, and sat down. He was horribly afraid of rats, so he did not try to sleep, but sat looking distrustfully at the dark, still terrified lest he might have awakened his father.

In such reactions, after one of the experiences which made days and nights out of the dreary blanks of the calendar, when his senses were deadened, Paul's head was always singularly clear. Suppose his father had heard him getting in at the window and had come down and shot him for a burglar? Then, again, suppose his father had come down, pistol in hand, and he had cried out in time to save himself, and his father had been horrified to think how nearly he had killed him? Then again, suppose a day should come when his father would remember that night, and wish there had been no warning cry to stay his hand? With this last supposition Paul entertained himself until daybreak.

The following Sunday was fine; the sodden November chill was broken by the last flash of autumnal summer. In the morning Paul had to go to church and Sabbath School, as always. On seasonable Sunday afternoons the burghers of Cordelia Street usually sat out on their front "stoops," and talked to their neighbors on the next stoop, or called to those across the street in neighborly fashion. The men sat placidly on gay cushions placed upon the steps that led down to the sidewalk, while the women, in their Sunday "waists," sat in rockers on the cramped porches, pretending to be greatly at their ease. The children played in the streets; there were so many of them that the place resembled the recreation grounds of a kindergarten. The men on the steps, all in their shirt-sleeves, their vests unbuttoned, sat with their legs well apart, their stomachs comfortably protruding, and talked of the prices of things, or told anecdotes of the sagacity of their various chiefs and overlords. They occasionally looked over the multitude of squabbling children, listened affectionately to their high-pitched, nasal voices, smiling to see their own proclivities reproduced in their offspring, and interspersed their legends of the iron kings with remarks about their sons' progress at school, their grades in arithmetic, and the amounts they had saved in their toy banks.

On this last Sunday of November, Paul sat all afternoon on the lowest step of his "stoop," staring into the street, while his sisters, in their rockers, were talking to the minister's daughters next door about how many shirtwaists they had made in the last week, and how many waffles someone had eaten at the last church supper. When the weather was warm, and his father was in a particularly jovial frame of mind the girls made lemonade, which was always brought out in a red-glass pitcher, ornamented with forget-me-nots in blue enamel. This the girls thought very fine, and the neighbors joked about the suspicious color of the pitcher.

25   Today Paul's father, on the top step, was talking to a young man who shifted a restless baby from knee to knee. He happened to be the young man who was daily held up to Paul as a model, and after whom it was his father's dearest hope that he would pattern. This young man was of a ruddy complexion, with a compressed, red mouth, and faded, nearsighted eyes, over which he wore thick spectacles, with gold bows that curved about his ears. He was clerk to one of the magnates of a great steel corporation, and was looked upon in Cordelia Street as a young man with a future. There was a story that, some five years ago—he was now barely twenty-six—he had been a trifle "dissipated," but in order to curb his appetites and save the loss of time and strength that a sowing of wild oats might have entailed, he had taken his chief's advice, oft reiterated to his employees, and at twenty-one had married the first woman whom he could persuade to share his fortunes. She happened to be an angular schoolmistress, much older than he, who also wore thick glasses, and who had now borne him four children, all nearsighted like herself.

The young man was relating how his chief, now cruising in the Mediterranean, kept in touch with all the details of the business, arranging his office hours on his yacht just as though he were at home, and "knocking off work enough to keep two stenographers busy." His father told, in turn, the plan his corporation was considering, of putting in an electric railway plant at Cairo. Paul snapped his teeth; he had an awful apprehension that they might spoil it all before he got there. Yet he rather liked to hear these legends of the iron kings, that were told and retold on Sundays and holidays; these stories of palaces in Venice, yachts on the Mediterranean, and high play at Monte Carlo appealed to his fancy, and he was interested in the triumphs of cash-boys who had become famous, though he had no mind for the cash-boy stage.

After supper was over, and he had helped to dry the dishes, Paul nervously asked his father whether he could go to George's to get some help in his geometry, and still more nervously asked for carfare. This latter request he had to repeat, as his father, on principle, did not like to hear requests for money, whether much or little. He asked Paul whether he could not go to some boy who lived nearer, and told him that he ought not to leave his school work until Sunday; but he gave him the dime. He was not a poor man, but he had a worthy ambition to come up in the world. His only reason for allowing Paul to usher was that he thought a boy ought to be earning a little.

Paul bounded upstairs, scrubbed the greasy odor of the dishwater from his hands with the ill-smelling soap he hated, and then shook over his fingers a few drops of violet water from the bottle he kept hidden in his drawer. He left the house with his geometry conspicuously under his arm, and the moment he got out of Cordelia Street and boarded a downtown car, he shook off the lethargy of two deadening days, and began to live again.

The leading juvenile of the permanent stock company which played at one of the downtown theaters was an acquaintance of Paul's and the boy had been invited to drop in at the Sunday-night rehearsals whenever he could. For more than a year Paul had spent every available moment loitering about Charley Edwards's dressing-room. He had won a place among Edwards's following not only because the young actor, who could not afford to employ a dresser, often found him useful, but because he recognized in Paul something akin to what churchmen term "vocation."

It was at the theater and at Carnegie Hall that Paul really lived; the rest was but a sleep and a forgetting. This was Paul's fairy tale, and it had for him all the allurement of a secret love. The moment he inhaled the gassy, painty, dusty odor behind the scenes, he breathed like a prisoner set free, and felt within him the possibility of doing or saying splendid, brilliant things. The moment the cracked orchestra beat out the overture from *Martha,* or jerked at the serenade from *Rigoletto,* all stupid and ugly things slid from him, and his senses were deliciously, yet delicately fired.

Perhaps it was because, in Paul's world, the natural nearly always wore the guise of ugliness, that a certain element of artificiality seemed to him necessary in beauty. Perhaps it was because his experience of life elsewhere was so full of Sabbath-School picnics, petty economies, wholesome advice as to how to succeed in life, and the unescapable odors of cooking, that he found this existence so alluring, these smartly clad men and women so attractive, that he was so moved by these starry apple orchards that bloomed perennially under the limelight. It would be difficult to put it strongly enough how convincingly the stage entrance of the theater was for Paul the actual portal of Romance. Certainly none of the company ever suspected it, least of all Charley Edwards. It was very like the old stories that used to float about London of fabulously rich Jews, who had subterranean halls, with palms, and fountains, and soft lamps and richly appareled women who never saw the disenchanting light of London day. So, in the midst of that smoke-palled city, enamored of figures and grimy oil, Paul had his secret temple, his wishing-carpet, his bit of blue-and-white Mediterranean shore bathed in perpetual sunshine.

Several of Paul's teachers had a theory that his imagination had been perverted by garish fiction; but the truth was he scarcely ever read at all. The books at home were not such as would either tempt or corrupt a youthful mind, and as for reading the novels that some of his friends urged upon him—well, he got what he wanted much more quickly from music; any sort of music, from an orchestra to a barrel-organ. He needed only the spark, the indescribable thrill that made his imagination master of his senses, and he could make plots and pictures enough of his own. It was equally true that he was not stage-struck—not, at any rate, in the usual acceptation of the expression. He had no desire to become an actor, any more than he had to become a musician. He felt no necessity to do any of these things; what he wanted was to see, to be in the atmosphere, float on the wave of it, to be carried out, blue league after league, away from everything.

After a night behind the scenes, Paul found the schoolroom more than ever repulsive; the bare floors and naked walls; the prosy men who never wore frock coats, or violets in their buttonholes; the women with their dull gowns, shrill voices, and pitiful seriousness about prepositions that govern the dative. He could not bear to have the other pupils think, for a moment, that he took these people seriously; he must convey to them that he considered it all trivial, and was there only by way of a joke, anyway. He had autographed pictures of all the members of the stock company which he showed his classmates, telling them the most incredible stories of his familiarity with these people, of his acquaintance with the soloists who came to Carnegie Hall, his suppers with them and the flowers he sent them. When these stories lost their effect, and his audience grew listless, he would bid all the boys goodbye, announcing that he was going to travel for a while; going to Naples, to California, to Egypt. Then, next Monday, he would slip back, conscious and nervously smiling; his sister was ill, and he would have to defer his voyage until spring.

Matters went steadily worse with Paul at school. In the itch to let his instructors know how heartily he despised them, and how thoroughly he was appreciated elsewhere, he mentioned once or twice that he had no time to fool with theorems; adding—with a twitch of the eyebrows and a touch of that nervous bravado which so perplexed them—that he was helping the people down at the stock company; they were old friends of his.

35   The upshot of the matter was that the Principal went to Paul's father, and Paul was taken out of school and put to work. The manager at Carnegie Hall was told to get another usher in his stead; the doorkeeper at the theater was warned not to admit him to the house; and Charley Edwards remorsefully promised the boy's father not to see him again.

The members of the stock company were vastly amused when some of Paul's stories reached them—especially the women. They were hard-working women, most of them supporting indolent husbands or brothers, and they laughed rather bitterly at having stirred the boy to such fervid and florid inventions. They agreed with the faculty and with his father, that Paul's was a bad case.

The east-bound train was plowing through a January snowstorm; the dull dawn was beginning to show grey when the engine whistled a mile out of Newark. Paul started up from the seat where he had lain curled in uneasy slumber, rubbed the breath-misted window-glass with his hand, and peered out. The snow was whirling in curling eddies above the white bottom lands, and the drifts lay already deep in the fields and along the fences, while here and there the tall dead grass and dried weed stalks protruded black above it. Lights shone from the scattered houses, and a gang of laborers who stood beside the track waved their lanterns.

Paul had slept very little, and he felt grimy and uncomfortable. He had made the all-night journey in a day coach because he was afraid if he took a Pullman he might be seen by some Pittsburgh business man who had noticed him in Denny and Carson's office. When the whistle woke him, he clutched quickly at his breast pocket, glancing about him with an uncertain smile. But the little, clay-bespattered Italians were still sleeping, the slatternly women across the aisle were in openmouthed oblivion, and even the crumby, crying babies were for the time stilled. Paul settled back to struggle with his impatience as best he could.

When he arrived at the Jersey City station, he hurried through his breakfast, manifestly ill at ease and keeping a sharp eye about him. After he reached the Twenty-Third Street station, he consulted a cabman, and had himself driven to a men's furnishing establishment which was just opening for the day. He spent upward of two hours there, buying with endless reconsidering and great care. His new street suit he put on in the fitting-room; the frock coat and dress clothes he had bundled into the cab with his new shirts. Then he drove to a hatter's and a shoe house. His next errand was at Tiffany's, where he selected silver-mounted brushes and a scarf-pin. He would not wait to have his silver marked, he said. Lastly, he stopped at a trunk shop on Broadway, and had his purchases packed into various traveling-bags.

It was a little after one o'clock when he drove up to the Waldorf, and, after set-tling with the cabman, went into the office. He registered from Washington; said his mother and father had been abroad, and that he had come down to await the arrival of their steamer. He told his story plausibly and had no trouble, since he offered to pay for them in advance, in engaging his rooms; a sleeping-room, sitting-room, and bath. 40

Not once, but a hundred times Paul had planned his entry into New York. He had gone over every detail of it with Charley Edwards, and in his scrapbook at home there were pages of description about New York hotels, cut from the Sunday papers.

When he was shown to his sitting-room on the eighth floor, he saw at a glance that everything was as it should be; there was but one detail in his mental picture that the place did not realize, so he rang for the bell-boy and sent him down for flowers. He moved about nervously until the boy returned, putting away his new linen and fingering it delightedly as he did so. When the flowers came, he put them hastily into water, and then tumbled into a hot bath. Presently he came out of his white bath-room, resplendent in his new silk underwear, and playing with the tassels of his red robe. The snow was whirling so fiercely outside his windows that he could scarcely see across the street; but within, the air was deliciously soft and fragrant. He put the violets and jonquils on the taboret beside the couch, and threw himself down with a long sigh, covering himself with a Roman blanket. He was thoroughly tired; he had been in such haste, he had stood up to such a strain, covered so much ground in the last twenty-four hours, that he wanted to think how it had all come about. Lulled by the sound of the wind, the warm air, and the cool fragrance of the flowers, he sank into deep, drowsy retrospection.

It had been wonderfully simple; when they had shut him out of the theater and concert hall, when they had taken away his bone, the whole thing was virtually de-termined. The rest was a mere matter of opportunity. The only thing that at all sur-prised him was his own courage—for he realized well enough that he had always been tormented by fear, a sort of apprehensive dread which, of late years, as the meshes of the lies he had told closed about him, had been pulling the muscles of his body tighter and tighter. Until now, he could not remember a time when he had not been dreading something. Even when he was a little boy, it was always there—behind him, or before, or on either side. There had always been the shadowed cor-ner, the dark place into which he dared not look, but from which something seemed always to be watching him—and Paul had done things that were not pretty to watch, he knew.

But now he had a curious sense of relief, as though he had at last thrown down the gauntlet to the thing in the corner.

Yet it was but a day since he had been sulking in the traces; but yesterday after-noon that he had been sent to the bank with Denny and Carson's deposit, as usual—but this time he was instructed to leave the book to be balanced. There was above two thousand dollars in checks, and nearly a thousand in the banknotes which he had 45 taken from the book and quietly transferred to his pocket. At the bank he had made out a new deposit slip. His nerves had been steady enough to permit of his returning to the office, where he had finished his work and asked for a full day's holiday tomorrow, Saturday, giving a perfectly reasonable pretext. The bank book, he knew, would not be returned before Monday or Tuesday, and his father would be out of town for the next week. From the time he slipped the banknotes into his pocket until he boarded the night train for New York, he had not known a moment's hesitation.

How astonishingly easy it had all been; here he was, the thing done; and this time there would be no awakening, no figure at the top of the stairs. He watched the snowflakes whirling by his window until he fell asleep.

When he awoke, it was four o'clock in the afternoon. He bounded up with a start; one of his precious days gone already! He spent nearly an hour in dressing, watching every stage of his toilet carefully in the mirror. Everything was quite perfect; he was exactly the kind of boy he had always wanted to be.

When he went downstairs, Paul took a carriage and drove up Fifth Avenue toward the Park. The snow had somewhat abated; carriages and tradesmen's wagons were hurrying soundlessly to and fro in the winter twilight; boys in woolen mufflers were shoveling off the doorsteps; the Avenue stages made fine spots of color against the white street. Here and there on the corners whole flower gardens bloomed behind glass windows, against which the snowflakes stuck and melted; violets, roses, carnations, lilies-of-the-valley—somehow vastly more lovely and alluring that they blossomed thus unnaturally in the snow. The Park itself was a wonderful stage winterpiece.

When he returned, the pause of the twilight had ceased, and the tune of the streets had changed. The snow was falling faster, lights streamed from the hotels that reared their many stories fearlessly up into the storm, defying the raging Atlantic winds. A long, black stream of carriages poured down the Avenue, intersected here and there by other streams, tending horizontally. There were a score of cabs about the entrance of his hotel, and his driver had to wait. Boys in livery were running in and out of the awning stretched across the sidewalk, up and down the red velvet carpet laid from the door to the street. Above, about, within it all, was the rumble and roar, the hurry and toss of thousands of human beings as hot for pleasure as himself, and on every side of him towered the glaring affirmation of the omnipotence of wealth.

50   The boy set his teeth and drew his shoulders together in a spasm of realization; the plot of all dramas, the text of all romances, the nerve-stuff of all sensations was whirling about him like the snowflakes. He burnt like a fagot in a tempest.

When Paul came down to dinner, the music of the orchestra floated up the elevator shaft to greet him. As he stepped into the thronged corridor, he sank back into one of the chairs against the wall to get his breath. The lights, the chatter, the perfumes, the bewildering medley of color—he had, for a moment, the feeling of not being able to stand it. But only for a moment; these were his own people, he told himself. He went slowly about the corridors, through the writing-rooms, smoking-rooms, reception-rooms, as though he were exploring the chambers of an enchanted palace, built and peopled for him alone.

When he reached the dining-room he sat down at a table near a window. The flowers, the white linen, the many-colored wine-glasses, the gay toilettes of the women, the low popping of corks, the undulating repetitions of the "Blue Danube" from the orchestra, all flooded Paul's dream with bewildering radiance. When the roseate tinge of his champagne was added—that cold, precious, bubbling stuff that creamed and foamed in his glass—Paul wondered that there were honest men in the world at all. This was what all the world was fighting for, he reflected; this was what all the struggle was about. He doubted the reality of his past. Had he ever known a place called Cordelia Street, a place where fagged-looking business men boarded the early car? Mere rivets in a machine they seemed to Paul—sickening men, with combings of children's hair always hanging to their coats, and the smell of cooking in their clothes. Cordelia Street—Ah, that belonged to another time and country! Had he not always been thus, had he not sat here night after night, from as far back as he could remember, looking pensively over just such shimmering textures, and slowly twirling the stem of a glass like this one between his thumb and middle finger? He rather thought he had.

He was not in the least abashed or lonely. He had no especial desire to meet or to know any of these people; all he demanded was the right to look on and conjecture, to watch the pageant. The mere stage properties were all he contended for. Nor was he lonely later in the evening, in his loge at the Opera. He was entirely rid of his nervous misgivings, of his forced aggressiveness, of the imperative desire to show himself different from his surroundings. He felt now that his surroundings explained him. Nobody questioned the purple; he had only to wear it passively. He had only to glance down at his dress coat to reassure himself that here it would be impossible for anyone to humiliate him.

He found it hard to leave his beautiful sitting-room to go to bed that night, and sat long watching the raging storm from his turret window. When he went to sleep, it was with the lights turned on in his bedroom; partly because of his old timidity, and partly so that, if he should wake in the night, there would be no wretched moment of doubt, no horrible suspicion of yellow wallpaper, or of Washington and Calvin above his bed.

On Sunday morning the city was practically snowbound. Paul breakfasted late, 55 and in the afternoon he fell in with a wild San Francisco boy, a freshman at Yale, who said he had run down for a "little flyer" over Sunday. The young man offered to show Paul the night side of the town, and the two boys went off together after dinner, not returning to the hotel until seven o'clock the next morning. They had started out in the confiding warmth of a champagne friendship, but their parting in the elevator was singularly cool. The freshman pulled himself together to make his train, and Paul went to bed. He awoke at two o'clock in the afternoon, very thirsty and dizzy, and rang for ice-water, coffee, and the Pittsburgh papers.

On the part of the hotel management, Paul excited no suspicion. There was this to be said for him, that he wore his spoils with dignity and in no way made himself conspicuous. His chief greediness lay in his ears and eyes, and his excesses were not offensive ones. His dearest pleasures were the grey winter twilights in his sitting-room; his quiet enjoyment of his flowers, his clothes, his wide divan, his cigarette, and his sense of power. He could not remember a time when he had felt so at peace with himself. The mere release from the necessity of petty lying, lying every day and every way, restored his self-respect. He had never lied for pleasure, even at school; but to make himself noticed and admired, to assert his difference from other Cordelia Street boys; and he felt a good deal more manly, more honest, even, now that he had no need for boastful pretensions, now that he could, as his actor friends used to say, "dress the part." It was characteristic that remorse did not occur to him. His golden days went by without a shadow, and he made each as perfect as he could.

On the eighth day after his arrival in New York, he found the whole affair exploited in the Pittsburgh papers, exploited with a wealth of detail which indicated that local news of a sensational nature was at a low ebb. The firm of Denny and Carson announced that the boy's father had refunded the full amount of his theft, and that they had no intention of prosecuting. The Cumberland minister had been interviewed, and expressed his hope of yet reclaiming the motherless lad, and Paul's Sabbath-School teacher declared that she would spare no effort to that end. The rumor had reached Pittsburgh that the boy had been seen in a New York hotel, and his father had gone East to find him and bring him home.

Paul had just come in to dress for dinner; he sank into the chair, weak in the knees, and clasped his head in his hands. It was to be worse than jail, even; the tepid waters of Cordelia Street were to close over him finally and forever. The grey monotony stretched before him in hopeless, unrelieved years;—Sabbath School, Young People's Meeting, the yellow-papered room, the damp dish-towels; it all rushed back upon him with sickening vividness. He had the old feeling that the orchestra had suddenly stopped, the sinking sensation that the play was over. The sweat broke out on his face, and he sprang to his feet, looked about him with his white, conscious smile, and winked at himself in the mirror. With something of the childish belief in miracles with which he had so often gone to class, all his lessons unlearned, Paul dressed and dashed whistling down the corridor to the elevator.

He had no sooner entered the dining-room and caught the measure of the music than his remembrance was lightened by his old elastic power of claiming the moment, mounting with it, and finding it all-sufficient. The glare and glitter about him, the mere scenic accessories had again, and for the last time, their old potency. He would show himself that he was game, he would finish the thing splendidly. He doubted, more than ever, the existence of Cordelia Street, and for the first time he drank his wine recklessly. Was he not, after all, one of these fortunate beings? Was he not still himself, and in his own place? He drummed a nervous accompaniment to the music and looked about him, telling himself over and over that it had paid.

60   He reflected drowsily, to the swell of the violin and the chill sweetness of his wine, that he might have done it more wisely. He might have caught an outbound steamer and been well out of their clutches before now. But the other side of the world had seemed too far away and too uncertain then; he could not have waited for it; his need had been too sharp. If he had to choose over again, he would do the same thing tomorrow. He looked affectionately about the dining-room, now gilded with a soft mist. Ah, it had paid indeed!

Paul was awakened next morning by a painful throbbing in his head and feet. He had thrown himself across the bed without undressing, and had slept with his shoes on. His limbs and hands were lead-heavy, and his tongue and throat were parched. There came upon him one of those fateful attacks of clear-headedness that never occurred except when he was physically exhausted and his nerves hung loose. He lay still and closed his eyes and let the tide of realities wash over him.

His father was in New York; "stopping at some joint or other," he told himself. The memory of successive summers on the front stoop fell upon him like a weight of black water. He had not a hundred dollars left; and he knew now, more than ever, that money was everything, the wall that stood between all he loathed and all he wanted. The thing was winding itself up; he had thought of that on his first glorious day in New York, and had even provided a way to snap the thread. It lay on his dressing-table now; he had got it out last night when he came blindly up from dinner—but the shiny metal hurt his eyes, and he disliked the look of it, anyway.

He rose and moved about with a painful effort, succumbing now and again to attacks of nausea. It was the old depression exaggerated; all the world had become Cordelia Street. Yet somehow he was not afraid of anything, was absolutely calm; perhaps because he had looked into the dark corner at last, and knew. It was bad enough, what he saw there; but somehow not so bad as his long fear of it had been. He saw everything clearly now. He had a feeling that he had made the best of it, that he had lived the sort of life he was meant to live, and for half an hour he sat staring at the revolver. But he told himself that was not the way, so he went downstairs and took a cab to the ferry.

When Paul arrived at Newark, he got off the train and took another cab, directing the driver to follow the Pennsylvania tracks out of town. The snow lay heavy on the roadways and had drifted deep in the open fields. Only here and there the dead grass or dried weed stalks projected, singularly black, above it.

Once well into the country, Paul dismissed the carriage and walked, floundering 65 along the tracks, his mind a medley of irrelevant things. He seemed to hold in his brain an actual picture of everything he had seen that morning. He remembered every feature of both his drivers, the toothless old woman from whom he had bought the red flowers in his coat, the agent from whom he had got his ticket, and all of his fellow-passengers on the ferry. His mind, unable to cope with vital matters near at hand, worked feverishly and deftly at sorting and grouping these images. They made for him a part of the ugliness of the world, of the ache in his head, and the bitter burning on his tongue. He stopped and put a handful of snow into his mouth as he walked, but that, too, seemed hot. When he reached a little hillside, where the tracks ran through a cut some twenty feet below him, he stopped and sat down.

The carnations in his coat were drooping with cold, he noticed; their red glory over. It occurred to him that all the flowers he had seen in the show windows that first night must have gone the same way, long before this. It was only one splendid breath they had, in spite of their brave mockery at the winter outside the glass. It was a losing game in the end, it seemed, this revolt against the homilies by which the world is run. Paul took one of the blossoms carefully from his coat and scooped a little hole in the snow, where he covered it up. Then he dozed awhile, from his weak condition, seeming insensible to the cold.

The sound of an approaching train woke him and he started to his feet, remembering only his resolution, and afraid lest he should be too late. He stood watching the approaching locomotive, his teeth chattering, his lips drawn away from them in a frightened smile; once or twice he glanced nervously sidewise, as though he were being watched. When the right moment came, he jumped. As he fell, the folly of his haste occurred to him with merciless clearness, the vastness of what he had left undone. There flashed through his brain, clearer than ever before, the blue of Adriatic water, the yellow of Algerian sands.

He felt something strike his chest—his body being thrown swiftly through the air, on and on, immeasurably far and fast, while his limbs gently relaxed. Then, because the picture-making mechanism was crushed, the disturbing visions flashed into black, and Paul dropped back into the immense design of things.

5

ELLEN   GILCHRIST

Among the Mourners

ELLEN GILCHRIST was born in 1935 in Vicksburg, Mississippi, and educated at Millsaps College and the University of Arkansas. She has worked as a reporter for *Vieux Carré Courier* and as a weekly commentator on National Public Radio's daily "Morning Edition" show. Gilchrist's first major publication was a collection of short stories, *In the Land of Dreamy Dreams* (1981), that focused on adolescents living in New Orleans and the Mississippi Delta. Her first novel, *The Annunciation* (1983), traces the life of a Mississippi girl from an early marriage to a wealthy New Orleans man to her membership in a hippie commune in the Ozarks. Gilchrist's next collection of stories, *Victory Over Japan* (1984), won the American Book Award for Fiction. Her other work includes a book of poems, *The Land Surveyor's Daughter* (1974), and a play, *A Season of Dreams,* based on short stories by Eudora Welty. In "Among the Mourners," reprinted from *The Age of Miracles* (1995), a young girl tries to interpret her reaction to a funeral.

The spring that I was thirteen years old a poet we knew died and we had to have the funeral. It was the most embarrassing thing that ever happened to me in my life. In the first place he killed himself and the police couldn't even get his briefcase open to find the suicide note, and in the second place it almost broke up my parents' marriage. Not that my mother minded my father offering to have the funeral. Somebody had to do it, I guess, and our house is always full of people anyway. She just goes back to her room and reads magazines until they go away. My dad is head of the English Department and there are always poets around telling Dad their problems. I'm used to them and so is she. But this was different. All those police cars pulling up in front of the house and my little sister running around in her pajamas in the front yard and everybody over there smoking cigarettes like it was going out of style. This was several years ago when a lot of people still smoked inside the house.

How would you feel if you had just gotten the first boyfriend you ever had and every time his parents drove by your house there were cars parked all over the yard and police cars in the driveway? I was mortified. His name is Giorgio and his mother is from Peru and his father is Jewish and they don't have things like that at their house. They are very religious. Giorgio goes to the Catholic church with his mom and goes to the temple with his dad. They teach in the Foreign Language Department and they don't always have to have crazy people around like you do if your father is head of the English Department.

Giorgio speaks about fifteen languages and he is so good-looking you wouldn't believe it. He's pretty short but I'm glad he is. I couldn't stand it if he was playing football and I had to get out there and cheer for him getting his nose broken or his teeth cracked. I'm on the Pep Squad. I didn't want to go out but my mother made me. She's always trying to make me have a normal life. Only how can I? With all my dad's crazy friends coming over all the time and my crazy little sister running around naked and failing the first grade. I think they got her mixed up in the nursery. I don't believe she's kin to me.

Anyway, this poet that used to come over all the time and talk to Dad shot himself because his girlfriend had talked his wife into divorcing him and the next thing I knew there were about a hundred cars parked all over the yard on the day after Giorgio finally told me he liked me. My cousin bet him ten dollars he wouldn't tell me, and he called me up that night and told me. I don't think he got the ten dollars but he didn't care. He was so glad to have me for a girlfriend. He's in Gifted and Talented and so am I. I've been liking him for ages but I didn't know it until he called me up. That was about six o'clock one afternoon. That night the poet shot himself and the people started showing up.

"Aurora," my dad says, when he called me into his office to tell me what was going on. "Mr. Alter has killed himself and the widow is going to stay here until we can figure out a way to bury him." 5

"Why'd he do that?" I asked.

"We don't know. We'll need your room if Mr. Seats comes in from Saint Louis. You remember Mr. Seats? He used to teach here."

"He can't have my room. I'm making a project for Swim Team. It's the decorations for the banquet next week." I backed off toward the door. If you get into my dad's office he can talk you into things. It's like there's not enough oxygen in there when he really gets something on his mind. "Take Annie's room. It's filthy anyway. She's such a pig."

"Aurora."

10   "Yes, sir."

"A man has killed himself. We have a civilized duty to mourn when someone dies. If Mr. Seats comes we will need your room."

"I didn't kill him. Why should I give up my room?"

"Aurora, I am deeply disappointed in you. It makes me very sad to hear you talk that way. Mr. Alter was a guest in this house. He was a friend of mine and your mother's. We are going to pay him the respect that's due."

"If someone kills themself they don't get my respect."

15   "Alice Armene! Come in here!" So he starts screaming for my mother. He always blames her when he gets mad at me. As if she can stop it. Sometimes I think I'm the one who was switched in the hospital. Here's what they do that drives me crazy. They preach all the time about reason. *Dharma,* my dad calls it. He is so big on dharma. Then the first time something happens they start acting like these big Christians or something and having all these rituals.

By ten o'clock the next morning the house was full. Mr. Seats caught the first plane he could get and came on down and put his suitcase in my room. I will say this, he didn't touch anything. He just put his suitcase down and went into the living room and started watching television with Mother. He used to be a poet but he had just got this job sending in dialogue for *Days of Our Lives* so he had to watch all the soap operas all day even while he was mourning. He was the best friend of Mr. Alter and had just seen him a few weeks ago. Also, he was suffering a broken heart because the person he loved in Saint Louis wouldn't get a divorce and marry him. He was telling Mother all about it the first day he was there and she's sitting on the sofa with him patting him on the hand. That's what almost broke up my parents' marriage, not to mention almost got the television taken out of our house for good.

So here they are, all sitting around the house drinking beer and iced tea and eating all the food everyone kept bringing over and waiting for the police to finish their investigation so they could bury the body. Giorgio's mother said she thought they should stop making a big deal out of someone young and in good health who would kill themself. "It ees an unholy act," she kept saying in this beautiful accent she has. They only live three blocks from us so I started staying over there all the time. I couldn't stand it at my house with all those people coming in and out the doors and Momma sitting in the living room with Mr. Seats holding his hand.

My dad is insanely jealous of my mother. He won't let anyone near her. He fell in love with her at first sight. She was second runner-up for Miss Tennessee and he met her when his roommate at the University of Kentucky had him up to visit one Thanksgiving vacation. She was good friends with his roommate's sister and she came walking into a room and he was instantly in love with her. Then he swept her off her feet and married her and brought her to Fayetteville, Arkansas, to live. As soon as they got here they had me on a freezing cold January night. I'm an Aquarius, born in my own time, only my parents don't like for me to talk about astrology. They say it's lower-middle-class superstition and not worthy of me. They are afraid I'll get into a coven or something when I grow up if I start believing in astrology.

They had Annie seven years later, although they didn't mean to. My mom is a sculptor although she hasn't had time to do it since Annie was born. Annie wouldn't even go to kindergarten half the time. Then she failed the first grade. All she wants to do is ride her stupid bike or run around with hardly any clothes on or just hang on Dad like some kind of monkey. She adores him.

So what does she do while this funeral is going on but run around in these little pink nylon pajamas that are about ten years old and too short for her and go from person to person being cute and getting people to talk about her to Dad. She's a slut if I ever saw one. She'll do anything for attention. That's why she failed the first grade. Just to get attention.

"It makes me sick," I told Giorgio. We were sitting on the front wall looking at the house. You've never seen so many people going in and out of a house in your life. Mom's going to have to throw the carpets away. There won't be any way to clean them. "He thinks it is his job," Giorgio says. He's sitting right next to me and I can smell the Peruvian perfume his mother puts on everything he wears. Just to think I waited all these years to have a boyfriend and the minute I get one they start having this six-day funeral at my house.

"A wake," my dad told me. "This is the wake."

"When are they going to bury him?" I ask. I don't say another word about Mr. Seats living in my room. He has barely opened his suitcase the whole time he's been here. He thinks Mr. Alter has been appearing to him. Like a ghost. But does my father start screaming and say don't start getting into that lower-middle-class superstition? No, of course not. He just gets this really serious look on his face and lets Mr. Seats talk all he wants about seeing Mr. Alter's ghost behind the rocking chair in the living room and also in the front yard near the maple tree. I bet Mr. Seats told that story about fifty times in one day. Every time I would walk through the room, trying to get something to eat or take a bath or finish my decorations for the Swimming Team banquet, there he would be, telling about the ghost behind the rocking chair.

"Are you coming to my banquet?" I asked my mother finally. She and Mr. Seats were in the living room watching *The Young and the Restless*. Mr. Snider was with them. He's my father's student assistant. Dad told him not to let them watch the television alone. I heard Mr. Snider laughing and telling that to the widow like he was trying to cheer her up. Anyway, I believed it because every time they were in there with the TV on, Mr. Snider was there too.

"They should not have eenvolved you in thees death," Giorgio's mother said to me. "Thees murder."

"I can't even take a bath," I told her. "It's a good thing I'm on the Swim Team. I might get impetigo or something. I was late to practice yesterday because my mother couldn't back out of the driveway. They had this man there from the radio station. They've been playing a special program of all the dead guy's favorite music on the student radio station. He was there getting everyone to tell him what to play."

"Thees ees so morbid, you poor baby girl." Giorgio's mother asked me to eat dinner with them that night so I called and they said I could and Giorgio and I went into his room and listened to music and played Scrabble. Just the two of us. No one bothered us or came in. Well, he's an only child, and his father is a workaholic so there wasn't anyone there but us and his mother and I could tell she wanted us to be in love. She was real excited because I'm in Gifted and Talented too.

"I want Giorgio to have friends who share hees interests so he won't get involved with thees football people." You should hear her say involved. She gives it about fourteen syllables. She grew up speaking French and Spanish and English and I could just live over there listening to her talk.

I guess you think we were in there kissing and making out but you are wrong. I would never take advantage of that woman. I wouldn't violate Mrs. Levine's trust for fifteen-carat diamonds in my ears. I wouldn't hurt that woman for all the money in the world. I love her with all my heart. Even if Giorgio did quit liking me I would never do one thing to make Mrs. Levine unhappy. If it hadn't been for her I would never have made it through that week.

30   Finally, on the Friday after he killed himself on Saturday, the police released the body and they all went up to the cemetery and buried him. He didn't have any parents. He was an orphan from the word go, which is what made it so tragic. The only one who had ever loved him was his wife and he betrayed her with another woman and then he couldn't face the consequences of what he had done.

"Thees happens every day in my country," Mrs. Levine told me. "We do not theeenk these things are tragedies. Tragedy ees for the poor widow or the child who loses his mother or when there is a war. Thees young man will have eternity to regret hees act. It would be better if the living walked off and forgot hees selfish life."

"Can Aurora spend the night tonight?" Giorgio asked. "She can sleep in the guest room. She hasn't had any sleep in days, Momma. She has to sleep with her little sister."

"I'm an insomniac anyway," I added. "But that's okay. I can take it another night."

"Of course not. Of course you can stay here with us. I will call your mother and see if thees is all right with her, then?"

35   So listen, my parents are so wrapped up in this funeral they said yes. They let me spend the night at a boy's house. I couldn't believe it. I was afraid to go home and get my pajamas and toothbrush. I was afraid my mom would change her mind if she saw me. Sometimes she can read my mind like a Gypsy.

I sneaked in the side door and grabbed some clothes and stuffed them in a bag and almost made it back out into the yard when Dad caught me. "Where are you going?" he says. By now they have buried Mr. Alter and are back at our house sitting around discussing the funeral. I'm in the back hall about four feet from the kitchen and Dad's blocking the way to the door.

"I'm going to church with the Levines," I said.

"You're doing what?" My father has spent his life listening to students. There is no fooling him. I raised my head and looked him in the eye. "I think they're going to the synagogue," I said. "Or maybe to St. Joseph's. I'm freaking out from this funeral, Dad. The Levines asked me to stay with them. Mom said I could."

"Mr. Harris?" It was this graduate student named Bellefontaine who's a big favorite of my dad's. He had a faded red corduroy shirt in his hand. "This was one of Francis's shirts. We thought you might like it for a souvenir. We cleaned out his closets like you said. We brought this to you. I don't know. Maybe you don't want it." He stood blocking the door to the kitchen with the dead poet's shirt in his hand. My dad reached out and took it. I went under their arms and made my escape. "I have to go," I said. "They're waiting for me in the car." I was out of the door. I had just told two lies in a row to a man who never forgets anything and is never fooled. I lit out across the patio and took the short cut to the Levines' house across the backyards of my piano teacher and some people from Indiana that no one ever sees.

Giorgio and his mother were waiting for me. They were making paella for din- 40
ner. Mr. Levine was going to be late. We weren't going to have to wait for him.

Everything went along just fine until Mr. Levine came home and he and Mrs. Levine went to bed, leaving Giorgio and me alone. "You want to go for a walk?" he asked. "They won't mind. They don't care what I do."

"It's ten-thirty at night. Sure. I'd love it. We can walk up to the store." I was about five feet away from him. He smelled like that perfume. He reached out and took my hand and we just walked on out the door. "We can go to the park," he said. "Sometimes I go there at night. It's not too far."

"I can walk a hundred miles. Who cares how far it is." So we started off down Washington Avenue. It was in between semesters at the college and the town was quiet. We walked down to Highway 71 and crossed at the IGA. There wasn't anyone around but old Donnie Hights, who is a lunatic that walks the streets all the time saying hello to people. He gives me the creeps but Dad says he is proof there is still freedom in the United States and to count my blessings and be polite.

Anyway, he was standing on the corner by the Shell station so I held on tighter to Giorgio's hand and we crossed 71 and started up toward Washington Elementary School.

"That's where I learned to read," I commented. "Right there in that corner room. 45
Mrs. Nordan taught me. She's the sweetest lady in the world. I adore her."

"I adore you," Giorgio says. He said that. Right there by the corner of the school on Maple Street. He got real near me and sort of breathed into my hair.

That's all that happened then. We walked up Maple and cut over at Doctor Wileman's house and went on down to the park. At the wooden bridge we stopped and sat down and started kissing. We just started kissing without saying a thing. I bet there wasn't a person left in the park. If it hadn't been for the lights in the houses on the hill there wouldn't have been any light except for the moon and stars. "This is just like the old shepherds in the Bible," I said at last. "Or else the Druids. It makes me think of death to be alone in the night. Does it you?"

But all Giorgio did was put his hand on my breast and keep it there. I would have made him move it but I wanted to know what it felt like. It felt good. I can tell you that much. If I hadn't had to think about what it would be like when my dad got me in his office and started screaming at me I might have just let him keep it there all night.

"We better get back," I said. I was kissing him as hard as I could in between talking but I still have my braces on and it hurts to kiss very hard with them. Besides, last week I got a free certificate to TCBY for not breaking any pieces off of them for a month and I was trying to get another one. "You better stop doing that," I added, and pushed his hand off of my breast.

50   He didn't fight me. He just ran it down my shorts and stuck his finger up inside my underpants. Just stuck it right up around the edge of my underpants. I don't know what would have happened but a car full of teenagers pulled up on Wilson Street and got out and started running for the swing sets which are only forty feet from the bridge where we were lying. Something crashed in the creek. It was probably just a beer can but it sounded like a hydrogen bomb.

I stood up and dusted myself off. I already had about five hundred chigger bites but luckily I wouldn't know that until morning.

That's all there is worth telling about that night. We walked back to the house. Giorgio was acting like he was mad at me. He was pouting if you want to know the truth. He was acting like he was about five years old. He's spoiled rotten, to tell the truth.

Besides, in another year he'll be too short for me. We're already the same height and my mom is five foot seven and my dad's six five. It wasn't going to last.

So I don't care if he told my best friend he doesn't like me anymore.

55   Mr. Seats has twin boys my age who live up in Minnesota. When he comes down next winter to be the Poet in Residence he's going to bring them with him. He thinks they will both fall in love with me. "They always fall in love together," he told me, while he was packing up his stuff to leave my room. "You can have them both, Aurora."

So what do you think? Do you think Giorgio quit liking me because I let him put his hand on my breast? Or because I didn't let him put it in my pants? Or because there were police cars outside my house for seven days?

My dad would say that's like trying to figure out why Mr. Alter killed himself. He believes in the theory of random acts. He thinks lightning strikes. He thinks we should just live every day and do the best we can.

Also, this is the last funeral we'll have to have. Before they left Dad called all the people into the living room and told them this was the last time he was going to a suicide's funeral. If anyone else killed themselves they were on their own for getting buried. "This has had a negative effect on my children," he said. He knew I was listening in the hall. "I am worried that I allowed them to witness it. Aside from that, I love you all and I wish you well." I noticed as soon as Dad made his announcement that Mr. Seats went into my room and took a shower and put on a shirt and tie and starting acting like a grown-up. My dad has the power to do things like that to people but he usually saves it up and only uses it at the end.

My parents are very cool people to tell the truth. They aren't even going to make Annie go to summer school. They're just going to let her run around all summer in her bathing suit and try again next year. This is very advanced behavior for academics and everyone was congratulating them on it when they were getting in their cars and leaving. You're right about Annie, people were saying. Let her be a child. Don't push her, and so forth.

Of course, why should they worry? They've got me. And I have them again. 60 More than I need. The television has a sign on it that says, GOODBYE, SEQUENTIAL THOUGHT, and a schedule of times when Annie and I are allowed to watch it. Although I think the sign is really just to remind my mother that Mr. Seats has whored himself by agreeing to write the dialogue for a soap opera.

Now that I know what it is they do when they go into their room at night I am looking at them with different eyes. I feel sorry for them, to tell the truth. If I had to do that stuff every night I might not be able to stay in Gifted and Talented or even be on the Swim Team. Here's the way I look when I start thinking about it. Very soft around the mouth and chin, like Bambi, sort of big-eyed and stupid, bowing my head to chew a little piece of grass.

Very helpless and half-asleep, while all around me for all I know the forest might be catching fire.

QUESTIONS FOR DISCUSSION AND WRITING

1. **Plot**   How does each protagonist's decision to leave home (Paul permanently, Aurora overnight) complicate the plots of these two stories? How does Paul resolve his conflict with his father? What conclusions does Aurora make about her relationship to her parents?

2. **Character**   How does Paul's animosity toward the clerk on Cordelia Street reveal his character? How does Aurora's admiration for Giorgio reveal her character? How are Paul's and Aurora's characters developed in their relationship with their fathers?

3. **Setting**   How do the economic and social classes of the two protagonists shape their characters? What external evidence suggests that Paul is a "bad case" and Aurora is "gifted and talented"?

4. **Point of View**   Why does Cather use a third-person narrator to speak for Paul? How might his "case" be read differently if he narrated his own story? Why does Gilchrist have Aurora tell her own story? How might her story be different if an adult third-person narrator interpreted her character?

5. **Theme**   What do these two stories imply about the possibility of free will? Does Paul really "choose" his fate? Does Aurora understand herself well enough to make "free" choices? Given your responses to these questions, explain why the tone of Cather's story is so dark and that of Gilchrist's story so bright.

SETTING

....

Katherine Mansfield's "Her First Ball"
Witi Ihimaera's "His First Ball"

Setting is even more important in these two stories than is ordinarily the case. If we fail to understand the nuances of the culture, the social class, and the particular occasion—the microcosmic worlds created—we have no way of really comprehending plot, character, or theme. Moreover, some of the most important meanings of the settings in both stories are implied rather than expressed, depending even more than is usual on the perception and knowledge of the readers and their ability to recognize and interpret subtexts.

Like Joyce Carol Oates in "The Lady with the Pet Dog," Witi Ihimaera alludes in his title to a classic short story, Katherine Mansfield's "Her First Ball." But while Oates incorporates much of Anton Chekhov's basic plot situation in her story, Ihimaera uses only the primary situation of a young person attending his or her first formal dance. However, Ihimaera does pay a kind of indirect homage to his notable predecessor: one of the delightful ironies in his story arises from the fact that the alien culture into which his protagonist stumbles is in fact an archaic remnant of the culture Mansfield depicts in her earlier story.

Although Mansfield says nothing directly about the social class to which her characters belong, she expects her readers to understand almost immediately that the young people in her story belong to a world of privilege and economic advantage. For example, the description of their dress suggests a lavish outlay of money and time: the boys' gloves are new, purchased for this particular dance; the girls are dressed in elaborate and expensive materials and furs; and their hair is coifed in styles that require great attention and time. Moreover, we soon come to understand that this ball is only one of many such affairs that they have attended and will continue to attend during this social season. The protagonist is exceptional only in that she is just entering this world, coming from "the country," the outside, but she is "ravished" by the charm and possibilities of this elaborate little universe—and obviously both she and others expect her to become part of it. Although her faith in this world and her joy in becoming a part of it are temporarily mitigated by the fat man's projection of her ordained future in it, she quickly forgets that challenge and is again swept into the irresistible rhythms of her world, a world that seems to her apart from the mundane realities of time and change.

The story also never mentions that these young people are English and that the world they inhabit is the aristocratic world that flourished in the nineteenth and early twentieth centuries, when England was the dominant economic and political power in the world and ruled a vast colonial empire that stretched around the globe.

Whether this particular party is taking place in London or in a colonial capital in New Zealand, the land of Mansfield's birth, is of no real consequence: the values, customs, and social expectations would be the same. They all grow from an absolute sense of the rightness of all things English, including the right to rule people in other cultures that have been incorporated into the empire and a smug belief that this empire is the final perfecting of the human possibility.

The wonderfully comic situational irony in Ihimaera's story arises directly from his protagonist's sudden confrontation with that world of colonial British respectability and privilege that Mansfield depicted. Mansfield's characters are all insiders who have no means or inclination to move beyond the boundaries of their world so that they might question it: it seems to them inevitable and right. Likewise, the world of the working-class Maoris seems to Tuta entirely natural and inevitable. We may be surprised by his easy acceptance of the hauteur of the British or would-be British superiors at work or by his relationship with the transvestite friends who teach him to dance, but for Tuta, the insider, these are simply facts of life.

However, we cannot understand Tuta's world unless we understand a most important part of the setting that is constantly implied but not directly expressed in the story itself, the whole history of colonialism as it developed in places like New Zealand. Western powers in the period after the discovery of the Americas entered a mad competition to seize and exploit the resources of the so-called "uncivilized" regions throughout the world. The British were particularly successful in claiming large parts of the globe as their own, including much of the South Pacific, the area that includes Australia and New Zealand. The Maoris were like most indigenous people in the empire who were dispossessed of land and political rights, at first violently and later by law, so that they became almost invisible to the ruling culture, insignificant inferiors first exploited and later patronized by their conquerors. This story is set in that moment in the middle of this century when it has become politically expedient for the British to pretend to acknowledge the basic humanity and rights of the displaced aboriginal peoples in the old empire, but Ihimaera of course makes stingingly clear that this "change" is entirely superficial and hypocritical.

These parallel universes of the old colonial empire and the subculture of the exploited people collide with the invitation to the ball, and as we watch Tuta's efforts to become acceptable in the other world, finally an impossible task given the historical reality, we are reminded humorously but strongly of the many absurdities of that world. The condescension of the "rulers" who invite the poor factory worker to a formal ball is amusingly exaggerated, especially in their ignorant substitution of an obscenity for Tuta's name, and it is with great relief that we see Tuta's natural good sense assert itself and transcend his original sense of inferiority. He sees the smallness of this great world, decides to have some fun in it, knowing "that, yes, he could beat them if he wanted to."

Tuta's triumph is by implication the triumph of his strong, enduring culture over the absurd ideal of empire, a theme that is common in what we now term postcolonial literature, the literature produced by once-exploited peoples in cultures once dominated by colonial powers. In all such literature the connection between setting and theme is emphatic, as it is in these two stories.

6

KATHERINE MANSFIELD

Her First Ball

KATHERINE MANSFIELD (1888–1923) was born in Wellington, New
Zealand, but came to England to study music at Queen's College in London.
In 1908, after a brief trip home to New Zealand, Mansfield returned to
London, where, with the help of her friends D. H. Lawrence and Aldous
Huxley, she embarked on a literary career. A disastrous marriage and an un-
planned pregnancy forced Mansfield to retreat to a German convent. After
suffering a miscarriage, Mansfield began writing stories and sketches, which
were published as *In a German Pension* (1911). In 1910 she returned to
London, where she contributed stories to *New Age* and met editor and critic
John Middleton Murry, whom she married in 1918. During this period she
published many of her stories in two magazines edited by Murry, *Rhythm* and
Blue Review. In 1916 she began writing a series of stories based on her life in
New Zealand. The first of these, *Prelude* (1918), was included in *Bliss and
Other Stories* (1920). Mansfield's other best-known collections are *The
Garden Party and Other Stories* (1922) and *The Dove's Nest and Other
Stories* (1923). In 1918 Mansfield contracted tuberculosis and began seeking
cures at health spas throughout southern Europe. She stopped writing in 1922
and died the next year at the age of thirty-five. "Her First Ball," reprinted
from *The Short Stories of Katherine Mansfield* (1937), is the story of a young
country girl's introduction to "the beginning of everything."

Exactly when the ball began Leila would have found it hard to say. Perhaps her
first real partner was the cab. It did not matter that she shared the cab with the
Sheridan girls and their brother. She sat back in her own little corner of it, and the bol-
ster on which her hand rested felt like the sleeve of an unknown young man's dress
suit; and away they bowled, past waltzing lampposts and houses and fences and trees.

"Have you really never been to a ball before, Leila? But, my child, how too
weird—" cried the Sheridan girls.

"Our nearest neighbor was fifteen miles," said Leila softly, gently opening and
shutting her fan.

Oh, dear, how hard it was to be indifferent like the others! She tried not to smile too
much; she tried not to care. But every single thing was so new and exciting . . . Meg's

tuberoses, Jose's long loop of amber, Laura's little dark head, pushing above her white fur like a flower through snow. She would remember for ever. It even gave her a pang to see her cousin Laurie throw away the wisps of tissue paper he pulled from the fastening of his new gloves. She would like to have kept those wisps as a keepsake, as a remembrance. Laurie leaned forward and put his hand on Laura's knee.

"Look here, darling," he said. "The third and the ninth as usual. Twig?"   5

Oh, how marvellous to have a brother! In her excitement Leila felt that if there had been time, if it hadn't been impossible, she couldn't have helped crying because she was an only child, and no brother had ever said "Twig?" to her; no sister would ever say, as Meg said to Jose that moment, "I've never known your hair go up more successfully than it has tonight!"

But, of course, there was no time. They were at the drill hall already; there were cabs in front of them and cabs behind. The road was bright on either side with moving fan-like lights, and on the pavement gay couples seemed to float through the air; little satin shoes chased each other like birds.

"Hold on to me, Leila; you'll get lost," said Laura.

"Come on, girls, let's make a dash for it," said Laurie.

Leila put two fingers on Laura's pink velvet cloak, and they were somehow   10 lifted past the big gold lantern, carried along the passage, and pushed into the little room marked "Ladies." Here the crowd was so great there was hardly space to take off their things; the noise was deafening. Two benches on either side were stacked high with wraps. Two old women in white aprons ran up and down tossing fresh armfuls. And everybody was pressing forward trying to get at the little dressing table and mirror at the far end.

A great quivering jet of gas lighted the ladies' room. It couldn't wait; it was dancing already. When the door opened again and there came a burst of tuning from the drill hall, it leaped almost to the ceiling.

Dark girls, fair girls were patting their hair, tying ribbons again, tucking handkerchiefs down the front of their bodices, smoothing marble-white gloves. And because they were all laughing it seemed to Leila that they were all lovely.

"Aren't there any invisible hairpins?" cried a voice. "How most extraordinary! I can't see a single invisible hairpin."

"Powder my back, there's a darling," cried some one else.

"But I must have a needle and cotton. I've torn simply miles and miles of the   15 frill," wailed a third.

Then, "Pass them along, pass them along!" The straw basket of programs was tossed from arm to arm. Darling little pink-and-silver programs, with pink pencils and fluffy tassels. Leila's fingers shook as she took one out of the basket. She wanted to ask someone, "Am I meant to have one too?" but she had just time to read: "Waltz 3. *Two, Two in a Canoe.* Polka 4. *Making the Feathers Fly,*" when Meg cried, "Ready, Leila?" and they pressed their way through the crush in the passage towards the big double doors of the drill hall.

Dancing had not begun yet, but the band had stopped tuning, and the noise was so great it seemed that when it did begin to play it would never be heard. Leila, pressing close to Meg, looking over Meg's shoulder, felt that even the little quivering colored flags strung across the ceiling were talking. She quite forgot to be shy; she forgot how in the middle of dressing she had sat down on the bed with one shoe off and one shoe on and begged her mother to ring up her cousins and say she couldn't go after all. And the rush of longing she had had to be sitting on the veranda of their forsaken upcountry home, listening to the baby owls crying "More pork" in the moonlight, was changed to a rush of joy so sweet that it was hard to bear alone. She clutched her fan, and, gazing at the gleaming, golden floor, the azaleas, the lanterns, the stage at one end with its red carpet and gilt chairs and the band in a corner, she thought breathlessly, "How heavenly; how simply heavenly!"

All the girls stood grouped together at one side of the doors, the men at the other, and the chaperones in dark dresses, smiling rather foolishly, walked with little careful steps over the polished floor towards the stage.

"This is my little country cousin Leila. Be nice to her. Find her partners; she's under my wing," said Meg, going up to one girl after another.

20   Strange faces smiled at Leila—sweetly, vaguely. Strange voices answered, "Of course, my dear." But Leila felt the girls didn't really see her. They were looking towards the men. Why didn't the men begin? What were they waiting for? There they stood, smoothing their gloves, patting their glossy hair and smiling among themselves. Then, quite suddenly, as if they had only just made up their minds that that was what they had to do, the men came gliding over the parquet. There was a joyful flutter among the girls. A tall, fair man flew up to Meg, seized her program, scribbled something; Meg passed him on to Leila. "May I have the pleasure?" He ducked and smiled. There came a dark man wearing an eyeglass, then cousin Laurie with a friend, and Laura with a little freckled fellow whose tie was crooked. Then quite an old man—fat, with a big bald patch on his head—took her program and murmured, "Let me see, let me see!" And he was a long time comparing his program, which looked black with names, with hers. It seemed to give him so much trouble that Leila was ashamed. "Oh, please don't bother," she said eagerly. But instead of replying the fat man wrote something, glanced at her again. "Do I remember this bright little face?" he said softly. "Is it known to me of yore?" At that moment the band began playing; the fat man disappeared. He was tossed away on a great wave of music that came flying over the gleaming floor, breaking the groups up into couples, scattering them, sending them spinning. . . .

Leila had learned to dance at boarding school. Every Saturday afternoon the boarders were hurried off to a little corrugated iron mission hall where Miss Eccles (of London) held her "select" classes. But the difference between that dusty-smelling hall—with calico texts on the walls, the poor terrified little woman in a brown velvet toque with rabbit's ears thumping the cold piano, Miss Eccles poking the girls' feet with her long white wand—and this was so tremendous that Leila was sure if her partner didn't come and she had to listen to that marvelous music and to watch the others sliding, gliding over the golden floor, she would die at least, or faint, or lift her arms and fly out of one of those dark windows that showed the stars.

"Ours, I think—" Some one bowed, smiled, and offered her his arm; she hadn't to die after all. Some one's hand pressed her waist, and she floated away like a flower that is tossed into a pool.

"Quite a good floor, isn't it?" drawled a faint voice close to her ear.

"I think it's most beautifully slippery," said Leila.

"Pardon!" The faint voice sounded surprised. Leila said it again. And there was 25 a tiny pause before the voice echoed, "Oh, quite!" and she was swung round again.

He steered so beautifully. That was the great difference between dancing with girls and men, Leila decided. Girls banged into each other, and stamped on each other's feet; the girl who was gentleman always clutched you so.

The azaleas were separate flowers no longer; they were pink and white flags streaming by.

"Were you at the Bells' last week?" the voice came again. It sounded tired. Leila wondered whether she ought to ask him if he would like to stop.

"No, this is my first dance," said she.

Her partner gave a little gasping laugh. "Oh, I say," he protested. 30

"Yes, it is really the first dance I've ever been to." Leila was most fervent. It was such a relief to be able to tell somebody. "You see, I've lived in the country all my life up until now. . . ."

At that moment the music stopped, and they went to sit on two chairs against the wall. Leila tucked her pink satin feet under and fanned herself, while she blissfully watched the other couples passing and disappearing through the swing doors.

"Enjoying yourself, Leila?" asked Jose, nodding her golden head.

Laura passed and gave her the faintest little wink; it made Leila wonder for a moment whether she was quite grown up after all. Certainly her partner did not say very much. He coughed, tucked his handkerchief away, pulled down his waistcoat, took a minute thread off his sleeve. But it didn't matter. Almost immediately the band started, and her second partner seemed to spring from the ceiling.

"Floor's not bad," said the new voice. Did one always begin with the floor? And 35 then, "Were you at the Neaves' on Tuesday?" And again Leila explained. Perhaps it was a little strange that her partners were not more interested. For it was thrilling. Her first ball! She was only at the beginning of everything. It seemed to her that she had never known what the night was like before. Up till now it had been dark, silent, beautiful very often—oh, yes—but mournful somehow. Solemn. And now it would never be like that again—it had opened dazzling bright.

"Care for an ice?" said her partner. And they went through the swing doors, down the passage, to the supper room. Her cheeks burned, she was fearfully thirsty. How sweet the ices looked on little glass plates, and how cold the frosted spoon was, iced too! And when they came back to the hall there was the fat man waiting for her by the door. It gave her quite a shock again to see how old he was; he ought to have been on the stage with the fathers and mothers. And when Leila compared him with her other partners he looked shabby. His waistcoat was creased, there was a button off his glove, his coat looked as if it was dusty with French chalk.

"Come along, little lady," said the fat man. He scarcely troubled to clasp her, and they moved away so gently, it was more like walking than dancing. But he said not a word about the floor. "Your first dance, isn't it?" he murmured.

"How *did* you know?"

"Ah," said the fat man, "that's what it is to be old!" He wheezed faintly as he steered her past an awkward couple. "You see, I've been doing this kind of thing for the last thirty years."

40   "Thirty years?" cried Leila. Twelve years before she was born!

"It hardly bears thinking about, does it?" said the fat man gloomily. Leila looked at his bald head, and she felt quite sorry for him.

"I think it's marvelous to be still going on," she said kindly.

"Kind little lady," said the fat man, and he pressed her a little closer, and hummed a bar of the waltz. "Of course," he said, "you can't hope to last anything like as long as that. No-o," said the fat man, "long before that you'll be sitting up there on the stage, looking on, in your nice black velvet. And these pretty arms will have turned into little short fat ones, and you'll beat time with such a different kind of fan—a black bony one." The fat man seemed to shudder. "And you'll smile away like the poor old dears up there, and point to your daughter, and tell the elderly lady next to you how some dreadful man tried to kiss her at the club ball. And your heart will ache, ache"—the fat man squeezed her closer still, as if he really was sorry for that poor heart—"because no one wants to kiss you now. And you'll say how unpleasant these polished floors are to walk on, how dangerous they are. Eh, Mademoiselle Twinkletoes?" said the fat man softly.

Leila gave a light little laugh, but she did not feel like laughing. Was it—could it all be true? It sounded terribly true. Was this first ball only the beginning of her last ball after all? At that the music seemed to change; it sounded sad, sad it rose upon a great sigh. Oh, how quickly things changed! Why didn't happiness last for ever? For ever wasn't a bit too long.

45   "I want to stop," she said in a breathless voice. The fat man led her to the door.

"No," she said, "I won't go outside. I won't sit down. I'll just stand here, thank you." She leaned against the wall, tapping with her foot, pulling up her gloves and trying to smile. But deep inside her a little girl threw her pinafore over her head and sobbed. Why had he spoiled it all?

"I say, you know," said the fat man, "you mustn't take me seriously, little lady."

"As if I should!" said Leila, tossing her small dark head and sucking her underlip. . . .

Again the couples paraded. The swing doors opened and shut. Now new music was given out by the bandmaster. But Leila didn't want to dance any more. She wanted to be home, or sitting on the veranda listening to those baby owls. When she looked through the dark windows at the stars, they had long beams like wings. . . .

50   But presently a soft, melting, ravishing tune began, and a young man with curly hair bowed before her. She would have to dance, out of politeness, until she could find Meg. Very stiffly she walked into the middle; very haughtily she put her hand on his sleeve. But in one minute, in one turn, her feet glided, glided. The lights, the azaleas, the dresses, the pink faces, the velvet chairs, all became one beautiful flying wheel. And when her next partner bumped her into the fat man and he said, "Par*don*," she smiled at him more radiantly than ever. She didn't even recognize him again.

7

WITI IHIMAERA

His First Ball

WITI IHIMAERA was born in 1944 in Gisborne, New Zealand, and educated at the University of Auckland. After working as a newspaper reporter, he accepted a position as a diplomatic officer in New Zealand's Ministry of Foreign Affairs. He began writing to document the two landscapes of New Zealand, the Maori (the indigenous people) and the Pakeha (the Europeans). In particular, he wanted to ensure that "my Maori people were taken into account." His short stories have been collected in *Pounamu, Pounamu* (1972) and *The New Net Goes Fishing* (1976). His novels include *Tangi* (1973) and *Whanau* (1974). He has also edited a collection of Maori writing, *Into the World of Light* (1978). "His First Ball," reprinted from *Dear Miss Mansfield* (1989), recalls a similar story by a Pakeha New Zealander who spent most of her life in England, Katherine Mansfield.

Just why it was that he, Tuta Wharepapa, should receive the invitation was a mystery to him. Indeed, when it came, in an envelope bearing a very imposing crest, his mother mistook it for something entirely different—notice of a traffic misdemeanour, a summons perhaps, or even worse, an overdue account. She fingered it gingerly, holding it as far away from her body as possible—just in case a pair of hands came out to grab her fortnightly cheque—and said, "Here, Tuta. It must be a bill." She thrust it quickly at her son before he could get away and, wriggling her fingers to get rid of the taint, waited for him to open it.

"Hey—" Tuta said as he stared down at the card. His face dropped such a long way that his mother—her name was Coral—became alarmed. Visions of pleading in court on his behalf flashed through her mind. "Oh, Tuta, how bad is it?" she said as she prepared to defend her son against all-comers. But Tuta remained speechless and Coral had to grab the card from his hands. "What's this?" she asked. The card was edged with gold:

The Aide-de-Camp in Waiting
Is Desired By Their Excellencies

"Oh, Tuta, what have you done?" Coral said. But Tuta was still in a state of shock. Then, "Read on, Mum," he said.

To Invite Mr Tuta Wharepapa
To A Dance At Government House

Coral's voice drifted away into speechlessness like her son's. Then she compressed her lips and jabbed Tuta with an elbow. "I'm tired of your jokes," she said. "It's not my joke, Mum," Tuta responded. "I know you, Tuta," Coral continued. "True, Mum, honest. One of the boys must be having me on." Coral looked at Tuta, unconvinced. "Who'd want to have *you* at their flash party?" she asked. "Just wait till I get the joker who sent this," Tuta swore to himself. Then Coral began to laugh. "You? Go to Government House? You don't even know how to bow!" And she laughed and laughed so much at the idea that Tuta couldn't take it. "Where are you going, Your Highness?" Coral asked. "To find out who sent this," Tuta replied, waving the offending invitation in her face. "By the time I finish with him—or her—" because he suddenly realised Coral herself might have sent it—"they'll be laughing on the other side of their face." With that, he strode out of the kitchen. "Oh, Tuta?" he heard Coral call, all la-di-da, "If you ore gooing pahst Government Howse please convay may regahrds to—" and she burst out laughing again.

Tuta leapt on to his motorbike and, over the rest of the day, roared around the city calling on his mates from the factory. "It wasn't me, Tuta," Crazy-Joe said as he sank a red ball in the billiard saloon, "but I tell you, man, you'll look great in a suit." Nor was it Blackjack over at the garage, who said, "But listen, mate, when you go grab some of those Diplo number plates for me, ay?" And neither was it Des, who moonlighted as Desirée Dawn at the strip club, or Sheree, who worked part time at the pinball parlour. "You couldn't take a partner, could you?" Desirée Dawn breathed hopefully. "Nah, you wouldn't be able to fit on my bike," Tuta said—apart from which he didn't think a six-foot transvestite with a passion for pink boas and slit satin dresses would enjoy it all that much. By the end of the day Tuta was no wiser, and when he arrived at Bigfoot's house and found his mate waiting for him in a tiara, he knew that word was getting around. Then it came to him that perhaps the invitation was real after all. Gloria Simmons would know—she was the boss's secretary and knew some lords.

"Oh," Mrs. Simmons whispered reverently as Tuta handed her the crested envelope. She led Tuta into the sitting-room. "It looks real," she said as she held it to the light. Then she opened the envelope and, incredulous, asked, "*You* received this?" Tuta nodded. "You didn't just pick it up on the street," Mrs. Simmons continued, "and put your name on it?" Offended, Tuta shook his head, saying "You don't think I want to go, do you?" Mrs. Simmons pursed her lips and said, "Perhaps there's another Tuta Wharepapa, and you got his invitation in error." And Mrs. Simmons's teeth smiled and said, "In that case, let me ring Government House and let them know." With that, Mrs. Simmons went into another room, where Tuta heard her dialling. Then *her* voice went all la-di-da too as she trilled, "Ooo, Gahverment Howse? May ay speak to the Aide-de-Camp? Ooo, har do yoo do. So sorry to trouble you but ay am ringing to advayse you—"Tuta rolled his eyes—how come everybody he told about the invitation got infected by some kind of disease! Then he became acutely aware that Mrs. Simmons had stopped talking. He heard her gasp. He heard her say in her own lingo, "You mean to tell me that this is for real? That you people actually sent an invite to a—a—boy who packs batteries in a factory?" She put down the telephone and returned to the sitting-room. She was pale but calm as she said, "Tuta dear, difficult though this may be, can you remember the woman who came to look at the factory about two months ago?" Tuta knitted his eyebrows. "Yeah, I think so. That must have been when we opened the new extension." Mrs. Simmons closed her eyes. "The woman, Tuta. The woman." Tuta thought again. "Oh yeah, there *was* a lady, come to think of it, a horsey-looking lady who—" Mrs. Simmons interrupted him. "Tuta, dear, that lady was the wife of the Governor-General."

Dazed, Tuta said, "But she didn't say who she was." And he listened as Mrs. ₅ Simmons explained that Mrs. Governor-General had been very impressed by the workers at the factory and that Tuta was being invited to represent them. "Of course you will have to go," Mrs. Simmons said. "One does not say 'No' to the Crown." Then Mrs. Simmons got up and telephoned Tuta's mother. "Coral? Gloria here. Listen, about Tuta, you and I should talk about what is required. What for? Why, when he goes to the ball of course! Now—" *Me? Go to a ball?* Tuta thought. *With all those flash people, all those flash ladies with their crowns and diamonds and emeralds? Not bloody likely—Bigfoot can go, he's already got a tiara, yeah. Not me. They'll have to drag me there. I'm not going. Not me. No fear. No WAY.* But he knew, when he saw the neighbours waiting for him at home that, of course, his mother had already flapped her mouth to everybody. "Oh yes," she was telling the neighbours when Tuta walked in, "it was delivered by special messenger. This dirty big black car came and a man, must have been a flunkey, knocked on the door and—" Then Coral saw Tuta and, "Oh Tuta," she cried, opening her arms to him as if she hadn't seen him for days.

After that, of course, there was no turning back. The boss from the factory called to put the hard word on Tuta. Mrs. Simmons RSVPeed by telephone and—"Just in case, Tuta dear"—by letter and, once that was done, he had to go. The rest of his mates at the factory got into the act, also, cancelling the airline booking he made to get out of town and, from thereon in, followed him everywhere. "Giz a break, fellas," Tuta pleaded as he tried to get out, cajole or bribe himself out of the predicament. But Crazy-Joe only said, "Lissen, if you don't get there then I'm—" and he drew a finger across his throat, and Blackjack said, "Hey, man, I know a man who knows a man who can get us a Rolls for the night—" and Bigfoot just handed him the tiara. And boy, did Coral ever turn out to be the walking compendium of What To Do And How To Do It At A Ball. "Gloria says that we have to take you to a tailor so you can hire a suit. Not just any suit and none of your purple numbers either. A black *conservative* suit. And then we have to get you a bowtie and you have to wear black shoes—so I reckon a paint job on your brown ones will do. You've got a white shirt, thank goodness, but we'll have to get some new socks—calf length so that when you sit down people won't see your hairy legs. Now, what else? Oh yes, I've already made an appointment for you to go to have your hair cut, no buts, Tuta, and the boys are taking you there, so don't think you're going to wriggle out of it. By the time that dance comes around we'll have you decked out like the Prince of Wales—" which was just what Tuta was afraid of.

But that was only the beginning. Not only did his appearance have to be radically altered, but his manners had to be brushed up also—and Mrs. Simmons was the first to have a go. "Tuta dear," she said when he knocked on her door, "Do come in. Yes, take your boots off but on THE NIGHT, the shoes stay *on*. Please, come this way. No, Tuta, *after* me, just a few steps behind. Never barge, Tuta and don't shamble along. Be PROUD, Tuta, be HAUGHTY"—and she showed him how to put his nose in the air. Tuta followed her, his nose so high that he almost tripped, into the dining-room. "Voila!" she said. "Ay?" Tuta answered. Mrs. Simmons then realised that this was going to be very difficult. "I said, 'Ta ra!'" She had set the table with a beautiful cloth—and it appeared to be laid with thousands of knives, forks and spoons. "This is what it will be like at the ball," she explained. "Oh boy," Tuta said. "Now, because I'm a lady you must escort me to my seat," Mrs. Simmons said. "Huh? Can't you walk there yourself?" Tuta asked. "Just *do* it," Mrs. Simmons responded dangerously, and *don't* push me all the way under the table, Tuta, just to the edge will do—" and then, under her breath "—Patience, Gloria dear, *patienza*." Once seated, she motioned Tuta to a chair opposite her. "Gee, thanks," he said. Mrs. Simmons paused, thoughtfully, and said, "Tuta dear, when in doubt don't say *anything*. Just shut your mouth." She shivered, but really, the boy would only understand common language, "—and keep it shut." Then she smiled. "Now follow every action that I make." Exaggerating the movements for Tuta's benefit, Mrs. Simmons said, "First, take up the spoon. No, not that one, *that* one. That's for your soup, that's for the second course, that's for the third course, that's for the fourth—" Tuta looked helplessly at her. "Can't I use the same knives and things all the time?" he asked. "*Never,*" Mrs. Simmons shivered. "Well, what's all these courses for?" Tuta objected. "Why don't they just stick all the kai on the table at once?" Mrs. Simmons deigned not to answer. Instead she motioned to the glasses, saying, "Now *this* is for white wine, this for red wine, this for champagne and this for cognac." Tuta sighed, saying "No beer? Thought as much." Refusing to hear him. Mrs. Simmons proceeded, "You sip your wine just like you sip the soup. Like *so*," and she showed him. "No, Tuta, not too fast. And leave the bowl *on* the table, *don't* put it to your lips. No, *don't* slurp. Oh my goodness. Very GOOD, Tuta! Now wipe your lips with the napkin." Tuta looked puzzled. "Ay?" he asked. "The paper napkin on your lap." Mrs. Simmons said. "This hanky thing?" Tuta responded. "Why, Tuta!" Mrs. Simmons's teeth said, "How clever of you to work that out. Shall we proceed to the second course? Good!" Mrs. Simmons felt quite sure that Professor Higgins didn't have it *this* bad.

Then, of course, there was the matter of learning how to dance—not hot rock but slow *slow* dancing, holding a girl, "You know," Mrs. Simmons said, "*together,*" adding, "and young ladies at the ball are never allowed to decline." So Tuta made a date with Desirée Dawn after hours at the club. Desirée was just overwhelmed to be asked for advice and told her friends Alexis Dynamite and Chantelle Derrier to help her. "Lissun, honey" Desirée said as she cracked her gum. "No matter what the dance is, there's always a basic rhythm." Chantelle giggled and said, "Yeah, very basic." Ignoring her, Desirée hauled Tuta on to the floor, did a few jeté's and, once she had limbered up, said, "Now *you* lead," and "Oo, honey, I didn't know you were so masterful." Alexis fluttered her false eyelashes and, "You two don't need music at *all*," she whispered. Nevertheless, Alexis ran the tape and the music boomed across the club floor. "This isn't ball music," Tuta said as he heard the raunch scream out of the saxes. "How do *you* know?" Chantelle responded. And Tuta had the feeling that he wasn't going to learn how to dance in any way except improperly. "Lissun," Desirée said, "Alexis and I will show you. Move your butt over here, Lexie. Now, Tuta honey, just watch. Can ya hear the rhythum? Well you go *boom* and a *boom* and a *boom boom boom.*" And Alexis screamed and yelled, "Desirée, he wants to dance with the girl, not *make* her in the middle of the floor." And Chantelle only made matters worse by laughing, "Yeah, you stupid slut, you want him to end up in prison like you?" At which Desirée gasped, walked over to Chantelle, peeled off both Chantelle's false eyelashes, said, "Can you see better? Good," and lammed her one in the mouth. As he exited, Tuta knew he would have better luck with Sheree at the pinball parlour—she used to be good at roller skating and could even do the splits in mid-air.

So it went on. The fitting at the tailor's was duly accomplished ("Hmm-mmnnnn," the tailor said as he measured Tuta up. "Your shoulders are too wide, your hips too large, you have shorter legs than you should have but—Hmmmmnnnn"), his hair was trimmed to within an inch of propriety, and he painted his brown shoes black. His lessons continued with Mrs. Simmons, Tuta's mother, the workers from the factory—even the boss—all pitching in to assist Tuta in the etiquette required. For instance: "If you're talking you ask about the weather. This is called polite conversation. You say "Isn't it lovely?" to everything, even if it isn't. You always say "Yes" if you're offered something, even if you don't want it. The man with the medals is *not* the waiter. He is His Excellency. The lady who looks like a horse is not in drag and you should *not* ask if her tiara fell off the same truck as Bigfoot's."

Then, suddenly it was time for Tuta to go to the ball. "Yes, Mum," he said to 10 Coral as she fussed around him with a clothes brush, "I've got a hanky, I've brushed my teeth three times already, the invite is in my pocket—" And when Tuta stepped out the door the whole world was there—the boss, Mrs. Simmons, Crazy-Joe, Blackjack, Bigfoot and others from the factory, Desirée Dawn and the neighbours. "Don't let us down ," the boss said. "Not too much food on the fork," Mrs. Simmons instructed. "The third boom is the one that does it," Desirée Dawn called. "Don't forget the Diplo plates," Blackjack whispered. "And don't drink too much of the beer," Coral said. Then, there was the car, a Jaguar festooned with white ribbons and two small dolls on the bonnet. "It's a ball I'm off to," Tuta said sarcastically, "not a wedding." Blackjack shrugged his shoulders. "Best I could do, mate, and this beauty was just sitting there outside the church and—" He got in and started the motor. Tuta sat in the back and, suddenly, Bigfoot and Crazy-Joe were in either side. "The boss's orders," they said. "We deliver you to the door or else—" Outside, Tuta saw the boss draw a line across their necks. The car drew away and as it did so, Mrs. Simmons gave a small scream. "Oh my goodness, I forgot to tell Tuta that if Nature calls he should not use the bushes," she said.

Looking back, Tuta never quite understood how he ever survived that journey. At one point a police car drew level on the motorway, but when they looked over at the Jaguar and saw Tuta he could just imagine their disbelief, Nah. Couldn't possibly . . . Nah. His head was whirling with all the etiquette he had learnt and all the instructions he had to remember. He trembled, squirmed, palpitated and sweated all over the seat. Then he was there, and Blackjack was showing the invitation, and the officer at the gate was looking doubtfully at the wedding decorations, and then "Proceed ahead, sir," the officer said. *What a long drive,* Tuta thought. *What a big palace. And look at all those flash people. And they're all going in.* "Well, mate," Blackjack said, "Good luck. Look for us in the car park." And Crazy-Joe said, "Hey, give the missus a whirl for me, ay?" and with that, and a squeal of tires (Blackjack was always such a show-off), they were gone.

He was alone. Him. Tuta Wharepapa. Standing there. At the entrance way. Inside he heard music and the laughter of the guests. Then someone grabbed his arm and said, "Come along!" and before he knew it he was inside and being propelled along a long hallway. And the young woman who had grabbed him was suddenly pulled away by her companion, and Tuta was alone again. *Oh boy,* he thought. *Look at this red carpet.* He felt quite sure that the paint was running off his shoes and that there were great big black footmarks all the way to where he was now standing. Then a voice BOOMED ahead, and Tuta saw that there was a line of people in front and they were handing their invitations in to the bouncer. Tuta joined them. The bouncer was very old and very dignified—he looked, though, as if he should have been retired from the job years ago. *Nah,* Tuta thought. *He couldn't be a bouncer. Must be a toff.* The toff looked Tuta up and down and thrust out his white-gloved hand. "I got an invitation," Tuta said. "True. I got one." The toff read the card and his eyebrows arched. "Your name?" he BOOMED. "Tuta." Couldn't he read? Then the toff turned away in the direction of a huge ballroom that stretched right to the end of the world. The room seemed to be hung with hundreds of chandeliers and *thousands* of people were either dancing or standing around the perimeter. There were steps leading down to the ballroom and, at the bottom, was a man wearing medals and a woman whose tiara wasn't as sparkly as Bigfoot's—*them.* And Tuta felt *sure,* when the Major-Domo—for that was who the toff was—stepped forward and opened his mouth to announce him, that *everybody* must have heard him BOOM—

"Your Excellencies, Mr. Tutae Tockypocka."

Tuta looked for a hole to disappear into. He tried to backpedal down the hallway but there were people behind him. "No, you got it wrong," he said between clenched teeth to the Major-Domo. "Tutae's a rude word." But the Major-Domo simply sniffed, handed back the invitation, and motioned Tuta down the stairs. Had *they* heard? In trembling anticipation Tuta approached the Governor-General. "Mr. Horrynotta?" the Governor-General smiled. "Splendid that you were able to come along. Dear? Here's Mr. Tutae." And in front of him was Mrs. Governor-General. "Mr. Forrimoppa, how kind of you to come. May I call you Tutae? Please let me introduce you to Lord Wells." And Lord Wells, too. "Mr. Mopperuppa, quite a mouthful, what. Not so with Tutae, what?" *You don't know the half of it,* Tuta thought gloomily. And then Mrs. Governor-General just *had* to, didn't she, giggle and pronounce to all and sundry, "Everybody, you must meet Mr. Tutae." And that's who Tuta became all that evening. "Have you met Mr. Tutae yet? No? Mr. Tutae, this is Mr.—" And Tuta would either shake hands or do a stiff little bow and look around for that hole in the floor. He once made an attempt to explain what "tutae" was but heard Mrs. Simmons's voice: "If in doubt, Tuta, *don't.*" So instead he would draw attention away from that word by asking about the weather. "Do you think it will rain?" he would ask. "Oh, not inside, Mr. Tutae!"—and the word got around that Mr. Tutae was such a wit, so funny, so quaint, that he soon found himself exactly where he didn't want to be—at the centre of attention. In desperation, he asked every woman to dance. "Why, certainly, Mr. Tutae!" they said, because ladies never said no. So he danced with them all—a fat lady, a slim lady, a lady whose bones cracked all the time—and, because he was nervous, he went *boom* at every third step, and *that* word got around too. And as the Governor-General waltzed past he shouted, "Well done, Tutae, jolly good show."

No matter what he tried to do Tuta could never get away from being at the cen- 15 tre of the crowd or at the centre of attention. Instead of being gratified, however, Tuta became more embarrassed. Everybody seemed to laugh at his every word, even when it wasn't funny, or to accept his way of dancing because it was so *daring.* It seemed as if he could get away with anything. At the same time, Tuta suddenly re- alised that he was the only Maori there and that perhaps people were mocking him. He wasn't a real person to them, but rather an Entertainment. Even when buffet din- ner was served, the crowd still seemed to mock him, pressing in upon him with "Have some hors d'oeuvres, Mr. Tutae. Some *escalope* of veal, perhaps? You must try the pâté de foie gras! A slice of *jambon?* What about some langouste? Oh, the raspberry gâteau is just divine!" It was as if the crowd knew very well his ignorance of such delicacies and, by referring to them, was putting him down. In desperation Tuta tried some caviar. "Oh, Mr. Tutae, we can see that you just love caviar!" Tuta gave a quiet, almost dangerous, smile. "Yes," he said. "I think it's just divine."

So it went on. But then, just after the buffet, a Very Important Person arrived and, relieved, Tuta found himself deserted. Interested, he watched as the one who had just arrived became the centre of attention. "It always happens this way," a voice said behind Tuta. "I wouldn't worry about it." Startled, Tuta turned around and saw a huge fern. "Before you," the fern continued, "it was me." Then Tuta saw that a young woman was sitting behind the fern. "I'm not worried," he said to her, "I'm glad." The woman sniffed and said, "You certainly looked as if you were enjoying it." Tuta parted the fronds to get a good look at the woman's face—it was a pleasant face, one which could be pretty if it didn't frown so much. "Shift over," Tuta said. "I'm coming to join you." He sidled around the plant and sat beside her. "My name is—" he began. "Yes, I know," the woman said quickly, "Mr. Tutae." Tuta shook his head vigorously, "*No,* not Tutae. Tuta." The woman looked at him curiously and, "Is there a difference?" she asked. "You better believe it," Tuta said. "Oh—" the woman sniffed. "I'm Joyce."

The music started to play again. Joyce squinted her eyes and Tuta sighed, "Why don't you put on your glasses?" Joyce squealed, "How did you know?" before pop- ping them on and parting the fronds. "I'm a sociology student," Joyce muttered. "Don't you think people's behaviour is just amazing? I mean ay-*may*zing?" Tuta shrugged his shoulders and wondered if Joyce was looking at something he couldn't see. "I mean," Joyce continued, "look at them out there, just *look* at them. This could be India under the Raj. All this British Imperial graciousness and yet the carpet is being pulled from right beneath their feet." Puzzled, Tuta tried to see the ball through Joyce's eyes, but failed. "Ah well," Joyce sighed. Then she put her hand out to Tuta so that he could shake it, saying "Goodbye, Mr. Tuta." Tuta looked at her and, "Are you going?" he asked. "Oh no," Joyce said, "I'm staying here until everybody leaves. But *you* must go out and reclaim attention." Tuta laughed. "That new guy's welcome," he said. "But don't you want to fulfil their expectations?" Joyce asked. Tuta paused, and "If that means what I think it means, no," he said. "Good," Joyce responded, "You are perfectly capable of beating them at their own game. Good luck."

Then, curious, Tuta asked, "What did you mean when you said that before me it had been *you?*" Joyce shifted uneasily, took off her glasses and said, "Well, I'm not a Maori, but I thought it would have been obvious—" *Oh,* Tuta thought, *she's a plain Jane and people have been making fun of her.* "But that doesn't matter to me," Tuta said gallantly. "Really?" Joyce asked. "I'll prove it," Tuta said. "How about having the next dance." Joyce gasped, "Are you *sure?*" Taken aback, Tuta said, "Of course, I'm sure." And Joyce said, "But are you *sure* you're sure!" To show her, Tuta stood up and took her hand. Joyce sighed and shook her head. "Well, don't say I didn't warn you." Then she stood up . . . and up . . . and UP.

"Oh," Tuta said as he parted the fronds to look up at Joyce's face. She must have been six feet six at least. He and Joyce regarded each other miserably. Joyce bit her lip. *Well you asked for it,* Tuta thought. "Come on," he said, "let's have a good time." He reached up, grabbed her waist, put his face against her chest, and they waltzed into the middle of the floor. There, Tuta stood as high on his toes as possible. *Oh, why did I come?* he thought. Then the music ended and he took Joyce back to the fern. "I'm sorry I'm such a bad dancer," she apologised. "I always took the man's part at school." Tuta smiled at her. "That's no sweat. Well—" And he was just about to leave her when he suddenly realised that after all he and Joyce were both outsiders really. And it came to him that, bloody hell, if you could not join them—as if he would really want to do *that*—then, yes, he could beat them if he wanted to. Not by giving in to them, but by being strong enough to stand up to them. Dance, perhaps, but using his own steps. Listen, also, not to the music of the band but to the music in his head. He owed it, after all, to generous but silly wonderful mixed-up Mum, Mrs. Simmons, Desirée Dawn, and the boys—Crazy-Joe, Blackjack and Bigfoot— who were out *there* but wanting to know enough to get *in.* But they needed to come in on their own terms—that's what they would have to learn—as the real people they were and not as carbon copies of the people already on the inside. Once they learnt that, *oh, world, watch out, for your walls will come down in a flash, like Jericho.*

20   "Look," Tuta said, "how about another dance!" Joyce looked at him in disbelief. "You're a sucker for punishment, aren't you!" she muttered. "Why?" Tuta bowed, mockingly. "Well, for one thing, it would be just divine." At that, Joyce let out a peal of laughter. She stood up again. "Thank you," Joyce whispered. Then, "You know, this is my first ball." And Tuta smiled and "It's *my* first ball too," he said. "From now on, balls like these will never be the same again." He took her hand and the band began to wail a sweet but *oh-so-mean* saxophone solo as he led her on to the floor.

QUESTIONS FOR DISCUSSION AND WRITING

1. **Plot**   An *epiphany* is a sudden illumination of a fundamental truth that one has not previously realized. What sort of epiphanies do Leila and Tuta experience at their dances? How do their responses to these epiphanies resolve the conflicts in their stories?

2. **Character**   How do the details that Leila notices at the beginning of the story justify Mansfield's characterization of her as a "country girl"? How do the details Tuta notices at the Government House reveal his differences from his hosts?

3. **Setting**   How does Mansfield use imagery and connotative language to describe the setting that Leila finds so appealing? How does Ihimaera use humor and slang to characterize Tuta's working-class world, the setting that he finds so familiar?

4. **Point of View**   How does the limited third-person point of view help readers understand the initiation of these young people into new and complex social worlds? What kinds of information would be missing from these stories if Leila and Tuta narrated their experiences in these unfamiliar settings?

5. **Theme**   In Mansfield's story, the fat man's age and weight make him an exception among the men at the dance; in Ihimaera's story, Joyce's height and academic interests make her different from the other guests. What truths do these "outsiders" provide for the protagonists? How do the protagonists' reactions to these truths underscore the themes of the stories?

POINT   OF   VIEW

Charlotte Perkins Gilman's "The Yellow Wallpaper" William Faulkner's "A Rose for Emily"

These two stories illustrate the power and interest that may be generated by the creation of unusual and challenging points of view in short fiction.

Charlotte Perkins Gilman's story creates particularly intriguing problems for the reader because it is narrated by a protagonist who, during the course of the narration, is apparently slipping further and further into madness. We can only know what she notices and chooses to tell us about the other characters, the setting, and her own interior reality, but we have no way to know for certain how many of her perceptions are accurate and which ones may be merely the products of her madness. The effect of this choice of point of view is to force readers to evaluate everything the narrator expresses and to come to considered conclusions about every important element in the story. To what extent is her husband responsible for her breakdown? Why does the narrator tend to express all thoughts and feelings in clipped, simple sentences? What exactly does the woman in the wallpaper represent to the narrator and to us? All such questions lead us back to the essential difficulty in the story: what can we know? How do we separate the worlds of the narrator's inner reality from our understanding of an implied objective reality? Gilman is, of course, not being merely perverse in choosing a point of view fraught with such difficulties, but is confronting us with the inescapable fact that all human reality is subjective and that madness and sanity have no clear boundary between them.

William Faulkner chooses an equally unusual and effective point of view from which to narrate "A Rose for Emily." The narrator is an anonymous resident of the town in which Miss Emily lives, but instead of expressing the uniquely individual point of view that we usually get from a first-person narrator, he or she purports to give us the town's view, the consensus among all the decent people who belong to this place. In a sense, Faulkner's narrator is the town itself. The collective common sense of the town, its sense of its own history, its certainty about its values, and even its pride in itself are inherent in the intelligent, ironic voice of the narrator.

Many of the themes in the story develop naturally from the point of view. When, for example, the genteel Southern tradition of protecting ladies leads Colonel Sartoris to lie to Emily to explain why she is not expected to pay taxes, the narrator asserts that "only a man of Colonel Sartoris' generation and thought could have invented it, and only a woman could have believed it." When the next generation tries to undo this bit of gallantry, the narrator reports with pride and humor that in ignoring the upstart demands of the later generation, "she vanquished them, horse and foot." The flashback account of the events thirty years earlier when Emily had found and then lost a suitor is delivered with the fondness and familiarity of a story long shared. Even the final shocking revelation in the story is muted by the mingling of pity and respect that the narrative voice inevitably conveys in its depiction of Emily.

As we read short fiction, our attention may be drawn first to such self-evident elements as plot and character, but as these two stories amply demonstrate, nothing is more important to the shaping of meaning and tone in a story than the choice of point of view.

8

··

C H A R L O T T E   P E R K I N S   G I L M A N

The Yellow Wallpaper

CHARLOTTE PERKINS GILMAN (1860–1935) was born in Hartford, Connecticut, the daughter of a family related to Lyman Beecher, the abolitionist; Henry Ward Beecher, the preacher; and Harriet Beecher Stowe, the author of *Uncle Tom's Cabin.* After briefly attending the Rhode Island School of Design, Gilman was forced to work as a commercial artist and art teacher because of her financial situation. In 1884 she married Charles Stetson, another artist. After the birth of her daughter the following year, she suffered a nervous breakdown. In 1888 she left her husband and moved with her daughter to Pasadena, where she began writing stories, poems, and political tracts. In 1900, she married her cousin George Gilman and began an active career as a lecturer on feminist and socialist issues. Her best-known work is *Women and Economics* (1898), which makes an appeal for the financial independence of women. In other books, such as *Concerning Children* (1900), *Human Work* (1904), and *The Man-Made World* (1911), she called for a re-examination of the traditional roles assigned to women in our culture. Her fiction includes *What Diantha Did* (1910), *The Crux* (1911), and short stories collected in *The Charlotte Perkins Gilman Reader* (1979). "The Yellow Wallpaper," first published in *The New England Magazine* (January 1892), is a study of a woman driven to madness.

It is very seldom that mere ordinary people like John and myself secure ancestral halls for the summer.

A colonial mansion, a hereditary estate, I would say a haunted house and reach the height of romantic felicity—but that would be asking too much of fate!

Still I will proudly declare that there is something queer about it.

Else, why should it be let so cheaply? And why have stood so long untenanted? John laughs at me, of course, but one expects that. 5

John is practical in the extreme. He has no patience with faith, an intense horror of superstition, and he scoffs openly at any talk of things not to be felt and seen and put down in figures.

John is a physician, and *perhaps*—(I would not say it to a living soul, of course, but this is dead paper and a great relief to my mind)—*perhaps* that is one reason I do not get well faster.

You see, he does not believe I am sick! And what can one do?

If a physician of high standing, and one's own husband, assures friends and relatives that there is really nothing the matter with one but temporary nervous depression—a slight hysterical tendency—what is one to do?

10   My brother is also a physician, and also of high standing, and he says the same thing.

So I take phosphates or phosphites—whichever it is—and tonics, and air and exercise, and journeys, and am absolutely forbidden to "work" until I am well again.

Personally, I disagree with their ideas.

Personally, I believe that congenial work, with excitement and change, would do me good.

But what is one to do?

15   I did write for a while in spite of them; but it *does* exhaust me a good deal—having to be so sly about it, or else meet with heavy opposition.

I sometimes fancy that in my condition, if I had less opposition and more society and stimulus—but John says the very worst thing I can do is to think about my condition, and I confess it always makes me feel bad.

So I will let it alone and talk about the house.

The most beautiful place! It is quite alone, standing well back from the road, quite three miles from the village. It makes me think of English places that you read about, for there are hedges and walls and gates that lock, and lots of separate little houses for the gardeners and people.

There is a *delicious* garden! I never saw such a garden—large and shady, full of box-bordered paths, and lined with long grape-covered arbors with seats under them.

20   There were greenhouses, but they are all broken now.

There was some legal trouble, I believe, something about the heirs and co-heirs; anyhow, the place has been empty for years.

That spoils my ghostliness, I am afraid, but I don't care—there is something strange about the house—I can feel it.

I even said so to John one moonlight evening, but he said what I felt was a draught, and shut the window.

I get unreasonably angry with John sometimes. I'm sure I never used to be so sensitive. I think it is due to this nervous condition.

25   But John says if I feel so I shall neglect proper self-control; so I take pains to control myself—before him, at least, and that makes me very tired.

I don't like our room a bit. I wanted one downstairs that opened onto the piazza and had roses all over the window, and such pretty old-fashioned chintz hangings! But John would not hear of it.

He said there was only one window and not room for two beds, and no near room for him if he took another.

He is very careful and loving, and hardly lets me stir without special direction.

I have a schedule prescription for each hour in the day; he takes all care from me, and so I feel basely ungrateful not to value it more.

He said he came here solely on my account, that I was to have perfect rest and all the air I could get. "Your exercise depends on your strength, my dear," said he, "and your food somewhat on your appetite; but air you can absorb all the time." So we took the nursery at the top of the house.

It is a big, airy room, the whole floor nearly, with windows that look all ways, and air and sunshine galore. It was nursery first, and then playroom and gymnasium, I should judge, for the windows are barred for little children, and there are rings and things in the walls.

The paint and paper look as if a boys' school had used it. It is stripped off—the paper—in great patches all around the head of my bed, about as far as I can reach, and in a great place on the other side of the room low down. I never saw a worse paper in my life. One of those sprawling, flamboyant patterns committing every artistic sin.

It is dull enough to confuse the eye in following, pronounced enough constantly to irritate and provoke study, and when you follow the lame uncertain curves for a little distance they suddenly commit suicide—plunge off at outrageous angles, destroy themselves in unheard-of contradictions.

The color is repellant, almost revolting: a smouldering unclean yellow, strangely faded by the slow-turning sunlight. It is a dull yet lurid orange in some places, a sickly sulphur tint in others.

No wonder the children hated it! I should hate it myself if I had to live in this room long.

There comes John, and I must put this away—he hates to have me write a word.

We have been here two weeks, and I haven't felt like writing before, since that first day.

I am sitting by the window now, up in this atrocious nursery, and there is nothing to hinder my writing as much as I please, save lack of strength.

John is away all day, and even some nights when his cases are serious.

I am glad my case is not serious!

But these nervous troubles are dreadfully depressing.

John does not know how much I really suffer. He knows there is no reason to suffer, and that satisfies him.

Of course it is only nervousness. It does weigh on me so not to do my duty in any way!

I meant to be such a help to John, such a real rest and comfort, and here I am a comparative burden already!

Nobody would believe what an effort it is to do what little I am able—to dress and entertain, and order things.

It is fortunate Mary is so good with the baby. Such a dear baby!

And yet I *cannot* be with him, it makes me so nervous.

I suppose John never was nervous in his life. He laughs at me so about this wallpaper!

At first he meant to repaper the room, but afterward he said that I was letting it get the better of me, and that nothing was worse for a nervous patient than to give way to such fancies.

50   He said that after the wallpaper was changed it would be the heavy bedstead, and then the barred windows, and then that gate at the end of the stairs, and so on.

"You know the place is doing you good," he said, "and really, dear, I don't care to renovate the house just for a three months' rental."

"Then do let us go downstairs," I said. "There are such pretty rooms there."

Then he took me in his arms and called me a blessed little goose, and said he would go down to the cellar, if I wished, and have it whitewashed into the bargain.

But he is right enough about the beds and windows and things.

55   It is as airy and comfortable a room as anyone need wish, and, of course, I would not be so silly as to make him uncomfortable just for a whim.

I'm really getting quite fond of the big room, all but that horrid paper.

Out of one window I can see the garden—those mysterious deep-shaded arbors, the riotous old-fashioned flowers, and bushes and gnarly trees.

Out of another I get a lovely view of the bay and a little private wharf belonging to the estate. There is a beautiful shaded lane that runs down there from the house. I always fancy I see people walking in these numerous paths and arbors, but John has cautioned me not to give way to fancy in the least. He says that with my imaginative power and habit of story-making, a nervous weakness like mine is sure to lead to all manner of excited fancies, and that I ought to use my will and good sense to check the tendency. So I try.

I think sometimes that if I were only well enough to write a little it would relieve the press of ideas and rest me.

60   But I find I get pretty tired when I try.

It is so discouraging not to have any advice and companionship about my work. When I get really well, John says we will ask Cousin Henry and Julia down for a long visit; but he says he would as soon put fireworks in my pillow-case as to let me have those stimulating people about now.

I wish I could get well faster.

But I must not think about that. This paper looks to me as if it *knew* what a vicious influence it had!

There is a recurrent spot where the pattern lolls like a broken neck and two bulbous eyes stare at you upside down.

65   I get positively angry with the impertinence of it and the everlastingness. Up and down and sideways they crawl, and those absurd unblinking eyes are everywhere. There is one place where two breadths didn't match, the eyes go all up and down the line, one a little higher than the other.

I never saw so much expression in an inanimate thing before, and we all know how much expression they have! I used to lie awake as a child and get more entertainment and terror out of blank walls and plain furniture than most children could find in a toy-store.

I remember what a kindly wink the knobs of our big old bureau used to have, and there was one chair that always seemed like a strong friend.

I used to feel that if any of the other things looked too fierce I could always hop into that chair and be safe.

The furniture in this room is no worse than inharmonious, however, for we had to bring it all from downstairs. I suppose when this was used as a playroom they had to take the nursery things out, and no wonder! I never saw such ravages as the children have made here.

The wallpaper, as I said before, is torn off in spots, and it sticketh closer than a brother—they must have had perseverance as well as hatred.

Then the floor is scratched and gouged and splintered, the plaster itself is dug out here and there, and this great heavy bed, which is all we found in the room, looks as if it had been through the wars.

But I don't mind it a bit—only the paper.

There comes John's sister. Such a dear girl as she is, and so careful of me! I must not let her find me writing.

She is a perfect and enthusiastic housekeeper, and hopes for no better profession. I verily believe she thinks it is the writing which makes me sick!

But I can write when she is out, and see her a long way off from these windows.

There is one that commands the road, a lovely shaded winding road, and one that just looks off over the country. A lovely country, too, full of great elms and velvet meadows.

This wallpaper has a kind of sub-pattern in a different shade, a particularly irritating one, for you can only see it in certain lights, and not clearly then.

But in the places where it isn't faded and where the sun is just so—I can see a strange provoking, formless sort of figure that seems to skulk about behind that silly and conspicuous front design.

There's sister on the stairs!

Well, the Fourth of July is over! The people are all gone, and I am tired out. John thought it might do me good to see a little company, so we just had Mother and Nellie and the children down for a week.

Of course I didn't do a thing. Jennie sees to everything now.

But it tired me all the same.

John says if I don't pick up faster he shall send me to Weir Mitchell in the fall.

But I don't want to go there at all. I had a friend who was in his hands once, and she says he is just like John and my brother, only more so!

Besides, it is such an undertaking to go so far.

I don't feel as if it was worthwhile to turn my hand over for anything, and I'm getting dreadfully fretful and querulous.

I cry at nothing, and cry most of the time.

Of course I don't when John is here, or anybody else, but when I am alone.

And I am alone a good deal just now. John is kept in town very often by serious cases, and Jennie is good and lets me alone when I want her to.

So I walk a little in the garden or down that lovely lane, sit on the porch under the roses, and lie down up here a good deal.

I'm getting really fond of the room in spite of the wallpaper. Perhaps *because* of the wallpaper.

It dwells in my mind so!

I lie here on this great immovable bed—it is nailed down, I believe—and follow that pattern about by the hour. It is as good as gymnastics, I assure you. I start, we'll say, at the bottom, down in the corner over there where it has not been touched, and

I determine for the thousandth time that I *will* follow that pointless pattern to some sort of a conclusion.

I know a little of the principle of design, and I know this thing was not arranged on any laws of radiation, or alternation, or repetition, or symmetry, or anything else that I ever heard of.

95   It is repeated, of course, by the breadths, but not otherwise.

Looked at in one way, each breadth stands alone; the bloated curves and flourishes—a kind of "debased Romanesque" with delirium tremens go waddling up and down in isolated columns of fatuity.

But, on the other hand, they connect diagonally, and the sprawling outlines run off in great slanting waves of optic horror, like a lot of wallowing sea-weeds in full chase.

The whole thing goes horizontally, too, at least it seems so, and I exhaust myself trying to distinguish the order of its going in that direction.

They have used a horizontal breadth for a frieze, and that adds wonderfully to the confusion.

100   There is one end of the room where it is almost intact, and there, when the cross-lights fade and the low sun shines directly upon it, I can almost fancy radiation after all—the interminable grotesque seems to form around a common center and rush off in headlong plunges of equal distraction.

It makes me tired to follow it. I will take a nap, I guess.

I don't know why I should write this.

I don't want to.

I don't feel able.

105   And I know John would think it absurd. But I *must* say what I feel and think in some way—it is such a relief!

But the effort is getting to be greater than the relief.

Half the time now I am awfully lazy, and lie down ever so much. John says I mustn't lose my strength, and has me take cod liver oil and lots of tonics and things, to say nothing of ale and wine and rare meat.

Dear John! He loves me very dearly, and hates to have me sick. I tried to have a real earnest reasonable talk with him the other day, and tell him how I wish he would let me go and make a visit to Cousin Henry and Julia.

But he said I wasn't able to go, nor able to stand it after I got there; and I did not make out a very good case for myself, for I was crying before I had finished.

110   It is getting to be a great effort for me to think straight. Just this nervous weakness, I suppose.

And dear John gathered me up in his arms, and just carried me upstairs and laid me on the bed, and sat by me and read to me till it tired my head.

He said I was his darling and his comfort and all he had, and that I must take care of myself for his sake, and keep well.

He says no one but myself can help me out of it, that I must use my will and self-control and not let any silly fancies run away with me.

There's one comfort—the baby is well and happy, and does not have to occupy this nursery with the horrid wallpaper.

If we had not used it, that blessed child would have! What a fortunate escape! Why, I wouldn't have a child of mine, an impressionable little thing, live in such a room for worlds.

I never thought of it before, but it is lucky that John kept me here after all; I can stand it so much easier than a baby, you see.

Of course I never mention it to them any more—I am too wise—but I keep watch for it all the same.

There are things in that wallpaper that nobody knows about but me, or ever will.

Behind that outside pattern the dim shapes get clearer every day.

It is always the same shape, only very numerous.

And it is like a woman stooping down and creeping about behind that pattern. I don't like it a bit. I wonder—I began to think—I wish John would take me away from here!

It is so hard to talk with John about my case, because he is so wise, and because he loves me so.

But I tried it last night.

It was moonlight. The moon shines in all around just as the sun does.

I hate to see it sometimes, it creeps so slowly, and always comes in by one window or another.

John was asleep and I hated to waken him, so I kept still and watched the moonlight on that undulating wallpaper till I felt creepy.

The faint figure behind seemed to shake the pattern, just as if she wanted to get out.

I got up softly and went to feel and see if the paper *did* move, and when I came back John was awake.

"What is it, little girl?" he said. "Don't go walking about like that—you'll get cold."

I thought it was a good time to talk, so I told him that I really was not gaining here, and that I wished he would take me away.

"Why, darling!" said he. "Our lease will be up in three weeks, and I can't see how to leave before.

"The repairs are not done at home, and I cannot possibly leave town just now. Of course, if you were in any danger, I could and would, but you really are better, dear, whether you can see it or not. I am a doctor, dear, and I know. You are gaining flesh and color, your appetite is better, I feel really much easier about you."

"I don't weigh a bit more," said I, "nor as much; and my appetite may be better in the evening when you are here but it is worse in the morning when you are away!"

"Bless her little heart!" said he with a big hug. "She shall be as sick as she pleases! But now let's improve the shining hours by going to sleep, and talk about it in the morning!"

"And you won't go away?" I asked gloomily.

"Why, how can I, dear? It is only three weeks more and then we will take a nice little trip of a few days while Jennie is getting the house ready. Really, dear, you are better!"

"Better in body perhaps—" I began, and stopped short, for he sat up straight and looked at me with such a stern, reproachful look that I could not say another word.

"My darling," said he, "I beg of you, for my sake and for our child's sake, as well as for your own, that you will never for one instant let that idea enter your mind! There is nothing so dangerous, so fascinating, to a temperament like yours. It is a false and foolish fancy. Can you not trust me as a physician when I tell you so?"

So of course I said no more on that score, and we went to sleep before long. He thought I was asleep first, but I wasn't, and lay there for hours trying to decide whether that front pattern and the back pattern really did move together or separately.

140   On a pattern like this, by daylight, there is a lack of sequence, a defiance of law, that is a constant irritant to a normal mind.

The color is hideous enough, and unreliable enough, and infuriating enough, but the pattern is torturing.

You think you have mastered it, but just as you get well under way in following, it turns a back-somersault and there you are. It slaps you in the face, knocks you down, and tramples upon you. It is like a bad dream.

The outside pattern is a florid arabesque, reminding one of a fungus. If you can imagine a toadstool in joints, an interminable string of toadstools, budding and sprouting in endless convolutions—why, that is something like it.

That is, sometimes!

145   There is one marked peculiarity about this paper, a thing nobody seems to notice but myself, and that is that it changes as the light changes.

When the sun shoots in through the east window—I always watch for that first long, straight ray—it changes so quickly that I never can quite believe it.

That is why I watch it always.

By moonlight—the moon shines in all night when there is a moon—I wouldn't know it was the same paper.

At night in any kind of light, in twilight, candlelight, lamplight, and worst of all by moonlight, it becomes bars! The outside pattern, I mean, and the woman behind it is as plain as can be.

150   I didn't realize for a long time what the thing was that showed behind, that dim sub-pattern, but now I am quite sure it is a woman.

By daylight she is subdued, quiet. I fancy it is the pattern that keeps her so still. It is so puzzling. It keeps me quiet by the hour.

I lie down ever so much now. John says it is good for me, and to sleep all I can. Indeed he started the habit by making me lie down for an hour after each meal.

It is a very bad habit, I am convinced, for you see, I don't sleep.

155   And that cultivates deceit, for I don't tell them I'm awake—oh, no!

The fact is I am getting a little afraid of John.

He seems very queer sometimes, and even Jennie has an inexplicable look.

It strikes me occasionally, just as a scientific hypothesis, that perhaps it is the paper!

I have watched John when he did not know I was looking, and come into the room suddenly on the most innocent excuses, and I've caught him several times *looking at the paper!* And Jennie too. I caught Jennie with her hand on it once.

She didn't know I was in the room, and when I asked her in a quiet, a very quiet voice, with the most restrained manner possible, what she was doing with the paper, she turned around as if she had been caught stealing, and looked quite angry—asked me why I should frighten her so!

Then she said that the paper stained everything it touched, that she had found yellow smooches on all my clothes and John's and she wished we would be more careful!

Did not that sound innocent? But I know she was studying that pattern, and I am determined that nobody shall find it out but myself!

Life is very much more exciting now than it used to be. You see, I have something more to expect, to look forward to, to watch. I really do eat better, and am more quiet than I was.

John is so pleased to see me improve! He laughed a little the other day, and said I seemed to be flourishing in spite of my wallpaper.

I turned it off with a laugh. I had no intention of telling him it was *because* of the wallpaper—he would make fun of me. He might even want to take me away.

I don't want to leave now until I have found it out. There is a week more, and I think that will be enough.

I'm feeling so much better!

I don't sleep much at night, for it is so interesting to watch developments; but I sleep a good deal during the daytime.

In the daytime it is tiresome and perplexing.

There are always new shoots on the fungus, and new shades of yellow all over it. I cannot keep count of them, though I have tried conscientiously.

It is the strangest yellow, that wallpaper! It makes me think of all the yellow things I ever saw—not beautiful ones like buttercups, but old, foul, bad yellow things.

But there is something else about that paper—the smell! I noticed it the moment we came into the room, but with so much air and sun it was not bad. Now we have had a week of fog and rain, and whether the windows are open or not, the smell is here.

It creeps all over the house.

I find it hovering in the dining-room, skulking in the parlor, hiding in the hall, lying in wait for me on the stairs.

It gets into my hair.

Even when I go to ride, if I turn my head suddenly and surprise it—there is that smell!

Such a peculiar odor, too! I have spent hours in trying to analyze it, to find what it smelled like.

It is not bad—at first—and very gentle, but quite the subtlest, most enduring odor I ever met.

In this damp weather it is awful. I wake up in the night and find it hanging over me.

It used to disturb me at first. I thought seriously of burning the house—to reach the smell.

But now I am used to it. The only thing I can think of that it is like is the *color* of the paper! A yellow smell.

There is a very funny mark on this wall, low down, near the mopboard. A streak that runs round the room. It goes behind every piece of furniture, except the bed, a long, straight, even *smooch,* as if it had been rubbed over and over.

I wonder how it was done and who did it, and what they did it for. Round and round and round—round and round and round—it makes me dizzy!

I really have discovered something at last.

185   Through watching so much at night, when it changes so, I have finally found out. The front pattern *does* move—and no wonder! The woman behind shakes it!

Sometimes I think there are a great many women behind, and sometimes only one, and she crawls around fast, and her crawling shakes it all over.

Then in the very bright spots she keeps still, and in the very shady spots she just takes hold of the bars and shakes them hard.

And she is all the time trying to climb through. But nobody could climb through that pattern—it strangles so; I think that is why it has so many heads.

190   They get through and then the pattern strangles them off and turns them upside down, and makes their eyes white!

If those heads were covered or taken off it would not be half so bad.

I think that woman gets out in the daytime!

And I'll tell you why—privately—I've seen her!

I can see her out of every one of my windows!

195   It is the same woman, I know, for she is always creeping, and most women do not creep by daylight.

I see her in that long shaded lane, creeping up and down. I see her in those dark grape arbors, creeping all around the garden.

I see her on that long road under the trees, creeping along, and when a carriage comes she hides under the blackberry vines.

I don't blame her a bit. It must be very humiliating to be caught creeping by daylight!

I always lock the door when I creep by daylight. I can't do it at night, for I know John would suspect something at once.

200   And John is so queer now that I don't want to irritate him. I wish he would take another room! Besides, I don't want anybody to get that woman out at night but myself.

I often wonder if I could see her out of all the windows at once.

But, turn as fast as I can, I can only see out of one at a time.

And though I always see her, she *may* be able to creep faster than I can turn! I have watched her sometimes away off in the open country, creeping as fast as a cloud shadow in a wind.

If only that top pattern could be gotten off from the under one! I mean to try it, little by little.

205   I have found out another funny thing, but I shan't tell this time! It does not do to trust people too much.

There are only two more days to get this paper off, and I believe John is beginning to notice. I don't like the look in his eyes.

And I heard him ask Jennie a lot of professional questions about me. She had a very good report to give.

She said I slept a good deal in the daytime.

John knows I don't sleep very well at night, for all I'm so quiet!

He asked me all sorts of questions, too, and pretended to be very loving and kind. 210
As if I couldn't see through him!

Still, I don't wonder he acts so, sleeping under this paper for three months.

It only interests me, but I feel sure John and Jennie are affected by it.

Hurray! This is the last day, but it is enough. John is to stay in town over night, and won't be out until this evening.

Jennie wanted to sleep with me—the sly thing; but I told her I should undoubt- 215
edly rest better for a night all alone.

That was clever, for really I wasn't alone a bit! As soon as it was moonlight and that poor thing began to crawl and shake the pattern, I got up and ran to help her.

I pulled and she shook. I shook and she pulled, and before morning we had peeled off yards of that paper.

A strip about as high as my head and half around the room.

And then when the sun came and that awful pattern began to laugh at me, I declared I would finish it today!

We go away tomorrow, and they are moving all my furniture down again to 220
leave things as they were before.

Jennie looked at the wall in amazement, but I told her merrily that I did it out of pure spite at the vicious thing.

She laughed and said she wouldn't mind doing it herself, but I must not get tired.

How she betrayed herself that time!

But I am here, and no person touches this paper but Me—not *alive!*

She tried to get me out of the room—it was too patent! But I said it was so quiet 225
and empty and clean now that I believed I would lie down again and sleep all I could, and not to wake me even for dinner—I would call when I woke.

So now she is gone, and the servants are gone, and the things are gone, and there is nothing left but that great bedstead nailed down, with the canvas mattress we found on it.

We shall sleep downstairs tonight, and take the boat home tomorrow.

I quite enjoy the room, now it is bare again.

How those children did tear about here!

This bedstead is fairly gnawed!   230

But I must get to work.

I have locked the door and thrown the key down into the front path.

I don't want to go out, and I don't want to have anybody come in, till John comes.

I want to astonish him.

235   I've got a rope up here that even Jennie did not find. If that woman does get out, and tries to get away, I can tie her!

But I forgot I could not reach far without anything to stand on!

This bed will *not* move!

I tried to lift and push it until I was lame, and then I got so angry I bit off a little piece at one corner—but it hurt my teeth.

Then I peeled off all the paper I could reach standing on the floor. It sticks horribly and the pattern just enjoys it! All those strangled heads and bulbous eyes and waddling fungus growths just shriek with derision!

240   I am getting angry enough to do something desperate. To jump out of the window would be admirable exercise, but the bars are too strong even to try.

Besides I wouldn't do it. Of course not. I know well enough that a step like that is improper and might be misconstrued.

I don't like to *look* out of the windows even—there are so many of those creeping women, and they creep so fast.

I wonder if they all come out of that wallpaper as I did?

But I am securely fastened now by my well-hidden rope—you don't get *me* out in the road there!

245   I suppose I shall have to get back behind the pattern when it comes night, and that is hard!

It is so pleasant to be out in this great room and creep around as I please!

I don't want to go outside. I won't, even if Jennie asks me to.

For outside you have to creep on the ground, and everything is green instead of yellow.

But here I can creep smoothly on the floor, and my shoulder just fits in that long smooch around the wall, so I cannot lose my way.

250   Why, there's John at the door!

It is no use, young man, you can't open it!

How he does call and pound!

Now he's crying to Jennie for an axe.

It would be a shame to break down that beautiful door!

255   "John, dear!" said I in the gentlest voice. "The key is down by the front steps, under a plantain leaf!"

That silenced him for a few moments.

Then he said, very quietly indeed, "Open the door, my darling!"

"I can't," said I. "The key is down by the front door under a plantain leaf!" And then I said it again, several times, very gently and slowly, and said it so often that he had to go and see, and he got it of course, and came in. He stopped short by the door.

"What is the matter?" he cried. "For God's sake, what are you doing?"

260   I kept on creeping just the same, but I looked at him over my shoulder.

"I've got out at last," said I, "in spite of you and Jane. And I've pulled off most of the paper, so you can't put me back."

Now why should that man have fainted? But he did, and right across my path by the wall, so that I had to creep over him every time!

9

W I L L I A M   F A U L K N E R

A Rose for Emily

WILLIAM FAULKNER (1897–1962) was born in New Albany, Mississippi, but soon moved to Oxford, Mississippi, where his father worked as the business manager of the University of Mississippi. Faulkner left high school to work in a local bank and then in 1918 enlisted in the Royal Canadian Air Force, before returning for a brief period to study at the University of Mississippi. During the early twenties, Faulkner began writing poetry and fiction and became acquainted with various members of the literary community in New Orleans, most notably Sherwood Anderson, who encouraged his endeavors. In 1929 Faulkner published *Sartoris,* the first of his novels dealing with the life and legends of Yoknapatawpha, an imaginary county in Mississippi. Although Faulkner wrote novels about this county at an astonishing pace—*The Sound and the Fury* (1929), *As I Lay Dying* (1930), *Light in August* (1932), *Absalom, Absalom* (1936), *The Hamlet* (1940), *Go Down, Moses* (1942)—and although he published his short stories in such commercially recognized magazines as *The Saturday Evening Post,* his literary reputation during this period was negligible. Faulkner's need for money forced him to accept many off-and-on assignments as a screenwriter in Hollywood, working on such films as *To Have and Have Not* and *The Big Sleep.* Faulkner was finally recognized as a major literary talent when he was awarded the Nobel Prize in 1949. He continued to produce novels such as *The Town* (1957), *The Mansion* (1959), and *The Reivers* (1963), and he collected many of his stories in a 1950 volume that won the National Book Award. "A Rose for Emily," reprinted from that volume, is a community's account of the life of one of its oldest citizens.

I

When Miss Emily Grierson died, our whole town went to her funeral: the men through a sort of respectful affection for a fallen monument, the women mostly out of curiosity to see the inside of her house, which no one save an old manservant—a combined gardener and cook—had seen in at least ten years.

It was a big, squarish frame house that had once been white, decorated with cupolas and spires and scrolled balconies in the heavily lightsome style of the seventies, set on what had once been our most select street. But garages and cotton gins had encroached and obliterated even the august names of that neighborhood; only Miss Emily's house was left, lifting its stubborn and coquettish decay above the cotton wagons and the gasoline pumps—an eyesore among eyesores. And now Miss Emily had gone to join the representatives of those august names where they lay in the cedar-bemused cemetery among the ranked and anonymous graves of Union and Confederate soldiers who fell at the battle of Jefferson.

Alive, Miss Emily had been a tradition, a duty, and a care; a sort of hereditary obligation upon the town, dating from that day in 1894 when Colonel Sartoris, the mayor—he who fathered the edict that no Negro woman should appear on the streets without an apron—remitted her taxes, the dispensation dating from the death of her father on into perpetuity. Not that Miss Emily would have accepted charity. Colonel Sartoris invented an involved tale to the effect that Miss Emily's father had loaned money to the town, which the town, as a matter of business, preferred this way of repaying. Only a man of Colonel Sartoris' generation and thought could have invented it, and only a woman could have believed it.

When the next generation, with its more modern ideas, became mayors and aldermen, this arrangement created some little dissatisfaction. On the first of the year they mailed her a tax notice. February came, and there was no reply. They wrote her a formal letter, asking her to call at the sheriff's office at her convenience. A week later the mayor wrote her himself, offering to call or to send his car for her, and received in reply a note on paper of an archaic shape, in a thin, flowing calligraphy in faded ink, to the effect that she no longer went out at all. The tax notice was also enclosed, without comment.

5   They called a special meeting of the Board of Aldermen. A deputation waited upon her, knocked at the door through which no visitor had passed since she ceased giving china-painting lessons eight or ten years earlier. They were admitted by the old Negro into a dim hall from which a stairway mounted into still more shadow. It smelled of dust and disuse—a close, dank smell. The Negro led them into the parlor. It was furnished in heavy, leather-covered furniture. When the Negro opened the blinds of one window, they could see that the leather was cracked; and when they sat down, a faint dust rose sluggishly about their thighs, spinning with slow motions in the single sun-ray. On a tarnished gilt easel before the fireplace stood a crayon portrait of Miss Emily's father.

They rose when she entered—a small, fat woman in black, with a thin gold chain descending to her waist and vanishing into her belt, leaning on an ebony cane with a tarnished gold head. Her skeleton was small and spare; perhaps that was why what would have been merely plumpness in another was obesity in her. She looked bloated, like a body long submerged in motionless water, and of that pallid hue. Her eyes, lost in the fatty ridges of her face, looked like two small pieces of coal pressed into a lump of dough as they moved from one face to another while the visitors stated their errand.

She did not ask them to sit. She just stood in the door and listened quietly until the spokesman came to a stumbling halt. Then they could hear the invisible watch ticking at the end of the gold chain.

Her voice was dry and cold. "I have no taxes in Jefferson. Colonel Sartoris explained it to me. Perhaps one of you can gain access to the city records and satisfy yourselves."

"But we have. We are the city authorities, Miss Emily. Didn't you get a notice from the sheriff, signed by him?"

"I received a paper, yes," Miss Emily said. "Perhaps he considers himself the   10 sheriff . . . I have no taxes in Jefferson."

"But there is nothing on the books to show that, you see. We must go by the—"

"See Colonel Sartoris." (Colonel Sartoris had been dead almost ten years.) "I have no taxes in Jefferson. Tobe!" The Negro appeared. "Show these gentlemen out."

2

So she vanquished them, horse and foot, just as she had vanquished their fathers thirty years before about the smell. That was two years after her father's death and a short time after her sweetheart—the one we believed would marry her—had deserted her. After her father's death she went out very little; after her sweetheart went away, people hardly saw her at all. A few of the ladies had the temerity to call, but were not received, and the only sign of life about the place was the Negro man—a young man then—going in and out with a market basket.

"Just as if a man—any man—could keep a kitchen properly," the ladies said; so they were not surprised when the smell developed. It was another link between the gross, teeming world and the high and mighty Griersons.

A neighbor, a woman, complained to the mayor, Judge Stevens, eighty years old.   15

"But what will you have me do about it, madam?" he said.

"Why, send her word to stop it," the woman said. "Isn't there a law?"

"I'm sure that won't be necessary," Judge Stevens said. "It's probably just a snake or a rat that nigger of hers killed in the yard. I'll speak to him about it."

The next day he received two more complaints, one from a man who came in diffident deprecation. "We really must do something about it, Judge. I'd be the last one in the world to bother Miss Emily, but we've got to do something." That night the Board of Aldermen met—three graybeards and one younger man, a member of the rising generation.

"It's simple enough," he said. "Send her word to have her place cleaned up. Give   20 her a certain time to do it in, and if she don't . . ."

"Dammit, sir," Judge Stevens said, "will you accuse a lady to her face of smelling bad?"

So the next night, after midnight, four men crossed Miss Emily's lawn and slunk about the house like burglars, sniffing along the base of the brickwork and at the cellar openings while one of them performed a regular sowing motion with his hand out of a sack slung from his shoulder. They broke open the cellar door and sprinkled lime there, and in all the outbuildings. As they recrossed the lawn, a window that had been dark was lighted and Miss Emily sat in it, the light behind her, and her upright torso motionless as that of an idol. They crept quietly across the lawn and into the shadow of the locusts that lined the street. After a week or two the smell went away.

That was when people had begun to feel really sorry for her. People in our town, remembering how old lady Wyatt, her great-aunt, had gone completely crazy at last, believed that the Griersons held themselves a little too high for what they really were. None of the young men were quite good enough for Miss Emily and such. We had long thought of them as a tableau, Miss Emily a slender figure in white in the background, her father a spraddled silhouette in the foreground, his back to her and clutching a horsewhip, the two of them framed by the back-flung front door. So when she got to be thirty and was still single, we were not pleased exactly, but vindicated; even with insanity in the family she wouldn't have turned down all of her chances if they had really materialized.

When her father died, it got about that the house was all that was left to her; and in a way, people were glad. At last they could pity Miss Emily. Being left alone, and a pauper, she had become humanized. Now she too would know the old thrill and the old despair of a penny more or less.

25   The day after his death all the ladies prepared to call at the house and offer condolence and aid, as is our custom. Miss Emily met them at the door, dressed as usual and with no trace of grief on her face. She told them that her father was not dead. She did that for three days, with the ministers calling on her, and the doctors, trying to persuade her to let them dispose of the body. Just as they were about to resort to law and force, she broke down, and they buried her father quickly.

We did not say she was crazy then. We believed she had to do that. We remembered all the young men her father had driven away, and we knew that with nothing left, she would have to cling to that which had robbed her, as people will.

3

She was sick for a long time. When we saw her again, her hair was cut short, making her look like a girl, with a vague resemblance to those angels in colored church windows—sort of tragic and serene.

The town had just let the contracts for paving the sidewalks, and in the summer after her father's death they began the work. The construction company came with niggers and mules and machinery, and a foreman named Homer Barron, a Yankee— a big, dark, ready man, with a big voice and eyes lighter than his face. The little boys would follow in groups to hear him cuss the niggers, and the niggers singing in time to the rise and fall of picks. Pretty soon he knew everybody in town. Whenever you heard a lot of laughing anywhere about the square, Homer Barron would be in the center of the group. Presently we began to see him and Miss Emily on Sunday afternoons driving in the yellow-wheeled buggy and the matched team of bays from the livery stable.

At first we were glad that Miss Emily would have an interest, because the ladies all said, "Of course a Grierson would not think seriously of a Northerner, a day laborer." But there were still others, older people, who said that even grief could not cause a real lady to forget *noblesse oblige*—without calling it *noblesse oblige*. They just said, "Poor Emily. Her kinsfolk should come to her." She had some kin in Alabama; but years ago her father had fallen out with them over the estate of old lady Wyatt, the crazy woman, and there was no communication between the two families. They had not even been represented at the funeral.

30   And as soon as the old people said, "Poor Emily," the whispering began. "Do you suppose it's really so?" they said to one another. "Of course it is. What else

could . . . " This behind their hands; rustling of craned silk and satin behind jalousies closed upon the sun of Sunday afternoon as the thin, swift clop-clop-clop of the matched team passed: "Poor Emily."

She carried her head high enough—even when we believed that she was fallen. It was as if she demanded more than ever the recognition of her dignity as the last Grierson; as if it had wanted that touch of earthiness to reaffirm her imperviousness. Like when she bought the rat poison, the arsenic. That was over a year after they had begun to say "Poor Emily," and while the two female cousins were visiting her.

"I want some poison," she said to the druggist. She was over thirty then, still a slight woman, though thinner than usual, with cold, haughty black eyes in a face the flesh of which was strained across the temples and about the eye-sockets as you imagine a lighthouse-keeper's face ought to look. "I want some poison," she said.

"Yes, Miss Emily. What kind? For rats and such? I'd recom—"

"I want the best you have. I don't care what kind."

The druggist named several. "They'll kill anything up to an elephant. But what 35 you want is—"

"Arsenic," Miss Emily said. "Is that a good one?"

"Is . . . arsenic? Yes, ma'am. But what you want—"

"I want arsenic."

The druggist looked down at her. She looked back at him, erect, her face like a strained flag. "Why, of course," the druggist said. "If that's what you want. But the law requires you to tell what you are going to use it for."

Miss Emily just stared at him, her head tilted back in order to look him eye for 40 eye, until he looked away and went and got the arsenic and wrapped it up. The Negro delivery boy brought her the package; the druggist didn't come back. When she opened the package at home there was written on the box, under the skull and bones: "For rats."

4

So the next day we all said, "She will kill herself"; and we said it would be the best thing. When she had first begun to be seen with Homer Barron, we had said, "She will marry him." Then we said, "She will persuade him yet," because Homer himself had remarked—he liked men, and it was known that he drank with the younger men in the Elks' Club—that he was not a marrying man. Later we said, "Poor Emily" behind the jalousies as they passed on Sunday afternoon in the glittering buggy, Miss Emily with her head high and Homer Barron with his hat cocked and a cigar in his teeth, reins and whip in a yellow glove.

Then some of the ladies began to say that it was a disgrace to the town and a bad example to the young people. The men did not want to interfere, but at last the ladies forced the Baptist minister—Miss Emily's people were Episcopal—to call upon her. He would never divulge what happened during that interview, but he refused to go back again. The next Sunday they again drove about the streets, and the following day the minister's wife wrote to Miss Emily's relations in Alabama.

So she had blood-kin under her roof again and we sat back to watch developments. At first nothing happened. Then we were sure that they were to be married. We learned that Miss Emily had been to the jeweler's and ordered a man's toilet set in silver, with the letters H.B. on each piece. Two days later we learned that she had bought a complete outfit of men's clothing, including a nightshirt, and we said, "They are married." We were really glad. We were glad because the two female cousins were even more Grierson than Miss Emily had ever been.

So we were not surprised when Homer Barron—the streets had been finished some time since—was gone. We were a little disappointed that there was not a public blowing-off, but we believed that he had gone on to prepare for Miss Emily's coming, or to give her a chance to get rid of the cousins. (By that time it was a cabal, and we were all Miss Emily's allies to help circumvent the cousins.) Sure enough, after another week they departed. And, as we had expected all along, within three days Homer Barron was back in town. A neighbor saw the Negro man admit him at the kitchen door at dusk one evening.

45   And that was the last we saw of Homer Barron. And of Miss Emily for some time. The Negro man went in and out with the market basket, but the front door remained closed. Now and then we would see her at a window for a moment, as the men did that night when they sprinkled the lime, but for almost six months she did not appear on the streets. Then we knew that this was to be expected too; as if that quality of her father which had thwarted her woman's life so many times had been too virulent and too furious to die.

When we next saw Miss Emily, she had grown fat and her hair was turning gray. During the next few years it grew grayer and grayer until it attained an even pepper-and-salt iron-gray, when it ceased turning. Up to the day of her death at seventy-four it was still that vigorous iron-gray, like the hair of an active man.

From that time on her front door remained closed, save for a period of six or seven years, when she was about forty, during which she gave lessons in china-painting. She fitted up a studio in one of the downstairs rooms, where the daughters and granddaughters of Colonel Sartoris' contemporaries were sent to her with the same regularity and in the same spirit that they were sent to church on Sundays with a twenty-five-cent piece for the collection plate. Meanwhile her taxes had been remitted.

Then the newer generation became the backbone and the spirit of the town, and the painting pupils grew up and fell away and did not send their children to her with boxes of color and tedious brushes and pictures cut from the ladies' magazines. The front door closed upon the last one and remained closed for good. When the town got free postal delivery, Miss Emily alone refused to let them fasten the metal numbers above her door and attach a mailbox to it. She would not listen to them.

Daily, monthly, yearly we watched the Negro grow grayer and more stooped, going in and out with the market basket. Each December we sent her a tax notice, which would be returned by the post office a week later, unclaimed. Now and then we would see her in one of the downstairs windows—she had evidently shut up the top floor of the house—like the carven torso of an idol in a niche, looking or not looking at us, we could never tell which. Thus she passed from generation to generation—dear, inescapable, impervious, tranquil, and perverse.

And so she died. Fell ill in the house filled with dust and shadows, with only a 50 doddering Negro man to wait on her. We did not even know she was sick; we had long since given up trying to get any information from the Negro. He talked to no one, probably not even to her, for his voice had grown harsh and rusty, as if from disuse.

She died in one of the downstairs rooms, in a heavy walnut bed with a curtain, her gray head propped on a pillow yellow and moldy with age and lack of sunlight.

5

The Negro met the first of the ladies at the front door and let them in, with their hushed, sibilant voices and their quick, curious glances, and then he disappeared. He walked right through the house and out the back and was not seen again.

The two female cousins came at once. They held the funeral on the second day, with the town coming to look at Miss Emily beneath a mass of bought flowers, with the crayon face of her father musing profoundly above the bier and the ladies sibilant and macabre; and the very old men—some in their brushed Confederate uniforms—on the porch and the lawn, talking of Miss Emily as if she had been a contemporary of theirs, believing that they had danced with her and courted her perhaps, confusing time with its mathematical progression, as the old do, to whom all the past is not a diminishing road but, instead, a huge meadow which no winter ever quite touches, divided from them now by the narrow bottle-neck of the most recent decade of years.

Already we knew that there was one room in that region above stairs which no one had seen in forty years, and which would have to be forced. They waited until Miss Emily was decently in the ground before they opened it.

The violence of breaking down the door seemed to fill this room with pervad- 55 ing dust. A thin, acrid pall as of the tomb seemed to lie everywhere upon this room decked and furnished as for a bridal: upon the valance curtains of faded rose color, upon the rose-shaded lights, upon the dressing table, upon the delicate array of crystal and the man's toilet things backed with tarnished silver, silver so tarnished that the monogram was obscured. Among them lay a collar and tie, as if they had just been removed, which, lifted, left upon the surface a pale crescent in the dust. Upon a chair hung the suit, carefully folded; beneath it the two mute shoes and the discarded socks.

The man himself lay in the bed.

For a long while we just stood there, looking down at the profound and fleshless grin. The body had apparently once lain in the attitude of an embrace, but now the long sleep that outlasts love, that conquers even the grimace of love, had cuckolded him. What was left of him, rotted beneath what was left of the nightshirt, had become inextricable from the bed in which he lay; and upon him and upon the pillow beside him lay that even coating of the patient and biding dust.

Then we noticed that in the second pillow was the indentation of a head. One of us lifted something from it, and leaning forward, that faint and invisible dust dry and acrid in the nostrils, we saw a long strand of iron-gray hair.

QUESTIONS FOR DISCUSSION AND WRITING

1. **Plot**   How does the point of view in each story contribute to the building of suspense in the plot? How does the first-person point of view in "The Yellow Wallpaper" shape the significance of the conclusion? How does the "we" point of view in "A Rose for Emily" emphasize the horror of the final scene?

2. **Character**   How does the choice of point of view in the two stories contribute to the characterization of the apparent madness of the two protagonists? Who is the implied audience for each narrative? What do the narrators reveal about their characters by telling their stories to this audience?

3. **Setting**   How do the narrators' description of the houses shape our initial response to the setting in the two stories? How do the narrators evoke the mystery of the two confining places, the room with the yellow wallpaper and the room "furnished for a bridal"?

4. **Point of view**   What important information would be lost if either story were told from another point of view? How might John interpret his wife's behavior? How might Emily explain her story?

5. **Theme**   In what ways are the protagonists in these two stories victims of their societies' attitudes toward women? How might stories with male protagonists represent the causes and effects of madness? In what ways do the narrator in Gilman's story and Emily maintain a sense of personal power in spite of their situation?

T H E M E

Kurt Vonnegut, Jr.'s "Harrison Bergeron"
Ursula K. Le Guin's
"The Ones Who Walk Away from Omelas"

Any good piece of short fiction is likely to develop a number of significant ideas about human experience and its meaning, but usually we will also find an integrating central theme, the core of what we think and feel as a result of the experience offered by the story.

As we have said earlier, it is difficult to isolate completely any one element of a story for purposes of analysis, but that difficulty is compounded in the case of theme because theme must grow directly out of the combination of all elements and techniques in the story. For that reason, we have chosen two stories for this section in which the other elements are deliberately simplified and muted so that theme is dramatically emphasized.

The plots in the two stories are simple; the characters obviously represent certain abstractions rather than complex human nature in action; and the settings are completely imagined and thus unambiguous, something that cannot be true of depictions of real places and cultures. Although the narrators refrain from any direct moral or political interpretation, most readers will quickly see that the stories are not really about other times and places, but about a few of the most powerful social and political questions in Western culture in the second half of this century, especially those involving the rights of minorities in a society that is more and more concerned with social equality and material progress.

In "Harrison Bergeron," Vonnegut's black humor belongs to a long tradition in literature written in English, a tradition that includes Jonathan Swift's *Gulliver's Travels* and Aldous Huxley's *Brave New World*. Like these earlier writers, Vonnegut creates a new world, this time in the distant future, in which the social values and political tendencies of our time reach their logical and horrifying final development. His question is fundamental: if, as a democratic society, we really want equality for all, must we purchase it at the price of limiting those of superior abilities?

Vonnegut's absurdly exaggerated world may at first appear merely to ridicule the folly of trying to engineer complete social equality, but a closer examination of the situation raises another equally difficult problem: Harrison Bergeron does not merely claim his right to be the most he can be; he insists that he is the natural ruler of all others, that he will make himself emperor. In the ultraliberal ideal of absolute equality for all on all levels and the fascistic notion of the right of the strong to seize power and rule, we face the concepts that have led to real twentieth-century atrocities such as China's Cultural Revolution and Hitler's rise to power in Germany.

Vonnegut offers no solutions. Like all great satirists, he simply confronts us with the full implications of our own thoughts and actions.

It seems hard to imagine a more powerful contrast to Vonnegut's dehumanizing future than the bright, celebratory world described in the first paragraphs of Ursula K. Le Guin's story. "Joyous! How is one to tell about joy?" her narrator exclaims. Finally, the narrator boggles at the task of describing so much happiness and invites the reader to construct an earthly paradise "as your own fancy bids." This reflexive technique strongly reminds the reader that this world is entirely an abstraction, a completely unified symbol of human joy. We already sense that in substance and style, Le Guin's story is very like those parables that all major religions use to teach moral and spiritual truths.

But beneath the glittering gaiety of this imagined world lies a reality as horrifying as anything in Vonnegut's dystopia. Le Guin meditates on the problem of mindless, endless human suffering and the connection of that suffering, always individual, to the mindless happiness of the larger group. If we could agree that one individual would bear the pain of all so that the rest might live in joy, would it not be absurd to throw away the joy of thousands to rescue one child from abject misery? The very fact that Omelas continues to exist in its splendor provides the answer to the question.

As the title suggests, however, the main theme is not focused on the suffering of the sacrificial child, or on those who are willing to inflict that suffering to benefit themselves, but on those who look, who know, and who walk away from both the splendid city and the hidden room where the child is tormented. Unlike the others, they have a quest, a journey through the darkness toward an unknown place difficult for them or us to imagine. They may escape, but Le Guin makes it clear that they have not mitigated the evil they reject. Their choice, like Harrison's, raises as many questions as it resolves.

Doesn't the greatest good for the greatest number justify a system that accepts the misery of the helpless and unprotected minority? Doesn't the ideal of true equality outweigh the rights of individuals to excel? Must we not protect the weak from the ruthless power of the strong? Vonnegut and Le Guin challenge us to face such issues squarely, unflinchingly, not as they exist in imagined worlds but as we live with them day to day in our own world.

IO

KURT VONNEGUT, JR.

Harrison Bergeron

KURT VONNEGUT, JR., was born in 1922 in Indianapolis, Indiana, and attended Cornell University, where he studied biochemistry before being drafted into the infantry in World War II. Vonnegut was captured by the Germans at the Battle of the Bulge and sent to Dresden, where he worked in the underground meat locker of a slaughterhouse. He miraculously survived the Allied firebombing of Dresden and, following the war, returned to the United States to study anthropology at the University of Chicago and to work for a local news bureau. In 1947 Vonnegut accepted a position writing publicity for the General Electric Research Laboratory in Schenectady, New York, but left the company in 1950 to work on his own writing. His first three novels, *Player Piano* (1952), a satire on the tyrannies of corporate automation, *The Sirens of Titan* (1959), a science-fiction comedy on the themes of free will and determination, and *Cat's Cradle* (1963), a science fantasy on the amorality of atomic scientists, established Vonnegut's reputation as a writer who could blend humor with serious insights into the human experience. His most successful novel, *Slaughterhouse-Five, or the Children's Crusade* (1969), is based on his wartime experiences in Dresden. His other works include *God Bless You, Mr. Rosewater* (1966), *Breakfast of Champions* (1973), *Jailbird* (1979), *Palm Sunday* (1981), *Galapagos* (1985), and *Hocus Pocus* (1990). His best-known short stories are collected in *Canary in the Cat House* (1961) and *Welcome to the Monkey House* (1968). "Harrison Bergeron," reprinted from the latter collection, is the story of the apparatus that a future society must create to make everyone equal.

T he year was 2081, and everybody was finally equal. They weren't only equal before God and the law. They were equal every which way. Nobody was smarter than anybody else. Nobody was better looking than anybody else. Nobody was stronger or quicker than anybody else. All this equality was due to the 211th, 212th, and 213th Amendments to the Constitution, and to the unceasing vigilance of agents of the United States Handicapper General.

Some things about living still weren't quite right, though. April, for instance, still drove people crazy by not being springtime. And it was in that clammy month that the H-G men took George and Hazel Bergeron's fourteen-year-old son, Harrison, away.

It was tragic, all right, but George and Hazel couldn't think about it very hard. Hazel had a perfectly average intelligence, which meant she couldn't think about anything except in short bursts. And George, while his intelligence was way above normal, had a little mental handicap radio in his ear. He was required by law to wear it at all times. It was tuned to a government transmitter. Every twenty seconds or so, the transmitter would send out some sharp noise to keep people like George from taking unfair advantage of their brains.

George and Hazel were watching television. There were tears on Hazel's cheeks, but she'd forgotten for the moment what they were about.

On the television screen were ballerinas. 5

A buzzer sounded in George's head. His thoughts fled in panic, like bandits from a burglar alarm.

"That was a real pretty dance, that dance they just did," said Hazel.

"Huh?" said George.

"That dance—it was nice," said Hazel.

"Yup," said George. He tried to think a little about the ballerinas. They weren't 10 really very good—no better than anybody else would have been, anyway. They were burdened with sashweights and bags of birdshot, and their faces were masked, so that no one, seeing a free and graceful gesture or a pretty face, would feel like something the cat drug in. George was toying with the vague notion that maybe dancers shouldn't be handicapped. But he didn't get very far with it before another noise in his ear radio scattered his thoughts.

George winced. So did two of the eight ballerinas.

Hazel saw him wince. Having no mental handicap herself, she had to ask George what the latest sound had been.

"Sounded like somebody hitting a milk bottle with a ball peen hammer," said George.

"I'd think it would be real interesting, hearing all the different sounds," said Hazel, a little envious. "All the things they think up."

15   "Um," said George.

"Only, if I was Handicapper General, you know what I would do?" said Hazel. Hazel, as a matter of fact, bore a strong resemblance to the Handicapper General, a woman named Diana Moon Glampers. "If I was Diana Moon Glampers," said Hazel, "I'd have chimes on Sunday—just chimes. Kind of in honor of religion."

"I could think, if it was just chimes," said George.

"Well—maybe make 'em real loud," said Hazel. "I think I'd make a good Handicapper General."

"Good as anybody else," said George.

20   "Who knows better'n I do what normal is?" said Hazel.

"Right," said George. He began to think glimmeringly about his abnormal son who was now in jail, about Harrison, but a twenty-one-gun salute in his head stopped that.

"Boy!" said Hazel, "that was a doozy, wasn't it?"

It was such a doozy that George was white and trembling, and tears stood on the rims of his red eyes. Two of the eight ballerinas had collapsed to the studio floor, were holding their temples.

"All of a sudden you look so tired," said Hazel. "Why don't you stretch out on the sofa, so's you can rest your handicap bag on the pillows, honeybunch." She was referring to the forty-seven pounds of birdshot in a canvas bag, which was padlocked around George's neck. "Go on and rest the bag for a little while," she said. "I don't care if you're not equal to me for a while."

25   George weighed the bag with his hands. "I don't mind it," he said. "I don't notice it any more. It's just a part of me."

"You been so tired lately—kind of wore out," said Hazel. "If there was just some way we could make a little hole in the bottom of the bag, and just take out a few of them lead balls. Just a few."

"Two years in prison and two thousand dollars fine for every ball I took out," said George. "I don't call that a bargain."

"If you could just take a few out when you came home from work," said Hazel. "I mean—you don't compete with anybody around here. You just set around."

"If I tried to get away with it," said George, "then other people'd get away with it—and pretty soon we'd be right back to the dark ages again, with everybody competing against everybody else. You wouldn't like that, would you?"

30   "I'd hate it," said Hazel.

"There you are," said George. "The minute people start cheating on laws, what do you think happens to society?"

If Hazel hadn't been able to come up with an answer to this question, George couldn't have supplied one. A siren was going off in his head.

"Reckon it'd fall all apart," said Hazel.

"What would?" said George blankly.

"Society," said Hazel uncertainly. "Wasn't that what you just said?"   35

"Who knows?" said George.

The television program was suddenly interrupted for a news bulletin. It wasn't clear at first as to what the bulletin was about, since the announcer, like all announcers, had a serious speech impediment. For about half a minute, and in a state of high excitement, the announcer tried to say, "Ladies and gentlemen—"

He finally gave up, handed the bulletin to a ballerina to read.

"That's all right—" Hazel said of the announcer, "he tried. That's the big thing. He tried to do the best he could with what God gave him. He should get a nice raise for trying so hard."

"Ladies and gentlemen—" said the ballerina, reading the bulletin. She must   40 have been extraordinarily beautiful, because the mask she wore was hideous. And it was easy to see that she was the strongest and most graceful of all the dancers, for her handicap bags were as big as those worn by two-hundred-pound men.

And she had to apologize at once for her voice, which was a very unfair voice for a woman to use. Her voice was a warm, luminous, timeless melody. "Excuse me—" she said, and she began again, making her voice absolutely uncompetitive.

"Harrison Bergeron, age fourteen," she said in a grackle squawk, "has just escaped from jail, where he was held on suspicion of plotting to overthrow the government. He is a genius and an athlete, is under-handicapped, and should be regarded as extremely dangerous."

A police photograph of Harrison Bergeron was flashed on the screen upside down, then sideways, upside down again, then right side up. The picture showed the full length of Harrison against a background calibrated in feet and inches. He was exactly seven feet tall.

The rest of Harrison's appearance was Halloween and hardware. Nobody had ever borne heavier handicaps. He had outgrown hindrances faster than the H-G men could think them up. Instead of a little ear radio for a mental handicap, he wore a tremendous pair of earphones, and spectacles with thick wavy lenses. The spectacles were intended to make him not only half blind, but to give him whanging headaches besides.

Scrap metal was hung all over him. Ordinarily, there was a certain symmetry, a   45 military neatness to the handicaps issued to strong people, but Harrison looked like a walking junkyard. In the race of life, Harrison carried three hundred pounds.

And to offset his good looks, the H-G men required that he wear at all times a red rubber ball for a nose, keep his eyebrows shaved off, and cover his even white teeth with black caps at snaggle-tooth random.

"If you see this boy," said the ballerina, "do not—I repeat, do not—try to reason with him."

There was the shriek of a door being torn from its hinges.

Screams and barking cries of consternation came from the television set. The photograph of Harrison Bergeron on the screen jumped again and again, as though dancing to the tune of an earthquake.

50   George Bergeron correctly identified the earthquake, and well he might have—for many was the time his own home had danced to the same crashing tune. "My God—" said George, "that must be Harrison!"

The realization was blasted from his mind instantly by the sound of an automobile collision in his head.

When George could open his eyes again, the photograph of Harrison was gone. A living, breathing Harrison filled the screen.

Clanking, clownish, and huge, Harrison stood in the center of the studio. The knob of the uprooted studio door was still in his hand. Ballerinas, technicians, musicians, and announcers cowered on their knees before him, expecting to die.

"I am the Emperor!" cried Harrison. "Do you hear? I am the Emperor! Everybody must do what I say at once!" He stamped his foot and the studio shook.

55   "Even as I stand here—" he bellowed, "crippled, hobbled, sickened—I am a greater ruler than any man who ever lived! Now watch me become what I *can* become!"

Harrison tore the straps of his handicap harness like wet tissue paper, tore straps guaranteed to support five thousand pounds.

Harrison's scrap-iron handicaps crashed to the floor.

Harrison thrust his thumbs under the bars of the padlock that secured his head harness. The bar snapped like celery. Harrison smashed his headphones and spectacles against the wall.

He flung away his rubber-ball nose, revealed a man that would have awed Thor, the god of thunder.

60   "I shall now select my Empress!" he said, looking down on the cowering people. "Let the first woman who dares rise to her feet claim her mate and her throne!"

A moment passed, and then a ballerina arose, swaying like a willow.

Harrison plucked the mental handicap from her ear, snapped off her physical handicaps with marvelous delicacy. Last of all, he removed her mask.

She was blindingly beautiful.

"Now—" said Harrison, taking her hand, "shall we show the people the meaning of the word dance? Music!" he commanded.

65   The musicians scrambled back into their chairs, and Harrison stripped them of their handicaps, too. "Play your best," he told them, "and I'll make you barons and dukes and earls."

The music began. It was normal at first—cheap, silly, false. But Harrison snatched two musicians from their chairs, waved them like batons as he sang the music as he wanted it played. He slammed them back into their chairs.

The music began again and was much improved.

Harrison and his Empress merely listened to the music for a while—listened gravely, as though synchronizing their heartbeats with it.

They shifted their weights to their toes.

70   Harrison placed his big hands on the girl's tiny waist, letting her sense the weightlessness that would soon be hers.

And then, in an explosion of joy and grace, into the air they sprang!

Not only were the laws of the land abandoned, but the law of gravity and the laws of motion as well.

They reeled, whirled, swiveled, flounced, capered, gamboled, and spun.

They leaped like deer on the moon.

The studio ceiling was thirty feet high, but each leap brought the dancers nearer 75 to it.

It became their obvious intention to kiss the ceiling.

They kissed it.

And then, neutralizing gravity with love and pure will, they remained suspended in air inches below the ceiling, and they kissed each other for a long, long time.

It was then that Diana Moon Glampers, the Handicapper General, came into the studio with a double-barreled ten-gauge shotgun. She fired twice, and the Emperor and the Empress were dead before they hit the floor.

Diana Moon Glampers loaded the gun again. She aimed it at the musicians and 80 told them they had ten seconds to get their handicaps back on.

It was then that the Bergerons' television tube burned out.

Hazel turned to comment about the blackout to George. But George had gone out into the kitchen for a can of beer.

George came back in with the beer, paused while a handicap signal shook him up. And then he sat down again. "You been crying?" he said to Hazel.

"Yup," she said.

"What about?" he said. 85

"I forgot," she said. "Something real sad on television."

"What was it?" he said.

"It's all kind of mixed up in my mind," said Hazel.

"Forget sad things," said George.

"I always do," said Hazel. 90

"That's my girl," said George. He winced. There was the sound of a rivetting gun in his head.

"Gee—I could tell that one was a doozy," said Hazel.

"You can say that again," said George.

"Gee—" said Hazel, "I could tell that one was a doozy."

II

···

URSULA K. LE GUIN

*The Ones Who Walk Away from Omelas**

URSULA K. LE GUIN was born in 1929 in Berkeley, California, and educated at Radcliffe College and Columbia University. In 1952 she obtained a Fulbright Fellowship to study in Paris, where she met her husband, historian Charles A. Le Guin. In the mid-fifties, she worked as a part-time writing instructor at Mercer University and the University of Idaho before moving to Portland, Oregon, where she was able to pursue a full-time career as a writer. She published her first novel, *Rocannon's World,* in 1964 and established herself as a leading writer of science fiction and fantasy. Le Guin has contributed short stories, essays, and reviews to numerous science fiction, scholarly, and popular journals, such as *Fantastic, Western Humanities Review,* and *The New Yorker.* Her novels include *The Left Hand of Darkness* (1969), *The Lathe of Heaven* (1970), and her "Earthsea" trilogy: *A Wizard of Earthsea* (1968), *The Tombs of Atuan* (1971), and *The Farthest Shore* (1972). The last volume was selected for a National Book Award. Le Guin's short fiction, which has won numerous prizes, is collected in *The Wind's Twelve Quarters* (1975) and *Orsinian Tales* (1976). Her more recent work includes *The Beginning Place* (1980), *Hard Words and Other Poems* (1981), *Always Coming Home* (1985), *Tehanu* (1990), and *Unlocking the Air and Other Stories* (1996). "The Ones Who Walk Away from Omelas," reprinted from *The Wind's Twelve Quarters,* depicts an idyllic community where the conditions for happiness are "strict and absolute."

With a clamor of bells that set the swallows soaring, the Festival of Summer came to the city Omelas, bright-towered by the sea. The rigging of the boats in harbor sparkled with flags. In the streets between houses with red roofs and painted walls, between old moss-grown gardens and under avenues of trees, past great parks and public buildings, processions moved. Some were decorous: old peo-

---

*The author says the name comes from "a road sign: Salem (Oregon) backwards.... Salem equals schelomo equals salaam equals Peace. Melas. O melas. Omelas. Homme hélas." The last phrase equals "Man, alas."

ple in long stiff robes of mauve and gray, grave master workmen, quiet, merry women carrying their babies and chatting as they walked. In other streets the music beat faster, a shimmering of gong and tambourine, and the people went dancing, the procession was a dance. Children dodged in and out, their high calls rising like the swallows' crossing flights over the music and the singing. All the processions wound towards the north side of the city, where on the great water-meadow called the Green Fields boys and girls, naked in the bright air, with mud-stained feet and ankles and long, lithe arms, exercised their restive horses before the race. The horses wore no gear at all but a halter without bit. Their manes were braided with streamers of silver, gold, and green. They flared their nostrils and pranced and boasted to one another; they were vastly excited, the horse being the only animal who has adopted our ceremonies as his own. Far off to the north and west the mountains stood up half encircling Omelas on her bay. The air of morning was so clear that the snow still crowning the Eighteen Peaks burned with white-gold fire across the miles of sunlit air, under the dark blue of the sky. There was just enough wind to make the banners that marked the racecourse snap and flutter now and then. In the silence of the broad green meadows one could hear the music winding through the city streets, farther and nearer and ever approaching, a cheerful faint sweetness of the air from time to time trembled and gathered together and broke out into the great joyous clanging of the bells.

Joyous! How is one to tell about joy? How describe the citizens of Omelas?

They were not simple folk, you see, though they were happy. But we do not say the words of cheer much any more. All smiles have become archaic. Given a description such as this one tends to make certain assumptions. Given a description such as this one tends to look next for the King, mounted on a splendid stallion and surrounded by his noble knights, or perhaps in a golden litter borne by great-muscled slaves. But there was no king. They did not use swords, or keep slaves. They were not barbarians. I do not know the rules and laws of their society, but I suspect that they were singularly few. As they did without monarchy and slavery, so they also got on without the stock exchange, the advertisement, the secret police, and the bomb. Yet I repeat that these were not simple folk, not dulcet shepherds, noble savages, bland utopians. They were not less complex than us. The trouble is that we have a bad habit, encouraged by pedants and sophisticates, of considering happiness as something rather stupid. Only pain is intellectual, only evil interesting. This is the treason of the artist: a refusal to admit the banality of evil and the terrible boredom of pain. If you can't lick 'em, join 'em. If it hurts, repeat it. But to praise despair is to condemn delight, to embrace violence is to lose hold of everything else. We have almost lost hold; we can no longer describe a happy man, nor make any celebration of joy. How can I tell you about the people of Omelas? They were not naïve and happy children—though their children were, in fact, happy. They were mature, intelligent, passionate adults whose lives were not wretched. O miracle! but I wish I could describe it better. I wish I could convince you. Omelas sounds in my words like a city in a fairy tale, long ago and far away, once upon a time. Perhaps it would be best if you imagined it as your own fancy bids, assuming it will rise to the occasion, for certainly I cannot suit you all. For instance, how about technology? I think that there would be no cars or helicopters in and above the streets; this follows from the fact that the people of Omelas are happy people. Happiness is based on a just discrimination of what is necessary, what is neither necessary nor destructive, and what is destructive. In the middle category, however—that of the unnecessary but undestructive, that of comfort, luxury, exuberance, etc.—they could perfectly well have central heating, subway trains, washing machines, and all kinds of marvelous devices not yet invented here, floating light-sources, fuelless power, a cure for the common cold. Or they could have none of that: it doesn't matter. As you like it. I incline to think that people from towns up and down the coast have been coming in to Omelas during the last days before the Festival on very fast little trains and double-decked trams, and that the train station of Omelas is actually the handsomest building in town, though plainer than the magnificent Farmers' Market. But even granted trains, I fear that Omelas so far strikes some of you as goody-goody. Smiles, bells, parades, horses, bleh. If so, please add an orgy. If an orgy would help, don't hesitate. Let us not, however, have temples from which issue beautiful nude priests and priestesses already half in ecstasy and ready to copulate with any man or woman, lover or stranger, who desires union with the deep godhead of the blood, although that was my first idea. But really it would be better not to have any temples in Omelas—at least, not manned temples. Religion yes, clergy no. Surely the beautiful nudes can just wander about, offering themselves like divine soufflés to the hunger of the needy and the rapture of the flesh. Let them join the processions. Let tambourines be struck above the copulations, and the glory of desire be proclaimed upon the gongs, and (a not unimportant point) let the offspring of these delightful rituals be beloved and looked after by all. One thing I know there is none of in Omelas is guilt. But what else should there be? I thought at first there were no drugs, but that is puritanical. For those who like it, the faint insistent sweetness of *drooz* may perfume the ways of the city, *drooz* which first brings a great lightness and brilliance to the mind and limbs, and then after some hours a dreamy languor, and wonderful visions at last of the very arcana and inmost secrets of the Universe, as well as exciting the pleasure of sex beyond all belief; and it is not habit-forming. For more modest tastes I think there ought to be beer. What else, what else belongs in the joyous city? The sense of victory, surely, the celebration of courage. But as we did without clergy, let us do without soldiers. The joy built upon successful slaughter is not the right kind of joy; it will not do; it is fearful and it is trivial. A boundless and generous contentment, a magnanimous triumph felt not against some outer enemy but in communion with the finest and fairest in the souls of all men everywhere and the splendor of the world's summer: this is what swells the hearts of the people of Omelas, and the victory they celebrate is that of life. I really don't think many of them need to take *drooz*.

Most of the processions have reached the Green Fields by now. A marvelous smell of cooking goes forth from the red and blue tents of the provisioners. The faces of small children are amiably sticky; in the benign gray beard of a man a couple of crumbs of rich pastry are entangled. The youths and girls have mounted their horses and are beginning to group around the starting line of the course. An old woman, small, fat, and laughing, is passing out flowers from a basket, and tall young men wear her flowers in their shining hair. A child of nine or ten sits at the edge of the crowd, alone, playing on a wooden flute. People pause to listen, and they smile, but they do not speak to him, for he never ceases playing and never sees them, his dark eyes wholly rapt in the sweet, thin magic of the tune.

He finishes, and slowly lowers his hands holding the wooden flute.   5

As if that little private silence were the signal, all at once a trumpet sounds from the pavilion near the starting line: imperious, melancholy, piercing. The horses rear on their slender legs, and some of them neigh in answer. Sober-faced, the young riders stroke the horses' necks and soothe them, whispering. "Quiet, quiet, there my beauty, my hope. . . ." They begin to form in rank along the starting line. The crowds along the racecourse are like a field of grass and flowers in the wind. The Festival of Summer has begun.

Do you believe? Do you accept the festival, the city, the joy? No? Then let me describe one more thing.

In a basement under one of the beautiful public buildings of Omelas, or perhaps in the cellar of one of its spacious private homes, there is a room. It has one locked door, and no window. A little light seeps in dustily between cracks in the boards, secondhand from a cobwebbed window somewhere across the cellar. In one corner of the little room a couple of mops, with stiff, clotted, foul-smelling heads, stand near a rusty bucket. The floor is dirt, a little damp to the touch, as cellar dirt usually is. The room is about three paces long and two wide: a mere broom closet or disused tool room. In the room a child is sitting. It could be a boy or a girl. It looks about six, but actually is nearly ten. It is feeble-minded. Perhaps it was born defective, or perhaps it has become imbecile through fear, malnutrition, and neglect. It picks its nose and occasionally fumbles vaguely with its toes or genitals, as it sits hunched in the corner farthest from the bucket and the two mops. It is afraid of the mops. It finds them horrible. It shuts its eyes, but it knows the mops are still standing there; and the door is locked; and nobody will come. The door is always locked; and nobody ever comes, except that sometimes—the child has no understanding of time or interval— sometimes the door rattles terribly and opens, and a person, or several people, are there. One of them may come in and kick the child to make it stand up. The others never come close, but peer in at it with frightened, disgusted eyes. The food bowl and the water jug are hastily filled, the door is locked; the eyes disappear. The people at the door never say anything, but the child, who has not always lived in the tool room, and can remember sunlight and its mother's voice, sometimes speaks. "I will be good," it says. "Please let me out. I will be good!" They never answer. The child used to scream for help at night, and cry a good deal, but now it only makes a kind of whining, "eh-haa, eh-haa," and it speaks less and less often. It is so thin there are no calves to its legs; its belly protrudes; it lives on a half-bowl of corn meal and grease a day. It is naked. Its buttocks and thighs are a mass of festered sores, as it sits in its own excrement continually.

They all know it is there, all the people of Omelas. Some of them have come to see it, others are content merely to know it is there. They all know that it has to be there. Some of them understand why, and some do not, but they all understand that their happiness, the beauty of their city, the tenderness of their friendships, the health of their children, the wisdom of their scholars, the skill of their makers, even the abundance of their harvest and the kindly weathers of their skies, depend wholly on this child's abominable misery.

10   This is usually explained to children when they are between eight and twelve, whenever they seem capable of understanding; and most of those who come to see the child are young people, though often enough an adult comes, or comes back, to see the child. No matter how well the matter has been explained to them, these young spectators are always shocked and sickened at the sight. They feel disgust, which they had thought themselves superior to. They feel anger, outrage, impotence, despite all the explanations. They would like to do something for the child. But there is nothing they can do. If the child were brought up into the sunlight out of that vile place, if it were cleaned and fed and comforted, that would be a good thing, indeed; but if it were done, in that day and hour all the prosperity and beauty and delight of Omelas would wither and be destroyed. Those are the terms. To exchange all the goodness and grace of every life in Omelas for that single, small improvement: to throw away the happiness of thousands for the chance of the happiness of one: that would be to let guilt within the walls indeed.

The terms are strict and absolute; there may not even be a kind word spoken to the child.

Often the young people go home in tears, or in a tearless rage, when they have seen the child and faced this terrible paradox. They may brood over it for weeks or years. But as time goes on they begin to realize that even if the child could be released, it would not get much good of its freedom: a little vague pleasure of warmth and food, no doubt, but little more. It is too degraded and imbecile to know any real joy. It has been afraid too long ever to be free of fear. Its habits are too uncouth for it to respond to humane treatment. Indeed, after so long it would probably be wretched without walls about it to protect it, and darkness for its eyes, and its own excrement to sit in. Their tears at the bitter injustice dry when they begin to perceive the terrible justice of reality, and to accept it. Yet it is their tears and anger, the trying of their generosity and the acceptance of their helplessness, which are perhaps the true source of the splendor of their lives. Theirs is no vapid, irresponsible happiness. They know that they, like the child, are not free. They know compassion. It is the existence of the child, and their knowledge of its existence, that makes possible the nobility of their architecture, the poignancy of their music, the profundity of their science. It is because of the child that they are so gentle with children. They know that if the wretched one were not there sniveling in the dark, the other one, the flute-player, could make no joyful music as the young riders line up in their beauty for the race in the sunlight of the first morning of summer.

Now do you believe in them? Are they not more credible? But there is one more thing to tell, and this is quite incredible.

At times one of the adolescent girls or boys who go to see the child does not go home to weep or rage, does not, in fact, go home at all. Sometimes also a man or woman much older falls silent for a day or two, and then leaves home. These people go out into the street, and walk down the street alone. They keep walking, and walk straight out of the city of Omelas, through the beautiful gates. They keep walking across the farmlands of Omelas. Each one goes alone, youth or girl, man or woman.

Night falls; the traveler must pass down village streets, between the houses with yellow-lit windows, and on out into the darkness of the fields. Each alone, they go west or north, towards the mountains. They go on. They leave Omelas, they walk ahead into the darkness, and they do not come back. The place they go towards is a place even less imaginable to most of us than the city of happiness. I cannot describe it at all. It is possible that it does not exist. But they seem to know where they are going, the ones who walk away from Omelas.

QUESTIONS FOR DISCUSSION AND WRITING

1. **Plot**   Why does Vonnegut frame Harrison's rebellion, the main action, with the account of his parents' ordinary lives? What are the three main parts of Le Guin's story, and what is accomplished in each of them? Why do both stories end without resolving the basic conflicts they represent?

2. **Characterization**   Who are the protagonists and antagonists in these stories? In what ways does Harrison represent both supremely heroic qualities and potentially destructive ones? Why does Le Guin deal only with the group of people who choose to walk away from Omelas and not particular individuals? How do both writers use their protagonists to develop the theme of the rights of the individual in conflict with the good of the group?

3. **Setting**   How do Vonnegut and Le Guin undermine the apparent reality of the worlds they create so that we focus on thematic implications rather than the places themselves? What do the two imagined worlds have in common? What specific issues in contemporary culture do you see implicitly depicted in the two worlds of the stories?

4. **Point of View**   Why does Vonnegut employ an objective narrator who offers no interpretation of judgments about the story he tells? Why does Le Guin create a narrator who is intrusive, who reminds us again and again that she is creating a world as we read? What are the advantages of each of these points of view in creating the themes of the stories?

5. **Theme**   How is the depiction of pain in the stories used to generate emotional as well as intellectual responses to the issues raised? What is morally ambiguous about the choice of a few to walk away from Omelas? What is the ambiguity in Harrison's heroic rebellion against his society? Why do Vonnegut and Le Guin leave the evil in their created worlds unreformed?

A COLLECTION OF STORIES

12

···

CHINUA   ACHEBE

Vengeful Creditor

CHINUA ACHEBE was born in 1930 in Ogidi, Nigeria, and educated at Government College, Umuahia; University College, Ibadan; and London University. After studying broadcasting at the BBC, he worked as a writer for the Nigerian Broadcasting Corporation and as the founder and director of Voice of Nigeria. His first novel, *Things Fall Apart* (1958), quickly established him as the most widely discussed contemporary African novelist. This modern classic was followed by *No Longer at Ease* (1960), *Arrow of God* (1964), and *A Man of the People* (1966). He has also written three books for children—*Chike and the River* (1966), *The Flute* (1978), and *The Drum* (1978); two volumes of poetry—*Beware, Soul Brother, and Other Poems* (1971) and *Christmas in Biafra, and Other Poems* (1973); and two collections of essays—*Morning Yet on Creation Day* (1975) and *Hopes and Impediments* (1988). His short stories have been collected in *The Sacrificial Egg, and Other Stories* (1962) and *Girls at War* (1973). Achebe has been a prominent spokesman for his own Igbo people, who tried to secede from Nigeria to form the independent nation of Biafra. His most recent novel, *Anthills of the Savannah* (1987), was nominated for the Booker Prize. In "Vengeful Creditor," reprinted from *Girls at War*, Achebe dramatizes the personal and public controversies created by the native African desire for education.

Madame, this way," sang the alert, high-wigged salesgirl minding one of a row of cash machines in the supermarket. Mrs. Emenike veered her full-stacked trolley ever so lightly to the girl.

"Madame, you were coming to me," complained the cheated girl at the next machine.

"Ah, sorry my dear. Next time."

"Good afternoon, Madame," sang the sweet-voiced girl already unloading Madame's purchases on to her counter.

"Cash or account, Madame?"   5

"Cash."

She punched the prices as fast as lightning and announced the verdict. Nine pounds fifteen and six. Mrs. Emenike opened her handbag, brought out from it a wallet, unzipped it and held out two clean and crisp five-pound notes. The girl punched again and the machine released a tray of cash. She put Madame's money away and gave her her change and a foot-long receipt. Mrs. Emenike glanced at the bottom of the long strip of paper where the polite machine had registered her total spending with the words THANK YOU COME AGAIN, and nodded.

It was at this point that the first hitch occurred. There seemed to be nobody around to load Madame's purchases into a carton and take them to her car outside.

"Where are these boys?" said the girl almost in distress. "Sorry, Madame. Many of our carriers have gone away because of this free primary . . . John!" she called out, as she caught sight of one of the remaining few, "Come and pack Madame's things!"

10   John was a limping forty-year-old boy sweating profusely even in the air-conditioned comfort of the supermarket. As he put the things into an empty carton he grumbled aloud.

"I don talk say make una tell Manager make e go fin' more people for dis monkey work."

"You never hear say everybody don go to free primary?" asked the wigged girl, jovially.

"All right-o. But I no go kill myself for sake of free primary."

Out in the car-park he stowed the carton away in the boot of Mrs. Emenike's grey Mercedes and then straightened up to wait while she opened her handbag and then her wallet and stirred a lot of coins there with one finger until she found a three-penny piece, pulled it out between two fingers and dropped it into the carrier's palm. He hesitated for a while and then limped away without saying a word.

15   Mrs. Emenike never cared for these old men running little boys' errands. No matter what you gave them they never seemed satisfied. Look at this grumbling cripple. How much did he expect to be given for carrying a tiny carton a few yards? That was what free primary education had brought. It had brought even worse to the homes. Mrs. Emenike had lost three servants including her baby-nurse since the beginning of the school year. The baby-nurse problem was of course the worst. What was a working woman with a seven-month-old baby supposed to do?

However the problem did not last. After only a term of free education the government withdrew the scheme for fear of going bankrupt. It would seem that on the advice of its experts the Education Ministry had planned initially for eight hundred thousand children. In the event one million and a half turned up on the first day of school. Where did all the rest come from? Had the experts misled the government? The chief statistician, interviewed on the radio, said it was nonsense to talk about a miscalculation. The trouble was simply that children from neighbouring states had been brought in in thousands and registered dishonestly by unscrupulous people, a clear case of sabotage.

Whatever the reason the government cancelled the scheme. The *New Age* wrote an editorial praising the Prime Minister for his statesmanship and courage but pointing out that the whole dismal affair could have been avoided if the government had listened in the first place to the warning of many knowledgeable and responsible citizens. Which was true enough, for these citizens had written on the pages of the

New Age to express their doubt and reservation about free education. The newspaper, on throwing open its pages to a thorough airing of views on the matter, had pointed out that it did so in the national cause and, mounting an old hobby-horse, challenged those of its critics who could see no merit whatever in a newspaper owned by foreign capital to come forward and demonstrate an equal or a higher order of national commitment and patriotism, a challenge that none of those critics took up. The offer of space by the *New Age* was taken up eagerly and in the course of ten days at the rate of two or even three articles a day a large number of responsible citizens—lawyers, doctors, merchants, engineers, salesmen, insurance brokers, university lecturers, etc.—had written in criticism of the scheme. No one was against education for the kids, they said, but free education was premature. Someone said that not even the United States of America in all its wealth and power had introduced it yet, how much less . . .

Mr. Emenike read the various contributions with boyish excitement. "I wish civil servants were free to write to the papers," he told his wife at least on three occasions during those ten days.

"This is not bad, but he should have mentioned that this country has made tremendous strides in education since independence because parents know the value of education and will make any sacrifice to find school fees for their children. We are not a nation of Oliver Twists."

His wife was not really interested in all the argument at that stage, because 20 somehow it all seemed to hang in the air. She had some vague, personal doubts about free education, that was all.

"Have you looked at the paper? Mike has written on this thing," said her husband on another occasion.

"Who is Mike?"

"Mike Ogudu."

"Oh, what does he say?"

"I haven't read it yet . . . Oh yes, you can trust Mike to call a spade a spade. See 25 how he begins: 'Free primary education is tantamount to naked Communism'? That's not quite true but that's Mike all over. He thinks someone might come up to nationalize his shipping line. He is so scared of Communism."

"But who wants Communism here?"

"Nobody. That's what I told him the other evening at the Club. But he is so scared. You know one thing? Too much money is bad-o."

The discussion in the Emenike family remained at this intellectual level until one day their "Small Boy," a very bright lad of twelve helping out the cook and understudying the steward, announced he must go home to see his sick father.

"How did you know your Father was sick?" asked Madame.

"My brodder come tell me." 30

"When did your brother come?"

"Yesterday for evening-time."

"Why didn't you bring him to see me?"

"I no no say Madame go wan see am."

"Why you no talk since yesterday?" asked Mr. Emenike looking up from his 35 newspaper.

"At first I tink say I no go go home. But today one mind tell me say make you go see-am-o; perhaps e de sick too much. So derefore . . ."

"All right. You can go but make sure you are back by tomorrow afternoon otherwise . . ."

"I must return back by morning-time sef."

He didn't come back. Mrs. Emenike was particularly angry because of the lies. She didn't like being outwitted by servants. Look at that little rat imagining himself clever. She should have suspected something from the way he had been carrying on of late. Now he had gone with a full month's pay which he should lose in lieu of notice. It went to show that kindness to these people did not pay in the least.

40   A week later the gardener gave notice. He didn't try to hide anything. His elder brother had sent him a message to return to their village and register for free education. Mr. Emenike tried to laugh him out of this ridiculous piece of village ignorance.

"Free primary education is for children. Nobody is going to admit an old man like you. How old are you?"

"I am fifteen years of old, sir."

"You are three," sneered Mrs. Emenike. "Come and suck breast."

"You are not fifteen," said Mr. Emenike. "You are at least twenty and no headmaster will admit you into a primary school. If you want to go and try, by all means do. But don't come back here when you've gone and failed."

45   "I no go fail, oga," said the gardener. "One man for our village wey old pass my fader sef done register everyting finish. He just go for Magistrate Court and pay dem five shilling and dey swear-am for Court juju wey no de kill porson; e no fit kill rat sef."

"Well it's entirely up to you. Your work here has been good but . . ."

"Mark, what is all that long talk for? He wants to go, let him go."

"Madame, no be say I wan go like dat. But my senior brodder . . ."

"We have heard. You can go now."

50   "But I no de go today. I wan give one week notice. And I fit find anoder gardener for Madame."

"Don't worry about notice or gardener. Just go away."

"I fit get my pay now or I go come back for afternoon-time?"

"What pay?"

"Madame, for dis ten days I don work for dis mont."

55   "Don't annoy me any further. Just go away."

But real annoyance was yet to come for Mrs. Emenike. Abigail, the baby-nurse, came up to her two mornings later as she was getting ready for work and dumped the baby in her lap and took off. Abigail of all people! After all she had done for her. Abigail who came to her full of craw-craw, who used rags for sanitary towels, who was so ignorant she gave the baby a full bowl of water to stop it crying and dropped some through its nose. Now Abigail was a lady; she could sew and bake, wear a bra and clean pants, put on powder and perfumes and stretch her hair; and she was ready to go.

From that day Mrs. Emenike hated the words "free primary" which had suddenly become part of everyday language, especially in the villages where they called it "free primadu." She was particularly angry when people made jokes about it and had a strong urge to hit them on the head for a lack of feeling and good taste. And she hated the Americans and the embassies (but particularly the Americans) who threw their money around and enticed the few remaining servants away from Africans. This began when she learnt later that her gardener had not gone to school at all but to a Ford Foundation man who had offered him seven pounds, and bought him a bicycle and a Singer sewing-machine for his wife.

"Why do they do it?" she asked. She didn't really want or need an answer but her husband gave one all the same.

"Because," said he, "back home in America they couldn't possibly afford a servant. So when they come out here and find them so cheap they go crazy. That's why."

Three months later free primary ended and school fees were brought back. The government was persuaded by then that its "piece of hare-brained socialism" as the *New Age* called it was unworkable in African conditions. This was a jibe at the Minister of Education who was notorious for his leftist sympathies and was perpetually at war with the formidable Minister of Finance.

"We cannot go through with this scheme unless we are prepared to impose new taxes," said the Finance Minister at a Cabinet meeting.

"Well then, let's impose the taxes," said the Minister of Education, which provoked derisive laughter from all his colleagues and even from Permanent Secretaries like Mr. Emenike who were in attendance and who in strict protocol should not participate in debate or laughter.

"We can't," said the Finance Minister indulgently with laughter still in his mouth. "I know my right honourable friend here doesn't worry whether or not this government lasts its full term, but some of us others do. At least I want to be here long enough to retire my election debts . . ."

This was greeted with hilarious laughter and cries of "Hear! Hear!" In debating skill Education was no match for Finance. In fact Finance had no equal in the entire Cabinet, the Prime Minister included.

"Let us make no mistake about it," he continued with a face and tone now serious, "if any one is so foolish as to impose new taxes now on our long-suffering masses . . ."

"I thought we didn't have masses in Africa," interrupted the Minister of Education starting a meagre laughter that was taken up in good sport by one or two others.

"I am sorry to trespass in my right honourable friend's territory; communist slogans are so infectious. But as I was saying we should not talk lightly about new taxes unless we are prepared to bring the Army out to quell tax riots. One simple fact of life which we have come to learn rather painfully and reluctantly—and I'm not so sure even now that we have all learnt it—is that people do riot against taxes but not against school fees. The reason is simple. Everybody, even a motor-park tout, knows what school fees are for. He can see his child going to school in the morning and coming back in the afternoon. But you go and tell him about general taxation and he immediately thinks that government is stealing his money from him. One other point, if a man doesn't want to pay school fees he doesn't have to. After all this is a democratic society. The worst that can happen is that his child stays at home which he probably doesn't mind at all. But taxes are different; everybody must pay whether they want to or not. The difference is pretty sharp. That's why mobs riot." A few people said "Hear! Hear!" Others just let out exhalations of relief or agreement. Mr. Emenike who had an unrestrainable admiration for the Finance Minister and had been nodding like a lizard through his speech shouted his "Hear! Hear!" too loud and got a scorching look from the Prime Minister.

A few desultory speeches followed and the government took its decision not to abolish free primary education but to suspend it until all the relevant factors had been thoroughly examined.

One little girl of ten, named Veronica, was brokenhearted. She had come to love school as an escape from the drabness and arduous demands of home. Her mother, a near-destitute widow who spent all hours of the day in the farm and, on market days, in the market, left Vero to carry the burden of caring for the younger children. Actually only the youngest, aged one, needed much looking after. The other two, aged seven and four, being old enough to fend for themselves, picking palm-kernels and catching grasshoppers to eat, were no problem at all to Vero. But Mary was different. She cried a lot even after she had been fed her midmorning foo-foo and soup saved for her (with a little addition of water to the soup) from breakfast, which was itself a diluted left-over from last night's supper. Mary could not manage palm-kernels on her own account yet so Vero half-chewed them first before passing them on to her. But even after the food and the kernels and grasshoppers and the bowls of water, Mary was rarely satisfied, even though her belly would be big and tight like a drum and shine like a mirror.

70   Their widowed mother, Martha, was a hard-luck woman. She had had an auspicious beginning long, long ago as a pioneer pupil at St. Monica's, then newly founded by white women-missionaries to train the future wives of native evangelists. Most of her schoolmates of those days had married young teachers and were now wives of pastors and one or two even of bishops. But Martha, encouraged by her teacher, Miss Robinson, had married a young carpenter trained by white artisan-missionaries at the Onitsha Industrial Mission, a trade school founded in the fervent belief that if the black man was to be redeemed he needed to learn the Bible alongside manual skills. (Miss Robinson was very keen on the Industrial Mission whose Principal she herself later married.) But in spite of the bright hopes of those early evangelical days carpentry never developed very much in the way teaching and clerical jobs were to develop. So when Martha's husband died (or as those missionary artisans who taught him long ago might have put it—when he was called to higher service in the heavenly mansions by Him who was Himself once a Carpenter on earth) he left her in complete ruins. It had been a bad-luck marriage from the start. To begin with she had had to wait twenty whole years after their marriage for her first child to be born, so that now she was virtually an old woman with little children to care for and little strength left for her task. Not that she was bitter about that. She was simply too overjoyed that God in His mercy had lifted her curse of barrenness to feel a need to grumble. What she nearly did grumble about was the disease that struck her husband and paralysed his right arm for five years before his death. It was a trial too heavy and unfair.

Soon after Vero withdrew from school Mr. Mark Emenike, the big government man of their village who lived in the capital, called on Martha. His Mercedes 220S pulled up on the side of the main road and he walked the 500 yards or so of a narrow unmotorable path to the widow's hut. Martha was perplexed at the visit of such a great man and as she bustled about for kolanut she kept wondering. Soon the great man himself in the hurried style of modern people cleared up the mystery.

"We have been looking for a girl to take care of our new baby and today someone told me to inquire about your girl . . ."

At first Martha was reluctant, but when the great man offered her £5 for the girl's services in the first year—plus feeding and clothing and other things—she began to soften.

"Of course it is not money I am concerned about," she said, "but whether my daughter will be well cared for."

"You don't have to worry about that, Ma. She will be treated just like one of our 75 own children. My wife is a Social Welfare Officer and she knows what it means to care for children. Your daughter will be happy in our home, I can tell you that. All she will be required to do is carry the little baby and give it its milk while my wife is away at the office and the older children at school."

"Vero and her sister Joy were also at school last term," said Martha without knowing why she said it.

"Yes, I know. That thing the government did is bad, very bad. But my belief is that a child who will be somebody will be somebody whether he goes to school or not. It is all written here, in the palm of the hand."

Martha gazed steadily at the floor and then spoke without raising her eyes. "When I married I said to myself: My daughters will do better than I did. I read Standard Three in those days and I said they will all go to College. Now they will not have even the little I had thirty years ago. When I think of it my heart wants to burst."

"Ma, don't let it trouble you too much. As I said before, what anyone of us is going to be is all written here, no matter what the difficulties."

"Yes, I pray God that what is written for these children will be better than what 80 He wrote for me and my husband."

"Amen! . . . And as for this girl if she is obedient and good in my house what stops my wife and me sending her to school when the baby is big enough to go about on his own? Nothing. And she is still a small girl. How old is she?"

"She is ten."

"You see? She is only a baby. There is plenty of time for her to go to school."

He knew that the part about sending her to school was only a manner of speaking. And Martha knew too. But Vero who had been listening to everything from a dark corner of the adjoining room did not. She actually worked out in her mind the time it would take the baby to go about on his own and it came out quite short. So she went happily to live in the capital in a great man's family and looked after a baby who would soon be big enough to go about on his own and then she would have a chance to go to school.

Vero was a good girl and very sharp. Mr. Emenike and his wife were very pleased 85 with her. She had the sense of a girl twice her age and was amazingly quick to learn.

Mrs. Emenike, who had almost turned sour over her recent difficulty in getting good servants, was now her old self again. She could now laugh about the fiasco of free primadu. She told her friends that now she could go anywhere and stay as long as she liked without worrying about her little man. She was so happy with Vero's work and manners that she affectionately nicknamed her "Little Madame." The nightmare of the months following Abigail's departure was mercifully at an end. She had sought high and low then for another baby-nurse and just couldn't find one. One rather over-ripe young lady had presented herself and asked for seven pounds a month. But it wasn't just the money. It was her general air—a kind of labour-exchange attitude which knew all the rights in the labour code, including presumably the right to have abortions in your servants' quarters and even have a go at your husband. Not that Mark was that way but the girl just wasn't right. After her no other person had turned up until now.

Every morning as the older Emenike children—three girls and a boy—were leaving for school in their father's Mercedes or their mother's little noisy Fiat, Vero would bring the baby out to the steps to say bye-bye. She liked their fine dresses and shoes—she'd never worn any shoes in her life—but what she envied them most was simply the going away every morning, going away from home, from familiar things and tasks. In the first months this envy was very, very mild. It lay beneath the joy of the big going away from the village, from her mother's drab hut, from eating palm-kernels that twisted the intestines at midday, from bitter-leaf soup without fish. That going away was something enormous. But as the months passed the hunger grew for these other little daily departures in fine dresses and shoes and sandwiches and biscuits wrapped in beautiful paper-napkins in dainty little school bags. One morning, as the Fiat took the children away and little Goddy began to cry on Vero's back, a song sprang into her mind to quieten him:

> Little noisy motor-car
> If you're going to the school
> Please carry me
> Pee—pee—pee!—poh—poh—poh!

All morning she sang her little song and was pleased with it. When Mr. Emenike dropped the other children home at one o'clock and took off again Vero taught them her new song. They all liked it and for days it supplanted "Baa Baa Black Sheep" and "Simple Simon" and the other songs they brought home from school.

"The girl is a genius," said Mr. Emenike when the new song finally got to him. His wife who heard it first had nearly died from laughter. She had called Vero and said to her, "So you make fun of my car, naughty girl." Vero was happy because she saw not anger but laughter in the woman's eyes.

90   "She is a genius," said her husband. "And she hasn't been to school."

"And besides she knows you ought to buy me a new car."

"Never mind, dear. Another year and you can have that sports car."

"Na so."

"So you don't believe me? Just you wait and see."

More weeks and months passed and little Goddy was beginning to say a few words but still no one spoke about Vero's going to school. She decided it was Goddy's fault, that he wasn't growing fast enough. And he was becoming rather too fond of riding on her back even though he could walk perfectly well. In fact his favourite words were "Cayi me." Vero made a song about that too and it showed her mounting impatience:

> Carry you! Carry you!
> Every time I carry you!
> If you no wan grow again
> I mus leave you and go school
> Because Vero e don tire!
> Tire, tire e don tire!

She sang it all morning until the other children returned from school and then she stopped. She only sang this one when she was alone with Goddy.

One afternoon Mrs. Emenike returned from work and noticed a redness on Vero's lips.

"Come here," she said, thinking of her expensive lipstick. "What is that?"

It turned out, however, not to be lipstick at all, only her husband's red ink. She couldn't help a smile then.

"And look at her finger-nails! And toes too! So, Little Madame, that's what you do when we go out and leave you at home to mind the baby? You dump him somewhere and begin to paint yourself. Don't ever let me catch you with that kind of nonsense again; do you hear?" It occurred to her to strengthen her warning somehow, if only to neutralize the smile she had smiled at the beginning.

"Do you know that red ink is poisonous? You want to kill yourself. Well, little lady you have to wait till you leave my house and return to your mother."

That did it, she thought in glowing self-satisfaction. She could see that Vero was suitably frightened. Throughout the rest of that afternoon she walked about like a shadow.

When Mr. Emenike came home she told him the story as he ate a late lunch. And she called Vero for him to see.

"Show him your finger-nails," she said. "And your toes, Little Madame!"

"I see," he said waving Vero away. "She is learning fast. Do you know the proverb which says that when mother-cow chews giant grass her little calves watch her mouth?"

"Who is a cow? You rhinoceros!"

"It is only a proverb, my dear."

A week or so later Mrs. Emenike just home from work noticed that the dress she had put on the baby in the morning had been changed into something much too warm.

"What happened to the dress I put on him?"

110   "He fell down and soiled it. So I changed him," said Vero. But there was something very strange in her manner. Mrs. Emenike's first thought was that the child must have had a bad fall.

"Where did he fall?" she asked in alarm. "Where did he hit on the ground? Bring him to me! What is all this? Blood? No? What is it? My God has killed me! Go and bring me the dress. At once!"

"I washed it," said Vero beginning to cry, a thing she had never done before. Mrs. Emenike rushed out to the line and brought down the blue dress and the white vest both heavily stained red!

She seized Vero and beat her in a mad frenzy with both hands. Then she got a whip and broke it all on her until her face and arms ran with blood. Only then did Vero admit making the child drink a bottle of red ink. Mrs. Emenike collapsed into a chair and began to cry.

Mr. Emenike did not wait to have lunch. They bundled Vero into the Mercedes and drove her the forty miles to her mother in the village. He had wanted to go alone but his wife insisted on coming, and taking the baby too. He stopped on the main road as usual. But he didn't go in with the girl. He just opened the door of the car, pulled her out and his wife threw her little bundle of clothes after her. And they drove away again.

115   Martha returned from the farm tired and grimy. Her children rushed out to meet her and to tell her that Vero was back and was crying in their bedroom. She practically dropped her basket and went to see; but she couldn't make any sense of her story.

"You gave the baby red ink? Why? So that you can go to school? How? Come on. Let's go to their place. Perhaps they will stay in the village overnight. Or else they will have told somebody there what happened. I don't understand your story. Perhaps you stole something. Not so?"

"Please Mama don't take me back there. They will kill me."

"Come on, since you won't tell me what you did."

She seized her wrist and dragged her outside. Then in the open she saw all the congealed blood on whip-marks all over her head, face, neck and arms. She swallowed hard.

120   "Who did this?"

"My Madame."

"And what did you say you did? You must tell me."

"I gave the baby red ink."

"All right, then let's go."

125   Vero began to wail louder. Martha seized her by the wrist again and they set off. She neither changed her work clothes nor even washed her face and hands. Every woman—and sometimes the men too—they passed on the way screamed on seeing Vero's whipmarks and wanted to know who did it. Martha's reply to all was "I don't know yet. I am going to find out."

She was lucky. Mr. Emenike's big car was there, so they had not returned to the capital. She knocked at their front door and walked in. Mrs. Emenike was sitting there in the parlour giving bottled food to the baby but she ignored the visitors completely neither saying a word to them nor even looking in their direction. It was her husband who descended the stairs a little later who told the story. As soon as the meaning dawned on Martha—that the red ink was given to the baby *to drink* and that the motive was to encompass its death—she screamed, with two fingers plugging her ears, that she wanted to hear no more. At the same time she rushed outside, tore a twig off a flowering shrub and by clamping her thumb and forefinger at one end and running them firmly along its full length stripped it of its leaves in one quick movement. Armed with the whip she rushed back to the house crying "I have heard an abomination!" Vero was now screaming and running round the room.

"Don't touch her here in my house," said Mrs. Emenike, cold and stern as an oracle, noticing her visitors for the first time. "Take her away from here at once. You want to show me your shock. Well I don't want to see. Go and show your anger in your own house. Your daughter did not learn murder here in my house."

This stung Martha deep in her spirit and froze her in mid-stride. She stood rooted to the spot, her whip-hand lifeless by her side. "My Daughter," she said finally addressing the younger woman, "as you see me here I am poor and wretched but I am not a murderer. If my daughter Vero is to become a murderer God knows she cannot say she learnt from me."

"Perhaps it's from me she learnt," said Mrs. Emenike showing her faultless teeth in a terrible false smile, "or maybe she snatched it from the air. That's right, she snatched it from the air. Look, woman, take your daughter and leave my house."

"Vero, let's go; come, let's go!"   130

"Yes, please go!"

Mr. Emenike who had been trying vainly to find an opening for the clearly needed male intervention now spoke.

"It is the work of the devil," he said. "I have always known that the craze for education in this country will one day ruin all of us. Now even children will commit murder in order to go to school."

This clumsy effort to mollify all sides at once stung Martha even more. As she jerked Vero homewards by the hand she clutched her unused whip in her other hand. At first she rained abuses on the girl, called her an evil child that entered her mother's womb by the back of the house.

"Oh God, what have I done?" Her tears began to flow now. "If I had had a child   135 with other women of my age, that girl that calls me murderer might have been no older than my daughter. And now she spits in my face. That's what you brought me to," she said to the crown of Vero's head, and jerked her along more violently.

"I will kill you today. Let's get home first."

Then a strange revolt, vague, undirected began to well up at first slowly inside her. "And that thing that calls himself a man talks to me about the craze for education. All his children go to school, even the one that is only two years; but that is no craze. Rich people have no craze. It is only when the children of poor widows like me want to go with the rest that it becomes a craze. What is this life? To God, what is it? And now my child thinks she must kill the baby she is hired to tend before she can get a chance. Who put such an abomination into her belly? God, you know I did not."

She threw away the whip and with her freed hand wiped her tears.

QUESTIONS FOR DISCUSSION AND WRITING

1. How does the possibility of free education create social crisis in the story? How does Martha's "strange revolt" bring that crisis to a climax?

2. How do Mrs. Emenike's behavior at the grocery store and Mr. Emenike's reaction to the newspaper stories reveal their attitudes toward race and class?

3. How does Achebe use the parliamentary debates to extend the social setting for the story?

4. How does the narrator's introduction of Veronica make it clear that his sympathy lies with her and her family?

5. How does Achebe want us to interpret Veronica's attempt to murder the baby? How does this episode fit into the larger political conflict?

Stories for Comparison

Nadine Gordimer's "Town and Country Lovers" (pages 594–607); Richard Wright's "The Man Who Was Almost a Man" (pages 1197–1207).

I3

....

A L I C E   A D A M S

Truth or Consequences

ALICE ADAMS was born in 1926 in Fredericksburg, Virginia, and educated at Radcliffe College. After twelve years of marriage, she began working at various office jobs, including secretary, clerk, and bookkeeper, while she mastered her skills as a writer. Adams published her first book of fiction, *Careless Love* (1966), at the age of forty. Since that time she has published several widely acclaimed novels including *Families and Survivors* (1975), *Listening to Billie* (1978)—the title refers to the legendary blues singer Billie Holiday—*Rich Rewards* (1980), and *Caroline's Daughters* (1991); and collections of short stories, *Beautiful Girl* (1979), *To See You Again* (1982), and *Return Trips* (1985). She has also contributed numerous short stories to magazines such as *The New Yorker, The Atlantic Monthly,* and *Paris Review.* In "Truth or Consequences," reprinted from *To See You Again,* the narrator tries to understand the "consequences" that resulted from her truthful answer in a childhood game.

This morning, when I read in a gossip column that a man named Carstairs Jones had married a famous former movie star, I was startled, thunderstruck, for I knew that he must certainly be the person whom I knew as a child, one extraordinary spring, as "Car Jones." He was a dangerous and disreputable boy, one of what were then called the "truck children," with whom I had a most curious, brief and frightening connection. Still, I noted that in a way I was pleased at such good fortune; I was "happy for him," so to speak, perhaps as a result of sheer distance, so many years. And before I could imagine Car as he might be now, Carstairs Jones, in Hollywood clothes, I suddenly saw, with the most terrific accuracy and bright sharpness of detail, the schoolyard of all those years ago, hard and bare, neglected. And I relived the fatal day, on the middle level of that schoolyard, when we were playing truth or consequences, and I said that I would rather kiss Car Jones than be eaten alive by ants.

Our school building then was three stories high, a formidable brick square. In front a lawn had been attempted, some years back; graveled walks led up to the broad, forbidding entranceway, and behind the school were the playing fields, the playground. This area was on three levels: on the upper level, nearest the school, were the huge polished steel frames for the creaking swings, the big green splintery wooden seesaws, the rickety slides—all for the youngest children. On the middle level older girls played hopscotch, various games, or jumped rope—or just talked and giggled. And out on the lowest level, the field, the boys practiced football, or baseball, in the spring.

To one side of the school was a parking space, usually filled with the bulging yellow trucks that brought children from out in the country in to town: truck children, country children. Sometimes they would go back to the trucks at lunchtime to eat their sandwiches, whatever; almost always there were several overgrown children, spilling out from the trucks. Or Car Jones, expelled from some class, for some new acts of rebelliousness. That area was always littered with trash, wrappings from sandwiches, orange peel, Coke bottles.

Beyond the parking space was an empty lot, overgrown with weeds, in the midst of which stood an abandoned trellis, perhaps once the support of wisteria; now wild honeysuckle almost covered it over.

The town was called Hilton, the seat of a distinguished university, in the middle South. My widowed mother, Charlotte Ames, had moved there the previous fall (with me, Emily, her only child). I am still not sure why she chose Hilton; she never much liked it there, nor did she really like the brother-in-law, a professor, into whose proximity the move had placed us.

An interesting thing about Hilton, at that time, was that there were three, and only three, distinct social classes. (Negroes could possibly make four, but they were so separate, even from the poorest whites, as not to seem part of the social system at

all; they were in effect invisible.) At the scale's top were professors and their families. Next were the townspeople, storekeepers, bankers, doctors and dentists, none of
whom had the prestige nor the money they were later to acquire. Country people
were the bottom group, families living out on the farms that surrounded the town,
people who sent their children in to school on the yellow trucks.

The professors' children of course had a terrific advantage, academically, coming from houses full of books, from parental respect for learning; many of those kids
read precociously and had large vocabularies. It was not so hard on most of the town
children; many of their families shared qualities with the faculty people; they too had
a lot of books around. But the truck children had a hard and very unfair time of it.
Not only were many of their parents near-illiterates, but often the children were kept
at home to help with chores, and sometimes, particularly during the coldest, wettest
months of winter, weather prevented the trucks' passage over the slithery red clay
roads of that countryside, that era. A child could miss out on a whole new skill, like
long division, and fail tests, and be kept back. Consequently many of the truck children were overage, oversized for the grades they were in.

In the seventh grade, when I was eleven, a year ahead of myself, having been
tested for and skipped the sixth (attesting to the superiority of Northern schools, my
mother thought, and probably she was right), dangerous Car Jones, in the same class,
was fourteen, and taller than anyone.

There was some overlapping, or crossing, among those three social groups;
there were hybrids, as it were. In fact, I was such a crossbreed myself: literally my
mother and I were town people—my dead father had been a banker, but since his
brother was a professor we too were considered faculty people. Also my mother had
a lot of money, making us further élite. To me, being known as rich was just embarrassing, more freakish than advantageous, and I made my mother stop ordering my
clothes from Best's; I wanted dresses from the local stores, like everyone else's.

10   Car Jones too was a hybrid child, although his case was less visible than mine:
his country family were distant cousins of the prominent and prosperous dean of the
medical school, Dean Willoughby Jones. (They seem to have gone in for fancy
names, in all the branches of that family.) I don't think his cousins spoke to him.

In any case, being richer and younger than the others in my class made me socially very insecure, and I always approached the playground with a sort of excited
dread: would I be asked to join in a game, and if it were dodge ball (the game I most
hated) would I be the first person hit with the ball, and thus eliminated? Or, if the
girls were just standing around and talking, would I get all the jokes, and know
which boys they were talking about?

Then, one pale-blue balmy April day, some of the older girls asked me if I
wanted to play truth or consequences with them. I wasn't sure how the game went,
but anything was better than dodge ball, and, as always, I was pleased at being asked.

"It's easy," said Jean, a popular leader, with curly red hair; her father was a dean
of the law school. "You just answer the questions we ask you, or you take the consequences."

I wasn't at all sure what consequences were, but I didn't like to ask.

15   They began with simple questions. How old are you? What's your middle name?

This led to more complicated (and crueler) ones.

"How much money does your mother have?"

"I don't know." I didn't, of course, and I doubt that she did either, that poor vague lady, too young to be a widow, too old for motherhood. "I think maybe a thousand dollars," I hazarded.

At this they all frowned, that group of older, wiser girls, whether in disbelief or disappointment, I couldn't tell. They moved a little away from me and whispered together.

It was close to the end of recess. Down on the playing field below us one of the boys threw the baseball and someone batted it out in a long arc, out to the farthest grassy edges of the field, and several other boys ran to retrieve it. On the level above us, a rutted terrace up, the little children stood in line for turns on the slide, or pumped with furious small legs on the giant swings.

The girls came back to me. "Okay, Emily," said Jean. "Just tell the truth. Would you rather be covered with honey and eaten alive by ants, in the hot Sahara Desert—or kiss Car Jones?"

Then, as now, I had a somewhat literal mind: I thought of honey, and ants, and hot sand, and quite simply I said I'd rather kiss Car Jones.

Well. Pandemonium: Did you hear what she said? Emily would kiss Car Jones! *Car Jones.* The truth—Emily would like to kiss Car Jones! Oh, Emily, if your mother only knew! Emily is going to kiss Car Jones! Emily said she would! Oh, Emily!

The boys, just then coming up from the baseball field, cast bored and pitying looks at the sources of so much noise; they had always known girls were silly. But Harry McGinnis, a glowing, golden boy, looked over at us and laughed aloud. I had been watching Harry timidly for months; that day I thought his laugh was friendly.

Recess being over, we all went back into the schoolroom, and continued with the civics lesson. I caught a few ambiguous smiles in my direction, which left me both embarrassed and confused.

That afternoon, as I walked home from school, two of the girls who passed me on their bikes called back to me, "Car Jones!" and in an automatic but for me new way I squealed out, "Oh no!" They laughed, and repeated, from their distance, "Car Jones!"

The next day I continued to be teased. Somehow the boys had got wind of what I had said, and they joined in with remarks about Yankee girls being fast, how you couldn't tell about quiet girls, that sort of wit. Some of the teasing sounded mean; I felt that Jean, for example, was really out to discomfit me, but most of it was high-spirited friendliness. I was suddenly discovered, as though hitherto I had been invisible. And I continued to respond with that exaggerated, phony squeal of embarrassment that seemed to go over so well. Harry McGinnis addressed me as Emily Jones, and the others took that up. (I wonder if Harry had ever seen me before.)

Curiously, in all this new excitement, the person I thought of least was the source of it all: Car Jones. Or, rather, when I saw the actual Car, hulking over the water fountain or lounging near the steps of a truck, I did not consciously connect him with what felt like social success, new popularity. (I didn't know about consequences.)

Therefore, when the first note from Car appeared on my desk, it felt like black-mail, although the message was innocent, was even kind. "You mustn't mind that they tease you. You are the prettiest one of the girls. C. Jones." I easily recognized his handwriting, those recklessly forward-slanting strokes, from the day when he had had to write on the blackboard, "I will not disturb the other children during Music." Twenty-five times. The note was real, all right.

30   Helplessly I turned around to stare at the back of the room, where the tallest boys sprawled in their too small desks. Truck children, all of them, bored and un-comfortable. There was Car, the tallest of all, the most bored, the least contained. Our eyes met, and even at that distance I saw that his were not black, as I had thought, but a dark slate blue; stormy eyes, even when, as he rarely did, Car smiled. I turned away quickly, and I managed to forget him for a while.

Having never witnessed a Southern spring before, I was astounded by its burst-ing opulence, that soft fullness of petal and bloom, everywhere the profusion of flowering shrubs and trees, the riotous flower beds. Walking home from school, I was enchanted with the yards of the stately houses (homes of professors) that I passed, the lush lawns, the rows of brilliant iris, the flowering quince and dogwood trees, crepe myrtle, wisteria vines. I would squint my eyes to see the tiniest pale-green leaves against the sky.

My mother didn't like the spring. It gave her hay fever, and she spent most of her time languidly indoors, behind heavily lined, drawn draperies. "I'm simply too old for such exuberance," she said.

"Happy" is perhaps not the word to describe my own state of mind, but I was tremendously excited, continuously. The season seemed to me so extraordinary in it-self, the colors, the enchanting smells, and it coincided with my own altered aware-ness of myself: I could command attention, I was pretty (Car Jones was the first person ever to say that I was, after my mother's long-ago murmurings to a late-arriving baby).

Now everyone knew my name, and called it out as I walked onto the play-ground. Last fall, as an envious, unknown new girl, I had heard other names, other greetings and teasing-insulting nicknames, "Hey, Red," Harry McGinnis used to shout, in the direction of popular Jean.

35   The next note from Car Jones said, "I'll bet you hate it down here. This is a cruddy town, but don't let it bother you. Your hair is beautiful. I hope you never cut it. C. Jones."

This scared me a little: the night before I had been arguing with my mother on just that point, my hair, which was long and straight. Why couldn't I cut and curl it, like the other girls? How had Car Jones known what I wanted to do? I forced myself not to look at him; I pretended that there was no Car Jones; it was just a name that certain people had made up.

I felt—I was sure—that Car Jones was an "abnormal" person. (I'm afraid "dif-ferent" would have been the word I used, back then.) He represented forces that were dark and strange, whereas I myself had just come out into the light. I had joined the world of the normal. (My "normality" later included three marriages to increasingly "rich and prominent" men; my current husband is a surgeon. Three children, and as many abortions. I hate the symmetry, but there you are. I haven't counted lovers. It comes to a normal life, for a woman of my age.) For years, at the time of our coming to Hilton, I had felt a little strange, isolated by my father's death, my older-than-most-parents mother, by money. By being younger than other children, and new in town. I could clearly afford nothing to do with Car, and at the same time my literal mind acknowledged a certain obligation.

Therefore, when a note came from Car telling me to meet him on a Saturday morning in the vacant lot next to the school, it didn't occur to me that I didn't have to go. I made excuses to my mother, and to some of the girls who were getting together for Cokes at someone's house. I'd be a little late, I told the girls. I had to do an errand for my mother.

It was one of the palest, softest, loveliest days of that spring. In the vacant lot weeds bloomed like the rarest of flowers; as I walked toward the abandoned trellis I felt myself to be a sort of princess, on her way to grant an audience to a courtier.

Car, lounging just inside the trellis, immediately brought me up short. "You're 40 several minutes late," he said, and I noticed that his teeth were stained (from tobacco?) and his hands were dirty: couldn't he have washed his hands, to come and meet me? He asked, "Just who do you think you are, the Queen of Sheba?"

I am not sure what I had imagined would happen between us, but this was wrong; I was not prepared for surliness, this scolding. Weakly I said that I was sorry I was late.

Car did not acknowledge my apology; he just stared at me, stormily, with what looked like infinite scorn.

Why had he insisted that I come to meet him? And now that I was here, was I less than pretty, seen close up?

A difficult minute passed, and then I moved a little away. I managed to say that I had to go; I had to meet some girls, I said.

At that Car reached and grasped my arm. "No, first we have to do it."   45

Do it? I was scared.

"You know what you said, as good as I do. You said kiss Car Jones, now didn't you?"

I began to cry.

Car reached for my hair and pulled me toward him; he bent down to my face and for an instant our mouths were mashed together. (Christ, my first kiss!) Then, so suddenly that I almost fell backward, Car let go of me. With a last look of pure rage he was out of the trellis and striding across the field, toward town, away from the school.

For a few minutes I stayed there in the trellis; I was no longer crying (that had 50 been for Car's benefit, I now think) but melodramatically I wondered if Car might come back and do something else to me—beat me up, maybe. Then a stronger fear took over: someone might find out, might have seen us, even. At that I got out of the trellis fast, out of the vacant lot. (I was learning conformity fast, practicing up for the rest of my life.)

I think, really, that my most serious problem was my utter puzzlement: what did it mean, that kiss? Car was mad, no doubt about that, but did he really hate me? In that case, why a kiss? (Much later in life I once was raped, by someone to whom I was married, but I still think that counts; in any case, I didn't know what he meant either.)

Not sure what else to do, and still in the grip of a monumental confusion, I went over to the school building, which was open on Saturdays for something called Story Hours, for little children. I went into the front entrance and up to the library where, to the surprise of the librarian, who may have thought me retarded, I listened for several hours to tales of the Dutch Twins, and Peter and Polly in Scotland. Actually it was very soothing, that long pasteurized drone, hard even to think about Car while listening to pap like that.

When I got home I found my mother for some reason in a livelier, more talkative mood than usual. She told me that a boy had called while I was out, three times. Even before my heart had time to drop—to think that it might be Car, she babbled on, "Terribly polite. Really, these *bien élevé* Southern boys." (No, not Car.) "Harry something. He said he'd call again. But, darling, where were you, all this time?"

I was beginning to murmur about the library, homework, when the phone rang. I answered, and it was Harry McGinnis, asking me to go to the movies with him the following Saturday afternoon. I said of course, I'd love to, and I giggled in a silly new way. But my giggle was one of relief; I was saved, I was normal, after all. I belonged in the world of light, of lightheartedness. Car Jones had not really touched me.

55   I spent the next day, Sunday, in alternating states of agitation and anticipation.

On Monday, on my way to school, I felt afraid of seeing Car, at the same time that I was both excited and shy at the prospect of Harry McGinnis—a combination of emotions that was almost too much for me, that dazzling, golden first of May, and that I have not dealt with too successfully in later life.

Harry paid even less attention to me than he had before; it was a while before I realized that he was conspicuously not looking in my direction, not teasing me, and that that in itself was a form of attention, as well as being soothing to my shyness.

I realized too, after a furtive scanning of the back row, that Car Jones was *not at school* that day. Relief flooded through my blood like oxygen, like spring air.

Absences among the truck children were so unremarkable, and due to so many possible causes, that any explanation at all for his was plausible. Of course it occurred to me, among other imaginings, that he had stayed home out of shame for what he did to me. Maybe he had run away to sea, had joined the Navy or the Marines? Coldheartedly, I hoped so. In any case, there was no way for me to ask.

60   Later that week the truth about Car Jones did come out—at first as a drifting rumor, then confirmed, and much more remarkable than joining the Navy: Car Jones had gone to the principal's office, a week or so back, and had demanded to be tested for entrance (immediate) into high school, a request so unprecedented (usually only pushy academic parents would ask for such a change) and so dumbfounding that it was acceded to. Car took the test and was put into the sophomore high-school class,

on the other side of town, where he by age and size—and intellect, as things turned out; he tested high—most rightfully belonged.

I went to a lot of Saturday movies with Harry McGinnis, where we clammily held hands, and for the rest of that spring, and into summer, I was teased about Harry. No one seemed to remember having teased me about Car Jones.

Considering the size of Hilton at that time, it seems surprising that I almost never saw Car again, but I did not, except for a couple of tiny glimpses, during the summer that I was still going to the movies with Harry. On both those occasions, seen from across the street, or on the other side of a dim movie house, Car was with an older girl, a high-school girl, with curled hair, and lipstick, all that. I was sure that his hands and teeth were clean.

By the time I had entered high school, along with all those others who were by now my familiar friends, Car was a freshman in the local university, and his family had moved into town. Then his name again was bruited about among us, but this time as an underground rumor: Car Jones was reputed to have "gone all the way"—to have "done it" with a pretty and most popular senior in our high school. (It must be remembered that this was more unusual among the young then than now.) The general (whispered) theory was that Car's status as a college boy had won the girl; traditionally, in Hilton, the senior high-school girls began to date the freshmen in the university, as many and as often as possible. But this was not necessarily true; maybe the girl was simply drawn to Car, his height and his shoulders, his stormy eyes. Or maybe they didn't do it after all.

The next thing I heard about Car, who was by then an authentic town person, a graduate student in the university, was that he had written a play which was to be produced by the campus dramatic society. (Maybe that is how he finally met his movie star, as a playwright? The column didn't say.) I think I read this item in the local paper, probably in a clipping forwarded to me by my mother; her letters were always thick with clippings, thin with messages of a personal nature.

My next news of Car came from my uncle, the French professor, a violent, en- 65 thusiastic partisan in university affairs, especially in their more traditional aspects. In scandalized tones, one family Thanksgiving, he recounted to me and my mother, that a certain young man, a graduate student in English, named Carstairs Jones, had been offered a special sort of membership in D.K.E., his own beloved fraternity, and "Jones had *turned it down.*" My mother and I laughed later and privately over this; we were united in thinking my uncle a fool, and I am sure that I added, Well, good for him. But I did not, at that time, reconsider the whole story of Car Jones, that most unregenerate and wicked of the truck children.

But now, with this fresh news of Carstairs Jones, and his wife the movie star, it occurs to me that we two, who at a certain time and place were truly misfits, although quite differently—we both have made it: what could be more American dream-y, more normal, than marriage to a lovely movie star? Or, in my case, marriage to the successful surgeon?

And now maybe I can reconstruct a little of that time; specifically, can try to see how it really was for Car, back then. Maybe I can even understand that kiss.

Let us suppose that he lived in a somewhat better than usual farmhouse; later events make this plausible—his family's move to town, his years at the university. Also, I wish him well. I will give him a dignified white house with a broad front porch, set back among pines and oaks, in the red clay countryside. The stability and size of his house, then, would have set Car apart from his neighbors, the other farm families, other truck children. Perhaps his parents too were somewhat "different," but my imagination fails at them; I can easily imagine and clearly see the house, but not its population. Brothers? sisters? Probably, but I don't know.

Car would go to school, coming out of his house at the honk of the stained and bulging, ugly yellow bus, which was crowded with his supposed peers, toward whom he felt both contempt and an irritation close to rage. Arrived at school, as one of the truck children, he would be greeted with a total lack of interest; he might as well have been invisible, or been black, *unless* he misbehaved in an outright, conspicuous way. And so he did: Car yawned noisily during history class, he hummed during study hall and after recess he dawdled around the playground and came in late. And for these and other assaults on the school's decorum he was punished in one way or another, and then, when all else failed to curb his ways, he would be *held back,* forced to repeat an already insufferably boring year of school.

70   One fall there was a minor novelty in school: a new girl (me), a Yankee, who didn't look much like the other girls, with long straight hair, instead of curled, and Yankee clothes, wool skirts and sweaters, instead of flowery cotton dresses worn all year round. A funny accent, a Yankee name: Emily Ames. I imagine that Car registered those facts about me, and possibly the additional information that I was almost as invisible as he, but without much interest.

Until the day of truth or consequences. I don't think Car was around on the playground while the game was going on; one of the girls would have seen him, and squealed out, "Oooh, there's Car, there *he is!*" I rather believe that some skinny little kid, an unnoticed truck child, overheard it all, and then ran over to where Car was lounging in one of the school buses, maybe peeling an orange and throwing the peel, in spirals, out the window. "Say, Car, that little Yankee girl, she says she'd like to kiss you."

"Aw, go on."

He is still not very interested; the little Yankee girl is as dumb as the others are.

And then he hears me being teased, everywhere, and teased with his name. "Emily would kiss Car Jones—Emily Jones!" Did he feel the slightest pleasure at such notoriety? I think he must have; a man who would marry a movie star must have at least a small taste for publicity. Well, at that point he began to write me those notes: "You are the prettiest one of the girls" (which I was not). I think he was casting us both in ill-fitting roles, me as the prettiest, defenseless girl, and himself as my defender.

75   He must have soon seen that it wasn't working out that way. I didn't need a defender, I didn't need him. I was having a wonderful time, at his expense, if you think about it, and I am pretty sure Car did think about it.

Interestingly, at the same time he had his perception of my triviality, Car must have got his remarkable inspiration in regard to his own life: there was a way out of those miserably boring classes, the insufferable children who surrounded him. He would demand a test, he would leave this place for the high school.

Our trellis meeting must have occurred after Car had taken the test, and had known that he did well. When he kissed me he was doing his last "bad" thing in that school, was kissing it off, so to speak. He was also insuring that I, at least, would remember him; he counted on its being my first kiss. And he may have thought that I was even sillier than I was, and that I would tell, so that what had happened would get around the school, waves of scandal in his wake.

For some reason, I would also imagine that Car is one of those persons who never look back; once kissed, I was readily dismissed from his mind, and probably for good. He could concentrate on high school, new status, new friends. Just as, now married to his movie star, he does not ever think of having been a truck child, one of the deprived, the disappointed. In his mind there are no ugly groaning trucks, no hopeless littered playground, no squat menacing school building.

But of course I could be quite wrong about Car Jones. He could be another sort of person altogether; he could be as haunted as I am by everything that ever happened in his life.

QUESTIONS FOR DISCUSSION AND WRITING

1. In what ways does Emily's answer to the question establish the conflict in the plot? In what ways does her meeting with Carstairs Jones bring the plot to its climax?

2. How does Emily characterize people as normal or abnormal? What "dark and strange" forces does Carstairs Jones represent? Why is she afraid of them? By contrast, how normal is her life, both as a girl and as an adult?

3. How is the setting of the playground—social and physical—important to an understanding of the main characters' school life and later life?

4. How does Emily present, reconsider, and wonder about her point of view on the events that she narrates?

5. Does Emily finally perceive any truth about herself and others from the *consequences* of her actions? Explain your answer.

Stories for Comparison

James Joyce's "Araby" (pages 723–728); Edna O'Brien's "A Scandalous Woman" (pages 948–966).

14

....

ISABEL ALLENDE

Phantom Palace

ISABEL ALLENDE was born in 1942 in Lima, Peru, the daughter of a
Chilean diplomat and the niece of Chile's former President Salvador Allende.
After completing her education at a private school in Santiago, Chile, she
first worked as a secretary for the United Nations Food and Agricultural
Organization and later as a journalist and television commentator. In 1973, as
part of a military coup, her uncle was assassinated and her family fled to
Venezuela. She began to contribute a newspaper column to *El Nacional*
(Caracas, Venezuela) and then completed her first novel, *The House of Spirits*
(1982), which has been adapted into a major film. Her subsequent novels include *Of Love and Shadows* (1984) and *Eva Luna* (1987). In 1985, Allende
began teaching creative writing at universities such as the University of
Virginia, Barnard College, and the University of California, Berkeley. Her
most recent novel, *The Infinite Plan* (1993), is set in the United States, and
her memoir, *Paula* (1995), is a personal narrative about her family. "Phantom
Palace," reprinted from *The Stories of Eva Luna* (1989), describes the creation and disappearance of a mysterious palace.

W hen five centuries earlier the bold renegades from Spain with their bone-
weary horses and armor candescent beneath an American sun stepped upon
the shores of Quinaroa, Indians had been living and dying in that same place for several thousand years. The conquistadors announced with heralds and banners the
"discovery" of a new land, declared it a possession of a remote emperor, set in place
the first cross, and named the place San Jerónimo, a name unpronounceable to the
natives. The Indians observed these arrogant ceremonies with some amazement, but
the news had already reached them of the bearded warriors who advanced across the
world with their thunder of iron and powder; they had heard that wherever these men
went they sowed sorrow and that no known people had been capable of opposing
them: all armies had succumbed before that handful of centaurs. These Indians were
an ancient tribe, so poor that not even the most befeathered chieftain had bothered
to exact taxes from them, and so meek that they had never been recruited for war.
They had lived in peace since the dawn of time and were not eager to change their

habits because of some crude strangers. Soon, nevertheless, they comprehended the magnitude of the enemy and they understood the futility of attempting to ignore them; their presence was overpowering, like a heavy stone bound to every back. In the years that followed, the Indians who had not died in slavery or as a result of the different tortures improvised to entrench the new gods, or as victims of unknown illnesses, scattered deep into the jungle and gradually lost even the name of their people. Always in hiding, like shadows among the foliage, they survived for centuries, speaking in whispers and mobilizing by night. They came to be so skillful in the art of dissimulation that history did not record them, and today there is no evidence of their passage through time. Books do not mention them, but the *campesinos* who live in the region say they have heard them in the forest, and every time the belly of a young unmarried woman begins to grow round and they cannot point to the seducer, they attribute the baby to the spirit of a lustful Indian. People of that place are proud of carrying a few drops of the blood of those invisible beings mingled with the torrential flow from English pirates, Spanish soldiers, African slaves, adventurers in search of El Dorado, and, later, whatever immigrant stumbled onto these shores with his pack on his back and his head filled with dreams.

Europe consumed more coffee, cocoa, and bananas than we as a nation could produce, but all that demand was no bonanza for us; we continued to be as poor as ever. Events took a sudden turn when a black man digging a well along the coast drove his pick deep into the ground and a stream of petroleum spurted over his face. Toward the end of the Great War there was a widely held notion that ours was a prosperous country, when in truth most of the inhabitants still squished mud between their toes. The fact was that gold flowed only into the coffers of El Benefactor and his retinue, but there was hope that someday a little would spill over for the people. Two decades passed under this democratic totalitarianism, as the President for Life called his government, during which any hint of subversion would have been crushed in the name of his greater glory. In the capital there were signs of progress: motorcars, movie houses, ice cream parlors, a hippodrome, and a theater that presented spectaculars from New York and Paris. Every day dozens of ships moored in the port, some carrying away petroleum and others bringing in new products, but the rest of the country drowsed in a centuries-long stupor.

One day the people of San Jerónimo awakened from their siesta to the deafening pounding that presaged the arrival of the steam engine. The railroad tracks would unite the capital with this small settlement chosen by El Benefactor as the site for his Summer Palace, which was to be constructed in the style of European royalty—no matter that no one knew how to distinguish summer from winter, since both were lived under nature's hot, humid breath. The sole reason for erecting such a monumental work on this precise spot was that a certain Belgian naturalist had affirmed that if there was any truth to the myth of the Earthly Paradise, this landscape of incomparable beauty would have been the location. According to his observations the forest harbored more than a thousand varieties of brightly colored birds and numerous species of wild orchids, from the *Brassia,* which is as large as a hat, to the tiny *Pleurothallis,* visible only under a magnifying glass.

The idea of the Palace had originated with some Italian builders who had called on His Excellency bearing plans for a hodgepodge of a villa, a labyrinth of countless columns, wide colonnades, curving staircases, arches, domes and capitals, salons, kitchens, bedchambers, and more than thirty baths decorated with gold and silver faucets. The railroad was the first stage in the enterprise, indispensable for transporting tons of materials and hundreds of workmen to this remote corner of the world, in addition to the supervisors and craftsmen brought from Italy. The task of putting together that jigsaw puzzle lasted four years: flora and fauna were transmuted in the process, and the cost was equivalent to that of all the warships of the nation's fleet, but it was paid for punctually with the dark mineral that flowed from the earth, and on the anniversary of the Glorious Ascent to Power the ribbon was cut to inaugurate the Summer Palace. For the occasion the locomotive of the train was draped in the colors of the flag, and the freight cars were replaced by parlor cars upholstered in plush and English leather; the formally attired guests included members of the oldest aristocracy who, although they detested the cold-blooded Andean who had usurped the government, did not dare refuse his invitation.

5   El Benefactor was a crude man with the comportment of a peon; he bathed in cold water and slept on a mat on the floor with his boots on and his pistol within arm's reach; he lived on roast meat and maize, and drank nothing but water and coffee. His black cigars were his one luxury; he considered anything else a vice befitting degenerates or homosexuals—including alcohol, which he disapproved of and rarely offered at his table. With time, nevertheless, he was forced to accept a few refinements, because he understood the need to impress diplomats and other eminent visitors if they were not to carry the report abroad that he was a barbarian. He did not have a wife to mend his Spartan ways. He believed that love was a dangerous weakness. He was convinced that all women, except his own mother, were potentially perverse and that the most prudent way to treat them was to keep them at arm's length. He had always said that a man asleep in an amorous embrace was as vulnerable as a premature baby; he demanded, therefore, that his generals sleep in the barracks and limit their family life to sporadic visits. No woman had ever spent the night in his bed or could boast of anything more than a hasty encounter. No woman, in fact, had ever made a lasting impression until Marcia Lieberman entered his life.

The celebration for the inauguration of the Summer Palace was a stellar event in the annals of El Benefactor's government. For two days and two nights alternating orchestras played the most current dance tunes and an army of chefs prepared an unending banquet. The most beautiful mulatto women in the Caribbean, dressed in sumptuous gowns created for the occasion, whirled through salons with officers who had never fought in a battle but whose chests were covered with medals. There was every sort of diversion: singers imported from Havana and New Orleans, flamenco dancers, magicians, jugglers and trapeze artists, card games and dominoes, and even a rabbit hunt. Servants released the rabbits from their cages, and the guests pursued the scampering pack with finely bred greyhounds; the chase came to an end when one wit blasted all the black-necked swans gliding across the lake. Some guests passed out in their chairs, drunk with dancing and liquor, while others jumped fully clothed into the swimming pool or drifted off in pairs to the bedchambers.

El Benefactor did not want to know the details. After greeting his guests with a brief speech, and beginning the dancing with the most aristocratic lady present, he had returned to the capital without a farewell. Parties put him in a bad humor. On the third day the train made the return journey, carrying home the enervated *bons vivants*. The Summer Palace was left in a calamitous state: the baths were dunghills, the curtains were dripping with urine, the furniture was gutted, and the plants drooped in their flowerpots. It took the servants a week to clean up the ravages of that hurricane.

The Palace was never again the scene of a bacchanal. Occasionally El Benefactor went there to get away from the pressures of his duties, but his repose lasted no more than three or four days, for fear that a conspiracy might be hatched in his absence. The government required eternal vigilance if power was not to slip through his fingers. The only people left in all that enormous edifice were the personnel entrusted with its maintenance. When the clatter of the construction equipment and the train had stilled, and the echoes of the inaugural festivities died down, the region was once again calm, and the orchids flowered and birds rebuilt their nests. The inhabitants of San Jerónimo returned to their habitual occupations and almost succeeded in forgetting the presence of the Summer Palace. That was when the invisible Indians slowly returned to occupy their territory.

The first signs were so subtle that no one paid attention to them; footsteps and whispers, fleeting silhouettes among the columns, the print of a hand on the clean surface of a table. Gradually food began to disappear from the kitchens, and bottles from the wine cellars; in the morning, some beds seemed to have been slept in. The servants blamed one another but never raised their voices because no one wanted the officer of the guard to take the matter into his hands. It was impossible to watch the entire expanse of that house, and while they were searching one room they would hear sighs in the adjoining one; but when they opened that door they would find only a curtain fluttering, as if someone had just stepped through it. The rumor spread that the Palace was under a spell, and soon the fear spread even to the soldiers, who stopped walking their night rounds and limited themselves to standing motionless at their post, eyes on the surrounding landscape, weapons at the ready. The frightened servants stopped going down to the cellars and, as a precaution, locked many of the rooms. They confined their activities to the kitchen and slept in one wing of the building. The remainder of the mansion was left unguarded, in the possession of the incorporeal Indians who had divided the rooms with invisible lines and taken up residence there like mischievous spirits. They had survived the passage of history, adapting to changes when they were inevitable, and when necessary taking refuge in a dimension of their own. In the rooms of the Palace they at last found refuge; there they noiselessly made love, gave birth without celebration, and died without tears. They learned so thoroughly all the twists and turns of that marble maze that they were able to exist comfortably in the same space with the guards and servants, never so much as brushing against them, as if they existed in a different time.

Ambassador Lieberman debarked in the port with his wife and a full cargo of personal belongings. He had traveled with his dogs, all his furniture, his library, his collection of opera recordings, and every imaginable variety of sports equipment, including a sailboat. From the moment his new destination had been announced, he had detested that country. He had left his post as Vice Consul in Vienna motivated by the ambition to obtain an ambassadorship, even if it meant South America, a bizarre continent for which he had not an ounce of sympathy. Marcia, his wife, took the appointment with better humor. She was prepared to follow her husband throughout his diplomatic pilgrimage—even though each day she felt more remote from him and had little interest in his mundane affairs—because she was allowed a great deal of freedom. She had only to fulfill certain minimal wifely requirements, and the remainder of her time was her own. In fact, her husband was so immersed in his work and his sports that he was scarcely aware of her existence; he noticed her only when she was not there. Lieberman's wife was an indispensable complement to his career; she lent brilliance to his social life and efficiently managed his complicated domestic staff. He thought of her as a loyal partner, but he had never been even slightly curious about her feelings. Marcia consulted maps and an encyclopedia to learn the particulars of that distant nation, and began studying Spanish. During the two weeks of the Atlantic crossing she read books by the famous Belgian naturalist and, even before arriving, was enamored of that heat-bathed geography. As she was a rather withdrawn woman, she was happier in her garden than in the salons where she had to accompany her husband, and she concluded that in the new post she would have fewer social demands and could devote herself to reading, painting, and exploring nature.

10   Lieberman's first act was to install fans in every room of his residence. Immediately thereafter he presented his credentials to the government authorities. When El Benefactor received him in his office, the couple had been in the city only a few days, but the gossip that the Ambassador's wife was a beautiful woman had already reached the caudillo's ears. For reasons of protocol he invited them to dinner, although he found the diplomat's arrogance and garrulity insufferable. On the appointed night Marcia Lieberman entered the Reception Hall on her husband's arm and, for the first time in a long lifetime, a woman caused El Benefactor to gasp for breath. He had seen more lithe figures, and faces more beautiful, but never such grace. She awakened memories of past conquests, fueling a heat in his blood that he had not felt in many years. He kept his distance that evening, observing the Ambassador's wife surreptitiously, seduced by the curve of her throat, the shadow in her eyes, the movement of her hands, the solemnity of her bearing. Perhaps it crossed his mind that he was more than forty years older than she and that any scandal would have repercussions far beyond the national boundaries, but that did not discourage him; on the contrary, it added an irresistible ingredient to his nascent passion.

Marcia Lieberman felt the man's eyes fastened on her like an indecent caress, and she was aware of the danger, but she did not have the strength to escape. At one moment she thought of telling her husband they should leave, but instead remained seated, hoping the old man would approach her and at the same time ready to flee if he did. She could not imagine why she was trembling. She had no illusions about her host; the signs of age were obvious from where she was sitting: the wrinkled and blemished skin, the dried-up body, the hesitant walk. She could imagine his stale odor and knew intuitively that his hands were claws beneath the white kid gloves.

But the dictator's eyes, clouded by age and the exercise of so much cruelty, still held a gleam of power that held her frozen in her chair.

El Benefactor did not know how to pay court to a woman; until that moment he had never had need to do so. That fact acted in his favor, for had he harassed Marcia with a Lothario's gallantries she would have found him repulsive and would have retreated with scorn. Instead she could not refuse him when a few days later he knocked at her door, dressed in civilian clothes and without his guards, looking like a dreary great-grandfather, to tell her that he had not touched a woman for ten years and that he was past temptations of that sort but, with all respect, he was asking her to accompany him that afternoon to a private place where he could rest his head in her queenly lap and tell her how the world had been when he was still a fine figure of a macho and she had not yet been born.

"And my husband?" Marcia managed to ask in a whisper-thin voice.

"Your husband does not exist, my child. Now only you and I exist," the President for Life replied as he led her to his black Packard.

Marcia did not return home, and before the month was out Ambassador Lieberman returned to his country. He had left no stone unturned in searching for his wife, refusing at first to accept what was no secret, but when the evidence of the abduction became impossible to ignore, Lieberman had asked for an audience with the Chief of State and demanded the return of his wife. The interpreter tried to soften his words in translation, but the President captured the tone and seized the excuse to rid himself once and for all of that imprudent husband. He declared that Lieberman had stained the honor of the nation with his absurd and unfounded accusations and gave him three days to leave the country. He offered him the option of withdrawing without a scandal, to protect the dignity of the country he represented, since it was to no one's interest to break diplomatic ties and obstruct the free movement of the oil tankers. At the end of the interview, with the expression of an injured father, he added that he could understand the Ambassador's dilemma and told him not to worry, because in his absence, he, El Benefactor, would continue the search for his wife. As proof of his good intents he called the Chief of Police and issued instructions in the Ambassador's presence. If at any moment Lieberman had thought of refusing to leave without Marcia, a second thought must have made clear to him that he was risking a bullet in the brain, so he packed his belongings and left the country before the three days were up.

Love had taken El Benefactor by surprise at an age when he no longer remembered the heart's impatience. This cataclysm rocked his senses and thrust him back into adolescence, but not sufficiently to dull his vulpine cunning. He realized that his was a passion of sensuality, and he could not imagine that Marcia returned his emotions. He did not know why she had followed him that afternoon, but his reason indicated that it was not for love, and, as he knew nothing about women, he supposed that she had allowed herself to be seduced out of a taste for adventure, or greed for power. In fact, she had fallen prey to compassion. When the old man embraced her, anxiously, his eyes watering with humiliation because his manhood did not respond as it once had, she undertook, patiently and with good will, to restore his pride. And thus after several attempts the poor man succeeded in passing through the gates and lingering a few brief instants in the proffered warm gardens, collapsing immediately thereafter with his heart filled with foam.

"Stay with me," El Benefactor begged, as soon as he had recovered from fear of succumbing upon her.

And Marcia had stayed, because she was moved by the aged caudillo's loneliness, and because the alternative of returning to her husband seemed less interesting than the challenge of slipping past the iron fence this man had lived behind for eighty years.

El Benefactor kept Marcia hidden on one of his estates, where he visited her daily. He never stayed the night with her. Their time together was spent in leisurely caresses and conversation. In her halting Spanish she told him about her travels and the books she had read; he listened, not understanding much, content simply with the cadence of her voice. In turn he told her stories of his childhood in the arid lands of the Andes, and of his life as a soldier; but if she formulated some question he immediately threw up his defenses, observing her from the corner of his eyes as if she were the enemy. Marcia could not fail to note this implacable stoniness and realized that his habit of distrust was much stronger than his need to yield to tenderness, and so, after a few weeks, she resigned herself to defeat. Once she had renounced any hope of winning him over with love, she lost interest in him and longed to escape the walls that sequestered her. But it was too late. El Benefactor needed her by his side because she was the closest thing to a companion he had known; her husband had returned to Europe and she had nowhere to turn in this land; and even her name was fading from memory. The dictator perceived the change in her and his mistrust intensified, but that did not cause him to stop loving her. To console her for the confinement to which she was now condemned—her appearance outside would have confirmed Lieberman's accusations and shot international relations to hell—he provided her with all the things she loved: music, books, animals. Marcia passed the hours in a world of her own, every day more detached from reality. When she stopped encouraging him, El Benefactor found it impossible to embrace her, and their meetings resolved into peaceful evenings of cookies and hot chocolate. In his desire to please her, El Benefactor invited her one day to go with him to the Summer Palace, so she could see the paradise of the Belgian naturalist she had read so much about.

20   The train had not been used since the inaugural celebration ten years before and was so rusted that they had to make the trip by automobile, escorted by a caravan of guards; a crew of servants had left a week before, taking everything needed to restore the Palace to its original luxury. The road was no more than a trail defended by chain gangs against encroaching vegetation. In some stretches they had to use machetes to clear the ferns, and oxen to haul the cars from the mud, but none of that diminished Marcia's enthusiasm. She was dazzled by the landscape. She endured the humid heat and the mosquitoes as if she did not feel them, absorbed by a nature that seemed to welcome her in its embrace. She had the impression that she had been there before, perhaps in dreams or in another life, that she belonged there, that until that moment she had been a stranger in the world, and that her instinct had dictated every step she had taken, including that of leaving her husband's house to follow a

trembling old man, for the sole purpose of leading her here. Even before she saw the Summer Palace, she knew that it would be her last home. When the edifice finally rose out of the foliage, encircled by palm trees and shimmering in the sun, Marcia breathed a deep sigh of relief, like a shipwrecked sailor when he sees home port.

Despite the frantic preparations that had been made to receive them, the mansion still seemed to be under a spell. The Roman-style structure, conceived as the center of a geometric park and grand avenues, was sunk in the riot of a gluttonous jungle growth. The torrid climate had changed the color of the building materials, covering them with a premature patina; nothing was visible of the swimming pool and gardens. The greyhounds had long ago broken their leashes and were running loose, a ferocious, starving pack that greeted the newcomers with a chorus of barking. Birds had nested in the capitals of the columns and covered the reliefs with droppings. On every side were signs of disorder. The Summer Palace had been transformed into a living creature defenseless against the green invasion that had surrounded and overrun it. Marcia leapt from the automobile and ran to the enormous doors where the servants awaited, oppressed by the heat of the dog days. One by one she explored all the rooms, the great salons decorated with crystal chandeliers that hung from the ceilings like constellations and French furniture whose tapestry upholstery was now home to lizards, bedchambers where bed canopies were blanched by intense sunlight, baths where moss had grown in the seams of the marble. Marcia never stopped smiling; she had the face of a woman recovering what was rightfully hers.

When El Benefactor saw Marcia so happy, a touch of the old vigor returned to warm his creaking bones, and he could embrace her as he had in their first meetings. Distractedly, she acceded. The week they had planned to spend there lengthened into two, because El Benefactor had seldom enjoyed himself so much. The fatigue accumulated in his years as tyrant disappeared, and several of his old man's ailments abated. He strolled with Marcia around the grounds, pointing out the many species of orchids climbing the tree trunks or hanging like grapes from the highest branches, the clouds of white butterflies that covered the ground, and the birds with iridescent feathers that filled the air with their song. He frolicked with her like a young lover, he fed her bits of the delicious flesh of wild mangoes, with his own hands he bathed her in herbal infusions, and he made her laugh by serenading her beneath her window. It had been years since he had been away from the capital, except for brief flights to provinces where his presence was required to put down some insurrection and to renew the people's belief that his authority was not to be questioned. This unexpected vacation had put him in a fine frame of mind; life suddenly seemed more fun, and he had the fantasy that with this beautiful woman beside him he could govern forever. One night he unintentionally fell asleep in her arms. He awoke in the early morning, terrified, with the clear sensation of having betrayed himself. He sprang out of bed, sweating, his heart galloping, and observed Marcia lying there, a white odalisque in repose, her copper hair spilling across her face. He informed his guards that he was returning to the city. He was not surprised when Marcia gave no sign of going with him. Perhaps in his heart he preferred it that way, since he understood that she represented his most dangerous weakness, that she was the only person who could make him forget his power.

El Benefactor returned to the capital without Marcia. He left behind a half-dozen soldiers to guard the property and a few employees to serve her, and he promised he would maintain the road so that she could receive his gifts, provisions, mail, and newspapers and magazines. He assured her that he would visit her often, as often as his duties as Chief of State permitted, but when he said goodbye they both knew they would never meet again. El Benefactor's caravan disappeared into the ferns and for a moment silence fell over the Summer Palace. Marcia felt truly free for the first time in her life. She removed the hairpins holding her hair in a bun, and shook out her long hair. The guards unbuttoned their jackets and put aside their weapons, while the servants went off to hang their hammocks in the coolest corners they could find.

For two weeks the Indians had observed the visitors from the shadows. Undeceived by Marcia Lieberman's fair skin and marvelous curly hair, they recognized her as one of their own but they had not dared materialize in her presence because of the habit of centuries of clandestinity. After the departure of the old man and his retinue, they returned stealthily to occupy the space where they had lived for generations. Marcia knew intuitively that she was never alone, that wherever she went a thousand eyes followed her, that she moved in a ferment of constant murmuring, warm breathing, and rhythmic pulsing, but she was not afraid; just the opposite, she felt protected by friendly spirits. She became used to petty annoyances: one of her dresses disappeared for several days, then one morning was back in a basket at the foot of her bed; someone devoured her dinner before she entered the dining room; her watercolors and books were stolen, but also she found freshly cut orchids on her table, and some evenings her bath waited with mint leaves floating in the cool water; she heard ghostly notes from pianos in the empty salons, the panting of lovers in the armoires, the voices of children in the attics. The servants had no explanation for those disturbances and she stopped asking, because she imagined they themselves were part of the benevolent conspiracy. One night she crouched among the curtains with a flashlight, and when she felt the thudding of feet on the marble, switched on the beam. She thought she saw shadowy, naked forms that for an instant gazed at her mildly and then vanished. She called in Spanish, but no one answered. She realized she would need enormous patience to uncover those mysteries, but it did not matter because she had the rest of her life before her.

25   A few years later the nation was jolted by the news that the dictatorship had come to an end for a most surprising reason: El Benefactor had died. He was a man in his dotage, a sack of skin and bones that for months had been decaying in life, and yet very few people imagined that he was mortal. No one remembered a time before him; he had been in power so many decades that people had become accustomed to thinking of him as an inescapable evil, like the climate. The echoes of the funeral were slow to reach the Summer Palace. By then most of the guards and servants, bored with waiting for replacements that never came, had deserted their posts. Marcia listened to the news without emotion. In fact, she had to make an effort to remember her past, what had happened beyond the jungle, and the hawk-eyed old man who had changed the course of her destiny. She realized that with the death of the tyrant the reasons for her remaining hidden had evaporated; she

could return to civilization, where now, surely, no one was concerned with the scandal of her kidnapping. She quickly discarded that idea, however, because there was nothing outside the snarl of the surrounding jungle that interested her. Her life passed peacefully among the Indians; she was absorbed in the greenness, clothed only in a tunic, her hair cut short, her body adorned with tattoos and feathers. She was utterly happy.

A generation later, when democracy had been established in the nation and nothing remained of the long history of dictators but a few pages in scholarly books, someone remembered the marble villa and proposed that they restore it and found an Academy of Art. The Congress of the Republic sent a commission to draft a report, but their automobiles were not up to the grueling trip, and when finally they reached San Jerónimo no one could tell them where the Summer Palace was. They tried to follow the railroad tracks, but the rails had been ripped from the ties and the jungle had erased all traces. Then the Congress sent a detachment of explorers and a pair of military engineers who flew over the area in a helicopter; the vegetation was so thick that not even they could find the site. Details about the Palace were misplaced in people's memories and the municipal archives; the notion of its existence became gossip for old women; reports were swallowed up in the bureaucracy and, since the nation had more urgent problems, the project of the Academy of Art was tabled.

Now a highway has been constructed that links San Jerónimo to the rest of the country. Travelers say that sometimes after a storm, when the air is damp and charged with electicity, a white marble palace suddenly rises up beside the road, hovers for a few brief moments in the air, like a mirage, and then noiselessly disappears.

QUESTIONS FOR DISCUSSION AND WRITING

1. Why does El Benefactor build the Summer Palace? How does Marcia tempt him to stay there? Why can't the new government convert it into an Academy of Art?

2. In what way is El Benefactor a "peon"? Why is Marcia attracted to him? Why does he consider her his "most dangerous weakness"? Why do the Indians consider her as "one of their own"?

3. How does the legacy of the Indians parallel the history of the Summer Palace? How does Marcia's reading of the Belgian naturalist prepare her to appreciate the setting of the palace?

4. Who narrates this story? What is the narrator's attitude toward El Benefactor, European explorers, and the Indians?

5. Which of the following themes seems most crucial to the story: the arrogance of power, the mystery of nature, the transience of human relationships? What other themes are evoked by the "magical realism" of this story?

Stories for Comparison

Gabriel García Márquez's "A Very Old Man with Enormous Wings" (pages 554–560); Franz Kafka's "In the Penal Colony" (pages 757–775).

15

··

RUDOLFO   ANAYA

B. Traven Is Alive and Well in Cuernavaca

RUDOLFO ANAYA was born in 1937 in Pastura, New Mexico, and
educated at the University of New Mexico. He was a public school teacher
in Albuquerque before joining the faculty of the University of New Mexico.
His most famous book, *Bless Me, Ultima* (1972), describes the life of a
Chicano boy in a small village in New Mexico. His other novels include
Heart of Aztlán (1976), *Tortuga* (1979), and *The Legend of La Llorona*
(1984). In "B. Traven Is Alive and Well in Cuernavaca," reprinted from *The
Anaya Reader,* a writer searches and finds a story in the magical landscape of
rumors, folk stories, and myth.

I didn't go to Mexico to find B. Traven. Why should I? I have enough to do
writing my own fiction, so I go to Mexico to write, not to search out writers.
B. Traven? you ask. Don't you remember *The Treasure of the Sierra Madre?* A real
classic. They made a movie from the novel. I remember seeing it when I was a kid.
It was set in Mexico, and it had all the elements of a real adventure story. B. Traven
was an adventurous man, traveled all over the world, then disappeared into Mexico
and cut himself off from society. He gave no interviews and allowed few photographs. While he lived he remained unapproachable, anonymous to his public, a
writer shrouded in mystery.

He's dead now, or they say he's dead. I think he's alive and well. At any
rate, he has become something of an institution in Mexico, a man honored for
his work. The cantineros and taxi drivers in Mexico City know about him as
well as the cantineros of Spain knew Hemingway, or they claim to. I never mention I'm a writer when I'm in a cantina, because inevitably some aficionado will
ask, "Do you know the work of B. Traven?" And from some dusty niche will
appear a yellowed, thumb-worn novel by Traven. Then if the cantinero knows
his business, and they all do in Mexico, he is apt to say, "Did you know that
B. Traven used to drink here?" If you show the slightest interest, he will follow
with, "Sure, he used to sit right over here. In this corner . . ." And if you don't
leave right then you will wind up hearing many stories about the mysterious
B. Traven while buying many drinks for the local patrons.

Everybody reads his novels, on the buses, on street corners, and if you look closely you'll spot one of his titles. One turned up for me, and that's how this story started. I was sitting in the train station in Juárez, waiting for the train to Cuernavaca, which would be an exciting title for this story except that there is no train to Cuernavaca. I was drinking beer to kill time, the erotic and sensitive Mexican time which is so different from the clean-packaged, well-kept time of the Americanos. Time in Mexico is at times cruel and punishing, but it is never indifferent. It permeates everything, it changes reality. Einstein would have loved Mexico because there time and space are one. I stare more often into empty space when I'm in Mexico. The past seems to infuse the present, and in the brown, wrinkled faces of the old people one sees the presence of the past. In Mexico I like to walk the narrow streets of the cities and the smaller pueblos, wandering aimlessly, feeling the sunlight which is so distinctively Mexican, listening to the voices which call in the streets, peering into the dark eyes which are so secretive and so proud. The Mexican people guard a secret. But in the end, one is never really lost in Mexico. All streets lead to a good cantina. All good stories start in a cantina.

At the train station, after I let the kids who hustle the tourists know that I didn't want chewing gum or cigarettes, and I didn't want my shoes shined, and I didn't want a woman at the moment, I was left alone to drink my beer. Luke-cold Dos Equis. I don't remember how long I had been there or how many Dos Equis I had finished when I glanced at the seat next to me and saw a book which turned out to be a B. Traven novel, old and used and obviously much read, but a novel nevertheless. What's so strange about finding a B. Traven novel in that dingy little corner of a bar in the Juárez train station? Nothing, unless you know that in Mexico one never finds anything. It is a country that doesn't waste anything, everything is recycled. Chevrolets run with patched-up Ford engines and Chrysler transmissions, buses are kept together, and kept running, with baling wire and homemade parts, yesterday's Traven novel is the pulp on which tomorrow's Fuentes story will appear. Time recycles in Mexico. Time returns to the past, and the Christian finds himself dreaming of ancient Aztec rituals. He who does not believe that Quetzalcóatl will return to save Mexico has little faith.

So the novel was the first clue. Later there was Justino. "Who is Justino?" you want to know. Justino was the jardinero who cared for the garden of my friend, the friend who had invited me to stay at his home in Cuernavaca while I continued to write. The day after I arrived I was sitting in the sun, letting the fatigue of the long journey ooze away, thinking nothing, when Justino appeared on the scene. He had finished cleaning the swimming pool and was taking his morning break, so he sat in the shade of the orange tree and introduced himself. Right away I could tell that he would rather be a movie actor or an adventurer, a real free spirit. But things didn't work out for him. He got married, children appeared, he took a couple of mistresses, more children appeared, so he had to work to support his family. "A man is like a rooster," he said after we talked awhile, "the more chickens he has the happier he is." Then he asked me what I was going to do about a woman while I was there, and I told him I hadn't thought that far ahead, that I would be happy if I could just get a damned story going.

This puzzled Justino, and I think for a few days it worried him. So on Saturday night he took me out for a few drinks and we wound up in some of the bordellos of Cuernavaca in the company of some of the most beautiful women in the world. Justino knew them all. They loved him, and he loved them.

I learned something more of the nature of this jardinero a few nights later when the heat and an irritating mosquito wouldn't let me sleep. I heard music from a radio, so I put on my pants and walked out into the Cuernavacan night, an oppressive, warm night heavy with the sweet perfume of the dama de la noche bushes which lined the wall of my friend's villa. From time to time I heard a dog cry in the distance, and I remembered that in Mexico many people die of rabies. Perhaps that is why the walls of the wealthy are always so high and the locks always secure. Or maybe it was because of the occasional gunshots which explode in the night. The news media tells us that Mexico is the most stable country in Latin America, and with the recent oil finds the bankers and the oil men want to keep it that way. I sense, and many know, that in the dark the revolution does not sleep. It is a spirit kept at bay by the high fences and the locked gates, yet it prowls the heart of every man. "Oil will create a new revolution," Justino had told me, "but it's going to be for our people. Mexicans are tired of building gas stations for the gringos from Gringolandia." I understood what he meant: there is much hunger in the country.

I lit a cigarette and walked towards my friend's car which was parked in the driveway near the swimming pool. I approached quietly and peered in. On the back seat with his legs propped on the front seat-back and smoking a cigar sat Justino. Two big, luscious women sat on either side of him, running their fingers through his hair and whispering in his ears. The doors were open to allow a breeze. He looked content. Sitting there he was that famous artist on his way to an afternoon reception in Mexico City, or he was a movie star on his way to the premiere of his most recent movie. Or perhaps it was Sunday and he was taking a Sunday drive in the country, towards Tepoztlán. And why shouldn't his two friends accompany him? I had to smile. Unnoticed I backed away and returned to my room. So there was quite a bit more than met the eye to this short, dark Indian from Ocosingo.

In the morning I asked my friend, "What do you know about Justino?"

10   "Justino? You mean Vitorino."

"Is that his real name?"

"Sometimes he calls himself Trinidad."

"Maybe his name is Justino Vitorino Trinidad," I suggested.

"I don't know and I don't care," my friend answered.

"He told me he used to be a guide in the jungle. Who knows? The Mexican Indian has an incredible imagination. Really gifted people. He's a good jardinero, and that's what matters to me. It's difficult to get good jardineros, so I don't ask questions."

15   "Is he reliable?" I wondered aloud.

"As reliable as a ripe mango," my friend nodded.

I wondered how much he knew, so I pushed a little further. "And the radio at night?"

"Oh, that. I hope it doesn't bother you. Robberies and break-ins are increasing here in the colonia. Something we never used to have. Vitorino said that if he keeps the radio on low the sound keeps thieves away. A very good idea, don't you think?"

I nodded. A very good idea.

"And I sleep very soundly," my friend concluded, "so I never hear it."   20

The following night when I awakened and heard the soft sound of the music from the radio and heard the splashing of water, I had only to look from my window to see Justino and his friends in the pool, swimming nude in the moonlight. They were joking and laughing softly as they splashed each other, being quiet so as not to awaken my friend, the patrón who slept so soundly. The women were beautiful. Brown skinned and glistening with water in the moonlight they reminded me of ancient Aztec maidens, swimming around Chac, their god of rain. They teased Justino, and he smiled as he floated on a rubber mattress in the middle of the pool, smoking his cigar, happy because they were happy. When he smiled the gold fleck of a filling glinted in the moonlight.

"¡Qué cabrón!" I laughed and closed my window.

Justino said a Mexican never lies. I believed him. If a Mexican says he will meet you at a certain time and place, he means he will meet you sometime at some place. Americans who retire in Mexico often complain of maids who swear they will come to work on a designated day, then don't show up. They did not lie, they knew they couldn't be at work, but they knew to tell the señora otherwise would make her sad or displease her, so they agree on a date so everyone would remain happy. What a beautiful aspect of character. It's a real virtue which Norteamericanos interpret as a fault in their character, because we are used to asserting ourselves on time and people. We feel secure and comfortable only when everything is neatly packaged in its proper time and place. We don't like the disorder of a free-flowing life.

Someday, I thought to myself, Justino will give a grand party in the sala of his patrón's home. His three wives, or his wife and two mistresses, and his dozens of children will be there. So will the women from the bordellos. He will preside over the feast, smoke his cigars, request his favorite beer-drinking songs from the mariachis, smile, tell stories and make sure everyone has a grand time. He will be dressed in a tuxedo, borrowed from the patrón's closet, of course, and he will act gallant and show everyone that a man who has just come into sudden wealth should share it with his friends. And in the morning he will report to the patrón that something has to be done about the poor mice that are coming in out of the streets and eating everything in the house.

"I'll buy some poison," the patrón will suggest.   25

"No, no," Justino will shake his head, "a little music from the radio and a candle burning in the sala will do."

And he will be right.

I liked Justino. He was a rogue with class. We talked about the weather, the lateness of the rainy season, women, the role of oil in Mexican politics. Like other workers, he believed nothing was going to filter down to the campesinos. "We could all be real Mexican greasers with all that oil," he said, "but the politicians will keep it all."

"What about the United States?" I asked.

30   "Oh, I have traveled in the estados unidos to the north. It's a country that's going to the dogs in a worse way than Mexico. The thing I liked the most was your cornflakes."

"Cornflakes?"

"Sí. You can make really good cornflakes."

"And women?"

"Ah, you better keep your eyes open, my friend. Those gringas are going to change the world just like the Suecas changed Spain."

35   "For better or for worse?"

"Spain used to be a nice country," he winked.

We talked, we argued, we drifted from subject to subject. I learned from him. I had been there a week when he told me the story which eventually led me to B. Traven. One day I was sitting under the orange tree reading the B. Traven novel I had found in the Juárez train station, keeping one eye on the ripe oranges which fell from time to time, my mind wandering as it worked to focus on a story so I could begin to write. After all, that's why I had come to Cuernavaca, to get some writing done, but nothing was coming, nothing. Justino wandered by and asked what I was reading and I replied it was an adventure story, a story of a man's search for the illusive pot of gold at the end of a make-believe rainbow. He nodded, thought awhile and gazed towards Popo, Popocatépetl, the towering volcano which lay to the south, shrouded in mist, waiting for the rains as we waited for the rains, sleeping, gazing at his female counterpart, Itza, who lay sleeping and guarding the valley of Cholula, there, where over four hundred years ago Cortés showed his wrath and executed thousands of Cholulans.

"I am going on an adventure," he finally said, and paused. "I think you might like to go with me."

I said nothing, but I put my book down and listened.

40   "I have been thinking about it for a long time, and now is the time to go. You see, it's like this. I grew up on the hacienda of Don Francisco Jiménez, it's to the south, just a day's drive on the carretera. In my village nobody likes Don Francisco, they fear and hate him. He has killed many men and he has taken their fortunes and buried them. He is a very rich man, muy rico. Many men have tried to kill him, but Don Francisco is like the devil, he kills them first."

I listened as I always listen, because one never knows when a word or a phrase or an idea will be the seed from which a story sprouts, but at first there was nothing interesting. It sounded like the typical patrón-peón story I had heard so many times before. A man, the patrón, keeps the workers enslaved, in serfdom, and because he wields so much power, soon stories are told about him and he begins to acquire super-human powers. He acquires a mystique, just like the divine right of old. The patrón wields a mean machete, like old King Arthur swung Excalibur. He chops off heads of dissenters and sits on top of the bones-and-skulls pyramid, the king of the mountain, the top macho.

"One day I was sent to look for lost cattle," Justino continued. "I rode back into the hills where I had never been. At the foot of a hill, near a ravine, I saw something move in the bush. I dismounted and moved forward quietly. I was afraid it might be bandidos who steal cattle, and if they saw me they would kill me. When I came near the place I heard a strange sound. Somebody was crying. My back shivered, just like a dog when he sniffs the devil at night. I thought I was going to see witches, brujas who like to go to those deserted places to dance for the devil, or La Llorona."

"La Llorona," I said aloud. My interest grew. I had been hearing Llorona stories since I was a kid, and I was always ready for one more. La Llorona was that archetypal woman of ancient legends who murdered her children, then repentant and demented she has spent the rest of eternity searching for them.

"Sí, La Llorona. You know that poor woman used to drink a lot. She played around with men, and when she had babies she got rid of them by throwing them into la barranca. One day she realized what she had done and went crazy. She started crying and pulling her hair and running up and down the sides of cliffs of the river looking for her children. It's a very sad story."

A new version, I thought, and yes, a sad story. And what of the men who made 45 love to the woman who became La Llorona? Did they ever cry for their children? It doesn't seem fair to have only her suffer, only her crying and doing penance. Perhaps a man should run with her, and in our legends we would call him "El Mero Chingón," he who screwed up everything. Then maybe the tale of love and passion and the insanity it can bring will be complete. Yes, I think someday I will write that story.

"What did you see?" I asked Justino.

"Something worse than La Llorona," he whispered.

To the south a wind mourned and moved the clouds off Popo's crown. The bald, snow-covered mountain thrust its power into the blue Mexican sky. The light glowed like liquid gold around the god's head. Popo was a god, an ancient god. Somewhere at his feet Justino's story had taken place.

"I moved closer, and when I parted the bushes I saw Don Francisco. He was sitting on a rock, and he was crying. From time to time he looked at the ravine in front of him, the hole seemed to slant into the earth. That pozo is called el Pozo de Mendoza. I had heard stories about it before, but I had never seen it. I looked into the pozo, and you wouldn't believe what I saw."

He waited, so I asked, "What?"   50

"Money! Huge piles of gold and silver coins! Necklaces and bracelets and crowns of gold, all loaded with all kinds of precious stones! Jewels! Diamonds! All sparkling in the sunlight that entered the hole. More money than I have ever seen! A fortune, my friend, a fortune which is still there, just waiting for two adventurers like us to take it!"

"Us? But what about Don Francisco? It's his land, his fortune."

"Ah," Justino smiled, "that's the strange thing about this fortune. Don Francisco can't touch it, that's why he was crying. You see, I stayed there, and I watched him closely. Every time he stood up and started to walk into the pozo the money disappeared. He stretched out his hand to grab the gold, and poof, it was gone! That's why he was crying! He murdered all those people and hid their wealth in the pozo, but now he can't touch it. He is cursed."

"El Pozo de Mendoza," I said aloud. Something began to click in my mind. I smelled a story.

55   "Who was Mendoza?" I asked.

"He was a very rich man. Don Francisco killed him in a quarrel they had over some cattle. But Mendoza must have put a curse on Don Francisco before he died, because now Don Francisco can't get to the money."

"So Mendoza's ghost haunts old Don Francisco."

"Many ghosts haunt him," Justino answered. "He has killed many men."

"And the fortune, the money . . ."

60   He looked at me and his eyes were dark and piercing. "It's still there. Waiting for us!"

"But it disappears as one approaches it, you said so yourself. Perhaps it's only an hallucination."

Justino shook his head. "No, it's real gold and silver, not hallucination money. It disappears for Don Francisco because the curse is on him, but the curse is not on us." He smiled. He knew he had drawn me into his plot. "We didn't steal the money, so it won't disappear for us. And you are not connected with the place. You are innocent. I've thought very carefully about it, and now is the time to go. I can lower you into the pozo with a rope, in a few hours we can bring out the entire fortune. All we need is a car. You can borrow the patrón's car, he is your friend. But he must not know where we're going. We can be there and back in one day, one night." He nodded as if to assure me, then he turned and looked at the sky. "It will not rain today. It will not rain for a week. Now is the time to go."

He winked and returned to watering the grass and flowers of the jardín, a wild Pan among the bougainvillea and the roses, a man possessed by a dream. The gold was not for him, he told me the next day, it was for his women, he would buy them all gifts, bright dresses, and he would take them on a vacation to the United States, he would educate his children, send them to the best colleges. I listened and the germ of a story cluttered my thoughts as I sat beneath the orange tree in the mornings. I couldn't write, nothing was coming, but I knew that there were elements for a good story in Justino's tale. In dreams I saw the lonely hacienda to the south. I saw the pathetic, tormented figure of Don Francisco as he cried over the fortune he couldn't touch. I saw the ghosts of the men he had killed, the lonely women who mourned over them and cursed the evil Don Francisco. In one dream I saw a man I took to be B. Traven, a gray-haired, distinguished-looking gentleman who looked at me and nodded approvingly.

"Yes, there's a story there, follow it, follow it . . ."

65   In the meantime, other small and seemingly insignificant details came my way. During a luncheon at the home of my friend, a woman I did not know leaned towards me and asked if I would like to meet the widow of B. Traven. The woman's hair was tinged orange, her complexion was ashen gray. I didn't know who she was or why she would mention B. Traven to me. How did she know Traven had come to haunt my thoughts? Was she a clue which would help unravel the mystery?

I didn't know, but I nodded. Yes, I would like to meet her. I had heard that Traven's widow, Rosa Elena, lived in Mexico City. But what would I ask her? What did I want to know? Would she know Traven's secret? Somehow he had learned that to keep his magic intact he had to keep away from the public.

Like the fortune in the pozo, the magic feel for the story might disappear if unclean hands reached for it. I turned to look at the woman, but she was gone. I wandered to the terrace to finish my beer. Justino sat beneath the orange tree. He yawned. I knew the literary talk bored him. He was eager to be on the way to el Pozo de Mendoza.

I was nervous, too, but I didn't know why. The tension for the story was there, but something was missing. Or perhaps it was just Justino's insistence that I decide whether I was going or not that drove me out of the house in the mornings. Time usually devoted to writing found me in a small cafe in the center of town. From there I could watch the shops open, watch the people cross the zócalo, the main square. I drank lots of coffee, I smoked a lot, I daydreamed, I wondered about the significance of the pozo, the fortune, Justino, the story I wanted to write and B. Traven. In one of these moods I saw a friend from whom I hadn't heard in years. Suddenly he was there, trekking across the square, dressed like an old rabbi, moss and green algae for a beard, and followed by a troop of very dignified Lacandones, Mayan Indians from Chiapas.

"Victor," I gasped, unsure if he was real or a part of the shadows which the sun created as it flooded the square with its light.

"I have no time to talk," he said as he stopped to munch on my pan dulce 70 and sip my coffee. "I only want you to know, for purposes of your story, that I was in a Lacandonian village last month, and a Hollywood film crew descended from the sky. They came in helicopters. They set up tents near the village, and big-bosomed, bikinied actresses emerged from them, tossed themselves on the cut trees which are the atrocity of the giant American lumber companies, and they cried while the director shot his film. Then they produced a gray-haired old man from one of the tents and took shots of him posing with the Indians. Herr Traven, the director called him."

He finished my coffee, nodded to his friends and they began to walk away.

"B. Traven?" I asked.

He turned. "No, an imposter, an actor. Be careful for imposters. Remember, even Traven used many disguises, many names!"

"Then he's alive and well?" I shouted. People around me turned to stare.

"His spirit is with us," were the last words I heard as they moved across the 75 zócalo, a strange troop of near naked Lacandon Mayans and my friend the Guatemalan Jew, returning to the rain forest, returning to the primal innocent land.

I slumped in my chair and looked at my empty cup. What did it mean? As their trees fall the Lacandones die. Betrayed as B. Traven was betrayed. Does each one of us also die as the trees fall in the dark depths of the Chiapas jungle? Far to the north, in Aztlán, it is the same where the earth is ripped open to expose and mine the yellow uranium. A few poets sing songs and stand in the way as the giant machines of the corporations rumble over the land and grind everything into dust. New holes are made in the earth, pozos full of curses, pozos with fortunes we cannot touch, should not touch. Oil, coal, uranium, from holes in the earth through which we suck the blood of the earth.

There were other incidents. A telephone call late one night, a voice with a German accent called my name, and when I answered the line went dead. A letter addressed to B. Traven came in the mail. It was dated March 26, 1969. My friend returned it to the post office. Justino grew more and more morose. He sat under the orange tree and stared into space, my friend complained about the garden drying up. Justino looked at me and scowled. He did a little work, then went back to daydreaming. Without the rains the garden withered. His heart was set on the adventure which lay at el pozo.

Finally I said "Yes, dammit, why not, let's go, neither one of us is getting anything done here," and Justino, cheering like a child, ran to prepare for the trip. But when I asked my friend for the weekend loan of the car he reminded me that we were invited to a tertulia, an afternoon reception, at the home of Señora Ana R. Many writers and artists would be there. It was in my honor, so I could meet the literati of Cuernavaca. I had to tell Justino I couldn't go.

Now it was I who grew morose. The story growing within would not let me sleep. I awakened in the night and looked out the window, hoping to see Justino and women bathing in the pool, enjoying themselves. But all was quiet. No radio played. The still night was warm and heavy. From time to time gunshots sounded in the dark, dogs barked, and the presence of a Mexico which never sleeps closed in on me.

80   Saturday morning dawned with a strange overcast. Perhaps the rains will come, I thought. In the afternoon I reluctantly accompanied my friend to the reception. I had not seen Justino all day, but I saw him at the gate as we drove out. He looked tired, as if he, too, had not slept. He wore the white shirt and baggy pants of a campesino. His straw hat cast a shadow over his eyes. I wondered if he had decided to go to the pozo alone. He didn't speak as we drove through the gate, he only nodded. When I looked back I saw him standing by the gate, looking after the car, and I had a vague, uneasy feeling that I had lost an opportunity.

The afternoon gathering was a pleasant affair, attended by a number of affectionate artists, critics and writers who enjoyed the refreshing drinks which quenched the thirst.

But my mood drove me away from the crowd. I wandered around the terrace and found a foyer surrounded by green plants, huge fronds and ferns and flowering bougainvillea. I pushed the green aside and entered a quiet, very private alcove. The light was dim, the air was cool, a perfect place for contemplation.

At first I thought I was alone, then I saw the man sitting in one of the wicker chairs next to a small wrought-iron table. He was an elderly white-haired gentleman. His face showed he had lived a full life, yet he was still very distinguished in his manner and posture. His eyes shone brightly.

"Perdón," I apologized, and turned to leave. I did not want to intrude.

85   "No, no, please," he motioned to the empty chair, "I've been waiting for you." He spoke English with a slight German accent. Or perhaps it was Norwegian, I couldn't tell the difference. "I can't take the literary gossip. I prefer the quiet."

I nodded and sat. He smiled and I felt at ease. I took the cigar he offered and we lit up. He began to talk and I listened. He was a writer also, but I had the good manners not to ask his titles. He talked about the changing Mexico, the change the new oil would bring, the lateness of the rains and how they affected the people and the land, and he talked about how important a woman was in a writer's life. He wanted to know about me, about the Chicanos, of Aztlán, about our work. It was the workers, he said, who would change society. The artist learned from the worker. I talked, and sometime during the conversation I told him the name of the friend with whom I was staying. He laughed and wanted to know if Vitorino was still working for him.

"Do you know Justino?" I asked.

"Oh, yes, I know that old guide. I met him many years ago, when I first came to Mexico," he answered. "Justino knows the campesino very well. He and I traveled many places together, he in search of adventure, I in search of stories."

I thought the coincidence strange, so I gathered the courage and asked, "Did he ever tell you the story of the fortune at el Pozo de Mendoza?"

"Tell me?" the old man smiled. "I went there."   90

"With Justino?"

"Yes, I went with him. What a rogue he was in those days, but a good man. If I remember correctly I even wrote a story based on that adventure. Not a very good story. Never came to anything. But we had a grand time. People like Justino are the writer's source. We met interesting people and saw fabulous places, enough to last me a lifetime. We were supposed to be gone for one day, but we were gone nearly three years. You see, I wasn't interested in the pots of gold he kept saying were just over the next hill. I went because there was a story to write."

"Yes, that's what interested me," I agreed.

"A writer has to follow a story if it leads him to hell itself. That's our curse. Ay, and each one of us knows our own private hell."

I nodded. I felt relieved. I sat back to smoke the cigar and sip from my drink.   95 Somewhere to the west the sun bronzed the evening sky. On a clear afternoon, Popo's crown would glow like fire.

"Yes," the old man continued, "a writer's job is to find and follow people like Justino. They're the source of life. The ones you have to keep away from are the dilettantes like the ones in there." He motioned in the general direction of the noise of the party. "I stay with people like Justino. They may be illiterate, but they understand our descent into the pozo of hell, and they understand us because they're willing to share the adventure with us. You seek fame and notoriety and you're dead as a writer."

I sat upright. I understood now what the pozo meant, why Justino had come into my life to tell me the story. It was clear. I rose quickly and shook the old man's hand. I turned and parted the palm leaves of the alcove. There, across the way, in one of the streets that led out of the maze of the town towards the south, I saw Justino. He was walking in the direction of Popo, and he was followed by women and children, a rag-tail army of adventurers, all happy, all singing. He looked up to where I stood on the terrace, and he smiled as he waved. He paused to light the stub of a cigar. The women turned, and the children turned, and all waved to me. Then they continued their walk, south, towards the foot of the volcano. They were going to the Pozo de Mendoza, to the place where the story originated.

I wanted to run after them, to join them in the glorious light which bathed the Cuernavaca valley and the majestic snow-covered head of Popo. The light was everywhere, a magnetic element which flowed from the clouds. I waved as Justino and his followers disappeared in the light. Then I turned to say something to the old man, but he was gone. I was alone in the alcove. Somewhere in the background I heard the tinkling of glasses and the laughter which came from the party, but that was not for me.

I left the terrace and crossed the lawn, found the gate and walked down the street. The sounds of Mexico filled the air. I felt light and happy. I wandered aimlessly through the curving, narrow streets, then I quickened my pace because suddenly the story was overflowing and I needed to write. I needed to get to my quiet room and write the story about B. Traven being alive and well in Cuernavaca.

QUESTIONS FOR DISCUSSION AND WRITING

1. In what sense is the plot of this story concerned with writing this story? How many other stories are embedded in the central plot? What revelation prompts the main story to reach its climax?

2. What are the arguments for seeing Justino as the protagonist in this story? In what sense is B. Traven or Mexico the protagonist? How are "stock" characters from Mexican folk stories represented—the patrón, the peon, La Llorona?

3. What details of the Mexican landscape does the narrator use to evoke the magic of the place? How does he use comparisons between Mexico and the United States to develop the story's settings?

4. Why is the writer an effective narrator for this story? How do the other guides (Justino) and advisors (man at party) in the story shape his point of view?

5. How might the following quotations be used to interpret the themes of the story? 1. "[Mexico] is a country [where] everything is recycled. . . . yesterday's Traven novel is pulp on which tomorrow's Fuentes story will appear." 2. "A writer's job is to find and follow people like Justino."

Stories for Comparison

Julio Cortázar's "We Love Glenda So Much" (pages 448–453); Charles Johnson's "The Sorcerer's Apprentice" (pages 714–723).

16

S H E R W O O D   A N D E R S O N

I'm a Fool

SHERWOOD ANDERSON (1876–1941) was born in Camden, Ohio, and spent most of his childhood in small Midwestern towns where his father worked intermittently as a harness maker and sign painter. Anderson's formal education ended at the age of fourteen when he began working as an errand boy and stable groom. At nineteen, he left home to work at a series of odd jobs in Chicago before enlisting in the Spanish-American War. After the war he worked as an advertising writer and then purchased an interest in a paint factory, trying for the next several years to combine his business interests with his growing aspirations to become a serious writer. In 1912, following a nervous breakdown, Anderson gave up his business to devote his full attention to writing. After three mildly successful books—*Windy McPherson's Son* (1916), *Marching Men* (1917), and *Mid-American Chants* (1918)—he published *Winesburg, Ohio* (1919), a set of related short stories exploring the deforming effects of disillusionment. Its innovative lyric style and psychological realism established Anderson's reputation as one of America's major writers. His later work includes two novels, *Poor White* (1920) and *Dark Laughter* (1925), and three volumes of short stories, *The Triumph of the Egg* (1921), *Horses and Men* (1923), and *Death in the Woods* (1933). In "I'm a Fool," reprinted from *Horses and Men,* a young man tries to explain what caused him to act like a "fool."

It was a hard jolt for me, one of the most bitterest I ever had to face. And it all came about through my own foolishness, too. Even yet sometimes, when I think of it, I want to cry or swear or kick myself. Perhaps, even now, after all this time, there will be a kind of satisfaction in making myself look cheap by telling of it.

It began at three o'clock one October afternoon as I sat in the grand stand at the fall trotting and pacing meet at Sandusky, Ohio.

To tell the truth, I felt a little foolish that I should be sitting in the grand stand at all. During the summer before I had left my home town with Harry Whitehead and, with a nigger named Burt, had taken a job as swipe with one of the two horses Harry was campaigning through the fall race meets that year. Mother cried and my sister Mildred, who wanted to get a job as a school teacher in our town that fall, stormed and scolded about the house all during the week before I left. They both thought it something disgraceful that one of our family should take a place as a swipe with race horses. I've an idea Mildred thought my taking the place would stand in the way of her getting the job she'd been working so long for.

But after all I had to work, and there was no other work to be got. A big lumbering fellow of nineteen couldn't just hang around the house and I had got too big to mow people's lawns and sell newspapers. Little chaps who could get next to people's sympathies by their sizes were always getting jobs away from me. There was one fellow who kept saying to everyone who wanted a lawn mowed or a cistern cleaned, that he was saving money to work his way through college, and I used to lay awake nights thinking up ways to injure him without being found out. I kept thinking of wagons running over him and bricks falling on his head as he walked along the street. But never mind him.

5   I got the place with Harry and I liked Burt fine. We got along splendid together. He was a big nigger with a lazy sprawling body and soft, kind eyes, and when it came to a fight he could hit like Jack Johnson. He had Bucephalus, a big black pacing stallion that could do 2.09 or 2.10, if he had to, and I had a little gelding named Doctor Fritz that never lost a race all fall when Harry wanted him to win.

We set out from home late in July in a box car with the two horses and after that, until late November, we kept moving along to the race meets and the fairs. It was a peachy time for me, I'll say that. Sometimes now I think that boys who are raised regular in houses, and never have a fine nigger like Burt for best friend, and go to high schools and college, and never steal anything, or get drunk a little, or learn to swear from fellows who know how, or come walking up in front of a grand stand in their shirt sleeves and with dirty horsey pants on when the races are going on and the grand stand is full of people all dressed up—What's the use of talking about it? Such fellows don't know nothing at all. They've never had no opportunity.

But I did. Burt taught me how to rub down a horse and put the bandages on after a race and steam a horse out and a lot of valuable things for any man to know. He could wrap a bandage on a horse's leg so smooth that if it had been the same color you would think it was his skin, and I guess he'd have been a big driver, too, and got to the top like Murphy and Walter Cox and the others if he hadn't been black.

Gee whizz, it was fun. You got to a county seat town, maybe say on a Saturday or Sunday, and the fair began the next Tuesday and lasted until Friday afternoon. Doctor Fritz would be, say in the 2.25 trot on Tuesday afternoon and on Thursday afternoon Bucephalus would knock 'em cold in the "free-for-all" pace. It left you a lot of time to hang around and listen to horse talk, and see Burt knock some yap cold that got too gay, and you'd find out about horses and men and pick up a lot of stuff you could use all the rest of your life, if you had some sense and salted down what you heard and felt and saw.

And then at the end of the week when the race meet was over, and Harry had run home to tend up to his livery stable business, you and Burt hitched the two horses to carts and drove slow and steady across country, to the place for the next meeting, so as to not over-heat the horses, etc., etc., you know.

Gee whizz, Gosh amighty, the nice hickorynut and beechnut and oaks and other 10
kinds of trees along the roads, all brown and red, and the good smells, and Burt
singing a song that was called Deep River, and the country girls at the windows of
houses and everything. You can stick your colleges up your nose for all me. I guess
I know where I got my education.

Why, one of those little burgs of towns you come to on the way, say now on a
Saturday afternoon, and Burt says, "let's lay up here." And you did.

And you took the horses to a livery stable and fed them, and you got your good
clothes out of a box and put them on.

And the town was full of farmers gaping, because they could see you were race
horse people, and the kids maybe never see a nigger before and was afraid and run
away when the two of us walked down their main street.

And that was before prohibition and all that foolishness, and so you went into a
saloon, the two of you, and all the yaps come and stood around, and there was always someone pretended he was horsey and knew things and spoke up and began
asking questions, and all you did was to lie and lie all you could about what horses
you had, and I said I owned them, and then some fellow said "will you have a drink
of whiskey" and Burt knocked his eye out the way he could say, off-hand like, "Oh
well, all right, I'm agreeable to a little nip. I'll split a quart with you." Gee whizz.

But that isn't what I want to tell my story about. We got home late in Novem- 15
ber and I promised mother I'd quit the race horses for good. There's a lot of things
you've got to promise a mother because she don't know any better.

And so, there not being any work in our town any more than when I left there
to go to the races, I went off to Sandusky and got a pretty good place taking care of
horses for a man who owned a teaming and delivery and storage and coal and real
estate business there. It was a pretty good place with good eats, and a day off each
week, and sleeping on a cot in a big barn, and mostly just shovelling in hay and oats
to a lot of big good-enough skates of horses, that couldn't have trotted a race with a
toad. I wasn't dissatisfied and I could send money home.

And then, as I started to tell you, the fall races come to Sandusky and I got the
day off and I went. I left the job at noon and had on my good clothes and my new
brown derby hat, I'd just bought the Saturday before, and a stand-up collar.

First of all I went down-town and walked about with the dudes. I've always
thought to myself, "put up a good front" and so I did it. I had forty dollars in my
pocket and so I went into the West House, a big hotel, and walked up to the cigar
stand. "Give me three twenty-five cent cigars," I said. There was a lot of horsemen
and strangers and dressed-up people from other towns standing around in the lobby
and in the bar, and I mingled amongst them. In the bar there was a fellow with a
cane and a Windsor tie on, that it made me sick to look at him. I like a man to be
a man and dress up, but not to go put on that kind of airs. So I pushed him aside, kind
of rough, and had me a drink of whiskey. And then he looked at me, as though he
thought maybe he'd get gay, but he changed his mind and didn't say anything. And
then I had another drink of whiskey, just to show him something, and went out and
had a hack out to the races, all to myself, and when I got there I bought myself the

best seat I could get up in the grand stand, but didn't go in for any of these boxes. That's putting on too many airs.

And so there I was, sitting up in the grand stand as gay as you please and looking down on the swipes coming out with their horses, and with their dirty horsey pants on and the horse blankets swung over their shoulders, same as I had been doing all the year before. I liked one thing about the same as the other, sitting up there and feeling grand and being down there and looking up at the yaps and feeling grander and more important, too. One thing's about as good as another, if you take it just right. I've often said that.

20   Well, right in front of me, in the grand stand that day, there was a fellow with a couple of girls and they was about my age. The young fellow was a nice guy all right. He was the kind maybe that goes to college and then comes to be a lawyer or maybe a newspaper editor or something like that, but he wasn't stuck on himself. There are some of that kind are all right and he was one of the ones.

He had his sister with him and another girl and the sister looked around over his shoulder, accidental at first, not intending to start anything—she wasn't that kind— and her eyes and mine happened to meet.

You know how it is. Gee, she was a peach! She had on a soft dress, kind of a blue stuff and it looked carelessly made, but was well sewed and made and everything. I knew that much. I blushed when she looked right at me and so did she. She was the nicest girl I've ever seen in my life. She wasn't stuck on herself and she could talk proper grammar without being like a school teacher or something like that. What I mean is, she was O.K. I think maybe her father was well-to-do, but not rich to make her chesty because she was his daughter, as some are. Maybe he owned a drug store or a drygoods store in their home town, or something like that. She never told me and I never asked.

My own people are all O.K. too, when you come to that. My grandfather was Welsh and over in the old country, in Wales he was—But never mind that.

The first heat of the first race come off and the young fellow setting there with the two girls left them and went down to make a bet. I knew what he was up to, but he didn't talk big and noisy and let everyone around know he was a sport, as some do. He wasn't that kind. Well, he come back and I heard him tell the two girls what horse he'd bet on, and when the heat was trotted they all half got to their feet and acted in the excited, sweaty way people do when they've got money down on a race, and the horse they bet on is up there pretty close at the end, and they think maybe he'll come on with a rush, but he never does because he hasn't got the old juice in him, come right down to it.

25   And then, pretty soon, the horses came out for the 2.18 pace and there was a horse in it I knew. He was a horse Bob French had in his string but Bob didn't own him. He was a horse owned by a Mr. Mathers down at Marietta, Ohio.

This Mr. Mathers had a lot of money and owned some coal mines or something, and he had a swell place out in the country, and he was stuck on race horses, but was a Presbyterian or something, and I think more than likely his wife was one, too, maybe a stiffer one than himself. So he never raced his horses hisself, and the story round the Ohio race tracks was that when one of his horses got ready to go to the races he turned him over to Bob French and pretended to his wife he was sold.

So Bob had the horses and he did pretty much as he pleased and you can't blame Bob, at least, I never did. Sometimes he was out to win and sometimes he wasn't. I never cared much about that when I was swiping a horse. What I did want to know was that my horse had the speed and could go out in front, if you wanted him to.

And, as I'm telling you, there was Bob in this race with one of Mr. Mathers' horses, was named "About Ben Ahem" or something like that, and was fast as a streak. He was a gelding and had a mark of 2.21, but could step in .08 or .09.

Because when Burt and I were out, as I've told you, the year before, there was a nigger, Burt knew, worked for Mr. Mathers and we went out there one day when we didn't have no race on at the Marietta Fair and our boss Harry was gone home.

And so everyone was gone to the fair but just this one nigger and he took us all through Mr. Mathers' swell house and he and Burt tapped a bottle of wine Mr. Mathers had hid in his bedroom, back in a closet, without his wife knowing, and he showed us this Ahem horse. Burt was always stuck on being a driver but didn't have much chance to get to the top, being a nigger, and he and the other nigger gulped that whole bottle of wine and Burt got a little lit up.

So the nigger let Burt take this About Ben Ahem and step him a mile in a track Mr. Mathers had all to himself, right there on the farm. And Mr. Mathers had one child, a daughter, kinda sick and not very good looking, and she came home and we had to hustle and get About Ben Ahem stuck back in the barn.

I'm only telling you to get everything straight. At Sandusky, that afternoon I was at the fair, this young fellow with the two girls was fussed, being with the girls and losing his bet. You know how a fellow is that way. One of them was his girl and the other his sister. I had figured that out.

"Gee whizz," I says to myself, "I'm going to give him the dope."

He was mighty nice when I touched him on the shoulder. He and the girls were nice to me right from the start and clear to the end. I'm not blaming them.

And so he leaned back and I give him the dope on About Ben Ahem. "Don't bet a cent on this first heat because he'll go like an oxen hitched to a plow, but when the first heat is over go right down and lay on your pile." That's what I told him.

Well, I never saw a fellow treat any one sweller. There was a fat man sitting beside the little girl, that had looked at me twice by this time, and I at her, and both blushing, and what did he do but have the nerve to turn and ask the fat man to get up and change places with me so I could set with his crowd.

Gee whizz, craps amighty. There I was. What a chump I was to go and get gay up there in the West House bar, and just because that dude was standing there with a cane and that kind of a necktie on, to go and get all balled up and drink that whiskey, just to show off.

Of course she would know, me setting right beside her and letting her smell of my breath. I could have kicked myself right down out of that grand stand and all around that race track and made a faster record than most of the skates of horses they had there that year.

Because that girl wasn't any mutt of a girl. What wouldn't I have give right then for a stick of chewing gum to chew, or a lozenger, or some liquorice, or most anything. I was glad I had those twenty-five cent cigars in my pocket and right away I give that fellow one and lit one myself. Then that fat man got up and we changed places and there I was, plunked right down beside her.

40   They introduced themselves and the fellow's best girl, he had with him, was named Miss Elinor Woodbury, and her father was a manufacturer of barrels from a place called Tiffin, Ohio. And the fellow himself was named Wilbur Wessen and his sister was Miss Lucy Wessen.

I suppose it was their having such swell names got me off my trolley. A fellow, just because he has been a swipe with a race horse, and works taking care of horses for a man in the teaming, delivery, and storage business, isn't any better or worse than any one else. I've often thought that, and said it too.

But you know how a fellow is. There's something in that kind of nice clothes, and the kind of nice eyes she had, and the way she had looked at me, awhile before, over her brother's shoulder, and me looking back at her, and both of us blushing.

I couldn't show her up for a boob, could I?

I made a fool of myself, that's what I did. I said my name was Walter Mathers from Marietta, Ohio, and then I told all three of them the smashingest lie you ever heard. What I said was that my father owned the horse About Ben Ahem and that he had let him out to this Bob French for racing purposes, because our family was proud and had never gone into racing that way, in our own name, I mean. Then I had got started and they were all leaning over and listening, and Miss Lucy Wessen's eyes were shining, and I went the whole hog.

45   I told about our place down at Marietta, and about the big stables and the grand brick house we had on a hill, up above the Ohio River, but I knew enough not to do it in no bragging way. What I did was to start things and then let them drag the rest out of me. I acted just as reluctant to tell as I could. Our family hasn't got any barrel factory, and, since I've known us, we've always been pretty poor, but not asking anything of any one at that, and my grandfather, over in Wales—but never mind that.

We set there talking like we had known each other for years and years, and I went and told them that my father had been expecting maybe this Bob French wasn't on the square, and had sent me up to Sandusky on the sly to find out what I could.

And I bluffed it through I had found out all about the 2.18 pace, in which About Ben Ahem was to start.

I said he would lose the first heat by pacing like a lame cow and then he would come back and skin 'em alive after that. And to back up what I said I took thirty dollars out of my pocket and handed it to Mr. Wilbur Wessen and asked him, would he mind, after the first heat, to go down and place it on About Ben Ahem for whatever odds he could get. What I said was that I didn't want Bob French to see me and none of the swipes.

Sure enough the first heat come off and About Ben Ahem went off his stride, up the back stretch, and looked like a wooden horse or a sick one, and come in to be last. Then this Wilbur Wessen went down to the betting place under the grand stand

and there I was with the two girls, and when that Miss Woodbury was looking the other way once, Lucy Wessen kinda, with her shoulder you know, kinda touched me. Not just tucking down, I don't mean. You know how a woman can do. They get close, but not getting gay either. You know what they do. Gee whizz.

And then they give me a jolt. What they had done, when I didn't know, was to get together, and they had decided Wilbur Wessen would bet fifty dollars, and the two girls had gone and put in ten dollars each, of their own money, too. I was sick then, but I was sicker later.

About the gelding, About Ben Ahem, and their winning their money, I wasn't worried a lot about that. It come out O.K. Ahem stepped the next three heats like a bushel of spoiled eggs going to market before they could be found out, and Wilbur Wessen had got nine to two for the money. There was something else eating at me.

Because Wilbur come back, after he had bet the money, and after that he spent most of his time talking to that Miss Woodbury, and Lucy Wessen and I was left alone together like on a desert island. Gee, if I'd only been on the square or if there had been any way of getting myself on the square. There ain't any Walter Mathers, like I said to her and them, and there hasn't ever been one, but if there was, I bet I'd go to Marietta, Ohio, and shoot him to-morrow.

There I was, big boob that I am. Pretty soon the race was over, and Wilbur had gone down and collected our money, and we had a hack down-town, and he stood us a swell supper at the West House, and a bottle of champagne beside.

And I was with that girl and she wasn't saying much, and I wasn't saying much either. One thing I know. She wasn't stuck on me because of the lie about my father being rich and all that. There's a way you know. . . . Craps amighty. There's a kind of girl, you see just once in your life, and if you don't get busy and make hay, then you're gone for good and all, and might as well go jump off a bridge. They give you a look from inside of them somewhere, and it ain't no vamping, and what it means is—you want that girl to be your wife, and you want nice things around her like flowers and swell clothes, and you want her to have the kids you're going to have, and you want good music played and no rag time. Gee whizz.

There's a place over near Sandusky, across a kind of bay, and it's called Cedar Point. And after we had supper we went over to it in a launch, all by ourselves. Wilbur and Miss Lucy and that Miss Woodbury had to catch a ten o'clock train back to Tiffin, Ohio, because, when you're out with girls like that you can't get careless and miss any trains and stay out all night, like you can with some kinds of Janes.

And Wilbur blowed himself to the launch and it cost him fifteen cold plunks, but I wouldn't never have knew if I hadn't listened. He wasn't no tin horn kind of a sport.

Over at the Cedar Point place, we didn't stay around where there was a gang of common kind of cattle at all.

There was big dance halls and dining places for yaps, and there was a beach you could walk along and get where it was dark, and we went there.

She didn't talk hardly at all and neither did I, and I was thinking how glad I was my mother was all right, and always made us kids learn to eat with a fork at table, and not swill soup, and not be noisy and rough like a gang you see around a race track that way.

60   Then Wilbur and his girl went away up the beach and Lucy and I sat down in a dark place, where there was some roots of old trees, the water had washed up, and after that the time, till we had to go back in the launch and they had to catch their trains, wasn't nothing at all. It went like winking your eye.

Here's how it was. The place we were setting in was dark, like I said, and there was the roots from that old stump sticking up like arms, and there was a watery smell, and the night was like—as if you could put your hand out and feel it—so warm and soft and dark and sweet like an orange.

I most cried and I most swore and I most jumped up and danced, I was so mad and happy and sad.

When Wilbur come back from being alone with his girl, and she saw him coming, Lucy she says, "we got to go to the train now," and she was most crying too, but she never knew nothing I knew, and she couldn't be so all busted up. And then, before Wilbur and Miss Woodbury got up to where we was, she put her face up and kissed me quick and put her head up against me and she was all quivering and— Gee whizz.

Sometimes I hope I have cancer and die. I guess you know what I mean. We went in the launch across the bay to the train like that, and it was dark, too. She whispered and said it was like she and I could get out of the boat and walk on the water, and it sounded foolish, but I knew what she meant.

65   And then quick we were right at the depot, and there was a big gang of yaps, the kind that goes to the fairs, and crowded and milling around like cattle, and how could I tell her? "It won't be long because you'll write and I'll write to you." That's all she said.

I got a chance like a hay barn afire. A swell chance I got.

And maybe she would write me, down at Marietta that way, and the letter would come back, and stamped on the front of it by the U.S.A. "there ain't any such guy," or something like that, whatever they stamp on a letter that way.

And me trying to pass myself off for a bigbug and a swell—to her, as decent a little body as God ever made. Craps amighty—a swell chance I got!

And then the train come in, and she got on it, and Wilbur Wessen he come and shook hands with me, and that Miss Woodbury was nice too and bowed to me, and I at her, and the train went and I busted out and cried like a kid.

70   Gee, I could have run after that train and made Dan Patch look like a freight train after a wreck but, socks amighty, what was the use? Did you ever see such a fool?

I'll bet you what—if I had an arm broke right now or a train had run over my foot—I wouldn't go to no doctor at all. I'd go set down and let her hurt and hurt— that's what I'd do.

I'll bet you what—if I hadn't a drunk that booze I'd a never been such a boob as to go tell such a lie—that couldn't never be made straight to a lady like her.

I wish I had that fellow right here that had on a Windsor tie and carried a cane. I'd smash him for fair. Gosh darn his eyes. He's a big fool—that's what he is.

And if I'm not another you just go find me one and I'll quit working and be a bum and give him my job. I don't care nothing for working, and earning money, and saving it for no such boob as myself.

QUESTIONS FOR DISCUSSION AND WRITING

1. What did the narrator have an *opportunity* to learn when he and Burt were on the circuit? How does his decision to lie prove that he hasn't learned what he was supposed to? In what ways does the narrator come to terms with the conflict he has created?

2. How does the narrator characterize himself, those who go to college, and those who show off at the races? How does he react to the man in the Windsor tie? How does he describe Lucy's special appeal?

3. What internal evidence in the story establishes its particular historical setting? How does Anderson condemn the racism in this world without ever mentioning it directly?

4. What do the narrator's own words—"gee whizz," etc.—reveal about his ability to interpret his own story? What is the difference between the narrator's interpretation of the events in the story and ours?

5. In what ways does this story depict the mistakes of any adolescent or the troubles of a young man filled with self-hatred? What evidence in the story supports each of these thematic readings?

Stories for Comparison

Willa Cather's "Paul's Case" (pages 78–92); John Updike's "A & P" (pages 1136–1141).

I7

....

M A R G A R E T A T W O O D

Dancing Girls

MARGARET ATWOOD was born in Ottawa, Ontario, in 1939, and educated
at the University of Toronto, Radcliffe College, and Harvard University. She
has taught at the University of British Columbia and York University and
served as writer-in-residence at the University of Alabama and Macquarie
University, Australia. Although she has written over a dozen volumes of poetry, several books for children and works of nonfiction, she is best known
for her novels, including *Surfacing* (1972), the best-selling and controversial
The Handmaid's Tale (1985), *Cat's Eye* (1989), and *The Robber Bride*
(1993). Her short stories have been collected in *Dancing Girls and Other
Stories* (1977), *Bluebird's Egg* (1983), *Murder in the Dark* (1983), and
Wilderness Tips (1991). In "Dancing Girls," a young student has difficulty
reconciling her idealized rearrangement of the world with the realities of life
in her boardinghouse.

The first sign of the new man was the knock on the door. It was the landlady,
knocking not at Ann's door, as she'd thought, but on the other door, the one east
of the bathroom. Knock, knock, knock; then a pause, soft footsteps, the sound of unlocking. Ann, who had been reading a book on canals, put it down and lit herself a
cigarette. It wasn't that she tried to overhear: in this house you couldn't help it.

"Hi!" Mrs. Nolan's voice loud, overly friendly. "I was wondering, my kids would
love to see your native costume. You think you could put it on, like, and come down?"

A soft voice, unintelligible.

"Gee, that's great! We'd sure appreciate it!"

5   Closing and locking, Mrs. Nolan slip-slopping along the hall in, Ann knew, her
mauve terry-cloth scuffies and flowered housecoat, down the stairs, hollering at
her two boys. "You get into this room right now!" Her voice came up through Ann's
hot air register as if the grate were a PA system. *It isn't those kids who want to see
him,* she thought. *It's her.* She put out the cigarette, reserving the other half for later,
and opened her book again. What costume? Which land, this time?

Unlocking, opening, soft feet down the hall. They sounded bare. Ann closed the
book and opened her own door. A white robe, the back of a brown head, moving with

a certain stealth or caution toward the stairs. Ann went into the bathroom and turned on the light. They would share it; the person in that room always shared her bathroom. She hoped he would be better than the man before, who always seemed to forget his razor and would knock on the door while Ann was having a bath. You wouldn't have to worry about getting raped or anything in this house though, that was one good thing. Mrs. Nolan was better than any burglar alarm, and she was always there.

That one had been from France, studying Cinema. Before him there had been a girl, from Turkey, studying Comparative Literature. Lelah, or that was how it was pronounced. Ann used to find her beautiful long auburn hairs in the washbasin fairly regularly; she'd run her thumb and index finger along them, enviously, before discarding them. She had to keep her own hair chopped off at ear level, as it was brittle and broke easily. Lelah also had a gold tooth, right at the front on the outside where it showed when she smiled. Curiously, Ann was envious of this tooth as well. It and the hair and the turquoise-studded earrings Lelah wore gave her a gypsy look, a wise look that Ann, with her beige eyebrows and delicate mouth, knew she would never be able to develop, no matter how wise she got. She herself went in for "classics," tailored skirts and Shetland sweaters; it was the only look she could carry off. But she and Lelah had been friends, smoking cigarettes in each other's rooms, commiserating with each other about the difficulties of their courses and the loudness of Mrs. Nolan's voice. So Ann was familiar with that room; she knew what it looked like inside and how much it cost. It was no luxury suite, certainly, and she wasn't surprised at the high rate of turnover. It had an even more direct pipeline to the sounds of the Nolan family than hers had. Lelah had left because she couldn't stand the noise.

The room was smaller and cheaper than her room, though painted the same depressing shade of green. Unlike hers, it did not have its own tiny refrigerator, sink and stove; you had to use the kitchen at the front of the house, which had been staked out much earlier by a small enclave of mathematicians, two men and one woman, from Hong Kong. Whoever took that room either had to eat out all the time or run the gamut of their conversation, which even when not in Chinese was so rarefied as to be unintelligible. And you could never find any space in the refrigerator, it was always full of mushrooms. This from Lelah; Ann herself never had to deal with them since she could cook in her own room. She could see them, though, as she went in and out. At mealtimes they usually sat quietly at their kitchen table, discussing surds, she assumed. Ann suspected that what Lelah had really resented about them was not the mushrooms: they simply made her feel stupid.

Every morning, before she left for classes, Ann checked the bathroom for signs of the new man—hairs, cosmetics—but there was nothing. She hardly ever heard him; sometimes there was that soft, barefooted pacing, the click of his lock, but there were no radio noises, no coughs, no conversations. For the first couple of weeks, apart from that one glimpse of a tall, billowing figure, she didn't even see him. He didn't appear to use the kitchen, where the mathematicians continued their mysteries undisturbed; or if he did, he cooked while no one else was there. Ann would have forgotten about him completely if it hadn't been for Mrs. Nolan.

"He's real nice, not like some you get," she said to Ann in her piercing whisper. 10 Although she shouted at her husband, when he was home, and especially at her children, she always whispered when she was talking to Ann, a hoarse, avid whisper, as if they shared disreputable secrets. Ann was standing in front of her door with the room key in her hand, her usual location during these confidences. Mrs. Nolan knew Ann's routine. It wasn't difficult for her to pretend to be cleaning the bathroom, to pop out and waylay Ann, Ajax and rag in hand, whenever she felt she had something to tell her. She was a short, barrel-shaped woman: the top of her head came only to Ann's nose, so she had to look up at Ann, which at these moments made her seem oddly childlike.

"He's from one of them Arabian countries. Though I thought they wore turbans, or not turbans, those white things, like. He just has this funny hat, sort of like the Shriners. He don't look much like an Arab to me. He's got these tattoo marks on his face. . . . But he's real nice."

Ann stood, her umbrella dripping onto the floor, waiting for Mrs. Nolan to finish. She never had to say anything much; it wasn't expected. "You think you could get me the rent on Wednesday?" Mrs. Nolan asked. Three days early; the real point of the conversation, probably. Still, as Mrs. Nolan had said back in September, she didn't have much of anyone to talk to. Her husband was away much of the time and her children escaped outdoors whenever they could. She never went out herself except to shop, and for Mass on Sundays.

"I'm glad it was you took the room," she'd said to Ann. "I can talk to you. You're not, like, foreign. Not like most of them. It was his idea, getting this big house to rent out. Not that he has to do the work or put up with them. You never know what they'll do."

Ann wanted to point out to her that she was indeed foreign, that she was just as foreign as any of the others, but she knew Mrs. Nolan would not understand. It would be like that fiasco in October. *Wear your native costumes.* She had responded to the invitation out of a sense of duty, as well as one of irony. Wait till they get a load of my native costume, she'd thought, contemplating snowshoes and a parka but actually putting on her good blue wool suit. There was only one thing *native costume* reminded her of: the cover picture on the Missionary Sunday School paper they'd once handed out, which showed children from all the countries of the world dancing in a circle around a smiling white-faced Jesus in a bedsheet. That, and the poem in the *Golden Windows Reader:*

> Little Indian, Sioux or Cree,
> Oh, don't you wish that you were me?

15   The awful thing, as she told Lelah later, was that she was the only one who'd gone. "She had all this food ready, and not a single other person was there. She was really upset, and I was so embarrassed for her. It was some Friends of Foreign Students thing, just for women: students and the wives of students. She obviously didn't think I was foreign enough, and she couldn't figure out why no one else came." Neither could Ann, who had stayed far too long and had eaten platefuls of crackers and cheese she didn't want in order to soothe her hostess' thwarted sense of hospitality. The woman, who had tastefully-streaked ash-blonde hair and a livingroom filled with polished and satiny traditional surfaces, had alternately urged her to eat

and stared at the door, as if expecting a parade of foreigners in their native costumes to come trooping gratefully through it.

Lelah smiled, showing her wise tooth. "Don't they know any better than to throw those things at night?" she said. "Those men aren't going to let their wives go out by themselves at night. And the single ones are afraid to walk on the streets alone, I know I am."

"I'm not," Ann said, "as long as you stay on the main ones, where it's lighted."

"Then you're a fool," Lelah said. "Don't you know there was a girl murdered three blocks from here? Left her bathroom window unlocked. Some man climbed through the window and cut her throat."

"I always carry my umbrella," Ann said. Of course there were certain places where you just didn't go. Scollay Square, for instance, where the prostitutes hung out and you might get followed, or worse. She tried to explain to Lelah that she wasn't used to this, to any of this, that in Toronto you could walk all over the city, well, almost anywhere, and never have any trouble. She went on to say that no one here seemed to understand that she wasn't like them, she came from a different country, it wasn't the same; but Lelah was quickly bored by this. She had to get back to Tolstoy, she said, putting out her cigarette in her unfinished cup of instant coffee. (*Not strong enough for her, I suppose,* Ann thought.)

"You shouldn't worry," she said. "You're well off. At least your family doesn't almost disown you for doing what you want to do." Lelah's father kept writing her letters, urging her to return to Turkey, where the family had decided on the perfect husband for her. Lelah had stalled them for one year, and maybe she could stall them for one more, but that would be her limit. She couldn't possibly finish her thesis in that time.

Ann hadn't seen much of her since she'd moved out. You lost sight of people quickly here, in the ever-shifting population of hopeful and despairing transients. No one wrote her letters urging her to come home, no one had picked out the perfect husband for her. On the contrary. She could imagine her mother's defeated look, the greying and sinking of her face, if she were suddenly to announce that she was going to quit school, trade in her ambitions for fate, and get married. Even her father wouldn't like it. *Finish what you start,* he'd say, *I didn't and look what happened to me.* The bungalow at the top of Avenue Road, beside a gas station, with the roar of the expressway always there, like the sea, and fumes blighting the Chinese elm hedge her mother had planted to conceal the pumps. Both her brothers had dropped out of high school; they weren't the good students Ann had been. One worked in a print shop now and had a wife; the other had drifted to Vancouver, and no one knew what he did. She remembered her first real boyfriend, beefy, easygoing Bill Decker, with his two-tone car that kept losing the muffler. They'd spent a lot of time parked on side streets, rubbing against each other through all those layers of clothes. But even in that sensual mist, the cocoon of breath and skin they'd spun around each other, those phone conversations that existed as a form of touch, she'd known this was not something she could get too involved in. He was probably flabby by now, settled. She'd had relationships with men since then, but she had treated them the same way. *Circumspect.*

Not that Mrs. Nolan's back room was any step up. Out one window there was a view of the funeral home next door; out the other was the yard, which the Nolan kids had scraped clean of grass and which was now a bog of half-frozen mud. Their dog, a mongrelized German Shepherd, was kept tied there, where the kids alternately hugged and tormented it. ("Jimmy! Donny! Now you leave that dog alone!" "Don't do that, he's filthy! Look at you!" Ann covering her ears, reading about underground malls.) She'd tried to fix the room up, she'd hung a Madras spread as a curtain in front of the cooking area, she'd put up several prints, Braque still-lifes of guitars and soothing Cubist fruit, and she was growing herbs on her windowsill; she needed surroundings that at least tried not to be ugly. But none of these things helped much. At night she wore earplugs. She hadn't known about the scarcity of good rooms, hadn't realized that the whole area was a student slum, that the rents would be so high, the available places so dismal. Next year would be different; she'd get here early and have the pick of the crop. Mrs. Nolan's was definitely a leftover. You could do much better for the money; you could even have a whole apartment, if you were willing to live in the real slum that spread in narrow streets of three-storey frame houses, fading mustard yellow and soot grey, nearer the river. Though Ann didn't think she was quite up to that. Something in one of the good old houses, on a quiet back street, with a little stained glass, would be more like it. Her friend Jetske had a place like that.

But she was doing what she wanted, no doubt of that. In high school she had planned to be an architect, but while finishing the preliminary courses at university she had realized that the buildings she wanted to design were either impossible— who could afford them?—or futile. They would be lost, smothered, ruined by all the other buildings jammed inharmoniously around them. This was why she had decided to go into Urban Design, and she had come here because this school was the best. Or rumoured to be the best. By the time she finished, she intended to be so well-qualified, so armoured with qualifications, that no one back home would dare turn her down for the job she coveted. She wanted to rearrange Toronto. Toronto would do for a start.

25   She wasn't yet too certain of the specific details. What she saw were spaces, beautiful green spaces, with water flowing through them, and trees. Not big golf-course lawns, though; something more winding, something with sudden turns, private niches, surprising vistas. And no formal flower beds. The houses, or whatever they were, set unobtrusively among the trees, the cars kept . . . where? And where would people shop, and who would live in these places? This was the problem: she could see the vistas, the trees and the streams or canals, quite clearly, but she could never visualize the people. Her green spaces were always empty.

She didn't see her next-door neighbour again until February. She was coming back from the small local supermarket where she bought the food for her cheap, carefully balanced meals. He was leaning in the doorway of what, at home, she would have called a vestibule, smoking a cigarette and staring out at the rain, through the glass panes at the side of the front door. He should have moved a little to give Ann room to put down her umbrella, but he didn't. He didn't even look at her. She squeezed in, shook her deflated umbrella and checked her mail box, which didn't have a key. There weren't usually any letters in it, and today was no exception. He was wearing a white shirt that was too big for him and some greenish trousers. His feet were not bare, in fact he was wearing a pair of prosaic brown shoes. He did have tattoo marks, though, or rather scars, a set of them running across each cheek. It was the first time she had seen him from the front. He seemed a little shorter than he had when she'd glimpsed him heading towards the stairs, but perhaps it was because he had no hat on. He was curved so listlessly against the doorframe, it was almost as if he had no bones.

There was nothing to see through the front of Mrs. Nolan's door except the traffic, sizzling by the way it did every day. He was depressed, it must be that. This weather would depress anyone. Ann sympathized with his loneliness, but she did not wish to become involved in it, implicated by it. She had enough trouble dealing with her own. She smiled at him, though since he wasn't looking at her this smile was lost. She went past him and up the stairs.

As she fumbled in her purse for her key, Mrs. Nolan stumped out of the bathroom. "You see him?" she whispered.

"Who?" Ann said.

"Him." Mrs. Nolan jerked her thumb. "Standing down there, by the door. He   30
does that a lot. He's bothering me, like. I don't have such good nerves."

"He's not doing anything," Ann said.

"That's what I mean," Mrs. Nolan whispered ominously. "He never does nothing. Far as I can tell, he never goes out much. All he does is borrow my vacuum cleaner."

"Your vacuum cleaner?" Ann said, startled into responding.

"That's what I said." Mrs. Nolan had a rubber plunger which she was fingering. "And there's more of them. They come in the other night, up to his room. Two more, with the same marks and everything, on their faces. It's like some kind of, like, a religion or something. And he never gave the vacuum cleaner back till the next day."

"Does he pay the rent?" Ann said, trying to switch the conversation to practical   35
matters. Mrs. Nolan was letting her imagination get out of control.

"Regular," Mrs. Nolan said. "Except I don't like the way he comes down, so quiet like, right into my house. With Fred away so much."

"I wouldn't worry," Ann said in what she hoped was a soothing voice. "He seems perfectly nice."

"It's always that kind," Mrs. Nolan said.

Ann cooked her dinner, a chicken breast, some peas, a digestive biscuit. Then she washed her hair in the bathroom and put it up in rollers. She had to do that, to give it body. With her head encased in the plastic hood of her portable dryer she sat at her table, drinking instant coffee, smoking her usual half cigarette, and attempting to read a book about Roman aqueducts, from which she hoped to get some novel ideas for her current project. (An aqueduct, going right through the middle of the obligatory shopping centre? Would anyone care?) Her mind kept flicking, though, to the problem of the man next door. Ann did not often try to think about what it would be like to be a man. But this particular man . . . Who was he, and what was happening to him? He must be a student, everyone here was a student. And he would be intelligent, that went without saying. Probably on scholarship. Everyone here in the graduate school was on scholarship, except the real Americans, who sometimes weren't. Or rather, the women were, but some of the men were still avoiding the draft, though President Johnson had announced he was going to do away with all that. She herself would never have made it this far without scholarships; her parents could not have afforded it.

40   So he was here on scholarship, studying something practical, no doubt, nuclear physics or the construction of dams, and, like herself and the other foreigners, he was expected to go away again as soon as he'd learned what he'd come for. But he never went out of the house; he stood at the front door and watched the brutish flow of cars, the winter rain, while those back in his own country, the ones that had sent him, were confidently expecting him to return some day, crammed with knowledge, ready to solve their lives. . . . *He's lost his nerve,* Ann thought. *He'll fail.* It was too late in the year for him ever to catch up. Such failures, such paralyses, were fairly common here, especially among the foreigners. He was far from home, from the language he shared, the wearers of his native costume; he was in exile, he was drowning. What did he do, alone by himself in his room at night?

Ann switched her hair dryer to COOL and wrenched her mind back to aqueducts. She could see he was drowning but there was nothing she could do. Unless you were good at it you shouldn't even try, she was wise enough to know that. All you could do for the drowning was to make sure you were not one of them.

The aqueduct, now. It would be made of natural brick, an earthy red; it would have low arches, in the shade of which there would be ferns and, perhaps, some delphiniums, in varying tones of blue. She must learn more about plants. Before entering the shopping complex (trust him to assign a shopping complex; before that he had demanded a public housing project), it would flow through her green space, in which, she could now see, there were people walking. Children? *But not children like Mrs. Nolan's.* They would turn her grass to mud, they'd nail things to her trees, their mangy dogs would shit on her ferns, they'd throw bottles and pop cans into her aqueduct. . . . And Mrs. Nolan herself, and her Noah's Ark of seedy, brilliant foreigners, where would she put them? For the houses of the Mrs. Nolans of this world would have to go; that was one of the axioms of Urban Design. She could convert them to small offices, or single-floor apartments; some shrubs and hanging plants and a new coat of paint would do wonders. But she knew this was temporizing. Around her green space, she could see, there was now a high wire fence. Inside it were trees, flowers and grass, outside the dirty snow, the endless rain, the grunting cars and the half-frozen mud of Mrs. Nolan's drab backyard. That was what *exclusive* meant, it meant that some people were excluded. Her parents stood in the rain outside the fence, watching with dreary pride while she strolled about in the eternal sunlight. Their one success.

Stop it, she commanded herself. *They want me to be doing this.* She unwound her hair and brushed it out. Three hours from now, she knew, it would be limp as ever because of the damp.

The next day, she tried to raise her new theoretical problem with her friend Jetske. Jetske was in Urban Design, too. She was from Holland, and could remember running through the devastated streets as a child, begging small change, first from the Germans, later from the American soldiers, who were always good for a chocolate bar or two.

"You learn how to take care of yourself," she'd said. "It didn't seem hard at the   45
time, but when you are a child, nothing is that hard. We were all the same, nobody
had anything." Because of this background, which was more exotic and cruel than
anything Ann herself had experienced (what was a gas pump compared to the
Nazis?), Ann respected her opinions. She liked her also because she was the only
person she'd met here who seemed to know where Canada was. There were a lot of
Canadian soldiers buried in Holland. This provided Ann with at least a shadowy
identity, which she felt she needed. She didn't have a native costume, but at least she
had some heroic dead bodies with which she was connected, however remotely.

"The trouble with what we're doing . . . ," she said to Jetske, as they walked towards the library under Ann's umbrella. "I mean, you can rebuild one part, but what
do you do about the rest?"

"Of the city?" Jetske said.

"No," Ann said slowly. "I guess I mean of the world."

Jetske laughed. She had what Ann now thought of as Dutch teeth, even and
white, with quite a lot of gum showing above them and below the lip. "I didn't know
you were a socialist," she said. Her cheeks were pink and healthy, like a cheese ad.

"I'm not," Ann said. "But I thought we were supposed to be thinking in total   50
patterns."

Jetske laughed again. "Did you know," she said, "that in some countries you
have to get official permission to move from one town to another?"

Ann didn't like this idea at all. "It controls the population flow," Jetske said.
"You can't really have Urban Design without that, you know."

"I think that's awful," Ann said.

"Of course you do," Jetske said, as close to bitterness as she ever got. "You've
never had to do it. Over here you are soft in the belly, you think you can always have
everything. You think there is freedom of choice. The whole world will come to it.
You will see." She began teasing Ann again about her plastic headscarf. Jetske never
wore anything on her head.

Ann designed her shopping complex, putting in a skylight and banks of indoor   55
plants, leaving out the aqueduct. She got an A.

In the third week of March, Ann went with Jetske and some of the others to a
Buckminster Fuller lecture. Afterwards they all went to the pub on the corner of the
Square for a couple of beers. Ann left with Jetske about eleven o'clock and walked
a couple of blocks with her before Jetske turned off towards her lovely old house
with the stained glass. Ann continued by herself, warily, keeping to the lighted
streets. She carried her purse under her elbow and held her furled umbrella at the
ready. For once it wasn't raining.

When she got back to the house and started to climb the stairs, it struck her that
something was different. Upstairs, she knew. Absolutely, something was out of line.
There was curious music coming from the room next door, a high flute rising over
drums, thumping noises, the sound of voices. The man next door was throwing a
party, it seemed. *Good for him,* Ann thought. He might as well do something. She
settled down for an hour's reading.

But the noises were getting louder. From the bathroom came the sound of retch-
ing. There was going to be trouble. Ann checked her door to make sure it was locked,

got out the bottle of sherry she kept in the cupboard next to the oven, and poured herself a drink. Then she turned out the light and sat with her back against the door,
drinking her sherry in the faint blue light from the funeral home next door. There was
no point in going to bed: even with her earplugs in, she could never sleep.

The music and thumpings got louder. After a while there was a banging on the
floor, then some shouting, which came quite clearly through Ann's hot-air register.
"I'm calling the police! You hear? I'm calling the police! You get them out of here
and get out yourself!" The music switched off, the door opened, and there was a clattering down the stairs. Then more footsteps—Ann couldn't tell whether they were
going up or down—and more shouting. The front door banged and the shouts continued on down the street. Ann undressed and put on her nightgown, still without
turning on the light, and crept into the bathroom. The bathtub was full of vomit.

60   This time Mrs. Nolan didn't even wait for Ann to get back from classes. She
waylaid her in the morning as she was coming out of her room. Mrs. Nolan was
holding a can of Drano and had dark circles under her eyes. Somehow this made her
look younger. *She's probably not much older than I am,* Ann thought. Until now she
had considered her middle-aged.

"I guess you saw the mess in there," she whispered.

"Yes, I did," Ann said.

"I guess you heard all that last night." She paused.

"What happened?" Ann asked. In fact she really wanted to know.

65   "He had some dancing girls in there! Three dancing girls, and two other men, in
that little room! I thought the ceiling was gonna come right down on our heads!"

"I did hear something like dancing," Ann said.

"Dancing! They was jumping, it sounded like they jumped right off the bed onto
the floor. The plaster was coming off. Fred wasn't home, he's not home yet. I was
afraid for the kids. Like, with those tattoos, who knows what they was working
themselves up to?" Her sibilant voice hinted of ritual murders, young Jimmy and
runny-nosed Donny sacrificed to some obscure god.

"What did you do?" Ann asked.

"I called the police. Well, the dancing girls, as soon as they heard I was calling
the police, they got out of here, I can tell you. Put on their coats and was down the
stairs and out the door like nothing. You can bet they didn't want no trouble with the
police. But not the others, they don't seem to know what police means."

70   She paused again, and Ann asked, "Did they come?"

"Who?"

"The police."

"Well, you know around here it always takes the police a while to get there, unless there's some right outside. I know that, it's not the first time I've had to call
them. So who knows what they would've done in the meantime? I could hear them
coming downstairs, like, so I just grabs the broom and I chased them out. I chased
them all the way down the street."

Ann saw that she thought she had done something very brave, which meant that
in fact she had. She really believed that the man next door and his friends were

dangerous, that they were a threat to her children. She had chased them single-handedly, yelling with fear and defiance. But he had only been throwing a party.

"Heavens," she said weakly.   75

"You can say that again," said Mrs. Nolan. "I went in there this morning, to get his things and put them out front where he could get them without me having to see him. I don't have such good nerves, I didn't sleep at all, even after they was gone. Fred is just gonna have to stop driving nights, I can't take it. But you know? He didn't have no things in there. Not one. Just an old empty suitcase?"

"What about his native costume?" Ann said.

"He had it on," Mrs. Nolan said. "He just went running down the street in it, like some kind of a loony. And you know what else I found in there? In one corner, there was this pile of empty bottles. Liquor. He must've been drinking like a fish for months, and never threw out the bottles. And in another corner, there was this pile of burnt matches. He could've burnt the house down, throwing them on the floor like that. But the worst thing was, you know all the times he borrowed my vacuum cleaner?"

"Yes," Ann said.

"Well, he never threw away the dirt. There it all was, in the other corner of the   80
room. He must've just emptied it out and left it there. I don't get it." Mrs. Nolan, by now, was puzzled rather than angry.

"Well," Ann said. "That certainly is strange."

"Strange?" Mrs. Nolan said. "I'll tell you it's strange. He always paid the rent though, right on time. Never a day late. Why would he put the dirt in a corner like that, when he could've put it out in a bag like everyone else? It's not like he didn't know. I told him real clear which were the garbage days, when he moved in."

Ann said she was going to be late for class if she didn't hurry. At the front door she tucked her hair under her plastic scarf. Today it was just a drizzle, not heavy enough for the umbrella. She started off, walking quickly along beside the double line of traffic.

She wondered where he had gone, chased down the street by Mrs. Nolan in her scuffies and flowered housecoat, shouting and flailing at him with a broom. She must have been at least as terrifying a spectacle to him as he was to her, and just as inexplicable. Why would this woman, this fat crazy woman, wish to burst in upon a scene of harmless hospitality, banging and raving? He and his friends could easily have overpowered her, but they would not even have thought about doing that. They would have been too frightened. What unspoken taboo had they violated? What would these cold, mad people do next?

Anyway, he did have some friends. They would take care of him, at least for the   85
time being. Which was a relief, she guessed. But what she really felt was a childish regret that she had not seen the dancing girls. If she had known they were there, she might even have risked opening her door. She knew they were not real dancing girls, they were probably just some whores from Scollay Square. Mrs. Nolan had called them that as a euphemism, or perhaps because of an unconscious association with the word *Arabian,* the vaguely Arabian country. She never had found out what it was. Nevertheless, she wished she had seen them. Jetske would find all of this quite

amusing, especially the image of her backed against the door, drinking sherry in the dark. It would have been better if she'd had the courage to look.

She began to think about her green space, as she often did during this walk. The green, perfect space of the future. She knew by now that it was cancelled in advance, that it would never come into being, that it was already too late. Once she was qualified, she would return to plan tasteful mixes of residential units and shopping complexes, with a lot of underground malls and arcades to protect people from the snow. But she could allow herself to see it one last time.

The fence was gone now, and the green stretched out endlessly, fields and trees and flowing water, as far as she could see. In the distance, beneath the arches of the aqueduct, a herd of animals, deer or something, was grazing. (She must learn more about animals.) Groups of people were walking happily among the trees, holding hands, not just in twos but in threes, fours, fives. The man from next door was there, in his native costume, and the mathematicians, they were all in their native costumes. Beside the stream a man was playing the flute; and around him, in long flowered robes and mauve scuffies, their auburn hair floating around their healthy pink faces, smiling their Dutch smiles, the dancing girls were sedately dancing.

QUESTIONS FOR DISCUSSION AND WRITING

1. In what ways does Atwood fill the story with apparent foreshadowing of violence that never occurs? How does the wild party serve as a climax of the conflicts in the story? In what ways does Ann's final vision of multicultural harmony resolve those conflicts?

2. How does Mrs. Nolan characterize her "foreign" tenants? Why does Ann object, silently, to Mrs. Nolan's characterization of her as "not, like, foreign"? In what ways does Ann distinguish herself from Lelah and Jetske?

3. How do Ann's imagined worlds contrast with the real world in which she finds herself? What is significant about the way she "rearranges Toronto"? Why does she have trouble "visualizing people" or figuring out what to do with "the rest of the world"?

4. How is the point of view in this story used to keep us at some emotional distance from the protagonist? How do Ann's statements about "loneliness" reveal her difficulty in interpreting her own story?

5. How does Ann's conversation with Jetske connect with Mrs. Nolan's reaction to the party? How does the repeated emphasis throughout the story on "native costumes" contrast with Ann's characterization of "the dancing girls . . . *sedately* dancing" in the last sentence of the story?

Stories for Comparison

Alice Munro's "Wild Swans" (pages 927–935); Edith Wharton's "Roman Fever" (pages 1187–1197).

18

JAMES BALDWIN

Sonny's Blues

JAMES BALDWIN (1924–1987) was born in New York City's Harlem and attended DeWitt Clinton High School. After working at a number of odd jobs, he moved in 1948 to Paris, where he felt the social and artistic environment gave him the freedom to pursue his career as a writer. He remained in self-exile for ten years, writing about his personal struggle to establish his identity as a black American man in novels such as *Go Tell It on the Mountain* (1953) and essays such as those collected in *Notes of a Native Son* (1955). In 1957, Baldwin returned to the United States and became actively involved in the civil rights movement. His essays during this period, *Nobody Knows My Name* (1961), *More Notes of a Native Son* (1961), and *The Fire Next Time* (1963), propelled Baldwin into the public spotlight as one of the most forceful and perceptive essayists of our time. His fiction includes the novels *Tell Me How Long the Train's Been Gone* (1968) and *If Beale Street Could Talk* (1974), and the short-story collections *Blues for Mister Charlie* (1964) and *The Amen Corner* (1965). His later publications include *The Devil Finds Work* (1976), *Just Above My Head* (1979), and a collection of poems, *Jimmy Blues* (1985). In "Sonny's Blues," excerpted from *Going to Meet the Man* (1957), an older brother begins to understand his own troubles as he watches his younger brother live and then play "the blues."

I read about it in the paper, in the subway, on my way to work. I read it, and I couldn't believe it, and I read it again. Then perhaps I just stared at it, at the newsprint spelling out his name, spelling out the story. I stared at it in the swinging lights of the subway car, and in the faces and bodies of the people, and in my own face, trapped in the darkness which roared outside.

It was not to be believed and I kept telling myself that, as I walked from the subway station to the high school. And at the same time I couldn't doubt it. I was scared, scared for Sonny. He became real to me again. A great block of ice got settled in my belly and kept melting there slowly all day long, while I taught my classes algebra. It was a special kind of ice. It kept melting, sending trickles of ice water all up and down my veins, but it never got less. Sometimes it hardened and seemed to expand until I felt my guts were going to come spilling out or that I was going to choke or scream. This would always be at a moment when I was remembering some specific thing Sonny had once said or done.

When he was about as old as the boys in my class his face had been bright and open, there was a lot of copper in it; and he'd had wonderfully direct brown eyes, and great gentleness and privacy. I wondered what he looked like now. He had been picked up, the evening before, in a raid on an apartment downtown, for peddling and using heroin.

I couldn't believe it: but what I mean by that is that I couldn't find any room for it anywhere inside me. I had kept it outside me for a long time. I hadn't wanted to know. I had had suspicions, but I didn't name them, I kept putting them away. I told myself that Sonny was wild, but he wasn't crazy. And he'd always been a good boy, he hadn't ever turned hard or evil or disrespectful, the way kids can, so quick, so quick, especially in Harlem. I didn't want to believe that I'd ever see my brother going down, coming to nothing, all that light in his face gone out, in the condition I'd already seen so many others. Yet it had happened and here I was, talking about algebra to a lot of boys who might, every one of them for all I knew, be popping off needles every time they went to the head. Maybe it did more for them than algebra could.

5   I was sure that the first time Sonny had ever had horse, he couldn't have been much older than these boys were now. These boys, now, were living as we'd been living then, they were growing up with a rush and their heads bumped abruptly against the low ceiling of their actual possibilities. They were filled with rage. All they really knew were two darknesses, the darkness of their lives, which was now closing in on them, and the darkness of the movies, which had blinded them to that other darkness, and in which they now, vindictively, dreamed, at once more together than they were at any other time, and more alone.

When the last bell rang, the last class ended, I let out my breath. It seemed I'd been holding it for all that time. My clothes were wet—I may have looked as though I'd been sitting in a steam bath, all dressed up, all afternoon. I sat alone in the classroom a long time. I listened to the boys outside, downstairs, shouting and cursing and laughing. Their laughter struck me for perhaps the first time. It was not the joyous laughter which—God knows why—one associates with children. It was mocking and insular, its intent was to denigrate. It was disenchanted, and in this, also, lay the authority of their curses. Perhaps I was listening to them because I was thinking about my brother and in them I heard my brother. And myself.

One boy was whistling a tune, at once very complicated and very simple, it seemed to be pouring out of him as though he were a bird, and it sounded very cool and moving through all that harsh, bright air, only just holding its own through all those other sounds.

I stood up and walked over to the window and looked down into the courtyard. It was the beginning of the spring and the sap was rising in the boys. A teacher passed through them every now and again, quickly, as though he or she couldn't wait to get out of that courtyard, to get those boys out of their sight and off their minds. I started collecting my stuff. I thought I'd better get home and talk to Isabel.

The courtyard was almost deserted by the time I got downstairs. I saw this boy standing in the shadow of a doorway, looking just like Sonny. I almost called his name. Then I saw that it wasn't Sonny, but somebody we used to know, a boy from around our block. He's been Sonny's friend. He's never been mine, having been too young for me, and, anyway, I'd never liked him. And now, even though he was a grown-up man, he still hung around that block, still spent hours on the street corners, was always high and raggy. I used to run into him from time to time and he'd often work around to asking me for a quarter or fifty cents. He always had some real good excuse, too, and I always gave it to him, I don't know why.   10

But now, abruptly, I hated him. I couldn't stand the way he looked at me, partly like a dog, partly like a cunning child. I wanted to ask him what the hell he was doing in the school courtyard.

He sort of shuffled over to me, and he said, "I see you got the papers. So you already know about it."

"You mean about Sonny? Yes, I already know about it. How come they didn't get you?"

He grinned. It made him repulsive and it also brought to mind what he'd looked like as a kid. "I wasn't there. I stay away from them people."

"Good for you." I offered him a cigarette and I watched him through the smoke. "You come all the way down here just to tell me about Sonny?"

"That's right." He was sort of shaking his head and his eyes looked strange, as   15
though they were about to cross. The bright sun deadened his damp dark brown skin and it made his eyes look yellow and showed up the dirt in his kinked hair. He smelled funky. I moved a little away from him and I said, "Well, thanks. But I already know about it and I got to get home."

"I'll walk you a little ways," he said. We started walking. There were a couple of kids still loitering in the courtyard and one of them said goodnight to me and looked strangely at the boy beside me.

"What're you going to do?" he asked me. "I mean, about Sonny?"

"Look. I haven't seen Sonny for over a year, I'm not sure I'm going to do anything. Anyway, what the hell *can* I do?"

"That's right," he said quickly, "ain't nothing you can do. Can't much help old Sonny no more, I guess."

It was what I was thinking and so it seemed to me he had no right to say it.   20

"I'm surprised at Sonny, though," he went on—he had a funny way of talking, he looked straight ahead as though he were talking to himself—"I thought Sonny was a smart boy, I thought he was too smart to get hung."

"I guess he thought so too," I said sharply, "and that's how he got hung. And how about you? You're pretty goddamn smart, I bet."

Then he looked directly at me, just for a minute. "I ain't smart," he said. "If I was smart, I'd have reached for a pistol a long time ago."

"Look. Don't tell *me* your sad story, if it was up to me, I'd give you one." Then I felt guilty—guilty, probably, for never having supposed that the poor bastard *had* a story of his own, much less a sad one, and I asked, quickly, "What's going to happen to him now?"

He didn't answer this. He was off by himself some place. "Funny thing," he   25
said, and from his tone we might have been discussing the quickest way to get to

Brooklyn, "when I saw the papers this morning, the first thing I asked myself was if I had anything to do with it. I felt sort of responsible."

I began to listen more carefully. The subway station was on the corner, just before us, and I stopped. He stopped, too. We were in front of a bar and he ducked slightly, peering in, but whoever he was looking for didn't seem to be there. The juke box was blasting away with something black and bouncy and I half watched the barmaid as she danced her way from the juke box to her place behind the bar. And I watched her face as she laughingly responded to something someone said to her, still keeping time to the music. When she smiled one saw the little girl, one sensed the doomed, still-struggling woman beneath the battered face of the semi-whore.

"I never *give* Sonny nothing," the boy said finally, "but a long time ago I come to school high and Sonny asked me how it felt." He paused, I couldn't bear to watch him, I watched the barmaid, and I listened to the music which seemed to be causing the pavement to shake. "I told him it felt great." The music stopped, the barmaid paused and watched the juke box until the music began again. "It did."

All this way carrying me some place I didn't want to go. I certainly didn't want to know how it felt. It filled everything, the people, the houses, the music, the dark, quicksilver barmaid, with menace; and this menace was their reality.

"What's going to happen to him now?" I asked again.

30   "They'll send him away some place and they'll try to cure him." He shook his head. "Maybe he'll even think he's kicked the habit. Then they'll let him loose"— he gestured, throwing his cigarette into the gutter. "That's all."

"What do you mean, that's *all?*"

But I knew what he meant.

"I *mean,* that's *all.*" He turned his head and looked at me, pulling down the corners of his mouth. "Don't you know what I mean?" he asked, softly.

"How the hell *would* I know what you mean?" I almost whispered it, I don't know why.

35   "That's right," he said to the air, "how would *he* know what I mean?" He turned toward me again, patient and calm, and yet I somehow felt him shaking, shaking as though he were going to fall apart. I felt that ice in my guts again, the dread I'd felt all afternoon; and again I watched the barmaid, moving about the bar, washing glasses, and singing. "Listen. They'll let him out and then it'll just start all over again. That's what I mean."

"You mean—they'll let him out. And then he'll just start working his way back in again. You mean he'll never kick the habit. Is that what you mean?"

"That's right," he said, cheerfully. "*You* see what I mean."

"Tell me," I said at last, "why does he want to die? He must want to die, he's killing himself, why does he want to die?"

He looked at me in surprise. He licked his lips. "He don't want to die. He wants to live. Don't nobody want to die, ever."

40   Then I wanted to ask him—too many things. He could not have answered, or if he had, I could not have borne the answers. I started walking. "Well, I guess it's none of my business."

"It's going to be rough on old Sonny," he said. We reached the subway station. "This is your station?" he asked. I nodded. I took one step down. "Damn!" he said, suddenly. I looked up at him. He grinned again. "Damn it if I didn't leave all my money home. You ain't got a dollar on you, have you? Just for a couple of days, is all."

All at once something inside gave and threatened to come pouring out of me. I didn't hate him any more. I felt that in another moment I'd start crying like a child.

"Sure," I said. "Don't swear." I looked in my wallet and didn't have a dollar, I only had a five. "Here," I said. "That hold you?"

He didn't look at it—he didn't want to look at it. A terrible, closed look came over his face, as though he were keeping the number on the bill a secret from him and me. "Thanks," he said, and now he was dying to see me go. "Don't worry about Sonny. Maybe I'll write him or something."

"Sure," I said. "You do that. So long."   45

"Be seeing you," he said. I went down the steps.

And I didn't write Sonny or send him anything for a long time. When I finally did, it was just after my little girl died, he wrote me back a letter which made me feel like a bastard.

Here's what he said:

Dear Brother,

You don't know how much I needed to hear from you. I wanted to write you many a time but I dug how much I must have hurt you and so I didn't write. But now I feel like a man who's been trying to climb up out of some deep, real deep and funky hole and just saw the sun up there, outside. I got to get outside.

I can't tell you much about how I got here. I mean I don't know how to tell you. I guess I was afraid of something or I was trying to escape from something and you know I have never been very strong in the head (smile). I'm glad Mama and Daddy are dead and can't see what's happened to their son and I swear if I'd known what I was doing I would never have hurt you so, you and a lot of other fine people who were nice to me and who believed in me.

I don't want you to think it had anything to do with me being a musician. It's more than that. Or maybe less than that. I can't get anything straight in my head down here and I try not to think about what's going to happen to me when I get outside again. Sometime I think I'm going to flip and *never* get outside and sometime I think I'll come straight back. I tell you one thing, though, I'd rather blow my brains out than go through this again. But that's what they all say, so they tell me. If I tell you when I'm coming to New York and if you could meet me, I sure would appreciate it. Give my love to Isabel and the kids and I was sure sorry to hear about little Gracie. I wish I could be like Mama and say the Lord's will be done, but I don't know it seems to me that trouble is the one thing that never does get stopped and I don't know what good it does to blame it on the Lord. But maybe it does some good if you believe it.

Your brother,
Sonny

Then I kept in constant touch with him and I sent him whatever I could and I went to meet him when he came back to New York. When I saw him many things I thought I had forgotten came flooding back to me. This was because I had begun, finally, to wonder about Sonny, about the life that Sonny lived inside. This life, whatever it was, had made him older and thinner and it had deepened the distant stillness in which he had always moved. He looked very unlike my baby brother. Yet, when he smiled, when we shook hands, the baby brother I'd never known looked out from the depths of his private life, like an animal waiting to be coaxed into the light.

50   "How you been keeping?" he asked me.

"All right. And you?"

"Just fine." He was smiling all over his face. "It's good to see you again."

"It's good to see you."

The seven years' difference in our ages lay between us like a chasm: I wondered if these years would ever operate between us as a bridge. I was remembering, and it made it hard to catch my breath, that I had been there when he was born; and I had heard the first words he had ever spoken. When he started to walk, he walked from our mother straight to me. I caught him just before he fell when he took the first steps he ever took in this world.

55   "How's Isabel?"

"Just fine. She's dying to see you."

"And the boys?"

"They're fine, too. They're anxious to see their uncle."

"Oh, come on. You know they don't remember me."

60   "Are you kidding? Of course they remember you."

He grinned again. We got into a taxi. We had a lot to say to each other, far too much to know how to begin.

As the taxi began to move, I asked, "You still want to go to India?"

He laughed. "You still remember that. Hell, no. This place is Indian enough for me."

"It used to belong to them," I said.

65   And he laughed again. "They damn sure knew what they were doing when they got rid of it."

Years ago, when he was around fourteen, he'd been all hipped on the idea of going to India. He read books about people sitting on rocks, naked, in all kinds of weather, but mostly bad, naturally, and walking barefoot through hot coals and arriving at wisdom. I used to say that it sounded to me as though they were getting away from wisdom as fast as they could. I think he sort of looked down on me for that.

"Do you mind," he asked, "if we have the driver drive alongside the park? On the west side—I haven't seen the city in so long."

"Of course not," I said. I was afraid that I might sound as though I were humoring him, but I hoped he wouldn't take it that way.

So we drove along, between the green of the park and the stony, lifeless elegance of hotels and apartment buildings, toward the vivid, killing streets of our childhood. These streets hadn't changed, though housing projects jutted up out of them now like rocks in the middle of a boiling sea. Most of the houses in which we had grown up had vanished, as had the stores from which we had stolen, the basements in which we had first tried sex, the rooftops from which we hurled tin cans and bricks. But houses exactly like the houses of our past yet dominated the landscape, boys exactly like the boys we once had been found themselves smothering in these houses, came down into the streets for light and air and found themselves encircled by disaster. Some escaped the trap, most didn't. Those who got out always left something of themselves behind, as some animals amputate a leg and leave it in the trap. It might be said, perhaps, that I had escaped, after all, I was a school teacher; or that Sonny had, he hadn't lived in Harlem for years. Yet, as the cab moved uptown through streets which seemed, with a rush, to darken with dark people, and as I covertly studied Sonny's face, it came to me that what we both were seeking through our separate cab windows was that part of ourselves which had been left behind. It's always at the hour of trouble and confrontation that the missing member aches.

We hit 110th Street and started rolling up Lenox Avenue. And I'd known this av- 70 enue all my life, but it seemed to me again, as it had seemed on the day I'd first heard about Sonny's trouble, filled with a hidden menace which was its very breath of life.

"We almost there," said Sonny.

"Almost." We were both too nervous to say anything more.

We lived in a housing project. It hasn't been up long. A few days after it was up it seemed uninhabitably new, now, of course, it's already rundown. It looks like a parody of the good, clean, faceless life—God knows the people who live in it do their best to make it a parody. The beat-looking grass lying around isn't enough to make their lives green, the hedges will never hold out the streets, and they know it. The big windows fool no one, they aren't big enough to make space out of no space. They don't bother with the windows, they watch the TV screen instead. The playground is most popular with the children who don't play at jacks, or skip rope, or roller skate, or swing, and they can be found in it after dark. We moved in partly because it's not too far from where I teach, and partly for the kids; but it's really just like the houses in which Sonny and I grew up. The same things happen, they'll have the same things to remember. The moment Sonny and I started into the house I had the feeling that I was simply bringing him back into the danger he had almost died trying to escape.

Sonny has never been talkative. So I don't know why I was sure he'd be dying to talk to me when supper was over the first night. Everything went fine, the oldest boy remembered him, and the youngest boy liked him, and Sonny had remembered to bring something for each of them; and Isabel, who is really much nicer than I am, more open and giving, had gone to a lot of trouble about dinner and was genuinely glad to see him. And she's always been able to tease Sonny in a way that I haven't. It was nice to see her face so vivid again and to hear her laugh and watch her make Sonny laugh. She wasn't, or, anyway, she didn't seem to be, at all uneasy or embarrassed. She chatted as though there were no subject which had to be avoided and she got Sonny past his first, faint stiffness. And thank God she was there, for I was filled with that icy dread again. Everything I did seemed awkward to me, and everything I said sounded freighted with hidden meaning. I was trying to remember everything

I'd heard about dope addiction and I couldn't help watching Sonny for signs. I wasn't doing it out of malice. I was trying to find out something about my brother. I was dying to hear him tell me he was safe.

75   "Safe!" my father grunted, whenever Mama suggested trying to move to a neighborhood which might be safer for children. "Safe, hell! Ain't no place safe for kids, nor nobody."

He always went on like this, but he wasn't, ever, really as bad as he sounded, not even on weekends, when he got drunk. As a matter of fact, he was always on the lookout for "something a little better," but he died before he found it. He died suddenly, during a drunken weekend in the middle of the war, when Sonny was fifteen. He and Sonny hadn't ever got on too well. And this was partly because Sonny was the apple of his father's eye. It was because he loved Sonny so much and was frightened for him, that he was always fighting with him. It doesn't do any good to fight with Sonny. Sonny just moves back, inside himself, where he can't be reached. But the principal reason that they never hit it off is that they were so much alike. Daddy was big and rough and loud-talking, just the opposite of Sonny, but they both had— that same privacy.

Mama tried to tell me something about this, just after Daddy died. I was home on leave from the army.

This was the last time I ever saw my mother alive. Just the same, this picture gets all mixed up in my mind with pictures I had of her when she was younger. The way I always see her is the way she used to be on a Sunday afternoon, say, when the old folks were talking after the big Sunday dinner. I always see her wearing pale blue. She'd be sitting on the sofa. And my father would be sitting in the easy chair, not far from her. And the living room would be full of church folks and relatives. There they sit, in chairs all around the living room, and the night is creeping up outside, but nobody knows it yet. You can see the darkness growing against the windowpanes and you hear the street noises every now and again, or maybe the jangling beat of a tambourine from one of the churches close by, but it's real quiet in the room. For a moment nobody's talking, but every face looks darkening, like the sky outside. And my mother rocks a little from the waist, and my father's eyes are closed. Everyone is looking at something a child can't see. For a minute they've forgotten the children. Maybe a kid is lying on the rug, half asleep. Maybe somebody's got a kid in his lap and is absent-mindedly stroking the kid's head. Maybe there's a kid, quiet and big-eyed, curled up in a big chair in the corner. The silence, the darkness coming, and the darkness in the faces frightens the child obscurely. He hopes that the hand which strokes his forehead will never stop—will never die. He hopes that there will never come a time when the old folks won't be sitting around the living room, talking about where they've come from, and what they've seen, and what's happened to them and their kinfolk.

But something deep and watchful in the child knows that this is bound to end, is already ending. In a moment someone will get up and turn on the light. Then the old folks will remember the children and they won't talk any more that day. And when light fills the room, the child is filled with darkness. He knows that every time this happens he's moved just a little closer to that darkness outside. The darkness outside is what the old folks have been talking about. It's what they've come from. It's what they endure. The child knows that they won't talk any more because if he knows too much about what's happened to *them,* he'll know too much too soon, about what's going to happen to *him.*

The last time I talked to my mother, I remember I was restless. I wanted to get 80 out and see Isabel. We weren't married then and we had a lot to straighten out between us.

There Mama sat, in black, by the window. She was humming an old church song, *Lord, you brought me from a long ways off.* Sonny was out somewhere. Mama kept watching the streets.

"I don't know," she said, "if I'll ever see you again, after you go off from here. But I hope you'll remember the things I tried to teach you."

"Don't talk like that," I said, and smiled. "You'll be here a long time yet."

She smiled, too, but she said nothing. She was quiet for a long time. And I said, "Mama, don't you worry about nothing. I'll be writing all the time, and you be getting the checks . . ."

"I want to talk to you about your brother," she said, suddenly. "If anything hap- 85 pens to me he ain't going to have nobody to look out for him."

"Mama," I said, "ain't nothing going to happen to you *or* Sonny. Sonny's all right. He's a good boy and he's got good sense."

"It ain't a question of his being a good boy," Mama said, "nor of his having good sense. It ain't only the bad ones, nor yet the dumb ones that gets sucked under." She stopped, looking at me. "Your Daddy once had a brother," she said, and she smiled in a way that made me feel she was in pain. "You didn't never know that, did you?"

"No," I said, "I never knew that," and I watched her face.

"Oh, yes," she said, "your Daddy had a brother." She looked out of the window again. "I know you never saw your Daddy cry. But *I* did—many a time, through all these years."

I asked her, "What happened to his brother? How come nobody's ever talked 90 about him?"

This was the first time I ever saw my mother look old.

"His brother got killed," she said, "when he was just a little younger than you are now. I knew him. He was a fine boy. He was maybe a little full of the devil, but he didn't mean nobody no harm."

Then she stopped and the room was silent, exactly as it had sometimes been on those Sunday afternoons. Mama kept looking out into the streets.

"He used to have a job in the mill," she said, "and, like all young folks, he just liked to perform on Saturday nights. Saturday nights, him and your father would drift around to different places, go to dances and things like that, or just sit around with people they knew, and your father's brother would sing, he had a fine voice, and play along with himself on his guitar. Well, this particular Saturday night, him and your father was coming home from some place, and they were both a little drunk and there was a moon that night, it was bright like day. Your father's brother was feeling kind of good, and he was whistling to himself, and he had his guitar slung over his shoulder. They was coming down a hill and beneath them was a road that turned off from the highway. Well, your father's brother, being always kind of frisky, decided to run down this hill, and he did, with that guitar banging and clanging behind him, and he ran across the road, and he was making water behind a tree. And your father was sort of amused at him and he was still coming down the hill, kind of slow. Then he heard a car motor and that same minute his brother stepped from behind the tree, into the road, in the moonlight. And he started to cross the road. And your father started to run down the hill, he says he don't know why. This car was full of white men. They was all drunk, and when they seen your father's brother they let out a great whoop and holler and they aimed the car straight at him. They was having fun, they just wanted to scare him, the way they do sometimes, you know. But they was drunk. And I guess the boy, being drunk, too, and scared, kind of lost his head. By the time he jumped it was too late. Your father says he heard his brother scream when the car rolled over him, and he heard the wood of that guitar when it give, and he heard them strings go flying, and he heard them white men shouting, and the car kept on a-going and it ain't stopped till this day. And, time your father got down the hill, his brother weren't nothing but blood and pulp."

95 Tears were gleaming on my mother's face. There wasn't anything I could say.

"He never mentioned it," she said, "because I never let him mention it before you children. Your Daddy was like a crazy man that night and for many a night thereafter. He says he never in his life seen anything as dark as that road after the lights of that car had gone away. Weren't nothing; weren't nobody on that road, just your Daddy and his brother and that busted guitar. Oh, yes. Your Daddy never did really get right again. Till the day he died he weren't sure but that every white man he saw was the man that killed his brother."

She stopped and took out her handkerchief and dried her eyes and looked at me.

"I ain't telling you all this," she said, "to make you scared or bitter or to make you hate nobody. I'm telling you this because you got a brother. And the world ain't changed."

I guess I didn't want to believe this. I guess she saw this in my face. She turned away from me, toward the window again, searching those streets.

100 "But I praise my Redeemer," she said at last, "that He called your Daddy home before me. I ain't saying it to throw no flowers at myself, but, I declare, it keeps me from feeling too cast down to know I helped your father get safely through this world. Your father always acted like he was the roughest, strongest man on earth. And everybody took him to be like that. But if he hadn't had *me* there—to see his tears!"

She was crying again. Still, I couldn't move. I said, "Lord, Lord, Mama, I didn't know it was like that."

"Oh, honey," she said, "There's a lot that you don't know. But you are going to find out." She stood up from the window and came over to me. "You got to hold on to your brother," she said, "and don't let him fall, no matter what it looks like is happening to him and no matter how evil you gets with him. You going to be evil with him many a time. But don't you forget what I told you, you hear?"

"I won't forget," I said. "Don't you worry, I won't forget. I won't let nothing happen to Sonny."

My mother smiled as though she were amused at something she saw in my face. Then, "You may not be able to stop nothing from happening. But you got to let him know you's *there*."

Two days later I was married, and then I was gone. And I had a lot of things on my mind and I pretty well forgot my promise to Mama until I got shipped home on a special furlough for her funeral.

And, after the funeral, with just Sonny and me alone in the empty kitchen, I tried to find out something about him.

"What do you want to do?" I asked him.

"I'm going to be a musician," he said.

For he had graduated, in the time I had been away, from dancing to the juke box to finding out who was playing what, and what they were doing with it, and he had bought himself a set of drums.

"You mean, you want to be a drummer?" I somehow had the feeling that being a drummer might be all right for other people but not for my brother Sonny.

"I don't know," he said, looking at me very gravely, "that I'll ever be a good drummer. But I think I can play a piano."

I frowned. I'd never played the role of the older brother quite so seriously before, had scarcely ever, in fact, *asked* Sonny a damn thing. I sensed myself in the presence of something I didn't really know how to handle, didn't understand. So I made my frown a little deeper as I asked: "What kind of musician do you want to be?"

He grinned. "How many kinds do you think there are?"

"Be *serious*," I said.

He laughed, throwing his head back, and then looked at me. "I *am* serious."

"Well, then, for Christ's sake, stop kidding around and answer a serious question. I mean, do you want to be a concert pianist, you want to play classical music and all that, or—or what?" Long before I finished he was laughing again. "For Christ's *sake,* Sonny!"

He sobered, but with difficulty. "I'm sorry. But you sound so—*scared!*" and he was off again.

"Well, you may think it's funny now, baby, but it's not going to be so funny when you have to make your living at it, let me tell you *that*." I was furious because I knew he was laughing at me and I didn't know why.

"No," he said, very sober now, and afraid, perhaps, that he'd hurt me, "I don't want to be a classical pianist. That isn't what interests me. I mean"—he paused, looking hard at me, as though his eyes would help me to understand, and then gestured helplessly, as though perhaps his hand would help—"I mean, I'll have a lot of studying to do, and I'll have to study *everything,* but, I mean, I want to play *with*—jazz musicians." He stopped. "I want to play jazz," he said.

Well, the word had never before sounded as heavy, as real, as it sounded that afternoon in Sonny's mouth. I just looked at him and I was probably frowning a real frown by this time. I simply couldn't see why on earth he'd want to spend his time hanging around nightclubs, clowning around on bandstands, while people pushed each other around a dance floor. It seemed—beneath him, somehow. I had never thought about it before, had never been forced to, but I suppose I had always put jazz musicians in a class with what Daddy called "goodtime people."

"Are you *serious?*"

"Hell, *yes,* I'm serious."

He looked more helpless than ever, and annoyed, and deeply hurt.

I suggested, helpfully: "You mean—like Louis Armstrong?"

125   His face closed as though I'd struck him. "No. I'm not talking about none of that old-time, down home crap."

"Well, look, Sonny, I'm sorry, don't get mad. I just don't altogether get it, that's all. Name somebody—you know, a jazz musician you admire."

"Bird."

"Who?"

"Bird! Charlie Parker! Don't they teach you nothing in the goddamn army?"

130   I lit a cigarette. I was surprised and then a little amused to discover that I was trembling. "I've been out of touch," I said. "You'll have to be patient with me. Now. Who's this Parker character?"

"He's just one of the greatest jazz musicians alive," said Sonny, sullenly, his hands in his pockets, his back to me. "Maybe *the* greatest," he added, bitterly, "that's probably why *you* never heard of him."

"All right," I said, "I'm ignorant. I'm sorry. I'll go out and buy all the cat's records right away, all right?"

"It don't," said Sonny, with dignity, "make any difference to me. I don't care what you listen to. Don't do me no favors."

I was beginning to realize that I'd never seen him so upset before. With another part of my mind I was thinking that this would probably turn out to be one of those things kids go through and that I shouldn't make it seem important by pushing it too hard. Still, I didn't think it would do any harm to ask: "Doesn't all this take a lot of time? Can you make a living at it?"

135   He turned back to me and half leaned, half sat, on the kitchen table. "Everything takes time," he said, "and—well, yes, sure, I can make a living at it. But what I don't seem to be able to make you understand is that it's the only thing I want to do."

"Well, Sonny," I said, gently, "you know people can't always do exactly what they *want* to do—"

"*No,* I don't know that," said Sonny, surprising me. "I think people *ought* to do what they want to do, what else are they alive for?"

"You getting to be a big boy," I said desperately, "it's time you started thinking about your future."

"I'm thinking about my future," said Sonny, grimly. "I think about it all the time."

140   I gave up. I decided, if he didn't change his mind, that we could always talk about it later. "In the meantime," I said, "you got to finish school." We had already decided that he'd have to move in with Isabel and her folks. I knew this wasn't the ideal arrangement because Isabel's folks are inclined to be dicty and they hadn't es-pecially wanted Isabel to marry me. But I didn't know what else to do. "And we have to get you fixed up at Isabel's."

There was a long silence. He moved from the kitchen table to the windows. "That's a terrible idea. You know it yourself."

"Do you have a *better* idea?"

He just walked up and down the kitchen for a minute. He was as tall as I was. He had started to shave. I suddenly had the feeling that I didn't know him at all.

He stopped at the kitchen table and picked up my cigarettes. Looking at me with a kind of mocking, amusing defiance, he put one between his lips. "You mind?"

"You smoking already?"   145

He lit the cigarette and nodded, watching me through the smoke. "I just wanted to see if I'd have the courage to smoke in front of you." He grinned and blew a great cloud of smoke to the ceiling. "It was easy." He looked at my face. "Come on, now. I bet you was smoking at my age, tell the truth."

I didn't say anything but the truth was on my face, and he laughed. But now there was something very strained in his laugh. "Sure. And I bet that ain't all you was doing."

He was frightening me a little. "Cut the crap," I said. "We already decided that you was going to go and live at Isabel's. Now what's got into you all of a sudden?"

"*You* decided it," he pointed out. "*I* didn't decide nothing." He stopped in front of me, leaning against the stove, arms loosely folded. "Look, brother. I don't want to stay in Harlem no more, I really don't." He was very earnest. He looked at me, then over toward the kitchen window. There was something in his eyes I'd never seen before, some thoughtfulness, some worry all his own. He rubbed the muscle of one arm. "It's time I was getting out of here."

"Where do you want to *go*, Sonny?"   150

"I want to join the army. Or the navy, I don't care. If I say I'm old enough, they'll believe me."

Then I got mad. It was because I was so scared. "You must be crazy. You goddamn fool, what the hell do you want to go and join the *army* for?"

"I just told you. To get out of Harlem."

"Sonny, you haven't even finished *school*. And if you really want to be a musician, how do you expect to study if you're in the *army?*"

He looked at me, trapped, and in anguish. "There's ways. I might be able to   155 work out some kind of deal. Anyway, I'll have the G.I. Bill when I come out."

"*If* you come out." We stared at each other. "Sonny, please. Be reasonable. I know the setup is far from perfect. But we got to do the best we can."

"I ain't learning nothing in school," he said. "Even when I go." He turned away from me and opened the window and threw his cigarette out into the narrow alley. I watched his back. "At least, I ain't learning nothing you'd want me to learn." He slammed the window so hard I thought the glass would fly out, and turned back to me. "And I'm sick of the stink of these garbage cans!"

"Sonny," I said, "I know how you feel. But if you don't finish school now, you're going to be sorry later that you didn't." I grabbed him by the shoulders. "And you only got another year. It ain't so bad. And I'll come back and I swear I'll help you do *whatever* you want to do. Just try to put up with it till I come back. Will you please do that? For me?"

He didn't answer and he wouldn't look at me.

160   "Sonny. You hear me?"

He pulled away. "I hear you. But you never hear anything *I* say."

I didn't know what to say to that. He looked out of the window and then back at me. "OK," he said, and sighed. "I'll try."

Then I said, trying to cheer him up a little, "They got a piano at Isabel's. You can practice on it."

And as a matter of fact, it did cheer him up for a minute. "That's right," he said to himself. "I forgot that." His face relaxed a little. But the worry, the thoughtfulness, played on it still, the way shadows play on a face which is staring into the fire.

165   But I thought I'd never hear the end of that piano. At first, Isabel would write me, saying how nice it was that Sonny was so serious about his music and how, as soon as he came in from school, or wherever he had been when he was supposed to be at school, he went straight to that piano and stayed there until suppertime. And, after supper, he went back to that piano and stayed there until everybody went to bed. He was at the piano all day Saturday and all day Sunday. Then he bought a record player and started playing records. He'd play one record over and over again, all day long sometimes, and he'd improvise along with it on the piano. Or he'd play one section of the record, one chord, one change, one progression, then he'd do it on the piano. Then back to the record. Then back to the piano.

Well, I really don't know how they stood it. Isabel finally confessed that it wasn't like living with a person at all, it was like living with sound. And the sound didn't make any sense to her, didn't make any sense to any of them—naturally. They began, in a way, to be afflicted by this presence that was living in their home. It was as though Sonny were some sort of god, or monster. He moved in an atmosphere which wasn't like theirs at all. They fed him and he ate, he washed himself, he walked in and out of their door; he certainly wasn't nasty or unpleasant or rude, Sonny isn't any of those things; but it was as though he were all wrapped up in some cloud, some fire, some vision all his own; and there wasn't any way to reach him.

At the same time, he wasn't really a man yet, he was still a child, and they had to watch out for him in all kinds of ways. They certainly couldn't throw him out. Neither did they dare to make a great scene about that piano because even they dimly sensed, as I sensed, from so many thousands of miles away, that Sonny was at that piano playing for his life.

But he hadn't been going to school. One day a letter came from the school board and Isabel's mother got it—there had, apparently, been other letters but Sonny had torn them up. This day, when Sonny came in, Isabel's mother showed him the letter and asked where he'd been spending his time. And she finally got it out of him that he'd been down in Greenwich Village, with musicians and other characters, in a white girl's apartment. And this scared her and she started to scream at him and what came up, once she began—though she denies it to this day—was what sacrifices they were making to give Sonny a decent home and how little he appreciated it.

Sonny didn't play the piano that day. By evening, Isabel's mother had calmed down but then there was the old man to deal with, and Isabel herself. Isabel says she did her best to be calm but she broke down and started crying. She says she just watched Sonny's face. She could tell, by watching him, what was happening with him. And what was happening was that they penetrated his cloud, they had reached him. Even if their fingers had been a thousand times more gentle than human fingers ever are, he could hardly help feeling that they had stripped him naked and were spitting on that nakedness. For he also had to see that his presence, that music, which was life or death to him, had been torture for them and that they had endured it, not at all for his sake, but only for mine. And Sonny couldn't take that. He can take it a little better today than he could then but he's still not very good at it and, frankly, I don't know anybody who is.

The silence of the next few days must have been louder than the sound of all the music ever played since time began. One morning, before she went to work, Isabel was in his room for something and she suddenly realized that all of his records were gone. And she knew for certain that he was gone. And he was. He went as far as the navy would carry him. He finally sent me a postcard from some place in Greece and that was the first I knew that Sonny was still alive. I didn't see him any more until we were both back in New York and the war had long been over. 170

He was a man by then, of course, but I wasn't willing to see it. He came by the house from time to time, but we fought almost every time we met. I didn't like the way he carried himself, loose and dreamlike all the time, and I didn't like his friends, and his music seemed to be merely an excuse for the life he led. It sounded just that weird and disordered.

Then we had a fight, a pretty awful fight, and I didn't see him for months. By and by I looked him up, where he was living, in a furnished room in the Village, and I tried to make it up. But there were lots of other people in the room and Sonny just lay on his bed, and he wouldn't come downstairs with me, and he treated these other people as though they were his family and I weren't. So I got mad and then he got mad, and then I told him that he might just as well be dead as live the way he was living. Then he stood up and he told me not to worry about him any more in life, that he *was* dead as far as I was concerned. Then he pushed me to the door and the other people looked on as though nothing were happening, and he slammed the door behind me. I stood in the hallway, staring at the door. I heard somebody laugh in the room and then the tears came to my eyes. I started down the steps, whistling to keep from crying, I kept whistling to myself, *You going to need me, baby, one of these cold, rainy days.*

I read about Sonny's trouble in the spring. Little Grace died in the fall. She was a beautiful little girl. But she only lived a little over two years. She died of polio and she suffered. She had a slight fever for a couple of days, but it didn't seem like anything and we just kept her in bed. And we would certainly have called the doctor, but the fever dropped, she seemed to be all right. So we thought it had just been a cold. Then, one day, she was up, playing, Isabel was in the kitchen fixing lunch for the two boys when they'd come in from school, and she heard Grace fall down in the living room. When you have a lot of children you don't always start running when one of them falls, unless they start screaming or something. And, this time, Grace was quiet.

Yet, Isabel says that when she heard that *thump* and then that silence, something happened in her to make her afraid. And she ran to the living room and there was little Grace on the floor, all twisted up, and the reason she hadn't screamed was that she couldn't get her breath. And when she did scream, it was the worst sound, Isabel says, that she'd ever heard in all her life, and she still hears it sometimes in her dreams. Isabel will sometimes wake me up with a low, moaning, strangled sound and I have to be quick to awaken her and hold her to me and where Isabel is weeping against me seems a mortal wound.

I think I may have written Sonny the very day that little Grace was buried. I was sitting in the living room in the dark, by myself, and I suddenly thought of Sonny. My trouble made his real.

175   One Saturday afternoon, when Sonny had been living with us, or, anyway, been in our house, for nearly two weeks, I found myself wandering aimlessly about the living room, drinking from a can of beer, and trying to work up the courage to search Sonny's room. He was out, he was usually out whenever I was home, and Isabel had taken the children to see their grandparents. Suddenly I was standing still in front of the living room window, watching Seventh Avenue. The idea of searching Sonny's room made me still. I scarcely dared to admit to myself what I'd be searching for. I didn't know what I'd do if I found it. Or if I didn't.

On the sidewalk across from me, near the entrance to a barbecue joint, some people were holding an old-fashioned revival meeting. The barbecue cook, wearing a dirty white apron, his conked hair reddish and metallic in the pale sun, and a cigarette between his lips, stood in the doorway, watching them. Kids and older people paused in their errands and stood there, along with some older men and a couple of very tough-looking women who watched everything that happened on the avenue, as though they owned it, or were maybe owned by it. Well, they were watching this, too. The revival was being carried on by three sisters in black, and a brother. All they had were their voices and their Bibles and a tambourine. The brother was testifying and while he testified two of the sisters stood together, seeming to say, amen, and the third sister walked around with the tambourine outstretched and a couple of people dropped coins into it. Then the brother's testimony ended and the sister who had been taking up the collection dumped the coins into her palm and transferred them to the pocket of her long black robe. Then she raised both hands, striking the tambourine against the air, and then against one hand, and she started to sing. And the two other sisters and the brother joined in.

It was strange, suddenly, to watch, though I had been seeing these street meetings all my life. So, of course, had everybody else down there. Yet, they paused and watched and listened and I stood still at the window. *"Tis the old ship of Zion,"* they sang, and the sister with the tambourine kept a steady, jangling beat, *"it has rescued many a thousand!"* Not a soul under the sound of their voices was hearing this song for the first time, not one of them had been rescued. Nor had they seen much in the way of rescue work being done around them. Neither did they especially believe in the holiness of the three sisters and the brother, they knew too much about them, knew where they lived, and how. The woman with the tambourine, whose voice dominated the air, whose face was bright with joy, was divided by very little from the woman who stood watching her, a cigarette between her heavy, chapped lips, her hair a cuckoo's nest, her face scarred and swollen from many beatings, and her black eyes glittering like coal. Perhaps they both knew this, which was why, when, as rarely, they addressed each other, they addressed each other as Sister. As the singing filled the air the watching, listening faces underwent a change, the eyes focusing on something within; the music seemed to soothe a poison out of them; and time seemed, nearly, to fall away from the sullen, belligerent, battered faces, as though they were fleeing back to their first condition, while dreaming of their last. The barbecue cook half shook his head and smiled, and dropped his cigarette and disappeared into his joint. A man fumbled in his pockets for change and stood holding it in his hand impatiently, as though he had just remembered a pressing appointment further up the avenue. He looked furious. Then I saw Sonny, standing on the edge of the crowd. He was carrying a wide, flat notebook with a green cover, and it made him look, from where I was standing, almost like a schoolboy. The coppery sun brought out the copper in his skin, he was very faintly smiling, standing very still. Then the singing stopped, the tambourine turned into a collection plate again. The furious man dropped in his coins and vanished, so did a couple of the women, and Sonny dropped some change in the plate, looking directly at the woman with a little smile. He started across the avenue, toward the house. He has a slow, loping walk, something like the way Harlem hipsters walk, only he's imposed on this his own half-beat. I had never really noticed it before.

I stayed at the window, both relieved and apprehensive. As Sonny disappeared from my sight, they began singing again. And they were still singing when his key turned in the lock.

"Hey," he said.

"Hey, youself. You want some beer?"   180

"No. Well, maybe." But he came up to the window and stood beside me, looking out. "What a warm voice," he said.

They were singing *If I could only hear my mother pray again!*

"Yes," I said, "and she can sure beat that tambourine."

"But what a terrible song," he said, and laughed. He dropped his notebook on the sofa and disappeared into the kitchen. "Where's Isabel and the kids?"

"I think they went to see their grandparents. You hungry?"   185

"No." He came back into the living room with his can of beer. "You want to come some place with me tonight?"

I sensed, I don't know how, that I couldn't possibly say no. "Sure. Where?"

He sat down on the sofa and picked up his notebook and started leafing through it. "I'm going to sit in with some fellows in a joint in the Village."

"You mean, you're going to play, tonight?"

"That's right." He took a swallow of his beer and moved back to the window.   190 He gave me a sidelong look. "If you can stand it."

"I'll try," I said.

He smiled to himself and we both watched as the meeting across the way broke up. The three sisters and the brother, heads bowed, were singing *God be with you till we meet again.* The faces around them were very quiet. Then the song ended. The small crowd dispersed. We watched the three women and the lone man walk slowly up the avenue.

"When she was singing before," said Sonny, abruptly, "her voice reminded me for a minute of what heroin feels like sometimes—when it's in your veins. It makes you feel sort of warm and cool at the same time. And distant. And—and sure." He sipped his beer, very deliberately not looking at me. I watched his face. "It makes you feel—in control. Sometimes you've got to have that feeling."

"Do you?" I sat down slowly in the easy chair.

195   "Sometimes." He went to the sofa and picked up his notebook again. "Some people do."

"In order," I asked, "to play?" And my voice was very ugly, full of contempt and anger.

"Well"—he looked at me with great, troubled eyes, as though, in fact, he hoped his eyes would tell me things he could never otherwise say—"they *think* so. And *if* they think so—!"

"And what do *you* think?" I asked.

He sat on the sofa and put his can of beer on the floor. "I don't know," he said, and I couldn't be sure if he were answering my question or pursuing his thoughts. His face didn't tell me. "It's not so much to *play*. It's to *stand* it, to be able to make it at all. On any level." He frowned and smiled: "In order to keep from shaking to pieces."

200   "But these friends of yours," I said, "they seem to shake themselves to pieces pretty goddamn fast."

"Maybe." He played with the notebook. And something told me that I should curb my tongue, that Sonny was doing his best to talk, that I should listen. "But of course you only know the ones that've gone to pieces. Some don't—or at least they haven't *yet* and that's just about all *any* of us can say." He paused. "And then there are some who just live, really, in hell, and they know it and they see what's happening and they go right on. I don't know." He sighed, dropped the notebook, folded his arms. "Some guys, you can tell from the way they play, they on something *all* the time. And you can see that, well, it makes something real for them. But of course," he picked up his beer from the floor and sipped it and put the can down again, "they *want* to, too, you've got to see that. Even some of them that say they don't—*some,* not all."

"And what about you?" I asked—I couldn't help it. "What about you? Do *you* want to?"

He stood up and walked to the window and remained silent for a long time. Then he sighed. "Me," he said. Then: "While I was downstairs before, on my way here, listening to that woman sing, it struck me all of a sudden how much suffering she must have had to go through—to sing like that. It's *repulsive* to think you have to suffer that much."

I said: "But there's no way not to suffer—is there, Sonny?"

205   "I believe not," he said and smiled, "but that's never stopped anyone from trying." He looked at me. "Has it?" I realized, with his mocking look, that there stood

between us, forever, beyond the power of time or forgiveness, the fact that I had held silence—so long!—when he had needed human speech to help him. He turned back to the window. "No, there's no way not to suffer. But you try all kinds of ways to keep from drowning in it, to keep on top of it, and to make it seem—well, like *you*. Like you did something, all right, and now you're suffering for it. You know?" I said nothing. "Well you know," he said, impatiently, "Why *do* people suffer? Maybe it's better to do something to give it a reason, *any* reason."

"But we just agreed," I said, "that there's no way not to suffer. Isn't it better, then, just to—take it?"

"But nobody just takes it," Sonny cried, "that's what I'm telling you! *Everybody* tries not to. You're just hung up on the *way* some people try—it's not *your* way!"

The hair on my face began to itch, my face felt wet. "That's not true," I said, "that's not true. I don't give a damn what other people do, I don't even care how they suffer. I just care how *you* suffer." And he looked at me. "Please believe me," I said, "I don't want to see you—die—trying not to suffer."

"I won't," he said, flatly, "die trying not to suffer. At least, not any faster than anybody else."

"But there's no need," I said, trying to laugh, "is there? in killing yourself."   210

I wanted to say more, but I couldn't. I wanted to talk about will power and how life could be—well, beautiful. I wanted to say that it was all within; but was it? or, rather, wasn't that exactly the trouble? And I wanted to promise that I would never fail him again. But it would all have sounded—empty words and lies.

So I made the promise to myself and prayed that I would keep it.

"It's terrible sometimes, inside," he said, "that's what's the trouble. You walk these streets, black and funky and cold, and there's not really a living ass to talk to, and there's nothing shaking, and there's no way of getting it out—that storm inside. You can't talk it and you can't make love with it, and when you finally try to get with it and play it, you realize *nobody's* listening. So *you've* got to listen. You got to find a way to listen."

And then he walked away from the window and sat on the sofa again, as though all the wind had suddenly been knocked out of him. "Sometimes you'll do *anything* to play, even cut your mother's throat." He laughed and looked at me. "Or your brother's." Then he sobered. "Or your own." Then: "Don't worry. I'm all right now and I think I'll *be* all right. But I can't forget—where I've been. I don't mean just the physical place I've been, I mean where I've *been*. And *what* I've been."

"What have you been, Sonny?" I asked.   215

He smiled—but sat sideways on the sofa, his elbow resting on the back, his fingers playing with his mouth and chin, not looking at me. "I've been something I didn't recognize, didn't know I could be. Didn't know anybody could be." He stopped, looking inward, looking helplessly young, looking old. "I'm not talking about it now because I feel *guilty* or anything like that—maybe it would be better if I did, I don't know. Anyway, I can't really talk about it. Not to you, not to anybody," and now he turned and faced me. "Sometimes, you know, and it was actually when I was most *out* of the world, I felt that I was in it, that I was *with* it, really, and I could play or I didn't really have to *play,* it just came out of me, it was there. And I don't know how

I played, thinking about it now, but I know I did awful things, those times, some-times, to people. Or it wasn't that I *did* anything to them—it was that they weren't real." He picked up the beer can; it was empty; he rolled it between his palms: "And other times—well, I needed a fix, I needed to find a place to lean, I needed to clear a space to *listen*—and I couldn't find it, and I—went crazy, I did terrible things to *me,* I was terrible *for* me." He began pressing the beer can between his hands, I watched the metal begin to give. It glittered, as he played with it, like a knife, and I was afraid he would cut himself, but I said nothing. "Oh well. I can never tell you. I was all by myself at the bottom of something, stinking and sweating and crying and shaking, and I smelled it, you know? *my* stink, and I thought I'd die if I couldn't get away from it and yet, all the same, I knew that everything I was doing was just lock-ing me in with it. And I didn't know," he paused, still flattening the beer can, "I didn't know, I still *don't* know, something kept telling me that maybe it was good to smell your own stink, but I didn't think that *that* was what I'd been trying to do—and—who can stand it?" and he abruptly dropped the ruined beer can, looking at me with a small, still smile, and then rose, walking to the window as though it were the lode-stone rock. I watched his face, he watched the avenue. "I couldn't tell you when Mama died—but the reason I wanted to leave Harlem so bad was to get away from drugs. And then, when I ran away, that's what I was running from—really. When I came back, nothing had changed. *I* hadn't changed, I was just—older." And he stopped, drumming with his fingers on the windowpane. The sun had vanished, soon darkness would fall. I watched his face. "It can come again," he said, almost as though speaking to himself. Then he turned to me. "It can come again," he repeated. "I just want you to know that."

"All right," I said, at last. "So it can come again, All right."

He smiled, but the smile was sorrowful. "I had to try to tell you," he said.

"Yes," I said. "I understand that."

220   "You're my brother," he said, looking straight at me, and not smiling at all.

"Yes," I repeated, "yes. I understand that."

He turned back to the window, looking out. "All that hatred down there," he said, "all that hatred and misery and love. It's a wonder it doesn't blow the avenue apart."

We went to the only nightclub on a short, dark street, downtown. We squeezed through the narrow, chattering, jam-packed bar to the entrance of the big room, where the bandstand was. And we stood there for a moment, for the lights were very dim in this room and we couldn't see. Then, "Hello, boy," said a voice and an enor-mous black man, much older than Sonny or myself, erupted out of all that atmos-pheric lighting and put an arm around Sonny's shoulder. "I been sitting right here," he said, "waiting for you."

He had a big voice, too, and heads in the darkness turned toward us.

225   Sonny grinned and pulled a little away, and said, "Creole, this is my brother. I told you about him."

Creole shook my hand. "I'm glad to meet you, son," he said, and it was clear that he was glad to meet me *there* for Sonny's sake. And he smiled, "You got a real musician in *your* family," and he took his arm from Sonny's shoulder and slapped him, lightly, affectionately, with the back of his hand.

"Well. Now I've heard it all," said a voice behind us. This was another musician, and a friend of Sonny's, a coal-black, cheerful-looking man, built close to the ground. He immediately began confiding to me, at the top of his lungs, the most terrible things about Sonny, his teeth gleaming like a lighthouse and his laugh coming up out of him like the beginning of an earthquake. And it turned out that everyone at the bar knew Sonny, or almost everyone; some were musicians, working there, or nearby, or not working, some were simply hangers-on, and some were there to hear Sonny play. I was introduced to all of them and they were all very polite to me. Yet, it was clear that, for them, I was only Sonny's brother. Here, I was in Sonny's world. Or, rather: his kingdom. Here, it was not even a question that his veins bore royal blood.

They were going to play soon and Creole installed me, by myself, at a table in a dark corner. Then I watched them, Creole, and the little black man, and Sonny, and the others, while they horsed around, standing just below the bandstand. The light from the bandstand spilled just a little short of them and, watching them laughing and gesturing and moving about, I had the feeling that they, nevertheless, were being most careful not to step into that circle of light too suddenly: that if they moved into the light too suddenly, without thinking, they would perish in flame. Then, while I watched, one of them, the small, black man, moved into the light and crossed the bandstand and started fooling around with his drums. Then—being funny and being, also, extremely ceremonious—Creole took Sonny by the arm and led him to the piano. A woman's voice called Sonny's name and a few hands started clapping. And Sonny, also being funny and being ceremonious, and so touched, I think, that he could have cried, but neither hiding it nor showing it, riding it like a man, grinned, and put both hands to his heart and bowed from the waist.

Creole then went to the bass fiddle and a lean, very bright-skinned brown man jumped up on the bandstand and picked up his horn. So there they were, and the atmosphere on the bandstand and in the room began to change and tighten. Someone stepped up to the microphone and announced them. Then there were all kinds of murmurs. Some people at the bar shushed others. The waitress ran around, frantically getting in the last orders, guys and chicks got closer to each other, and the lights on the bandstand, on the quartet, turned to a kind of indigo. Then they all looked different there. Creole looked about him for the last time, as though he were making certain that all his chickens were in the coop, and then he—jumped and struck the fiddle. And there they were.

All I know about music is that not many people ever really hear it. And even then, on the rare occasions when something opens within, and the music enters, what we mainly hear, or hear corroborated, are personal, private, vanishing evocations. But the man who creates the music is hearing something else, is dealing with the roar rising from the void and imposing order on it as it hits the air. What is evoked in him, then, is of another order, more terrible because it has no words, and triumphant, too, for that same reason. And his triumph, when he triumphs, is ours. I just watched Sonny's face. His face was troubled, he was working hard, but he wasn't with it. And

I had the feeling that, in a way, everyone on the bandstand was waiting for him, both waiting for him and pushing him along. But as I began to watch Creole, I realized that it was Creole who held them all back. He had them on a short rein. Up there, keeping the beat with his whole body, wailing on the fiddle, with his eyes half closed, he was listening to everything, but he was listening to Sonny. He was having a dialogue with Sonny. He wanted Sonny to leave the shoreline and strike out for the deep water. He was Sonny's witness that deep water and drowning were not the same thing—he had been there, and he knew. And he wanted Sonny to know. He was waiting for Sonny to do the things on the keys which would let Creole know that Sonny was in the water.

And, while Creole listened, Sonny moved, deep within, exactly like someone in torment. I had never before thought of how awful the relationship must be between the musician and his instrument. He has to fill it, this instrument, with the breath of life, his own. He has to make it do what he wants it to do. And a piano is just a piano. It's made out of so much wood and wires and little hammers and big ones, and ivory. While there's only so much you can do with it, the only way to find this out is to try; to try and make it do everything.

And Sonny hadn't been near a piano for over a year. And he wasn't on much better terms with his life, not the life that stretched before him now. He and the piano stammered, started one way, got scared, stopped; started another way, panicked, marked time, started again; then seemed to have found a direction, panicked again, got stuck. And the face I saw on Sonny I'd never seen before. Everything had been burned out of it, and, at the same time, things usually hidden were being burned in, by the fire and fury of the battle which was occurring in him up there.

Yet, watching Creole's face as they neared the end of the first set, I had the feeling that something had happened, something I hadn't heard. Then they finished, there was scattered applause, and then, without an instant's warning, Creole started into something else, it was almost sardonic, it was *Am I Blue*. And, as though he commanded, Sonny began to play. Something began to happen. And Creole let out the reins. The dry, low, black man said something awful on the drums, Creole answered, and the drums talked back. Then the horn insisted, sweet and high, slightly detached perhaps, and Creole listened, commenting now and then, dry, and driving, beautiful and calm and old. Then they all came together again, and Sonny was part of the family again. I could tell this from his face. He seemed to have found, right there beneath his fingers, a damn brand-new piano. It seemed that he couldn't get over it. Then, for awhile, just being happy with Sonny, they seemed to be agreeing with him that brand-new pianos certainly were a gas.

Then Creole stepped forward to remind them that what they were playing was the blues. He hit something in all of them, he hit something in me, myself, and the music tightened and deepened, apprehension began to beat the air. Creole began to tell us what the blues were all about. They were not about anything very new. He and his boys up there were keeping it new, at the risk of ruin, destruction, madness, and death, in order to find new ways to make us listen. For, while the tale of how we suffer, and how we are delighted, and how we may triumph is never new, it always must be heard. There isn't any other tale to tell, it's the only light we've got in all this darkness.

And this tale, according to that face, that body, those strong hands on those strings, has another aspect in every country, and a new depth in every generation. Listen, Creole seemed to be saying, listen. Now these are Sonny's blues. He made the little black man on the drums know it, and the bright, brown man on the horn. Creole wasn't trying any longer to get Sonny in the water. He was wishing him Godspeed. Then he stepped back, very slowly, filling the air with the immense suggestion that Sonny speak for himself.

Then they all gathered around Sonny and Sonny played. Every now and again one of them seemed to say, amen. Sonny's fingers filled the air with life, his life. But that life contained so many others. And Sonny went all the way back, he really began with the spare, flat statement of the opening phrase of the song. Then he began to make it his. It was very beautiful because it wasn't hurried and it was no longer a lament. I seemed to hear with what burning he had made it his, with what burning we had yet to make it ours, how we could cease lamenting. Freedom lurked around us and I understood, at last, that he could help us to be free if we would listen, that he would never be free until we did. Yet, there was no battle in his face now. I heard what he had gone through, and would continue to go through until he came to rest in earth. He had made it his: that long line, of which we knew only Mama and Daddy. And he was giving it back, as everything must be given back, so that, passing through death, it can live forever. I saw my mother's face again, and felt, for the first time, how the stones of the road she had walked on must have bruised her feet. I saw the moonlit road where my father's brother died. And it brought something else back to me, and carried me past it, I saw my little girl again and felt Isabel's tears again, and I felt my own tears begin to rise. And I was yet aware that this was only a moment, that the world waited outside, as hungry as a tiger, and that trouble stretched above us, longer than the sky.

Then it was over. Creole and Sonny let out their breath, both soaking wet, and grinning. There was a lot of applause and some of it was real. In the dark, the girl came by and I asked her to take drinks to the bandstand. There was a long pause, while they talked up there in the indigo light and after awhile I saw the girl put a Scotch and milk on top of the piano for Sonny. He didn't seem to notice it, but just before they started playing again, he sipped from it and looked toward me, and nodded. Then he put it back on top of the piano. For me, then, as they began to play again, it glowed and shook above my brother's head like the very cup of trembling.

QUESTIONS FOR DISCUSSION AND WRITING

1. How does Mama's story about Sonny's uncle help prepare us for the events of the story? In what way does the promise she extracts from the older brother complicate the plot?

2. How would you contrast the characters of Sonny and his brother? In what unexpected ways are they similar?

3. How does Baldwin characterize the risks and the rewards of living in Harlem? How does this setting shape the characters in the story?

4. How does the older brother's point of view change during the course of the story? How is his point of view toward his brother deepened by his own personal problems?

5. What relationship does Baldwin suggest exists among heroin, religion, and music? What do they promise? What do they provide? How do they help define "the blues"?

Stories for Comparison

Philip Roth's "Defender of the Faith" (pages 1036–1058); Alice Walker's "Everyday Use" (pages 1151–1158).

19

T O N I   C A D E   B A M B A R A

The Lesson

TONI CADE BAMBARA (1939–1995) was born in New York City and educated at Queens College, the University of Florence, the École de Mme. Étienne Decroux in Paris, and the City College of the City University of New York. She attended post-degree courses at the New School for Social Research, the Katherine Dunham Dance Studio, and the Studio Museum of Harlem Film Institute. Bambara's work experience has been extremely varied: a social investigator for the New York State Department of Welfare, a director of recreation in the psychiatry department of New York's Metropolitan Hospital, a visiting professor of Afro-American studies (Stephens College), a consultant on women's studies (Emory University), and a writer-in-residence (Spelman College in Atlanta). Bambara has contributed stories and essays to magazines as diverse as *Negro Digest, Prairie Schooner,* and *Redbook.* Her collections of short stories—*Gorilla, My Love* (1972), *The Sea Birds Are Still Alive: Collected Stories* (1977), and *The Salt Eaters* (1980)—and novel,

If Blessing Comes (1987), deal with the emerging sense of self of black women. "The Lesson," reprinted from *Gorilla, My Love,* focuses on the experiences of several black children who learn how much things "cost."

Back in the days when everyone was old and stupid or young and foolish and me and Sugar were the only ones just right, this lady moved on our block with nappy hair and proper speech and no makeup. And quite naturally we laughed at her, laughed the way we did at the junk man who went about his business like he was some big-time president and his sorry-ass horse his secretary. And we kinda hated her too, hated the way we did the winos who cluttered up our parks and pissed on our handball walls and stank up our hallways and stairs so you couldn't halfway play hide-and-seek without a goddamn gas mask. Miss Moore was her name. The only woman on the block with no first name. And she was black as hell, cept for her feet, which were fish-white and spooky. And she was always planning these boring-ass things for us to do, us being my cousin, mostly, who lived on the block cause we all moved North the same time and to the same apartment then spread out gradual to breathe. And our parents would yank our heads into some kinda shape and crisp up our clothes so we'd be presentable for travel with Miss Moore, who always looked like she was going to church, though she never did. Which is just one of the things the grownups talked about when they talked behind her back like a dog. But when she came calling with some sachet she'd sewed up or some gingerbread she'd made or some book, why then they'd all be too embarrassed to turn her down and we'd get handed over all spruced up. She'd been to college and said it was only right that she should take responsibility for the young ones' education, and she not even related by marriage or blood. So they'd go for it. Specially Aunt Gretchen. She was the main gofer in the family. You got some ole dumb shit foolishness you want somebody to go for, you send for Aunt Gretchen. She been screwed into the go-along for so long, it's a blood-deep natural thing with her. Which is how she got saddled with me and Sugar and Junior in the first place while our mothers were in a la-de-da apartment up the block having a good ole time.

So this one day, Miss Moore rounds us all up at the mailbox and it's puredee hot and she's knockin herself out about arithmetic. And school suppose to let up in summer I heard, but she don't never let up. And the starch in my pinafore scratching the shit outta me and I'm really hating this nappy-head bitch and her goddamn college degree. I'd much rather go to the pool or to the show where it's cool. So me and Sugar leaning on the mailbox being surly, which is a Miss Moore word. And Flyboy checking out what everybody brought for lunch. And Fat Butt already wasting his peanut-butter-and-jelly sandwich like the pig he is. And Junebug punchin on Q.T.'s arm for potato chips. And Rosie Giraffe shifting from one hip to the other waiting for somebody to step on her foot or ask her if she from Georgia so she can kick ass, preferably Mercedes'. And Miss Moore asking us do we know what money is, like we a bunch of retards. I mean real money, she say, like it's only poker chips or monopoly papers we lay on the grocer. So right away I'm tired of this and say so. And would much rather snatch Sugar and go to the Sunset and terrorize the West Indian kids and take their hair ribbons and their money too. And Miss Moore files that remark away for next week's lesson on brotherhood, I can tell. And finally I say we oughta get to the subway cause it's cooler and besides we might meet some cute boys. Sugar done swiped her mama's lipstick, so we ready.

So we heading down the street and she's boring us silly about what things cost and what our parents make and how much goes for rent and how money ain't divided up right in this country. And then she gets to the part about we all poor and live in the slums, which I don't feature. And I'm ready to speak on that, but she steps out in the street and hails two cabs just like that. Then she hustles half the crew in with her and hands me a five-dollar bill and tells me to calculate 10 percent tip for the driver. And we're off. Me and Sugar and Junebug and Flyboy hangin out the window and hollering to everybody, putting lipstick on each other cause Flyboy a faggot anyway, and making farts with our sweaty armpits. But I'm mostly trying to figure how to spend this money. But they all fascinated with the meter ticking and Junebug starts laying bets as to how much it'll read when Flyboy can't hold his breath no more. Then Sugar lays bets as to how much it'll be when we get there. So I'm stuck. Don't nobody want to go for my plan, which is to jump out at the next light and run off to the first bar-b-que we can find. Then the driver tells us to get the hell out cause we there already. And the meter reads eighty-five cents. And I'm stalling to figure out the tip and Sugar say give him a dime. And I decide he don't need it bad as I do, so later for him. But then he tries to take off with Junebug foot still in the door so we talk about his mamma something ferocious. Then we check out that we on Fifth Avenue and everybody dressed up in stockings. One lady in a fur coat, hot as it is. White folks crazy.

"This is the place," Miss Moore say, presenting it to us in the voice she uses at the museum. "Let's look in the windows before we go in."

5   "Can we steal?" Sugar asks very serious like she's getting the ground rules squared away before she plays. "I beg your pardon," say Miss Moore, and we fall out. So she leads us around the windows of the toy store and me and Sugar screamin, "This is mine, that's mine, I gotta have that, that was made for me, I was born for that," till Big Butt drowns us out.

"Hey, I'm goin to buy that there."

"That there? You don't even know what it is, stupid."

"I do so," he say punchin on Rosie Giraffe. "It's a microscope."

"Whatcha gonna do with a microscope, fool?"

10   "Look at things."

"Like what, Ronald?" ask Miss Moore. And Big Butt ain't got the first notion. So here go Miss Moore gabbing about the thousands of bacteria in a drop of water and the somethinorother in a speck of blood and the million and one living things in the air around us is invisible to the naked eye. And what she say that for? Junebug go to town on that "naked" and we rolling. Then Miss Moore ask what it cost. So we all jam into the window smudgin it up and the price tag say $300. So then she ask how long'd take for Big Butt and Junebug to save up their allowances. "Too long," I say. "Yeh," adds Sugar, "outgrown it by that time." And Miss Moore say no, you never outgrow learning instruments. "Why, even medical students and interns and," blah, blah, blah. And we ready to choke Big Butt for bringing it up in the first damn place.

"This here costs four hundred eighty dollars," say Rosie Giraffe. So we pile up all over her to see what she pointin out. My eyes tell me it's a chunk of glass cracked with something heavy, and different-color inks dripped into the splits, then the whole thing put into a oven or something. But for $480 it don't make sense.

"That's a paperweight made of semi-precious stones fused together under tremendous pressure," she explains slowly, with her hands doing the mining and all the factory work.

"So what's a paperweight?" ask Rosie Giraffe.

"To weigh paper with, dumbbell," say Flyboy, the wise man from the East.   15

"Not exactly," say Miss Moore, which is what she say when you warm or way off too. "It's to weigh paper down so it won't scatter and make your desk untidy." So right away me and Sugar curtsy to each other and then to Mercedes who is more the tidy type.

"We don't keep paper on top of the desk in my class," say Junebug, figuring Miss Moore crazy or lyin one.

"At home, then," she say. "Don't you have a calendar and a pencil case and a blotter and a letter-opener on your desk at home where you do your homework?" And she know damn well what our homes look like cause she nosys around in them every chance she gets.

"I don't even have a desk," say Junebug. "Do we?"

"No. And I don't get no homework neither," says Big Butt.   20

"And I don't even have a home," says Flyboy like he do at school to keep the white folks off his back and sorry for him. Send this poor kid to camp posters, is his specialty.

"I do," says Mercedes. "I have a box of stationery on my desk and a picture of my cat. My godmother bought the stationery and the desk. There's a big rose on each sheet and the envelopes smell like roses."

"Who wants to know about your smelly-ass stationery," say Rosie Giraffe fore I can get my two cents in.

"It's important to have a work area all your own so that . . ."

"Will you look at this sailboat, please," say Flyboy, cutting her off and pointin   25 to the thing like it was his. So once again we tumble all over each other to gaze at this magnificent thing in the toy store which is just big enough to maybe sail two kittens across the pond if you strap them to the posts tight. We all start reciting the price tag like we in assembly. "Handcrafted sailboat of fiberglass at one thousand one hundred ninety-five dollars."

"Unbelievable," I hear myself say and am really stunned. I read it again for myself just in case the group recitation put me in a trance. Same thing. For some reason this pisses me off. We look at Miss Moore and she lookin at us, waiting for I dunno what.

"Who'd pay all that when you can buy a sailboat set for a quarter at Pop's, a tube of glue for a dime, and a ball of string for eight cents? It must have a motor and a whole lot else besides," I say. "My sailboat cost me about fifty cents."

"But will it take water?" say Mercedes with her smart ass.

"Took mine to Alley Pond Park once," say Flyboy. "String broke. Lost it. Pity."

30   "Sailed mine in Central Park and it keeled over and sank. Had to ask my father for another dollar."

"And you got the strap," laugh Big Butt. "The jerk didn't even have a string on it. My old man wailed on his behind."

Little Q.T. was staring hard at the sailboat and you could see he wanted it bad. But he too little and somebody'd just take it from him. So what the hell. "This boat for kids, Miss Moore?"

"Parents silly to buy something like that just to get all broke up," say Rosie Giraffe.

"That much money it should last forever," I figure.

35   "My father'd buy it for me if I wanted it."

"Your father, my ass," say Rosie Giraffe getting a chance to finally push Mercedes.

"Must be rich people shop here," say Q.T.

"You are a very bright boy," say Flyboy. "What was your first clue?" And he rap him on the head with the back of his knuckles, since Q.T. the only one he could get away with. Though Q.T. liable to come up behind you years later and get his licks in when you half expect it.

"What I want to know is," I says to Miss Moore though I never talk to her, I wouldn't give the bitch that satisfaction, "is how much a real boat costs? I figure a thousand'd get you a yacht any day."

40   "Why don't you check that out," she says, "and report back to the group?" Which really pains my ass. If you gonna mess up a perfectly good swim day least you could do is have some answers. "Let's go in," she say like she got something up her sleeve. Only she don't lead the way. So me and Sugar turn the corner to where the entrance is, but when we get there I kinda hang back. Not that I'm scared, what's there to be afraid of, just a toy store. But I feel funny, shame. But what I got to be shamed about? Got as much right to go in as anybody. But somehow I can't seem to get hold of the door, so I step away from Sugar to lead. But she hangs back too. And I look at her and she looks at me and this is ridiculous. I mean, damn, I have never ever been shy about doing nothing or going nowhere. But then Mercedes steps up and then Rosie Giraffe and Big Butt crowd in behind and shove, and next thing we all stuffed into the doorway with only Mercedes squeezing past us, smoothing out her jumper and walking right down the aisle. Then the rest of us tumble in like a glued-together jigsaw done all wrong. And people lookin at us. And it's like the time me and Sugar crashed into the Catholic church on a dare. But once we got in there and everything so hushed and holy and the candles and the bowin and the handkerchiefs on all the drooping heads, I just couldn't go through with the plan. Which was for me to run up to the altar and do a tap dance while Sugar played the nose flute and messed around in the holy water. And Sugar kept given me the elbow. Then later teased me so bad I tied her up in the shower and turned it on and locked her in. And she'd be there till this day if Aunt Gretchen hadn't finally figured I was lyin about the boarder takin a shower.

Same thing in the store. We all walkin on tiptoe and hardly touchin the games and puzzles and things. And I watched Miss Moore who is steady watchin us like she waitin for a sign. Like Mama Drewery watches the sky and sniffs the air and takes note of just how much slant is in the bird formation. Then me and Sugar bump smack into each other, so busy gazing at the toys, 'specially the sailboat. But we don't laugh and go into our fat-lady bump-stomach routine. We just stare at that price tag. Then Sugar run a finger over the whole boat. And I'm jealous and want to hit her. Maybe not her, but I sure want to punch somebody in the mouth.

"Watcha bring us here for, Miss Moore?"

"You sound angry, Sylvia. Are you mad about something?" Givin me one of them grins like she tellin a grown-up joke that never turns out to be funny. And she's lookin very closely at me like maybe she plannin to do my portrait from memory. I'm mad, but I won't give her that satisfaction. So I slouch around the store bein very bored and say, "Let's go."

Me and Sugar at the back of the train watchin the tracks whizzin by large then small then getting gobbled up in the dark. I'm thinkin about this tricky toy I saw in the store. A clown that somersaults on a bar then does chin-ups just cause you yank lightly at his leg. Cost $35. I could see me askin my mother for a $35 birthday clown. "You wanna who that costs what?" she'd say, cocking her head to the side to get a better view of the hole in my head. Thirty-five dollars could buy new bunk beds for Junior and Gretchen's boy. Thirty-five dollars and the whole household could go visit Granddaddy Nelson in the country. Thirty-five dollars would pay for the rent and the piano bill too. Who are these people that spend that much for performing clowns and $1000 for toy sailboats? What kinda work they do and how they live and how come we ain't in on it? Where we are is who we are, Miss Moore always pointin out. But it don't necessarily have to be that way, she always adds then waits for somebody to say that poor people have to wake up and demand their share of the pie and don't none of us know what kind of pie she talking about in the first damn place. But she ain't so smart cause I still got her four dollars from the taxi and she sure ain't gettin it. Messin up my day with this shit. Sugar nudges me in my pocket and winks.

Miss Moore lines us up in front of the mailbox where we started from, seem like years ago, and I got a headache for thinkin so hard. And we lean all over each other so we can hold up under the draggy-ass lecture she always finishes us off with at the end before we thank her for borin us to tears. But she just looks at us like she readin tea leaves. Finally she say, "Well, what did you think of F. A. O. Schwarz?"

Rosie Giraffe mumbles, "White folks crazy."

"I'd like to go there again when I get my birthday money," says Mercedes, and we shove her out the pack so she has to lean on the mailbox by herself.

"I'd like a shower. Tiring day," say Flyboy.

Then Sugar surprises me by sayin, "You know, Miss Moore, I don't think all of us here put together eat in a year what that sailboat costs." And Miss Moore lights up like somebody goosed her. "And?" she say, urging Sugar on. Only I'm standin on her foot so she don't continue.

"Imagine for a minute what kind of society it is in which some people can spend on a toy what it would cost to feed a family of six or seven. What do you think?"

"I think," say Sugar pushing me off her feet like she never done before, cause I whip her ass in a minute, "that this is not much of a democracy if you ask me. Equal chance to pursue happiness means an equal crack at the dough, don't it?" Miss Moore is besides herself and I am disgusted with Sugar's treachery. So I stand on her foot one more time to see if she'll shove me. She shuts up, and Miss Moore looks at me, sorrowfully I'm thinkin. And somethin weird is goin on, I can feel it in my chest.

"Anybody else learn anything today?" lookin dead at me. I walk away and Sugar has to run to catch up and don't even seem to notice when I shrug her arm off my shoulder.

"Well, we got four dollars anyway," she says.

"Uh, hunh."

55   "We could go to Hascombs and get a half a chocolate layer and then go to the Sunset and still have plenty money for potato chips and ice cream sodas."

"Uh hunh."

"Race you to Hascombs," she say.

We start down the block and she gets ahead which is O.K. by me cause I'm going to the West End and then over to the Drive to think this day through. She can run if she want to and even run faster. But ain't nobody gonna beat me at nuthin.

QUESTIONS FOR DISCUSSION AND WRITING

1. How does the cost of the sailboat help establish the conflict in the story?

2. How do the language and behavior of the children in this story help characterize them? How do their reactions to Miss Moore help characterize her?

3. Why does Miss Moore take the children out of their neighborhood to Fifth Avenue to teach them "the lesson"?

4. How does the narrator's point of view change once she enters the toy store? What emotions does she say she feels? How do these emotions affect her behavior?

5. What sign is Miss Moore waiting for as she watches the children in the toy store? What evidence can you find that she has seen the sign?

Stories for Comparison

Ellen Gilchrist's "Traceleen, She's Still Talking" (pages 569–583); Paule Marshall's "To Da-duh, In Memoriam" (pages 863–871).

20

RUSSELL BANKS

Sarah Cole: A Type of Love Story

RUSSELL BANKS was born in 1940 in Newton, Massachusetts, and was educated at Colgate University and the University of North Carolina. From 1966 to 1975 Banks worked as the publisher and editor of a small press, Lillabulero Press, before moving on to a series of writer-in-residence positions at Emerson College, Princeton University, and New York University. Many of his early stories, such as those collected in *Trailerpark* (1981), were perceived as experimental, concerned with "re-inventing the narrator." Banks continued these experiments in his first major novel, *Hamilton Stark* (1978), the story of a "misanthropic New Hampshire pipefitter." His more recent fiction is concerned with the themes of travel and self-discovery. The settings in *The Book of Jamaica* (1980), the critically acclaimed *Continental Drift* (1985), and *Rule of the Bone* (1995) contrast the bleak environment of New England with the warmth and mystery of the Caribbean. In "Sarah Cole: A Type of Love Story," reprinted from *Success Stories* (1986), the narrator shifts his point of view several times in trying to explain an unusual love story.

I

To begin, then, here is a scene in which I am the man and my friend Sarah Cole is the woman. I don't mind describing it now, because I'm a decade older and don't look the same now as I did then, and Sarah Cole is dead. That is to say, on hearing this story you might think me vain if I looked the same now as I did then, because I must tell you that I was extremely handsome then. And if Sarah were not dead, you'd think I was cruel, for I must tell you that Sarah was very homely. In fact, she was the homeliest woman I have ever known. Personally, I mean. I've *seen* a few women who were more unattractive than Sarah, but they were clearly freaks of nature or had been badly injured or had been victimized by some grotesque, disfiguring disease. Sarah, however, was quite normal, and I knew her well, because for three and a half months we were lovers.

Here is the scene. You can put it in the present, even though it took place ten years ago, because nothing that matters to the story depends on when it took place, and you can put it in Concord, New Hampshire, even though that is indeed where it took place, because it doesn't matter where it took place, so it might as well be Concord, New Hampshire, a place I happen to know well and can therefore describe with sufficient detail to make the story believable. Around six o'clock on a Wednesday evening in late May, a man enters a bar. The bar, a cocktail lounge at street level, with a restaurant upstairs, is decorated with hanging plants and unfinished wood paneling, butcher-block tables and captain's chairs, with a half-dozen darkened, thickly upholstered booths along one wall. Three or four men between the ages of twenty-five and thirty-five are drinking at the bar and, like the man who has just entered, wear three-piece suits and loosened neckties. They are probably lawyers, young, unmarried lawyers gossiping with their brethren over martinis so as to postpone arriving home alone at their whitewashed town-house apartments, where they will fix their evening meals in radar ranges and afterwards, while their TVs chuckle quietly in front of them, sit on their couches and do a little extra work for tomorrow. They are, for the most part, honorable, educated, hard-working, shallow and moderately unhappy young men.

Our man, call him Ronald, Ron, in most ways is like these men, except that he is unusually good-looking, and that makes him a little less unhappy than they. Ron is effortlessly attractive, a genetic wonder, tall, slender, symmetrical and clean. His flaws—a small mole on the left corner of his square, not-too-prominent chin, a slight excess of blond hair on the tops of his tanned hands, and somewhat underdeveloped buttocks—insofar as they keep him from resembling too closely a men's store mannequin, only contribute to his beauty, for he is beautiful, the way we usually think of a woman as being beautiful. And he is nice too, the consequence, perhaps, of his seeming not to know how beautiful he is, to men as well as women, to young people (even children) as well as old, to attractive people (who realize immediately that he is so much more attractive than they as not to be competitive with them) as well as unattractive people.

Ron takes a seat at the bar, unfolds the evening paper in front of him, and before he can start reading, the bartender asks to help him, calling him "Sir," even though Ron has come into this bar numerous times at this time of day, especially since his divorce last fall. Ron got divorced because, after three years of marriage, his wife chose to pursue the career that his had interrupted, that of a fashion designer, which meant that she had to live in New York City while he had to continue to live in New Hampshire, where his career got its start. They agreed to live apart until he could continue his career near New York City, but after a few months, between conjugal visits, he started sleeping with other women and she started sleeping with other men, and that was that. "No big deal," he explained to friends, who liked both Ron and his wife, even though he was slightly more beautiful than she. "We really were too young when we got married, college sweethearts. But we're still best friends," he assured them. They understood. Most of Ron's friends were divorced by then too.

5   Ron orders a Scotch and soda with a twist and goes back to reading his paper. When his drink comes, before he takes a sip of it, he first carefully finishes reading an article about the recent reappearance of coyotes in northern New Hampshire and Vermont. He lights a cigarette. He goes on reading. He takes a second sip of his

drink. Everyone in the room—the three or four men scattered along the bar, the tall, thin bartender and several people in the booths at the back—watches him do these ordinary things.

He has got to the classified section, is perhaps searching for someone willing to come in once a week and clean his apartment, when the woman who will turn out to be Sarah Cole leaves a booth in the back and approaches him. She comes up from the side and sits next to him. She's wearing heavy tan cowboy boots and a dark brown suede cowboy hat, lumpy jeans and a yellow T-shirt that clings to her arms, breasts and round belly like the skin of a sausage. Though he will later learn that she is thirty-eight years old, she looks older by about ten years, which makes her look about twenty years older than he actually is. (It's difficult to guess accurately how old Ron is; he looks anywhere from a mature twenty-five to a youthful forty, so his actual age doesn't seem to matter.)

"It's not bad here at the bar," she says, looking around. "More light, anyhow. Whatcha readin'?" she asks brightly, planting both elbows on the bar.

Ron looks up from his paper with a slight smile on his lips, sees the face of a woman homelier than any he has ever seen or imagined before, and goes on smiling lightly. He feels himself falling into her tiny, slightly crossed, dark brown eyes, pulls himself back, and studies for a few seconds her mottled, pocked complexion, bulbous nose, loose mouth, twisted and gapped teeth and heavy but receding chin. He casts a glance over her thatch of dun-colored hair and along her neck and throat, where acne burns against gray skin, and returns to her eyes and again feels himself falling into her.

"What did you say?" he asks.

She knocks a mentholated cigarette from her pack, and Ron swiftly lights it. 10
Blowing smoke from her large, wing-shaped nostrils, she speaks again. Her voice is thick and nasal, a chocolate-colored voice. "I asked you whatcha readin', but I can see now." She belts out a single, loud laugh. "The paper!"

Ron laughs too. "The paper! The *Concord Monitor!*" He is not hallucinating, he clearly sees what is before him and admits—no, he asserts—to himself that he is speaking to the most unattractive woman he has ever seen, a fact that fascinates him, as if instead he were speaking to the most beautiful woman he has ever seen or perhaps ever will see, so he treasures the moment, attempts to hold it as if it were a golden ball, a disproportionately heavy object which—if he does not hold it lightly, with precision and firmness—will slip from his hand and roll across the lawn to the lip of the well and down, down to the bottom of the well, lost to him forever. It will be a memory, that's all, something to speak of wistfully and with wonder as over the years the image fades and comes in the end to exist only in the telling. His mind and body waken from their sleepy self-absorption, and all his attention focuses on the woman, Sarah Cole, her ugly face, like a warthog's, her thick, rapid speech, her dumpy, off-center wreck of a body. To keep this moment here before him, he begins to ask questions of her, he buys her a drink, he smiles, until soon it seems, even to him, that he is taking her and her life, its vicissitudes and woe, quite seriously.

He learns her name, of course, and she volunteers the information that she spoke to him on a dare from one of the two women still sitting in the booth behind her. She turns on her stool and smiles brazenly, triumphantly, at her friends, two women, also homely (though nowhere as homely as she), and dressed, like her, in cowboy boots, hats and jeans. One of the women, a blond with an underslung jaw and wearing heavy eye makeup, flips a little wave at her, and as if embarrassed, she and the other woman at the booth turn back to their drinks and sip fiercely at straws.

Sarah returns to Ron and goes on telling him what he wants to know, about her job at Rumford Press, about her divorced husband, who was a bastard and stupid and "sick," she says, as if filling suddenly with sympathy for the man. She tells Ron about her three children, the youngest, a girl, in junior high school and boy-crazy, the other two, boys, in high school and almost never at home anymore. She speaks of her children with genuine tenderness and concern and Ron is touched. He can see with what pleasure and pain she speaks of her children; he watches her tiny eyes light up and water over when he asks their names.

"You're a nice woman," he informs her.

15   She smiles, looks at her empty glass. "No. No, I'm not. But you're a nice man, to tell me that."

Ron, with a gesture, asks the bartender to refill Sarah's glass. She is drinking white Russians. Perhaps she has been drinking them for an hour or two, for she seems very relaxed, more relaxed than women usually do when they come up and without introduction or invitation speak to Ron.

She asks him about himself, his job, his divorce, how long he has lived in Concord, but he finds that he is not at all interested in telling her about himself. He wants to know about her, even though what she has to tell him about herself is predictable and ordinary and the way she tells it unadorned and clichéd. He wonders about her husband. What kind of man would fall in love with Sarah Cole?

2

That scene, at Osgood's Lounge in Concord, ended with Ron's departure, alone, after having bought Sarah a second drink, and Sarah's return to her friends in the booth. I don't know what she told them, but it's not hard to imagine. The three women were not close friends, merely fellow workers at Rumford Press, where they stood at the end of a long conveyor belt day after day packing *TV Guides* into cartons. They all hated their jobs, and frequently after work, when they worked the day shift, they would put on their cowboy hats and boots, which they kept all day in their lockers, and stop for a drink or two on their way home. This had been their first visit to Osgood's, however, a place that, prior to this, they had avoided out of a sneering belief that no one went there but lawyers and insurance men. It had been Sarah who had asked the others why that should keep them away, and when they had no answer for her, the three had decided to stop at Osgood's. Ron was right, they had been there over an hour when he came in, and Sarah was a little drunk. "We'll hafta come in here again," she said to her friends, her voice rising slightly.

Which they did, that Friday, and once again Ron appeared with his evening newspaper. He put his briefcase down next to his stool and ordered a drink and proceeded to read the front page, slowly, deliberately, clearly a weary, unhurried, solitary man.

He did not notice the three women in cowboy hats and boots in the booth in back, but they saw him, and after a few minutes Sarah was once again at his side.

"Hi."   20

He turned, saw her, and instantly regained the moment he had lost when, two nights ago, once outside the bar and on his way home, he had forgotten about the ugliest woman he had ever seen. She seemed even more grotesque to him now than before, which made the moment all the more precious to him, and so once again he held the moment as if in his hands and began to speak with her, to ask questions, to offer his opinions and solicit hers.

I said earlier that I am the man in this story and my friend Sarah Cole, now dead, is the woman. I think back to that night, the second time I had seen Sarah, and I tremble, not with fear but in shame. My concern then, when I was first becoming involved with Sarah, was merely with the moment, holding on to it, grasping it wholly, as if its beginning did not grow out of some other prior moment in her life and my life separately and at the same time did not lead into future moments in our separate lives. She talked more easily than she had the night before, and I listened as eagerly and carefully as I had before, again with the same motives, to keep her in front of me, to draw her forward from the context of her life and place her, as if she were an object, into the context of mine. I did not know how cruel this was. When you have never done a thing before and that thing is not simply and clearly right or wrong, you frequently do not know if it is a cruel thing, you just go ahead and do it and maybe later you'll be able to determine whether you acted cruelly. That way you'll know if it was right or wrong of you to have done it in the first place; too late, of course, but at least you'll know.

While we drank, Sarah told me that she hated her ex-husband because of the way he treated the children. "It's not so much the money," she said, nervously wagging her booted feet from her perch on the high barstool. "I mean, I get by, barely, but I get them fed and clothed on my own okay. It's because he won't even write them a letter or anything. He won't call them on the phone, all he calls for is to bitch at me because I'm trying to get the state to take him to court so I can get some of the money he's s'posed to be paying for child support. And he won't even think to talk to the kids when he calls. Won't even ask about them."

"He sounds like a sonofabitch."

"He is, he is!" she said. "I don't know why I married him. Or stayed married.   25 Fourteen years, for Christ's sake. He put a spell over me or something. I don't know," she said, with a note of wistfulness in her voice. "He wasn't what you'd call good-looking."

After her second drink, she decided she had to leave. Her children were at home, it was Friday night and she liked to make sure she ate supper with them and knew where they were going and who they were with when they went out on their dates. "No dates on school nights," she said to me. "I mean, you gotta have rules, you know."

I agreed, and we left together, everyone in the place following us with his or her gaze. I was aware of that, I knew what they were thinking, and I didn't care, because I was simply walking her to her car.

It was a cool evening, dusk settling onto the lot like a gray blanket. Her car, a huge, dark green Buick sedan at least ten years old, was battered almost beyond use. She reached for the door handle on the driver's side and yanked. Nothing. The door wouldn't open. She tried again. Then I tried. Still nothing.

Then I saw it, a V-shaped dent in the left front fender, binding the metal of the door against the metal of the fender in a large crimp that held the door fast. "Someone must've backed into you while you were inside," I said to her.

30   She came forward and studied the crimp for a few seconds, and when she looked back at me, she was weeping. "Jesus, Jesus, Jesus!" she wailed, her large, froglike mouth wide open and wet with spit, her red tongue flopping loosely over gapped teeth. "I can't pay for this! I *can't!*" Her face was red, and even in the dusky light I could see it puff out with weeping, her tiny eyes seeming almost to disappear behind wet cheeks. Her shoulders slumped, and her hands fell limply to her sides.

Placing my briefcase on the ground, I reached out to her and put my arms around her body and held her close to me, while she cried wetly into my shoulder. After a few seconds, she started pulling herself back together and her weeping got reduced to snuffling. Her cowboy hat had been pushed back and now clung to her head at a precarious, absurdly jaunty angle. She took a step away from me and said, "I'll get in the other side."

"Okay," I said, almost in a whisper. "That's fine."

Slowly, she walked around the front of the huge, ugly vehicle and opened the door on the passenger's side and slid awkwardly across the seat until she had positioned herself behind the steering wheel. Then she started the motor, which came to life with a roar. The muffler was shot. Without saying another word to me or even waving, she dropped the car into reverse gear and backed it loudly out of the parking space and headed out of the lot to the street.

I turned and started for my car, when I happened to glance toward the door of the bar, and there, staring after me, were the bartender, the two women who had come in with Sarah, and two of the men who had been sitting at the bar. They were lawyers, and I knew them slightly. They were grinning at me. I grinned back and got into my car, and then, without looking at them again, I left the place and drove straight to my apartment.

3

35   One night several weeks later, Ron meets Sarah at Osgood's, and after buying her three white Russians and drinking three Scotches himself, he takes her back to his apartment in his car—a Datsun fastback coupe that she says she admires—for the sole purpose of making love to her.

I'm still the man in this story, and Sarah is still the woman, but I'm telling it this way because what I have to tell you now confuses me, embarrasses me and makes me sad, and consequently I'm likely to tell it falsely. I'm likely to cover the truth by making Sarah a better woman than she actually was, while making me appear worse than I actually was or am; or else I'll do the opposite, make Sarah worse than she was and me better. The truth is, I was pretty, extremely so, and she was not, extremely so, and

I knew it and she knew it. She walked out the door of Osgood's determined to make love to a man much prettier than any she had seen up close before, and I walked out determined to make love to a woman much homelier than any I had made love to before. We were, in a sense, equals.

No, that's not exactly true. (You see? This is why I have to tell the story the way I'm telling it.) I'm not at all sure she feels as Ron does. That is to say, perhaps she genuinely likes the man, in spite of his being the most physically attractive man she has ever known. Perhaps she is more aware of her homeliness than of his beauty, for Ron, despite what I may have implied, does not think of himself as especially beautiful. He merely knows that other people think of him that way. As I said before, he is a nice man.

Ron unlocks the door to his apartment, walks in ahead of her and flicks on the lamp beside the couch. It's a small, single-bedroom, modern apartment, one of thirty identical apartments in a large brick building on the Heights just east of downtown Concord. Sarah stands nervously at the door, peering in.

"Come in, come in," Ron says.

She steps timidly in and closes the door behind her. She removes her cowboy hat, then quickly puts it back on, crosses the living room and plops down in a blond easy chair, seeming to shrink in its hug out of sight to safety. Behind her, Ron, at the entry to the kitchen, places one hand on her shoulder, and she stiffens. He removes his hand.

"Would you like a drink?"

"No . . . I guess not," she says, staring straight ahead at the wall opposite, where a large framed photograph of a bicyclist advertises in French the Tour de France. Around a corner, in an alcove off the living room, a silver-gray ten-speed bicycle leans casually against the wall, glistening and poised, slender as a thoroughbred racehorse.

"I don't know," she says. Ron is in the kitchen now, making himself a drink. "I don't know . . . I don't know."

"What? Change your mind? I can make a white Russian for you. Vodka, cream, Kahlua and ice, right?"

Sarah tries to cross her legs, but she is sitting too low in the chair and her legs are too thick at the thigh, so she ends, after a struggle, with one leg in the air and the other twisted on its side. She looks as if she has fallen from a great height.

Ron steps out from the kitchen, peers over the back of the chair, and watches her untangle herself, then ducks back into the kitchen. After a few seconds, he returns. "Seriously. Want me to fix you a white Russian?"

"No."

Ron, again from behind and above her, places one hand on Sarah's shoulder, and this time she does not stiffen, though she does not exactly relax, either. She sits there, a block of wood, staring straight ahead.

"Are you scared?" he asks gently. Then he adds, "*I* am."

"Well, no. I'm not scared." She remains silent for a moment. "You're scared? Of what?" She turns to face him but avoids his blue eyes.

"Well . . . I don't do this all the time, you know. Bring home a woman I . . . ," he trails off.

"Picked up in a bar."

"No. I mean, I like you, Sarah. I really do. And I didn't just pick you up in a bar, you know that. We've gotten to be friends, you and me."

"You want to sleep with me?" she asks, still not meeting his steady gaze.

55   "Yes." He seems to mean it. He does not take a gulp or even a sip from his drink. He just says, "Yes," straight out, and cleanly, not too quickly, either, and not after a hesitant delay. A simple statement of a simple fact. The man wants to make love to the woman. She asked him, and he told her. What could be simpler?

"Do you want to sleep with *me?*" he asks.

She turns around in the chair, faces the wall again, and says in a low voice, "Sure I do, but . . . it's hard to explain."

"What? But what?" Placing his glass down on the table between the chair and the sofa, he puts both hands on her shoulders and lightly kneads them. He knows he can be discouraged from pursuing this, but he is not sure how easily. Having got this far without bumping against obstacles (except the ones he has placed in his way himself), he is not sure what it will take to turn him back. He does not know, therefore, how assertive or how seductive he should be with her. He suspects that he can be stopped very easily, so he is reluctant to give her a chance to try. He goes on kneading her doughy shoulders.

"You and me . . . we're real different." She glances at the bicycle in the corner.

60   "A man . . . and a woman," he says.

"No, not that. I mean, different. That's all. Real different. More than you . . . You're nice, but you don't know what I mean, and that's one of the things that makes you so nice. But we're different. Listen," she says, "I gotta go. I gotta leave now."

The man removes his hands and retrieves his glass, takes a sip and watches her over the rim of the glass, as, not without difficulty, the woman rises from the chair and moves swiftly toward the door. She stops at the door, squares her hat on her head, and glances back at him.

"We can be friends, okay?"

"Okay. Friends."

65   "I'll see you again down at Osgood's, right?"

"Oh, yeah, sure."

"Good. See you," she says, opening the door.

The door closes. The man walks around the sofa, snaps on the television set, and sits down in front of it. He picks up a *TV Guide* from the coffee table and flips through it, stops, runs a finger down the listings, stops, puts down the magazine and changes the channel. He does not once connect the magazine in his hand to the woman who has just left his apartment, even though he knows she spends her days packing *TV Guides* into cartons that get shipped to warehouses in distant parts of New England. He'll think of the connection some other night, but by then the connection will be merely sentimental. It'll be too late for him to understand what she meant by "different."

4

But that's not the point of my story. Certainly, it's an aspect of the story, the political aspect, if you want, but it's not the reason I'm trying to tell the story in the first place. I'm trying to tell the story so that I can understand what happened between me and Sarah Cole that summer and early autumn ten years ago. To say we were lovers says very little about what happened; to say we were friends says even less. No, if I'm to understand the whole thing, I'll have to say the whole thing, for, in the end, what I need to know is whether what happened between me and Sarah Cole was right or wrong. Character is fate, which suggests that if a man can know and then to some degree control his character, he can know and to that same degree control his fate.

But let me go on with my story. The next time Sarah and I were together we were at her apartment in the south end of Concord, a second-floor flat in a tenement building on Perley Street. I had stayed away from Osgood's for several weeks, deliberately trying to avoid running into Sarah there, though I never quite put it that way to myself. I found excuses and generated interest in and reasons for going elsewhere after work. Yet I was obsessed with Sarah by then, obsessed with the idea of making love to her, which, because it was not an actual *desire* to make love to her, was an unusually complex obsession. Passion without desire, if it gets expressed, may in fact be a kind of rape, and perhaps I sensed the danger that lay behind my obsession and for that reason went out of my way to avoid meeting Sarah again.

Yet I did meet her, inadvertently, of course. After picking up shirts at the cleaner's on South Main and Perley streets, I'd gone down Perley on my way to South State and the post office. It was a Saturday morning, and this trip on my bicycle was part of my regular Saturday routine. I did not remember that Sarah lived on Perley Street, although she had told me several times in a complaining way—it's a rough neighborhood, packed-dirt yards, shabby apartment buildings, the carcasses of old, half-stripped cars on cinder blocks in the driveways, broken red and yellow plastic tricycles on the cracked sidewalks—but as soon as I saw her, I remembered. It was too late to avoid meeting her. I was riding my bike, wearing shorts and T-shirt, the package containing my folded and starched shirts hooked to the carrier behind me, and she was walking toward me along the sidewalk, lugging two large bags of groceries. She saw me, and I stopped. We talked, and I offered to carry her groceries for her. I took the bags while she led the bike, handling it carefully, as if she were afraid she might break it.

At the stoop we came to a halt. The wooden steps were cluttered with half-opened garbage bags spilling eggshells, coffee grounds and old food wrappers to the walkway. "I can't get the people downstairs to take care of their garbage," she explained. She leaned the bike against the banister and reached for her groceries.

"I'll carry them up for you," I said. I directed her to loop the chain lock from the bike to the banister rail and snap it shut and told her to bring my shirts up with her.

"Maybe you'd like a beer?" she said as she opened the door to the darkened hallway. Narrow stairs disappeared in front of me into heavy, damp darkness, and the air smelled like old newspapers.

75   "Sure," I said, and followed her up.

"Sorry there's no light. I can't get them to fix it."

"No matter. I can see you and follow along," I said, and even in the dim light of the hall I could see the large, dark blue veins that cascaded thickly down the backs of her legs. She wore tight, white-duck Bermuda shorts, rubber shower sandals and a pink sleeveless sweater. I pictured her in the cashier's line at the supermarket. I would have been behind her, a stranger, and on seeing her, I would have turned away and studied the covers of the magazines, *TV Guide, People,* the *National Enquirer,* for there was nothing of interest in her appearance that in the hard light of day would not have slightly embarrassed me. Yet here I was inviting myself into her home, eagerly staring at the backs of her ravaged legs, her sad, tasteless clothing, her poverty. I was not detached, however, was not staring at her with scientific curiosity, and because of my passion, did not feel or believe that what I was doing was perverse. I felt warmed by her presence and was flirtatious and bold, a little pushy, even.

Picture this. The man, tanned, limber, wearing red jogging shorts, Italian leather sandals, a clinging net T-shirt of Scandinavian design and manufacture, enters the apartment behind the woman, whose dough-colored skin, thick, short body and homely, uncomfortable face all try, but fail, to hide themselves. She waves him toward the table in the kitchen, where he sets down the bags and looks good-naturedly around the room. "What about the beer you bribed me with?" he asks.

The apartment is dark and cluttered with old, oversized furniture, yard sale and secondhand stuff bought originally for a large house in the country or a spacious apartment on a boulevard forty or fifty years ago, passed down from antique dealer to used-furniture store to yard sale to thrift shop, where it finally gets purchased by Sarah Cole and gets hauled over to Perley Street and shoved up the narrow stairs, she and her children grunting and sweating in the darkness of the hallway—overstuffed armchairs and couch, huge, ungainly dressers, upholstered rocking chairs, and in the kitchen, an old flat-topped maple desk for a table, a half-dozen heavy oak dining room chairs, a high, glass-fronted cabinet, all peeling, stained, chipped and squatting heavily on a dark green linoleum floor.

80   The place is neat and arranged in a more or less orderly way, however, and the man seems comfortable there. He strolls from the kitchen to the living room and peeks into the three small bedrooms that branch off a hallway behind the living room. "Nice place!" he calls to the woman. He is studying the framed pictures of her three children arranged as if on an altar atop the buffet. "Nice-looking kids!" he calls out. They are. Blond, round-faced, clean and utterly ordinary-looking, their pleasant faces glance, as instructed, slightly off camera and down to the right, as if they are trying to remember the name of the capital of Montana.

When he returns to the kitchen, the woman is putting away her groceries, her back to him. "Where's that beer you bribed me with?" he asks again. He takes a position against the doorframe, his weight on one hip, like a dancer resting. "You sure are quiet today, Sarah," he says in a low voice. "Everything okay?"

Silently, she turns away from the grocery bags, crosses the room to the man, reaches up to him, and holding him by the head, kisses his mouth, rolls her torso against his, drops her hands to his hips and yanks him tightly to her and goes on kissing him, eyes closed, working her face furiously against his. The man places his hands on her shoulders and pulls away, and they face each other, wide-eyed, as if amazed and frightened. The man drops his hands, and the woman lets go of his hips. Then, after a few seconds, the man silently turns, goes to the door, and leaves. The last thing he sees as he closes the door behind him is the woman standing in the kitchen doorframe, her face looking down and slightly to one side, wearing the same pleasant expression on her face as her children in their photographs, trying to re-member the capital of Montana.

5

Sarah appeared at my apartment door the following morning, a Sunday, cool and rainy. She had brought me the package of freshly laundered shirts I'd left in her kitchen, and when I opened the door to her, she simply held the package out to me, as if it were a penitent's gift. She wore a yellow rain slicker and cap and looked more like a disconsolate schoolgirl facing an angry teacher than a grown woman dropping a package off at a friend's apartment. After all, she had nothing to be ashamed of.

I invited her inside, and she accepted my invitation. I had been reading the Sun-day *New York Times* on the couch and drinking coffee, lounging through the gray morning in bathrobe and pajamas. I told her to take off her wet raincoat and hat and hang them in the closet by the door and started for the kitchen to get her a cup of coffee, when I stopped, turned and looked at her. She closed the closet door on her yellow raincoat and hat, turned around and faced me.

What else can I do? I must describe it. I remember that moment of ten years ago as if it occurred ten minutes ago, the package of shirts on the table behind her, the newspapers scattered over the couch and floor, the sound of wind-blown rain wash-ing the side of the building outside and the silence of the room, as we stood across from one another and watched, while we each simultaneously removed our own clothing, my robe, her blouse and skirt, my pajama top, her slip and bra, my pajama bottom, her underpants, until we were both standing naked in the harsh gray light, two naked members of the same species, a male and a female, the male somewhat younger and less scarred than the female, the female somewhat less delicately con-structed than the male, both individuals pale-skinned, with dark thatches of hair in the area of their genitals, both individuals standing slackly, as if a great, protracted tension between them had at last been released. 85

6

We made love that morning in my bed for long hours that drifted easily into after-noon. And we talked, as people usually do when they spend half a day or half a night in bed together. I told her of my past, named and described the people whom I had loved and had loved me, my ex-wife in New York, my brother in the air force, my mother in San Diego, and I told her of my ambitions and dreams and even confessed some of my fears. She listened patiently and intelligently throughout and talked much less than I. She had already told me many of these things about herself, and perhaps whatever she had to say to me now lay on the next inner circle of intimacy or else could not be spoken of at all.

During the next few weeks, we met and made love often, and always at my apartment. On arriving home from work, I would phone her, or if not, she would phone me, and after a few feints and dodges, one would suggest to the other that we get together tonight, and a half hour later she'd be at my door. Our lovemaking was passionate, skillful, kindly and deeply satisfying. We didn't often speak of it to one another or brag about it, the way some couples do when they are surprised by the ease with which they have become contented lovers. We did occasionally joke and tease each other, however, playfully acknowledging that the only thing we did together was make love but that we did it so frequently there was no time for anything else.

Then one hot night, a Saturday in August, we were lying in bed atop the tangled sheets, smoking cigarettes and chatting idly, and Sarah suggested that we go out for a drink.

"Out? Now?"

90   "Sure. It's early. What time is it?"

I scanned the digital clock next to the bed. "Nine forty-nine."

"There. See?"

"That's not so early. You usually go home by eleven, you know. It's almost ten."

"No, it's only a little after nine. Depends on how you look at things. Besides, Ron, it's Saturday night. Don't you want to go out and dance or something? Or is this the only thing you know how to do?" she said, and poked me in the ribs. "You know how to dance? You like to dance?"

95   "Yeah, sure . . . sure, but not tonight. It's too hot. And I'm tired."

But she persisted, happily pointing out that an air-conditioned bar would be as cool as my apartment, and we didn't have to go to a dance bar, we could go to Osgood's. "As a compromise," she said.

I suggested a place called the El Rancho, a restaurant with a large, dark cocktail lounge and dance bar located several miles from town on the old Portsmouth highway. Around nine the restaurant closed and the bar became something of a roadhouse, with a small country-and-western band and a clientele drawn from the four or five villages that adjoined Concord on the north and east. I had eaten at the restaurant once but had never gone to the bar, and I didn't know anyone who had.

Sarah was silent for a moment. Then she lighted a cigarette and drew the sheet over her naked body. "You don't want anybody to know about us, do you? Do you?"

"That's not it. . . . I just don't like gossip, and I work with a lot of people who show up sometimes at Osgood's. On a Saturday night especially."

100   "No," she said firmly. "You're ashamed of being seen with me. You'll sleep with me, all right, but you won't go out in public with me."

"That's not true, Sarah."

She was silent again. Relieved, I reached across her to the bed table and got my cigarettes and lighter.

"You owe me, Ron," she said suddenly, as I passed over her. "You owe me."

"What?" I lay back, lighted a cigarette, and covered my body with the sheet.

"I said, 'You owe me.'"

"I don't know what you're talking about, Sarah. I just don't like a lot of gossip going around, that's all. I like keeping my private life private, that's all. I don't *owe* you anything."

"Friendship you owe me. And respect. Friendship and respect. A person can't do what you've done with me without owing them friendship and respect."

"Sarah, I really don't know what you're talking about," I said. "I am your friend, you know that. And I respect you. I do."

"You really think so, don't you?"

"Yes. Of course."

She said nothing for several long moments. Then she sighed and in a low, almost inaudible voice said, "Then you'll have to go out in public with me. I don't care about Osgood's or the people you work with, we don't have to go there or see any of them," she said. "But you're gonna have to go to places like the El Rancho with me, and a few other places I know, too, where there's people *I* know, people *I* work with, and maybe we'll even go to a couple of parties, because *I* get invited to parties sometimes, you know. I have friends, and I have some family, too, and you're gonna have to meet my family. My kids think I'm just going around barhopping when I'm over here with you, and I don't like that, so you're gonna have to meet them so I can tell them where I am when I'm not at home nights. And sometimes you're gonna come over and spend the evening at my place!" Her voice had risen as she heard her demands and felt their rightness, until now she was almost shouting at me. "You *owe* that to me. Or else you're a bad man. It's that simple, Ron."

It was.

7

The handsome man is overdressed. He is wearing a navy blue blazer, taupe shirt open at the throat, white slacks, white loafers. Everyone else, including the homely woman with the handsome man, is dressed appropriately—that is, like everyone else—jeans and cowboy boots, blouses or cowboy shirts or T-shirts with catchy sayings or the names of country-and-western singers printed across the front, and many of the women are wearing cowboy hats pushed back and tied under their chins.

The man doesn't know anyone at the bar or, if they're at a party, in the room, but the woman knows most of the people there, and she gladly introduces him. The men grin and shake his hand, slap him on his jacketed shoulder, ask him where he works, what's his line, after which they lapse into silence. The women flirt briefly with their faces, but they lapse into silence even before the men do. The woman with the man in the blazer does most of the talking for everyone. She talks for the man in the blazer, for the men standing around the refrigerator, or if they're at a bar, for the other men at the table, and for the other women too. She chats and rambles aimlessly through loud monologues, laughs uproariously at trivial jokes and drinks too much, until soon she is drunk, thick-tongued, clumsy, and the man has to say her goodbyes and ease her out the door to his car and drive her home to her apartment on Perley Street.

115   This happens twice in one week and then three times the next—at the El Rancho, at the Ox Bow in Northwood, at Rita and Jimmy's apartment on Thorndike Street, out in Warner at Betsy Beeler's new house and, the last time, at a cottage on Lake Sunapee rented by some kids in shipping at Rumford Press. Ron no longer calls Sarah when he gets home from work; he waits for her call, and sometimes, when he knows it's she, he doesn't answer the phone. Usually, he lets it ring five or six times, and then he reaches down and picks up the receiver. He has taken his jacket and vest off and loosened his tie and is about to put his supper, frozen manicotti, into the radar range.

"Hello?"

"Hi."

"How're you doing?"

"Okay, I guess. A little tired."

120   "Still hung over?"

"Naw. Not really. Just tired. I hate Mondays."

"You have fun last night?"

"Well, yeah, sorta. It's nice out there, at the lake. Listen," she says, brightening. "Whyn't you come over here tonight? The kids're all going out later, but if you come over before eight, you can meet them. They really want to meet you."

"You told them about me?"

125   "Sure. Long time ago. I'm not supposed to tell my own kids?"

Ron is silent.

She says, "You don't want to come over here tonight. You don't want to meet my kids. No, you don't want my kids to meet *you,* that's it."

"No, no, it's just . . . I've got a lot of work to do. . . ."

"We should talk," she announces in a flat voice.

130   "Yes," he says. "We should talk."

They agree that she will meet him at his apartment, and they'll talk, and they say goodbye and hang up.

While Ron is heating his supper and then eating it alone at his kitchen table and Sarah is feeding her children, perhaps I should admit, since we are nearing the end of my story, that I don't actually know that Sarah Cole is dead. A few years ago I happened to run into one of her friends from the press, a blond woman with an underslung jaw. Her name, she reminded me, was Glenda; she had seen me at Osgood's a couple of times and we had met at the El Rancho once when I had gone there with Sarah. I was amazed that she could remember me and a little embarrassed that I did not recognize her at all, and she laughed at that and said, "You haven't changed much, mister!" I pretended to recognize her then, but I think she knew she was a stranger to me. We were standing outside the Sears store on South Main Street, where I had gone to buy paint. I had recently remarried, and my wife and I were redecorating my apartment.

"Whatever happened to Sarah?" I asked Glenda. "Is she still down at the press?"

"Jeez, no! She left a long time ago. Way back. I heard she went back with her ex-husband. I can't remember his name, something Cole. Eddie Cole, maybe."

135   I asked her if she was sure of that, and she said no, she had only heard it around the bars and down at the press, but she had assumed it was true. People said Sarah

had moved back with her ex-husband and was living for a while with him and the kids in a trailer in a park near Hooksett, and then when the kids, or at least the boys, got out of school, the rest of them moved down to Florida or someplace because he was out of work. He was a carpenter, she thought.

"He was mean to her," I said. "I thought he used to beat her up and everything. I thought she hated him."

"Oh, well, yeah, he was a bastard, all right. I met him a couple times, and I didn't like him. Short, ugly and mean when he got drunk. But you know what they say."

"What do they say?"

"Oh, you know, about water seeking its own level and all."

"Sarah wasn't mean when she was drunk."   140

The woman laughed. "Naw, but she sure was short and ugly!"

I said nothing.

"Hey, don't get me wrong," Glenda said. "I liked Sarah. But you and her . . . well, you sure made a funny-looking couple. She probably didn't feel so self-conscious and all with her husband," she said somberly. "I mean, with you, all tall and blond, and poor old Sarah . . . I mean, the way them kids in the press room used to kid her about her looks, it was embarrassing just to have to hear it."

"Well . . . I loved her," I said.

The woman raised her plucked eyebrow in disbelief. She smiled. "Sure, you did,   145
honey," she said, and she patted me on the arm. "Sure, you did." Then she let the smile drift off her face, turned and walked away from me.

When someone you have loved dies, you accept the fact of his or her death, but then the person goes on living in your memory, dreams and reveries. You have imaginary conversations with him or her, you see something striking and remind yourself to tell your loved one about it and then get brought up short by the knowledge of the fact of his or her death, and at night, in your sleep, the dead person visits you. With Sarah, none of that happened. When she was gone from my life, she was gone absolutely, as if she had never existed in the first place. It was only later, when I could think of her as dead and could come out and say it, my friend Sarah Cole is dead, that I was able to tell this story, for that is when she began to enter my memories, my dreams and my reveries. In that way, I learned that I truly did love her, and now I have begun to grieve over her death, to wish her alive again, so that I can say to her the things I could not know or say when she was alive, when I did not know that I loved her.

8

The woman arrives at Ron's apartment around eight. He hears her car, because of the broken muffler, blat and rumble into the parking lot below, and he crosses quickly from the kitchen and peers out the living room window and, as if through a telescope, watches her shove herself across the seat to the passenger's side to get out of the car, then walk slowly in the dusky light toward the apartment building. It's a warm evening, and she's wearing her white Bermuda shorts, pink sleeveless sweater and shower sandals. Ron hates those clothes. He hates the way the shorts cut into her flesh at the crotch and thigh, hates the large, dark caves below her arms that get exposed by the sweater, hates the sucking noise made by the sandals.

Shortly, there is a soft knock at his door. He opens it, turns away and crosses to the kitchen, where he turns back, lights a cigarette and watches her. She closes the door. He offers her a drink, which she declines, and somewhat formally, he invites her to sit down. She sits carefully on the sofa, in the middle, with her feet close together on the floor, as if she were being interviewed for a job. Then he comes around and sits in the easy chair, relaxed, one leg slung over the other at the knee, as if he were interviewing her for the job.

"Well," he says, "you wanted to talk."

150   "Yes. But now you're mad at me. I can see that. I didn't do anything, Ron."

"I'm not mad at you."

They are silent for a moment. Ron goes on smoking his cigarette.

Finally, she sighs and says, "You don't want to see me anymore, do you?"

He waits a few seconds and answers, "Yes. That's right." Getting up from the chair, he walks to the silver-gray bicycle and stands before it, running a fingertip along the slender crossbar from the saddle to the chrome-plated handlebars.

155   "You're a sonofabitch," she says in a low voice. "You're worse than my exhusband." Then she smiles meanly, almost sneers, and soon he realizes that she is telling him that she won't leave. He's stuck with her, she informs him with cold precision. "You think I'm just so much meat, and all you got to do is call up the butcher shop and cancel your order. Well, now you're going to find out different. You *can't* cancel your order. I'm not meat, I'm not one of your pretty little girlfriends who come running when you want them and go away when you get tired of them. I'm *different!* I got nothing to lose, Ron. Nothing. So you're stuck with me, Ron."

He continues stroking his bicycle. "No, I'm not."

She sits back in the couch and crosses her legs at the ankles. "I think I *will* have that drink you offered."

"Look, Sarah, it would be better if you go now."

"No," she says flatly. "You offered me a drink when I came in. Nothing's changed since I've been here. Not for me and not for you. I'd like that drink you offered," she says haughtily.

160   Ron turns away from the bicycle and takes a step toward her. His face has stiffened into a mask. "Enough is enough," he says through clenched teeth. "I've given you enough."

"Fix me a drink, will you, honey?" she says with a phony smile.

Ron orders her to leave.

She refuses.

He grabs her by the arm and yanks her to her feet.

165   She starts crying lightly. She stands there and looks up into his face and weeps, but she does not move toward the door, so he pushes her. She regains her balance and goes on weeping.

He stands back and places his fists on his hips and looks at her. "Go on, go on and leave, you ugly bitch," he says to her, and as he says the words, as one by one they leave his mouth, she's transformed into the most beautiful woman he has ever seen. He says the words again, almost tenderly. "Leave, you ugly bitch." Her hair is golden, her brown eyes deep and sad, her mouth full and affectionate, her tears the tears of love and loss, and her pleading, outstretched arms, her entire body, the arms and body of a devoted woman's cruelly rejected love. A third time he says the words. "Leave me now, you disgusting, ugly bitch." She is wrapped in an envelope of golden light, a warm, dense haze that she seems to have stepped into, as into a carriage. And then she is gone, and he is alone again.

He looks around the room, as if searching for her. Sitting down in the easy chair, he places his face in his hands. It's not as if she has died; it's as if he has killed her.

QUESTIONS FOR DISCUSSION AND WRITING

1. How does the narrator's decision to be seen in public with Sarah mark a change in the plot? Why can the narrator tell this story only after he imagines that Sarah is dead?

2. Why does the narrator insist on providing so much physical detail about the characters, especially Sarah? To what extent does he live up to his characterization of himself as "nice"?

3. How do the descriptions of the two apartments reveal the characters' lives, values, and inevitable conflict? What does the bicycle come to symbolize in the story?

4. How are the shifting points of view in the story marked by *I, Ron,* and *the man?* Why does the narrator admit that he is likely to "tell [the story] falsely"?

5. What does the title suggest about the theme of love in the story? What does Ron think he has learned about love? Is his explanation convincing?

Stories for Comparison

Elizabeth Bowen's "The Demon Lover" (pages 299–304); Doris Lessing's "A Woman on a Roof" (pages 804–811).

21

·····································

F I O N A   B A R R

The Wall-Reader

FIONA BARR was born in 1952 in Derry, Northern Ireland, and currently
works as television critic for the *Irish News.* She has published numerous
short stories, many of them adapted for broadcast. "Sisters," first published in
a collection of the same name by Blackstaff Press, is being adapted for the
BBC. "The Wall-Reader," which received first place in the Maxwell House
Women Writer's Competition in 1978, reveals how a young woman's attempt
at ordinary conversation has extraordinary consequences.

S hall only our rivers run free?" The question jumped out from the cobbled wall in
huge white letters, as The People's taxi swung round the corner at Beechmount.
"Looks like paint is running freely enough down here," she thought to herself, as
other slogans glided past in rapid succession. Reading Belfast's grim graffiti had become an entertaining hobby for her, and she often wondered, was it in the dead of
night that groups of boys huddled round a paint tin daubing walls and gables with
tired political slogans and clichés? Did anyone ever see them? Was the guilty brush
ever found? The brush is mightier than the bomb, she declared inwardly, as she
thought of how celebrated among journalists some lines had become. "Is there a life
before death?" Well, no one had answered that one yet, at least, not in this city.

The shapes of Belfast crowded in on her as the taxi rattled over the ramps outside the fortressed police barracks. Dilapidated houses, bricked-up terraces. Rosy-
cheeked soldiers, barely out of school, and quivering with high-pitched fear. She
thought of the thick-lipped youth who came to hijack the car, making his point by
showing his revolver under his anorak, and of the others, jigging and taunting every
July, almost sexual in their arrogance and hatred. Meanwhile, passengers climbed in
and out at various points along the road, maneuvering between legs, bags of shopping and umbrellas. The taxi swerved blindly into the road. No Highway Code here.
As the woman's stop approached, the taxi swung up to the pavement, and she
stepped out.

She thought of how she read walls—like tea-cups, she smiled to herself. Pushing her baby in the pram to the supermarket, she had to pass under a motorway

bridge that was peppered with lines, some in irregular lettering with the paint dribbling down the concrete, others written with felt-tip pen in minute secretive hand. A whole range of human emotions splayed itself with persistent anarchy on the walls. "One could do worse than be a reader of walls," she thought, twisting Frost's words. Instead, though, the pram was rushed past the intriguing mural with much gusto. Respectable housewives don't read walls!

The "Troubles," as they were euphemistically named, remained for this couple as a remote, vaguely irritating wart on their life. They were simply ordinary (she often groaned at the oppressive banality of the word), middle-class, and hoping the baby would marry a doctor, thereby raising them in their autumn days to the select legions of the upper class. Each day their lives followed the same routine—no harm in that sordid little detail, she thought. It helps structure one's existence. He went to the office, she fed the baby, washed the rapidly growing mound of nappies, prepared the dinner and looked forward to the afternoon walk. She had convinced herself she was happy with her lot, and yet felt disappointed at the pangs of jealousy endured on hearing of a friend's glamorous job or another's academic and erudite husband. If only someone noticed her from time to time, or even wrote her name on a wall declaring her existence worthwhile; "A fine mind" or "I was once her lover." That way, at least, she would have evidence she was having impact on others. As it was, she was perpetually bombarded with it. Marital successes, even marital failures evoked a response from her. All one-way traffic.

That afternoon she dressed the baby and started out for her walk. "Fantasy 5 time" her husband called it. "Wall-reading time" she knew it to be. On this occasion, however, she decided to avoid those concrete temptations and, instead, visit the park. Out along the main road she trundled, pushing the pram, pausing to gaze into the hardware store's window, hearing the whine of the Saracen as it thundered by, waking the baby and making her feel uneasy. A foot patrol of soldiers strolled past, their rifles, lethal even in the brittle sunlight of this March day, lounged lovingly and relaxed in the arms of their men. One soldier stood nonchalantly, almost impertinent, against a corrugated railing and stared at her. She always blushed on passing troops.

The park is ugly, stark and hostile. Even in summer, when courting couples seek out secluded spots like mating cats, they reject Musgrave. There are a few trees, clustered together, standing like skeletons, ashamed of their nakedness. The rest is grass, a green wasteland speckled with puddles of gulls squawking over a worm patch. The park is bordered by a hospital with a military wing which is guarded by an army billet. The beauty of the place, it has only this, is its silence.

The hill up to the park bench was not the precipice it seemed, but the baby and pram were heavy. Ante-natal self-indulgence had taken its toll—her midriff was now most definitely a bulge. With one final push, pram, baby and mother reached the green wooden seat, and came to rest. The baby slept soundly with the soother touching her velvet pink cheeks, hand on pillow, a picture of purity. The woman heard a coughing noise coming from the nearby gun turret, and managed to see the tip of a rifle and a face peering out from the darkness. Smells of cabbage and burnt potatoes wafted over from behind the slanting sheets of protective steel.

"Is that your baby?" an English voice called out. She could barely see the face belonging to the voice. She replied yes, and smiled. The situation reminded her of the confessional. Dark and supposedly anonymous, "Is that you, my child?" She knew the priest personally. Did he identify her sins with his "Good morning, Mary," and think to himself, "and I know what you were up to last night!" She blushed at the secrets given away during the ceremony. Yes, she nervously answered again, it was her baby, a little girl. First-time mothers rarely resist the temptation to talk about their offspring. Forgetting her initial shyness, she told the voice of when the baby was born, the early problems of all-night crying, now teething, how she could crawl backwards and gurgle.

The voice responded. It too had a son, a few months older than her child, away in Germany at the army base at Munster. Factory pipes, chimney tops, church spires, domes all listened impassively to the Englishman's declaration of paternal love. The scene was strange, for although Belfast's sterile geography slipped into classical forms with dusk and heavy rain-clouds, the voice and the woman knew the folly of such innocent communication. They politely finished their conversation, said good-bye, and the woman pushed her pram homewards. The voice remained in the turret, watchful and anxious. Home she went, past vanloads of workers leering out at the pavement, past the uneasy presence of foot patrols, past the church. "Let us give each other the sign of peace," they said at Mass. The only sign Belfast knew was two fingers pointing towards Heaven. Life was self-contained, the couple often declared, just like flats. No need to go outside.

10   She did go outside, however. Each week the voice and the woman learned more of each other. No physical contact was needed, no face-to-face encounter to judge reaction, no touching to confirm amity, no threat of dangerous intimacy. It was a meeting of minds, as she explained later to her husband, a new opinion, a common bond, an opening of vistas. He disclosed his ambitions to become a pilot, to watching the land, fields and horizons spread out beneath him—a patchwork quilt of dappled colors and textures. She wanted to be remembered by writing on walls, about them that is, a world-shattering thesis on their psychological complexities, their essential truths, their witticisms and intellectual genius. And all this time the city's skyline and distant buildings watched and listened.

It was April now. More slogans had appeared, white and dripping, on the city walls. "Brits out. Peace in." A simple equation for the writer. "Loose talk claims lives," another shouted menacingly. The messages, the woman decided, had acquired a more ominous tone. The baby had grown and could sit up without support. New political solutions had been proposed and rejected, inter-paramilitary feuding had broken out and subsided, four soldiers and two policemen had been blown to smithereens in separate incidents, and a building a day had been bombed by the Provos. It had been a fairly normal month by Belfast's standards. The level of violence was no more or less acceptable than at other times.

One day—it was, perhaps, the last day in April—her husband returned home panting and trembling a little. He asked had she been to the park, and she replied she had. Taking her by the hand, he led her to the wall on the left of their driveway. She felt her heart sink and thud against her. She felt her face redden. Her mouth was suddenly dry. She could not speak. In huge angry letters the message spat itself out,

"TOUT."

The four-letter word covered the whole wall. It clanged in her brain, its venom rushed through her body. Suspicion was enough to condemn. The job itself was not well done, she had seen better. The letters were uneven, paint splattered down from the cross T, the U looked a misshapen O. The workmanship was poor, the impact perfect.

Her husband led her back into the kitchen. The baby was crying loudly in the living-room but the woman did not seem to hear. Like sleepwalkers, they sat down on the settee. The woman began to sob. Her shoulders heaved in bursts as she gasped hysterically. Her husband took her in his arms gently and tried to make her sorrow his. Already he shared her fear.

"What did you talk about? Did you not realize how dangerous it was? We must leave." He spoke quickly, making plans. Selling the house and car, finding a job in London or Dublin, far away from Belfast, mortgages, removals, savings, the tawdry affairs of normal living stunned her, making her more confused. "I told him nothing," she sobbed, "what could I tell? We talked about life, everything, but not about here." She trembled, trying to control herself. "We just chatted about reading walls, families, anything at all. Oh Sean, it was as innocent as that. A meeting of minds we called it, for it was little else."

She looked into her husband's face and saw he did not fully understand. There was a hint of jealousy, of resentment at not being part of their communication. Her hands fell on her lap, resting in resignation. What was the point of explanation? She lifted her baby from the floor. Pressing the tiny face and body to her breast, she felt all her hopes and desires for a better life become one with the child's struggle for freedom. The child's hands wandered over her face, their eyes met. At once that moment of maternal and filial love eclipsed her fear, gave her the impetus to escape.

For nine months she had been unable to accept the reality of her condition. Absurd, for the massive bump daily shifted position and thumped against her. When her daughter was born, she had been overwhelmed by love for her and amazed at her own ability to give life. By nature she was a dreamy person, given to moments of fancy. She wondered at her competence in fulfilling the role of mother. Could it be measured? This time she knew it could. She really did not care if they maimed her or even murdered her. She did care about her daughter. She was her touchstone, her anchor to virtue. Not for her child a legacy of fear, revulsion or hatred. With the few hours respite the painters had left between judgment and sentence she determined to leave Belfast's walls behind.

The next few nights were spent in troubled, restless sleep. The message remained on the wall outside. The neighbors pretended not to notice and refused to discuss the matter. She and the baby remained indoors despite the refreshing May breezes and blue skies. Her husband had given in his notice at the office, for health reasons, he suggested to his colleagues. An aunt had been contacted in Dublin. The couple did not answer knocks at the door. They carefully examined the shape and size of mail delivered and always paused when they answered the telephone.

The mini-van was to call at eleven on Monday night, when it would be dark enough to park, and pack their belongings and themselves without too much suspicion being aroused. The firm had been very understanding when the nature of their work had been explained. They were Protestant so there was no conflict of loyalties involved in the exercise. They agreed to drive them to Dublin at extra cost, changing drivers at Newry on the way down.

20   Monday finally arrived. The couple nervously laughed about how smoothly everything had gone. Privately, they each expected something to go wrong. The baby was fed, and played with, the radio listened to and the clock watched. They listened to the news at nine. Huddled together in their anxiety, they kept vigil in the darkening room. Rain had begun to pour from black thunderclouds. Everywhere it was quiet and still. Hushed and cold they waited. Ten o'clock, and it was now dark. A blustery wind had risen, making the lattice separation next door bang and clatter. At ten to eleven, her husband went into the sitting-room to watch for the mini-van. His footsteps clamped noisily on the floorboards as he paced back and forth. The baby slept.

A black shape glided slowly up the street and backed into the driveway. It was eleven. The van had arrived. Her husband asked to see their identification and then they began to load up the couple's belongings. Settee, chairs, television, washing machine—all were dumped hastily, it was no time to worry about breakages. She stood holding the sleeping baby in the living-room as the men worked anxiously between van and house. The scene was so unreal, the circumstances absolutely incredible. She thought, "What have I done?" Recollections of her naivety, her insensibility to historical fact and political climate were stupefying. She had seen women who had been tarred and feathered, heard of people who had been shot in the head, boys who had been knee-capped, all for suspected fraternizing with troops. The catalog of violence spilled out before her as she realized the gravity and possible repercussions of her alleged misdemeanor.

A voice called her, "Mary, come on now. We have to go. Don't worry, we're all together." Her husband led her to the locked and waiting van. Handing the baby to him, she climbed up beside the driver, took back the baby as her husband sat down beside her and waited for the engine to start. The van slowly maneuvered out onto the street and down the main road. They felt more cheerful now, a little like refugees seeking safety and freedom not too far away. As they approached the motorway bridge, two figures with something clutched in their hands stood side by side in the darkness. She closed her eyes tightly, expecting bursts of gunfire. The van shot past. Relieved, she asked her husband what they were doing at this time of night. "Writing slogans on the wall," he replied.

The furtiveness of the painters seemed ludicrous and petty as she recalled the heroic and literary characteristics with which she had endowed them. What did they matter? The travelers sat in silence as the van sped past the city suburbs, the glare of police and army barracks, on out and further out into the countryside. Past sleeping villages and silent fields, past whitewashed farmhouses and barking dogs. On to Newry where they said goodbye to their driver as the new one stepped in. Far along the coast with Rostrevor's twinkling lights opposite the bay down to the Border check and a drowsy soldier waving them through. Out of the North, safe, relieved and heading for Dublin.

Some days later in Belfast the neighbors discovered the house vacant, the people next door received a letter and a check from Dublin. Remarks about the peculiar couple were made over hedges and cups of coffee, the message on the wall was painted over by the couple who had bought the house when it went up for sale. They too were ordinary people, living a self-contained life, worrying over finance and babies, promotion and local gossip. He too had an office job, but his wife was merely a housekeeper for him. She was sensible, down to earth, and not in the least inclined to wall-reading.

QUESTIONS FOR DISCUSSION AND WRITING

1. How do the various wall paintings mark the development of the plot? How does the painting of the word *tout* ("informer") mark the climax of the plot? In what ways does painting over this word resolve the conflicts in the plot?

2. What are the protagonist's motives for "going to the park" to talk with "the voice"? What do the woman and the voice reveal about themselves during their "meeting of the minds"?

3. What are the "Troubles"? How does the description of the park help clarify the effect of the "Troubles" on "ordinary" life in Northern Ireland?

4. Why did Barr choose a third-person narrator when the internal conflicts in the story seem especially well-suited to first-person narration? What is the effect of the narrator's repeated use of such words as *tired, sordid,* and *banality?*

5. What are the thematic implications of the revision of the line from Robert Frost's "Birches"—"one could do worse than be a *reader* of walls"?

Stories for Comparison

Alice Adams's "Truth or Consequences" (pages 164–173); Frank O'Connor's "Guests of the Nation" (pages 995–1004).

22

....

J O H N   B A R T H

Lost in the Funhouse

JOHN BARTH was born in Cambridge, Maryland, in 1930. After attending
the Juilliard School of Music, he completed his education at Johns Hopkins
University. He held academic appointments in the English departments of
Pennsylvania State University and the State University of New York at
Buffalo before becoming writer-in-residence at Johns Hopkins, a position he
has held since 1973. Barth's novels, which include *The Floating Opera*
(1956), *The End of the Road* (1958), *The Sot-Weed Factor* (1960), and *Giles
Goat-Boy* (1966), examine and parody major philosophical themes and traditional literary forms. *Chimera* (1972), a novel that recalls the storytelling in
Tales of the Arabian Nights, won the National Book Award. He has also published several collections of essays, such as *Friday Book Essays* (1984), and
collections of stories, such as *On with the Story* (1996). "Lost in the Funhouse," the title story from a collection of short stories (1968), intersperses
discussion of the craft of fiction with the problem of creating a story.

For whom is the funhouse fun? Perhaps for lovers. For Ambrose it is *a place of
fear and confusion.* He has come to the seashore with his family for the holiday,
*the occasion of their visit is Independence Day, the most important secular holiday
of the United States of America.* A single straight underline is the manuscript mark
for italic type, *which in turn* is the printed equivalent to oral emphasis of words and
phrases as well as the customary type for titles of complete works, not to mention.
Italics are also employed, in fiction stories especially, for "outside," intrusive, or artificial voices, such as radio announcements, the texts of telegrams and newspaper
articles, et cetera. They should be used *sparingly.* If passages originally in roman
type are italicized by someone repeating them, it's customary to acknowledge the
fact. *Italics mine.*

Ambrose was "at that awkward age." His voice came out high-pitched as a
child's if he let himself get carried away; to be on the safe side, therefore, he moved
and spoke with *deliberate calm* and *adult gravity.* Talking soberly of unimportant or
irrelevant matters, and listening consciously to the sound of your own voice are useful habits for maintaining control in this difficult interval. *En route* to Ocean City he

sat in the back seat of the family car with his brother Peter, age fifteen, and Magda G———, age fourteen, a pretty girl an exquisite young lady, who lived not far from them on B——— Street in the Town of D———, Maryland. Initials, blanks, or both were often substituted for proper names in nineteenth-century fiction to enhance the illusion of reality. It is as if the author felt it necessary to delete the names for reasons of tact or legal liability. Interestingly, as with other aspects of realism, it is an *illusion* that is being enhanced, by purely artificial means. Is it likely, does it violate the principle of verisimilitude, that a thirteen-year-old boy could make such a sophisticated observation? A girl of fourteen is the *psychological coeval* of a boy of fifteen or sixteen; a thirteen-year-old boy, therefore, even one precocious in some other respects, might be three years *her emotional junior.*

Thrice a year—on Memorial, Independence, and Labor Days—the family visits Ocean City for the afternoon and evening. When Ambrose and Peter's father was their age, the excursion was made by train, as mentioned in the novel *The 42nd Parallel* by John Dos Passos. Many families from the same neighborhood used to travel together, with dependent relatives and often with Negro servants; schoolfuls of children swarmed through the railway cars; everyone shared everyone else's Maryland fried chicken, Virginia ham, deviled eggs, potato salad, beaten biscuits, iced tea. Nowadays (that is, in 19—, the year of our story) the journey is made by automobile—more comfortably and quickly though without the extra fun though without the *camaraderie* of a general excursion. It's all part of the deterioration of American life, their father declares; Uncle Karl supposes that when the boys take *their* families to Ocean City for the holidays they'll fly in Autogiros. Their mother, sitting in the middle of the front seat like Magda in the second, only with her arms on the seat-back behind the men's shoulders, wouldn't want the good old days back again, the steaming trains and stuffy long dresses; on the other hand she can do without Autogiros, too, if she has to become a grandmother to fly in them.

Description of physical appearance and mannerisms is one of several standard methods of characterization used by writers of fiction. It is also important to "keep the senses operating"; when a detail from one of the five senses, say visual, is "crossed" with a detail from another, say auditory, the reader's imagination is oriented to the scene, perhaps unconsciously. This procedure may be compared to the way surveyors and navigators determine their positions by two or more compass bearings, a process known as triangulation. The brown hair on Ambrose's mother's forearms gleamed in the sun like. Though right-handed, she took her left arm from the seat-back to press the dashboard cigar lighter for Uncle Karl. When the glass bead in its handle glowed red, the lighter was ready for use. The smell of Uncle Karl's cigar smoke reminded one of. The fragrance of the ocean came strong to the picnic ground where they always stopped for lunch, two miles inland from Ocean City. Having to pause for a full hour almost within sound of the breakers was difficult for Peter and Ambrose when they were younger; even at their present age it was not easy to keep their anticipation, *stimulated by the briny spume,* from turning into short temper. The Irish author James Joyce, in his unusual novel entitled *Ulysses,* now available in this country, uses the adjectives *snot-green* and *scrotum-tightening* to describe the sea. Visual, auditory, tactile, olfactory, gustatory. Peter and Ambrose's father, while steering their black 1936 LaSalle sedan with one hand, could with the other remove the first cigarette from a white pack of Lucky Strikes and, more remarkably, light it with a match forefingered from its book and thumbed against the flint paper without being detached. The matchbook cover merely advertised U.S. War Bonds and Stamps. A fine metaphor, simile, or other figure of speech, in addition to its obvious "first-order" relevance to the thing it describes, will be seen upon reflection to have a second order of significance: it may be drawn from the *milieu* of the action, for example, or be particularly appropriate to the sensibility of the narrator, even hinting to the reader things of which the narrator is unaware; or it may cast further and subtler lights upon the thing it describes, sometimes ironically qualifying the more evident sense of the comparison.

5   To say that Ambrose's and Peter's mother was *pretty* is to accomplish nothing; the reader may acknowledge the proposition, but his imagination is not engaged. Besides, Magda was also pretty, yet in an altogether different way. Although she lived on B——— Street she had very good manners and did better than average in school. Her figure was very well developed for her age. Her right hand lay casually on the plush upholstery of the seat, very near Ambrose's left leg, on which his own hand rested. The space between their legs, between her right and his left leg, was out of the line of sight of anyone sitting on the other side of Magda, as well as anyone glancing into the rearview mirror. Uncle Karl's face resembled Peter's—rather, vice versa. Both had dark hair and eyes, short husky statures, deep voices. Magda's left hand was probably in a similar position on her left side. The boy's father is difficult to describe; no particular feature of his appearance or manner stood out. He wore glasses and was principal of a T——— County grade school. Uncle Karl was a masonry contractor.

Although Peter must have known as well as Ambrose that the latter, because of his position in the car, would be the first to see the electrical towers of the power plant at V———, the halfway point of their trip, he leaned forward and slightly toward the center of the car and pretended to be looking for them through the flat pinewoods and tuckahoe creeks along the highway. For as long as the boys could remember, "looking for the Towers" had been a feature of the first half of their excursions to Ocean City, "looking for the standpipe" of the second. Though the game was childish, their mother preserved the tradition of rewarding the first to see the Towers with a candy-bar or piece of fruit. She insisted now that Magda play the game; the prize, she said, was "something hard to get nowadays." Ambrose decided not to join in; he sat far back in his seat. Magda, like Peter, leaned forward. Two sets of straps were discernible through the shoulders of her sun dress; the inside right one, a brassiere-strap, was fastened or shortened with a small safety pin. The right armpit of her dress, presumably the left as well, was damp with perspiration. The simple strategy for being first to espy the Towers, which Ambrose had understood by the age of four, was to sit on the right-hand side of the car. Whoever sat there, however, had also to put up with the worst of the sun, and so Ambrose, without mentioning the matter, chose sometimes the one and sometimes the other. Not impossibly Peter had never caught on to the trick, or thought that his brother hadn't simply because Ambrose on occasion preferred shade to a Baby Ruth or tangerine.

The shade-sun situation didn't apply to the front seat, owing to the windshield; if anything the driver got more sun, since the person on the passenger side not only was shaded below by the door and dashboard but might swing down his sunvisor all the way too.

"Is that them?" Magda asked. Ambrose's mother teased the boys for letting Magda win, insinuating that "somebody [had] a girlfriend." Peter and Ambrose's father reached a long thin arm across their mother to butt his cigarette in the dashboard ashtray, under the lighter. The prize this time for seeing the Towers first was a banana. Their mother bestowed it after chiding their father for wasting a half-smoked cigarette when everything was so scarce. Magda, to take the prize, moved her hand from so near Ambrose's that he could have touched it as though accidentally. She offered to share the prize, things like that were so hard to find; but everyone insisted it was hers alone. Ambrose's mother sang an iambic trimeter couplet from a popular song, femininely rhymed:

> "What's good is in the Army;
> What's left will never harm me."

Uncle Karl tapped his cigar ash out the ventilator window; some particles were sucked by the slipstream back into the car through the rear window on the passenger side. Magda demonstrated her ability to hold a banana in one hand and peel it with her teeth. She still sat forward; Ambrose pushed his glasses back onto the bridge of his nose with his left hand, which he then negligently let fall to the seat cushion immediately behind her. He even permitted the single hair, gold, on the second joint of his thumb to brush the fabric of her skirt. Should she have sat back at that instant, his hand would have been caught under her.

Plush upholstery prickles uncomfortably through gabardine slacks in the July sun. The function of the *beginning* of a story is to introduce the principal characters, establish their initial relationships, set the scene for the main action, expose the background of the situation if necessary, plant motifs and foreshadowings where appropriate, and initiate the first complication or whatever of the "rising action." Actually, if one imagines a story called "The Funhouse," or "Lost in the Funhouse," the details of the drive to Ocean City don't seem especially relevant. The *beginning* should recount the events between Ambrose's first sight of the funhouse early in the afternoon and his entering it with Magda and Peter in the evening. The *middle* would narrate all relevant events from the time he goes in to the time he loses his way; middles have the double and contradictory function of delaying the climax while at the same time preparing the reader for it and fetching him to it. Then the *ending* would tell what Ambrose does while he's lost, how he finally finds his way out, and what everybody makes of the experience. So far there's been no real dialogue, very little sensory detail, and nothing in the way of a *theme*. And a long time has gone by already without anything happening; it makes a person wonder. We haven't even reached Ocean City yet: we will never get out of the funhouse.

The more closely an author identifies with the narrator, literally or metaphorically, the less advisable it is, as a rule, to use the first-person narrative viewpoint.

Once three years previously the young people *aforementioned* played Niggers and Masters in the backyard; when it was Ambrose's turn to be Master and theirs to be Niggers, Peter had to go serve his evening papers; Ambrose was afraid to punish Magda alone, but she led him to the whitewashed Torture Chamber between the woodshed and the privy in the Slaves Quarters; there she knelt sweating among bamboo rakes and dusty Mason jars, pleadingly embraced his knees, and while bees droned in the lattice as if on an ordinary summer afternoon, purchased clemency at a surprising price set by herself. Doubtless she remembered nothing of this event; Ambrose on the other hand seemed unable to forget the least detail of his life. He even recalled how, standing beside himself with awed impersonality in the reeky heat, he'd stared the while at an empty cigar box in which Uncle Karl kept stone-cutting chisels: beneath the words *El Producto,* a laureled, loose-toga'd lady regarded the sea from a marble bench; beside her, forgotten or not yet turned to, was a five-stringed lyre. Her chin reposed on the back of her right hand; her left depended negligently from the bencharm. The lower half of scene and lady was peeled away; the words EXAMINED BY——— were inked there into the wood. Nowadays cigar boxes are made of pasteboard. Ambrose wondered what Magda would have done, Ambrose wondered what Magda would do when she sat back on his hand as he resolved she should. Be angry. Make a teasing joke of it. Give no sign at all. For a long time she leaned forward, playing cow-poker with Peter against Uncle Karl and Mother and watching for the first sign of Ocean City. At nearly the same instant, picnic ground and Ocean City standpipe hove into view; an Amoco filling station on their side of the road cost Mother and Uncle Karl fifty cows and the game; Magda bounced back, clapping her right hand on Mother's right arm; Ambrose moved clear "in the nick of time."

At this rate our hero, at this rate our protagonist will remain in the funhouse forever. Narrative ordinarily consists of alternating dramatization and summarization. One symptom of nervous tension, paradoxically, is repeated and violent yawning; neither Peter nor Magda nor Uncle Karl nor Mother reacted in this manner. Although they were no longer small children, Peter and Ambrose were each given a dollar to spend on boardwalk amusements in addition to what money of their own they'd brought along. Magda too, though she protested she had ample spending money. The boys' mother made a little scene out of distributing the bills; she pretended that her sons and Magda were small children and cautioned them not to spend the sum too quickly or in one place. Magda promised with a merry laugh and, having both hands free, took the bill with her left. Peter laughed also and pledged in a falsetto to be a good boy. His imitation of a child was not clever. The boys' father was tall and thin, balding, fair-complexioned. Assertions of that sort are not effective; the reader may acknowledge the proposition, but. We should be much farther along than we are; something has gone wrong; not much of this preliminary rambling seems relevant. Yet everyone begins in the same place; how is it that most go along without difficulty but a few lose their way?

"Stay out from under the boardwalk," Uncle Karl growled from the side of his mouth. The boys' mother pushed his shoulder in *mock annoyance.* They were all standing before Fat May the Laughing Lady who advertised the funhouse. Larger than life, Fat May mechanically shook, rocked on her heels, slapped her thighs while recorded laughter—uproarious, female—came amplified from a hidden loudspeaker. It chuckled, wheezed, wept; tried in vain to catch its breath; tittered, groaned, exploded raucous and anew. You couldn't hear it without laughing yourself, no matter how you felt. Father came back from talking to a Coast-Guardsman on duty and reported that the surf was spoiled with crude oil from tankers recently torpedoed offshore. Lumps of it, difficult to remove, made tarry tidelines on the beach and stuck on swimmers. Many bathed in the surf nevertheless and came out speckled; others paid to use a municipal pool and only sunbathed on the beach. We would do the latter. We would do the latter. We would do the latter.

Under the boardwalk, matchbook covers, grainy other things. What is the story's theme? Ambrose is ill. He perspires in the dark passages; candied apples-on-a-stick, delicious-looking, disappointing to eat. Funhouses need men's and ladies' rooms at intervals. Others perhaps have also vomited in corners and corridors; may even have had bowel movements liable to be stepped in in the dark. The word *fuck* suggests suction and/or and/or flatulence. Mother and Father; grandmothers and grandfathers on both sides; great-grandmothers and great-grandfathers on four sides, et cetera. Count a generation as thirty years: in approximately the year when Lord Baltimore was granted charter to the province of Maryland by Charles I, five hundred twelve women—English, Welsh, Bavarian, Swiss—of every class and character, received into themselves the penises the intromittent organs of five hundred twelve men, ditto, in every circumstance and posture, to conceive the five hundred twelve ancestors of the two hundred fifty-six ancestors of the et cetera et cetera et cetera et cetera et cetera et cetera et cetera et cetera of the author, of the narrator, of this story, *Lost in the Funhouse.* In alleyways, ditches, canopy beds, pinewoods, bridal suites, ship's cabins, coach-and-fours, coaches-and-four, sultry toolsheds; on the cold sand under boardwalks, littered with *El Producto* cigar butts, treasured with Lucky Strike cigarette stubs, Coca-Cola caps, gritty turds, cardboard lollipop sticks, matchbook covers warning that A Slip of the Lip Can Sink a Ship. The shluppish whisper, continuous as seawash round the globe, tidelike falls and rises with the circuit of dawn and dusk.

Magda's teeth. She *was* left-handed. Perspiration. They've gone all the way through, Magda and Peter, they've been waiting for hours with Mother and Uncle Karl while Father searches for his lost son; they draw french-fried potatoes from a paper cup and shake their heads. They've named the children they'll one day have and bring to Ocean City on holidays. Can spermatozoa properly be thought of as male animalcules when there are no female spermatozoa? They grope through hot, dark windings, past Love's Tunnel's fearsome obstacles. Some perhaps lose their way.

Peter suggested then and there that they do the funhouse; he had been 15 through it before, so had Magda, Ambrose hadn't and suggested, his voice cracking on account of Fat May's laughter, that they swim first. All were chuckling, couldn't help it; Ambrose's father, Ambrose's and Peter's father came up grinning like a lunatic with two boxes of syrup-coated popcorn, one for Mother, one for Magda; the men were to help themselves. Ambrose walked on Magda's right;

being by nature left-handed, she carried the box in her left hand. Up front the situation was reversed.

"What are you limping for?" Magda inquired of Ambrose. He supposed in a husky tone that his foot had gone to sleep in the car. Her teeth flashed. "Pins and needles?" It was the honeysuckle on the lattice of the former privy that drew the bees. Imagine being stung there. How long is this going to take?

The adults decided to forgo the pool; but Uncle Karl insisted they change into swimsuits and do the beach. "He wants to watch the pretty girls," Peter teased, and ducked behind Magda from Uncle Karl's pretended wrath. "You've got all the pretty girls you need right here," Magda declared, and Mother said: "Now that's the gospel truth." Magda scolded Peter, who reached over her shoulder to sneak some popcorn. "Your brother and father aren't getting any." Uncle Karl wondered if they were going to have fireworks that night, what with the shortages. It wasn't the shortages, Mr. M——— replied; Ocean City had fireworks from pre-war. But it was too risky on account of the enemy submarines, some people thought.

"Don't seem like Fourth of July without fireworks," said Uncle Karl. The inverted tag in dialogue writing is still considered permissible with proper names or epithets, but sounds old-fashioned with personal pronouns. "We'll have 'em again soon enough," predicted the boys' father. Their mother declared she could do without fireworks: they reminded her too much of the real thing. Their father said all the more reason to shoot off a few now and again. Uncle Karl asked *rhetorically* who needed reminding, just look at people's hair and skin.

"The oil, yes," said Mrs. M———.

20   Ambrose had a pain in his stomach and so didn't swim but enjoyed watching the others. He and his father burned red easily. Magda's figure was exceedingly well developed for her age. She too declined to swim, and got mad, and became angry when Peter attempted to drag her into the pool. She always swam, he insisted; what did she mean not swim? Why did a person come to Ocean City?

"Maybe I want to lay here with Ambrose," Magda teased.

Nobody likes a pedant.

"Aha," said Mother. Peter grabbed Magda by one ankle and ordered Ambrose to grab the other. She squealed and rolled over on the beach blanket. Ambrose pretended to help hold her back. Her tan was darker than even Mother's and Peter's. "Help out, Uncle Karl!" Peter cried. Uncle Karl went to seize the other ankle. Inside the top of her swimsuit, however, you could see the line where the sunburn ended and, when she hunched her shoulders and squealed again, one nipple's auburn edge. Mother made them behave themselves. "*You* should certainly know," she said to Uncle Karl. Archly. "That when a lady says she doesn't feel like swimming, a gentleman doesn't ask questions." Uncle Karl said excuse *him;* Mother winked at Magda; Ambrose blushed; stupid Peter kept saying "Phooey on *feel like!*" and tugging at Magda's ankle; then even he got the point, and cannonballed with a holler into the pool.

"I swear," Magda said, in mock *in feigned* exasperation.

25   The diving would make a suitable literary symbol. To go off the high board you had to wait in a line along the poolside and up the ladder. Fellows tickled girls and

goosed one another and shouted to the ones at the top to hurry up, or razzed them for bellyfloppers. Once on the springboard some took a great while posing or clowning or deciding on a dive or getting up their nerve; others ran right off. Especially among the younger fellows the idea was to strike the funniest pose or do the craziest stunt as you fell, a thing that got harder to do as you kept on and kept on. But whether you hollered *Geronimo!* or *Sieg heil!*, held your nose or "rode a bicycle," pretended to be shot or did a perfect jackknife or changed your mind halfway down and ended up with nothing, it was over in two seconds, after all that wait. Spring, pose, splash. Spring, neat-o, splash. Spring, aw fooey, splash.

The grown-ups had gone on; Ambrose wanted to converse with Magda; she was remarkably well developed for her age; it was said that that came from rubbing with a turkish towel, and there were other theories. Ambrose could think of nothing to say except how good a diver Peter was, who was showing off for her benefit. You could pretty well tell by looking at their bathing suits and arm muscles how far along the different fellows were. Ambrose was glad he hadn't gone in swimming, the cold water shrank you up so. Magda pretended to be uninterested in the diving; she probably weighed as much as he did. If you knew your way around in the funhouse like your own bedroom, you could wait until a girl came along and then slip away without ever getting caught, even if her boyfriend was right with her. She'd think *he* did it! It would be better to be the boyfriend, and act outraged, and tear the funhouse apart.

Not act; *be*.

"He's a master diver," Ambrose said. In feigned admiration. "You really have to slave away at it to get that good." What would it matter anyhow if he asked her right out whether she remembered, even teased her with it as Peter would have?

There's no point in going farther; this isn't getting anybody anywhere; they haven't even come to the funhouse yet. Ambrose is off the track, in some new or old part of the place that's not supposed to be used; he strayed into it by some one-in-a-million chance, like the time the roller-coaster car left the tracks in the nineteen-teens against all the laws of physics and sailed over the boardwalk in the dark. And they can't locate him because they don't know where to look. Even the designer and operator have forgotten this other part, that winds around on itself like a whelk shell. That winds around the right part like the snakes on Mercury's caduceus. Some people, perhaps, don't "hit their stride" until their twenties, when the growing-up business is over and women appreciate other things besides wisecracks and teasing and strutting. Peter didn't have one-tenth the imagination *he* had, not one-tenth. Peter did this naming-their-children thing as a joke, making up names like Aloysius and Murgatroyd, but Ambrose knew *exactly* how it would feel to be married and have children of your own, and be a loving husband and father, and go comfortably to work in the mornings and to bed with your wife at night, and wake up with her there. With a breeze coming through the sash and birds and mockingbirds singing in the Chinese-cigar trees. His eyes watered, there aren't enough ways to say that. He would be quite famous in his line of work. Whether Magda was his wife or not, one evening when he was wise-lined and gray at the temples he'd smile gravely, at a fashionable dinner party, and remind her of his youthful passion. The time they went with his family to Ocean City; the *erotic fantasies* he used to have about her. How long ago it seemed, and childish! Yet tender, too, *n'est-ce pas?* Would she have imagined that the world-famous whatever remembered how many strings were on the lyre on the bench beside the girl on the label of the cigar box he'd stared at in the toolshed at age ten while she, age eleven. Even then he had felt *wise beyond his years;* he'd stroked her hair and said in his deepest voice and correctest English, as to a dear child: "I shall never forget this moment."

30   But though he had breathed heavily, groaned as if ecstatic, what he'd really felt throughout was an odd detachment, as though someone else were Master. Strive as he might to be transported, he heard his mind take notes upon the scene: *This is what they call* passion. *I am experiencing it.* Many of the digger machines were out of order in the penny arcades and could not be repaired or replaced for the duration. Moreover the prizes, made now in USA, were less interesting than formerly, pasteboard items for the most part, and some of the machines wouldn't work on white pennies. The gypsy fortuneteller machine might have provided a foreshadowing of the climax of this story if Ambrose had operated it. It was even dilapidateder than most: the silver coating was worn off the brown metal handles, the glass windows around the dummy were cracked and taped, her kerchiefs and silks long-faded. If a man lived by himself, he could take a department-store mannequin with flexible joints and modify her in certain ways. *However:* by the time he was that old he'd have a real woman. There was a machine that stamped your name around a white-metal coin with a star in the middle: A————. His son would be the second, and when the lad reached thirteen or so he would put a strong arm around his shoulder and tell him calmly: "It is perfectly normal. We have all been through it. It will not last forever." Nobody knew how to be what they were right. He'd smoke a pipe, teach his son how to fish and softcrab, assure him he needn't worry about himself. Magda would certainly give, Magda would certainly yield a great deal of milk, although guilty of occasional solecisms. It don't taste so bad. Suppose the lights come on now!

The day wore on. You think you're yourself, but there are other persons in you. Ambrose gets hard when Ambrose doesn't want to, *and obversely.* Ambrose watches them disagree; Ambrose watches him watch. In the funhouse mirror-room you can't see yourself go on forever, because no matter how you stand, your head gets in the way. Even if you had a glass periscope, the image of your eye would cover up the thing you really wanted to see. The police will come; there'll be a story in the papers. That must be where it happened. Unless he can find a surprise exit, an unofficial backdoor or escape hatch opening on an alley, say, and then stroll up to the family in front of the funhouse and ask where everybody's been; *he's* been out of the place for ages. That's just where it happened, in that last lighted room: Peter and Magda found the right exit; he found one that you weren't supposed to find and strayed off into the works somewhere. In a perfect funhouse you'd be able to go only one way, like the divers off the high-board; getting lost would be impossible; the doors and halls would work like minnow traps or the valves in veins.

On account of German U-boats, Ocean City was "browned out": streetlights were shaded on the seaward side; shop-windows and boardwalk amusement places were kept dim, not to silhouette tankers and Liberty-ships for torpedoing. In a short story about Ocean City, Maryland, during World War II, the author could make use of the image of sailors on leave in the penny arcades and shooting galleries, sighting through the crosshairs of toy machine guns at swastika'd subs, while out in the black Atlantic a U-boat skipper squints through his periscope at real ships outlined by the glow of penny arcades. After dinner the family strolled back to the amusement end of the boardwalk. The boys' father had burnt red as always and was masked with Noxzema, a minstrel in reverse. The grown-ups stood at the end of the boardwalk where the Hurricane of '33 had cut an inlet from the ocean to Assawoman Bay.

"Pronounced with a long *o*," Uncle Karl reminded Magda with a wink. His shirt sleeves were rolled up; Mother punched his brown biceps with the arrowed heart on it and said his mind was naughty. Fat May's laugh came suddenly from the funhouse, as if she'd just got the joke; the family laughed too at the coincidence. Ambrose went under the boardwalk to search for out-of-town matchbook covers with the aid of his pocket flashlight; he looked out from the edge of the North American continent and wondered how far their laughter carried over the water. Spies in rubber rafts; survivors in lifeboats. If the joke had been beyond his understanding, he could have said: *"The laughter was over his head."* And let the reader see the serious wordplay on second reading.

He turned the flashlight on and then off at once even before the woman whooped. He sprang away, heart athud, dropping the light. What had the man grunted? Perspiration drenched and chilled him by the time he scrambled up to the family. "See anything?" his father asked. His voice wouldn't come; he shrugged and violently brushed sand from his pants legs.

"Let's ride the old flying horses!" Magda cried. I'll never be an author. It's been 35 forever already, everybody's gone home, Ocean City's deserted, the ghost-crabs are tickling across the beach and down the littered cold streets. And the empty halls of clapboard hotels and abandoned funhouses. A tidal wave; an enemy air raid; a monster-crab swelling like an island from the sea. *The inhabitants fled in terror.* Magda clung to his trouser leg; he alone knew the maze's secret. "He gave his life that we might live," said Uncle Karl with a scowl of pain, as he. The fellow's hands had been tattooed; the woman's legs, the woman's fat white legs had. *An astonishing coincidence.* He yearned to tell Peter. He wanted to throw up for excitement. They hadn't even chased him. He wished he were dead.

One possible ending would be to have Ambrose come across another lost person in the dark. They'd match their wits together against the funhouse, struggle like Ulysses past obstacle after obstacle, help and encourage each other. Or a girl. By the time they found the exit they'd be closest friends, sweethearts if it were a girl; they'd know each other's inmost souls, be bound together *by the cement of shared adventure;* then they'd emerge into the light and it would turn out that his friend was a Negro. A blind girl. President Roosevelt's son. Ambrose's former archenemy.

Shortly after the mirror room he'd groped along a musty corridor, his heart already misgiving him at the absence of phosphorescent arrows and other signs. He'd found a crack of light—not a door, it turned out, but a seam between the plyboard wall panels—and squinting up to it, espied a small old man, *in appearance not unlike* the photographs at home of Ambrose's late grandfather, nodding upon a stool beneath a bare, speckled bulb. A crude panel of toggle- and knife-switches hung beside the open fuse box near his head; elsewhere in the little room were wooden levers and ropes belayed to boat cleats. At the time, Ambrose wasn't lost enough to rap or call; later he couldn't find that crack. Now it seemed to him that he'd possibly dozed off for a few minutes somewhere along the way; certainly he was exhausted from the afternoon's sunshine and the evening's problems; he couldn't be sure he hadn't dreamed part or all of the sight. Had an old black wall fan droned like bees and shimmied two flypaper streamers? Had the funhouse operator—gentle, somewhat sad and tired-appearing, in expression not unlike the photographs at home of Ambrose's late Uncle Konrad—murmured in his sleep? Is there really such a person as Ambrose, or is he a figment of the author's imagination? Was it Assawoman Bay or Sinepuxent? Are there other errors of fact in this fiction? Was there another sound besides the little slap slap of thigh on ham, like water sucking at the chine-board of a skiff?

When you're lost, the smartest thing to do is stay put till you're found, hollering if necessary. But to holler guarantees humiliation as well as rescue; keeping silent permits some saving of face—you can act surprised at the fuss when your rescuers find you and swear you weren't lost, if they do. What's more you might find your own way yet, *however belatedly.*

"Don't tell me your foot's still asleep!" Magda exclaimed as the three young people walked from the inlet to the area set aside for ferris wheels, carrousels, and other carnival rides, they having decided in favor of the vast and ancient merry-go-round instead of the funhouse. What a sentence, everything was wrong from the outset. People don't know what to make of him, he doesn't know what to make of himself, he's only thirteen, *athletically and socially inept,* not astonishingly bright, but there are antennae; he has . . . some sort of receivers in his head; things speak to him, he understands more than he should, the world winks at him through its objects, grabs grinning at his coat. Everybody else is in on some secret he doesn't know; they've forgotten to tell him. Through simple *procrastination* his mother put off his baptism until this year. Everyone else had it done as a baby; he'd assumed the same of himself, as had his mother, so she claimed, until it was time for him to join Grace Methodist-Protestant and the oversight came out. He was mortified, but pitched sleepless through his private catechizing, intimidated by the ancient mysteries, a thirteen year old would never say that, resolved to experience conversion like St. Augustine. When the water touched his brow and Adam's sin left him, he contrived by a strain like defecation to bring tears into his eyes—but felt nothing. There was some simple, radical difference about him; he hoped it was genius, feared it was madness, devoted himself to amiability and inconspicuousness. Alone on the seawall near his house he was seized by the terrifying transports he'd thought to find in toolshed, in Communion-cup. The grass was alive! The town, the river, himself, were not imaginary; time roared in his ears like wind; the world was *going on!* This part ought to be dramatized. The Irish author James Joyce once wrote. Ambrose M———is going to scream.

40   There is no *texture of rendered sensory detail,* for one thing. The faded distorting mirrors beside Fat May; the impossibility of choosing a mount when one had but

a single ride on the great carrousel; the *vertigo attendant on his recognition* that Ocean City was worn out, the place of fathers and grandfathers, straw-boatered men and parasoled ladies survived by their amusements. Money spent, the three paused at Peter's insistence beside Fat May to watch the girls get their skirts blown up. The object was to tease Magda, who said: "I swear, Peter M———, you've got a one-track mind! Amby and me aren't *interested* in such things." In the tumbling-barrel, too, just inside the Devil's-mouth entrance to the funhouse, the girls were upended and their boyfriends and others could see up their dresses if they cared to. Which was the whole point, Ambrose realized. Of the entire funhouse! If you looked around, you noticed that almost all the people on the boardwalk were paired off into couples except the small children; in a way, that was the whole point of Ocean City! If you had X-ray eyes and could see everything going on at that instant under the board-walk and in all the hotel rooms and cars and alleyways, you'd realize that all that normally *showed,* like restaurants and dance halls and clothing and test-your-strength machines, was merely preparation and intermission. Fat May screamed.

Because he watched the goings-on from the corner of his eye, it was Ambrose who spied the half-dollar on the boardwalk near the tumbling-barrel. Losers weepers. The first time he'd heard some people moving through a corridor not far away, just after he'd lost sight of the crack of light, he'd decided not to call to them, for fear they'd guess he was scared and poke fun; it sounded like roughnecks; he'd hoped they'd come by and he could follow in the dark without their knowing. Another time he'd heard just one person, unless he imagined it, bumping along as if on the other side of the plywood; perhaps Peter coming back for him, or Father, or Magda lost too. Or the owner and operator of the funhouse. He'd called out once, as though merrily: "Anybody know where the heck we are?" But the query was too stiff, his voice cracked, when the sounds stopped he was terrified: maybe it was a queer who waited for fellows to get lost, or a longhaired filthy monster that lived in some cranny of the funhouse. He stood rigid for hours it seemed like, scarcely respiring. His future was shockingly clear, in outline. He tried holding his breath to the point of unconsciousness. There ought to be a button you could push to end your life absolutely without pain; disappear in a flick, like turning out a light. He would push it instantly! He despised Uncle Karl. But he despised his father too, for not being what he was supposed to be. Perhaps his father hated *his* father, and so on, and his son would hate him, and so on. Instantly!

Naturally he didn't have nerve enough to ask Magda to go through the funhouse with him. With incredible nerve and to everyone's surprise he invited Magda, quietly and politely, to go through the funhouse with him. "I warn you, I've never been through it before," he added, *laughing easily;* "but I reckon we can manage some-how. The important thing to remember, after all, is that it's meant to be a *fun*house; that is, a place of amusement. If people really got lost or injured or too badly fright-ened in it, the owner'd go out of business. There'd even be lawsuits." No character in a work of fiction can make a speech this long without interruption or acknowl-edgment from the other characters.

Mother teased Uncle Karl: "Three's a crowd, I always heard." But actually Ambrose was relieved that Peter now had a quarter too. Nothing was what it looked

like. Every instant, under the surface of the Atlantic Ocean, millions of living animals devoured one another. Pilots were falling in flames over Europe; women were
being forcibly raped in the South Pacific. His father should have taken him aside and
said: "There is a simple secret to getting through the funhouse, as simple as being
first to see the Towers. Here it is. Peter does not know it; neither does your Uncle
Karl. You and I are different. Not surprisingly, you've often wished you weren't.
Don't think I haven't noticed how unhappy your childhood has been! But you'll understand, when I tell you, why it had to be kept secret until now. And you won't regret not being like your brother and your uncle. *On the contrary!*" If you knew all
the stories behind all the people on the boardwalk, you'd see that *nothing* was what
it looked like. Husbands and wives often hated each other; parents didn't necessarily love their children; et cetera. A child took things for granted because he had nothing to compare his life to and everybody acted as if things were as they should be.
Therefore each saw himself as the hero of the story, when the truth might turn out
to be that he's the villain, or the coward. And there wasn't one thing you could do
about it!

Hunchbacks, fat ladies, fools—that no one chose what he was was unbearable.
In the movies he'd meet a beautiful young girl in the funhouse; they'd have hairs-
breadth escapes from real dangers; he'd do and say the right things; she also; in the
end they'd be lovers; their dialogue lines would match up; he'd be perfectly at ease;
she'd not only like him well enough, she'd think he was *marvelous;* she'd lie awake
thinking about *him,* instead of vice versa—the way *his* face looked in different lights
and how he stood and exactly what he'd said—and yet that would be only one small
episode in his wonderful life, among many many others. Not a *turning point* at all.
What had happened in the toolshed was nothing. He hated, he loathed his parents!
One reason for not writing a lost-in-the-funhouse story is that either everybody's felt
what Ambrose feels, in which case it goes without saying, or else no normal person
feels such things, in which case Ambrose is a freak. "Is anything more tiresome, in
fiction, than the problems of sensitive adolescents?" And it's all too long and rambling, as if the author. For all a person knows the first time through, the end could be
just around any corner; perhaps, *not impossibly* it's been within reach any number of
times. On the other hand he may be scarcely past the start, with everything yet to get
through, an intolerable idea.

45   *Fill in:* His father's raised eyebrows when he announced his decision to do the
funhouse with Magda. Ambrose understands now, but didn't then, that his father was
wondering whether he knew what the funhouse was *for*—especially since he didn't
object, as he should have, when Peter decided to come along too. The ticket-woman,
witchlike, mortifying him when inadvertently he gave her his name-coin instead of
the half-dollar, then unkindly calling Magda's attention to the birthmark on his temple: "Watch out for him, girlie, he's a marked man!" She wasn't even cruel, he understood, only vulgar and insensitive. Somewhere in the world there was a young
woman with such splendid understanding that she'd see him entire, like a poem or
story, and find his words so valuable after all that when he confessed his apprehensions she would explain why they were in fact the very things that made him precious to her . . . and to Western Civilization! There was no such girl, the simple truth

being. Violent yawns as they approached the mouth. Whispered advice from an old-timer on a bench near the barrel: "Go crabwise and ye'll get an eyeful without upsetting!" Composure vanished at the first pitch: Peter hollered joyously, Magda tumbled, shrieked, clutched her skirt; Ambrose scrambled crabwise, tight-lipped with terror, was soon out, watched his dropped name-coin slide among the couples. Shamefaced he saw that to get through expeditiously was not the point; Peter feigned assistance in order to trip Magda up, shouted "I see Christmas!" when her legs went flying. The old man, his latest betrayer, cackled approval. A dim hall then of black-thread cobwebs and recorded gibber: he took Magda's elbow to steady her against revolving discs set in the slanted floor to throw your feet out from under, and explained to her in a calm, deep voice his theory that each phase of the funhouse was triggered either automatically, by a series of photoelectric devices, or else manually by operators stationed at peepholes. But he lost his voice thrice as the discs unbalanced him; Magda was anyhow squealing; but at one point she clutched him about the waist to keep from falling, and her right cheek pressed for a moment against his belt-buckle. Heroically he drew her up, it was his chance to clutch her close as if for support and say: "I love you." He even put an arm lightly about the small of her back before a sailor-and-girl pitched into them from behind, sorely treading his left big toe and knocking Magda asprawl with them. The sailor's girl was a string-haired hussy with a loud laugh and light blue drawers; Ambrose realized that he wouldn't have said "I love you" anyhow, and was smitten with self-contempt. How much better it would be to be that common sailor! A wiry little Seaman 3rd, the fellow squeezed a girl to each side and stumbled hilarious into the mirror room, closer to Magda in thirty seconds than Ambrose had got in thirteen years. She giggled at something the fellow said to Peter; she drew her hair from her eyes with a movement so womanly it struck Ambrose's heart; Peter's smacking her backside then seemed particularly coarse. But Magda made a pleased indignant face and cried, "All right for *you*, mister!" and pursued Peter into the maze without a backward glance. The sailor followed after, leisurely, drawing his girl against his hip; Ambrose understood not only that they were all so relieved to be rid of his burdensome company that they didn't even notice his absence, but that he himself shared their relief. Stepping from the treacherous passage at last into the mirror-maze, he saw once again, more clearly than ever, how readily he deceived himself into supposing he was a person. He even foresaw, wincing at his dreadful self-knowledge, that he would repeat the deception, at ever-rarer intervals, all his wretched life, so fearful were the alternatives. Fame, madness, suicide; perhaps all three. It's not believable that so young a boy could articulate that reflection, and in fiction the merely true must always yield to the plausible. Moreover, the symbolism is in places heavy-footed. Yet Ambrose M——— understood, as few adults do, that the famous loneliness of the great was no popular myth but a general truth—furthermore, that it was as much cause as effect.

All the preceding except the last few sentences is exposition that should've been done earlier or interspersed with the present action instead of lumped together. No reader would put up with so much with such *prolixity*. It's interesting that Ambrose's father, though presumably an intelligent man (as indicated by his role as grade-school principal), neither encouraged nor discouraged his sons at all in any way—as if he either didn't care about them or cared all right but didn't know how to act. If this fact should contribute to one of them's becoming a celebrated but wretchedly unhappy scientist, was it a good thing or not? He too might someday face the question; it would be useful to know whether it had tortured his father for years, for example, or never once crossed his mind.

In the maze two important things happened. First, our hero found a name-coin someone else had lost or discarded: *AMBROSE,* suggestive of the famous lightship and of his late grandfather's favorite dessert, which his mother used to prepare on special occasions out of coconut, oranges, grapes, and what else. Second, as he wondered at the endless replication of his image in the mirrors, second, as he *lost himself in the reflection* that the necessity for an observer makes perfect observation impossible, better make him eighteen at least, yet that would render other things unlikely, he heard Peter and Magda chuckling somewhere together in the maze. "Here!" "No, here!" they shouted to each other; Peter said, "Where's Amby?" Magda murmured. "Amb?" Peter called. In a pleased, friendly voice. He didn't reply. The truth was, his brother was a *happy-go-lucky youngster* who'd've been better off with a regular brother of his own, but who seldom complained of his lot and was generally cordial. Ambrose's throat ached; there aren't enough different ways to say that. He stood quietly while the two young people giggled and thumped through the glittering maze, hurrah'd their discovery of its exit, cried out in joyful alarm at what next beset them. Then he set his mouth and followed after, as he supposed, took a wrong turn, strayed into the pass *wherein he lingers yet.*

The action of conventional dramatic narrative may be represented by a diagram called Freitag's Triangle:

or more accurately by a variant of that diagram:

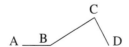

in which *AB* represents the exposition, *B* the introduction of conflict, *BC* the "rising action," complication, or development of the conflict, *C* the climax, or turn of the action, *CD* the dénouement, or resolution of the conflict. While there is no reason to regard this pattern as an absolute necessity, like many other conventions it became conventional because great numbers of people over many years learned by trial and error that it was effective; one ought not to forsake it, therefore, unless one wishes to forsake as well the effect of drama or has clear cause to feel that deliberate violation of the "normal" pattern can better can better effect that effect. This can't go on much longer; it can go on forever. He died telling stories to himself in the dark; years later, when that vast unsuspected area of the funhouse came to light, the first expedition found his skeleton in one of its labyrinthine corridors and mistook it for part of the entertainment. He died of starvation telling himself stories in the dark; but un-beknownst unbeknownst to him, an assistant operator of the funhouse, happening to overhear him, crouched just behind the plyboard partition and wrote down his every word. The operator's daughter, an exquisite young woman with a figure unusually well developed for her age, crouched just behind the partition and transcribed his every word. Though she had never laid eyes on him, she recognized that here was one of Western Culture's truly great imaginations, the eloquence of whose suffering would be an inspiration to unnumbered. And her heart was torn between her love for the misfortunate young man (yes, she loved him, though she had never laid though she knew him only—but how well!—through his words, and the deep, calm voice in which he spoke them) between her love et cetera and her womanly intuition that only in suffering and isolation could he give voice et cetera. Lone dark dying. Quietly she kissed the rough plywood, and a tear fell upon the page. Where she had written in shorthand *Where she had written in shorthand* Where she had written in shorthand *Where she* et cetera. A long time ago we should have passed the apex of Freitag's Triangle and made brief work of the *dénouement;* the plot doesn't rise by meaning-ful steps but winds upon itself, digresses, retreats, hesitates, sighs, collapses, expires. The climax of the story must be its protagonist's discovery of a way to get through the funhouse. But he has found none, may have ceased to search.

What relevance does the war have to the story? Should there be fireworks out-side or not?

Ambrose wandered, languished, dozed. Now and then he fell into his habit ₅₀ of rehearsing to himself the unadventurous story of his life, narrated from the third-person point of view, from his earliest memory parenthesis of maple leaves stirring in the summer breath of tidewater Maryland end of parenthesis to the present moment. Its principal events, on this telling, would appear to have been *A, B, C,* and *D.*

He imagined himself years hence, successful, married, at ease in the world, the trials of his adolescence far behind him. He has come to the seashore with his fam-ily for the holiday: how Ocean City has changed! But at one seldom at one ill-frequented end of the boardwalk a few derelict amusements survive from times gone by: the great carrousel from the turn of the century, with its monstrous griffins and mechanical concert band; the roller coaster rumored since 1916 to have been con-demned; the mechanical shooting gallery in which only the image of our enemies changed. His own son laughs with Fat May and wants to know what a funhouse is; Ambrose hugs the sturdy lad close and smiles around his pipestem at his wife.

The family's going home. Mother sits between Father and Uncle Karl, who teases him good-naturedly who chuckles over the fact that the comrade with whom he'd fought his way shoulder to shoulder through the funhouse had turned out to be a blind Negro girl—to their mutual discomfort, as they'd opened their souls. But such are the walls of custom, which even. Whose arm is where? How must it feel. He dreams of a funhouse vaster by far than any yet constructed; but by then they may be out of fashion, like steamboats and excursion trains. Already quaint and seedy: the draperied ladies on the frieze of the carrousel are his father's father's mooncheeked dreams; if he thinks of it more he will vomit his apple-on-a-stick.

He wonders: will he become a regular person? Something has gone wrong; his vaccination didn't take; at the Boy-Scout initiation campfire he only pretended to be deeply moved, as he pretends to this hour that it is not so bad after all in the funhouse, and that he has a little limp. How long will it last? He envisions a truly astonishing funhouse, incredibly complex yet utterly controlled from a great central switchboard like the console of a pipe organ. Nobody had enough imagination. He could design such a place himself, wiring and all, and he's only thirteen years old. He would be its operator: panel lights would show what was up in every cranny of its cunning of its multifarious vastness; a switch-flick would ease this fellow's way, complicate that's, to balance things out; if anyone seemed lost or frightened, all the operator had to do was.

He wishes he had never entered the funhouse. But he has. Then he wishes he were dead. But he's not. Therefore he will construct funhouses for others and be their secret operator—though he would rather be among the lovers for whom funhouses are designed.

QUESTIONS FOR DISCUSSION AND WRITING

1. How does Freitag's triangle illustrate the plots of most stories? Why doesn't it explain the plot of this story?

2. How does the setting of the story, "the funhouse," affect the way events are presented and interpreted in the story?

3. How many methods of characterization does the author of the story explain? How many does he use? Which ones seem most effective?

4. How would you describe the difference between the author's and Ambrose's point of view? In what ways are they the same?

5. What does Ambrose learn about himself in the funhouse? How does the last paragraph help us understand the theme of the story?

Stories for Comparison

Jorge Luis Borges's "The Garden of Forking Paths" (pages 291–298); Rudolfo Anaya's "B. Traven Is Alive and Well in Cuernavaca" (pages 184–194).

23

....

A N N   B E A T T I E

The Working Girl

ANN BEATTIE was born in 1947 in Washington, D.C., and educated at
American University and the University of Connecticut. She has worked as a
writer-in-residence at the University of Virginia and Harvard University, and
has contributed numerous short stories to *The New Yorker.* She has published
these stories in collections such as *Distortions* (1976), *Secrets and Surprises*
(1979), *What Was Mine* (1991), and *Where You'll Find Me* (1996). She has
also published critically acclaimed novels such as *Chilly Scenes of Winter*
(1976) and *Another You* (1995). In "The Working Girl," reprinted from *What
Was Mine,* the author speculates on how various details contribute to her
story about "a working girl."

This is a story about Jeanette, who is a working girl. She sometimes thinks of herself as a traveler, a seductress, a secret gourmet. She takes a one-week vacation
in the summer to see her sister in Michigan, buys lace-edged silk underpants from a
mail-order catalogue, and has improvised a way, in America, to make crème fraîche,
which is useful on so many occasions.
   Is this another story in which the author knows the main character all too well?
   Let's suppose, for a moment, that the storyteller is actually mystified by
Jeanette, and only seems to stand in judgment because words come easily. Let's
imagine that in real life there is, or once was, a person named Jeanette, and that from
a conversation the storyteller had with her, it could be surmised that Jeanette has a
notion of freedom, though the guilty quiver of the mouth when she says "Lake
Michigan" is something of a giveaway about how she really feels. If the storyteller
is a woman, Jeanette might readily confide that she is a seductress, but if the author is
a man, Jeanette will probably keep quiet on that count. Crème fraîche is crème
fraîche, and not worth thinking about. But back to the original supposition: Let's say
that the storyteller is a woman, and that Jeanette discusses the pros and cons of the
working life, calling a spade a spade, and greenbacks greenbacks, and if Jeanette is
herself a good storyteller, Lake Michigan sounds exciting, and if she isn't, it doesn't.
Let's say that Jeanette talks about the romance in her life, and that the storyteller
finds it credible. Even interesting. That there are details: Jeanette's lover makes a

photocopy of his hand and drops the piece of paper in her in-box; Jeanette makes a copy of her hand and has her trusted friend Charlie hang it in the men's room, where it is allowed to stay until Jeanette's lover sees it, because it means nothing to anyone else. If the storyteller is lucky, they will exchange presents small enough to be put in a breast pocket or the pocket of a skirt. Also a mini French-English/English-French dictionary (France is the place they hope to visit); a finger puppet; an ad that is published in the "personals" column, announcing, by his initials, whom he loves (her), laminated in plastic and made useful as well as romantic by its conversion into a keyring. Let's hope, for the sake of a good story, they are wriggling together in the elevator, sneaking kisses as the bubbles rise in the watercooler, and she is tying his shoelaces together at night, to delay his departure in the morning.

Where is the wife?

5   In North Dakota or Memphis or Paris, let's say. Let's say she's out of the picture even if she isn't out of the picture.

No no no. Too expedient. The wife has to be there: a presence, even if she's gone off somewhere. There has to be a wife, and she has to be either determined and brave, vile and addicted, or so ordinary that with a mere sentence of description, the reader instantly knows that she is a prototypical wife.

There is a wife. She is a pretty, dark-haired girl who married young, and who won a trip to Paris and is therefore out of town.

Nonsense. *Paris?*

She won a beauty contest.

10   But she can't be beautiful. She has to be ordinary.

It suddenly becomes apparent that she is extraordinary. She's quite beautiful, and she's in Paris, and although there's no reason to bring this up, the people who sponsored the contest do not know that she's married.

If this is what the wife is like, she'll be more interesting than the subject of the story.

Not if the working girl is believable, and the wife's exit has been made credible.

But we know how that story will end.

15   How will it end?

It will end badly—which means predictably—because either the beautiful wife will triumph, and then it will be just another such story, or the wife will turn out to be not so interesting after all, and by default the working girl will triumph.

When is the last time you heard of a working girl triumphing?

They do it every day. They are executives, not "working girls."

No, not those. This is about a real working girl. One who gets very little money or vacation time, who periodically rewards herself for life's injustices by buying cream and charging underwear she'll spend a year paying off.

20   All right, then. What is the story?

Are you sure you want to hear it? Apparently you are already quite shaken, to have found out that the wife, initially ordinary, is in fact extraordinary, and has competed in a beauty pageant and won a trip to Paris.

But this was to be a story about the working girl. What's the scoop with her?

This is just the way the people in the office think: the boss wants to know what's going on in his secretary's mind, the secretary wonders if the mail boy is gay, the mail boy is cruising the elevator operator, and every day the working girl walks into this tense, strange situation. She does it because she needs the money, and also because it's the way things are. It isn't going to be much different wherever she works.

Details. Make the place seem real.

In the winter, when the light disappears early, the office has a very strange aura. The ficus trees cast shadows on the desks. The water in the watercooler looks golden—more like wine than water.

How many people are there?

There are four people typing in the main room, and there are three executives, who share an executive secretary. She sits to the left of the main room.

Which one is the working girl in love with?

Andrew Darby, the most recently hired executive. He has prematurely gray hair, missed two days of work when his dog didn't pull through surgery, and was never drafted because of a deteriorating disc which causes him much pain, though it is difficult to predict when the pain will come on. Once it seemed to coincide with the rising of a bubble in the watercooler. The pain shot up his spine as though mimicking the motion of the bubble.

And he's married?

We just finished discussing his wife.

He's really married, right?

There are no tricks here. He's been married for six years.

Is there more information about his wife?

No. You can find out what the working girl thinks of her, but as far as judging for yourself, you can't, because she is in Paris. What good would it do to overhear a phone conversation between the wife and Andrew? None of us generalizes from phone conversations. Other than that, there's only a postcard. It's a close-up of a column, and she says on the back that she loves and misses him. That if love could be embodied in columns, her love for him would be Corinthian.

That's quite something. What is his reaction to that?

He receives the postcard the same day his ad appears in the "personals" column. He has it in his pocket when he goes to laminate the ad, punch a hole in the plastic, insert a chain, and make a keyring of it.

Doesn't he go through a bad moment?

A bit of one, but basically he is quite pleased with himself. He and Jeanette are going to lunch together. Over lunch, he gives her the keyring. She is slightly scandalized, amused, and touched. They eat sandwiches. He can't sit in a booth because of his back. They sit at a table.

Ten years later, where is Andrew Darby?

Dead. He dies of complications following surgery. A blood clot that went to his brain.

Why does he have to die?

This is just reporting, now. In point of fact, he dies.

Is Jeanette still in touch with him when he dies?

She's his wife. Married men do leave their wives. Andrew Darby didn't have that rough a go of it. After a while, he and his former wife developed a fairly cordial relationship. She spoke to him on the phone the day he checked into the hospital.

What happened then?

At what point?

When he died.

He saw someone beckoning to him. But that isn't what you mean. What happened is that Jeanette was in a cab on her way to the hospital, and when she got there, one of the nurses was waiting by the elevator. The nurse knew that Jeanette was on her way, because she came at the same time every day. Also, Andrew Darby had been on that same floor, a year or so before, for surgery that was successful. That nurse took care of him then, also. It isn't true that the nurse you have one year will be gone the next.

50   This isn't a story about the working girl anymore.

It is, because she went right on working. She worked during the marriage and for quite a few years after he died. Toward the end, she wasn't working because she needed the money. She wanted the money, but that's different from needing the money.

What kind of a life did they have together?

He realized that he had something of a problem with alcohol and gave it up. She kept her figure. They went to Bermuda and meant to return, but never did. Every year she reordered perfume from a catalogue she had taken from the hotel room in Bermuda. She tried to find another scent that she liked, but always ended up reordering the one she was so pleased with. They didn't have children. He didn't have children with his first wife either, so that by the end it was fairly certain that the doctor had been right, and that the problem was with Andrew, although he never would agree to be tested. He had two dogs in his life, and one cat. Jeanette's Christmas present to him, the year he died, was a Rolex. He gave her a certificate that entitled her to twenty free tanning sessions and a monthly massage.

What was it like when she was a working girl?

55   Before she met him, or afterwards?

Before and afterwards.

Before, she often felt gloomy, although she entertained more in those days, and she enjoyed that. Her charge card bills were always at the limit, and if she had been asked, even at the time, she would have admitted that a sort of overcompensation was taking place. She read more before she met him, but after she met him he read the same books, and it was nice to have someone to discuss them with. She was convinced that she had once broken someone's heart: a man she dated for a couple of years, who inherited his parents' estate when they died. He wanted to marry Jeanette and take care of her. His idea was to commute into New York from the big estate in Connecticut. She felt that she didn't know how to move comfortably into someone else's life. Though she tried to explain carefully, he was bitter and always maintained that she didn't marry him because she didn't like the furniture.

Afterwards?

You've already heard some things about afterwards. Andrew had a phobia about tollbooths, so when they were driving on the highway, he'd pull onto the shoulder when he saw the sign for a tollbooth, and she'd drive through it. On the Jersey Turnpike, of course, she just kept the wheel. They knew only one couple that they liked equally well—they liked the man as well as they liked the woman, that is. They tended to like the same couples.

What was it like, again, in the office?   60

The plants and the watercooler.

Besides that.

That's really going back in time. It would seem like a digression at this point.

But what about understanding the life of the working girl?

She turned a corner, and it was fall. With a gigantic intake of breath, her feet 65
lifted off the ground.

Explain.

Nothing miraculous happened, but still things did happen, and life changed. She lost touch with some friends, became quite involved in reading the classics. In Bermuda, swimming, she looked up and saw a boat and remembered very distinctly, and much to her surprise, that the man she had been involved with before Andrew had inherited a collection of ships in bottles from his great-great-grandfather. And that day, as she came out of the water, she cut her foot on something. Whatever it was was as sharp as glass, if it was not glass. And that seemed to sum up something. She was quite shaken. She and Andrew sat in the sand, and the boat passed by, and Andrew thought that it was the pain alone that had upset her.

In the office, when the light dimmed early in the day. In the winter. Before they were together. She must have looked at the shadows on her desk and felt like a person lost in the forest.

If she thought that, she never said it.

Did she confide in Charlie?   70

To some extent. She and Charlie palled around together before she became involved with Andrew. Afterwards, too, a little. She was always consulted when he needed to buy a new tie.

Did Charlie go to the wedding?

There was no wedding. It was a civil ceremony.

Where did they go on their honeymoon?

Paris. He always wanted to see Paris.   75

But his wife went to Paris.

That was just coincidence, and besides, she wasn't there at the same time. By then she was his ex-wife. Jeanette never knew that his wife had been to Paris.

What things did he not know?

That she once lost two hundred dollars in a cab. That she did a self-examination of her breasts twice a day. She hid her dislike of the dog, which they had gotten at his insistence, from the pound. The dog was a chewer.

When an image of Andrew came to mind, what was it?   80

Andrew at forty, when she first met him. She felt sorry that he had a mole on his cheekbone, but later came to love it. Sometimes, after his death, the mole would fill the whole world of her dream. At least that is what she thought it was—a gray mass like a mountain, seen from the distance, then closer and closer until it became amorphous and she was awake, gripping the sheet. It was a nightmare, obviously, not a dream. Though she called it a dream.

Who is Berry McKenn?

A woman he had a brief flirtation with. Nothing of importance.

Why do storytellers start to tell one story and then tell another?

85   Life is a speeding train. Storytellers get derailed too.

What did Andrew see when he conjured up Jeanette?

Her green eyes. That startled look, as if the eyes had a life of their own, and were surprised to be bracketing so long a nose.

What else is there to say about their life together?

There is something of an anecdote about the watercooler. It disappeared once, and it was noticeably absent, as if someone had removed a geyser. The surprise on people's faces when they stared at the empty corner of the corridor was really quite astonishing. Jeanette went to meet Andrew there the day the repairman took it away. They made it a point, several times a day, to meet there as if by accident. One of the other girls who worked there—thinking Charlie was her friend, which he certainly was not: he was Jeanette's friend—had seen the watercooler being removed, and she whispered slyly to Charlie that it would be amusing when Jeanette strolled away from her desk, and Andrew left his office moments later with great purpose in his step and holding his blue pottery mug, because they would be standing in an empty corridor, with their prop gone and their cover blown.

90   What did Charlie say?

Jeanette asked him that too, when he reported the conversation. "They're in love," he said. "You might not want to think it, but a little thing like that isn't going to be a setback at all." He felt quite triumphant about taking a stand, though there's room for skepticism, of course. What people say is one thing, and what they later report they have said is another.

QUESTIONS FOR DISCUSSION AND WRITING

1. Is Beattie a "derailed storyteller," or is there actually a well-constructed plot in the apparent randomness of this story? What is the real subject of this plot? What are its major conflicts?

2. How does the narrator become an actual character within the story? How does her characterization of the first wife become a meditation on the creator of a fictional character? In what ways does Jeanette emerge as a fully developed character in spite of the apparent fragmentation of her presentation?

3. How does Beattie use details to make the office setting "seem real"? For example, how does she use the water cooler to evoke the conflicts, conversations, and conspiracies of office life?

4. In what sense does "the author know the main character all too well"? How does her use of point of view make it impossible for the reader to "know" anything for certain in the story? Who is the "character" that interrogates the "narrator"?

5. What does the title of the story suggest about the nature of Jeanette's life? How does Beattie's sharing of the fiction-making process with the reader suggest a major thematic point about the nature of life itself?

Stories for Comparison

Jamaica Kincaid's "Girl" (pages 776–777); Tillie Olsen's "I Stand Here Ironing" (pages 1004–1011).

24

JORGE LUIS BORGES

The Garden of Forking Paths

TRANSLATED BY DONALD A. YATES

For Victoria Ocampo

JORGE LUIS BORGES (1899–1986) was born in Buenos Aires, Argentina, and educated at the College de Geneve, Switzerland. After World War I, he traveled throughout Europe and associated with a Spanish literary movement called *Ultraisme.* Borges returned to Argentina in 1921 to lead various avant-garde literary movements and to publish his poems and essays. In the 1930s he began composing fiction that revealed the influence of Kafka and Joyce. In addition to writing, Borges worked as an editor, teacher, and librarian. In 1946 dictator Juan Perón demoted him for political reasons to the rank of chicken inspector. With the fall of Perón's government in 1955, Borges was reappointed director of the National Library and professor of English and American Literature at the University of Buenos Aires. During the next thirty years Borges continued to teach and write in Europe, America, and Argentina. His writings include *Ficciones* (1944), *Labyrinths* (1962), *The Aleph and Other Stories* (1970), *Doctor Brodie's Report* (1972), *The Book of Sand* (1977), and *Six Problems for Don Isidro Parodi* (1981). In "The Garden of Forking Paths," reprinted from *Labyrinths,* Borges meditates on the infinitely complex relationship between writing history and writing fiction.

On page 22 of Liddell Hart's *History of World War I* you will read that an attack against the Serre-Montauban line by thirteen British divisions (supported by

1,400 artillery pieces), planned for the 24th of July, 1916, had to be postponed until the morning of the 29th. The torrential rains, Captain Liddell Hart comments, caused this delay, an insignificant one, to be sure.

The following statement, dictated, reread and signed by Dr. Yu Tsun, former professor of English at the *Hochschule* at Tsingtao, throws an unsuspected light over the whole affair. The first two pages of the document are missing.

". . . and I hung up the receiver. Immediately afterwards, I recognized the voice that had answered in German. It was that of Captain Richard Madden. Madden's presence in Viktor Runeberg's apartment meant the end of our anxieties and—but this seemed, *or should have seemed,* very secondary to me—also the end of our lives. It meant that Runeberg had been arrested or murdered.[1] Before the sun set on that day, I would encounter the same fate. Madden was implacable. Or rather, he was obliged to be so. An Irishman at the service of England, a man accused of laxity and perhaps of treason, how could he fail to seize and be thankful for such a miraculous opportunity: the discovery, capture, maybe even the death of two agents of the German Reich? I went up to my room; absurdly I locked the door and threw myself on my back on the narrow iron cot. Through the window I saw the familiar roofs and the cloud-shaded six o'clock sun. It seemed incredible to me that that day without premonitions or symbols should be the one of my inexorable death. In spite of my dead father, in spite of having been a child in a symmetrical garden of Hai Feng, was I—now—going to die? Then I reflected that everything happens to a man precisely, precisely *now.* Centuries of centuries and only in the present do things happen; countless men in the air, on the face of the earth and the sea, and all that really is happening is happening to me . . . The almost intolerable recollection of Madden's horselike face banished these wanderings. In the midst of my hatred and terror (it means nothing to me now to speak of terror, now that I have mocked Richard Madden, now that my throat yearns for the noose) it occurred to me that that tumultuous and doubtless happy warrior did not suspect that I possess the Secret. The name of the exact location of the new British artillery park on the River Ancre. A bird streaked across the gray sky and blindly I translated it into an airplane and that airplane into many (against the French sky) annihilating the artillery station with vertical bombs. If only my mouth, before a bullet shattered it, could cry out that secret name so it could be heard in Germany . . . My human voice was very weak. How might I make it carry to the ear of the Chief? To the ear of that sick and hateful man who knew nothing of Runeberg and me save that we were in Staffordshire and who was waiting in vain for our report in his arid office in Berlin, endlessly examining newspapers . . . I said out loud: *I must flee.* I sat up noiselessly, in a useless perfection of silence, as if Madden were already lying in wait for me. Something—perhaps the mere vain ostentation of proving my resources were nil—made me look through my pockets. I found what I knew I would find. The American watch, the nickel chain and the square coin, the key ring with the incriminating useless keys to Runeberg's apartment, the notebook, a letter which I resolved to destroy immediately (and which I did not

---

[1] An hypothesis both hateful and odd. The Prussian spy Hans Rabener, alias Viktor Runeberg, attacked with drawn automatic the bearer of the warrant for his arrest, Captain Richard Madden. The latter, in self-defense, inflicted the wound which brought about Runeberg's death. (Borges's note.)

destroy), a crown, two shillings and a few pence, the red and blue pencil, the handkerchief, the revolver with one bullet. Absurdly, I took it in my hand and weighed it in order to inspire courage within myself. Vaguely I thought that a pistol report can be heard
at a great distance. In ten minutes my plan was perfected. The telephone book listed the
name of the only person capable of transmitting the message; he lived in a suburb of
Fenton, less than a half hour's train ride away.

I am a cowardly man. I say it now, now that I have carried to its end a plan whose
perilous nature no one can deny. I know its execution was terrible. I didn't do it for Germany, no. I care nothing for a barbarous country which imposed upon me the abjection
of being a spy. Besides, I know of a man from England—a modest man—who for me is
no less great than Goethe. I talked with him for scarcely an hour, but during that hour he
was Goethe . . . I did it because I sensed that the Chief somehow feared people of my
race—for the innumerable ancestors who merge within me. I wanted to prove to him
that a yellow man could save his armies. Besides, I had to flee from Captain Madden.
His hands and his voice could call at my door at any moment. I dressed silently, bade
farewell to myself in the mirror, went downstairs, scrutinized the peaceful street and
went out. The station was not far from my home, but I judged it wise to take a cab. I argued that in this way I ran less risk of being recognized; the fact is that in the deserted
street I felt myself visible and vulnerable, infinitely so. I remember that I told the cab
driver to stop a short distance before the main entrance. I got out with voluntary, almost
painful slowness; I was going to the village of Ashgrove but I bought a ticket for a more
distant station. The train left within a very few minutes, at eight-fifty. I hurried; the next
one would leave at nine-thirty. There was hardly a soul on the platform. I went through
the coaches; I remember a few farmers, a woman dressed in mourning, a young boy
who was reading with fervor the *Annals* of Tacitus, a wounded and happy soldier. The
coaches jerked forward at last. A man whom I recognized ran in vain to the end of the
platform. It was Captain Richard Madden. Shattered, trembling, I shrank into the far
corner of the seat, away from the dreaded window.

From this broken state I passed into an almost abject felicity. I told myself that   5
the duel had already begun and that I had won the first encounter by frustrating, even
if for forty minutes, even if by a stroke of fate, the attack of my adversary. I argued
that this slightest of victories foreshadowed a total victory. I argued (no less falla-
ciously) that my cowardly felicity proved that I was a man capable of carrying out the
adventure successfully. From this weakness I took strength that did not abandon me.
I foresee that man will resign himself each day to more atrocious undertakings; soon
there will be no one but warriors and brigands; I give them this counsel: *The author
of an atrocious undertaking ought to imagine that he has already accomplished it,
ought to impose upon himself a future as irrevocable as the past.* Thus I proceeded as
my eyes of a man already dead registered the elapsing of that day, which was perhaps
the last, and the diffusion of the night. The train ran gently along, amid ash trees. It
stopped, almost in the middle of the fields. No one announced the name of the station.
"Ashgrove?" I asked a few lads on the platform. "Ashgrove," they replied. I got off.

A lamp enlightened the platform but the faces of the boys were in shadow. One
questioned me, "Are you going to Dr. Stephen Albert's house?" Without waiting for
my answer, another said, "The house is a long way from here, but you won't get lost
if you take this road to the left and at every crossroads turn again to your left."

I tossed them a coin (my last), descended a few stone steps and started down the solitary road. It went downhill, slowly. It was of elemental earth; overhead the branches were tangled; the low, full moon seemed to accompany me.

For an instant, I thought that Richard Madden in some way had penetrated my desperate plan. Very quickly, I understood that that was impossible. The instructions to turn always to the left reminded me that such was the common procedure for discovering the central point of certain labyrinths. I have some understanding of labyrinths: not for nothing am I the great grandson of that Ts'ui Pên who was governor of Yunnan and who renounced worldly power in order to write a novel that might be even more populous than the *Hung Lu Meng* and to construct a labyrinth in which all men would become lost. Thirteen years he dedicated to these heterogeneous tasks, but the hand of a stranger murdered him—and his novel was incoherent and no one found the labyrinth. Beneath English trees I meditated on that lost maze: I imagined it inviolate and perfect at the secret crest of a mountain; I imagined it erased by rice fields or beneath the water; I imagined it infinite, no longer composed of octagonal kiosks and returning paths, but of rivers and provinces and kingdoms . . . I thought of a labyrinth of labyrinths, of one sinuous spreading labyrinth that would encompass the past and the future and in some way involve the stars. Absorbed in these illusory images, I forgot my destiny of one pursued. I felt myself to be, for an unknown period of time, an abstract perceiver of the world. The vague, living countryside, the moon, the remains of the day worked on me, as well as the slope of the road which eliminated any possibility of weariness. The afternoon was intimate, infinite. The road descended and forked among the now confused meadows. A high-pitched, almost syllabic music approached and receded in the shifting of the wind, dimmed by leaves and distance. I though that a man can be an enemy of other men, of the moments of other men, but not of a country: not of fireflies, words, gardens, streams of water, sunsets. Thus I arrived before a tall, rusty gate. Between the iron bars I made out a poplar grove and a pavilion. I understood suddenly two things, the first trivial, the second almost unbelievable: the music came from the pavilion, and the music was Chinese. For precisely that reason I had openly accepted it without paying it any heed. I do not remember whether there was a bell or whether I knocked with my hand. The sparkling of the music continued.

From the rear of the house within a lantern approached: a lantern that the trees sometimes striped and sometimes eclipsed, a paper lantern that had the form of a drum and the color of the moon. A tall man bore it. I didn't see his face for the light blinded me. He opened the door and said slowly, in my own language: "I see that the pious Hsi P'êng persists in correcting my solitude. You no doubt wish to see the garden?"

I recognized the name of one of our consuls and I replied, disconcerted, "The garden?"

10   "The garden of forking paths."

Something stirred in my memory and I uttered with incomprehensible certainty, "The garden of my ancestor Ts'ui Pên."

"Your ancestor? Your illustrious ancestor? Come in."

The damp path zigzagged like those of my childhood. We came to a library of Eastern and Western books. I recognized bound in yellow silk several volumes of the

Lost Encyclopedia, edited by the Third Emperor of the Luminous Dynasty but never printed. The record on the phonograph revolved next to a bronze phoenix. I also recall a *famille rose* vase and another, many centuries older, of that shade of blue which our craftsmen copied from the potters of Persia . . .

Stephen Albert observed me with a smile. He was, as I have said, very tall, sharp-featured, with gray eyes and a gray beard. He told me that he had been a missionary in Tientsin "before aspiring to become a Sinologist."

We sat down—I on a long, low divan, he with his back to the window and a tall circular clock. I calculated that my pursuer, Richard Madden, could not arrive for at least an hour. My irrevocable determination could wait.

"An astounding fate, that of Ts'ui Pên," Stephen Albert said. "Governor of his native province, learned in astronomy, in astrology and in the tireless interpretation of the canonical books, chess player, famous poet and calligrapher—he abandoned all this in order to compose a book and a maze. He renounced the pleasures of both tyranny and justice, of his populous couch, of his banquets and even of erudition— all to close himself up for thirteen years in the Pavilion of the Limpid Solitude. When he died, his heirs found nothing save chaotic manuscripts. His family, as you may be aware, wished to condemn them to the fire; but his executor—a Taoist or Buddhist monk—insisted on their publication."

"We descendants of Ts'ui Pên," I replied, "continue to curse that monk. Their publication was senseless. The book is an indeterminate heap of contradictory drafts. I examined it once: in the third chapter the hero dies, in the fourth he is alive. As for the other undertaking of Ts'ui Pên, his labyrinth . . ."

"Here is Ts'ui Pên's labyrinth," he said, indicating a tall lacquered desk.

"An ivory labyrinth!" I exclaimed. "A minimum labyrinth."

"A labyrinth of symbols," he corrected. "An invisible labyrinth of time. To me, a barbarous Englishman, has been entrusted the revelation of this diaphanous mystery. After more than a hundred years, the details are irretrievable; but it is not hard to conjecture what happened. Ts'ui Pên must have said once: *I am withdrawing to write a book.* And another time: *I am withdrawing to construct a labyrinth.* Every one imagined two works; to no one did it occur that the book and the maze were one and the same thing. The Pavilion of the Limpid Solitude stood in the center of a garden that was perhaps intricate; that circumstance could have suggested to the heirs a physical labyrinth. Ts'ui Pên died; no one in the vast territories that were his came upon the labyrinth; the confusion of the novel suggested to me that *it* was the maze. Two circumstances gave me the correct solution of the problem. One: the curious legend that Ts'ui Pên had planned to create a labyrinth which would be strictly infinite. The other: a fragment of a letter I discovered."

Albert rose. He turned his back on me for a moment; he opened a drawer of the black and gold desk. He faced me and in his hands he held a sheet of paper that had once been crimson, but was now pink and tenuous and cross-sectioned. The fame of Ts'ui Pên as a calligrapher had been justly won. I read, uncomprehendingly and with fervor, these words written with a minute brush by a man of my blood: *I leave to the various futures (not to all) my garden of forking paths.* Wordlessly, I returned the sheet. Albert continued:

"Before unearthing this letter, I had questioned myself about the ways in which a book can be infinite. I could think of nothing other than a cyclic volume, a circular one. A book whose last page was identical with the first, a book which had the possibility of continuing indefinitely. I remembered too that night which is at the middle of the Thousand and One Nights when Scheherazade (through a magical oversight of the copyist) begins to relate word for word the story of the Thousand and One Nights, establishing the risk of coming once again to the night when she must repeat it, and thus on to infinity. I imagined as well a Platonic, hereditary work, transmitted from father to son, in which each new individual adds a chapter or corrects with pious care the pages of his elders. These conjectures diverted me; but none seemed to correspond, not even remotely, to the contradictory chapters of Ts'ui Pên. In the midst of this perplexity, I received from Oxford the manuscript you have examined. I lingered, naturally, on the sentence: *I leave to the various futures (not to all) my garden of forking paths.* Almost instantly, I understood: 'the garden of forking paths' was the chaotic novel; the phrase 'the various futures (not to all)' suggested to me the forking in time, not in space. A broad rereading of the work confirmed the theory. In all fictional works, each time a man is confronted with several alternatives, he chooses one and eliminates the others; in the fiction of Ts'ui Pên, he chooses—simultaneously—all of them. *He creates,* in this way, diverse futures, diverse times which themselves also proliferate and fork. Here, then, is the explanation of the novel's contradictions. Fang, let us say, has a secret; a stranger calls at his door; Fang resolves to kill him. Naturally, there are several possible outcomes: Fang can kill the intruder, the intruder can kill Fang, they both can escape, they both can die, and so forth. In the work of Ts'ui Pên, all possible outcomes occur; each one is the point of departure for other forkings. Sometimes, the paths of this labyrinth converge: for example, you arrive at this house, but in one of the possible pasts you are my enemy, in another, my friend. If you will resign yourself to my incurable pronunciation, we shall read a few pages."

His face, within the vivid circle of the lamplight, was unquestionably that of an old man, but with something unalterable about it, even immortal. He read with slow precision two versions of the same epic chapter. In the first, an army marches to a battle across a lonely mountain; the horror of the rocks and shadows makes the men undervalue their lives and they gain an easy victory. In the second, the same army traverses a palace where a great festival is taking place; the resplendent battle seems to them a continuation of the celebration and they win the victory. I listened with proper veneration to these ancient narratives, perhaps less admirable in themselves than the fact that they had been created by my blood and were being restored to me by a man of a remote empire, in the course of a desperate adventure, on a Western isle. I remember the last words, repeated in each version like a secret commandment: *Thus fought the heroes, tranquil their admirable hearts, violent their swords, resigned to kill and to die.*

From that moment on, I felt about me and within my dark body an invisible, intangible swarming. Not the swarming of the divergent, parallel and finally coalescent armies, but a more inaccessible, more intimate agitation that they in some manner prefigured. Stephen Albert continued:

"I don't believe that your illustrious ancestor played idly with these variations. 25
I don't consider it credible that he would sacrifice thirteen years to the infinite execution of a rhetorical experiment. In your country, the novel is a subsidiary form of
literature; in Ts'ui Pên's time it was a despicable form. Ts'ui Pên was a brilliant novelist, but he was also a man of letters who doubtless did not consider himself a mere
novelist. The testimony of his contemporaries proclaims—and his life fully con-
firms—his metaphysical and mystical interests. Philosophic controversy usurps a
good part of the novel. I know that of all problems, none disturbed him so greatly
nor worked upon him so much as the abysmal problem of time. Now then, the latter
is the only problem that does not figure in the pages of the *Garden.* He does not even
use the word that signifies *time.* How do you explain this voluntary omission?"

I proposed several solutions—all unsatisfactory. We discussed them. Finally,
Stephen Albert said to me:

"In a riddle whose answer is chess, what is the only prohibited word?"

I thought a moment and replied, "The word *chess.*"

"Precisely," said Albert. "*The Garden of Forking Paths* is an enormous riddle, or
parable, whose theme is time; this recondite cause prohibits its mention. To omit a
word always, to resort to inept metaphors and obvious periphrases, is perhaps the
most emphatic way of stressing it. That is the tortuous method preferred, in each of
the meanderings of his indefatigable novel, by the oblique Ts'ui Pên. I have compared
hundreds of manuscripts. I have corrected the errors that the negligence of the copyists has introduced. I have guessed the plan of this chaos, I have re-established—
I believe I have re-established—the primordial organization, I have translated the entire work: it is clear to me that not once does he employ the word 'time.' The explanation is obvious: *The Garden of Forking Paths* is an incomplete, but not false, image of the universe as Ts'ui Pên conceived it. In contrast to Newton and Schopenhauer,
your ancestor did not believe in a uniform, absolute time. He believed in an infinite
series of times, in a growing, dizzying net of divergent, convergent and parallel
times. This network of times which approached one another, forked, broke off,
or were unaware of one another for centuries, embraces *all* possibilities of time. We
do not exist in the majority of these times; in some you exist, and not I; in others I,
and not you; in others, both of us. In the present one, which a favorable fate has
granted me, you have arrived at my house; in another, while crossing the garden, you
found me dead; in still another, I utter these same words, but I am a mistake, a
ghost."

"In every one," I pronounced, not without a tremble to my voice, "I am grateful 30
to you and revere you for your re-creation of the garden of Ts'ui Pên."

"Not in all," he murmured with a smile. "Time forks perpetually toward innumerable futures. In one of them I am your enemy."

Once again I felt the swarming sensation of which I have spoken. It seemed to me
that the humid garden that surrounded the house was infinitely saturated with invisible persons. Those persons were Albert and I, secret, busy and multiform in other dimensions of time. I raised my eyes and the tenuous nightmare dissolved. In the yellow and black garden there was only one man; but this man was as strong as a statue
. . . this man was approaching along the path and he was Captain Richard Madden.

"The future already exists," I replied, "but I am your friend. Could I see the letter again?"

Albert rose. Standing tall, he opened the drawer of the tall desk; for the moment his back was to me. I had readied the revolver. I fired with extreme caution. Albert fell uncomplainingly, immediately. I swear his death was instantaneous—a lightning stroke.

35   The rest is unreal, insignificant. Madden broke in, arrested me. I have been condemned to the gallows. I have won out abominably; I have communicated to Berlin the secret name of the city they must attack. They bombed it yesterday; I read it in the same papers that offered to England the mystery of the learned Sinologist Stephen Albert who was murdered by a stranger, one Yu Tsun. The Chief had deciphered this mystery. He knew my problem was to indicate (through the uproar of the war) the city called Albert, and that I had found no other means to do so than to kill a man of that name. He does not know (no one can know) my innumerable contrition and weariness.

QUESTIONS FOR DISCUSSION AND WRITING

1. Arrange the major events of the story in chronological order. Does this arrangement help explain the events narrated in the first two paragraphs? Explain your answer.

2. How do you explain the narrator's intense commitment to completing his mission in spite of the fact that he has no patriotic concern about the outcome of the war? How does the narrator characterize the man who means to prevent him from completing this mission?

3. In what ways do the house, garden, and study provide an appropriate setting for the discussion of the concept of forking paths?

4. How does Tsun's acknowledgment that "everything happens to a man precisely, precisely *now*" influence his point of view toward the events he narrates? What advice does he offer other people who attempt "atrocious undertakings"?

5. How is the concept of a labyrinth crucial to an understanding of the theme of the story? For example, how do the past accomplishments of Tsun's ancestor prefigure his present choices?

Stories for Comparison

John Barth's "Lost in the Funhouse" (pages 268–284); Italo Calvino's "The Form of Space" (pages 322–328).

25

ELIZABETH BOWEN

The Demon Lover

ELIZABETH BOWEN (1899–1973) was born in Dublin, Ireland, and educated in England. During World War I she worked as a nurse in a military
hospital in Dublin. Bowen returned to England and became a student at the
London Council of Art. In 1923 she married Alan Cameron, a teacher in a
school near Oxford. In the same year, Bowen published her first collection of
short stories, *Encounters.* For the next twelve years she lived and wrote in
Oxford, publishing *The Hotel* (1927), *The Last September* (1929), *Friends
and Relations* (1931), and *The House in Paris* (1935). In 1935 the couple
moved to London, where Bowen became acquainted with the Bloomsbury
Group and, in particular, Virginia Woolf. During World War II Bowen
worked for the Ministry of Information and contributed reviews and essays to
The New Statesman. Her most acclaimed novel, *Death of the Heart* (1938),
was followed by a series of short-story collections including *Look at All
Those Roses* (1941), *The Demon Lover* (1945), and *Day in the Dark* (1965).
"The Demon Lover," reprinted from *The Collected Stories of Elizabeth
Bowen* (1974), recounts a woman's fateful encounter with a former lover.

Towards the end of her day in London Mrs. Drover went round to her shut-up
house to look for several things she wanted to take away. Some belonged to herself, some to her family, who were by now used to their country life. It was late August; it had been a steamy, showery day: at the moment the trees down the pavement
glittered in an escape of humid yellow afternoon sun. Against the next batch of
clouds, already piling up ink-dark, broken chimneys and parapets stood out. In her
once familiar street, as in any unused channel, an unfamiliar queerness had silted up;
a cat wove itself in and out of railings, but no human eye watched Mrs. Drover's return. Shifting some parcels under her arm, she slowly forced round her latchkey in
an unwilling lock, then gave the door, which had warped, a push with her knee. Dead
air came out to meet her as she went in.

The staircase window having been boarded up, no light came down into the hall.
But one door, she could just see, stood ajar, so she went quickly through into the
room and unshuttered the big window in there. Now the prosaic woman, looking

about her, was more perplexed than she knew by everything that she saw, by traces of her long former habit of life—the yellow smoke-stain up the white marble mantelpiece, the ring left by a vase on the top of the escritoire; the bruise in the wallpaper where, on the door being thrown open widely, the china handle had always hit the wall. The piano, having gone away to be stored, had left what looked like claw-marks on its part of the parquet. Though not much dust had seeped in, each object wore a film of another kind; and, the only ventilation being the chimney, the whole drawing-room smelled of the cold hearth. Mrs. Drover put down her parcels on the escritoire and left the room to proceed upstairs; the things she wanted were in a bed-room chest.

She had been anxious to see how the house was—the part-time caretaker she shared with some neighbours was away this week on his holiday, known to be not yet back. At the best of times he did not look in often, and she was never sure that she trusted him. There were some cracks in the structure, left by the last bombing, on which she was anxious to keep an eye. Not that one could do anything—

A shaft of refracted daylight now lay across the hall. She stopped dead and stared at the hall table—on this lay a letter addressed to her.

5   She thought first—then the caretaker *must* be back. All the same, who, seeing the house shuttered, would have dropped a letter in at the box? It was not a circular, it was not a bill. And the post office redirected, to the address in the country, everything for her that came through the post. The caretaker (even if he *were* back) did not know she was due in London today—her call here had been planned to be a surprise—so his negligence in the manner of this letter, leaving it to wait in the dusk and the dust, annoyed her. Annoyed, she picked up the letter, which bore no stamp. But it cannot be important, or they would know . . . She took the letter rapidly upstairs with her, without a stop to look at the writing till she reached what had been her bedroom, where she let in light. The room looked over the garden and other gardens: the sun had gone in; as the clouds sharpened and lowered, the trees and rank lawns seemed already to smoke with dark. Her reluctance to look again at the letter came from the fact that she felt intruded upon—and by someone contemptuous of her ways. However, in the tenseness preceding the fall of rain she read it: it was a few lines.

Dear Kathleen: You will not have forgotten that today is our anniversary, and the day we said. The years have gone by at once slowly and fast. In view of the fact that nothing has changed, I shall rely upon you to keep your promise. I was sorry to see you leave London, but was satisfied that you would be back in time. You may expect me, therefore, at the hour arranged. Until then . . .

K.

Mrs. Drover looked for the date: it was today's. She dropped the letter on to the bed-springs, then picked it up to see the writing again—her lips, beneath the remains of lipstick, beginning to go white. She felt so much the change in her own face that she went to the mirror, polished a clear patch in it and looked at once urgently and stealthily in. She was confronted by a woman of forty-four, with eyes starting out under a hat-brim that had been rather carelessly pulled down. She had not put on any more powder since she left the shop where she ate her solitary tea. The pearls her husband had given her on their marriage hung loose round her now rather thinner throat, slipping in the V of the pink wool jumper her sister knitted last autumn as they sat round the fire. Mrs. Drover's most normal expression was one of controlled worry, but of assent. Since the birth of the third of her little boys, attended by a quite serious illness, she had had an intermittent muscular flicker to the left of her mouth, but in spite of this she could always sustain a manner that was at once energetic and calm.

Turning from her own face as precipitately as she had gone to meet it, she went to the chest where the things were, unlocked it, threw up the lid and knelt to search. But as rain began to come crashing down she could not keep from looking over her shoulder at the stripped bed on which the letter lay. Behind the blanket of rain the clock of the church that still stood struck six—with rapidly heightening apprehension she counted each of the slow strokes. "The hour arranged . . . My God," she said, "*what* hour? How should I . . .? After twenty-five years . . ."

The young girl talking to the soldier in the garden had not ever completely seen his face. It was dark; they were saying goodbye under a tree. Now and then—for it felt, from not seeing him at this intense moment, as though she had never seen him at all—she verified his presence for these few moments longer by putting out a hand, which he each time pressed, without very much kindness, and painfully, on to one of the breast buttons of his uniform. That cut of the button on the palm of her hand was, principally, what she was to carry away. This was so near the end of a leave from France that she could only wish him already gone. It was August 1916. Being not kissed, being drawn away from and looked at intimidated Kathleen till she imagined spectral glitters in the place of his eyes. Turning away and looking back up the lawn she saw, through branches of trees, the drawing-room window light: she caught a breath for the moment when she could go running back there into the safe arms of her mother and sister, and cry: "What shall I do, what shall I do? He has gone."

Hearing her catch her breath, her fiancé said, without feeling: "Cold?"

"You're going away such a long way."

"Not so far as you think."   10

"I don't understand?"

"You don't have to," he said. "You will. You know what we said."

"But that was—suppose you—I mean, suppose."

"I shall be with you," he said, "sooner or later. You won't forget that. You need do nothing but wait."

Only a little more than a minute later she was free to run up the silent lawn. 15 Looking in through the window at her mother and sister, who did not for the moment perceive her, she already felt that unnatural promise drive down between her and the rest of all human kind. No other way of having given herself could have made her feel so apart, lost and foresworn. She could not have plighted a more sinister troth.

Kathleen behaved well when, some months later, her fiancé was reported missing, presumed killed. Her family not only supported her but were able to praise her courage without stint because they could not regret, as a husband for her, the man they knew almost nothing about. They hoped she would, in a year or two, console herself—and had it been only a question of consolation things might have gone much straighter ahead. But her trouble, behind just a little grief, was a complete dislocation from everything. She did not reject other lovers, for these failed to appear: for years she failed to attract men—and with the approach of her thirties she became natural enough to share her family's anxiousness on this score. She began to put herself out, to wonder; and at thirty-two she was very greatly relieved to find herself being courted by William Drover. She married him, and the two of them settled down in this quiet, arboreal part of Kensington: in this house the years piled up, her children were born and they all lived till they were driven out by the bombs of the next war. Her movements as Mrs. Drover were circumscribed, and she dismissed any idea that they were still watched.

As things were—dead or living the letter-writer sent her only a threat. Unable, for some minutes, to go on kneeling with her back exposed to the empty room, Mrs. Drover rose from the chest to sit on an upright chair whose back was firmly against the wall. The desuetude of her former bedroom, her married London home's whole air of being a cracked cup from which memory, with its reassuring power, had either evaporated or leaked away, made a crisis—and at just this crisis the letter-writer had, knowledgeably, struck. The hollowness of the house this evening cancelled years on years of voices, habits and steps. Through the shut windows she only heard rain fall on the roofs around. To rally herself, she said she was in a mood—and for two or three seconds shutting her eyes, told herself that she had imagined the letter. But she opened them—there it lay on the bed.

On the supernatural side of the letter's entrance she was not permitting her mind to dwell. Who, in London, knew she meant to call at the house today? Evidently, however, this had been known. The caretaker, *had* he come back, had had no cause to expect her: he would have taken the letter in his pocket, to forward it, at his own time, through the post. There was no other sign that the caretaker had been in—but, if not? Letters dropped in at doors of deserted houses do not fly or walk to tables in halls. They do not sit on the dust of empty tables with the air of certainty that they will be found. There is needed some human hand—but nobody but the caretaker had a key. Under circumstances she did not care to consider, a house can be entered without a key. It was possible that she was not alone now. She might be being waited for, downstairs. Waited for—until when? Until "the hour arranged." At least that was not six o'clock: six has struck.

She rose from the chair and went over and locked the door.

20   The thing was, to get out. To fly? No, not that: she had to catch her train. As a woman whose utter dependability was the keystone of her family life she was not willing to return to the country, to her husband, her little boys and her sister, without the objects she had come up to fetch. Resuming work at the chest she set about making up a number of parcels in a rapid, fumbling-decisive way. These, with her shopping parcels, would be too much to carry; these meant a taxi—at the thought of the taxi her heart went up and her normal breathing resumed. I will ring up the taxi now; the taxi cannot come too soon: I shall hear the taxi out there running its engine,

till I walk calmly down to it through the hall. I'll ring up—But no: the telephone is cut off . . . She tugged at a knot she had tied wrong.

The idea of flight . . . He was never kind to me, not really. I don't remember him kind at all. Mother said he never considered me. He was set on me, that was what it was—not love. Not love, not meaning a person well. What did he do, to make me promise like that? I can't remember—But she found that she could.

She remembered with such dreadful acuteness that the twenty-five years since then dissolved like smoke and she instinctively looked for the weal left by the button on the palm of her hand. She remembered not only all that he said and did but the complete suspension of *her* existence during that August week. I was not myself—they all told me so at the time. She remembered—but with one white burning blank as where acid has dropped on a photograph: *under no conditions* could she remember his face.

So, wherever he may be waiting, I shall not know him. You have no time to run from a face you do not expect.

The thing was to get to the taxi before any clock struck what could be the hour. She would slip down the street and round the side of the square to where the square gave on the main road. She would return in the taxi, safe, to her own door, and bring the solid driver into the house with her to pick up the parcels from room to room. The idea of the taxi driver made her decisive, bold: she unlocked her door, went to the top of the staircase and listened down.

She heard nothing—but while she was hearing nothing the *passé* air of the stair- 25 case was disturbed by a draught that travelled up to her face. It emanated from the basement: down there a door or window was being opened by someone who chose this moment to leave the house.

The rain had stopped; the pavements steamily shone as Mrs. Drover let herself out by inches from her own front door into the empty street. The unoccupied houses opposite continued to meet her look with their damaged stare. Making towards the thoroughfare and the taxi, she tried not to keep looking behind. Indeed, the silence was so intense—one of those creeks of London silence exaggerated this summer by the damage of war—that no tread could have gained on hers unheard. Where her street debouched on the square where people went on living, she grew conscious of, and checked, her unnatural pace. Across the open end of the square two buses impassively passed each other: women, a perambulator, cyclists, a man wheeling a barrow signalized, once again, the ordinary flow of life. At the square's most populous corner should be—and was—the short taxi rank. This evening, only one taxi—but this, although it presented its blank rump, appeared already to be alertly waiting for her. Indeed, without looking round the driver started his engine as she panted up from behind and put her hand on the door. As she did so, the clock struck seven. The taxi faced the main road: to make the trip back to her house it would have to turn— she had settled back on the seat and the taxi *had* turned before she, surprised by its knowing movement, recollected that she had not "said where." She leaned forward to scratch at the glass panel that divided the driver's head from her own.

The driver braked to what was almost a stop, turned round and slid the glass panel back: the jolt of this flung Mrs. Drover forward till her face was almost into the glass. Through the aperture driver and passenger, not six inches between them, remained for an eternity eye to eye. Mrs. Drover's mouth hung open for some seconds before she could issue her first scream. After that she continued to scream freely and to beat with her gloved hands on the glass all round as the taxi, accelerating without mercy, made off with her into the hinterland of deserted streets.

QUESTIONS FOR DISCUSSION AND WRITING

1. In what ways does the middle section of the story explain Mrs. Drover's "controlled worry" during the first part of the story? How does it prepare for the dramatic ending?

2. How does Mrs. Drover characterize her demon lover? In what way does Mrs. Drover's house characterize her life since the war?

3. How is the setting of the shut-up house and the deserted street important to our understanding of the story? For example, how does Mrs. Drover explain the appearance of the letter?

4. What is Mrs. Drover's point of view toward this experience? Is she really surprised by the appearance of her demon lover, or has she been looking for him? Explain your answer.

5. What is the theme of this story? Can you explain it in realistic terms, or do you have to consider the "supernatural side"?

Stories for Comparison

Joyce Carol Oates's "Where Are You Going, Where Have You Been?" (pages 935–948); Edgar Allan Poe's "The Cask of Amontillado" (pages 1011–1017).

26

T. C O R A G H E S S A N B O Y L E

Heart of a Champion

T. CORAGHESSAN BOYLE was born in 1948 in Peekskill, New York, and educated at the State University of New York at Potsdam and the University of Iowa. After a brief career as a high school teacher, Boyle became professor of creative writing at the University of Southern California. He has published his short stories in such provocative collections as *The Descent of Man* (1979), *Greasy Lake and Other Stories* (1985), and *If the River Was Whiskey* (1990). His novels, equally bizarre and humorous, include *Water Music* (1981), *World's End* (1987), *The Road to Wellville* (1993)—adapted into a major film—and *The Tortilla Curtain* (1995). "Heart of a Champion, reprinted from *The Descent of Man,* is a humorous reworking of the exploits of the popular television dog Lassie.

We scan the cornfields and the wheatfields winking gold and goldbrown and yellowbrown in the midday sun, on up the grassy slope to the barn redder than red against the sky bluer than blue, across the smooth stretch of the barnyard with its pecking chickens, and then right on up to the screen door at the back of the house. The door swings open, a black hole in the sun, and Timmy emerges with his cornsilk hair, corn-fed face. He is dressed in crisp overalls, striped T-shirt, stubby blue Keds. There'd have to be a breeze—and we're not disappointed—his clean fine cupcut hair waves and settles as he scuffs across the barnyard and out to the edge of the field. The boy stops there to gaze out over the nodding wheat, eyes unsquinted despite the sun, and blue as tinted lenses. Then he brings three fingers to his lips in a neat triangle and whistles long and low, sloping up sharp to cut off at the peak. A moment passes: he whistles again. And then we see it—way out there at the far corner of the field—the ripple, the dashing furrow, the blur of the streaking dog, white chest, flashing feet.

They're in the woods now. The boy whistling, hands in pockets, kicking along with his short baby-fat strides; the dog beside him wagging the white tip of her tail like an all-clear flag. They pass beneath an arching old black-barked oak. It creaks. And suddenly begins to fling itself down on them: immense, brutal: a panzer strike.

The boy's eyes startle and then there's a blur, a smart snout clutching his pantleg, the thunderblast of the trunk, the dust and spinning leaves. "Golly, Lassie . . . I didn't even see it," says the boy sitting safe in a mound of moss. The collie looks up at him (the svelte snout, the deep gold logician's eyes), and laps at his face.

And now they're down by the river. The water is brown with angry suppurations, spiked with branches, fence posts, tires and logs. It rushes like the sides of boxcars— and chews deep and insidious at the bank under Timmy's feet. The roar is like a jet-port: little wonder he can't hear the dog's warning bark. We watch the crack appear, widen to a ditch; then the halves separating (snatch of red earth, writhe of worm), the poise and pitch, and Timmy crushing down with it. Just a flash—but already he's way downstream, his head like a plastic jug, dashed and bobbed, spinning toward the nasty mouth of the falls. But there's the dog—fast as a struck match—bursting along the bank all white and gold melded in motion, hair sleeked with the wind of it, legs beating time to the panting score. . . . Yet what can she hope to do?—the current surges on, lengths ahead, sure bet to win the race to the falls. Timmy sweeps closer, sweeps closer, the falls loud now as a hundred tympani, the war drums of the Sioux, Africa gone bloodlust mad! The dog strains, lashing over the wet earth like a whipcrack; strains every last ganglion and dendrite until finally she draws abreast of him. Then she's in the air, the foaming yellow water. Her paws churning like pistons, whiskers chuffing with the exertion—oh the roar!—and there, she's got him, her sure jaws clamping down on the shirt collar, her eyes fixed on the slip of rock at the falls' edge. Our blood races, organs palpitate. The black brink of the falls, the white paws digging at the rock—and then they're safe. The collie sniffs at Timmy's inert little form, nudges his side until she manages to roll him over. Then clears his tongue and begins mouth-to-mouth.

Night: the barnyard still, a bulb burning over the screen door. Inside, the family sit at dinner, the table heaped with pork chops, mashed potatoes, applesauce and peas, a pitcher of clean white milk. Home-baked bread. Mom and Dad, their faces sexless, bland, perpetually good-humored and sympathetic, poise stiff-backed, forks in midswoop, while Timmy tells his story: "So then Lassie grabbed me by the collar and golly I musta blanked out cause I don't remember anything more till I woke up on the rock—"

5   "Well I'll be," says Mom.

"You're lucky you've got such a good dog, son," says Dad, gazing down at the collie where she lies patiently, snout over paw, tail wapping the floor. She is combed and washed and fluffed, her lashes mascaraed and curled, her chest and paws white as dishsoap. She looks up humbly. But then her ears leap, her neck jerks round—and she's up at the door, head cocked, alert. A high yipping yowl like a stuttering fire whistle shudders through the room. And then another. The dog whines.

"Darn," says Dad. "I thought we were rid of those coyotes—next thing they'll be after the chickens again."

The moon blanches the yard, leans black shadows on the trees, the barn. Up-stairs in the house, Timmy lies sleeping in the pale light, his hair fastidiously mussed, his breathing gentle. The collie lies on the throw rug beside the bed. We see that her eyes are open. Suddenly she rises and slips to the window, silent as a shadow. And looks down the long elegant snout to the barnyard below, where the coyote slinks from shade to shade, a limp pullet dangling from his jaws. He is stunted, scabious, syphilitic, his forepaw trap-twisted, his eyes running. The collie whimpers softly from behind the window. And the coyote stops in mid-trot, frozen in a cold shard of light, ears high on his head. Then drops the chicken at his feet, leers up at the window and begins a soft, crooning, sad-faced song.

The screen door slaps behind Timmy as he bolts from the house, Lassie at his heels. Mom's head emerges on the rebound. "Timmy!" (He stops as if jerked by a rope, turns to face her.) "You be home before lunch, hear?"

"Sure, Mom," he says, already spinning off, the dog by his side. We get a close-up of Mom's face: she is smiling a benevolent boys-will-be-boys smile. Her teeth are perfect. 10

In the woods Timmy steps on a rattler and the dog bites its head off. "Gosh," he says. "Good girl, Lassie." Then he stumbles and slips over an embankment, rolls down the brushy incline and over a sudden precipice, whirling out into the breath-taking blue space like a sky diver. He thumps down on a narrow ledge twenty feet below. And immediately scrambles to his feet, peering timorously down the sheer wall to the heap of bleached bone at its base. Small stones break loose, shoot out like asteroids. Dirt-slides begin. But Lassie yarps reassuringly from above, sprints back to the barn for a winch and cable, hoists the boy to safety.

On their way back for lunch Timmy leads them through a still and leaf-darkened copse. We remark how odd it is that the birds and crickets have left off their cheeping, how puzzling that the background music has begun to rumble so. Suddenly, round a bend in the path before them, the coyote appears. Nose to the ground, intent, unaware of them. But all at once he jerks to a halt, shudders like an epileptic, the hackles rising, tail dipping between his legs. The collie too stops short, just yards away, her chest proud and shaggy and white. The coyote cowers, bunches like a cat, glares at them. Timmy's face sags with alarm. The coyote lifts his lip. But then, instead of leaping at her adversary's throat, the collie prances up and stretches her nose out to him, her eyes soft as a leading lady's, round as a doe's. She's balsamed and perfumed; her full chest tapers a lovely S to her sleek haunches and sculpted legs. He is puny, runted, half her size, his coat like a discarded door-mat. She circles him now, sniffing. She whimpers, he growls: throaty and tough, the bad guy. And stands stiff while she licks at his whiskers, noses at his rear, the bald black scrotum. Timmy is horror-struck. Then, the music sweeping off in birdtrills of flute and harpstring, the coyote slips round behind, throat thrown back, black lips tight with anticipation.

"What was she doing, Dad?" Timmy asks over his milk and sandwich.

"The sky was blue today, son," he says.

"But she had him trapped, Dad—they were stuck together end to end and I 15 thought we had that wicked old coyote but then she went and let him go—what's got into her, Dad?"

"The barn was red today, son," he says.

Late afternoon: the sun mellow, more orange than white. Purpling clots of shadow hang from the branches, ravel out from the tree trunks. Bees and wasps and flies saw away at the wet full-bellied air. Timmy and the dog are far out beyond the north pasture, out by the old Indian burial mound, where the boy stoops now to search for arrowheads. Oddly, the collie is not watching him: instead she's pacing the crest above, whimpering softly, pausing from time to time to stare out across the forest, her eyes distant and moonstruck. Behind her, storm clouds squat on the horizon like dark kidneys or brains.

We observe the wind kicking up: leaves flapping like wash, saplings quivering, weeds whipping. It darkens quickly now, the clouds scudding low and smoky over the treetops, blotting the sun from view. Lassie's white is whiter than ever, highlighted against the dark horizon, the wind-whipped hair foaming around her. Still she doesn't look down at the boy: he digs, dirty-kneed, stoop-backed, oblivious. Then the first fat random drops, a flash, the volcanic blast of thunder. Timmy glances over his shoulder at the noise: he's just in time to watch the scorched pine plummeting toward the constellated freckles in the center of his forehead. Now the collie turns—too late!—the *swoosh-whack!* of the tree, the trembling needles. She's there in an instant, tearing at the green welter, struggling through to his side. He lies unconscious in the muddying earth, hair artistically arranged, a thin scratch painted on his cheek. The trunk lies across the small of his back like the tail of a brontosaurus. The rain falls.

Lassie tugs doggedly at a knob in the trunk, her pretty paws slipping in the wet—but it's no use—it would take a block and tackle, a crane, an army of Bunyans to shift that stubborn bulk. She falters, licks at his ear, whimpers. We observe the troubled look in her eyes as she hesitates, uncertain, priorities warring: should she stand guard, or dash for help? The decision is sure and swift—her eyes firm with purpose and she's off like a shard of shrapnel, already up the hill, shooting past the dripping trees, over the river, already cleaving through the high wet banks of wheat.

20   A moment later she's dashing through the puddled and rain-screened barnyard, barking right on up to the back door, where she pauses to scratch daintily, her voice high-pitched and insistent. Mom swings open the door and the collie pads in, claws clacking on the shiny linoleum. "What is it girl? What's the matter? Where's Timmy?"

"Yarf! Yarfata-yarf-yarf!"

"Oh my! Dad! Dad, come quickly!"

Dad rushes in, his face stolid and reassuring as the Lincoln Memorial. "What is it, dear? . . . Why, Lassie?"

"Oh Dad, Timmy's trapped under a pine tree out by the old Indian burial ground—"

25   "Arpit-arp."

"—a mile and a half past the north pasture."

Dad is quick, firm, decisive. "Lassie—you get back up there and stand watch over Timmy . . . Mom and I'll go for Doc Walker. Hurry now!"

The collie hesitates at the door: "Rarf-arrar-ra!"

"Right," says Dad. "Mom, fetch the chain saw."

We're back in the woods now. A shot of the mud-running burial mound locates 30 us—yes, there's the fallen pine, and there: Timmy. He lies in a puddle, eyes closed, breathing slow. The hiss of the rain is loud as static. We see it at work: scattering leaves, digging trenches, inciting streams to swallow their banks. It lies deep now in the low areas, and in the mid areas, and in the high areas. Then a shot of the dam, some indeterminate (but short we presume) distance off, the yellow water churning over its lip like urine, the ugly earthen belly distended, blistered with the pressure. Raindrops pock the surface like a plague.

Suddenly the music plunges to those thunderous crouching chords—we're back at the pine now—what is it? There: the coyote. Sniffing, furtive, the malicious eyes, the crouch and slink. He stiffens when he spots the boy—but then slouches closer, a rubbery dangle drooling from between his mismeshed teeth. Closer. Right over the prone figure now, those ominous chords setting up ominous vibrations in our bowels. He stoops, head dipping between his shoulders, irises caught in the corners of his eyes: wary, sly, predatory: the vulture slavering over the fallen fawn.

But wait!—here comes the collie, sprinting out of the wheatfield, bounding rock to rock across the crazed river, her limbs contourless with sheer speed and purpose, the music racing in a mad heroic prestissimo!

The jolting front seat of a Ford. Dad, Mom and the Doctor, all dressed in rain slickers and flap-brimmed rain hats, sitting shoulder to shoulder behind the clapping wipers. Their jaws set with determination, eyes aflicker with pioneer gumption.

The coyote's jaws, serrated grinders, work at the tough bone and cartilage of Timmy's left hand. The boy's eyelids flutter with the pain, and he lifts his head feebly—but almost immediately it slaps down again, flat and volitionless, in the mud. At that instant Lassie blazes over the hill like a cavalry charge, show-dog indignation aflame in her eyes. The scrag of a coyote looks up at her, drooling blood, choking down frantic bits of flesh. Looks up at her from eyes that go back thirty million years, savage and bloodlustful and free. Looks up unmoved, uncringing, the bloody snout and steady yellow eyes less a physical challenge than philosophical. We watch the collie's expression alter in midbound—the look of offended AKC morality giving way, dissolving. She skids to a halt, drops her tail and approaches him, a buttery gaze in her golden eyes. She licks the blood from his lips.

The dam. Impossibly swollen, rain festering the yellow surface, a hundred new 35 streams a minute rampaging in, the pressure of those millions of gallons hard-punching those millions more. There! the first gap, the water spewing out, a burst bubo. And now the dam shudders, splinters, falls to pieces like so much cheap pottery. The roar is devastating.

The two animals start at that terrible rumbling, and still working their gummy jaws, they dash up the far side of the hill. We watch the white-tipped tail retreating side by side with the hacked and tick-blistered gray one—wagging like raggled banners as they disappear into the trees at the top of the rise. We're left with a tableau: the rain, the fallen pine in the crotch of the valley's V, the spot of the boy's head. And that chilling roar in our ears. Suddenly the wall of water appears at the far end of the V, smashing through the little declivity like a god-sized fist, prickling with shattered trunks and boulders, grinding along like a quick-melted glacier, like planets in collision. We cut to Timmy: eyes closed, hair plastered, his left arm looking as though it should be wrapped in butcher's paper. How? we wonder. How will they ever get him out of this? But then we see them—Mom, Dad and the Doctor—struggling up that same rise, rushing with the frenetic music now, the torrent seething closer, booming and howling. Dad launches himself in full charge down the hillside—but the water is already sweeping over the fallen pine, lifting it like paper—there's a blur, a quick clip of a typhoon at sea (is that a flash of blond hair?), and it's over. The valley is filled to the top of the rise, the water ribbed and rushing like the Colorado in adolescence. Dad's pants are wet to the crotch.

Mom's face, the Doctor's. Rain. And then the opening strains of the theme song, one violin at first, swelling in mournful mid-American triumph as the full orchestra comes in, tearful, beautiful, heroic, sweeping us up and out of the dismal rain, back to the golden wheatfields in the midday sun. The boy cups his hands to his mouth and pipes: "Laahh-sie! Laahh-sie!" And then we see it—way out there at the end of the field—the ripple, the dashing furrow, the blur of the streaking dog, white chest, flashing feet.

QUESTIONS FOR DISCUSSION AND WRITING

1. How do Timmy's near-mishaps prepare us for the climax of the plot? In what way does the coyote create tension in this plot? What do the opening and closing scenes contribute to the plot?

2. In what ways is Lassie, the protagonist, characterized in this story? What does the coyote come to represent as a character? How does Boyle use dialogue to characterize Timmy and his family?

3. How do we know that the setting for this story is a fiction? To what extent does our knowledge of this setting depend on our familiarity with images from the television series?

4. How does Boyle use the first-person plural (we) point of view to render this story? How does this narrator use exaggerated poetic diction and allusions to music to dramatize the story?

5. How does the story satirize the values we ascribe to the relationship between animals and children in our culture? How does Boyle "trick" us into accepting a satire that includes us as part of that culture?

Stories for Comparison

James Thurber's "The Greatest Man in the World" (pages 1090–1096); W. D. Wetherell's "The Bass, the River, and Sheila Mant" (pages 1181–1186).

27

LARRY BROWN

Kubuku Rides (This Is It)

LARRY BROWN was born in 1951 in Oxford, Mississippi, where he attended the University of Mississippi. He has worked as a carpenter, lumberjack, house painter, and as a member of the Oxford Fire Department. He has contributed short stories to journals such as the *Mississippi Review, Fiction International,* and *Paris Review.* He has published three novels, *Dirty Work* (1989), *Joe* (1991), and *Father and Son* (1996), and two collections of short stories, *Facing the Music* (1988) and *Big Bad Love* (1990). He is currently at work on a book of nonfiction, *Fire Notes.* "Kubuku Rides (This Is It)," reprinted from *Facing the Music,* portrays the destructive power of alcoholism.

A ngel hear the back door slam. It Alan, in from work. She start to hide the glass and then she don't hide the glass, he got a nose like a bloodhound and gonna smell it anyway, so she just keep sitting on the couch. She gonna act like nothing happening, like everything cool. Little boy in the yard playing, he don't know nothing. He think Mama in here watching Andy Griffith. Cooking supper. She better now anyway. Just wine, beer, no whiskey, no vodka. No gin. She getting well, she gonna make it. He have to be patient with her. She trying. He no rose garden himself anyway.

She start to get up and then she don't, it better if she stay down like nothing going on. She nervous, though. She know he looking, trying to catch her messing up. He watch her like a hawk, like somebody with eyes in the back of they head. He don't miss much. He come into the room and he see her. She smile, try to, but it wrong, she know it wrong, she guilty. He see it. He been out loading lumber or something all day long, he tired and ready for supper. But ain't no supper yet. She know all this and ain't said nothing. She scared to speak because she so guilty. But she mad over having to *feel* guilty, because some of this guilt *his* fault. Not all his fault. But some of it. Maybe half. Maybe less. This thing been going on a while. This thing nothing new.

"Hey honey," she say.

"I done unloaded two tons of two-by-fours today," he say.

⁵   "You poor baby," she say. "Come on and have a little drink with Mama." That the wrong thing to say.

"What?" he say. "You drinkin again? I done told you and told you and told you."

"It's just wine," she say.

"Well woman how many you done had?"

"This just my first one," she say, but she lying. She done had five and ain't even took nothing out the deep freeze. Wind up having a turkey pot pie or something. Something don't nobody want. She can't cook while she trying to figure out what to do. Don't know what to do. Ain't gonna drink nothing at all when she get up. Worries all day about drinking, then in the evening she done worried so much over *not* drinking she starts *in* drinking. She in one of them vicious circles. She done even thought about doing away with herself, but she hate to leave her husband and her little boy alone in the world. Probably mess her little boy up for the rest of his life. She don't want to die anyway. Angel ain't but about thirty years old. She still good-looking too. And love her husband like God love Jesus. Ain't no answer, that's it.

¹⁰   "Where that bottle?" he say.

Now she gonna act like she don't know what he talking about. "What bottle?" she say.

"Hell, woman. Bottle you drinkin from. What you mean what bottle?"

She scared now, frightened of his wrath. He don't usually go off. But he go off on her drinking in a minute. He put up with anything but her drinking.

"It's in the fridge," she say.

¹⁵   He run in there. She hear him open the door. He going to bust it in a million pieces. She get up and go after him, wobbly. She grabbing for doors and stuff, trying to get in there. He done took her money away, she can't have no more. He don't let her write no checks. He holding the bottle up where she can see it good. The contents of that bottle done trashed.

He say, "First glass my ass."

"Oh, Alan," she say. "That a old bottle."

"Old bottle? That what you say, old bottle?"

"I found it," she say.

²⁰   "Lyin!" he say.

She shake her head no no no no no. She wanting that last drink because everything else hid.

"What you mean goin out buying some more?" he say. He got veins standing up in his neck. He mad, he madder than she ever seen him.

"Oh, Alan, please," she say. She hate herself begging like this. She ready to get down on her knees if she have to, though.

"I found it," she say.

²⁵   "You been to the liquor store. Come on, now," he say. "You been to the liquor store, ain't you?"

Angel start to say something, start to scream something, but she see Randy come in from the front yard. He stop behind his daddy. Mama fixing to get down in the floor for that bottle. Daddy yelling stuff. Ain't no good time to come in. He eight year old but he know what going on. He tiptoe back out.

"Don't pour it out," she say. "Just let me finish it and I'll quit. Start supper," she say.

"Lie to me," he say. "Lie to me and take money and promise. How many times you promised?"

She go to him. He put the bottle behind his back, saying, "Don't, now, baby." He moaning, like.

"Alan *please,*" she say. She put one arm around his waist and try for that bottle. He stronger than her. It ain't fair! They stumble around in the kitchen. She trying for the bottle, he heading for the sink, she trying to get it. Done done this before. Ain't no fun no more.

He say, "I done told you what I'm goin to do."

She say, "Just let me finish it, Alan. Don't make me beg," she say. Ain't no way she hold him, he too strong. Lift weights three days a week. Runs. Got muscles like concrete. Know how to box but don't never hit her. She done hit him plenty with her little drunk fists, ain't hurt him, though. He turn away and start taking the cap off the bottle. She grab for it. She got both hands on it. He trying to pull it away. She panting. He pulling the bottle away, down in the sink so he can pour it out. They going to break it. Somebody going to get cut. May be him, may be her. Don't matter who. They tugging, back and forth, up and down. Ain't nobody in they right mind.

"Let go!" she say. She know Randy hearing it. He done run away once. Ain't enough for her. Ought to be but ain't.

He jerk it away and it hit the side of the sink and break. Blood gushing out of his hand. Mixing with the wine. Blood and wine all over the sink. Don't look good. Look bad. Look like maybe somebody have to kill theirself before it all get over with. Can't keep on like this. Done gone on too long.

"Godomightydamn," he say. Done sliced his hand wide open. It bad, she don't know how bad. Angel don't want to see. She run back to the living room for the rest of that glass. She don't drink it, he'll get it. She grab it. Pour it down. Two inches of wine. Then it all gone. She throw the glass into the mirror and everything break. Alan yell something in the kitchen and she run back in there and look. He got a bloody towel wrap around his hand. Done unloaded two tons of wood today and hospital bill gonna be more than he made. Won't take fifteen minutes. Emergency room robbery take longer than plain robbery but don't require no gun.

He shout, "This is it!" He crying and he don't cry. "Can't stand it! Sick of it!"

She sick too. He won't leave her alone. He love her. He done cut his hand wide open because of this love. He crying, little boy terrified. He run off again, somebody liable to snatch him up and they never see him again. Ought to be enough but ain't. Ain't never enough.

She flashing back now. She done had a wreck a few weeks ago. She done went out with some friends of hern, Betty and Glynnis and Sue. She done bought clothes for Randy and towels for her mama and cowboy boots for Alan. Pretty ones. Rhino's hide and hippo's toes. She working then, she still have a job then. It a Saturday. Randy and Alan at Randy's Little League game. She think she going over later, but she never make it. She get drunk instead.

They gone have just one little drink, her and Betty and Sue and them. One little drink ain't gone hurt nothing or nobody. Betty telling about her divorce and new men she checking out. She don't give no details, though. They drinking a light white wine but Angel having a double One Fifty-One and Coke. She ain't messing around. This a few weeks ago, she ain't got time for no wine. And she drink hers off real quick and order and get another one before they even get they wines down. She think maybe they won't even notice she done had two, they all so busy listening to Betty telling about these wimps she messing with. But it ain't even interesting and they notice right away. Angel going to the game, though. She definitely going to the game. She done promised everybody in the country. Time done come where she have to be straight. She got to quit breaking these promises. She got to quit all this lying and conniving.

40   Then before long they start talking about leaving. She ask them to stay, say Please, ya'll just stay and have one more. But naw, they got to go. Glynnis, she claim she got this hot date tonight. She talk like she got a hot date every night. Betty got this new man she going out with and she got to roll her hair and stuff. But Sue now is true. Angel done went to high school with her. They was in school together back when they was wearing hot pants and stuff. This like a old relationship. But Sue know what going on. She just hate to say anything. She just hate to bring it out in the wide open. She got to say something, though. She wait till the rest of them go and then she speak up.

She say, "I thought you goin to the ball game, girl." She look at her watch.

"Yeah," Angel say. "Honey, I'm goin. I wouldn't miss it for the world. But first I got to have me some more One Fifty-One and Coke."

Sue know she lying. She done lied to everybody about everything. This thing a problem can't keep quiet. She done had troubles at work. She done called in late, and sick, done called in and lied like a dog about her physical condition with these hungovers.

Now Angel hurting. She know Sue know the truth but too good to nag. She know Sue one good person she can depend on the rest of her life, but she know too Sue ain't putting up with her killing herself in her midst. She know Sue gone say something, but Sue don't say nothing until she finish her second wine. This after Angel ask her to have a third wine. Somebody got to stop her. She keep on, she be asking to stay for a eighth and a ninth wine. She be asking to stay till the place close down.

45   So Sue say, "You gone miss that ball game, girl."

She say she already late. She motion for another drink. Sue reach over and put her hand over Angel's glass and say, "Don't do that, girl."

"Late already," she say. "One more won't make no difference."

She know her speech and stuff messed up. It embarrassing, but the barmaid, she bring the drink. And Sue reach out, put her hand over the glass and say, "Don't you give her that shit, woman."

Girl back up and say, "*Ma'am?*" Real nice like.

50   "Don't you give her that," say Sue.

Girl say, "Yes'm, but ma'am, she order it, ma'am."

Girl look at Angel.

"Thank you, hon," she say. She reach and take the drink and give the girl some money. Then she tip her a dollar and the girl walk away. Angel grab this drink and slosh some of it out on her. She know it but she can't help it. She don't know what went wrong. She shopping and going to the ball game and now this done happened again. She ain't making no ball game. Ball game done shot to hell. She be in perhaps two three in the morning.

Sue now, she tired of this.

"When you goin to admit it?" she say.   55

"Admit what?"

"Girl, *you* know. Laying drunk. Runnin around here drinkin every night. Stayin out."

She say, "I don't know what you talkin about," like she huffy. She drinking every day. Even Sunday. Especially Sunday. Sunday the worst because ain't nothing open. She don't hit the liquor store Saturday night she climbing the walls Sunday afternoon. She done even got drunk and listened to the services on TV Sunday morning and got all depressed and passed out before dinnertime. Then Alan and Randy have to eat them turkey pot pies again.

"Alan and Randy don't understand me," she say.

"They love you," Sue say.   60

"And I love them," she say.

"Listen now," Sue tell her, "you gonna lose that baby and that man if you don't stop this messin around."

"Ain't gonna do that no such of a thing," she say, but she know Sue right. She still pouring that rum down, she ain't slacked off. She just have to deny the truth because old truth hurt too much to face.

Sue get up, she got tears in her eye and stuff, she dabbing with Kleenexes. Can't nobody talk sense to this fool.

"Yes you will," she say, and she leave. She ain't gone hang around and 65 watch this self-destruction. Woman done turned into a time bomb ticking. She got to get away from here, so she run out the door. She booking home. Everybody looking.

Angel all alone now. She order two more singles and drink both of them. But she shitfaced time she drink that last one, she done been in the booth a hour and a half. Which has done caused some men to think about hitting on her, they done seen them thin legs and stuff she got. This one wimp done even come over to the table, he just assume she lonesome and want some male company, he think he gonna come over like he Robert Goulet or somebody and just invite himself to sit down. He done seen her wedding ring, but he thinking, Man, this woman horny or something, she wouldn't be sitting here all by her lonesome. And this fool almost sit down in the booth with her, he gonna buy her a drink, talk some trash to her, when he really thinking is he gonna get her in some motel room and take her panties off. But she done recognized his act, she ain't having nothing to do with this fool. She tell him off right quick. Of course he get huffy and leave. That's fine. Ain't asked that fool to sit down with her anyway.

Now she done decided she don't want to have another drink in this place. Old depression setting in. People coming in now to eat seafood with they families, little kids and stuff, grandmamas, she don't need to be hanging around in here no more. Waiters looking at her. She know they wanting her to leave before she give their place a bad name. Plus she taking up room in this booth where some family wanting to eat some filet catfish. She know all this stuff. She know she better leave before they ask her to. She done had embarrassment enough, don't need no more.

Ain't eat nothing yet. Don't want nothing to eat. Don't even eat at home much. Done lost weight, breasts done come down, was fine and full, legs even done got skinny. She know Alan notice it when she undress. She don't even weigh what she weigh on they wedding night when she give herself to Alan. She know he worried sick about her. He get her in the bed and squeeze her so tight he hurt her, but she don't say Let go.

She trying to walk straight when she go out to her car, but she look like somebody afflicted. Bumping into hoods and stuff. She done late already. Ball game over. It after six and Randy and Alan already home by now. Ain't no way she going home right now. She ain't gonna face them crying faces. And, too, she go home, Alan ain't letting her drink another drop. So she decide to get her a bottle and just ride around a while. She gonna ride around and sober up, then she gonna go home. And she need to do this anyway because this give her time to think something up like say the car tore up or something, why she late.

70   Only thing, she done gone in the liquor store so many times she ashamed to. She see these same people and she know they thinking: Damn, this woman done been in here four times this week. Drinking like a fish. She don't like to look in they eyes. So she hunt her up another store on the other side of town. She don't want to get too drunk, so she just get a sixer of beers and some schnapps. She going to ride around, cruise a little and sober up. That what she thinking.

She driving okay. Hitting them beers occasionally, hitting that peach schnapps every few minutes because it so good and ain't but forty-eight proof. It so weak it ain't gonna make her drunk. Not no half pint. She ain't gonna ride around but a hour. Then she gonna go home.

She afraid to take a drink when anybody behind her. She thinking the police gonna see her and throw them blue lights on her. Then she be in jail calling Alan to come bail her out. Which he already done twice before. She don't want to stay in town. She gonna drive out on the lake road. They not as much traffic out there. So she go off out there, on this blacktop road. She gonna ride out to the boat landing. Ain't nobody out there, it too cold to fish. She curve around through the woods three or four miles. She done finished one of them beers and throwed the bottle out the window. She get her another one and drink some more of that schnapps. That stuff go down so easy and so hard to stop on. Usually when she open a half pint, she throw the cap far as she can.

Angel weaving a little, but she ain't drunk. She just a little tired. She wishing she home in the bed right now. She know they gonna have a big argument when she get home. She dreading that. Alan, he have to fix supper for Randy and his mama ain't taught him nothing about cooking. Only thing he know how to do is warm up a TV dinner, and Randy just sull up when he have to eat one of them. She wishing now she'd just gone on home. Wouldn't have been so bad then. Going to be worse now, much worser than if she'd just gone on home after them double One Fifty-Ones. Way it is, though. Get started, can't stop. Take that first drink, she ain't gonna stop till she pass out or run out. She don't know what it is. She ain't even understand it herself. Didn't start out like this. Didn't use to be this way. Use to be a beer once in a while, little wine at New Year's. Things just get out of hand. Don't mean to be this way. Just can't help it. Alan used to would drink a little beer on weekends and it done turned him flat against it. He don't even want to be around nobody drinking now. Somebody offer him a drink now he tell em to get it out of his face. He done even lost some of his friends over this thing.

Angel get down to the boat ramp, ain't a soul there. Windy out there, water dark, scare her to death just to see it. What would it be to be out in them waves, them black waves closing over your head, ain't nobody around to hear you screaming. Coat be waterlogged and pulling you down. Hurt just a little and that's all. Just a brief pain. Be dead then, won't know nothing. Won't have no hurts. Easy way out. They get over it eventually. Could make it look like an accident. Drive her car right off in the water, everybody think it a mistake. Just a tragedy, that's all, a unfortunate thing. Don't want to hurt nobody. What so wrong with her life she do the things she do? Killing her baby and her man little at a time. And her ownself. But have to have it. Thinking things when she drinking she wouldn't think at all when she not drinking. But now she drinking all the time, and she thinking same way all the time.

She drink some more beer and schnapps, and then she pass out or go to sleep, 75 she don't know which. Same thing. Sleeping she don't have to think no more. Ain't no hurting when she sleeping. Sleeping good, but can't sleep forever. Somebody done woke her up, knocking on the glass. Some boy out there. High school boy. Truck parked beside, some more kids in it. She scared at first, think something bad. But they look all right. Don't look mean or nothing. Just look worried. She get up and roll her window down just a little, just crack it.

"Ma'am?" this boy say. "You all right, ma'am?"

"Yes," she say. "Fine, thank you."

"Seen you settin here," he say. "Thought your car tore up maybe."

"No," Angel say. "Just sleepy," she say. "Leaving now," she say, and she roll the window up. She turn the lights on, car still running, ain't even shut it off. Out in the middle of nowhere asleep, ain't locked the door. Somebody walk up and slit her throat, she not even know it. She crazy. She got to get home. She done been asleep no telling how long.

She afraid they gonna follow her out. They do. She can't stand for nobody to get 80 behind her like that. Make her nervous. She decide she gonna speed up and leave them behind. She get up to about sixty-five. She start to pull away. She sobered up a little while she asleep. Be okay to get another one of them beers out the sack now. Beer sack down in the floor. Have to lean over and take her eyes off the road just a second to get that beer, no problem.

Her face hit the windshield, the seat slam her up. Too quick. Lights shining up against a tree. Don't even know what happened. Windshield broke all to pieces.

Smoke coming out the hood. She wiping her face. Interior light on, she got blood all over her hands. Face bleeding. She look in the rearview mirror, she don't know her own self. Look like something in a monster movie. She screaming now. Face cut all to pieces. She black out again. She come to, she out on the ground. People helping her up. She screaming I'm ruint I'm ruint. Lights in her eyes, legs moving in front of her. Kids talking. One of them say she just drive right off the road into that tree. She don't believe it. Road move or something. Tree jump out in front of her. She a good driver. She drive too good for something like this.

Cost three thousand dollars to fix the car this time. Don't even drive right no more. Alan say the frame bent. Alan say it won't never drive right no more. And ain't even paid for. She don't know about no frame. She just know it jerk going down the road.

She in the hospital a while. She don't remember exactly, three or four days. They done had to sew her face up. People see them scars even through thick makeup the rest of her life. She bruised so bad she don't get out the bed for a week. Alan keep saying they lucky she ain't dead. He keep praising God his wife ain't dead. She know she just gonna have to go through it again now sometime, till a worse one happen. Police done come and talked to her. She lie her way out of it, though. Can't prove nothing. Alan keep saying we lucky.

Ain't lucky. Boss call, want to know when she coming back to work. She hem and haw. Done missed all them Mondays. She can't give no definite answer. He clear his throat. Maybe he should find somebody else for her position since she so vague. Well yessir, she say, yessir, if you think that the best thing.

85   Alan awful quiet after this happen. He just sit and stare. She touch him out on the porch, he just draw away. Like her hand a bad thing to feel on him. This go on about a week. Then he come home from work one evening and she sitting in the living room with a glass of wine in her hand.

He back now from having his hand sewed up. He sitting in the kitchen drinking coffee, he done bought some cigarettes and he smoking one after another. Done been quit two years, say it the hardest thing he ever done. He say he never stop wanting one, that he have to brace himself every day. Now he done started back. She know: This what she done to him.

Angel not drinking anything. Don't mean she don't have nothing. Just can't have it right now. He awake now. Later he be asleep. He think the house clean. House ain't clean. Lots of places to hide things, you want to hide them bad enough. Ain't like Easter eggs, like Christmas presents. Like life and death.

Wouldn't never think on her wedding night it ever be like this. She in the living room by herself, he in the kitchen by himself. TV on, she ain't watching it, some fool on Johnny Carson telling stuff ain't even funny. She ain't got the sound on. Ain't hear nothing, ain't see nothing. She hear him like choke in there once in a while. Randy in the bed asleep. Want so bad to get up and go in there and tell Alan, Baby I promise I will quit. Again. But ain't no use in saying it, she don't mean it. Just words. Don't mean nothing. Done lost trust anyway. Lose trust, a man and wife, done lost everything. Even if she quit now, stay quit, he always be looking over that shoulder, he always be smelling her breath. Lost his trust she won't never get it back.

He come in there where she at finally. He been crying, she tell it by looking at him. He not hurting for himself, he not hurting for his hand. He cut off his hand and throw it away she ask him to. He hurting for her. She know all this, don't nobody have to tell her. Why it don't do no good to talk to her. She know it all already.

"Baby," he say. "I goin to bed. Had a long day today."   90

His face look like he about sixty years old. He thirty-one. Weigh one sixty-five and bench press two-ninety. "You comin?" he say.

She want to. Morning be soon enough to drink something else. He be gone to work, Randy be gone to school. House be quiet by seven-thirty. She do what she want to then. Whole day be hers to do what she want to. Things be better tomorrow maybe. She cook them something good for supper, she make them a good old pie and have ice cream. She get better. They know she trying. She just weak, she just need some time. This thing not something you throw off like a cold. This thing deep, this thing beat more good people than her.

Angel say, "Not just yet, baby. I going to sit in here in the livin room a while. I so sorry you cut your hand," she say.

"You want to move?" he say. "Another state? Another country? You say the word I quit my job tomorrow. Don't matter. Just a job," he say.

"Don't want to move," she say. She trembling.   95

"Don't matter what people thinks," he say.

She think he gonna come over and get down on the floor and hug her knees and cry, but he don't. He look like he holding back to keep from doing that. And she glad he don't. He do that, she make them promises again. She promise anything if he just stop.

"Okay," he say. "I goin to bed now." He look beat.

He go. She by herself. It real quiet now. Hear anything. Hear walls pop, hear mice move. They eating something in the cabinet, she need to set some traps.

Time go by so slow. She know he in there listening. He listen for any step she   100
make, which room she move into, which furniture she reach for. She have to wait. It risky now. He think she in here drinking, they gonna have it all over again. One time a night enough. Smart thing is go to bed. Get next to him. That what he want. Ought to be what she want. Use to be she did.

Thirty minutes a long time like this. She holding her breath when she go in there to look at him. He just a lump in the dark. Can't tell if he sleeping or not. Could be laying there looking at her. Too dark to tell. He probably asleep, though. He tired, he give out. He work so hard for them.

Tomorrow be better. Tomorrow she have to try harder. She know she can do it, she got will power. Just need a little time. They have to be patient with her. Ain't built Rome in a day. And she gonna be so good in the future, it ain't gonna hurt nothing to have a few cold beers tonight. Ain't drinking no whiskey now. Liquor store done closed anyway. Big Star still open. She just run down get some beer and then run right back. Don't need to drink what she got hid anyway. Probably won't need none later, she gonna quit anyway, but just in case.

She know where the checkbook laying. She ain't making no noise. If he awake he ain't saying nothing. If he awake he'd be done said something. He won't know she ever been gone. Won't miss no three dollar check no way. Put it in with groceries sometime.

Side door squeak every time. Don't never notice it in daytime. Squeak like hell at night. Porch light on. He always leave it on if she going to be out. Ain't no need to turn it off. She be back in ten minutes. He never know she gone. Car in the driveway. It raining. A little.

105   Ain't cold. Don't need no coat.

She get in, ease the door to. Trying to be quiet. He so tired, he need his rest. She look at the bedroom window when she turn the key. And the light come on in there.

Caught now. Wasn't even asleep. Trying to just catch her on purpose. Laying in there in the dark just making out like he asleep. Don't trust her. Won't never trust her. It like he making her slip around. Damn him anyway.

Ain't nothing to do but talk to him. He standing on the step in his underwear. She put it in reverse and back on up. She stop beside him and roll down the window. She hate to. Neighbors gonna see him out here in his underwear. What he think he doing anyway, can't leave her alone. Treat her like some baby he can't take his eye off of for five minutes.

"I just goin to the store," she say. "I be right back."

110   "Don't care for you goin to the store," he say. "Long as you come back. You comin back?"

He got his arms wrapped around him, he shivering in the night air. He look like he been asleep.

"I just goin after some cigarettes," she say. "I be back in ten minutes. Go on back to bed. I be right back. I promise."

He step off the porch and come next the car. He hugging himself and shaking, barefooted. Standing in the driveway getting wet.

"I won't say nothin about you drinkin if you just do it at home," he say. "Go git you somethin to drink. But come back home," he say. "Please," he say.

115   It hit her now, this enough. This enough to stop anything, anybody, everything. He done give up.

"Baby," he say, "know you ain't gone stop. Done said all I can say. Just don't get out on the road drinkin. Don't care about the car. Just don't hurt yourself."

"I done told you I be back in ten minutes," she say. "I be *back* in ten minutes."

Something cross his face. Can't tell rain from tears in this. But what he shivering from she don't think is cold.

"Okay, baby," he say, "okay," and he turn away. She relieved. Now maybe won't be no argument. Now maybe won't be no dread. She telling the truth anyway. Ain't going nowhere but Big Star. Be back in ten minutes. All this fussing for nothing. Neighbors probably looking out the windows.

120   He go up on the porch and put his hand on the door. He watching her back out the driveway, she watching him standing there half naked. All this foolishness over a little trip to Big Star. She shake her head while she backing out the driveway. It almost like he ain't even expecting her to come back. She almost laugh at this. Ain't

nothing even open this late but bars, and she *ain't* going to none of them, no ma'am. She see him watch her again, and then she see him step inside. What he need to do. Go on back to bed, get him some rest. He got to go to work in the morning. All she got to do is sleep.

She turn the wipers on to see better. The porch light shining out there, yellow light showing rain, it slanting down hard. It shine on the driveway and on Randy's bicycle and on they barbecue grill setting there getting wet. It make her feel good to know this all hers, that she always got this to come back to. This light show her home, this warm place she own that mean everything to her. This light, it always on for her. That what she thinking when it go out.

QUESTIONS FOR DISCUSSION AND WRITING

1. How is the basic conflict in the story established in the first paragraph? How are flashback and foreshadowing used to suggest the likely outcome of Angel's story?

2. How does Brown maintain our sympathy for Angel even as she portrays her own self-destructiveness? What does our last glimpse of Alan reveal about his character?

3. How is the social and economic situation of the family established in the details of the story? For example, what will Alan's trip to the emergency room mean to the family?

4. Although this story appears to be told in the third person, what evidence can you supply that Angel is telling her own story?

5. What does Angel's self-assessment reveal about the power of addiction? How does her assessment suggest that mutual trust is essential to overcoming addiction? What thematic meaning do you find in the title of the story?

Stories for Comparison

James Baldwin's "Sonny's Blues" (pages 215–238); Dennis McFarland's "Nothing to Ask For" (pages 832–843).

28

ITALO CALVINO

The Form of Space

ITALO CALVINO (1923–1985) was born in Cuba but was brought up in
Italy, where he was educated at the University of Turin. During World War II,
he participated in the Resistance against Fascism in Italy; his early novel
The Path to the Nest of Spiders (1947) and his first story collection, *Adam,
One Afternoon and Other Stories* (1949), were based on this experience.
He first became well-known to American readers for *Italian Folktales* (1956),
a collection of fables he wrote and edited. His later writing continued to
explore the fusion of reality and fantasy in books such as *Cosmicomics*
(1965), which won the National Book Award, and *Invisible Cities* (1972),
which relates an imaginary conversation between explorer Marco Polo
and the emperor Kubla Khan. In "The Form of Space," reprinted from
Cosmicomics, a narrator tries to understand a fall through space where
"nobody really knew anything."

*The equations of the gravitational field which relate the curve of space to the
distribution of matter are already becoming common knowledge.*

To fall in the void as I fell: none of you knows what that means. For you, to fall
means to plunge perhaps from the twenty-sixth floor of a skyscraper, or from an airplane which breaks down in flight: to fall headlong, grope in the air a moment, and
then the Earth is immediately there, and you get a big bump. But I'm talking about
the time when there wasn't any Earth underneath or anything else solid, not even a
celestial body in the distance capable of attracting you into its orbit. You simply fell,
indefinitely, for an indefinite length of time. I went down into the void, to the most
absolute bottom conceivable, and once there I saw that the extreme limit must have
been much, much farther below, very remote, and I went on falling, to reach it. Since
there were no reference points, I had no idea whether my fall was fast or slow. Now
that I think about it, there weren't even any proofs that I was really falling: perhaps
I had always remained immobile in the same place, or I was moving in an upward
direction; since there was no above or below these were only nominal questions and
so I might just as well go on thinking I was falling, as I was naturally led to think.

Assuming then that one was falling, everyone fell with the same speed and rate of acceleration; in fact we were always more or less on the same level: I, Ursula H'x, Lieutenant Fenimore. I didn't take my eyes off Ursula H'x: she was very beautiful to see, and in falling she had an easy, relaxed attitude. I hoped I would be able sometimes to catch her eye, but as she fell, Ursula H'x was always intent on filing and polishing her nails or running her comb through her long, smooth hair, and she never glanced toward me. Nor toward Lieutenant Fenimore, I must say, though he did everything he could to attract her attention.

Once I caught him—he thought I couldn't see him—as he was making some signals to Ursula H'x: first he struck his two index fingers, outstretched, one against the other, then he made a rotating gesture with one hand, then he pointed down. I mean, he seemed to hint at an understanding with her, an appointment for later on, in some place down there, where they were to meet. All nonsense, I knew perfectly well: there were no meetings possible among us, because our falls were parallel and the same distance always remained between us. But the mere fact that Lieutenant Fenimore had got such ideas into his head—and tried to put them into the head of Ursula H'x—was enough to get on my nerves, even though she paid no attention to him, indeed she made a slight blurting sound with her lips, directed—I felt there was no doubt—at him. (Ursula H'x fell, revolving with lazy movements as if she were turning in her bed and it was hard to say whether her gestures were directed at someone else or whether she was playing for her own benefit, as was her habit.)

I too, naturally, dreamed only of meeting Ursula H'x, but since, in my fall, I was following a straight line absolutely parallel to the one she followed, it seemed inappropriate to reveal such an unattainable desire. Of course, if I chose to be an optimist, there was always the possibility that, if our two parallels continued to infinity, the moment would come when they would touch. This eventuality gave me some hope; indeed, it kept me in a state of constant excitement. I don't mind telling you I had dreamed so much of a meeting of our parallels, in great detail, that it was now a part of my experience, as if I had actually lived it. Everything would happen suddenly, with simplicity and naturalness: after the long separate journey, unable to move an inch closer to each other, after having felt her as an alien being for so long, a prisoner of her parallel route, then the consistency of space, instead of being impalpable as it had always been, would become more taut and, at the same time, looser, a condensing of the void which would seem to come not from outside but from within us, and would press me and Ursula H'x together (I had only to shut my eyes to see her come forward, in an attitude I recognized as hers even if it was different from all her habitual attitudes: her arms stretched down, along her sides, twisting her wrists as if she were stretching and at the same time writhing and leaning forward), and then the invisible line I was following would become a single line, occupied by a mingling of her and me where her soft and secret nature would be penetrated or rather would enfold and, I would say, almost absorb the part of myself that till then had been suffering at being alone and separate and barren.

Even the most beautiful dreams can suddenly turn into nightmares, and it then occurred to me that the meeting point of our two parallels might also be the point at which all parallels existing in space eventually meet, and so it would mark not only my meeting with Ursula H'x but also—dreadful prospect—a meeting with Lieutenant Fenimore. At the very moment when Ursula H'x would cease to be alien to me, another alien with his thin black mustache would share our intimacies in an inextricable way: this thought was enough to plunge me into the most tormented jealous hallucinations: I heard the cry that our meeting—hers and mine—tore from us melt in a spasmodically joyous unison and then—I was aghast at the presentiment—from that sound burst her piercing cry as she was violated—so, in my resentful bias, I imagined—from behind, and at the same time the Lieutenant's vulgar shout of triumph, but perhaps—and here my jealousy became delirium—these cries of theirs, hers and his—might also not be so different or so dissonant, they might also achieve a unison, be joined in a single cry of downright pleasure, distinct from the sobbing, desperate moan that would burst from my lips.

In this alternation of hopes and apprehensions I continued to fall, constantly peering into the depths of space to see if anything heralded an immediate or future change in our condition. A couple of times I managed to glimpse a universe, but it was far away and seemed very tiny, well off to the right or to the left; I barely had time to make out a certain number of galaxies like shining little dots collected into superimposed masses which revolved with a faint buzz, when everything would vanish as it had appeared, upwards or to one side, so that I began to suspect it had only been a momentary glare in my eyes.

"There! Look! There's a universe! Look over there! There's something!" I shouted to Ursula H'x, motioning in that direction; but, tongue between her teeth, she was busy caressing the smooth, taut skin of her legs, looking for those very rare and almost invisible excess hairs she could uproot with a sharp tug of her pincerlike nails, and the only sign she had heard my call might be the way she stretched one leg upwards, as if to exploit—you would have said—for her methodical inspection the dim light reflected from that distant firmament.

I don't have to tell you the contempt Lieutenant Fenimore displayed toward what I might have discovered on those occasions: he gave a shrug—shaking his epaulettes, his bandoleer, and the decorations with which he was pointlessly arrayed—and turned in the other direction, snickering. Unless he was the one (when he was sure I was looking elsewhere) who tried to arouse Ursula's curiosity (and then it was my turn to laugh, seeing that her only response was to revolve in a kind of somersault, turning her behind to him: a gesture no doubt disrespectful but lovely to see, so that, after rejoicing in my rival's humiliation, I caught myself envying him this, as a privilege), indicating a labile point fleeing through space, shouting: "There! There! A universe! This big! I saw it! It's a universe!"

10   I won't say he was lying: statements of that sort, as far as I know, were as likely to be true as false. It was a proved fact that, every now and then, we skirted a universe (or else a universe skirted us), but it wasn't clear whether these were a number of universes scattered through space or whether it was always the same universe we kept passing, revolving in a mysterious trajectory, or whether there was no universe at all and what we thought we saw was the mirage of a universe which perhaps had once existed and whose image continued to rebound from the walls of space like the rebounding of an echo. But it could also be that the universes had always been there,

dense around us, and had no idea of moving, and we weren't moving, either, and everything was arrested forever, without time, in a darkness punctuated only by rapid flashes when something or someone managed for a moment to free himself from that sluggish timelessness and indicate the semblance of a movement.

All these hypotheses were equally worth considering, but they interested me only insofar as they concerned our fall and the possibility of touching Ursula H'x. In other words, nobody really knew anything. So why did that pompous Fenimore sometimes assume a superior manner, as if he were certain of things? He had realized that when he wanted to infuriate me the surest system was to pretend to a long-standing familiarity with Ursula H'x. At a certain point Ursula took to swaying as she came down, her knees together, shifting the weight of her body this way and that, as if wavering in an ever-broader zigzag: just to break the monotony of that endless fall. And the Lieutenant then also started swaying, trying to pick up her rhythm, as if he were following the same invisible track, or rather as if he were dancing to the sound of the same music, audible only to the two of them, which he even pretended to whistle, putting into it, on his own, a kind of unspoken understanding, as if alluding to a private joke among old boozing companions. It was all a bluff—I knew that, of course—but still it gave me the idea that a meeting between Ursula H'x and Lieutenant Fenimore might already have taken place, who knows how long ago, at the beginning of their trajectories, and this suspicion gnawed at me painfully, as if I had been the victim of an injustice. On reflecting, however, I reasoned that if Ursula and the Lieutenant had once occupied the same point in space, this meant that their respective lines of fall had since been moving apart and presumably were still moving apart. Now, in this slow but constant removal from the Lieutenant, it was more than likely that Ursula was coming closer to me; so the Lieutenant had little to boast of in his past conjunctions: I was the one at whom the future smiled.

The process of reasoning that led me to this conclusion was not enough to reassure me at heart: the possibility that Ursula H'x had already met the Lieutenant was in itself a wrong which, if it had been done to me, could no longer be redeemed. I must add that past and future were vague terms for me, and I couldn't make much distinction between them: my memory didn't extend beyond the interminable present of our parallel fall, and what might have been before, since it couldn't be remembered, belonged to the same imaginary world as the future, and was confounded with the future. So I could also suppose that if two parallels had ever set out from the same point, these were the lines that Ursula H'x and I were following (in this case it was nostalgia for a lost oneness that fed my eager desire to meet her); however, I was reluctant to believe in this hypothesis, because it might imply a progressive separation and perhaps her future arrival in the braid-festooned arms of Lieutenant Fenimore, but chiefly because I couldn't get out of the present except to imagine a different present, and none of the rest counted.

Perhaps this was the secret: to identify oneself so completely with one's own state of fall that one could realize the line followed in falling wasn't what it seemed but another, or rather to succeed in changing that line in the only way it could be changed, namely, by making it become what it had really always been. It wasn't through concentrating on myself that this idea came to me, though, but through observing, with my loving eye, how beautiful Ursula H'x was even when seen from behind, and noting, as we passed in sight of a very distant system of constellations, an arching of her back and a kind of twitch of her behind, but not so much the behind itself as an external sliding that seemed to rub past the behind and cause a not unpleasant reaction from the behind itself. This fleeting impression was enough to make me see our situation in a new way: if it was true that space with something inside is different from empty space because the matter causes a curving or a tautness which makes all the lines contained in space curve or tauten, then the line each of us was following was straight in the only way a straight line can be straight: namely, deformed to the extent that the limpid harmony of the general void is deformed by the clutter of matter, in other words, twisting all around this bump or pimple or excrescence which is the universe in the midst of space.

My point of reference was always Ursula and, in fact, a certain way she had of proceeding as if twisting could make more familiar the idea that our fall was like a winding and unwinding in a sort of spiral that tightened and then loosened. However, Ursula—if you watched her carefully—wound first in one direction, then in the other, so the pattern we were tracing was more complicated. The universe, therefore, had to be considered not a crude swelling placed there like a turnip, but as an angular, pointed figure where every dent or bulge or facet corresponded to other cavities and projections and notchings of space and of the lines we followed. This, however, was still a schematic image, as if we were dealing with a smooth-walled solid, a compenetration of polyhedrons, a cluster of crystals; in reality the space in which we moved was all battlemented and perforated, with spires and pinnacles which spread out on every side, with cupolas and balustrades and peristyles, with rose windows, with double- and triple-arched fenestrations, and while we felt we were plunging straight down, in reality we were racing along the edge of moldings and invisible friezes, like ants who, crossing a city, follow itineraries traced not on the street cobbles but along walls and ceilings and cornices and chandeliers. Now if I say city it amounts to suggesting figures that are, in some way, regular, with right angles and symmetrical proportions, whereas instead, we should always bear in mind how space breaks up around every cherry tree and every leaf of every bough that moves in the wind, and at every indentation of the edge of every leaf, and also it forms along every vein of the leaf, and on the network of veins inside the leaf, and on the piercings made every moment by the riddling arrows of light, all printed in negative in the dough of the void, so that there is nothing now that does not leave its print, every possible print of every possible thing, and together every transformation of these prints, instant by instant, so the pimple growing on a caliph's nose or the soap bubble resting on a laundress's bosom changes the general form of space in all its dimensions.

15   All I had to do was understand that space was made in this way and I realized there were certain soft cavities hollowed in it as welcoming as hammocks where I could lie joined with Ursula H'x, the two of us swaying together, biting each other in turn along all our persons. The properties of space, in fact, were such that one parallel went one way, and another in another way: I for

example was plunging within a tortuous cavern while Ursula H'x was being sucked along a passage communicating with that same cavern so that we found ourselves rolling together on a lawn of algae in a kind of subspatial island, writhing, she and I, in every pose, upright and capsized, until all of a sudden our two straight lines resumed their distance, the same as always, and each continued on its own as if nothing had happened.

The grain of space was porous and broken with crevasses and dunes. If I looked carefully, I could observe when Lieutenant Fenimore's course passed through the bed of a narrow, winding canyon; then I placed myself on the top of a cliff and, at just the right moment, I hurled myself down on him, careful to strike him on the cervical vertebrae with my full weight. The bottom of such precipices in the void was stony as the bed of a dried-up stream, and Lieutenant Fenimore, sinking to the ground, remained with his head stuck between two spurs of rock; I pressed one knee into his stomach, but he meanwhile was crushing my knuckles against a cactus's thorns—or the back of a porcupine? (spikes, in any case, of the kind corresponding to certain sharp contractions of space)—to prevent me from grabbing the pistol I had kicked from his hand. I don't know how I happened, a moment later, to find myself with my head thrust into the stifling granulosity of the strata where space gives way, crumbling like sand; I spat, blinded and dazed; Fenimore had managed to collect his pistol; a bullet whistled past my ear, ricocheting off a proliferation of the void that rose in the shape of an anthill. And I fell upon him, my hands at his throat, to strangle him, but my hands slammed against each other with a "plop!": our paths had become parallel again, and Lieutenant Fenimore and I were descending, maintaining our customary distance, ostentatiously turning our backs on each other, like two people who pretend they have never met, haven't even seen each other before.

What you might consider straight, one-dimensional lines were similar, in effect, to lines of handwriting made on a white page by a pen that shifts words and fragments of sentences from one line to another, with insertions and cross-references, in the haste to finish an exposition which has gone through successive, approximate drafts, always unsatisfactory; and so we pursued each other, Lieutenant Fenimore and I, hiding behind the loops of the *l*'s, especially the *l*'s of the word "parallel," in order to shoot and take cover from the bullets and pretend to be dead and wait, say, till Fenimore went past in order to trip him up and drag him by his feet, slamming his chin against the bottoms of the *v*'s and the *u*'s and the *m*'s and the *n*'s which, written all evenly in an italic hand, became a bumpy succession of holes in the pavement (for example, in the expression "unmeasurable universe"), leaving him stretched out in a place all trampled with erasings and x-ings, then standing up there again, stained with clotted ink, to run toward Ursula H'x, who was trying to act sly, slipping behind the tails of the *f* which trail off until they become wisps, but I could seize her by the hair and bend her against a *d* or a *t* just as I write them now, in haste, bent, so you can recline against them, then we might dig a niche for ourselves down in a *g,* in the *g* of "big," a subterranean den which can be adapted as we choose to our dimensions, being made more cozy and almost invisible or else arranged more horizontally so you can stretch out in it. Whereas naturally the same lines, rather than remain series of letters and words, can easily be drawn out in their black thread and unwound in continuous, parallel, straight lines which mean nothing beyond themselves in their constant flow, never meeting, just as we never meet in our constant fall: I, Ursula H'x, Lieutenant Fenimore, and all the others.

QUESTIONS FOR DISCUSSION AND WRITING

1. Why is there no beginning to this story, a section in which we would be told how the characters came to be falling? How does the sexual rivalry serve as the main conflict in the story? How does writing serve as a way of resolving that conflict?

2. How much does the narrator understand about anyone else in the story? How does he describe Ursula H'x and Lieutenant Fenimore? How would you describe his personality? Is he a flat or a round character?

3. In what sense is the fall itself the basic setting in this story? What do universes, cities, and lives contribute to this setting? What is the emotional effect of the void as setting?

4. Who is the implied audience (the "you") in this story? What is the evidence *for* and *against* seeing this narrator as reliable?

5. How are the various interpretations of existence implied in the narrator's discussions of the forms of space? What does the scientific information about gravitational field that opens the story contribute to our understanding of the story's theme?

Stories for Comparison

Jorge Luis Borges's "The Garden of Forking Paths" (pages 291–298); Pamela Zoline's "The Heat Death of the Universe" (pages 1207–1218).

29

ALBERT   CAMUS

The Guest

TRANSLATED BY JUSTIN O'BRIEN

ALBERT CAMUS (1913–1960) was born in Mondovi, Algeria, then still a colony of France, and was educated at the University of Algeria, where he majored in philosophy and participated in the activities of a small theatrical company. During World War II he moved to France, joined the Resistance, and wrote for and edited the underground magazine *Combat.* His three novels, *The Stranger* (1942), *The Plague* (1947), and *The Fall* (1956), together with his first collection of philosophical essays, *The Myth of Sisyphus* (1942), established Camus as one of the primary spokespersons for existentialist philosophy. During the Algerian war in the 1950s, Camus's loyalties were divided between the Arab nationalists and the French colonists. His attempt to find a reasonable middle position between these extremes resulted in his major philosophical work, *The Rebel: An Essay on Man in Revolt* (1954), and in his selection for the Nobel Prize for Literature in 1957. Camus was killed in an automobile accident near Paris in 1960. "The Guest," reprinted from Camus's collection of short stories, *Exile and the Kingdom* (1957), portrays the dilemma of a man trying to decide between conflicting responsibilities.

The schoolmaster was watching the two men climb toward him. One was on horseback, the other on foot. They had not yet tackled the abrupt rise leading to the schoolhouse built on the hillside. They were toiling onward, making slow progress in the snow, among the stones, on the vast expanse of the high, deserted plateau. From time to time the horse stumbled. Without hearing anything yet, he could see the breath issuing from the horse's nostrils. One of the men, at least, knew the region. They were following the trail although it had disappeared days ago under a layer of dirty white snow. The schoolmaster calculated that it would take them half an hour to get onto the hill. It was cold; he went back into the school to get a sweater.

He crossed the empty, frigid classroom. On the blackboard the four rivers of France, drawn with four different colored chalks, had been flowing toward their estuaries for the past three days. Snow had suddenly fallen in mid-October after eight months of drought without the transition of rain, and the twenty pupils, more or less, who lived in the villages scattered over the plateau had stopped coming. With fair weather they would return. Daru now heated only the single room that was his lodging, adjoining the classroom and giving also onto the plateau to the east. Like the class windows, his window looked to the south too. On that side the school was a few kilometers from the point where the plateau began to slope toward the south. In clear weather could be seen the purple mass of the mountain range where the gap opened onto the desert.

Somewhat warmed, Daru returned to the window from which he had first seen the two men. They were no longer visible. Hence they must have tackled the rise. The sky was not so dark, for the snow had stopped falling during the night. The morning had opened with a dirty light which had scarcely become brighter as the ceiling of clouds lifted. At two in the afternoon it seemed as if the day were merely beginning. But still this was better than those three days when the thick snow was falling amidst unbroken darkness with little gusts of wind that rattled the double door of the classroom. Then Daru had spent long hours in his room, leaving it only to go to the shed and feed the chickens or get some coal. Fortunately the delivery truck from Tadjid, the nearest village to the north, had brought his supplies two days before the blizzard. It would return in forty-eight hours.

Besides, he had enough to resist a siege, for the little room was cluttered with bags of wheat that the administration left as a stock to distribute to those of his pupils whose families had suffered from the drought. Actually they had all been victims because they were all poor. Every day Daru would distribute a ration to the children. They had missed it, he knew, during these bad days. Possibly one of the fathers or big brothers would come this afternoon and he could supply them with grain. It was just a matter of carrying them over to the next harvest. Now shiploads of wheat were arriving from France and the worst was over. But it would be hard to forget that poverty, that army of ragged ghosts wandering in the sunlight, the plateaus burned to a cinder month after month, the earth shriveled up little by little, literally scorched, every stone bursting into dust under one's foot. The sheep had died then by thousands and even a few men, here and there, sometimes without anyone's knowing.

5   In contrast with such poverty, he who lived almost like a monk in his remote schoolhouse, nonetheless satisfied with the little he had and with the rough life, had felt like a lord with his whitewashed walls, his narrow couch, his unpainted shelves, his well, and his weekly provision of water and food. And suddenly this snow, without warning, without the foretaste of rain. This is the way the region was, cruel to live in, even without men—who didn't help matters either. But Daru had been born here. Everywhere else, he felt exiled.

He stepped out onto the terrace in front of the schoolhouse. The two men were now halfway up the slope. He recognized the horseman as Balducci, the old gendarme he had known for a long time. Balducci was holding on the end of a rope an Arab who was walking behind him with hands bound and head lowered. The gendarme waved a greeting to which Daru did not reply, lost as he was in contemplation of the Arab dressed in a faded blue jellaba, his feet in sandals but covered with socks of heavy raw wool, his head surmounted by a narrow, short *chèche.* They were approaching. Balducci was holding back his horse in order not to hurt the Arab, and the group was advancing slowly.

Within earshot, Balducci shouted: "One hour to do the three kilometers from El Ameur!" Daru did not answer. Short and square in his thick sweater, he watched them climb. Not once had the Arab raised his head. "Hello," said Daru when they got up onto the terrace. "Come in and warm up." Balducci painfully got down from his horse without letting go the rope. From under his bristling mustache he smiled at the schoolmaster. His little dark eyes, deep-set under a tanned forehead, and his mouth surrounded with wrinkles made him look attentive and studious. Daru took the bridle, led the horse to the shed, and came back to the two men, who were now waiting for him in the school. He led them into his room. "I am going to heat up the classroom," he said. "We'll be more comfortable there." When he entered the room again, Balducci was on the couch. He had undone the rope tying him to the Arab, who had squatted near the stove. His hands still bound, the *chèche* pushed back on his head, he was looking toward the window. At first Daru noticed only his huge lips, fat, smooth, almost Negroid; yet his nose was straight, his eyes were dark and full of fever. The *chèche* revealed an obstinate forehead and, under the weathered skin now rather discolored by the cold, the whole face had a restless and rebellious look that struck Daru when the Arab, turning his face toward him, looked him straight in the eyes. "Go into the other room," said the schoolmaster, "and I'll make you some mint tea." "Thanks," Balducci said. "What a chore! How I long for retirement." And addressing his prisoner in Arabic: "Come on, you." The Arab got up and, slowly, holding his bound wrists in front of him, went into the classroom.

With the tea, Daru brought a chair. But Balducci was already enthroned on the nearest pupil's desk and the Arab had squatted against the teacher's platform facing the stove, which stood between the desk and the window. When he held out the glass of tea to the prisoner, Daru hesitated at the sight of his bound hands. "He might perhaps be untied." "Sure," said Balducci. "That was for the trip." He started to get to his feet. But Daru, setting the glass on the floor, had knelt beside the Arab. Without saying anything, the Arab watched him with his feverish eyes. Once his hands were free, he rubbed his swollen wrists against each other, took the glass of tea, and sucked up the burning liquid in swift little sips.

"Good," said Daru. "And where are you headed?"

Balducci withdrew his mustache from the tea. "Here, son."   10

"Odd pupils! And you're spending the night?"

"No. I'm going back to El Ameur. And you will deliver this fellow to Tinguit. He is expected at police headquarters."

Balducci was looking at Daru with a friendly little smile.

"What's this story?" asked the schoolmaster. "Are you pulling my leg?"

"No, son. Those are the orders."   15

"The orders? I'm not . . ." Daru hesitated, not wanting to hurt the old Corsican. "I mean, that's not my job."

"What! What's the meaning of that? In wartime people do all kinds of jobs."

"Then I'll wait for the declaration of war!"

Balducci nodded.

20   "O.K. But the orders exist and they concern you too. Things are brewing, it appears. There is talk of a forthcoming revolt. We are mobilized, in a way."

Daru still had his obstinate look.

"Listen, son," Balducci said. "I like you and you must understand. There's only a dozen of us at El Ameur to patrol throughout the whole territory of a small department and I must get back in a hurry. I was told to hand this guy over to you and return without delay. He couldn't be kept there. His village was beginning to stir; they wanted to take him back. You must take him to Tinguit tomorrow before the day is over. Twenty kilometers shouldn't faze a husky fellow like you. After that, all will be over. You'll come back to your pupils and your comfortable life."

Behind the wall the horse could be heard snorting and pawing the earth. Daru was looking out the window. Decidedly, the weather was clearing and the light was increasing over the snowy plateau. When all the snow was melted, the sun would take over again and once more would burn the fields of stone. For days, still, the unchanging sky would shed its dry light on the solitary expanse where nothing had any connection with man.

"After all," he said, turning around toward Balducci, "what did he do?" And, before the gendarme had opened his mouth, he asked: "Does he speak French?"

25   "No, not a word. We had been looking for him for a month, but they were hiding him. He killed his cousin."

"Is he against us?"

"I don't think so. But you can never be sure."

"Why did he kill?"

"A family squabble, I think. One owed the other grain, it seems. It's not at all clear. In short, he killed his cousin with a billhook. You know, like a sheep, *kreezk!*"

30   Balducci made the gesture of drawing a blade across his throat and the Arab, his attention attracted, watched him with a sort of anxiety. Daru felt a sudden wrath against the man, against all men with their rotten spite, their tireless hates, their blood lust.

But the kettle was singing on the stove. He served Balducci more tea, hesitated, then served the Arab again, who a second time, drank avidly. His raised arms made the jellaba fall open and the schoolmaster saw his thin, muscular chest.

"Thanks, kid," Balducci said. "And now, I'm off."

He got up and went toward the Arab, taking a small rope from his pocket.

"What are you doing?" Daru asked dryly.

35   Balducci, disconcerted, showed him the rope.

"Don't bother."

The old gendarme hesitated. "It's up to you. Of course, you are armed?"

"I have my shotgun."

"Where?"

40   "In the trunk."

"You ought to have it near your bed."

"Why? I have nothing to fear."

"You're crazy, son. If there's an uprising, no one is safe, we're all in the same boat."

"I'll defend myself. I'll have time to see them coming."

Balducci began to laugh, then suddenly the mustache covered the white teeth. ⁴⁵

"You'll have time? O.K. That's just what I was saying. You have always been a little cracked. That's why I like you, my son was like that."

At the same time he took out his revolver and put it on the desk.

"Keep it; I don't need two weapons from here to El Ameur."

The revolver shone against the black paint of the table. When the gendarme turned toward him, the schoolmaster caught the smell of leather and horseflesh.

"Listen, Balducci," Daru said suddenly, "every bit of this disgusts me, and ⁵⁰ first of all your fellow here. But I won't hand him over. Fight, yes, if I have to. But not that."

The old gendarme stood in front of him and looked at him severely.

"You're being a fool," he said slowly. "I don't like it either. You don't get used to putting a rope on a man even after years of it, and you're even ashamed—yes, ashamed. But you can't let them have their way."

"I won't hand him over," Daru said again.

"It's an order, son, and I repeat it."

"That's right. Repeat to them what I've said to you: I won't hand him over." ⁵⁵

Balducci made a visible effort to reflect. He looked at the Arab and at Daru. At last he decided.

"No, I won't tell them anything. If you want to drop us, go ahead; I'll not denounce you. I have an order to deliver the prisoner and I'm doing so. And now you'll just sign this paper for me."

"There's no need. I'll not deny that you left him with me."

"Don't be mean with me. I know you'll tell the truth. You're from hereabouts and you are a man. But you must sign, that's the rule."

Daru opened his drawer, took out a little square bottle of purple ink, the red ⁶⁰ wooden penholder with the "sergeant-major" pen he used for making models of penmanship, and signed. The gendarme carefully folded the paper and put it into his wallet. Then he moved toward the door.

"I'll see you off," Daru said.

"No," said Balducci. "There's no use being polite. You insulted me."

He looked at the Arab, motionless in the same spot, sniffed peevishly, and turned away toward the door. "Good-by, son," he said. The door shut behind him. Balducci appeared suddenly outside the window and then disappeared. His footsteps were muffled by the snow. The horse stirred on the other side of the wall and several chickens fluttered in fright. A moment later Balducci reappeared outside the window leading the horse by the bridle. He walked toward the little rise without turning around and disappeared from sight with the horse following him. A big stone could be heard bouncing down. Daru walked back toward the prisoner, who, without stirring, never took his eyes off him. "Wait," the schoolmaster said in Arabic and went toward the bedroom. As he was going through the door, he had a second thought, went to the desk, took the revolver, and stuck it in his pocket. Then, without looking back, he went into his room.

For some time he lay on his couch watching the sky gradually close over, listening to the silence. It was this silence that had seemed painful to him during the first days here, after the war. He had requested a post in the little town at the base of the foothills separating the upper plateaus from the desert. There, rocky walls, green and black to the north, pink and lavender to the south, marked the frontier of eternal summer. He had been named to a post farther north, on the plateau itself. In the beginning, the solitude and the silence had been hard for him on these wastelands peopled only by stones. Occasionally, furrows suggested cultivation, but they had been dug to uncover a certain kind of stone good for building. The only plowing here was to harvest rocks. Elsewhere a thin layer of soil accumulated in the hollows would be scraped out to enrich paltry village gardens. This is the way it was: bare rock covered three quarters of the region. Towns sprang up, flourished, then disappeared; men came by, loved one another or fought bitterly, then died. No one in this desert, neither he nor his guest, mattered. And yet, outside this desert neither of them, Daru knew, could have really lived.

65   When he got up, no noise came from the classroom. He was amazed at the unmixed joy he derived from the mere thought that the Arab might have fled and that he would be alone with no decision to make. But the prisoner was there. He had merely stretched out between the stove and the desk. With eyes open, he was staring at the ceiling. In that position, his thick lips were particularly noticeable, giving him a pouting look. "Come," said Daru. The Arab got up and followed him. In the bedroom, the schoolmaster pointed to a chair near the table under the window. The Arab sat down without taking his eyes off Daru.

"Are you hungry?"

"Yes," the prisoner said.

Daru set the table for two. He took flour and oil, shaped a cake in a frying-pan, and lighted the little stove that functioned on bottled gas. While the cake was cooking, he went out to the shed to get cheese, eggs, dates, and condensed milk. When the cake was done he sat it on the window sill to cool, heated some condensed milk diluted with water, and beat up the eggs into an omelette. In one of his motions he knocked against the revolver stuck in his right pocket. He set the bowl down, went into the classroom, and put the revolver in his desk drawer. When he came back to the room, night was falling. He put on the light and served the Arab. "Eat," he said. The Arab took a piece of the cake, lifted it eagerly to his mouth, and stopped short.

"And you?" he asked.

70   "After you. I'll eat too."

The thick lips opened slightly. The Arab hesitated, then bit into the cake determinedly.

The meal over, the Arab looked at the schoolmaster. "Are you the judge?"

"No, I'm simply keeping you until tomorrow."

"Why do you eat with me?"

75   "I'm hungry."

The Arab fell silent. Daru got up and went out. He brought back a folding bed from the shed, set it up between the table and the stove, perpendicular to his own bed. From a large suitcase which, upright in a corner, served as a shelf for papers, he took two blankets and arranged them on the camp bed. Then he stopped, felt useless, and sat down on his bed. There was nothing more to do or to get ready. He had to look at this man. He looked at him, therefore, trying to imagine his face bursting with rage. He couldn't do so. He could see nothing but the dark yet shining eyes and the animal mouth.

"Why did you kill him?" he asked in a voice whose hostile tone surprised him.

The Arab looked away.

"He ran away. I ran after him."

He raised his eyes to Daru again and they were full of a sort of woeful interro- 80 gation. "Now what will they do to me?"

"Are you afraid?"

He stiffened, turning his eyes away.

"Are you sorry?"

The Arab stared at him openmouthed. Obviously he did not understand. Daru's annoyance was growing. At the same time he felt awkward and self-conscious with his big body wedged between the two beds.

"Lie down there," he said impatiently. "That's your bed."   85

The Arab didn't move. He called to Daru:

"Tell me!"

The schoolmaster looked at him.

"Is the gendarme coming back tomorrow?"

"I don't know."   90

"Are you coming with us?"

"I don't know. Why?"

The prisoner got up and stretched out on top of the blankets, his feet toward the window. The light from the electric bulb shone straight into his eyes and he closed them at once.

"Why?" Daru repeated, standing beside the bed.

The Arab opened his eyes under the blinding light and looked at him, trying not 95 to blink.

"Come with us," he said.

In the middle of the night, Daru was still not asleep. He had gone to bed after undressing completely; he generally slept naked. But when he suddenly realized that he had nothing on, he hesitated. He felt vulnerable and the temptation came to him to put his clothes back on. Then he shrugged his shoulders; after all, he wasn't a child and, if need be, he could break his adversary in two. From his bed he could observe him, lying on his back, still motionless with his eyes closed under the harsh light. When Daru turned out the light, the darkness seemed to coagulate all of a sudden. Little by little, the night came back to life in the window where the starless sky was stirring gently. The schoolmaster soon made out the body lying at his feet. The Arab still did not move, but his eyes seemed open. A faint wind was prowling around the schoolhouse. Perhaps it would drive away the clouds and the sun would reappear.

During the night the wind increased. The hens fluttered a little and then were silent. The Arab turned over on his side with his back to Daru, who thought he heard him moan. Then he listened for his guest's breathing, become heavier and more regular. He listened to that breath so close to him and mused without being able to go to sleep. In this room where he had been sleeping alone for a year, this presence bothered him. But it bothered him also by imposing on him a sort of brotherhood he knew well but refused to accept in the present circumstances. Men who share the same rooms, soldiers or prisoners, develop a strange alliance as if, having cast off their armor with their clothing, they fraternized every evening, over and above their differences, in the ancient community of dream and fatigue. But Daru shook himself; he didn't like such musings, and it was essential to sleep.

A little later, however, when the Arab stirred slightly, the schoolmaster was still not asleep. When the prisoner made a second move, he stiffened, on the alert. The Arab was lifting himself slowly on his arms with almost the motion of a sleepwalker. Seated upright in bed, he waited motionless without turning his head toward Daru, as if he were listening attentively. Daru did not stir; it had just occurred to him that the revolver was still in the drawer of his desk. It was better to act at once. Yet he continued to observe the prisoner, who, with the same slithery motion, put his feet on the ground, waited again, then began to stand up slowly. Daru was about to call out to him when the Arab began to walk, in a quite natural but extraordinarily silent way. He was heading toward the door at the end of the room that opened into the shed. He lifted the latch with precaution and went out, pushing the door behind him but without shutting it. Daru had not stirred. "He is running away," he merely thought. "Good riddance!" Yet he listened attentively. The hens were not fluttering; the guest must be on the plateau. A faint sound of water reached him, and he didn't know what it was until the Arab again stood framed in the doorway, closed the door carefully, and came back to bed without a sound. Then Daru turned his back on him and fell asleep. Still later he seemed, from the depths of his sleep, to hear furtive steps around the schoolhouse. "I'm dreaming! I'm dreaming!" he repeated to himself. And he went on sleeping.

100   When he awoke, the sky was clear; the loose window let in a cold, pure air. The Arab was asleep, hunched up under the blankets now, his mouth open, utterly relaxed. But when Daru shook him, he started dreadfully, staring at Daru with wild eyes as if he had never seen him and such a frightened expression that the schoolmaster stepped back. "Don't be afraid. It's me. You must eat." The Arab nodded his head and said yes. Calm had returned to his face, but his expression was vacant and listless.

The coffee was ready. They drank it seated together on the folding bed as they munched their pieces of the cake. Then Daru led the Arab under the shed and showed him the faucet where he washed. He went back into the room, folded the blankets and the bed, made his own bed and put the room in order. Then he went through the classroom and out onto the terrace. The sun was already rising in the blue sky; a soft, bright light was bathing the deserted plateau. On the ridge the snow was melting in spots. The stones were about to reappear. Crouched on the edge of the plateau, the schoolmaster looked at the deserted expanse. He thought of Balducci. He had hurt him, for he had sent him off in a way as if he didn't want to be associated with him. He could still hear the gendarme's farewell and, without knowing why, he felt strangely empty and vulnerable. At that moment, from the other side of the schoolhouse, the prisoner coughed. Daru listened to him almost despite himself and then, furious, threw a pebble that whistled through the air before sinking into the snow. That man's stupid crime revolted him, but to hand him over was contrary to honor. Merely thinking of it made him smart with humiliation. And he cursed at one and the same time his own people who had sent him this Arab and the Arab too who had dared to kill and not managed to get away. Daru got up, walked in a circle on the terrace, waited motionless, and then went back into the schoolhouse.

The Arab, leaning over the cement floor of the shed, was washing his teeth with two fingers. Daru looked at him and said: "Come." He went back into the room ahead of the prisoner. He slipped a hunting-jacket on over his sweater and put on walking-shoes. Standing, he waited until the Arab had put on his *chèche* and sandals. They went into the classroom and the schoolmaster pointed to the exit, saying: "Go ahead." The fellow didn't budge. "I'm coming," said Daru. The Arab went out. Daru went back into the room and made a package of pieces of rusk, dates, and sugar. In the classroom, before going out, he hesitated a second in front of his desk, then crossed the threshold and locked the door. "That's the way," he said. He started toward the east, followed by the prisoner. But, a short distance from the schoolhouse, he thought he heard a slight sound behind them. He retraced his steps and examined the surroundings of the house; there was no one there. The Arab watched him without seeming to understand. "Come on," said Daru.

They walked for an hour and rested beside a sharp peak of limestone. The snow was melting faster and faster and the sun was drinking up the puddles at once, rapidly cleaning the plateau, which gradually dried and vibrated like the air itself. When they resumed walking, the ground rang under their feet. From time to time a bird rent the space in front of them with a joyful cry. Daru breathed in deeply the fresh morning light. He felt a sort of rapture before the vast familiar expanse, now almost entirely yellow under its dome of blue sky. They walked an hour more, descending toward the south. They reached a level height made up of crumbly rocks. From there on, the plateau sloped down, eastward, toward a low plain where there were a few spindly trees and, to the south, toward outcroppings of rock that gave the landscape a chaotic look.

Daru surveyed the two directions. There was nothing but the sky on the horizon. Not a man could be seen. He turned toward the Arab, who was looking at him blankly. Daru held out the package to him. "Take it," he said. "There are dates, bread, and sugar. You can hold out for two days. Here are a thousand francs too." The Arab took the package and the money but kept his full hands at chest level as if he didn't know what to do with what was being given him. "Now look," the schoolmaster said as he pointed in the direction of the east, "there's the way to Tinguit. You have a two-hour walk. At Tinguit you'll find the administration and the police. They are expecting you." The Arab looked toward the east, still holding the package and the money against his chest. Daru took his elbow and turned him rather roughly toward the south. At the foot of the height on which they stood could be seen a faint path. "That's the trail across the plateau. In a day's walk from here you'll find pasturelands and the first nomads. They'll take you in and shelter you according to their law." The Arab had now turned toward Daru and a sort of panic was visible in his expression. "Listen," he said. Daru shook his head: "No, be quiet. Now I'm leaving you." He turned his back on him, took two long steps in the direction of the school, looked hesitantly at the motionless Arab, and started off again. For a few minutes he heard nothing but his own step resounding on the cold ground and did not turn his head. A moment later, however, he turned around. The Arab was still there on the edge of the hill, his arms hanging now, and he was looking at the schoolmaster. Daru felt something rise in his throat. But he swore with impatience, waved vaguely, and started off again. He had already gone some distance when he again stopped and looked. There was no longer anyone on the hill.

105   Daru hesitated. The sun was now rather high in the sky and was beginning to beat down on his head. The schoolmaster retraced his steps, at first somewhat uncertainly, then with decision. When he reached the little hill, he was bathed in sweat. He climbed it as fast as he could and stopped, out of breath, at the top. The rock-fields to the south stood out sharply against the blue sky, but on the plain to the east a steamy heat was already rising. And in that slight haze, Daru, with heavy heart, made out the Arab walking slowly on the road to prison.

A little later, standing before the window of the classroom, the schoolmaster was watching the clear light bathing the whole surface of the plateau, but he hardly saw it. Behind him on the blackboard, among the winding French rivers, sprawled the clumsily chalked-up words he had just read: "You handed over our brother. You will pay for this." Daru looked at the sky, the plateau, and, beyond, the invisible lands stretching all the way to the sea. In this vast landscape he had loved so much, he was alone.

QUESTIONS FOR DISCUSSION AND WRITING

1. The conflicts in this story arise from the choices Daru is forced to make. Which choice forms the climax of the story? Explain your answer.

2. How does Daru's request for an isolated post establish his character? What does Daru's attitude toward firearms reveal about him? How would Balducci characterize Daru and his motives?

3. In what ways do the three major characters differ in their understanding of their common environment?

4. Why does Camus choose a third-person omniscient rather than a first-person point of view for this story? How does this technique further emphasize Daru's isolation?

5. Why does Daru free the Arab to make his own choice? Has he, in fact, betrayed his "brother"? Explain your answer.

Stories for Comparison:

Herman Melville's "Bartleby, the Scrivener" (pages 883–909); Frank O'Connor's "Guests of the Nation" (pages 995–1004).

30

···

E T H A N   C A N I N

We Are Nighttime Travelers

ETHAN CANIN was born in 1960 in Ann Arbor, Michigan, and educated at Stanford University, the University of Iowa, and Harvard Medical School. Among the first to recognize Canin's talent was Danielle Steel, who taught at Canin's private school before her own novels began to sell widely. Her praise inspired Canin to write fiction throughout college and at the University of Iowa Writer's Workshop, where he drafted stories that were included in Houghton Mifflin's annual collection, *Best American Short Stories.* Despite this early success, Canin decided to pursue a more practical career in medicine. He was in the middle of exams when an editor from Houghton Mifflin called, suggesting that he publish a collection of his stories. *Emperor of the Air* (1988) became a best-seller, and Canin reclaimed his life as a writer. He continues to write stories for periodicals such as *The Atlantic Monthly* and *Esquire,* and novels such as *Blue River* (1991) and *Palace Thief* (1994). In "We Are Nighttime Travelers," reprinted from *Emperor of the Air,* an old man moves toward a reassessment of his relationship with his wife.

Where are we going? Where, I might write, is this path leading us? Francine is asleep and I am standing downstairs in the kitchen with the door closed and the light on and a stack of mostly blank paper on the counter in front of me. My dentures are in a glass by the sink. I clean them with a tablet that bubbles in the water, and although they were clean already I just cleaned them again because the bubbles are agreeable and I thought their effervescence might excite me to action. By action, I mean I thought they might excite me to write. But words fail me.

This is a love story. However, its roots are tangled and involve a good bit of my life, and when I recall my life my mood turns sour and I am reminded that no man makes truly proper use of his time. We are blind and small-minded. We are dumb as snails and as frightened, full of vanity and misinformed about the importance of things. I'm an average man, without great deeds except maybe one, and that has been to love my wife.

I have been more or less faithful to Francine since I married her. There has been one transgression—leaning up against a closet wall with a red-haired purchasing agent at a sales meeting once in Minneapolis twenty years ago; but she was buying auto upholstery and I was selling it and in the eyes of judgment this may bear a key weight. Since then, though, I have ambled on this narrow path of life bound to one woman. This is a triumph and a regret. In our current state of affairs it is a regret because in life a man is either on the uphill or on the downhill, and if he isn't procreating he is on the downhill. It is a steep downhill indeed. These days I am tumbling, falling headlong among the scrub oaks and boulders, tearing my knees and abrading all the bony parts of the body. I have given myself to gravity.

Francine and I are married now forty-six years, and I would be a bamboozler to say that I have loved her for any more than half of these. Let us say that for the last year I haven't; let us say this for the last ten, even. Time has made torments of our small differences and tolerance of our passions. This is our state of affairs. Now I stand by myself in our kitchen in the middle of the night; now I lead a secret life. We wake at different hours now, sleep in different corners of the bed. We like different foods and different music, keep our clothing in different drawers, and if it can be said that either of us has aspirations, I believe that they are to a different bliss. Also, she is healthy and I am ill. And as for conversation—that feast of reason, that flow of the soul—our house is silent as the bone yard.

5   Last week we did talk. "Frank," she said one evening at the table, "there is something I must tell you."

The New York game was on the radio, snow was falling outside, and the pot of tea she had brewed was steaming on the table between us. Her medicine and my medicine were in little paper cups at our places.

"Frank," she said, jiggling her cup, "what I must tell you is that someone was around the house last night."

I tilted my pills onto my hand. "Around the house?"

"Someone was at the window."

10   On my palm the pills were white, blue, beige, pink: Lasix, Diabinese, Slow-K, Lopressor. "What do you mean?"

She rolled her pills onto the tablecloth and fidgeted with them, made them into a line, then into a circle, then into a line again. I don't know her medicine so well. She's healthy, except for little things. "I mean," she said, "there was someone in the yard last night."

"How do you know?"

"Frank, will you really, please?"

"I'm asking how you know."

15   "I heard him," she said. She looked down. "I was sitting in the front room and I heard him outside the window."

"You heard him?"

"Yes."

"The front window?"

She got up and went to the sink. This is a trick of hers. At that distance I can't see her face.

20   "The front window is ten feet off the ground," I said.

"What I know is that there was a man out there last night, right outside the glass." She walked out of the kitchen.

"Let's check," I called after her. I walked into the living room, and when I got there she was looking out the window.

"What is it?"

She was peering out at an angle. All I could see was snow, blue-white.

"Footprints," she said.   25

I built the house we live in with my two hands. That was forty-nine years ago, when, in my foolishness and crude want of learning, everything I didn't know seemed like a promise. I learned to build a house and then I built one. There are copper fixtures on the pipes, sanded edges on the struts and queen posts. Now, a half-century later, the floors are flat as a billiard table but the man who laid them needs two hands to pick up a woodscrew. This is the diabetes. My feet are gone also. I look down at them and see two black shapes when I walk, things I can't feel. Black clubs. No connection with the ground. If I didn't look, I could go to sleep with my shoes on.

Life takes its toll, and soon the body gives up completely. But it gives up the parts first. This sugar in the blood: God says to me: "Frank Manlius—codger, man of prevarication and half-truth—I shall take your life from you, as from all men. But first—" But first! Clouds in the eyeball, a heart that makes noise, feet cold as un-cooked roast. And Francine, beauty that she was—now I see not much more than the dark line of her brow and the intersections of her body: mouth and nose, neck and shoulders. Her smells have changed over the years so that I don't know what's her own anymore and what's powder.

We have two children, but they're gone now too, with children of their own. We have a house, some furniture, small savings to speak of. How Francine spends her day I don't know. This is the sad truth, my confession. I am gone past nightfall. She wakes early with me and is awake when I return, but beyond this I know almost nothing of her life.

I myself spend my days at the aquarium. I've told Francine something else, of course, that I'm part of a volunteer service of retired men, that we spend our days setting young businesses afoot: "Immigrants," I told her early on, "newcomers to the land." I said it was difficult work. In the evenings I could invent stories, but I don't, and Francine doesn't ask.

I am home by nine or ten. Ticket stubs from the aquarium fill my coat pocket.   30 Most of the day I watch the big sea animals—porpoises, sharks, a manatee—turn their saltwater loops. I come late morning and move a chair up close. They are wait-ing to eat then. Their bodies skim the cool glass, full of strange magnifications. I think, if it is possible, that they are beginning to know me: this man—hunched at the shoulder, cataractic of eye, breathing through water himself—this man who sits and watches. I do not pity them. At lunchtime I buy coffee and sit in one of the hotel lob-bies or in the cafeteria next door, and I read poems. Browning, Whitman, Eliot. This is my secret. It is night when I return home. Francine is at the table, four feet across from my seat, the width of two dropleaves. Our medicine is in cups. There have been three Presidents since I held her in my arms.

The cafeteria moves the men along, old or young, who come to get away from the cold. A half-hour for a cup, they let me sit. Then the manager is at my table. He is nothing but polite. I buy a pastry then, something small. He knows me—I have seen him nearly every day for months now—and by his slight limp I know he is a man of mercy. But business is business.

"What are you reading?" he asks me as he wipes the table with a wet cloth. He touches the saltshaker, nudges the napkins in their holder. I know what this means.

"I'll take a cranberry roll," I say. He flicks the cloth and turns back to the counter.

This is what:

> Shall I say, I have gone at dusk through narrow streets
> And watched the smoke that rises from the pipes
> Of lonely men in shirt-sleeves, leaning out of windows?

35   Through the magnifier glass the words come forward, huge, two by two. With spectacles, everything is twice enlarged. Still, though, I am slow to read it. In a half-hour I am finished, could not read more, even if I bought another roll. The boy at the register greets me, smiles when I reach him. "What are you reading today?" he asks, counting out the change.

The books themselves are small and fit in the inside pockets of my coat. I put one in front of each breast, then walk back to see the fish some more. These are the fish I know: the gafftopsail pompano, sixgill shark, the starry flounder with its up-turned eyes, queerly migrated. He rests half-submerged in sand. His scales are platey and flat-hued. Of everything upward he is wary, of the silvery seabass and the bluefin tuna that pass above him in the region of light and open water. For a life he lies on the bottom of the tank. I look at him. His eyes are dull. They are ugly and an aber-ration. Above us the bony fishes wheel at the tank's corners. I lean forward to the glass. "*Platichthys stellatus,*" I say to him. The caudal fin stirs. Sand moves and re-settles, and I see the black and yellow stripes. "Flatfish," I whisper, "we are, you and I, observers of this life."

"A man on our lawn," I say a few nights later in bed.

"Not just that."

I breathe in, breathe out, look up at the ceiling. "What else?"

40   "When you were out last night he came back."

"He came back."

"Yes."

"What did he do?"

"Looked in at me."

45   Later, in the early night, when the lights of cars are still passing and the walked dogs still jingle their collar chains out front, I get up quickly from bed and step into

the hall. I move fast because this is still possible in short bursts and with concentration. The bed sinks once, then rises. I am on the landing and then downstairs without Francine waking. I stay close to the staircase joists.

In the kitchen I take out my almost blank sheets and set them on the counter. I write standing up because I want to take more than an animal's pose. For me this is futile, but I stand anyway. The page will be blank when I finish. This I know. The dreams I compose are the dreams of others, remembered bits of verse. Songs of greater men than I. In months I have written few more than a hundred words. The pages are stacked, sheets of different sizes.

If I could

one says.

It has never seemed

says another. I stand and shift them in and out. They are mostly blank, sheets from months of nights. But this doesn't bother me. What I have is patience.

Francine knows nothing of the poetry. She's a simple girl, toast and butter. I myself am hardly the man for it: forty years selling (anything—steel piping, heater elements, dried bananas). Didn't read a book except one on sales. Think victory, the book said. Think *sale*. It's a young man's bag of apples, though; young men in pants that nip at the waist. Ten years ago I left the Buick in the company lot and walked home, dye in my hair, cotton rectangles in the shoulders of my coat. Francine was in the house that afternoon also, the way she is now. When I retired we bought a camper and went on a trip. A traveling salesman retires, so he goes on a trip. Forty miles out of town the folly appeared to me, big as a balloon. To Francine, too. "Frank," she said in the middle of a bend, a prophet turning to me, the camper pushing sixty and rocking in the wind, trucks to our left and right big as trains—"Frank," she said, "these roads must be familiar to you."

So we sold the camper at a loss and a man who'd spent forty years at highway speed looked around for something to do before he died. The first poem I read was in a book on a table in a waiting room. My eyeglasses made half-sense of things.

THESE
are the desolate, dark weeks

I read

when nature in its barrenness
equals the stupidity of man.

Gloom, I thought, and nothing more, but then I reread the words, and suddenly there I was, hunched and wheezing, bald as a trout, and tears were in my eye. I don't know where they came from.

In the morning an officer visits. He has muscles, mustache, skin red from the cold. He leans against the door frame.

50   "Can you describe him?" he says.

"It's always dark," says Francine.

"Anything about him?"

"I'm an old woman. I can see that he wears glasses."

"What kind of glasses?"

55   "Black."

"Dark glasses?"

"Black glasses."

"At a particular time?"

"Always when Frank is away."

60   "Your husband has never been here when he's come?"

"Never."

"I see." He looks at me. This look can mean several things, perhaps that he thinks Francine is imagining. "But never at a particular time?"

"No."

"Well," he says. Outside on the porch his partner is stamping his feet. "Well," he says again. "We'll have a look." He turns, replaces his cap, heads out to the snowy steps. The door closes. I hear him say something outside.

65   "Last night—" Francine says. She speaks in the dark. "Last night I heard him on the side of the house."

We are in bed. Outside, on the sill, snow has been building since morning.

"You heard the wind."

"Frank." She sits up, switches on the lamp, tilts her head toward the window. Through a ceiling and two walls I can hear the ticking of our kitchen clock.

"I heard him climbing," she says. She has wrapped her arms about her own waist. "He was on the house. I heard him. He went up the drainpipe." She shivers as she says this. "There was no wind. He went up the drainpipe and then I heard him on the porch roof."

70   "Houses make noise."

"I heard him. There's gravel there."

I imagine the sounds, amplified by hollow walls, rubber heels on timber. I don't say anything. There is an arm's length between us, cold sheet, a space uncrossed since I can remember.

"I have made the mistake in my life of not being interested in enough people," she says then. "If I'd been interested in more people, I wouldn't be alone now."

"Nobody's alone," I say.

75   "I mean that if I'd made more of an effort with people I would have friends now. I would know the postman and the Giffords and the Kohlers, and we'd be together in this, all of us. We'd sit in each other's living rooms on rainy days and talk about the children. Instead we've kept to ourselves. Now I'm alone."

"You're not alone," I say.

"Yes, I am." She turns the light off and we are in the dark again. "You're alone, too."

My health has gotten worse. It's slow to set in at this age, not the violent shaking grip of death; instead—a slow leak, nothing more. A bicycle tire: rimless, thready, worn treadless already and now losing its fatness. A war of attrition. The tall camels of the spirit steering for the desert. One morning I realized I hadn't been warm in a year.

And there are other things that go, too. For instance, I recall with certainty that it was on the 23rd of April, 1945, that, despite German counteroffensives in the Ardennes, Eisenhower's men reached the Elbe; but I cannot remember whether I have visited the savings and loan this week. Also, I am unable to produce the name of my neighbor, though I greeted him yesterday in the street. And take, for example, this: I am at a loss to explain whole decades of my life. We have children and photographs, and there is an understanding between Francine and me that bears the weight of nothing less than half a century, but when I gather my memories they seem to fill no more than an hour. Where has my life gone?

It has gone partway to shoddy accumulations. In my wallet are credit cards, a license ten years expired, twenty-three dollars in cash. There is a photograph but it depresses me to look at it, and a poem, half-copied and folded into the billfold. The leather is pocked and has taken on the curve of my thigh. The poem is from Walt Whitman. I copy only what I need.

But of all things to do last, poetry is a barren choice. Deciphering other men's riddles while the world is full of procreation and war. A man should go out swinging an axe. Instead, I shall go out in a coffee shop.

But how can any man leave this world with honor? Despite anything he does, it grows corrupt around him. It fills with locks and sirens. A man walks into a store now and the microwaves announce his entry; when he leaves, they make electronic peeks into his coat pockets, his trousers. Who doesn't feel like a thief? I see a policeman now, any policeman, and I feel a fright. And the things I've done wrong in my life haven't been crimes. Crimes of the heart perhaps, but nothing against the state. My soul may turn black but I can wear white trousers at any meeting of men. Have I loved my wife? At one time, yes—in rages and torrents. I've been covered by the pimples of ecstasy and have rooted in the mud of despair; and I've lived for months, for whole years now, as mindless of Francine as a tree of its mosses.

And this is what kills us, this mindlessness. We sit across the tablecloth now with our medicines between us, little balls and oblongs. We sit, sit. This has become our view of each other, a tableboard apart. We sit.

"Again?" I say.

"Last night."

We are at the table. Francine is making a twisting motion with her fingers. She coughs, brushes her cheek with her forearm, stands suddenly so that the table bumps and my medicines move in the cup.

"Francine," I say.

The half-light of dawn is showing me things outside the window: silhouettes, our maple, the eaves of our neighbor's garage. Francine moves and stands against the glass, hugging her shoulders.

"You're not telling me something," I say.

90   She sits and makes her pills into a circle again, then into a line. Then she is crying.

I come around the table, but she gets up before I reach her and leaves the kitchen. I stand there. In a moment I hear a drawer open in the living room. She moves things around, then shuts it again. When she returns she sits at the other side of the table. "Sit down," she says. She puts two folded sheets of paper onto the table. "I wasn't hiding them," she says.

"What weren't you hiding?"

"These," she says. "He leaves them."

"He leaves them?"

95   "They say he loves me."

"Francine."

"They're inside the windows in the morning." She picks one up, unfolds it. Then she reads:

> Ah, I remember well (and how can I
> But evermore remember well) when first

She pauses, squint-eyed, working her lips. It is a pause of only faint understanding. Then she continues:

> Our flame began, when scarce we knew what was
> The flame we felt.

When she finishes she refolds the paper precisely. "That's it," she says. "That's one of them."

At the aquarium I sit, circled by glass and, behind it, the senseless eyes of fish. I have never written a word of my own poetry but can recite the verse of others. This is the culmination of a life. *Coryphaena hippurus,* says the plaque on the dolphin's tank, words more beautiful than any of my own. The dolphin circles, circles, approaches with alarming speed, but takes no notice of, if he even sees, my hands. I wave them in front of his tank. What must he think has become of the sea? He turns and his slippery proboscis nudges the glass. I am every part sore from life.

> Ah, silver shrine, here will I take my rest
> After so many hours of toil and quest,
> A famished pilgrim—saved by miracle.

100   There is nothing noble for either of us here, nothing between us, and no miracles. I am better off drinking coffee. Any fluid refills the blood. The counter boy knows me and later at the café he pours the cup, most of a dollar's worth. Refills are free but my heart hurts if I drink more than one. It hurts no different from a bone, bruised or cracked. This amazes me.

Francine is amazed by other things. She is mystified, thrown beam ends by the romance. She reads me the poems now at breakfast, one by one. I sit. I roll my pills. "Another came last night," she says, and I see her eyebrows rise. "Another this morning." She reads them as if every word is a surprise. Her tongue touches teeth, shows between lips. These lips are dry. She reads:

> Kiss me as if you made believe
> You were not sure, this eve,
> How my face, your flower, had pursed
> Its petals up

That night she shows me the windowsill, second story, rimmed with snow, where she finds the poems. We open the glass. We lean into the air. There is ice below us, sheets of it on the trellis, needles hanging from the drainwork.

"Where do you find them?"

"Outside," she says. "Folded, on the lip."

"In the morning?"

"Always in the morning."

"The police should know about this."

"What will they be able to do?"

I step away from the sill. She leans out again, surveying her lands, which are the yard's-width spit of crusted ice along our neighbor's chain link and the three maples out front, now lost their leaves. She peers as if she expects this man to appear. An icy wind comes inside. "Think," she says. "Think. He could come from anywhere."

One night in February, a month after this began, she asks me to stay awake and stand guard until the morning. It is almost spring. The earth has reappeared in patches. During the day, at the borders of yards and driveways, I see glimpses of brown—though I know I could be mistaken. I come home early that night, before dusk, and when darkness falls I move a chair by the window downstairs. I draw apart the outer curtain and raise the shade. Francine brings me a pot of tea. She turns out the light and pauses next to me, and as she does, her hand on the chair's backbrace, I am so struck by the proximity of elements—of the night, of the teapot's heat, of the sounds of water outside—that I consider speaking. I want to ask her what has become of us, what has made our breathed air so sorry now, and loveless. But the timing is wrong and in a moment she turns and climbs the stairs. I look out into the night. Later, I hear the closet shut, then our bed creak.

There is nothing to see outside, nothing to hear. This I know. I let hours pass. Behind the window I imagine fish moving down to greet me: broomtail grouper, surfperch, sturgeon with their prehistoric rows of scutes. It is almost possible to see them. The night is full of shapes and bits of light. In it the moon rises, losing the colors of the horizon, so that by early morning it is high and pale. Frost has made a ring around it.

A ringed moon above, and I am thinking back on things. What have I regretted in my life? Plenty of things, mistakes enough to fill the car showroom, then a good deal of the back lot. I've been a man of gains and losses. What gains? My marriage, certainly, though it has been no knee-buckling windfall but more like a split decision in the end, a stock risen a few points since bought. I've certainly enjoyed certain things about the world, too. These are things gone over and over again by the writers and probably enjoyed by everybody who ever lived. Most of them involve air. Early morning air, air after a rainstorm, air through a car window. Sometimes I think the cerebrum is wasted and all we really need is the lower brain, which I've been told is what makes the lungs breathe and the heart beat and what lets us smell pleasant things. What about the poetry? That's another split decision, maybe going the other way if I really made a tally. It's made me melancholy in old age, sad when if I'd stuck with motor homes and the national league standings I don't think I would have been rooting around in regret and doubt at this point. Nothing wrong with sadness, but this is not the real thing—not the death of a child but the feelings of a college student reading *Don Quixote* on a warm afternoon before going out to the lake.

Now, with Francine upstairs, I wait for a night prowler. He will not appear. This I know, but the window glass is ill-blown and makes moving shadows anyway, shapes that change in the wind's rattle. I look out and despite myself am afraid.

Before me, the night unrolls. Now the tree leaves turn yellow in moonshine. By two or three, Francine sleeps, but I get up anyway and change into my coat and hat. The books weigh against my chest. I don gloves, scarf, galoshes. Then I climb the stairs and go into our bedroom, where she is sleeping. On the far side of the bed I see her white hair and beneath the blankets the uneven heave of her chest. I watch the bedcovers rise. She is probably dreaming at this moment. Though we have shared this bed for most of a lifetime I cannot guess what her dreams are about. I step next to her and touch the sheets where they lie across her neck.

115   "Wake up," I whisper. I touch her cheek, and her eyes open. I know this though I cannot really see them, just the darkness of their sockets.

"Is he there?"

"No."

"Then what's the matter?"

"Nothing's the matter," I say. "But I'd like to go for a walk."

120   "You've been outside," she says. "You saw him, didn't you?"

"I've been at the window."

"Did you see him?"

"No. There's no one there."

"Then why do you want to walk?" In a moment she is sitting aside the bed, her feet in slippers. "We don't ever walk," she says.

125   I am warm in all my clothing. "I know we don't," I answer. I turn my arms out, open my hands toward her. "But I would like to. I would like to walk in air that is so new and cold."

She peers up at me. "I haven't been drinking," I say. I bend at the waist, and though my head spins, I lean forward enough so that the effect is of a bow. "Will you come with me?" I whisper. "Will you be queen of this crystal night?" I recover from my bow, and when I look up again she has risen from the bed, and in another moment she has dressed herself in her wool robe and is walking ahead of me to the stairs.

Outside, the ice is treacherous. Snow has begun to fall and our galoshes squeak and slide, but we stay on the plowed walkway long enough to leave our block and enter a part of the neighborhood where I have never been. Ice hangs from the lamps. We pass unfamiliar houses and unfamiliar trees, street signs I have never seen, and as we walk the night begins to change. It is becoming liquor. The snow is banked on either side of the walk, plowed into hillocks at the corners. My hands are warming from the exertion. They are the hands of a younger man now, someone else's fingers in my gloves. They tingle. We take ten minutes to cover a block but as we move through this neighborhood my ardor mounts. A car approaches and I wave, a boatman's salute, because here we are together on these rare and empty seas. We are nighttime travelers. He flashes his headlamps as he passes, and this fills me to the gullet with celebration and bravery. The night sings to us. I am Bluebeard now, Lindbergh, Genghis Khan.

No, I am not.

I am an old man. My blood is dark from hypoxia, my breaths singsong from disease. It is only the frozen night that is splendid. In it we walk, stepping slowly, bent forward. We take steps the length of table forks. Francine holds my elbow.

I have mean secrets and small dreams, no plans greater than where to buy groceries and what rhymes to read next, and by the time we reach our porch again my foolishness has subsided. My knees and elbows ache. They ache with a mortal ache, tired flesh, the cartilage gone sandy with time. I don't have the heart for dreams. We undress in the hallway, ice in the ends of our hair, our coats stiff from cold. Francine turns down the thermostat. Then we go upstairs and she gets into her side of the bed and I get into mine. 130

It is dark. We lie there for some time, and then, before dawn, I know she is asleep. It is cold in our bedroom. As I listen to her breathing I know my life is coming to an end. I cannot warm myself. What I would like to tell my wife is this:

What the
imagination
seizes
as beauty must be truth. What holds you
to what you see of me is
that grasp alone.

But I do not say anything. Instead I roll in the bed, reach across, and touch her, and because she is surprised she turns to me.

When I kiss her the lips are dry, cracking against mine, unfamiliar as the ocean floor. But then the lips give. They part. I am inside her mouth, and there, still, hidden from the world, as if ruin had forgotten a part, it is wet—Lord! I have the feeling of a miracle. Her tongue comes forward. I do not know myself then, what man I am, who I lie with in embrace. I can barely remember her beauty. She touches my chest and I bite lightly on her lip, spread moisture to her cheek and then kiss there. She makes something like a sigh. "Frank," she says. "Frank." We are lost now in seas and deserts. My hand finds her fingers and grips them, bone and tendon, fragile things.

QUESTIONS FOR DISCUSSION AND WRITING

1. What are the major conflicts in this love story? How are they resolved?

2. How does the reader's view of Frank differ from his characterization of himself? How do the passages he quotes from the poems reveal his true character?

3. Why does Frank feel more at home in the aquarium and the cafeteria than in the house he built with his own hands?

4. What details convince us that we are seeing the story from the perspective of an old man? How does the narrator's voice change during and after the walk?

5. Why does the narrator begin the story with the question "Where are we going?" Is the question personal or universal? In what ways does the story answer the question?

Stories for Comparison:

Katherine Anne Porter's "The Jilting of Granny Weatherall" (pages 1017–1025); James Joyce's "The Dead" (pages 728–757).

3I

· ·

R A Y M O N D   C A R V E R

A Small, Good Thing

RAYMOND CARVER (1938–1988) was born in Clatskanie, Oregon, and educated at Humboldt State College (now Humboldt State University, Arcata). After further study at the University of Iowa, Carver worked briefly as an editor for Science Research Associates before accepting several positions as lecturer in creative writing at the University of California, Berkeley, the Writing Workshop at the University of Iowa, and the University of Texas at El Paso. In 1980 he became a Professor of English at Syracuse University. He died in the summer of 1988, at the age of 50, at his home in Port Angeles, Washington. He contributed poems and stories to many literary periodicals and such national magazines as *Esquire* and *Harper's*. His poems are collected in *Near Klamath* (1968), *Winter Insomnia* (1970), and *At Night the Salmon Move* (1976). Carver's stories, which received many awards, are collected in *Will You Please Be Quiet, Please?* (1976), *Furious Seasons* (1977), *What We Talk About When We Talk About Love* (1981), *Cathedral* (1983), *The Stories of Raymond Carver* (1985), and *Where I'm Calling From,* completed shortly before his death. In "A Small, Good Thing," reprinted from *Cathedral,* Carver dramatizes the reactions of a mother and father when their son is struck down by a hit-and-run driver.

Saturday afternoon she drove to the bakery in the shopping center. After looking through a loose-leaf binder with photographs of cakes taped onto the pages, she ordered chocolate, the child's favorite. The cake she chose was decorated with a space ship and launching pad under a sprinkling of white stars, and a planet made of red frosting at the other end. His name, SCOTTY, would be in green letters beneath the planet. The baker, who was an older man with a thick neck, listened without saying anything when she told him the child would be eight years old next Monday. The baker wore a white apron that looked like a smock. Straps cut under his arms, went around in back and then to the front again, where they were secured under his heavy waist. He wiped his hands on his apron as he listened to her. He kept his eyes down on the photographs and let her talk. He let her take her time. He'd just come to work and he'd be there all night, baking, and he was in no real hurry.

She gave the baker her name, Ann Weiss, and her telephone number. The cake would be ready on Monday morning, just out of the oven, in plenty of time for the child's party that afternoon. The baker was not jolly. There were no pleasantries between them, just the minimum exchange of words, the necessary information. He made her feel uncomfortable, and she didn't like that. While he was bent over the counter with the pencil in his hand, she studied his coarse features and wondered if he'd ever done anything else with his life besides be a baker. She was a mother and thirty-three years old, and it seemed to her that everyone, especially someone the baker's age—a man old enough to be her father—must have children who'd gone through this special time of cakes and birthday parties. There must be that between them, she thought. But he was abrupt with her—not rude, just abrupt. She gave up trying to make friends with him. She looked into the back of the bakery and could see a long, heavy wooden table with aluminum pie pans stacked at one end; and beside the table a metal container filled with empty racks. There was an enormous oven. A radio was playing country-Western music.

The baker finished printing the information on the special order card and closed up the binder. He looked at her and said, "Monday morning." She thanked him and drove home.

On Monday morning, the birthday boy was walking to school with another boy. They were passing a bag of potato chips back and forth and the birthday boy was trying to find out what his friend intended to give him for his birthday that afternoon. Without looking, the birthday boy stepped off the curb at an intersection and was immediately knocked down by a car. He fell on his side with his head in the gutter and his legs out in the road. His eyes were closed, but his legs moved back and forth as if he were trying to climb over something. His friend dropped the potato chips and started to cry. The car had gone a hundred feet or so and stopped in the middle of the road. The man in the driver's seat looked back over his shoulder. He waited until the boy got unsteadily to his feet. The boy wobbled a little. He looked dazed, but okay. The driver put the car into gear and drove away.

5   The birthday boy didn't cry, but he didn't have anything to say about anything either. He wouldn't answer when his friend asked him what it felt like to be hit by a car. He walked home, and his friend went on to school. But after the birthday boy was inside his house and was telling his mother about it—she sitting beside him on the sofa, holding his hands in her lap, saying, "Scotty, honey, are you sure you feel all right, baby?" thinking she would call the doctor anyway—he suddenly lay back on the sofa, closed his eyes, and went limp. When she couldn't wake him up, she hurried to the telephone and called her husband at work. Howard told her to remain calm, remain calm, and then he called an ambulance for the child and left for the hospital himself.

Of course, the birthday party was canceled. The child was in the hospital with a mild concussion and suffering from shock. There'd been vomiting, and his lungs had taken in fluid which needed pumping out that afternoon. Now he simply seemed to be in a very deep sleep—but no coma, Dr. Francis had emphasized, no coma, when he saw the alarm in the parents' eyes. At eleven o'clock that night, when the boy seemed to be resting comfortably enough after the many X-rays and the lab work, and it was just a matter of his waking up and coming around, Howard left the hospital. He and Ann had been at the hospital with the child since that afternoon, and he was going home for a short while to bathe and change clothes. "I'll be back in an hour," he said. She nodded. "It's fine," she said. "I'll be right here." He kissed her on the forehead, and they touched hands. She sat in the chair beside the bed and looked at the child. She was waiting for him to wake up and be all right. Then she could begin to relax.

Howard drove home from the hospital. He took the wet, dark streets very fast, then caught himself and slowed down. Until now, his life had gone smoothly and to his satisfaction—college, marriage, another year of college for the advanced degree in business, a junior partnership in an investment firm. Fatherhood. He was happy and, so far, lucky—he knew that. His parents were still living, his brothers and his sister were established, his friends from college had gone out to take their places in the world. So far, he had kept away from any real harm, from those forces he knew existed and that could cripple or bring down a man if the luck went bad, if things suddenly turned. He pulled into the driveway and parked. His left leg began to tremble. He sat in the car for a minute and tried to deal with the present situation in a rational manner. Scotty had been hit by a car and was in the hospital, but he was going to be all right. Howard closed his eyes and ran his hand over his face. He got out of the car and went up to the front door. The dog was barking inside the house. The telephone rang and rang while he unlocked the door and fumbled for the light switch. He shouldn't have left the hospital, he shouldn't have. "Goddamn it!" he said. He picked up the receiver and said, "I just walked in the door!"

"There's a cake here that wasn't picked up," the voice on the other end of the line said.

"What are you saying?" Howard asked.

"A cake," the voice said. "A sixteen-dollar cake." 10

Howard held the receiver against his ear, trying to understand. "I don't know anything about a cake," he said. "Jesus, what are you talking about?"

"Don't hand me that," the voice said.

Howard hung up the telephone. He went into the kitchen and poured himself some whiskey. He called the hospital. But the child's condition remained the same; he was still sleeping and nothing had changed there. While water poured into the tub, Howard lathered his face and shaved. He'd just stretched out in the tub and closed his eyes when the telephone rang again. He hauled himself out, grabbed a towel, and hurried through the house, saying, "Stupid, stupid," for having left the hospital. But when he picked up the receiver and shouted, "Hello!" there was no sound at the other end of the line. Then the caller hung up.

He arrived back at the hospital a little after midnight. Ann still sat in the chair beside the bed. She looked up at Howard, and then she looked back at the child. The child's eyes stayed closed, the head was still wrapped in bandages. His breathing was quiet and regular. From an apparatus over the bed hung a bottle of glucose with a tube running from the bottle to the boy's arm.

"How is he?" Howard said. "What's all this?" waving at the glucose and the tube. 15

"Dr. Francis's orders," she said. "He needs nourishment. He needs to keep up his strength. Why doesn't he wake up, Howard? I don't understand, if he's all right."

Howard put his hand against the back of her head. He ran his fingers through her hair. "He's going to be all right. He'll wake up in a little while. Dr. Francis knows what's what."

After a time, he said, "Maybe you should go home and get some rest. I'll stay here. Just don't put up with this creep who keeps calling. Hang up right away."

"Who's calling?" she asked.

"I don't know who, just somebody with nothing better to do than call up peo- 20 ple. You go on now."

She shook her head. "No," she said, "I'm fine."

"Really," he said. "Go home for a while, and then come back and spell me in the morning. It'll be all right. What did Dr. Francis say? He said Scotty's going to be all right. We don't have to worry. He's just sleeping now, that's all."

A nurse pushed the door open. She nodded at them as she went to the bedside. She took the left arm out from under the covers and put her fingers on the wrist, found the pulse, then consulted her watch. In a little while, she put the arm back under the covers and moved to the foot of the bed, where she wrote something on a clipboard attached to the bed.

"How is he?" Ann said. Howard's hand was a weight on her shoulder. She was aware of the pressure from his fingers.

25   "He's stable," the nurse said. Then she said, "Doctor will be in again shortly. Doctor's back in the hospital. He's making rounds right now."

"I was saying maybe she'd want to go home and get a little rest," Howard said. "After the doctor comes," he said.

"She could do that," the nurse said. "I think you should both feel free to do that, if you wish." The nurse was a big Scandinavian woman with blond hair. There was the trace of an accent in her speech.

"We'll see what the doctor says," Ann said. "I want to talk to the doctor. I don't think he should keep sleeping like this. I don't think that's a good sign." She brought her hand up to her eyes and let her head come forward a little. Howard's grip tightened on her shoulder, and then his hand moved up to her neck, where his fingers began to knead the muscles there.

"Dr. Francis will be here in a few minutes," the nurse said. Then she left the room.

30   Howard gazed at his son for a time, the small chest quietly rising and falling under the covers. For the first time since the terrible minutes after Ann's telephone call to him at his office, he felt a genuine fear starting in his limbs. He began shaking his head. Scotty was fine, but instead of sleeping at home in his own bed, he was in a hospital bed with bandages around his head and a tube in his arm. But this help was what he needed right now.

Dr. Francis came in and shook hands with Howard, though they'd just seen each other a few hours before. Ann got up from the chair. "Doctor?"

"Ann," he said and nodded. "Let's just first see how he's doing," the doctor said. He moved to the side of the bed and took the boy's pulse. He peeled back one eyelid and then the other. Howard and Ann stood beside the doctor and watched. Then the doctor turned back the covers and listened to the boy's heart and lungs with his stethoscope. He pressed his fingers here and there on the abdomen. When he was finished, he went to the end of the bed and studied the chart. He noted the time, scribbling something on the chart, and then looked at Howard and Ann.

"Doctor, how is he?" Howard said. "What's the matter with him exactly?"

"Why doesn't he wake up?" Ann said.

35   The doctor was a handsome, big-shouldered man with a tanned face. He wore a three-piece blue suit, a striped tie, and ivory cufflinks. His gray hair was combed along the sides of his head, and he looked as if he had just come from a concert. "He's all right," the doctor said. "Nothing to shout about, he could be better, I think. But he's all right. Still, I wish he'd wake up. He should wake up pretty soon." The doctor looked at the boy again. "We'll know some more in a couple of hours, after the results of a few more tests are in. But he's all right, believe me, except for the hairline fracture of the skull. He does have that."

"Oh, no," Ann said.

"And a bit of a concussion, as I said before. Of course, you know he's in shock," the doctor said. "Sometimes you see this in shock cases. This sleeping."

"But he's out of any real danger?" Howard said. "You said before he's not in a coma. You wouldn't call this a coma, then—would you, doctor?" Howard waited. He looked at the doctor.

"No, I don't want to call it a coma," the doctor said and glanced over at the boy once more. "He's just in a very deep sleep. It's a restorative measure the body is taking on its own. He's out of any real danger, I'd say that for certain, yes. But we'll know more when he wakes up and the other tests are in," the doctor said.

"It's a coma," Ann said. "Of sorts."   40

"It's not a coma yet, not exactly," the doctor said. "I wouldn't want to call it coma. Not yet, anyway. He's suffered shock. In shock cases, this kind of reaction is common enough; it's a temporary reaction to bodily trauma. Coma. Well, coma is a deep, prolonged unconsciousness, something that could go on for days, or weeks even. Scotty's not in that area, not as far as we can tell. I'm certain his condition will show improvement by morning. I'm betting that it will. We'll know more when he wakes up, which shouldn't be long now. Of course, you may do as you like, stay here or go home for a time. But by all means feel free to leave the hospital for a while if you want. This is not easy, I know." The doctor gazed at the boy again, watching him, and then he turned to Ann and said, "You try not to worry, little mother. Believe me, we're doing all that can be done. It's just a question of a little more time now." He nodded at her, shook hands with Howard again, and then he left the room.

Ann put her hands over the child's forehead. "At least he doesn't have a fever," she said. Then she said, "My God, he feels so cold, though. Howard? Is he supposed to feel like this? Feel his head."

Howard touched the child's temples. His own breathing had slowed. "I think he's supposed to feel this way right now," he said. "He's in shock, remember? That's what the doctor said. The doctor was just in here. He would have said something if Scotty wasn't okay."

Ann stood there a while longer, working her lip with her teeth. Then she moved over to her chair and sat down.

Howard sat in the chair next to her chair. They looked at each other. He wanted   45
to say something else and reassure her, but he was afraid, too. He took her hand and put it in his lap, and this made him feel better, her hand being there. He picked up her hand and squeezed it. Then he just held her hand. They sat like that for a while, watching the boy and not talking. From time to time, he squeezed her hand. Finally, she took her hand away.

"I've been praying," she said.

He nodded.

She said, "I almost thought I'd forgotten how, but it came back to me. All I had to do was close my eyes and say, 'Please God, help us—help Scotty,' and the rest was easy. The words were right there. Maybe if you prayed, too," she said to him.

"I've already prayed," he said. "I prayed this afternoon—yesterday afternoon, I mean—after you called, while I was driving to the hospital. I've been praying," he said.

"That's good," she said. For the first time, she felt they were together in it, this   50
trouble. She realized with a start that, until now, it had only been happening to her and to Scotty. She hadn't let Howard into it, though he was there and needed all along. She felt glad to be his wife.

The same nurse came in and took the boy's pulse again and checked the flow from the bottle hanging above the bed.

In an hour, another doctor came in. He said his name was Parsons, from Radiology. He had a bushy mustache. He was wearing loafers, a Western shirt, and a pair of jeans.

"We're going to take him downstairs for more pictures," he told them. "We need to do some more pictures, and we want to do a scan."

"What's that?" Ann said. "A scan?" She stood between this new doctor and the bed. "I thought you'd already taken all your X-rays."

55   "I'm afraid we need some more," he said. "Nothing to be alarmed about. We just need some more pictures, and we want to do a brain scan on him."

"My God," Ann said.

"It's perfectly normal procedure in cases like this," this new doctor said. "We just need to find out for sure why he isn't back awake yet. It's normal medical procedure, and nothing to be alarmed about. We'll be taking him down in a few minutes," this doctor said.

In a little while, two orderlies came into the room with a gurney. They were black-haired, dark-complexioned men in white uniforms, and they said a few words to each other in a foreign tongue as they unhooked the boy from the tube and moved him from his bed to the gurney. Then they wheeled him from the room. Howard and Ann got on the same elevator. Ann gazed at the child. She closed her eyes as the elevator began its descent. The orderlies stood at either end of the gurney without saying anything, though once one of the men made a comment to the other in their own language, and the other man nodded slowly in response.

Later that morning, just as the sun was beginning to lighten the windows in the waiting room outside the X-ray department, they brought the boy out and moved him back up to his room. Howard and Ann rode up on the elevator with him once more, and once more they took up their places beside the bed.

60   They waited all day, but still the boy did not wake up. Occasionally, one of them would leave the room to go downstairs to the cafeteria to drink coffee and then, as if suddenly remembering and feeling guilty, get up from the table and hurry back to the room. Dr. Francis came again that afternoon and examined the boy once more and then left after telling them he was coming along and could wake up at any minute now. Nurses, different nurses from the night before, came in from time to time. Then a young woman from the lab knocked and entered the room. She wore white slacks and a white blouse and carried a little tray of things which she put on the stand beside the bed. Without a word to them, she took blood from the boy's arm. Howard closed his eyes as the woman found the right place on the boy's arm and pushed the needle in.

"I don't understand this," Ann said to the woman.

"Doctor's orders," the young woman said. "I do what I'm told. They say draw that one, I draw. What's wrong with him, anyway?" she said. "He's a sweetie."

"He was hit by a car," Howard said. "A hit-and-run."

The young woman shook her head and looked again at the boy. Then she took her tray and left the room.

"Why won't he wake up?" Ann said. "Howard? I want some answers from these 65 people."

Howard didn't say anything. He sat down again in the chair and crossed one leg over the other. He rubbed his face. He looked at his son and then he settled back in the chair, closed his eyes, and went to sleep.

Ann walked to the window and looked out at the parking lot. It was night, and cars were driving into and out of the parking lot with their lights on. She stood at the window with her hands gripping the sill, and knew in her heart that they were into something now, something hard. She was afraid, and her teeth began to chatter until she tightened her jaws. She saw a big car stop in front of the hospital and someone, a woman in a long coat, get into the car. She wished she were that woman and some-body, anybody, was driving her away from here to somewhere else, a place where she would find Scotty waiting for her when she stepped out of the car, ready to say *Mom* and let her gather him in her arms.

In a little while, Howard woke up. He looked at the boy again. Then he got up from the chair, stretched, and went over to stand beside her at the window. They both stared out at the parking lot. They didn't say anything. But they seemed to feel each other's insides now, as though the worry had made them transparent in a perfectly natural way.

The door opened and Dr. Francis came in. He was wearing a different suit and tie this time. His gray hair was combed along the sides of his head, and he looked as if he had just shaved. He went straight to the bed and examined the boy. "He ought to have come around by now. There's just no good reason for this," he said. "But I can tell you we're all convinced he's out of any danger. We'll just feel better when he wakes up. There's no reason, absolutely none, why he shouldn't come around. Very soon. Oh, he'll have himself a dilly of a headache when he does, you can count on that. But all of his signs are fine. They're as normal as can be."

"It is a coma, then?" Ann said. 70

The doctor rubbed his smooth cheek. "We'll call it that for the time being, until he wakes up. But you must be worn out. This is hard. I know this is hard. Feel free to go out for a bite," he said. "It would do you good. I'll put a nurse in here while you're gone if you'll feel better about going. Go and have yourselves something to eat."

"I couldn't eat anything," Ann said.

"Do what you need to do, of course," the doctor said. "Anyway, I wanted to tell you that all the signs are good, the tests are negative, nothing showed up at all, and just as soon as he wakes up he'll be over the hill."

"Thank you, doctor," Howard said. He shook hands with the doctor again. The doctor patted Howard's shoulder and went out.

"I suppose one of us should go home and check on things," Howard said. "Slug 75 needs to be fed, for one thing."

"Call one of the neighbors," Ann said. "Call the Morgans. Anyone will feed a dog if you ask them to."

"All right," Howard said. After a while, he said, "Honey, why don't *you* do it? Why don't you go home and check on things, and then come back? It'll do you good. I'll be right here with him. Seriously," he said. "We need to keep up our strength on this. We'll want to be here for a while even after he wakes up."

"Why don't *you* go?" she said. "Feed Slug. Feed yourself."

"I already went," he said. "I was gone for exactly an hour and fifteen minutes. You go home for an hour and freshen up. Then come back."

80   She tried to think about it, but she was too tired. She closed her eyes and tried to think about it again. After a time, she said, "Maybe I *will* go home for a few minutes. Maybe if I'm not just sitting right here watching him every second, he'll wake up and be all right. You know? Maybe he'll wake up if I'm not here. I'll go home and take a bath and put on clean clothes. I'll feed Slug. Then I'll come back."

"I'll be right here," he said. "You go on home, honey. I'll keep an eye on things here." His eyes were bloodshot and small, as if he'd been drinking for a long time. His clothes were rumpled. His beard had come out again. She touched his face, and then she took her hand back. She understood he wanted to be by himself for a while, not have to talk or share his worry for a time. She picked her purse up from the nightstand, and he helped her into her coat.

"I won't be gone long," she said.

"Just sit and rest for a little while when you get home," he said. "Eat something. Take a bath. After you get out of the bath, just sit for a while and rest. It'll do you a world of good, you'll see. Then come back," he said. "Let's try not to worry. You heard what Dr. Francis said."

She stood in her coat for a minute trying to recall the doctor's exact words, looking for any nuances, any hint of something behind his words other than what he had said. She tried to remember if his expression had changed any when he bent over to examine the child. She remembered the way his features had composed themselves as he rolled back the child's eyelids and then listened to his breathing.

85   She went to the door, where she turned and looked back. She looked at the child, and then she looked at the father. Howard nodded. She stepped out of the room and pulled the door closed behind her.

She went past the nurses' station and down to the end of the corridor, looking for the elevator. At the end of the corridor, she turned to her right and entered a little waiting room where a Negro family sat in wicker chairs. There was a middle-aged man in a khaki shirt and pants, a baseball cap pushed back on his head. A large woman wearing a housedress and slippers was slumped in one of the chairs. A teenaged girl in jeans, hair done in dozens of little braids, lay stretched out in one of the chairs smoking a cigarette, her legs crossed at the ankles. The family swung their eyes to Ann as she entered the room. The little table was littered with hamburger wrappers and Styrofoam cups.

"Franklin," the large woman said as she roused herself. "Is it about Franklin?" Her eyes widened. "Tell me now, lady," the woman said. "Is it about Franklin?" She was trying to rise from her chair, but the man had closed his hand over her arm.

"Here, here," he said. "Evelyn."

"I'm sorry," Ann said. "I'm looking for the elevator. My son is in the hospital, and now I can't find the elevator."

90   "Elevator is down that way, turn left," the man said as he aimed a finger.

The girl drew on her cigarette and stared at Ann. Her eyes were narrowed to slits, and her broad lips parted slowly as she let the smoke escape. The Negro woman let her head fall on her shoulder and looked away from Ann, no longer interested.

"My son was hit by a car," Ann said to the man. She seemed to need to explain herself. "He has a concussion and a little skull fracture, but he's going to be all right. He's in shock now, but it might be some kind of coma, too. That's what really worries us, the coma part. I'm going out for a little while, but my husband is with him. Maybe he'll wake up while I'm gone."

"That's too bad," the man said and shifted in the chair. He shook his head. He looked down at the table, and then he looked back at Ann. She was still standing there. He said, "Our Franklin, he's on the operating table. Somebody cut him. Tried to kill him. There was a fight where he was at. At this party. They say he was just standing and watching. Not bothering nobody. But that don't mean nothing these days. Now he's on the operating table. We're just hoping and praying, that's all we can do now." He gazed at her steadily.

Ann looked at the girl again, who was still watching her, and at the older woman, who kept her head down, but whose eyes were now closed. Ann saw the lips moving silently, making words. She had an urge to ask what those words were. She wanted to talk more with these people who were in the same kind of waiting she was in. She was afraid, and they were afraid. They had that in common. She would have liked to have said something else about the accident, told them more about Scotty, that it had happened on the day of his birthday, Monday, and that he was still unconscious. Yet she didn't know how to begin. She stood looking at them without saying anything more.

She went down the corridor the man had indicated and found the elevator. She 95 waited a minute in front of the closed doors, still wondering if she was doing the right thing. Then she put out her finger and touched the button.

She pulled into the driveway and cut the engine. She closed her eyes and leaned her head against the wheel for a minute. She listened to the ticking sounds the engine made as it began to cool. Then she got out of the car. She could hear the dog barking inside the house. She went to the front door, which was unlocked. She went inside and turned on lights and put on a kettle of water for tea. She opened some dog-food and fed Slug on the back porch. The dog ate in hungry little smacks. It kept running into the kitchen to see that she was going to stay. As she sat down on the sofa with her tea, the telephone rang.

"Yes!" she said as she answered. "Hello!"

"Mrs. Weiss," a man's voice said. It was five o'clock in the morning, and she thought she could hear machinery or equipment of some kind in the background.

"Yes, yes! What is it?" she said. "This is Mrs. Weiss. This is she. What is it please?" She listened to whatever it was in the background. "Is it Scotty, for Christ's sake?"

"Scotty," the man's voice said. "It's about Scotty, yes. It has to do with Scotty, 100 that problem. Have you forgotten about Scotty?" the man said. Then he hung up.

She dialed the hospital's number and asked for the third floor. She demanded information about her son from the nurse who answered the telephone. Then she asked to speak to her husband. It was, she said, an emergency.

She waited, turning the telephone cord in her fingers. She closed her eyes and felt sick at her stomach. She would have to make herself eat. Slug came in from the back porch and lay down near her feet. He wagged his tail. She pulled at his ear while he licked her fingers. Howard was on the line.

"Somebody just called here," she said. She twisted the telephone cord. "He said it was about Scotty," she cried.

"Scotty's fine," Howard told her. "I mean, he's still sleeping. There's been no change. The nurse has been in twice since you've been gone. A nurse or else a doctor. He's all right."

105   "This man called. He said it was about Scotty," she told him.

"Honey, you rest for a little while, you need the rest. It must be that same caller I had. Just forget it. Come back down here after you've rested. Then we'll have breakfast or something."

"Breakfast," she said. "I don't want any breakfast."

"You know what I mean," he said. "Juice, something. I don't know. I don't know anything, Ann. Jesus, I'm not hungry, either. Ann, it's hard to talk now. I'm standing here at the desk. Dr. Francis is coming again at eight o'clock this morning. He's going to have something to tell us then, something more definite. That's what one of the nurses said. She didn't know any more than that. Ann? Honey, maybe we'll know something more then. At eight o'clock. Come back here before eight. Meanwhile, I'm right here and Scotty's all right. He's still the same," he added.

"I was drinking a cup of tea," she said, "when the telephone rang. They said it was about Scotty. There was a noise in the background. Was there a noise in the background on that call you had, Howard?"

110   "I don't remember," he said. "Maybe the driver of the car, maybe he's a psychopath and found out about Scotty somehow. But I'm here with him. Just rest like you were going to do. Take a bath and come back by seven or so, and we'll talk to the doctor together when he gets here. It's going to be all right, honey. I'm here, and there are doctors and nurses around. They say his condition is stable."

"I'm scared to death," she said.

She ran water, undressed, and got into the tub. She washed and dried quickly, not taking the time to wash her hair. She put on clean underwear, wool slacks, and a sweater. She went into the living room, where the dog looked up at her and let its tail thump once against the floor. It was just starting to get light outside when she went out to the car.

She drove into the parking lot of the hospital and found a space close to the front door. She felt she was in some obscure way responsible for what had happened to the child. She let her thoughts move to the Negro family. She remembered the name Franklin and the table that was covered with hamburger papers, and the teenaged girl staring at her as she drew on her cigarette. "Don't have children," she told the girl's image as she entered the front door of the hospital. "For God's sake, don't."

She took the elevator up to the third floor with two nurses who were just going on duty. It was Wednesday morning, a few minutes before seven. There was a page for a Dr. Madison as the elevator doors slid open on the third floor. She got off behind the nurses, who turned in the other direction and continued the conversation she had interrupted when she'd gotten into the elevator. She walked down the corridor to the little alcove where the Negro family had been waiting. They were gone now, but the chairs were scattered in such a way that it looked as if people had just jumped up from them the minute before. The tabletop was cluttered with the same cups and papers, the ashtray was filled with cigarette butts.

She stopped at the nurses' station. A nurse was standing behind the counter, brushing her hair and yawning.

"There was a Negro boy in surgery last night," Ann said. "Franklin was his name. His family was in the waiting room. I'd like to inquire about his condition."

A nurse who was sitting at a desk behind the counter looked up from a chart in front of her. The telephone buzzed and she picked up the receiver, but she kept her eyes on Ann.

"He passed away," said the nurse at the counter. The nurse held the hairbrush and kept looking at her. "Are you a friend of the family or what?"

"I met the family last night," Ann said. "My own son is in the hospital. I guess he's in shock. We don't know for sure what's wrong. I just wondered about Franklin, that's all. Thank you." She moved down the corridor. Elevator doors the same color as the walls slid open and a gaunt, bald man in white pants and white canvas shoes pulled a heavy cart off the elevator. She hadn't noticed these doors last night. The man wheeled the cart out into the corridor and stopped in front of the room nearest the elevator and consulted a clipboard. Then he reached down and slid a tray out of the cart. He rapped lightly on the door and entered the room. She could smell the unpleasant odors of warm food as she passed the cart. She hurried on without looking at any of the nurses and pushed open the door to the child's room.

Howard was standing at the window with his hands behind his back. He turned around as she came in.

"How is he?" she said. She went over to the bed. She dropped her purse on the floor beside the nightstand. It seemed to her she had been gone a long time. She touched the child's face. "Howard?"

"Dr. Francis was here a little while ago," Howard said. She looked at him closely and thought his shoulders were bunched a little.

"I thought he wasn't coming until eight o'clock this morning," she said quickly.

"There was another doctor with him. A neurologist."

"A neurologist," she said.

Howard nodded. His shoulders were bunching, she could see that. "What'd they say, Howard? For Christ's sake, what'd they say? What is it?"

"They said they're going to take him down and run more tests on him, Ann. They think they're going to operate, honey. Honey, they *are* going to operate. They can't figure out why he won't wake up. It's more than just shock or concussion, they know that much now. It's in his skull, the fracture, it has something, something to do with that, they think. So they're going to operate. I tried to call you, but I guess you'd already left the house."

"Oh, God," she said. "Oh, please, Howard, please," she said, taking his arms.

"Look!" Howard said. "Scotty! Look, Ann!" He turned her toward the bed.

130   The boy had opened his eyes, then closed them. He opened them again now. The eyes stared straight ahead for a minute, then moved slowly in his head until they rested on Howard and Ann, then traveled away again.

"Scotty," his mother said, moving to the bed.

"Hey, Scott," his father said. "Hey, son."

They leaned over the bed. Howard took the child's hand in his hands and began to pat and squeeze the hand. Ann bent over the boy and kissed his forehead again and again. She put her hands on either side of his face. "Scotty, honey, it's Mommy and Daddy," she said. "Scotty?"

The boy looked at them, but without any sign of recognition. Then his mouth opened, his eyes scrunched closed, and he howled until he had no more air in his lungs. His face seemed to relax and soften then. His lips parted as his last breath was puffed through his throat and exhaled gently through the clenched teeth.

135   The doctors called it a hidden occlusion and said it was a one-in-a-million circumstance. Maybe if it could have been detected somehow and surgery undertaken immediately, they could have saved him. But more than likely not. In any case, what would they have been looking for? Nothing had shown up in the tests or in the X-rays.

Dr. Francis was shaken. "I can't tell you how badly I feel. I'm so very sorry, I can't tell you," he said as he led them into the doctors' lounge. There was a doctor sitting in a chair with his legs hooked over the back of another chair, watching an early-morning TV show. He was wearing a green delivery-room outfit, loose green pants and green blouse, and a green cap that covered his hair. He looked at Howard and Ann and then looked at Dr. Francis. He got to his feet and turned off the set and went out of the room. Dr. Francis guided Ann to the sofa, sat down beside her, and began to talk in a low, consoling voice. At one point, he leaned over and embraced her. She could feel his chest rising and falling evenly against her shoulder. She kept her eyes open and let him hold her. Howard went into the bathroom, but he left the door open. After a violent fit of weeping, he ran water and washed his face. Then he came out and sat down at the little table that held a telephone. He looked at the telephone as though deciding what to do first. He made some calls. After a time, Dr. Francis used the telephone.

"Is there anything else I can do for the moment?" he asked them.

Howard shook his head. Ann stared at Dr. Francis as if unable to comprehend his words.

The doctor walked them to the hospital's front door. People were entering and leaving the hospital. It was eleven o'clock in the morning. Ann was aware of how slowly, almost reluctantly, she moved her feet. It seemed to her that Dr. Francis was making them leave when she felt they should stay, when it would be more the right thing to do to stay. She gazed out into the parking lot and then turned around and looked back at the front of the hospital. She began shaking her head. "No, no," she said. "I can't leave him here, no." She heard herself say that and thought how unfair it was that the only words that came out were the sort of words used on TV shows where people were stunned by violent or sudden deaths. She wanted her words to be her own. "No," she said, and for some reason the memory of the Negro woman's head lolling on the woman's shoulder came to her. "No," she said again.

"I'll be talking to you later in the day," the doctor was saying to Howard. "There are still some things that have to be done, things that have to be cleared up to our satisfaction. Some things that need explaining." 140

"An autopsy," Howard said.

Dr. Francis nodded.

"I understand," Howard said. Then he said, "Oh, Jesus. No, I don't understand, doctor. I can't, I can't. I just can't."

Dr. Francis put his arm around Howard's shoulders. "I'm sorry. God, how I'm sorry." He let go of Howard's shoulders and held out his hand. Howard looked at the hand, and then he took it. Dr. Francis put his arms around Ann once more. He seemed full of some goodness she didn't understand. She let her head rest on his shoulder, but her eyes stayed open. She kept looking at the hospital. As they drove out of the parking lot, she looked back at the hospital.

At home, she sat on the sofa with her hands in her coat pockets. Howard closed the door to the child's room. He got the coffee-maker going and then he found an empty box. He had thought to pick up some of the child's things that were scattered around the living room. But instead he sat down beside her on the sofa, pushed the box to one side, and leaned forward, arms between his knees. He began to weep. She pulled his head over into her lap and patted his shoulder. "He's gone," she said. She kept patting his shoulder. Over his sobs, she could hear the coffee-maker hissing in the kitchen. "There, there," she said tenderly. "Howard, he's gone. He's gone and now we'll have to get used to that. To being alone." 145

In a little while, Howard got up and began moving aimlessly around the room with the box, not putting anything into it, but collecting some things together on the floor at one end of the sofa. She continued to sit with her hands in her coat pockets. Howard put the box down and brought coffee into the living room. Later, Ann made calls to relatives. After each call had been placed and the party had answered, Ann would blurt out a few words and cry for a minute. Then she would quietly explain, in a measured voice, what had happened and tell them about arrangements. Howard took the box out to the garage, where he saw the child's bicycle. He dropped the box and sat down on the pavement beside the bicycle. He took hold of the bicycle awkwardly so that it leaned against his chest. He held it, the rubber pedal sticking into his chest. He gave the wheel a turn.

Ann hung up the telephone after talking to her sister. She was looking up another number when the telephone rang. She picked it up on the first ring.

"Hello," she said, and she heard something in the background, a humming noise. "Hello!" she said. "For God's sake," she said. "Who is this? What is it you want?"

"Your Scotty, I got him ready for you," the man's voice said. "Did you forget him?"

"You evil bastard!" she shouted into the receiver. "How can you do this, you evil son of a bitch?" 150

"Scotty," the man said. "Have you forgotten about Scotty?" Then the man hung up on her.

Howard heard the shouting and came in to find her with her head on her arms over the table, weeping. He picked up the receiver and listened to the dial tone.

Much later, just before midnight, after they had dealt with many things, the telephone rang again.

"You answer it," she said. "Howard, it's him, I know." They were sitting at the kitchen table with coffee in front of them. Howard had a small glass of whiskey beside his cup. He answered on the third ring.

155   "Hello," he said. "Who is this? Hello! Hello!" The line went dead. "He hung up," Howard said. "Whoever it was."

"It was him," she said. "That bastard. I'd like to kill him," she said. "I'd like to shoot him and watch him kick," she said.

"Ann, my God," he said.

"Could you hear anything?" she said. "In the background? A noise, machinery, something humming?"

"Nothing, really. Nothing like that," he said. "There wasn't much time. I think there was some radio music. Yes, there was a radio going, that's all I could tell. I don't know what in God's name is going on," he said.

160   She shook her head. "If I could, could get my hands on him." It came to her then. She knew who it was. Scotty, the cake, the telephone number. She pushed the chair away from the table and got up. "Drive me down to the shopping center," she said. "Howard."

"What are you saying?"

"The shopping center. I know who it is who's calling. I know who it is. It's the baker, the son-of-a-bitching baker, Howard. I had him bake a cake for Scotty's birthday. That's who's calling. That's who has the number and keeps calling us. To harass us about that cake. The baker, that bastard."

They drove down to the shopping center. The sky was clear and stars were out. It was cold, and they ran the heater in the car. They parked in front of the bakery. All of the shops and stores were closed, but there were cars at the far end of the lot in front of the movie theater. The bakery windows were dark, but when they looked through the glass they could see a light in the back room and, now and then, a big man in an apron moving in and out of the white, even light. Through the glass, she could see the display cases and some little tables with chairs. She tried the door. She rapped on the glass. But if the baker heard them, he gave no sign. He didn't look in their direction.

They drove around behind the bakery and parked. They got out of the car. There was a lighted window too high up for them to see inside. A sign near the back door said THE PANTRY BAKERY, SPECIAL ORDERS. She could hear faintly a radio playing inside and something creak—an oven door as it was pulled down? She knocked on the door and waited. Then she knocked again, louder. The radio was turned down and there was a scraping sound now, the distinct sound of something, a drawer, being pulled open and then closed.

Someone unlocked the door and opened it. The baker stood in the light and ¹⁶⁵
peered out at them: "I'm closed for business," he said. "What do you want at this
hour? It's midnight. Are you drunk or something?"

She stepped into the light that fell through the open door. He blinked his heavy
eyelids as he recognized her. "It's you," he said.

"It's me," she said. "Scotty's mother. This is Scotty's father. We'd like to
come in."

The baker said, "I'm busy now. I have work to do."

She had stepped inside the doorway anyway. Howard came in behind her. The
baker moved back. "It smells like a bakery in here. Doesn't it smell like a bakery in
here, Howard?"

"What do you want?" the baker said. "Maybe you want your cake? That's it, you ¹⁷⁰
decided you want your cake. You ordered a cake, didn't you?"

"You're pretty smart for a baker," she said. "Howard, this is the man who's been
calling us." She clenched her fists. She stared at him fiercely. There was a deep burning inside her, an anger that made her feel larger than herself, larger than either of
these men.

"Just a minute here," the baker said. "You want to pick up your three-day-old
cake? That it? I don't want to argue with you, lady. There it sits over there, getting
stale. I'll give it to you for half of what I quoted you. No. You want it? You can have
it. It's no good to me, no good to anyone now. It cost me time and money to make
that cake. If you want it, okay, if you don't, that's okay, too. I have to get back to
work." He looked at them and rolled his tongue behind his teeth.

"More cakes," she said. She knew she was in control of it, of what was increasing in her. She was calm.

"Lady, I work sixteen hours a day in this place to earn a living," the baker said.
He wiped his hands on his apron. "I work night and day in here, trying to make ends
meet." A look crossed Ann's face that made the baker move back and say, "No trouble, now." He reached to the counter and picked up a rolling pin with his right hand
and began to tap it against the palm of his other hand. "You want the cake or not? I
have to get back to work. Bakers work at night," he said again. His eyes were small,
mean-looking, she thought, nearly lost in the bristly flesh around his cheeks. His
neck was thick with fat.

"I know bakers work at night," Ann said. "They make phone calls at night, too. ¹⁷⁵
You bastard," she said.

The baker continued to tap the rolling pin against his hand. He glanced at
Howard. "Careful, careful," he said to Howard.

"My son's dead," she said with a cold, even finality. "He was hit by a car Monday morning. We've been waiting with him until he died. But, of course, you couldn't
be expected to know that, could you? Bakers can't know everything—can they,
Mr. Baker? But he's dead. He's dead, you bastard!" Just as suddenly as it had welled
in her, the anger dwindled, gave way to something else, a dizzy feeling of nausea.
She leaned against the wooden table that was sprinkled with flour, put her hands over
her face, and began to cry, her shoulders rocking back and forth. "It isn't fair," she
said. "It isn't, isn't fair."

Howard put his hand at the small of her back and looked at the baker. "Shame on you," Howard said to him. "Shame."

The baker put the rolling pin back on the counter. He undid his apron and threw it on the counter. He looked at them, and then he shook his head slowly. He pulled a chair out from under the card table that held papers and receipts, an adding machine, and a telephone directory. "Please sit down," he said. "Let me get you a chair," he said to Howard. "Sit down now, please." The baker went into the front of the shop and returned with two little wrought-iron chairs. "Please sit down, you people."

180   Ann wiped her eyes and looked at the baker. "I wanted to kill you," she said. "I wanted you dead."

The baker had cleared a space for them at the table. He shoved the adding machine to one side, along with the stacks of notepaper and receipts. He pushed the telephone directory onto the floor, where it landed with a thud. Howard and Ann sat down and pulled their chairs up to the table. The baker sat down, too.

"Let me say how sorry I am," the baker said, putting his elbows on the table. "God alone knows how sorry. Listen to me. I'm just a baker. I don't claim to be anything else. Maybe once, maybe years ago, I was a different kind of human being. I've forgotten, I don't know for sure. But I'm not any longer, if I ever was. Now I'm just a baker. That don't excuse my doing what I did, I know. But I'm deeply sorry. I'm sorry for your son, and sorry for my part in this," the baker said. He spread his hands out on the table and turned them over to reveal his palms. "I don't have any children myself, so I can only imagine what you must be feeling. All I can say to you now is that I'm sorry. Forgive me, if you can," the baker said. "I'm not an evil man, I don't think. Not evil, like you said on the phone. You got to understand what it comes down to is I don't know how to act anymore, it would seem. Please," the man said, "let me ask you if you can find it in your hearts to forgive me?"

It was warm inside the bakery. Howard stood up from the table and took off his coat. He helped Ann from her coat. The baker looked at them for a minute and then nodded and got up from the table. He went to the oven and turned off some switches. He found cups and poured coffee from an electric coffee-maker. He put a carton of cream on the table, and a bowl of sugar.

"You probably need to eat something," the baker said. "I hope you'll eat some of my hot rolls. You have to eat and keep going. Eating is a small, good thing in a time like this," he said.

185   He served them warm cinnamon rolls just out of the oven, the icing still runny. He put butter on the table and knives to spread the butter. Then the baker sat down at the table with them. He waited. He waited until they each took a roll from the platter and began to eat. "It's good to eat something," he said, watching them. "There's more. Eat up. Eat all you want. There's all the rolls in the world in here."

They ate rolls and drank coffee. Ann was suddenly hungry, and the rolls were warm and sweet. She ate three of them, which pleased the baker. Then he began to talk. They listened carefully. Although they were tired and in anguish, they listened to what the baker had to say. They nodded when the baker began to speak of loneliness, and of the sense of doubt and limitation that had come to him in his middle years. He told them what it was like to be childless all these years. To repeat the days with the ovens endlessly full and endlessly empty. The party food, the celebrations he'd worked over. Icing knuckle-deep. The tiny wedding couples stuck into cakes. Hundreds of them, no, thousands by now. Birthdays. Just imagine all those candles burning. He had a necessary trade. He was a baker. He was glad he wasn't a florist. It was better to be feeding people. This was a better smell anytime than flowers.

"Smell this," the baker said, breaking open a dark loaf. "It's a heavy bread, but rich." They smelled it, then he had them taste it. It had the taste of molasses and coarse grains. They listened to him. They ate what they could. They swallowed the dark bread. It was like daylight under the fluorescent trays of light. They talked on into the early morning, the high, pale cast of light in the windows, and they did not think of leaving.

QUESTIONS FOR DISCUSSION AND WRITING

1. How do the following scenes contribute to the development of the plot—the opening scene in the bakery, the scene at the hospital with the black family, and the final scene in the bakery?

2. What insight into character is revealed by Howard's associating the accident with the luck upon which his whole life has been based? How is Ann's character revealed through her relationship to Dr. Francis and his choice of words?

3. What details give us a sense of the reality of the hospital, the home, and the bakery?

4. Why does the narrator shift his point of view between Howard and Ann throughout the story? How does his objective approach emphasize their emotional ordeal?

5. In how many different ways does the title of the story suggest its themes? How are the themes developed in Ann and Howard's experience with the baker at the end of the story?

Stories for Comparison

F. Scott Fitzgerald's "Babylon Revisited" (pages 505–520); Gail Godwin's "Dream Children" (pages 583–593).

<h1 style="text-align:center">32</h1>

....

<h2 style="text-align:center">J O H N   C H E E V E R</h2>

<h1 style="text-align:center">The Swimmer</h1>

JOHN CHEEVER (1912–1982) was born in Quincy, Massachusetts, and attended Thayer Academy until he was expelled at the age of seventeen for being, according to his own account, a "quarrelsome, intractable and lousy student." He moved to New York City and began writing, publishing his first story, "Expelled," in *The New Republic* at the age of eighteen. For the next ten years, Cheever published his stories in magazines such as *Collier's, The Atlantic Monthly,* and *The New Yorker.* His first collection of stories, *The Way Some People Live,* was published in 1942. His next collection, *The Enormous Radio and Other Stories* (1953), established his reputation as one of America's most accomplished writers of short fiction. Cheever's first novel, *The Wapshot Chronicle* (1957), and its sequel, *The Wapshot Scandal* (1964), were critically acclaimed, as were subsequent novels such as *Bullet Park* (1969) and *Falconer* (1977). Despite these successes, Cheever will probably be remembered best for his short stories, superbly represented in *The Stories of John Cheever* (1978), which won the Pulitzer Prize. "The Swimmer," reprinted from *The Brigadier and the Golf Widow* (1964), examines the surfaces and realities of affluent suburbia.

I t was one of those midsummer Sundays when everyone sits around saying, "I *drank* too much last night." You might have heard it whispered by the parishioners leaving church, heard it from the lips of the priest himself, struggling with his cassock in the *vestiarium,* heard it from the golf links and the tennis courts, heard it from the wildlife preserve where the leader of the Audubon group was suffering from a terrible hangover. "I *drank* too much," said Donald Westerhazy. "We all *drank* too much," said Lucinda Merrill. "It must have been the wine," said Helen Westerhazy. "I *drank* too much of that claret."

This was at the edge of the Westerhazys' pool. The pool, fed by an artesian well with a high iron content, was a pale shade of green. It was a fine day. In the west there was a massive stand of cumulus cloud so like a city seen from a distance— from the bow of an approaching ship—that it might have had a name. Lisbon. Hackensack. The sun was hot. Neddy Merrill sat by the green water, one hand in it, one around a glass of gin. He was a slender man—he seemed to have the especial slenderness of youth—and while he was far from young he had slid down his banister that morning and given the bronze backside of Aphrodite on the hall table a smack, as he jogged toward the smell of coffee in his dining room. He might have been compared to a summer's day, particularly the last hours of one, and while he lacked a tennis racket or a sail bag the impression was definitely one of youth, sport, and clement weather. He had been swimming and now he was breathing deeply, stertorously as if he could gulp into his lungs the components of that moment, the heat of the sun, the intenseness of his pleasure. It all seemed to flow into his chest. His own house stood in Bullet Park, eight miles to the south, where his four beautiful daughters would have had their lunch and might be playing tennis. Then it occurred to him that by taking a dogleg to the southwest he could reach his home by water.

His life was not confining and the delight he took in this observation could not be explained by its suggestion of escape. He seemed to see, with a cartographer's eye, that string of swimming pools, that quasi-subterranean stream that curved across the county. He had made a discovery, a contribution to modern geography; he would name the stream Lucinda after his wife. He was not a practical joker nor was he a fool but he was determinedly original and had a vague and modest idea of himself as a legendary figure. The day was beautiful and it seemed to him that a long swim might enlarge and celebrate its beauty.

He took off a sweater that was hung over his shoulders and dove in. He had an inexplicable contempt for men who did not hurl themselves into pools. He swam a choppy crawl, breathing either with every stroke or every fourth stroke and counting somewhere well in the back of his mind the one-two one-two of a flutter kick. It was not a serviceable stroke for long distances but the domestication of swimming had saddled the sport with some customs and in his part of the world a crawl was customary. To be embraced and sustained by the light green water was less a pleasure, it seemed, than the resumption of a natural condition, and he would have liked to swim without trunks, but this was not possible, considering his project. He hoisted himself up on the far curb—he never used the ladder—and started across the lawn. When Lucinda asked where he was going he said he was going to swim home.

The only maps and charts he had to go by were remembered or imaginary but 5 these were clear enough. First there were the Grahams, the Hammers, the Lears, the Howlands, and the Crosscups. He would cross Ditmar Street to the Bunkers and come, after a short portage, to the Levys, the Welchers, and the public pool in Lancaster. Then there were the Hallorans, the Sachses, the Biswangers, Shirley Adams, the Gilmartins, and the Clydes. The day was lovely, and that he lived in a world so generously supplied with water seemed like a clemency, a beneficence. His heart was high and he ran across the grass. Making his way home by an uncommon route gave him the feeling that he was a pilgrim, an explorer, a man with a destiny, and he knew that he would find friends all along the way; friends would line the banks of the Lucinda River.

He went through a hedge that separated the Westerhazys' land from the Grahams', walked under some flowering apple trees, passed the shed that housed their pump and filter, and came out at the Grahams' pool. "Why, Neddy," Mrs. Graham said, "what a marvelous surprise. I've been trying to get you on the phone all morning. Here, let me get you a drink." He saw then, like an explorer, that the hospitable customs and traditions of the natives would have to be handled with diplomacy if he was ever going to reach his destination. He did not want to mystify or seem rude to the Grahams nor did he have the time to linger there. He swam the length of their pool and joined them in the sun and was rescued, a few minutes later, by the arrival of two carloads of friends from Connecticut. During the uproarious reunions he was able to slip away. He went down by the front of the Grahams' house, stepped over a thorny hedge, and crossed a vacant lot to the Hammers'. Mrs. Hammer, looking up from her roses, saw him swim by although she wasn't quite sure who it was. The Lears heard him splashing past the open windows of their living room. The Howlands and the Crosscups were away. After leaving the Howlands' he crossed Ditmar Street and started for the Bunkers', where he could hear, even at the distance, the noise of a party.

The water refracted the sound of voices and laughter and seemed to suspend it in midair. The Bunkers' pool was on a rise and he climbed some stairs to a terrace where twenty-five or thirty men and women were drinking. The only person in the water was Rusty Towers, who floated there on a rubber raft. Oh, how bonny and lush were the banks of the Lucinda River! Prosperous men and women gathered by the sapphire-colored waters while caterer's men in white coats passed them cold gin. Overhead a red de Haviland trainer was circling around and around and around in the sky with something like the glee of a child in a swing. Ned felt a passing affection for the scene, a tenderness for the gathering, as if it was something he might touch. In the distance he heard thunder. As soon as Enid Bunker saw him she began to scream: "Oh, look who's here! What a marvelous surprise! When Lucinda said that you couldn't come I thought I'd *die*." She made her way to him through the crowd, and when they had finished kissing she led him to the bar, a progress that was slowed by the fact that he stopped to kiss eight or ten other women and shake the hands of as many men. A smiling bartender he had seen at a hundred parties gave him a gin and tonic and he stood by the bar for a moment, anxious not to get stuck in any conversation that would delay his voyage. When he seemed about to be surrounded he dove in and swam close to the side to avoid colliding with Rusty's raft. At the far end of the pool he bypassed the Tomlinsons with a broad smile and jogged up the garden path. The gravel cut his feet but this was the only unpleasantness. The party was confined to the pool, and as he went toward the house he heard the brilliant, watery sound of voices fade, heard the noise of a radio from the Bunkers' kitchen, where someone was listening to a ball game. Sunday afternoon. He made his way through the parked cars and down the grassy border of their driveway to Alewives Lane. He did not want to be seen on the road in his bathing trunks but there was no traffic and he made the short distance to the Levys' driveway, marked with a PRIVATE PROPERTY sign and green tube for *The New York Times*. All the doors and windows of the big house were open but there were no signs of life; not even a dog barked. He went around the side of the house to the pool and saw that the Levys had only recently left. Glasses and bottles and dishes of nuts were on a table at the deep end, where there was a bathhouse or gazebo, hung with Japanese lanterns. After swimming the pool he got himself a glass and poured a drink. It was his fourth or fifth drink and he had swum nearly half the length of the Lucinda River. He felt tired, clean, and pleased at that moment to be alone; pleased with everything.

It would storm. The stand of cumulus cloud—that city—had risen and darkened, and while he sat there he heard the percussiveness of thunder again. The de Haviland trainer was still circling overhead and it seemed to Ned that he could almost hear the pilot laugh with pleasure in the afternoon; but when there was another peal of thunder he took off for home. A train whistle blew and he wondered what time it had gotten to be. Four? Five? He thought of the provincial station at that hour, where a waiter, his tuxedo concealed by a raincoat, a dwarf with some flowers wrapped in newspaper, and a woman who had been crying would be waiting for the local. It was suddenly growing dark; it was that moment when the pin-headed birds seem to organize their song into some acute and knowledgeable recognition of the storm's approach. Then there was a fine noise of rushing water from the crown of an oak at his back, as if a spigot there had been turned. Then the noise of fountains came from the crowns of all the tall trees. Why did he love storms, what was the meaning of his excitement when the door sprang open and the rain wind fled rudely up the stairs, why had the simple task of shutting the windows of an old house seemed fitting and urgent, why did the first watery notes of a storm wind have for him the unmistakable sound of good news, cheer, glad tidings? Then there was an explosion, a smell of cordite, and rain lashed the Japanese lanterns that Mrs. Levy had bought in Kyoto the year before last, or was it the year before that?

He stayed in the Levys' gazebo until the storm had passed. The rain had cooled the air and he shivered. The force of the wind had stripped a maple of its red and yellow leaves and scattered them over the grass and the water. Since it was midsummer the tree must be blighted, and yet he felt a peculiar sadness at this sign of autumn. He braced his shoulders, emptied his glass, and started for the Welchers' pool. This meant crossing the Lindleys' riding ring and he was surprised to find it overgrown with grass and all the jumps dismantled. He wondered if the Lindleys had sold their horses or gone away for the summer and put them out to board. He seemed to remember having heard something about the Lindleys and their horses but the memory was unclear. On he went, barefoot through the wet grass, to the Welchers', where he found their pool was dry.

This breach in his chain of water disappointed him absurdly, and he felt like 10 some explorer who seeks a torrential headwater and finds a dead stream. He was disappointed and mystified. It was common enough to go away for the summer but no one ever drained his pool. The Welchers had definitely gone away. The pool furniture was folded, stacked, and covered with a tarpaulin. The bathhouse was locked. All the windows of the house were shut, and when he went around to the driveway in front he saw a FOR SALE sign nailed to a tree. When had he last heard from the Welchers—when, that is, had he and Lucinda last regretted an invitation to dine with them? It seemed only a week or so ago. Was his memory failing or had he so disciplined it in the repression of unpleasant facts that he had damaged his sense of the truth? Then in the distance he heard the sound of a tennis game. This cheered him, cleared away all his apprehensions and let him regard the overcast sky and the cold air with indifference. This was the day that Neddy Merrill swam across the county. That was the day! He started off then for his most difficult portage.

Had you gone for a Sunday afternoon ride that day you might have seen him, close to naked, standing on the shoulders of Route 424, waiting for a chance to cross. You might have wondered if he was the victim of foul play, had his car broken down, or was he merely a fool. Standing barefoot in the deposits of the highway—beer cans, rags, and blowout patches—exposed to all kinds of ridicule, he seemed pitiful. He had known when he started that this was a part of his journey—it had been on his maps—but confronted with the lines of traffic, worming through the summery light, he found himself unprepared. He was laughed at, jeered at, a beer can was thrown at him, and he had no dignity or humor to bring to the situation. He could have gone back, back to the Westerhazys', where Lucinda would still be sitting in the sun. He had signed nothing, vowed nothing, pledged nothing, not even to himself. Why, believing as he did, that all human obduracy was susceptible to common sense, was he unable to turn back? Why was he determined to complete his journey even if it meant putting his life in danger? At what point had this prank, this joke, this piece of horseplay become serious? He could not go back, he could not even recall with any clearness the green water at the Westerhazys', the sense of inhaling the day's components, the friendly and relaxed voices saying that they had *drunk* too much. In the space of an hour, more or less, he had covered a distance that made his return impossible.

An old man, tooling down the highway at fifteen miles an hour, let him get to the middle of the road, where there was a grass divider. Here he was exposed to the ridicule of the northbound traffic, but after ten or fifteen minutes he was able to cross. From here he had only a short walk to the Recreation Center at the edge of the village of Lancaster, where there were some handball courts and a public pool.

The effect of the water on voices, the illusion of brilliance and suspense, was the same here as it had been at the Bunkers' but the sounds here were louder, harsher, and more shrill, and as soon as he entered the crowded enclosure he was confronted with regimentation. "ALL SWIMMERS MUST TAKE A SHOWER BEFORE USING THE POOL. ALL SWIMMERS MUST USE THE FOOTBATH, ALL SWIMMERS MUST WEAR THEIR IDENTIFICATION DISKS." He took a shower, washed his feet in a cloudy and bitter solution, and made his way to the edge of the water. It stank of chlorine and looked to him like a sink. A pair of lifeguards in a pair of towers blew police whistles at what seemed to be regular intervals and abused the swimmers through a public address system. Neddy remembered the sapphire water at the Bunkers' with longing and thought that he might contaminate himself—damage his own prosperousness and charm—by swimming in this murk, but he reminded himself that he was an explorer, a pilgrim, and that this was merely a stagnant bend in the Lucinda River. He dove, scowling with distaste, into the chlorine and had to swim with his head above water to avoid collisions, but even so he was bumped into, splashed, and jostled. When he got to the shallow end both lifeguards were shouting at him: "Hey, you, you without the identification disk, get outa the water." He did, but they had no way of pursuing him and he went through the reek of suntan oil and chlorine out through the hurricane fence and passed the handball courts. By crossing the road he entered the wooded part of the Halloran estate. The woods were not cleared and the footing was treacherous and difficult until he reached the lawn and the clipped beech hedge that encircled their pool.

The Hallorans were friends, an elderly couple of enormous wealth who seemed to bask in the suspicion that they might be Communists. They were zealous reformers but they were not Communists, and yet when they were accused, as they sometimes were, of subversion, it seemed to gratify and excite them. Their beech hedge was yellow and he guessed this had been blighted like the Levys' maple. He called hullo, hullo, to warn the Hallorans of his approach, to palliate his invasion of their privacy. The Hallorans, for reasons that had never been explained to him, did not wear bathing suits. No explanations were in order, really. Their nakedness was a detail in their uncompromising zeal for reform and he stepped politely out of his trunks before he went through the opening in the hedge.

Mrs. Halloran, a stout woman with white hair and a serene face, was reading the 15
Times, Mr. Halloran was taking beech leaves out of the water with a scoop. They seemed not surprised or displeased to see him. Their pool was perhaps the oldest in the county, a fieldstone rectangle, fed by a brook. It had no filter or pump and its waters were the opaque gold of the stream.

"I'm swimming across the county," Ned said.

"Why, I didn't know one could," exclaimed Mrs. Halloran.

"Well, I've made it from the Westerhazys'," Ned said. "That must be about four miles."

He left his trunks at the deep end, walked to the shallow end, and swam this stretch. As he was pulling himself out of the water he heard Mrs. Halloran say, "We've been *terribly* sorry to hear about all your misfortunes, Neddy."

"My misfortunes?" Ned asked. "I don't know what you mean."   20

"Why, we heard that you'd sold the house and that your poor children . . ."

"I don't recall having sold the house," Ned said, "and the girls are at home."

"Yes," Mrs. Halloran sighed. "Yes . . ." Her voice filled the air with an unseasonable melancholy and Ned spoke briskly. "Thank you for the swim."

"Well, have a nice trip," said Mrs. Halloran.

Beyond the hedge he pulled on his trunks and fastened them. They were loose 25
and he wondered if, during the space of an afternoon, he could have lost some weight. He was cold and he was tired and the naked Hallorans and their dark water had depressed him. The swim was too much for his strength but how could he have guessed this, sliding down the banister that morning and sitting in the Westerhazys' sun? His arms were lame. His legs felt rubbery and ached at the joints. The worst of it was the cold in his bones and the feeling that he might never be warm again. Leaves were falling down around him and he smelled wood smoke on the wind. Who would be burning wood at this time of year?

He needed a drink. Whiskey would warm him, pick him up, carry him through the last of his journey, refresh his feeling that it was original and valorous to swim across the county. Channel swimmers took brandy. He needed a stimulant. He crossed the lawn in front of the Hallorans' house and went down a little path to where they had built a house for their only daughter, Helen, and her husband, Eric Sachs. The Sachses' pool was small and he found Helen and her husband there.

"Oh, *Neddy,*" Helen said. "Did you lunch at Mother's?"

"Not *really,*" Ned said. "I *did* stop to see your parents." This seemed to be explanation enough. "I'm terribly sorry to break in on you like this but I've taken a chill and I wonder if you'd give me a drink."

"Why, I'd *love* to," Helen said, "but there hasn't been anything in this house to drink since Eric's operation. That was three years ago."

30   Was he losing his memory, had his gift for concealing painful facts let him forget that he had sold his house, that his children were in trouble, and that his friend had been ill? His eyes slipped from Eric's face to his abdomen, where he saw three pale, sutured scars, two of them at least a foot long. Gone was his naval, and what, Neddy thought, would the roving hand, bed-checking one's gifts at 3 A.M., make of a belly with no navel, no link to birth, this breach in the succession?

"I'm sure you can get a drink at the Biswangers'," Helen said. "They're having an enormous do. You can hear it from here. Listen!"

She raised her head and from across the road, the lawns, the gardens, the woods, the fields, he heard again the brilliant noise of voices over water. "Well, I'll get wet," he said, still feeling that he had no freedom of choice about his means of travel. He dove into the Sachses' cold water and, gasping, close to drowning, made his way from one end of the pool to the other. "Lucinda and I want *terribly* to see you," he said over his shoulder, his face set toward the Biswangers'. "We're sorry it's been so long and we'll call you *very* soon."

He crossed some fields to the Biswangers' and the sounds of revelry there. They would be honored to give him a drink, they would be happy to give him a drink. The Biswangers invited him and Lucinda for dinner four times a year, six weeks in advance. They were always rebuffed and yet they continued to send out their invitations, unwilling to comprehend the rigid and undemocratic realities of their society. They were the sort of people who discussed the price of things at cocktails, exchanged market tips during dinner, and after dinner told dirty stories to mixed company. They did not belong to Neddy's set—they were not even on Lucinda's Christmas-card list. He went toward their pool with feelings of indifference, charity, and some unease, since it seemed to be getting dark and these were the longest days of the year. The party when he joined it was noisy and large. Grace Biswanger was the kind of hostess who asked the optometrist, the veterinarian, the real-estate dealer, and the dentist. No one was swimming and the twilight, reflected on the water of the pool, had a wintry gleam. There was a bar and he started for this. When Grace Biswanger saw him she came toward him, not affectionately as he had every right to expect, but bellicosely.

"Why, this party has everything," she said loudly, "including a gate crasher."

35   She could not deal him a social blow—there was no question about this and he did not flinch. "As a gate crasher," he asked politely, "do I rate a drink?"

"Suit yourself," she said. "You don't seem to pay much attention to invitations."

She turned her back on him and joined some guests, and he went to the bar and ordered a whiskey. The bartender served him but he served him rudely. His was a world in which the caterer's men kept the social score, and to be rebuffed by a part-time barkeep meant that he had suffered some loss of social esteem. Or perhaps the man was new and uninformed. Then he heard Grace at his back say: "They went for broke overnight—nothing but income—and he showed up drunk one Sunday and asked us to loan him five thousand dollars. . . ." She was always talking about money. It was worse than eating your peas off a knife. He dove into the pool, swam its length and went away.

The next pool on his list, the last but two, belonged to his old mistress, Shirley Adams. If he had suffered any injuries at the Biswangers' they would be cured here. Love—sexual roughhouse in fact—was the supreme elixir, the pain killer, the brightly colored pill that would put the spring back into his step, the joy of life in his heart. They had had an affair last week, last month, last year. He couldn't re-member. It was he who had broken it off, his was the upper hand, and he stepped through the gate of the wall that surrounded her pool with nothing so considered as self-confidence. It seemed in a way to be his pool, as the lover, particularly the illicit lover, enjoys the possessions of his mistress with an authority unknown to holy matrimony. She was there, her hair the color of brass, but her figure, at the edge of the lighted, cerulean water, excited in him no profound memories. It had been, he thought, a lighthearted affair, although she had wept when he broke it off. She seemed confused to see him and he wondered if she was still wounded. Would she, God forbid, weep again?

"What do you want?" she asked.

"I'm swimming across the county."   40

"Good Christ. Will you ever grow up?"

"What's the matter?"

"If you've come here for money," she said, "I won't give you another cent."

"You could give me a drink."

"I could but I won't. I'm not alone."   45

"Well, I'm on my way."

He dove in and swam the pool, but when he tried to haul himself up onto the curb he found that the strength in his arms and shoulders had gone, and he paddled to the ladder and climbed out. Looking over his shoulder he saw, in the lighted bath-house, a young man. Going out onto the dark lawn he smelled chrysanthemums or marigolds—some stubborn autumnal fragrance—on the night air, strong as gas. Looking overhead he saw that the stars had come out, but why should he seem to see Andromeda, Cepheus, and Cassiopeia? What had become of the constellations of midsummer? He began to cry.

It was probably the first time in his adult life that he had ever cried, certainly the first time in his life that he had ever felt so miserable, cold, tired, and bewildered. He could not understand the rudeness of the caterer's barkeep or the rudeness of a mis-tress who had come to him on her knees and showered his trousers with tears. He had swum too long, he had been immersed too long, and his nose and his throat were sore from the water. What he needed then was a drink, some company, and some clean, dry clothes, and while he could have cut directly across the road to his house he went on to the Gilmartins' pool. Here, for the first time in his life, he did not dive but went down the steps into the icy water and swam a hobbled sidestroke that he might have learned as a youth. He staggered with fatigue on his way to the Clydes' and paddled the length of their pool, stopping again and again with his hand on the curb to rest. He climbed up the ladder and wondered if he had the strength to get home. He had done what he wanted, he had swum the county, but he was so stupe-fied with exhaustion that his triumph seemed vague. Stooped, holding on to the gateposts for support, he turned up the driveway of his own house.

The place was dark. Was it so late that they had all gone to bed? Had Lucinda stayed at the Westerhazys' for supper? Had the girls joined her there or gone some-place else? Hadn't they agreed, as they usually did on Sundays, to regret all their in-vitations and stay at home? He tried the garage doors to see what cars were in but the doors were locked and rust came off the handles onto his hands. Going toward the house, he saw that the force of the thunderstorm had knocked one of the rain gut-ters loose. It hung down over the front door like an umbrella rib, but it could be fixed in the morning. The house was locked, and he thought that the stupid cook or the stu-pid maid must have locked the place up until he remembered that it had been some time since they had employed a maid or a cook. He shouted, pounded on the door, tried to force it with his shoulder, and then, looking in at the windows, saw that the place was empty.

QUESTIONS FOR DISCUSSION AND WRITING

1. How does Cheever's opening paragraph help explain Neddy Merrill's plan to swim across the county?

2. At the beginning of the story, how does Neddy see himself and his pilgrimage? How is he seen by others at different points on his journey? How does Cheever mean for us to see Neddy by the end of the story?

3. How does each pool provide a different kind of setting? In what ways do these settings change as Neddy gets closer to home?

4. What major shift in point of view is marked by the storm?

5. What themes are implied in Cheever's description of this society as "rigid and un-democratic"? Does this world have any redeeming qualities?

Stories for Comparison

T. Coraghessan Boyle's "Heart of a Champion" (pages 305–310); Ethan Canin's "We Are Nighttime Travelers" (pages 339–349).

33

··

S A N D R A   C I S N E R O S

One Holy Night

About the truth, if you give it to a person, then he has power over you.
And if someone gives it to you, then they have made themselves your slave.
It is a strong magic. You can never take it back.
—Chaq Uxmal Paloquín

SANDRA CISNEROS was born in 1954 in Chicago, Illinois, and spent much of her childhood living in Chicago and Mexico City. A graduate of the University of Iowa Writer's Workshop, she has taught writing at the University of California, Berkeley, and the University of Michigan. She has also taught in the San Antonio Public Schools and worked as Literary Director of the Guadalupe Cultural Arts Center. She has contributed stories and poems to periodicals such as *Imagine, Contact II,* and *Revista Chicano-Riquena.* Her poems appear in *Bad Boys* (1980), *The Rodrigo Poems* (1985), and *My Wicked, Wicked Ways* (1992); her stories are collected in *Woman Hollering Creek* (1991). Cisneros's book for young adults, *The House on Mango Street* (1983), won the American Book Award. In "One Holy Night," reprinted from *Woman Hollering Creek,* Cisneros's narrator describes the consequences of her "holy night" with a man who claims to be descended from Mayan kings.

H E SAID HIS name was Chaq. Chaq Uxmal Paloquín. That's what he told me. He was of an ancient line of Mayan kings. Here, he said, making a map with the heel of his boot, this is where I come from, the Yucatán, the ancient cities. This is what Boy Baby said.

It's been eighteen weeks since Abuelita chased him away with the broom, and what I'm telling you I never told nobody, except Rachel and Lourdes, who know everything. He said he would love me like a revolution, like a religion. Abuelita burned the pushcart and sent me here, miles from home, in this town of dust, with one wrinkled witch woman who rubs my belly with jade, and sixteen nosy cousins.

I don't know how many girls have gone bad from selling cucumbers. I know I'm not the first. My mother took the crooked walk too, I'm told, and I'm sure my Abuelita has her own story, but it's not my place to ask.

Abuelita says it's Uncle Lalo's fault because he's the man of the family and if he had come home on time like he was supposed to and worked the pushcart on the days he was told to and watched over his goddaughter, who is too foolish to look after herself, nothing would've happened, and I wouldn't have to be sent to Mexico. But Uncle Lalo says if they had never left Mexico in the first place, shame enough would have kept a girl from doing devil things.

5   I'm not saying I'm not bad. I'm not saying I'm special. But I'm not like the Allport Street girls, who stand in doorways and go with men into alleys.

All I know is I didn't want it like that. Not against the bricks or hunkering in somebody's car. I wanted it to come undone like gold thread, like a tent full of birds. The way it's supposed to be, the way I knew it would be when I met Boy Baby.

But you must know, I was no girl back then. And Boy Baby was no boy. Chaq Uxmal Paloquín. Boy Baby was a man. When I asked him how old he was he said he didn't know. The past and the future are the same thing. So he seemed boy and baby and man all at once, and the way he looked at me, how do I explain?

I'd park the pushcart in front of the Jewel food store Saturdays. He bought a mango on a stick the first time. Paid for it with a new twenty. Next Saturday he was back. Two mangoes, lime juice, and chili powder, keep the change. The third Saturday he asked for a cucumber spear and ate it slow. I didn't see him after that till the day he brought me Kool-Aid in a plastic cup. Then I knew what I felt for him.

Maybe you wouldn't like him. To you he might be a bum. Maybe he looked it. Maybe. He had broken thumbs and burnt fingers. He had thick greasy fingernails he never cut and dusty hair. And all his bones were strong ones like a man's. I waited every Saturday in my same blue dress. I sold all the mango and cucumber, and then Boy Baby would come finally.

10   What I knew of Chaq was only what he told me, because nobody seemed to know where he came from. Only that he could speak a strange language that no one could understand, said his name translated into boy, or boy-child, and so it was the street people nicknamed him Boy Baby.

I never asked about his past. He said it was all the same and didn't matter, past and the future all the same to his people. But the truth has a strange way of following you, of coming up to you and making you listen to what it has to say.

Night time. Boy Baby brushes my hair and talks to me in his strange language because I like to hear it. What I like to hear him tell is how he is Chaq, Chaq of the people of the sun, Chaq of the temples, and what he says sounds sometimes like broken clay, and at other times like hollow sticks, or like the swish of old feathers crumbling into dust.

He lived behind Esparza & Sons Auto Repair in a little room that used to be a closet—pink plastic curtains on a narrow window, a dirty cot covered with newspapers, and a cardboard box filled with socks and rusty tools. It was there, under one bald bulb, in the back room of the Esparza garage, in the single room with pink curtains, that he showed me the guns—twenty-four in all. Rifles and pistols, one rusty musket, a machine gun, and several tiny weapons with mother-of-pearl handles that looked like toys. So you'll see who I am, he said, laying them all out on the bed of newspapers. So you'll understand. But I didn't want to know.

The stars foretell everything, he said. My birth. My son's. The boy-child who will bring back the grandeur of my people from those who have broken the arrows, from those who have pushed the ancient stones off their pedestals.

Then he told how he had prayed in the Temple of the Magician years ago as a 15 child when his father had made him promise to bring back the ancient ways. Boy Baby had cried in the temple dark that only the bats made holy. Boy Baby who was man and child among the great and dusty guns lay down on the newspaper bed and wept for a thousand years. When I touched him, he looked at me with the sadness of stone.

You must not tell anyone what I am going to do, he said. And what I remember next is how the moon, the pale moon with its one yellow eye, the moon of Tikal, and Tulum, and Chichén, stared through the pink plastic curtains. Then something inside bit me, and I gave out a cry as if the other, the one I wouldn't be anymore, leapt out.

So I was initiated beneath an ancient sky by a great and mighty heir—Chaq Uxmal Paloquín. I, Ixchel, his queen.

The truth is, it wasn't a big deal. It wasn't any deal at all. I put my bloody panties inside my T-shirt and ran home hugging myself. I thought about a lot of things on the way home. I thought about all the world and how suddenly I became a part of history and wondered if everyone on the street, the sewing machine lady and the *panadería* saleswomen and the woman with two kids sitting on the bus bench didn't all know. *Did I look any different? Could they tell?* We were all the same somehow, laughing behind our hands, waiting the way all women wait, and when we find out, we wonder why the world and a million years made such a big deal over nothing.

I know I was supposed to feel ashamed, but I wasn't ashamed. I wanted to stand on top of the highest building, the top-top floor, and yell, *I know.*

Then I understood why Abuelita didn't let me sleep over at Lourdes's house full 20 of too many brothers, and why the Roman girl in the movies always runs away from the soldier, and what happens when the scenes in love stories begin to fade, and why brides blush, and how it is that sex isn't simply a box you check *M* or *F* on in the test we get at school.

I was wise. The corner girls were still jumping into their stupid little hopscotch squares. I laughed inside and climbed the wooden stairs two by two to the second floor rear where me and Abuelita and Uncle Lalo live. I was still laughing when I opened the door and Abuelita asked, Where's the pushcart?

And then I didn't know what to do.

It's a good thing we live in a bad neighborhood. There are always plenty of bums to blame for your sins. If it didn't happen the way I told it, it really could've. We looked and looked all over for the kids who stole my pushcart. The story wasn't the best, but since I had to make it up right then and there with Abuelita staring a hole through my heart, it wasn't too bad.

For two weeks I had to stay home. Abuelita was afraid the street kids who had stolen the cart would be after me again. Then I thought I might go over to the Esparza garage and take the pushcart out and leave it in some alley for the police to find, but I was never allowed to leave the house alone. Bit by bit the truth started to seep out like a dangerous gasoline.

25   First the nosy woman who lives upstairs from the laundromat told my Abuelita she thought something was fishy, the pushcart wheeled into Esparza & Sons every Saturday after dark, how a man, the same dark Indian one, the one who never talks to anybody, walked with me when the sun went down and pushed the cart into the garage, that one there, and yes we went inside, there where the fat lady named Concha, whose hair is dyed a hard black, pointed a fat finger.

I prayed that we would not meet Boy Baby, and since the gods listen and are mostly good, Esparza said yes, a man like that had lived there but was gone, had packed a few things and left the pushcart in a corner to pay for his last week's rent.

We had to pay $20 before he would give us our pushcart back. Then Abuelita made me tell the real story of how the cart had disappeared, all of which I told this time, except for that one night, which I would have to tell anyway, weeks later, when I prayed for the moon of my cycle to come back, but it would not.

When Abuelita found out I was going to *dar a luz,* she cried until her eyes were little, and blamed Uncle Lalo, and Uncle Lalo blamed this country, and Abuelita blamed the infamy of men. That is when she burned the cucumber pushcart and called me a *sinvergüenza* because I *am* without shame.

Then I cried too—Boy Baby was lost from me—until my head was hot with headaches and I fell asleep. When I woke up, the cucumber pushcart was dust and Abuelita was sprinkling holy water on my head.

30   Abuelita woke up early every day and went to the Esparza garage to see if news about that *demonio* had been found, had Chaq Uxmal Paloquín sent any letters, any, and when the other mechanics heard that name they laughed, and asked if we had made it up, that we could have some letters that had come for Boy Baby, no forwarding address, since he had gone in such a hurry.

There were three. The first, addressed "Occupant," demanded immediate payment for a four-month-old electric bill. The second was one I recognized right away—a brown envelope fat with cake-mix coupons and fabric-softener samples—because we'd gotten one just like it. The third was addressed in a spidery Spanish to a Señor C. Cruz, on paper so thin you could read it unopened by the light of the sky. The return address a convent in Tampico.

This was to whom my Abuelita wrote in hopes of finding the man who could correct my ruined life, to ask if the good nuns might know the whereabouts of a certain Boy Baby—and if they were hiding him it would be of no use because God's eyes see through all souls.

We heard nothing for a long time. Abuelita took me out of school when my uniform got tight around the belly and said it was a shame I wouldn't be able to graduate with the other eighth graders.

Except for Lourdes and Rachel, my grandma and Uncle Lalo, nobody knew about my past. I would sleep in the big bed I share with Abuelita same as always. I could hear Abuelita and Uncle Lalo talking in low voices in the kitchen as if they were praying the rosary, how they were going to send me to Mexico, to San Dionisio de Tlaltepango, where I have cousins and where I was conceived and would've been born had my grandma not thought it wise to send my mother here to the United States so that neighbors in San Dionisio de Tlaltepango wouldn't ask why her belly was suddenly big.

I was happy. I liked staying home. Abuelita was teaching me to crochet the way 35 she had learned in Mexico. And just when I had mastered the tricky rosette stitch, the letter came from the convent which gave the truth about Boy Baby—however much we didn't want to hear.

He was born on a street with no name in a town called Miseria. His father, Eusebio, is a knife sharpener. His mother, Refugia, stacks apricots into pyramids and sells them on a cloth in the market. There are brothers. Sisters too of which I know little. The youngest, a Carmelite, writes me all this and prays for my soul, which is why I know it's all true.

Boy Baby is thirty-seven years old. His name is Chato which means fat-face. There is no Mayan blood.

I don't think they understand how it is to be a girl. I don't think they know how it is to have to wait your whole life. I count the months for the baby to be born, and it's like a ring of water inside me reaching out and out until one day it will tear from me with its own teeth.

Already I can feel the animal inside me stirring in his own uneven sleep. The witch woman says it's the dreams of weasels that make my child sleep the way he sleeps. She makes me eat white bread blessed by the priest, but I know it's the ghost of him inside me that circles and circles, and will not let me rest.

Abuelita said they sent me here just in time, because a little later Boy Baby 40 came back to our house looking for me, and she had to chase him away with the broom. The next thing we hear, he's in the newspaper clippings his sister sends. A picture of him looking very much like stone, police hooked on either arm . . . *on the road to* Las Grutas de Xtacumbilxuna, *the Caves of the Hidden Girl . . . eleven female bodies . . . the last seven years . . .*

Then I couldn't read but only stare at the little black-and-white dots that make up the face I am in love with.

All my girl cousins here either don't talk to me, or those who do, ask questions they're too young to know *not* to ask. What they want to know really is how it is to have a man, because they're too ashamed to ask their married sisters.

They don't know what it is to lay so still until his sleep breathing is heavy, for the eyes in the dim dark to look and look without worry at the man-bones and the neck, the man-wrist and man-jaw thick and strong, all the salty dips and hollows, the stiff hair of the brow and sour swirl of sideburns, to lick the fat earlobes that taste of smoke, and stare at how perfect is a man.

I tell them, "It's a bad joke. When you find out you'll be sorry."

I'm going to have five children. Five. Two girls. Two boys. And one baby. 45

The girls will be called Lisette and Maritza. The boys I'll name Pablo and Sandro.

And my baby. My baby will be named Alegre, because life will always be hard.

Rachel says that love is like a big black piano being pushed off the top of a three-story building and you're waiting on the bottom to catch it. But Lourdes says it's not that way at all. It's like a top, like all the colors in the world are spinning so fast they're not colors anymore and all that's left is a white hum.

There was a man, a crazy who lived upstairs from us when we lived on South Loomis. He couldn't talk, just walked around all day with this harmonica in his mouth. Didn't play it. Just sort of breathed through it, all day long, wheezing, in and out, in and out.

50   This is how it is with me. Love I mean.

QUESTIONS FOR DISCUSSION AND WRITING

1. How do the movements of the characters from Mexico to the United States and back again provide the basic structure of the plot? How do the narrator's changing attitudes toward sex create the conflicts in the story?

2. How does the narrator use different names to characterize her lover? How do her choices characterize her? For example, why does she refuse to read the story in the newspaper?

3. How are the details of setting used to develop character? How does the description of Chato's room behind the garage, and especially the guns, explain "who I am"? How does the narrator's attitude toward the pushcart reveal who she is?

4. How does the narrator reveal her youth and naivete by the way she interprets her "holy night"? What is ironic about her proclamation that she is "wise"?

5. What does the quotation at the beginning of the story suggest about the major theme of the story? What does the narrator's comparison of love to the insistent playing of a tuneless harmonica suggest that she has learned as a result of her experience?

Stories for Comparison

Ann Beattie's "The Working Girl" (pages 285–290); Mary Hood's "How Far She Went" (pages 664–670).

34

···

A R T H U R   C .   C L A R K E

The Star

ARTHUR C. CLARKE was born in 1917 in Somerset, England. Although he was interested in science at an early age, building his first telescope at the age of thirteen, he could not afford a formal university education. He went to work for the British Civil Service as an auditor and became treasurer for the British Interplanetary Society. During World War II, he was a radar specialist with the Royal Air Force. Following the war he received educational assistance and entered King's College, University of London, where in two years he graduated with honorary degrees in math and physics. He worked briefly as an editor for *Science Abstracts,* but soon devoted his full attention to his lifetime vocation, writing about science. His nonfiction publications, such as *Interplanetary Flight* (1950), *The Exploration of Space* (1951), and *The Making of a Moon* (1957), explained space travel, but his science fiction concerned the complex effect of such travel on human emotions and values. His hundreds of short stories are collected in such volumes as *The Other Side of the Story* (1958) and *The Wind from the Sun* (1972). His novels include *The Sounds of Mars* (1951), *A Fall of Moondust* (1961), and *Rendezvous with Rama* (1974), and his screenplay for Stanley Kubrik's *2001: A Space Odyssey* is considered a classic. In "The Star," reprinted from *The Nine Billion Names of God* (1955), a Jesuit astronomer tells of a space journey that challenges his faith in God.

It is three thousand light-years to the Vatican. Once, I believed that space could have no power over faith, just as I believed that the heavens declared the glory of God's handiwork. Now I have seen that handiwork, and my faith is sorely troubled. I stare at the crucifix that hangs on the cabin wall above the Mark VI Computer, and for the first time in my life I wonder if it is no more than an empty symbol.

I have told no one yet, but the truth cannot be concealed. The facts are there for all to read, recorded on the countless miles of magnetic tape and the thousands of photographs we are carrying back to Earth. Other scientists can interpret them as easily as I can, and I am not one who would condone that tampering with the truth which often gave my order a bad name in the olden days.

The crew were already sufficiently depressed: I wonder how they will take this ultimate irony. Few of them have any religious faith, yet they will not relish using this final weapon in their campaign against me—that private, good-natured, but fundamentally serious war which lasted all the way from Earth. It amused them to have a Jesuit as chief astrophysicist: Dr. Chandler, for instance, could never get over it. (Why are medical men such notorious atheists?) Sometimes he would meet me on the observation deck, where the lights are always low so that the stars shine with undiminished glory. He would come up to me in the gloom and stand staring out of the great oval port, while the heavens crawled slowly around us as the ship turned end over end with the residual spin we had never bothered to correct.

"Well, Father," he would say at last, "it goes on forever and forever, and perhaps *Something* made it. But how you can believe that Something has a special interest in us and our miserable little world—that just beats me." Then the argument would start, while the stars and nebulae would swing around us in silent, endless arcs beyond the flawlessly clear plastic of the observation port.

5   It was, I think, the apparent incongruity of my position that caused most amusement to the crew. In vain I would point to my three papers in the *Astrophysical Journal,* my five in the *Monthly Notices of the Royal Astronomical Society.* I would remind them that my order has long been famous for its scientific works. We may be few now, but ever since the eighteenth century we have made contributions to astronomy and geophysics out of all proportion to our numbers. Will my report on the Phoenix Nebula end our thousand years of history? It will end, I fear, much more than that.

I do not know who gave the nebula its name, which seems to me a very bad one. If it contains a prophecy, it is one that cannot be verified for several billion years. Even the word "nebula" is misleading: this is a far smaller object than those stupendous clouds of mist—the stuff of unborn stars—that are scattered throughout the length of the Milky Way. On the cosmic scale, indeed, the Phoenix Nebula is a tiny thing—a tenuous shell of gas surrounding a single star.

Or what is left of a star . . .

The Rubens engraving of Loyola seems to mock me as it hangs there above the spectrophotometer tracings. What would *you,* Father, have made of this knowledge that has come into my keeping, so far from the little world that was all the Universe you knew? Would your faith have risen to the challenge, as mine has failed to do?

You gaze into the distance, Father, but I have traveled a distance beyond any that you could have imagined when you founded our order a thousand years ago. No other survey ship has been so far from Earth: we are at the very frontiers of the explored Universe. We set out to reach the Phoenix Nebula, we succeeded, and we are homeward bound with our burden of knowledge. I wish I could lift that burden from my shoulders, but I call to you in vain across the centuries and the light-years that lie between us.

10   On the book you are holding the words are plain to read. AD MAIOREM DEI GLORIAM, the message runs, but it is a message I can no longer believe. Would you still believe it, if you could see what we have found?

We knew, of course, what the Phoenix Nebula was. Every year, in our Galaxy alone, more than a hundred stars explode, blazing for a few hours or days with thousands of times their normal brilliance before they sink back into death and obscurity. Such are the ordinary novae—the commonplace disasters of the Universe. I have recorded the spectrograms and light curves of dozens since I started working at the Lunar Observatory.

But three or four times in every thousand years occurs something beside which even a nova pales into total insignificance.

When a star becomes a *supernova,* it may for a little while outshine all the massed suns of the Galaxy. The Chinese astronomers watched this happen in A.D. 1054, not knowing what it was they saw. Five centuries later, in 1572, a supernova blazed in Cassiopeia so brilliantly that it was visible in the daylight sky. There have been three more in the thousand years that have passed since then.

Our mission was to visit the remnants of such a catastrophe, to reconstruct the events that led up to it, and, if possible, to learn its cause. We came slowly in through the concentric shells of gas that had been blasted out six thousand years before, yet were expanding still. They were immensely hot, radiating even now with a fierce violet light, but were far too tenuous to do us any damage. When the star had exploded, its outer layers had been driven upward with such speed that they had escaped completely from its gravitational field. Now they formed a hollow shell large enough to engulf a thousand solar systems, and at its center burned the tiny, fantastic object which the star had now become—a White Dwarf, smaller than the Earth, yet weighing a million times as much.

The glowing gas shells were all around us, banishing the normal night of interstellar space. We were flying into the center of the cosmic bomb that had detonated millennia ago and whose incandescent fragments were still hurtling apart. The immense scale of the explosion, and the fact that the debris already covered a volume of space many billions of miles across, robbed the scene of any visible movement. It would take decades before the unaided eye could detect any motion in these tortured wisps and eddies of gas, yet the sense of turbulent expansion was overwhelming.

We had checked our primary drive hours before, and were drifting slowly toward the fierce little star ahead. Once it had been a sun like our own, but it had squandered in a few hours the energy that should have kept it shining for a million years. Now it was a shrunken miser, hoarding its resources as if trying to make amends for its prodigal youth.

No one seriously expected to find planets. If there had been any before the explosion, they would have been boiled into puffs of vapor, and their substance lost in the greater wreckage of the star itself. But we made the automatic search, as we always do when approaching an unknown sun, and presently we found a single small world circling the star at an immense distance. It must have been the Pluto of this vanished Solar System, orbiting on the frontiers of the night. Too far from the central sun ever to have known life, its remoteness had saved it from the fate of all its lost companions.

The passing fires had seared its rocks and burned away the mantle of frozen gas that must have covered it in the days before the disaster. We landed, and we found the Vault.

Its builders had made sure that we should. The monolithic marker that stood above the entrance was now a fused stump, but even the first long-range photographs told us that here was the work of intelligence. A little later we detected the continent-wide pattern of radioactivity that had been buried in the rock. Even if the pylon above the vault had been destroyed, this would have remained, an immovable and all but eternal beacon calling to the stars. Our ship fell toward this gigantic bull's-eye like an arrow into its target.

20   The pylon must have been a mile high when it was built, but now it looked like a candle that had melted down into a puddle of wax. It took us a week to drill through the fused rock, since we did not have the proper tools for a task like this. We were astronomers, not archaeologists, but we could improvise. Our original purpose was forgotten: this lonely monument, reared with such labor at the greatest possible distance from the doomed sun, could have only one meaning. A civilization that knew it was about to die had made its last bid for immortality.

It will take us generations to examine all the treasures that were placed in the Vault. They had plenty of time to prepare, for their sun must have given its first warnings many years before the final detonation. Everything that they wished to preserve, all the fruit of their genius, they brought here to this distant world in the days before the end, hoping that some other race would find it and that they would not be utterly forgotten. Would we have done as well, or would we have been too lost in our own misery to give thought to a future we could never see or share?

If only they had had a little more time! They could travel freely enough between the planets of their own sun, but they had not yet learned to cross the interstellar gulfs, and the nearest Solar System was a hundred light-years away. Yet even had they possessed the secret of the Transfinite Drive, no more than a few millions could have been saved. Perhaps it was better thus.

Even if they had not been so disturbingly human as their sculpture shows, we could not have helped admiring them and grieving for their fate. They left thousands of visual records and the machines for projecting them, together with elaborate pictorial instructions from which it will not be difficult to learn their written language. We have examined many of these records, and brought to life for the first time in six thousand years the warmth and beauty of a civilization that in many ways must have been superior to our own. Perhaps they only showed us the best, and one can hardly blame them. But their worlds were very lovely, and their cities were built with a grace that matches anything of man's. We have watched them at work and play, and listened to their musical speech sounding across the centuries. One scene is still before my eyes—a group of children on a beach of strange blue sand, playing in the waves as children play on Earth. Curious whiplike trees line the shore, and some very large animal is wading in the shallows yet attracting no attention at all.

And sinking into the sea, still warm and friendly and life-giving, is the sun that will soon turn traitor and obliterate all this innocent happiness.

25   Perhaps if we had not been so far from home and so vulnerable to loneliness, we should not have been so deeply moved. Many of us had seen the ruins of ancient civilizations on other worlds, but they had never affected us so profoundly.

This tragedy was unique. It is one thing for a race to fail and die, as nations and cultures have done on Earth. But to be destroyed so completely in the full flower of its achievement, leaving no survivors—how could that be reconciled with the mercy of God?

My colleagues have asked me that, and I have given what answers I can. Perhaps you could have done better, Father Loyola, but I have found nothing in the *Exercitia Spiritualia* that helps me here. They were not an evil people: I do not know what gods they worshiped, if indeed they worshiped any. But I have looked back at them across the centuries, and have watched while the loveliness they used their last strength to preserve was brought forth again into the light of their shrunken sun. They could have taught us much: why were they destroyed?

I know the answers that my colleagues will give when they get back to Earth. They will say that the Universe has no purpose and no plan, that since a hundred suns explode every year in our Galaxy, at this very moment some race is dying in the depths of space. Whether that race has done good or evil during its lifetime will make no difference in the end: there is no divine justice, for there is no God.

Yet, of course, what we have seen proves nothing of the sort. Anyone who argues thus is being swayed by emotion, not logic. God has no need to justify His actions to man. He who built the Universe can destroy it when He chooses. It is arrogance—it is perilously near blasphemy—for us to say what He may or may not do.

This I could have accepted, hard though it is to look upon whole worlds and peoples thrown into the furnace. But there comes a point when even the deepest faith must falter, and now, as I look at the calculations lying before me, I know I have reached that point at last.

We could not tell, before we reached the nebula, how long ago the explosion 30 took place. Now, from the astronomical evidence and the record in the rocks of that one surviving planet, I have been able to date it very exactly. I know in what year the light of this colossal conflagration reached our Earth. I know how brilliantly the supernova whose corpse now dwindles behind our speeding ship once shone in terrestrial skies. I know how it must have blazed low in the east before sunrise, like a beacon in that oriental dawn.

There can be no reasonable doubt: the ancient mystery is solved at last. Yet, oh God, there were so many stars you could have used. What was the need to give these people to the fire, that the symbol of their passing might shine above Bethlehem?

QUESTIONS FOR DISCUSSION AND WRITING

1. How do the narrator's questions about the information he has discovered sustain the suspense of the plot? Where does the conflict in the story reach its climax?

2. How does the narrator characterize himself? How must he attempt to establish his credentials in two conflicting areas of knowledge?

3. How effective are the techniques the narrator uses to describe the setting of the spaceship, outer space, and the life of a lost civilization? Why does he devote so much attention to portraying the "loveliness" of the lost civilization?

4. What effect is achieved by having the narrator tell his story retrospectively? For example, how did he defend his beliefs on the way to the Phoenix Nebula? How has the discovery of the date of the explosion of the nebula challenged his beliefs?

5. Although the discovery does not challenge the existence of God, it does raise a major question about God's intentions. Explain the implications of the question at the end of the story.

Stories for Comparison:

Italo Calvino's "The Form of Space" (pages 322–328); Ursula K. Le Guin's "The Ones Who Walk Away from Omelas" (pages 144–150).

35

JOSEPH   CONRAD

Heart of Darkness

JOSEPH CONRAD (1857–1924) was born Josef Teodor Konrad Korzeniowski, in Berdyczew, Poland, the son of a patriot who was exiled to Russia. Conrad spent most of his early adult life in the French mercantile marine, visiting Africa, South America, and Australia, surviving two shipwrecks, and eventually rising to the position of captain. As a commander of British ships in the Orient, Conrad mastered the English language and developed a love for the novels of Charles Dickens. When his health failed, he turned to fiction, writing in his second language, English, and drawing upon his many experiences at sea. For the next thirty years Conrad wrote stories about physical and psychological journeys. His longer novels include such masterpieces as *Lord Jim* (1900), *Nostromo* (1904), and *Victory* (1915). His shorter works include *The Nigger of the Narcissus* (1898), *Youth* (1903), and "The Secret Sharer" (1912). "Heart of Darkness," reprinted from *Youth,* is based on Conrad's own expedition up the Congo River. The narrator, Marlow, uses the circumstances of the expedition to explore the moral ambiguities of human existence.

The *Nellie,* a cruising yawl, swung to her anchor without a flutter of the sails, and was at rest. The flood had made, the wind was nearly calm, and being bound down the river, the only thing for it was to come to and wait for the turn of the tide.

The sea-reach of the Thames stretched before us like the beginning of an interminable waterway. In the offing the sea and the sky were welded together without a joint, and in the luminous space the tanned sails of the barges drifting up with the tide seemed to stand still in red clusters of canvas sharply peaked, with gleams of varnished spirits. A haze rested on the low shores that ran out to sea in vanishing flatness. The air was dark above Gravesend, and farther back still seemed condensed into a mournful gloom, brooding motionless over the biggest, and the greatest, town on earth.

The Director of Companies was our captain and our host. We four affectionately watched his back as he stood in the bows looking to seaward. On the whole river there was nothing that looked half so nautical. He resembled a pilot, which to a seaman is trustworthiness personified. It was difficult to realize his work was not out there in the luminous estuary, but behind him, within the brooding gloom.

Between us there was, as I have already said somewhere, the bond of the sea. Besides holding our hearts together through long periods of separation, it had the effect of making us tolerant of each other's yarns—and even convictions. The Lawyer—the best of old fellows—had, because of his many years and many virtues, the only cushion on deck, and was lying on the only rug. The Accountant had brought out already a box of dominoes, and was toying architecturally with the bones. Marlow sat cross-legged right aft, leaning against the mizzenmast. He had sunken cheeks, a yellow complexion, a straight back, an ascetic aspect, and, with his arms dropped, the palms of hands outwards, resembled an idol. The director, satisfied the anchor had good hold, made his way aft and sat down amongst us. We exchanged a few words lazily. Afterwards there was silence on board the yacht. For some reason or other we did not begin that game of dominoes. We felt meditative, and fit for nothing but placid staring. The day was ending in a serenity of still and exquisite brilliance. The water shone pacifically; the sky, without a speck, was a benign immensity of unstained light; the very mist on the Essex marshes was like a gauzy and radiant fabric, hung from the wooded rises inland, and draping the low shores in diaphanous folds. Only the gloom to the west, brooding over the upper reaches, became more sombre every minute, as if angered by the approach of the sun.

And at last, in its curved and imperceptible fall, the sun sank low, and from glowing white changed to a dull red without rays and without heat, as if about to go out suddenly, stricken to death by the touch of that gloom brooding over a crowd of men.

Forthwith a change came over the waters, and the serenity became less brilliant but more profound. The old river in its broad reach rested unruffled at the decline of day, after ages of good service done to the race that peopled its banks, spread out in the tranquil dignity of a waterway leading to the uttermost ends of the earth. We looked at the venerable stream not in the vivid flush of a short day that comes and departs forever, but in the august light of abiding memories. And indeed nothing is easier for a man who has, as the phrase goes, "followed the sea" with reverence and affection, than to evoke the great spirit of the past upon the lower reaches of the Thames. The tidal current runs to and fro in its unceasing service, crowded with memories of men and ships it had borne to the rest of home or to the battles of the sea. It had known and served all the men of whom the nation is proud, from Sir Francis Drake to Sir John Franklin, knights all, titled and untitled—the great knights-errant of the sea. It had borne all the ships whose names are like jewels flashing in the night of time, from the *Golden Hind* returning with her round flanks full of treasure, to be visited by the Queen's Highness and thus pass out of the gigantic tale, to the *Erebus* and *Terror,* bound on other conquests—and that never returned. It had known the ships and the men. They had sailed from Deptford, from Greenwich, from Erith—the adventurers and the settlers; kings' ships and the ships of men on 'Change; captains, admirals, the dark "interlopers" of the Eastern trade, and the commissioned "generals" of East India fleets. Hunters for gold or pursuers of fame, they all had gone out on that stream, bearing the sword, and often the torch, messengers of the might within the land, bearers of a spark from the sacred fire. What greatness had not floated on the ebb of that river into the mystery of an unknown earth! . . . The dreams of men, the seed of commonwealths, the germs of empires.

The sun set; the dusk fell on the stream, and lights began to appear along the shore. The Chapman lighthouse, a three-legged thing erect on a mudflat, shone strongly. Lights of ships moved in the fairway—a great stir of lights going up and going down. And farther west on the upper reaches the place of the monstrous town was still marked ominously on the sky, a brooding gloom in sunshine, a lurid glare under the stars.

"And this also," said Marlow suddenly, "has been one of the dark places of the earth."

He was the only man of us who still "followed the sea." The worst that could be said of him was that he did not represent his class. He was a seaman, but he was a wanderer, too, while most seamen lead, if one may so express it, a sedentary life. Their minds are of the stay-at-home order, and their home is always with them—the ship; and so is their country—the sea. One ship is very much like another, and the sea is always the same. In the immutability of their surroundings the foreign shores, the foreign faces, the changing immensity of life, glide past, veiled not by a sense of mystery but by a slight disdainful ignorance; for there is nothing mysterious to a seaman unless it be the sea itself, which is the mistress of his existence and as inscrutable as Destiny. For the rest, after his hours of work, a casual stroll or a casual spree on shore suffices to unfold for him the secret of a whole continent, and generally he finds the secret not worth knowing. The yarns of seamen have a direct simplicity, the whole meaning of which lies within the shell of a cracked nut. But Marlow was not typical (if his propensity to spin yarns be excepted), and to him the meaning of an episode was not inside like a kernel but outside, enveloping the tale which brought it out only as a glow brings out a haze, in the likeness of one of these misty halos that sometimes are made visible by the spectral illumination of moonshine.

10   His remark did not seem at all surprising. It was just like Marlow. It was accepted in silence. No one took the trouble to grunt even; and presently he said, very slow—

"I was thinking of very old times, when the Romans first came here, nineteen hundred years ago—the other day. . . . Light came out of this river since—you say Knights? Yes; but it is like a running blaze on a plain, like a flash of lightning in the clouds. We live in the flicker—may it last as long as the old earth keeps rolling! But darkness was here yesterday. Imagine the feelings of a commander of a fine—what d'ye call 'em?—trireme in the Mediterranean, ordered suddenly to the north; run overland across the Gauls in a hurry; put in charge of one of these craft the legionaries—a wonderful lot of handy men they must have been, too—used to build, apparently by the hundred, in a month or two, if we may believe what we read. Imagine him here—the very end of the world, a sea the colour of lead, a sky the colour of smoke, a kind of ship about as rigid as a concertina—and going up this river with stores, or orders, or what you like. Sand-banks, marshes, forests, savages,—precious little to eat fit for a civilized man, nothing but Thames water to drink. No Falernian wine here, no going ashore. Here and there a military camp lost in a wilderness, like a needle in a bundle of hay—cold, fog, tempests, disease, exile, and death,—death skulking in the air, in the water, in the bush. They must have been dying like flies here. Oh, yes—he did it. Did it very well, too, no doubt, and without thinking much about it either, except afterwards to brag of what he had gone through in his time, perhaps. They were men enough to face the darkness. And perhaps he was cheered by keeping his eye on a chance of promotion to the fleet at Ravenna by-and-by, if he had good friends in Rome and survived the awful climate. Or think of a decent young citizen in a toga—perhaps too much dice, you know—coming out here in the train of some prefect, or tax-gatherer, or trader even, to mend his fortunes. Land in a swamp, march through the woods, and in some inland post feel the savagery, the utter savagery, had closed round him,—all that mysterious life of the wilderness that stirs in the forest, in the jungles, in the hearts of wild men. There's no initiation either into such mysteries. He has to live in the midst of the incomprehensible, which is also detestable. And it has a fascination, too, that goes to work upon him. The fascination of the abomination—you know, imagine the growing regrets, the longing to escape, the powerless disgust, the surrender, the hate."

He paused.

"Mind," he began again, lifting one arm from the elbow, the palm of the hand outwards, so that, with his legs folded before him, he had the pose of a Buddha preaching in European clothes and without a lotusflower—"Mind, none of us would feel exactly like this. What saves us is efficiency—the devotion to efficiency. But these chaps were not much account, really. They were no colonists; their administration was merely a squeeze, and nothing more, I suspect. They were conquerors, and for that you want only brute force—nothing to boast of, when you have it, since your strength is just an accident arising from the weakness of others. They grabbed what they could get for the sake of what was to be got. It was just robbery with violence, aggravated murder on a great scale, and men going at it blind—as is very proper for those who tackle a darkness. The conquest of the earth, which mostly means the taking it away from those who have a different complexion or slightly flatter noses than ourselves, is not a pretty thing when you look into it too much. What redeems it is the idea only. An idea at the back of it; not a sentimental pretence but an idea; and an unselfish belief in the idea—something you can set up, and bow down before, and offer a sacrifice to. . . ."

He broke off. Flames glided in the river, small green flames, red flames, white flames, pursuing, overtaking, joining, crossing each other—then separating slowly or hastily. The traffic of the great city went on in the deepening night upon the sleepless river. We looked on, waiting patiently—there was nothing else to do till the end of the flood; but it was only after a long silence, when he said, in a hesitating voice, "I suppose you fellows remember I did once turn fresh-water sailor for a bit," that we knew we were fated, before the ebb began to run, to hear about one of Marlow's inconclusive experiences.

15   "I don't want to bother you much with what happened to me personally," he began, showing in this remark the weakness of many tellers of tales who seem so often unaware of what their audience would best like to hear; "yet to understand the effect of it on me you ought to know how I got out there, what I saw, how I went up that river to the place where I first met the poor chap. It was the farthest point of navigation and the culminating point of my experience. It seemed somehow to throw a kind of light on everything about me—and into my thoughts. It was sombre enough, too—and pitiful—not extraordinary in any way—not very clear either. No, not very clear. And yet it seemed to throw a kind of light.

"I had then, as you remember, just returned to London after a lot of Indian Ocean, Pacific, China Seas—a regular dose of the East—six years or so, and I was loafing about, hindering you fellows in your work and invading your homes, just as though I had got a heavenly mission to civilize you. It was very fine for a time, but after a bit I did get tired of resting. Then I began to look for a ship—I should think the hardest work on earth. But the ships wouldn't even look at me. And I got tired of that game, too.

"Now when I was a little chap I had a passion for maps. I would look for hours at South America, or Africa, or Australia, and lose myself in all the glories of exploration. At that time there were many blank spaces on the earth, and when I saw one that looked particularly inviting on a map (but they all look that) I would put my finger on it and say, When I grow up I will go there. The North Pole was one of these places, I remember. Well, I haven't been there yet, and shall not try now. The glamour's off. Other places were scattered about the Equator, and in every sort of latitude all over the two hemispheres. I have been in some of them, and . . . well, we won't talk about that. But there was one yet—the biggest, the most blank, so to speak—that I had a hankering after.

"True, by this time it was not a blank space any more. It had got filled since my boyhood with rivers and lakes and names. It had ceased to be a blank space of delightful mystery—a white patch for a boy to dream gloriously over. It had become a place of darkness. But there was in it one river especially, a mighty big river, that you could see on the map, resembling an immense snake uncoiled, with its head in the sea, its body at rest curving afar over a vast country, and its tail lost in the depths of the land. And as I looked at the map of it in a shop-window, it fascinated me as a snake would a bird—a silly little bird. Then I remembered there was a big concern, a Company for trade on that river. Dash it all! I thought to myself, they can't trade without using some kind of craft on that lot of fresh water—steamboats! Why shouldn't I try to get charge of one?

I went on along Fleet Street, but could not shake off the idea. The snake had charmed me.

"You understand it was a Continental concern, that Trading society; but I have a lot of relations living on the Continent, because it's cheap and not so nasty as it looks, they say.

"I am sorry to own I began to worry them. This was already a fresh departure 20 for me. I was not used to get things that way, you know. I always went my own road and on my own legs where I had a mind to go. I wouldn't have believed it of myself; but, then—you see—I felt somehow I must get there by hook or by crook. So I worried them. The men said 'My dear fellow,' and did nothing. Then—would you believe it?—I tried the women. I, Charles Marlow, set the women to work—to get a job. Heavens! Well, you see, the notion drove me. I had an aunt, a dear enthusiastic soul. She wrote: 'It will be delightful. I am ready to do anything, anything for you. It is a glorious idea, I know the wife of a very high personage in the Administration, and also a man who has lots of influence with,' etc, etc. She was determined to make no end of fuss to get me appointed skipper of a river steamboat, if such was my fancy.

"I got my appointment—of course; and I got it very quick. It appears the Company had received news that one of their captains had been killed in a scuffle with the natives. This was my chance, and it made me the more anxious to go. It was only months and months afterwards, when I made the attempt to recover what was left of the body, that I heard the original quarrel arose from a misunderstanding about some hens. Yes, two black hens. Fresleven—that was the fellow's name, a Dane—thought himself wronged somehow in the bargain, so he went ashore and started to hammer the chief of the village with a stick. Oh, it didn't surprise me in the least to hear this, and at the same time to be told that Fresleven was the gentlest, quietest creature that ever walked on two legs. No doubt he was; but he had been a couple of years already out there engaged in the noble cause, you know, and he probably felt the need at last of asserting his self-respect in some way. Therefore he whacked the old nigger mercilessly, while a big crowd of his people watched him, thunderstruck, till some man—I was told the chief's son—in desperation at hearing the old chap yell, made a tentative jab with a spear at the white man—and of course it went quite easy between the shoulderblades. Then the whole population cleared into the forest, expecting all kinds of calamities to happen, while, on the other hand, the steamer Fresleven commanded left also in a bad panic, in charge of the engineer, I believe. Afterwards nobody seemed to trouble much about Fresleven's remains, till I got out and stepped into his shoes. I couldn't let it rest, though; but when an opportunity offered at last to meet my predecessor, the grass growing through his ribs was tall enough to hide his bones. They were all there. The supernatural being had not been touched after he fell. And the village was deserted, the huts gaped black, rotting, all askew within the fallen enclosures. A calamity had come to it, sure enough. The people had vanished. Mad terror had scattered them, men, women, and children, through the bush, and they had never returned. What became of the hens I don't know either. I should think the cause of progress got them, anyhow. However, through this glorious affair I got my appointment, before I had fairly begun to hope for it.

"I flew around like mad to get ready, and before forty-eight hours I was crossing the Channel to show myself to my employers, and sign the contract. In a very few hours I arrived in a city that always makes me think of a whited sepulchre. Prejudice no doubt. I had no difficulty in finding the Company's offices. It was the biggest thing in the town, and everybody I met was full of it. They were going to run an over-sea empire, and make no end of coin by trade.

"A narrow and deserted street in deep shadow, high houses, innumerable windows with venetian blinds, a dead silence, grass sprouting between the stones, imposing carriage archways right and left, immense double doors standing ponderously ajar. I slipped through one of these cracks, went up a swept and ungarnished staircase, as arid as a desert, and opened the first door I came to. Two women, one fat and the other slim, sat on straw-bottomed chairs, knitting black wool. The slim one got up and walked straight at me—still knitting with down-cast eyes—and only just as I began to think of getting out of her way, as you would a somnambulist, stood still, and looked up. Her dress was as plain as an umbrella-cover, and she turned round without a word and preceded me into a waiting-room. I gave my name, and looked about. Deal table in the middle, plain chairs all round the walls, on one end a large shining map, marked with all the colours of a rainbow. There was a vast amount of red—good to see at any time, because one knows that some real work is done in there, a deuce of a lot of blue, a little green, smears of orange, and, on the East Coast, a purple patch, to show where the jolly pioneers of progress drink the jolly lager-beer. However, I wasn't going into any of these. I was going into the yellow. Dead in the centre. And the river was there—fascinating—deadly—like a snake. Ough! A door opened, a white-haired secretarial head, but wearing a compassionate expression, appeared, and a skinny forefinger beckoned me into the sanctuary. Its light was dim, and a heavy writing-desk squatted in the middle. From behind that structure came out an impression of pale plumpness in a frock-coat. The great man himself. He was five feet six, I should judge, and had his grip on the handle-end of ever so many millions. He shook hands, I fancy, murmured vaguely, was satisfied with my French. *Bon voyage.*

"In about forty-five seconds I found myself again in the waiting-room with the compassionate secretary, who, full of desolation and sympathy, made me sign some document. I believe I undertook amongst other things not to disclose any trade secrets. Well, I am not going to.

25   "I began to feel slightly uneasy. You know I am not used to such ceremonies, and there was something ominous in the atmosphere. It was just as though I had been let into some conspiracy—I don't know—something not quite right; and I was glad to get out. In the outer room the two women knitted black wool feverishly. People were arriving, and the younger one was walking back and forth introducing them. The old one sat on her chair. Her flat cloth slippers were propped up on a foot-warmer, and a cat reposed on her lap. She wore a starched white affair on her head, had a wart on one cheek, and silver-rimmed spectacles hung on the tip of her nose. She glanced at me above the glasses. The swift and indifferent placidity of that look troubled me. Two youths with foolish and cheery countenances were being piloted over, and she threw at them the same quick glance of unconcerned wisdom. She seemed to know all about

them and about me, too. An eerie feeling came over me. She seemed uncanny and fateful. Often far away there I thought of these two, guarding the door of Darkness, knitting black wool as for a warm pall, one introducing, introducing continuously to the unknown, the other scrutinizing the cheery and foolish faces with unconcerned old eyes. *Ave!* Old knitter of black wool. *Morituri te salutant.* Not many of those she looked at ever saw her again—not half, by a long way.

"There was yet a visit to the doctor. 'A simple formality,' assured me the secretary, with an air of taking an immense part in all my sorrows. Accordingly a young chap wearing his hat over the left eyebrow, some clerk I suppose,—there must have been clerks in the business, though the house was as still as a house in a city of the dead—came from somewhere up-stairs, and led me forth. He was shabby and careless, with inkstains on the sleeves of his jacket, and his cravat was large and billowy, under a chin shaped like the toe of an old boot. It was a little too early for the doctor, so I proposed a drink, and thereupon he developed a vein of joviality. As we sat over our vermouths he glorified the Company's business, and by-and-by I expressed casually my surprise at him not going out there. He became very cool and collected all at once. 'I am not such a fool as I look, quoth Plato to his disciples,' he said sententiously, emptied his glass with great resolution, and we rose.

"The old doctor felt my pulse, evidently thinking of something else the while. 'Good, good for there,' he mumbled, and then with a certain eagerness asked me whether I would let him measure my head. Rather surprised, I said Yes, when he produced a thing like calipers and got the dimensions back and front and every way, taking notes carefully. He was an unshaven little man in a threadbare coat like a gaberdine with his feet in slippers, and I thought him a harmless fool. 'I always ask leave, in the interests of science, to measure the crania of those going back out there,' he said. 'And when they come back, too?' I asked. 'Oh. I never see them,' he remarked; 'and, moreover, the changes take place inside, you know.' He smiled, as if at some quiet joke. 'So you are going out there. Famous. Interesting, too.' He gave me a searching glance, and made another note. 'Ever any madness in your family?' he asked, in a matter-of-fact tone. I felt very annoyed. 'Is that question in the interests of science, too?' 'It would be,' he said, without taking notice of my irritation, 'interesting for science to watch the mental changes of individuals, on the spot, but . . .' 'Are you an alienist?' I interrupted. 'Every doctor should be—a little,' answered that original, imperturbably. 'I have a little theory which you Messieurs who go out there must help me to prove. This is my share in the advantages my country shall reap from the possession of such a magnificent dependency. The mere wealth I leave to others. Pardon my questions, but you are the first Englishman coming under my observation . . .' I hastened to assure him I was not in the least typical. 'If I were,' said I, 'I wouldn't be talking like this with you.' 'What you say is rather profound, and probably erroneous,' he said, with a laugh. 'Avoid irritation more than exposure to the sun. Adieu. How do you English say, eh? Goodbye. Ah! Goodbye. Adieu. In the tropics one must before everything keep calm.' . . . He lifted a warning forefinger. . . . *'Du calme, du calme. Adieu.'*

"One thing more remained to do—say good-bye to my excellent aunt. I found her triumphant. I had a cup of tea—that last decent cup of tea for many days—and in a room that most soothingly looked just as you would expect a lady's drawing-room to look, we had a long quiet chat by the fireside. In the course of these confidences it became quite plain to me I had been represented to the wife of the high dignitary, and goodness knows how many more people besides, as an exceptional and gifted creature—a piece of good fortune for the Company—a man you don't get hold of every day. Good heavens! and I was going to take charge of a two-penny-half-penny river-steamboat with a penny whistle attached! It appeared, however, I was also one of the Workers, with a capital—you know. Something like an emissary of light, something like a lower sort of apostle. There had been a lot of such rot let loose in print and talk just about that time, and the excellent woman, living right in the rush of all that humbug, got carried off her feet. She talked about 'weaning those ignorant millions from their horrid ways,' till, upon my words, she made me quite uncomfortable. I ventured to hint that the Company was run for profit.

"'You forget, dear Charlie, that the labourer is worthy of his hire,' she said, brightly. It's queer how out of touch with truth women are. They live in a world of their own, and there had never been anything like it, and never can be. It is too beautiful altogether, and if they were to set it up it would go to pieces before the first sunset. Some confounded fact we men have been living contentedly with ever since the day of creation would start up and knock the whole thing over.

30   "After this I got embraced, told to wear flannel, be sure to write often, and so on—and I left. In the street—I don't know why—a queer feeling came to me that I was an impostor. Odd thing that I, who used to clear out for any part of the world at twenty-four hours' notice, with less thought than most men give to the crossing of a street, had a moment—I won't say of hesitation, but of startled pause, before this commonplace affair. The best way I can explain it to you is by saying that, for a second or two, I felt as though, instead of going to the centre of a continent, I were about to set off for the centre of the earth.

"I left in a French steamer, and she called in every blamed port they have out there, for, as far as I could see, the sole purpose of landing soldiers and custom-house officers. I watched the coast. Watching a coast as it slips by the ship is like thinking about an enigma. There it is before you—smiling, frowning, inviting, grand, mean, insipid, or savage, and always mute with an air of whispering, Come and find out. This one was almost featureless, as if still in the making, with an aspect of monotonous grimness. The edge of a colossal jungle, so dark-green as to be almost black, fringed with white surf, ran straight, like a ruled line, far, far away along a blue sea whose glitter was blurred by a creeping mist. The sun was fierce, the land seemed to glisten and drip with steam. Here and there grayish-whitish specks showed up clustered inside the white surf, with a flag flying above them perhaps. Settlements some centuries old, and still no bigger than pinheads on the untouched expanse of their background. We pounded along, stopped, landed soldiers; went on, landed custom-house clerks to levy toll in what looked like a God-forsaken wilderness, with a tin shed and a flag-pole lost in it; landed more soldiers—to take care of the custom-house clerks, presumably. Some, I heard, got drowned in the surf; but whether they did or not, nobody seemed particularly to care. They were just flung out there, and on we went. Every day the coast looked the same, as though we had not moved; but we passed various places—trading places—with names like Gran'Bassam, Little Popo; names that seemed to belong to some sordid farce acted in front of a sinister back-cloth. The idleness of a passenger, my isolation amongst all these men with whom I had no point of contact, the oily and languid sea, the uniform sombreness of the coast, seemed to keep me away from the truth of things, within the toil of a mournful and senseless delusion. The voice of the surf heard now and then was a positive pleasure, like the speech of a brother. It was something natural, that had its reason, that had a meaning. Now and then a boat from the shore gave one a momentary contact with reality. It was paddled by black fellows. You could see from afar the white of their eyeballs glistening. They shouted, sang; their bodies streamed with perspiration; they had faces like grotesque masks—these chaps; but they had bone, muscle, a wild vitality, an intense energy of movement, that was as natural and true as the surf along their coast. They wanted no excuse for being there. They were a great comfort to look at. For a time I would feel I belonged still to a world of straight-forward facts; but the feeling would not last long. Something would turn up to scare it away. Once, I remember, we came upon a man-of-war anchored off the coast. There wasn't even a shed there, and she was shelling the bush. It appears the French had one of their wars going on thereabouts. Her ensign dropped limp like a rag; the muzzles of the long six-inch guns stuck out all over the low hull; the greasy, slimy swell swung her up lazily and let her down, swaying her thin masts. In the empty immensity of earth, sky, and water, there she was, incomprehensible, firing into a continent. Pop, would go one of the six-inch guns; a small flame would dart and vanish, a little white smoke would disappear, a tiny projectile would give a feeble screech—and nothing happened. Nothing could happen. There was a touch of insanity in the proceeding, a sense of lugubrious drollery in the sight; and it was not dissipated by somebody on board assuring me earnestly there was a camp of natives—he called them enemies!—hidden out of sight somewhere.

"We gave her letters (I heard the men in that lonely ship were dying of fever at the rate of three a-day) and went on. We called at some more places with farcical names, where the merry dance of death and trade goes on in a still and earthy atmosphere as of an overheated catacomb; all along the formless coast bordered by dangerous surf, as if Nature herself had tried to ward off intruders; in and out of rivers, streams of death in life, whose banks were rotting into mud, whose waters, thickened into slime, invaded the contorted mangroves, that seemed to writhe at us in the extremity of an impotent despair. Nowhere did we stop long enough to get a particularized impression, but the general sense of vague and oppressive wonder grew upon me. It was like a weary pilgrimage amongst hints for nightmares.

"It was upward of thirty days before I saw the mouth of the big river. We anchored off the seat of the government. But my work would not begin till some two hundred miles farther on. So as soon as I could I made a start for a place thirty miles higher up.

"I had my passage on a little sea-going steamer. Her captain was a Swede, and knowing me for a seaman, invited me on the bridge. He was a young man, lean, fair, and morose, with lanky hair and a shuffling gait. As we left the miserable little wharf, he tossed his head contemptuously at the shore. 'Been living there?' he asked.

I said, 'Yes.' 'Fine lot these government chaps—are they not?' he went on, speaking English with great precision and considerable bitterness. 'It is funny what some people will do for a few francs a-month. I wonder what becomes of that kind when it goes up country?' I said to him I expected to see that soon. 'So-o-o!' he exclaimed. He shuffled athwart, keeping one eye ahead vigilantly. 'Don't be too sure,' he continued. 'The other day I took up a man who hanged himself on the road. He was a Swede, too.' 'Hanged himself! Why, in God's name?' I cried. He kept on looking out watchfully. 'Who knows? The sun too much for him, or the country perhaps.'

35   "At last we opened a reach. A rocky cliff appeared, mounds of turned-up earth by the shore, houses on a hill, others with iron roofs, amongst a waste of excavations, or hanging to the declivity. A continuous noise of the rapids above hovered over this scene of inhabited devastation. A lot of people, mostly black and naked, moved about like ants. A jetty projected into the river. A blinding sunlight drowned all this at times in a sudden recrudescence of glare. 'There's your Company's station,' said the Swede, pointing to three wooden barrack-like structures on the rocky slope. 'I will send your things up. Four boxes did you say? So. Farewell.'

"I came upon a boiler wallowing in the grass, then found a path leading up the hill. It turned aside for the boulders, and also for an undersized railway-truck lying there on its back with its wheels in the air. One was off. The thing looked as dead as the carcass of some animal. I came upon more pieces of decaying machinery, a stack of rusty nails. To the left a clump of trees made a shady spot, where dark things seemed to stir feebly. I blinked, the path was steep. A horn tooted to the right, and I saw the black people run. A heavy and dull detonation shook the ground, a puff of smoke came out of the cliff, and that was all. No change appeared on the face of the rock. They were building a railway. The cliff was not in the way or anything; but this objectless blasting was all the work going on.

"A slight clinking behind me made me turn my head. Six black men advanced in a file, toiling up the path. They walked erect and slow, balancing small baskets full of earth on their heads, and the clink kept time with their footsteps. Black rags were wound round their loins, and the short ends behind waggled to and fro like tails. I could see every rib, the joints of their limbs were like knots in a rope; each had an iron collar on his neck, and all were connected together with a chain whose bights swung between them, rhythmically clinking. Another report from the cliff made me think suddenly of that ship of war I had seen firing into a continent. It was the same kind of ominous voice; but these men could by no stretch of imagination be called enemies. They were called criminals, and the outraged law, like the bursting shells, had come to them, an insoluble mystery from the sea. All their meagre breasts panted together, the violently dilated nostrils quivered, the eyes stared stonily up-hill. They passed me within six inches, without a glance, with that complete, deathlike indifference of unhappy savages. Behind this raw matter one of the reclaimed, the product of the new forces at work, strolled despondently, carrying a rifle by its middle. He had a uniform jacket with one button off, and seeing a white man on the path, hoisted his weapon to his shoulder with alacrity. This was simple prudence, white men being so much alike at a distance that he could not tell who I might be. He was speedily reassured, and with a large, white, rascally grin, and a glance at his charge, seemed to take me into partnership in his exalted trust. After all, I also was a part of the great cause of these high and just proceedings.

"Instead of going up, I turned and descended to the left. My idea was to let that chain-gang get out of sight before I climbed the hill. You know I am not particularly tender; I've had to strike and to fend off. I've had to resist and attack sometimes—that's only one way of resisting—without counting the exact cost, according to the demands of such sort of life as I had blundered into. I've seen the devil of violence, and the devil of greed, and the devil of hot desire; but, by all the stars! these were strong, lusty, red-eyed devils, that swayed and drove men—men, I tell you. But as I stood on this hillside, I foresaw that in the blinding sunshine of that land I would become acquainted with a flabby, pretending, weak-eyed devil of a rapacious and pitiless folly. How insidious he could be, too, I was only to find out several months later and a thousand miles farther. For a moment I stood appalled, as though by a warning. Finally I descended the hill, obliquely, towards the trees I had seen.

"I avoided a vast artificial hole somebody had been digging on the slope, the purpose of which I found it impossible to divine. It wasn't a quarry or a sandpit, anyhow. It was just a hole. It might have been connected with the philanthropic desire of giving the criminals something to do. I don't know. Then I nearly fell into a very narrow ravine, almost no more than a scar in the hillside. I discovered that a lot of imported drainage-pipes for a settlement had been tumbled in there. There wasn't one that was not broken. It was a wanton smash-up. At last I got under the trees. My purpose was to stroll into the shade for a moment; but no sooner within than it seemed to me I had stepped into the gloomy circle of some Inferno. The rapids were near, and an uninterrupted, uniform, headlong, rushing noise filled the mournful stillness of the grove, where not a breath stirred, not a leaf moved with a mysterious sound—as though the tearing pace of the launched earth had suddenly become audible.

"Black shapes crouched, lay, sat between the trees leaning against the trunks, clinging to the earth, half coming out, half effaced within the dim light, in all the attitudes of pain, abandonment, and despair. Another mine on the cliff went off, followed by a slight shudder of the soil under my feet. The work was going on. The work! And this was the place where some of the helpers had withdrawn to die.

"They were dying slowly—it was very clear. They were not enemies, they were not criminals, they were nothing earthly now,—nothing but the black shadows of disease and starvation, lying confusedly in the greenish gloom. Brought from all the recesses of the coast in all the legality of time contracts, lost in uncongenial surroundings, fed on unfamiliar food, they sickened, became inefficient, and were then allowed to crawl away and rest. These moribund shapes were free as air—and nearly as thin. I began to distinguish the gleam of the eyes under the trees. Then, glancing down, I saw a face near my hand. The black bones reclined at full length with one shoulder against the tree, and slowly the eyelids rose and the sunken eyes looked up at me, enormous and vacant, a kind of blind, white flicker in the depths of the orbs, which died out slowly. The man seemed young—almost a boy—but you know with them it's hard to tell. I found nothing else to do but to offer him one of my good Swede's ship's biscuits I had in my pocket. The fingers closed slowly on it and held—there was no other movement and no other glance. He had tied a bit of white worsted round his neck—Why? Where did he get it? Was it a badge—an ornament—a charm—a propitiatory act? Was there any idea at all connected with it? It looked startling round his black neck, this bit of white thread from beyond the seas.

"Near the same tree two more bundles of acute angles sat with their legs drawn up. One, with his chin propped on his knees, stared at nothing, in an intolerable and appalling manner: his brother phantom rested its forehead, as if overcome with a great weariness; and all about others were scattered in every pose of contorted collapse, as in some picture of a massacre or a pestilence. While I stood horror-struck, one of these creatures rose to his hands and knees, and went off on all-fours towards the river to drink. He lapped out of his hand, then sat up in the sunlight, crossing his shins in front of him, and after a time let his woolly head fall on his breastbone.

"I didn't want any more loitering in the shade, and I made haste towards the station. When near the buildings I met a white man, in such an unexpected elegance of get-up that in the first moment I took him for a sort of vision. I saw a high starched collar, white cuffs, a light alpaca jacket, snowy trousers, a clear necktie, and varnished boots. No hat. Hair parted, brushed, oiled, under a green-lined parasol held in a big white hand. He was amazing, and had a penholder behind his ear.

"I shook hands with this miracle, and I learned he was the Company's chief accountant, and that all the book-keeping was done at this station. He had come out for a moment, he said, 'to get a breath of fresh air.' The expression sounded wonderfully odd, with its suggestion of sedentary desk-life. I wouldn't have mentioned the fellow to you at all, only it was from his lips that I first heard the name of the man who is so indissolubly connected with the memories of that time. Moreover, I respected the fellow. Yes; I respected his collars, his vast cuffs, his brushed hair. His appearance was certainly that of a hairdresser's dummy; but in the great demoralization of the land he kept up his appearance. That's backbone. His starched collars and got-up shirt-fronts were achievements of character. He had been out nearly three years; and, later, I could not help asking him how he managed to sport such linen. He had just the faintest blush, and said modestly, 'I've been teaching one of the native women about the station. It was difficult. She had a distaste for the work.' Thus this man had verily accomplished something. And he was devoted to his books, which were in apple-pie order.

45   "Everything else in the station was in a muddle,—heads, things, buildings. Strings of dusty niggers with splay feet arrived and departed; a stream of manufactured goods, rubbishy cottons, beads, and brass-wire set into the depths of darkness, and in return came a precious trickle of ivory.

"I had to wait in the station for ten days—an eternity. I lived in a hut in the yard, but to be out of the chaos I would sometimes get into the accountant's office. It was built of horizontal planks, and so badly put together that, as he bent over his high desk, he was barred from neck to heels with narrow strips of sunlight. There was no need to open the big shutter to see. It was hot there, too; big flies buzzed fiendishly, and did not sting, but stabbed. I sat generally on the floor, while of faultless appearance (and even slightly scented), perching on a high stool, he wrote, he wrote. Sometimes he stood up for exercise. When a trucklebed with a sick man (some invalid agent from upcountry) was put in there, he exhibited a gentle annoyance. 'The groans of this sick person,' he said, 'distract my attention. And without that it is extremely difficult to guard against clerical errors in this climate.'

"One day he remarked, without lifting his head, 'In the interior you will no doubt meet Mr. Kurtz.' On my asking who Mr. Kurtz was, he said he was a first-class agent; and seeing my disappointment at this information, he added slowly, laying down his pen, 'He is a very remarkable person.' Further questions elicited from him that Kurtz was at present in charge of a trading post, a very important one, in the true ivory-country, at 'the very bottom of there. Sends in as much ivory as all the others put together . . .' He began to write again. The sick man was too ill to groan. The flies buzzed in a great peace.

"Suddenly there was a growing murmur of voices and a great tramping of feet. A caravan had come in. A violent babble of uncouth sounds burst out on the other side of the planks. All the carriers were speaking together, and in the midst of the uproar the lamentable voice of the chief agent was heard 'giving it up' tearfully for the twentieth time that day. . . . He rose slowly. 'What a frightful row,' he said. He crossed the room gently to look at the sick man, and returning, said to me, 'He does not hear.' 'What! Dead?' I asked, startled. 'No, not yet,' he answered, with great composure. Then, alluding with a toss of the head to the tumult in the station-yard. 'When one has got to make correct entries, one comes to hate those savages—hate them to the death.' He remained thoughtful for a moment. 'When you see Mr. Kurtz,' he went on, 'tell him from me that everything here'—he glanced at the desk—'is very satisfactory. I don't like to write him—with those messengers of ours you never know who may get hold of your letter—at that Central Station.' He stared at me for a moment with his mild, bulging eyes. 'Oh, he will go far, very far,' he began again. 'He will be a somebody in the Administration before long. They, above—the Council in Europe, you know—mean him to be.'

"He turned to his work. The noise outside had ceased, and presently in going out I stopped at the door. In the steady buzz of flies the homeward-bound agent was lying flushed and insensible; the other, bent over his books, was making correct entries of perfectly correct transactions; and fifty feet below the doorstep I could see the still tree-tops of the grove of death.

"Next day I left that station at last, with a caravan of sixty men, for a two- hundred-mile tramp.

"No use telling you much about that. Paths, paths, everywhere; a stamped-in network of paths spreading over the empty land, through long grass, through burnt grass, through thickets, down and up chilly ravines, up and down stony hills ablaze with heat; and a solitude, a solitude, nobody, not a hut. The population had cleared out a long time ago. Well, if a lot of mysterious niggers armed with all kinds of fearful weapons suddenly took to travelling on the road between Deal and Gravesend, catching the yokels right and left to carry heavy loads for them, I fancy every farm and cottage thereabouts would get empty very soon. Only here the dwellings were gone, too. Still I passed through several abandoned villages. There's something pathetically childish in the ruins of grass walls. Day after day, with the stamp and shuffle of sixty pairs of bare feet behind me, each pair under a 60-lb. load. Camp, cook, sleep, strike camp, march. Now and then a carrier dead in harness, at rest in the long grass near the path, with an empty water-gourd and his long staff lying by his side. A great silence around and above. Perhaps on some quiet night the tremor of far-off drums, sinking, swelling, a tremor vast, faint; a sound weird, appealing, suggestive, and wild—and perhaps with as profound a meaning as the sound of bells in a Christian country. Once a white man in an unbuttoned uniform, camping on the path with an armed escort of lank Zanzibaris, very hospitable and festive—not to say drunk. Was looking after the upkeep of the road he declared. Can't say I saw any road or any upkeep, unless the body of a middle-aged negro, with a bullet-hole in the forehead, upon which I absolutely stumbled three miles farther on, may be considered as a permanent improvement. I had a white companion, too, not a bad chap, but rather too fleshy and with the exasperating habit of fainting on the hot hillsides, miles away from the least bit of shade and water. Annoying, you know, to hold your own coat like a parasol over a man's head while he is coming-to. I couldn't help asking him once what he meant by coming there at all. 'To make money, of course. What do you think?' he said, scornfully. Then he got fever, and had to be carried in a hammock slung under a pole. As he weighed sixteen stone I had no end of rows with the carriers. They jibbed, ran away, sneaked off with their loads in the night—quite a mutiny. So, one evening, I made a speech in English with gestures, not one of which was lost to the sixty pairs of eyes before me, and the next morning I started the hammock off in front all right. An hour afterwards I came upon the whole concern wrecked in a bush—man, hammock, groans, blankets, horrors. The heavy pole had skinned his poor nose. He was very anxious for me to kill somebody, but there wasn't the shadow of a carrier near. I remember the old doctor,—'It would be interesting for science to watch the mental changes of individuals, on the spot.' I felt I was becoming scientifically interesting. However, all that is to no purpose. On the fifteenth day I came in sight of the big river again, and hobbled into the Central Station. It was on a back water surrounded by scrub and forest, with a pretty border of smelly mud on one side, and on the three others enclosed by a crazy fence of rushes. A neglected gap was all the gate it had, and the first glance at the place was enough to let you see the flabby devil was running that show. White men with long staves in their hands appeared languidly from amongst the buildings, strolling up to take a look at me, and then retired out of sight somewhere. One of them, a stout, excitable chap with black moustaches, informed me with great volubility and many digressions, as soon as I told him who I was, that my steamer was at the bottom of the river. I was thunderstruck. What, how, why? Oh, it was 'all right.' The 'manager himself' was there. All quite correct. 'Everybody had behaved splendidly! splendidly!'—'you must,' he said in agitation, 'go and see the general manager at once. He is waiting!'

"I did not see the real significance of that wreck at once. I fancy I see it now, but I am not sure—not at all. Certainly the affair was too stupid—when I think of it—to be altogether natural. Still . . . But at the moment it presented itself simply as a confounded nuisance. The steamer was sunk. They had started two days before in a sudden hurry up the river with the manager on board, in charge of some volunteer skipper, and before they had been out three hours they tore the bottom out of her on stones, and she sank near the south bank. I asked myself what I was to do there, now my boat was lost. As a matter of fact, I had plenty to do in fishing my command out of the river. I had to set about it the very next day. That, and the repairs when I brought the pieces to the station, took some months.

"My first interview with the manager was curious. He did not ask me to sit down after my twenty-mile walk that morning. He was commonplace in complexion, in feature, in manners, and in voice. He was of middle size and of ordinary build. His eyes, of the usual blue, were perhaps remarkably cold, and he certainly could make his glance fall on one as trenchant and heavy as an axe. But even at these times the rest of his person seemed to disclaim the intention. Otherwise there was only an indefinable, faint expression of his lips, something stealthy—a smile—not a smile—I remember it, but I can't explain. It was unconscious, this smile was, though just after he had said something it got intensified for an instant. It came at the end of his speeches like a seal applied on the words to make the meaning of the commonest phrase appear absolutely inscrutable. He was a common trader, from his youth up employed in these parts—nothing more. He was obeyed, yet he inspired neither love nor fear, nor even respect. He inspired uneasiness. That was it! Uneasiness. Not a definite mistrust—just uneasiness—nothing more. You have no idea how effective such a . . . a . . . faculty can be. He had no genius for organizing, for initiative, or for order even. That was evident in such things as the deplorable state of the station. He had no learning, and no intelligence. His position had come to him—why? Perhaps because he was never ill . . . He had served three terms of three years out there . . . Because triumphant health in the general rout of constitutions is a kind of power in itself. When he went home on leave he rioted on a large scale—pompously. Jack ashore—with a difference—in externals only. This one could gather from his casual talk. He originated nothing, he could keep the routine going—that's all. But he was great. He was great by this little thing that it was impossible to tell what could control such a man. He never gave that secret away. Perhaps there was nothing within him. Such a suspicion made one pause—for out there there were no external checks. Once when various tropical diseases had laid low almost every 'agent' in the station, he was heard to say, 'Men who come out here should have no entrails.' He sealed the utterance with that smile of his, as though it had been a door opening into a darkness he had in his keeping. You fancied you had seen things—but the seal was on. When annoyed at meal-times by the constant quarrels of the white men about precedence, he ordered an immense round table to be made, for which a special house had to be built. This was the station's mess-room. Where he sat was the first place—the rest were nowhere. One felt this to be his unalterable conviction. He was neither civil nor uncivil. He was quiet. He allowed his 'boy'—an overfed young negro from the coast—to treat the white men, under his very eyes, with provoking insolence.

"He began to speak as soon as he saw me. I had been very long on the road. He could not wait. Had to start without me. The up-river stations had to be relieved. There had been so many delays already that he did not know who was dead and who was alive, and how they got on—and so on, and so on. He paid no attention to my explanations, and, playing with a stick of sealing-wax, repeated several times that the situation was 'very grave, very grave.' There were rumours that a very important station was in jeopardy, and its chief, Mr. Kurtz, was ill. Hoped it was not true.

Mr. Kurtz was . . . I felt weary and irritable. Hang Kurtz, I thought. I interrupted him by saying I had heard of Mr. Kurtz on the coast. 'Ah! So they talk of him down there,' he murmured to himself. Then he began again, assuring me Mr. Kurtz was the best agent he had, an exceptional man, of the greatest importance to the Company; therefore I could understand his anxiety. He was, he said, 'very, very uneasy.' Certainly he fidgeted on his chair a good deal, exclaimed, 'Ah, Mr. Kurtz!' broke the stick of sealing-wax and seemed dumbfounded by the accident. Next thing he wanted to know 'how long it would take to' . . . I interrupted him again. Being hungry, you know, and kept on my feet, too, I was getting savage. 'How could I tell?' I said. "I hadn't even seen the wreck yet—some months, no doubt.' All this talk seemed to me so futile. 'Some months,' he said. 'Well, let us say three months before we can make a start. Yes. That ought to do the affair.' I flung out of his hut (he lived all alone in a clay hut with a sort of verandah) muttering to myself my opinion of him. He was a chattering idiot. Afterwards I took it back when it was borne in upon me startlingly with what extreme nicety he had estimated the time requisite for the 'affair.'

55   "I went to work the next day, turning, so to speak, my back on that station. In that way only it seemed to me I could keep my hold on the redeeming facts of life. Still, one must look about sometimes; and then I saw this station, these men strolling aimlessly about in the sunshine of the yard. I asked myself sometimes what it all meant. They wandered here and there with their absurd long staves in their hands, like a lot of faithless pilgrims bewitched inside a rotten fence. The word 'ivory' rang in the air, was whispered, was sighed. You would think they were praying to it. A taint of imbecile rapacity blew through it all, like a whiff from some corpse. By Jove! I've never seen anything so unreal in my life. And outside, the silent wilderness surrounding this cleared speck on the earth struck me as something great and invincible, like evil or truth, waiting patiently for the passing away of this fantastic invasion.

"Oh, these months! Well, never mind. Various things happened. One evening a grass shed full of calico, cotton prints, beads, and I don't know what else, burst into a blaze so suddenly that you would have thought the earth had opened to let an avenging fire consume all that trash. I was smoking my pipe quietly by my dismantled steamer, and saw them all cutting capers in the light, with their arms lifted high, when the stout man with moustaches came tearing down to the river, a tin pail in his hand, assured me that everybody was 'behaving splendidly, splendidly,' dipped about a quart of water and tore back again. I noticed there was a hole in the bottom of his pail.

"I strolled up. There was no hurry. You see the thing had gone off like a box of matches. It had been hopeless from the very first. The flame had leaped high, driven everybody back, lighted up everything—and collapsed. The shed was already a heap of embers glowing fiercely. A nigger was being beaten near by. They said he had caused the fire in some way; be that as it may, he was screeching most horribly. I saw him, later, for several days, sitting in a bit of shade looking very sick and trying to recover himself: afterwards he arose and went out—and the wilderness without a sound took him into its bosom again. As I approached the glow from the dark I found myself at the back of two men, talking. I heard the name of Kurtz pronounced, then the words, 'take advantage of this unfortunate accident.' One of the men was the manager. I wished him a good evening. 'Did you ever see anything like it—eh? it is incredible,' he said, and walked off. The other man remained. He was a first-class agent, young, gentlemanly, a bit reserved, with a forked little beard and a hooked nose. He was stand-offish with the other agents, and they on their side said he was the manager's spy upon them. As to me, I had hardly ever spoken to him before. We got into talk, and by-and-by we strolled away from the hissing ruins. Then he asked me to his room, which was in the main building of the station. He struck a match, and I perceived that this young aristocrat had not only a silver-mounted dressing-case but also a whole candle all to himself. Just at that time the manager was the only man supposed to have any right to candles. Native mats covered the clay walls; a collection of spears, assegais, shields, knives, was hung up in trophies. The business intrusted to this fellow was the making of bricks—so I had been informed; but there wasn't a fragment of a brick anywhere in the station, and he had been there more than a year—waiting. It seems he could not make bricks without something, I don't know what—straw maybe. Anyways, it could not be found there, and as it was not likely to be sent from Europe, it did not appear clear to me what he was waiting for. An act of special creation perhaps. However, they were all waiting—all the sixteen or twenty pilgrims of them—for something; and upon my word it did not seem an uncongenial occupation, from the way they took it, though the only thing that ever came to them was disease—as far as I could see. They beguiled the time by back-biting and intriguing against each other in a foolish kind of way. There was an air of plotting about this station, but nothing came of it, of course. It was as unreal as everything else—as the philanthropic pretence of the whole concern, as their talk, as their government, as their show of work. The only real feeling was a desire to get appointed to a trading-post where ivory was to be had, so that they could earn percentages. They intrigued and slandered and hated each other only on that account,—but as to effectually lifting a little finger—oh, no. By heavens! there is something after all in the world allowing one man to steal a horse while another must not look at a halter. Steal a horse straight out. Very well. He has done it. Perhaps he can ride. But there is a way of looking at a halter that would provoke the most charitable of saints into a kick.

"I had no idea why he wanted to be sociable, but as we chatted in there it suddenly occurred to me the fellow was trying to get at something—in fact, pumping me. He alluded constantly to Europe, to the people I was supposed to know there—putting leading questions as to my acquaintances in the sepulchral city, and so on. His little eyes glittered like mica discs—with curiosity—though he tried to keep up a bit of superciliousness. At first I was astonished, but very soon I became awfully curious to see what he would find out from me. I couldn't possibly imagine what I had in me to make it worth his while. It was very pretty to see how he baffled himself, for in truth my body was full only of chills, and my head had nothing in it but that wretched steamboat business. It was evident he took me for a perfectly shameless prevaricator. At last he got angry, and, to conceal a movement of furious annoyance, he yawned. I rose. Then I noticed a small sketch in oils, on a panel, representing a woman, draped and blindfolded, carrying a lighted torch. The background was sombre—almost black. The movement of the woman was stately, and the effect of the torch-light on the face was sinister.

"It arrested me, and he stood by civilly, holding an empty half-pint champagne bottle (medical comforts) with the candle stuck in it. To my question he said Mr. Kurtz had painted this—in this very station more than a year ago—while waiting for means to go to his trading-post. 'Tell me, pray,' said I, 'who is this Mr. Kurtz?'

60 "'The chief of the Inner Station,' he answered in a short tone, looking away. 'Much obliged,' I said, laughing. 'And you are the brickmaker of the Central Station. Everyone knows that.' He was silent for a while. 'He is a prodigy,' he said at last. 'He is an emissary of pity, and science, and progress, and devil knows what else. We want,' he began to declaim suddenly, 'for the guidance of the cause intrusted to us by Europe, so to speak, higher intelligence, wide sympathies, a singleness of purpose.' 'Who says that?' I asked. 'Lots of them,' he replied. 'Some even write that; and so *he* comes here, a special being, as you ought to know.' 'Why ought I to know?' I interrupted, really surprised. He paid no attention. 'Yes. To-day he is chief of the best station, next year he will be assistant-manager, two years more and . . . but I daresay you know what he will be in two years' time. You are of the new gang—the gang of virtue. The same people who sent him specially also recommended you. Oh, don't say no. I've my own eyes to trust.' Light dawned upon me. My dear aunt's influential acquaintances were producing an unexpected effect upon that young man. I nearly burst into a laugh. 'Do you read the Company's confidential correspondence?' I asked. He hadn't a word to say. It was great fun. 'When Mr. Kurtz,' I continued, severely, 'is General Manager, you won't have the opportunity.'

"He blew the candle out suddenly, and we went outside. The moon had risen. Black figures strolled about listlessly, pouring water on the glow, whence proceeded a sound of hissing; steam ascended in the moonlight, the beaten nigger groaned somewhere. 'What a row the brute makes!' said the indefatigable man with the moustaches, appearing near us. 'Serve him right. Transgression—punishment—bang! Pitiless, pitiless. That's the only way. This will prevent all conflagrations for the future. I was just telling the manager . . .' He noticed my companion, and became crestfallen all at once. 'Not in bed yet,' he said, with a kind of servile heartiness; 'it's so natural. Ha! Danger—agitation.' He vanished. I went on to the river-side and the other followed me. I heard a scathing murmur at my ear. 'Heap of muffs—go to.' The pilgrims could be seen in knots gesticulating, discussing. Several had still their staves in their hands. I verily believe they took these sticks to bed with them. Beyond the fence the forest stood up spectrally in the moonlight, and through the dim stir, through the faint sounds of that lamentable courtyard, the silence of the land went home to one's very heart—its mystery, its greatness, the amazing reality of its concealed life. The hurt nigger moaned feebly somewhere near by, and then fetched a deep sigh that made me mend my pace away from there. I felt a hand introducing itself under my arm. 'My dear sir,' said the fellow. 'I don't want to be misunderstood, and especially by you, who will see Mr. Kurtz long before I can have that pleasure. I wouldn't like him to get a false idea of my disposition. . . .'

"I let him run on, this papier-maché Mephistopheles, and it seemed to me that if I tried I could poke my forefinger through him, and would find nothing inside but a little loose dirt, maybe. He, don't you see, had been planning to be assistant-manager by-and-by under the present man, and I could see that the coming of that Kurtz had upset them both not a little. He talked precipitately, and I did not try to stop him. I had my shoulders against the wreck of my steamer, hauled up on the slope like a carcass of some big river animal. The smell of mud, of primeval mud, by Jove! was in my nostrils, the high stillness of primeval forest was before my eyes; there were shiny patches on the black creek. The moon had spread over every-thing a thin layer of silver—over the rank grass, over the mud, upon the wall of matted vegetation standing higher than the wall of a temple, over the great river I could see through a sombre gap glittering, glittering, as it flowed broadly by with-out a murmur. All this was great, expectant, mute, while the man jabbered about himself. I wondered whether the stillness on the face of the immensity looking at us two were meant as an appeal or as a menace. What were we who had strayed in here? Could we handle that dumb thing, or would it handle us? I felt how big, how confoundly big, was that thing that couldn't talk, and perhaps was deaf as well. What was in there? I could see a little ivory coming out from there, and I had heard Mr. Kurtz was in there. I had heard enough about it, too—God knows! Yet some-how it didn't bring any image with it—no more than if I had been told an angel or a fiend was in there. I believed it in the same way one of you might believe there are inhabitants in the planet Mars. I knew once a Scotch sailmaker who was cer-tain, dead sure, there were people in Mars. If you asked him for some idea how they looked and behaved, he would get shy and mutter something about 'walking on all-fours.' If you as much as smiled, he would—though a man of sixty—offer to fight you. I would not have gone so far as to fight for Kurtz, but I went for him near enough to a lie. You know I hate, detest, and can't bear a lie, not because I am straighter than the rest of us, but simply because it appalls me. There is a taint of death, a flavour of mortality in lies—which is exactly what I hate and detest in the world—what I want to forget. It makes me miserable and sick, like biting some-thing rotten would do. Temperament, I suppose. Well, I went near enough to it by letting the young fool there believe anything he liked to imagine as to my influence in Europe. I became in an instant as much of a pretence as the rest of the bewitched pilgrims. This simply because I had a notion it somehow would be of help to that Kurtz whom at the time I did not see—you understand. He was just a word for me. I did not see the man in the name any more than you do. Do you see him? Do you see the story? Do you see anything? It seems to me I am trying to tell you a dream—making a vain attempt, because no relation of a dream can convey the dream-sensation, that commingling of absurdity, surprise, and bewilderment in a tremor of struggling revolt, that notion of being captured by the incredible which is of the very essence of dreams. . . ."

He was silent for a while.

". . . No, it is impossible; it is impossible to convey the life-sensation of any given epoch of one's existence—that which makes its truth, its meaning—its subtle and penetrating essence. It is impossible. We live, as we dream—alone. . . ."

He paused again as if reflecting, then added—

"Of course in this you fellows see more than I could then. You see me now, whom you know. . . ."

It had become so pitch dark that we listeners could hardly see one another. For a long time already he, sitting apart, had been no more to us than a voice. There was not a word from anybody. The others might have been asleep, but I was awake. I listened. I listened on the watch for the sentence, for the word, that would give me the clue to the faint uneasiness inspired by this narrative that seemed to shape itself without human lips in the heavy night-air of the river.

". . . Yes—I let him run on," Marlow began again, "and think what he pleased about the powers that were behind me. I did! And there was nothing behind me! There was nothing but that wretched, old, mangled steamboat I was leaning against, while he talked fluently about 'the necessity for every man to get on.' 'And when one comes out here, you conceive, it is not to gaze at the moon.' Mr. Kurtz was a 'universal genius,' but even a genius would find it easier to work with 'adequate tools—intelligent men.' He did not make bricks—why, there was a physical impossibility in the way—as I was well aware; and if he did secretarial work for the manager, it was because 'no sensible man rejects wantonly the confidence of his superiors.' Did I see it? I saw it. What more did I want? What I really wanted was rivets, by heaven! Rivets. To get on with the work—to stop the hole. Rivets I wanted. There were cases of them down at the coast—cases—piled up—burst—split! You kicked a loose rivet at every second step in that station yard on the hillside. Rivets had rolled into the grove of death. You could fill your pockets with rivets for the trouble of stooping down—and there wasn't one rivet to be found where it was wanted. We had plates that would do, but nothing to fasten them with. And every week the messenger, a lone negro, letter-bag on shoulder and staff in hand, left our station for the coast. And several times a week a coast caravan came in with trade goods—ghastly glazed calico that made you shudder only to look at it, glass beads value about a penny a quart, confounded spotted cotton handkerchiefs. And no rivets. Three carriers could have brought all that was wanted to see that steamboat afloat.

"He was becoming confidential now, but I fancy my unresponsive attitude must have exasperated him at last, for he judged it necessary to inform me he feared neither God nor the devil, let alone any mere man. I said I could see that very well, but what I wanted was a certain quantity of rivets—and rivets were what really Mr. Kurtz wanted, if he had only known it. Now letters went to the coast every week. . . . 'My dear sir,' he cried, 'I write from dictation.' I demanded rivets. There was a way—for an intelligent man. He changed his manner; became very cold, and suddenly began to talk about a hippopotamus; wondered whether sleeping on board the steamer (I stuck to my salvage night and day) I wasn't disturbed. There was an old hippo that had the bad habit of getting out on the bank and roaming at night over the station grounds. The pilgrims used to turn out in a body and empty every rifle they could lay hands on at him. Some even had sat up o'nights for him. All this energy was wasted, though. 'That animal has a charmed life,' he said; 'but you can say this only of brutes in this country. No man—you apprehend me?—no man here bears a charmed life.' He stood there for a moment in the moonlight with his delicate hooked nose set a little askew, and his mica eyes glittering without a wink, then, with a curt Good-night, he strode off. I could see he was disturbed and considerably puzzled, which made me feel more hopeful than I had been for days. It was a great comfort to turn from that chap to my influential friend, the battered, twisted, ruined, tin-pot steamboat. I clambered on board. She rang under my feet like an empty Huntley & Palmer biscuit-tin kicked along a gutter; she was nothing so solid in make, and rather less pretty in shape, but I had expended enough hard work on her to make me love her. No influential friend would have served me better. She had given me a chance to come out a bit—to find out what I could do. No, I don't like work. I had rather laze about and think of all the fine things that can be done. I don't like work—no man does—but I like what is in the work,—the chance to find yourself. Your own reality—for yourself, not for others—what no other man can ever know. They can only see the mere show, and never can tell what it really means.

"I was not surprised to see somebody sitting aft, on the deck, with his legs dangling over the mud. You see I rather chummed with the few mechanics there were in that station, whom the other pilgrims naturally despised—on account of their imperfect manners, I suppose. This was the foreman—a boiler-maker by trade—a good worker. He was a lank, bony, yellow-faced man, with big intense eyes. His aspect was worried, and his head was as bald as the palm of my hand; but his hair in falling seemed to have stuck to his chin, and had prospered in the new locality, for his beard hung down to his waist. He was a widower with six young children (he had left them in charge of a sister of his to come out there), and the passion of his life was pigeon-flying. He was an enthusiast and a connoisseur. He would rave about pigeons. After work hours he used sometimes to come over from his hut for a talk about his children and his pigeons; at work, when he had to crawl in the mud under the bottom of the steamboat, he would tie up that beard of his in a kind of white serviette he brought for the purpose. It had loops to go over his ears. In the evening he could be seen squatted on the bank rinsing that wrapper in the creek with great care, then spreading it solemnly on a bush to dry.

"I slapped him on the back and shouted 'We shall have rivets!' He scrambled to his feet exclaiming 'No! Rivets!' as though he couldn't believe his ears. Then in a low voice, 'You . . . eh?' I don't know why we behaved like lunatics. I put my finger to the side of my nose and nodded mysteriously. 'Good for you!' he cried, snapped his fingers above his head, lifting one foot. I tried a jig. We capered on the iron deck. A frightful clatter came out of that hulk, and the virgin forest on the other bank of the creek sent it back in a thundering roll upon the sleeping station. It must have made some of the pilgrims sit up in their hovels. A dark figure obscured the lighted doorway of the manager's hut, vanished, then, a second or so after, the doorway itself vanished, too. We stopped, and the silence driven away by the stamping of our feet flowed back again from the recesses of the land. The great wall of vegetation, an exuberant and entangled mass of trunks, branches, leaves, boughs, festoons, motionless in the moonlight, was like a rioting invasion of soundless life, a rolling wave of plants, piled up, crested, ready to topple over the creek, to sweep every little man of us out of his little existence. And it moved not. A deadened burst of mighty splashes and snorts reached us from afar, as though an ichthyosaurus had been taking a bath of glitter in the great river. 'After all,' said the boiler-maker in a reasonable tone, 'why shouldn't we get the rivets?' Why not, indeed! I did not know of any reason why we shouldn't. 'They'll come in three weeks,' I said, confidently.

"But they didn't. Instead of rivets there came an invasion, an infliction, a visitation. It came in sections during the next three weeks, each section headed by a donkey carrying a white man in new clothes and tan shoes, bowing from that elevation right and left to the impressed pilgrims. A quarrelsome band of footsore sulky niggers trod on the heels of the donkey; a lot of tents, campstools, tin boxes, white cases, brown bales would be shot down in the courtyard, and the air of mystery would deepen a little over the muddle of the station. Five such installments came, with their absurd air of disorderly flight with the loot of innumerable outfit shops and provision stores, that, one would think, they were lugging, after a raid, into the wilderness for equitable division. It was an inextricable mess of things decent in themselves but that human folly made look like spoils of thieving.

"This devoted band called itself the Eldorado Exploring Expedition, and I believe they were sworn to secrecy. Their talk, however, was the talk of sordid buccaneers: it was reckless without hardihood, greedy without audacity, and cruel without courage; there was not an atom of foresight or of serious intention in the whole batch of them, and they did not seem aware these things are wanted for the work of the world. To tear treasure out of the bowels of the land was their desire, with no more moral purpose at the back of it than there is in burglars breaking into a safe. Who paid the expenses of the noble enterprise I don't know; but the uncle of our manager was leader of that lot.

"In exterior he resembled a butcher in a poor neighbourhood, and his eyes had a look of sleepy cunning. He carried his fat paunch with ostentation on his short legs, and during the time his gang infested the station spoke to no one but his nephew. You could see these two roaming about all day long with their heads together in an everlasting confab.

75   "I had given up worrying myself about the rivets. One's capacity for that kind of folly is more limited than you would suppose. I said Hang!—and let things slide. I had plenty of time for meditation, and now and then I would give some thought to Kurtz. I wasn't very interested in him. No. Still, I was curious to see whether this man, who had come out equipped with moral ideas of some sort, would climb to the top after all and how he would set about his work when there."

2

"One evening as I was lying flat on the deck of my steamboat, I heard voices approaching—and there were the nephew and the uncle strolling along the bank. I laid my head on my arm again, and had nearly lost myself in a doze, when somebody said in my ear, as it were: 'I am as harmless as a little child, but I don't like to be dictated to. Am I the manager—or am I not? I was ordered to send him there. It's incredible.' . . . I became aware that the two were standing on the shore alongside the forepart of the steamboat, just below my head. I did not move; it did not occur to me to move: I was sleepy. 'It *is* unpleasant,' grunted the uncle. 'He has asked the Administration to be sent there,' said the other, 'with the idea of showing what he could do; and I was instructed accordingly. Look at the influence that man must have. Is it not frightful?' They both agreed it was frightful, then made several bizarre remarks:

'Make rain and fine weather—one man—the Council—by the nose'—bits of absurd sentences that got the better of my drowsiness, so that I had pretty near the whole of my wits about me when the uncle said, 'The climate may do away with this difficulty for you. Is he alone there?' 'Yes,' answered the manager; 'he sent his assistant down the river with a note to me in these terms: "Clear this poor devil out of the country, and don't bother sending more of that sort. I had rather be alone than have the kind of men you can dispose of with me." It was more than a year ago. Can you imagine such impudence!' 'Anything since then?' asked the other, hoarsely. 'Ivory,' jerked the nephew; 'lots of it—prime sort—lots—most annoying, from him.' 'And with that?' questioned the heavy rumble. 'Invoice,' was the reply fired out, so to speak. Then silence. They had been talking about Kurtz.

"I was broad awake by this time, but, lying perfectly at ease, remained still, having no inducement to change my position. 'How did that ivory come all this way?' growled the elder man, who seemed very vexed. The other explained that it had come with a fleet of canoes in charge of an English half-caste clerk Kurtz had with him; that Kurtz had apparently intended to return himself, the station being by that time bare of goods and stores, but after coming three hundred miles, had suddenly decided to go back, which he started to do alone in a small dugout with four paddlers, leaving the half-caste to continue down the river with the ivory. The two fellows there seemed astounded at anybody attempting such a thing. They were at a loss for an adequate motive. As to me, I seemed to see Kurtz for the first time. It was a distinct glimpse; the dugout, four paddling savages, and the lone white man turning his back suddenly on the headquarters, on relief, on thoughts of home—perhaps; setting his face towards the depths of the wilderness, towards his empty and desolate station. I did not know the motive. Perhaps he was just simply a fine fellow who stuck to his work for its own sake. His name, you understand, had not been pronounced once. He was 'that man.' The half-caste, who, as far as I could see, had conducted a difficult trip with great prudence and pluck, was invariably alluded to as 'that scoundrel.' The 'scoundrel' had reported that the 'man' had been very ill—had recovered imperfectly. . . . The two below me moved away then a few paces, and strolled back and forth at some little distance. I heard: 'Military post—doctor—two hundred miles—quite alone now—unavoidable, delays—nine months—no news—strange rumours.' They approached again, just as the manager was saying, 'No one, as far as I know, unless a species of wandering trader—a pestilential fellow, snapping ivory from the natives.' Who was it they were talking about now? I gathered in snatches that this was some man supposed to be in Kurtz's district, and of whom the manager did not approve. 'We will not be free from unfair competition till one of these fellows is hanged for an example,' he said. 'Certainly,' grunted the other; 'get him hanged! Why not? Anything—anything can be done in this country. That's what I say; nobody here, you understand, *here,* can endanger your position. And why? You stand the climate—you outlast them all. The danger is in Europe; but there before I left I took care to————' They moved off and whispered, then their voices rose again. 'The extraordinary series of delays is not my fault. I did my best.' The fat man sighed. 'Very sad.' 'And the pestiferous absurdity of his talk,' continued the other; 'he bothered me enough when he was here. "Each station should be like a beacon on the road towards better things, a centre for trade of course, but also for humanizing, improving, instructing." Conceive you—that ass! And he wants to be manager! No, it's——' Here he got choked by excessive indignation, and I lifted my head the least bit. I was surprised to see how near they were—right under me. I could have spat upon their hats. They were looking on the ground, absorbed in thought. The manager was switching his leg with a slender twig: his sagacious relative lifted his head. 'You have been well since you came out this time?' he asked. The other gave a start. 'Who? I? Oh! Like a charm—like a charm. But the rest—oh, my goodness! All sick. They die so quick, too, that I haven't the time to send them out of the country—it's incredible!' 'H'm. Just so,' grunted the uncle. 'Ah! my boy, trust to this—I say, trust to this.' I saw him extend his short flipper of an arm for a gesture that took in the forest, the creek, the mud, the river,—seemed to beckon with a dishonouring flourish before the sunlit face of the land a treacherous appeal to the lurking death, to the hidden evil, to the profound darkness of its heart. It was so startling that I leaped to my feet and looked back at the edge of the forest, as though I had expected an answer of some sort to that black display of confidence. You know the foolish notions that come to one sometimes. The high stillness confronted these two figures with its ominous patience, waiting for the passing away of a fantastic invasion.

"They swore aloud together—out of sheer fright, I believe—then pretending not to know anything of my existence, turned back to the station. The sun was low; and leaning forward side by side, they seemed to be tugging painfully uphill their two ridiculous shadows of unequal length, that trailed behind them slowly over the tall grass without bending a single blade.

"In a few days the Eldorado Expedition went into the patient wilderness, that closed upon it as the sea closes over a diver. Long afterwards the news came that all the donkeys were dead. I know nothing as to the fate of the less valuable animals. They, no doubt, like the rest of us, found what they deserved. I did not inquire. I was then rather excited at the prospect of meeting Kurtz very soon. When I say very soon I mean it comparatively. It was just two months from the day we left the creek when we came to the bank below Kurtz's station.

80   "Going up that river was like travelling back to the earliest beginnings of the world, when vegetation rioted on the earth and the big trees were kings. An empty stream, a great silence, an impenetrable forest. The air was warm, thick, heavy, sluggish. There was no joy in the brilliance of sunshine. The long stretches of the waterway ran on, deserted, into the gloom of overshadowed distances. On silvery sandbanks hippos and alligators sunned themselves side by side. The broadening waters flowed through a mob of wooded islands; you lost your way on that river as you would in a desert, and butted all day long against shoals, trying to find the channel, till you thought yourself bewitched and cut off for ever from everything you had known once—somewhere—far away—in another existence perhaps. There were moments when one's past came back to one, as it will sometimes when you have not a moment to spare to yourself; but it came in the shape of an unrestful and noisy dream, remembered with wonder amongst the overwhelming realities of this strange world of plants, and water, and silence. And this stillness of life did not in the least resemble a peace. It was the stillness of an implacable force brooding over an

inscrutable intention. It looked at you with a vengeful aspect. I got used to it after-wards; I did not see it any more; I had no time. I had to keep guessing at the chan-nel; I had to discern, mostly by inspiration, the signs of hidden banks; I watched for sunken stones; I was learning to clap my teeth smartly before my heart flew out, when I shaved by a fluke some infernal sly old snag that would have ripped the life out of the tin-pot steamboat and drowned all the pilgrims; I had to keep a look-out for the signs of dead wood we could cut up in the night for next day's steaming. When you have to attend to things of that sort, to the mere incidents of the surface, the reality—the reality, I tell you—fades. The inner truth is hidden—luckily, luckily. But I felt it all the same; I felt often its mysterious stillness watching me at my mon-key tricks, just as it watches you fellows performing on your respective tight-ropes for—what is it? half a-crown a tumble————"

"Try to be civil, Marlow," growled a voice, and I knew there was at least one lis-tener awake besides myself.

"I beg your pardon. I forgot the heartache which makes up the rest of the price. And indeed what does the price matter, if the trick be well done? You do your tricks very well. And I didn't do badly either, since I managed not to sink that steamboat on my first trip. It's a wonder to me yet. Imagine a blindfolded man set to drive a van over a bad road. I sweated and shivered over that business considerably, I can tell you. After all, for a seaman, to scrape the bottom of the thing that's supposed to float all the time under his care is the unpardonable sin. No one may know of it, but you never forget the thump—eh? A blow on the very heart. You remember it, you dream of it, you wake up at night and think of it—years after—and go hot and cold all over. I don't pretend to say that steamboat floated all the time. More than once she had to wade for a bit, with twenty cannibals splashing around and pushing. We had enlisted some of these chaps on the way for a crew. Fine fellows—cannibals—in their place. They were men one could work with, and I am grateful to them. And, after all, they did not eat each other before my face: they had brought along a provision of hippo-meat which went rotten, and made the mystery of the wilderness stink in my nos-trils. Phoo! I can sniff it now. I had the manager on board and three or four pilgrims with their staves—all complete. Sometimes we came upon a station close by the bank, clinging to the skirts of the unknown, and the white men rushing out of a tum-bledown hovel, with great gestures of joy and surprise and welcome, seemed very strange—had the appearance of being held there captive by a spell. The word ivory would ring in the air for a while—and on we went again into the silence, along empty reaches, round the still bends, between the high walls of our winding way, re-verberating in hollow claps the ponderous beat of the stern-wheel. Trees, trees, mil-lions of trees, massive, immense, running up high; and at their foot, hugging the bank against the stream, crept the little begrimed steamboat, like a sluggish beetle crawling on the floor of a lofty portico. It made you feel very small, very lost, and yet it was not altogether depressing, that feeling. After all, if you were small, the grimy beetle crawled on—which was just what you wanted it to do. Where the pil-grims imagined it crawled to I don't know. To some place where they expected to get something. I bet! For me it crawled towards Kurtz—exclusively; but when the steam-pipes started leaking we crawled very slow. The reaches opened before us and closed behind, as if the forest had stepped leisurely across the water to bar the way for our return. We penetrated deeper and deeper into the heart of darkness. It was very quiet there. At night sometimes the roll of drums behind the curtain of trees would run up the river and remain sustained faintly, as if hovering in the air high over our heads, till the first break of day. Whether it meant war, peace, or prayer we could not tell. The dawns were heralded by the descent of a chill stillness; the wood-cutters slept, their fires burned low; the snapping of a twig would make you start. We were wanderers on prehistoric earth, on an earth that wore the aspect of an unknown planet. We could have fancied ourselves the first of men taking possession of an ac-cursed inheritance, to be subdued at the cost of profound anguish and of excessive toil. But suddenly, as we struggled round a bend, there would be a glimpse of rush walls, of peaked grass-roofs, a burst of yells, a whirl of black limbs, a mass of hands clapping, of feet stamping, of bodies swaying, of eyes rolling, under the droop of heavy and motionless foliage. The steamer toiled along slowly on the edge of a black and incomprehensible frenzy. The prehistoric man was cursing us, praying to us, welcoming us—who could tell? We were cut off from the comprehension of our sur-roundings; we glided past like phantoms, wondering and secretly appalled, as sane men would be before an enthusiastic outbreak in a madhouse. We could not under-stand because we were too far and could not remember, because we were travelling in the night of first ages, of those ages that are gone, leaving hardly a sign—and no memories.

"The earth seemed unearthly. We are accustomed to look upon the shackled form of a conquered monster, but there—there you could look at a thing monstrous and free. It was unearthly, and the men were——No, they were not inhuman. Well, you know, that was the worst of it—this suspicion of their not being inhuman. It would come slowly to one. They howled and leaped, and spun, and made horrid faces; but what thrilled you was just the thought of their humanity—like yours—the thought of your remote kinship with this wild and passionate uproar. Ugly. Yes, it was ugly enough; but if you were man enough you would admit to yourself that there was in you just the faintest trace of a response to the terrible frankness of that noise, a dim suspicion of there being a meaning in it which you—you so remote from the night of first ages—could comprehend. And why not? The mind of man is capable of anything—because everything is in it, all the past as well as all the future. What was there after all? Joy, fear, sorrow, devotion, valour, rage—who can tell?—but truth—truth stripped of its cloak of time. Let the fool gape and shudder—the man knows, and can look on without a wink. But he must at least be as much of a man as these on the shore. He must meet that truth with his own true stuff—with his own in-born strength. Principles won't do. Acquisitions, clothes, pretty rags—rags that would fly off at the first good shake. No; you want a deliberate belief. An appeal to me in this fiendish row—is there? Very well; I hear; I admit, but I have a voice, too, and for good or evil mine is the speech that cannot be silenced. Of course, a fool, what with sheer fright and fine sentiments, is always safe. Who's that grunting? You wonder I didn't go ashore for a howl and a dance? Well, no—I didn't. Fine senti-ments, you say? Fine sentiments, be hanged! I had not time. I had to mess about with white-lead and strips of woollen blanket helping to put bandages on those leaky steampipes—I tell you. I had to watch the steering, and circumvent those snags, and get the tin-pot along by hook or by crook. There was surface-truth enough in these things to save a wiser man. And between whiles I had to look after the savage who was fireman. He was an improved specimen; he could fire up a vertical boiler. He was there below me, and, upon my word, to look at him was as edifying as seeing a dog in a parody of breeches and a feather hat, walking on his hind-legs. A few months of training had done for that really fine chap. He squinted at the steam-gauge and at the water-gauge with an evident effort of intrepidity—and he had filed teeth, too, the poor devil, and the wool of his pate shaved into queer patterns, and three ornamental scars on each of his cheeks. He ought to have been clapping his hands and stamping his feet on the bank, instead of which he was hard at work, a thrall to strange witchcraft, full of improving knowledge. He was useful because he had been instructed; and what he knew was this—that should the water in that transparent thing disappear, the evil spirit inside the boiler would get angry through the greatness of his thirst, and take a terrible vengeance. So he sweated and fired up and watched the glass fearfully (with an impromptu charm, made of rags, tied to his arm, and a piece of polished bone, as big as a watch, stuck flatways through his lower lip), while the wooded banks slipped past us slowly, the short noise was left behind, the interminable miles of silence—and we crept on, towards Kurtz. But the snags were thick, the water was teacherous and shallow, the boiler seemed indeed to have a sulky devil in it, and thus neither that fireman nor I had any time to peer into our creepy thoughts.

"Some fifty miles below the Inner Station we came upon a hut of reeds, an inclined and melancholy pole, with the unrecognizable tatters of what had been a flag of some sort flying from it, and a neatly stacked wood-pile. This was unexpected. We came to the bank, and on the stack of firewood found a flat piece of board with some faded pencil-writing on it. When deciphered it said: 'Wood for you. Hurry up. Approach cautiously.' There was a signature, but it was illegible—not Kurtz—a much longer word. Hurry up. Where? Up the river? 'Approach cautiously.' We had not done so. But the warning could not have been meant for the place where it could be only found after approach. Something was wrong above. But what—and how much? That was the question. We commented adversely upon the imbecility of that telegraphic style. The bush around said nothing, and would not let us look very far, either. A torn curtain of red twill hung in the doorway of the hut, and flapped sadly in our faces. The dwelling was dismantled; but we could see a white man had lived there not very long ago. There remained a rude table—a plank on two posts; a heap of rubbish reposed in a dark corner, and by the door I picked up a book. It had lost its covers, and the pages had been thumbed into a state of extremely dirty softness; but the back had been lovingly stitched afresh with white cotton thread, which looked clean yet. It was an extraordinary find. Its title was, *An Inquiry into some Points of Seamanship,* by a man Tower, Towson—some such name—Master in his Majesty's Navy. The matter looked dreary reading enough, with illustrative diagrams and repulsive tables of figures, and the copy was sixty years old. I handled this amazing antiquity with the greatest possible tenderness, lest it should dissolve in my hands. Within, Towson or Towser was inquiring earnestly into the breaking strain of ships' chains and tackle, and other such matters. Not a very enthralling book; but at the first glance you could see there a singleness of intention, an honest concern for the right way of going to work, which made these humble pages, thought out so many years ago, luminous with another than a professional light. The simple old sailor, with his talk of chains and purchases, made me forget the jungle and the pilgrims in a delicious sensation of having come upon something unmistakably real. Such a book being there was wonderful enough; but still more astounding were the notes pencilled in the margin, and plainly referring to the text. I couldn't believe my eyes! They were in cipher! Yes, it looked like cipher. Fancy a man lugging with him a book of that description into this nowhere and studying it—and making notes—in cipher at that! It was an extravagant mystery.

85   "I had been dimly aware for some time of a worrying noise, and when I lifted my eyes I saw the wood-pile was gone, and the manager, aided by all the pilgrims, was shouting at me from the river-side. I slipped the book into my pocket. I assure you to leave off reading was like tearing myself away from the shelter of an old and solid friendship.

"I started the lame engine ahead. 'It must be this miserable trader—this intruder,' exclaimed the manager, looking back malevolently at the place we had left. 'He must be English,' I said. 'It will not save him from getting into trouble if he is not careful,' muttered the manager darkly. I observed with assumed innocence that no man was safe from trouble in this world.

"The current was more rapid now, the steamer seemed at her last gasp, the stern-wheel flopped languidly, and I caught myself listening on tiptoe for the next beat of the boat, for in sober truth I expected the wretched thing to give up every moment. It was like watching the last flickers of a life. But still we crawled. Sometimes I would pick out a tree a little way ahead to measure our progress towards Kurtz by, but I lost it invariably before we got abreast. To keep the eyes so long on one thing was too much for human patience. The manager displayed a beautiful resignation. I fretted and fumed and took to arguing with myself whether or no I would talk openly with Kurtz; but before I could come to any conclusion it occurred to me that my speech or my silence, indeed any action of mine, would be a mere futility. What did it matter what any one knew or ignored? What did it matter who was manager? One gets sometimes such a flash of insight. The essentials of this affair lay deep under the surface, beyond my reach, and beyond my power of meddling.

"Towards the evening of the second day we judged ourselves about eight miles from Kurtz's station. I wanted to push on; but the manager looked grave, and told me the navigation up there was so dangerous that it would be advisable, the sun being very low already, to wait where we were till next morning. Moreover, he pointed out that if the warning to approach cautiously were to be followed, we must approach in daylight—not at dusk, or in the dark. This was sensible enough. Eight miles meant nearly three hours' steaming for us, and I could also see suspicious ripples at the upper end of the reach. Nevertheless, I was annoyed beyond expression at the delay, and most unreasonably, too, since one night more could not matter much after so many months. As we had plenty of wood, and caution was the word, I brought up in the middle of the stream. The reach was narrow, straight, and had high sides like a railway cutting. The dusk came gliding into it long before the sun had set. The current ran smooth and swift, but a dumb immobility sat on the banks. The living trees, lashed together by the creepers and every living bush of the undergrowth, might have been changed into stone, even to the slenderest twig, to the lightest leaf. It was not sleep—it seemed unnatural, like a state of trance. Not the faintest sound of any kind could be heard. You looked on amazed, and began to suspect yourself of being deaf—then the night came suddenly, and struck you blind as well. About three in the morning some large fish leaped, and the loud splash made me jump as though a gun had been fired. When the sun rose there was a white fog, very warm and clammy, and more blinding than the night. It did not shift or drive; it was just there, standing all round you like something solid. At eight or nine, perhaps, it lifted as a shutter lifts. We had a glimpse of the towering multitude of trees, of the immense matted jungle, with the blazing little ball of the sun hanging over it—all perfectly still—and then the white shutter came down again, smoothly, as if sliding in greased grooves. I ordered the chain, which we had begun to heave in, to be paid out again. Before it stopped running with a muffled rattle, a cry, a very loud cry, as of infinite desolation, soared slowly in the opaque air. It ceased. A complaining clamour, modulated in savage discords, filled our ears. The sheer unexpectedness of it made my hair stir under my cap. I don't know how it struck the others; to me it seemed as though the mist itself had screamed, so suddenly, and apparently from all sides at once, did this tumultuous and mournful uproar arise. It culminated in a hurried outbreak of almost intolerably excessive shrieking, which stopped short, leaving us stiffened in a variety of silly attitudes, and obstinately listening to the nearly as appalling and excessive silence. 'Good God! What is the meaning————' stammered at my elbow one of the pilgrims,—a little fat man, with sandy hair and red whiskers, who wore sidespring boots, and pink pyjamas tucked into his socks. Two others remained open-mouthed a whole minute, then dashed into the little cabin, to rush out incontinently and stand darting scared glances, with Winchesters at 'ready' in their hands. What we could see was just the steamer we were on, her outlines blurred as though she had been on the point of dissolving, and a misty strip of water, perhaps two feet broad, around her—and that was all. The rest of the world was nowhere, as far as our eyes and ears were concerned. Just nowhere. Gone, disappeared; swept off without leaving a whisper or a shadow behind.

"I went forward, and ordered the chain to be hauled in short, so as to be ready to trip the anchor and move the steamboat at once if necessary. 'Will they attack?' whispered an awed voice. 'We will be all butchered in this fog,' murmured another. The faces twitched with the strain, the hands trembled slightly, the eyes forgot to wink. It was very curious to see the contrast of expressions of the white men and of the black fellows of our crew, who were as much strangers to that part of the river as we, though their homes were only eight hundred miles away. The whites, of course greatly discomposed, had besides a curious look of being painfully shocked by such an outrageous row. The others had an alert, naturally interested expression; but their faces were essentially quiet, even those of the one or two who grinned as they hauled at the chain. Several exchanged short, grunting phrases, which seemed to settle the matter to their satisfaction. Their headman, a young, broad-chested black, severely draped in dark-blue fringed cloths, with fierce nostrils and his hair all done up art-fully in oily ringlets, stood near me. 'Aha!' I said, just for good fellowship's sake. 'Catch 'im,' he snapped, with a bloodshot widening of his eyes and a flash of sharp teeth—'catch 'im. Give 'im to us.' 'To you, eh?' I asked; 'what would you do with them?' 'Eat 'im!' he said, curtly, and, leaning his elbow on the rail, looked out into the fog in a dignified and profoundly pensive attitude. I would no doubt have been properly horrified, had it not occurred to me that he and his chaps must be very hungry: that they must have been growing increasingly hungry for at least this month past. They had been engaged for six months (I don't think a single one of them had any clear idea of time, as we at the end of countless ages have. They still belonged to the beginnings of time—had no inherited experience to teach them as it were), and of course, as long as there was a piece of paper written over in accordance with some farcical law or other made down the river, it didn't enter anybody's head to trouble how they would live. Certainly they had brought with them some rotten hippo-meat, which couldn't have lasted very long, anyway, even if the pilgrims hadn't, in the midst of a shocking hullabaloo, thrown a considerable quantity of it overboard. It looked like a high-handed proceeding; but it was really a case of legitimate self-defence. You can't breathe dead hippo waking, sleeping, and eating, and at the same time keep your precarious grip on existence. Besides that, they had given them every week three pieces of brass wire, each about nine inches long; and the theory was they were to buy their provisions with that currency in river-side villages. You can see how *that* worked. There were either no villages, or the people were hostile, or the director, who like the rest of us fed out of tins, with an occasional old he-goat thrown in, didn't want to stop the steamer for some more or less recondite reason. So, unless they swallowed the wire itself, or made loops of it to snare the fishes with, I don't see what good their extravagant salary could be to them. I must say it was paid with a regularity worthy of a large and honourable trading company. For the rest, the only thing to eat—though it didn't look eatable in the least—I saw in their possession was a few lumps of some stuff like half-cooked dough, of a dirty lavender colour, they kept wrapped in leaves, and now and then swallowed a piece of, but so small that it seemed done more for the looks of the thing than for any serious purpose of sustenance. Why in the name of all the gnawing devils of hunger they didn't go for us—they were thirty to five—and have a good tuck-in for once, amazes me now when I think of it. They were big powerful men, with not much capacity to weigh the consequences, with courage, with strength, even yet, though their skins were no longer glossy and their muscles no longer hard. And I saw that something restraining, one of those human secrets that baffle probability, had come into play there. I looked at them with a swift quickening of interest—not because it occurred to me I might be eaten by them before very long, though I own to you that just then I perceived—in a new light, as it were—how unwholesome the pilgrims looked, and I hoped, yes, I positively hoped, that my aspect was not so—what shall I say?—so—unappetizing: a touch of fantastic vanity which fitted well with the dream-sensation that pervaded all my days at that time. Perhaps I had a little fever, too. One can't live with one's finger everlasting on one's pulse. I had often 'a little fever,' or a little touch of other things—the playful paw-strokes of the wilderness, the preliminary trifling before the more serious onslaught which came in due course. Yes; I looked at them as you would on any human being, with a curiosity of their impulses, motives, capacities, weaknesses, when brought to the test of an inexorable physical necessity. Restraint! What possible restraint? Was it superstition, disgust, patience, fear—or some kind of primitive honour? No fear can stand up to hunger, no patience can wear it out, disgust simply does not exist where hunger is; and as to superstition, beliefs, and what you may call principles, they are less than chaff in a breeze. Don't you know that devilry of lingering starvation, its exasperating torment, its black thoughts, its sombre and brooding ferocity? Well, I do. It takes a man all his inborn strength to fight hunger properly. It's really easier to face bereavement, dishonour, and the perdition of one's soul—than this kind of prolonged hunger. Sad, but true. And these chaps, too, had no earthly reason for any kind of scruple. Restraint! I would just as soon have expected restraint from a hyena prowling amongst the corpses of a battlefield. But there was the fact facing me—the fact dazzling, to be seen, like the foam on the depths of the sea, like a ripple on an unfathomable enigma, a mystery greater—when I thought of it—than the curious, inexplicable note of desperate grief in this savage clamour that had swept by us on the river-bank, behind the blind whiteness of the fog.

"Two pilgrims were quarrelling in hurried whispers as to which bank. 'Left.' ⁹⁰ 'No, no; how can you? Right, right, of course.' 'It is very serious,' said the manager's voice behind me; 'I would be desolated if anything should happen to Mr. Kurtz before we came up.' I looked at him, and had not the slightest doubt he was sincere. He was just the kind of man who would wish to preserve appearances. That was his restraint. But when he muttered something about going on at once, I did not even take the trouble to answer him. I knew, and he knew, that it was impossible. Were we to let go our hold of the bottom, we would be absolutely in the air—in space. We wouldn't be able to tell where we were going to—whether up or down stream, or across—till we fetched against one bank or the other,—and then we wouldn't know at first which it was. Of course I made no move. I had no mind for a smash-up. You couldn't imagine a more deadly place for a shipwreck. Whether drowned at once or not, we were sure to perish speedily in one way or another. 'I authorize you to take all the risks,' he said, after a short silence. 'I refuse to take any,' I said, shortly; which was just the answer he expected, though its tone might have surprised him. 'Well, I must defer to your judgment. You are captain,' he said, with marked civility. I turned my shoulder to him in sign of my appreciation, and looked into the fog. How long would it last? It was the most hopeless look-out. The approach to this Kurtz grubbing for ivory in the wretched bush was beset by as many dangers as though he had been an enchanted princess sleeping in a fabulous castle. 'Will they attack, do you think?' asked the manager, in a confidential tone.

"I did not think they would attack, for several obvious reasons. The thick fog was one. If they left the bank in their canoes they would get lost in it, as we would be if we attempted to move. Still, I had also judged the jungle of both banks quite impenetrable—and yet eyes were in it, eyes that had seen us. The river-side bushes were certainly very thick; but the undergrowth behind was evidently penetrable. However, during the short lift I had seen no canoes anywhere in the reach—certainly not abreast of the steamer. But what made the idea of attack inconceivable to me was the nature of the noise—of the cries we had heard. They had not the fierce character boding of immediate hostile intention. Unexpected, wild, and violent as they had been, they had given me an irresistible impression of sorrow. The glimpse of the steamboat had for some reason filled those savages with unrestrained grief. The danger, if any, I expounded, was from our proximity to a great human passion let loose. Even extreme grief may ultimately vent itself in violence—but more generally takes the form of apathy. . . .

"You should have seen the pilgrims stare! They had no heart to grin, or even to revile me: but I believe they thought me gone mad—with fright, maybe. I delivered a regular lecture. My dear boys, it was no good bothering. Keep a look-out? Well, you may guess I watched the fog for the signs of lifting as a cat watches a mouse; but for anything else our eyes were of no more use to us than if we had been buried miles deep in a heap of cotton-wool. It felt like it, too—choking, warm, stifling. Besides, all I said, though it sounded extravagant, was absolutely true to fact. What we afterwards alluded to as an attack was really an attempt at repulse. The action was very far from being aggressive—it was not even defensive, in the usual sense: it was undertaken under the stress of desperation, and in its essence was purely protective.

"It developed itself, I should say, two hours after the fog lifted, and its commencement was at a spot, roughly speaking, about a mile and a half below Kurtz's station. We had just floundered and flopped round a bend, when I saw an islet, a mere grassy hummock of bright green, in the middle of the stream. It was the only thing of the kind; but as we opened the reach more, I perceived it was the head of a long sandbank, or rather of a chain of shallow patches stretching down the middle of the river. They were discoloured, just awash, and the whole lot was seen just under the water, exactly as a man's backbone is seen running down the middle of his back under the skin. Now, as far as I did see, I could go to the right or to the left of this. I didn't know either channel, of course. The banks looked pretty well alike, the depth appeared the same; but as I had been informed the station was on the west side, I naturally headed for the western passage.

"No sooner had we fairly entered it than I became aware it was much narrower than I had supposed. To the left of us there was the long uninterrupted shoal, and to the right a high, steep bank heavily overgrown with bushes. Above the bush the trees stood in serried ranks. The twigs overhung the current thickly, and from distance to distance a large limb of some tree projected rigidly over the stream. It was then well on in the afternoon, the face of the forest was gloomy, and a broad strip of shadow had already fallen on the water. In this shadow we steamed up—very slowly, as you may imagine. I sheered her well inshore—the water being deepest near the bank, as the sounding-pole informed me.

95   "One of my hungry and forebearing friends was sounding in the bows just below me. This steamboat was exactly like a decked scow. On the deck, there were two little teak-wood houses, with doors and windows. The boiler was in the fore-end, and the machinery right astern. Over the whole there was a light roof, supported on stanchions. The funnel projected through that roof, and in front of the funnel a small cabin built of light planks served for a pilot-house. It contained a

couch, two camp-stools, a loaded Martini-Henry leaning in one corner, a tiny table, and the steering-wheel. It had a wide door in front and a broad shutter at each side. All these were always thrown open, of course. I spent my days perched up there on the extreme fore-end of that roof, before the door. At night I slept, or tried to, on the couch. An athletic black belonging to some coast tribe, and educated by my poor predecessor, was the helmsman. He sported a pair of brass earrings, wore a blue cloth wrapper from the waist to the ankles, and thought all the world of himself. He was the most unstable kind of fool I had ever seen. He steered with no end of a swagger while you were by; but if he lost sight of you, he became instantly the prey of an abject funk, and would let that cripple of a steamboat get the upper hand of him in a minute.

"I was looking down at the sounding-pole, and feeling much annoyed to see at each try a little more of it stick out of that river, when I saw my poleman give up the business suddenly, and stretch himself flat on the deck, without even taking the trouble to haul his pole in. He kept hold on it though, and it trailed in the water. At the same time the fireman, whom I could also see below me, sat down abruptly before his furnace and ducked his head. I was amazed. Then I had to look at the river mighty quick, because there was a snag in the fairway. Sticks, little sticks, were flying about—thick: they were whizzing before my nose, dropping below me, striking behind me against my pilot-house. All this time the river, the shore, the woods, were very quiet—perfectly quiet. I could only hear the heavy splashing thump of the stern-wheel and the patter of these things. We cleared the snag clumsily. Arrows, by Jove! We were being shot at! I stepped in quickly to close the shutter on the land-side. That fool-helmsman, his hands on the spokes, was lifting his knees high, stamping his feet, champing his mouth, like a reined-in horse. Confound him! And we were staggering within ten feet of the bank. I had to lean right out to swing the heavy shutter, and I saw a face amongst the leaves on the level with my own, looking at me very fierce and steady; and then suddenly, as though a veil had been removed from my eyes, I made out, deep in the tangled gloom, naked breasts, arms, legs, glaring eyes,—the bush was swarming with human limbs in movement, glistening, of bronze colour. The twigs shook, swayed, and rustled, the arrows flew out of them, and then the shutter came to. 'Steer her straight,' I said to the helmsman. He held his head rigid, face forward; but his eyes rolled, he kept on, lifting and setting down his feet gently, his mouth foamed a little. 'Keep quiet!' I said in a fury. I might just as well have ordered a tree not to sway in the wind. I darted out. Below me there was a great scuffle of feet on the iron deck; confused exclamations; a voice screamed, 'Can you turn back?' I caught sight of a V-shaped ripple on the water ahead. What? Another snag! A fusillade burst out under my feet. The pilgrims had opened with their Winchesters and were simply squirting lead into that bush. A deuce of a lot of smoke came up and drove slowly forward. I swore at it. Now I couldn't see the ripple or the snag either. I stood in the doorway, peering, and the arrows came in swarms. They might have been poisoned, but they looked as though they wouldn't kill a cat. The bush began to howl. Our wood-cutters raised a warlike whoop; the report of a rifle just at my back deafened me. I glanced over my shoulder, and the pilot-house was yet full of noise and smoke when I made a dash at the wheel. The fool-nigger had dropped everything, to throw the shutter open and let off that Martini-Henry. He stood before the wide opening, glaring, and I yelled at him to come back, while I straightened the sudden twist out of that steamboat. There was no room to turn even if I had wanted to, the snag was somewhere very near ahead in that confounded smoke, there was no time to lose, so I just crowded her into the bank—right into the bank, where I knew the water was deep.

"We tore slowly along the overhanging bushes in a whirl of broken twigs and flying leaves. The fusillade below stopped short, as I had foreseen it would when the squirts got empty. I threw my head back to a glinting whizz that traversed the pilot-house, in at one shutter-hole and out at the other. Looking past that mad helmsman, who was shaking the empty rifle and yelling at the shore, I saw vague forms of men running bent double, leaping, gliding, distinct, incomplete, evanescent. Something big appeared in the air before the shutter, the rifle went overboard, and the man stepped back swiftly, looked at me over his shoulder in an extraordinary, profound, familiar manner, and fell upon my feet. The side of his head hit the wheel twice, and the end of what appeared a long cane clattered round and knocked over a little camp-stool. It looked as though after wrenching that thing from somebody ashore he had lost his balance in the effort. The thin smoke had blown away, we were clear of the snag, and looking ahead I could see that in another hundred yards or so I would be free to sheer off, away from the bank; but my feet felt so very warm and wet that I had to look down. The man had rolled on his back and stared straight up at me; both his hands clutched that cane. It was the shaft of a spear that, either thrown or lunged through the opening, had caught him in the side just below the ribs; the blade had gone in out of sight, after making a frightful gash; my shoes were full; a pool of blood lay very still, gleaming dark-red under the wheel; his eyes shone with an amazing lustre. The fusillade burst out again. He looked at me anxiously, gripping the spear like something precious, with an air of being afraid I would try to take it away from him. I had to make an effort to free my eyes from his gaze and attend to the steering. With one hand I felt above my head for the line of the steam whistle, and jerked out screech after screech hurriedly. The tumult of angry and warlike yells was checked instantly, and then from the depths of the woods went out such a tremulous and prolonged wail of mournful fear and utter despair as may be imagined to follow the flight of the last hope from the earth. There was a great commotion in the bush; the shower of arrows stopped, a few dropping shots rang out sharply—then silence, in which the languid beat of the stern-wheel came plainly to my ears. I put the helm hard a-star-board at the moment when the pilgrim in pink pyjamas, very hot and agitated, appeared in the doorway. 'The manager sends me———' he began in an official tone, and stopped short. 'Good God!' he said, glaring at the wounded man.

"We two whites stood over him, and his lustrous and inquiring glance enveloped us both. I declare it looked as though he would presently put to us some question in an understandable language; but he died without uttering a sound, without moving a limb, without twitching a muscle. Only in the very last moment, as though in response to some sign we could not see, to some whisper we could not hear, he frowned heavily, and that frown gave to his black death-mask an inconceivably sombre, brooding, and menacing expression. The lustre of inquiring glance faded swiftly into vacant glassiness. 'Can you steer?' I asked the agent eagerly. He looked very dubious; but I made a grab at his arm, and he understood at once I meant him to steer whether or no. I tell you the truth, I was morbidly anxious to change my shoes and socks. 'He is dead,' murmured the fellow, immensely impressed. 'No doubt about it,' said I, tugging like mad at the shoe-laces. 'And by the way, I suppose Mr. Kurtz is dead as well by this time.'

"For the moment that was the dominant thought. There was a sense of extreme disappointment, as though I had found out I had been striving after something altogether without a substance. I couldn't have been more disgusted if I had travelled all this way for the sole purpose of talking with Mr. Kurtz. Talking with. . . . I flung one shoe overboard, and became aware that that was exactly what I had been looking forward to—a talk with Kurtz. I made the strange discovery that I had never imagined him as doing, you know, but as discoursing. I didn't say to myself, 'Now I will never see him,' or 'Now I will never shake him by the hand,' but, 'now I will never hear him.' The man presented himself as a voice. Not of course that I did not connect him with some sort of action. Hadn't I been told in all the tones of jealousy and admiration that he had collected, bartered, swindled, or stolen more ivory than all the other agents together? That was not the point. The point was in his being a gifted creature, and that of all his gifts the one that stood out preëminently, that carried with it a sense of real presence, was his ability to talk, his words—the gift of expression, the bewildering, the illuminating, the most exalted and the most contemptible, the pulsating stream of light, or the deceitful flow from the heart of an impenetrable darkness.

"The other shoe went flying unto the devil-god of that river. I thought, By Jove! It's all over. We are too late; he has vanished—the gift has vanished, by means of some spear, arrow, or club. I will never hear that chap speak after all,—and my sorrow had a startling extravagance of emotion, even such as I had noticed in the howling sorrow of these savages in the bush. I couldn't have felt more of lonely desolation somehow, had I been robbed of a belief or had missed my destiny in life. . . . Why do you sigh in this beastly way, somebody? Absurd? Well, absurd. Good Lord! mustn't a man ever———Here, give me some tobacco." . . .

There was a pause of profound stillness, then a match flared, and Marlow's lean face appeared, worn, hollow, with downward folds and dropped eyelids, with an aspect of concentrated attention; and as he took vigorous draws at his pipe, it seemed to retreat and advance out of the night in the regular flicker of the tiny flame. The match went out.

"Absurd!" he cried. "This is the worst of trying to tell. . . . Here you all are, each moored with two good addresses, like a hulk with two anchors, a butcher round one corner, a policeman round another, excellent appetites, and temperature normal—you hear—normal from year's end to year's end. And you say, Absurd! Absurd be—exploded! Absurd! My dear boys, what can you expect from a man who out of sheer nervousness had just flung overboard a pair of new shoes! Now I think of it, it is amazing I did not shed tears. I am, upon the whole, proud of my fortitude. I was cut to the quick at the idea of having lost the inestimable privilege of listening to the gifted Kurtz. Of course I was wrong. The privilege was waiting for me. Oh, yes, I heard more than enough. And I was right, too. A voice. He was very little more than a voice. And I heard—him—it—this voice—other voices—all of them were so little more than voices—and the memory of that time itself lingers around me, impalpable, like a dying vibration of one immense jabber, silly, atrocious, sordid, savage, or simply mean, without any kind of sense. Voices, voices—even the girl herself—now—"

He was silent for a long time.

"I laid the ghost of his gifts at last with a lie," he began, suddenly. "Girl! What? Did I mention a girl? Oh, she is out of it—completely. They—the women I mean—are out of it—should be out of it. We must help them to stay in that beautiful world of their own, lest ours get worse. Oh, she had to be out of it. You should have heard the disinterred body of Mr. Kurtz saying, 'My Intended.' You would have perceived directly then how completely she was out of it. And the lofty frontal bone of Mr. Kurtz! They say the hair goes on growing sometimes, but this—ah—specimen, was impressively bald. The wilderness had patted him on the head, and, behold, it was like a ball—an ivory ball; it had caressed him, and—lo!—he had withered; it had taken him, loved him, embraced him, got into his veins, consumed his flesh, and sealed his soul to its own by the inconceivable ceremonies of some devilish initiation. He was its spoiled and pampered favourite. Ivory? I should think so. Heaps of it, stacks of it. The old mud shanty was bursting with it. You would think there was not a single tusk left either above or below the ground in the whole country. 'Mostly fossil,' the manager had remarked, disparagingly. It was no more fossil than I am; but they call it fossil when it is dug up. It appears these niggers do bury the tusks sometimes—but evidently they couldn't bury this parcel deep enough to save the gifted Mr. Kurtz from his fate. We filled the steamboat with it, and had to pile a lot on the deck. Thus he could see and enjoy as long as he could see, because the appreciation of this favour had remained with him to the last. You should have heard him say, 'My ivory.' Oh yes, I heard him. 'My Intended, my ivory, my station, my river, my———' everything belonged to him. It made me hold my breath in expectation of hearing the wilderness burst into a prodigious peal of laughter that would shake the fixed stars in their places. Everything belonged to him—but that was a trifle. The thing was to know what he belonged to, how many powers of darkness claimed him for their own. That was the reflection that made you creepy all over. It was impossible—it was not good for one either—trying to imagine. He had taken a high seat amongst the devils of the land—I mean literally. You can't understand. How could you?—with solid pavement under your feet, surrounded by kind neighbours ready to cheer you or to fall on you, stepping delicately between the butcher and the policeman, in the holy terror of scandal and gallows and lunatic asylums—how can you imagine what particular region of the first ages a man's untrammelled feet may take him into by the way of solitude—utter solitude without a policeman—by the way of silence—utter silence, where no warning voice of a kind neighbour can be heard whispering of public opinion? These little things make all the great difference. When they are gone you must fall back upon your own innate strength, upon your own capacity for faithfulness. Of course you may be too much of a fool to go wrong—too dull even to know you are being assaulted by the powers of darkness. I take it, no fool ever made a bargain for his soul with the devil: the fool is too much of a fool, or the devil too much of a devil—I don't know which. Or you may be such a thunderingly exalted creature as to be altogether deaf and blind to anything but heavenly sights and sounds. Then the earth for you is only a standing place—and whether to be like this is your loss or your gain I won't pretend to say. But most of us are neither one nor the other. The earth for us is a place to live in, where we must put up with sights, with sounds, with smells, too, by Jove!—breathe dead hippo, so to speak, and not be contaminated. And there, don't you see? your strength comes in, the faith in your ability for the digging of unostentatious holes to bury the stuff in—your power of devotion, not to yourself, but to an obscure, back-breaking business. And that's difficult enough. Mind, I am not trying to excuse or even explain—I am trying to account to myself for—for—Mr. Kurtz—for the shade of Mr. Kurtz. This initiated wraith from the back of Nowhere honoured me with its amazing confidence before it vanished altogether. This was because it could speak English to me. The original Kurtz had been educated partly in England, and—as he was good enough to say himself—his sympathies were in the right place. His mother was half-English, his father was half-French. All Europe contributed to the making of Kurtz; and by-and-by I learned that, most appropriately, the International Society for the Suppression of Savage Customs had intrusted him with the making of a report, for its future guidance. And he had written it, too. I've seen it. I've read it. It was eloquent, vibrating with eloquence, but too high-strung, I think. Seventeen pages of close writing he had found time for! But this must have been before his—let us say—nerves, went wrong, and caused him to preside at certain midnight dances ending with unspeakable rites, which—as far as I reluctantly gathered from what I heard at various times—were offered up to him—do you understand?—to Mr. Kurtz himself. But it was a beautiful piece of writing. The opening paragraph, however, in the light of later information, strikes me now as ominous. He began with the argument that we whites, from the point of development we had arrived at, 'must necessarily appear to him [savages] in the nature of supernatural beings—we approach them with the might as of a deity,' and so on, and so on. 'By the simple exercise of our will we can exert a power for good practically unbounded,' etc., etc. From that point he soared and took me with him. The peroration was magnificent, though difficult to remember, you know. It gave me the notion of an exotic immensity ruled by an august Benevolence. It made me tingle with enthusiasm. This was the unbounded power of eloquence—of words—of burning noble words. There were no practical hints to interrupt the magic current of phrases, unless a kind of note at the foot of the last page, scrawled evidently much later, in an unsteady hand, may be regarded as the exposition of a method. It was very simple, and at the end of that moving appeal to every altruistic sentiment it blazed at you, luminous and terrifying, like a flash of lightning in a serene sky: 'Exterminate all the brutes!' The curious part was that he had apparently forgotten all about that valuable postscriptum, because, later on, when he in a sense came to himself, he repeatedly entreated me to take good care of 'my pamphlet' (he called it), as it was sure to have in the future a good influence upon his career. I had full information about all these things, and, besides, as it turned out, I was to have the care of his memory. I've done enough for it to give me the indisputable right to lay it, if I choose, for an everlasting rest in the dust-bin of progress, amongst all the sweepings and, figuratively speaking, all the dead cats of civilization. But then, you see, I can't choose. He won't be forgotten. Whatever he was, he was not common. He had the power to charm or frighten rudimentary souls into an aggravated witch-dance in his honour; he could also fill the small souls of the pilgrims with bitter misgivings: he had one devoted friend at least, and he had conquered one soul in the world that was neither rudimentary nor tainted with self-seeking. No; I can't forget him, though I am not prepared to affirm the fellow was exactly worth the life we lost in getting to him. I missed my late helmsman awfully,—I missed him even while his body was still lying in the pilot-house. Perhaps you will think it passing strange this regret for a savage who was no more account than a grain of sand in a black Sahara. Well, don't you see, he had done something, he had steered; for months I had him at my back—a help—an instrument. It was a kind of partnership. He steered for me—I had to look after him, I worried about his deficiencies, and thus a subtle bond had been created, of which I only became aware when it was suddenly broken. And the intimate profundity of that look he gave me when he received his hurt remains to this day in my memory—like a claim of distant kinship affirmed in a supreme moment.

105   "Poor fool! If he had only left that shutter alone. He had no restraint, no restraint—just like Kurtz—a tree swayed by the wind. As soon as I had put on a dry pair of slippers, I dragged him out, after first jerking the spear out of his side, which operation I confess I performed with my eyes shut tight. His heels leaped together over the little door-step; his shoulders were pressed to my breast; I hugged him from behind desperately. Oh! he was heavy, heavy; heavier than any man on earth, I should imagine. Then without more ado I tipped him overboard. The current snatched him as though he had been a wisp of grass, and I saw the body roll over twice before I lost sight of it for ever. All the pilgrims and the manager were then congregated on the awning-deck about the pilot-house, chattering at each other like a flock of excited magpies, and there was a scandalized murmur at my heartless promptitude. What they wanted to keep that body hanging about for I can't guess. Embalm it, maybe. But I had also heard another, and a very ominous, murmur on the deck below. My friends the wood-cutters were likewise scandalized, and with a better show of reason—though I admit that the reason itself was quite inadmissible. Oh, quite! I had made up my mind that if my late helmsman was to be eaten, the fishes alone should have him. He had been a very second-rate helmsman while alive, but now he was dead he might have become a first-class temptation, and possibly cause some startling trouble. Besides, I was anxious to take the wheel, the man in pink pyjamas showing himself a hopeless duffer at the business.

"This I did directly after the simple funeral was over. We were going half-speed, keeping right in the middle of the stream, and I listened to the talk about me. They had given up Kurtz, they had given up the station; Kurtz was dead, and the station had been burnt—and so on—and so on. The red-haired pilgrim was beside himself with the thought that at least this poor Kurtz had been properly avenged. 'Say! We must have made a glorious slaughter of them in the bush. Eh? What do you think? Say?' He positively danced, the bloodthirsty little gingery beggar. And he had nearly fainted when he saw the wounded man! I could not help saying, 'You made a

glorious lot of smoke, anyhow.' I had seen, from the way the tops of the bushes rustled and flew, that almost all the shots had gone too high. You can't hit anything unless you take aim and fire from the shoulder; but these chaps fired from the hip with
their eyes shut. The retreat, I maintained—and I was right—was caused by the
screeching of the steam-whistle. Upon this they forgot Kurtz, and began to howl at
me with indignant protests.

"The manager stood by the wheel murmuring confidentially about the necessity
of getting well away down the river before dark at all events, when I saw in the distance a clearing on the river-side and the outlines of some sort of building. 'What's
this?' I asked. He clapped his hands in wonder. 'The station!' he cried. I edged in at
once, still going half-speed.

"Through my glasses I saw the slope of a hill interspersed with rare trees and
perfectly free from undergrowth. A long decaying building on the summit was half
buried in the high grass; the large holes in the peaked roof gaped black from afar;
the jungle and the woods made a background. There was no enclosure or fence of
any kind; but there had been one apparently, for near the house half-a-dozen slim
posts remained in a row, roughly trimmed, and with their upper ends ornamented
with round carved balls. The rails, or whatever there had been between, had disappeared. Of course the forest surrounded all that. The river-bank was clear, and on the
water-side I saw a white man under a hat like a cart-wheel beckoning persistently
with his whole arm. Examining the edge of the forest above and below, I was almost
certain I could see movements—human forms gliding here and there. I steamed past
prudently, then stopped the engines and let her drift down. The man on the shore began to shout, urging us to land, 'We have been attacked,' screamed the manager. 'I
know—I know. It's all right,' yelled back the other, as cheerful as you please. 'Come
along. It's all right. I am glad.'

"His aspect reminded me of something I had seen—something funny I had seen
somewhere. As I manœuvred to get alongside, I was asking myself, 'What does this
fellow look like?' Suddenly I got it. He looked like a harlequin. His clothes had been
made of some stuff that was brown holland probably, but it was covered with patches
all over, with bright patches, blue, red, and yellow,—patches on the back, patches on
the front, patches on the elbows, on knees; coloured binding around his jacket, scarlet edging at the bottom of his trousers; and the sunshine made him look extremely
gay and wonderfully neat withal, because you could see how beautifully all this
patching had been done. A beardless, boyish face, very fair, no features to speak of,
nose peeling, little blue eyes, smiles and frowns chasing each other over that open
countenance like sunshine and shadow on a wide-swept plain. 'Look out, captain!'
he cried; 'there's a snag lodged in here last night.' What! Another snag? I confess I
swore shamefully. I had nearly holed my cripple, to finish off that charming trip. The
harlequin on the bank turned his little pug-nose up to me. 'You English?' he asked,
all smiles. 'Are you?' I shouted from the wheel. The smiles vanished, and he shook
his head as if sorry for my disappointment. Then he brightened up. 'Never mind!' he
cried, encouragingly. 'Are we in time?' I asked. 'He is up there,' he replied, with a
toss of the head up the hill, and becoming gloomy all of a sudden. His face was like
the autumn sky, overcast one moment and bright the next.

110   "When the manager, escorted by the pilgrims, all of them armed to the teeth, had gone to the house this chap came on board. 'I say, I don't like this, these natives are in the bush,' I said. He assured me earnestly it was all right. 'They are simple people,' he added; 'well, I am glad you came. It took me all my time to keep them off.' 'But you said it was all right,' I cried. 'Oh, they meant no harm,' he said; and as I stared he corrected himself, 'Not exactly.' Then vivaciously, 'My faith, your pilot-house wants a clean up!' In the next breath he advised me to keep enough steam on the boiler to blow the whistle in case of any trouble. 'One good screech will do more for you than all your rifles. They are simple people,' he repeated. He rattled away at such a rate he quite overwhelmed me. He seemed to be trying to make up for lots of silence, and actually hinted, laughing, that such was the case. 'Don't you talk with Mr. Kurtz?' I said. 'You don't talk with that man—you listen to him,' he exclaimed with severe exaltation. 'But now————' he waved his arm, and in the twinkling of an eye was in the uttermost depths of despondency. In a moment he came up again with a jump, possessed himself of both my hands, shook them continuously, while he gabbled: 'Brother sailor . . . honour . . . pleasure . . . delight . . . introduce myself . . . Russian . . . son of an arch-priest . . . Government of Tambov . . . What? Tobacco! English tobacco; the excellent English tobacco! Now, that's brotherly. Smoke? Where's a sailor that does not smoke?'

"The pipe soothed him, and gradually I made out he had run away from school, had gone to sea in a Russian ship; ran away again; served some time in English ships; was now reconciled with the arch-priest. He made a point of that. 'But when one is young one must see things, gather experience, ideas; enlarge the mind.' 'Here!' I interrupted. 'You can never tell! Here I met Mr. Kurtz,' he said, youthfully solemn and reproachful. I held my tongue after that. It appears he had persuaded a Dutch trading-house on the coast to fit him out with stores and goods, and had started for the interior with a light heart, and no more idea of what would happen to him than a baby. He had been wandering about that river for nearly two years alone, cut off from everybody and everything. 'I am not so young as I look. I am twenty-five,' he said. 'At first old Van Shuyten would tell me to go to the devil,' he narrated with keen enjoyment; 'but I stuck to him, and talked and talked, till at last he got afraid I would talk the hind-leg off his favourite dog, so he gave me some cheap things and a few guns, and told me he hoped he would never see my face again. Good old Dutchman, Van Shuyten. I've sent him one small lot of ivory a year ago, so that he can't call me a little thief when I get back. I hope he got it. And for the rest I don't care. I had some wood stacked for you. That was my old house. Did you see?'

"I gave him Towson's book. He made as though he would kiss me, but restrained himself. 'The only book I had left, and I thought I had lost it,' he said, looking at it ecstatically. 'So many accidents happen to a man going about alone, you know. Canoes get upset sometimes—and sometimes you've got to clear out so quick when the people get angry.' He thumbed the pages. 'You made notes in Russian?' I asked. He nodded. 'I thought they were written in cipher,' I said. He laughed, then became serious. 'I had lots of trouble to keep these people off,' he said. 'Did they want to kill you?' I asked. 'Oh, no!' he cried, and checked himself. 'Why did they attack us?' I pursued. He hesitated, then said shamefacedly, 'They don't want him to go.' 'Don't they?' I said, curiously. He nodded a nod full of mystery and wisdom. 'I tell you,' he cried, 'this man has enlarged my mind.' He opened his arms wide, staring at me with his little blue eyes that were perfectly round."

3

"I looked at him, lost in astonishment. There he was before me, in motley, as though he had absconded from a troupe of mimes, enthusiastic, fabulous. His very existence was improbable, inexplicable, and altogether bewildering. He was an insoluble problem. It was inconceivable how he had existed, how he had succeeded in getting so far, how he had managed to remain—why he did not instantly disappear. 'I went a little farther,' he said, 'then still a little farther—till I had gone so far that I don't know how I'll ever get back. Never mind. Plenty time. I can manage. You take Kurtz away quick—quick—I tell you.' The glamour of youth enveloped his particoloured rags, his destitution, his loneliness, the essential desolation of his futile wanderings. For months—for years—his life hadn't been worth a day's purchase; and there he was gallantly, thoughtlessly alive, to all appearance indestructible solely by the virtue of his few years and of his unreflecting audacity. I was seduced into something like admiration—like envy. Glamour urged him on, glamour kept him unscathed. He surely wanted nothing from the wilderness but space to breathe in and to push on through. His need was to exist, and to move onwards at the greatest possible risk, and with a maximum of privation. If the absolutely pure, uncalculating, unpractical spirit of adventure had ever ruled a human being, it ruled this be-patched youth. I almost envied him the possession of this modest and clear flame. It seemed to have consumed all thought of self so completely, that even while he was talking to you, you forgot that it was he—the man before your eyes—who had gone through these things. I did not envy him his devotion to Kurtz, though. He had not meditated over it. It came to him, and he accepted it with a sort of eager fatalism. I must say that to me it appeared about the most dangerous thing in every way he had come upon so far.

"They had come together unavoidably, like two ships becalmed near each other, and lay rubbing sides at last. I suppose Kurtz wanted an audience, because on a certain occasion, when encamped in the forest, they had talked all night, or more probably Kurtz had talked. 'We talked of everything,' he said, quite transported at the recollection. 'I forgot there was such a thing as sleep. The night did not seem to last an hour. Everything! Everything! . . . Of love, too.' 'Ah, he talked to you of love!' I said, much amused. 'It isn't what you think,' he cried, almost passionately. 'It was in general. He made me see things—things.'

"He threw his arms up. We were on deck at the time, and the headman of my wood-cutters, lounging nearby, turned upon him his heavy and glittering eyes. I looked around, and I don't know why, but I assure you that never, never before, did this land, this river, this jungle, the very arch of this blazing sky, appear to me so hopeless and so dark, so impenetrable to human thought, so pitiless to human weakness. 'And ever since, you have been with him, of course?' I said.

"On the contrary. It appears their intercourse had been very much broken by various causes. He had, as he informed me proudly, managed to nurse Kurtz through two illnesses (he alluded to it as you would to some risky feat), but as a rule Kurtz wandered alone, far in the depths of the forest. 'Very often coming to this station, I had to wait days and days before he would turn up,' he said. 'Ah, it was worth waiting for!—sometimes.' 'What was he doing? exploring or what?' I asked. 'Oh, yes, of course;' he had discovered lots of villages, a lake, too—he did not know exactly in what direction; it was dangerous to inquire too much—but mostly his expeditions had been for ivory. 'But he had no goods to trade with by that time,' I objected. 'There's a good lot of cartridges left even yet,' he answered, looking away. 'To speak plainly, he raided the country,' I said. He nodded. 'Not alone, surely!' He muttered something about the villages round that lake. 'Kurtz got the tribe to follow him, did he?' I suggested. He fidgeted a little. 'They adored him,' he said. The tone of these words was so extraordinary that I looked at him searchingly. It was curious to see his mingled eagerness and reluctance to speak of Kurtz. The man filled his life, occupied his thoughts, swayed his emotions. 'What can you expect?' he burst out; 'he came to them with thunder and lightning, you know—and they had never seen anything like it—and very terrible. He could be very terrible. You can't judge Mr. Kurtz as you would an ordinary man. No, no, no! Now—just to give you an idea—I don't mind telling you, he wanted to shoot me, too, one day—but I don't judge him.' 'Shoot you!' I cried. 'What for?' 'Well, I had a small lot of ivory the chief of that village near my house gave me. You see I used to shoot game for them. Well, he wanted it, and wouldn't hear reason. He declared he would shoot me unless I gave him the ivory and then cleared out of the country, because he could do so, and had a fancy for it, and there was nothing on earth to prevent him killing whom he jolly well pleased. And it was true, too. I gave him the ivory. What did I care! But I didn't clear out. No, no. I couldn't leave him. I had to be careful, of course, till we got friendly again for a time. He had his second illness then. Afterwards I had to keep out of the way; but I didn't mind. He was living for the most part in those villages on the lake. When he came down to the river, sometimes he would take to me, and sometimes it was better for me to be careful. This man suffered too much. He hated all this, and somehow he couldn't get away. When I had a chance I begged him to try and leave while there was time; I offered to go back with him. And he would say yes, and then he would remain; go off on another ivory hunt; disappear for weeks; forget himself amongst these people—forget himself—you know.' 'Why! he's mad,' I said. He protested indignantly. Mr. Kurtz couldn't be mad. If I had heard him talk, only two days ago, I wouldn't dare hint at such a thing. . . . I had taken up my binoculars while we talked, and was looking at the shore, sweeping the limit of the forest at each side and at the back of the house. The consciousness of there being people in that bush, so silent, so quiet—as silent and quiet as the ruined house on the hill—made me uneasy. There was no sign on the face of nature of this amazing tale that was not so much told as suggested to me in desolate exclamations, completed by shrugs, in interrupted phrases, in hints ending in deep sighs. The woods were unmoved, like a mask—heavy, like the closed door of a prison—they looked with their air of hidden knowledge, of patient expectation, of unapproachable silence. The Russian was explaining to me that it was only lately that Mr. Kurtz had come down to the river, bringing along with him all the fighting men of that lake tribe. He had been absent for several months—getting himself adored, I suppose—and had come down unexpectedly, with the intention to all appearance of making a raid either across the river or down stream. Evidently the appetite for more ivory had got the better of the— what shall I say?—less material aspirations. However he had got much worse suddenly. 'I heard he was laying helpless, and so I came up—took my chance,' said the Russian. 'Oh, he is bad, very bad.' I directed my glass to the house. There were no signs of life, but there was the ruined roof, the long mud wall peeping above the grass, with three little square window-holes, no two of the same size; all this brought within reach of my hand, as it were. And then I made a brusque movement, and one of the remaining posts of that vanished fence leaped up in the field of my glass. You remember I told you I had been struck at the distance by certain attempts at ornamentation, rather remarkable in the ruinous aspect of the place. Now I had suddenly a nearer view, and its first result was to make me throw my head back as if before a blow. Then I went carefully from post to post with my glass, and I saw my mistake. These round knobs were not ornamental but symbolic; they were expressive and puzzling, striking and disturbing—food for thought and also for the vultures if there had been any looking down from the sky; but at all events for such ants as were industrious enough to ascend the pole. They would have been even more impressive, those heads on the stakes, if their faces had not been turned to the house. Only one, the first I had made out, was facing my way. I was not so shocked as you may think. The start back I had given was really nothing but a movement of surprise. I had expected to see a knob of wood there, you know. I returned deliberately to the first I had seen—and there it was, black, dried, sunken, with closed eyelids,—a head that seemed to sleep at the top of that pole, and, with the shrunken dry lips showing a narrow white line of the teeth, was smiling, too, smiling continuously at some endless and jocose dream of that eternal slumber.

"I am not disclosing any trade secrets. In fact, the manager said afterwards that Mr. Kurtz's methods had ruined the district. I have no opinion on that point, but I want you clearly to understand that there was nothing exactly profitable in these heads being there. They only showed that Mr. Kurtz lacked restraint in the gratification of his various lusts, that there was something wanting in him—some small matter which, when the pressing need arose, could not be found under his magnificent eloquence. Whether he knew of this deficiency himself I can't say. I think the knowledge came to him at last—only at the very last. But the wilderness had found him out early, and had taken on him a terrible vengeance for the fantastic invasion. I think it had whispered to him things about himself which he did not know, things of which he had no conception till he took counsel with this great solitude—and the whisper had proved irresistibly fascinating. It echoed loudly within him because he was hollow at the core. . . . I put down the glass, and the head that had appeared near enough to be spoken to seemed at once to have leaped away from me into inaccessible distance.

"The admirer of Mr. Kurtz was a bit crestfallen. In a hurried, indistinct voice he began to assure me he had not dared to take these—say, symbols—down. He was not afraid of the natives; they would not stir till Mr. Kurtz gave the word. His ascendancy was extraordinary. The camps of these people surrounded the place, and the chiefs came every day to see him. They would crawl. . . . 'I don't want to know anything of the ceremonies used when approaching Mr. Kurtz,' I shouted. Curious, this feeling that came over me that such details would be more intolerable than those heads drying on the stakes under Mr. Kurtz's windows. After all, that was only a savage sight, while I seemed at one bound to have been transported into some lightless region of subtle horrors, where pure, uncomplicated savagery was a positive relief, being something that had a right to exist—obviously—in the sunshine. The young man looked at me with surprise. I suppose it did not occur to him that Mr. Kurtz was no idol of mine. He forgot I hadn't heard any of these splendid monologues on, what was it? on love, justice, conduct of life—or what not. If it had come to crawling before Mr. Kurtz, he crawled as much as the veriest savage of them all. I had no idea of the conditions, he said: these heads were the heads of rebels. I shocked him excessively by laughing. Rebels! What would be the next definition I was to hear? There had been enemies, criminals, workers—and these were rebels. Those rebellious heads looked very subdued to me on their sticks. 'You don't know how such a life tries a man like Kurtz,' cried Kurtz's last disciple. 'Well, and you?' I said. 'I! I! I am a simple man. I have no great thoughts. I want nothing from anybody. How can you compare me to? . . .' His feelings were too much for speech, and suddenly he broke down. 'I don't understand,' he groaned. 'I've been doing my best to keep him alive, and that's enough. I had no hand in all this. I have no abilities. There hasn't been a drop of medicine or a mouthful of invalid food for months here. He was shamefully abandoned. A man like this, with such ideas. Shamefully! Shamefully! I—I—haven't slept for the last ten nights. . . .'

"His voice lost itself in the calm of the evening. The long shadows of the forest had slipped down hill while we talked, had gone far beyond the ruined hovel, beyond the symbolic row of stakes. All this was in the gloom, while we down there were yet in the sunshine, and the stretch of the river abreast of the clearing glittered in a still and dazzling splendour, with a murky and overshadowed bend above and below. Not a living soul was seen on the shore. The bushes did not rustle.

120   "Suddenly round the corner of the house a group of men appeared, as though they had come up from the ground. They waded waist-deep in the grass, in a compact body, bearing an improvised stretcher in their midst. Instantly, in the emptiness of the landscape, a cry arose whose shrillness pierced the still air like a sharp arrow flying straight to the very heart of the land; and, as if by enchantment, streams of human beings—of naked human beings—with spears in their hands, with bows, with shields, with wild glances and savage movements, were poured into the clearing by the dark-faced and pensive forest. The bushes shook, the grass swayed for a time, and then everything stood still in attentive immobility.

"'Now, if he does not say the right thing to them we are all done for,' said the Russian at my elbow. The knot of men with the stretcher had stopped, too, halfway to the steamer, as if petrified. I saw the man on the stretcher sit up, lank and with an uplifted arm, above the shoulders of the bearers. 'Let us hope that the man who can talk so well of love in general will find some particular reason to spare us this time,' I said. I resented bitterly the absurd danger of our situation, as if to be at the mercy of that atrocious phantom had been a dishonouring necessity. I could not hear a sound, but through my glasses I saw the thin arm extended commandingly, the lower jaw moving, the eyes of that apparition shining darkly far in its bony head that nodded with grotesque jerks. Kurtz—Kurtz—that means short in German—don't it? Well, the name was as true as everything else in his life—and death. He looked at least seven feet long. His covering had fallen off, and his body emerged from it pitiful and appalling as from a winding-sheet. I could see the cage of his ribs all astir, the bones of his arm waving. It was as though an animated image of death carved out of old ivory had been shaking its hand with menaces at a motionless crowd of men made of dark and glittering bronze. I saw him open his mouth wide—it gave him a weirdly voracious aspect, as though he had wanted to swallow all the air, all the earth, all the men before him. A deep voice reached me faintly. He must have been shouting. He fell back suddenly. The stretcher shook as the bearers staggered forward again, and almost at the same time I noticed that the crowd of savages was vanishing without any perceptible movement of retreat, as if the forest that had ejected these beings so suddenly had drawn them in again as the breath is drawn in a long aspiration.

"Some of the pilgrims behind the stretcher carried his arms—two shot-guns, a heavy rifle, and a light revolver-carbine—the thunderbolts of that pitiful Jupiter. The manager bent over him murmuring as he walked beside his head. They laid him down in one of the little cabins—just a room for a bedplace and a camp-stool or two, you know. We had brought his belated correspondence, and a lot of torn envelopes and open letters littered his bed. His hand roamed feebly amongst these papers. I was struck by the fire of his eyes and the composed languor of his expression. It was not so much the exhaustion of disease. He did not seem in pain. This shadow looked satiated and calm, as though for the moment it had had its fill of all the emotions.

"He rustled one of the letters, and looking straight in my face said, 'I am glad.' Somebody had been writing to him about me. These special recommendations were turning up again. The volume of tone he emitted without effort, almost without the trouble of moving his lips, amazed me. A voice! a voice! It was grave, profound, vibrating, while the man did not seem capable of a whisper. However, he had enough strength in him—factitious no doubt—to very nearly make an end of us, as you shall hear directly.

"The manager appeared silently in the doorway; I stepped out at once and he drew the curtain after me. The Russian, eyed curiously by the pilgrims, was staring at the shore. I followed the direction of his glance.

"Dark human shapes could be made out in the distance, flitting indistinctly 125 against the gloomy border of the forest, and near the river two bronze figures, leaning on tall spears, stood in the sunlight under fantastic head-dresses of spotted skins, warlike and still in statuesque repose. And from right to left along the lighted shore moved a wild and gorgeous apparition of a woman.

"She walked with measured steps, draped in striped and fringed cloths, treading the earth proudly, with a slight jingle and flash of barbarous ornaments. She carried her head high; her hair was done in the shape of a helmet; she had brass leggings to the knee, brass wire gauntlets to the elbow, a crimson spot on her tawny cheek, innumerable necklaces of glass beads on her neck; bizarre things, charms, gifts of witch-men, that hung about her, glittered and trembled at every step. She must have had the value of several elephant tusks upon her. She was savage and superb, wild-eyed and magnificent; there was something ominous and stately in her deliberate progress. And in the hush that had fallen suddenly upon the whole sorrowful land, the immense wilderness, the colossal body of the fecund and mysterious life seemed to look at her, pensive, as though it had been looking at the image of its own tene-brous and passionate soul.

"She came abreast of the steamer, stood still, and faced us. Her long shadow fell to the water's edge. Her face had a tragic and fierce aspect of wild sorrow and of dumb pain mingled with the fear of some struggling, half-shaped resolve. She stood looking at us without a stir, and like the wilderness itself, with an air of brooding over an inscrutable purpose. A whole minute passed, and then she made a step forward. There was a long jingle, a glint of yellow metal, a sway of fringed draperies, and she stopped as if her heart had failed her. The young fellow by my side growled. The pilgrims murmured at my back. She looked at us all as if her life had depended upon the unswerving steadiness of her glance. Suddenly she opened her bared arms and threw them up rigid above her head, as though in an uncontrollable desire to touch the sky, and at the same time the swift shadows darted out on the earth, swept around on the river, gathering the steamer into a shadowy embrace. A formidable si-lence hung over the scene.

"She turned away slowly, walked on, following the bank, and passed into the bushes to the left. Once only her eyes gleamed back at us in the dusk of the thickets before she disappeared.

"'If she had offered to come aboard I really think I would have tried to shoot her,' said the man of patches, nervously. 'I had been risking my life every day for the last fortnight to keep her out of the house. She got in one day and kicked up a row about those miserable rags I picked up in the storeroom to mend my clothes with. I wasn't decent. At least it must have been that, for she talked like a fury to Kurtz for an hour, pointing at me now and then. I don't understand the dialect of this tribe. Luckily for me, I fancy Kurtz felt too ill that day to care, or there would have been mischief. I don't understand. . . . No—it's too much for me. Ah, well, it's all over now.'

130   "At this moment I heard Kurtz's deep voice behind the curtain: 'Save me!—save the ivory, you mean. Don't tell me. Save *me*! Why, I've had to save you. You are in-terrupting my plans now. Sick! Sick! Not so sick as you would like to believe. Never mind. I'll carry my ideas out yet—I will return. I'll show you what can be done. You with your little peddling notions—you are interfering with me. I will return. I. . . .'

"The manager came out. He did me the honour to take me under the arm and lead me aside. 'He is very low, very low,' he said. He considered it necessary to sigh, but neglected to be consistently sorrowful. 'We have done all we could for him—haven't we? But there is no disguising the fact, Mr. Kurtz has done more harm than good to the Company. He did not see the time was not ripe for vigorous action. Cau-tiously, cautiously—that's my principle. We must be cautious yet. The district is closed to us for a time. Deplorable! Upon the whole, the trade will suffer, I don't deny there is a remarkable quantity of ivory—mostly fossil. We must save it, at all events—but look how precarious the position is—and why? Because the method is unsound.' 'Do you,' said I, looking at the shore, 'call it "unsound method?"' 'Without doubt,' he exclaimed hotly. 'Don't you?' . . . 'No method at all,' I murmured after a while. 'Exactly,' he exulted. 'I anticipated this. Shows a complete want of judgment. It is my duty to point it out in the proper quarter.' 'Oh,' said I, 'that fellow—what's his name?—the brickmaker, will make a readable report for you.' He appeared confounded for a moment. It seemed to me I had never breathed an atmosphere so vile, and I turned mentally to Kurtz for relief—positively for relief. 'Nevertheless I think Mr. Kurtz is a remarkable man,' I said with emphasis. He started, dropped on me a cold heavy glance, said very quietly, "he *was*,' and turned his back on me. My hour of favour was over; I found myself lumped along with Kurtz as a partisan of methods for which the time was not ripe; I was unsound! Ah! but it was something to have at least a choice of nightmares.

"I had turned to the wilderness really, not to Mr. Kurtz, who, I was ready to admit, was as good as buried. And for a moment it seemed to me as if I also were buried in a vast grave full of unspeakable secrets. I felt an intolerable weight oppressing my breast, the smell of the damp earth, the unseen presence of victorious corruption, the darkness of an impenetrable night. . . . The Russian tapped me on the shoulder. I heard him mumbling and stammering something about 'brother seaman—couldn't conceal—knowledge of matters that would affect Mr. Kurtz's reputation.' I waited. For him evidently Mr. Kurtz was not in his grave; I suspect that for him Mr. Kurtz was one of the immortals. 'Well!' said I at last, 'speak out. As it happens, I am Mr. Kurtz's friend—in a way.'

"He stated with a good deal of formality that had we not been 'of the same profession,' he would have kept the matter to himself without regard to consequences. 'He suspected there was an active ill will towards him on the part of these white men that———' 'You are right,' I said, remembering a certain conversation I had overheard. 'The manager thinks you ought to be hanged.' He showed a concern at this intelligence which amused me at first. 'I had better get out of the way quietly,' he said, earnestly. 'I can do no more for Kurtz now, and they would soon find some excuse. What's to stop them? There's a military post three hundred miles from here.' 'Well, upon my word,' said I, 'perhaps you had better go if you have any friends amongst the savages near by.' 'Plenty,' he said. 'They are simple people—and I want nothing, you know.' He stood biting his lip, then: 'I don't want any harm to happen to these whites here, but of course I was thinking of Mr. Kurtz's reputation—but you are a brother seaman and———' 'All right,' said I, after a time. 'Mr. Kurtz's reputation is safe with me.' I did not know how truly I spoke.

"He informed me, lowering his voice, that it was Kurtz who had ordered the attack to be made on the steamer. 'He hated sometimes the idea of being taken away—and then again. . . . But I don't understand these matters. I am a simple man. He thought it would scare you away—that you would give it up, thinking him dead. I could not stop him. Oh, I had an awful time of it this last month.' 'Very well,' I said. 'He is all right now.' 'Ye-e-es,' he muttered, not very convinced apparently. 'Thanks,' said I; 'I shall keep my eyes open.' 'But quiet—eh?' he urged, anxiously. 'It would be awful for his reputation if anybody here———' I promised a complete discretion with great gravity. 'I have a canoe and three black fellows waiting not very far. I am off. Could you give me a few Martini-Henry cartridges?' I could, and did, with proper secrecy. He helped himself, with a wink at me, to a handful of my tobacco. 'Between sailors—you know—good English tobacco.' At the door of the pilot-house he turned round—'I say, haven't you a pair of shoes you could spare?' He raised one leg. 'Look.' The soles were tied with knotted strings sandal-wise under his bare feet. I rooted out an old pair, at which he looked with admiration before tucking it under his left arm. One of his pockets (bright red) was bulging with cartridges, from the other (dark blue) peeped 'Towson's Inquiry,' etc., etc. He seemed to think himself ex-cellently well equipped for a renewed encounter with the wilderness. 'Ah! I'll never, never meet such a man again. You ought to have heard him recite poetry—his own, too, it was, he told me. Poetry!' He rolled his eyes at the recollection of these de-lights, 'Oh, he enlarged my mind!' 'Goodbye,' said I. He shook hands and vanished in the night. Sometimes I ask myself whether I had ever really seen him—whether it was possible to meet such a phenomenon! . . .

135   "When I woke up shortly after midnight his warning came to my mind with its hint of danger that seemed, in the starred darkness, real enough to make me get up for the purpose of having a look round. On the hill a big fire burned, illuminating fit-fully a crooked corner of the station-house. One of the agents with a picket of a few of our blacks, armed for the purpose, was keeping guard over the ivory; but deep within the forest, red gleams that wavered, that seemed to sink and rise from the ground amongst confused columnar shapes of intense blackness, showed the exact position of the camp where Mr. Kurtz's adorers were keeping their uneasy vigil. The monotonous beating of a big drum filled the air with muffled shocks and a lingering vibration. A steady droning sound of many men chanting each to himself some weird incantation came out from the black, flat wall of the woods as the humming of bees comes out of a hive, and had a strange narcotic effect upon my half-awake senses. I believe I dozed off leaning over the rail, till an abrupt burst of yells, an overwhelm-ing outbreak of a pent-up and mysterious frenzy, woke me up in a bewildered won-der. It was cut short all at once, and the low droning went on with an effect of audi-ble and soothing silence. I glanced casually into the little cabin. A light was burning within, but Mr. Kurtz was not there.

        "I think I would have raised an outcry if I had believed my eyes. But I didn't be-lieve them at first—the thing seemed so impossible. The fact is I was completely un-nerved by a sheer blank fright, pure abstract terror, unconnected with any distinct shape of physical danger. What made this emotion so overpowering was—how shall I define it?—the moral shock I received, as if something altogether monstrous, in-tolerable to thought and odious to the soul, had been thrust upon me unexpectedly. This lasted of course the merest fraction of a second, and then the usual sense of commonplace, deadly danger, the possibility of a sudden onslaught and massacre, or something of the kind, which I saw impending, as positively welcome and compos-ing. It pacified me, in fact, so much, that I did not raise an alarm.

        "There was an agent buttoned up inside an ulster and sleeping on a chair on deck within three feet of me. The yells had awakened him; he snored very slightly; I left him to his slumbers and leaped ashore. I did not betray Mr. Kurtz—it was ordered I should never betray him—it was written I should be loyal to the nightmare of my choice. I was anxious to deal with this shadow by myself alone,—and to this day I don't know why I was so jealous of sharing with any one the peculiar blackness of that experience.

"As soon as I got on the bank I saw a trail—a broad trail through the grass. I remember the exultation with which I said to myself, 'He can't walk—he is crawling on all-fours—I've got him.' The grass was wet with dew. I strode rapidly with clenched fists. I fancy I had some vague notion of falling upon him and giving him a drubbing. I don't know. I had some imbecile thoughts. The knitting old woman with the cat obtruded herself upon my memory as a most improper person to be sitting at the other end of such an affair. I saw a row of pilgrims squirting lead in the air out of Winchesters held to the hip. I thought I would never get back to the steamer, and imagined myself living alone and unarmed in the woods to an advanced age. Such silly things—you know. And I remember I confounded the beat of the drum with the beating of my heart, and was pleased at its calm regularity.

"I kept to the track though—then stopped to listen. The night was very clear; a dark blue space, sparkling with dew and starlight, in which black things stood very still. I thought I could see a kind of motion ahead of me. I was strangely cocksure of everything that night. I actually left the track and ran in a wide semicircle (I verily believe chuckling to myself) so as to get in front of that stir, of that motion I had seen—if indeed I had seen anything. I was circumventing Kurtz as though it had been a boyish game.

"I came upon him, and, if he had not heard me coming, I would have fallen over 140 him, too, but he got up in time. He rose, unsteady, long, pale, indistinct, like a vapour exhaled by the earth, and swayed slightly, misty and silent before me; while at my back the fires loomed between the trees, and the murmur of many voices issued from the forest. I had cut him off cleverly; but when actually confronting him I seemed to come to my senses. I saw the danger in its right proportion. It was by no means over yet. Suppose he began to shout? Though he could hardly stand, there was plenty of vigour in his voice. 'Go away—hide yourself,' he said, in that profound tone. It was very awful. I glanced back. We were within thirty yards from the nearest fire. A black figure stood up, strode on long black legs, waving long black arms, across the glow. It had horns—antelope horns, I think—on its head. Some sorcerer, some witch-man, no doubt: it looked fiend-like enough. 'Do you know what you are doing?' I whispered. 'Perfectly,' he answered, raising his voice for that single word: it sounded to me far off and yet loud, like a hail through a speaking-trumpet. If he makes a row we are lost, I thought to myself. This clearly was not a case for fisticuffs, even apart from the very natural aversion I had to beat that Shadow—this wandering and tormented thing. 'You will be lost,' I said—'utterly lost.' One gets sometimes such a flash of inspiration, you know. I did say the right thing, though indeed he could not have been more irretrievably lost than he was at this very moment, when the foundations of our intimacy were being laid—to endure—to endure—even to the end—even beyond.

"'I had immense plans,' he muttered irresolutely. 'Yes,' said I; 'but if you try to shout I'll smash your head with————' There was not a stick or a stone near. 'I will throttle you for good,' I corrected myself. 'I was on the threshold of great things,' he pleaded, in a voice of longing, with a wistfulness of tone that made my blood run cold. 'And now for this stupid scoundrel—' 'Your success in Europe is assured in any case,' I affirmed, steadily. I did not want to have the throttling of him, you understand—and indeed it would have been very little use for any practical purpose. I tried to break the spell—the heavy, mute spell of the wilderness—that seemed to draw him to its pitiless breast by the awakening of forgotten and brutal instincts, by the memory of gratified and monstrous passions. This alone, I was convinced, had driven him out to the edge of the forest, to the bush, towards the gleam of fires, the throb of drums, the drone of weird incantations; this alone had beguiled his unlawful soul beyond the bounds of permitted aspirations. And, don't you see, the terror of the position was not in being knocked on the head—though I had a very lively sense of that danger, too—but in this, that I had to deal with a being to whom I could not appeal in the name of anything high or low. I had, even like the niggers, to invoke him—himself—his own exalted and incredible degradation. There was nothing either above or below him, and I knew it. He had kicked himself loose of the earth. Confound the man! he had kicked the very earth to pieces. He was alone, and I before him did not know whether I stood on the ground or floated in the air. I've been telling you what we said—repeating the phrases we pronounced—but what's the good? They were common everyday words—the familiar, vague sounds exchanged on every waking day of life. But what of that? They had behind them, to my mind, the terrific suggestiveness of words heard in dreams, of phrases spoken in nightmares. Soul! If anybody had ever struggled with a soul, I am the man. And I wasn't arguing with a lunatic either. Believe me or not, his intelligence was perfectly clear—concentrated, it is true, upon himself with horrible intensity, yet clear; and therein was my only chance—barring, of course, the killing him there and then, which wasn't so good, on account of unavoidable noise. But his soul was mad. Being alone in the wilderness, it had looked within itself, and, by heavens! I tell you, it had gone mad. I had—for my sins, I suppose—to go through the ordeal of looking into it myself. No eloquence could have been so withering to one's belief in mankind as his final burst of sincerity. He struggled with himself, too. I saw it,—I heard it. I saw the inconceivable mystery of a soul that knew no restraint, no faith, and no fear, yet struggling blindly with itself. I kept my head pretty well; but when I had him at last stretched on the couch, I wiped my forehead, while my legs shook under me as though I had carried half a ton on my back down that hill. And yet I had only supported him, his bony arm clasped round my neck—and he was not much heavier than a child.

"When next day we left at noon, the crowd, of whose presence behind the curtain of trees I had been acutely conscious all the time, flowed out of the woods again, filled the clearing, covered the slope with a mass of naked, breathing, quivering, bronze bodies. I steamed up a bit, then swung downstream, and two thousand eyes followed the evolutions of the splashing, thumping, fierce river-demon beating the water with its terrible tail and breathing black smoke into the air. In front of the first rank, along the river, three men, plastered with bright red earth from head to foot, strutted to and fro restlessly. When we came abreast again, they faced the river, stamped their feet, nodded their horned heads, swayed their scarlet bodies; they shook towards the fierce river-demon a bunch of black feathers, a mangy skin with a pendent tail—something that looked like a dried gourd; they shouted periodically together strings of amazing words that resembled no sounds of human language; and the deep murmurs of the crowd, interrupted suddenly, were like the responses of some satanic litany.

"We had carried Kurtz into the pilot-house: there was more air there. Lying on the couch, he stared through the open shutter. There was an eddy in the mass of human bodies, and the woman with helmeted head and tawny cheeks rushed out to the very brink of the stream. She put out her hands, shouted something, and all that wild mob took up the shout in a roaring chorus of articulated, rapid breathless utterance.

"'Do you understand this?' I asked.

"He kept on looking out past me with fiery, longing eyes, with a mingled expression of wistfulness and hate. He made no answer, but I saw a smile, a smile of indefinable meaning, appear on his colourless lips that a moment after twitched convulsively. 'Do I not?' he said slowly, gasping, as if the words had been torn out of him by a supernatural power. 145

"I pulled the string of the whistle, and I did this because I saw the pilgrims on deck getting out their rifles with an air of anticipating a jolly lark. At the sudden screech there was a movement of abject terror through that wedged mass of bodies. 'Don't! don't you frighten them away,' cried someone on deck disconsolately. I pulled the string time after time. They broke and ran, they leaped, they crouched, they swerved, they dodged the flying terror of the sound. The three red chaps had fallen flat, face down on the shore, as though they had been shot dead. Only the barbarous and superb woman did not so much as flinch, and stretched tragically her bare arms after us over the sombre and glittering river.

"And then that imbecile crowd down on the deck started their little fun, and I could see nothing more for smoke.

"The brown current ran swiftly out of the heart of darkness, bearing us down toward the sea with twice the speed of our upward progress; and Kurtz's life was running swiftly, too, ebbing, ebbing out of his heart into the sea of inexorable time. The manager was very placid, he had no vital anxieties now, he took us both in with a comprehensive and satisfied glance: the 'affair' had come off as well as could be wished. I saw the time approaching when I would be left alone of the party of 'unsound method.' The pilgrims looked up me with disfavour. I was, so to speak, numbered with the dead. It is strange how I accepted this unforeseen partnership, this choice of nightmares forced upon me in the tenebrous land invaded by these mean and greedy phantoms.

"Kurtz discoursed. A voice! a voice! It rang deep to the very last. It survived his strength to hide in the magnificent folds of eloquence the barren darkness of his heart. Oh, he struggled! he struggled! The wastes of his weary brain were haunted by shadowy images now—images of wealth and fame revolving obsequiously round his unextinguishable gift of noble and lofty expression. My Intended, my station, my career, my ideas—these were the subjects for the occasional utterances of elevated sentiments. The shade of the original Kurtz frequented the bedside of the hollow sham, whose fate it was to be buried presently in the mould of primeval earth. But both the diabolic love and the unearthly hate of the mysteries it had penetrated fought for the possession of that soul satiated with primitive emotions, avid of lying fame, of sham distinction, of all the appearances of success and power.

150   "Sometimes he was contemptibly childish. He desired to have kings meet him at railway-stations on his return from some ghastly Nowhere, where he intended to accomplish great things. 'You show them you have in you something that is really profitable, and then there will be no limits to the recognition of your ability,' he would say. 'Of course you must take care of the motives—right motives—always.' The long reaches that were like one and the same reach, monotonous bends that were exactly alike, slipped past the steamer with their multitude of secular trees looking patiently after this grimy fragment of another world, the forerunner of change, of conquest, of trade, of massacres, of blessings. I looked ahead—piloting. 'Close the shutter,' said Kurtz suddenly one day; 'I can't bear to look at this.' I did so. There was a silence. 'Oh, but I will wring your heart yet!' he cried at the invisible wilderness.

"We broke down—as I had expected—and had to lie up for repairs at the head of an island. This delay was the first thing that shook Kurtz's confidence. One morning he gave me a packet of papers and a photograph—the lot tied together with a shoe-string. 'Keep this for me,' he said. 'This noxious fool' (meaning the manager) 'is capable of prying into my boxes when I am not looking.' In the afternoon I saw him. He was lying on his back with closed eyes, and I withdrew quietly, but I heard him mutter, 'Live rightly, die, die . . .' I listened. There was nothing more. Was he rehearsing some speech in his sleep, or was it a fragment of a phrase from some newspaper article? He had been writing for the papers and meant to do so again, 'for the furthering of my ideas. It's a duty.'

"His was an impenetrable darkness. I looked at him as you peer down at a man who is lying at the bottom of a precipice where the sun never shines. But I had not much time to give him, because I was helping the engine-driver to take to pieces the leaky cylinders, to straighten a bent connecting-rod, and in other such matters. I lived in an infernal mess of rust, filings, nuts, bolts, spanners, hammers, ratchet-drills—things I abominate, because I don't get on with them. I tended the little forge we fortunately had aboard; I toiled wearily in a wretched scrap-heap—unless I had the shakes too bad to stand.

"One evening coming in with a candle I was startled to hear him say a little tremulously, 'I am lying here in the dark waiting for death.' The light was within a foot of his eyes. I forced myself to murmur, 'Oh, nonsense!' and stood over him as if transfixed.

"Anything approaching the change that came over his features I have never seen before, and hope never to see again. Oh, I wasn't touched. I was fascinated. It was as though a veil had been rent. I saw on that ivory face the expression of sombre pride, of ruthless power, of craven terror—of an intense and hopeless despair. Did he live his life again in every detail of desire, temptation, and surrender during that supreme moment of complete knowledge? He cried in a whisper at some image, at some vision—he cried out twice, a cry that was no more than a breath—"'The horror! The horror!'

"I blew the candle out and left the cabin. The pilgrims were dining in the mess- 155
room, and I took my place opposite the manager, who lifted his eyes to give me a
questioning glance, which I successfully ignored. He leaned back, serene, with that
peculiar smile of his sealing the unexpressed depths of his meanness. A continuous
shower of small flies streamed upon the lamp, upon the cloth, upon our hands and
faces. Suddenly the manager's boy put his insolent black head in the doorway, and
said in a tone of scathing contempt—

"'Mistah Kurtz—he dead.'

"All the pilgrims rushed out to see. I remained, and went on with my dinner.
I believe I was considered brutally callous. However, I did not eat much. There
was a lamp in there—light, don't you know—and outside it was so beastly, beastly
dark. I went no more near the remarkable man who had pronounced a judgment
upon the adventures of his soul on this earth. The voice was gone. What else had
been there? But I am of course aware that next day the pilgrims buried something
in a muddy hole.

"And then they very nearly buried me.

"However, as you see, I did not go to join Kurtz there and then. I did not. I re- 160
mained to dream the nightmare out to the end, and to show my loyalty to Kurtz
once more. Destiny. My destiny! Droll thing life is—that mysterious arrangement
of merciless logic for a futile purpose. The most you can hope from it is some
knowledge of yourself—that comes too late—a crop of unextinguishable regrets. I
have wrestled with death. It is the most unexciting contest you can imagine. It takes
place in an impalpable grayness, with nothing underfoot, with nothing around, without spectators, without clamour, without glory, without the great desire of victory,
without the great fear of defeat, in a sickly atmosphere of tepid scepticism, without much belief in your own right, and still less in that of your adversary. If such
is the form of ultimate wisdom, then life is a greater riddle than some of us think
it to be. I was within a hair's-breadth of the last opportunity for pronouncement,
and I found with humiliation that probably I would have nothing to say. This is the
reason why I affirm that Kurtz was a remarkable man. He had something to say.
He said it. Since I had peeped over the edge myself, I understand better the meaning of his stare, that could not see the flame of the candle, but was wide enough to
embrace the whole universe, piercing enough to penetrate all the hearts that beat in
the darkness. He had summed up—he had judged. 'The horror!' He was a remarkable man. After all, this was the expression of some sort of belief; it had candour,
it had conviction, it had a vibrating note of revolt in its whisper, it had the appalling
face of a glimpsed truth—the strange commingling of desire and hate. And it is not
my own extremity I remember best—a vision of grayness without form filled with
physical pain, and a careless contempt for the evanescence of all things—even of
this pain itself. No! It is his extremity that I seem to have lived through. True, he
had made that last stride, he had stepped over the edge, while I had been permitted to draw back my hesitating foot. And perhaps in this is the whole difference;
perhaps all the wisdom, and all truth, and all sincerity, are just compressed into that
inappreciable moment of time in which we step over the threshold of the invisible.
Perhaps! I like to think my summing-up would not have been a word of careless

contempt. Better his cry—much better. It was an affirmation, a moral victory paid for by innumerable defeats, by abominable terrors, by abominable satisfactions. But it was a victory! That is why I have remained loyal to Kurtz to the last, and even beyond, when a long time after I heard once more, not his own voice, but the echo of his magnificent eloquence thrown to me from a soul as translucently pure as a cliff of crystal.

"No, they did not bury me, though there is a period of time which I remember mistily, with a shuddering wonder, like a passage through some inconceivable world that had no hope in it and no desire. I found myself in the sepulchral city resenting the sight of people hurrying through the streets to filch a little money from each other, to devour their infamous cookery, to gulp their unwholesome beer, to dream their insignificant and silly dreams. They trespassed upon my thoughts. They were intruders whose knowledge of life was to me an irritating pretence, because I felt so sure they could not possibly know the things I knew. Their bearing, which was simply the bearing of commonplace individuals going about their business in the assurance of perfect safety, was offensive to me like the outrageous flauntings of folly in the face of a danger it is unable to comprehend. I had no particular desire to enlighten them, but I had some difficulty in restraining myself from laughing in their faces, so full of stupid importance. I daresay I was not very well at that time. I tottered about the streets—there were various affairs to settle—grinning bitterly at perfectly respectable persons. I admit my behaviour was inexcusable, but then my temperature was seldom normal in these days. My dear aunt's endeavours to 'nurse up my strength' seemed altogether beside the mark. It was not my strength that wanted nursing, it was my imagination that wanted soothing. I kept the bundle of papers given me by Kurtz, not knowing exactly what to do with it. His mother had died lately, watched over, as I was told, by his Intended. A clean-shaved man, with an official manner and wearing goldrimmed spectacles, called on me one day and made inquiries, at first circuitous, afterwards suavely pressing, about what he was pleased to denominate certain 'documents.' I was not surprised, because I had had two rows with the manager on the subject out there. I had refused to give up the smallest scrap out of that package, and I took the same attitude with the spectacled man. He became darkly menacing at last, and with much heat argued that the Company had the right to every bit of information about its 'territories.' And said he, 'Mr. Kurtz's knowledge of unexplored regions must have been necessarily extensive and peculiar—owing to his great abilities and to the deplorable circumstances in which he had been placed: therefore—' I assured him Mr. Kurtz's knowledge, however extensive, did not bear upon the problems of commerce or administration. He invoked then the name of science. 'It would be an incalculable loss if,' etc., etc. I offered him the report on the 'Suppression of Savage Customs,' with the postscriptum torn off. He took it up eagerly, but ended by sniffing at it with an air of contempt. 'This is not what we had a right to expect,' he remarked. 'Expect nothing else,' I said. 'There are only private letters.' He withdrew upon some threat of legal proceedings, and I saw him no more; but another fellow, calling himself Kurtz's cousin, appeared two days later, and was anxious to hear all the details about his dear relative's last moments. Incidentally he gave me to understand that Kurtz had been essentially a great musician.

'There was the making of an immense success,' said the man, who was an organist, I believe, with lank gray hair flowing over a greasy coat-collar. I had no reason to doubt his statement; and to this day I am unable to say what was Kurtz's profession, whether he ever had any—which was the greatest of his talents. I had taken him for a painter who wrote for the papers, or else for a journalist who could paint—but even the cousin (who took snuff during the interview) could not tell me what he had been—exactly. He was a universal genius—on that point I agreed with the old chap, who thereupon blew his nose noisily into a large cotton handkerchief and withdrew in senile agitation, bearing off some family letters and memoranda without importance. Ultimately a journalist anxious to know something of the fate of his 'dear colleague' turned up. This visitor informed me Kurtz's proper sphere ought to have been politics 'on the popular side.' He had furry straight eyebrows, bristly hair cropped short, an eye-glass on a broad ribbon, and, becoming expansive, confessed his opinion that Kurtz really couldn't write a bit—'but heavens! how that man could talk. He electrified large meetings. He had faith—don't you see?—he had the faith. He could get himself to believe anything—anything. He would have been a splendid leader of an extreme party.' 'What party?' I asked. 'Any party,' answered the other. 'He was an—an—extremist.' Did I not think so? I assented. Did I know, he asked, with a sudden flash of curiosity, 'what it was that had induced him to go out there?' 'Yes,' said I, and forthwith handed him the famous Report for publication, if he thought fit. He glanced through it hurriedly, mumbling all the time, judged 'it would do,' and took himself off with this plunder.

"Thus I was left at last with a slim packet of letters and the girl's portrait. She struck me as beautiful—I mean she had a beautiful expression. I know that the sunlight can be made to lie, too, yet one felt that no manipulation of light and pose could have conveyed the delicate shade of truthfulness upon those features. She seemed ready to listen without mental reservation, without suspicion, without a thought for herself. I concluded I would go and give her back her portrait and those letters myself. Curiosity? Yes; and also some other feelings perhaps. All that had been Kurtz's had passed out of my hands: his soul, his body, his station, his plans, his ivory, his career. There remained only his memory and his Intended—and I wanted to give that up, too, to the past, in a way—to surrender personally all that remained of him with me to that oblivion which is the last word of our common fate. I don't defend myself. I had no clear perception of what it was I really wanted. Perhaps it was an impulse of unconscious loyalty, or the fulfilment of one of these ironic necessities that lurk in the facts of human existence. I don't know. I can't tell. But I went.

"I thought his memory was like the other memories of the dead that accumulate in every man's life—a vague impress on the brain of shadows that had fallen on it in their swift and final passage; but before the high and ponderous door, between the tall houses of a street as still and decorous as a well-kept alley in a cemetery, I had a vision of him on the stretcher, opening his mouth voraciously, as if to devour all the earth with all its mankind. He lived then before me; he lived as much as he had ever lived—a shadow insatiable of splendid appearances, of frightful realities; a shadow darker than the shadow of the night, and draped nobly in the folds of a gorgeous eloquence. The vision seemed to enter the house with me—the stretcher, the phantom-bearers, the wild crowd of obedient worshippers, the gloom of the forests, the glitter of the reach between the murky bends, the beat of the drum, regular and muffled like the beating of a heart—the heart of a conquering darkness. It was a moment of triumph for the wilderness, an invading and vengeful rush which, it seemed to me, I would have to keep back alone for the salvation of another soul. And the memory of what I had heard him say afar there, with the horned shapes stirring at my back, in the glow of fires, within the patient woods, those broken phrases came back to me, were heard again in their ominous and terrifying simplicity. I remembered his abject pleading, his abject threats, the colossal scale of his vile desires, the meanness, the torment, the tempestuous anguish of his soul. And later on I seemed to see his collected languid manner, when he said one day, 'This lot of ivory now is really mine. The Company did not pay for it. I collected it myself at a very great personal risk. I am afraid they will try to claim it as theirs though. H'm. It is a difficult case. What do you think I ought to do—resist? Eh? I want no more than justice.' . . . He wanted no more than justice—no more than justice. I rang the bell before a mahogany door on the first floor, and while I waited he seemed to stare at me out of the glassy panel—stare with that wide and immense stare embracing, condemning, loathing all the universe. I seemed to hear the whispered cry, 'The horror! The horror!'

"The dusk was falling. I had to wait in a lofty drawing-room with three long windows from floor to ceiling that were like three luminous and bedraped columns. The bent gilt legs and backs of the furniture shone in indistinct curves. The tall marble fireplace had a cold and monumental whiteness. A grand piano stood massively in a corner; with dark gleams on the flat surfaces like a sombre and polished sarcophagus. A high door opened—closed. I rose.

165   "She came forward, all in black, with a pale head, floating towards me in the dusk. She was in mourning. It was more than a year since his death, more than a year since the news came; she seemed as though she would remember and mourn for ever. She took both my hands in hers and murmured, 'I had heard you were coming.' I noticed she was not very young—I mean not girlish. She had a mature capacity for fidelity, for belief, for suffering. The room seemed to have grown darker, as if all the sad light of the cloudy evening had taken refuge on her forehead. This fair hair, this pale visage, this pure brow, seemed surrounded by an ashy halo from which the dark eyes looked out at me. Their glance was guileless, profound, confident, and trustful. She carried her sorrowful head as though she were proud of that sorrow, as though she would say, I—I alone know how to mourn for him as he deserves. But while we were still shaking hands, such a look of awful desolation came upon her face that I perceived she was one of those creatures that are not the playthings of Time. For her he had died only yesterday. And, by Jove! the impression was so powerful that for me, too, he seemed to have died only yesterday—nay, this very minute. I saw her and him in the same instant of time—his death and her sorrow—I saw her sorrow in the very moment of his death. Do you understand? I saw them together—I heard them together. She had said, with a deep catch of the breath, 'I have survived' while my strained ears seemed to hear distinctly, mingled with her tone of despairing regret, the summing up whisper of his eternal condemnation. I asked myself what I was

doing there, with a sensation of panic in my heart as though I had blundered into a place of cruel and absurd mysteries not fit for a human being to behold. She motioned me to a chair. We sat down. I laid the packet gently on the little table, and she put her hand over it. . . . 'You knew him well,' she murmured, after a moment of mourning silence.

"'Intimacy grows quickly out there,' I said. 'I knew him as well as it is possible for one man to know another.'

"'And you admired him,' she said. 'It was impossible to know him and not to admire him. Was it?'

"'He was a remarkable man,' I said, unsteadily. Then before the appealing fixity of her gaze, that seemed to watch for more words on my lips, I went on. 'It was impossible not to———'

"'Love him,' she finished eagerly, silencing me into an appalled dumbness. 'How true! how true! But when you think that no one knew him so well as I! I had all his noble confidence. I knew him best.'

"'You knew him best,' I repeated. And perhaps she did. But with every word 170 spoken the room was growing darker, and only her forehead, smooth and white, remained illumined by the unextinguishable light of belief and love.

"'You were his friend,' she went on. 'His friend,' she repeated, a little louder. 'You must have been, if he had given you this, and sent you to me. I feel I can speak to you—and oh! I must speak. I want you—you who have heard his last words—to know I have been worthy of him. . . . It is not pride. . . . Yes! I am proud to know I understood him better than any one on earth—he told me so himself. And since his mother died I have had no one—no one—to—to———'

"I listened. The darkness deepened. I was not even sure whether he had given me the right bundle. I rather suspect he wanted me to take care of another batch of his papers which, after his death, I saw the manager examining under the lamp. And the girl talked, easing her pain in the certitude of my sympathy; she talked as thirsty men drink. I had heard that her engagement with Kurtz had been disapproved by her people. He wasn't rich enough or something. And indeed I don't know whether he had not been a pauper all his life. He had given me some reason to infer that it was his impatience of comparative poverty that drove him out there.

"'. . . Who was not his friend who had heard him speak once?' she was saying. 'He drew men towards him by what was best in them.' She looked at me with intensity. 'It is the gift of the great,' she went on, and the sound of her low voice seemed to have the accompaniment of all the other sounds, full of mystery, desolation, and sorrow, I had ever heard—the ripple of the river, the soughing of the trees swayed by the wind, the murmurs of the crowds, the faint ring of incomprehensible words cried from afar, the whisper of a voice speaking from beyond the threshold of an eternal darkness. 'But you have heard him! You know!' she cried.

"'Yes, I know,' I said with something like despair in my heart, but bowing my head before the faith that was in her, before that great and saving illusion that shone with an unearthly glow in the darkness, in the triumphant darkness from which I could not have defended her—from which I could not even defend myself.

175   "'What a loss to me—to us!'—she corrected herself with beautiful generosity; then added in a murmur, 'To the world.' By the last gleams of twilight I could see the glitter of her eyes, full of tears—of tears that would not fall.

    "'I have been very happy—very fortunate—very proud,' she went on. 'Too fortunate. Too happy for a little while. And now I am unhappy for—for life.'

    "She stood up; her fair hair seemed to catch all the remaining light in a glimmer of gold. I rose, too.

    "'And of all this,' she went on, mournfully, 'of all his promise, and of all his greatness, of his generous mind, of his noble heart, nothing remains—nothing but a memory. You and I———'

    "'We shall always remember him,' I said, hastily.

180   "'No!' she cried. 'It is impossible that all this should be lost—that such a life should be sacrificed to leave nothing—but sorrow. You know what vast plans he had. I knew of them, too—I could not perhaps understand—but others knew of them. Something must remain. His words, at least, have not died.'

    "'His words will remain,' I said.

    "'And his example,' she whispered to herself. 'Men looked up to him—his goodness shone in every act. His example———'

    "'True,' I said; 'his example, too. Yes, his example. I forgot that.'

    "'But I do not. I cannot—I cannot believe—not yet. I cannot believe that I shall never see him again, that nobody will see him again, never, never, never.'

185   "She put out her arms as if after a retreating figure, stretching them back and with clasped pale hands across the fading and narrow sheen of the window. Never see him! I saw him clearly enough then. I shall see this eloquent phantom as long as I live, and I shall see her, too, a tragic and familiar Shade, resembling in this gesture another one, tragic also, and bedecked with powerless charms, stretching bare brown arms over the glitter of the infernal stream, the stream of darkness. She said suddenly very low, 'He died as he lived.'

    "'His end,' said I, with dull anger stirring in me, 'was in every way worthy of his life.'

    "'And I was not with him,' she murmured. My anger subsided before a feeling of infinite pity.

    "'Everything that could be done———' I mumbled.

    "'Ah, but I believed in him more than any one on earth—more than his own mother, more than—himself. He needed me! Me! I would have treasured every sigh, every word, every sign, every glance.'

190   "I felt like a chill grip on my chest. 'Don't,' I said, in a muffled voice.

    "'Forgive me. I—I—have mourned so long in silence—in silence. . . . You were with him—to the last? I think of his loneliness. Nobody near to understand him as I would have understood. Perhaps no one to hear . . . .'

    "'To the very end,' I said, shakily. 'I heard his very last words. . . .' I stopped in a fright.

    "'Repeat them,' she murmured in a heart-broken tone. 'I want—I want—something—something—to—to live with.'

"I was on the point of crying at her, 'Don't you hear them?' The dusk was repeating them in a persistent whisper all around us, in a whisper that seemed to swell menacingly like the first whisper of a rising wind. 'The horror! the horror!'

"'His last word—to live with,' she insisted. 'Don't you understand I loved 195 him—I loved him—I loved him!'

"I pulled myself together and spoke slowly.

"'The last word he pronounced was—your name.'

"I heard a light sigh and then my heart stood still, stopped dead short by an exulting and terrible cry, by the cry of inconceivable triumph and of unspeakable pain. 'I knew it—I was sure! . . .' She knew. She was sure. I heard her weeping; she had hidden her face in her hands. It seemed to me that the house would collapse before I could escape, that the heavens would fall upon my head. But nothing happened. The heavens do not fall for such a trifle. Would they have fallen, I wonder, if I had rendered Kurtz that justice which was his due? Hadn't he said he wanted only justice? But I couldn't. I could not tell her. It would have been too dark—too dark altogether. . . .'"

Marlow ceased, and sat apart, indistinct and silent, in the pose of a meditating Buddha. Nobody moved for a time. "We have lost the first of the ebb," said the Director, suddenly. I raised my head. The offing was barred by a black bank of clouds, and the tranquil waterway leading to the uttermost ends of the earth flowed sombre under an overcast sky—seemed to lead into the heart of an immense darkness.

QUESTIONS FOR DISCUSSION AND WRITING

1. What are the most important choices that Marlow has to make in the story? How does Marlow's decision to lie to the Intended about Kurtz's last words serve as the climax of the story?

2. What preconception does Marlow form about Kurtz based on the assessment and rumors of others? How does the man Marlow finally meets fulfill or contradict that preconception?

3. What surprising similarities does Marlow discover between the civilized Thames River and the savage Congo? In what sense has the whole world become a dark place for Marlow? What has darkness come to mean to him?

4. How does the first narrator of the story introduce the difference between a typical sea yarn and the kind of story Marlow tells? How does Marlow's statement, "We live, as we dream—alone," explain his difficulty in telling his story to his listeners?

5. What is "the horror, the horror" that Kurtz perceives in the heart of darkness? What restrains Marlow from falling into that horror?

Stories for Comparison

Nathaniel Hawthorne's "Young Goodman Brown" (pages 640–650); William Gass's "In the Heart of the Heart of the Country" (pages 560–568).

36

JULIO CORTÁZAR

We Love Glenda So Much

JULIO CORTÁZAR (1914–1984) was born in Brussels, Belgium, educated at Buenos Aires University, and held dual citizenship in Argentina and (beginning in 1981) France. He worked as a teacher of French literature in Argentina, publishing many of the poems, plays, and stories that established his literary reputation in South America. In the 1950s the political turmoil in his country prompted Cortázar to move to Paris, where he wrote and worked as a freelance translator for UNESCO. In the mid-1960s much of his work began to be translated into English, and critics proclaimed *Hopscotch* (1966) one of the best novels written by a South American. His other work of the period, *Cronopios and Famas* (1964), *The Winners* (1973), *62: A Model Kit* (1972), *A Manual for Manual* (1978), reveals Cortázar's experiments with fictional form, preoccupations with fantasy and reality, and commitment to radical politics. His last books translated into English before his death include *A Change of Light and Other Stories* (1980) and *We Love Glenda So Much* (1983). The title story from the latter volume provides an ironic commentary on the mixture of fantasy and reality.

I n those days it was hard to know. You go to the movies or the theater and live your night without thinking about the people who have already gone through the same ceremony, choosing the place and the time, getting dressed and telephoning and row eleven or five, the darkness and the music, territory that belongs to nobody and to everybody there where everybody is nobody, the men or women in their seats, maybe a word of apology for arriving late, a murmured comment that someone picks up or ignores, almost always silence, looks pouring onto the stage or the screen, fleeing from what's beside them, from what's on this side. It was really hard to know that there were so many of us—beyond the ads, the endless lines, the posters, and the reviews—so many who loved Glenda.

It took three or four years, and it would not be bold to assert that the nucleus had its start with Irazusta or Diana Rivero; they themselves didn't know how at some moment, over drinks with friends after the movies, things were said or left unsaid that suddenly would form the alliance, what afterward we all called the nucleus and the younger ones called the club. There was nothing of a club about it, we simply loved Glenda Garson, and that was enough to set us apart from those who only admired her. Just like them, we admired Glenda too, and also Anouk, Marilyn, Annie, Silvana, and why not Marcello, Yves, Vittorio, or Dirk, but only we loved Glenda so much, and the nucleus was formed because of that and out of that, it was something that only we knew, and we trusted in those who all during our conversations had shown little by little that they loved Glenda too.

Starting with Diana or Irazusta, the nucleus was slowly expanding. In the year of *Snow Fire* there couldn't have been more than six or seven of us; with the premiere of *The Uses of Elegance* the nucleus broadened and we felt that it was growing at an almost unbearable rate and that we were threatened with snobbish imitation or seasonal sentimentality. The first, Irazusta and Diana and two or three more of us, decided to close ranks, not to admit anyone without a test, without an examination disguised under the whiskey and a show of erudition (so Buenos Aires, so London and Mexico, those midnight exams). At the time of the opening of *Fragile Returns,* we had to admit, melancholically triumphant, that there were many of us who loved Glenda. The chance meetings at the movies, the glances exchanged as we came out, that kind of lost look on the women and the painful silence of the men, showed us better than any insignia or password. Mechanics that defied investigation led us to the same downtown café, the isolated tables began to draw closer together, there was the gracious custom of ordering the same cocktail so as to lay aside any useless skirmishing, and finally looking each other in the eyes, there where Glenda's last image in the last scene of the last movie still breathed.

Twenty, maybe thirty, we never knew how many we had come to be, because sometimes Glenda would go on for months at one theater or was in two or three at the same time, and there was also that exceptional moment when she appeared onstage to play the young murderess in *The Lunatics* and her success broke the dikes and created a momentary enthusiasm that we never accepted. By that time we already knew each other; a lot of us would visit each other to talk about Glenda. From the very beginning Irazusta seemed to exercise a tacit command that he had never asked for, and Diana Rivero played her slow chess game of acceptance and rejection that assured us a total authenticity without the risk of infiltrators or boobs. What had begun as a free association was now attaining the structure of a clan, and the casual interrogations of early times had been succeeded by concrete questions, the stumbling scene in *The Uses of Elegance,* the final retort in *Snow Fire,* the second erotic scene in *Fragile Returns.* We loved Glenda so much that we couldn't tolerate parvenus, rowdy lesbians, erudite aestheticians. It was even (we'll never know how) taken for granted that we would go to the café on Fridays when a Glenda movie was playing downtown, and with the reruns in neighborhood theaters we would let a week go by before getting together in order to give everybody the necessary time; like a rigorous regulation, the obligations were defined without error; not respecting them would have meant provoking Irazusta's contemptuous smile or that graciously horrible look with which Diana Rivero denounced and punished treason.

At that time the gatherings were only Glenda, her dazzling presence in every 5 one of us, and we knew nothing of discrepancies or misgivings. Only gradually, at first with a feeling of guilt, did some dare to let partial criticisms slip, disillusion or disappointment with an unfortunate scene, descents into the conventional or the predictable. We knew that Glenda wasn't responsible for the weaknesses that at certain moments clouded the splendid crystal of *The Lash* or the ending of *You Never Know Why.* We found out about other films by the directors, where the stories and the scripts came from, we were implacable with them because we were beginning to feel that our love for Glenda was going beyond the merely artistic terrain and that she alone was saved from what the rest did imperfectly. Diana was the first to talk about a mission; she did it in her tangential way, not stating outright what really counted for her. We saw the joy of a double whiskey, of a satisfied smile in her when we admitted openly that it was true, that we couldn't just stay like that, the movies and the café and loving Glenda so much.

Not even then were clear words spoken; we didn't need them. All that counted was Glenda's happiness in each one of us, and that happiness could only come from perfection. Suddenly the mistakes, the misses, became unbearable for us; we couldn't accept the way *You Never Know Why* ended, or that *Snow Fire* should include the infamous poker scene (in which Glenda didn't take part, but which in some way stained her like vomit—that expression of Nancy Phillips's) and the inadmissible arrival of the repentant son. As almost always, it was up to Irazusta to give a clear definition of the mission that awaited us, and that night we went home as if crushed by the responsibility we had just recognized and assumed, catching a glimpse at the same time of the happiness of a flawless future, of Glenda without blunders or betrayals.

Instinctively, the nucleus closed ranks, the task wouldn't allow for a hazy plurality. Irazusta spoke of the laboratory after it had already been set up in a country house in Recife de Lobos. We divided up the tasks equitably among those who were to collect all the prints of *Fragile Returns,* chosen for its relatively few imperfections. No one had thought to raise the question of money; Irazusta had been Howard Hughes's partner in the Pichincha tin mines, an extremely simple mechanism put the necessary power in our hands, jets and connections and bribes. We didn't even have an office; Hagar Loss's computer programmed the tasks and the stages. Two months after Diana Rivero's remark the laboratory was all set up to replace the ineffective bird scene in *Fragile Returns* with a different one that gave Glenda back the perfect rhythm and the exact feeling of the dramatic action. The film was already several years old and its rerun on international circuits didn't cause the slightest surprise; memory plays with its repositories and makes them accept their own permutations and variants, perhaps Glenda herself wouldn't have noticed the change but would have noticed, because we all had, the marvel of perfect coincidence with a memory washed clean of slag, precisely in tune with desire.

The mission was being accomplished without surcease; as soon as we felt sure that the laboratory was in working order we brought off the rescue of *Snow Fire* and *The Prism:* the other films entered into the process with the exact rhythm foreseen by Hagar Loss's personnel and the people in the laboratory. We had problems with *The Uses of Elegance* because people in the oil-producing emirates owned copies for their personal enjoyment and extraordinary maneuvers and procedures were necessary in order to steal them (there's no reason to use any other word) and to steal them without their owners' noticing. The laboratory was functioning at a level of perfection that had seemed unattainable to us at the start, even though we hadn't dared say so to Irazusta; curiously, the most doubtful one had been Diana; but when Irazusta showed us *You Never Know Why* and we saw the real ending, we saw Glenda, who instead of going back to Romano's house, headed her car toward the cliff and destroyed us with her splendid, necessary fall into the torrent, we knew that there could be perfection in this world and that now it belonged to Glenda, to Glenda for us forever.

The most difficult part was, of course, deciding on the changes, the cuts, the modifications in montage and rhythm; our different ways of feeling Glenda brought on harsh confrontations that calmed down only after long analyses and in some cases the imposition of majority rule in the nucleus. But while some of us, defeated, watched the new version with bitterness over the fact that it wasn't completely up to our dreams, I don't think anyone was disappointed with the finished work, we loved Glenda so much that the results were always justifiable, often beyond what had been foreseen. There were even a few scares, a letter from a reader of the inevitable *Times* of London showing surprise that three scenes in *Snow Fire* had been shown in a different order from how the writer thought he remembered, and also an article in *La Opinión* protesting a supposed cut in *The Prism,* imagining the hand of bureaucratic prudishness. In every case rapid arrangements were made in order to avoid possible follow-ups; it wasn't hard, people are fickle and forget or accept or are in search of what's new, the movie world is ephemeral, like the historical present, except for those of us who love Glenda so much.

Basically more dangerous were the arguments within the nucleus, risking schism or diaspora. Even though we felt more united than ever because of the mission, there were nights when analytical voices contaminated by political philosophies were raised, bringing up moral problems in the midst of the work, asking if we weren't surrendering to an onanistic hall of mirrors, foolishly carving a piece of baroque madness on an ivory tusk or a grain of rice. It wasn't easy to turn our backs on them because the nucleus had only been able to do its work in the way a heart or an airplane does: by maintaining a perfectly coherent rhythm. It wasn't easy to listen to criticism that accused us of escapism, that suspected a waste of strength that was being turned away from a more pressing reality, one that was more in need of agreement in the times we were living. And yet it wasn't necessary to crush summarily a heresy that was only hinted at, as even its protagonists limited themselves to a partial objection, they and we loved Glenda so much that above and beyond ethical or historical disagreements the feeling that would always unite us remained, the certainty that perfecting Glenda was perfecting us and perfecting the world. We even had splendid recompense in the fact that one of the philosophers re-established the equilibrium after overcoming that period of inane scruples; from his mouth we heard that all partial works are also history, that something as immense as the invention of the printing press had been born of the most individual and particular of desires—to repeat and perpetuate a woman's name.

10   In that way we came to the day on which we got proof that Glenda's image was now being projected without the slightest weakness; the screens of the world were presenting her in just the way that she herself—we were sure—would have wanted to be presented, and perhaps that was why it didn't surprise us too much to read in the press that she had just announced her retirement from movies and the theater. Glenda's involuntary and marvelous contribution to our work couldn't have been either coincidence or miracle, it was simply that something in her had unknowingly respected our anonymous love, from the depths of her being came the only answer that she could give us, the act of love that included us in one last act of giving, the one that ordinary people would only understand as an absence. We were living the happiness of the seventh day, of the rest after the creation; now we would be able to see every one of Glenda's works without the agonizing threat of a tomorrow plagued by mistakes and blunders; now we could come together with the lightness of angels or birds, in an absolute presence that was like eternity.

Yes, but a poet had said under Glenda's same skies that eternity is in love with the works of time, and it was for Diana to discover and give us the news a year later. Ordinary and human, Glenda was announcing her return to the screen, the usual reasons, the frustration of a professional with nothing to do, a role that was made to order, an imminent filming. No one can have forgotten that night at the café, precisely after seeing *The Uses of Elegance,* which was returning to downtown theaters. It almost wasn't necessary for Irazusta to say what we were all experiencing, a bitter taste of injustice and rebellion. We loved Glenda so much that our discouragement didn't touch her, it was no fault of hers, being an actress and being Glenda, the horror was in the ruptured mechanism, in the reality of figures and awards and Oscars entering our so hard-won heaven like a hidden fissure. When Diana laid her hand on Irazusta's arm and said "Yes, it's the only thing left to do," she was speaking for all of us with no need for consultation. Never had the nucleus had such a fearsome drive, never had it needed fewer words to put it into motion. We separated, undone, already living what would happen on a day that only one of us would know ahead of time. We were sure we wouldn't meet again at the café, that each of us from then on would hide the solitary perfection of our realm. We knew that Irazusta was going to do what was necessary, nothing simpler for someone like him. We didn't even say good-bye the way we usually did, with the nice security of meeting again after the movies some night with *Fragile Returns* or *The Lash.* It was rather a turning your back, with the pretext that it was late, that you had to leave; we went off separately, each one bearing his or her desire to forget until everything was consummated, and knowing it wouldn't be that way, that we would still have to open the newspaper some morning and read the news, the stupid phrases of professional consternation. We would never talk about that with anybody, we would courteously avoid each other in theaters and on the street; it would be the only way that the nucleus could remain true to its faith, could silently guard the finished work. We loved Glenda so much that we would offer her one last inviolable perfection. On the untouchable heights to which we had raised her in exaltation, we would save her from the fall, her faithful could go on adoring her without any decrease; one does not come down from a cross alive.

QUESTIONS FOR DISCUSSION AND WRITING

1. How do the opening sections of the story explain the evolution of the group that "loved Glenda so much"? How does Glenda's decision to return to the screen lead to the climax of the story?

2. How does the group's love for Glenda reveal its characteristics? What characteristics separate the nucleus of the group from the rest?

3. Why does the created world of film become more real to the group than ordinary reality?

4. Why does the narrator use *we* rather than *I* in this narration?

5. How does Cortázar clarify that he is writing about the development of cults in general as well as this cult in particular? How does the last sentence, for example, connect the representation of this cult to the larger issues of religion?

Stories for Comparison:

T. Coraghessan Boyle's "Heart of a Champion" (pages 305–310); James Thurber's "The Greatest Man in the World" (pages 1090–1096).

37

....

S T E P H E N   C R A N E

The Open Boat

*A Tale Intended to be after the Fact: Being the Experience
of Four Men from the Sunk Steamer* Commodore

STEPHEN CRANE (1871–1900) was born in Newark, New Jersey, and spent a term each at Lafayette College and Syracuse University. After this disappointing year, Crane discontinued his university education to work as a free-lance journalist in New York City. More interested in creating moods and examining motives, Crane became disenchanted with routine factual reporting, turning his attention more and more to fiction. His first novel, *Maggie: A Girl of the Streets* (1893), based on his knowledge of New York slum life, was not successful, but his second, *The Red Badge of Courage* (1895), a vivid account of an imaginary episode from the Civil War, won him international acclaim. Crane's newly acquired literary reputation enabled him to travel to various parts of the world as a feature reporter. One such tour of the West, in 1895, produced such memorable stories as "The Blue Hotel" and "The Bride Comes to Yellow Sky." In 1897 Crane was assigned to cover the insurrection in Cuba, but his ship wrecked off the coast of Florida, leading to the adventures he revealed in "The Open Boat." In that same year, Crane covered the Greco-Turkish War, and in 1898 returned to report on the Spanish-American War in Cuba. After a brief residence in England, Crane checked into a sanatorium in Bodenweiler, Germany, where he died of tuberculosis at the age of twenty-eight. In "The Open Boat," reprinted from *The Open Boat and Other Tales of Adventure* (1898), Crane portrays the human struggle in an indifferent universe.

I

N one of them knew the colour of the sky. Their eyes glanced level, and were fastened upon the waves that swept toward them. These waves were of the hue of slate, save for the tops, which were of foaming white, and all of the men knew the colours of the sea. The horizon narrowed and widened, and dipped and rose, and at all times its edge was jagged with waves that seemed thrust up in points like rocks.

Many a man ought to have a bathtub larger than the boat which here rode upon the sea. These waves were most wrongfully and barbarously abrupt and tall, and each froth-top was a problem in small-boat navigation.

The cook squatted in the bottom, and looked with both eyes at the six inches of gunwale which separated him from the ocean. His sleeves were rolled over his fat forearms, and the two flaps of his unbuttoned vest dangled as he bent to bail out the boat. Often he said, "Gawd! that was a narrow clip." As he remarked it he invariably gazed eastward over the broken sea.

The oiler, steering with one of the two oars in the boat, sometimes raised himself suddenly to keep clear of water that swirled in over the stern. It was a thin little oar, and it seemed often ready to snap.

5   The correspondent, pulling at the other oar, watched the waves and wondered why he was there.

The injured captain, lying in the bow, was at this time buried in that profound dejection and indifference which comes, temporarily at least, to even the bravest and most enduring when, willy-nilly, the firm fails, the army loses, the ship goes down. The mind of the master of a vessel is rooted deep in the timbers of her, though he command for a day or a decade; and this captain had on him the stern impression of a scene in the greys of dawn of seven turned faces, and later a stump of a topmast with a white ball on it, that slashed to and fro at the waves, went low and lower, and down. Thereafter there was something strange in his voice. Although steady, it was deep with mourning, and of a quality beyond oration or tears.

"Keep 'er a little more south, Billie," said he.

"A little more south, sir," said the oiler in the stern.

A seat in this boat was not unlike a seat upon a bucking broncho, and by the same token a broncho is not much smaller. The craft pranced and reared and plunged like an animal. As each wave came, and she rose for it, she seemed like a horse making at a fence outrageously high. The manner of her scramble over these walls of water is a mystic thing, and, moreover, at the top of them were ordinarily these problems in white water, the foam racing down from the summit of each wave requiring a new leap, and a leap from the air. Then, after scornfully bumping a crest, she would slide and race and splash down a long incline, and arrive bobbing and nodding in front of the next menace.

A singular disadvantage of the sea lies in the fact that after successfully surmounting one wave you discover that there is another behind it just as important and just as nervously anxious to do something effective in the way of swamping boats. In a ten-foot dinghy one can get an idea of the resources of the sea in the line of waves that is not probable to the average experience which is never at sea in a dinghy. As each slaty wall of water approached, it shut all else from the view of the men in the boat, and it was not difficult to imagine that this particular wave was the final outburst of the ocean, the last effort of the grim water. There was a terrible grace in the move of the waves, and they came in silence, save for the snarling of the crests.

In the wan light the faces of the men must have been grey. Their eyes must have glinted in strange ways as they gazed steadily astern. Viewed from a balcony, the whole thing would doubtless have been weirdly picturesque. But the men in the boat had no time to see it, and if they had had leisure, there were other things to occupy their minds. The sun swung steadily up the sky, and they knew it was broad day because the colour of the sea changed from slate to emerald green streaked with amber lights, and the foam was like tumbling snow. The process of the breaking day was unknown to them. They were aware only of this effect upon the colour of the waves that rolled toward them.

In disjointed sentences the cook and the correspondent argued as to the difference between a life-saving station and a house of refuge. The cook had said: "There's a house of refuge just north of the Mosquito Inlet Light, and as soon as they see us they'll come off in their boat and pick us up."

"As soon as who see us?" said the correspondent.

"The crew," said the cook.

"Houses of refuge don't have crews," said the correspondent. "As I understand them, they are only places where clothes and grub are stored for the benefit of shipwrecked people. They don't carry crews."

"Oh, yes, they do," said the cook.

"No, they don't," said the correspondent.

"Well, we're not there yet, anyhow," said the oiler, in the stern.

"Well," said the cook, "perhaps it's not a house of refuge that I'm thinking of as being near Mosquito Inlet Light; perhaps it's a life-saving station."

"We're not there yet," said the oiler in the stern.

2

As the boat bounced from the top of each wave the wind tore through the hair of the hatless men, and as the craft plopped her stern down again the spray slashed past them. The crest of each of these waves was a hill, from the top of which the men surveyed for a moment a broad tumultuous expanse, shining and wind-riven. It was probably splendid, it was probably glorious, this play of the free sea, wild with lights of emerald and white and amber.

"Bully good thing it's an on-shore wind," said the cook. "If not, where would we be? Wouldn't have a show."

"That's right," said the correspondent.

The busy oiler nodded his assent.

25   Then the captain, in the bow, chuckled in a way that expressed humour, contempt, tragedy, all in one. "Do you think we've got much of a show now, boys?" said he.

Whereupon the three were silent, save for a trifle of hemming and hawing. To express any particular optimism at this time they felt to be childish and stupid, but they all doubtless possessed this sense of the situation in their minds. A young man thinks doggedly at such times. On the other hand, the ethics of their condition was decidedly against any open suggestion of hopelessness. So they were silent.

"Oh, well," said the captain, soothing his children, "we'll get ashore all right."

But there was that in his tone which made them think; so the oiler quoth, "Yes! if this wind holds."

The cook was bailing, "Yes! if we don't catch hell in the surf."

30   Canton-flannel gulls flew near and far. Sometimes they sat down on the sea, near patches of brown seaweed that rolled over the waves with a movement like carpets on a line in a gale. The birds sat comfortably in groups, and they were envied by some in the dinghy, for the wrath of the sea was no more to them than it was to a covey of prairie chickens a thousand miles inland. Often they came very close and stared at the men with black bead-like eyes. At these times they were uncanny and sinister in their unblinking scrutiny, and the men hooted angrily at them, telling them to be gone. One came, and evidently decided to alight on the top of the captain's head. The bird flew parallel to the boat and did not circle, but made short sidelong jumps in the air in chicken-fashion. His black eyes were wistfully fixed upon the captain's head. "Ugly brute," said the oiler to the bird. "You look as if you were made with a jackknife." The cook and the correspondent swore darkly at the creature. The captain naturally wished to knock it away with the end of the heavy painter, but he did not dare do it, because anything resembling an emphatic gesture would have capsized this freighted boat; and so, with his open hand, the captain gently and carefully waved the gull away. After it had been discouraged from the pursuit the captain breathed easier on account of his hair, and others breathed easier because the bird struck their minds at this time as being somehow gruesome and ominous.

In the meantime the oiler and the correspondent rowed. And also they rowed. They sat together in the same seat, and each rowed an oar. Then the oiler took both oars; then the correspondent took both oars; then the oiler; then the correspondent. They rowed and they rowed. The very ticklish part of the business was when the time came for the reclining one in the stern to take his turn at the oars. By the very last star of truth, it is easier to steal eggs from under a hen than it was to change seats in the dinghy. First the man in the stern slid his hand along the thwart and moved with care, as if he were of Sèvres. Then the man in the rowing-seat slid his hand along the other thwart. It was all done with the most extraordinary care. As the two sidled past each other, the whole party kept watchful eyes on the coming wave, and the captain cried: "Look out, now! Steady, there!"

The brown mats of seaweed that appeared from time to time were like islands, bits of earth. They were travelling, apparently, neither one way nor the other. They were, to all intents, stationary. They informed the men in the boat that it was making progress slowly toward the land.

The captain, rearing cautiously in the bow after the dinghy soared on a great swell, said that he had seen the lighthouse at Mosquito Inlet. Presently the cook remarked that he had seen it. The correspondent was at the oars then, and for some reason he too wished to look at the lighthouse; but his back was toward the far shore, and the waves were important, and for some time he could not seize an opportunity to turn his head. But at last there came a wave more gentle than the others and when at the crest of it he swiftly scoured the western horizon.

"See it?" said the captain.

"No," said the correspondent, slowly; "I didn't see anything."   35

"Look again," said the captain. He pointed. "It's exactly in that direction."

At the top of another wave the correspondent did as he was bid, and this time his eyes chanced on a small, still thing on the edge of the swaying horizon. It was precisely like the point of a pin. It took an anxious eye to find a lighthouse so tiny.

"Think we'll make it, Captain?"

"If this wind holds and the boat don't swamp, we can't do much else," said the captain.

The little boat, lifted by each towering sea and splashed viciously by the crests, 40 made progress that in the absence of seaweed was not apparent to those in her. She seemed just a wee thing wallowing, miraculously top up, at the mercy of five oceans. Occasionally a great spread of water, like white flames, swarmed into her.

"Bail her, cook," said the captain, serenely.

"All right, Captain," said the cheerful cook.

3

It would be difficult to describe the subtle brotherhood of men that was here established on the seas. No one said that it was so. No one mentioned it. But it dwelt in the boat, and each man felt it warm him. They were a captain, an oiler, a cook, and a correspondent, and they were friends—friends in a more curiously iron-bound degree than may be common. The hurt captain, lying against the water-jar in the bow, spoke always in a low voice and calmly; but he could never command a more ready and swiftly obedient crew than the motley three of the dinghy. It was more than a mere recognition of what was best for the common safety. There was surely in it a quality that was personal and heart-felt. And after this devotion to the commander of the boat, there was this comradeship, that the correspondent, for instance, who had been taught to be cynical of men, knew even at the time was the best experience of his life. But no one said that it was so. No one mentioned it.

"I wish we had a sail," remarked the captain. "We might try my overcoat on the end of an oar, and give you two boys a chance to rest." So the cook and the correspondent held the mast and spread wide the overcoat; the oiler steered; and the little boat made good way with her new rig. Sometimes the oiler had to scull sharply to keep a sea from breaking into the boat, but otherwise sailing was a success.

45   Meanwhile the lighthouse had been growing slowly larger. It had now almost assumed colour, and appeared like a little grey shadow on the sky. The man at the oars could not be prevented from turning his head rather often to try for a glimpse of this little grey shadow.

At last, from the top of each wave, the men in the tossing boat could see land. Even as the lighthouse was an upright shadow on the sky, this land seemed but a long black shadow on the sea. It certainly was thinner than paper. "We must be about opposite New Smyrna," said the cook, who had coasted this shore often in schooners. "Captain, by the way, I believe they abandoned that life-saving station there about a year ago."

"Did they?" said the captain.

The wind slowly died away. The cook and the correspondent were not now obliged to slave in order to hold high the oar. But the waves continued their old impetuous swooping at the dinghy, and the little craft, no longer under way, struggled woundily over them. The oiler or the correspondent took the oars again.

Shipwrecks are apropos of nothing. If men could only train for them and have them occur when the men had reached pink condition, there would be less drowning at sea. Of the four in the dinghy none had slept any time worth mentioning for two days and two nights previous to embarking in the dinghy, and in the excitement of clambering about the deck of a foundering ship they had also forgotten to eat heartily.

50   For these reasons, and for others, neither the oiler nor the correspondent was fond of rowing at this time. The correspondent wondered ingenuously how in the name of all that was sane could there be people who thought it amusing to row a boat. It was not an amusement; it was a diabolical punishment, and even a genius of mental aberrations could never conclude that it was anything but a horror to the muscles and a crime against the back. He mentioned to the boat in general how the amusement of rowing struck him, and the weary-faced oiler smiled in full sympathy. Previously to the foundering, by the way, the oiler had worked a double watch in the engine-room of the ship.

"Take her easy now, boys," said the captain. "Don't spend yourselves. If we have to run a surf you'll need all your strength, because we'll sure have to swim for it. Take your time."

55   Slowly the land arose from the sea. From a black line it became a line of black and a line of white—trees and sand. Finally the captain said that he could make out a house on the shore. "That's the house of refuge, sure," said the cook. "They'll see us before long, and come out after us."

The distant lighthouse reared high. "The keeper ought to be able to make us out now, if he's looking through a glass," said the captain. "He'll notify the life-saving people."

"None of those other boats could have got ashore to give word of this wreck," said the oiler, in a low voice, "else the life-boat would be out hunting us."

Slowly and beautifully the land loomed out of the sea. The wind came again. It had veered from the north-east to the south-east. Finally a new sound struck the ears of the men in the boat. It was the low thunder of the surf on the shore. "We'll never be able to make the lighthouse now," said the captain. "Swing her head a little more north, Billie."

"A little more north, sir," said the oiler.

Whereupon the little boat turned her nose once more down the wind, and all but the oarsman watched the shore grow. Under the influence of this expansion doubt and direful apprehension were leaving the minds of the men. The management of the boat was still most absorbing, but it could not prevent a quiet cheerfulness. In an hour, perhaps, they would be ashore.

Their backbones had become thoroughly used to balancing in the boat, and they now rode this wild colt of a dinghy like circus men. The correspondent thought that he had been drenched to the skin, but happening to feel in the top pocket of his coat, he found therein eight cigars. Four of them were soaked with sea-water; four were perfectly scatheless. After a search, somebody produced three dry matches; and thereupon the four waifs rode impudently in their little boat and, with an assurance of an impending rescue shining in their eyes, puffed at the big cigars, and judged well and ill of all men. Everybody took a drink of water.

4

"Cook," remarked the captain, "there don't seem to be any signs of life about your house of refuge."

"No," replied the cook. "Funny they don't see us!"

A broad stretch of lowly coast lay before the eyes of the men. It was of low dunes topped with dark vegetation. The roar of the surf was plain, and sometimes they could see the white lip of a wave as it spun up the beach. A tiny house was blocked out black upon the sky. Southward, the slim lighthouse lifted its little grey length.

Tide, wind, and waves were swinging the dinghy northward. "Funny they don't see us," said the men.

The surf's roar was here dulled, but its tone was nevertheless thunderous and mighty. As the boat swam over the great rollers the men sat listening to this roar. "We'll swamp sure," said everybody.

It is fair to say here that there was not a life-saving station within twenty miles in either direction; but the men did not know this fact, and in consequence they made dark and opprobrious remarks concerning the eyesight of the nation's life-savers. Four scowling men sat in the dinghy and surpassed records in the invention of epithets.

65   "Funny they don't see us."

The light-heartedness of a former time had completely faded. To their sharpened minds it was easy to conjure pictures of all kinds of incompetency and blindness and, indeed, cowardice. There was the shore of the populous land, and it was bitter and bitter to them that from it came no sign.

"Well," said the captain, ultimately, "I suppose we'll have to make a try for ourselves. If we stay out here too long, we'll none of us have strength left to swim after the boat swamps."

And so the oiler, who was at the oars, turned the boat straight for the shore. There was a sudden tightening of muscles. There was some thinking.

"If we don't all get ashore," said the captain—"if we don't all get ashore, I suppose you fellows know where to send news of my finish?"

70   They then briefly exchanged some addresses and admonitions. As for the reflections of the men, there was a great deal of rage in them. Perchance they might be formulated thus: "If I am going to be drowned—if I am going to be drowned—if I am going to be drowned, why, in the name of the seven mad gods who rule the sea, was I allowed to come thus far and contemplate sand and trees? Was I brought here merely to have my nose dragged away as I was about to nibble the sacred cheese of life? It is preposterous. If this old ninny-woman, Fate, cannot do better than this, she should be deprived of the management of men's fortunes. She is an old hen who knows not her intention. If she has decided to drown me, why did she not do it in the beginning and save me all this trouble? The whole affair is absurd.—But no; she cannot mean to drown me. She dare not drown me. She cannot drown me. Not after all this work." Afterward the man might have had an impulse to shake his fist at the clouds. "Just you drown me, now, and then hear what I call you!"

The billows that came at this time were more formidable. They seemed always just about to break and roll over the little boat in a turmoil of foam. There was a preparatory and long growl in the speech of them. No mind unused to the sea would have concluded that the dinghy could ascend these sheer heights in time. The shore was still afar. The oiler was a wily surfman. "Boys," he said swiftly, "she won't live three minutes more, and we're too far out to swim. Shall I take her to sea again, Captain?"

"Yes; go ahead!" said the captain.

This oiler, by a series of quick miracles and fast and steady oarsmanship, turned the boat in the middle of the surf and took her safely to sea again.

There was a considerable silence as the boat bumped over the furrowed sea to deeper water. Then somebody in gloom spoke: "Well, anyhow, they must have seen us from the shore by now."

75   The gulls went in slanting flight up the wind toward the grey, desolate east. A squall, marked by dingy clouds and clouds brick-red like smoke from a burning building, appeared from the south-east.

"What do you think of those life-saving people? Ain't they peaches?"

"Funny they haven't seen us."

"Maybe they think we're out here for sport! Maybe they think we're fishin'. Maybe they think we're damned fools."

It was a long afternoon. A changed tide tried to force them southward, but wind and wave said northward. Far ahead, where coast-line, sea, and sky formed their mighty angle, there were little dots which seemed to indicate a city on the shore.

"St. Augustine?"   80

The captain shook his head. "Too near Mosquito Inlet."

And the oiler rowed, and then the correspondent rowed; then the oiler rowed. It was a weary business. The human back can become the seat of more aches and pains than are registered in books for the composite anatomy of a regiment. It is a limited area, but it can become the theatre of innumerable muscular conflicts, tangles, wrenches, knots, and other comforts.

"Did you ever like to row, Billie?" said the correspondent.

"No," said the oiler; "hang it!"

When one exchanged the rowing-seat for a place in the bottom of the boat, he   85 suffered a bodily depression that caused him to be careless of everything save an obligation to wiggle one finger. There was cold sea-water swashing to and fro in the boat, and he lay in it. His head, pillowed on a thwart, was within an inch of the swirl of a wave-crest, and sometimes a particularly obstreperous sea came inboard and drenched him once more. But these matters did not annoy him. It is almost certain that if the boat had capsized he would have tumbled comfortably out upon the ocean as if he felt sure that it was a great soft mattress.

"Look! There's a man on the shore!"

"Where?"

"There! See 'im? See 'im?"

"Yes, sure! He's walking along."

"Now he's stopped. Look! He's facing us!"   90

"He's waving at us!"

"So he is! By thunder!"

"Ah, now we're all right! Now we're all right! There'll be a boat out here for us in half an hour."

"He's going on. He's running. He's going up to that house there."

The remote beach seemed lower than the sea, and it required a searching glance   95 to discern the little black figure. The captain saw a floating stick, and they rowed to it. A bath towel was by some weird chance in the boat, and, tying this on the stick, the captain waved it. The oarsman did not dare turn his head, so he was obliged to ask questions.

"What's he doing now?"

"He's standing still again. He's looking, I think.—There he goes again—toward the house.—Now he's stopped again."

"Is he waving at us?"

"No, not now; he was, though."

"Look! There comes another man!"   100

"He's running."

"Look at him go, would you!"

"Why, he's on a bicycle. Now he's met the other man. They're both waving at us. Look!"

"There comes something up the beach."

105   "What the devil is that thing?"

"Why, it looks like a boat."

"Why, certainly, it's a boat."

"No; it's on wheels."

"Yes, so it is. Well, that must be the life-boat. They drag them along shore on a wagon."

110   "That's the life-boat, sure."

"No, by God, it's—it's an omnibus."

"I tell you it's a life-boat."

"It is not! It's an omnibus. I can see it plain. See. One of these big hotel omnibuses."

"By thunder, you're right. It's an omnibus, sure as fate. What do you suppose they are doing with an omnibus? Maybe they are going around collecting the life-crew, hey?"

115   "That's it, likely. Look! There's a fellow waving a little black flag. He's standing on the steps of the omnibus. There come those other two fellows. Now they're all talking together. Look at the fellow with the flag. Maybe he ain't waving it!"

"That ain't a flag, is it? That's his coat. Why, certainly, that's his coat."

"So it is; it's his coat. He's taken it off and is waving it around his head. But would you look at him swing it!"

"Oh, say, there isn't any life-saving station there. That's just a winter-resort hotel omnibus that has brought over some of the boarders to see us drown."

"What's that idiot with the coat mean? What's he signalling, anyhow?"

120   "It looks as if he were trying to tell us to go north. There must be a life-saving station up there."

"No; he thinks we're fishing. Just giving us a merry hand. See? Ah, there, Willie!"

"Well, I wish I could make something out of those signals. What do you suppose he means?"

"He don't mean anything; he's just playing."

"Well, if he'd just signal us to try the surf again, or to go to sea and wait, or go north, or go south, or go to hell, there would be some reason in it. But look at him! He just stands there and keeps his coat revolving like a wheel. The ass!"

125   "There come more people."

"Now there's quite a mob. Look! Isn't that a boat?"

"Where? Oh, I see where you mean. No, that's no boat."

"That fellow is still waving his coat."

"He must think we like to see him do that. Why don't he quit it? It don't mean anything."

130   "I don't know. I think he is trying to make us go north. It must be that there's a life-saving station there somewhere."

"Say, he ain't tired yet. Look at 'im wave!"

"Wonder how long he can keep that up. He's been revolving his coat ever since he caught sight of us. He's an idiot. Why aren't they getting men to bring a boat out?

A fishing boat—one of those big yawls—could come out here all right. Why don't he do something?"

"Oh, it's all right now."

"They'll have a boat out here for us in less than no time, now that they've seen us."

A faint yellow tone came into the sky over the low land. The shadows on the sea 135 slowly deepened. The wind bore coldness with it, and the men began to shiver.

"Holy smoke!" said one, allowing his voice to express his impious mood, "if we keep on monkeying out here! If we've got to flounder out here all night!"

"Oh, we'll never have to stay here all night! Don't you worry. They've seen us now, and it won't be long before they'll come chasing out after us."

The shore grew dusky. The man waving a coat blended gradually into this gloom, and it swallowed in the same manner the omnibus and the group of people. The spray, when it dashed uproariously over the side, made the voyagers shrink and swear like men who were being branded.

"I'd like to catch the chump who waved the coat. I feel like socking him one, just for luck."

"Why? What did he do?"   140

"Oh, nothing, but then he seemed so damned cheerful."

In the meantime the oiler rowed, and then the correspondent rowed, and then the oiler rowed. Grey-faced and bowed forward, they mechanically, turn by turn, plied the leaden oars. The form of the lighthouse had vanished from the southern horizon, but finally a pale star appeared, just lifting from the sea. The streaked saffron in the west passed before the all-merging darkness, and the sea to the east was black. The land had vanished, and was expressed only by the low and drear thunder of the surf.

"If I am going to be drowned—if I am going to be drowned—if I am going to be drowned, why, in the name of the seven mad gods who rule the sea, was I allowed to come thus far and contemplate sand and trees? Was I brought here merely to have my nose dragged away as I was about to nibble the sacred cheese of life?"

The patient captain, drooped over the water-jar, was sometimes obliged to speak to the oarsman.

"Keep her head up! Keep her head up!"   145

"Keep her head up, sir." The voices were weary and low.

This was surely a quiet evening. All save the oarsman lay heavily and listlessly in the boat's bottom. As for him, his eyes were just capable of noting the tall black waves that swept forward in a most sinister silence, save for an occasional subdued growl of a crest.

The cook's head was on a thwart, and he looked without interest at the water under his nose. He was deep in other scenes. Finally he spoke. "Billie," he murmured, dreamfully, "what kind of pie do you like best?"

5

"Pie!" said the oiler and correspondent, agitatedly. "Don't talk about those things, blast you!"

"Well," said the cook, "I was just thinking about ham sandwiches, and—"   150

A night on the sea in an open boat is a long night. As darkness settled finally, the shine of the light, lifting from the sea in the south, changed to full gold. On the northern horizon a new light appeared, a small bluish gleam on the edge of the waters. These two lights were the furniture of the world. Otherwise there was nothing but waves.

Two men huddled in the stern, and distances were so magnificent in the dinghy that the rower was enabled to keep his feet partly warm by thrusting them under his companions. Their legs indeed extended far under the rowing-seat until they touched the feet of the captain forward. Sometimes, despite the efforts of the tired oarsman, a wave came piling into the boat, an icy wave of the night, and the chilling water soaked them anew. They would twist their bodies for a moment and groan, and sleep the dead sleep once more, while the water in the boat gurgled about them as the craft rocked.

The plan of the oiler and the correspondent was for one to row until he lost the ability, and then arouse the other from his sea-water couch in the bottom of the boat.

The oiler plied the oars until his head drooped forward and the overpowering sleep blinded him; and he rowed yet afterward. Then he touched a man in the bottom of the boat, and called his name. "Will you spell me for a little while?" he said meekly.

155   "Sure, Billie," said the correspondent, awaking and dragging himself to a sitting position. They exchanged places carefully, and the oiler, cuddling down in the sea-water at the cook's side, seemed to go to sleep instantly.

The particular violence of the sea had ceased. The waves came without snarling. The obligation of the man at the oars was to keep the boat headed so that the tilt of the rollers would not capsize her, and to preserve her from filling when the crests rushed past. The black waves were silent and hard to be seen in the darkness. Often one was almost upon the boat before the oarsman was aware.

In a low voice the correspondent addressed the captain. He was not sure that the captain was awake, although this iron man seemed to be always awake. "Captain, shall I keep her making for that light north, sir?"

The same steady voice answered him. "Yes. Keep it about two points off the port bow."

The cook had tied a life-belt around himself in order to get even the warmth which this clumsy cork contrivance could donate, and he seemed almost stove-like when a rower, whose teeth invariably chattered wildly as soon as he ceased his labour, dropped down to sleep.

160   The correspondent, as he rowed, looked down at the two men sleeping underfoot. The cook's arm was around the oiler's shoulders, and, with their fragmentary clothing and haggard faces, they were the babes of the sea—a grotesque rendering of the old babes in the wood.

Later he must have grown stupid at his work, for suddenly there was a growling of water, and a crest came with a roar and a swash into the boat, and it was a wonder that it did not set the cook afloat in his life-belt. The cook continued to sleep, but the oiler sat up, blinking his eyes and shaking with the new cold.

"Oh, I'm awful sorry, Billie," said the correspondent contritely.

"That's all right, old boy," said the oiler, and lay down again and was asleep.

Presently it seemed that even the captain dozed, and the correspondent thought that he was the one man afloat on all the ocean. The wind had a voice as it came over the waves, and it was sadder than the end.

There was a long, loud swishing astern of the boat, and a gleaming trail of phos-   165
phorescence, like blue flame, was furrowed on the black waters. It might have been made by a monstrous knife.

Then there came a stillness, while the correspondent breathed with open mouth and looked at the sea.

Suddenly there was another swish and another long flash of bluish light, and this time it was alongside the boat, and might almost have been reached with an oar. The correspondent saw an enormous fin speed like a shadow through the water, hurling the crystalline spray, and leaving the long glowing trail.

The correspondent looked over his shoulder at the captain. His face was hidden, and he seemed to be asleep. He looked at the babes of the sea. They certainly were asleep. So, being bereft of sympathy, he leaned a little way to one side and swore softly into the sea.

But the thing did not then leave the vicinity of the boat. Ahead or astern, on one side or the other, at intervals long or short, fled the long sparkling streak, and there was to be heard the *whirroo* of the dark fin. The speed and power of the thing was greatly to be admired. It cut the water like a gigantic and keen projectile.

The presence of this biding thing did not affect the man with the same horror   170
that it would if he had been a picnicker. He simply looked at the sea dully and swore in an undertone.

Nevertheless, it is true that he did not wish to be alone with the thing. He wished one of his companions to awake by chance and keep him company with it. But the captain hung motionless over the water-jar, and the oiler and the cook in the bottom of the boat were plunged in slumber.

6

"If I am going to be drowned—if I am going to be drowned—if I am going to be drowned, why, in the name of the seven mad gods who rule the sea, was I allowed to come thus far and contemplate sand and trees?"

During this dismal night, it may be remarked that a man would conclude that it was really the intention of the seven mad gods to drown him, despite the abominable injustice of it. For it was certainly an abominable injustice to drown a man who had worked so hard, so hard. The man felt it would be a crime most unnatural. Other people had drowned at sea since galleys swarmed with painted sails, but still—

When it occurs to a man that nature does not regard him as important, and that she feels she would not maim the universe by disposing of him, he at first wishes to throw bricks at the temple, and he hates deeply the fact that there are no bricks and no temples. Any visible expression of nature would surely be pelleted with his jeers.

175   Then, if there be no tangible thing to hoot, he feels, perhaps, the desire to confront a personification and indulge in pleas, bowed to one knee, and with hands supplicant, saying, "Yes, but I love myself."

A high cold star on a winter's night is the word he feels that she says to him. Thereafter he knows the pathos of his situation.

The men in the dinghy had not discussed these matters, but each had, no doubt, reflected upon them in silence and according to his mind. There was seldom any expression upon their faces save the general one of complete weariness. Speech was devoted to the business of the boat.

To chime the notes of his emotion, a verse mysteriously entered the correspondent's head. He had even forgotten that he had forgotten this verse, but it suddenly was in his mind.

> A soldier of the Legion lay dying in Algiers;
> There was lack of woman's nursing, there was dearth of woman's tears;
> But a comrade stood beside him, and he took that comrade's hand,
> And he said, "I never more shall see my own, my native land."

In his childhood the correspondent had been made acquainted with the fact that a soldier of the Legion lay dying in Algiers, but he had never regarded the fact as important. Myriads of his school-fellows had informed him of the soldier's plight, but the dinning had naturally ended by making him perfectly indifferent. He had never considered it his affair that a soldier of the Legion lay dying in Algiers, nor had it appeared to him as a matter for sorrow. It was less to him than the breaking of a pencil's point.

180   Now, however, it quaintly came to him as a human, living thing. It was no longer merely a picture of a few throes in the breast of a poet, meanwhile drinking tea and warming his feet at the grate; it was an actuality—stern, mournful, and fine.

The correspondent plainly saw the soldier. He lay on the sand with his feet out straight and still. While his pale left hand was upon his chest in an attempt to thwart the going of his life, the blood came between his fingers. In the far Algerian distance, a city of low square forms was set against a sky that was faint with the last sunset hues. The correspondent, plying the oars and dreaming of the slow and slower movements of the lips of the soldier, was moved by a profound and perfectly impersonal comprehension. He was sorry for the soldier of the Legion who lay dying in Algiers.

The thing which had followed the boat and waited had evidently grown bored at the delay. There was no longer to be heard the slash of the cutwater, and there was no longer the flame of the long trail. The light in the north still glimmered, but it was apparently no nearer to the boat. Sometimes the boom of the surf rang in the correspondent's ears, and he turned the craft seaward then and rowed harder. Southward, some one had evidently built a watch-fire on the beach. It was too low and too far to be seen, but it made a shimmering, roseate reflection upon the bluff in back of it, and this could be discerned from the boat. The wind came stronger, and sometimes a wave suddenly raged out like a mountain cat, and there was to be seen the sheen and sparkle of a broken crest.

The captain, in the bow, moved on his water-jar and sat erect. "Pretty long night," he observed to the correspondent. He looked at the shore. "Those life-saving people take their time."

"Did you see that shark playing around?"

"Yes, I saw him. He was a big fellow, all right."   185

"Wish I had known you were awake."

Later the correspondent spoke into the bottom of the boat. "Billie!" There was a slow and gradual disentanglement. "Billie, will you spell me?"

"Sure," said the oiler.

As soon as the correspondent touched the cold, comfortable sea-water in the bottom of the boat and had huddled close to the cook's life-belt he was deep in sleep, despite the fact that his teeth played all the popular airs. This sleep was so good to him that it was but a moment before he heard a voice call his name in a tone that demonstrated the last stages of exhaustion. "Will you spell me?"

"Sure, Billie."   190

The light in the north had mysteriously vanished, but the correspondent took his course from the wide-awake captain.

Later in the night they took the boat farther out to sea, and the captain directed the cook to take one oar at the stern and keep the boat facing the seas. He was to call out if he should hear the thunder of the surf. This plan enabled the oiler and the correspondent to get respite together. "We'll give those boys a chance to get into shape again," said the captain. They curled down and, after a few preliminary chatterings and trembles, slept once more the dead sleep. Neither knew they had bequeathed to the cook the company of another shark, or perhaps the same shark.

As the boat caroused on the waves, spray occasionally bumped over the side and gave them a fresh soaking, but this had no power to break their repose. The ominous slash of the wind and the water affected them as it would have affected mummies.

"Boys," said the cook, with the notes of every reluctance in his voice, "she's drifted in pretty close. I guess one of you had better take her to sea again." The correspondent, aroused, heard the crash of the toppled crests.

As he was rowing, the captain gave him some whiskey-and-water, and this 195 steadied the chills out of him. "If I ever get ashore and anybody shows me even a photograph of an oar—"

At last there was a short conversation.

"Billie!—Billie, will you spell me?"

"Sure," said the oiler.

7

When the correspondent again opened his eyes, the sea and the sky were each of the grey hue of the dawning. Later, carmine and gold was painted upon the waters. The morning appeared finally, in its splendour, with a sky of pure blue, and the sunlight flamed on the tips of the waves.

200   On the distant dunes were set many little black cottages, and a tall white wind-mill reared above them. No man, nor dog, nor bicycle appeared on the beach. The cottages might have formed a deserted village.

The voyagers scanned the shore. A conference was held in the boat. "Well," said the captain, "if no help is coming, we might better try a run through the surf right away. If we stay out here much longer we will be too weak to do anything for ourselves at all." The others silently acquiesced in this reasoning. The boat was headed for the beach. The correspondent wondered if none ever ascended the tall wind-tower, and if then they never looked seaward. This tower was a giant, standing with its back to the plight of the ants. It represented in a degree, to the correspondent, the serenity of nature amid the struggles of the individual—nature in the wind, and nature in the vision of men. She did not seem cruel to him then, nor beneficent, nor treacherous, nor wise. But she was indifferent, flatly indifferent. It is, perhaps, plausible that a man in this situation, impressed with the unconcern of the universe, should see the innumerable flaws of his life, and have them taste wickedly in his mind, and wish for another chance. A distinction between right and wrong seems absurdly clear to him, then, in this new ignorance of the grave-edge, and he understands that if he were given another opportunity he would mend his conduct and his words, and be better and brighter during an introduction or at a tea.

"Now, boys," said the captain, "she is going to swamp sure. All we can do is to work her in as far as possible, and then when she swamps, pile out and scramble for the beach. Keep cool now, and don't jump until she swamps sure."

The oiler took the oars. Over his shoulders he scanned the surf. "Captain," he said, "I think I'd better bring her about and keep her head-on to the seas and back her in."

"All right, Billie," said the captain. "Back her in." The oiler swung the boat then, and, seated in the stern, the cook and the correspondent were obliged to look over their shoulders to contemplate the lonely and indifferent shore.

205   The monstrous inshore rollers heaved the boat high until the men were again en-abled to see the white sheets of water scudding up the slanted beach. "We won't get in very close," said the captain. Each time a man could wrest his attention from the rollers, he turned his glance toward the shore, and in the expression of the eyes dur-ing this contemplation there was a singular quality. The correspondent, observing the others, knew that they were not afraid, but the full meaning of their glances was shrouded.

As for himself, he was too tired to grapple fundamentally with the fact. He tried to coerce his mind into thinking of it, but the mind was dominated at this time by the muscles, and they did not care. It merely occurred to him that if he should drown it would be a shame.

There were no hurried words, no pallor, no plain agitation. The men simply looked at the shore. "Now, remember to get well clear of the boat when you jump," said the captain.

Seaward the crest of a roller suddenly fell with a thunderous crash, and the long white comber came roaring down upon the boat.

"Steady now," said the captain. The men were silent. They turned their eyes from the shore to the comber and waited. The boat slid up the incline, leaped at the furious top, bounced over it, and swung down the long back of the wave. Some water had been shipped, and the cook bailed it out.

But the next crest crashed also. The tumbling, boiling flood of white water 210 caught the boat and whirled it almost perpendicular. Water swarmed in from all sides. The correspondent had his hands on the gunwale at this time, and when the water entered at that place he swiftly withdrew his fingers, as if he objected to wetting them.

The little boat, drunken with this weight of water, reeled and snuggled deeper into the sea.

"Bail her out, cook! Bail her out!" said the captain.

"All right, Captain," said the cook.

"Now, boys, the next one will do for us sure," said the oiler. "Mind to jump clear of the boat."

The third wave moved forward, huge, furious, implacable. It fairly swallowed 215 the dinghy, and almost simultaneously the men tumbled into the sea. A piece of life-belt had lain in the bottom of the boat, and as the correspondent went overboard he held this to his chest with his left hand.

The January water was icy, and he reflected immediately that it was colder than he had expected to find it off the coast of Florida. This appeared to his dazed mind as a fact important enough to be noted at the time. The coldness of the water was sad; it was tragic. This fact was somehow mixed and confused with his opinion of his own situation, so that it seemed almost a proper reason for tears. The water was cold.

When he came to the surface he was conscious of little but the noisy water. Afterward he saw his companions in the sea. The oiler was ahead in the race. He was swimming strongly and rapidly. Off to the correspondent's left, the cook's great white and corked back bulged out of the water; and in the rear the captain was hanging with his one good hand to the keel of the overturned dinghy.

There is a certain immovable quality to a shore, and the correspondent wondered at it amid the confusion of the sea.

It seemed also very attractive; but the correspondent knew that it was a long journey, and he paddled leisurely. The piece of life-preserver lay under him, and sometimes he whirled down the incline of a wave as if he were on a hand-sled.

But finally he arrived at a place in the sea where travel was beset with difficulty. 220 He did not pause swimming to inquire what manner of current had caught him, but there his progress ceased. The shore was set before him like a bit of scenery on a stage, and he looked at it and understood with his eyes each detail of it.

As the cook passed, much farther to the left, the captain was calling to him. "Turn over on your back, cook! Turn over on your back and use the oar."

"All right, sir." The cook turned on his back, and paddling with an oar, went ahead as if he were a canoe.

Presently the boat also passed to the left of the correspondent, with the captain clinging with one hand to the keel. He would have appeared like a man raising himself to look over a board fence if it were not for the extraordinary gymnastics of the boat. The correspondent marvelled that the captain could still hold to it.

They passed on nearer to shore—the oiler, the cook, the captain—and following them went the water-jar, bouncing gaily over the seas.

225   The correspondent remained in the grip of this strange new enemy—a current. The shore, with its white slope of sand and its green bluff topped with little silent cottages, was spread like a picture before him. It was very near to him then, but he was impressed as one who, in a gallery, looks at a scene from Brittany or Algiers.

He thought: "I'm going to drown? Can it be possible? Can it be possible? Can it be possible?" Perhaps an individual must consider his own death to be the final phenomenon of nature.

But later a wave perhaps whirled him out of this small deadly current, for he found suddenly that he could again make progress toward the shore. Later still he was aware that the captain, clinging with one hand to the keel of the dinghy, had his face turned away from the shore and toward him, and was calling his name. "Come to the boat! Come to the boat!"

In his struggle to reach the captain and the boat, he reflected that when one gets properly wearied drowning must really be a comfortable arrangement—a cessation of hostilities accompanied by a large degree of relief; and he was glad of it, for the main thing in his mind for some moments had been horror of the temporary agony. He did not wish to be hurt.

Presently he saw a man running along the shore. He was undressing with most remarkable speed. Coat, trousers, shirt, everything flew magically off him.

230   "Come to the boat!" called the captain.

"All right, Captain." As the correspondent paddled, he saw the captain let himself down to bottom and leave the boat. Then the correspondent performed his own little marvel of the voyage. A large wave caught him and flung him with ease and supreme speed completely over the boat and far beyond it. It struck him even then as an event in gymnastics and a true miracle of the sea. An overturned boat in the surf is not a plaything to a swimming man.

The correspondent arrived in water that reached only to his waist, but his condition did not enable him to stand for more than a moment. Each wave knocked him into a heap, and the undertow pulled at him.

Then he saw the man who had been running and undressing, and undressing and running, come bounding into the water. He dragged ashore the cook, and then waded toward the captain; but the captain waved him away and sent him to the correspondent. He was naked—naked as a tree in winter; but a halo was about his head, and he shone like a saint. He gave a strong pull, and a long drag, and a bully heave at the correspondent's hand. The correspondent, schooled in the minor formulae, said, "Thanks, old man." But suddenly the man cried, "What's that?" He pointed a swift finger. The correspondent said, "Go."

In the shallows, face downward, lay the oiler. His forehead touched sand that was periodically, between each wave, clear of the sea.

The correspondent did not know all that transpired afterward. When he achieved 235
safe ground he fell, striking the sand with each particular part of his body. It was as
if he had dropped from a roof, but the thud was grateful to him.

It seems that instantly the beach was populated with men with blankets, clothes,
and flasks, and women with coffee-pots and all the remedies sacred to their minds.
The welcome of the land to the men from the sea was warm and generous; but a still
and dripping shape was carried slowly up the beach, and the land's welcome for it
could only be the different and sinister hospitality of the grave.

When it came night, the white waves paced to and fro in the moonlight, and the
wind brought the sound of the great sea's voice to the men on the shore, and they felt
that they could then be interpreters.

QUESTIONS FOR DISCUSSION AND WRITING

1. This story alternates between extended moments of boredom and intense moments of physical exertion. How do these alternating rhythms sustain the plot?
   What unifies each of the seven sections of the story?

2. At first, what special quality distinguishes each of the four men in the boat? In
   what surprising ways do the characters change during the course of the story?

3. How does Crane describe the environment of the open sea? How do the attitudes
   of the men toward the sea change during the story?

4. Although this story is told from an objective point of view, the correspondent
   seems to speak for the other men in the boat. How is this essential point of view
   established in his repeated question: "Why, in the name of the seven mad gods
   who rule the sea, was I allowed to come this far and contemplate sand and trees?"

5. What do the verse about "a soldier of the Legion" and the death of the oiler reveal about the nature of existence? How might the three survivors interpret the
   "sound of the great sea's voice"?

Stories for Comparison

Joseph Conrad's "Heart of Darkness" (pages 388–447); Jack London's
"To Build a Fire" (pages 812–823).

38

···

RALPH ELLISON

Battle Royal

RALPH ELLISON (1914–1994) was born in Oklahoma City and studied music
for three years at Tuskegee Institute in Alabama, a school founded by the black
educator Booker T. Washington. In 1936 Ellison went to New York City, met
Langston Hughes and Richard Wright, and began working with the Federal
Writers Project. In 1942 he became editor of *Negro Quarterly* before serving in
the Merchant Marine during World War II. During this period, Ellison published
short stories and essays in magazines such as *New Challenge* and *New Masses,*
and with the help of several fellowships, began writing his major epic of the
black experience in America, *Invisible Man* (1952). The novel was widely acclaimed, winning the 1953 National Book Award and named in a 1965 *Book
Week* poll of prominent authors, critics, and editors as "the most distinguished
single work published in the last twenty years." Ellison subsequently received a
number of fellowships and lectureships, and in 1970 was appointed Albert
Schweitzer Professor of Humanities at New York University. Although Ellison
published a collection of his essays, *Shadow and Act* in 1964, he never published another novel. Two collections have been published since his death,
Collected Essays (1995), and *Flying Home and Other Stories* (1996). "Battle
Royal," first published as a short story in 1947, appears in slightly altered form
as the opening chapter of *Invisible Man.* The story portrays a young black man's
initiation into the rituals of white repression.

It goes a long way back, some twenty years. All my life I had been looking for
something, and everywhere I turned someone tried to tell me what it was. I accepted their answers too, though they were often in contradiction and even self-
contradictory. I was naïve. I was looking for myself and asking everyone except myself questions which I, and only I, could answer. It took me a long time and much
painful boomeranging of my expectations to achieve a realization everyone else appears to have been born with: That I am nobody but myself. But first I had to discover that I am an invisible man!

And yet I am no freak of nature, nor of history. I was in the cards, other things
having been equal (or unequal) eighty-five years ago. I am not ashamed of my grandparents for having been slaves. I am only ashamed of myself for having at one time

been ashamed. About eighty-five years ago they were told they were free, united with others of our country in everything pertaining to the common good, and, in everything social, separate like the fingers of the hand. And they believed it. They exulted in it. They stayed in their place, worked hard, and brought up my father to do the same. But my grandfather is the one. He was an odd old guy, my grandfather, and I am told I take after him. It was he who caused the trouble. On his deathbed he called my father to him and said, "Son, after I'm gone I want you to keep up the good fight. I never told you, but our life is a war and I have been a traitor all my born days, a spy in the enemy's country ever since I give up my gun back in the Reconstruction. Live with your head in the lion's mouth. I want you to overcome 'em with yeses, undermine 'em with grins, agree 'em to death and destruction, let 'em swoller you till they vomit or bust wide open." They thought the old man had gone out of his mind. He had been the meekest of men. The younger children were rushed from the room, the shades drawn and the flame of the lamp turned so low that it sputtered on the wick like the old man's breathing. "Learn it to the younguns," he whispered fiercely; then he died.

But my folks were more alarmed over his last words than over his dying. It was as though he had not died at all, his words caused so much anxiety. I was warned emphatically to forget what he had said and, indeed, this is the first time it has been mentioned outside the family circle. It had a tremendous effect upon me, however. I could never be sure of what he meant. Grandfather had been a quiet old man who never made any trouble, yet on his deathbed he had called himself a traitor and a spy, and he had spoken of his meekness as a dangerous activity. It became a constant puzzle which lay unanswered in the back of my mind. And whenever things went well for me I remembered my grandfather and felt guilty and uncomfortable. It was as though I was carrying out his advice in spite of myself. And to make it worse, everyone loved me for it. I was praised by the most lily-white men in town. I was considered an example of desirable conduct—just as my grandfather had been. And what puzzled me was that the old man had defined it as *treachery*. When I was praised for my conduct I felt a guilt that in some way I was doing something that was really against the wishes of the white folks, that if they had understood they would have desired me to act just the opposite, that I should have been sulky and mean, and that that really would have been what they wanted, even though they were fooled and thought they wanted me to act as I did. It made me afraid that some day they would look upon me as a traitor and I would be lost. Still I was more afraid to act any other way because they didn't like that at all. The old man's words were like a curse. On my graduation day I delivered an oration in which I showed that humility was the secret, indeed, the very essence of progress. (Not that I believed this—how could I, remembering my grandfather?—I only believed that it worked.) It was a great success. Everyone praised me and I was invited to give the speech at a gathering of the town's leading white citizens. It was a triumph for the whole community.

It was in the main ballroom of the leading hotel. When I got there I discovered that it was on the occasion of a smoker, and I was told that since I was to be there anyway I might as well take part in the battle royal to be fought by some of my schoolmates as part of the entertainment. The battle royal came first.

5   All of the town's big shots were there in their tuxedoes, wolfing down the buffet foods, drinking beer and whiskey and smoking black cigars. It was a large room with a high ceiling. Chairs were arranged in neat rows around three sides of a portable boxing ring. The fourth side was clear, revealing a gleaming space of polished floor. I had some misgivings over the battle royal, by the way. Not from a distaste for fighting but because I didn't care too much for the other fellows who were to take part. They were tough guys who seemed to have no grandfather's curse worrying their minds. No one could mistake their toughness. And besides, I suspected that fighting a battle royal might distract from the dignity of my speech. In those pre-invisible days I visualized myself as a potential Booker T. Washington. But the other fellows didn't care too much for me either, and there were nine of them. I felt superior to them in my way, and I didn't like the manner in which we were all crowded together in the servants' elevator. Nor did they like my being there. In fact, as the warmly lighted floors flashed past the elevator we had words over the fact that I, by taking part in the fight, had knocked one of their friends out of a night's work.

We were led out of the elevator through a rococo hall into an anteroom and told to get into our fighting togs. Each of us was issued a pair of boxing gloves and ushered out into the big mirrored hall, which we entered looking cautiously about us and whispering, lest we might accidentally be heard above the noise of the room. It was foggy with cigar smoke. And already the whiskey was taking effect. I was shocked to see some of the most important men of the town quite tipsy. They were all there—bankers, lawyers, judges, doctors, fire chiefs, teachers, merchants. Even one of the more fashionable pastors. Something we could not see was going on up front. A clarinet was vibrating sensuously and the men were standing up and moving eagerly forward. We were a small tight group, clustered together, our bare upper bodies touching and shining with anticipatory sweat; while up front the big shots were becoming increasingly excited over something we still could not see. Suddenly I heard the school superintendent, who had told me to come, yell, "Bring up the shines, gentlemen! Bring up the little shines!"

We were rushed up to the front of the ballroom, where it smelled even more strongly of tobacco and whiskey. Then we were pushed into place. I almost wet my pants. A sea of faces, some hostile, some amused, ringed around us, and in the center, facing us, stood a magnificent blonde—stark naked. There was dead silence. I felt a blast of cold air chill me. I tried to back away, but they were behind me and around me. Some of the boys stood with lowered heads, trembling. I felt a wave of irrational guilt and fear. My teeth chattered, my skin turned to goose flesh, my knees knocked. Yet I was strongly attracted and looked in spite of myself. Had the price of looking been blindness, I would have looked. The hair was yellow like that of a circus kewpie doll, the face heavily powdered and rouged, as though to form an abstract mask, the eyes hollow and smeared a cool blue, the color of a baboon's butt. I felt a desire to spit upon her as my eyes brushed slowly over her body. Her breasts were firm and round as the domes of East Indian temples, and I stood so close as to see the fine skin texture and beads of pearly perspiration glistening like dew around the pink and erected buds of her nipples. I wanted at one and the same time to run from the room, to sink through the floor, or go to her and cover her from my eyes and the eyes of the others with my body; to feel the soft thighs, to caress her and destroy her, to love her and to murder her, to hide from her, and yet to stroke where below the small American flag tattooed upon her belly her thighs formed a capital V. I had a notion that of all in the room she saw only me with her impersonal eyes.

And then she began to dance, a slow sensuous movement; the smoke of a hundred cigars clinging to her like the thinnest of veils. She seemed like a fair bird-girl girdled in veils calling to me from the angry surface of some gray and threatening sea. I was transported. Then I became aware of the clarinet playing and the big shots yelling at us. Some threatened us if we looked and others if we did not. On my right I saw one boy faint. And now a man grabbed a silver pitcher from a table and stepped close as he dashed ice water upon him and stood him up and forced two of us to support him as his head hung and moans issued from his thick bluish lips. Another boy began to plead to go home. He was the largest of the group, wearing dark red fighting trunks much too small to conceal the erection which projected from him as though in answer to the insinuating low-registered moaning of the clarinet. He tried to hide himself with his boxing gloves.

And all the while the blonde continued dancing, smiling faintly at the big shots who watched her with fascination, and faintly smiling at our fear. I noticed a certain merchant who followed her hungrily, his lips loose and drooling. He was a large man who wore diamond studs in a shirtfront which swelled with the ample paunch underneath, and each time the blonde swayed her undulating hips he ran his hand through the thin hair of his bald head and, with his arms upheld, his posture clumsy like that of an intoxicated panda, wound his belly in a slow and obscene grind. This creature was completely hypnotized. The music had quickened. As the dancer flung herself about with a detached expression on her face, the men began reaching out to touch her. I could see their beefy fingers sink into her soft flesh. Some of the others tried to stop them and she began to move around the floor in graceful circles, as they gave chase, slipping and sliding over the polished floor. It was mad. Chairs went crashing, drinks were spilt, as they ran laughing and howling after her. They caught her just as she reached a door, raised her from the floor, and tossed her as college boys are tossed at a hazing, and above her red, fixed-smiling lips I saw the terror and disgust in her eyes, almost like my own terror and that which I saw in some of the other boys. As I watched, they tossed her twice and her soft breasts seemed to flatten against the air and her legs flung wildly as she spun. Some of the more sober ones helped her to escape. And I started off the floor, heading for the anteroom with the rest of the boys.

Some were still crying and in hysteria. But as we tried to leave we were stopped 10 and ordered to get into the ring. There was nothing to do but what we were told. All ten of us climbed under the ropes and allowed ourselves to be blindfolded with broad bands of white cloth. One of the men seemed to feel a bit sympathetic and tried to cheer us up as we stood with our backs against the ropes. Some of us tried to grin. "See that boy over there?" one of the men said. "I want you to run across at the bell and give it to him right in the belly. If you don't get him, I'm going to get you. I don't like his looks." Each of us was told the same. The blindfolds were put on. Yet even then I had been going over my speech. In my mind each word was as bright as a flame. I felt the cloth pressed into place, and frowned so that it would be loosened when I relaxed.

But now I felt a sudden fit of blind terror. I was unused to darkness. It was as though I had suddenly found myself in a dark room filled with poisonous cottonmouths. I could hear the bleary voices yelling insistently for the battle royal to begin.

"Get going in there!"

"Let me at that big nigger!"

I strained to pick up the school superintendent's voice, as though to squeeze some security out of that slightly more familiar sound.

"Let me at those black sonabitches!" someone yelled.

"No, Jackson, no!" another voice yelled. "Here, somebody, help me hold Jack."

"I want to get at that ginger-colored nigger. Tear him limb from limb," the first voice yelled.

I stood against the ropes trembling. For in those days I was what they called ginger-colored, and he sounded as though he might crunch me between his teeth like a crisp ginger cookie.

Quite a struggle was going on. Chairs were being kicked about and I could hear voices grunting as with terrific effort. I wanted to see, to see more desperately than ever before. But the blindfold was as tight as a thick skin-puckering scab and when I raised my gloved hand to push the layers of white aside a voice yelled, "Oh, no you don't, black bastard! Leave that alone!"

"Ring the bell before Jackson kills him a coon!" someone boomed in the sudden silence. And I heard the bell clang and the sound of the feet scuffling forward.

A glove smacked against my head. I pivoted, striking out stiffly as someone went past, and felt the jar ripple along the length of my arm to my shoulder. Then it seemed as though all nine of the boys had turned upon me at once. Blows pounded me from all sides while I struck out as best I could. So many blows landed upon me that I wondered if I were not the only blindfolded fighter in the ring, or if the man called Jackson hadn't succeeded in getting me after all.

Blindfolded, I could no longer control my motions. I had no dignity. I stumbled about like a baby or a drunken man. The smoke had become thicker and with each new blow it seemed to sear and further restrict my lungs. My saliva became like hot bitter glue. A glove connected with my head, filling my mouth with warm blood. It was everywhere. I could not tell if the moisture I felt upon my body was sweat or blood. A blow landed hard against the nape of my neck. I felt myself going over, my head hitting the floor. Streaks of blue light filled the black world behind the blindfold. I lay prone, pretending that I was knocked out, but felt myself seized by hands and yanked to my feet. "Get going, black boy! Mix it up!" My arms were like lead, my head smarting from blows. I managed to feel my way to the ropes and held on, trying to catch my breath. A glove landed in my midsection and I went over again, feeling as though the smoke had become a knife jabbed into my guts. Pushed this way and that by the legs milling around me, I finally pulled erect and discovered that I could see the black, sweat-washed forms weaving in the smoky-blue atmosphere like drunken dancers weaving to the rapid drum-like thuds of blows.

Everyone fought hysterically. It was complete anarchy. Everybody fought everybody else. No group fought together for long. Two, three, four, fought one, then turned to fight each other, were themselves attacked. Blows landed below the belt and in the kidney, with the gloves open as well as closed, and with my eye partly opened now there was not so much terror. I moved carefully, avoiding blows, although not too many to attract attention, fighting group to group. The boys groped about like blind, cautious crabs crouching to protect their midsections, their heads pulled in short against their shoulders, their arms stretched nervously before them, with their fists testing the smoke-filled air like the knobbed feelers of hypersensitive snails. In one corner I glimpsed a boy violently punching the air and heard him scream in pain as he smashed his hand against a ring post. For a second I saw him bent over holding his hand, then going down as a blow caught his unprotected head. I played one group against the other, slipping in and throwing a punch then stepping out of range while pushing the others into the melee to take the blows blindly aimed at me. The smoke was agonizing and there were no rounds, no bells at three minute intervals to relieve our exhaustion. The room spun round me, a swirl of lights, smoke, sweating bodies surrounded by tense white faces. I bled from both nose and mouth, the blood spattering upon my chest.

The men kept yelling, "Slug him, black boy! Knock his guts out!"

"Uppercut him! Kill him! Kill that big boy!"   25

Taking a fake fall, I saw a boy going down heavily beside me as though we were felled by a single blow, saw a sneaker-clad foot shoot into his groin as the two who had knocked him down stumbled upon him. I rolled out of range, feeling a twinge of nausea.

The harder we fought the more threatening the men became. And yet, I had begun to worry about my speech again. How would it go? Would they recognize my ability? What would they give me?

I was fighting automatically when suddenly I noticed that one after another of the boys were leaving the ring. I was surprised, filled with panic, as though I had been left alone with an unknown danger. Then I understood. The boys had arranged it among themselves. It was the custom for the two men left in the ring to slug it out for the winner's prize. I discovered this too late. When the bell sounded two men in tuxedoes leaped into the ring and removed the blindfold. I found myself facing Tatlock, the biggest of the gang. I felt sick at my stomach. Hardly had the bell stopped ringing in my ears than it clanged again and I saw him moving swiftly toward me. Thinking of nothing else to do I hit him smash on the nose. He kept coming, bringing the rank sharp violence of stale sweat. His face was a black blank of a face, only his eyes alive—with hate of me and aglow with a feverish terror from what had happened to us all. I became anxious. I wanted to deliver my speech and he came at me as though he meant to beat it out of me. I smashed him again and again, taking his blows as they came. Then on a sudden impulse I struck him lightly and we clinched. I whispered, "Fake like I knocked you out, you can have the prize."

"I'll break your behind," he whispered hoarsely.

"For *them?*"   30

"For *me,* sonafabitch!"

They were yelling for us to break it up and Tatlock spun me half around with a blow, and as a joggled camera sweeps in a reeling scene, I saw the howling red faces crouching tense beneath the cloud of blue-gray smoke. For a moment the world wavered, unraveled, flowed, then my head cleared and Tatlock bounced before me. That fluttering shadow before my eyes was his jabbing left hand. Then falling forward, my head against his damp shoulder, I whispered,

"I'll make it five dollars more."

"Go to hell!"

35   But his muscles relaxed a trifle beneath my pressure and I breathed, "Seven?"

"Give it to your ma," he said, ripping me beneath the heart.

And while I still held him I butted him and moved away. I felt myself bombarded with punches. I fought back with hopeless desperation. I wanted to deliver my speech more than anything else in the world, because I felt that only these men could judge truly my ability, and now this stupid clown was ruining my chances. I began fighting carefully now, moving in to punch him and out again with my greater speed. A lucky blow to his chin and I had him going too—until I heard a loud voice yell, "I got my money on the big boy."

Hearing this, I almost dropped my guard. I was confused: Should I try to win against the voice out there? Would not this go against my speech, and was not this a moment for humility, for nonresistance? A blow to my head as I danced about sent my right eye popping like a jack-in-the-box and settled my dilemma. The room went red as I fell. It was a dream fall, my body languid and fastidious as to where to land, until the floor became impatient and smashed up to meet me. A moment later I came to. An hypnotic voice said FIVE emphatically. And I lay there, hazily watching a dark red spot of my own blood shaping itself into a butterfly, glistening and soaking into the soiled gray world of the canvas.

When the voice drawled TEN I was lifted up and dragged to a chair. I sat dazed. My eye pained and swelled with each throb of my pounding heart and I wondered if now I would be allowed to speak. I was wringing wet, my mouth still bleeding. We were grouped along the wall now. The other boys ignored me as they congratulated Tatlock and speculated as to how much they would be paid. One boy whimpered over his smashed hand. Looking up front, I saw attendants in white jackets rolling the portable ring away and placing a small square rug in the vacant space surrounded by chairs. Perhaps, I thought, I will stand on the rug to deliver my speech.

40   Then the M.C. called to us, "Come on up here boys and get your money."

We ran forward to where the men laughed and talked in their chairs, waiting. Everyone seemed friendly now.

"There it is on the rug," the man said. I saw the rug covered with coins of all dimensions and a few crumpled bills. But what excited me, scattered here and there, were the gold pieces.

"Boys, it's all yours," the man said. "You get all you grab."

"That's right, Sambo," a blond man said, winking at me confidentially.

45   I trembled with excitement, forgetting my pain. I would get the gold and the bills, I thought. I would use both hands. I would throw my body against the boys nearest me to block them from the gold.

"Get down around the rug now," the man commanded, "and don't anyone touch it until I give the signal."

"This ought to be good," I heard.

As told, we got around the square rug on our knees. Slowly the man raised his freckled hand as we followed it upward with our eyes.

I heard, "These niggers look like they're about to pray!"

Then, "Ready," the man said. "Go!"   50

I lunged for a yellow coin lying on the blue design of the carpet, touching it and sending a surprised shriek to join those around me. I tried frantically to remove my hand but could not let go. A hot, violent force tore through my body, shaking me like a wet rat. The rug was electrified. The hair bristled up on my head as I shook myself free. My muscles jumped, my nerves jangled, writhed. But I saw that this was not stopping the other boys. Laughing in fear and embarrassment, some were holding back and scooping up the coins knocked off by the painful contortions of others. The men roared above us as we struggled.

"Pick it up, goddamnit, pick it up!" someone called like a bass-voiced parrot. "Go on, get it!"

I crawled rapidly around the floor, picking up the coins, trying to avoid the coppers and to get greenbacks and the gold. Ignoring the shock by laughing, as I brushed the coins off quickly, I discovered that I could contain the electricity—a contradiction but it works. Then the men began to push us onto the rug. Laughing embarrassedly, we struggled out of their hands and kept after the coins. We were all wet and slippery and hard to hold. Suddenly I saw a boy lifted into the air, glistening with sweat like a circus seal, and dropped, his wet back landing flush upon the charged rug, heard him yell and saw him literally dance upon his back, his elbows beating a frenzied tattoo upon the floor, his muscles twitching like the flesh of a horse stung by many flies. When he finally rolled off, his face was gray and no one stopped him when he ran from the floor amid booming laughter.

"Get the money," the M.C. called. "That's good hard American cash!"

And we snatched and grabbed, snatched and grabbed. I was careful not to come   55
too close to the rug now, and when I felt the hot whiskey breath descend upon me like a cloud of foul air I reached out and grabbed the leg of a chair. It was occupied and I held on desperately.

"Leggo, nigger! Leggo!"

The huge face wavered down to mine as he tried to push me free. But my body was slippery and he was too drunk. It was Mr. Colcord, who owned a chain of movie houses and "entertainment palaces." Each time he grabbed me I slipped out of his hands. It became a real struggle. I feared the rug more than I did the drunk, so I held on, surprising myself for a moment by trying to *topple* him upon the rug. It was such an enormous idea that I found myself actually carrying it out. I tried not to be obvious, yet when I grabbed his leg, trying to tumble him out of the chair, he raised up roaring with laughter, and, looking at me with soberness dead in the eye, kicked me viciously in the chest. The chair leg flew out of my hand and I felt myself going and rolled. It was as though I had rolled through a bed of hot coals. It seemed a whole century would pass before I would roll free, a century in which I was seared through the deepest levels of my body to the fearful breath within me and the breath seared and heated to the point of explosion. It'll all be over in a flash, I thought as I rolled clear. It'll all be over in a flash.

But not yet, the men on the other side were waiting, red faces swollen as though from apoplexy as they bent forward in their chairs. Seeing their fingers coming toward me I rolled away as a fumbled football rolls off the receiver's fingertips, back into the coals. That time I luckily sent the rug sliding out of place and heard the coins ringing against the floor and the boys scuffling to pick them up and the M.C. calling, "All right, boys, that's all. Go get dressed and get your money."

I was limp as a dish rag. My back felt as though it had been beaten with wires.

60   When we had dressed the M.C. came in and gave us each five dollars, except Tatlock, who got ten for being the last in the ring. Then he told us to leave. I was not to get a chance to deliver my speech, I thought. I was going out into the dim alley in despair when I was stopped and told to go back. I returned to the ballroom, where the men were pushing back their chairs and gathering in small groups to talk.

The M.C. knocked on a table for quiet. "Gentlemen," he said, "we almost forgot an important part of the program. A most serious part, gentlemen. This boy was brought here to deliver a speech which he made at his graduation yesterday. . . ."

"Bravo!"

"I'm told that he is the smartest boy we've got out there in Greenwood. I'm told that he knows more big words than a pocket-sized dictionary."

Much applause and laughter.

65   "So now, gentlemen, I want you to give him your attention."

There was still laughter as I faced them, my mouth dry, my eyes throbbing. I began slowly, but evidently my throat was tense, because they began shouting, "Louder! Louder!"

"We of the younger generation extol the wisdom of that great leader and educator," I shouted, "who first spoke these flaming words of wisdom: 'A ship lost at sea for many days suddenly sighted a friendly vessel. From the mast of the unfortunate vessel was seen a signal: "Water, water; we die of thirst!" The answer from the friendly vessel came back: "Cast down your bucket where you are." The captain of the distressed vessel, at last heeding the injunction, cast down his bucket, and it came up full of fresh sparkling water from the mouth of the Amazon River.' And like him I say, and in his words, 'To those of my race who depend upon bettering their condition in a foreign land, or who underestimate the importance of cultivating friendly relations with the Southern white man, who is his next-door neighbor, I would say: "Cast down your bucket where you are"—cast it down in making friends in every manly way of the people of all races by whom we are surrounded. . . .'"

I spoke automatically and with such fervor that I did not realize that the men were still talking and laughing until my dry mouth, filling up with blood from the cut, almost strangled me. I coughed, wanting to stop and go to one of the tall brass, sand-filled spittoons to relieve myself, but a few of the men, especially the superintendent, were listening and I was afraid. So I gulped it down, blood, saliva and all, and continued. (What power of endurance I had during those days! What enthusiasm! What a belief in the rightness of things!) I spoke even louder in spite of the pain. But still they talked and still they laughed, as though deaf with cotton in dirty ears. So I spoke with greater emotional emphasis. I closed my ears and swallowed blood until I was nauseated. The speech seemed a hundred times as long as before, but I could not leave out a single word. All had to be said, each memorized nuance considered, rendered. Nor was that all. Whenever I uttered a word of three or more syllables a group of voices would yell for me to repeat it. I used the phrase "social responsibility" and they yelled:

"What's the word you say, boy?"

"Social responsibility," I said.   70

"What?"

"Social . . ."

"Louder."

". . . responsibility."

"More!"   75

"Respon—"

"Repeat!"

"—sibility."

The room filled with the uproar of laughter until, no doubt, distracted by having to gulp down my blood, I made a mistake and yelled a phrase I had often seen denounced in newspaper editorials, heard debated in private.

"Social . . ."   80

"What?" they yelled.

". . . equality—"

The laughter hung smokelike in the sudden stillness. I opened my eyes, puzzled. Sounds of displeasure filled the room. The M.C. rushed forward. They shouted hostile phrases at me. But I did not understand.

A small dry mustached man in the front row blared out, "Say that slowly, son!"

"What, sir?"   85

"What you just said!"

"Social responsibility, sir," I said.

"You weren't being smart, were you boy?" he said, not unkindly.

"No, sir!"

"You sure that about 'equality' was a mistake?"   90

"Oh, yes, sir," I said. "I was swallowing blood."

"Well, you had better speak more slowly so we can understand. We mean to do right by you, but you've got to know your place at all times. All right, now, go on with your speech."

I was afraid. I wanted to leave but I wanted also to speak and I was afraid they'd snatch me down.

"Thank you sir," I said, beginning where I had left off, and having them ignore me as before.

Yet when I finished there was a thunderous applause. I was surprised to see the 95 superintendent come forth with a package wrapped in white tissue paper, and, gesturing for quiet, address the men.

"Gentlemen, you see that I did not overpraise the boy. He makes a good speech and some day he'll lead his people in the proper paths. And I don't have to tell you that this is important in these days and times. This is a good, smart boy, and so to encourage him in the right direction, in the name of the Board of Education I wish to present him a prize in the form of this . . ."

He paused, removing the tissue paper and revealing a gleaming calfskin briefcase.

". . . in the form of this first-class article from Shad Whitmore's shop."

"Boy," he said, addressing me, "take this prize and keep it well. Consider it a badge of office. Prize it. Keep developing as you are and some day it will be filled with important papers that will help shape the destiny of your people."

100   I was so moved that I could hardly express my thanks. A rope of bloody saliva forming a shape like an undiscovered continent drooled upon the leather and I wiped it quickly away. I felt an importance that I had never dreamed.

"Open it and see what's inside," I was told.

My fingers a-tremble, I complied, smelling fresh leather and finding an official-looking document inside. It was a scholarship to the state college for Negroes. My eyes filled with tears and I ran awkwardly off the floor.

I was overjoyed; I did not even mind when I discovered the gold pieces I had scrambled for were brass pocket tokens advertising a certain make of automobile.

When I reached home everyone was excited. Next day the neighbors came to congratulate me. I even felt safe from grandfather, whose deathbed curse usually spoiled my triumphs. I stood beneath his photograph with my briefcase in hand and smiled triumphantly into his stolid black peasant's face. It was a face that fascinated me. The eyes seemed to follow everywhere I went.

105   That night I dreamed I was at a circus with him and that he refused to laugh at the clowns no matter what they did. Then later he told me to open my briefcase and read what was inside and I did, finding an official envelope stamped with the state seal; and inside the envelope I found another and another, endlessly, and I thought I would fall of weariness. "Them's years," he said. "Now open that one." And I did and in it I found an engraved stamp containing a short message in letters of gold. "Read it," my grandfather said. "Out loud."

"To Whom It May Concern," I intoned. "Keep This Nigger-Boy Running."

I awoke with the old man's laughter ringing in my ears.

QUESTIONS FOR DISCUSSION AND WRITING

1. How do the dying words of the narrator's grandfather establish the various conflicts in the story? In what sense does the narrator's dream about his grandfather bring those conflicts to a satisfactory conclusion?

2. How does the narrator characterize himself? In what way does he characterize the other participants in the battle royal? How does the behavior of these "leading white citizens" contrast with the behavior expected of men in their social position?

3. What kind of setting does the narrator expect when he is invited to give his speech at "a gathering of the town's leading citizens"? What kind of setting does he discover at the smoker? What does this contrast suggest about the setting promised by his scholarship?

4. How does the opening paragraph of the story establish the point of view of the narrator? What has the narrator presumably learned since the time of the events he is describing? How does this knowledge influence the way he tells his tale?

5. What are the specific events portrayed in the story designed to demonstrate? In what ways do these "rituals" symbolize the relationships between blacks and whites in our culture?

Stories for Comparison

Ernest Gaines's "The Sky Is Gray" (pages 533–554); Zora Neale Hurston's "Sweat" (pages 671–680).

39

L O U I S E   E R D R I C H

The Red Convertible

LOUISE ERDRICH was born in 1954 in Little Falls, Minnesota, and grew up in Wahpeton, North Dakota, as a member of the Turtle Mountain Band of Chippewa. She was educated at Dartmouth College and Johns Hopkins University, taught poetry in both schools and prisons, and edited the Boston *Indian Council* newspaper before accepting a position as writer-in-residence at Dartmouth College. Her first work of fiction, *Love Medicine* (1984), won the National Book Critics Circle Award. Her recent novels, continuing the saga she began in *Love Medicine,* include *The Beet Queen* (1986), *Tracks* (1998), and *The Bingo Palace* (1994). She has also published several collections of poetry, including *Jacklight* (1984) and *Baptism of Desire* (1989), and a personal narrative, *The Blue Jay's Dance: A Birth Year* (1995). In "The Red Convertible," reprinted from *Love Medicine,* two brothers reveal their affection for each other through their car.

I was the first one to drive a convertible on my reservation. And of course it was red, a red Olds. I owned that car along with my brother Henry Junior. We owned it together until his boots filled with water on a windy night and he bought out my share. Now Henry owns the whole car, and his younger brother Lyman (that's myself), Lyman walks everywhere he goes.

How did I earn enough money to buy my share in the first place? My one talent was I could always make money. I had a touch for it, unusual in a Chippewa. From the first I was different that way, and everyone recognized it. I was the only kid they let in the American Legion Hall to shine shoes, for example, and one Christmas I sold spiritual bouquets for the mission door to door. The nuns let me keep a percentage. Once I started, it seemed the more money I made the easier the money came. Everyone encouraged it. When I was fifteen I got a job washing dishes at the Joliet Café, and that was where my first big break happened.

It wasn't long before I was promoted to bussing tables, and then the short-order cook quit and I was hired to take her place. No sooner than you know it I was managing the Joliet. The rest is history. I went on managing. I soon become part owner, and of course there was no stopping me then. It wasn't long before the whole thing was mine.

After I'd owned the Joliet for one year, it blew over in the worst tornado ever seen around here. The whole operation was smashed to bits. A total loss. The fryalator was up in a tree, the grill torn in half like it was paper. I was only sixteen. I had it all in my mother's name, and I lost it quick, but before I lost it I had every one of my relatives, and their relatives, to dinner, and I also bought that red Olds I mentioned, along with Henry.

5   The first time we saw it! I'll tell you when we first saw it. We had gotten a ride up to Winnipeg, and both of us had money. Don't ask me why, because we never mentioned a car or anything, we just had all our money. Mine was cash, a big bankroll from the Joliet's insurance. Henry had two checks—a week's extra pay for being laid off, and his regular check from the Jewel Bearing Plant.

We were walking down Portage anyway, seeing the sights, when we saw it. There it was, parked, large as life. Really as *if* it was alive. I thought of the word *repose,* because the car wasn't simply stopped, parked, or whatever. That car reposed, calm and gleaming, a FOR SALE sign in its left front window. Then, before we had thought it over at all, the car belonged to us and our pockets were empty. We had just enough money for gas back home.

We went places in that car, me and Henry. We took off driving all one whole summer. We started off toward the Little Knife River and Mandaree in Fort Berthold and then we found ourselves down in Wakpala somehow, and then suddenly we were over in Montana on the Rocky Boys, and yet the summer was not even half over. Some people hang on to details when they travel, but we didn't let them bother us and just lived our everyday lives here to there.

I do remember this one place with willows. I remember I laid under those trees and it was comfortable. So comfortable. The branches bent down all around me like a tent or a stable. And quiet, it was quiet, even though there was a powwow close enough so I could see it going on. The air was not too still, not too windy either. When the dust rises up and hangs in the air around the dancers like that, I feel good.

Henry was asleep with his arms thrown wide. Later on, he woke up and we started driving again. We were somewhere in Montana, or maybe on the Blood Reserve—it could have been anywhere. Anyway it was where we met the girl.

All her hair was in buns around her ears, that's the first thing I noticed about her. She was posed alongside the road with her arm out, so we stopped. That girl was short, so short her lumber shirt looked comical on her, like a nightgown. She had jeans on and fancy moccasins and she carried a little suitcase.

"Hop on in," says Henry. So she climbs in between us.   10

"We'll take you home," I says. "Where do you live?"

"Chicken," she says.

"Where the hell's that?" I ask her.

"Alaska."

"Okay," says Henry, and we drive.   15

We got up there and never wanted to leave. The sun doesn't truly set there in summer, and the night is more a soft dusk. You might doze off, sometimes, but before you know it you're up again, like an animal in nature. You never feel like you have to sleep hard or put away the world. And things would grow up there. One day just dirt or moss, the next day flowers and long grass. The girl's name was Susy. Her family really took to us. They fed us and put us up. We had our own tent to live in by their house, and the kids would be in and out of there all day and night. They couldn't get over me and Henry being brothers, we looked so different. We told them we knew we had the same mother, anyway.

One night Susy came in to visit us. We sat around in the tent talking of this thing and that. The season was changing. It was getting darker by that time, and the cold was even getting just a little mean. I told her it was time for us to go. She stood up on a chair.

"You never seen my hair," Susy said.

That was true. She was standing on a chair, but still, when she unclipped her buns the hair reached all the way to the ground. Our eyes opened. You couldn't tell how much hair she had when it was rolled up so neatly. Then my brother Henry did something funny. He went up to the chair and said, "Jump on my shoulders." So she did that, and her hair reached down past his waist, and he started twirling, this way and that, so her hair was flung out from side to side.

"I always wondered what it was like to have long pretty hair," Henry says. Well   20 we laughed. It was a funny sight, the way he did it. The next morning we got up and took leave of those people.

On to greener pastures, as they say. It was down through Spokane and across Idaho then Montana and very soon we were racing the weather right along under the Canadian border through Columbus, Des Lacs, and then we were in Bottineau County and soon home. We'd made most of the trip, that summer, without putting up the car hood at all. We got home just in time, it turned out, for the army to remember Henry had signed up to join it.

I don't wonder that the army was so glad to get my brother that they turned him into a Marine. He was built like a brick outhouse anyway. We liked to tease him that they really wanted him for his Indian nose. He had a nose big and sharp as a hatchet, like the nose on Red Tomahawk, the Indian who killed Sitting Bull, whose profile is on signs all along the North Dakota highways. Henry went off to training camp, came home once during Christmas, then the next thing you know we got an overseas letter from him. It was 1970, and he said he was stationed up in the northern hill country. Whereabouts I did not know. He wasn't such a hot letter writer, and only got off two before the enemy caught him. I could never keep it straight, which direction those good Vietnam soldiers were from.

I wrote him back several times, even though I didn't know if those letters would get through. I kept him informed all about the car. Most of the time I had it up on blocks in the yard or half taken apart, because that long trip did a hard job on it under the hood.

I always had good luck with numbers, and never worried about the draft myself. I never even had to think about what my number was. But Henry was never lucky in the same way as me. It was at least three years before Henry came home. By then I guess the whole war was solved in the government's mind, but for him it would keep on going. In those years I'd put his car into almost perfect shape. I always thought of it as his car while he was gone, even though when he left he said, "Now it's yours," and threw me his key.

25   "Thanks for the extra key," I'd said. "I'll put it up in your drawer just in case I need it." He laughed.

When he came home, though, Henry was very different, and I'll say this: the change was no good. You could hardly expect him to change for the better, I know. But he was quiet, so quiet, and never comfortable sitting still anywhere but always up and moving around. I thought back to times we'd sat still for whole afternoons, never moving a muscle, just shifting our weight along the ground, talking to whoever sat with us, watching things. He'd always had a joke, then, too, and now you couldn't get him to laugh, or when he did it was more the sound of a man choking, a sound that stopped up the throats of other people around him. They got to leaving him alone most of the time, and I didn't blame them. It was a fact: Henry was jumpy and mean.

I'd bought a color TV set for my mom and the rest of us while Henry was away. Money still came very easy. I was sorry I'd ever bought it though, because of Henry. I was also sorry I'd bought color, because with black-and-white the pictures seem older and farther away. But what are you going to do? He sat in front of it, watching it, and that was the only time he was completely still. But it was the kind of stillness that you see in a rabbit when it freezes and before it will bolt. He was not easy. He sat in his chair gripping the armrests with all his might, as if the chair itself was moving at a high speed and if he let go at all he would rocket forward and maybe crash right through the set.

Once I was in the room watching TV with Henry and I heard his teeth click at something. I looked over, and he'd bitten through his lip. Blood was going down his chin. I tell you right then I wanted to smash that tube to pieces. I went over to it but Henry must have known what I was up to. He rushed from his chair and shoved me out of the way, against the wall. I told myself he didn't know what he was doing.

My mom came in, turned the set off real quiet, and told us she had made something for supper. So we went and sat down. There was still blood going down

Henry's chin, but he didn't notice it and no one said anything, even though every time he took a bite of his bread his blood fell onto it until he was eating his own blood mixed in with the food.

While Henry was not around we talked about what was going to happen to him. 30 There were no Indian doctors on the reservation, and my mom was afraid of trusting Old Man Pillager because he courted her long ago and was jealous of her husbands. He might take revenge through her son. We were afraid that if we brought Henry to a regular hospital they would keep him.

"They don't fix them in those places," Mom said; "they just give them drugs."

"We wouldn't get him there in the first place," I agreed, "so let's just forget about it."

Then I thought about the car.

Henry had not even looked at the car since he'd gotten home, though like I said, it was in tip-top condition and ready to drive. I thought the car might bring the old Henry back somehow. So I bided my time and waited for my chance to interest him in the vehicle.

One night Henry was off somewhere. I took myself a hammer. I went out to that 35 car and I did a number on its underside. Whacked it up. Bent the tail pipe double. Ripped the muffler loose. By the time I was done with the car it looked worse than any typical Indian car that has been driven all its life on reservation roads, which they always say are like government promises—full of holes. It just about hurt me, I'll tell you that! I threw dirt in the carburetor and I ripped all the electric tape off the seats. I made it look just as beat up as I could. Then I sat back and waited for Henry to find it.

Still, it took him over a month. That was all right, because it was just getting warm enough, not melting, but warm enough to work outside.

"Lyman," he says, walking in one day, "that red car looks like shit."

"Well it's old," I says. "You got to expect that."

"No way!" says Henry. "That car's a classic! But you went and ran the piss right out of it, Lyman, and you know it don't deserve that. I kept that car in A-one shape. You don't remember. You're too young. But when I left, that car was running like a watch. Now I don't even know if I can get it to start again, let alone get it anywhere near its old condition."

"Well you try," I said, like I was getting mad, "but I say it's a piece of junk."   40

Then I walked out before he could realize I knew he'd strung together more than six words at once.

After that I thought he'd freeze himself to death working on that car. He was out there all day, and at night he rigged up a little lamp, ran a cord out the window, and had himself some light to see by while he worked. He was better than he had been before, but that's still not saying much. It was easier for him to do the things the rest of us did. He ate more slowly and didn't jump up and down during the meal to get this or that or look out the window. I put my hand in the back of the TV set, I admit, and fiddled around with it good, so that it was almost impossible now to get a clear picture. He didn't look at it very often anyway. He was always out with that car or going off to get parts for it. By the time it was really melting outside, he had it fixed.

I had been feeling down in the dumps about Henry around this time. We had always been together before. Henry and Lyman. But he was such a loner now that I didn't know how to take it. So I jumped at the chance one day when Henry seemed friendly. It's not that he smiled or anything. He just said, "Let's take that old shitbox for a spin." Just the way he said it made me think he could be coming around.

We went out to the car. It was spring. The sun was shining very bright. My only sister, Bonita, who was just eleven years old, came out and made us stand together for a picture. Henry leaned his elbow on the red car's windshield, and he took his other arm and put it over my shoulder, very carefully, as though it was heavy for him to lift and he didn't want to bring the weight down all at once.

45   "Smile," Bonita said, and he did.

That picture. I never look at it anymore. A few months ago, I don't know why, I got his picture out and tacked it on the wall. I felt good about Henry at the time, close to him. I felt good having his picture on the wall, until one night when I was looking at television. I was a little drunk and stoned. I looked up at the wall and Henry was staring at me. I don't know what it was, but his smile had changed, or maybe it was gone. All I know is I couldn't stay in the same room with that picture. I was shaking. I got up, closed the door, and went into the kitchen. A little later my friend Ray came over and we both went back into that room. We put the picture in a brown bag, folded the bag over and over tightly, then put it way back in a closet.

I still see that picture now, as if it tugs at me, whenever I pass that closet door. The picture is very clear in my mind. It was so sunny that day Henry had to squint against the glare. Or maybe the camera Bonita held flashed like a mirror, blinding him, before she snapped the picture. My face is right out in the sun, big and round. But he might have drawn back, because the shadows on his face are deep as holes. There are two shadows curved like little hooks around the ends of his smile, as if to frame it and try to keep it there—that one, first smile that looked like it might have hurt his face. He has his field jacket on and the worn-in clothes he'd come back in and kept wearing ever since. After Bonita took the picture, she went into the house and we got into the car. There was a full cooler in the trunk. We started off, east, toward Pembina and the Red River because Henry said he wanted to see the high water.

The trip over there was beautiful. When everything starts changing, drying up, clearing off, you feel like your whole life is starting. Henry felt it, too. The top was down and the car hummed like a top. He'd really put it back in shape, even the tape on the seats was very carefully put down and glued back in layers. It's not that he smiled again or even joked, but his face looked to me as if it was clear, more peaceful. It looked as though he wasn't thinking of anything in particular except the bare fields and windbreaks and houses we were passing.

The river was high and full of winter trash when we got there. The sun was still out, but it was colder by the river. There were still little clumps of dirty snow here and there on the banks. The water hadn't gone over the banks yet, but it would, you could tell. It was just at its limit, hard swollen, glossy like an old gray scar. We made ourselves a fire, and we sat down and watched the current go. As I watched it I felt something squeezing inside me and tightening and trying to let go all at the same time. I knew I was not just feeling it myself; I knew I was feeling what Henry was going through at that moment. Except that I couldn't stand it, the closing and opening. I jumped to my feet. I took Henry by the shoulders and I started shaking him. "Wake up," I says, "wake up, wake up, wake up!" I didn't know what had come over me. I sat down beside him again.

His face was totally white and hard. Then it broke, like stones break all of a sudden when water boils up inside them.

"I know it," he says. "I know it. I can't help it. It's no use."

We start talking. He said he knew what I'd done with the car. It was obvious that it had been whacked out of shape and not just neglected. He said he wanted to give the car to me for good now, it was no use. He said he'd fixed it just to give it back and I should take it.

"No way," I says, "I don't want it."

"That's okay," he says, "you take it."

"I don't want it, though," I says back to him, and then to emphasize, just to emphasize, you understand, I touch his shoulder. He slaps my hand off.

"Take that car," he says.

"No," I say, "make me," I say, and then he grabs my jacket and rips the arm loose. That jacket is a class act, suede with tags and zippers. I push Henry backwards, off the log. He jumps up and bowls me over. We go down in a clinch and come up swinging hard, for all we're worth, with our fists. He socks my jaw so hard I feel like it swings loose. Then I'm at his ribcage and land a good one under his chin so his head snaps back. He's dazzled. He looks at me and I look at him and then his eyes are full of tears and blood and at first I think he's crying. But no, he's laughing. "Ha! Ha!" he says. "Ha! Ha! Take good care of it."

"Okay," I says, "okay, no problem. Ha! Ha!"

I can't help it, and I start laughing, too. My face feels fat and strange, and after a while I get a beer from the cooler in the trunk, and when I hand it to Henry he takes his shirt and wipes my germs off. "Hoof-and-mouth disease," he says. For some reason this cracks me up, and so we're really laughing for a while, and then we drink all the rest of the beers one by one and throw them in the river and see how far, how fast, the current takes them before they fill up and sink.

"You want to go on back?" I ask after a while. "Maybe we could snag a couple nice Kashpaw girls."

He says nothing. But I can tell his mood is turning again.

"They're all crazy, the girls up here, every damn one of them."

"You're crazy too," I say, to jolly him up. "Crazy Lamartine boys!"

He looks as though he will take this wrong at first. His face twists, then clears, and he jumps up on his feet. "That's right!" he says. "Crazier 'n hell. Crazy Indians!"

I think it's the old Henry again. He throws off his jacket and starts swinging his legs out from the knees like a fancy dancer. He's down doing something between a grouse dance and a bunny hop, no kind of dance I ever saw before, but neither has anyone else on all this green growing earth. He's wild. He wants to pitch whoopee!

He's up and at me and all over. All this time I'm laughing so hard, so hard my belly is getting tied up in a knot.

"Got to cool me off!" he shouts all of a sudden. Then he runs over to the river and jumps in.

There's boards and other things in the current. It's so high. No sound comes from the river after the splash he makes, so I run right over. I look around. It's getting dark. I see he's halfway across the water already, and I know he didn't swim there but the current took him. It's far. I hear his voice, though, very clearly across it.

"My boots are filling," he says.

He says this in a normal voice, like he just noticed and he doesn't know what to think of it. Then he's gone. A branch comes by. Another branch. And I go in.

70   By the time I get out of the river, off the snag I pulled myself onto, the sun is down. I walk back to the car, turn on the high beams, and drive it up the bank. I put it in first gear and then I take my foot off the clutch. I get out, close the door, and watch it plow softly into the water. The headlights reach in as they go down, searching, still lighted even after the water swirls over the back end. I wait. The wires short out. It is all finally dark. And then there is only the water, the sound of it going and running and going and running and running.

QUESTIONS FOR DISCUSSION AND WRITING

1. How is the convertible used as a structuring device throughout the story? Which moment serves as the climax of the story? How does the sacrifice of the car serve as an appropriate denouement?

2. How do Lyman and Henry act as foils for each other? How does Lyman describe his own character? How does Vietnam change Henry's character?

3. What qualities does Lyman associate with Native Americans and their culture? How does the family's discussion about "what to do about Henry" reveal the differences between Indian and American culture?

4. How does Lyman's love for his brother affect the way he remembers the events in this story? For example, how does Lyman describe Henry's relationship with Susy, his television watching, and their fight at the river?

5. What is the symbolic significance of the photograph? What themes grow directly out of this symbol? What are the thematic implications of the first paragraph when one comes back to it after having read the story?

Stories for Comparison

Carson McCullers's "Sucker" (pages 824–831); Leslie Marmon Silko's "Storyteller" (pages 1058–1070).

40

WILLIAM FAULKNER

Barn Burning

WILLIAM FAULKNER (1897–1962) was born in New Albany, Mississippi, but soon moved to Oxford, Mississippi, where his father worked as the business manager of the University of Mississippi. Faulkner left high school to work in a local bank and then in 1918 enlisted in the Royal Canadian Air Force, before returning for a brief period to study at the University of Mississippi. During the early twenties, Faulkner began writing poetry and fiction and became acquainted with various members of the literary community in New Orleans, most notably Sherwood Anderson, who encouraged his endeavors. In 1929 Faulkner published *Sartoris,* the first of his novels dealing with the life and legends of Yoknapatawpha, a fictional county in Mississippi. Although Faulkner wrote novels about this county at an astonishing pace— *The Sound and the Fury* (1929), *As I Lay Dying* (1930), *Light in August* (1932), *Absalom, Absalom* (1936), *The Hamlet* (1940), *Go Down, Moses* (1942)—and although he published his short stories in such commercially recognized magazines as *The Saturday Evening Post,* his literary reputation during this period was negligible. Faulkner's need for money forced him to accept many off-and-on assignments as a screenwriter in Hollywood, working on such films as *To Have and Have Not* and *The Big Sleep.* Faulkner was finally recognized as a major literary talent when he was awarded the Nobel Prize in 1949. He continued to produce novels such as *The Town* (1957), *The Mansion* (1959), and *The Reivers* (1963), and collected many of his stories in a 1950 volume that won the National Book Award. "Barn Burning," reprinted from that volume, describes the complex social and psychological causes that lead the father of a poor family to commit acts of revenge.

The store in which the Justice of the Peace's court was sitting smelled of cheese. The boy, crouched on his nail keg at the back of the crowded room, knew he smelled cheese, and more: from where he sat he could see the ranked shelves close-packed with the solid, squat, dynamic shapes of tin cans whose labels his stomach read, not from the lettering which meant nothing to his mind but from the scarlet devils and the silver curve of fish—this, the cheese which he knew he smelled and the hermetic meat which his intestines believed he smelled coming in intermittent gusts momentary and brief between the other constant one, the smell and sense just a little of fear because mostly of despair and grief, the old fierce pull of blood. He could not see the table where the Justice sat and before which his father and his father's enemy (*our enemy* he thought in that despair; *ourn! mine and hisn both! He's my father!*) stood, but he could hear them, the two of them that is, because his father had said no word yet:

"But what proof have you, Mr. Harris?"

"I told you. The hog got into my corn. I caught it up and sent it back to him. He had no fence that would hold it. I told him so, warned him. The next time I put the hog in my pen. When he came to get it I gave him enough wire to patch up his pen. The next time I put the hog up and kept it. I rode down to his house and saw the wire I gave him still rolled on to the spool in his yard. I told him he could have the hog when he paid me a dollar pound fee. That evening a nigger came with the dollar and got the hog. He was a strange nigger. He said, 'He say to tell you wood and hay kin burn.' I said, 'What?' 'That whut he say to tell you,' the nigger said. 'Wood and hay kin burn.' That night my barn burned. I got the stock out but I lost the barn."

"Where is the nigger? Have you got him?"

5   "He was a strange nigger, I tell you. I don't know what became of him."

"But that's not proof. Don't you see that's not proof?"

"Get that boy up here. He knows." For a moment the boy thought too that the man meant his older brother until Harris said, "Not him. The little one. The boy," and, crouching, small for his age, small and wiry like his father, in patched and faded jeans even too small for him, with straight, uncombed, brown hair and eyes gray and wild as storm scud, he saw the men between himself and the table part and become a lane of grim faces, at the end of which he saw the Justice, a shabby, collarless, graying man in spectacles, beckoning him. He felt no floor under his bare feet; he seemed to walk beneath the palpable weight of the grim turning faces. His father, stiff in his black Sunday coat donned not for the trial but for the moving, did not even look at him. *He aims for me to lie,* he thought, again with that frantic grief and despair. *And I will have to do hit.*

"What's your name, boy?" the Justice said.

"Colonel Sartoris Snopes," the boy whispered.

10   "Hey?" the Justice said. "Talk louder, Colonel Sartoris? I reckon anybody named for Colonel Sartoris in this country can't help but tell the truth, can they?" The boy said nothing. *Enemy! Enemy!* he thought; for a moment he could not even see, could not see that the Justice's face was kindly nor discern that his voice was troubled when he spoke to the man named Harris: "Do you want me to question this boy?" But he could hear, and during those subsequent long seconds while there was absolutely no sound in the crowded little room save that of quiet and intent breathing it was as if he had swung outward at the end of a grape vine, over a ravine, and at the top of the swing had been caught in a prolonged instant of mesmerized gravity, weightless in time.

"No!" Harris said violently, explosively. "Damnation! Send him out of here!" Now time, the fluid world, rushed beneath him again, the voices coming to him again through the smell of cheese and sealed meat, the fear and despair and the old grief of blood:

"This case is closed. I can't find against you, Snopes, but I can give you advice. Leave this country and don't come back to it."

His father spoke for the first time, his voice cold and harsh, level, without emphasis: "I aim to. I don't figure to stay in a country among people who . . ." he said something unprintable and vile, addressed to no one.

"That'll do," the Justice said. "Take your wagon and get out of this country before dark. Case dismissed."

His father turned, and he followed the stiff black coat, the wiry figure walking 15 a little stiffly from where a Confederate provost's man's musket ball had taken him in the heel on a stolen horse thirty years ago, followed the two backs now, since his older brother had appeared from somewhere in the crowd, no taller than the father but thicker, chewing tobacco steadily, between the two lines of grim-faced men and out of the store and across the worn gallery and down the sagging steps and among the dogs and half-grown boys in the mild May dust, where as he passed a voice hissed:

"Barn burner!"

Again he could not see, whirling; there was a face in a red haze, moonlike, bigger than the full moon, the owner of it half again his size, he leaping in the red haze toward the face, feeling no blow, feeling no shock when his head struck the earth, scrabbling up and leaping again, feeling no blow this time either and tasting no blood, scrabbling up to see the other boy in full flight and himself already leaping into pursuit as his father's hand jerked him back, the harsh, cold voice speaking above him: "Go get in the wagon."

It stood in a grove of locusts and mulberries across the road. His two hulking sisters in their Sunday dresses and his mother and her sister in calico and sunbonnets were already in it, sitting on and among the sorry residue of the dozen and more movings which even the boy could remember—and battered stove, the broken beds and chairs, the clock inlaid with mother-of-pearl, which would not run, stopped at some fourteen minutes past two o'clock of a dead and forgotten day and time, which had been his mother's dowry. She was crying, though when she saw him she drew her sleeve across her face and began to descend from the wagon. "Get back," the father said.

"He's hurt. I got to get some water and wash his . . ."

"Get back in the wagon," his father said. He got in too, over the tail-gate. His 20 father mounted to the seat where the older brother already sat and struck the gaunt mules two savage blows with the peeled willow, but without heat. It was not even sadistic; it was exactly that same quality which in later years would cause his descendants to over-run the engine before putting a motor car into motion, striking and reining back in the same movement. The wagon went on, the store with its quiet crowd of grimly watching men dropped behind; a curve in the road hid it. *Forever* he thought. *Maybe he's done satisfied now, now that he has* . . . stopping himself, not to say it aloud even to himself. His mother's hand touched his shoulder.

"Does hit hurt?" she said.

"Naw," he said. "Hit don't hurt. Lemme be."

"Can't you wipe some of the blood off before hit dries?"

"I'll wash to-night," he said. "Lemme be, I tell you."

25   The wagon went on. He did not know where they were going. None of them ever did or ever asked, because it was always somewhere, always a house of sorts waiting for them a day or two days or even three days away. Likely his father had already arranged to make a crop on another farm before he . . . Again he had to stop himself. He (the father) always did. There was something about his wolflike independence and even courage when the advantage was at least neutral which impressed strangers, as if they got from his latent ravening ferocity not so much a sense of dependability as a feeling that his ferocious conviction in the rightness of his own actions would be of advantage to all whose interest lay with his.

That night they camped, in a grove of oaks and beeches where a spring ran. The nights were still cool and they had a fire against it, of a rail lifted from a nearby fence and cut into lengths—a small fire, neat, niggard almost, a shrewd fire; such fires were his father's habit and custom always, even in freezing weather. Older, the boy might have remarked this and wondered why not a big one; why should not a man who had not only seen the waste and extravagance of war, but who had in his blood an inherent voracious prodigality with material not his own, have burned everything in sight? Then he might have gone a step farther and thought that that was the reason: that niggard blaze was the living fruit of nights passed during those four years in the woods hiding from all men, blue or gray, with his strings of horses (captured horses, he called them). And older still, he might have divined the true reason: that the element of fire spoke to some deep mainspring of his father's being, as the element of steel or of powder spoke to other men, as the one weapon for the preservation of integrity, else breath were not worth the breathing, and hence to be regarded with respect and used with discretion.

But he did not think this now and he had seen those same niggard blazes all his life. He merely ate his supper beside it and was already half asleep over his iron plate when his father called him, and once more he followed the stiff back, the stiff and ruthless limp, up the slope and on to the starlit road where, turning, he could see his father against the stars but without face or depth—a shape black, flat, and bloodless as though cut from tin in the iron folds of the frockcoat which had not been made for him, the voice harsh like tin and without heat like tin:

"You were fixing to tell him. You would have told him." He didn't answer. His father struck him with the flat of his hand on the side of the head, hard but without heat, exactly as he had struck the two mules at the store, exactly as he would strike either of them with any stick in order to kill a horse fly, his voice still without heat or anger: "You're getting to be a man. You got to learn. You got to learn to stick to your own blood or you ain't going to have any blood to stick to you. Do you think either of them, any man there this morning, would? Don't you know all they wanted was a chance to get at me because they knew I had them beat? Eh?" Later, twenty years later, he was to tell himself, "If I said they wanted only truth, justice, he would have hit me again." But now he said nothing. He was not crying. He just stood there. "Answer me," his father said.

"Yes," he whispered. His father turned.

"Get on to bed. We'll be there to-morrow."   30

To-morrow they were there. In the early afternoon the wagon stopped before a paintless two-room house identical almost with the dozen others it had stopped before even in the boy's ten years, and again, as on the other dozen occasions, his mother and aunt got down and began to unload the wagon, although his two sisters and his father and brother had not moved.

"Likely hit ain't fitten for hawgs," one of the sisters said.

"Nevertheless, fit it will and you'll hog it and like it," his father said. "Get out of them chairs and help your Ma unload."

The two sisters got down, big, bovine, in a flutter of cheap ribbons; one of them drew from the jumbled wagon bed a battered lantern, the other a worn broom. His father handed the reins to the older son and began to climb stiffly over the wheel. "When they get unloaded, take the team to the barn and feed them." Then he said, and at first the boy thought he was still speaking to his brother: "Come with me."

"Me?" he said.   35

"Yes," his father said. "You."

"Abner," his mother said. His father paused and looked back—the harsh level stare beneath the shaggy, graying, irascible brows.

"I reckon I'll have a word with the man that aims to begin to-morrow owning me body and soul for the next eight months."

They went back up the road. A week ago—or before last night, that is—he would have asked where they were going, but not now. His father had struck him before last night but never before had he paused afterward to explain why; it was as if the blow and the following calm, outrageous voice still range, repercussed, divulging nothing to him save the terrible handicap of being young, the light weight of his few years, just heavy enough to prevent his soaring free of the world as it seemed to be ordered but not heavy enough to keep him footed solid in it, to resist it and try to change the course of its events.

Presently he could see the grove of oaks and cedars and the other flowering trees 40
and shrubs where the house would be, though not the house yet. They walked beside a fence massed with honeysuckle and Cherokee roses and came to a gate swinging open between two brick pillars, and now, beyond a sweep of drive, he saw the house for the first time and at that instant he forgot his father and the terror and despair both, and even when he remembered his father again (who had not stopped) the terror and despair did not return. Because, for all the twelve movings, they had sojourned until now in a poor country, a land of small farms and fields and houses, and he had never seen a house like this before. *Hit's big as a courthouse* he thought quietly, with a surge of peace and joy whose reason he could not have thought into words, being too young for that: *They are safe from him. People whose lives are a part of this peace and dignity are beyond his touch, he no more to them than a buzzing wasp: capable of stinging for a little moment but that's all; the spell of this peace and dignity rendering even the barns and stable and cribs which belong to it impervious to the puny flames he might contrive . . .* this, the peace and joy, ebbing for an instant as he looked again at the stiff black back, the stiff and implacable limp

of the figure which was not dwarfed by the house, for the reason that it had never looked big anywhere and which now, against the serene columned backdrop, had more than ever that impervious quality of something cut ruthlessly from tin, depthless, as though, sidewise to the sun, it would cast no shadow. Watching him, the boy remarked the absolutely undeviating course which his father held and saw the stiff foot come squarely down in a pile of fresh droppings where a horse had stood in the drive and which his father could have avoided by a simple change of stride. But it ebbed only for a moment, though he could not have thought this into words either, walking on in the spell of the house, which he could even want but without envy, without sorrow, certainly never with that ravening and jealous rage which unknown to him walked in the ironlike black coat before him: *Maybe he will feel it too. Maybe it will even change him now from what maybe he couldn't help but be.*

They crossed the portico. Now he could hear his father's stiff foot as it came down on the boards with clocklike finality, a sound out of all proportion to the displacement of the body it bore and which was not dwarfed either by the white door before it, as though it had attained to a sort of vicious and ravening minimum not to be dwarfed by anything—the flat, wide, black hat, the formal coat of broadcloth which had once been black but which had now that friction-glazed greenish cast of the bodies of old house flies, the lifted sleeve which was too large, the lifted hand like a curled claw. The door opened so promptly that the boy knew the Negro must have been watching them all the time, an old man with neat grizzled hair, in a linen jacket, who stood barring the door with his body, saying, "Wipe yo foots, white man, fo you come in here. Major ain't home nohow."

"Get out of my way, nigger," his father said, without heat too, flinging the door back and the Negro also and entering, his hat still on his head. And now the boy saw the prints of the stiff foot on the doorjamb and saw them appear on the pale rug behind the machinelike deliberation of the foot which seemed to bear (or transmit) twice the weight which the body compassed. The Negro was shouting "Miss Lula! Miss Lula!" somewhere behind them, then the boy, deluged as though by a warm wave by a suave turn of carpeted stairs and a pendant glitter of chandeliers and a mute gleam of gold frames, heard the swift feet and saw her too, a lady—perhaps he had never seen her like before either—in a gray, smooth gown with lace at the throat and an apron tied at the waist and the sleeves turned back, wiping cake or biscuit dough from her hands with a towel as she came up the hall, looking not at his father at all but at the tracks on the blond rug with an expression of incredulous amazement.

"I tried," the Negro cried. "I tole him to . . ."

"Will you please go away?" she said in a shaking voice. "Major de Spain is not at home. Will you please go away?"

45   His father had not spoken again. He did not speak again. He did not even look at her. He just stood stiff in the center of the rug, in his hat, the shaggy iron-gray brows twitching slightly above the pebble-colored eyes as he appeared to examine the house with brief deliberation. Then with the same deliberation he turned; the boy watched him pivot on the good leg and saw the stiff foot drag round the arc of the turning, leaving a final long and fading smear. His father never looked at it, he never

once looked down at the rug. The Negro held the door. It closed behind them, upon the hysteric and indistinguishable woman-wail. His father stopped at the top of the steps and scraped his boot clean on the edge of it. At the gate he stopped again. He stood for a moment, planted stiffly on the stiff foot, looking back at the house. "Pretty and white, ain't it?" he said. "That's sweat. Nigger sweat. Maybe it ain't white enough yet to suit him. Maybe he wants to mix some white sweat with it."

Two hours later the boy was chopping wood behind the house within which his mother and aunt and the two sisters (the mother and aunt, not the two girls, he knew that; even at this distance and muffled by walls the flat loud voices of the two girls emanated an incorrigible idle inertia) were setting up the stove to prepare a meal, when he heard the hooves and saw the linen-clad man on a fine sorrel mare, whom he recognized even before he saw the rolled rug in front of the Negro youth following on a fat bay carriage horse—a suffused, angry face vanishing, still at full gallop, beyond the corner of the house where his father and brother were sitting in the two tilted chairs; and a moment later, almost before he could have put the axe down, he heard the hooves again and watched the sorrel mare go back out of the yard, already galloping again. Then his father began to shout one of the sisters' names, who presently emerged backward from the kitchen door dragging the rolled rug along the ground by one end while the other sister walked behind it.

"If you ain't going to tote, go on and set up the wash pot," the first said.

"You, Sarty!" the second shouted. "Set up the wash pot!" His father appeared at the door, framed against that shabbiness, as he had been against that other bland perfection, impervious to either, the mother's anxious face at his shoulder.

"Go on," the father said. "Pick it up." The two sisters stooped, broad, lethargic; stooping, they presented an incredible expanse of pale cloth and a flutter of tawdry ribbons.

"If I thought enough of a rug to have to git hit all the way from France I wouldn't   50 keep hit where folks coming in would have to tromp on hit," the first said. They raised the rug.

"Abner," the mother said. "Let me do it."

"You go back and git dinner," his father said. "I'll tend to this."

From the woodpile through the rest of the afternoon the boy watched them, the rug spread flat in the dust beside the bubbling wash-pot, the two sisters stooping over it with that profound and lethargic reluctance, while the father stood over them in turn, implacable and grim, driving them though never raising his voice again. He could smell the harsh homemade lye they were using; he saw his mother come to the door once and look toward them with an expression not anxious now but very like despair; he saw his father turn, and he fell to with the axe and saw from the corner of his eye his father raise from the ground a flattish fragment of field stone and examine it and return to the pot, and this time his mother actually spoke: "Abner. Abner. Please don't. Please, Abner."

Then he was done too. It was dusk; the whippoorwills had already begun. He could smell coffee from the room where they would presently eat the cold food remaining from the mid-afternoon meal, though when he entered the house he realized they were having coffee again probably because there was a fire on the hearth, before which the rug now lay spread over the backs of the two chairs. The tracks of his father's foot were gone. Where they had been were now long, water-cloudy scoriations resembling the sporadic course of a lilliputian mowing machine.

55   It still hung there while they ate the cold food and then went to bed, scattered without order or claim up and down the two rooms, his mother in one bed, where his father would later lie, the older brother in the other, himself, the aunt, and the two sisters on pallets on the floor. But his father was not in bed yet. The last thing the boy remembered was the depthless, harsh silhouette of the hat and coat bending over the rug and it seemed to him that he had not even closed his eyes when the silhouette was standing over him, the fire almost dead behind it, the stiff foot prodding him awake. "Catch up the mule," his father said.

When he returned with the mule his father was standing in the back door, the rolled rug over his shoulder. "Ain't you going to ride?" he said.

"No. Give me your foot."

He bent his knee into his father's hand, the wiry, surprising power flowed smoothly, rising, he rising with it, on to the mule's bare back (they had owned a saddle once; the boy could remember it though not when or where) and with the same effortlessness his father swung the rug up in front of him. Now in the starlight they retraced the afternoon's path, up the dusty road rife with honeysuckle, through the gate and up the black tunnel of the drive to the lightless house, where he sat on the mule and felt the rough warp of the rug drag across his thighs and vanish.

"Don't you want me to help?" he whispered. His father did not answer and now he heard again that stiff foot striking the hollow portico with that wooden and clock-like deliberation, that outrageous overstatement of the weight it carried. The rug, hunched, not flung (the boy could tell that even in the darkness) from his father's shoulder struck the angle of wall and floor with a sound unbelievably loud, thunderous, then the foot again, unhurried and enormous; a light came on in the house and the boy sat, tense, breathing steadily and quietly and just a little fast, though the foot itself did not increase its beat at all, descending the steps now; now the boy could see him.

60   "Don't you want to ride now?" he whispered. "We kin both ride now," the light within the house altering now, flaring up and sinking. *He's coming down the stairs now,* he thought. He had already ridden the mule up beside the horse block; presently his father was up behind him and he doubled the reins over and slashed the mule across the neck, but before the animal could begin to trot the hard, thin arm came round him, the hard, knotted hand jerking the mule back to a walk.

In the first red rays of the sun they were in the lot, putting plow gear on the mules. This time the sorrel mare was in the lot before he heard it at all, the rider collarless and even bareheaded, trembling, speaking in a shaking voice as the woman in the house had done. His father merely looking up once before stooping again to the hame he was buckling, so that the man on the mare spoke to his stooping back:

"You must realize you have ruined that rug. Wasn't there anybody here, any of your women? . . ." he ceased, shaking, the boy watching him, the older brother leaning now in the stable door, chewing, blinking slowly and steadily at nothing apparently. "It cost a hundred dollars. But you never had a hundred dollars. You never will.

So I'm going to charge you twenty bushels of corn against your crop. I'll add it in your contract and when you come to the commissary you can sign it. That won't keep Mrs. de Spain quiet but maybe it will teach you to wipe your feet off before you enter her house again."

Then he was gone. The boy looked at his father, who still had not spoken or even looked up again, who was now adjusting the loggerhead in the hame.

"Pap," he said. His father looked at him—the inscrutable face, the shaggy brows beneath which the gray eyes glinted coldly. Suddenly the boy went toward him, fast, stopping as suddenly. "You done the best you could!" he cried. "If he wanted hit done different why didn't he wait and tell you how? He won't git no twenty bushels! He won't git none! We'll gether hit and hide hit! I kin watch . . ."

"Did you put the cutter back in that straight stock like I told you?"   65

"No, sir," he said.

"Then go do it."

That was Wednesday. During the rest of that week he worked steadily, at what was within his scope and some which was beyond it, with an industry that did not need to be driven nor even commanded twice; he had this from his mother, with the difference that some at least of what he did he liked to do, such as splitting wood with the half-size axe which his mother and aunt had earned, or saved money somehow, to present him with at Christmas. In company with the two older women (and on one afternoon, even one of the sisters), he built pens for the shoat and the cow which were a part of his father's contract with the landlord, and one afternoon, his father being absent, gone somewhere on one of the mules, he went to the field.

They were running a middle buster now, his brother holding the plow straight while he handled the reins, and walking beside the straining mule, the rich black soil shearing cool and damp against his bare ankles, he thought *Maybe this is the end of it. Maybe even that twenty bushels that seems hard to have to pay for just a rug will be a cheap price for him to stop forever and always from being what he used to be;* thinking, dreaming now, so that his brother had to speak sharply to him to mind the mule: *Maybe he even won't collect the twenty bushels. Maybe it will all add up and balance and vanish—corn, rug, fire; the terror and grief, the being pulled two ways like between two teams of horses—gone, done with for ever and ever.*

Then it was Saturday; he looked up from beneath the mule he was harnessing 70 and saw his father in the black coat and hat. "Not that," his father said. "The wagon gear." And then, two hours later, sitting in the wagon bed behind his father and brother on the seat, the wagon accomplished a final curve, and he saw the weathered paintless store with its tattered tobacco- and patent-medicine posters and the tethered wagons and saddle animals below the gallery. He mounted the gnawed steps behind his father and brother, and there again was the lane of quiet, watching faces for the three of them to walk through. He saw the man in spectacles sitting at the plank table and he did not need to be told this was a Justice of the Peace; he sent one glare of fierce, exultant, partisan defiance at the man in collar and cravat now, whom he had seen but twice before in his life, and that on a galloping horse, who now wore on his face an expression not of rage but of amazed unbelief which the boy could not have known was at the incredible circumstance of being sued by one of his own tenants, and came and stood against his father and cried at the Justice: "He ain't done it! He ain't burnt . . ."

"Go back to the wagon," his father said.

"Burnt?" the Justice said. "Do I understand this rug was burned too?"

"Does anybody here claim it was?" his father said. "Go back to the wagon." But he did not, he merely retreated in the rear of the room, crowded as that other had been, but not to sit down this time, instead, to stand pressing among the motionless bodies, listening to the voices:

"And you claim twenty bushels of corn is too high for the damage you did to the rug?"

75   "He brought the rug to me and said he wanted the tracks washed out of it. I washed the tracks out and took the rug back to him."

"But you didn't carry the rug back to him in the same condition it was in before you made the tracks on it."

His father did not answer, and now for perhaps half a minute there was no sound at all save that of breathing, the faint, steady suspiration of complete and intent listening.

"You decline to answer that, Mr. Snopes?" Again his father did not answer. "I'm going to find against you, Mr. Snopes. I'm going to find that you were responsible for the injury to Major de Spain's rug and hold you liable for it. But twenty bushels of corn seems a little high for a man in your circumstances to have to pay. Major de Spain claims it cost a hundred dollars. October corn will be worth about fifty cents. I figure that if Major de Spain can stand a ninety-five-dollar loss on something he paid cash for, you can stand a five-dollar loss you haven't earned yet. I hold you in damages to Major de Spain to the amount of ten bushels of corn over and above your contract with him, to be paid to him out of your crop at gathering time. Court adjourned."

It had taken no time hardly, the morning was but half begun. He thought they would return home and perhaps back to the field, since they were late, far behind all other farmers. But instead his father passed on behind the wagon, merely indicating with his hand for the older brother to follow with it, and crossed the road toward the blacksmith shop opposite, pressing on after his father, overtaking him, speaking, whispering up at the harsh, calm face beneath the weathered hat: "He won't git no ten bushels neither. He won't git one. We'll . . ." until his father glanced for an instant down at him, the face absolutely calm, the grizzled eyebrows tangled above the cold eyes, the voice almost pleasant, almost gentle:

80   "You think so? Well, we'll wait till October anyway."

The matter of the wagon—the setting of a spoke or two and the tightening of the tires—did not take long either, the business of the tires accomplished by driving the wagon into the spring branch behind the shop and letting it stand there, the mules nuzzling into the water from time to time, and the boy on the seat with the idle reins, looking up the slope and through the sooty tunnel of the shed where the slow hammer rang and where his father sat on an upended cypress bolt, easily, either talking or listening, still sitting there when the boy brought the dripping wagon up out of the branch and halted it before the door.

"Take them on to the shade and hitch," his father said. He did so and returned. His father and the smith and a third man squatting on his heels inside the door were talking, about crops and animals; the boy, squatting too in the ammoniac dust and hoof-parings and scales of rust, heard his father tell a long and unhurried story out of the time before the birth of the older brother even when he had been a professional horsetrader. And then his father came up beside him where he stood before a tattered last year's circus poster on the other side of the store, gazing rapt and quiet at the scarlet horses, the incredible poisings and convolutions of tulle and tights and the painted leers of comedians, and said, "It's time to eat."

But not at home. Squatting beside his brother against the front wall, he watched his father emerge from the store and produce from a paper sack a segment of cheese and divide it carefully and deliberately into three with his pocket knife and produce crackers from the same sack. They all three squatted on the gallery and ate, slowly, without talking; then in the store again, they drank from a tin dipper tepid water smelling of the cedar bucket and of living beech trees. And still they did not go home. It was a horse lot this time, a tall rail fence upon and along which men stood and sat and out of which one by one horses were led, to be walked and trotted and then cantered back and forth along the road while the slow swapping and buying went on and the sun began to slant westward, they—the three of them—watching and listening, the older brother with his muddy eyes and his steady, inevitable tobacco, the father commenting now and then on certain of the animals, to no one in particular.

It was after sundown when they reached home. They ate supper by lamplight, then, sitting on the doorstep, the boy watched the night fully accomplish, listening to the whippoorwills and the frogs, when he heard his mother's voice: "Abner! No! No! Oh, God. Oh, God. Abner!" and he rose, whirled, and saw the altered light through the door where a candle stub now burned in a bottle neck on the table and his father, still in the hat and coat, at once formal and burlesque as though dressed carefully for some shabby and ceremonial violence, emptying the reservoir of the lamp back into the five-gallon kerosene can from which it had been filled, while the mother tugged at his arm until he shifted the lamp to the other hand and flung her back, not savagely or vicious, just hard, into the wall, her hands flung out against the wall for balance, her mouth open and in her face the same quality of hopeless despair as had been in her voice. Then his father saw him standing in the door.

"Go to the barn and get that can of oil we were oiling the wagon with," he said. 85 The boy did not move. Then he could speak.

"What . . ." he cried. "What are you . . ."

"Go get that oil," his father said. "Go."

Then he was moving, running, outside the house, toward the stable: this the old habit, the old blood which he had not been permitted to choose for himself, which had been bequeathed him willy nilly and which had run for so long (and who knew where, battening on what of outrage and savagery and lust) before it came to him. *I could keep on,* he thought. *I could run on and on and never look back, never need to see his face again. Only I can't. I can't,* the rusted can in his hand now, the liquid sploshing in it as he ran back to the house and into it, into the sound of his mother's weeping in the next room, and handed the can to his father.

"Ain't you going to even send a nigger?" he cried. "At least you sent a nigger before!"

90   This time his father didn't strike him. The hand came even faster than the blow had, the same hand which had set the can on the table with almost excruciating care flashing from the can toward him too quick for him to follow it, gripping him by the back of his shirt and on to tiptoe before he had seen it quit the can, the face stooping at him in breathless and frozen ferocity, the cold, dead voice speaking over him to the older brother who leaned against the table, chewing with that steady, curious, sidewise motion of cows:

"Empty the can into the big one and go on. I'll catch up with you."

"Better tie him up to the bedpost," the brother said.

"Do like I told you," the father said. Then the boy was moving, his bunched shirt and the hard, bony hand between his shoulderblades, his toes just touching the floor, across the room and into the other one, past the sisters sitting with spread heavy thighs in the two chairs over the cold hearth, and to where his mother and aunt sat side by side on the bed, the aunt's arms about his mother's shoulders.

"Hold him," the father said. The aunt made a startled movement. "Not you," the father said. "Lennie. Take hold of him. I want to see you do it." His mother took him by the wrist. "You'll hold him better than that. If he gets loose don't you know what he is going to do? He will go up yonder." He jerked his head toward the road. "Maybe I'd better tie him."

95   "I'll hold him," his mother whispered.

"See you do then." Then his father was gone, the stiff foot heavy and measured upon the boards, ceasing at last.

Then he began to struggle. His mother caught him in both arms, he jerking and wrenching at them. He would be stronger in the end, he knew that. But he had no time to wait for it. "Lemme go!" he cried. "I don't want to have to hit you!"

"Let him go!" the aunt said. "If he don't go, before God, I am going up there myself!"

"Don't you see I can't?" his mother cried. "Sarty! Sarty! No! No! Help me, Lizzie!"

100   Then he was free. His aunt grasped at him but it was too late. He whirled, running, his mother stumbled forward on to her knees behind him, crying to the nearer sister: "Catch him, Net! Catch him!" But that was too late too, the sister (the sisters were twins, born at the same time, yet either of them now gave the impression of being, encompassing as much living meat and volume and weight as any other two of the family) not yet having begun to rise from the chair, her head, face, alone merely turned, presenting to him in the flying instant an astonishing expanse of young female features untroubled by any surprise even, wearing only an expression of bovine interest. Then he was out of the room, out of the house, in the mild dust of the starlit road and the heavy rifeness of honeysuckle, the pale ribbon unspooling with terrific slowness under his running feet, reaching the gate at last and turning in, running, his heart and lungs drumming, on up the drive toward the lighted house, the

lighted door. He did not knock, he burst in, sobbing for breath, incapable for the moment of speech; he saw the astonished face of the Negro in the linen jacket without knowing when the Negro had appeared.

"De Spain!" he cried, panted. "Where's . . ." then he saw the white man too emerging from a white door down the hall. "Barn!" he cried. "Barn!"

"What?" the white man said. "Barn?"

"Yes!" the boy cried. "Barn!"

"Catch him!" the white man shouted.

But it was too late this time too. The Negro grasped his shirt, but the entire sleeve, rotten with washing, carried away, and he was out that door too and in the drive again, and had actually never ceased to run even while he was screaming into the white man's face.

Behind him the white man was shouting. "My horse! Fetch my horse!" and he thought for an instant of cutting across the park and climbing the fence into the road, but he did not know the park nor how high the vine-massed fence might be and he dared not risk it. So he ran on down the drive, blood and breath roaring; presently he was in the road again though he could not see it. He could not hear either: the galloping mare was almost upon him before he heard her, and even then he held his course, as if the very urgency of his wild grief and need must in a moment more find him wings, waiting until the ultimate instant to hurl himself aside and into the weed-choked roadside ditch as the horse thundered past and on, for an instant in furious silhouette against the stars, the tranquil early summer night sky which, even before the shape of the horse and rider vanished, stained abruptly and violently upward: a long, swirling roar incredible and soundless, blotting the stars, and he springing up and into the road again, running again, knowing it was too late yet still running even after he heard the shot and, an instant later, two shots, pausing now without knowing he had ceased to run, crying "Pap! Pap!", running again before he knew he had begun to run, stumbling, tripping over something and scrabbling up again without ceasing to run, looking backward over his shoulder at the glares as he got up, running on among the invisible trees, panting, sobbing, "Father! Father!"

At midnight he was sitting on the crest of a hill. He did not know it was midnight and he did not know how far he had come. But there was no glare behind him now and he sat now, his back toward what he had called home for four days anyhow, his face toward the dark woods which he would enter when breath was strong again, small, shaking steadily in the chill darkness, hugging himself into the remainder of this thin, rotten shirt, the grief and despair now no longer terror and fear but just grief and despair. *Father. My father,* he thought. "He was brave!" He cried suddenly, aloud but not loud, no more than a whisper: "He was! He was in the war! He was in Colonel Sartoris' cav'ry!" not knowing that his father had gone to that war a private in the fine old European sense, wearing no uniform, admitting the authority of and giving fidelity to no man or army or flag, going to war as Malbrouck himself did: for booty—it meant nothing and less than nothing to him if it were enemy booty or his own.

The slow constellations wheeled on. It would be dawn and then sun-up after a while and he would be hungry. But that would be to-morrow and now he was only cold, and walking would cure that. His breathing was easier now and he decided to get up and go on, and then he found that he had been asleep because he knew it was almost dawn, the night almost over. He could tell that from the whippoorwills. They were everywhere now among the dark trees below him, constant and inflectioned and ceaseless, so that, as the instant for giving over to the day birds drew nearer and nearer, there was no interval at all between them. He got up. He was a little stiff, but walking would cure that too as it would the cold, and soon there would be the sun. He went on down the hill, toward the dark woods within which the liquid silver voices of the birds called unceasing—the rapid and urgent beating of the urgent and quiring heart of the late spring night. He did not look back.

QUESTIONS FOR DISCUSSION AND WRITING

1. How does the opening courtroom scene establish the many conflicts in the story? For example, how does Sarty attempt to clarify the external conflict by calling Harris an enemy? What internal conflict does Sarty feel when he thinks he will have to testify?

2. How does Faulkner characterize the father? Explain how the phrase "barn burner" stereotypes the father in the eyes of the community. In what ways does his fierce independence alter that stereotype?

3. In what ways does the Snopes wagon establish the setting of the story? In what kind of houses do the Snopeses live? How often has the family moved and why? What do the "big houses" seem to represent for the family?

4. What device does Faulkner use to emphasize Sarty's thoughts throughout the story? What does Sarty think about his father? How does his thinking lead to his final decision?

5. What is the difference between the community's definition of justice and the family's definition?

Stories for Comparison

Graham Greene's "The Destructors" (pages 607–618); D. H. Lawrence's "The Rocking-Horse Winner" (pages 793–803).

41

....

F. SCOTT FITZGERALD

Babylon Revisited

F. SCOTT FITZGERALD (1896–1940) was born in St. Paul, Minnesota, and attended Princeton University until he left in 1917 to enlist in the Army. World War I ended before he received an assignment overseas, but while he was stationed at Camp Sheridan in Alabama, he began writing his first novel, *This Side of Paradise* (1920), and fell in love with Zelda Sayre, the belle of Montgomery, Alabama. The financial success of his first novel enabled Scott and Zelda to marry and to begin living the high life of the Jazz Age in New York, Paris, and the French Riviera. Most of their income came from stories published in magazines such as *The Saturday Evening Post* and later collected in volumes such as *Flappers and Philosophers* (1921), *Tales of the Jazz Age* (1922), and *All the Sad Young Men* (1926). His finest novel, *The Great Gatsby* (1925), portrays a man whose search for a romantic dream is rivaled only by Fitzgerald's own quest. His wife's mental breakdown in 1930, together with his ensuing alcoholism and financial difficulties, led to the dissipation of his talents and an early death in Hollywood while working as a screenwriter. He wrote about his wife's tragedy in *Tender Is the Night* (1934) and his own in two posthumously published works edited by Edmund Wilson, *The Last Tycoon* (1941) and *The Crack-Up* (1945). In "Babylon Revisited," reprinted from *Taps at Reveille* (1935), Fitzgerald records the attempts of a broken man to reclaim his child and his honor.

I

And where's Mr. Campbell?" Charlie asked.

"Gone to Switzerland. Mr. Campbell's a pretty sick man, Mr. Wales."

"I'm sorry to hear that. And George Hardt?" Charlie inquired.

"Back in America, gone to work."

"And where is the Snow Bird?"

"He was in here last week. Anyway, his friend, Mr. Schaeffer, is in Paris."

Two familiar names from the long list of a year and a half ago. Charlie scribbled an address in his notebook and tore out the page.

"If you see Mr. Schaeffer, give him this," he said. "It's my brother-in-law's ad-dress. I haven't settled on a hotel yet."

He was not really disappointed to find Paris was so empty. But the stillness in the Ritz bar was strange and portentous. It was not an American bar any more—he felt polite in it, and not as if he owned it. It had gone back into France. He felt the stillness from the moment he got out of the taxi and saw the doorman, usually in a frenzy of activity at this hour, gossiping with a *chasseur* by the servants' entrance.

10   Passing through the corridor, he heard only a single, bored voice in the once-clamorous women's room. When he turned into the bar he traveled the twenty feet of green carpet with his eyes fixed straight ahead by old habit; and then, with his foot firmly on the rail, he turned and surveyed the room, encountering only a single pair of eyes that fluttered up from a newspaper in the corner. Charlie asked for the head barman, Paul, who in the latter days of the bull market had come to work in his own custom-built car—disembarking, however, with due nicety at the nearest corner. But Paul was at his country house today and Alix giving him information.

"No, no more," Charlie said. "I'm going slow these days."

Alix congratulated him: "You were going pretty strong a couple of years ago."

"I'll stick to it all right," Charlie assured him. "I've stuck to it for over a year and a half now."

"How do you find conditions in America?"

15   "I haven't been to America for months. I'm in business in Prague, representing a couple of concerns there. They don't know about me down there."

Alix smiled.

"Remember the night of George Hardt's bachelor dinner here?" said Charlie. "By the way, what's become of Claude Fessenden?"

Alix lowered his voice confidentially: "He's in Paris, but he doesn't come here any more. Paul doesn't allow it. He ran up a bill of thirty thousand francs, charging all his drinks and his lunches, and usually his dinner, for more than a year. And when Paul finally told him he had to pay, he gave him a bad check."

Alix shook his head sadly.

20   "I don't understand it, such a dandy fellow. Now he's all bloated up—" He made a plump apple of his hands.

Charlie watched a group of strident queens installing themselves in a corner.

"Nothing affects them," he thought. "Stocks rise and fall, people loaf or work, but they go on forever." The place oppressed him. He called for the dice and shook with Alix for the drink.

"Here for long, Mr. Wales?"

"I'm here for four or five days to see my little girl."

25   "Oh-h! You have a little girl?"

Outside, the fire-red, gas-blue, ghost-green signs shone smokily through the tranquil rain. It was late afternoon and the streets were in movement; the bistros gleamed. At the corner of the Boulevard des Capucines he took a taxi. The Place de la Concorde moved by in pink majesty; they crossed the logical Seine, and Charlie felt the sudden provincial quality of the Left Bank.

Charlie directed his taxi to the Avenue de l'Opéra, which was out of his way. But he wanted to see the blue hour spread over the magnificent façade, and imagine that the cab horns, playing endlessly the first few bars of *Le Plus que Lent,* were the trumpets of the Second Empire. They were closing the iron grill in front of Brentano's Bookstore, and people were already at dinner behind the trim little bourgeois hedge of Duval's. He had never eaten at a really cheap restaurant in Paris. Five-course dinner, four francs fifty, eighteen cents, wine included. For some odd reason he wished that he had.

As they rolled on to the Left Bank, and he felt its sudden provincialism, he thought, "I spoiled this city for myself. I didn't realize it, but the days came along one after another, and then two years were gone, and everything was gone, and I was gone."

He was thirty-five, and good to look at. The Irish mobility of his face was sobered by a deep wrinkle between his eyes. As he rang his brother-in-law's bell in the Rue Palatine, the wrinkle deepened till it pulled down his brows; he felt a cramping sensation in his belly. From behind the maid who opened the door darted a lovely little girl of nine who shrieked "Daddy!" and flew up, struggling like a fish, into his arms. She pulled his head around by one ear and set her cheek against his.

"My old pie," he said.   30

"Oh, daddy, daddy, daddy, daddy, dads, dads, dads!"

She drew him into the salon, where the family waited, a boy and a girl his daughter's age, his sister-in-law and her husband. He greeted Marion with his voice pitched carefully to avoid either feigned enthusiasm or dislike, but her response was more frankly tepid though she minimized her expression of unalterable distrust by directing her regard toward his child. The two men clasped hands in a friendly way and Lincoln Peters rested his for a moment on Charlie's shoulder.

The room was warm and comfortably American. The three children moved intimately about, playing through the yellow oblongs that led to other rooms; the cheer of six o'clock spoke in the eager smacks of the fire and the sounds of French activity in the kitchen. But Charlie did not relax; his heart sat up rigidly in his body and he drew confidence from his daughter, who from time to time came close to him, holding in her arms the doll he had brought.

"Really extremely well," he declared in answer to Lincoln's question. "There's a lot of business there that isn't moving at all, but we're doing even better than ever. In fact, damn well. I'm bringing my sister over from America next month to keep house for me. My income last year was bigger than it was when I had money. You see, the Czechs——"

His boasting was for a specific purpose; but after a moment, seeing a faint 35 restiveness in Lincoln's eye, he changed the subject:

"Those are fine children of yours, well brought up, good manners."

"We think Honoria's a great little girl too."

Marion Peters came back from the kitchen. She was a tall woman with worried eyes, who had once possessed a fresh American loveliness. Charlie had never been sensitive to it and was always surprised when people spoke of how pretty she had been. From the first there had been an instinctive antipathy between them.

"Well, how do you find Honoria?" she asked.

"Wonderful. I was astonished how much she's grown in ten months. All the chil- 40 dren are looking well."

"We haven't had a doctor for a year. How do you like being back in Paris?"

"It seems very funny to see so few Americans around."

"I'm delighted," Marion said vehemently. "Now at least you can go into a store without their assuming you're a millionaire. We've suffered like everybody, but on the whole it's a good deal pleasanter."

"But it was nice while it lasted," Charlie said. "We were a sort of royalty, almost infallible, with a sort of magic around us. In the bar this afternoon"—he stumbled, seeing his mistake—"there wasn't a man I knew."

45   She looked at him keenly. "I should think you'd have had enough of bars."

"I only stayed a minute. I take one drink every afternoon, and no more."

"Don't you want a cocktail before dinner?" Lincoln asked.

"I take only one drink every afternoon, and I've had that."

"I hope you keep to it," said Marion.

50   Her dislike was evident in the coldness with which she spoke, but Charlie only smiled; he had larger plans. Her very aggressiveness gave him an advantage, and he knew enough to wait. He wanted them to initiate the discussion of what they knew had brought him to Paris.

At dinner he couldn't decide whether Honoria was most like him or her mother. Fortunate if she didn't combine the traits of both that had brought them to disaster. A great wave of protectiveness went over him. He thought he knew what to do for her. He believed in character; he wanted to jump back a whole generation and trust in character again as the eternally valuable element. Everything else wore out.

He left soon after dinner, but not to go home. He was curious to see Paris by night with clearer and more judicious eyes than those of other days. He bought a *strapontin* for the Casino and watched Josephine Baker go through her chocolate arabesques.

After an hour he left and strolled toward Montmartre, up the Rue Pigalle into the Place Blanche. The rain had stopped and there were a few people in evening clothes disembarking from taxis in front of cabarets, and *cocottes* prowling singly or in pairs, and many Negroes. He passed a lighted door from which issued music, and stopped with the sense of familiarity; it was Bricktop's, where he had parted with so many hours and so much money. A few doors farther on he found another ancient rendezvous and incautiously put his head inside. Immediately an eager orchestra burst into sound, a pair of professional dancers leaped to their feet and a maître d'hôtel swooped toward him, crying, "Crowd just arriving, sir!" But he withdrew quickly.

"You have to be damn drunk," he thought.

55   Zelli's was closed, the bleak and sinister cheap hotels surrounding it were dark; up in the Rue Blanche there was more light and a local, colloquial French crowd. The Poet's Cave had disappeared, but the two great mouths of the Café of Heaven and the Café of Hell still yawned—even devoured, as he watched, the meager contents of a tourist bus—a German, a Japanese, and an American couple who glanced at him with frightened eyes.

So much for the effort and ingenuity of Montmartre. All the catering to vice and waste was on an utterly childish scale, and he suddenly realized the meaning of the word "dissipate"—to dissipate into thin air; to make nothing out of something. In the little hours of the night every move from place to place was an enormous human jump, an increase of paying for the privilege of slower and slower motion.

He remembered thousand-franc notes given to an orchestra for playing a single number, hundred-franc notes tossed to a doorman for calling a cab.

But it hadn't been given for nothing.

It had been given, even the most wildly squandered sum, as an offering to destiny that he might not remember the things most worth remembering, the things that now he would always remember—his child taken from his control, his wife escaped to a grave in Vermont.

In the glare of a *brasserie* a woman spoke to him. He bought her some eggs and 60 coffee, and then, eluding her encouraging stare, gave her a twenty-franc note and took a taxi to his hotel.

2

He woke upon a fine fall day—football weather. The depression of yesterday was gone and he liked the people on the streets. At noon he sat opposite Honoria at Le Grand Vatel, the only restaurant he could think of not reminiscent of champagne dinners and long luncheons that began at two and ended in a blurred and vague twilight.

"Now, how about vegetables? Oughtn't you to have some vegetables?"

"Well, yes."

"Here's *épinards* and *chou-fleur* and carrots and *haricots.*"

"I'd like *chou-fleur.*"   65

"Wouldn't you like to have two vegetables?"

"I usually only have one at lunch."

The waiter was pretending to be inordinately fond of children. *"Qu'elle est mignonne la petite! Elle parle exactement comme une française."*

"How about dessert? Shall we wait and see?"

The waiter disappeared. Honoria looked at her father expectantly.   70

"What are we going to do?"

"First, we're going to that toy store in the Rue Saint-Honoré and buy you anything you like. And then we're going to the vaudeville at the Empire."

She hesitated. "I like it about the vaudeville, but not the toy store."

"Why not?"

"Well, you brought me this doll." She had it with her. "And I've got lots of 75 things. And we're not rich any more, are we?"

"We never were. But today you are to have anything you want."

"All right," she agreed resignedly.

When there had been her mother and a French nurse he had been inclined to be strict; now he extended himself, reached out for a new tolerance; he must be both parents to her and not shut any of her out of communication.

"I want to get to know you," he said gravely. "First let me introduce myself. My name is Charles J. Wales, of Prague."

"Oh, daddy!" her voice cracked with laughter.   80

"And who are you, please?" he persisted, and she accepted a role immediately: "Honoria Wales, Rue Palatine, Paris."

"Married or single?"

"No, not married. Single."

He indicated the doll. "But I see you have a child, madame."

85   Unwilling to disinherit it, she took it to her heart and thought quickly: "Yes, I've been married, but I'm not married now. My husband is dead."

He went on quickly, "And the child's name?"

"Simone. That's after my best friend at school."

"I'm very pleased that you're doing so well at school."

"I'm third this month," she boasted. "Elsie"—that was her cousin—"is only about eighteenth, and Richard is about at the bottom."

90   "You like Richard and Elsie, don't you?"

"Oh, yes. I like Richard quite well and I like her all right."

Cautiously and casually he asked: "And Aunt Marion and Uncle Lincoln— which do you like best?"

"Oh, Uncle Lincoln, I guess."

He was increasingly aware of her presence. As they came in, a murmur of ". . . adorable" followed them, and now the people at the next table bent all their silences upon her, staring as if she were something no more conscious than a flower.

95   "Why don't I live with you?" she asked suddenly. "Because mamma's dead?"

"You must stay here and learn more French. It would have been hard for daddy to take care of you so well."

"I don't really need much taking care of any more. I do everything for myself."

Going out of the restaurant, a man and a woman unexpectedly hailed him.

"Well, the old Wales!"

100   "Hello there, Lorraine. . . . Dunc."

Sudden ghosts out of the past: Duncan Schaeffer, a friend from college. Lorraine Quarrles, a lovely, pale blonde of thirty; one of a crowd who had helped him make months into days in the lavish times of three years ago.

"My husband couldn't come this year," she said, in answer to his question. "We're poor as hell. So he gave me two hundred a month and told me I could do my worst on that. . . . This your little girl?"

"What about coming back and sitting down?" Duncan asked.

"Can't do it." He was glad for an excuse. As always, he felt Lorraine's passionate, provocative attraction, but his own rhythm was different now.

105   "Well, how about dinner?" she asked.

"I'm not free. Give me your address and let me call you."

"Charlie, I believe you're sober," she said judicially. "I honestly believe he's sober, Dunc. Pinch him and see if he's sober."

Charlie indicated Honoria with his head. They both laughed.

"What's your address?" said Duncan skeptically.

110   He hesitated, unwilling to give the name of his hotel.

"I'm not settled yet. I'd better call you. We're going to see the vaudeville at the Empire."

"There! That's what I want to do," Lorraine said. "I want to see some clowns and acrobats and jugglers. That's just what we'll do, Dunc."

"We've got to do an errand first," said Charlie. "Perhaps we'll see you there."

"All right, you snob. . . . Good-by, beautiful little girl."

"Good-by."   115

Honoria bobbed politely.

Somehow, an unwelcome encounter. They liked him because he was functioning, because he was serious; they wanted to see him, because he was stronger than they were now, because they wanted to draw a certain sustenance from his strength.

At the Empire, Honoria proudly refused to sit upon her father's folded coat. She was already an individual with a code of her own, and Charlie was more and more absorbed by the desire of putting a little of himself into her before she crystallized utterly. It was hopeless to try to know her in so short a time.

Between the acts they came upon Duncan and Lorraine in the lobby where the band was playing.

"Have a drink?"   120

"All right, but not up at the bar. We'll take a table."

"The perfect father."

Listening abstractly to Lorraine, Charlie watched Honoria's eyes leave their table, and he followed them wistfully about the room, wondering what they saw. He met her glance and she smiled.

"I liked that lemonade," she said.

What had she said? What had he expected? Going home in a taxi afterward, he 125
pulled her over until her head rested against his chest.

"Darling, do you ever think about your mother?"

"Yes, sometimes," she answered vaguely.

"I don't want you to forget her. Have you got a picture of her?"

"Yes, I think so. Anyhow, Aunt Marion has. Why don't you want me to forget her?"

"She loved you very much."   130

"I loved her too."

They were silent for a moment.

"Daddy, I want to come and live with you," she said suddenly.

His heart leaped; he had wanted it to come like this.

"Aren't you perfectly happy?"   135

"Yes, but I love you better than anybody. And you love me better than anybody, don't you, now that mummy's dead?"

"Of course I do. But you won't always like me best, honey. You'll grow up and meet somebody your own age and go marry him and forget you ever had a daddy."

"Yes, that's true, " she agreed tranquilly.

He didn't go in. He was coming back at nine o'clock and he wanted to keep himself fresh and new for the thing he must say then.

"When you're safe inside, just show yourself in that window."   140

"All right. Good-by, dads, dads, dads, dads."

He waited in the dark street until she appeared, all warm and glowing, in the window above and kissed her fingers out into the night.

3

They were waiting. Marion sat behind the coffee service in a dignified black dinner dress that just faintly suggested mourning. Lincoln was walking up and down with the animation of one who had already been talking. They were as anxious as he was to get into the question. He opened it almost immediately.

"I suppose you know what I want to see you about—why I really came to Paris."

145   Marion played with the black stars on her necklace and frowned.

"I'm awfully anxious to have a home," he continued. "And I'm awfully anxious to have Honoria in it. I appreciate your taking in Honoria for her mother's sake, but things have changed now"—he hesitated and then continued more forcibly— "changed radically with me, and I want to ask you to reconsider the matter. It would be silly for me to deny that about three years ago I was acting badly———"

Marion looked up at him with hard eyes.

"—but all that's over. As I told you, I haven't had more than a drink a day for over a year, and I take that drink deliberately, so that the idea of alcohol won't get too big in my imagination. You see the idea?"

"No," said Marion succinctly.

150   "It's a sort of stunt I set myself. It keeps the matter in proportion."

"I get you," said Lincoln. "You don't want to admit it's got any attraction for you."

"Something like that. Sometimes I forget and don't take it. But I try to take it. Anyhow, I couldn't afford to drink in my position. The people I represent are more than satisfied with what I've done, and I'm bringing my sister over from Burlington to keep house for me, and I want awfully to have Honoria too. You know that even when her mother and I weren't getting along well we never let anything that happened touch Honoria. I know she's fond of me and I know I'm able to take care of her and—well, there you are. How do you feel about it?"

He knew that now he would have to take a beating. It would last an hour or two hours, and it would be difficult, but if he modulated his inevitable resentment to the chastened attitude of the reformed sinner, he might win his point in the end.

Keep your temper, he told himself. You don't want to be justified. You want Honoria.

155   Lincoln spoke first: "We've been talking it over ever since we got your letter last month. We're happy to have Honoria here. She's a dear little thing, and we're glad to be able to help her, but of course that isn't the question———"

Marion interrupted suddenly. "How long are you going to stay sober, Charlie?" she asked.

"Permanently, I hope."

"How can anybody count on that?"

"You know I never did drink heavily until I gave up business and came over here with nothing to do. Then Helen and I began to run around with———"

"Please leave Helen out of it. I can't bear to hear you talk about her like that."   160

He stared at her grimly; he had never been certain how fond of each other the sisters were in life.

"My drinking only lasted about a year and a half—from the time we came over until I—collapsed."

"It was time enough."

"It was time enough," he agreed.

"My duty is entirely to Helen," she said. "I try to think what she would have   165 wanted me to do. Frankly, from the night you did that terrible thing you haven't really existed for me. I can't help that. She was my sister."

"Yes."

"When she was dying she asked me to look out for Honoria. If you hadn't been in a sanitarium then, it might have helped matters."

He had no answer.

"I'll never in my life be able to forget the morning when Helen knocked at my door, soaked to the skin and shivering, and said you'd locked her out."

Charlie gripped the sides of the chair. This was more difficult than he expected;   170 he wanted to launch out into a long expostulation and explanation, but he only said: "The night I locked her out—" and she interrupted, "I don't feel up to going over that again."

After a moment's silence Lincoln said: "We're getting off the subject. You want Marion to set aside her legal guardianship and give you Honoria. I think the main point for her is whether she has confidence in you or not."

"I don't blame Marion," Charlie said slowly, "but I think she can have entire confidence in me. I had a good record up to three years ago. Of course, it's within human possibilities I might go wrong any time. But if we wait much longer I'll lose Honoria's childhood and my chance for a home." He shook his head. "I'll simply lose her, don't you see?"

"Yes, I see," said Lincoln.

"Why didn't you think of all this before?" Marion asked.

"I suppose I did, from time to time, but Helen and I were getting along badly.   175 When I consented to the guardianship, I was flat on my back in a sanitarium and the market had cleaned me out. I knew I'd acted badly, and I thought if it would bring any peace to Helen, I'd agree to anything. But now it's different. I'm functioning. I'm behaving damn well, so far as————"

"Please don't swear at me," Marion said.

He looked at her, startled. With each remark the force of her dislike became more and more apparent. She had built up her fear of life into one wall and faced it toward him. This trivial reproof was possibly the result of some trouble with the cook several hours before. Charlie became increasingly alarmed at leaving Honoria in this atmosphere of hostility against himself; sooner or later it would come out, in a word here, a shake of the head there, and some of that distrust would be irrevocably implanted in Honoria. But he pulled his temper down out of his face and shut it up inside him; he had won a point, for Lincoln realized the absurdity of Marion's remark and asked her lightly since when she had objected to the word "damn."

"Another thing," Charlie said: "I'm able to give her certain advantages now. I'm going to take a French governess to Prague with me. I've got a lease on a new apartment———"

He stopped, realizing that he was blundering. They couldn't be expected to accept with equanimity the fact that his income was again twice as large as their own.

180   "I suppose you can give her more luxuries than we can," said Marion. "When you were throwing away money we were living along watching every ten francs. . . . I suppose you'll start doing it again."

"Oh, no," he said. "I've learned. I worked hard for ten years, you know—until I got lucky in the market, like so many people. Terribly lucky. It won't happen again."

There was a long silence. All of them felt their nerves straining, and for the first time in a year Charlie wanted a drink. He was sure now that Lincoln Peters wanted him to have his child.

Marion shuddered suddenly; part of her saw that Charlie's feet were planted on the earth now, and her own maternal feeling recognized the naturalness of his desire; but she had lived for a long time with a prejudice—a prejudice founded on a curious disbelief in her sister's happiness, which, in the shock of one terrible night, had turned to hatred for him. It had all happened at a point in her life where the discouragement of ill health and adverse circumstances made it necessary for her to believe in tangible villainy and a tangible villain.

"I can't help what I think!" she cried out suddenly. "How much you were responsible for Helen's death, I don't know. It's something you'll have to square with your own conscience."

185   An electric current of agony surged through him; for a moment he was almost on his feet, an unuttered sound echoing in his throat. He hung on to himself for a moment, another moment.

"Hold on there," said Lincoln uncomfortably. "I never thought you were responsible for that."

"Helen died of heart trouble," Charlie said dully.

"Yes, heart trouble." Marion spoke as if the phrase had another meaning for her.

Then, in the flatness that followed her outburst, she saw him plainly and she knew he had somehow arrived at control over the situation. Glancing at her husband, she found no help from him, and as abruptly as if it were a matter of no importance, she threw up the sponge.

190   "Do what you like!" she cried, springing up from her chair. "She's your child. I'm not the person to stand in your way. I think if it were my child I'd rather see her—" She managed to check herself. "You two decide it. I can't stand this. I'm sick. I'm going to bed."

She hurried from the room; after a moment Lincoln said:

"This has been a hard day for her. You know how strongly she feels—" His voice was almost apologetic: "When a woman gets an idea in her head."

"Of course."

"It's going to be all right. I think she sees now that you—can provide for the child, and so we can't very well stand in your way or Honoria's way."

195   "Thank you, Lincoln."

"I'd better go along and see how she is."

"I'm going."

He was still trembling when he reached the street, but a walk down the Rue Bonaparte to the *quais* set him up, and as he crossed the Seine, fresh and new by the *quai* lamps, he felt exultant. But back in his room he couldn't sleep. The image of Helen haunted him. Helen whom he had loved so until they had senselessly begun to abuse each other's love, tear it into shreds. On that terrible February night that Marion remembered so vividly, a slow quarrel had gone on for hours. There was a scene at the Florida, and then he attempted to take her home, and then she kissed young Webb at a table; after that there was what she had hysterically said. When he arrived home alone he turned the key in the lock in wild anger. How could he know she would arrive an hour later alone, that there would be a snow storm in which she wandered about in slippers, too confused to find a taxi? Then the aftermath, her escaping pneumonia by a miracle, and all the attendant horror. They were "reconciled," but that was the beginning of the end, and Marion, who had seen with her own eyes and who imagined it to be one of many scenes from her sister's martyrdom, never forgot.

Going over it again brought Helen nearer, and in the white, soft light that steals upon half sleep near morning he found himself talking to her again. She said that he was perfectly right about Honoria and that she wanted Honoria to be with him. She said she was glad he was being good and doing better. She said a lot of other things— very friendly things—but she was in a swing in a white dress, and swinging faster and faster all the time, so that at the end he could not hear clearly all that she said.

4

He woke up feeling happy. The door of the world was open again. He made plans, 200 vistas, futures for Honoria and himself, but suddenly he grew sad, remembering all the plans he and Helen had made. She had not planned to die. The present was the thing—work to do and someone to love. But not to love too much, for he knew the injury that a father can do to a daughter or a mother to a son by attaching them too closely: afterward, out in the world, the child would seek in the marriage partner the same blind tenderness and, failing probably to find it, turn against love and life.

It was another bright, crisp day. He called Lincoln Peters at the bank where he worked and asked if he could count on taking Honoria when he left for Prague. Lincoln agreed that there was no reason for delay. One thing—the legal guardianship. Marion wanted to retain that a while longer. She was upset by the whole matter, and it would oil things if she felt that the situation was still in her control for another year. Charlie agreed, wanting only the tangible, visible child.

Then the question of a governess. Charlie sat in a gloomy agency and talked to a cross Béarnaise and to a buxom Breton peasant, neither of whom he could have endured. There were others whom he would see tomorrow.

He lunched with Lincoln Peters at Griffons, trying to keep down his exultation.

"There's nothing quite like your own child," Lincoln said. "But you understand how Marion feels too."

205   "She's forgotten how hard I worked for seven years there," Charlie said. "She just remembers one night."

"There's another thing," Lincoln hesitated. "When you and Helen were tearing around Europe throwing money away, we were just getting along. I didn't touch any of the prosperity because I never got ahead enough to carry anything but my insurance. I think Marion felt there was some kind of injustice in it—you not even working toward the end, and getting richer and richer."

"It went just as quick as it came," said Charlie.

"Yes, a lot of it stayed in the hands of *chasseurs* and saxophone players and maitres d'hôtel—well, the big party's over now. I just said that to explain Marion's feeling about those crazy years. If you drop in about six o'clock tonight before Marion's too tired, we'll settle the details on the spot."

Back at his hotel, Charlie found a *pneumatique* that had been redirected from the Ritz bar, where Charlie had left his address for the purpose of finding a certain man.

DEAR CHARLIE: You were so strange when we saw you the other day I wondered if I did something to offend you. If so, I'm not conscious of it. In fact, I have thought about you much for the last year, and it's always been in the back of my mind that I might see you if I came over here. We *did* have such good times that crazy spring, like the night you and I stole the butcher's tricycle, and the time we tried to call on the president and you had the old derby rim and the wire cane. Everybody seems so old lately, but I don't feel old a bit. Couldn't we get together some time today for old time's sake? I've got a vile hangover for the moment, but will be feeling better this afternoon and will look for you about five in the sweatshop at the Ritz.

Always devotedly,
Lorraine

210   His first feeling was one of awe that he had actually, in his mature years, stolen a tricycle and pedaled Lorraine all over the Étoile between the small hours and dawn. In retrospect it was a nightmare. Locking out Helen didn't fit in with any other act of his life, but the tricycle incident did—it was one of many. How many weeks or months of dissipation to arrive at that condition of utter irresponsibility?

He tried to picture how Lorraine had appeared to him then—very attractive; Helen was unhappy about it, though she said nothing. Yesterday, in the restaurant, Lorraine had seemed trite, blurred, worn away. He emphatically did not want to see her, and he was glad Alix had not given away his hotel address. It was a relief to think, instead, of Honoria, to think of Sundays spent with her and of saying good morning to her and of knowing she was there in his house at night, drawing her breath in the darkness.

At five he took a taxi and bought presents for all the Peterses—a piquant cloth doll, a box of Roman soldiers, flowers for Marion, big linen handkerchiefs for Lincoln.

He saw, when he arrived in the apartment, that Marion had accepted the inevitable. She greeted him now as though he were a recalcitrant member of the

family, rather than a menacing outsider. Honoria had been told she was going;
Charlie was glad to see that her tact made her conceal her excessive happiness.
Only on his lap did she whisper her delight and the question "When?" before
she slipped away with the other children.

He and Marion were alone for a minute in the room, and on an impulse he spoke
out boldly:

"Family quarrels are bitter things. They don't go according to any rules. They're   215
not like aches or wounds; they're more like splits in the skin that won't heal because
there's not enough material. I wish you and I could be on better terms."

"Some things are hard to forget," she answered. "It's a question of confidence."
There was no answer to this and presently she asked, "When do you propose to
take her?"

"As soon as I can get a governess. I hoped the day after tomorrow."

"That's impossible. I've got to get her things in shape. Not before Saturday."

He yielded. Coming back into the room, Lincoln offered him a drink.

"I'll take my daily whiskey," he said.   220

It was warm here, it was a home, people together by a fire. The children felt very
safe and important; the mother and father were serious, watchful. They had things to
do for the children more important than his visit here. A spoonful of medicine was,
after all, more important than the strained relations between Marion and himself.
They were not dull people, but they were very much in the grip of life and circumstances. He wondered if he couldn't do something to get Lincoln out of his rut at
the bank.

A long peal at the doorbell; the *bonne à tout faire* passed through and went
down the corridor. The door opened upon another long ring, and then voices,
and the three in the salon looked up expectantly; Richard moved to bring the
corridor within his range of vision, and Marion rose. Then the maid came back
along the corridor, closely followed by the voices, which developed under the
light into Duncan Schaeffer and Lorraine Quarrles.

They were gay, they were hilarious, they were roaring with laughter. For a moment Charlie was astounded; unable to understand how they ferreted out the
Peterses' address.

"Ah-h-h!" Duncan wagged his finger roguishly at Charlie, "Ah-h-h!"

They both slid down another cascade of laughter. Anxious and at a loss, Charlie   225
shook hands with them quickly and presented them to Lincoln and Marion. Marion
nodded, scarcely speaking. She had drawn back a step toward the fire; her little girl
stood beside her, and Marion put an arm about her shoulder.

With growing annoyance at the intrusion, Charlie waited for them to explain
themselves. After some concentration Duncan said:

"We came to invite you out to dinner. Lorraine and I insist that all this shishi,
cagy business 'bout your address got to stop."

Charlie came closer to them, as if to force them backward down the corridor.

"Sorry, but I can't. Tell me where you'll be and I'll phone you in half an hour."

This made no impression. Lorraine sat down suddenly on the side of a chair, and   230
focusing her eyes on Richard, cried, "Oh, what a nice little boy! Come here, little

boy." Richard glanced at his mother, but did not move. With a perceptible shrug of her shoulder, Lorraine turned back to Charlie:

"Come and dine. Sure your cousins won' mine. See you so sel'om. Or solemn."

"I can't," said Charlie sharply. "You two have dinner and I'll phone you."

Her voice became suddenly unpleasant. " All right, we'll go. But I remember once when you hammered on my door at four A.M. I was enough of a good sport to give you a drink. Come on, Dunc."

Still in slow motion, with blurred, angry faces, with uncertain feet, they retired along the corridor.

235   "Good night," Charlie said.

"Good night!" responded Lorraine emphatically.

When he went back into the salon Marion had not moved, only now her son was standing in the circle of her other arm. Lincoln was still swinging Honoria back and forth like a pendulum from side to side.

"What an outrage!" Charlie broke out. "What an absolute outrage!"

Neither of them answered. Charlie dropped into an armchair, picked up his drink, set it down again and said:

240   "People I haven't seen for two years having the colossal nerve————"

He broke off. Marion had made the sound "Oh!" in one swift, furious breath, turned her body from him with a jerk and left the room.

Lincoln set down Honoria carefully.

"You children go in and start your soup," he said, and when they obeyed, he said to Charlie:

"Marion's not well and she can't stand shocks. That kind of people make her really physically sick."

245   "I didn't tell them to come here. They wormed your name out of somebody. They deliberately————"

"Well, it's too bad. It doesn't help matters. Excuse me a minute."

Left alone, Charlie sat tense in his chair. In the next room he could hear the children eating, talking in monosyllables, already oblivious to the scene between their elders. He heard a murmur of conversation from a farther room and then the ticking bell of a telephone receiver picked up, and in a panic he moved to the other side of the room and out of earshot.

In a minute Lincoln came back. "Look here, Charlie. I think we'd better call off dinner for tonight. Marion's in bad shape."

"Is she angry with me?"

250   "Sort of," he said, almost roughly. "She's not strong and————"

"You mean she's changed her mind about Honoria?"

"She's pretty bitter right now. I don't know. You phone me at the bank tomorrow."

"I wish you'd explain to her I never dreamed these people would come here. I'm just as sore as you are."

"I couldn't explain anything to her now."

Charlie got up. He took his coat and hat and started down the corridor. Then 255
he opened the door of the dining room and said in a strange voice, "Good night,
children."

Honoria rose and ran around the table to hug him.

"Good night, sweetheart," he said vaguely, and then trying to make his voice
more tender, trying to conciliate something, "Good night, dear children."

5

Charlie went directly to the Ritz bar with the furious idea of finding Lorraine and
Duncan, but they were not there, and he realized that in any case there was nothing
he could do. He had not touched his drink at the Peters, and now he ordered a
whiskey-and-soda. Paul came over to say hello.

"It's a great change," he said sadly. "We do about half the business we did. So
many fellows I hear about back in the States lost everything, maybe not in the first
crash, but then in the second. Your friend George Hardt lost every cent, I hear. Are
you back in the States?"

"No, I'm in business in Prague."   260

"I heard that you lost a lot in the crash."

"I did," and he added grimly, "but I lost everything I wanted in the boom."

"Selling short."

"Something like that."

Again the memory of those days swept over him like a nightmare—the people 265
they had met traveling; then people who couldn't add a row of figures or speak a coherent sentence. The little man Helen had consented to dance with at the ship's party,
who had insulted her ten feet from the table; the women and girls carried screaming
with drink or drugs out of public places————

The men who locked their wives out in the snow, because the snow of twenty-
nine wasn't real snow. If you didn't want it to be snow, you just paid some money.

He went to the phone and called the Peterses' apartment; Lincoln answered.

"I called up because this thing is on my mind. Has Marion said anything definite?"

"Marion's sick," Lincoln answered shortly. "I know this thing isn't altogether
your fault, but I can't have her go to pieces about it. I'm afraid we'll have to let it
slide for six months; I can't take the chance of working her up to this state again."

"I see."   270

"I'm sorry, Charlie."

He went back to his table. His whiskey glass was empty, but he shook his
head when Alix looked at it questioningly. There wasn't much he could do now
except send Honoria some things; he would send her a lot of things tomorrow.
He thought rather angrily that this was just money—he had given so many people money. . . .

"No, no more," he said to another waiter. "What do I owe you?"

He would come back some day; they couldn't make him pay forever. But he
wanted his child, and nothing was much good now, beside that fact. He wasn't young

any more, with a lot of nice things and dreams to have by himself. He was absolutely sure Helen wouldn't have wanted him to be so alone.

QUESTIONS FOR DISCUSSION AND WRITING

1. How does Fitzgerald present the events that took place before the beginning of the action of this story? Contrast the way Charlie and Marion remember those events.

2. How do the various characters help define Charlie's character? For example, compare and contrast the way Marion, Lorraine, and Honoria portray Charlie's character.

3. What kind of setting is evoked by the word *Babylon?* In what sense does the Ritz bar represent Charlie's former life? How does Prague represent his present life?

4. How does the third-person point of view enable us to raise questions about the accuracy of Charlie's current view of himself? Has he changed as much as he believes he has? Explain your answer.

5. Many of the metaphors in this story are economic. What has Charlie lost? What has he sold short? Can they "make him pay forever"?

Stories for Comparison

John Cheever's "The Swimmer" (pages 368–376); Mary Hood's "How Far She Went (pages 664–670).

42

....

MARY   WILKINS   FREEMAN

The Revolt of "Mother"

MARY WILKINS FREEMAN (1852–1930) was born in Randolph, Massachusetts, and was educated at Mt. Holyoke Female Seminary and West Brattleboro Seminary. In the early 1880s she established herself as an author of literature for children with the publication of a collection of poems, *Decorative Plaques* (1883). She soon began publishing adult fiction in magazines such as *Harper's Bazaar* and *Harper's Weekly.* Her best stories, focusing on the endurance and pride of the people in New England, are collected in *A Humble Romance and Other Stories* (1887) and *A New England Nun and Other Stories* (1891). In her best novel, *Pembroke* (1894), Freeman is able to reveal "the pathos in the comedy" of the New England character. "The Revolt of 'Mother,'" reprinted from *A New England Nun,* demonstrates how individual victories can be won over entrenched habits and values.

F ather!"

"What is it?"

"What are them men diggin' over there in the field for?"

There was a sudden dropping and enlarging of the lower part of the old man's face, as if some heavy weight had settled therein; he shut his mouth tight, and went on harnessing the great bay mare. He hustled the collar on to her neck with a jerk.

"Father!"   5

The old man slapped the saddle upon the mare's back.

"Look here, father, I want to know what them men are diggin' over in the field for, an' I'm goin' to know."

"I wish you'd go into the house, mother, an' 'tend to your own affairs," the old man said then. He ran his words together, and his speech was almost as inarticulate as a growl.

But the woman understood; it was her most native tongue. "I ain't goin' into the house till you tell me what them men are doin' over there in the field," said she.

Then she stood waiting. She was a small woman, short and straight-waisted like 10 a child in her brown cotton gown. Her forehead was mild and benevolent between the smooth curves of gray hair; there were meek downward lines about her nose and mouth; but her eyes, fixed upon the old man, looked as if the meekness had been the result of her own will, never of the will of another.

They were in the barn, standing before the wide open doors. The spring air, full of the smell of growing grass and unseen blossoms, came in their faces. The deep yard in front was littered with farm wagons and piles of wood; on the edges, close to the fence and the house, the grass was a vivid green, and there were some dandelions.

The old man glanced doggedly at his wife as he tightened the last buckles on the harness. She looked as immovable to him as one of the rocks in his pasture-land, bound to the earth with generations of blackberry vines. He slapped the reins over the horse, and started forth from the barn.

"Father!" said she.

The old man pulled up. "What is it?"

"I want to know what them men are diggin' over there in that field for."   15

"They're diggin' a cellar, I s'pose, if you've got to know."

"A cellar for what?"

"A barn."

"A barn? You ain't goin' to build a barn over there where we was goin' to have a house, father?"

20   The old man said not another word. He hurried the horse into the farm wagon, and clattered out of the yard, jouncing as sturdily on his seat as a boy.

The woman stood a moment looking after him, then she went out of the barn across a corner of the yard to the house. The house, standing at right angles with the great barn and a long reach of sheds and out-buildings, was infinitesimal compared with them. It was scarcely as commodious for people as the little boxes under the barn eaves were for doves.

A pretty girl's face, pink and delicate as a flower, was looking out of one of the house windows. She was watching three men who were digging over in the field which bounded the yard near the road line. She turned quietly when the woman entered.

"What are they digging for, mother?" said she. "Did he tell you?"

"They're diggin' for—a cellar for a new barn."

25   "Oh, mother, he ain't going to build another barn?"

"That's what he says."

A boy stood before the kitchen glass combing his hair. He combed slowly and painstakingly, arranging his brown hair in a smooth hillock over his forehead. He did not seem to pay any attention to the conversation.

"Sammy, did you know father was going to build a new barn?" asked the girl.

The boy combed assiduously.

30   "Sammy!"

He turned, and showed a face like his father's under his smooth crest of hair. "Yes, I s'pose I did," he said, reluctantly.

"How long have you known it?" asked his mother.

"'Bout three months, I guess."

"Why didn't you tell of it?"

35   "Didn't think 'twould do no good."

"I don't see what father wants another barn for," said the girl, in her sweet, slow voice. She turned again to the window, and stared out at the digging men in the field. Her tender, sweet face was full of a gentle distress. Her forehead was as bald and innocent as a baby's, with the light hair strained back from it in a row of curl-papers. She was quite large, but her soft curves did not look as if they covered muscles.

Her mother looked sternly at the boy. "Is he goin' to buy more cows?" said she.

The boy did not reply; he was tying his shoes.

"Sammy, I want you to tell me if he's goin' to buy more cows."

40   "I s'pose he is."

"How many?"

"Four, I guess."

His mother said nothing more. She went into the pantry, and there was a clatter of dishes. The boy got his cap from a nail behind the door, took an old arithmetic from the shelf, and started for school. He was lightly built, but clumsy. He went out of the yard with a curious spring in the hips, that made his loose home-made jacket tilt up in the rear.

The girl went to the sink, and began to wash the dishes that were piled up there. Her mother came promptly out of the pantry, and shoved her aside. "You wipe 'em," said she; "I'll wash. There's a good many this mornin'."

The mother plunged her hands vigorously into the water, the girl wiped the 45 plates slowly and dreamily. "Mother," said she, "don't you think it's too bad father's going to build that new barn, much as we need a decent house to live in?"

Her mother scrubbed a dish fiercely. "You ain't found out yet we're women-folks, Nanny Penn," said she. "You ain't seen enough of men-folks yet to. One of these days you'll find it out, an' then you'll know that we know only what men-folks think we do, so far as any use of it goes, an' how we'd ought to reckon men-folks in with Providence, an' not complain of what they do any more than we do of the weather."

"I don't care; I don't believe George is anything like that, anyhow," said Nanny. Her delicate face flushed pink, her lips pouted softly, as if she were going to cry.

"You wait an' see. I guess George Eastman ain't no better than other men. You hadn't ought to judge father, though. He can't help it, 'cause he don't look at things jest the way we do. An' we've been pretty comfortable here, after all. The roof don't leak—ain't never but once—that's one thing. Father's kept it shingled right up."

"I do wish we had a parlor."

"I guess it won't hurt George Eastman any to come to see you in a nice clean 50 kitchen. I guess a good many girls don't have as good a place as this. Nobody's ever heard me complain."

"I ain't complained either, mother."

"Well, I don't think you'd better, a good father an' a good home as you've got. S'pose your father made you go out an' work for your livin'? Lots of girls have to that ain't no stronger an' better able to than you be."

Sarah Penn washed the frying-pan with a conclusive air. She scrubbed the outside of it as faithfully as the inside. She was a masterly keeper of her box of a house. Her one living-room never seemed to have in it any of the dust which the friction of life with inanimate matter produces. She swept, and there seemed to be no dirt to go before the broom; she cleaned, and one could see no difference. She was like an artist so perfect that he has apparently no art. To-day she got out a mixing bowl and a board, and rolled some pies, and there was no more flour upon her than upon her daughter who was doing finer work. Nanny was to be married in the fall, and she was sewing on some white cambric and embroidery. She sewed industriously while her mother cooked, her soft milk-white hands and wrists showed whiter than her delicate work.

"We must have the stove moved out in the shed before long," said Mrs. Penn. "Talk about not havin' things, it's been a real blessin' to be able to put a stove up in that shed in hot weather. Father did one good thing when he fixed that stove-pipe out there."

Sarah Penn's face as she rolled her pies had that expression of meek vigor 55 which might have characterized one of the New Testament saints. She was making mince-pies. Her husband, Adoniram Penn, liked them better than any other kind. She baked twice a week. Adoniram often liked a piece of pie between meals. She hurried this morning. It had been later than usual when she began, and she wanted to have a pie baked for dinner. However deep a resentment she might be forced to hold against her husband, she would never fail in sedulous attention to his wants.

Nobility of character manifests itself in loop-holes when it is not provided with large doors. Sarah Penn's showed itself to-day in flaky dishes of pastry. So she made the pies faithfully, while across the table she could see, when she glanced up from her work, the sight that rankled in her patient and steadfast soul—the digging of the cellar of the new barn in the place where Adoniram forty years ago had promised her their new house should stand.

The pies were done for dinner. Adoniram and Sammy were home a few minutes after twelve o'clock. The dinner was eaten with serious haste. There was never much conversation at the table in the Penn family. Adoniram asked a blessing, and they ate promptly, then rose up and went about their work.

Sammy went back to school, taking soft sly lopes out of the yard like a rabbit. He wanted a game of marbles before school, and feared his father would give him some chores to do. Adoniram hastened to the door and called after him, but he was out of sight.

"I don't see what you let him go for, mother," said he. "I wanted him to help me unload that wood."

60   Adoniram went to work out in the yard unloading wood from the wagon. Sarah put away the dinner dishes, while Nanny took down her curl-papers and changed her dress. She was going down to the store to buy some more embroidery and thread.

When Nanny was gone, Mrs. Penn went to the door. "Father!" she called.

"Well, what is it!"

"I want to see you jest a minute, father."

"I can't leave this wood nohow. I've got to git it unloaded an' go for a load of gravel afore two o'clock. Sammy had ought to helped me. You hadn't ought to let him go to school so early."

65   "I want to see you jest a minute."

"I tell ye I can't, nohow, mother."

"Father, you come here." Sarah Penn stood in the door like a queen; she held her head as if it bore a crown; there was that patience which makes authority royal in her voice. Adoniram went.

Mrs. Penn led the way into the kitchen, and pointed to a chair. "Sit down, father," said she; "I've got somethin' I want to say to you."

He sat down heavily; his face was quite stolid, but he looked at her with restive eyes. "Well, what is it, mother?"

70   "I want to know what you're buildin' that new barn for, father?"

"I ain't got nothin' to say about it."

"It can't be you think you need another barn?"

"I tell ye I ain't got nothin' to say about it, mother; an' I ain't goin' to say nothin'."

"Be you goin' to buy more cows?"

75   Adoniram did not reply; he shut his mouth tight.

"I know you be, as well as I want to. Now, father, look here"—Sarah Penn had not sat down; she stood before her husband in the humble fashion of a Scripture woman—"I'm goin' to talk real plain to you; I never have since I married you, but I'm goin' to now. I ain't never complained, an' I ain't goin' to complain now, but I'm goin' to talk plain. You see this room here, father; you look at it well. You see there ain't no carpet on the floor, an' you see the paper is all dirty, an' droppin' off the walls. We ain't had no new paper on it for ten year, an' then I put it on myself, an' it didn't cost but ninepence a roll. You see this room, father; it's all the one I've had to work in an' eat in an' sit in since we was married. There ain't another woman in the whole town whose husband ain't got half the means you have but what's got better. It's all the room Nanny's got to have her company in; an' there ain't one of her mates but what's got better, an' their fathers not so able as hers is. It's all the room she'll have to be married in. What would you have thought, father, if we had had our weddin' in a room no better than this? I was married in my mother's parlor, with a carpet on the floor, an' stuffed furniture, an' a mahogany card-table. An' this is all the room my daughter will have to be married in. Look here, father!"

Sarah Penn went across the room as though it were a tragic stage. She flung open a door and disclosed a tiny bedroom, only large enough for a bed and bureau, with a path between. "There, father," said she—"there's all the room I've had to sleep in forty year. All my children were born there—the two that died, an' the two that's livin'. I was sick with a fever there."

She stepped to another door and opened it. It led into the small, ill-lighted pantry. "Here," said she, "is all the buttery I've got—every place I've got for my dishes, to set away my victuals in, an' to keep my milk-pans in. Father, I've been takin' care of the milk of six cows in this place, an' now you're goin' to build a new barn, an' keep more cows, an' give me more to do in it."

She threw open another door. A narrow crooked flight of stairs wound upward from it. "There, father," said she, "I want you to look at the stairs that go up to them two unfinished chambers that are all the places our son an' daughter have had to sleep in all their lives. There ain't a prettier girl in town nor a more ladylike one than Nanny, an' that's the place she has to sleep in. It ain't so good as your horse's stall; it ain't so warm an' tight."

Sarah Penn went back and stood before her husband. "Now, father," said she, "I want to know if you think you're doin' right an' accordin' to what you profess. Here, when we was married, forty year ago, you promised me faithful that we should have a new house built in that lot over in the field before the year was out. You said you had money enough, an' you wouldn't ask me to live in no such place as this. It is forty year now, an' you've been makin' more money, an' I've been savin' of it for you ever since, an' you ain't built no house yet. You've built sheds an' cow-houses an' one new barn, an' now you're goin' to build another. Father, I want to know if you think it's right. You're lodgin' your dumb beasts better than you are your own flesh an' blood. I want to know if you think it's right."

"I ain't got nothin' to say."

"You can't say nothin' without ownin' it ain't right, father. An' there's another thing—I ain't complained; I've got along forty year, an' I s'pose I should forty more, if it wa'n't for that—if we don't have another house. Nanny she can't live with us after she's married. She'll have to go somewheres else to live away from us, an' it don't seem as if I could have it so, noways, father. She wa'n't ever strong. She's got considerable color, but there wa'n't never any backbone to her. I've always took the heft of everything off her, an' she ain't fit to keep house an' do everything herself. She'll be all worn out inside of a year. Think of her doin' all the washin' an' ironin' an' bakin' with them soft white hands an' arms, an' sweepin'! I can't have it so, noways, father."

Mrs. Penn's face was burning; her mild eyes gleamed. She had pleaded her little cause like a Webster; she had ranged from severity to pathos; but her opponent employed that obstinate silence which makes eloquence futile with mocking echoes. Adoniram arose clumsily.

"Father, ain't you got nothin' to say?" said Mrs. Penn.

85   "I've got to go off after that load of gravel. I can't stan' here talkin' all day."

"Father, won't you think it over, an' have a house built there instead of a barn?"

"I ain't got nothin' to say."

Adoniram shuffled out. Mrs. Penn went into her bedroom. When she came out, her eyes were red. She had a roll of unbleached cotton cloth. She spread it out on the kitchen table, and began cutting out some shirts for her husband. The men over in the field had a team to help them this afternoon; she could hear their halloos. She had a scanty pattern for the shirts; she had to plan and piece the sleeves.

Nanny came home with her embroidery, and sat down with her needlework. She had taken down her curl-papers, and there was a soft roll of fair hair like an aureole over her forehead; her face was as delicately fine and clear as porcelain. Suddenly she looked up, and the tender red flamed all over her face and neck. "Mother," said she.

90   "What say?"

"I've been thinking—I don't see how we're goin' to have any—wedding in this room. I'd be ashamed to have his folks come if we didn't have anybody else."

"Mebbe we can have some new paper before then; I can put it on. I guess you won't have no call to be ashamed of your belongin's."

"We might have the wedding in the new barn," said Nanny, with gentle pettishness. "Why, mother, what makes you look so?"

Mrs. Penn had started, and was staring at her with a curious expression. She turned again to her work, and spread out a pattern carefully on the cloth. "Nothin'," said she.

95   Presently Adoniram clattered out of the yard in his two-wheeled dump cart, standing as proudly upright as a Roman charioteer. Mrs. Penn opened the door and stood there a minute looking out; the halloos of the men sounded louder.

It seemed to her all through the spring months that she heard nothing but the halloos and the noises of saws and hammers. The new barn grew fast. It was a fine edifice for this little village. Men came on pleasant Sundays, in their meeting suits and clean shirt bosoms, and stood around it admiringly. Mrs. Penn did not speak of it, and Adoniram did not mention it to her, although sometimes, upon a return from inspecting it, he bore himself with injured dignity.

"It's a strange thing how your mother feels about the new barn," he said, confidentially, to Sammy one day.

Sammy only grunted after an odd fashion for a boy; he had learned it from his father.

The barn was all completed ready for use by the third week in July. Adoniram had planned to move his stock in on Wednesday; on Tuesday he received a letter which changed his plans. He came in with it early in the morning. "Sammy's been to the post-office," said he, "an' I've got a letter from Hiram." Hiram was Mrs. Penn's brother, who lived in Vermont.

"Well," said Mrs. Penn, "what does he say about the folks?"   100

"I guess they're all right. He says he thinks if I come up country right off there's a chance to buy jest the kind of a horse I want." He stared reflectively out of the window at the new barn.

Mrs. Penn was making pies. She went on clapping the rolling-pin into the crust, although she was very pale, and her heart beat loudly.

"I dun' know but what I'd better go," said Adoniram. "I hate to go off jest now, right in the midst of hayin', but the ten-acre lot's cut, an' I guess Rufus an' the others can git along without me three or four days. I can't get a horse round here to suit me, nohow, an' I've got to have another for all that wood-haulin' in the fall. I told Hiram to watch out, an' if he got wind of a good horse to let me know. I guess I'd better go."

"I'll get out your clean shirt an' collar," said Mrs. Penn calmly.

She laid out Adoniram's Sunday suit and his clean clothes on the bed in the lit-   105
tle bedroom. She got his shaving-water and razor ready. At last she buttoned on his collar and fastened his black cravat.

Adoniram never wore his collar and cravat except on extra occasions. He held his head high, with a rasped dignity. When he was all ready, with his coat and hat brushed, and a lunch of pie and cheese in a paper bag, he hesitated on the threshold of the door. He looked at his wife, and his manner was defiantly apologetic. "*If* them cows come to-day, Sammy can drive 'em into the new barn," said he; "an' when they bring the hay up, they can pitch it in there."

"Well," replied Mrs. Penn.

Adoniram set his shaven face ahead and started. When he had cleared the doorstep, he turned and looked back with a kind of nervous solemnity. "I shall be back by Saturday if nothin' happens," said he.

"Do be careful, father," returned his wife.

She stood in the door with Nanny at her elbow and watched him out of sight.   110
Her eyes had a strange, doubtful expression in them; her peaceful forehead was contracted. She went in, and about her baking again. Nanny sat sewing. Her wedding-day was drawing nearer, and she was getting pale and thin with her steady sewing. Her mother kept glancing at her.

"Have you got that pain in your side this mornin'?" she asked.

"A little."

Mrs. Penn's face, as she worked, changed, her perplexed forehead smoothed, her eyes were steady, her lips firmly set. She formed a maxim for herself, although incoherently with her unlettered thoughts. "Unsolicited opportunities are the guide-posts of the Lord to the new roads of life," she repeated in effect, and she made up her mind to her course of action.

"S'posin' I *had* wrote to Hiram," she muttered once, when she was in the pantry—"s'posin' I had wrote, an' asked him if he knew of any horse? But I didn't, an' father's goin' wa'n't none of my doin'. It looks like a providence." Her voice rang out quite loud at the last.

115   "What you talkin' about, mother?" called Nanny.

"Nothin'."

Mrs. Penn hurried her baking; at eleven o'clock it was all done. The load of hay from the west field came slowly down the cart track, and drew up at the new barn. Mrs. Penn ran out. "Stop!" she screamed—"stop!"

The men stopped and looked; Sammy upreared from the top of the load, and stared at his mother.

"Stop!" she cried out again. "Don't you put the hay in that barn; put it in the old one."

120   "Why, he said to put it in here," returned one of the haymakers, wonderingly. He was a young man, a neighbor's son, whom Adoniram hired by the year to help on the farm.

"Don't you put the hay in the new barn; there's room enough in the old one, ain't there?" said Mrs. Penn.

"Room enough," returned the hired man, in his thick, rustic tones. "Didn't need the new barn, nohow, far as room's concerned. Well, I s'pose he changed his mind." He took hold of the horses' bridles.

Mrs. Penn went back to the house. Soon the kitchen windows were darkened, and a fragrance like warm honey came into the room.

Nanny laid down her work. "I thought father wanted them to put the hay into the new barn?" she said, wonderingly.

125   "It's all right," replied her mother.

Sammy slid down from the load of hay, and came in to see if dinner was ready.

"I ain't goin' to get a regular dinner to-day, as long as father's gone," said his mother. "I've let the fire go out. You can have some bread an' milk an' pie. I thought we could get along." She set out some bowls of milk, some bread, and a pie on the kitchen table. "You'd better eat your dinner now," said she. "You might jest as well get through with it. I want you to help me afterward."

Nanny and Sammy stared at each other. There was something strange in their mother's manner. Mrs. Penn did not eat anything herself. She went into the pantry, and they heard her moving dishes while they ate. Presently she came out with a pile of plates. She got the clothesbasket out of the shed, and packed them in it. Nanny and Sammy watched. She brought out cups and saucers, and put them in with the plates.

"What you goin' to do, mother?" inquired Nanny, in a timid voice. A sense of something unusual made her tremble, as if it were a ghost. Sammy rolled his eyes over his pie.

"You'll see what I'm goin' to do," replied Mrs. Penn. "If you're through, Nanny, 130 I want you to go up-stairs an' pack up your things; an' I want you, Sammy, to help me take down the bed in the bedroom."

"Oh, mother, what for?" gasped Nanny.

"You'll see."

During the next few hours a feat was performed by this simple, pious New England mother which was equal in its way to Wolfe's storming of the Heights of Abraham. It took no more genius and audacity of bravery for Wolfe to cheer his wondering soldiers up those steep precipices, under the sleeping eyes of the enemy, than for Sarah Penn, at the head of her children, to move all their little household goods into the new barn while her husband was away.

Nanny and Sammy followed their mother's instructions without a murmur; indeed, they were overawed. There is a certain uncanny and superhuman quality about all such purely original undertakings as their mother's was to them. Nanny went back and forth with her light loads, and Sammy tugged with sober energy.

At five o'clock in the afternoon the little house in which the Penns had lived for 135 forty years had emptied itself into the new barn.

Every builder builds somewhat for unknown purposes, and is in a measure a prophet. The architect of Adoniram Penn's barn, while he designed it for the comfort of four-footed animals, had planned better than he knew for the comfort of humans. Sarah Penn saw at a glance its possibilities. Those great box-stalls, with quilts hung before them, would make better bedrooms than the one she had occupied for forty years, and there was a tight carriage-room. The harness-room, with its chimney and shelves, would make a kitchen of her dreams. The great middle space would make a parlor, by-and-by, fit for a palace. Up stairs there was as much room as down. With partitions and windows, what a house would there be! Sarah looked at the row of stanchions before the allotted space for cows, and reflected that she would have her front entry there.

At six o'clock the stove was up in the harness-room, the kettle was boiling, and the table set for tea. It looked almost as home-like as the abandoned house across the yard had ever done. The young hired man milked, and Sarah directed him calmly to bring the milk to the new barn. He came gaping, dropping little blots of foam from the brimming pails on the grass. Before the next morning he had spread the story of Adoniram Penn's wife moving into the new barn all over the little village. Men assembled in the store and talked it over, women with shawls over their heads scuttled into each other's houses before their work was done. Any deviation from the ordinary course of life in this quiet town was enough to stop all progress in it. Everybody paused to look at the staid, independent figure on the side track. There was a difference of opinion with regard to her. Some held her to be insane; some, of a lawless and rebellious spirit.

Friday the minister went to see her. It was in the forenoon, and she was at the barn door shelling peas for dinner. She looked up and returned his salutation with dignity, then she went on with her work. She did not invite him in. The saintly expression of her face remained fixed, but there was an angry flush over it.

The minister stood awkwardly before her, and talked. She handled the peas as if they were bullets. At last she looked up, and her eyes showed the spirit that her meek front had covered for a lifetime.

140   "There ain't no use talkin', Mr. Hersey," said she. "I've thought it all over an' over, an' I believe I'm doin' what's right. I've made it the subject of prayer, an' it's betwixt me an' the Lord an' Adoniram. There ain't no call for nobody else to worry about it."

"Well, of course, if you have brought it to the Lord in prayer, and feel satisfied that you are doing right, Mrs. Penn," said the minister, helplessly. His thin gray-bearded face was pathetic. He was a sickly man; his youthful confidence had cooled; he had to scourge himself up to some of his pastoral duties as relentlessly as a Catholic ascetic, and then he was prostrated by the smart.

"I think it's right jest as much as I think it was right for our forefathers to come over from the old country 'cause they didn't have what belonged to 'em," said Mrs. Penn. She arose. The barn threshold might have been Plymouth Rock from her bearing. "I don't doubt you mean well, Mr. Hersey," said she, "but there are things people hadn't ought to interfere with. I've been a member of the church for over forty year. I've got my own mind an' my own feet, an' I'm goin' to think my own thoughts an' go my own ways, an' nobody but the Lord is goin' to dictate to me un-less I've a mind to have him. Won't you come in an' set down? How is Mis' Hersey?"

"She is well, I thank you," replied the minister. He added some more perplexed apologetic remarks; then he retreated.

He could expound the intricacies of every character study in the Scriptures, he was competent to grasp the Pilgrim Fathers and all historical innovators, but Sarah Penn was beyond him. He could deal with primal cases, but parallel ones worsted him. But, after all, although it was aside from his province, he wondered more how Adoniram Penn would deal with his wife than how the Lord would. Everybody shared the wonder. When Adoniram's four new cows arrived, Sarah ordered three to be put in the old barn, the other in the house shed where the cooking-stove had stood. That added to the excitement. It was whispered that all four cows were domiciled in the house.

145   Towards sunset on Saturday, when Adoniram was expected home, there was a knot of men in the road near the new barn. The hired man had milked, but he still hung around the premises. Sarah Penn had supper all ready. There were brown-bread and baked beans and a custard pie; it was the supper that Adoniram loved on a Saturday night. She had on a clean calico, and she bore herself imperturbably. Nanny and Sammy kept close at her heels. Their eyes were large, and Nanny was full of nervous tremors. Still there was to them more pleasant excitement than anything else. An inborn confidence in their mother over their father asserted itself.

Sammy looked out of the harness-room window. "There he is," he announced, in an awed whisper. He and Nanny peeped around the casing. Mrs. Penn kept on about her work. The children watched Adoniram leave the new horse standing in the drive while he went to the house door. It was fastened. Then he went around to the shed. That door was seldom locked, even when the family was away. The thought how her father would be confronted by the cow flashed upon Nanny. There was a hysterical sob in her throat. Adoniram emerged from the shed and stood looking around in a dazed fashion. His lips moved; he was saying something, but they could not hear what it was. The hired man was peeping around a corner of the old barn, but nobody saw him.

Adoniram took the new horse by the bridle and led him across the yard to the new barn. Nanny and Sammy slunk close to their mother. The barn doors rolled back, and there stood Adoniram, with the long mild face of the great Canadian farm horse looking over his shoulder.

Nanny kept behind her mother, but Sammy stepped suddenly forward, and stood in front of her.

Adoniram stared at the group. "What on airth you all down here for?" said he. "What's the matter over to the house?"

"We've come here to live, father," said Sammy. His shrill voice quavered out   150 bravely.

"What"—Adoniram sniffed—"what is it smells like cookin'?" said he. He stepped forward and looked in the open door of the harness-room. Then he turned to his wife. His old bristling face was pale and frightened. "What on airth does this mean, mother?" he gasped.

"You come in here, father," said Sarah. She led the way into the harness-room and shut the door. "Now, father," said she, "you needn't be scared. I ain't crazy. There ain't nothin' to be upset over. But we've come here to live, an' we're goin' to live here. We've got jest as good a right here as new horses an' cows. The house wa'n't fit for us to live in any longer, an' I made up my mind I wa'n't goin' to stay there. I've done my duty by you forty year, an' I'm goin' to do it now; but I'm goin' to live here. You've got to put in some windows and partitions; an' you'll have to buy some furniture."

"Why, mother!" the old man gasped.

"You'd better take your coat off an' get washed—there's the wash-basin—an' then we'll have supper."

"Why, mother!"   155

Sammy went past the window, leading the new horse to the old barn. The old man saw him, and shook his head speechlessly. He tried to take off his coat, but his arms seemed to lack the power. His wife helped him. She poured some water into the tin basin, and put in a piece of soap. She got the comb and brush, and smoothed his thin gray hair after he had washed. Then she put the beans, hot bread, and tea on the table. Sammy came in and the family drew up. Adoniram sat looking dazedly at his plate, and they waited.

"Ain't you goin' to ask a blessin', father?" said Sarah.

And the old man bent his head and mumbled.

All through the meal he stopped eating at intervals, and stared furtively at his wife; but he ate well. The home food tasted good to him, and his old frame was too sturdily healthy to be affected by his mind. But after supper he went out, and sat down on the step of the smaller door at the right of the barn, through which he had meant his Jerseys to pass in stately file, but which Sarah designed for her front house door, and he leaned his head on his hands.

160   After the supper dishes were cleared away and the milkpans washed, Sarah went out to him. The twilight was deepening. There was a clear green glow in the sky. Before them stretched the smooth level of field; in the distance was a cluster of haystacks like the huts of a village; the air was very cool and calm and sweet. The landscape might have been an ideal one of peace.

Sarah bent over and touched her husband on one of his thin, sinewy shoulders. "Father!"

The old man's shoulders heaved: he was weeping.

"Why, don't do so, father," said Sarah.

"I'll—put up the—partitions, an'—everything you—want, mother."

165   Sarah put her apron up to her face; she was overcome by her own triumph.

Adoniram was like a fortress whose walls had no active resistance, and went down the instant the right besieging tools were used. "Why, mother," he said, hoarsely, "I hadn't no idee you was so set on't as all this comes to."

QUESTIONS FOR DISCUSSION AND WRITING

1. How does the major conflict in the story illustrate a clash of gender roles and expectations?

2. How do the physical descriptions in the first few paragraphs reveal the characters? How does the father's refusal to respond to his wife's questions suggest his sense of power?

3. How does the description of the buildings on the farm reflect the values of the people who live there? To what extent does the community share these values?

4. How does the narrator's use of allusion—e.g., General James Wolfe's "storming the Heights of Abraham"—suggest her distance from the people she writes about?

5. Why is it thematically important that Freeman titles her story "The Revolt of 'Mother'" rather than "The Revolt of Sarah"?

Stories for Comparison

William Faulkner's "Barn Burning" (pages 491–504); Sarah Orne Jewett's "A White Heron" (pages 706–713).

43

....

E R N E S T   J.   G A I N E S

The Sky Is Gray

ERNEST J. GAINES was born in 1933 in Oscar, Louisiana, and educated at
Valley's Junior College, San Francisco State University, and Stanford Univer-
sity. He has worked as a writer-in-residence at Denison University, Stanford
University, and the University of Southwestern Louisiana. Gaines's boyhood
experiences growing up in Louisiana provide the setting for many of his novels, such as *Of Love and Dust* (1967), *The Autobiography of Miss Jane
Pittman* (1971), *A Gathering of Old Men* (1983), and his most recent work,
A Lesson Before Dying (1993). The best of his short stories are collected in
Bloodline (1968). "The Sky Is Gray," reprinted from *Bloodline,* documents a
young boy's growing awareness of what it means to be a man in a world full
of poverty and prejudice.

I

G o'n be coming in a few minutes. Coming round that bend down there full speed.
And I'm go'n get out my handkerchief and wave it down, and we go'n get on
it and go.

I keep on looking for it, but Mama don't look that way no more. She's looking
down the road where we just come from. It's a long old road, and far's you can see
you don't see nothing but gravel. You got dry weeds on both sides, and you got trees
on both sides, and fences on both sides, too. And you got cows in the pastures and
they standing close together. And when we was coming out here to catch the bus I
seen the smoke coming out of the cows's noses.

I look at my mama and I know what she's thinking. I been with Mama so much,
just me and her, I know what she's thinking all the time. Right now it's home—
Auntie and them. She's thinking if they got enough wood—if she left enough there
to keep them warm till we get back. She's thinking if it go'n rain and if any of them
go'n have to go out in the rain. She's thinking 'bout the hog—if he go'n get out, and
if Ty and Val be able to get him back in. She always worry like that when she leaves
the house. She don't worry too much if she leave me there with the smaller ones,
'cause she know I'm go'n look after them and look after Auntie and everything else.
I'm the oldest and she say I'm the man.

I look at my mama and I love my mama. She's wearing that black coat and that black hat and she's looking sad. I love my mama and I want put my arm round her and tell her. But I'm not supposed to do that. She say that's weakness and that's crybaby stuff, and she don't want no crybaby round her. She don't want you to be scared, either. 'Cause Ty's scared of ghosts and she's always whipping him. I'm scared of the dark, too, but I make 'tend I ain't. I make 'tend I ain't 'cause I'm the oldest, and I got to set a good sample for the rest. I can't ever be scared and I can't ever cry. And that's why I never said nothing 'bout my teeth. It's been hurting me and hurting me close to a month now, but I never said it. I didn't say it 'cause I didn't want act like a crybaby, and 'cause I know we didn't have enough money to go have it pulled. But, Lord, it been hurting me. And look like it wouldn't start till at night when you was trying to get yourself little sleep. Then soon 's you shut your eyes— ummm-ummm, Lord, look like it go right down to your heartstring.

5 "Hurting, hanh?" Ty'd say.

I'd shake my head, but I wouldn't open my mouth for nothing. You open your mouth and let that wind in, and it almost kill you.

I'd just lay there and listen to them snore. Ty there, right 'side me, and Auntie and Val over by the fireplace. Val younger than me and Ty, and he sleeps with Auntie. Mama sleeps round the other side with Louis and Walker.

I'd just lay there and listen to them, and listen to that wind out there, and listen to that fire in the fireplace. Sometimes it'd stop long enough to let me get little rest. Sometimes it just hurt, hurt, hurt. Lord, have mercy.

2

Auntie knowed it was hurting me. I didn't tell nobody but Ty, 'cause we buddies and he ain't go'n tell nobody. But some kind of way Auntie found out. When she asked me, I told her no, nothing was wrong. But she knowed it all the time. She told me to mash up a piece of aspirin and wrap it in some cotton and jugg it down in that hole. I did it, but it didn't do no good. It stopped for a little while, and started right back again. Auntie wanted to tell Mama, but I told her, "Uh-uh." 'Cause I knowed we didn't have any money, and it just was go'n make her mad again. So Auntie told Monsieur Bayonne, and Monsieur Bayonne came over to the house and told me to kneel down 'side him on the fireplace. He put his finger in his mouth and made the Sign of the Cross on my jaw. The tip of Monsieur Bayonne's finger is some hard, 'cause he's always playing on that guitar. If we sit outside at night we can always hear Monsieur Bayonne playing on his guitar. Sometimes we leave him out there playing on the guitar.

10 Monsieur Bayonne made the Sign of the Cross over and over on my jaw, but that didn't do no good. Even when he prayed and told me to pray some, too, that tooth still hurt me.

"How you feeling?" he say.

"Same," I say.

He kept on praying and making the Sign of the Cross and I kept on praying, too.

"Still hurting?" he say.

"Yes, sir."

Monsieur Bayonne mashed harder and harder on my jaw. He mashed so hard he almost pushed me over on Ty. But then he stopped.

"What kind of prayers you praying, boy?" he say.

"Baptist," I say.

"Well, I'll be—no wonder that tooth still killing him. I'm going one way and he pulling the other. Boy, don't you know any Catholic prayers?"

"I know 'Hail Mary,'" I say.

"Then you better start saying it."

"Yes, sir."

He started mashing on my jaw again, and I could hear him praying at the same time. And, sure enough, after while it stopped hurting me.

Me and Ty went outside where Monsieur Bayonne's two hounds was and we started playing with them. "Let's go hunting," Ty say. "All right," I say; and we went on back in the pasture. Soon the hounds got on a trail, and me and Ty followed them all 'cross the pasture and then back in the woods, too. And then they cornered this little old rabbit and killed him, and me and Ty made them get back, and we picked up the rabbit and started on back home. But my tooth had started hurting me again. It was hurting me plenty now, but I wouldn't tell Monsieur Bayonne. That night I didn't sleep a bit, and first thing in the morning Auntie told me to go back and let Monsieur Bayonne pray over me some more. Monsieur Bayonne was in his kitchen making coffee when I got there. Soon 's he seen me he knowed what was wrong.

"All right, kneel down there 'side that stove," he say. "And this time make sure you pray Catholic. I don't know nothing 'bout that Baptist, and I don't want know nothing 'bout him."

3

Last night Mama say, "Tomorrow we going to town."

"It ain't hurting me no more," I say. "I can eat anything on it."

"Tomorrow we going to town," she say.

And after she finished eating, she got up and went to bed. She always go to bed early now. 'Fore Daddy went in the Army, she used to stay up late. All of us sitting out on the gallery or round the fire. But now, look like soon 's she finish eating she go to bed.

This morning when I woke up, her and Auntie was standing 'fore the fireplace. She say: "Enough to get there and get back. Dollar and a half to have it pulled. Twenty-five for me to go, twenty-five for him. Twenty-five for me to come back, twenty-five for him. Fifty cents left. Guess I get little piece of salt meat with that."

"Sure can use it," Auntie say. "White beans and no salt meat ain't white beans."

"I do the best I can," Mama say.

They was quiet after that, and I made 'tend I was still asleep.

"James, hit the floor," Auntie say.

I still made 'tend I was asleep. I didn't want them to know I was listening.

"All right," Auntie say, shaking me by the shoulder. "Come on. Today's the day."

I pushed the cover down to get out, and Ty grabbed it and pulled it back.

"You, too, Ty," Auntie say.

"I ain't getting no teef pulled," Ty say.

40   "Don't mean it ain't time to get up," Auntie say. "Hit it, Ty."

Ty got up grumbling.

"James, you hurry up and get in your clothes and eat your food," Auntie say. "What time y'all coming back?" she say to Mama.

"That 'leven o'clock bus," Mama say. "Got to get back in that field this evening."

"Get a move on you, James," Auntie say.

45   I went in the kitchen and washed my face, then I ate my breakfast. I was having bread and syrup. The bread was warm and hard and tasted good. And I tried to make it last a long time.

Ty came back there grumbling and mad at me.

"Got to get up," he say. "I ain't having no teefes pulled. What I got to be getting up for?"

Ty poured some syrup in his pan and got a piece of bread. He didn't wash his hands, neither his face, and I could see that white stuff in his eyes.

"You the one getting your teef pulled," he say. "What I got to get up for. I bet if I was getting a teef pulled, you wouldn't be getting up. Shucks; syrup again. I'm getting tired of this old syrup. Syrup, syrup, syrup. I'm go'n take with the sugar diabetes. I want me some bacon sometime."

50   "Go out in the field and work and you can have your bacon," Auntie say. She stood in the middle door looking at Ty. "You better be glad you got syrup. Some people ain't got that—hard's time is."

"Shucks," Ty say. "How can I be strong."

"I don't know too much 'bout your strength," Auntie say; "but I know where you go'n be hot at, you keep that grumbling up. James, get a move on you; your mama waiting."

I ate my last piece of bread and went in the front room. Mama was standing 'fore the fireplace warming her hands. I put on my coat and my cap, and we left the house.

4

I look down there again, but it still ain't coming. I almost say, "It ain't coming yet," but I keep my mouth shut. 'Cause that's something else she don't like. She don't like for you to say something just for nothing. She can see it ain't coming, I can see it ain't coming, so why say it ain't coming. I don't say it, I turn and look at the river that's back of us. It's so cold the smoke's just raising up from the water. I see a bunch of pool-doos not too far out—just on the other side the lilies. I'm wondering if you can eat pool-doos. I ain't too sure, 'cause I ain't never ate none. But I done ate owls and blackbirds, and I done ate redbirds, too. I didn't want kill the redbirds, but she made me kill them. They had two of them back there. One in my trap, one in Ty's trap. Me and Ty was go'n play with them and let them go, but she made me kill them 'cause we needed the food.

"I can't," I say. "I can't."   55

"Here," she say. "Take it."

"I can't," I say. "I can't. I can't kill him, Mama, please."

"Here," she say. "Take this fork, James."

"Please, Mama, I can't kill him," I say.

I could tell she was go'n hit me. I jerked back, but I didn't jerk back soon   60
enough.

"Take it," she say.

I took it and reached in for him, but he kept on hopping to the back.

"I can't, Mama," I say. The water just kept on running down my face. "I can't,"
I say.

"Get him out of there," she say.

I reached in for him and he kept on hopping to the back. Then I reached in far-   65
ther, and he pecked me on the hand.

"I can't, Mama," I say.

She slapped me again.

I reached in again, but he kept on hopping out my way. Then he hopped to one
side and I reached there. The fork got him on the leg and I heard his leg pop. I pulled
my hand out 'cause I had hurt him.

"Give it here," she say, and jerked the fork out my hand.

She reached in and got the little bird right in the neck. I heard the fork go in his   70
neck, and I heard it go in the ground. She brought him out and helt him right in front
of me.

"That's one," she say. She shook him off and gived me the fork. "Get the
other one."

"I can't, Mama," I say. "I'll do anything, but don't make me do that."   75

She went to the corner of the fence and broke the biggest switch over there she
could find. I knelt 'side the trap, crying.

"Get him out of there," she say.

"I can't, Mama."

She started hitting me 'cross the back. I went down on the ground, crying.

"Get him," she say.

"Octavia?" Auntie say.

'Cause she had come out of the house and she was standing by the tree looking
at us.

"Get him out of there," Mama say.   80

"Octavia," Auntie say, "explain to him. Explain to him. Just don't beat him. Explain to him."

But she hit me and hit me and hit me.

I'm still young—I ain't no more than eight; but I know now; I know why I had
to do it. (They was so little, though. They was so little. I 'member how I picked
the feathers off them and cleaned them and helt them over the fire. Then we all ate

them. Ain't had but a little bitty piece each, but we all had a little bitty piece, and everybody just looked at me 'cause they was so proud.) Suppose she had to go away? That's why I had to do it. Suppose she had to go away like Daddy went away? Then who was go'n look after us? They had to be somebody left to carry on. I didn't know it then, but I know it now. Auntie and Monsieur Bayonne talked to me and made me see.

5

Time I see it I get out my handkerchief and start waving. It's still 'way down there, but I keep waving anyhow. Then it come up and stop and me and Mama get on. Mama tell me go sit in the back while she pay. I do like she say, and the people look at me. When I pass the little sign that say "White" and "Colored," I start looking for a seat. I just see one of them back there, but I don't take it, 'cause I want my mama to sit down herself. She comes in the back and sit down, and I lean on the seat. They got seats in the front, but I know I can't sit there, 'cause I have to sit back of the sign. Anyhow, I don't want sit there if my mama go'n sit back here.

85 They got a lady sitting 'side my mama and she looks at me and smiles little bit. I smile back, but I don't open my mouth, 'cause the wind'll get in and make that tooth ache. The lady take out a pack of gum and reach me a slice, but I shake my head. The lady just can't understand why a little boy'll turn down gum, and she reach me a slice again. This time I point to my jaw. The lady understands and smiles little bit, and I smile little bit, but I don't open my mouth, though.

They got a girl sitting 'cross from me. She got on a red overcoat and her hair's plaited in one big plait. First, I make 'tend I don't see her over there, but then I start looking at her little bit. She make 'tend she don't see me, either, but I catch her looking that way. She got a cold, and every now and then she h'ist that little handkerchief to her nose. She ought to blow it, but she don't. Must think she's too much a lady or something.

Every time she h'ist that little handkerchief, the lady 'side her say something in her ear. She shakes her head and lays her hands in her lap again. Then I catch her kind of looking where I'm at. I smile at her little bit. But think she'll smile back? Uh-uh. She just turn up her little old nose and turn her head. Well, I show her both of us can turn us head. I turn mine too and look out at the river.

The river is gray. The sky is gray. They have pool-doos on the water. The water is wavy, and the pool-doos go up and down. The bus go round a turn, and you got plenty trees hiding the river. Then the bus go round another turn, and I can see the river again.

I look toward the front where all the white people sitting. Then I look at that little old gal again. I don't look right at her, 'cause I don't want all them people to know I love her. I just look at her little bit, like I'm looking out that window over there. But she knows I'm looking that way, and she kind of look at me, too. The lady sitting 'side her catch her this time, and she leans over and says something in her ear.

90 "I don't love him nothing," that little old gal says out loud.

Everybody back there hear her mouth, and all of them look at us and laugh.

"I don't love you, either," I say. "So you don't have to turn up your nose, Miss."

"You the one looking," she say.

"I wasn't looking at you," I say. "I was looking out that window, there."

"Out that window, my foot," she say. "I seen you. Everytime I turned round you ^{95} was looking at me."

"You must of been looking yourself if you seen me all them times," I say.

"Shucks," she say, "I got me all kind of boyfriends."

"I got girlfriends, too," I say.

"Well, I just don't want you getting your hopes up," she say.

I don't say no more to that little old gal 'cause I don't want have to bust her in ^{100} the mouth. I lean on the seat where Mama sitting, and I don't even look that way no more. When we get to Bayonne, she jugg her little old tongue out at me. I make 'tend I'm go'n hit her, and she duck down 'side her mama. And all the people laugh at us again.

6

Me and Mama get off and start walking in town. Bayonne is a little bitty town. Baton Rouge is a hundred times bigger than Bayonne. I went to Baton Rouge once—me, Ty, Mama, and Daddy. But that was 'way back yonder, 'fore Daddy went in the Army. I wonder when we go'n see him again. I wonder when. Look like he ain't ever coming back home. . . . Even the pavement all cracked in Bayonne. Got grass shooting right out the sidewalk. Got weeds in the ditch, too; just like they got at home.

It's some cold in Bayonne. Look like it's colder than it is home. The wind blows in my face, and I feel that stuff running down my nose. I sniff. Mama says use that handkerchief. I blow my nose and put it back.

We pass a school and I see them white children playing in the yard. Big old red school, and them children just running and playing. Then we pass a café, and I see a bunch of people in there eating. I wish I was in there 'cause I'm cold. Mama tells me keep my eyes in front where they belong.

We pass stores that's got dummies, and we pass another café, and then we pass a shoe shop, and that bald-head man in there fixing on a shoe. I look at him and I butt into that white lady, and Mama jerks me in front and tells me stay there.

We come up to the courthouse, and I see the flag waving there. This flag ain't ^{105} like the one we got at school. This one here ain't got but a handful of stars. One at school got a big pile of stars—one for every state. We pass it and we turn and there it is—the dentist office. Me and Mama go in, and they got people sitting everywhere you look. They even got a little boy in there younger than me.

Me and Mama sit on that bench, and a white lady come in there and ask me what my name is. Mama tells her and the white lady goes on back. Then I hear somebody hollering in there. Soon 's that little boy hear him hollering, he starts hollering, too. His mama pats him and pats him, trying to make him hush up, but he ain't thinking 'bout his mama.

The man that was hollering in there comes out holding his jaw. He is a big old man and he's wearing overalls and a jumper.

"Got it, hanh?" another man asks him.

The man shakes his head—don't want open his mouth.

110 "Man, I thought they was killing you in there," the other man says. "Hollering like a pig under a gate."

The man don't say nothing. He just heads for the door, and the other man follows him.

"John Lee," the white lady says. "John Lee Williams."

The little boy juggs his head down in his mama's lap and holler more now. His mama tells him go with the nurse, but he ain't thinking 'bout his mama. His mama tells him again, but he don't even hear her. His mama picks him up and takes him in there, and even when the white lady shuts the door I can still hear little old John Lee.

"I often wonder why the Lord let a child like that suffer," a lady says to my mama. The lady's sitting right in front of us on another bench. She's got on a white dress and a black sweater. She must be a nurse or something herself, I reckon.

115 "Not us to question," a man says.

"Sometimes I don't know if we shouldn't," the lady says.

"I know definitely we shouldn't," the man says. The man looks like a preacher. He's big and fat and he's got on a black suit. He's got a gold chain, too.

"Why?" the lady says.

"Why anything?" the preacher says.

120 "Yes," the lady says. "Why anything?"

"Not us to question," the preacher says.

The lady looks at the preacher a little while and looks at Mama again.

"And look like it's the poor who suffers the most," she says. "I don't understand it."

"Best not to even try," the preacher says. "He works in mysterious ways—wonders to perform."

125 Right then little John Lee bust out hollering, and everybody turn they head to listen.

"He's not a good dentist," the lady says. "Dr. Robillard is much better. But more expensive. That's why most of the colored people come here. The white people go to Dr. Robillard. Y'all from Bayonne?"

"Down the river," my mama says. And that's all she go'n say, 'cause she don't talk much. But the lady keeps on looking at her, and so she says, "Near Morgan."

"I see," the lady says.

7

"That's the trouble with the black people in this country today," somebody else says. This one here's sitting on the same side me and Mama's sitting, and he is kind of sitting in front of that preacher. He looks like a teacher or somebody that goes to college. He's got on a suit, and he's got a book that he's been reading. "We don't question is exactly our problem," he says. "We should question and question and question—question everything."

130 The preacher just looks at him a long time. He done put a toothpick or something in his mouth, and he just keeps on turning it and turning it. You can see he don't like that boy with that book.

"Maybe you can explain what you mean," he says.

"I said what I meant," the boy says. "Question everything. Every stripe, every star, every word spoken. Everything."

"It 'pears to me that this young lady and I was talking 'bout God, young man," the preacher says.

"Question Him, too," the boy says.

"Wait," the preacher says. "Wait now."   135

"You heard me right," the boy says. "His existence as well as everything else. Everything."

The preacher just looks across the room at the boy. You can see he's getting madder and madder. But mad or no mad, the boy ain't thinking 'bout him. He looks at that preacher just 's hard 's the preacher looks at him.

"Is this what they coming to?" the preacher says. "Is this what we educating them for?"

"You're not educating me," the boy says. "I wash dishes at night so that I can go to school in the day. So even the words you spoke need questioning."

The preacher just looks at him and shakes his head.   140

"When I come in this room and seen you there with your book, I said to myself, 'There's an intelligent man.' How wrong a person can be."

"Show me one reason to believe in the existence of a God," the boys says.

"My heart tells me," the preacher says.

"'My heart tells me,'" the boy says, "'My heart tells me.' Sure, 'My heart tells me.' And as long as you listen to what your heart tells you, you will have only what the white man gives you and nothing more. Me, I don't listen to my heart. The purpose of the heart is to pump blood throughout the body, and nothing else."

"Who's your paw, boy?" the preacher says.   145

"Why?"

"Who is he?"

"He's dead."

"And your mom?"

"She's in Charity Hospital with pneumonia. Half killed herself, working for   150
nothing."

"And 'cause he's dead and she's sick, you mad at the world?"

"I'm not mad at the world. I'm questioning the world. I'm questioning it with cold logic, sir. What do words like Freedom, Liberty, God, White, Colored mean? I want to know. That's why *you* are sending us to school, to read and to ask questions. And because we ask these questions, you call us mad. No sir, it is not us who are mad."

"You keep saying 'us'?"

"'Us.' Yes—us. I'm not alone."

The preacher just shakes his head. Then he looks at everybody in the room—   155
everybody. Some of the people look down at the floor, keep from looking at him. I kind of look 'way myself, but soon 's I know he done turn his head, I look that way again.

"I'm sorry for you," he says to the boy.

"Why?" the boy says. "Why not be sorry for yourself? Why are you so much better off than I am? Why aren't you sorry for these other people in here? Why not be sorry for the lady who had to drag her child into the dentist office? Why not be sorry for the lady sitting on that bench over there? Be sorry for them. Not for me. Some way or the other I'm going to make it."

"No, I'm sorry for you," the preacher says.

"Of course, of course," the boy says, nodding his head. "You're sorry for me because I rock that pillar you're leaning on."

160   "You can't ever rock the pillar I'm leaning on, young man. It's stronger than anything man can ever do."

"You believe in God because a man told you to believe in God," the boy says. "A white man told you to believe in God. And why? To keep you ignorant so he can keep his feet on your neck."

"So now we the ignorant?" the preacher says.

"Yes," the boy says. "Yes." And he opens his book again.

The preacher just looks at him sitting there. The boy done forgot all about him. Everybody else make 'tend they done forgot the squabble, too.

165   Then I see that preacher getting up real slow. Preacher's a great big old man and he got to brace himself to get up. He comes over where the boy is sitting. He just stands there a little while looking down at him, but the boy don't raise his head.

"Get up, boy," preacher says.

The boy looks up at him, then he shuts his book real slow and stands up. Preacher just hauls back and hit him in the face. The boy falls back 'gainst the wall, but he straightens himself up and looks right back at that preacher.

"You forgot the other cheek," he says.

The preacher hauls back and hit him again on the other side. But this time the boy braces himself and don't fall.

170   "That hasn't changed a thing," he says.

The preacher just looks at the boy. The preacher's breathing real hard like he just run up a big hill. The boy sits down and opens his book again.

"I feel sorry for you," the preacher says. "I never felt so sorry for a man before."

The boy makes 'tend he don't even hear that preacher. He keeps on reading his book. The preacher goes back and gets his hat off the chair.

"Excuse me," he says to us. "I'll come back some other time. Y'all, please excuse me."

175   And he looks at the boy and goes out the room. The boy h'ist his hand up to his mouth one time to wipe 'way some blood. All the rest of the time he keeps on reading. And nobody else in there say a word.

8

Little John Lee and his mama come out the dentist office, and the nurse calls somebody else in. Then little bit later they come out, and the nurse calls another name. But fast 's she calls somebody in there, somebody else comes in the place where we sitting, and the room stays full.

The people coming in now, all of them wearing big coats. One of them says something 'bout sleeting, another one says he hope not. Another one says he think it ain't nothing but rain. 'Cause, he says, rain can get awful cold this time of year.

All round the room they talking. Some of them talking to people right by them, some of them talking to people clear 'cross the room, some of them talking to anybody'll listen. It's a little bitty room, no bigger than us kitchen, and I can see everybody in there. The little old room's full of smoke, 'cause you got two old men smoking pipes over by that side door. I think I feel my tooth thumping me some, and I hold my breath and wait. I wait and wait, but it don't thump me no more. Thank God for that.

I feel like going to sleep, and I lean back 'gainst the wall. But I'm scared to go to sleep. Scared 'cause the nurse might call my name and I won't hear her. And Mama might go to sleep, too, and she'll be mad if neither one of us heard the nurse.

I look up at Mama. I love my mama. I love my mama. And when cotton come 180 I'm go'n get her a new coat. And I ain't go'n get a black one, either. I think I'm go'n get her a red one.

"They got some books over there," I say. "Want read one of them?"

Mama looks at the books, but she don't answer me.

"You got yourself a little man there," the lady says.

Mama don't say nothing to the lady, but she must've smiled, 'cause I seen the lady smiling back. The lady looks at me a little while, like she's feeling sorry for me.

"You sure got that preacher out here in a hurry," she says to that boy.   185

The boy looks up at her and looks in his book again. When I grow up I want be just like him. I want clothes like that and I want keep a book with me, too.

"You really don't believe in God?" the lady says.

"No," he says.

"But why?" the lady says.

"Because the wind is pink," he says.   190

"What?" the lady says.

The boy don't answer her no more. He just reads in his book.

"Talking 'bout the wind is pink," that old lady says. She's sitting on the same bench with the boy and she's trying to look in his face. The boy makes 'tend the old lady ain't even there. He just keeps on reading. "Wind is pink," she says again. "Eh, Lord, what children go'n be saying next?"

The lady 'cross from us bust out laughing.

"That's a good one," she says. "The wind is pink. Yes sir, that's a good one."   195

"Don't you believe the wind is pink?" the boy says. He keeps his head down in the book.

"Course I believe it, honey," the lady says. "Course I do." She looks at us and winks her eye. "And what color is grass, honey?"

"Grass? Grass is black."

She bust out laughing again. The boy looks at her.

"Don't you believe grass is black?" he says.   200

The lady quits her laughing and looks at him. Everybody else looking at him, too. The place quiet, quiet.

"Grass is green, honey," the lady says. "It was green yesterday, it's green today, and it's go'n be green tomorrow."

"How do you know it's green?"

"I know because I know."

205   "You don't know it's green," the boy says. "You believe it's green because someone told you it was green. If someone had told you it was black you'd believe it was black."

"It's green," the lady says. "I know green when I see green."

"Prove it's green," the boy says.

"Sure, now," the lady says. "Don't tell me it's coming to that."

"It's coming to just that," the boy says. "Words mean nothing. One means no more than the other."

210   "That's what it all coming to?" that old lady says. That old lady got on a turban and she got on two sweaters. She got a green sweater under a black sweater. I can see the green sweater 'cause some of the buttons on the other sweater's missing.

"Yes ma'am," the boy says. "Words mean nothing. Action is the only thing. Doing. That's the only thing."

"Other words, you want the Lord to come down here and show Hisself to you?" she says.

"Exactly, ma'am," he says.

"You don't mean that, I'm sure?" she says.

215   "I do, ma'am," he says.

"Done, Jesus," the old lady says, shaking her head.

"I didn't go 'long with that preacher at first," the other lady says; "but now—I don't know. When a person say the grass is black, he's either a lunatic or something's wrong."

"Prove to me that it's green," the boy says.

"It's green because the people say it's green."

220   "Those same people say we're citizens of these United States," the boy says.

"I think I'm a citizen," the lady says.

"Citizens have certain rights," the boy says. "Name me one right that you have. One right, granted by the Constitution, that you can exercise in Bayonne."

The lady don't answer him. She just looks at him like she don't know what he's talking 'bout. I know I don't.

225   "Things changing," she says.

"Things are changing because some black men have begun to think with their brains and not their hearts," the boy says.

"You trying to say these people don't believe in God?"

"I'm sure some of them do. Maybe most of them do. But they don't believe that God is going to touch these white people's hearts and change things tomorrow. Things change through action. By no other way."

Everybody sit quiet and look at the boy. Nobody says a thing. Then the lady 'cross the room from me and Mama just shakes her head.

"Let's hope that not all your generation feel the same way you do," she says.

"Think what you please, it doesn't matter," the boy says. "But it will be men 230 who listen to their heads and not their hearts who will see that your children have a better chance than you had."

"Let's hope they ain't all like you, though," the old lady says. "Done forgot the heart absolutely."

"Yes ma'am, I hope they aren't all like me," the boy says. "Unfortunately, I was born too late to believe in your God. Let's hope that the ones who come after will have your faith—if not in your God, then in something else, something definitely that they can lean on. I haven't anything. For me, the wind is pink, the grass is black."

9

The nurse comes in the room where we all sitting and waiting and says the doctor won't take no more patients till one o'clock this evening. My mama jumps up off the bench and goes up to the white lady.

"Nurse, I have to go back in the field this evening," she says.

"The doctor is treating his last patient now," the nurse says. "One o'clock this 235 evening."

"Can I at least speak to the doctor?" my mama asks.

"I'm his nurse," the lady says.

"My little boy's sick," my mama says. "Right now his tooth almost killing him."

The nurse looks at me. She's trying to make up her mind if to let me come in. I look at her real pitiful. The tooth ain't hurting me at all, but Mama say it is, so I make 'tend for her sake.

"This evening," the nurse says, and goes on back in the office.   240

"Don't feel 'jected, honey," the lady says to Mama. "I been round them a long time—they take you when they want to. If you was white, that's something else; but we the wrong color."

Mama don't say nothing to the lady, and me and her go outside and stand 'gainst the wall. It's cold out there. I can feel that wind going through my coat. Some of the other people come out of the room and go up the street. Me and Mama stand there a little while and we start walking. I don't know where we going. When we come to the other street we just stand there.

"You don't have to make water, do you?" Mama says.

"No, ma'am," I say.

We go on up the street. Walking real slow. I can tell Mama don't know where 245 she's going. When we come to a store we stand there and look at the dummies. I look at a little boy wearing a brown overcoat. He's got on brown shoes, too. I look at my old shoes and look at his'n again. You wait till summer, I say.

Me and Mama walk away. We come up to another store and we stop and look at them dummies, too. Then we go on again. We pass a café where the white people in there eating. Mama tells me keep my eyes in front where they belong, but I can't help from seeing them people eat. My stomach starts to growling 'cause I'm hungry. When I see people eating, I get hungry; when I see a coat, I get cold.

A man whistles at my mama when we go by a filling station. She makes 'tend she don't even see him. I look back and I feel like hitting him in the mouth. If I was bigger, I say; if I was bigger, you'd see.

We keep on going. I'm getting colder and colder, but I don't say nothing. I feel that stuff running down my nose and I sniff.

"That rag," Mama says.

250   I get it out and wipe my nose. I'm getting cold all over now—my face, my hands, my feet, everything. We pass another little café, but this'n for white people, too, and we can't go in there, either. So we just walk. I'm so cold now I'm 'bout ready to say it. If I knowed where we was going I wouldn't be so cold, but I don't know where we going. We go, we go, we go. We walk clean out of Bayonne. Then we cross the street and we come back. Same thing I seen when I got off the bus this morning. Same old trees, same old walk, same old weeds, same old cracked pave— same old everything.

I sniff again.

"That rag," Mama says.

I wipe my nose real fast and jugg that handkerchief back in my pocket 'fore my hand gets too cold. I raise my head and I can see David's hardware store. When we come up to it, we go in. I don't know why, but I'm glad.

It's warm in there. It's so warm in there you don't ever want to leave. I look for the heater, and I see it over by them barrels. Three white men standing round the heater talking in Creole. One of them comes over to see what my mama want.

255   "Got any axe handles?" she says.

Me, Mama and the white man start to the back, but Mama stops me when we come up to the heater. She and the white man go on. I hold my hands over the heater and look at them. They go all the way to the back, and I see the white man pointing to the axe handles 'gainst the wall. Mama takes one of them and shakes it like she's trying to figure how much it weighs. Then she rubs her hand over it from one end to the other end. She turns it over and looks at the other side, then she shakes it again, and shakes her head and puts it back. She gets another one and she does it just like she did the first one, then she shakes her head. Then she gets a brown one and do it that, too. But she don't like this one, either. Then she gets another one, but 'fore she shakes it or anything, she looks at me. Look like she's trying to say something to me, but I don't know what it is. All I know is I done got warm now and I'm feeling right smart better. Mama shakes this axe handle just like she did the others, and shakes her head and says something to the white man. The white man just looks at his pile of axe handles, and when Mama pass him to come to the front, the white man just scratch his head and follows her. She tells me come on and we go on out and start walking again.

We walk and walk, and no time at all I'm cold again. Look like I'm colder now 'cause I can still remember how good it was back there. My stomach growls and I suck it in to keep Mama from hearing it. She's walking right 'side me, and it growls so loud you can hear it a mile. But Mama don't say a word.

10

When we come up to the courthouse, I look at the clock. It's got quarter to twelve. Mean we got another hour and a quarter to be out here in the cold. We go and stand 'side a building. Something hits my cap and I look up at the sky. Sleet's falling.

I look at Mama standing there. I want stand close 'side her, but she don't like that. She say that's crybaby stuff. She say you got to stand for yourself, by yourself.

"Let's go back to that office," she says.   260

We cross the street. When we get to the dentist office I try to open the door, but I can't. I twist and twist, but I can't. Mama pushes me to the side and she twist the knob, but she can't open the door, either. She turns 'way from the door. I look at her, but I don't move and I don't say nothing. I done seen her like this before and I'm scared of her.

"You hungry?" she says. She says it like she's mad at me, like I'm the cause of everything.

"No, ma'am," I say.

"You want eat and walk back, or you rather don't eat and ride?"

"I ain't hungry," I say.   265

I ain't just hungry, but I'm cold, too. I'm so hungry and cold I want to cry. And look like I'm getting colder and colder. My feet done got numb. I try to work my toes, but I don't even feel them. Look like I'm go'n die. Look like I'm go'n stand right here and freeze to death. I think 'bout home. I think 'bout Val and Auntie and Ty and Louis and Walker. It's 'bout twelve o'clock and I know they eating dinner now. I can hear Ty making jokes. He done forgot 'bout getting up early this morning and right now he's probably making jokes. Always trying to make somebody laugh. I wish I was right there listening to him. Give anything in the world if I was home round the fire.

"Come on," Mama says.

We start walking again. My feet so numb I can't hardly feel them. We turn the corner and go on back up the street. The clock on the courthouse starts hitting for twelve.

The sleet's coming down plenty now. They hit the pave and bounce like rice. Oh, Lord; oh, Lord, I pray. Don't let me die, don't let me die, don't let me die, Lord.

11

Now I know where we going. We going back of town where the colored peo-   270
ple eat. I don't care if I don't eat. I been hungry before. I can stand it. But I can't stand the cold.

I can see we go'n have a long walk. It's 'bout a mile down there. But I don't mind. I know when I get there I'm go'n warm myself. I think I can hold out. My hands numb in my pockets and my feet numb, too, but if I keep moving I can hold out. Just don't stop no more, that's all.

The sky's gray. The sleet keeps on falling. Falling like rain now—plenty, plenty. You can hear it hitting the pave. You can see it bouncing. Sometimes it bounces two times 'fore it settles.

We keep on going. We don't say nothing. We just keep on going, keep on going.

I wonder what Mama's thinking. I hope she ain't mad at me. When summer come I'm go'n pick plenty cotton and get her a coat. I'm go'n get her a red one.

275   I hope they'd make it summer all the time. I'd be glad if it was summer all the time—but it ain't. We got to have winter, too. Lord, I hate the winter. I guess everybody hate the winter.

I don't sniff this time. I get out my handkerchief and wipe my nose. My hands's so cold I can hardly hold the handkerchief.

I think we getting close, but we ain't there yet. I wonder where everybody is. Can't see a soul but us. Look like we the only two people moving round today. Must be too cold for the rest of the people to move round in.

I can hear my teeth. I hope they don't knock together too hard and make that bad one hurt. Lord, that's all I need, for that bad one to start off.

I hear a church bell somewhere. But today ain't Sunday. They must be ringing for a funeral or something.

280   I wonder what they doing at home. They must be eating. Monsieur Bayonne might be there with his guitar. One day Ty played with Monsieur Bayonne's guitar and broke one of the strings. Monsieur Bayonne was some mad with Ty. He say Ty wasn't go'n ever 'mount to nothing. Ty can go just like Monsieur Bayonne when he ain't there. Ty can make everybody laugh when he starts to mocking Monsieur Bayonne.

I used to like to be with Mama and Daddy. We used to be happy. But they took him in the Army. Now, nobody happy no more. . . . I be glad when Daddy comes home.

Monsieur Bayonne say it wasn't fair for them to take Daddy and give Mama nothing and give us nothing. Auntie say, "Shhh, Etienne. Don't let them hear you talk like that." Monsieur Bayonne say, "It's God truth. What they giving his children? They have to walk three and a half miles to school hot or cold. That's anything to give for a paw? She's got to work in the field rain or shine just to make ends meet. That's anything to give for a husband?" Auntie say, "Shhh, Etienne, shhh." "Yes, you right," Monsieur Bayonne say. "Best don't say it in front of them now. But one day they go'n find out. One day." "Yes, I suppose so," Auntie say. "Then what, Rose Mary?" Monsieur Bayonne say. "I don't know, Etienne," Auntie say. "All we can do is us job, and leave everything else in His hand. . . ."

We getting closer, now. We getting closer. I can even see the railroad tracks.

We cross the tracks, and now I see the café. Just to get in there, I say. Just to get in there. Already I'm starting to feel little better.

12

285   We go in. Ahh, it's good. I look for the heater; there 'gainst the wall. One of them little brown ones. I just stand there and hold my hands over it. I can't open my hands too wide 'cause they almost froze.

Mama's standing right 'side me. She done unbuttoned her coat. Smoke rises out of the coat, and the coat smells like a wet dog.

I move to the side so Mama can have more room. She opens out her hands and rubs them together. I rub mine together, too, 'cause this keep them from hurting. If you let them warm too fast, they hurt you sure. But if you let them warm just little bit at a time, and you keep rubbing them, they be all right every time.

They got just two more people in the café. A lady back of the counter, and a man on this side the counter. They been watching us ever since we come in.

Mama gets out the handkerchief and count up the money. Both of us know how much money she's got there. Three dollars. No, she ain't got three dollars, 'cause she had to pay us way up here. She ain't got but two dollars and a half left. Dollar and a half to get my tooth pulled, and fifty cents for us to go back on, and fifty cents worth of salt meat.

She stirs the money round with her finger. Most of the money is change 'cause 290
I can hear it rubbing together. She stirs it and stirs it. Then she looks at the door. It's still sleeting. I can hear it hitting 'gainst the wall like rice.

"I ain't hungry, Mama," I say.

"Got to pay them something for they heat," she says.

She takes a quarter out the handkerchief and ties the handkerchief up again. She looks over her shoulder at the people, but she still don't move. I hope she don't spend the money. I don't want her spending it on me. I'm hungry, I'm almost starving I'm so hungry, but I don't want her spending the money on me.

She flips the quarter over like she's thinking. She's must be thinking 'bout us walking back home. Lord, I sure don't want walk home. If I thought it'd do any good to say something, I'd say it. But Mama makes up her own mind 'bout things.

She turns 'way from the heater right fast, like she better hurry up and spend the 295
quarter 'fore she change her mind. I watch her go toward the counter. The man and the lady look at her, too. She tells the lady something and the lady walks away. The man keeps on looking at her. Her back's turned to the man, and she don't even know he's standing there.

The lady puts some cakes and a glass of milk on the counter. Then she pours up a cup of coffee and sets it 'side the other stuff. Mama pays her for the things and comes on back where I'm standing. She tells me sit down at the table 'gainst the wall.

The milk and the cakes's for me; the coffee's for Mama. I eat slow and I look at her. She's looking outside at the sleet. She's looking real sad. I say to myself, I'm go'n make all this up one day. You see, one day, I'm go'n make all this up. I want say it now; I want tell her how I feel right now; but Mama don't like for us to talk like that.

"I can't eat all this," I say.

They ain't got but just three little old cakes there. I'm so hungry right now, the Lord knows I can eat a hundred times three, but I want my mama to have one.

Mama don't even look my way. She knows I'm hungry, she knows I want it. I 300
let it stay there a little while, then I get it and eat it. I eat just on my front teeth, though, 'cause if cake touch that back tooth I know what'll happen. Thank God it ain't hurt me at all today.

After I finish eating I see the man go to the juke box. He drops a nickel in it, then he just stand there a little while looking at the record. Mama tells me keep my eyes in front where they belong. I turn my head like she say, but then I hear the man coming toward us.

"Dance, pretty?" he says.

Mama gets up to dance with him. But 'fore you know it, she done grabbed the little man in the collar and done heaved him 'side the wall. He hit the wall so hard he stop the juke box from playing.

"Some pimp," the lady back of the counter says. "Some pimp."

305   The little man jumps up off the floor and starts toward my mama. 'Fore you know it, Mama done sprung open her knife and she's waiting for him.

"Come on," she says. "Come on. I'll gut you from your neighbo to your throat. Come on."

I go up to the little man to hit him, but Mama makes me come and stand 'side her. The little man looks at me and Mama and goes on back to the counter.

"Some pimp," the lady back of the counter says. "Some pimp." She starts laughing and pointing at the little man. "Yes sir, you a pimp, all right. Yes sir-ree."

13

"Fasten that coat, let's go," Mama says.

310   "You don't have to leave," the lady says.

Mama don't answer the lady, and we right out in the cold again. I'm warm right now—my hands, my ears, my feet—but I know this ain't go'n last too long. It done sleet so much now you got ice everywhere you look.

We cross the railroad tracks, and soon's we do, I get cold. That wind goes through this little old coat like it ain't even there. I got on a shirt and a sweater under the coat, but that wind don't pay them no mind. I look up and I can see we got a long way to go. I wonder if we go'n make it 'fore I get too cold.

We cross over to walk on the sidewalk. They got just one sidewalk back here, and it's over there.

After we go just a little piece, I smell bread cooking. I look, then I see a baker shop. When we get closer, I can smell it more better. I shut my eyes and make 'tend I'm eating. But I keep them shut too long and I butt up 'gainst a telephone post. Mama grabs me and see if I'm hurt. I ain't bleeding or nothing and she turns me loose.

315   I can feel I'm getting colder and colder, and I look up to see how far we still got to go. Uptown is 'way up yonder. A half mile more, I reckon. I try to think of something. They say think and you won't get cold. I think of that poem, "Annabel Lee." I ain't been to school in so long—this bad weather—I reckon they done passed "Annabel Lee" by now. But passed it or not, I'm sure Miss Walker go'n make me recite it when I get there. That woman don't never forget nothing. I ain't never seen nobody like that in my life.

I'm still getting cold. "Annabel Lee" or no "Annabel Lee," I'm still getting cold. But I can see we getting closer. We getting there gradually.

Soon 's we turn the corner, I see a little old white lady up in front of us. She's the only lady on the street. She's all in black and she's got a long black rag over her head.

"Stop," she says.

Me and Mama stop and look at her. She must be crazy to be out in all this bad weather. Ain't got but a few other people out there, and all of them's men.

"Y'all done ate?" she says.   320

"Just finish," Mama says.

"Y'all must be cold then?" she says.

"We headed for the dentist," Mama says. "We'll warm up when we get there."

"What dentist?" the old lady says. "Mr. Bassett?"

"Yes, ma'am," Mama says.   325

"Come on in," the old lady says. "I'll telephone him and tell him y'all coming."

Me and Mama follow the old lady in the store. It's a little bitty store, and it don't have much in there. The old lady takes off her head rag and folds it up.

"Helena?" somebody calls from the back.

"Yes, Alnest?" the old lady says.

"Did you see them?"   330

"They're here. Standing beside me."

"Good. Now you can stay inside."

The old lady looks at Mama. Mama's waiting to hear what she brought us in here for. I'm waiting for that, too.

'I saw y'all each time you went by," she says. "I came out to catch you, but you were gone."

"We went back of town," Mama says.   335

"Did you eat?"

"Yes, ma'am."

The old lady looks at Mama a long time, like she's thinking Mama might be just saying that. Mama looks right back at her. The old lady looks at me to see what I have to say. I don't say nothing. I sure ain't going 'gainst my mama.

"There's food in the kitchen," she says to Mama. "I've been keeping it warm."

Mama turns right around and starts for the door.   340

"Just a minute," the old lady says. Mama stops. "The boy'll have to work for it. It isn't free."

"We don't take no handout," Mama says.

"I'm not handing out anything," the old lady says. "I need my garbage moved to the front. Ernest has a bad cold and can't go out there."

"James'll move it for you," Mama says.

"Not unless you eat," the old lady says. "I'm old, but I have my pride, too, 345 you know."

Mama can see she ain't go'n beat this old lady down, so she just shakes her head.

"All right," the old lady says. "Come into the kitchen."

She leads the way with that rag in her hand. The kitchen is a little bitty little old thing, too. The table and the stove just 'bout fill it up. They got a little room to the side. Somebody in there laying 'cross the bed—'cause I can see one of his feet. Must be the person she was talking to: Ernest or Alnest—something like that.

"Sit down," the old lady says to Mama. "Not you," she says to me. "You have to move the cans."

350 "Helena?" the man says in the other room.

"Yes, Alnest?" the old lady says.

"Are you going out there again?"

"I must show the boy where the garbage is, Alnest," the old lady says.

"Keep that shawl over your head," the old man says.

355 "You don't have to remind me, Alnest. Come, boy," the old lady says.

We go out in the yard. Little old back yard ain't no bigger than the store or the kitchen. But it can sleet here just like it can sleet in any big back yard. And 'fore you know it, I'm trembling.

"There," the old lady says, pointing to the cans. I pick up one of the cans and set it right back down. The can's so light, I'm go'n see what's inside of it.

"Here," the old lady says. "Leave that can alone."

I look back at her standing there in the door. She's got that black rag wrapped round her shoulders, and she's pointing one of her little old fingers at me.

360 "Pick it up and carry it to the front," she says. I go by her with the can, and she's looking at me all the time. I'm sure the can's empty. I'm sure she could've carried it herself—maybe both of them at the same time. "Set it on the sidewalk by the door and come back for the other one," she says.

I go and come back, and Mama looks at me when I pass her. I get the other can and take it to the front. It don't feel a bit heavier than that first one. I tell myself I ain't go'n be nobody's fool, and I'm go'n look inside this can to see just what I been hauling. First, I look up the street, then down the street. Nobody coming. Then I look over my shoulder toward the door. That little old lady done slipped up there quiet 's mouse, watching me again. Look like she knowed what I was go'n do.

"Ehh, Lord," she says. "Children, children. Come in here, boy, and go wash your hands."

I follow her in the kitchen. She points toward the bathroom, and I go in there and wash up. Little bitty old bathroom, but it's clean, clean. I don't use any of her towels; I wipe my hands on my pants legs.

When I come back in the kitchen, the old lady done dished up the food. Rice, gravy, meat—and she even got some lettuce and tomato in a saucer. She even got a glass of milk and a piece of cake there, too. It looks so good, I almost start eating 'fore I say my blessing.

365 "Helena?" the old man says.

"Yes, Alnest?"

"Are they eating?"

"Yes," she says.

"Good," he says. "Now you'll stay inside."

370 The old lady goes in there where he is and I can hear them talking. I look at Mama. She's eating slow like she's thinking. I wonder what's the matter now. I reckon she's thinking 'bout home.

The old lady comes back in the kitchen.

"I talked to Dr. Bassett's nurse," she says. "Dr. Bassett will take you as soon as you get there."

"Thank you, ma'am," Mama says.

"Perfectly all right," the old lady says. "Which one is it?"

Mama nods toward me. The old lady looks at me real sad. I look sad, too.   375

"You're not afraid, are you?" she says.

"No, ma'am," I say.

"That's a good boy," the old lady says. "Nothing to be afraid of. Dr. Bassett will not hurt you."

When me and Mama get through eating, we thank the old lady again.

"Helena, are they leaving?" the old man says.   380

"Yes, Alnest."

"Tell them I say good-bye."

"They can hear you, Alnest."

"Good-bye both mother and son," the old man says. "And may God be with you."

Me and Mama tell the old man good-bye, and we follow the old lady in the   385
front room. Mama opens the door to go out, but she stops and comes back in the store.

"You sell salt meat?" she says.

"Yes."

"Give me two bits worth."

"That isn't very much salt meat," the old lady says.

"That's all I have," Mama says.   390

The old lady goes back of the counter and cuts a big piece off the chunk. Then she wraps it up and puts it in a paper bag.

"Two bits," she says.

"That looks like awful lot of meat for a quarter," Mama says.

"Two bits," the old lady says. "I've been selling salt meat behind this counter twenty-five years. I think I know what I'm doing."

"You got a scale there," Mama says.   395

"What?" the old lady says.

"Weigh it," Mama says.

"What?" the old lady says. "Are you telling me how to run my business?"

"Thanks very much for the food," Mama says.

"Just a minute," the old lady says.   400

"James," Mama says to me. I move toward the door.

"Just one minute, I said," the old lady says.

Me and Mama stop again and look at her. The old lady takes the meat out of the bag and unwraps it and cuts 'bout half of it off. Then she wraps it up again and juggs it back in the bag and gives the bag to Mama. Mama lays the quarter on the counter.

"Your kindness will never be forgotten," she says. "James," she says to me.

We go out, and the old lady comes to the door to look at us. After we go a little   405
piece I look back, and she's still there watching us.

The sleet's coming down heavy, heavy now, and I turn up my coat collar to keep my neck warm. My mama tells me turn it right back down.

"You not a bum," she says. "You a man."

QUESTIONS FOR DISCUSSION AND WRITING

1. How are the conflicts in the story personified in the characters of the preacher, the young man with the book, the pimp, and the old couple?

2. How does the reader's view of the mother's motives and behavior change as the story develops? Why does the narrator want to be like the young man with the book?

3. Why is the winter setting important to the development of the story? What details does Gaines use to document the social context of the story?

4. Is the narrator in this story—James—reliable even though he is only eight years old? Explain your answer. How might the narrator and the reader interpret the events in this story differently?

5. How does the story lead the reader to believe that James will become a man of both reason and faith?

Stories for Comparison

Ralph Ellison's "Battle Royal" (pages 472–483); Eudora Welty's "A Worn Path" (pages 1174–1180).

44

....

GABRIEL   GARCÍA   MÁRQUEZ

A Very Old Man with Enormous Wings
A Tale for Children
TRANSLATED BY GREGORY RABASSA

GABRIEL GARCÍA MÁRQUEZ was born in 1928 in Aracataca, Colombia, a remote town near the Caribbean seacoast. Although he was brought up in considerable poverty, García Márquez was sent away to school at the age of eight to attend the Liceo Nacional near Bogotá. After his graduation in 1946, he began studying at Bogotá University until the civil war forced the university to close in 1948. García Márquez moved to Cartagena and began his career as a journalist, moving on to Barranquilla in 1950, where he wrote a daily column for *El Heraldo* and lived in a four-story brothel called "The Skyscraper." In 1954 he returned to Bogotá to work as a reporter and film critic for *El Espectador.* After the publication of his first collection of stories, *Leaf Storm and Other Stories* (1955), García Márquez traveled to Europe as a foreign correspondent, but political turmoil at home closed down *El Espectador,* putting him out of work. He spent the next few years in Paris, living in great poverty and writing two short novels, *No One Writes to the Colonel* (1958) and *In Evil Hour* (1961). After living for a time in Havana, he moved to Mexico City to begin a new career as a screenwriter. It was during this period that García Márquez wrote his masterpiece, *One Hundred Years of Solitude* (1967). His later works include a collection of short stories, *The Incredible and Sad Story of Innocent Eréndira and Her Heartless Grandmother* (1972), and three novels, *The Autumn of the Patriarch* (1975), *Chronicle of a Death Foretold* (1982), and *The Story of the Shipwrecked Sailor: Who . . .* (1986). In 1982, García Márquez was awarded the Nobel Prize for literature. "A Very Old Man with Enormous Wings," reprinted from *Leaf Storm and Other Stories,* documents the reactions of a community to a strange visitor.

O n the third day of rain they had killed so many crabs inside the house that Pelayo had to cross his drenched courtyard and throw them into the sea, because the newborn child had a temperature all night and they thought it was due to the stench. The world had been sad since Tuesday. Sea and sky were a single ashgray thing and the sands of the beach, which on March nights glimmered like powdered light, had become a stew of mud and rotten shellfish. The light was so weak at noon that when Pelayo was coming back to the house after throwing away the crabs, it was hard for him to see what it was that was moving and groaning in the rear of the courtyard. He had to go very close to see that it was an old man, a very old man, lying face down in the mud, who, in spite of his tremendous efforts, couldn't get up, impeded by his enormous wings.

Frightened by that nightmare, Pelayo ran to get Elisenda, his wife, who was putting compresses on the sick child, and he took her to the rear of the courtyard. They both looked at the fallen body with mute stupor. He was dressed like a ragpicker. There were only a few faded hairs left on his bald skull and very few teeth in his mouth, and his pitiful condition of a drenched great-grandfather had taken away any sense of grandeur he might have had. His huge buzzard wings, dirty and half-plucked, were forever entangled in the mud. They looked at him so long and so closely that Pelayo and Elisenda very soon overcame their surprise and in the end found him familiar. Then they dared speak to him, and he answered in an incomprehensible dialect with a strong sailor's voice. That was how they skipped over the inconvenience of the wings and quite intelligently concluded that he was a lonely castaway from some foreign ship wrecked by the storm. And yet, they called in a neighbor woman who knew everything about life and death to see him, and all she needed was one look to show them their mistake.

"He's an angel," she told them. "He must have been coming for the child, but the poor fellow is so old that the rain knocked him down."

On the following day everyone knew that a flesh-and-blood angel was held captive in Pelayo's house. Against the judgment of the wise neighbor woman, for whom angels in those times were the fugitive survivors of a celestial conspiracy, they did not have the heart to club him to death. Pelayo watched over him all afternoon from the kitchen, armed with his bailiff's club, and before going to bed he dragged him out of the mud and locked him up with the hens in the wire chicken coop. In the middle of the night, when the rain stopped, Pelayo and Elisenda were still killing crabs. A short time afterward the child woke up without a fever and with a desire to eat. Then they felt magnanimous and decided to put the angel on a raft with fresh water and provisions for three days and leave him to his fate on the high seas. But when they went out into the courtyard with the first light of dawn, they found the whole neighborhood in front of the chicken coop having fun with the angel, without the slightest reverence, tossing him things to eat through the openings in the wire as if he weren't a supernatural creature but a circus animal.

5   Father Gonzaga arrived before seven o'clock, alarmed at the strange news. By that time onlookers less frivolous than those at dawn had already arrived and they were making all kinds of conjectures concerning the captive's future. The simplest among them thought that he should be named mayor of the world. Others of sterner mind felt that he should be promoted to the rank of five-star general in order to win all wars. Some visionaries hoped that he could be put to stud in order to implant on earth a race of winged wise men who could take charge of the universe. But Father Gonzaga, before becoming a priest, had been a robust woodcutter. Standing by the wire, he reviewed his catechism in an instant and asked them to open the door so that he could take a close look at that pitiful man who looked more like a huge decrepit hen among the fascinated chickens. He was lying in a corner drying his open wings in the sunlight among the fruit peels and breakfast leftovers that the early risers had thrown him. Alien to the impertinences of the world, he only lifted his antiquarian eyes and murmured something in his dialect when Father Gonzaga went into the chicken coop and said good morning to him in Latin. The parish priest had his first suspicion of an impostor when he saw that he did not understand the language of God or know how to greet His ministers. Then he noticed that seen close up he was much too human; he had an unbearable smell of the outdoors, the back side of his wings was strewn with parasites and his main feathers had been mistreated by terrestrial winds, and nothing about him measured up to the proud dignity of angels. Then he came out of the chicken coop and in a brief sermon warned the curious against the risks of being ingenuous. He reminded them that the devil had the bad habit of making use of carnival tricks in order to confuse the unwary. He argued that if wings were not the essential element in determining the difference between a hawk and an airplane, they were even less so in the recognition of angels. Nevertheless, he promised to write a letter to his bishop so that the latter would write to his primate so that the latter would write to the Supreme Pontiff in order to get the final verdict from the highest courts.

His prudence fell on sterile hearts. The news of the captive angel spread with such rapidity that after a few hours the courtyard had the bustle of a marketplace and they had to call in troops with fixed bayonets to disperse the mob that was about to knock the house down. Elisenda, her spine all twisted from sweeping up so much marketplace trash, then got the idea of fencing in the yard and charging five cents admission to see the angel.

The curious came from far away. A traveling carnival arrived with a flying acrobat who buzzed over the crowd several times, but no one paid any attention to him because his wings were not those of an angel but, rather, those of a sidereal bat. The most unfortunate invalids on earth came in search of health: a poor woman who since childhood had been counting her heartbeats and had run out of numbers; a Portuguese man who couldn't sleep because the noise of the stars disturbed him; a sleepwalker who got up at night to undo the things he had done while awake; and many others with less serious ailments. In the midst of that shipwreck disorder that made the earth tremble, Pelayo and Elisenda were happy with fatigue, for in less than a week they had crammed their rooms with money and the line of pilgrims waiting their turn to enter still reached beyond the horizon.

The angel was the only one who took no part in his own act. He spent his time trying to get comfortable in his borrowed nest, befuddled by the hellish heat of the oil lamps and sacramental candles that had been placed along the wire. At first they tried to make him eat some mothballs, which, according to the wisdom of the wise neighbor woman, were the food prescribed for angels. But he turned them down, just as he turned down the papal lunches that the penitents brought him, and they never found out whether it was because he was an angel or because he was an old man that in the end he ate nothing but eggplant mush. His only supernatural virtue seemed to be patience. Especially during the first days, when the hens pecked at him, searching for the stellar parasites that proliferated in his wings, and the cripples pulled out feathers to touch their defective parts with, and even the most merciful threw stones at him, trying to get him to rise so they could see him standing. The only time they succeeded in arousing him was when they burned his side with an iron for branding steers, for he had been motionless for so many hours that they thought he was dead. He awoke with a start, ranting in his hermetic language and with tears in his eyes, and he flapped his wings a couple of times, which brought on a whirlwind of chicken dung and lunar dust and a gale of panic that did not seem to be of this world. Although many thought that his reaction had been one not of rage but of pain, from then on they were careful not to annoy him, because the majority understood that his passivity was not that of a hero taking his ease but that of a cataclysm in repose.

Father Gonzaga held back the crowd's frivolity with formulas of maidservant inspiration while awaiting the arrival of a final judgment on the nature of the captive. But the mail from Rome showed no sense of urgency. They spent their time finding out if the prisoner had a navel, if his dialect had any connection with Aramaic, how many times he could fit on the head of a pin, or whether he wasn't just a Norwegian with wings. Those meager letters might have come and gone until the end of time if a providential event had not put an end to the priest's tribulations.

It so happened that during those days, among so many other carnival attractions, there arrived in town the traveling show of the woman who had been changed into a spider for having disobeyed her parents. The admission to see her was not only less than the admission to see the angel, but people were permitted to ask her all manner of questions about her absurd state and to examine her up and down so that no one would ever doubt the truth of her horror. She was a frightful tarantula the size of a ram and with the head of a sad maiden. What was most heart-rending, however, was not her outlandish shape but the sincere affliction with which she recounted the details of her misfortune. While still practically a child she had sneaked out of her parents' house to go to a dance, and while she was coming back through the woods after having danced all night without permission, a fearful thunderclap rent the sky in two and through the crack came the lightning bolt of brimstone that changed her into a spider. Her only nourishment came from the meatballs that charitable souls chose to toss into her mouth. A spectacle like that, full of so much human truth and with such a fearful lesson, was bound to defeat without even trying that of a haughty angel who scarcely deigned to look at mortals. Besides, the few miracles attributed to the angel showed a certain mental disorder, like the blind man who didn't recover his sight but grew three new teeth, or the paralytic who didn't get to walk but almost won the lottery, and the leper whose sores sprouted sunflowers. Those consolation miracles, which were more like mocking fun, had already ruined the angel's reputation when the woman who had been changed into a spider finally crushed him completely. That was how Father Gonzaga was cured forever of his insomnia and Pelayo's courtyard went back to being as empty as during the time it had rained for three days and crabs walked through the bedrooms.

The owners of the house had no reason to lament. With the money they saved they built a two-story mansion with balconies and gardens and high netting so that crabs wouldn't get in during the winter, and with iron bars on the windows so that angels wouldn't get in. Pelayo also set up a rabbit warren close to town and gave up his job as bailiff for good, and Elisenda bought some satin pumps with high heels and many dresses of iridescent silk, the kind worn on Sunday by the most desirable women in those times. The chicken coop was the only thing that didn't receive any attention. If they washed it down with creolin and burned tears of myrrh inside it every so often, it was not in homage to the angel but to drive away the dung heap stench that still hung everywhere like a ghost and was turning the new house into an old one. At first, when the child learned to walk, they were careful that he not get too close to the chicken coop. But then they began to lose their fears and got used to the smell, and before the child got his second teeth he'd gone inside the chicken coop to play, where the wires were falling apart. The angel was no less standoffish with him than with other mortals, but he tolerated the most ingenious infamies with the patience of a dog who had no illusions. They both came down with chicken pox at the same time. The doctor who took care of the child couldn't resist the temptation to listen to the angel's heart, and he found so much whistling in the heart and so many sounds in his kidneys that it seemed impossible for him to be alive. What surprised him most, however, was the logic of his wings. They seemed so natural on that completely human organism that he couldn't understand why other men didn't have them too.

When the child began school it had been some time since the sun and rain had caused the collapse of the chicken coop. The angel went dragging himself about here and there like a stray dying man. They would drive him out of the bedroom with a broom and a moment later find him in the kitchen. He seemed to be in so many places at the same time that they grew to think that he'd been duplicated, that he was reproducing himself all through the house, and the exasperated and unhinged Elisenda shouted that it was awful living in that hell full of angels. He could scarcely eat and his antiquarian eyes had also become so foggy that he went about bumping into posts. All he had left were the bare cannulae of his last feathers. Pelayo threw a blanket over him and extended him the charity of letting him sleep in the shed, and only then did they notice that he had a temperature at night, and was delirious with the tongue twisters of an old Norwegian. That was one of the few times they became alarmed, for they thought he was going to die and not even the wise neighbor woman had been able to tell them what to do with dead angels.

And yet he not only survived his worst winter, but seemed improved with the first sunny days. He remained motionless for several days in the farthest corner of the courtyard, where no one would see him, and at the beginning of December some large, stiff feathers began to grow on his wings, the feathers of a scarecrow, which looked more like another misfortune of decrepitude. But he must have known the reason for those changes, for he was quite careful that no one should notice them, that no one should hear the sea chanteys that he sometimes sang under the stars. One morning Elisenda was cutting some bunches of onions for lunch when a wind that seemed to come from the high seas blew into the kitchen. Then she went to the window and caught the angel in his first attempts at flight. They were so clumsy that his fingernails opened a furrow in the vegetable patch and he was on the point of knocking the shed down with the ungainly flapping that slipped on the light and couldn't get a grip on the air. But he did manage to gain altitude. Elisenda let out a sigh of relief, for herself and for him, when she saw him pass over the last houses, holding himself up in some way with the risky flapping of a senile vulture. She kept watching him even when she was through cutting the onions and she kept on watching until it was no longer possible for her to see him, because then he was no longer an annoyance in her life but an imaginary dot on the horizon of the sea.

QUESTIONS FOR DISCUSSION AND WRITING

1. What expectations does the "angel" produce within the community and surrounding territories? How does the spider woman revise those expectations? What events enable the angel to depart?

2. What is Pelayo's first impression of the old man with wings? How does his impression change once the neighbor woman identifies his visitor as an angel? Why does the priest suspect the angel is an impostor? What single virtue characterizes the angel during the story?

3. How does the opening sentence establish an appropriate setting for the appearance of the angel? What kind of world is represented in a story where people believe in angels, celestial conspiracies, and consolation miracles?

4. How does the subtitle suggest the author's point of view toward the story? To what extent do the various characters in the story exhibit a childlike point of view toward the events they witness?

5. What is the "fearful lesson" of the angel's story? How does it compare with the "human truth" of the spider woman?

Stories for Comparison

Isabel Allende's "Phantom Palace" (pages 174–183); Bernard Malamud's "The Magic Barrel" (pages 850–863).

45

....

W I L L I A M   G A S S

In the Heart of the Heart of the Country

WILLIAM GASS was born in 1924 in Fargo, North Dakota, and educated at Kenyon College and Cornell University. Although he is best known for his experimental works of fiction, he has spent most of his career as a professor of philosophy—at College of Wooster, Purdue University, and Washington University, St. Louis. His novels include *Omensetter's Luck* (1966) and *Tunnel* (1995), and his stories are collected in *In the Heart of the Heart of the Country* (1968). He is also the author of *On Being Blue: A Philosophical Inquiry* (1975) and several collections of nonfiction, including *Fiction and the Figures of Life* (1970) and *The Habitation of the Word* (1985). The following excerpt from "In the Heart of the Heart of the Country" provides a complex view of a place and the writer's reading of its predicaments.

A Place

S o I have sailed the seas and come . . .
                            to B . . .
a small town fastened to a field in Indiana. Twice there have been twelve hundred people here to answer to the census. The town is outstandingly neat and shady, and always puts its best side to the highway. On one lawn there's even a wood or plastic iron deer.

You can reach us by crossing a creek. In the spring the lawns are green, the for-sythia is singing, and even the railroad that guts the town has straight bright rails which hum when the train is coming, and the train itself has a welcome horning sound.

Down the back streets the asphalt crumbles into gravel. There's Westbrook's, with the geraniums, Horsefall's, Mott's. The sidewalk shatters. Gravel dust rises like breath behind the wagons. And I am in retirement from love.

Weather

In the Midwest, around the lower Lakes, the sky in the winter is heavy and close, and it is a rare day, a day to remark on, when the sky lifts and allows the heart up. I am keeping count, and as I write this page, it is eleven days since I have seen the sun.

My House

There's a row of headless maples behind my house, cut to free the passage of elec- 5 tric wires. High stumps, ten feet tall, remain, and I climb these like a boy to watch the country sail away from me. They are ordinary fields, a little more uneven than they should be, since in the spring they puddle. The topsoil's thin, but only moder-ately stony. Corn is grown one year, soybeans another. At dusk starlings darken the single tree—a larch—which stands in the middle. When the sky moves, fields move under it. I feel, on my perch, that I've lost my years. It's as though I were living at last in my eyes, as I have always dreamed of doing, and I think then I know why I've come here: to see, and so to go out against new things—oh god how easily—like air in a breeze. It's true there are moments—foolish moments, ecstasy on a tree stump—when I'm all but gone, scattered I like to think like seed, for I'm the sort now in the fool's position of having love left over which I'd like to lose; what good is it now to me, candy ungiven after Halloween?

A Person

There are vacant lots on either side of Billy Holsclaw's house. As the weather im-proves, they fill with hollyhocks. From spring through fall, Billy collects coal and wood and puts the lumps and pieces in piles near his door, for keeping warm is his one work. I see him most often on mild days sitting on his doorsill in the sun. I notice he's squinting a little, which is perhaps the reason he doesn't cackle as I pass. His house is the size of a single garage, and very old. It shed its paint with its youth, and its boards are a warped and weathered gray. So is Billy. He wears a short lumpy faded black coat when it's cold, otherwise he always goes about in the same loose, grease-spotted shirt and trousers. I suspect his galluses were yellow once, when they were new.

Wires

These wires offend me. Three trees were maimed on their account, and now these wires deface the sky. They cross like a fence in front of me, enclosing the crows with the clouds. I can't reach in, but like a stick, I throw my feelings over. What is it that offends me? I am on my stump, I've built a platform there and the wires prevent my going out. The cut trees, the black wires, all the beyond birds therefore anger me. When I've wormed through a fence to reach a meadow, do I ever feel the same about the field? . . .

My House

Leaves move in the windows. I cannot tell you yet how beautiful it is, what it means. But they do move. They move in the glass.

People

Their hair in curlers and their heads wrapped in loud scarves, young mothers, fattish in trousers, lounge about in the speedwash, smoking cigarettes, eating candy, drinking pop, thumbing magazines, and screaming at their children above the whir and rumble of the machines.

10   At the bank a young man freshly pressed is letting himself in with a key. Along the street, delicately teetering, many grandfathers move in a dream. During the murderous heat of summer, they perch on window ledges, their feet dangling just inside the narrow shelf of shade the store has made, staring steadily into the street. Where their consciousness has gone I can't say. It's not in the eyes. Perhaps it's diffuse, all temperature and skin, like an infant's, though more mild. Near the corner there are several large overalled men employed in standing. A truck turns to be weighed on the scales at the Feed and Grain. Images drift on the drugstore window. The wind has blown the smell of cattle into town. Our eyes have been driven in like the eyes of the old men. And there's no one to have mercy on us.

Vital Data

There are two restaurants here and a tearoom, two bars, one bank, three barbers, one with a green shade with which he blinds his window, two groceries, a dealer in Fords, one drug, one hardware, and one appliance store, several that sell feed, grain, and farm equipment, an antique shop, a poolroom, a laundromat, three doctors, a dentist, a plumber, a vet, a funeral home in elegant repair the color of a buttercup, numerous beauty parlors which open and shut like night-blooming plants, a tiny dime and department store of no width but several floors, a hutch, homemade, where you can order, after lying down or squirming in, furniture that's been fashioned from bent lengths of stainless tubing, glowing plastic, metallic thread, and clear shellac, an American Legion Post and a root beer stand, little agencies for this and that: cosmetics, brushes, insurance, greeting cards and garden produce—anything—sample shoes—which do their business out of hats and satchels, over coffee cups and dissolving sugar, a factory for making paper sacks and pasteboard boxes that's lodged in an old brick building bearing the legend OPERA HOUSE, still faintly golden, on its roof, a library given by Carnegie, a post office, a school, a railroad station, fire station, lumberyard, telephone company, welding shop, garage . . . and spotted through the town from one end to the other in a line along the highway, gas stations to the number five.

My House, This Place and Body

I have met with some mischance, wings withering, as Plato says obscurely, and across the breadth of Ohio, like heaven on a table, I've fallen as far as the poet, to the sixth sort of body, this house in B, in Indiana, with its blue and gray bewitching windows, holy magical insides. Great thick evergreens protect its entry. And I live *in*.

Lost in the corn rows, I remember feeling just another stalk, and thus this country takes me over in the way I occupy myself when I am well . . . completely—to the edge of both my house and body. No one notices, when they walk by, that I am brimming in the doorways. My house, this place and body, I've come in mourning to be born in. To anybody else it's pretty silly: love. Why should I feel a loss? How am I bereft? She was never mine; she was a fiction, always a golden tomgirl, barefoot, with an adolescent's slouch and a boy's taste for sports and fishing, a figure out of Twain, or worse, in Riley. Age cannot be kind.

There's little hand-in-hand here . . . not in B. No one touches except in rage. Occasionally girls will twine their arms about each other and lurch along, school out, toward home and play. I dreamed my lips would drift down your back like a skiff on a river. I'd follow a vein with the point of my finger, hold your bare feet in my naked hands.

My House, My Cat, My Company

I must organize myself. I must, as they say, pull myself together, dump this cat from my lap, stir—yes, resolve, move, do. But do what? My will is like the rosy dustlike light in this room: soft, diffuse, and gently comforting. It lets me do . . . anything . . . nothing. My ears hear what they happen to; I eat what's put before me; my eyes see what blunders into them; my thoughts are not thoughts, they are dreams. I'm empty or I'm full . . . depending; and I cannot choose. I sink my claws in Tick's fur and scratch the bones of his back until his rear rises amorously. Mr. Tick, I murmur, I must organize myself. I must pull myself together. And Mr. Tick rolls over on his belly, all ooze.

I spill Mr. Tick when I've rubbed his stomach. Shoo. He steps away slowly, his long tail rhyming with his paws. How beautifully he moves, I think; how beautifully, like you, he commands his loving, how beautifully he accepts. So I rise and wander from room to room, up and down, gazing through most of my forty-one windows. How well this house receives its loving too. Let out like Mr. Tick, my eyes sink in the shrubbery. I am not here; I've passed the glass, passed second-story spaces, flown by branches, brilliant berries, to the ground, grass high in seed and leafage every season; and it is the same as when I passed above you in my aged, ardent body; it's, in short, a kind of love; and I am learning to restore myself, my house, my body, by paying court to gardens, cats, and running water, and with neighbors keeping company.

Mrs. Desmond is my right-hand friend; she's eighty-five. A thin white mist of hair, fine and tangled, manifests the climate of her mind. She is habitually suspicious, fretful, nervous. Burglars break in at noon. Children trespass. Even now they are shaking the pear tree, stealing rhubarb, denting lawn. Flies caught in the screens and numbed by frost awake in the heat to buzz and scrape the metal cloth and frighten her, though she is deaf to me, and consequently cannot hear them. Boards creak, the wind whistles across the chimney mouth, drafts cruise like fish through the hollow rooms. It is herself she hears, her own flesh failing, for only death will preserve her from those daily chores she climbs like stairs, and all that anxious waiting. Is it now, she wonders. No? Then: is it now?

We do not converse. She visits me to talk. My task to murmur. She talks about her grandsons, her daughter who lives in Delphi, her sister or her husband—both gone—obscure friends—dead—obscurer aunts and uncles—lost—ancient neighbors, members of her church or of her clubs—passed or passing on; and in this way she brings the ends of her life together with a terrifying rush: she is a girl, a wife, a mother, widow, all at once. . . . Her talk's a fence—a shade drawn, window fastened, door that's locked—for no one dies taking tea in a kitchen; and as her years compress and begin to jumble, I really believe in the brevity of life; I sweat in my wonder; death is the dog down the street, the angry gander, bedroom spider, goblin who's come to get her; and it occurs to me that in my listening posture I'm the boy who suffered the winds of my grandfather with an exactly similar politeness, that I am, right now, all my ages, out in elbows, as angular as badly stacked cards. Thus was I, when I loved you, every man I could be, youth and child—far from enough—and you, so strangely ambiguous a being, met me, heart for spade, play after play, the whole run of our suits.

Mr. Tick, you do me honor. You not only lie in my lap, but you remain alive there, coiled like a fetus. Through your deep nap, I feel you hum. You are, and are not, a machine. You are alive, alive exactly, and it means nothing to you—much to me. You are a cat—you cannot understand—you are a cat so easily. Your nature is not something you must rise to. You, not I, live in: in house, in skin, in shrubbery. Yes. I think I shall hat my head with a steeple; turn church; devour people. Mr. Tick, though, has a tail he can twitch, he need not fly his Fancy. Claws, not metrical schema, poetry his paws; while smoothing . . . smoothing . . . smoothing roughly, his tongue laps its neatness.

More Vital Data

20 The town is exactly fifty houses, trailers, stores, and miscellaneous buildings long, but in places no streets deep. It takes on width as you drive south, always adding to the east. Most of the dwellings are fairly spacious farm houses in the customary white, with wide wraparound porches and tall narrow windows, though there are many of the grander kind—fretted, scalloped, turreted, and decorated with clapboards set at angles or on end, with stained-glass windows at the stair landings and lots of wrought iron full of fancy curls—and a few of these look like castles in their rarer brick. Old stables serve as garages now, and the lots are large to contain them

and the vegetable and flower gardens which, ultimately, widows plant and weed and then entirely disappear in. The shade is ample, the grass is good, the sky a glorious fall violet; the apple trees are heavy and red, the roads are calm and empty; corn has sifted from the chains of tractored wagons to speckle the streets with gold and with the russet fragments of the cob, and a man would be a fool who wanted, blessed with this, to live anywhere else in the world.

Wires

Where sparrows sit like fists. Doves fly the steeple. In mist the wires change perspective, rise and twist. If they led to you, I would know what they were. Thoughts passing often, like the starlings who flock these fields at evening to sleep in the trees beyond, would form a family of paths like this; they'd foot down the natural height of air to just about a bird's perch. But they do not lead to you.

> Of whose beauty it was sung
> She shall make the old man young.

They fasten me.

If I walked straight on, in my present mood, I would reach the Wabash. It's not a mood in which I'd choose to conjure you. Similes dangle like baubles from me. This time of the year the river is slow and shallow, the clay banks crack in the sun, weeds surprise the sandbars. The air is moist and I am sweating. It's impossible to rhyme in this dust. Everything—sky, the cornfield, stump, wild daisies, my old clothes and pressless feelings—seems fabricated for installment purchase. Yes, Christ, I am suffering a summer Christmas; and I cannot walk under the wires. The sparrows scatter like handfuls of gravel. Really, wires are voices in thin strips. They are words wound in cables. Bars of connection.

Weather

I would rather it were the weather that was to blame for what I am and what my friends and neighbors are—we who live here in the heart of the country. Better the weather, the wind, the pale dying snow . . . the snow—why not the snow? There's never much really, not around the lower Lakes anyway, not enough to boast about, not enough to be useful. . . .

Place

I would rather it were the weather. It drives us in upon ourselves—an unlucky fate. Of course there is enough to stir our wonder anywhere; there's enough to love, any-where, if one is strong enough, if one is diligent enough, if one is perceptive, patient, kind enough—whatever it takes; and surely it's better to live in the country, to live on a prairie by a drawing of rivers, in Iowa or Illinois or Indiana, say, than in any city. . . .

People

25 Aunt Pet's still able to drive her car—a high square Ford—even though she walks with difficulty and a stout stick. She has a watery gaze, a smooth plump face despite her age, and jet black hair in a bun. She has the slowest smile of anyone I ever saw, but she hates dogs, and not very long ago cracked the back of one she cornered in her garden. To prove her vigor she will tell you this, her smile breaking gently while she raises the knob of her stick to the level of your eyes.

Final Vital Data

The Modern Homemakers' Demonstration Club. The Prairie Home Demonstration Club. The Night-outers' Home Demonstration Club. The IOOF, FFF, VFW, WCTU, WSCS, 4-H, 40 and 8, Psi Iota Chi, and PTA. The Boy and Girl Scouts, Rainbows, Masons, Indians and Rebekah Lodge. Also the Past Noble Grand Club of the Rebekah Lodge. As well as the Moose and the Ladies of the Moose. The Elks, the Eagles, the Jaynettes and the Eastern Star. The Women's Literary Club, the Hobby Club, the Art Club, the Sunshine Society, the Dorcas Society, the Pythian Sisters, the Pilgrim Youth Fellowship, the American Legion, the American Legion Auxiliary, the American Legion Junior Auxiliary, the Garden Club, the Bridge for Fun Club, the What-can-you-do? Club, the Get Together Club, the Coterie Club, the Worth-while Club, the Let's Help Our Town Club, the No Name Club, the Forget-me-not Club, the Merry-go-round Club . . .

[Elementary] Education

Has a quarter disappeared from Paula Frosty's pocket book? Imagine the landscape of that face: no crayon could engender it; soft wax is wrong; thin wire in trifling snips might do the trick. Paula Frosty and Christopher Roger accuse the pale and splotchy Cheryl Pipes. But Miss Jakes, I *saw* her. Miss Jakes is so extremely vexed she snaps her pencil. What else is missing? I appoint you a detective, John: search her desk. Gum, candy, paper, pencils, marble, round eraser—whose? A thief. I can't watch her all the time. I'm here to teach. . . .

Another Person

I was raking leaves when Uncle Halley introduced himself to me. He said his name came from the comet, and that his mother had borne him prematurely in her fright of it. I thought of Hobbes, whom fear of the Spanish Armada had hurried into birth, and so I believed Uncle Halley to honor the philosopher, though Uncle Halley is a liar, and neither the one hundred twenty-nine nor the fifty-three he ought to be. That fall the leaves had burned themselves out on the trees, the leaf lobes had curled, and now they flocked noisily down the street and were broken in the wires of my rake. Uncle Halley was himself (like Mrs. Desmond and history generally) both deaf and implacable, and he shooed me down his basement stairs to a room set aside there for

stacks of newspapers reaching to the ceiling, boxes of leaflets and letters and programs, racks of photo albums, scrapbooks, bundles of rolled-up posters and maps,
flags and pennants and slanting piles of dusty magazines devoted mostly to motor-
ing and the Christian ethic. I saw a bird cage, a tray of butterflies, a bugle, a stiff
straw boater, and all kinds of tassels tied to a coat tree. He still possessed and had on
display the steering lever from his first car, a linen duster, driving gloves and gog-
gles, photographs along the wall of himself, his friends, and his various machines, a
shell from the first war, a record of "Ramona" nailed through its hole to a post, walking sticks and fanciful umbrellas, shoes of all sorts (his baby shoes, their counters
broken, were held in sorrow beneath my nose—they had not been bronzed, but he
might have them done someday before he died, he said), countless boxes of medals,
pins, beads, trinkets, toys, and keys (I scarcely saw—they flowed like jewels from
his palms), pictures of downtown when it was only a path by the railroad station, a
brightly colored globe of the world with a dent in Poland, antique guns, belt buckles, buttons, souvenir plates and cups and saucers (I can't remember all of it—I
won't), but I recall how shamefully, how rudely, how abruptly, I fled, a good story in
my mouth but death in my nostrils; and how afterward I busily, righteously, burned
my leaves as if I were purging the world of its years. I still wonder if this town—its
life, and mine now—isn't really a record like the one of "Ramona" that I used to
crank around on my grandmother's mahogany Victrola through lonely rainy days as
a kid.

[Basketball at] The Church [Gymnasium]

Friday night. Girls in dark skirts and white blouses sit in ranks and scream in concert. They carry funnels loosely stuffed with orange and black paper which they
shake wildly, and small megaphones through which, as drilled, they direct and mag-
nify their shouting. Their leaders, barely pubescent girls, prance and shake and whirl
their skirts above their bloomers. The young men, leaping, extend their arms and
race through puddles of amber light, their bodies glistening. In a lull, though it rarely
occurs, you can hear the squeak of tennis shoes against the floor. Then the yelling
begins again, and then continues; fathers, mothers, neighbors joining in to form a
single pulsing ululation—a cry of the whole community—for in this gymnasium
each body becomes the bodies beside it, pressed as they are together, thigh to thigh,
and the same shudder runs through all of them, and runs toward the same release.
Only the ball moves serenely through this dazzling din. Obedient to law it scarcely
speaks but caroms quietly and lives at peace.

Business

It is the week of Christmas and the stores, to accommodate the rush they hope for, 30
are remaining open in the evening. You can see snow falling in the cones of the street
lamps. The roads are filling—undisturbed. Strings of red and green lights droop over
the principal highway, and the water tower wears a star. The windows of the stores
have been bedizened. Shamelessly they beckon. But I am alone, leaning against a

pole—no . . . there is no one in sight. They're all at home, perhaps by their instruments, tuning in on their evenings, and like Ramona, tirelessly playing and replaying themselves. There's a speaker perched in the tower, and through the boughs of falling snow and over the vacant streets, it drapes the twisted and metallic strains of a tune that can barely be distinguished—yes, I believe it's one of the jolly ones, it's "Joy to the World." There's no one to hear the music but myself, and though I'm listening, I'm no longer certain. Perhaps the record's playing something else.

QUESTIONS FOR DISCUSSION AND WRITING

1. Is there a central plot in this story? How does the narrator use the divisions and headings as structuring devices? How are the seasons used to provide rhythm and structure in the story?

2. How is the narrator characterized by his reactions to those townspeople he returns to again and again? What do we know about him as poet and as lover?

3. How does the narrator mean for his readers to feel about the rural Midwest, its geography and culture? Does a unified sense of place emerge out of the apparent fragments he presents?

4. How does the narrator break down the distance between narrator and reader that one ordinarily expects in fiction? What is the effect of the intimacy between narrator and audience?

5. In how many different ways can one interpret the title of the story? The story begins with an allusion to William Butler Yeats's poem "Sailing to Byzantium," in which an old man renounces the world of flesh and reality for an idealized world of spiritual beauty. How does the story lead us to respond to that particular idea?

Stories for Comparison

Ernest Hemingway's "Big Two-Hearted River" (pages 650–663); William Faulkner's "A Rose for Emily" (pages 129–135).

46

ELLEN GILCHRIST

Traceleen, She's Still Talking

ELLEN GILCHRIST was born in 1935 in Vicksburg, Mississippi, and educated at Millsaps College and the University of Arkansas. She has worked as a reporter for *Vieux Carré Courier* and as a weekly commentator on National Public Radio's daily "Morning Edition" show. Gilchrist's first major publication was a collection of short stories, *In the Land of Dreamy Dreams* (1981), that focused on adolescents living in New Orleans and the Mississippi Delta. Her first novel, *The Annunciation* (1983), traces the life of a Mississippi girl from an early marriage to a wealthy New Orleans man to her membership in a hippie commune in the Ozarks. Gilchrist's next collection of stories, *Victory Over Japan* (1984), won the American Book Award for Fiction. Her other works include a book of poems, *The Land Surveyor's Daughter* (1974), a play, *A Season of Dreams,* based on the short stories by Eudora Welty, and several novels, including *Net of Jewels* (1992) and *Anabasis: A Journey to the Interior* (1994). In "Traceleen, She's Still Talking," reprinted from *Victory Over Japan,* a black maid recounts the comic adventures of a trip to Texas.

A nother time, Miss Crystal's brother Phelan bought this car in Germany and shipped it to New Orleans and we had to get it off the boat. There's more to getting a car off a boat than you'd imagine. In the end Miss Crystal had to call her cousin Harry that's a lawyer, and get him to call the owner of the shipyards and I don't know what all. That was just to get it off the boat. Before we even started driving it to Texas.

Miss Crystal is the lady I work for. I nurse her little girl, Crystal Anne, and I run the house. They're rich people, all the ones I'm talking about. Not that it does them much good that I can see. Miss Crystal's married to this man she can't stand. All the money in the world will not make up for that.

I'll say one thing for her though, she manages to have herself a good time. Her and her cousin Harry are always up to something. And Mr. Phelan, her brother that bought the car. He's always in on it too whenever he's in town. He's this big barrel-chested man that talks real low and looks at you out of the bottom of his eyes. Looks like he's sighting you down the barrel of a gun. He's always in Africa or getting married or something, sending Miss Crystal these clothes she don't wear. Lace dresses and negligees, satin pants, tennis dresses with little flowers appliquéd on them, like that. That's not her style. She like plain things. She never has flowers or writing on anything she wears.

I never had been to Texas before this trip. I'd heard all about it though. One time Mr. Phelan was in town and he got this screen and showed pictures of Texas, where he's got his ranch, and some of Brazil, where he'd been shooting jaguars. He had just got home from Brazil and he had all this jewelry with him made out of jaguar parts. He give Miss Crystal a necklace with a jaguar claw on it to make her play tennis better. She tried it a number of times but it never worked. She was so busy rubbing the claw for luck she forgot to look at the ball.

5   Finally she got so mad one day she just tore it off her neck, chain and all, and gave it to me. I put it away with the other stuff she gives me, newspaper clippings from when we get our name in the paper for having parties, silver spoons that get caught in the disposal, her old wedding ring. From her other marriage, to King's daddy. King's her son that smokes dope. She gave me the ring one day when she was drunk. I tried and tried to give it back but she made me keep it.

Anyway, it was Mr. Phelan that sent this car. He's her brother but they're not a thing alike. Miss Crystal don't like him very much. She's always badmouthing him to Mr. Harry behind his back. Saying her daddy give him all her money. So now it's nine o'clock in the morning and they're calling her to come down to the docks and get this car he shipped over here. Then Mr. Phelan he calls from Texas and begs her to do it. "I can't," she says into the phone. "I've got a match at ten. I can't leave people standing on the court to be your errand boy, Phelan. It's like car, you come and get it."

Well, he finally talked her into it and she puts me in the car with the baby, Crystal Anne, and off we go to the docks. First we have to go in this little smelly office and this Cajun wants her to fill out some forms about who owns the car. Act like he think we're trying to steal it or something.

Well, she raises Cain about the forms and then she calls her cousin Harry and he comes over and gets it straightened out. Mr. Harry's a lawyer, but he only works part time. He doesn't keep regular hours or go in an office or anything. He just does enough to get by. So he dresses and comes on down, all the time we're sitting in that office and I'm trying to keep Crystal Anne from touching anything, everything's so dirty. So finally Mr. Harry comes in wearing this good-looking white suit, all shaved and looking like he owns the world. Miss Crystal's crazy about Mr. Harry. She's always in a good mood when he's around. So he comes and makes all these calls, then everything is okay. Crystal Anne, she's rubbed her hands all over the back of his pants but he doesn't notice it. Miss Crystal's in a better mood now that Mr. Harry has put the Cajun in his place.

What really cheers her up though is the car. "Look at that goddamn car," she says. "Isn't that car just like Phelan. Isn't that the tackiest thing you've ever seen in your life?" We're in a warehouse. Right down on the docks. It's noisy as it can be and this Cajun is driving down a gangplank in the biggest, shinest dark green car you have ever seen in your life. A Mercedes Benz number six hundred. It's as big as a hearse and heavy looking. "Just look at it," Miss Crystal says. She's laughing her head off. The driver had got out and was letting her look inside. "Where in the name of God did he get this car?"

"It's the biggest one they make," the Cajun said. "I've never seen one bigger and 10 I unload them all the time." Mr. Harry had the explanation. "He got it from the head of the Mercedes company. It was being custom made for the president of the company. Phelan bought it right off the line and he needs someone to drive it down to Texas. Come on, leave the other cars here. Let's take it for a spin." He gave the Cajun a check and a twenty-dollar tip for putting up with Miss Crystal and the four of us got in the car. Crystal Anne needed changing in the worst way. As soon as we got inside I whipped off the old diaper and put on a new one. She'd been happy as she could be all morning, just as good as gold, watching everything the way she do and chewing on her pacifier.

"How much do you think Phelan paid for this thing?" Miss Crystal said. "I bet it cost a fortune. He's gone too far this time, Harry. Even Phelan can't justify this car." She was playing with the radio dials, running the automatic antenna up and down outside the window.

"He needs it for his hunts," Mr. Harry said. "To meet planes when people come down for the hunts. And he needs someone to get it down to Texas right away."

"Well, it won't be me," she said. "I'm not his errand boy. Let him fly up here and get it himself if he needs it so bad."

"He can't. Some men from Jackson are going down this weekend. They're paying two thousand dollars apiece to shoot a wild Russian boar. Phelan's got everything he owns in this operation, Crystal. You ought to want to see him make a go of it. Those animals he imported cost a lot of money."

"My money, Harry. My money. Every cent he spends is one more I'll never in- 15 herit. What kind of hunt? What's he up to now?" She turns her head and raises her eyes at me like only I can understand what she really means by anything.

"He's got the Lost Horizon stocked with game animals," Mr. Harry says, getting a serious expression on his face now he's talking hunting. All the men in Miss Crystal's family got that look. They put their elbows on their knees and their chins in their hand and put on that look whenever they got to talk about hunting anything, whether it's animals or King the time he ran away to the hippie commune. Scare me to death when they look like that. "He's got antelope and water buffalo and Russian boar. Well, the water buffalo aren't there yet but they're on their way. He's arranging African safaris for people that don't have time to go to Africa. It could be big, Crystal. He could get back all the money he lost in the duck decoy factory. He could make up for that land deal in Joberg."

"He's having safaris at the Lost Horizon? That little scraggly piece of land? There aren't even any trees. I don't believe anybody would pay two thousand dollars to go down there for anything."

"You'd be surprised what people will do. I put some of my own money into it. So I think I'll just drive the car on down there for him, to protect my investment."

"Russian boar?" she said, like she couldn't believe she heard right. "He's importing Russian boar?"

20   "We better be getting Crystal Anne on home now," I say from the back seat. "I need to be putting her down for a nap." We were out in Jefferson Parish, almost to the lake, cruising along, it's like riding in a big green cloud, air conditioning so quiet you can hear yourself breathe, big old tires going thump, thump.

"I think I'll go with you to Texas," Miss Crystal says. "I'll take Traceleen and Crystal Anne and go along. It's a perfect time. Manny's out of town and King's in Meridian with Big King. I want to see this operation. This boar hunt. Honest to God, Harry, Phelan's outside the limits. He really is, you know he is."

"You just can't resist the car," Mr. Harry says, laughing and smiling, laying his hand on her knee. "You want to keep riding in it as much as I do."

"Let's don't forget to stock the bar," she says. "I want to really fill it up. Fix it the way it ought to be."

So the upshot of it is the very next morning Miss Crystal and Crystal Anne and Mr. Harry and me are driving out of town on eye-ten headed for San Antonio. "I've never been to Texas in my life," I said to Mark, getting my permission to go. Mark's my husband, sweetest man you'll ever know. He don't stand in anybody's way. "Go ahead," he says. "See the country. I'll be right here when you get back, right where you left me." That's how it always is with Mark and me. Miss Crystal, she can't believe my luck in men. My first husband was just as sweet as Mark. I've had two since Miss Crystal knew me, one just as sweet as the other. "Your turn'll come," I tell her when she gets low. "You'll find your true love before it's over." Well, it didn't happen on this trip to Texas.

25   The first thing that happened was we stopped on the outskirts of Baton Rouge and stocked up the bar. They must have put two hundred dollars' worth of whiskey in the car. One hundred ninety-six, seventy-eight, to be exact. I saw it on the cash register when Mr. Harry paid the bill. Crystal Anne, she picks up a plastic lemon and starts sucking on the cap so he bought that too. I started getting worried when I saw all that whiskey. Mr. Harry, he's got a bad head for whiskey and much as I hate to say it Miss Crystal's not much better. They started mixing drinks in these little silver cups that come with the car and by the time we're to Lafayette I'm driving. Miss Crystal and Mr. Harry in the back seat drinking and singing country songs and me up front with Crystal Anne strapped in her seat sucking on the lemon. "Don't let her swallow the cap, Traceleen," Miss Crystal said. "Keep an eye on her." As if I didn't have enough to do driving the number six hundred down the road and it starting to rain. I mean rain. We were just outside of Crowley when it started coming down. Coming down in sheets!

People from other parts of the country they see us on television having our rains and floods and sometimes I wonder what they think it's like. Because the thing the television can't show them is the smell. Not a bad smell, a cold clean smell like breathing in water. We're below the sea in south Louisiana and when the rains come we're in the sea. The rain that day was the worst I've ever seen. I hadn't been driving ten minutes outside of Crowley when I knew we'd have to stop. "I can't see a thing," I said. "I can't see the road before me."

"Pull over," Mr. Harry said. "Let me take the wheel. Pull over on the side." I tried to. Crystal Anne was screaming and standing up in her seat belt. And the rain was coming straight at us like a hurricane. I thought I saw a place to pull over beside a bridge. I turned the wheel and the next thing I knew we were sliding down a wall of mud headed for an oak tree. We hit it broadside and came to a stop not ten feet from a river. "It's the Lacassine!" Mr. Harry yelled. "Goddamn, I've fished this river."

"Oh, my God," Miss Crystal said. She set down the glass she was holding and pulled Crystal Anne into the back seat. I'll say one thing for Miss Crystal. She's a good mother when she wants to be. "What are we going to do now, Harry?" she said. "What in the name of hell are we going to do?"

"I bet that door'll cost a couple of grand," he said. "At least two."

"To hell with the door," she said. "How are we getting out of here?"   30

"I'm not sure," he said. "Fix me another drink and let me think it over." So, there we were and it kept on raining. Every now and then I'd feel the car squench down in the mud, like it was settling. You could see me shudder every time it did it. Miss Crystal, she fixed me a bourbon and Coke. That helped a little. Crystal Anne had fallen asleep on her momma, just screamed a few minutes and went on off.

I guess this would be as good a time as any to tell you about the inside of the car. It was all made of leather, everything was leather. There wasn't anything that wasn't covered with leather but the dials. Even the refrigerator had a leather cover, softest, sweetest-smelling leather you could dream of in a million years, dark tan with here and there a black stripe.

Every place you turned there was a little hidden mirror. One beside each seat. I couldn't help but think of Mr. Phelan looking himself over while he'd be driving. The bar was in the middle so you could fix drinks from the front or the back and underneath was this nice little refrigerator that makes cubes the size of table dice. Net bags on the back of the seats for holding things. Just like on a Pullman. Oh, it was some car. And there we were, rammed up against a live oak and the rain coming down and no one knowing what to do next. "I'm for getting out and trying to make it up the bank," I said. "It's too big a chance to take, getting washed into the Lacassine inside a car."

"This car's not going anywhere," Mr. Harry said. "It weighs a ton. The best thing we can do is stay right here. Just sit tight till it stops raining."

"I think he's right," Miss Crystal said. "Let's just make another drink and eat   35 some of this lunch you had the sense to bring." It *was* thanks to me there was anything to eat. I'd fixed a lunch of cream cheese sandwiches on Boston bread and radish roses and a little pie made of chicken scraps. Food tastes so good when you're in danger. We ate it every bite.

The highway patrol finally came and got us out. I never have been so glad to see a policeman. A black man, black as me, not coffee colored. "How you doing, ma'am," he said in the sweetest voice, sticking his head into the car. It was still raining but it was passing. "You hold on. We're bringing a rope for you all to hold on to going up the hill. We'll have you out of here before you know it." Then they came with ropes and took us one by one up the hill, Crystal Anne first, awake now and screaming her head off and in a while we're all up on the road and the policemen are writing everything down. The rain's slacking up but it's still falling.

Getting the car out was something else. They had to send for a wrecker and when they didn't pull it they had to get a tractor and lay boards on the hill and I don't know what all. Crystal Anne and I were sitting in the policeman's car watching and talking to him about everything. His people are from Boutte where Mark's from. Know everybody we know. Finally they got the wrecker and the boards all lined up and here come the car inching up the hill and back out onto the highway. Everybody clapping and cheering. The side that hit the tree didn't look too bad after all. Not as bad as I thought it was going to. Of course the doors won't open. All the men and policemen they're walking around the car, admiring it and commenting on it, talking about how much it cost and after a while Mr. Harry got into the driver's seat and turned the key and it started right up. Everybody cheered. "They make these things out of old tanks," Mr. Harry said, laughing up at the policemen. "Those Krauts can make a car. You got to hand it to them. They can make a car."

"Let's get going then," Miss Crystal said. She was starting to look pretty bad, her hair all coming out of her pageboy and her pants covered with mud. I can't stand to see her like that, hard as I work ironing everything she owns.

"Get in," Mr. Harry called out. "We're back on the road. We're on our way." So we all piled back into the car, this time I'm in the back with Crystal Anne and they're up front and as soon as we're out of sight of the policeman Miss Crystal tells me to reach in the refrigerator and hand her a bottle of wine. "No more hard liquor till we get to Texas," she said. "We've had enough trouble for one day."

40   Then it seem like we're driving forever. Like driving into a dream. First Beaumont, then Liberty, then Houston and we got to stop and let Mr. Harry get some Mexican food and call Mr. Phelan and tell him what's going on. Then someplace called Clear Lake where Crystal Anne went to sleep for the third time, this time for good. Then Almeda, then Salt Lick, then Seville. I'm memorizing the names to tell Mark. Then we're only six miles away on an asphalt road, then we turn onto gravel, then to dirt and we're there. Country as flat as a pancake and dry, hardly a tree in sight. It's the middle of the night and we're at this Mexican-style house all sprawled out in the moonlight, must have twenty rooms. Mr. Phelan's waiting for us in the yard, about six dogs with him. These big red dogs with skinny faces, like the ones Judge Winn have over on Henry Clay, look like they'd take your arm off. The minute I saw them I just held Crystal Anne closer to me.

"There he is," Miss Crystal said. "Wearing black. Look at those pants, Harry. Can you believe he's kin to us?"

Mr. Phelan always wears black. Every time he come up to New Orleans he's got on black. Look like that's his only style. This night he's got on a long-sleeve shirt with a big collar and his pants are sewn up the side with white stitching. His hair all cut off real short. Look like it's been shaved, and he's standing with his hands in his pockets, standing real still and not letting anything show on his face. If he's seen the side of the car he's not letting on. Mr. Harry, he turn off the motor and get out and hug his cousin. "Goddammit, Phelan," he says. "Put those dogs up. I've had enough trouble for one day without fooling with your dogs."

"They won't hurt you, Harry. They won't move unless I tell them to. Sit," he says to the dog pack. "Show Uncle Harry your manners." Every last one of them sit down on their hindquarters the second he say it.

"Hello, Phelan," Miss Crystal says, getting out. "Look in the back seat. There's your niece. Well, come on, stop acting like a movie star and look at what we did. It isn't all that bad." She walked around to the bashed-in side and he followed her.

"Who was driving?" he says. He still hasn't let on that he even cares.   45

"Traceleen," Miss Crystal says. "And Crystal Anne was in the front seat with her. It's a wonder she didn't crack her head open. It's a wonder we aren't all at the bottom of the river."

"You were letting Traceleen drive?" He let out his breath and moved in to put his hand on the bashed-in door. I moved back deeper into the back seat, keeping Crystal Anne between me and him. "Holy Christ, Crystal. You let the nigger maid drive my car? This goddamn car isn't even insured. Well, Jesus fucking H. Christ . . . I don't believe it . . . I can't understand . . ." He stopped and stuck his hands back into his pockets. He looked off into the sky, this look coming onto his face like he is surrounded by a bunch of people that don't know what to do and he is tired of fooling with it and might just disappear into the night some day. "Never mind," he says. "I guess I'm lucky that it drives. I've got to use it tomorrow to pick up a party in San Antonio." He bent over and tried to stick a piece of chrome back on that was falling off. I felt sort of sorry for him for a moment. He'd been having a rough time lately from all I hear Mr. Harry and Miss Crystal say. Up to his ears in debt and all like that.

"Well, come on in," he was saying. "Come in and see the place." We all went in together. You've never seen such a sight as was in that house. No words will describe it. Every animal you ever heard of was in there. A full-sized baby giraffe, that's one thing. A big pile of elephant tusks. I don't know how many. Lion heads and leopards and some kind of curved-horn sheep and several deer and this caped buffalo that almost killed him when he shot it. In between the animal heads was pictures of Mr. Phelan on his hunts. He's kneeling over animals in every picture. Like a preacher. Every way you'd turn there's another picture of him kneeling over something. I was thinking maybe if he was so broke he might think of starting him a museum.

"I want to go with you on the hunt tomorrow," I heard Miss Crystal saying. "I want to watch you hunt a Russian boar."

In the morning some new troubles started. Miss Lauren Gail. They were all   50
around this big Mexican table eating breakfast and Miss Lauren Gail's with them now. She's Mr. Phelan's new wife. And her little girls, Teresa and Lisalee. Miss Lauren Gail's in a bad mood about the car. "He told me he bought a secondhand car over there," she's saying to Mr. Harry. "He didn't tell me he bought it from the

president of Mercedes-Benz. All he does is lie to me. He lies when he could tell the truth. Crystal, remember that ring I wanted in that antique store in New Orlens, that I called you about? It was only eight hundred dollars. Eight hundred dollars, that's all, and he said we couldn't afford it and now he turns up with this car. How much did it cost, Phelan? I want to know how much it cost."

"I don't want to hear any more about the car," Mr. Phelan said. "That's a business car, Lauren Gail. And anytime you don't like what's going on around here you just take your feet out from underneath my table and hit the road . . . I mean it, Lauren . . . and take that expression off your face. I'm not going to watch you pout all day. That's it . . . start crying . . . because then I'll just go pack for you myself."

She straightened up her face and Mr. Harry tried to change the subject. He always is the peacemaker. "How many groups you had down here, Phelan?" he said. "Enough to start paying expenses?"

"We're doing okay. Rainey's got so much work he can't get caught up. He's got four heads waiting in the freezer. It's going to go, Harry, don't worry about that . . . I mean it, Lauren Gail," he says, looking her way again. "Don't pull that stuff on me when I have company." He's looking at her with his mouth set in a line.

Miss Lauren Gail she don't say any more after that and it all passes. In a little while she take her little girls and go off to her end of the house and Mr. Phelan he leads the way to show us around the ranch. We got to go see the stables and the cisterns and the lookout tower and then he takes us to see the hunt animals. First we got to go look at the antelope. They're in this corral with a barn behind it. "Haldeston shipped them from Wyoming," Mr. Phelan's saying. "We lost three on the truck and a couple since they got here. But they're all right. I think this crowd's going to make it. See that stallion over there. That's the horse. That's the ringleader. I'm saving him for myself."

55 "I thought you were letting them run," Mr. Harry said. "You told me you were going to keep them on the range."

"In time," Mr. Phelan said. "All in good time. Got to get them fattened up first. Come on, let's go look at the boar. That's the cash crop this year." He had the Russian boars in a special pen about a mile from the house. We got to drive across a field to get there. It's this pen behind a stand of pine trees, all surrounded by barb wire with some dogs outside and another fence around them. These dogs called mastiffs, all dusty and mean looking. Russian boar on the inside and mastiffs on the outside.

There are six boar altogether. Two real small looking, the other ones look okay. They're all milling around. They don't look like anything worth two thousand dollars to me, dead or alive. Just look like old wild pigs anybody can see up around Crowley. Only these boar got gray fur, with black hair around their faces and legs. Where you get them from? I kept wanting to ask but I don't say it, I just hold on to Crystal Anne and keep my eyes and ears open.

"You're charging people two thousand dollars to shoot one of those things?" Miss Crystal says. "You've got to be kidding."

"It costs a lot to keep them," he says. "Have to air-condition the shed and God knows what else. They're very delicate. It's hard to keep them healthy."

60 "You've lost your mind, Phelan," she says. "Do you realize that?"

"Well, Sister," he says, shutting the door to the pen and turning around to take us back. "Nobody asked you to come down here and tell me how to live my life. I don't come up to New Orleans and stick my nose in your business, do I?"

"You've gone too far, Phelan. These pigs are just too far." She was right up to him now, almost touching. There couldn't have been an inch between them. It's busting loose, I thought. It's getting out of hand. I held on to the baby, holding in my breath. It was terrible, those mean-looking dogs leaning up against the fence and Miss Crystal, she's got this bad hangover anyway, she's right up in his face threatening him on his own ranch.

"I'm not the same person you used to kick around, Phelan," she says. "I'm a powerful woman, strong and powerful. I wouldn't mess around with me if I was you. I'm a different person than the one you used to know."

"That may all be so, little sister," he says. He hasn't moved on inch. He is still as he can be. "On the other hand, it's the same wall you're up against." I looked at him then and he did sort of look like a wall. I guess Miss Crystal thought so too because she took the baby out of my arms and started walking back to the car, holding up her head and swaying from side to side kind of devil-may-care.

We weren't in the big car this time. We were in a little steel-covered jeep made in England. It was fitted out with all kinds of hunting things. We all squeezed back into it and headed back to the ranch. Jack was driving. He's this black man Mr. Phelan took off to college with him when he was young. Call himself a chauffeur but he ain't no better than a slave. "Jack was the first black man to go to Ole Miss," Mr. Phelan's saying. "He was there a long time before James Meredith, weren't you, Jack? Jack was a KA, lived in the house with me. We even had him a pin made. Jack, you still got your KA pin? I want you to show it to Traceleen when we get back." Jack didn't say a word, just grinning from ear to ear.

Then Mr. Phelan and Mr. Harry took the new car and drove off to San Antonio to get the men for the hunt and the rest of us spent the afternoon in the air conditioning listening to Miss Lauren Gail talk about Mr. Phelan won't buy her anything. "Don't say anything to the visitors about the pen with the boars in it," he had said to me, taking me aside when he was leaving. "We pretend the boar just comes charging out of nowhere. It makes it more exciting."

"Don't worry about me," I said. "I just came along to ride in the car."

Later that afternoon Mr. Phelan and Mr. Harry come back with these two men and they all sit around and have drinks and hot pepper cheese and then they have this Mexican dinner. You ought to see that dining room. Forty feet long, fireplace on either end. Every wall covered with animal heads, this big brown bear standing in one corner with his teeth showing and his claws out. Mr. Phelan's third wife shot it in Tennessee. Got her picture in a gun magazine for doing it. They got the story framed beside the bear in this glass frame that's really for holding recipe books. "Lauren Gail thought that up," Mr. Phelan said. "She should have been a decorator. Then she could have been in stores buying things all day long." He hugged her to his side and she put on this sad look like what's she supposed to do but take it.

In the middle of the room there's this big mahogany table and hand-carved chairs with chairseats embroidered with Mr. Phelan's coat-of-arms. He had a picture of it on the wall too, painted to match the chairseats. He kept asking Mr. Harry didn't he wanted him to get him a coat-of-arms for his house but Mr. Harry said no, he already had everything on his walls he needed.

70   These two men from Jackson they're having the time of their lives. One of the men was in the shoemaking business. He'd been playing chess with Mr. Phelan before dinner and he kept talking about how smart Mr. Phelan was. That he hadn't ever played anybody could beat him so fast. The other man, he used to have a tent factory but the government closed it down by driving him crazy telling him what all to do. He kept complaining about the government doing different things to him and getting drunker and drunker and Mr. Phelan kept pouring him wine and egging him on. "So I just closed the goddamn place and went to Vegas," he kept saying. "Fuck 'em. Fuck 'em. I just closed it down and went to Vegas. Fuck 'em. That's all I've got to say. Fuck 'em."

I took Crystal Anne and went off to bed as soon as I could. I don't like her listening to talk like that. "Fock em, fock em, fock em," she's saying. "Fock em, fock em, fock em." She parrot everthing she hear. What's going to happen when she shows up at nursery school talking like that? I could still hear them yelling while I'm walking down the hallway, talking all about the government and hunts they'd been on and what a wild Russian boar will do to you if you only wound it and don't kill it right and how you have got to shoot it just so or you'll mess it up for being stuffed. Mr. Phelan he was standing up when I left showing them a Russian boar nailed to a board, showing them where you have to make the bullets go in so you won't mess up the face.

"We're going on that hunt tomorrow, Traceleen," Miss Crystal said when she came to get in bed with Crystal Anne and me. She just climbed right in with us. First time I'd ever sleep with a lady I work for. That's how Miss Crystal is. Just act like she thinks she can make up the world. So she and Crystal Anne and me snuggle down into the covers. "Tomorrow you will see me in action, Traceleen," she said. "Crystal Anne, I want you to remember what's going to happen next." I thought it was the whiskey talking.

Now morning comes and they all have a breakfast of tequila and lemons and bread and butter. Mr. Phelan insist that's the right thing for hunters to have before they start a hunt. Miss Crystal, she's drinking it with them. Then she and Mr. Harry and one of the men from Jackson get into the English truck and Mr. Phelan and the other man and this one named Rainey that's the one stuffs the animals, they're next in the jeep and Jack and me and Crystal Anne bringing up the rear in the number six hundred. Jack, he's got on his cowboy hat and an African hunter's vest and he's been working on the bar. Got it fixed up more Mexican than we had it. Beer and tequila and some homemade drinks I never did learn the name of. So then we're ready and the sun's lighting up this big Texas field, looked like they hadn't had any rain in a year. Crystal Anne's she's real excited to be going somewhere so early in the morning and she's reaching up in the front seat trying to get Jack's attention and pulling on his hat.

Off we go down that dirt road and out onto the asphalt and then back onto dirt and up in front I can see Mr. Phelan standing up behind the wheel pointing out things and talking. We come to a little used-up house by the road and we all stop and they come back to our car to get some more to drink and he's talking all about the boar and how tricky they are. Them men from Jackson hanging on to his every word. He should have been a preacher. I've thought that before.

So we packed back up and this time we take off across a stubble-covered field 75 and across a little ditch on top of some two by fours don't look like they'd hold a man much less a car, then we follow the ditch, it's supposed to be a creek but there's no water in it. It looks to me like we're just driving around the ranch. I can't see that we've gone three miles from home. We have another stop beside an old chimney that used to be a house and Mr. Phelan's got the binoculars out now, sighting through them and letting the men use them and they're sweeping the country he calls it. Then Mr. Phelan keeps on looking and looking at a spot over near a stand of pine trees and finally he takes down the binoculars and looks around on the ground for a while walking around and around in a circle looking for tracks. After a while he puts his arms around the tent man's shoulders and the two of them come over to our car and fix a drink. "We'll use that stand over there by the ridge. They've got to come this way sooner or later to get to water." He pointed east. "Over there's the only water source, a pond about a mile away. So we'll lay for them on the rise." He licked his finger and stuck it up into the air. "Yeah, the breeze is with us. They won't be able to smell us until they're here. They'll come before too long. They've got to have water. The only tracks are two days old. You're lucky, Charlie. This breeze is going to win you a shot. You're a lucky man. I can tell that. I feel lucky just being with you." He leaned into the car. "Jack, you come over when we get set. Traceleen, you and the baby stay in the car. We're going up to the stand." His voice is real low now and he's pointing over to the east where the sun is getting up above the ground. There's this little rise of land look like it was pushed up by a tractor. With a board screen like for a bullfight in a movie. They're all real quiet now and put all the tequila glasses back in the car and take out all the guns and the men and Miss Crystal go walking off to the rise. Miss Crystal, she's at the edge, look like she's holding back. Off in the distance is the stand of pine trees in front of the wild Russian boar pen. I'm just hoping nobody will make a mistake and shoot at the car. "Now what's going to happen?" I ask Jack.

"Now the boys will let 'em wait awhile and get all hot and bothered. Then they'll let one of the boars go, back behind the trees, and it'll come charging out and as soon as it sees people it'll come running at them. Them boars go crazy when you let 'em loose, they'll run at anything."

"Then what?" I said.

"Then Mr. Phelan'll let somebody shoot and he'll shoot too in case they miss and then they'll keep letting them loose till everybody that paid gets to shoot one. Then they'll be through and Rainey'll put the boars in a tarp and take them off to be stuffed unless somebody wants to drive home with it tied to the hood of the jeep.

Sometimes they do that." He stretched his arms and opened up the door. "Well, let me get my rifle out the trunk. He likes me to be standing by in case he should miss. You excuse me, Miss Traceleen. I got to get my gun out the trunk and load it up. I forgot to have it loaded." Then Jack pushes a button to open the trunk and he get out and goes around the back of the car to get his gun.

"Here's what's going to happen," I say to Crystal Anne, thinking I'd better tell her what it's going to sound like when they start shooting. So she won't be surprised. But I never got time to tell her because about that time it all busted loose. Someone at the pen has let a boar loose and he's coming across that field like a baseball. He's coming so fast my heart almost stopped. I feel Jack jump into the trunk of the car. He let out a big yell and jump right in on top of his gun and here comes Miss Crystal running down off the hill and she jump into the driver's seat and starts honking the horn as loud as she can and starts the car and then the car's moving she she's chasing the pig. Trying to save him or run over him one, I can't decide. Then the pig he takes off in the direction of the sun and we're chasing him in the car. Jack's in the back with the trunk top flopping up and down and Crystal Anne's laughing her head off, she thinks it's wonderful. I look out the window and there's Mr. Phelan, running after us with his gun in his hand. He's sprinting like a deer, heavy as he is. He's as mad as he can be.

80   Then we're on the asphalt and Miss Crystal's yelling. "Traceleen, roll up the window. Lock the doors." Jack's jumped out by then but the trunk top's still waving up and down and we're on the road. "Where're we going?" I say. "What's happening now?"

"Were going for the antelope pen," she says. "We're going to ram it down." Sure enough, she press her foot down on the pedal, lean into the wheel, the seat's too far back for her but she doesn't even stop to adjust it, and we're headed for the ranch. Mr. Phelan's still running after us, then I see him stop and help Jack up off the ground. We bust on down the road and turn on the gravel, one tire's sliding off in the ditch but Miss Crystal, she holds it on the road. I wish you could have seen her, sitting there behind the steering wheel in her fringed vest and her hunting pants with sandpaper on the knees and her khaki-colored hunting shirt, her hair all messed up and wild looking. If I live a million years I won't ever forget the look on her face that morning or the ride we had.

First we come to the automatic gate. What you call a Kentucky gate, you have to stop and pull a chain and it opens, then you got to close it by hand from the other side, but we don't close it this time. We bust on down the road over the cattle gaps and go on past the house without even slowing up, almost run over a couple of dogs, then we're to the antelope pen and Miss Crystal she just drive the car right into the gate, just ram it down. The she backs up and rams it again. I could see it giving in and the radiator on the front of the car starting to smoke. This is no way to treat a Mercedes-Benz number six hundred that cost twenty-six thousand dollars I couldn't help thinking. It would have been just as good to do it with the English truck. "Don't hit it on the front," I said, but she wasn't listening. "Hit it more to the side, with the fender." She don't even hear me. She just back up and ram it one more time. This time the whole gate and half the fence fall forward like they was made out of paper.

Then antelope are everywhere, all around us. For a minute it seem like the windows are covered with antelope faces, then they're gone, spreading out in every direction, their little white tails waving behind them.

The biggest one, the one Mr. Phelan call the horse, is taking off across the field behind the boar pen, two more following him. It's a field that stretches way off and ends in a wood beside where that little dry river runs. I watched those ones until they disappeared into the trees.

Then we're backing out over the boards and Miss Lauren Gail and her little girls 85 and all the kitchen help are running out into the yard to see what's happened. The radiator's really smoking now, but Miss Crystal she backs and turns and pulls up in front of the kitchen stairs to yell to Miss Lauren Gail. "Send my clothes to New Orleans," she yells out the window. "Tell Harry I'm sorry I had to leave him here." Then we're barreling back down the dirt road and through the gate and onto the asphalt.

"You think we ought to drive it with that steam coming out in front?" I said.

"It will run," she says. "If we don't stop it will get us where we're going." We make it through the gate and turn onto the main road and here comes Mr. Phelan in the jeep headed right at us. "God in Heaven," I'm yelling. "Here he comes. What if he shoots?"

"I'll run over him if he shoots at me," she says. "I'll knock his goddamn jeep off the road." She was gripping the wheel like it was a horse she was riding. She was *driving* that car. I held Crystal Anne in my lap. When we passed Mr. Phelan I laid my head down so I wouldn't have to see him. I was sure he would shoot out our tires but I guess even Mr. Phelan knows better than to shoot at people. We passed him on that narrow road with a swoosh, so close I could hear him screaming. I guess he could see the steam coming out the radiator. I was wondering if Miss Crystal caught his eye.

She had planned it all before it happened. Well, not the exact way but near enough. She had put a bag for Crystal Anne into the car and had her pockets stuffed with money and credit cards and we drove to San Antonio at ninety miles an hour and cruised into the parking lot at the airport and got out and left the car sitting there with steam coming out the bottom and the top. It had made it to San Antonio but I heard later that all it was good for after that was to sell in Mexico. I sure hated to leave that car like that. I ran my hand across the leather dashboard as I was getting out, admiring one last time the way the leather parts fit into the steel so fine you couldn't tell where one began and the other ended. Even the button on the dashboard looked special, like it had grown there. Look like a navel on a baby, I was thinking. Or a navel orange.

We got a ticket on a United Airlines 747 and started for home. We were travel- 90 ing first class, traveling in style. That's how Miss Crystal does things. She's always saying she's going to stop and save some money but she can't ever seem to find the right place to stop.

We strapped ourselves into these nice big seats, with Crystal Anne sitting in the middle and Miss Crystal leaned back and took a moment's rest for the first time since she'd opened her eyes that morning. She still had on her hunting clothes. Looked like some famous actress that had been on a location shot. She reached over and touched me on the arm. "We're going home in triumph, Traceleen. What a trip. I could never have followed my conscience today if you hadn't been there to help, you know that, don't you?"

I accepted the compliment. I knew it was the truth. Nobody can get anything done by theirself. That's not the way the world is set up.

"It is very sad," she said to me later, when the plane was in the air, and we had been served some French Columbard wine and were having our lunch. "When you cannot love your one and only brother. It breaks my heart, Traceleen, here he is in the modern world and still killing things all the time. Like he was from another century. He was such a smart little boy. He was destined for better things."

"I wouldn't waste too much time feeling sorry for Mr. Phelan," I said. "He looks to me like he does about what he wants to do."

95   "You're right," she says. "That wine was making my mind soft. Listen, Traceleen, let me tell you a story about what he did to me one time. I was thinking about it this morning while I was getting up my courage, waiting for the boar to come. This was a long time ago, when I was eight years old and he was twelve." She took a big sip of her French Columbard wine and started telling the story.

"It was one Sunday, in Indiana, right in the middle of the Second World War. It was in this Spanish house we had. There was this living room, with very high cathedral ceilings, and I came downstairs one Sunday and there was Phelan, sitting at Momma's cardtable driving an airplane. There were footpedals for his feet and a steering wheel and a dashboard with all sorts of dials on it. It was a special kind of plane where the pilot is also the bombardier and Phelan was flying over Japan, dropping bombs on cities and ammunition dumps.

"Ack, ack, ack, his guns would roar. Ziiiiiinnnnnnngggggg, as the bombs fell. Then he would lift up into the clouds barely escaping the zeroes. I almost fainted with envy when I saw him. It drove me crazy. Finally I went over and asked him if I could fly it and he said no, it was against the law because I wasn't a pilot.

"So I went to my room and got my new Monopoly set and brought it out and offered to trade. 'No,' he said. Then I went back into my room and got my butterfly collecting kit and I brought that out and still he wouldn't let me have a turn.

"All day I kept adding to the pile of things beside the fireplace and still Phelan flew on and on as if I wasn't even there. Ack, ack, ack, the guns would roar. Ziiiinnnnnnnggggggggggg.

100   "Finally I went to my room and came out with the binoculars my great-uncle Philip Phillips had used in World War I and I said, 'Phelan, I will trade you these binoculars for the plane.'

"He got up from the pilot's seat and took the binoculars and the Monopoly set and my rubber printing stamps and several other things that interested him and we shook hands on the deal. At our house a deal was a deal forever. If you shook hands it was over. So Phelan took my stuff and I sat down at the plane and reached for the steering wheel. It was only an old piece of cardboard he had painted. I put my feet down on the pedals. They were two old shoeboxes with cardboard springs.

Traceleen," she said. Her voice was rising. "Traceleen, are you listening? Can you hear me? This is everything I know about love I'm telling you. Everything I know about everything."

"Momma," Crystal Anne said, laying her hand on her momma's cheek to calm her down. "Momma's talking."

QUESTIONS FOR DISCUSSION AND WRITING

1. What conflicts prompt Crystal to make the trip to Texas? How are these conflicts brought to a climax when Crystal drives the Mercedes through the gate, freeing the antelope? Why has the trip been a "triumph"?

2. In what ways does Traceleen display her superiority to the other characters in the story? How does Traceleen provide insights into the behavior of other characters— such as Harry, Phelan, and Lauren Gail?

3. In what way do the car and the ranch reveal the values of Phelan's world? How does this world differ from Crystal's and Traceleen's?

4. Who is Traceleen's apparent audience for this story? Why does her position in the world make her an effective narrator?

5. How does Crystal's story about her childhood conflicts with her brother explain everything she knows "about love. . . . Everything [she] know[s] about anything"?

Stories for Comparison

Toni Cade Bambara's "The Lesson" (pages 238–244); Eudora Welty's "Why I Live at the P.O." (pages 1164–1173).

47

GAIL GODWIN

Dream Children

GAIL GODWIN was born in Birmingham, Alabama, in 1937 and was educated at the University of North Carolina and the University of Iowa. She has worked as a journalist for the *Miami Herald,* as a travel consultant with the

United States Embassy in London, and as an English instructor at the University of Iowa, Vassar College, and Columbia University. Godwin's essays and short stories have appeared in magazines such as *Harper's, Esquire, Cosmopolitan, Mademoiselle,* and *Ms.* She has also written librettos for four musical compositions by Robert Starer. Her novels, *The Perfectionists* (1970), *Glass People* (1972), *The Odd Woman* (1974), *Violet Clay* (1978), *A Mother and Two Daughters* (1981), *The Finishing School* (1985), *Father's Melancholy Daughter* (1991), and *Good Husband* (1994), capture the consciousness of contemporary women. In "Dream Children," the title story from her 1976 collection, Godwin recounts a young woman's attempts to find happiness after she has been victimized by a terrible, freakish mistake.

T *he worst thing. Such a terrible thing to happen to a young woman. It's a wonder she didn't go mad.*

As she went about her errands, a cheerful, neat young woman, a wife, wearing pants with permanent creases and safari jackets and high-necked sweaters that folded chastely just below the line of the small gold hoops she wore in her ears, she imagined people saying this, or thinking it to themselves. But nobody knew. Nobody knew anything, other than that she and her husband had moved here a year ago, as so many couples were moving farther away from the city, the husband commuting, or staying in town during the week—as hers did. There was nobody here, in this quaint, unspoiled village, nestled in the foothills of the mountains, who could have looked at her and guessed that anything out of the ordinary, predictable, auspicious spectrum of things that happen to bright, attractive young women had happened to her. She always returned her books to the local library on time; she bought liquor at the local liquor store only on Friday, before she went to meet her husband's bus from the city. He was something in television, a producer? So many ambitious young couples moving to this Dutch farming village, founded in 1690, to restore ruined fieldstone houses and plant herb gardens and keep their own horses and discover the relief of finding oneself insignificant in Nature for the first time!

A terrible thing. So freakish. If you read it in a story or saw it on TV, you'd say no, this sort of thing could never happen in an American hospital.

DePuy, who owned the Old Patroon farm adjacent to her land, frequently glimpsed her racing her horse in the early morning, when the mists still lay on the fields, sometimes just before the sun came up and there was a frost on everything. "One woodchuck hole and she and that stallion will both have to be put out of their misery," he told his wife. "She's too reckless. I'll bet you her old man doesn't know she goes streaking to hell across the field like that." Mrs. DePuy nodded, silent, and went about her business. She, too, watched that other woman ride, a woman not much younger than herself, but with an aura of romance—of tragedy, perhaps. The way she looked: like those heroines in English novels who ride off their bad tempers and unrequited love affairs, clenching their thighs against the flanks of spirited horses with murderous red eyes. Mrs. DePuy, who had ridden since the age of three, recognized something beyond recklessness in that elegant young woman, in her crisp checked shirts and her dove-gray jodhpurs. *She has nothing to fear anymore,* thought the farmer's wife, with sure feminine instinct; she both envied and pitied her. "What she needs is children," remarked DePuy.

"A Dry Sack, a Remy Martin, and . . . let's see, a half-gallon of the Chablis, and ₅ I think I'd better take a Scotch . . . and the Mouton-Cadet . . . and maybe a dry vermouth." Mrs. Frye, another farmer's wife, who runs the liquor store, asks if her husband is bringing company for the weekend. "He sure is; we couldn't drink all that by ourselves," and the young woman laughs, her lovely teeth exposed, her small gold earrings quivering in the light. "You know, I saw his name—on the television the other night," says Mrs. Frye. "It was at the beginning of that new comedy show, the one with the woman who used to be on another show with her husband and little girl, only they divorced, you know the one?" "Of course I do. It's one of my husband's shows. I'll tell him you watched it." Mrs. Frye puts the bottles in an empty box, carefully inserting wedges of cardboard between them. Through the window of her store she sees her customer's pert bottle-green car, some sort of little foreign car with the engine running, filled with groceries and weekend parcels, and that big silver-blue dog sitting up in the front seat just like a human being. "I think that kind of thing is so sad," says Mrs. Frye; "families breaking up, poor little children having to divide their loyalties." "I couldn't agree more," replies the young woman, nodding gravely. Such a personable, polite girl! "Are you sure you can carry that, dear? I can get Earl from the back. . . ." But the girl has it hoisted on her shoulder in a flash, is airily maneuvering between unopened cartons stacked in the aisle, in her pretty boots. Her perfume lingers in Mrs. Frye's store for a half-hour after she has driven away.

After dinner, her husband and his friends drank brandy. She lay in front of the fire, stroking the dog, and listening to Victoria Darrow, the news commentator, in person. A few minutes ago, they had all watched Victoria on TV. "That's right; thirty-nine!" Victoria now whispered to her. "What? That's kind of you. I'm photogenic, thank God, or I'd have been put out to pasture long before. . . . I look five, maybe seven years younger on the screen . . . but the point I'm getting at is, I went to this doctor and he said, 'If you want to do this thing, you'd better go home today and get started.' He told me—did you know this? Did you know that a woman is born with all the eggs she'll ever have, and when she gets to my age, the ones that are left have been rattling around so long they're a little shopworn; then every time you fly you get an extra dose of radioactivity, so those poor eggs. He told me when a woman over forty comes into his office pregnant, his heart sinks; that's why he quit practicing obstetrics, he said; he could still remember the screams of a woman whose baby he delivered . . . she was having natural childbirth and she kept saying, 'Why won't you let me see it, I insist on seeing it,' and so he had to, and he says he can still hear her screaming."

"Oh, what was—what was wrong with it?"

But she never got the answer. Her husband, white around the lips, was standing over Victoria ominously, offering the Remy Martin bottle. "Vicky, let me pour you some more," he said. And to his wife, "I think Blue Boy needs to go out."

"Yes, yes, of course. Please excuse me, Victoria. I'll just be . . ."

10   Her husband followed her to the kitchen, his hand on the back of her neck. "Are you okay? That stupid yammering bitch. She and her twenty-six-year-old lover! I wish I'd never brought them, but she's been hinting around the studio for weeks."

"But I like them, I like having them. I'm fine. Please go back. I'll take the dog out and come back. Please . . ."

"All right. If you're sure you're okay." He backed away, hands dangling at his sides. A handsome man, wearing a pink shirt with Guatemalan embroidery. Thick black hair and a face rather boyish, but cunning. Last weekend she had sat beside him, alone in this house, just the two of them, and watched him on television: a documentary, in several parts, in which TV "examines itself." There was his double, sitting in an armchair in his executive office, coolly replying to the questions of Victoria Darrow. *"Do you personally watch all the programs you produce, Mr. McNair?"* She watched the man on the screen, how he moved his lips when he spoke, but kept the rest of his face, his body perfectly still. Funny, she had never noticed this before. He managed to say that he did not watch all the programs he produced.

Now, in the kitchen, she looked at him backing away, a little like a renegade in one of his own shows—a desperate man, perhaps, who had just killed somebody and is backing away, hands dangling loosely at his sides, Mr. McNair, her husband. That man on the screen. Once a lover above her in bed. That friend who held her hand in the hospital. One hand in hers, the other holding the stopwatch. For a brief instant, all the images coalesce and she feels something again. But once outside, under the galaxies of autumn-sharp stars, the intelligent dog at her heels like some smart gray ghost, she is glad to be free of all that. She walks quickly over the damp grass to the barn, to look in on her horse. She understands something: her husband, Victoria Darrow lead double lives that seem perfectly normal to them. But if she told her husband that she, too, is in two lives, he would become alarmed; he would sell this house and make her move back to the city where he could keep an eye on her welfare.

She is discovering people like herself, down through the centuries, all over the world. She scours books with titles like *The Timeless Moment, The Sleeping Prophet, Between Two Worlds, Silent Union: A Record of Unwilled Communication;* collecting evidence, weaving a sort of underworld net of colleagues around her.

15   A rainy fall day. Too wet to ride. The silver dog asleep beside her in her special alcove, a padded window seat filled with pillows and books. She is looking down on the fields of dried lithrium, and the fir trees beyond, and the mountains gauzy with fog and rain, thinking, in a kind of terror and ecstasy, about all these connections. A book lies face down on her lap. She has just read the following:

Theodore Dreiser and his friend John Cowper Powys had been dining at Dreiser's place on West Fifty Seventh Street. As Powys made ready to leave and catch his train to the little town up the Hudson, where he was then living, he told Dreiser, "I'll appear before you here, later in the evening."

Dreiser laughed. "Are you going to turn yourself into a ghost, or have you a spare key?" he asked. Powys said he would return "in some form," he didn't know exactly what kind.

After his friend left, Dreiser sat up and read for two hours. Then he looked up and saw Powys standing in the doorway to the living room. It was Powys' features, his tall stature, even the loose tweed garments which he wore. Dreiser rose at once and strode toward the figure, saying, "Well, John, you kept your word. Come on in and tell me how you did it." But the figure vanished when Dreiser came within three feet of it.

Dreiser then went to the telephone and called Powys' house in the country. Powys answered. Dreiser told him what had happened and Powys said, "I told you I'd be there and you oughtn't to be surprised." But he refused to discuss how he had done it, if, indeed, he knew how.

"But don't you get frightened, up here all by yourself, alone with all these creaky sounds?" asked Victoria, the next morning.

"No, I guess I'm used to them," she replied, breaking eggs into a bowl. "I know what each one means. The wood expanding and contracting . . . the wind getting caught between the shutter and the latch . . . Sometimes small animals get lost in the stone walls and scratch around till they find their way out . . . or die."

"Ugh. But don't you imagine things? I would, in a house like this. How old? That's almost three hundred years of lived lives, people suffering and shouting and making love and giving birth, under this roof. . . . You'd think there'd be a few ghosts around."

"I don't know," said her hostess blandly. "I haven't heard any. But of course, I have Blue Boy, so I don't get scared." She whisked the eggs, unable to face Victoria. She and her husband had lain awake last night, embarrassed at the sounds coming from the next room. No ghostly moans, those. "Why can't that bitch control herself, or at least lower her voice," he said angrily. He stroked his wife's arm, both of them pretending not to remember. She had bled for an entire year afterward, until the doctor said they would have to remove everything. "I'm empty," she had said when her husband had tried again, after she was healed. "I'm sorry, I just don't feel anything." Now they lay tenderly together on these weekends, like childhood friends, like effigies on a lovers' tomb, their mutual sorrow like a sword between them. She assumed he had another life, or lives, in town. As she had here. Nobody is just one person, she had learned.

"I'm sure I would imagine things," said Victoria. "I would see things and hear things inside my head much worse than an ordinary murderer or rapist." [20]

The wind caught in the shutter latch . . . a small animal dislodging pieces of fieldstone in its terror, sending them tumbling down the inner walls, from attic to cellar . . . a sound like a child rattling a jar full of marbles, or small stones . . .

"I have so little imagination," she said humbly, warming the butter in the omelet pan. She could feel Victoria Darrow's professional curiosity waning from her dull country life, focusing elsewhere.

Cunning!

As a child of nine, she had gone through a phase of walking in her sleep. One summer night, they found her bed empty, and after an hour's hysterical search they had found her in her nightgown, curled up on the flagstones beside the fishpond. She woke, baffled, in her father's tense clutch, the stars all over the sky, her mother repeating over and over again to the night at large, "Oh, my God, she could have drowned!" They took her to a child psychiatrist, a pretty Austrian woman who spoke to her with the same vocabulary she used on grownups, putting the child instantly at ease. "It is not at all uncommon what you did. I have known so many children who take little night journeys from their beds, and then they awaken and don't know what all the fuss is about! Usually these journeys are quite harmless, because children are surrounded by a magical reality that keeps them safe. Yes, the race of children possesses magically sagacious powers! But the grownups, they tend to forget how it once was for them. They worry, they are afraid of so many things. You do not want your mother and father, who love you so anxiously, to live in fear of you going to live with the fishes." She had giggled at the thought. The woman's steady gray-green eyes were trained on her carefully, suspending her in a kind of bubble. Then she had rejoined her parents, a dutiful "child" again, holding a hand up to each of them. The night journeys had stopped.

25   A thunderstorm one night last spring. Blue Boy whining in his insulated house below the garage. She had lain there, strangely elated by the nearness of the thunderclaps that tore at the sky, followed by instantaneous flashes of jagged light. Wondering shouldn't she go down and let the dog in; he hated storms. Then dozing off again . . .

She woke. The storm had stopped. The dark air was quiet. Something had changed, some small thing—what? She had to think hard before she found it: the hall light, which she kept burning during the week-nights when she was there alone, had gone out. She reached over and switched the button on her bedside lamp. Nothing. A tree must have fallen and hit a wire, causing the power to go off. This often happened here. No problem. The dog had stopped crying. She felt herself sinking into a delicious, deep reverie, the kind that sometimes came just before morning, as if her being broke slowly into tiny pieces and spread itself over the world. It was a feeling she had not known until she had lived by herself in this house: this weightless though conscious state in which she lay, as if in a warm bath, and yet was able to send her thoughts anywhere, as if her mind contained the entire world.

And as she floated in this silent world, transparent and buoyed upon the dream layers of the mind, she heard a small rattling sound, like pebbles being shaken in a jar. The sound came distinctly from the guest room, a room so chosen by her husband and herself because it was the farthest room from their bedroom on this floor. It lay above what had been the old side of the house, built seventy-five years before the new side, which was completed in 1753. There was a bed in it, and a chair, and some plants in the window. Sometimes on weekends when she could not sleep, she went and read there, or meditated, to keep from waking her husband. It was the room where Victoria Darrow and her young lover would not sleep the following fall, because she would say quietly to her husband, "No . . . not that room. I—I've made up the bed in the other room," "What?" he would want to know. "The one next to ours? Right under our noses?"

She did not lie long listening to this sound before she understood it was one she had never heard in the house before. It had a peculiar regularity to its rhythm; there was nothing accidental about it, nothing influenced by the wind, or the nerves of some lost animal. *K-chunk, k-chunk, k-chunk,* it went. At intervals of exactly a half-minute apart. She still remembered how to time such things, such intervals. She was as good as any stopwatch when it came to timing certain intervals.

K-chunk, k-chunk, k-chunk. That determined regularity. Something willed, something poignantly repeated, as though the repetition was a means of consoling someone in the dark. Her skin began to prickle. Often, lying in such states of weight-less reverie, she had practiced the trick of sending herself abroad, into rooms of the house, out into the night to check on Blue Boy, over to the barn to look in on her horse, who slept standing up. Once she had heard a rather frightening noise, as if someone in the basement had turned on a faucet, and so she forced herself to "go down," floating down two sets of stairs into the darkness, only to discover what she had known all the time: the hookup system between the hot-water tank and the pump, which sounded like someone turning on the water.

Now she went through the palpable, prickly darkness, without lights, down the 30 chilly hall in her sleeveless gown, into the guest room. Although there was no light, not even a moon shining through the window, she could make out the shape of the bed and then the chair, the spider plants on the window, and a small dark shape in one corner, on the floor, which she and her husband had painted a light yellow.

K-chunk, k-chunk, k-chunk. The shape moved with the noise.

Now she knew what they meant, that "someone's hair stood on end." It was true. As she forced herself across the borders of a place she had never been, she felt, dis-tinctly, every single hair on her head raise itself a millimeter or so from her scalp.

She knelt down and discovered him. He was kneeling, a little cold and scared, 35 shaking a small jar filled with some kind of pebbles. (She later found out, in a sub-sequent visit, that they were small colored shells, of a triangular shape, called co-quinas: she found them in a picture in a child's nature book at the library.) He was wearing pajamas a little too big for him, obviously hand-me-downs, and he was ex-actly two years older than the only time she had ever held him in her arms.

The two of them knelt in the corner of the room, taking each other in. His large eyes were the same as before: dark and unblinking. He held the small jar close to him, watching her. He was not afraid, but she knew better than to move too close.

She knelt, the tears streaming down her cheeks, but she made no sound, her eyes fastened on that small form. And then the hall light came on silently, as well as the lamp beside her bed, and with wet cheeks and pounding heart she could not be sure whether or not she had actually been out of the room.

But what did it matter, on the level where they had met? He traveled so much farther than she to reach that room. (*"Yes, the race of children possesses magically sagacious powers!"*)

She and her husband sat together on the flowered chintz sofa, watching the last of the series in which TV purportedly examined itself. She said, "Did you ever think that the whole thing is really a miracle? I mean, here we sit, eighty miles away from your studios, and we turn on a little machine and there is Victoria, speaking to us as clearly as she did last weekend when she was in this very room. Why, it's magic, it's time travel and space travel right in front of our eyes, but because it's been 'discovered,' because the world understands that it's only little dots that transmit Victoria electrically to us, it's *all right.* We can bear it. Don't you sometimes wonder about all the miracles that haven't been officially approved yet? I mean, who knows, maybe in a hundred years everybody will take it for granted that they can send an image of themselves around in space by some perfectly natural means available to us now. I mean, when you think about it, what *is* space? What *is* time? Where do the so-called boundaries of each of us begin and end? Can anyone explain it?"

He was drinking Scotch and thinking how they had decided not to renew Victoria Darrow's contract. Somewhere on the edges of his mind hovered an anxious, growing certainty about his wife. At the local grocery store this morning, when he went to pick up a carton of milk and the paper, he had stopped to chat with DePuy. "I don't mean to interfere, but she doesn't know those fields," said the farmer. "Last year we had to shoot a mare, stumbled into one of those holes. . . . It's madness, the way she rides."

And look at her now, her face so pale and shining, speaking of miracles and space travel, almost on the verge of tears. . . .

40   And last night, his first night up from the city, he had wandered through the house, trying to drink himself into this slower weekend pace, and he had come across a pile of her books, stacked in the alcove where, it was obvious, she lay for hours, escaping into science fiction, and the occult.

Now his own face appeared on the screen. "I want to be fair," he was telling Victoria Darrow. "I want to be objective. . . . Violence has always been part of the human makeup. I don't like it anymore than you do, but there it is. I think it's more a question of whether we want to face things as they are or escape into fantasies of how we would like them to be."

Beside him, his wife uttered a sudden bell-like laugh.

(". . . *It's madness, the way she rides.*")

He did want to be fair, objective. She had told him again and again that she liked her life here. And he—well, he had to admit he liked his own present setup.

45   "I am a pragmatist," he was telling Victoria Darrow on the screen. He decided to speak to his wife about her riding and leave her alone about the books. She had the right to some escape, if anyone did. But the titles: *Marvelous Manifestations, The Mind Travellers, A Doctor Looks at Spiritualism, The Other Side* . . . Something revolted in him, he couldn't help it; he felt an actual physical revulsion at this kind of thinking. Still it was better than some other escapes. His friend Barnett, the actor, who said at night he went from room to room, after his wife was asleep, collecting empty glasses. ("Once I found one by the Water Pik, a second on the ledge beside the tub, a third on the back of the john, and a fourth on the floor beside the john. . . .")

He looked sideways at his wife, who was absorbed, it seemed, in watching him on the screen. Her face was tense, alert, animated. She did not look mad. She wore slim gray pants and a loose-knit pullover made of some silvery material, like a knight's chain mail. The lines of her profile were clear and silvery themselves, somehow sexless and pure, like a child's profile. He no longer felt lust when he looked at her, only a sad determination to protect her. He had a mistress in town, whom he loved, but he had explained, right from the beginning, that he considered himself married for the rest of his life. He told this woman the whole story. "And I am implicated in it. I could never leave her." An intelligent, sensitive woman, she had actually wept and said, "Of course not."

He always wore the same pajamas, a shade too big, but always clean. Obviously washed again and again in a machine that went through its cycles frequently. She imagined his "other mother," a harassed woman with several children, short on money, on time, on dreams—all the things she herself had too much of. The family lived, she believed, somewhere in Florida, probably on the west coast. She had worked that out from the little coquina shells: their bright colors, even in moonlight shining through a small window with spider plants in it. His face and arms had been suntanned early in the spring and late into the autumn. They never spoke or touched. She was not sure how much of this he understood. She tried and failed to remember where she herself had gone, in those little night journeys to the fishpond. Perhaps he never remembered afterward, when he woke up, clutching his jar, in a roomful of brothers and sisters. Or with a worried mother or father come to collect him, asleep by the sea. Once she had a very clear dream of the whole family, living in a trailer, with palm trees. But that was a dream; she recognized its difference in quality from those truly magic times when, through his own childish powers, he somehow found a will strong enough, or innocent enough, to project himself upon her still-floating consciousness, as clearly and as believably as her own husband's image on the screen.

There had been six of those times in six months. She dared to look forward to more. So unafraid he was. The last time was the day after Victoria Darrow and her young lover and her own good husband had returned to the city. She had gone farther with the child than ever before. On a starry-clear, cold September Monday, she had coaxed him down the stairs and out of the house with her. He held to the banisters, a child unused to stairs, and yet she knew there was no danger; he floated in his own dream with her. She took him to see Blue Boy. Who disappointed her by whining and backing away in fear. And then to the barn to see the horse. Who perked up his ears and looked interested. There was no touching, of course, no touching or speaking. Later she wondered if horses, then, were more magical than dogs. If dogs were more "realistic." She was glad the family was poor, the mother harassed. They could not afford any expensive child psychiatrist who would hypnotize him out of his night journeys.

He loved her. She knew that. Even if he never remembered her in his other life.

"At last I was beginning to understand what Teilhard de Chardin meant when he said that man's true home is the mind. I understood that when the mystics tell us that the mind is a place, they *don't mean it as a metaphor.* I found these new powers developed with practice. I had to detach myself from my ordinary physical personality. The intelligent part of me had to remain wide awake, and move down into this world of thoughts, dreams and memories. After several such journeyings I understood something else: dream and reality aren't competitors, but reciprocal sources of consciousness." This she read in a "respectable book," by a "respectable man," a scientist, alive and living in England, only a few years older than herself. She looked down at the dog, sleeping on the rug. His lean silvery body actually ran as he slept! Suddenly his muzzle lifted, the savage teeth snapped. Where was he "really" now? Did the dream rabbit in his jaws know it was a dream? There was much to think about, between her trips to the nursery.

Would the boy grow, would she see his body slowly emerging from its child's shape, the arms and legs lengthening, the face thinning out into a man's—like a certain advertisement for bread she had seen on TV where a child grows up, in less than a half-minute of sponsor time, right before the viewer's eyes. Would he grow into a man, grow a beard . . . outgrow the nursery region of his mind where they had been able to meet?

And yet, some daylight part of his mind must have retained an image of her from that single daylight time they had looked into each other's eyes.

The worst thing, such an awful thing to happen to a young woman . . . She was having this natural childbirth, you see, her husband in the delivery room with her, and the pains were coming a half-minute apart, and the doctor had just said, "This is going to be a breeze, Mrs. McNair," and they never knew exactly what went wrong, but all of a sudden the pains stopped and they had to go in after the baby without even time to give her a saddle block or any sort of anesthetic. . . . They must have practically had to tear it out of her . . . the husband fainted. The baby was born dead, and they gave her a heavy sedative to put her out all night.

When she woke the next morning, before she had time to remember what had happened, a nurse suddenly entered the room and laid a baby in her arms. "Here's your little boy," she said cheerfully, and the woman thought, with a profound, religious relief, *So that other nightmare was a dream,* and she had the child at her breast feeding him before the nurse realized her mistake and rushed back into the room, but they had to knock the poor woman out with more sedatives before she would let the child go. She was screaming and so was the little baby and they clung to each other till she passed out.

55   They would have let the nurse go, only it wasn't entirely her fault. The hospital was having a strike at the time; some of the nurses were outside picketing and this nurse had been working straight through for forty-eight hours, and when she was questioned afterward she said she had just mixed up the rooms, and yet, she said, when she had seen the woman and the baby clinging to each other like that, she had undergone a sort of revelation in her almost hallucinatory exhaustion: the nurse said she saw that all children and mothers were interchangeable, that nobody could own anybody or anything, anymore than you could own an idea that happened to be passing through the air and caught on your mind, or anymore than you owned the rosebush that grew in your back yard. There were only mothers and children, she realized; though, afterward, the realization faded.

It was the kind of freakish thing that happens once in a million times, and it's a wonder the poor woman kept her sanity.

In the intervals, longer than those measured by any stopwatch, she waited for him. In what the world accepted as "time," she shopped for groceries, for clothes; she read; she waved from her bottle-green car to Mrs. Frye, trimming the hedge in front of the liquor store, to Mrs. DePuy, hanging out her children's pajamas in the back yard of the old Patroon farm. She rode her horse through the fields of the waning season, letting him have his head; she rode like the wind, a happy, happy woman. She rode faster than fear because she was a woman in a dream, a woman anxiously awaiting her child's sleep. The stallion's hoofs pounded the earth. Oiling his tractor, DePuy resented the foolish woman and almost wished for a woodchuck hole to break that arrogant ride. Wished deep in a violent level of himself he never knew he had. For he was a kind, distracted father and husband, a practical, hard-working man who would never descend deeply into himself. Her body, skimming through time, felt weightless to the horse.

Was she a woman riding a horse and dreaming she was a mother who anxiously awaited her child's sleep; or was she a mother dreaming of herself as a free spirit who could ride her horse like the wind because she had nothing to fear?

I am a happy woman, that's all I know. Who can explain such things?

QUESTIONS FOR DISCUSSION AND WRITING

1. How do Mrs. McNair's reading and her childhood sessions with her psychiatrist help establish the conflict in this story? What justifies the narrator's resolution of this conflict?

2. How do neighbors characterize Mrs. McNair? In what ways does Victoria serve as a direct contrast to her? How does such a contrast help characterize the two women?

3. In what ways do the Dutch farming village and the old house provide an appropriate setting for this story? In particular, how does the guest room provide an appropriate setting for Victoria?

4. Godwin tells this story primarily from the wife's point of view, but occasionally she switches to the point of view of a neighbor or of Mr. McNair. How do they help verify the wife's assumption that everyone lives a double life?

5. In what sense does this story demonstrate that "man's true home is the mind"? What produces Mrs. McNair's sense of complete freedom and joy in the final scene of the story?

Stories for Comparison

Raymond Carver's "A Small, Good Thing" (pages 350–368); Tillie Olsen's "I Stand Here Ironing" (pages 1004–1011).

48

NADINE GORDIMER

Town and Country Lovers

NADINE GORDIMER was born in 1923 in Springs, South Africa, and attended private preparatory schools as well as the University of Witwatersrand in Johannesburg. Although Gordimer has held teaching positions at Harvard, Northwestern, Michigan, and Columbia universities, she has devoted most of her time to writing about life in her native South Africa. Her stories have appeared in magazines such as *The New Yorker, Atlantic Monthly, Harper's,* and *Holiday,* and have been collected in several volumes such as *Face to Face* (1949), *The Soft Voice of the Serpent* (1952), *Friday's Footprint* (1960), *Not for Publication* (1965), *Livingstone's Companions* (1971), *A Soldier's Embrace* (1980), and *Something Out There* (1984). Some of her best nonfiction appears in *The Essential Gordimer* (1988). Her novels, widely acclaimed for their sensitive examination of the effects of apartheid on the people of her politically troubled homeland, include *Occasion for Loving* (1963), *The Burgher's Daughter* (1979), *July's People* (1981), and *None to Accompany Me* (1994). Gordimer was awarded the Nobel Prize for Literature in 1991. "Town and Country Lovers," reprinted from *A Soldier's Embrace,* documents the complications, private and public, of two interracial romances.

One

Dr Franz-Josef von Leinsdorf is a geologist absorbed in his work; wrapped up in it, as the saying goes—year after year the experience of this work enfolds him, swaddling him away from the landscapes, the cities and the people, wherever he lives: Peru, New Zealand, the United States. He's always been like that, his mother could confirm from their native Austria. There, even as a handsome small boy he presented only his profile to her: turned away to his bits of rock and stone. His few relaxations have not changed much since then. An occasional skiing trip, listening to music, reading poetry—Rainer Maria Rilke once stayed in his grandmother's hunting lodge in the forests of Styria and the boy was introduced to Rilke's poems while very young.

Layer upon layer, country after country, wherever his work takes him—and now he has been almost seven years in Africa. First the Côte d'Ivoire, and for the past five years, South Africa. The shortage of skilled manpower brought about his recruitment here. He has no interest in the politics of the countries he works in. His private preoccupation-within-the-preoccupation of his work has been research into underground water-courses, but the mining company that employs him in a senior though not executive capacity is interested only in mineral discovery. So he is much out in the field—which is the veld, here—seeking new gold, copper, platinum and uranium deposits. When he is at home—on this particular job, in this particular country, this city—he lives in a two-roomed flat in a suburban block with a landscaped garden, and does his shopping at a supermarket conveniently across the street. He is not married—yet. That is how his colleagues, and the typists and secretaries at the mining company's head office, would define his situation. Both men and women would describe him as a good-looking man, in a foreign way, with the lower half of the face dark and middle-aged (his mouth is thin and curving, and no matter how close-shaven his beard shows like fine shot embedded in the skin round mouth and chin) and the upper half contradictorily young, with deep-set eyes (some would say grey, some black), thick eyelashes and brows. A tangled gaze: through which concentration and gleaming thoughtfulness perhaps appear as fire and languor. It is this that the women in the office mean when they remark he's not unattractive. Although the gaze seems to promise, he has never invited any one of them to go out with him. There is the general assumption he probably has a girl who's been picked for him, he's bespoken by one of his own kind, back home in Europe where he comes from. Many of these well-educated Europeans have no intention of becoming permanent immigrants; neither the remnant of white colonial life nor idealistic involvement with Black Africa appeals to them.

One advantage, at least, of living in underdeveloped or half-developed countries is that flats are serviced. All Dr von Leinsdorf has to do for himself is buy his own supplies and cook an evening meal if he doesn't want to go to a restaurant. It is simply a matter of dropping in to the supermarket on his way from his car to his flat after work in the afternoon. He wheels a trolley up and down the shelves, and his simple needs are presented to him in the form of tins, packages, plastic-wrapped meat, cheeses, fruit and vegetables, tubes, bottles . . . At the cashiers' counters where customers must converge and queue there are racks of small items uncategorized, for last-minute purchase. Here, as the coloured girl cashier punches the adding machine, he picks up cigarettes and perhaps a packet of salted nuts or a bar of nougat. Or razor-blades, when he remembers he's running short. One evening in winter he saw that the cardboard display was empty of the brand of blades he preferred, and he drew the cashier's attention to this. These young coloured girls are usually pretty unhelpful, taking money and punching their machines in a manner that asserts with the time-serving obstinacy of the half-literate the limit of any responsibility towards customers, but this one ran an alert glance over the selection of razor-blades, apologized that she was not allowed to leave her post, and said she would see that the stock was replenished "next time." A day or two later she recognized him, gravely, as he took his turn before her counter—"I ahssed them, but it's out of stock. You can't get it. I did ahss about it." He said this didn't matter. "When it comes in, I can keep a few packets for you." He thanked her.

He was away with the prospectors the whole of the next week. He arrived back in town just before nightfall on Friday, and was on his way from car to flat with his arms full of briefcase, suitcase and canvas bags when someone stopped him by standing timidly in his path. He was about to dodge round unseeingly on the crowded pavement but she spoke. "We got the blades in now. I didn't see you in the shop this week, but I kept some for when you come. So . . ."

5   He recognized her. He had never seen her standing before, and she was wearing a coat. She was rather small and finely-made, for one of them. The coat was skimpy but no big backside jutted. The cold brought an apricot-graining of warm colour to her cheekbones, beneath which a very small face was quite delicately hollowed, and the skin was smooth, the subdued satiny colour of certain yellow wood. That crêpey hair, but worn drawn back flat and in a little knot pushed into one of the cheap wool chignons that (he recognized also) hung in the miscellany of small goods along with the razor-blades, at the supermarket. He said thanks, he was in a hurry, he'd only just got back from a trip—shifting the burdens he carried, to demonstrate. "Oh shame." She acknowledged his load. "But if you want I can run in and get it for you quickly. If you want."

He saw at once it was perfectly clear that all the girl meant was that she would go back to the supermarket, buy the blades and bring the packet to him there where he stood, on the pavement. And it seemed that it was this certainty that made him say, in the kindly tone of assumption used for an obliging underling, "I live just across there—*Atlantis*—that flat building. Could you drop them by, for me—number seven-hundred-and-eighteen, seventh floor—"

She had not before been inside one of these big flat buildings near where she worked. She lived a bus- and train-ride away to the West of the city, but this side of the black townships, in a township for people her tint. There was a pool with ferns, not plastic, and even a little waterfall pumped electrically over rocks, in the entrance of the building *Atlantis;* she didn't wait for the lift marked GOODS but took the one meant for whites and a white woman with one of those sausage-dogs on a lead got in with her but did not pay her any attention. The corridors leading to the flats were nicely glassed-in, not draughty.

He wondered if he should give her a twenty-cent piece for her trouble—ten cents would be right for a black; but she said, "Oh no—please, here—" standing outside his open door and awkwardly pushing back at his hand the change from the money he'd given her for the razor-blades. She was smiling, for the first time, in the dignity of refusing a tip. It was difficult to know how to treat these people, in this country; to know what they expected. In spite of her embarrassing refusal of the coin, she stood there, completely unassuming, fists thrust down the pockets of her cheap coat against the cold she'd come in from, rather pretty thin legs neatly aligned, knee to knee, ankle to ankle.

"Would you like a cup of coffee or something?"

10   He couldn't very well take her into his study-cum-living-room and offer her a drink. She followed him to his kitchen, but at the sight of her pulling out the single chair to drink her cup of coffee at the kitchen table, he said, "No—bring it in here—" and led the way into the big room where, among his books and his papers, his files

of scientific correspondence (and the cigar boxes of stamps from the envelopes), his racks of records, his specimens of minerals and rocks, he lived alone.

It was no trouble to her; she saved him the trips to the supermarket and brought him his groceries two or three times a week. All he had to do was to leave a list and the key under the doormat, and she would come up in her lunch-hour to collect them, returning to put his supplies in the flat after work. Sometimes he was home and sometimes not. He bought a box of chocolates and left it, with a note, for her to find; and that was acceptable, apparently, as a gratuity.

Her eyes went over everything in the flat although her body tried to conceal its sense of being out of place by remaining as still as possible, holding its contours in the chair offered her as a stranger's coat is set aside and remains exactly as left until the owner takes it up to go. "You collect?"

"Well, these are specimens—connected with my work."

"My brother used to collect. Miniatures. With brandy and whisky and that, in them. From all over. Different countries."

The second time she watched him grinding coffee for the cup he had offered her 15 she said, "You always do that? Always when you make coffee?"

"But of course. Is it no good, for you? Do I make it too strong?"

"Oh it's just I'm not used to it. We buy it ready—you know, it's in a bottle, you just add a bit to the milk or water."

He laughed, instructive: "That's not coffee, that's a synthetic flavouring. In my country we drink only real coffee, fresh, from the beans—you smell how good it is as it's being ground?"

She was stopped by the caretaker and asked what she wanted in the building? Heavy with the *bona fides* of groceries clutched to her body, she said she was working at number 718, on the seventh floor. The caretaker did not tell her not to use the whites' lift; after all, she was not black; her family was very light-skinned.

There was the item "grey button for trousers" on one of his shopping lists. She 20 said as she unpacked the supermarket carrier, "Give me the pants, so long, then," and sat on his sofa that was always gritty with fragments of pipe tobacco, sewing in and out through the four holes of the button with firm, fluent movements of the right hand, gestures supplying the articulacy missing from her talk. She had a little yokel's, peasant's (he thought of it) gap between her two front teeth when she smiled that he didn't much like, but, face ellipsed to three-quarter angle, eyes cast down in concentration with soft lips almost closed, this didn't matter. He said, watching her sew, "You're a good girl"; and touched her.

She remade the bed every late afternoon when they left it and she dressed again before she went home. After a week there was a day when late afternoon became evening, and they were still in the bed.

"Can't you stay the night?"

"My mother," she said.

"Phone her. Make an excuse." He was a foreigner. He had been in the country five years, but he didn't understand that people don't usually have telephones in their houses, where she lived. She got up to dress. He didn't want that tender body to go out in the night cold and kept hindering her with the interruption of his hands; saying nothing. Before she put on her coat, when the body had already disappeared, he spoke. "But you must make some arrangement."

25   "Oh my mother!" Her face opened to fear and vacancy he could not read.

He was not entirely convinced the woman would think of her daughter as some pure and unsullied virgin . . . "Why?"

The girl said, "S'e'll be scared. S'e'll be scared we get caught."

"Don't tell her anything. Say I'm employing you." In this country he was working in now there were generally rooms on the roofs of flat buildings for tenants' servants.

She said: "That's what I told the caretaker."

30   She ground fresh coffee beans every time he wanted a cup while he was working at night. She never attempted to cook anything until she had watched in silence while he did it the way he liked, and she learned to reproduce exactly the simple dishes he preferred. She handled his pieces of rock and stone, at first admiring the colours—"It'd make a beautiful ring or a necklace, ay." Then he showed her the striations, the formation of each piece, and explained what each was, and how, in the long life of the earth, it had been formed. He named the mineral it yielded, and what that was used for. He worked at his papers, writing, writing, every night, so it did not matter that they could not go out together to public places. On Sundays she got into his car in the basement garage and they drove to the country and picnicked away up in the Magaliesberg, where there was no one. He read or poked about among the rocks; they climbed together, to the mountain pools. He taught her to swim. She had never seen the sea. She squealed and shrieked in the water, showing the gap between her teeth, as—it crossed his mind—she must do when among her own people. Occasionally he had to go out to dinner at the houses of colleagues from the mining company; she sewed and listened to the radio in the flat and he found her in the bed, warm and already asleep, by the time he came in. He made his way into her body without speaking; she made him welcome without a word. Once he put on evening dress for a dinner at his country's consulate; watching him brush one or two fallen hairs from the shoulders of the dark jacket that sat so well on him, she saw a huge room, all chandeliers and people dancing some dance from a costume film—stately, hand-to-hand. She supposed he was going to fetch, in her place in the car, a partner for the evening. They never kissed when either left the flat; he said, suddenly, kindly, pausing as he picked up cigarettes and keys, "Don't be lonely." And added, "Wouldn't you like to visit your family sometimes, when I have to go out?"

He had told her he was going home to his mother in the forests and mountains of his country near the Italian border (he showed her on the map) after Christmas. She had not told him how her mother, not knowing there was any other variety, assumed he was a medical doctor, so she had talked to her about the doctor's children and the doctor's wife who was a very kind lady, glad to have someone who could help out in the surgery as well as the flat.

She remarked wonderingly on his ability to work until midnight or later, after a day at work. She was so tired when she came home from her cash register at the supermarket that once dinner was eaten she could scarcely keep awake. He explained in a way she could understand that while the work she did was repetitive, undemanding of any real response from her intelligence, requiring little mental or physical effort and therefore unrewarding, his work was his greatest interest, it taxed his mental capacities to their limit, exercised all his concentration, and rewarded him constantly as much with the excitement of a problem presented as with the satisfaction of a problem solved. He said later, putting away his papers, speaking out of a silence: "Have you done other kinds of work?" She said, "I was in a clothing factory before. Sportbeau shirts; you know? But the pay's better in the shop."

Of course. Being a conscientious newspaper-reader in every country he lived in, he was aware that it was only recently that the retail consumer trade in this one had been allowed to employ coloureds as shop assistants; even punching a cash register represented advancement. With the continuing shortage of semi-skilled whites a girl like this might be able to edge a little farther into the white-collar category. He began to teach her to type. He was aware that her English was poor, even though, as a foreigner, in his ears her pronunciation did not offend, nor categorize her as it would in those of someone of his education whose mother tongue was English. He corrected her grammatical mistakes but missed the less obvious ones because of his own sometimes exotic English usage—she continued to use the singular pronoun "it" when what was required was the plural "they." Because he was a foreigner (although so clever, as she saw) she was less inhibited than she might have been by the words she knew she misspelled in her typing. While she sat at the typewriter she thought how one day she would type notes for him, as well as making coffee the way he liked it, and taking him inside her body without saying anything, and sitting (even if only through the empty streets of quiet Sundays) beside him in his car, like a wife.

On a summer night near Christmas—he had already bought and hidden a slightly showy but nevertheless good watch he thought she would like—there was a knocking at the door that brought her out of the bathroom and him to his feet, at his work-table. No one ever came to the flat at night; he had no friends intimate enough to drop in without warning. The summons was an imperious banging that did not pause and clearly would not stop until the door was opened.

She stood in the open bathroom doorway gazing at him across the passage into the living-room; her bare feet and shoulders were free of a big bath-towel. She said nothing, did not even whisper. The flat seemed to shake with the strong unhurried blows. 35

He made as if to go to the door, at last, but now she ran and clutched him by both arms. She shook her head wildly; her lips drew back but her teeth were clenched, she didn't speak. She pulled him into the bedroom, snatched some clothes from the clean laundry laid out on the bed and got into the wall-cupboard, thrusting the key at his hand. Although his arms and calves felt weakly cold he was horrified, distastefully embarrassed at the sight of her pressed back crouching there under his suits and coat; it was horrible and ridiculous. *Come out!* he whispered. *No! Come out!* She hissed: *Where? Where can I go?*

Never mind! Get out of there!

He put out his hand to grasp her. At bay, she said with all the force of her terrible whisper, baring the gap in her teeth: *I'll throw myself out the window.*

She forced the key into his hand like the handle of a knife. He closed the door on her face and drove the key home in the lock, then dropped it among coins in his trouser pocket.

40   He unslotted the chain that was looped across the flat door. He turned the serrated knob of the Yale lock. The three policemen, two in plain clothes, stood there without impatience although they had been banging on the door for several minutes. The big dark one with an elaborate moustache held out in a hand wearing a plaited gilt ring some sort of identity card.

Dr von Leinsdorf said quietly, the blood coming strangely back to legs and arms, "What is it?"

The sergeant told him they knew there was a coloured girl in the flat. They had had information; "I been watching this flat three months, I know."

"I am alone here." Dr von Leinsdorf did not raise his voice.

"I know, I know who is here. Come—" And the sergeant and his two assistants went into the living-room, the kitchen, the bathroom (the sergeant picked up a bottle of after-shave cologne, seemed to study the French label) and the bedroom. The assistants removed the clean laundry that was laid upon the bed and then turned back the bedding, carrying the sheets over to be examined by the sergeant under the lamp. They talked to one another in Afrikaans, which the Doctor did not understand. The sergeant himself looked under the bed, and lifted the long curtains at the window. The wall cupboard was of the kind that has no knobs; he saw that it was locked and began to ask in Afrikaans, then politely changed to English, "Give us the key."

45   Dr von Leinsdorf said, "I'm sorry, I left it at my office—I always lock and take my keys with me in the mornings."

"It's no good, man, you better give me the key."

He smiled a little, reasonably. "It's on my office desk."

The assistants produced a screwdriver and he watched while they inserted it where the cupboard doors met, gave it quick, firm but not forceful leverage. He heard the lock give.

She had been naked, it was true, when they knocked. But now she was wearing a long-sleeved T-shirt with an appliquéd butterfly motif on one breast, and a pair of jeans. Her feet were still bare; she had managed, by feel, in the dark, to get into some of the clothing she had snatched from the bed, but she had no shoes. She had perhaps been weeping behind the cupboard door (her cheeks looked stained) but now her face was sullen and she was breathing heavily, her diaphragm contracting and expanding exaggeratedly and her breasts pushing against the cloth. It made her appear angry; it might simply have been that she was half-suffocated in the cupboard and needed oxygen. She did not look at Dr von Leinsdorf. She would not reply to the sergeant's questions.

50   They were taken to the police station where they were at once separated and in turn led for examination by the district surgeon. The man's underwear was taken away and examined, as the sheets had been, for signs of his seed. When the girl was

undressed, it was discovered that beneath her jeans she was wearing a pair of men's briefs with his name on the neatly-sewn laundry tag; in her haste, she had taken the wrong garment to her hiding-place.

Now she cried, standing there before the district surgeon in a man's underwear.

He courteously pretended not to notice. He handed briefs, jeans and T-shirt round the door, and motioned her to lie on a white-sheeted high table where he placed her legs apart, resting in stirrups, and put into her where the other had made his way so warmly a cold hard instrument that expanded wider and wider. Her thighs and knees trembled uncontrollably while the doctor looked into her and touched her deep inside with more hard instruments, carrying wafers of gauze.

When she came out of the examining room back to the charge office, Dr von Leinsdorf was not there; they must have taken him somewhere else. She spent what was left of the night in a cell, as he must be doing; but early in the morning she was released and taken home to her mother's house in the coloured township by a white man who explained he was the clerk of the lawyer who had been engaged for her by Dr von Leinsdorf. Dr von Leinsdorf, the clerk said, had also been bailed out that morning. He did not say when, or if she would see him again.

A statement made by the girl to the police was handed in to Court when she and the man appeared to meet charges of contravening the Immorality Act in a Johannesburg flat on the night of—December, 19—. *I lived with the white man in his flat. He had intercourse with me sometimes. He gave me tablets to take to prevent me becoming pregnant.*

Interviewed by the Sunday papers, the girl said, "I'm sorry for the sadness brought to my mother." She said she was one of nine children of a female laundry worker. She had left school in Standard Three because there was no money at home for gym clothes or a school blazer. She had worked as a machinist in a factory and a cashier in a supermarket. Dr von Leinsdorf taught her to type his notes.

Dr Franz-Josef von Leinsdorf, described as the grandson of a baroness, a cultured man engaged in international mineralogical research, said he accepted social distinctions between people but didn't think they should be legally imposed. "Even in my own country it's difficult for a person from a higher class to marry one from a lower class."

The two accused gave no evidence. They did not greet or speak to each other in Court. The Defence argued that the sergeant's evidence that they had been living together as man and wife was hearsay. (The woman with the dachshund, the caretaker?) The magistrate acquitted them because the State failed to prove carnal intercourse had taken place on the night of—December, 19—.

The girl's mother was quoted, with photograph, in the Sunday papers: "I won't let my daughter work as a servant for a white man again."

Two

The farm children play together when they are small; but once the white children go away to school they soon don't play together any more, even in the holidays.

Although most of the black children get some sort of schooling, they drop every year farther behind the grades passed by the white children; the childish vocabulary, the child's exploration of the adventurous possibilities of dam, koppies, mealie lands and veld—there comes a time when the white children have surpassed these with the vocabulary of boarding-school and the possibilities of inter-school sports matches and the kind of adventures seen at the cinema. This usefully coincides with the age of twelve or thirteen; so that by the time early adolescence is reached, the black children are making, along with the bodily changes common to all, an easy transition to adult forms of address, beginning to call their old playmates *missus* and *baasie*— little master.

60   The trouble was Paulus Eysendyck did not seem to realize that Thebedi was now simply one of the crowd of farm children down at the kraal, recognizable in his sisters' old clothes. The first Christmas holidays after he had gone to boarding-school he brought home for Thebedi a painted box he had made in his wood-work class. He had to give it to her secretly because he had nothing for the other children at the kraal. And she gave him, before he went back to school, a bracelet she had made of thin brass wire and the grey-and-white beans of the castor-oil crop his father cultivated. (When they used to play together, she was the one who had taught Paulus how to make clay oxen for their toy spans.) There was a craze, even in the *platteland* towns like the one where he was at school, for boys to wear elephant-hair and other bracelets beside their watch-straps; his was admired, friends asked him to get similar ones for them. He said the natives made them on his father's farm and he would try.

When he was fifteen, six feet tall, and tramping round at school dances with the girls from the "sister" school in the same town; when he had learnt how to tease and flirt and fondle quite intimately these girls who were the daughters of prosperous farmers like his father; when he had even met one who, at a wedding he had attended with his parents on a nearby farm, had let him do with her in a locked storeroom what people did when they made love—when he was as far from his childhood as all this, he still brought home from a shop in town a red plastic belt and gilt hoop ear-rings for the black girl, Thebedi. She told her father the missus had given these to her as a reward for some work she had done—it was true she sometimes was called to help out in the farmhouse. She told the girls in the kraal that she had a sweetheart nobody knew about, far away, away on another farm, and they giggled, and teased, and admired her. There was a boy in the kraal called Njabulo who said he wished he could have bought her a belt and ear-rings.

When the farmer's son was home for the holidays she wandered far from the kraal and her companions. He went for walks alone. They had not arranged this; it was an urge each followed independently. He knew it was she, from a long way off. She knew that his dog would not bark at her. Down at the dried-up river-bed where five or six years ago the children had caught a leguaan one great day—a creature that combined ideally the size and ferocious aspect of the crocodile with the harmlessness of the lizard—they squatted side by side on the earth bank. He told her traveller's tales: about school, about the punishments at school, particularly, exaggerating both their nature and his indifference to them. He told her about the town of Middleburg, which she had never seen. She had nothing to tell but she prompted with many questions, like any good listener. While he talked he twisted and tugged at the roots of white stinkwood and Cape willow trees that looped out of the eroded earth around them. It had always been a good spot for children's games, down there hidden by the mesh of old, ant-eaten trees held in place by vigorous ones, wild asparagus bushing up between the trunks, and here and there prickly-pear cactus sunken-skinned and bristly, like an old man's face, keeping alive sapless until the next rainy season. She punctured the dry hide of a prickly-pear again and again with a sharp stick while she listened. She laughed a lot at what he told her, sometimes dropping her face on her knees, sharing amusement with the cool shady earth beneath her bare feet. She put on her pair of shoes—white sandals, thickly Blanco-ed against the farm dust—when he was on the farm, but these were taken off and laid aside, at the river-bed.

One summer afternoon when there was water flowing there and it was very hot she waded in as they used to do when they were children, her dress bunched modestly and tucked into the legs of her pants. The schoolgirls he went swimming with at dams or pools on neighbouring farms wore bikinis but the sight of their dazzling bellies and thighs in the sunlight had never made him feel what he felt now, when the girl came up the bank and sat beside him, the drops of water beading off her dark legs the only points of light in the earth-smelling, deep shade. They were not afraid of one another, they had known one another always; he did with her what he had done that time in the storeroom at the wedding, and this time it was so lovely, so lovely, he was surprised . . . and she was surprised by it, too—he could see in her dark face that was part of the shade, with her big dark eyes, shiny as soft water, watching him attentively: as she had when they used to huddle over their teams of mud oxen, as she had when he told her about detention weekends at school.

They went to the river-bed often through those summer holidays. They met just before the light went, as it does quite quickly, and each returned home with the dark—she to her mother's hut, he to the farmhouse—in time for the evening meal. He did not tell her about school or town any more. She did not ask questions any longer. He told her, each time, when they would meet again. Once or twice it was very early in the morning; the lowing of the cows being driven to graze came to them where they lay, dividing them with unspoken recognition of the sound read in their two pairs of eyes, opening so close to each other.

He was a popular boy at school. He was in the second, then the first soccer team. The head girl of the "sister" school was said to have a crush on him; he didn't particularly like her, but there was a pretty blonde who put up her long hair into a kind of doughnut with a black ribbon round it, whom he took to see films when the schoolboys and girls had a free Saturday afternoon. He had been driving tractors and other farm vehicles since he was ten years old, and as soon as he was eighteen he got a driver's licence and in the holidays, this last year of his school life, he took neighbours' daughters to dances and to the drive-in cinema that had just opened twenty kilometres from the farm. His sisters were married, by then; his parents often left him in charge of the farm over the weekend while they visited the young wives and grandchildren.

When Thebedi saw the farmer and his wife drive away on a Saturday afternoon, the boot of their Mercedes filled with fresh-killed poultry and vegetables from the garden that it was part of her father's work to tend, she knew that she must come not to the river-bed but up to the house. The house was an old one, thick-walled, dark against the heat. The kitchen was its lively thoroughfare, with servants, food supplies, begging cats and dogs, pots boiling over, washing being damped for ironing, and the big deep-freeze the missus had ordered from town, bearing a crocheted mat and a vase of plastic irises. But the dining-room with the bulging-legged heavy table was shut up in its rich, old smell of soup and tomato sauce. The sitting-room curtains were drawn and the T.V. set silent. The door of the parents' bedroom was locked and the empty rooms where the girls had slept had sheets of plastic spread over the beds. It was in one of these that she and the farmer's son stayed together whole nights—almost: she had to get away before the house servants, who knew her, came in at dawn. There was a risk someone would discover her or traces of her presence if he took her to his own bedroom, although she had looked into it many times when she was helping out in the house and knew well, there, the row of silver cups he had won at school.

When she was eighteen and the farmer's son nineteen and working with his father on the farm before entering a veterinary college, the young man Njabulo asked her father for her. Njabulo's parents met with hers and the money he was to pay in place of the cows it is customary to give a prospective bride's parents was settled upon. He had no cows to offer; he was a labourer on the Eysendyck farm, like her father. A bright youngster; old Eysendyck had taught him brick-laying and was using him for odd jobs in construction, around the place. She did not tell the farmer's son that her parents had arranged for her to marry. She did not tell him, either, before he left for his first term at the veterinary college, that she thought she was going to have a baby. Two months after her marriage to Njabulo, she gave birth to a daughter. There was no disgrace in that; among her people it is customary for a young man to make sure, before marriage, that the chosen girl is not barren, and Njabulo had made love to her then. But the infant was very light and did not quickly grow darker as most African babies do. Already at birth there was on its head a quantity of straight, fine floss, like that which carries the seeds of certain weeds in the veld. The unfocused eyes it opened were grey flecked with yellow. Njabulo was the matt, opaque coffee-grounds colour that has always been called black; the colour of Thebedi's legs on which beaded water looked oyster-shell blue, the same colour as Thebedi's face, where the black eyes, with their interested gaze and clear whites, were so dominant.

Njabulo made no complaint. Out of his farm labourer's earnings he bought from the Indian store a cellophane-windowed pack containing a pink plastic bath, six napkins, a card of safety pins, a knitted jacket, cap and bootees, a dress, and a tin of Johnson's Baby Powder, for Thebedi's baby.

When it was two weeks old Paulus Eysendyck arrived home from the veterinary college for the holidays. He drank a glass of fresh, still-warm milk in the childhood familiarity of his mother's kitchen and heard her discussing with the old house-servant where they could get a reliable substitute to help out now that the girl Thebedi had had a baby. For the first time since he was a small boy he came right into the kraal. It was eleven o'clock in the morning. The men were at work in the lands. He looked about him, urgently; the women turned away, each not wanting to be the one approached to point out where Thebedi lived. Thebedi appeared, coming slowly from the hut Njabulo had built in white man's style, with a tin chimney, and a proper window with glass panes set in straight as walls made of unfired bricks would allow. She greeted him with hands brought together and a token movement representing the respectful bob with which she was accustomed to acknowledge she was in the presence of his father or mother. He lowered his head under the doorway of her home and went in. He said, "I want to see. Show me."

She had taken the bundle off her back before she came out into the light to face him. She moved between the iron bedstead made up with Njabulo's checked blankets and the small wooden table where the pink plastic bath stood among food and kitchen pots, and picked up the bundle from the snugly-blanketed grocer's box where it lay. The infant was asleep; she revealed the closed, pale, plump tiny face, with a bubble of spit at the corner of the mouth, the spidery pink hands stirring. She took off the woollen cap and the straight fine hair flew up after it in static electricity, showing gilded strands here and there. He said nothing. She was watching him as she had done when they were little, and the gang of children had trodden down a crop in their games or transgressed in some other way for which he, as the farmer's son, the white one among them, must intercede with the farmer. She disturbed the sleeping face by scratching or tickling gently at a cheek with one finger, and slowly the eyes opened, saw nothing, were still asleep, and then, awake, no longer narrowed, looked out at them, grey with yellowish flecks, his own hazel eyes.

He struggled for a moment with a grimace of tears, anger and self-pity. She could not put out her hand to him. He said, "You haven't been near the house with it?"

She shook her head.

"Never?"

Again she shook her head.

"Don't take it out. Stay inside. Can't you take it away somewhere. You must give it to someone—"

She moved to the door with him.

He said, "I'll see what I will do. I don't know." And then he said: "I feel like killing myself."

Her eyes began to glow, to thicken with tears. For a moment there was the feeling between them that used to come when they were alone down at the river-bed.

He walked out.

Two days later, when his mother and father had left the farm for the day, he appeared again. The women were away on the lands, weeding, as they were employed to do as casual labour in summer; only the very old remained, propped up on the ground outside the huts in the flies and the sun. Thebedi did not ask him in. The child had not been well; it had diarrhoea. He asked where its food was. She said, "The milk comes from me." He went into Njabulo's house, where the child lay; she did not follow but stayed outside the door and watched without seeing an old crone who had lost her mind, talking to herself, talking to the fowls who ignored her.

She thought she heard small grunts from the hut, the kind of infant grunt that indicates a full stomach, a deep sleep. After a time, long or short she did not know, he

came out and walked away with plodding stride (his father's gait) out of sight, towards his father's house.

The baby was not fed during the night and although she kept telling Njabulo it
was sleeping, he saw for himself in the morning that it was dead. He comforted her
with words and caresses. She did not cry but simply sat, staring at the door. Her
hands were cold as dead chickens' feet to his touch.

Njabulo buried the little baby where farm workers were buried, in the place in
the veld the farmer had given them. Some of the mounds had been left to weather
away unmarked, others were covered with stones and a few had fallen wooden
crosses. He was going to make a cross but before it was finished the police came and
dug up the grave and took away the dead baby: someone—one of the other labourers? their women?—had reported that the baby was almost white, that, strong and
healthy, it had died suddenly after a visit by the farmer's son. Pathological tests on
the infant corpse showed intestinal damage not always consistent with death by natural causes.

Thebedi went for the first time to the country town where Paulus had been to
school, to give evidence at the preparatory examination into the charge of murder
brought against him. She cried hysterically in the witness box, saying yes, yes (the
gilt hoop ear-rings swung in her ears), she saw the accused pouring liquid into the
baby's mouth. She said he had threatened to shoot her if she told anyone.

85   More than a year went by before, in that same town, the case was brought
to trial. She came to Court with a new-born baby on her back. She wore gilt
hoop ear-rings; she was calm; she said she had not seen what the white man did
in the house.

Paulus Eysendyck said he had visited the hut but had not poisoned the child.

The Defence did not contest that there had been a love relationship between the
accused and the girl, or that intercourse had taken place, but submitted there was no
proof that the child was the accused's.

The judge told the accused there was strong suspicion against him but not
enough proof that he had committed the crime. The Court could not accept the girl's
evidence because it was clear she had committed perjury either at this trial or at the
preparatory examination. There was the suggestion in the mind of the Court that she
might be an accomplice in the crime; but, again, insufficient proof.

The judge commended the honourable behaviour of the husband (sitting in court
in a brown-and-yellow-quartered golf cap bought for Sundays) who had not rejected
his wife and had "even provided clothes for the unfortunate infant out of his slender
means."

90   The verdict on the accused was "not guilty."

The young white man refused to accept the congratulations of press and public
and left the Court with his mother's raincoat shielding his face from photographers.
His father said to the press, "I will try and carry on as best I can to hold up my head
in the district."

Interviewed by the Sunday papers, who spelled her name in a variety of ways,
the black girl, speaking in her own language, was quoted beneath her photograph:
"It was a thing of our childhood, we don't see each other any more."

QUESTIONS FOR DISCUSSION AND WRITING

1. How does Gordimer unify the two narratives into a single story? In what ways are the major conflicts in the two narratives different? How does the intervention of the legal system serve as the climax in each narrative?

2. How does Gordimer make the female protagonist in each narrative more sympathetic than her lover? How does his career as a geologist characterize von Leinsdorf? How does his schooling shape Paulus Eysendyck's character?

3. Why does Gordimer set the first narrative in the white man's urban world and the second part of the story in the black girl's rural world? How do the apartment and the river serve as symbolic settings for lovemaking? How does Gordimer lead her readers to understand the inhumanity of South Africa's social and legal system without directly criticizing it?

4. Why does Gordimer create an objective narrator in these two narratives? In what ways does the flat objectivity of this point of view add to or detract from the emotional power of the story?

5. How does Gordimer use both halves of this narrative to criticize the cruelty and folly of apartheid? How does Gordimer show us that the system is sexist as well as racist? How does the press report the events represented in the two stories?

Stories for Comparison

Chinua Achebe's "Vengeful Creditor" (pages 153–163); Ralph Ellison's "Battle Royal" (pages 472–482).

49

GRAHAM GREENE

The Destructors

GRAHAM GREENE (1904–1991) was born in Berkhamsted, Hertfordshire, England, and attended Balliol College, Oxford University. He began his career as a journalist, working as an editor for the London *Times* and writing film criticism for *The Spectator.* During the 1940s he worked as an editor for several publishers in London and as a correspondent with the British Foreign

Office in Africa. Greene published his first novel, *The Man Within,* in 1929, but he did not establish his reputation as a writer until *Stamboul Train* (1932), one of six works of fiction he called "entertainments" to distinguish them from his more serious novels. Greene also wrote several books of travel, such as *Journey Without Maps* (1936), *The Lawless Roads* (1939), and *Travels with My Aunt* (1969), and numerous screenplays based on his books and stories. He is best known for his serious novels, such as *Brighton Rock* (1938), *The Power and the Glory* (1940), *The Heart of the Matter* (1948), *The Quiet American* (1955), *A Burnt-Out Case* (1961), *The Comedians* (1966), *The Honorary Consul* (1973), *The Human Factor* (1978), and *Monsignor Quixote* (1982). "The Destructors," reprinted from *Collected Stories* (1973), describes how a gang of boys plan and complete the destruction of a house.

I

It was the eve of August Bank Holiday that the latest recruit became the leader of the Wormsley Common Gang. No one was surprised except Mike, but Mike at the age of nine was surprised by everything. "If you don't shut your mouth," somebody once said to him, "you'll get a frog down it." After that Mike had kept his teeth tightly clamped except when the surprise was too great.

The new recruit had been with the gang since the beginning of the summer holidays, and there were possibilities about his brooding silence that all recognized. He never wasted a word even to tell his name until that was required of him by the rules. When he said "Trevor" it was a statement of fact, not as it would have been with the others a statement of shame or defiance. Nor did anyone laugh except Mike, who finding himself without support and meeting the dark gaze of the newcomer opened his mouth and was quiet again. There was every reason why T., as he was afterwards referred to, should have been an object of mockery—there was his name (and they substituted the initial because otherwise they had no excuse not to laugh at it), the fact that his father, a former architect and present clerk, had "come down in the world" and that his mother considered herself better than the neighbors. What but an odd quality of danger, of the unpredictable, established him in the gang without any ignoble ceremony of initiation?

The gang met every morning in an impromptu car-park, the site of the last bomb of the first blitz. The leader, who was known as Blackie, claimed to have heard it fall, and no one was precise enough in his dates to point out that he would have been one year old and fast asleep on the down platform of Wormsley Common Underground Station. On one side of the car-park leant the first occupied house, No. 3, of the shattered Northwood Terrace—literally leant, for it had suffered from the blast of the bomb and the side walls were supported on wooden struts. A smaller bomb and some incendiaries had fallen beyond, so that the house stuck up like a jagged tooth and carried on the further wall relics of its neighbor, a dado, the remains of a fireplace. T., whose words were almost confined to voting "Yes" or "No" to the plan of operations proposed each day by Blackie, once startled the whole gang by saying broodingly, "Wren built that house, father says."

"Who's Wren?"

"The man who built St. Paul's."   5

"Who cares?" Blackie said. "It's only Old Misery's."

Old Misery—whose real name was Thomas—had once been a builder and decorator. He lived alone in the crippled house, doing for himself: once a week you could see him coming back across the common with bread and vegetables, and once as the boys played in the car-park he put his head over the smashed wall of his garden and looked at them.

"Been to the lav," one of the boys said, for it was common knowledge that since the bombs fell something had gone wrong with the pipes of the house and Old Misery was too mean to spend money on the property. He could do the redecorating himself at cost price, but he had never learnt plumbing. The lav was a wooden shed at the bottom of the narrow garden with a star-shaped hole in the door: it had escaped the blast which had smashed the house next door and sucked out the window-frames of No. 3.

The next time the gang became aware of Mr. Thomas was more surprising. Blackie, Mike and a thin yellow boy, who for some reason was called by his surname Summers, met him on the common coming back from the market. Mr. Thomas stopped them. He said glumly, "You belong to the lot that play in the car-park?"

Mike was about to answer when Blackie stopped him. As the leader he had re- 10 sponsibilities. "Suppose we are?" he said ambiguously.

"I got some chocolates," Mr. Thomas said. "Don't like 'em myself. Here you are. Not enough to go round, I don't suppose. There never is," he added with somber conviction. He handed over three packets of Smarties.

The gang were puzzled and perturbed by this action and tried to explain it away. "Bet someone dropped them and he picked 'em up," somebody suggested.

"Pinched 'em and then got in a bleeding funk," another thought aloud.

"It's a bribe," Summers said. "He wants us to stop bouncing balls on his wall."

"We'll show him we don't take bribes," Blackie said, and they sacrificed the 15 whole morning to the game of bouncing that only Mike was young enough to enjoy. There was no sign from Mr. Thomas.

Next day T. astonished them all. He was late at the rendezvous, and the voting for the day's exploit took place without him. At Blackie's suggestion the gang was to disperse in pairs, take buses at random and see how many free rides could be snatched from unwary conductors (the operation was to be carried out in pairs to avoid cheating). They were drawing lots for their companions when T. arrived.

"Where you been, T.?" Blackie asked. "You can't vote now. You know the rules."

"I've been *there*," T. said. He looked at the ground, as though he had thoughts to hide.

"Where?"

"At Old Misery's." Mike's mouth opened and then hurriedly closed again with 20 a click. He had remembered the frog.

"At Old Misery's?" Blackie said. There was nothing in the rules against it, but he had a sensation that T. was treading on dangerous ground. He asked hopefully, "Did you break in?"

"No. I rang the bell."

"And what did you say?"

"I said I wanted to see his house."

25 "What did he do?"

"He showed it to me."

"Pinch anything?"

"No."

"What did you do it for then?"

30 The gang had gathered round: it was as though an impromptu court were about to form and to try some case of deviation. T. said, "It's a beautiful house," and still watching the ground, meeting no one's eyes, he licked his lips first one way, then the other.

"What do you mean, a beautiful house?" Blackie asked with scorn.

"It's got a staircase two hundred years old like a corkscrew. Nothing holds it up."

"What do you mean, nothing holds it up. Does it float?"

"It's to do with opposite forces, Old Misery said."

35 "What else?"

"There's paneling."

"Like in the Blue Boar?"

"Two hundred years old."

"Is Old Misery two hundred years old?"

40 Mike laughed suddenly and then was quiet again. The meeting was in a serious mood. For the first time since T. had strolled into the car-park on the first day of the holidays his position was in danger. It only needed a single use of his real name and the gang would be at his heels.

"What did you do it for?" Blackie asked. He was just, he had no jealousy, he was anxious to retain T. in the gang if he could. It was the word "beautiful" that worried him—that belonged to a class world that you could still see parodied at the Wormsley Common Empire by a man wearing a top hat and a monocle, with a haw-haw accent. He was tempted to say, "My dear Trevor, old chap," and unleash his hell hounds. "If you'd broken in," he said sadly—that indeed would have been an exploit worthy of the gang.

"This was better," T. said. "I found out things." He continued to stare at his feet, not meeting anybody's eye, as though he were absorbed in some dream he was un-willing—or ashamed—to share.

"What things?"

"Old Misery's going to be away all tomorrow and Bank Holiday."

45 Blackie said with relief, "You mean we could break in?"

"And pinch things?" somebody asked.

Blackie said, "Nobody's going to pinch things. Breaking in—that's good enough, isn't it? We don't want any court stuff."

"I don't want to pinch anything," T. said. "I've got a better idea."

"What is it?"

T. raised eyes, as grey and disturbed as the drab August day. "We'll pull it 50 down," he said. "We'll destroy it."

Blackie gave a single hoot of laughter and then, like Mike, fell quiet, daunted by the serious implacable gaze. "What'd the police be doing all the time?" he asked.

"They'd never know. We'd do it from inside. I've found a way in." He said with a sort of intensity, "We'd be like worms, don't you see, in an apple. When we came out again there'd be nothing there, no staircase, no panels, nothing but just walls, and then we'd make the walls fall down—somehow."

"We'd go to jug," Blackie said.

"Who's to prove? And anyway we wouldn't have pinched anything." He added without the smallest flicker of glee, "There wouldn't be anything to pinch after we'd finished."

"I've never heard of going to prison for breaking things," Summers said.   55

"There wouldn't be time," Blackie said. "I've seen housebreakers at work."

"There are twelve of us," T. said. "We'd organize."

"None of us know how . . ."

"I know," T. said. He looked across at Blackie. "Have you got a better plan?"

"Today," Mike said tactlessly, "we're pinching free rides . . ."   60

"Free rides," T. said. "You can stand down, Blackie, if you'd rather . . ."

"The gang's got to vote."

"Put it up then."

Blackie said uneasily, "It's proposed that tomorrow and Monday we destroy Old Misery's house."

"Here, here," said a fat boy called Joe.   65

"Who's in favor?"

T. said, "It's carried."

"How do we start?" Summers asked.

"He'll tell you," Blackie said. It was the end of his leadership. He went away to the back of the car-park and began to kick a stone, dribbling it this way and that. There was only one old Morris in the park, for few cars were left there except lorries: without an attendant there was no safety. He took a flying kick at the car and scraped a little paint off the rear mudguard. Beyond, paying no more attention to him than to a stranger, the gang had gathered round T.; Blackie was dimly aware of the fickleness of favor. He thought of going home, of never returning, of letting them all discover the hollowness of T.'s leadership, but suppose after all what T. proposed was possible—nothing like it had ever been done before. The fame of the Wormsley Common car-park gang would surely reach around London. There would be headlines in the papers. Even the grown-up gangs who ran the betting at the all-in wrestling and the barrow-boys would hear with respect of how Old Misery's house had been destroyed. Driven by the pure, simple and altruistic ambition of fame for the gang, Blackie came back to where T. stood in the shadow of Misery's wall.

T. was giving his orders with decision: it was as though this plan had been with 70 him all his life, pondered through the seasons, now in his fifteenth year crystallized with the pain of puberty. "You," he said to Mike, "bring some big nails, the biggest you can find, and a hammer. Anyone else who can better bring a hammer and a screwdriver. We'll need plenty of them. Chisels too. We can't have too many chisels. Can anybody bring a saw?"

"I can," Mike said.

"Not a child's saw," T. said. "A real saw."

Blackie realized he had raised his hand like any ordinary member of the gang.

"Right, you bring one, Blackie. But now there's a difficulty. We want a hacksaw."

75   "What's a hacksaw?" someone asked.

"You can get 'em at Woolworth's," Summers said.

The fat boy called Joe said gloomily, "I knew it would end in a collection."

"I'll get one myself," T. said. "I don't want your money. But I can't buy a sledge-hammer."

Blackie said, "They are working on No. 15. I know where they'll leave their stuff for Bank Holiday."

80   "Then that's all," T. said. "We meet here at nine sharp."

"I've got to go to church," Mike said.

"Come over the wall and whistle. We'll let you in."

2

On Sunday morning all were punctual except Blackie, even Mike. Mike had had a stroke of luck. His mother felt ill, his father was tired after Saturday night, and he was told to go to church alone with many warnings of what would happen if he strayed. Blackie had had difficulty in smuggling out the saw, and then in finding the sledge-hammer at the back of No. 15. He approached the house from a lane at the rear of the garden, for fear of the policeman's beat along the main road. The tired evergreens kept off a stormy sun: another wet Bank Holiday was being prepared over the Atlantic, beginning in swirls of dust under the trees. Blackie climbed the wall into Misery's garden.

There was no sign of anybody anywhere. The lav stood like a tomb in a neglected graveyard. The curtains were drawn. The house slept. Blackie lumbered nearer with the saw and the sledge-hammer. Perhaps after all nobody had turned up: the plan had been a wild invention: they had woken wiser. But when he came close to the back door he could hear a confusion of sound hardly louder than a hive in swarm: a clickety-clack, a bang bang, a scraping, a creaking, a sudden painful crack. He thought: it's true, and whistled.

85   They opened the back door to him and he came in. He had at once the impression of organization, very different from the old happy-go-lucky ways under his leadership. For a while he wandered up and down stairs looking for T. Nobody addressed him: he had a sense of great urgency, and already he could begin to see the plan. The interior of the house was being carefully demolished without touching the outer walls. Summers with hammer and chisel was ripping out the skirting-boards in the ground floor dining-room: he had already smashed the panels of the door. In the

same room Joe was heaving up the parquet blocks, exposing the soft wood floor-boards over the cellar. Coils of wire came out of the damaged skirting and Mike sat happily on the floor clipping the wires.

On the curved stairs two of the gang were working hard with an inadequate child's saw on the banisters—when they saw Blackie's big saw they signaled for it wordlessly. When he next saw them a quarter of the banisters had been dropped into the hall. He found T. at last in the bathroom—he sat moodily in the least cared-for room in the house, listening to the sounds coming up from below.

"You've really done it," Blackie said with awe. "What's going to happen?"

"We've only just begun," T. said. He looked at the sledge-hammer and gave his instructions. "You stay here and break the bath and the wash-basin. Don't bother about the pipes. They come later."

Mike appeared at the door. "I've finished the wires, T.," he said.

"Good. You've just got to go wandering round now. The kitchen's in the base-   90 ment. Smash all the china and glass and bottles you can lay hold of. Don't turn on the taps—we don't want a flood—yet. Then go into all the rooms and turn out draw-ers. If they are locked get one of the others to break them open. Tear up any papers you find and smash all the ornaments. Better take a carving-knife with you from the kitchen. The bedroom's opposite here. Open the pillows and tear up the sheets. That's enough for the moment. And you, Blackie, when you've finished in here crack the plaster in the passage up with your sledge-hammer."

"What are you going to do?" Blackie asked.

"I'm looking for something special," T. said.

It was nearly lunch-time before Blackie had finished and went in search of T. Chaos had advanced. The kitchen was a shambles of broken glass and china. The dining-room was stripped of parquet, the skirting was up, the door had been taken off its hinges, and the destroyers had moved up a floor. Streaks of light came in through the closed shutters where they worked with the seriousness of creators—and destruction after all is a form of creation. A kind of imagination had seen this house as it had now become.

Mike said, "I've got to go home for dinner."

"Who else?" T. asked, but all the others on one excuse or another had brought   95 provisions with them.

They squatted in the ruins of the room and swapped unwanted sandwiches. Half an hour for lunch and they were at work again. By the time Mike returned, they were on the top floor, and by six the superficial damage was completed. The doors were all off, all the skirtings raised, the furniture pillaged and ripped and smashed—no one could have slept in the house except on a bed of broken plaster. T. gave his orders—eight o'clock next morning, and to escape notice they climbed singly over the garden wall, into the car-park. Only Blackie and T. were left: the light had nearly gone, and when they touched a switch, nothing worked—Mike had done his job thoroughly.

"Did you find anything special?" Blackie asked.

T. nodded. "Come over here," he said, "and look." Out of both pockets he drew bundles of pound notes. "Old Misery's savings," he said. "Mike ripped out the mat-tress, but he missed them."

"What are you going to do? Share them?"

100   "We aren't thieves," T. said. "Nobody's going to steal anything from this house. I kept these for you and me—a celebration." He knelt down on the floor and counted them out—there were seventy in all. "We'll burn them," he said, "one by one," and taking it in turns they held a note upwards and lit the top corner, so that the flame burnt slowly towards their fingers. The grey ash floated above them and fell on their heads like age. "I'd like to see Old Misery's face when we are through," T. said.

"You hate him a lot?" Blackie asked.

"Of course I don't hate him," T. said. "There'd be no fun if I hated him." The last burning note illuminated his brooding face. "All this hate and love," he said, "it's soft, it's hooey. There's only things, Blackie," and he looked round the room crowded with the unfamiliar shadows of half things, broken things, former things. "I'll race you home, Blackie," he said.

3

Next morning the serious destruction started. Two were missing—Mike and another boy whose parents were off to Southend and Brighton in spite of the slow warm drops that had begun to fall and the rumble of thunder in the estuary like the first guns of the old blitz. "We've got to hurry," T. said.

Summers was restive. "Haven't we done enough?" he said. "I've been given a bob for slot machines. This is like work."

105   "We've hardly started," T. said. "Why, there's all the floor left, and the stairs. We haven't taken out a single window. You voted like the others. We are going to *destroy* this house. There won't be anything left when we've finished."

They began again on the first floor picking up the top floor-boards next the outer wall, leaving the joists exposed. Then they sawed through the joists and retreated into the hall, as what was left of the floor heeled and sank. They had learnt with practice, and the second floor collapsed more easily. By the evening an odd exhilaration seized them as they looked down the great hollow of the house. They ran risks and made mistakes: when they thought of the windows it was too late to reach them. "Cor," Joe said, and dropped a penny down into the dry rubble-filled well. It cracked and span among the broken glass.

"Why did we start this?" Summers asked with astonishment; T. was already on the ground, digging at the rubble, clearing a space along the outer wall. "Turn on the taps," he said. "It's too dark for anyone to see now, and in the morning it won't matter." The water overtook them on the stairs and fell through the floor-less rooms.

It was then they heard Mike's whistle at the back. "Something's wrong," Blackie said. They could hear his urgent breathing as they unlocked the door.

"The bogies?" Summers asked.

110   "Old Misery," Mike said. "He's on his way." He put his head between his knees and retched. "Ran all the way," he said with pride.

"But why?" T. said. "He told me . . ." He protested with the fury of the child he had never been, "It isn't fair."

"He was down at Southend," Mike said, "and he was on the train coming back. Said it was too cold and wet." He paused and gazed at the water. "My, you've had a storm here. Is the roof leaking?"

"How long will he be?"

"Five minutes. I gave Ma the slip and ran."

"We better clear," Summers said. "We've done enough, anyway." 115

"Oh no, we haven't. Anybody could do this—" "this" was the shattered hollowed house with nothing left but the walls. Yet the walls could be preserved. Façades were valuable. They could build inside again more beautifully than before. This could again be a home. He said angrily, "We've got to finish. Don't move. Let me think."

"There's no time," a boy said.

"There's got to be a way," T. said. "We couldn't have got this far . . ."

"We've done a lot," Blackie said.

"No. No, we haven't. Somebody watch the front." 120

"We can't do any more."

"He may come in at the back."

"Watch the back too." T. began to plead. "Just give me a minute and I'll fix it. I swear I'll fix it." But his authority had gone with his ambiguity. He was only one of the gang. "Please," he said.

"Please," Summers mimicked him, and then suddenly struck home with the fatal name. "Run along home, Trevor."

T. stood with his back to the rubble like a boxer knocked groggy against the 125 ropes. He had no words as his dreams shook and slid. Then Blackie acted before the gang had time to laugh, pushing Summers backward. "I'll watch the front, T.," he said, and cautiously he opened the shutters of the hall. The grey wet common stretched ahead, and the lamps gleamed in the puddles. "Someone's coming, T. No, it's not him. What's your plan, T.?"

"Tell Mike to go out to the lav and hide close beside it. When he hears me whistle he's got to count ten and start to shout."

"Shout what?"

"Oh, 'Help,' anything."

"You hear, Mike," Blackie said. He was the leader again. He took a quick look between the shutters. "He's coming, T."

"Quick, Mike. The lav. Stay here, Blackie, all of you till I yell." 130

"Where are you going, T.?"

"Don't worry. I'll see to this. I said I would, didn't I?"

Old Misery came limping off the common. He had mud on his shoes and he stopped to scrape them on the pavement's edge. He didn't want to soil his house, which stood jagged and dark between the bomb-sites, saved so narrowly, as he believed, from destruction. Even the fanlight had been left unbroken by the bomb's blast. Somewhere somebody whistled. Old Misery looked sharply round. He didn't trust whistles. A child was shouting: it seemed to come from his own garden. Then a boy ran into the road from the car-park. "Mr. Thomas," he called, "Mr. Thomas."

"What is it?"

135   "I'm terribly sorry, Mr. Thomas. One of us got taken short, and we thought you wouldn't mind, and now he can't get out."

"What do you mean, boy?"

"He's got stuck in your lav."

"He'd no business . . . Haven't I seen you before?"

"You showed me your house."

140   "So I did. So I did. That doesn't give you the right to . . ."

"Do hurry, Mr. Thomas. He'll suffocate."

"Nonsense. He can't suffocate. Wait till I put my bag in."

"I'll carry your bag."

"Oh no, you don't. I carry my own."

145   "This way, Mr. Thomas."

"I can't get in the garden that way. I've got to go through the house."

"But you *can* get in the garden this way, Mr. Thomas. We often do."

"You often do?" He followed the boy with a scandalized fascination. "When? What right? . . ."

"Do you see . . . ? The wall's low."

150   "I'm not going to climb walls into my own garden. It's absurd."

"This is how we do it. One foot here, one foot there, and over." The boy's face peered down, an arm shot out, and Mr. Thomas found his bag taken and deposited on the other side of the wall.

"Give me back my bag," Mr. Thomas said. From the loo a boy yelled and yelled. "I'll call the police."

"Your bag's all right, Mr. Thomas. Look. One foot there. On your right. Now just above. To your left." Mr. Thomas climbed over his own garden wall. "Here's your bag, Mr. Thomas."

"I'll have the wall built up," Mr. Thomas said, "I'll not have you boys coming over here, using my loo." He stumbled on the path, but the boy caught his elbow and supported him. "Thank you, thank you, my boy," he murmured automatically. Somebody shouted again through the dark. "I'm coming, I'm coming," Mr. Thomas called. He said to the boy beside him, "I'm not unreasonable. Been a boy myself. As long as things are done regular. I don't mind you playing round the place Saturday mornings. Sometimes I like company. Only it's got to be regular. One of you asks leave and I say Yes. Sometimes I'll say No. Won't feel like it. And you come in at the front door and out at the back. No garden walls."

155   "Do get him out, Mr. Thomas."

"He won't come to any harm in my loo," Mr. Thomas said, stumbling slowly down the garden. "Oh, my rheumatics," he said. "Always get 'em on Bank Holiday. I've got to go careful. There's loose stones here. Give me your hand. Do you know what my horoscope said yesterday? 'Abstain from any dealings in first half of week. Danger of serious crash.' That might be on this path," Mr. Thomas said. "They speak in parables and double meanings." He paused at the door of the loo. "What's the matter in there?" he called. There was no reply.

"Perhaps he's fainted," the boy said.

"Not in my loo. Here, you come out," Mr. Thomas said, and giving a great jerk at the door he nearly fell on his back when it swung easily open. A hand first supported him and then pushed him hard. His head hit the opposite wall and he sat heavily down. His bag hit his feet. A hand whipped the key out of the lock and the door slammed. "Let me out," he called, and heard the key turn in the lock. "A serious crash," he thought, and felt dithery and confused and old.

A voice spoke to him softly through the star-shaped hole in the door. "Don't worry, Mr. Thomas," it said, "we won't hurt you, not if you stay quiet."

Mr. Thomas put his head between his hands and pondered. He had noticed that 160 there was only one lorry in the car-park, and he felt certain that the driver would not come for it before the morning. Nobody could hear him from the road in front, and the lane at the back was seldom used. Anyone who passed there would be hurrying home and would not pause for what they would certainly take to be drunken cries. And if he did call "Help," who, on a lonely Bank Holiday evening, would have the courage to investigate? Mr. Thomas sat on the loo and pondered with the wisdom of age.

After a while it seemed to him that there were sounds in the silence—they were faint and came from the direction of his house. He stood up and peered through the ventilation-hole—between the cracks in one of the shutters he saw a light, not the light of a lamp, but the wavering light that a candle might give. Then he thought he heard the sound of hammering and scraping and chipping. He thought of burglars—perhaps they had employed the boy as a scout, but why should burglars engage in what sounded more and more like a stealthy form of carpentry? Mr. Thomas let out an experimental yell, but nobody answered. The noise could not even have reached his enemies.

4

Mike had gone home to bed, but the rest stayed. The question of leadership no longer concerned the gang. With nails, chisels, screwdrivers, anything that was sharp and penetrating, they moved around the inner walls worrying at the mortar between the bricks. They started too high, and it was Blackie who hit on the damp course and realized the work could be halved if they weakened the joints immediately above. It was a long, tiring, unamusing job, but at last it was finished. The gutted house stood there balanced on a few inches of mortar between the damp course and the bricks.

There remained the most dangerous task of all, out in the open at the edge of the bomb-site. Summers was sent to watch the road for passers-by, and Mr. Thomas, sitting on the loo, heard clearly now the sound of sawing. It no longer came from his house, and that a little reassured him. He felt less concerned. Perhaps the other noises too had no significance.

A voice spoke to him through the hole. "Mr. Thomas."

"Let me out," Mr. Thomas said sternly.   165

"Here's a blanket," the voice said, and a long grey sausage was worked through the hole and fell in swathes over Mr. Thomas' head.

"There's nothing personal," the voice said. "We want you to be comfortable tonight."

"Tonight," Mr. Thomas repeated incredulously.

"Catch," the voice said. "Penny buns—we've buttered them, and sausage-rolls. We don't want you to starve, Mr. Thomas."

170   Mr. Thomas pleaded desperately. "A joke's a joke, boy. Let me out and I won't say a thing. I've got rheumatics. I got to sleep comfortable."

"You wouldn't be comfortable, not in your house, you wouldn't. Not now."

"What do you mean, boy?" but the footsteps receded. There was only the silence of night: no sound of sawing. Mr. Thomas tried one more yell, but he was daunted and rebuked by the silence—a long way off an owl hooted and made away again on its muffled flight through the soundless world.

At seven next morning the driver came to fetch his lorry. He climbed into the seat and tried to start the engine. He was vaguely aware of a voice shouting, but it didn't concern him. At last the engine responded and he backed the lorry until it touched the great wooden shore that supported Mr. Thomas' house. That way he could drive right out and down the street without reversing. The lorry moved forward, was momentarily checked as though something were pulling it from behind, and then went on to the sound of a long rumbling crash. The driver was astonished to see bricks bouncing ahead of him, while stones hit the roof of his cab. He put on his brakes. When he climbed out the whole landscape had suddenly altered. There was no house beside the car-park, only a hill of rubble. He went round and examined the back of his car for damage, and found a rope tied there that was still twisted at the other end round part of a wooden strut.

The driver again became aware of somebody shouting. It came from the wooden erection which was the nearest thing to a house in that desolation of broken brick. The driver climbed the smashed wall and unlocked the door. Mr. Thomas came out of the loo. He was wearing a grey blanket to which flakes of pastry adhered. He gave a sobbing cry. "My house," he said. "Where's my house?"

175   "Search me," the driver said. His eye lit on the remains of a bath and what had once been a dresser and he began to laugh. There wasn't anything left anywhere.

"How dare you laugh," Mr. Thomas said. "It was my house. My house."

"I'm sorry," the driver said, making heroic efforts, but when he remembered the sudden check to his lorry, the crash of bricks falling, he became convulsed again. One moment the house had stood there with such dignity between the bomb-sites like a man in a top hat, and then, bang, crash, there wasn't anything left—not anything. He said, "I'm sorry. I can't help it, Mr. Thomas. There's nothing personal, but you got to admit it's funny."

QUESTIONS FOR DISCUSSION AND WRITING

1. How does Trevor's plan help focus the plot of the story? How does Trevor resolve the complication caused by Mr. Thomas's early return?

2. How is Trevor characterized in the second paragraph of the story? How does his description of his tour of Mr. Thomas's house add to that characterization? What qualities does he possess that inspire the gang to accept his leadership?

3. The setting for this story is London nine years after the city survived a series of bombing attacks during World War II. How does this setting contribute to the development of the story? For example, what do the gang's other activities suggest about life in postwar England?

4. Because the point of view in this story is objective, we see the events from different perspectives. How do Trevor, Blackie, Mr. Thomas, and the driver see the destruction of the house?

5. How does the phrase "nothing personal" contribute to an understanding of the events in the story? If it is not personal, what is the point of the destruction? How does the success of the gang's mission comment on the success (and destruction) caused by war?

Stories for Comparison

William Faulkner's "Barn Burning" (pages 491–504); Flannery O'Connor's "A Good Man Is Hard to Find" (pages 967–979).

50

....

N A T H A N I E L   H A W T H O R N E

Rappaccini's Daughter
From the Writings of Aubépine

NATHANIEL HAWTHORNE (1804–1864) was born in Salem, Massachusetts, the descendant of a prominent Puritan family that included a judge at the Salem witchcraft trials. After graduating from Bowdoin College in 1825, Hawthorne returned to Salem to live a life of almost total seclusion for twelve years as he mastered his skills as a writer. His first novel, *Fanshawe* (1828), based on his experiences at Bowdoin, was an embarrassing failure, but he soon published enough stories in magazines to collect his first volume of stories, *Twice-Told Tales* (1837). The volume was a critical but not a commercial success, so Hawthorne was forced to support himself by working in the United States Custom House in Boston. He invested his savings in a communal experiment at Brook Farm, but soon withdrew from the community to marry and take up residence in Concord, Massachusetts, where he rented the "Old Manse," a house built by Ralph Waldo Emerson's grandfather. Another collection of stories, *Mosses from an Old Manse* (1846), was followed by his masterpiece, *The Scarlet Letter* (1850). The sales from this novel allowed him to move to the Berkshires in western Massachusetts, where he wrote two novels—*The House of the Seven Gables* (1851) and *The Blithedale Romance* (1852)—collected another volume of his stories, *The Snow-Image* (1852), and completed a campaign biography, *The Life of Franklin Pierce* (1852). When Pierce was elected president of the United States in 1852, Hawthorne was rewarded with a consulship first in England, and then in Italy. He returned to the United States in 1860 to live in Concord. "Rappaccini's Daughter," from *Mosses from an Old Manse,* dramatizes the conflict between love and science. "Young Goodman Brown," also reprinted from *Mosses from an Old Manse,* tells of a young man's journey into the wilderness on a mysterious errand.

W e do not remember to have seen any translated specimens of the productions of M. de l'Aubépine; a fact the less to be wondered at, as his very name is unknown to many of his own countrymen, as well as to the student of foreign literature. As a writer, he seems to occupy an unfortunate position between the Transcendentalists (who, under one name or another, have their share in all the current literature of the world), and the great body of pen-and-ink men who address the intellect and sympathies of the multitude. If not too refined, at all events too remote, too shadowy and unsubstantial in his modes of development, to suit the taste of the latter class, and yet too popular to satisfy the spiritual or metaphysical requisitions of the former, he must necessarily find himself without an audience; except here and there an individual, or possibly an isolated clique. His writings, to do them justice, are not altogether destitute of fancy and originality; they might have won him greater reputation but for an inveterate love of allegory, which is apt to invest his plots and characters with the aspect of scenery and people in the clouds, and to steal away the human warmth out of his conceptions. His fictions are sometimes historical, sometimes of the present day, and sometimes, so far as can be discovered, have little or no reference either to time or space. In any case, he generally contents himself with a very slight embroidery of outward manners,—the faintest possible counterfeit of real life—and endeavors to create an interest by some less obvious peculiarity of the subject. Occasionally, a breath of nature, a rain-drop of pathos and tenderness, or a gleam of humor, will find its way into the midst of his fantastic imagery, and make us feel as if, after all, we were yet within the limits of our native earth. We will only add to this very cursory notice, that M. de l'Aubépine's productions, if the reader chance to take them in precisely the proper point of view, may amuse a leisure hour as well as those of a brighter man; if otherwise, they can hardly fail to look excessively like nonsense.

Our author is voluminous; he continues to write and publish with as much praise-worthy and indefatigable prolixity, as if his efforts were crowned with the brilliant success that so justly attends those of Eugene Sue. His first appearance was by a collection of stories, in a long series of volumes, entitled *"Contes deux fois racontées."* The titles of some of his more recent works (we quote from memory) are as follows:—*"Le Voyage Céleste à Chemin de Fer,"* 3 tom. 1838. *"Le nouveau Père Adam et la nouvelle Mère Eve,"* 2 tom. 1839. *"Roderic; ou le Serpent à l'estomac,"* 2 tom. 1840. *"Le Culte du Feu,"* a folio volume of ponderous research into the religion and ritual of the old Persian Ghebers, published in 1841. *"La Soirée du Chateau en Espagne,"* 1 tom. 8vo. 1842; and *"L'Artiste du Beau; ou le Papillon Mécanique,"* 5 tom. 4to. 1843. Our somewhat wearisome perusal of this startling catalogue of volumes has left behind it a certain personal affection and sympathy, though by no means admiration, for M. de l'Aubépine; and we would fain do the little in our power towards introducing him favorably to the American public. The ensuing tale is a translation of his *"Beatrice; ou la Belle Empoisonneuse,"* recently published in *"La Revue Anti-Aristocratique."* This journal, edited by the Comte de Bearhaven, has, for some years past, led the defence of liberal principles and popular rights, with a faithfulness and ability worthy of all praise.

A young man, named Giovanni Guasconti, came, very long ago, from the more southern region of Italy, to pursue his studies at the University of Padua. Giovanni, who had but a scanty supply of gold ducats in his pocket, took lodgings in a high and gloomy chamber of an old edifice, which looked not unworthy to have been the palace of a Paduan noble, and which, in fact, exhibited over its entrance the armorial bearings of a family long since extinct. The young stranger, who was not unstudied in the great poem of his country, recollected that one of the ancestors of this family, and perhaps an occupant of this very mansion, had been pictured by Dante as a partaker of the immortal agonies of his Inferno. These reminiscences and associations, together with the tendency to heart-break natural to a young man for the first time out of his native sphere, caused Giovanni to sigh heavily, as he looked around the desolate and ill-furnished apartment.

"Holy Virgin, Signor," cried old dame Lisabetta, who, won by the youth's remarkable beauty of person, was kindly endeavoring to give the chamber a habitable air, "what a sigh was that to come out of a young man's heart! Do you find this old mansion gloomy? For the love of heaven, then, put your head out of the window, and you will see as bright sunshine as you have left in Naples."

Guasconti mechanically did as the old woman advised, but could not quite agree ₅ with her that the Paduan sunshine was as cheerful as that of southern Italy. Such as it was, however, it fell upon a garden beneath the window, and expended its fostering influences on a variety of plants, which seemed to have been cultivated with exceeding care.

"Does this garden belong to the house?" asked Giovanni.

"Heaven forbid, Signor!—unless it were fruitful of better pot-herbs than any that grow there now," answered old Lisabetta. "No; that garden is cultivated by the own hands of Signor Giacomo Rappaccini, the famous Doctor, who, I warrant him, has been heard of as far as Naples. It is said that he distils these plants into medicines that are as potent as a charm. Oftentimes you may see the Signor Doctor at work, and perchance the Signora his daughter, too, gathering the strange flowers that grow in the garden."

The old woman had now done what she could for the aspect of the chamber, and, commending the young man to the protection of the saints, took her departure.

Giovanni still found no better occupation than to look down into the garden beneath his window. From its appearance, he judged it to be one of those botanic gardens, which were of earlier date in Padua than elsewhere in Italy, or in the world. Or, not improbably, it might once have been the pleasure-place of an opulent family; for there was the ruin of a marble fountain in the centre, sculptured with rare art, but so wofully shattered that it was impossible to trace the original design from the chaos of remaining fragments. The water, however, continued to gush and sparkle into the sunbeams as cheerfully as ever. A little gurgling sound ascended to the young man's window, and made him feel as if the fountain were an immortal spirit, that sung its song unceasingly, and without heeding the vicissitudes around it; while one century embodied it in marble, and another scattered the perishable garniture on the soil. All about the pool into which the water subsided, grew various plants, that seemed to require a plentiful supply of moisture for the nourishment of gigantic leaves, and, in some instances, flowers gorgeously magnificent. There was one shrub in particular, set in a marble vase in the midst of the pool, that bore a profusion of purple blossoms, each of which had the lustre and richness of a gem; and the whole together made a show so resplendent that it seemed enough to illuminate the garden, even had there been no sunshine. Every portion of the soil was peopled with plants and herbs, which, if less beautiful, still bore tokens of assiduous care; as if all had their individual virtues, known to the scientific mind that fostered them. Some were placed in urns, rich with old carving, and others in common garden-pots; some crept serpent-like along the ground, or climbed on high, using whatever means of ascent was offered them. One plant had wreathed itself round a statue of Vertumnus, which was thus quite veiled and shrouded in a drapery of hanging foliage, so happily arranged that it might have served a sculptor for a study.

10   While Giovanni stood at the window, he heard a rustling behind a screen of leaves, and became aware that a person was at work in the garden. His figure soon emerged into view, and showed itself to be that of no common laborer, but a tall, emaciated, sallow, and sickly-looking man, dressed in a scholar's garb of black. He was beyond the middle term of life, with grey hair, a thin grey beard, and a face singularly marked with intellect and cultivation, but which could never, even in his more youthful days, have expressed much warmth of heart.

Nothing could exceed the intentness with which this scientific gardener examined every shrub which grew in his path; it seemed as if he was looking into their inmost nature, making observations in regard to their creative essence, and discovering why one leaf grew in this shape, and another in that, and wherefore such and such flowers differed among themselves in hue and perfume. Nevertheless, in spite of this deep intelligence on his part, there was no approach to intimacy between himself and these vegetable existences. On the contrary, he avoided their actual touch, or the direct inhaling of their odors, with a caution that impressed Giovanni most disagreeably; for the man's demeanor was that of one walking among malignant influences, such as savage beasts, or deadly snakes, or evil spirits, which, should he allow them one moment of license, would wreak upon him some terrible fatality. It

was strangely frightful to the young man's imagination, to see this air of insecurity in a person cultivating a garden, that most simple and innocent of human toils, and which had been alike the joy and labor of the unfallen parents of the race. Was this garden, then, the Eden of the present world?—and this man, with such a perception of harm in what his own hands caused to grow, was he the Adam?

The distrustful gardener, while plucking away the dead leaves or pruning the too luxuriant growth of the shrubs, defended his hands with a pair of thick gloves. Nor were these his only armor. When, in his walk through the garden, he came to the magnificent plant that hung its purple gems beside the marble fountain, he placed a kind of mask over his mouth and nostrils, as if all this beauty did but conceal a deadlier malice. But finding his task still too dangerous, he drew back, removed the mask, and called loudly, but in the infirm voice of a person affected with inward disease:

"Beatrice!—Beatrice!"

"Here am I, my father! What would you?" cried a rich and youthful voice from the window of the opposite house; a voice as rich as a tropical sunset, and which made Giovanni, though he knew not why, think of deep hues of purple or crimson, and of perfumes heavily delectable.—"Are you in the garden?"

"Yes, Beatrice," answered the gardener, "and I need your help."   15

Soon there emerged from under a sculptured portal the figure of a young girl, arrayed with as much richness of taste as the most splendid of the flowers, beautiful as the day, and with a bloom so deep and vivid that one shade more would have been too much. She looked redundant with life, health, and energy; all of which attributes were bound down and compressed, as it were, and girdled tensely, in their luxuriance, by her virgin zone. Yet Giovanni's fancy must have grown morbid, while he looked down into the garden; for the impression which the fair stranger made upon him was as if here were another flower, the human sister of those vegetable ones, as beautiful as they—more beautiful than the richest of them—but still to be touched only with a glove, nor to be approached without a mask. As Beatrice came down the garden path, it was observable that she handled and inhaled the odor of several of the plants, which her father had most sedulously avoided.

"Here, Beatrice," said the latter,—"see how many needful offices require to be done to our chief treasure. Yet, shattered as I am, my life might pay the penalty of approaching it so closely as circumstances demand. Henceforth, I fear, this plant must be consigned to your sole charge."

"And gladly will I undertake it," cried again the rich tones of the young lady, as she bent towards the magnificent plant, and opened her arms as if to embrace it. "Yes, my sister, my splendor, it shall be Beatrice's task to nurse and serve thee; and thou shalt reward her with thy kisses and perfumed breath, which to her is as the breath of life!"

Then, with all the tenderness in her manner that was so strikingly expressed in her words, she busied herself with such attentions as the plant seemed to require; and Giovanni, at his lofty window, rubbed his eyes, and almost doubted whether it were a girl tending her favorite flower, or one sister performing the duties of affection to another. The scene soon terminated. Whether Doctor Rappaccini had finished his labors in the garden, or that his watchful eye had caught the stranger's face, he now

took his daughter's arm and retired. Night was already closing in; oppressive exhalations seemed to proceed from the plants, and steal upward past the open window; and Giovanni, closing the lattice, went to his couch, and dreamed of a rich flower and beautiful girl. Flower and maiden were different and yet the same, and fraught with some strange peril in either shape.

20   But there is an influence in the light of morning that tends to rectify whatever errors of fancy, or even of judgment, we may have incurred during the sun's decline, or among the shadows of the night, or in the less wholesome glow of moonshine. Giovanni's first movement on starting from sleep, was to throw open the window, and gaze down into the garden which his dreams had made so fertile of mysteries. He was surprised, and a little ashamed, to find how real and matter-of-fact an affair it proved to be, in the first rays of the sun, which gilded the dewdrops that hung upon leaf and blossom, and, while giving a brighter beauty to each rare flower, brought everything within the limits of ordinary experience. The young man rejoiced, that, in the heart of the barren city, he had the privilege of overlooking this spot of lovely and luxuriant vegetation. It would serve, he said to himself, as a symbolic language, to keep him in communion with Nature. Neither the sickly and thought-worn Doctor Giacomo Rappaccini, it is true, nor his brilliant daughter, were now visible; so that Giovanni could not determine how much of the singularity which he attributed to both, was due to their own qualities, and how much to his wonder-working fancy. But he was inclined to take a most rational view of the whole matter.

In the course of the day, he paid his respects to Signor Pietro Baglioni, professor of medicine in the University, a physician of eminent repute, to whom Giovanni had brought a letter of introduction. The Professor was an elderly personage, apparently of genial nature, and habits that might almost be called jovial; he kept the young man to dinner, and made himself very agreeable by the freedom and liveliness of his conversation, especially when warmed by a flask or two of Tuscan wine. Giovanni, conceiving that men of science, inhabitants of the same city, must needs be on familiar terms with one another, took an opportunity to mention the name of Doctor Rappaccini. But the Professor did not respond with so much cordiality as he had anticipated.

"Ill would it become a teacher of the divine art of medicine," said Professor Pietro Baglioni, in answer to a question of Giovanni, "to withhold due and well-considered praise of a physician so eminently skilled as Rappaccini. But, on the other hand, I should answer it but scantily to my conscience, were I to permit a worthy youth like yourself, Signor Giovanni, the son of an ancient friend, to imbibe erroneous ideas respecting a man who might hereafter chance to hold your life and death in his hands. The truth is, our worshipful Doctor Rappaccini has as much science as any member of the faculty—with perhaps one single exception—in Padua, or all Italy. But there are certain grave objections to his professional character."

"And what are they?" asked the young man.

"Has my friend Giovanni any disease of body or heart, that he is so inquisitive about physicians?" said the Professor, with a smile. "But as for Rappaccini, it is said of him—and I, who know the man well, can answer for its truth—that he cares infinitely more for science than for mankind. His patients are interesting to him only as

subjects for some new experiment. He would sacrifice human life, his own among the rest, or whatever else was dearest to him, for the sake of adding so much as a grain of mustard-seed to the great heap of his accumulated knowledge."

"Methinks he is an awful man, indeed," remarked Guasconti, mentally recall- 25 ing the cold and purely intellectual aspect of Rappaccini. "And yet, worshipful Professor, is it not a noble spirit? Are there many men capable of so spiritual a love of science?"

"God forbid," answered the Professor, somewhat testily—"at least, unless they take sounder views of the healing art than those adopted by Rappaccini. It is his the-ory, that all medicinal virtues are comprised within those substances which we term vegetable poisons. These he cultivates with his own hands, and is said even to have produced new varieties of poison, more horribly deleterious than Nature, without the assistance of this learned person, would ever have plagued the world withal. That the Signor Doctor does less mischief than might be expected, with such dangerous sub-stances, is undeniable. Now and then, it must be owned, he has effected—or seemed to effect—a marvellous cure. But, to tell you my private mind, Signor Giovanni, he should receive little credit for such instances of success—they being probably the work of chance—but should be held strictly accountable for his failures, which may justly be considered his own work."

The youth might have taken Baglioni's opinions with many grains of allowance, had he known that there was a professional warfare of long continuance between him and Doctor Rappaccini, in which the latter was generally thought to have gained the advantage. If the reader be inclined to judge for himself, we refer him to certain black-letter tracts on both sides, preserved in the medical department of the Univer-sity of Padua.

"I know not, most learned Professor," returned Giovanni, after musing on what had been said of Rappaccini's exclusive zeal for science—"I know not how dearly this physician may love his art; but surely there is one object more dear to him. He has a daughter."

"Aha!" cried the Professor with a laugh. "So now our friend Giovanni's secret is out. You have heard of this daughter, whom all the young men in Padua are wild about, though not half a dozen have ever had the good hap to see her face. I know little of the Signora Beatrice, save that Rappaccini is said to have instructed her deeply in his science, and that, young and beautiful as fame reports her, she is al-ready qualified to fill a professor's chair. Perchance her father destines her for mine! Other absurd rumors there be, not worth talking about, or listening to. So now, Signor Giovanni, drink off your glass of Lacryma."

Guasconti returned to his lodgings somewhat heated with the wine he had 30 quaffed, and which caused his brain to swim with strange fantasies in reference to Doctor Rappaccini and the beautiful Beatrice. On his way, happening to pass by a florist's, he bought a fresh bouquet of flowers.

Ascending to his chamber, he seated himself near the window, but within the shadow thrown by the depth of the wall, so that he could look down into the garden with little risk of being discovered. All beneath his eye was a solitude. The strange plants were basking in the sunshine, and now and then nodding gently to one

another, as if in acknowledgement of sympathy and kindred. In the midst, by the shattered fountain, grew the magnificent shrub, with its purple gems clustering all over it; they glowed in the air, and gleamed back again out of the depths of the pool, which thus seemed to overflow with colored radiance from the rich reflection that was steeped in it. At first, as we have said, the garden was a solitude. Soon, however,—as Giovanni had half-hoped, half-feared, would be the case,—a figure appeared beneath the antique sculptured portal, and came down between the rows of plants, inhaling their various perfumes, as if she were one of those beings of old classic fable, that lived upon sweet odors. On again beholding Beatrice, the young man was even startled to perceive how much her beauty exceeded his recollection of it; so brilliant, so vivid was its character, that she glowed amid the sunlight, and, as Giovanni whispered to himself, positively illuminated the more shadowy intervals of the garden path. Her face being now more revealed than on the former occasion, he was struck by its expression of simplicity and sweetness; qualities that had not entered into his idea of her character, and which made him ask anew, what manner of mortal she might be. Nor did he fail again to observe, or imagine, an analogy between the beautiful girl and the gorgeous shrub that hung its gem-like flowers over the fountain; a resemblance which Beatrice seemed to have indulged a fantastic humor in heightening, both by the arrangement of her dress and the selection of its hues.

Approaching the shrub, she threw open her arms, as with a passionate ardor, and drew its branches into an intimate embrace; so intimate, that her features were hidden in its leafy bosom, and her glistening ringlets all intermingled with the flowers.

"Give me thy breath, my sister," exclaimed Beatrice; "for I am faint with common air! And give me this flower of thine, which I separate with gentlest fingers from the stem, and place it close beside my heart."

With these words, the beautiful daughter of Rappaccini plucked one of the richest blossoms of the shrub, and was about to fasten it in her bosom. But now, unless Giovanni's draughts of wine had bewildered his senses, a singular incident occurred. A small orange-colored reptile, of the lizard or chameleon species, chanced to be creeping along the path, just at the feet of Beatrice. It appeared to Giovanni—but, at the distance from which he gazed, he could scarcely have seen anything so minute—it appeared to him, however, that a drop or two of moisture from the broken stem of the flower descended upon the lizard's head. For an instant, the reptile contorted itself violently, and then lay motionless in the sunshine. Beatrice observed this remarkable phenomenon, and crossed herself, sadly, but without surprise; nor did she therefore hesitate to arrange the fatal flower in her bosom. There it blushed, and almost glimmered with the dazzling effect of a precious stone, adding to her dress and aspect the one appropriate charm, which nothing else in the world could have supplied. But Giovanni, out of the shadow of his window, bent forward and shrank back, and murmured and trembled.

35   "Am I awake? Have I my senses?" said he to himself. "What is this being?—beautiful, shall I call her?—or inexpressibly terrible?"

Beatrice now strayed carelessly through the garden, approaching closer beneath Giovanni's window, so that he was compelled to thrust his head quite out of its

concealment in order to gratify the intense and painful curiosity which she excited. At this moment, there came a beautiful insect over the garden wall; it had perhaps wandered through the city and found no flowers nor verdure among those antique haunts of men, until the heavy perfumes of Doctor Rappaccini's shrubs had lured it from afar. Without alighting on the flowers, this winged brightness seemed to be attracted by Beatrice, and lingered in the air and fluttered about her head. Now, here it could not be but that Giovanni Guasconti's eyes deceived him. Be that as it might, he fancied that while Beatrice was gazing at the insect with childish delight, it grew faint and fell at her feet;—its brightwings shivered; it was dead—from no cause that he could discern, unless it were the atmosphere of her breath. Again Beatrice crossed herself and sighed heavily, as she bent over the dead insect.

An impulsive movement of Giovanni drew her eyes to the window. There she beheld the beautiful head of the young man—rather a Grecian than an Italian head, with fair, regular features, and a glistening of gold among his ringlets—gazing down upon her like a being that hovered in mid-air. Scarcely knowing what he did, Giovanni threw down the bouquet which he had hitherto held in his hand.

"Signora," said he, "there are pure and healthful flowers. Wear them for the sake of Giovanni Guasconti!"

"Thanks, Signor," replied Beatrice, with her rich voice, that came forth as it were like a gush of music; and with a mirthful expression half childish and half woman-like. "I accept your gift, and would fain recompense it with this precious purple flower; but if I toss it into the air, it will not reach you. So Signor Guasconti must even content himself with my thanks."

She lifted the bouquet from the ground, and then as if inwardly ashamed at having stepped aside from her maidenly reserve to respond to a stranger's greeting, passed swiftly homeward through the garden. But, few as the moments were, it seemed to Giovanni when she was on the point of vanishing beneath the sculptured portal, that his beautiful bouquet was already beginning to wither in her grasp. It was an idle thought; there could be no possibility of distinguishing a faded flower from a fresh one at so great a distance.

For many days after this incident, the young man avoided the window that looked into Doctor Rappaccini's garden, as if something ugly and monstrous would have blasted his eye-sight, had he been betrayed into a glance. He felt conscious of having put himself, to a certain extent, within the influence of an unintelligible power, by the communication which he had opened with Beatrice. The wisest course would have been, if his heart were in any real danger, to quit his lodgings and Padua itself, at once; the next wiser, to have accustomed himself, as far as possible, to the familiar and day-light view of Beatrice; thus bringing her rigidly and systematically within the limits of ordinary experience. Least of all, while avoiding her sight, ought Giovanni to have remained so near this extraordinary being, that the proximity and possibility even of intercourse, should give a kind of substance and reality to the wild vagaries which his imagination ran riot continually in producing. Guasconti had not a deep heart—or at all events, its depths were not sounded now—but he had a quick fancy, and an ardent southern temperament, which rose every instant to a higher fever-pitch. Whether or no Beatrice possessed those terrible attributes—that fatal breath—the affinity with those so beautiful and deadly flowers—which were indicated by what Giovanni had witnessed, she had at least instilled a fierce and subtle poison into his system. It was not love, although her rich beauty was a madness to him; nor horror, even while he fancied her spirit to be imbued with the same baneful essence that seemed to pervade her physical frame; but a wild offspring of both love and horror that had each parent in it, and burned like one and shivered like the other. Giovanni knew not what to dread; still less did he know what to hope; yet hope and dread kept a continual warfare in his breast, alternately vanquishing one another and starting up afresh to renew the contest. Blessed are all simple emotions, be they dark or bright! It is the lurid intermixture of the two that produces the illuminating blaze of the infernal regions.

Sometimes he endeavored to assuage the fever of his spirit by a rapid walk through the streets of Padua, or beyond its gates; his footsteps kept time with the throbbings of his brain, so that the walk was apt to accelerate itself to a race. One day, he found himself arrested; his arm was seized by a portly personage who had turned back on recognizing the young man, and expended much breath in overtaking him.

"Signor Giovanni!—stay, my young friend!" cried he. "Have you forgotten me? That might well be the case, if I were as much altered as yourself."

It was Baglioni, whom Giovanni had avoided, ever since their first meeting, from a doubt that the Professor's sagacity would look too deeply into his secrets. Endeavoring to recover himself, he stared forth wildly from his inner world into the outer one, and spoke like a man in a dream:

45   "Yes; I am Giovanni Guasconti. You are Professor Pietro Baglioni. Now let me pass!"

"Not yet—not yet, Signor Giovanni Guasconti," said the Professor, smiling, but at the same time scrutinizing the youth with an earnest glance—"What; did I grow up side by side with your father, and shall his son pass me like a stranger, in these old streets of Padua? Stand still, Signor Giovanni; for we must have a word or two, before we part."

"Speedily, then, most worshipful Professor, speedily!" said Giovanni, with feverish impatience. "Does not your worship see that I am in haste?"

Now, while he was speaking, there came a man in black along the street, stooping and moving feebly, like a person in inferior health. His face was all overspread with a most sickly and sallow hue, but yet so pervaded with an expression of piercing and active intellect, that an observer might easily have overlooked the merely physical attributes, and have seen only this wonderful energy. As he passed, this person exchanged a cold and distant salutation with Baglioni, but fixed his eyes upon Giovanni with an intentness that seemed to bring out whatever was within him worthy of notice. Nevertheless, there was a peculiar quietness in the look, as if taking merely a speculative, not a human, interest in the young man.

"It is Doctor Rappaccini!" whispered the Professor, when the stranger had passed—"Has he ever seen your face before?"

50   "Not that I know," answered Giovanni, starting at the name.

"He *has* seen you!—he must have seen you!" said Baglioni, hastily. "For some purpose or other, this man of science is making a study of you. I know that look of his! It is the same that coldly illuminates his face, as he bends over a bird, a mouse, or a butterfly, which, in pursuance of some experiment, he has killed by the perfume of a flower;—a look as deep as Nature itself, but without Nature's warmth of love. Signor Giovanni, I will stake my life upon it, you are the subject of one of Rappaccini's experiments!"

"Will you make a fool of me?" cried Giovanni, passionately. "*That*, Signor Professor, were an untoward experiment."

"Patience, patience!" replied the imperturbable Professor.—"I tell thee, my poor Giovanni, that Rappaccini has a scientific interest in thee. Thou hast fallen into fearful hands! And the Signora Beatrice? What part does she act in this mystery?"

But Guasconti, finding Baglioni's pertinacity intolerable, here broke away, and was gone before the Professor could again seize his arm. He looked after the young man intently, and shook his head.

"This must not be," said Baglioni to himself. "The youth is the son of my old friend, and shall not come to any harm from which the arcana of medical science can preserve him. Besides, it is too insufferable an impertinence in Rappaccini, thus to snatch the lad out of my own hands, as I may say, and make use of him for his infernal experiments. This daughter of his! It shall be looked to. Perchance, most learned Rappaccini, I may foil you where you little dream of it!"

Meanwhile, Giovanni had pursued a circuitous route, and at length found himself at the door of his lodgings. As he crossed the threshold, he was met by old Lisabetta, who smirked and smiled, and was evidently desirous to attract his attention; vainly, however, as the ebullition of his feelings had momentarily subsided into a cold and dull vacuity. He turned his eyes full upon the withered face that was puckering itself into a smile, but seemed to behold it not. The old dame, therefore, laid her grasp upon his cloak.

"Signor!—Signor!" whispered she, still with a smile over the whole breadth of her visage, so that it looked not unlike a grotesque carving in wood, darkened by centuries—"Listen, Signor! There is a private entrance into the garden!"

"What do you say?" exclaimed Giovanni, turning quickly about, as if an inanimate thing should start into feverish life—"A private entrance into Doctor Rappaccini's garden!"

"Hush! hush!—not so loud!" whispered Lisabetta, putting her hand over his mouth. "Yes; into the worshipful Doctor's garden, where you may see all his fine shrubbery. Many a young man in Padua would give gold to be admitted among those flowers."

Giovanni put a piece of gold into her hand.

"Show me the way," said he.

A surmise, probably excited by his conversation with Baglioni, crossed his mind, that this interposition of old Lisabetta might perchance be connected with the intrigue, whatever were its nature, in which the Professor seemed to suppose that Doctor Rappaccini was involving him. But such a suspicion, though it disturbed Giovanni, was inadequate to restrain him. The instant that he was aware of the possibility of approaching Beatrice, it seemed an absolute necessity of his existence to do so. It mattered not whether she were angel or demon; he was irrevocably within her sphere, and must obey the law that whirled him onward, in ever lessening circles, towards a result which he did not attempt to foreshadow. And yet, strange to say, there came across him a sudden doubt, whether this intense interest on his part were not delusory—whether it were really of so deep and positive a nature as to justify him in now thrusting himself into an incalculable position—whether it were not merely the fantasy of a young man's brain, only slightly, or not at all, connected with his heart!

He paused—hesitated—turned half about—but again went on. His withered guide led him along several obscure passages, and finally undid a door, through which, as it was opened, there came the sight and sound of rustling leaves, with the broken sunshine glimmering among them. Giovanni stepped forth, and forcing himself through the entanglement of a shrub that wreathed its tendrils over the hidden entrance, he stood beneath his own window, in the open area of Doctor Rappaccini's garden.

How often is it the case, that, when impossibilities have come to pass, and dreams have condensed their misty substance into tangible realities, we find ourselves calm, and even coldly self-possessed, amid circumstances which it would have been a delirium of joy or agony to anticipate! Fate delights to thwart us thus. Passion will choose his own time to rush upon the scene, and lingers sluggishly behind, when an appropriate adjustment of events would seem to summon his appearance. So was it now with Giovanni. Day after day, his pulses had throbbed with feverish blood, at the improbable idea of an interview with Beatrice, and of standing with her, face to face, in this very garden, basking in the Oriental sunshine of her beauty, and snatching from her full gaze the mystery which he deemed the riddle of his own existence. But now there was a singular and untimely equanimity within his breast. He threw a glance around the garden to discover if Beatrice or her father were present, and perceiving that he was alone, began a critical observation of the plants.

65   The aspect of one and all of them dissatisfied him; their gorgeousness seemed fierce, passionate, and even unnatural. There was hardly an individual shrub which a wanderer, straying by himself through a forest, would not have been startled to find growing wild, as if an unearthly face had glared at him out of the thicket. Several, also, would have shocked a delicate instinct by an appearance of artificialness, indicating that there had been such commixture, and, as it were, adultery of various vegetable species, that the production was no longer of God's making, but the monstrous offspring of man's depraved fancy, glowing with only an evil mockery of beauty. They were probably the result of experiment, which, in one or two cases, had succeeded in mingling plants individually lovely into a compound possessing the questionable and ominous character that distinguished the whole growth of the garden. In fine, Giovanni recognized but two or three plants in the collection, and those of a kind that he well knew to be poisonous. While busy with these contemplations, he heard the rustling of a silken garment, and turning, beheld Beatrice emerging from beneath the sculptured portal.

Giovanni had not considered with himself what should be his deportment; whether he should apologize for his intrusion into the garden, or assume that he was there with the privity, at least, if not by the desire, of Doctor Rappaccini or his daughter. But Beatrice's manner placed him at his ease, though leaving him still in doubt by what agency he had gained admittance. She came lightly along the path, and met him near the broken fountain. There was surprise in her face, but brightened by a simple and kind expression of pleasure.

"You are a connoisseur in flowers, Signor," said Beatrice with a smile, alluding to the bouquet which he had flung her from the window. "It is no marvel, therefore, if the sight of my father's rare collection has tempted you to take a nearer view. If he were here, he could tell you many strange and interesting facts as to the nature and habits of these shrubs, for he has spent a life-time in such studies, and this garden is his world."

"And yourself, lady"—observed Giovanni—"if fame says true—you, likewise, are deeply skilled in the virtues indicated by these rich blossoms, and these spicy perfumes. Would you deign to be my instructress, I should prove an apter scholar than if taught by Signor Rappaccini himself."

"Are there such idle rumors?" asked Beatrice, with the music of a pleasant laugh. "Do people say that I am skilled in my father's science of plants? What a jest is there! No; though I have grown up among these flowers, I know no more of them than their hues and perfume; and sometimes, methinks I would fain rid myself of even that small knowledge. There are many flowers here, and those not the least brilliant, that shock and offend me, when they meet my eye. But, pray, Signor, do not believe these stories about my science. Believe nothing of me save what you see with your own eyes."

"And must I believe all that I have seen with my own eyes?" asked Giovanni ₇₀ pointedly, while the recollection of former scenes made him shrink. "No, Signora, you demand too little of me. Bid me believe nothing, save what comes from your own lips."

It would appear that Beatrice understood him. There came a deep flush to her cheek; but she looked full into Giovanni's eyes, and responded to his gaze of uneasy suspicion with a queen-like haughtiness.

"I do so bid you, Signor!" she replied. "Forget whatever you may have fancied in regard to me. If true to the outward senses, still it may be false in its essence. But the words of Beatrice Rappaccini's lips are true from the depths of the heart outward. Those you may believe!"

A fervor glowed in her whole aspect, and beamed upon Giovanni's consciousness like the light of truth itself. But while she spoke, there was a fragrance in the atmosphere around her, rich and delightful, though evanescent, yet which the young man, from an indefinable reluctance, scarcely dared to draw into his lungs. It might be the odor of the flowers. Could it be Beatrice's breath, which thus embalmed her words with a strange richness, as if by steeping them in her heart? A faintness passed like a shadow over Giovanni, and flitted away; he seemed to gaze through the beautiful girl's eyes into her transparent soul, and felt no more doubt or fear.

The tinge of passion that had colored Beatrice's manner vanished; she became gay, and appeared to derive a pure delight from her communion with the youth, not unlike what the maiden of a lonely island might have felt, conversing with a voyager from the civilized world. Evidently her experience of life had been confined within the limits of that garden. She talked now about matters as simple as the daylight or summer-clouds, and now asked questions in reference to the city, or Giovanni's distant home, his friends, his mother, and his sisters; questions indicating such seclusion, and such lack of familiarity with modes and forms, that Giovanni responded as if to an infant. Her spirit gushed out before him like a fresh rill, that was just catching its first glimpse of the sunlight, and wondering at the reflections of earth and sky which were flung into its bosom. There came thoughts, too, from a deep source, and fantasies of a gemlike brilliancy, as if diamonds and rubies sparkled upward among the bubbles of the fountain. Ever and anon, there gleamed across the young man's mind a sense of wonder, that he should be walking side by side with the being who had so wrought upon his imagination—whom he had idealized in such hues of terror—in whom he had positively witnessed such manifestations of dreadful attributes—that he should be conversing with Beatrice like a brother, and should find her so human and so maiden-like. But such reflections were only momentary; the effect of her character was too real, not to make itself familiar at once.

75   In this free intercourse, they had strayed through the garden, and now, after many turns among its avenues, were come to the shattered fountain, beside which grew the magnificent shrub with its treasury of glowing blossoms. A fragrance was diffused from it, which Giovanni recognized as identical with that which he had attributed to Beatrice's breath, but incomparably more powerful. As her eyes fell upon it, Giovanni beheld her press her hand to her bosom, as if her heart were throbbing suddenly and painfully.

"For the first time in my life," murmured she, addressing the shrub, "I had forgotten thee!"

"I remember, Signora," said Giovanni, "that you once promised to reward me with one of these living gems for the bouquet, which I had the happy boldness to fling to your feet. Permit me now to pluck it as a memorial of this interview."

He made a step towards the shrub, with extended hand. But Beatrice darted forward, uttering a shriek that went through his heart like a dagger. She caught his hand, and drew it back with the whole force of her slender figure. Giovanni felt her touch thrilling through his fibres.

"Touch it not!" exclaimed she, in a voice of agony. "Not for thy life! It is fatal!"

80   Then, hiding her face, she fled from him, and vanished beneath the sculptured portal. As Giovanni followed her with his eyes, he beheld the emaciated figure and pale intelligence of Doctor Rappaccini, who had been watching the scene, he knew not how long, within the shadow of the entrance.

No sooner was Guasconti alone in his chamber, than the image of Beatrice came back to his passionate musings, invested with all the witchery that had been gathering around it ever since his first glimpse of her, and now likewise imbued with a tender warmth of girlish womanhood. She was human: her nature was endowed with all gentle and feminine qualities; she was worthiest to be worshipped; she was capable, surely, on her part, of the height and heroism of love. Those tokens, which he had hitherto considered as proofs of a frightful peculiarity in her physical and moral system, were now either forgotten, or, by the subtle sophistry of passion, transmuted into a golden crown of enchantment, rendering Beatrice the more admirable, by so much as she was the more unique. Whatever had looked ugly, was now beautiful; or, if incapable of such a change, it stole away and hid itself among those shapeless half-ideas, which throng the dim region beyond the daylight of our perfect consciousness. Thus did he spend the night, nor fell asleep, until the dawn had begun to awake the slumbering flowers in Doctor Rappaccini's garden, whither Giovanni's dreams doubtless led him. Up rose the sun in his due season, and flinging his beams upon the young man's eyelids, awoke him to a sense of pain. When thoroughly aroused, he became sensible of a burning and tingling agony in his hand—in his right hand—the very hand which Beatrice had grasped in her own, when he was on the point of plucking one of the gem-like flowers. On the back of that hand there was now a purple print, like that of four small fingers, and the likeness of a slender thumb upon his wrist.

Oh, how stubbornly does love—or even that cunning semblance of love which flourishes in the imagination, but strikes no depth of root into the heart—how stubbornly does it hold its faith, until the moment come, when it is doomed to vanish into thin mist! Giovanni wrapt a handkerchief about his hand, and wondered what evil thing had stung him, and soon forgot his pain in a reverie of Beatrice.

After the first interview, a second was in the inevitable course of what we call fate. A third; a fourth; and a meeting with Beatrice in the garden was no longer an incident in Giovanni's daily life, but the whole space in which he might be said to live; for the anticipation and memory of that ecstatic hour made up the remainder. Nor was it otherwise with the daughter of Rappaccini. She watched for the youth's appearance, and flew to his side with confidence as unreserved as if they had been playmates from early infancy—as if they were such playmates still. If, by any unwonted chance, he failed to come at the appointed moment, she stood beneath the window, and sent up the rich sweetness of her tones to float around him in his chamber, and echo and reverberate throughout his heart—"Giovanni! Giovanni! Why tarriest thou? Come down!"—And down he hastened into that Eden of poisonous flowers.

But, with all this intimate familiarity, there was still a reserve in Beatrice's demeanor, so rigidly and invariably sustained, that the idea of infringing it scarcely occurred to his imagination. By all appreciable signs, they loved; they had looked love, with eyes that conveyed the holy secret from the depths of one soul into the depths of the other, as if it were too sacred to be whispered by the way; they had even spoken love, in those gushes of passion when their spirits darted forth in articulated breath, like tongues of long-hidden flame; and yet there had been no seal of lips, no clasp of hands, nor any slightest caresses, such as love claims and hallows. He had never touched one of the gleaming ringlets of her hair; her garment—so marked was the physical barrier between them—had never been waved against him by a breeze. On the few occasions when Giovanni had seemed tempted to overstep the limit, Beatrice grew so sad, so stern, and withal wore such a look of desolate separation, shuddering at itself, that not a spoken word was requisite to repel him. At such times, he was startled at the horrible suspicions that rose, monster-like, out of the caverns of his heart, and stared him in the face; his love grew thin and faint as the morning-mist; his doubts alone had substance. But when Beatrice's face brightened again, after the momentary shadow, she was transformed at once from the mysterious, questionable being, whom he had watched with so much awe and horror; she was now the beautiful and unsophisticated girl, whom he felt that his spirit knew with a certainty beyond all other knowledge.

85   A considerable time had now passed since Giovanni's last meeting with Baglioni. One morning, however, he was disagreeably surprised by a visit from the Professor, whom he had scarcely thought of for whole weeks, and would willingly have forgotten still longer. Given up, as he had long been, to a pervading excitement, he could tolerate no companions, except upon condition of their perfect sympathy with his present state of feeling. Such sympathy was not to be expected from Professor Baglioni.

The visitor chatted carelessly, for a few moments, about the gossip of the city and the University, and then took up another topic.

"I have been reading an old classic author lately," said he, "and met with a story that strangely interested me. Possibly you may remember it. It is of an Indian prince, who sent a beautiful woman as a present to Alexander the Great. She was as lovely as the dawn, and gorgeous as the sunset; but what especially distinguished her was a certain rich perfume in her breath—richer than a garden of Persian roses. Alexander, as was natural to a youthful conqueror, fell in love at first sight with this magnificent stranger. But a certain sage physician, happening to be present, discovered a terrible secret in regard to her."

"And what was that?" asked Giovanni, turning his eyes downward to avoid those of the Professor.

"That this lovely woman," continued Baglioni, with emphasis, "had been nourished with poisons from her birth upward, until her whole nature was so imbued with them, that she herself had become the deadliest poison in existence. Poison was her element of life. With that rich perfume of her breath, she blasted the very air. Her love would have been poison!—her embrace death! Is not this a marvelous tale?"

90   "A childish fable," answered Giovanni, nervously starting from his chair. "I marvel how your worship finds time to read such nonsense, among your graver studies."

"By the bye," said the Professor, looking uneasily about him, "what singular fragrance is this in your apartment? Is it the perfume of your gloves? It is faint, but delicious, and yet, after all, by no means agreeable. Were I to breathe it long, methinks it would make me ill. It is like the breath of a flower—but I see no flowers in the chamber."

"Nor are there any," replied Giovanni, who had turned pale as the Professor spoke; "nor, I think, is there any fragrance, except in your worship's imagination. Odors, being a sort of element combined of the sensual and the spiritual, are apt to deceive us in this manner. The recollection of a perfume—the bare idea of it—may easily be mistaken for a present reality."

"Aye; but my sober imagination does not often play such tricks," said Baglioni; "and were I to fancy any kind of odor, it would be that of some vile apothecary drug, wherewith my fingers are likely enough to be imbued. Our worshipful friend Rappaccini, as I have heard, tinctures his medicaments with odors richer than those of Araby. Doubtless, likewise, the fair and learned Signora Beatrice would minister to her patients with draughts as sweet as a maiden's breath. But wo to him that sips them!"

Giovanni's face evinced many contending emotions. The tone in which the Professor alluded to the pure and lovely daughter of Rappaccini was a torture to his soul; and yet, the intimation of a view of her character, opposite to his own, gave instantaneous distinctness to a thousand dim suspicions, which now grinned at him like so many demons. But he strove hard to quell them, and to respond to Baglioni with a true lover's perfect faith.

"Signor Professor," said he, "you were my father's friend—perchance, too, it is   95 your purpose to act a friendly part towards his son. I would fain feel nothing towards you, save respect and deference. But I pray you to observe, Signor, that there is one subject on which we must not speak. You know not the Signora Beatrice. You cannot, therefore, estimate the wrong—the blasphemy, I may even say—that is offered to her character by a light or injurious word."

"Giovanni!—my poor Giovanni!" answered the Professor, with a calm expression of pity, "I know this wretched girl far better than yourself. You shall hear the truth in respect to the poisoner Rappaccini, and his poisonous daughter. Yes; poisonous as she is beautiful! Listen; for even should you do violence to my grey hairs, it shall not silence me. That old fable of the Indian woman has become a truth, by the deep and deadly science of Rappaccini, and in the person of the lovely Beatrice!"

Giovanni groaned and hid his face.

"Her father," continued Baglioni, "was not restrained by natural affection from offering up his child, in this horrible manner, as the victim of his insane zeal for science. For—let us do him justice—he is as true a man of science as ever distilled his own heart in an alembic. What, then, will be your fate? Beyond a doubt, you are selected as the material of some new experiment. Perhaps the result is to be death— perhaps a fate more awful still! Rappaccini, with what he calls the interest of science before his eyes, will hesitate at nothing."

"It is a dream!" muttered Giovanni to himself, "surely it is a dream!"

"But," resumed the Professor, "be of good cheer, son of my friend! It is not yet   100 too late for the rescue. Possibly, we may even succeed in bringing back this miserable child within the limits of ordinary nature, from which her father's madness has estranged her. Behold this little silver vase! It was wrought by the hands of the renowned Benvenuto Cellini, and is well worthy to be a love-gift to the fairest dame in Italy. But its contents are invaluable. One little sip of this antidote would have rendered the most virulent poisons of the Borgias innocuous. Doubt not that it will be as efficacious against those of Rappaccini. Bestow the vase, and the precious liquid within it, on your Beatrice, and hopefully await the result."

Baglioni laid a small exquisitely wrought silver phial on the table, and withdrew, leaving what he had said to produce its effect upon the young man's mind.

"We will thwart Rappaccini yet!" thought he, chuckling to himself, as he descended the stairs. "But, let us confess the truth of him, he is a wonderful man!—a wonderful man indeed! A vile empiric, however, in his practice, and therefore not to be tolerated by those who respect the good old rules of the medical profession!"

Throughout Giovanni's whole acquaintance with Beatrice, he had occasionally, as we have said, been haunted by dark surmises as to her character. Yet, so thoroughly had she made herself felt by him as a simple, natural, most affectionate and guileless creature, that the image now held up by Professor Baglioni, looked as strange and incredible, as if it were not in accordance with his own original conception. True, there were ugly recollections connected with his first glimpses of the beautiful girl; he could not quite forget the bouquet that withered in her grasp, and the insect that perished amid the sunny air, by no ostensible agency, save the fragrance of her breath. These incidents, however, dissolving in the pure light of her character, had no longer the efficacy of facts, but were acknowledged as mistaken fantasies, by whatever testimony of the senses they might appear to be substantiated. There is something truer and more real, than what we can see with the eyes, and touch with the finger. On such better evidence, had Giovanni founded his confidence in Beatrice, though rather by the necessary force of her high attributes, than by any deep and generous faith, on his part. But, now, his spirit was incapable of sustaining itself at the height to which the early enthusiasm of passion had exalted it; he fell down, grovelling among earthly doubts, and defiled therewith the pure whiteness of Beatrice's image. Not that he gave her up; he did but distrust. He resolved to institute some decisive test that should satisfy him, once for all, whether there were those dreadful peculiarities in her physical nature, which could not be supposed to exist without some corresponding monstrosity of soul. His eyes, gazing down afar, might have deceived him as to the lizard, the insect, and the flowers. But if he could witness, at the distance of a few paces, the sudden blight of one fresh and healthful flower in Beatrice's hand, there would be room for no further question. With this idea, he hastened to the florist's, and purchased a bouquet that was still gemmed with the morning dewdrops.

It was now the customary hour of his daily interview with Beatrice. Before descending into the garden, Giovanni failed not to look at his figure in the mirror; a vanity to be expected in a beautiful young man, yet, as displaying itself at that troubled and feverish moment, the token of a certain shallowness of feeling and insincerity of character. He did gaze, however, and said to himself, that his features had never before possessed so rich a grace, nor his eyes such vivacity, nor his cheeks so warm a hue of superabundant life.

105 "At least," thought he, "her poison has not yet insinuated itself into my system. I am no flower to perish in her grasp!"

With that thought, he turned his eyes on the bouquet, which he had never once laid aside from his hand. A thrill of indefinable horror shot through his frame, on perceiving that those dewy flowers were already beginning to droop; they wore the aspect of things that had been fresh and lovely, yesterday. Giovanni grew white as marble, and stood motionless before the mirror, staring at his own reflection there, as at the likeness of something frightful. He remembered Baglioni's remark about the fragrance that seemed to pervade the chamber. It must have been the poison in his breath! Then he shuddered—shuddered at himself! Recovering from his stupor, he began to watch, with curious eye, a spider that was busily at work, hanging its web from the antique cornice of the apartment, crossing and re-crossing the artful system of interwoven lines, as vigorous and active a spider as ever dangled from an old ceiling. Giovanni bent towards the insect, and emitted a deep, long breath. The spider suddenly ceased its toil; the web vibrated with a tremor originating in the body of the small artisan. Again

Giovanni sent forth a breath, deeper, longer, and imbued with a venomous feeling out of his heart; he knew not whether he were wicked or only desperate. The spider made a convulsive gripe with his limbs, and hung dead across the window.

"Accursed! Accursed!" muttered Giovanni, addressing himself. "Hast thou grown so poisonous, that this deadly insect perishes by thy breath?"

At that moment, a rich, sweet voice came floating up from the garden:—

"Giovanni! Giovanni! It is past the hour! Why tarriest thou! Come down!"

"Yes," muttered Giovanni again. "She is the only being whom my breath may not slay! Would that it might!" 110

He rushed down, and in an instant, was standing before the bright and loving eyes of Beatrice. A moment ago, his wrath and despair had been so fierce that he could have desired nothing so much as to wither her by a glance. But, with her actual presence, there came influences which had too real an existence to be at once shaken off; recollections of the delicate and benign power of her feminine nature, which had so often enveloped him in a religious calm; recollections of many a holy and passionate outgush of her heart, when the pure fountain had been unsealed from its depths, and made visible in its transparency to his mental eye; recollections which, had Giovanni known how to estimate them, would have assured him that all this ugly mystery was but an earthly illusion, and that, whatever mist of evil might seem to have gathered over her, the real Beatrice was a heavenly angel. Incapable as he was of such high faith, still her presence had not utterly lost its magic. Giovanni's rage was quelled into an aspect of sullen insensibility. Beatrice, with a quick spiritual sense, immediately felt that there was a gulf of blackness between them, which neither he nor she could pass. They walked on together, sad and silent, and came thus to the marble fountain, and to its pool of water on the ground, in the midst of which grew the shrub that bore gem-like blossoms. Giovanni was affrighted at the eager enjoyment—the appetite, as it were—with which he found himself inhaling the fragrance of the flowers.

"Beatrice," asked he abruptly, "whence came this shrub?"

"My father created it," answered she, with simplicity.

"Created it! created it!" repeated Giovanni. "What mean you, Beatrice?"

"He is a man fearfully acquainted with the secrets of nature," replied Beatrice; 115 "and, at the hour when I first drew breath, this plant sprang from the soil, the offspring of his science, of his intellect, while I was but his earthly child. Approach it not!" continued she, observing with terror that Giovanni was drawing nearer to the shrub. "It has qualities that you little dream of. But I, dearest Giovanni—I grew up and blossomed with the plant, and was nourished with its breath. It was my sister, and I loved it with a human affection: for—alas! hast thou not suspected it? there was an awful doom."

Here Giovanni frowned so darkly upon her that Beatrice paused and trembled. But her faith in his tenderness reassured her, and made her blush that she had doubted for an instant.

"There was an awful doom," she continued,—"the effect of my father's fatal love of science—which estranged me from all society of my kind. Until Heaven sent thee, dearest Giovanni, Oh! how lonely was thy poor Beatrice!"

"Was it a hard doom?" asked Giovanni, fixing his eyes upon her.

"Only of late have I known how hard it was," answered she tenderly. "Oh, yes; but my heart was torpid, and therefore quiet."

120   Giovanni's rage broke forth from his sullen gloom like a lightning-flash out of a dark cloud.

"Accursed one!" cried he, with venomous scorn and anger. "And finding thy solitude wearisome, thou hast severed me, likewise, from all the warmth of life, and enticed me into thy region of unspeakable horror!"

"Giovanni!" exclaimed Beatrice, turning her large bright eyes upon his face. The force of his words had not found its way into her mind; she was merely thunder-struck.

"Yes, poisonous thing!" repeated Giovanni, beside himself with passion. "Thou hast done it! Thou hast blasted me! Thou hast filled my veins with poison! Thou hast made me as hateful, as ugly, as loathsome and deadly a creature as thyself,— a world's wonder of hideous monstrosity! Now—if our breath be happily as fatal to ourselves as to all others—let us join our lips in one kiss of unutterable hatred, and so die!"

"What has befallen me?" murmured Beatrice, with a low moan out of her heart. "Holy Virgin pity me, a poor heartbroken child!"

125   "Thou! Dost thou pray?" cried Giovanni, still with the same fiendish scorn. "Thy very prayers, as they come from thy lips, taint the atmosphere with death. Yes, yes; let us pray! Let us to church, and dip our fingers in the holy water at the portal! They that come after us will perish as by a pestilence. Let us sign crosses in the air! It will be scattering curses abroad in the likeness of holy symbols!"

"Giovanni," said Beatrice calmly, for her grief was beyond passion, "why dost thou join thyself with me thus in those terrible words? I, it is true, am the horrible thing thou namest me. But thou!—what hast thou to do, save with one other shudder at my hideous misery, to go forth out of the garden and mingle with thy race, and forget that there ever crawled on earth such a monster as poor Beatrice?"

"Dost thou pretend ignorance?" asked Giovanni, scowling upon her. "Behold! This power have I gained from the pure daughter of Rappaccini!"

There was a swarm of summer-insects flitting through the air, in search of the food promised by the flower-odors of the fatal garden. They circled round Giovanni's head, and were evidently attracted towards him by the same influence which had drawn them, for an instant, within the sphere of several of the shrubs. He sent forth a breath among them, and smiled bitterly at Beatrice, as at least a score of the insects fell dead upon the ground.

"I see it! I see it!" shrieked Beatrice. "It is my father's fatal science! No, no, Giovanni; it was not I! Never, never! I dreamed only to love thee, and be with thee a little time, and so to let thee pass away, leaving but thine image in mine heart. For, Giovanni—believe it—though my body be nourished with poison, my spirit is God's creature, and craves love as its daily food. But my father!—he has united us in this fearful sympathy. Yes; spurn me!—tread upon me!—kill me! Oh, what is death, after such words as thine? But it was not I! Not for a world of bliss would I have done it!"

Giovanni's passion had exhausted itself in its outburst from his lips. There now   130
came across him a sense, mournful, and not without tenderness, of the intimate and
peculiar relationship between Beatrice and himself. They stood, as it were, in an utter solitude, which would be made none the less solitary by the densest throng of human life. Ought not, then, the desert of humanity around them to press this insulated
pair closer together? If they should be cruel to one another, who was there to be kind
to them? Besides, thought Giovanni, might there not still be a hope of his returning
within the limits of ordinary nature, and leading Beatrice—the redeemed Beatrice—
by the hand? Oh, weak, and selfish, and unworthy spirit, that could dream of an
earthly union and earthly happiness as possible, after such deep love had been so bitterly wronged as was Beatrice's love by Giovanni's blighting words! No, no; there
could be no such hope. She must pass heavily, with that broken heart, across the borders of Time—she must bathe her hurts in some fount of Paradise, and forget her
grief in the light of immortality—and *there* be well!

But Giovanni did not know it.

"Dear Beatrice," said he, approaching her, while she shrank away, as always at
his approach, but now with a different impulse—"dearest Beatrice, our fate is not
yet so desperate. Behold! There is a medicine, potent, as a wise physician has assured me, and almost divine in its efficacy. It is composed of ingredients the most
opposite to those by which thy awful father has brought this calamity upon thee
and me. It is distilled of blessed herbs. Shall we not quaff it together, and thus be
purified from evil?"

"Give it me!" said Beatrice, extending her hand to receive the little silver phial
which Giovanni took from his bosom. She added, with a peculiar emphasis: "I will
drink—but do thou await the result."

She put Baglioni's antidote to her lips; and, at the same moment, the figure of
Rappaccini emerged from the portal, and came slowly towards the marble fountain.
As he drew near, the pale man of science seemed to gaze with a triumphant expression at the beautiful youth and maiden, as might an artist who should spend his life
in achieving a picture or a group of statuary, and finally be satisfied with his success.
He paused—his bent form grew erect with conscious power, he spread out his hands
over them, in the attitude of a father imploring a blessing upon his children. But
those were the same hands that had thrown poison into the stream of their lives!
Giovanni trembled. Beatrice shuddered nervously, and pressed her hand upon her
heart.

"My daughter," said Rappaccini, "thou art no longer lonely in the world! Pluck   135
one of those precious gems from thy sister shrub, and bid thy bridegroom wear it in
his bosom. It will not harm him now! My science, and the sympathy between thee
and him, have so wrought within his system, that he now stands apart from common
men, as thou dost, daughter of my pride and triumph, from ordinary women. Pass
on, then, through the world, most dear to one another, and dreadful to all besides!"

"My father," said Beatrice, feebly—and still, as she spoke, she kept her hand
upon her heart—"wherefore didst thou inflict this miserable doom upon thy child?"

"Miserable!" exclaimed Rappaccini. "What mean you, foolish girl? Dost thou
deem it misery to be endowed with marvellous gifts, against which no power nor

strength could avail an enemy? Misery, to be able to quell the mightiest with a breath? Misery, to be as terrible as thou art beautiful? Wouldst thou, then, have preferred the condition of a weak woman, exposed to all evil, and capable of none?"

"I would fain have been loved, not feared," murmured Beatrice, sinking down upon the ground—"But now it matters not; I am going, father, where the evil, which thou hast striven to mingle with my being, will pass away like a dream—like the fragrance of these poisonous flowers, which will no longer taint my breath among the flowers of Eden. Farewell, Giovanni! Thy words of hatred are like lead within my heart—but they, too, will fall away as I ascend. Oh, was there not, from the first, more poison in thy nature than in mine?"

To Beatrice—so radically had her earthly part been wrought upon by Rappaccini's skill—as poison had been life, so the powerful antidote was death. And thus the poor victim of man's ingenuity and of thwarted nature, and of the fatality that attends all such efforts of perverted wisdom, perished there, at the feet of her father and Giovanni. Just at that moment, Professor Pietro Baglioni looked forth from the window, and called loudly, in a tone of triumph mixed with horror, to the thunderstricken man of science:

140   "Rappaccini! Rappaccini! And is *this* the upshot of your experiment?"

QUESTIONS FOR DISCUSSION AND WRITING

1. How do Baglioni's appearances mark important stages in the development of the plot?

2. What qualities do the male characters in the story have in common? In what ways is Beatrice like the flower she calls "sister"?

3. How does the Italian setting make possible the rich allusiveness of this story—as in the references to Roman gods, Dante, and Beatrice?

4. How would you characterize the attitude of the narrator toward the story he tells? How do the first two paragraphs establish the qualities of this narrator?

5. Because the narrator confesses to an "inveterate love of allegory," the reader expects a moral truth to emerge from the narrative. How would you state the moral truth in the story?

Stories for Comparison

Arthur C. Clarke's "The Star" (pages 383–387); Bernard Malamud's "The Magic Barrel" (pages 850–863).

51

....

N A T H A N I E L   H A W T H O R N E

Young Goodman Brown

Young Goodman Brown came forth at sunset into the street at Salem village; but put his head back, after crossing the threshold, to exchange a parting kiss with his young wife. And Faith, as the wife was aptly named, thrust her own pretty head into the street, letting the wind play with the pink ribbons on her cap while she called to Goodman Brown.

"Dearest heart," whispered she, softly and rather sadly, when her lips were close to his ear, "prithee put off your journey until sunrise and sleep in your own bed to-night. A lone woman is troubled with such dreams and such thoughts that she's afeard of herself sometimes. Pray tarry with me this night, dear husband, of all nights in the year."

"My love and my Faith," replied young Goodman Brown, "of all nights in the year, this one night must I tarry away from thee. My journey, as thou callest it, forth and back again, must needs be done 'twixt now and sunrise. What, my sweet, pretty wife, dost thou doubt me already, and we but three months married?"

"Then God bless you!" said Faith, with the pink ribbons; "and may you find all well when you come back."

"Amen!" cried Goodman Brown. "Say thy prayers, dear Faith, and go to bed at 5 dusk, and no harm will come to thee."

So they parted; and the young man pursued his way until, being about to turn the corner by the meeting-house, he looked back and saw the head of Faith still peeping after him with a melancholy air, in spite of her pink ribbons.

"Poor little Faith!" thought he, for his heart smote him. "What a wretch am I to leave her on such an errand! She talks of dreams, too. Methought as she spoke there was trouble in her face, as if a dream had warned her what work is to be done to-night. But no, no; 'twould kill her to think it. Well, she's a blessed angel on earth; and after this one night I'll cling to her skirts and follow her to heaven."

With this excellent resolve for the future, Goodman Brown felt himself justified in making more haste on his present evil purpose. He had taken a dreary road, darkened by all the gloomiest trees of the forest, which barely stood aside to let the narrow path creep through, and closed immediately behind. It was all as lonely as could be; and there is this peculiarity in such a solitude, that the traveller knows not who may be concealed by the innumerable trunks and the thick boughs overhead; so that with lonely footsteps he may yet be passing through an unseen multitude.

"There may be a devilish Indian behind every tree," said Goodman Brown to himself; and he glanced fearfully behind him as he added, "What if the devil himself should be at my very elbow!"

His head being turned back, he passed a crook of the road, and, looking forward again, beheld the figure of a man, in grave and decent attire, seated at the foot of an old tree. He arose at Goodman Brown's approach and walked onward side by side with him.

"You are late, Goodman Brown," said he. "The clock of the Old South was striking as I came through Boston, and that is full fifteen minutes agone."

"Faith kept me back a while," replied the young man, with a tremor in his voice, caused by the sudden appearance of his companion, though not wholly unexpected.

It was now deep dusk in the forest, and deepest in that part of it where these two were journeying. As nearly as could be discerned, the second traveller was about fifty years old, apparently in the same rank of life as Goodman Brown, and bearing a considerable resemblance to him, though perhaps more in expression than features. Still they might have been taken for father and son. And yet, though the elder person was as simply clad as the younger, and as simple in manner too, he had an indescribable air of one who knew the world, and who would not have felt abashed at the governor's dinner table or in King William's court, were it possible that his affairs should call him thither. But the only thing about him that could be fixed upon as remarkable was his staff, which bore the likeness of a great black snake, so curiously wrought that it might almost be seen to twist and wriggle itself like a living serpent. This, of course, must have been an ocular deception, assisted by the uncertain light.

"Come, Goodman Brown," cried his fellow-traveller, "this is a dull pace for the beginning of a journey. Take my staff, if you are so soon weary."

"Friend," said the other, exchanging his slow pace for a full stop, "having kept convenant by meeting thee here, it is my purpose now to return whence I came. I have scruples touching the matter thou wot'st of."

"Sayest thou so?" replied he of the serpent, smiling apart. "Let us walk on, nevertheless, reasoning as we go; and if I convince thee not thou shalt turn back. We are but a little way in the forest yet."

"Too far! too far!" exclaimed the goodman, unconsciously resuming his walk. "My father never went into the woods on such an errand, nor his father before him. We have been a race of honest men and good Christians since the days of the martyrs; and shall I be the first of the name of Brown that ever took this path and kept"—

"Such company, thou wouldst say," observed the elder person, interpreting his pause. "Well said, Goodman Brown! I have been as well acquainted with your family as with ever a one among the Puritans; and that's no trifle to say. I helped your grandfather, the constable, when he lashed the Quaker woman so smartly through the streets of Salem; and it was I that brought your father a pitch-pine knot, kindled at my own hearth, to set fire to an Indian village, in King Philip's war. They were my good friends, both; and many a pleasant walk have we had along this path, and returned merrily after midnight. I would fain be friends with you for their sake."

"If it be as thou sayest," replied Goodman Brown, "I marvel they never spoke of these matters; or, verily, I marvel not, seeing that the least rumor of the sort would have driven them from New England. We are a people of prayer, and good works to boot, and abide no such wickedness."

"Wickedness or not," said the traveller with the twisted staff, "I have a very gen- 20 eral acquaintance here in New England. The deacons of many a church have drunk the communion wine with me; the selectmen of divers towns make me their chairman; and a majority of the Great and General Court are firm supporters of my interest. The governor and I, too—But these are state secrets."

"Can this be so?" cried Goodman Brown, with a stare of amazement at his undisturbed companion. "Howbeit, I have nothing to do with the governor and council; they have their own ways, and are no rule for a simple husbandman like me. But, were I to go on with thee, how should I meet the eye of that good old man, our minister, at Salem village? Oh, his voice would make me tremble both Sabbath day and lecture day."

Thus far the elder traveller had listened with due gravity; but now burst into a fit of irrepressible mirth, shaking himself so violently that his snake-like staff actually seemed to wriggle in sympathy.

"Ha! ha! ha!" shouted he again and again; then composing himself, "Well, go on, Goodman Brown, go on; but, prithee, don't kill me with laughing."

"Well, then, to end the matter at once," said Goodman Brown, considerably nettled, "there is my wife, Faith. It would break her dear little heart; and I'd rather break my own."

"Nay, if that be the case," answered the other, "e'en go thy ways, Goodman 25 Brown. I would not for twenty old women like the one hobbling before us that Faith should come to any harm."

As he spoke he pointed his staff at a female figure on the path, in whom Goodman Brown recognized a very pious and exemplary dame, who had taught him his catechism in youth, and was still his moral and spiritual adviser, jointly with the minister and Deacon Gookin.

"A marvel, truly, that Goody Cloyse should be so far in the wilderness at nightfall," said he. "But with your leave, friend, I shall take a cut through the woods until we have left this Christian woman behind. Being a stranger to you, she might ask whom I was consorting with and whither I was going."

"Be it so," said his fellow-traveller. "Betake you to the woods, and let me keep the path."

Accordingly the young man turned aside, but took care to watch his companion, who advanced softly along the road until he had come within a staff's length of the old dame. She, meanwhile, was making the best of her way, with singular speed for so aged a woman, and mumbling some indistinct words—a prayer, doubtless—as she went. The traveller put forth his staff and touched her withered neck with what seemed the serpent's tail.

"The devil!" screamed the pious old lady. 30

"Then Goody Cloyse knows her old friend?" observed the traveller, confronting her and leaning on his writhing stick.

"Ah, forsooth, and is it your worship indeed?" cried the good dame. "Yes, truly is it, and in the very image of my old gossip, Goodman Brown, the grandfather of the silly fellow that now is. But—would your worship believe it?—my broomstick hath strangely disappeared, stolen, as I suspect, by that unhanged witch, Goody Cory, and that, too, when I was all anointed with the juice of smallage, and cinque-foil, and wolf's bane"—

"Mingled with fine wheat and the fat of a new-born babe," said the shape of old Goodman Brown.

"Oh, your worship knows the recipe," cried the old lady, cackling aloud. "So, as I was saying, being all ready for the meeting, and no horse to ride on, I made up my mind to foot it, for they tell me there is a nice young man to be taken into communion tonight. But now your good worship will lend me your arm, and we shall be there in a twinkling."

35   "That can hardly be," answered her friend. "I may not spare you my arm, Goody Cloyse; but here is my staff, if you will."

So saying, he threw it down at her feet, where, perhaps, it assumed life, being one of the rods which its owner had formerly lent to the Egyptian magi. Of this fact, however, Goodman Brown can not take cognizance. He had cast up his eyes in astonishment, and, looking down again, beheld neither Goody Cloyse nor the serpentine staff, but his fellow-traveller alone, who waited for him as calmly as if nothing had happened.

"That old woman taught me my catechism," said the young man; and there was a world of meaning in this simple comment.

They continued to walk onward, while the elder traveller exhorted his companion to make good speed and persevere in the path, discoursing so aptly that his arguments seemed rather to spring up in the bosom of his auditor than to be suggested by himself. As they went, he plucked a branch of maple to serve for a walking stick, and began to strip it of the twigs and little boughs, which were wet with evening dew. The moment his fingers touched them they became strangely withered and dried up as with a week's sunshine. Thus the pair proceeded, at a good free pace, until suddenly, in a gloomy hollow of the road, Goodman Brown sat himself down on the stump of a tree and refused to go any farther.

"Friend," said he, stubbornly, "my mind is made up. Not another step will I budge on this errand. What if a wretched old woman do choose to go to the devil when I thought she was going to heaven: is that any reason why I should quit my dear Faith and go after her?"

40   "You will think better of this by and by," said his acquaintance, composedly. "Sit here and rest yourself a while; and when you feel like moving again, there is my staff to help you along."

Without words, he threw his companion the maple stick, and was as speedily out of sight as if he had vanished into the deepening gloom. The young man sat a few moments by the roadside, applauding himself greatly, and thinking with how clear a conscience he should meet the minister in his morning walk, nor shrink from the eye of good old Deacon Gookin. And what calm sleep would be his that very night, which was to have been spent so wickedly, but so purely and sweetly now, in the arms of Faith! Amidst these pleasant and praiseworthy meditations, Goodman Brown heard the tramp of horses along the road, and deemed it advisable to conceal himself within the verge of the forest, conscious of the guilty purpose that had brought him thither, though now so happily turned from it.

On came the hoof tramps and the voices of the riders, two grave old voices, conversing soberly as they drew near. These mingled sounds appeared to pass along the road, within a few yards of the young man's hiding-place; but, owing doubtless to the depth of the gloom at that particular spot, neither the travellers nor their steeds were visible. Though their figures brushed the small boughs by the wayside, it could not be seen that they intercepted, even for a moment; the faint gleam from the strip of bright sky athwart which they must have passed. Goodman Brown alternately crouched and stood on tiptoe, pulling aside the branches and thrusting forth his head as far as he durst without discerning so much as a shadow. It vexed him the more, because he could have sworn, were such a thing possible, that he recognized the voices of the minister and Deacon Gookin, jogging along quietly, as they were wont to do, when bound to some ordination or ecclesiastical council. While yet within hearing one of the riders stopped to pluck a switch.

"Of the two, reverend sir," said the voice like the deacon's, "I had rather miss an ordination dinner than to-night's meeting. They tell me that some of our community are to be here from Falmouth and beyond, and others from Connecticut and Rhode Island besides several of Indian powwows, who, after their fashion, know almost as much deviltry as the best of us. Moreover, there is a goodly young woman to be taken into communion."

"Mighty well, Deacon Gookin!" replied the solemn old tones of the minister. "Spur up, or we shall be late. Nothing can be done you know until I get on the ground."

The hoofs clattered again; and the voices, talking so strangely in the empty air, 45 passed on through the forest, where no church had ever been gathered or solitary Christian prayed. Whither, then, could these holy men be journeying so deep into the heathen wilderness? Young Goodman Brown caught hold of a tree for support, being ready to sink down on the ground, faint and overburdened with the heavy sickness of his heart. He looked up to the sky, doubting whether there really was a heaven above him. Yet there was the blue arch, and the stars brightening in it.

"With heaven above and Faith below, I will yet stand firm against the devil!" cried Goodman Brown.

While he still gazed upward into the deep arch of the firmament and had lifted his hands to pray, a cloud, though no wind was stirring, hurried across the zenith and hid the brightening stars. The blue sky was still visible, except directly overhead, where this black mass of cloud was sweeping swiftly northward. Aloft in the air, as if from the depths of the cloud, came a confused and doubtful sound of voices. Once the listener fancied that he could distinguish the accents of townspeople of his own, men, and women, both pious and ungodly, many of whom he had met at the communion table, and had seen others rioting at the tavern. The next moment, so indistinct were the sounds, he doubted whether he had heard aught but the murmur of the old forest, whispering without a wind. Then came a stronger swell of those familiar tones, heard daily in the sunshine at Salem village, but never until now from a cloud of night. There was one voice of a young woman uttering lamentations, yet with an uncertain sorrow, and entreating for some favor, which perhaps, it would grieve her to obtain; and all the unseen multitude, both saints and sinners, seemed to encourage her onward.

"Faith!" shouted Goodman Brown, in a voice of agony and desperation; and the echoes of the forest mocked him, crying, "Faith! Faith!" as if bewildered wretches were seeking her all through the wilderness.

The cry of grief, rage, and terror was yet piercing the night, when the unhappy husband held his breath for a response. There was a scream, drowned immediately in a loud murmur of voices, fading into far-off laughter, as the dark cloud swept away, leaving the clear and silent sky above Goodman Brown. But something fluttered lightly down through the air and caught on the branch of a tree. The young man seized it, and beheld a pink ribbon.

50   "My Faith is gone!" cried he, after one stupefied moment. "There is no good on earth; and sin is but a name. Come, devil; for to thee is this world given."

And, maddened with despair, so that he laughed loud and long, did Goodman Brown grasp his staff and set forth again, at such a rate that he seemed to fly along the forest path rather than to walk or run. The road grew wilder and drearier and more faintly traced, and vanished at length, leaving him in the heart of the dark wilderness, still rushing onward with the instinct that guides mortal man to evil. The whole forest was peopled with frightful sounds—the creaking of the trees, the howling of wild beasts, and the yells of Indians; while sometimes the wind tolled like a distant church bell, and sometimes gave a broad roar around the traveller, as if all Nature were laughing him to scorn. But he was himself the chief horror of the scene, and shrank not from its other horrors.

"Ha! ha! ha!" roared Goodman Brown when the wind laughed at him. "Let us hear which will laugh loudest. Think not to frighten me with your deviltry. Come witch, come wizard, come Indian powwow, come devil himself, and here comes Goodman Brown. You may as well fear him as he fear you."

In truth, all through the haunted forest there could be nothing more frightful than the figure of Goodman Brown. On he flew among the black pines, brandishing his staff with frenzied gestures, now giving vent to an inspiration of horrid blasphemy, and now shouting forth such laughter as set all the echoes of the forest laughing like demons around him. The fiend in his own shape is less hideous than when he rages in the breast of man. Thus sped the demoniac on his course, until, quivering among the trees, he saw a red light before him, as when the felled trunks and branches of a clearing have been set on fire, and throw up their lurid blaze against the sky, at the hour of midnight. He paused, in a lull of the tempest that had driven him onward, and heard the swell of what seemed a hymn, rolling solemnly from a distance with the weight of many voices. He knew the tune; it was a familiar one in the choir of the village meeting-house. The verse died heavily away, and was lengthened by a chorus, not of human voices, but of all the sounds of the benighted wilderness pealing in awful harmony together. Goodman Brown cried out, and his cry was lost to his own ear by its unison with the cry of the desert.

In the interval of silence he stole forward until the light glared full upon his eyes. At one extremity of an open space, hemmed in by the dark wall of the forest, arose a rock, bearing some rude, natural resemblance either to an altar or a pulpit, and surrounded by four blazing pines, their tops aflame, their stems untouched, like candles at an evening meeting. The mass of foliage that had overgrown the summit of the rock was all on fire, blazing into the night and fitfully illuminating the whole field. Each pendant twig and leafy festoon was in a blaze. As the red light arose and fell, a numerous congregation alternately shone forth, then disappeared in shadow, and again grew, as it were, out of the darkness, peopling the heart of the solitary woods at once.

"A grave and dark-clad company," quoth Goodman Brown.   55

In truth they were such. Among them, quivering to and fro between gloom and splendor, appeared faces that would be seen next day at the council board of the province, and others which, Sabbath after Sabbath, looked devoutly heavenward, and benignantly over the crowded pews, from the holiest pulpits in the land. Some affirm that the lady of the governor was there. At least there were high dames well known to her, and wives of honored husbands, and widows, a great multitude, and ancient maidens, all of excellent repute, and fair young girls, who trembled lest their mothers should espy them. Either the sudden gleams of light flashing over the obscure field bedazzled Goodman Brown, or he recognized a score of the church members of Salem village famous for their special sanctity. Good old Deacon Gookin had arrived, and waited at the skirts of that venerable saint, his revered pastor. But, irreverently consorting with these grave, reputable, and pious people, these elders of the church, these chaste dames and dewy virgins, there were men of dissolute lives and women of spotted fame, wretches given over to all mean and filthy vice, and suspected even of horrid crimes. It was strange to see that the good shrank not from the wicked, nor were the sinners abashed by the saints. Scattered also among their pale-faced enemies were the Indian priests, or powwows, who had often scared their native forest with more hideous incantations than any known to English witchcraft.

"But where is Faith?" thought Goodman Brown; and, as hope came into his heart, he trembled.

Another verse of the hymn arose, a slow and mournful strain, such as the pious love, but joined to words which expressed all that our nature can conceive of sin, and darkly hinted at far more. Unfathomable to mere mortals is the lore of fiends. Verse after verse was sung; and still the chorus of the desert swelled between like the deepest tone of a mighty organ; and with the final peal of that dreadful anthem there came a sound, as if the roaring wind, the rushing streams, the howling beasts, and every other voice of the unconcerted wilderness were mingling and according with the voice of guilty man in homage to the prince of all. The four blazing pines threw up a loftier flame, and obscurely discovered shapes and visages of horror on the smoke wreaths above the impious assembly. At the same moment the fire on the rock shot redly forth and formed a glowing arch above its base, where now appeared a figure.

With reverence be it spoken, the figure bore no slight similitude, both in garb and manner, to some grave divine of the New England churches.

"Bring forth the converts!" cried a voice that echoed through the field and rolled into the forest.

60   At the word, Goodman Brown stepped forth from the shadow of the trees and approached the congregation, with whom he felt a loathful brotherhood by the sympathy of all that was wicked in his heart. He could have well-nigh sworn that the shape of his own dead father beckoned him to advance, looking downward from a smoke wreath, while a woman, with dim features of despair, threw out her hand to warn him back. Was it his mother? But he had no power to retreat one step, nor to resist, even in thought, when the minister and good old Deacon Gookin seized his arms and led him to the blazing rock. Thither came also the slender form of a veiled female, led between Goody Cloyse, that pious teacher of the catechism, and Martha Carrier, who had received the devil's promise to be queen of hell. A rampant hag was she. And there stood the proselytes beneath the canopy of fire.

"Welcome, my children," said the dark figure, "to the communion of your race. Ye have found thus young your nature and your destiny. My children, look behind you!"

They turned; and flashing forth, as it were, in a sheet of flame, the fiend worshippers were seen; the smile of welcome gleamed darkly on every visage.

"There," resumed the sable form, "are all whom ye have reverenced from youth. Ye deemed them holier than yourself, and shrank from your own sins, contrasting it with their lives of righteousness and prayerful aspirations heavenward. Yet here are they all in my worshipping assembly. This night it shall be granted you to know their secret deeds: how hoary-bearded elders of the church have whispered wanton words to the young maids of their households; how many a woman, eager for widow's weeds, has given her husband a drink at bedtime and let him sleep his last sleep in her bosom; how beardless youths have made haste to inherit their fathers' wealth, and how fair damsels—blush not, sweet ones—have dug little graves in the garden, and bidden me, the sole guest to an infant's funeral. By the sympathy of your human hearts for sin ye shall scent out all the places—whether in church, bed-chamber, street, field, or forest—where crime has been committed, and shall exult to behold the whole earth one stain of guilt, one mighty blood spot. Far more than this. It shall be yours to penetrate, in every bosom, the deep mystery of sin, the fountain of all wicked arts, and which inexhaustibly supplies more evil impulses than human power—than my power at its utmost—can make manifest in deeds. And now, my children, look upon each other."

They did so; and, by the blaze of the hell-kindled torches, the wretched man beheld his Faith, and the wife her husband, trembling before that unhallowed altar.

65   "Lo, there ye stand, my children," said the figure, in a deep and solemn tone, almost sad with its despairing awfulness, as if his once angelic nature could yet mourn for our miserable race. "Depending upon one another's hearts, ye had still hoped that virtue were not all a dream. Now are ye undeceived. Evil is the nature of mankind. Evil must be your only happiness. Welcome again, my children, to the communion of your race."

"Welcome," repeated the fiend worshippers, in one cry of despair and triumph.

And there they stood, the only pair, as it seemed, who were yet hesitating on the verge of wickedness in this dark world. A basin was hollowed, naturally, in the rock. Did it contain water, reddened by the lurid light? or was it blood? or, perchance, a liquid flame? Herein did the shape of evil dip his hand and prepare to lay the mark of baptism upon their foreheads, that they might be partakers of the mystery of sin, more conscious of the secret guilt of others, both in deed and thought, than they could now be of their own. The husband cast one look at his pale wife, and Faith at him. What polluted wretches would the next glance show them to each other, shuddering alike at what they disclosed and what they saw!

"Faith! Faith!" cried the husband, "look up to heaven, and resist the wicked one."

Whether Faith obeyed he knew not. Hardly had he spoken when he found himself amid calm night and solitude, listening to a roar of the wind which died heavily away through the forest. He staggered against the rock, and felt it chill and damp; while a hanging twig, that had been all on fire, besprinkled his cheek with the coldest dew.

The next morning young Goodman Brown came slowly into the street of Salem 70 village, staring around him like a bewildered man. The good old minister was taking a walk along the graveyard to get an appetite for breakfast and meditate his sermon, and bestowed a blessing, as he passed, on Goodman Brown. He shrank from the venerable saint as if to avoid an anathema. Old Deacon Gookin was at domestic worship, and the holy words of his prayer were heard through the open window. "What God does the wizard pray to?" quoth Goodman Brown. Goody Cloyse, that excellent old Christian, stood in the early sunshine at her own lattice, catechizing a little girl who had brought her a pint of morning's milk. Goodman Brown snatched away the child as from the grasp of the fiend himself. Turning the corner by the meeting-house, he spied the head of Faith, with the pink ribbons, gazing anxiously forth, and bursting into such joy at sight of him that she skipped along the street and almost kissed her husband before the whole village. But Goodman Brown looked sternly and sadly into her face, and passed on without a greeting.

Had Goodman Brown fallen asleep in the forest and only dreamed a wild dream of a witch-meeting?

Be it so if you will; but, alas! it was a dream of evil omen for young Goodman Brown. A stern, a sad, a darkly meditative, a distrustful, if not a desperate man did he become from the night of that fearful dream. On the Sabbath day, when the congregation were singing a holy psalm, he could not listen because an anthem of sin rushed loudly upon his ears and drowned all the blessed strain. When the minister spoke from the pulpit with power and fervid eloquence, and, with his hand on the open Bible, of the sacred truths of our religion, and of saint-like lives and triumphant death and of future bliss or misery unutterable, then did Goodman Brown turn pale, dreading lest the roof should thunder down upon the gray blasphemer and his hearers. Often, waking suddenly at midnight, he shrank from the bosom of Faith; and at morning or eventide, when the family knelt down at prayer, he scowled and muttered to himself, and gazed sternly at his wife, and turned away. And when he had lived long, and was borne to his grave a hoary corpse, followed by Faith, an aged woman, and children and grandchildren, a goodly procession, besides neighbors not a few, they carved no hopeful verse upon his tombstone, for his dying hour was gloom.

QUESTIONS FOR DISCUSSION AND WRITING

1. What is significant about the order in which Brown meets the people in the woods? What is the greatest danger he faces? Does the denouement suggest that he has escaped that danger? Explain your answer.

2. In what ways do the names *Young Goodman Brown* and *Faith* characterize the young couple? How does Hawthorne's assertion that "the fiend in his own shape is less hideous than when he rages in the breast of man" characterize the devil?

3. Why is the forest an appropriate setting for Brown's journey? How does Brown perceive the setting of the town? How does that perception change after his night in the woods?

4. How does Hawthorne's omniscient point of view help establish the dreamlike quality of the story? Does it finally matter, from Brown's point of view, whether he attended or merely dreamed about the meeting of the witches?

5. What is the theme of the devil's sermon? In what sense do the final three paragraphs of the story demonstrate that the devil was right?

Stories for Comparison

Joseph Conrad's "Heart of Darkness" (pages 388–447); Charles Johnson's "The Sorcerer's Apprentice" (pages 714–722).

52

....

ERNEST HEMINGWAY

Big Two-Hearted River

ERNEST HEMINGWAY (1899–1961) was born in Oak Park, Illinois, but spent most of his summers in upper Michigan, where he developed his skills in hunting and fishing. After high school, Hemingway worked as a journalist for the *Kansas City Star* until the outbreak of World War I. He then served as an ambulance driver, first in France and then in Italy, where he was seriously wounded. After the war, Hemingway lived in Paris, working as a foreign correspondent for the *Toronto Star* and writing the stories and novels that eventually earned him the 1954 Nobel Prize and a legendary place in American literature. His novels include *The Sun Also Rises* (1926), *A Farewell to Arms* (1929), *For Whom the Bell Tolls* (1940), and his Pulitzer Prize novel, *The Old Man and the Sea* (1953). On July 2, 1961, Hemingway, plagued by the sense that his health and literary ability were failing, used his favorite shotgun to take his life. Hemingway was fascinated by war, sports, bullfighting, and other moments of extreme adventure that provided men with the opportunity to perform acts of courage with grace and poise. "Big Two-Hearted River," reprinted from *The Short Stories of Ernest Hemingway* (1938), recounts the details of a fishing trip and suggests other conflicts beneath the surface.

I

The train went on up the track out of sight, around one of the hills of burnt timber. Nick sat down on the bundle of canvas and bedding the baggage man had pitched out of the door of the baggage car. There was no town, nothing but the rails and the burned-over country. The thirteen saloons that had lined the one street of Seney had not left a trace. The foundations of the Mansion House hotel stuck up above the ground. The stone was chipped and split by the fire. It was all that was left of the town of Seney. Even the surface had been burned off the ground.

Nick looked at the burned-over stretch of hillside, where he had expected to find the scattered houses of the town and then walked down the railroad track to the bridge over the river. The river was there. It swirled against the log spiles of the bridge. Nick looked down into the clear, brown water, colored from the pebbly bottom, and watched the trout keeping themselves steady in the current with wavering fins. As he watched them they changed their positions by quick angles, only to hold steady in the fast water again. Nick watched them a long time.

He watched them holding themselves with their noses into the current, many trout in deep, fast-moving water, slightly distorted as he watched far down through the glassy convex surface of the pool, its surface pushing and swelling smooth against the resistance of the log-driven spiles of the bridge. At the bottom of the pool were the big trout. Nick did not see them at first. Then he saw them at the bottom of the pool, big trout looking to hold themselves on the gravel bottom in a varying mist of gravel and sand, raised in spurts by the current.

Nick looked down into the pool from the bridge. It was a hot day. A kingfisher flew up the stream. It was a long time since Nick had looked into a stream and seen trout. They were very satisfactory. As the shadow of the kingfisher moved up the stream, a big trout shot upstream in a long angle, only his shadow marking the angle, then lost his shadow as he came through the surface of the water, caught the sun, and then, as he went back into the stream under the surface, his shadow seemed to float down the stream with the current, unresisting, to his post under the bridge, where he tightened, facing up into the current.

5   Nick's heart tightened as the trout moved. He felt all the old feeling.

He turned and looked down the stream. It stretched away, pebbly-bottomed with shallows and big boulders and a deep pool as it curved away around the foot of a bluff.

Nick walked back up the ties to where his pack lay in the cinders beside the railway track. He was happy. He adjusted the pack harness around the bundle, pulling straps tight, slung the pack on his back, got his arms through the shoulder straps and took some of the pull off his shoulders by leaning his forehead against the wide band of the tumpline. Still, it was too heavy. It was much too heavy. He had his leather rod-case in his hand and leaning forward to keep the weight of the pack high on his shoulders he walked along the road that paralleled the railway track, leaving the burned town behind in the heat, and then turned off around a hill with a high, fire-scarred hill on either side onto a road that went back into the country. He walked along the road feeling the ache from the pull of the heavy pack. The road climbed steadily. It was hard work walking uphill. His muscles ached and the day was hot, but Nick felt happy. He felt he had left everything behind, the need for thinking, the need to write, other needs. It was all back of him.

From the time he had gotten down off the train and the baggage man had thrown his pack out of the open car door things had been different. Seney was burned, the country was burned over and changed, but it did not matter. It could not all be burned. He knew that. He hiked along the road, sweating in the sun, climbing to cross the range of hills that separated the railway from the pine plains.

The road ran on, dipping occasionally, but always climbing. Nick went on up. Finally the road, after going parallel to the burnt hillside, reached the top. Nick leaned back against a stump and slipped out of the pack harness. Ahead of him, as far as he could see, was the pine plain. The burned country stopped off at the left with the range of hills. On ahead islands of dark pine trees rose out of the plain. Far off to the left was the line of the river. Nick followed it with his eye and caught glints of the water in the sun.

10   There was nothing but the pine plain ahead of him, until the far blue hills that marked the Lake Superior height of land. He could hardly see them, faint and far away in the heat-light over the plain. If he looked too steadily they were gone. But if he only half-looked they were there, the far-off hills of the height of land.

Nick sat down against the charred stump and smoked a cigarette. His pack balanced on the top of the stump, harness holding ready, a hollow molded in it from his back. Nick sat smoking, looking out over the country. He did not need to get his map out. He knew where he was from the position of the river.

As he smoked, his legs stretched out in front of him, he noticed a grasshopper walk along the ground and up onto his woolen sock. The grasshopper was black. As he had walked along the road, climbing, he had started many grasshoppers from the dust. They were all black. They were not the big grasshoppers with yellow and black or red and black wings whirring out from their black wing sheathing as they fly up. These were just ordinary hoppers, but all a sooty black in color. Nick had wondered about them as he walked, without really thinking about them. Now, as he watched the black hopper that was nibbling at the wool of his sock with its four-way lip, he

realized that they had all turned black from living in the burned-over land. He realized that the fire must have come the year before, but the grasshoppers were all black
now. He wondered how long they would stay that way.

Carefully he reached his hand down and took hold of the hopper by the wings.
He turned him up, all his legs walking in the air, and looked at his jointed belly. Yes,
it was black too, iridescent where the back and head were dusty.

"Go on, hopper," Nick said, speaking out loud for the first time. "Fly away
somewhere."

He tossed the grasshopper up into the air and watched him sail away to a char-   15
coal stump across the road.

Nick stood up. He leaned his back against the weight of his pack where it rested
upright on the stump and got his arms through the shoulder straps. He stood with the
pack on his back on the brow of the hill looking out across the country, toward the
distant river and then struck down the hillside away from the road. Underfoot
the ground was good walking. Two hundred yards down the hillside the fire line
stopped. Then it was sweet fern, growing ankle-high, to walk through, and clumps
of jack pines; a long undulating country with frequent rises and descents, sandy underfoot and the country alive again.

Nick kept his direction by the sun. He knew where he wanted to strike the river
and he kept on through the pine plain, mounting small rises to see other rises ahead
of him and sometimes from the top of a rise a great solid island of pines off to his
right or his left. He broke off some sprigs of the heathery sweet fern and put them
under his pack straps. The chafing crushed it and he smelled it as he walked.

He was tired and very hot, walking across the uneven, shadeless pine plain. At
any time he knew he could strike the river by turning off to his left. It could not be
more than a mile away. But he kept on toward the north to hit the river as far upstream as he could go in one day's walking.

For some time as he walked Nick had been in sight of one of the big islands of
pine standing out above the rolling high ground he was crossing. He dipped down
and then as he came slowly up to the crest of the ridge he turned and made toward
the pine trees.

There was no underbrush in the island of pine trees. The trunks of the trees went   20
straight up or slanted toward each other. The trunks were straight and brown without
branches. The branches were high above. Some interlocked to make a solid shadow
on the brown forest floor. Around the grove of trees was a bare space. It was brown
and soft underfoot as Nick walked on it. This was the overlapping of the pine needle floor, extending out beyond the width of the high branches. The trees had grown
tall and the branches moved high, leaving in the sun this bare space they had once
covered with shadow. Sharp at the edge of this extension of the forest floor commenced the sweet fern.

Nick slipped off his pack and lay down in the shade. He lay on his back and
looked up into the pine trees. His neck and back and the small of his back rested as
he stretched. The earth felt good against his back. He looked up at the sky, through
the branches, and then shut his eyes. He opened them and looked up again. There
was a wind high up in the branches. He shut his eyes again and went to sleep.

Nick woke stiff and cramped. The sun was nearly down. His pack was heavy and the straps painful as he lifted it on. He leaned over with the pack on and picked up the leather rod-case and started out from the pine trees across the sweet fern swale, toward the river. He knew it could not be more than a mile.

He came down a hillside covered with stumps into a meadow. At the edge of the meadow flowed the river. Nick was glad to get to the river. He walked upstream through the meadow. His trousers were soaked with the dew as he walked. After the hot day, the dew had come quickly and heavily. The river made no sound. It was too fast and smooth. At the edge of the meadow, before he mounted to a piece of high ground to make camp, Nick looked down the river at the trout rising. They were rising to insects come from the swamp on the other side of the stream when the sun went down. The trout jumped out of water to take them. While Nick walked through the little stretch of meadow alongside the stream, trout had jumped high out of water. Now as he looked down the river, the insects must be settling on the surface, for the trout were feeding steadily all down the stream. As far down the long stretch as he could see, the trout were rising, making circles all down the surface of the water, as though it were starting to rain.

The ground rose, wooded and sandy, to overlook the meadow, the stretch of river and the swamp. Nick dropped his pack and rod-case and looked for a level piece of ground. He was very hungry and he wanted to make his camp before he cooked. Between two jack pines, the ground was quite level. He took the ax out of the pack and chopped out two projecting roots. That leveled a piece of ground large enough to sleep on. He smoothed out the sandy soil with his hand and pulled all the sweet fern bushes by their roots. His hands smelled good from the sweet fern. He smoothed the uprooted earth. He did not want anything making lumps under the blankets. When he had the ground smooth, he spread his three blankets. One he folded double, next to the ground. The other two he spread on top.

25   With the ax he slit off a bright slab of pine from one of the stumps and split it into pegs for the tent. He wanted them long and solid to hold in the ground. With the tent unpacked and spread on the ground, the pack, leaning against a jack pine, looked much smaller. Nick tied the rope that served the tent for a ridgepole to the trunk of one of the pine trees and pulled the tent up off the ground with the other end of the rope and tied it to the other pine. The tent hung on the rope like a canvas blanket on a clothesline. Nick poked a pole he had cut up under the back peak of the canvas and then made it a tent by pegging out the sides. He pegged the sides out taut and drove the pegs deep, hitting them down into the ground with the flat of the ax until the rope loops were buried and the canvas was drum tight.

Across the open mouth of the tent Nick fixed cheesecloth to keep out mosquitoes. He crawled inside under the mosquito bar with various things from the pack to put at the head of the bed under the slant of the canvas. Inside the tent the light came through the brown canvas. It smelled pleasantly of canvas. Already there was something mysterious and home-like. Nick was happy as he crawled inside the tent. He had not been unhappy all day. This was different though. Now things were done. There had been this to do. Now it was done. It had been a hard trip. He was very tired. That was done. He had made his camp. He was settled. Nothing could touch him. It was a good place to camp. He was there, in the good place. He was in his home where he had made it. Now he was hungry.

He came out, crawling under the cheesecloth. It was quite dark outside. It was lighter in the tent.

Nick went over to the pack and found, with his fingers, a long nail in a paper sack of nails, in the bottom of the pack. He drove it into the pine tree, holding it close and hitting it gently with the flat of the ax. He hung the pack up on the nail. All his supplies were in the pack. They were off the ground and sheltered now.

Nick was hungry. He did not believe he had ever been hungrier. He opened and emptied a can of pork and beans and a can of spaghetti into the frying pan.

"I've got a right to eat this kind of stuff, if I'm willing to carry it," Nick said. 30 His voice sounded strange in the darkening woods. He did not speak again.

He started a fire with some chunks of pine he got with the ax from a stump. Over the fire he stuck a wire grill, pushing the four legs down into the ground with his boot. Nick put the frying pan on the grill over the flames. He was hungrier. The beans and spaghetti warmed. Nick stirred them and mixed them together. They began to bubble, making little bubbles that rose with difficulty to the surface. There was a good smell. Nick got out a bottle of tomato catchup and cut four slices of bread. The little bubbles were coming faster now. Nick sat down beside the fire and lifted the frying pan off. He poured about half the contents out into the tin plate. It spread slowly on the plate. Nick knew it was too hot. He poured on some tomato catchup. He knew the beans and spaghetti were still too hot. He looked at the fire, then at the tent, he was not going to spoil it all by burning his tongue. For years he had never enjoyed fried bananas because he had never been able to wait for them to cool. His tongue was very sensitive. He was very hungry. Across the river in the swamp, in the almost dark, he saw a mist rising. He looked at the tent once more. All right. He took a full spoonful from the plate.

"Chrise," Nick said, "Geezus Chrise," he said happily.

He ate the whole plateful before he remembered the bread. Nick finished the second plateful with the bread, mopping the plate shiny. He had not eaten since a cup of coffee and a ham sandwich in the station restaurant at St. Ignace. It had been a very fine experience. He had been that hungry before, but had not been able to satisfy it. He could have made camp hours before if he had wanted to. There were plenty of good places to camp on the river. But this was good.

Nick tucked two big chips of pine under the grill. The fire flared up. He had forgotten to get water for the coffee. Out of the pack he got a folding canvas bucket and walked down the hill, across the edge of the meadow, to the stream. The other bank was in the white mist. The grass was wet and cold as he knelt on the bank and dipped the canvas bucket into the stream. It bellied and pulled hard in the current. The water was ice cold. Nick rinsed the bucket and carried it full up to the camp. Up away from the stream it was not so cold.

Nick drove another big nail and hung up the bucket full of water. He dipped the 35 coffeepot half full, put some more chips under the grill onto the fire and put the pot on. He could not remember which way he made coffee. He could remember an argument about it with Hopkins, but not which side he had taken. He decided to bring it to a boil. He remembered now that was Hopkins's way. He had once argued about everything with Hopkins. While he waited for the coffee to boil, he opened a small can of apricots. He liked to open cans. He emptied the can of apricots out into a tin cup. While he watched the coffee on the fire, he drank the juice syrup of the apricots, carefully at first to keep from spilling, then meditatively, sucking the apricots down. They were better than fresh apricots.

The coffee boiled as he watched. The lid came up and coffee and grounds ran down the side of the pot. Nick took it off the grill. It was a triumph for Hopkins. He put sugar in the empty apricot cup and poured some of the coffee out to cool. It was too hot to pour and he used his hat to hold the handle of the coffeepot. He would not let it steep in the pot at all. Not the first cup. It should be straight Hopkins all the way. Hop deserved that. He was a very serious coffee maker. He was the most serious man Nick had ever known. Not heavy, serious. That was a long time ago. Hopkins spoke without moving his lips. He had played polo. He made millions of dollars in Texas. He had borrowed carfare to go to Chicago, when the wire came that his first big well had come in. He could have wired for money. That would have been too slow. They called Hop's girl the Blonde Venus. Hop did not mind because she was not his real girl. Hopkins said very confidently that none of them would make fun of his real girl. He was right. Hopkins went away when the telegram came. That was on the Black River. It took eight days for the telegram to reach him. Hopkins gave away his .22 caliber Colt automatic pistol to Nick. He gave his camera to Bill. It was to remember him always by. They were all going fishing again next summer. The Hop Head was rich. He would get a yacht and they would all cruise along the north shore of Lake Superior. He was excited but serious. They said good-by and all felt bad. It broke up the trip. They never saw Hopkins again. That was a long time ago on the Black River.

Nick drank the coffee, the coffee according to Hopkins. The coffee was bitter. Nick laughed. It made a good ending to the story. His mind was starting to work. He knew he could choke it because he was tired enough. He spilled the coffee out of the pot and shook the grounds loose into the fire. He lit a cigarette and went inside the tent. He took off his shoes and trousers, sitting on the blankets, rolled the shoes up inside the trousers for a pillow and got in between the blankets.

Out through the front of the tent he watched the glow of the fire when the night wind blew on it. It was a quiet night. The swamp was perfectly quiet. Nick stretched under the blanket comfortably. A mosquito hummed close to his ear. Nick sat up and lit a match. The mosquito was on the canvas, over his head. Nick moved the match quickly up to it. The mosquito made a satisfactory hiss in the flame. The match went out. Nick lay down again under the blankets. He turned on his side and shut his eyes. He was sleepy. He felt sleep coming. He curled up under the blanket and went to sleep.

2

In the morning the sun was up and the tent was starting to get hot. Nick crawled out under the mosquito netting stretched across the mouth of the tent to look at the morning. The grass was wet on his hands as he came out. He held his trousers and his shoes in his hands. The sun was just up over the hill. There was the meadow, the river and the swamp. There were birch trees in the green of the swamp on the other side of the river.

The river was clear and smoothly fast in the early morning. Down about two 40 hundred yards were three logs all the way across the stream. They made the water smooth and deep above them. As Nick watched, a mink crossed the river on the logs and went into the swamp. Nick was excited. He was excited by the early morning and the river. He was really too hurried to eat breakfast, but he knew he must. He built a little fire and put on the coffeepot. While the water was heating in the pot he took an empty bottle and went down over the edge of the high ground to the meadow. The meadow was wet with dew and Nick wanted to catch grasshoppers for bait before the sun dried the grass. He found plenty of good grasshoppers. They were at the base of the grass stems. Sometimes they clung to a grass stem. They were cold and wet with the dew and could not jump until the sun warmed them. Nick picked them up, taking only the medium-sized brown ones, and put them into the bottle. He turned over a log and just under the shelter of the edge were several hundred hoppers. It was a grasshopper lodging house. Nick put about fifty of the medium browns into the bottle. While he was picking up the hoppers the others warmed in the sun and commenced to hop away. They flew when they hopped. At first they made one flight and stayed stiff when they landed, as though they were dead.

Nick knew that by the time he was through with breakfast they would be as lively as ever. Without dew in the grass it would take him all day to catch a bottle full of good grasshoppers and he would have to crush many of them, slamming at them with his hat. He washed his hands at the stream. He was excited to be near it. Then he walked up to the tent. The hoppers were already jumping stiffly in the grass. In the bottle, warmed by the sun, they were jumping in a mass. Nick put in a pine stick as a cork. It plugged the mouth of the bottle enough so the hoppers could not get out, and left plenty of air passage.

He had rolled the log back and knew he could get grasshoppers there every morning.

Nick laid the bottle full of jumping grasshoppers against a pine trunk. Rapidly he mixed some buckwheat flour with water and stirred it smooth, one cup of flour, one cup of water. He put a handful of coffee in the pot and dipped a lump of grease out of a can and slid it sputtering across the hot skillet. On the smoking skillet he poured smoothly the buckwheat batter. It spread like lava, the grease spitting sharply. Around the edges the buckwheat cake began to firm, then brown, then crisp. The surface was bubbling slowly to porousness. Nick pushed under the browned undersurface with a fresh pine chip. He shook the skillet sideways and the cake was loose on the surface. I won't try and flop it, he thought. He slid the chip of clean wood all the way under the cake, and flopped it over onto its face. It sputtered in the pan.

When it was cooked Nick regreased the skillet. He used all the batter. It made another big flapjack and one smaller one.

Nick ate a big flapjack and a smaller one, covered with apple butter. He put ap- 45 ple butter on the third cake, folded it over twice, wrapped it in oiled paper and put it in his shirt pocket. He put the apple butter jar back in the pack and cut bread for two sandwiches.

In the pack he found a big onion. He sliced it in two and peeled the silky outer skin. Then he cut one half into slices and made onion sandwiches. He wrapped them in oiled paper and buttoned them in the other pocket of his khaki shirt. He turned the skillet upside down on the grill, drank the coffee, sweetened and yellow brown with the condensed milk in it, and tidied up the camp. It was a nice little camp.

Nick took his fly rod out of the leather rod-case, jointed it, and shoved the rod-case back into the tent. He put on the reel and threaded the line through the guides. He had to hold it from hand to hand, as he threaded it, or it would slip back through its own weight. It was a heavy, double-tapered fly line. Nick had paid eight dollars for it a long time ago. It was made heavy to lift back in the air and come forward flat and heavy and straight to make it possible to cast a fly which has no weight. Nick opened the aluminum leader box. The leaders were coiled between the damp flannel pads. Nick had wet the pads at the water cooler on the train up to St. Ignace. In the damp pads the gut leaders had softened and Nick unrolled one and tied it by a loop at the end to the heavy fly line. He fastened a hook on the end of the leader. It was a small hook, very thin and springy.

Nick took it from his hook book, sitting with the rod across his lap. He tested the knot and the spring of the rod by pulling the line taut. It was a good feeling. He was careful not to let the hook bite into his finger.

He started down to the stream, holding his rod, the bottle of grasshoppers hung from his neck by a thong tied in half hitches around the neck of the bottle. His landing net hung by a hook from his belt. Over his shoulder was a long flour sack tied at each corner into an ear. The cord went over his shoulder. The sack flapped against his legs.

50   Nick felt awkward and professionally happy with all his equipment hanging from him. The grasshopper bottle swung against his chest. In his shirt the breast pockets bulged against him with the lunch and his fly book.

He stepped into the stream. It was a shock. His trousers clung tight to his legs. His shoes felt the gravel. The water was a rising cold shock.

Rushing, the current sucked against his legs. Where he stepped in, the water was over his knees. He waded with the current. The gravel slid under his shoes. He looked down at the swirl of water below each leg and tipped up the bottle to get a grasshopper.

The first grasshopper gave a jump in the neck of the bottle and went out into the water. He was sucked under in the whirl by Nick's right leg and came to the surface a little way down stream. He floated rapidly, kicking. In a quick circle, breaking the smooth surface of the water, he disappeared. A trout had taken him.

Another hopper poked his head out of the bottle. His antennae wavered. He was getting his front legs out of the bottle to jump. Nick took him by the head and held him while he threaded the slim hook under his chin, down through his thorax and into the last segments of his abdomen. The grasshopper took hold of the hook with his front feet, spitting tobacco juice on it. Nick dropped him into the water.

55   Holding the rod in his right hand he let out line against the pull of the grasshopper in the current. He stripped off line from the reel with his left hand and let it run free. He could see the hopper in the little waves of the current. It went out of sight.

There was a tug on the line. Nick pulled against the taut line. It was his first strike. Holding the now living rod across the current, he brought in the line with his left hand. The rod bent in jerks, the trout pumping against the current. Nick knew it was a small one. He lifted the rod straight up in the air. It bowed with the pull.

He saw the trout in the water jerking with his head and body against the shifting tangent of the line in the stream.

Nick took the line in his left hand and pulled the trout, thumping tiredly against the current, to the surface. His back was mottled the clear, water-over-gravel color, his side flashing in the sun. The rod under his right arm, Nick stooped, dipping his right hand into the current. He held the trout, never still, with his moist right hand, while he unhooked the barb from his mouth, then dropped him back into the stream.

He hung unsteadily in the current, then settled to the bottom beside a stone. Nick reached down his hand to touch him, his arm to the elbow underwater. The trout was steady in the moving stream, resting on the gravel, beside a stone. As Nick's fingers touched him, touched his smooth, cool, underwater feeling, he was gone, gone in a shadow across the bottom of the stream.

He's all right, Nick thought. He was only tired.   60

He had wet his hand before he touched the trout, so he would not disturb the delicate mucus that covered him. If a trout was touched with a dry hand, a white fungus attacked the unprotected spot. Years before when he had fished crowded streams, with fly fishermen ahead of him and behind him, Nick had again and again come on dead trout, furry with white fungus, drifted against a rock, or floating belly up in some pool. Nick did not like to fish with other men on the river. Unless they were of your party, they spoiled it.

He wallowed down the stream, above his knees in the current, through the fifty yards of shallow water above the pile of logs that crossed the stream. He did not rebait his hook and held it in his hand as he waded. He was certain he could catch small trout in the shallows, but he did not want them. There would be no big trout in the shallows this time of day.

Now the water deepened up his thighs sharply and coldly. Ahead was the smooth dammed-back flood of water above the logs. The water was smooth and dark; on the left, the lower edge of the meadow; on the right, the swamp.

Nick leaned back against the current and took a hopper from the bottle. He threaded the hopper on the hook and spat on him for good luck. Then he pulled several yards of line from the reel and tossed the hopper out ahead onto the fast, dark water. It floated down toward the logs, then the weight of the line pulled the bait under the surface. Nick held the rod in his right hand, letting the line run out through his fingers.

There was a long tug. Nick struck and the rod came alive and dangerous, bent   65 double, the line tightening, coming out of water, tightening, all in a heavy, dangerous, steady pull. Nick felt the moment when the leader would break if the strain increased and let the line go.

The reel ratcheted into a mechanical shriek as the line went out in a rush. Too fast. Nick could not check it, the line rushing out, the reel note rising as the line ran out.

With the core of the reel showing, his heart feeling stopped with the excitement, leaning back against the current that mounted icily his thighs, Nick thumbed the reel hard with his left hand. It was awkward getting his thumb inside the fly reel frame.

As he put on pressure the line tightened into sudden hardness and beyond the logs a huge trout went high out of water. As he jumped, Nick lowered the tip of the rod. But he felt, as he dropped the tip to ease the strain, the moment when the strain was too great, the hardness too tight. Of course, the leader had broken. There was no mistaking the feeling when all spring left the line and it became dry and hard. Then it went slack.

His mouth dry, his heart down, Nick reeled in. He had never seen so big a trout. There was a heaviness, a power not to be held, and then the bulk of him, as he jumped. He looked as broad as a salmon.

70   Nick's hand was shaky. He reeled in slowly. The thrill had been too much. He felt, vaguely, a little sick, as though it would be better to sit down.

The leader had broken where the hook was tied to it. Nick took it in his hand. He thought of the trout somewhere on the bottom, holding himself steady over the gravel, far down below the light, under the logs, with the hook in his jaw. Nick knew the trout's teeth would cut through the snell of the hook. The hook would imbed itself in his jaw. He'd bet the trout was angry. Anything that size would be angry. That was a trout. He had been solidly hooked. Solid as a rock. He felt like a rock, too, before he started off. By God, he was a big one. By God, he was the biggest one I ever heard of.

Nick climbed out onto the meadow and stood, water running down his trousers and out of his shoes, his shoes squlchy. He went over and sat on the logs. He did not want to rush his sensations any.

He wriggled his toes in the water, in his shoes, and got out a cigarette from his breast pocket. He lit it and tossed the match into the fast water below the logs. A tiny trout rose at the match, as it swung around in the fast current. Nick laughed. He would finish the cigarette.

He sat on the logs, smoking, drying in the sun, the sun warm on his back, the river shallow ahead, entering the woods, curving into the woods, shallows, light glittering, big watersmooth rocks, cedars along the bank and white birches, the logs warm in the sun, smooth to sit on, without bark, gray to the touch; slowly the feeling of disappointment left him. It went away slowly, the feeling of disappointment that came sharply after the thrill that made his shoulders ache. It was all right now. His rod lying out on the logs, Nick tied a new hook on the leader, pulling the gut tight until it grimped into itself in a hard knot.

75   He baited up, then picked up the rod and walked to the far end of the logs to get into the water, where it was not too deep. Under and beyond the logs was a deep pool. Nick walked around the shallow shelf near the swamp shore until he came out on the shallow bed of the stream.

On the left, where the meadow ended and the woods began, a great elm tree was uprooted. Gone over in a storm, it lay back into the woods, its roots clotted with dirt, grass growing in them, rising a solid bank beside the stream. The river cut to the edge of the uprooted tree. From where Nick stood he could see deep channels, like ruts, cut in the shallow bed of the stream by the flow of the current. Pebbly where he stood and pebbly and full of boulders beyond; where it curved near the tree roots, the bed of the stream was marly and between the ruts of deep water green weed fronds swung in the current.

Nick swung the rod back over his shoulder and forward, and the line, curving forward, laid the grasshopper down on one of the deep channels in the weeds. A trout struck and Nick hooked him.

Holding the rod far out toward the uprooted tree and sloshing backward in the current, Nick worked the trout, plunging, the rod bending alive, out of the danger of the weeds into the open river. Holding the rod, pumping alive against the current, Nick brought the trout in. He rushed, but always came, the spring of the rod yielding to the rushes, sometimes jerking underwater, but always bringing him in. Nick eased downstream with the rushes. The rod above his head, he led the trout over the net, then lifted.

The trout hung heavy in the net, mottled trout back and silver sides in the meshes. Nick unhooked him; heavy sides, good to hold, big undershot jaw; and slipped him, heaving and big, sliding, into the long sack that hung from his shoulders in the water.

Nick spread the mouth of the sack against the current and it filled, heavy with water. He held it up, the bottom in the stream, and the water poured out through the sides. Inside at the bottom was the big trout, alive in the water.

Nick moved downstream. The sack out ahead of him, sunk, heavy in the water, pulling from his shoulders.

It was getting hot, the sun hot on the back of his neck.

Nick had one good trout. He did not care about getting many trout. Now the stream was shallow and wide. There were trees along both banks. The trees of the left bank made short shadows on the current in the forenoon sun. Nick knew there were trout in each shadow. In the afternoon, after the sun had crossed toward the hills, the trout would be in the cool shadows on the other side of the stream.

The very biggest ones would lie up close to the bank. You could always pick them up there on the Black. When the sun was down they all moved out into the current. Just when the sun made the water blinding in the glare before it went down, you were liable to strike a big trout anywhere in the current. It was almost impossible to fish then, the surface of the water was blinding as a mirror in the sun. Of course, you could fish upstream, but in a stream like the Black, or this, you had to wallow against the current and in a deep place, the water piled up on you. It was no fun to fish upstream with this much current.

Nick moved along through the shallow stretch, watching the banks for deep holes. A beech tree grew close beside the river, so that the branches hung down into the water. The stream went back in under the leaves. There were always trout in a place like that.

Nick did not care about fishing that hole. He was sure he would get hooked in the branches.

It looked deep, though. He dropped the grasshopper so the current took it underwater, back in under the overhanging branch. The line pulled hard and Nick struck. The trout threshed heavily, half out of water in the leaves and branches. The line was caught. Nick pulled hard and the trout was off. He reeled in and, holding the hook in his hand, walked down the stream.

Ahead, close to the left bank, was a big log. Nick saw it was hollow; pointing up river the current entered it smoothly, only a little ripple spread each side of the log. The water was deepening. The top of the hollow log was gray and dry. It was partly in the shadow.

Nick took the cork out of the grasshopper bottle and a hopper clung to it. He picked him off, hooked him and tossed him out. He held the rod far out so that the hopper on the water moved into the current flowing into the hollow log. Nick lowered the rod and the hopper floated in. There was a heavy strike. Nick swung the rod against the pull. It felt as though he were hooked into the log itself, except for the live feeling.

90   He tried to force the fish out into the current. It came, heavily.

The line went slack and Nick thought the trout was gone. Then he saw him, very near, in the current, shaking his head, trying to get the hook out. His mouth was clamped shut. He was fighting the hook in the clear flowing current.

Looping in the line with his left hand, Nick swung the rod to make the line taut and tried to lead the trout toward the net, but he was gone, out of sight, the line pumping. Nick fought him against the current, letting him thump in the water against the spring of the rod. He shifted the rod to his left hand, worked the trout upstream, holding his weight, fighting on the rod, and then let him down into the net. He lifted him clear of the water, a heavy half circle in the net, the net dripping, unhooked him and slid him into the sack.

He spread the mouth of the sack and looked down in at the two big trout alive in the water.

Through the deepening water, Nick waded over to the hollow log. He took the sack off, over his head, the trout flopping as it came out of water, and hung it so the trout were deep in the water. Then he pulled himself up on the log and sat, the water from his trousers and boots running down into the stream. He laid his rod down, moved along to the shady end of the log and took the sandwiches out of his pocket. He dipped the sandwiches in the cold water. The current carried away the crumbs. He ate the sandwiches and dipped his hat full of water to drink, the water running out through his hat just ahead of his drinking.

95   It was cool in the shade, sitting on the log. He took a cigarette out and struck a match to light it. The match sunk into the gray wood, making a tiny furrow. Nick leaned over the side of the log, found a hard place and lit the match. He sat smoking and watching the river.

Ahead the river narrowed and went into a swamp. The river became smooth and deep and the swamp looked solid with cedar trees, their trunks close together, their branches solid. It would not be possible to walk through a swamp like that. The branches grew so low. You would have to keep almost level with the ground to move at all. You could not crash through the branches. That must be why the animals that lived in swamps were built the way they were, Nick thought.

He wished he had brought something to read. He felt like reading. He did not feel like going on into the swamp. He looked down the river. A big cedar slanted all the way across the stream. Beyond that the river went into the swamp.

Nick did not want to go in there now. He felt a reaction against deep wading with the water deepening up under his armpits, to hook big trout in places impossible to land them. In the swamp the banks were bare, the big cedars came together overhead, the sun did not come through, except in patches; in the fast deep water, in the half light, the fishing would be tragic. In the swamp fishing was a tragic adventure. Nick did not want it. He did not want to go down the stream any farther today.

He took out his knife, opened it and stuck it in the log. Then he pulled up the sack, reached into it and brought out one of the trout. Holding him near the tail, hard to hold, alive, in his hand, he whacked him against the log. The trout quivered, rigid. Nick laid him on the log in the shade and broke the neck of the other fish the same way. He laid them side by side on the log. They were fine trout.

Nick cleaned them, slitting them from the vent to the tip of the jaw. All the insides and the gills and tongue came out in one piece. They were both males; long gray-white strips of milt, smooth and clean. All the insides clean and compact, coming out all together. Nick tossed the offal ashore for the minks to find. 100

He washed the trout in the stream. When he held them back up in the water they looked like live fish. Their color was not gone yet. He washed his hands and dried them on the log. Then he laid the trout on the sack spread out on the log, rolled them up in it, tied the bundle and put it in the landing net. His knife was still standing, blade stuck in the log. He cleaned it on the wood and put it in his pocket.

Nick stood up on the log, holding his rod, the landing net hanging heavy, then stepped into the water and splashed ashore. He climbed the bank and cut up into the woods, toward the high ground. He was going back to camp. He looked back. The river just showed through the trees. There were plenty of days coming when he could fish the swamp.

QUESTIONS FOR DISCUSSION AND WRITING

1. How do words such as *look, see,* and *watch* suggest the kind of action in the first part of the story? How do the descriptions of the battles with the trout in the second part of the story change the pace of the narrative?

2. How is Nick's character revealed by his knowledge of the outdoors? For example, why is he careful to wet his hand before freeing the undersized trout? How do his differences with Hopkins reveal his character?

3. How does Hemingway establish the significance of the major settings in the story—the burned-over land, the camp, the river, and the swamp? Why does Nick avoid the swamp?

4. What evidence suggests that Nick is the storyteller even though the story is told in the third person? For example, what does Nick say about the big fish that got away?

5. How does the flat, unadorned style of the story reinforce the theme that anything one does should be done deliberately and well? How do allusions to the burned-over land, the kingfisher, and tragic adventures in the swamp suggest the reworking of mythic themes in this story?

Stories for Comparison

Jack London's "To Build a Fire" (pages 812–823); W. D. Wetherell's "The Bass, the River, and Sheila Mant" (pages 1181–1186).

53

....

M A R Y   H O O D

How Far She Went

MARY HOOD was born in 1946 in Brunswick, Georgia, and educated at Georgia State University. She frequently contributes short stories and essays to magazines such as *Georgia Review, North American Review,* and *Harper's.* Hood's first collection of short stories, *How Far She Went* (1984), won both the Flannery O'Connor Award for short fiction and the *Southern Review/* Louisiana State University Short Fiction Award for its re-creation of the people and places of backwoods Georgia. *And Venus Is Blue* (1986), Hood's second collection, again portrays tough, determined characters who fight hard for what they want but don't usually succeed. In "How Far She Went," the title story of Hood's prize-winning collection, a grandmother has to make a difficult choice to save her granddaughter.

They had quarreled all morning, squalled all summer about the incidentals: how tight the girl's cut-off jeans were, the "Every Inch a Woman" T-shirt, her choice of music and how loud she played it, her practiced inattention, her sullen look. Her granny wrung out the last boiled dishcloth, pinched it to the line, giving the basin a sling and a slap, the water flying out in a scalding arc onto the Queen Anne's lace by the path, never mind if it bloomed, that didn't make it worth anything except to chiggers, but the girl would cut it by the everlasting armload and cherish it in the old churn, going to that much trouble for a weed but not bending once—unbegged—to pick the nearest bean; she was sulking now. Bored. Displaced.

"And what do you think happens to a chigger if nobody ever walks by his weed?" her granny asked, heading for the house with that sidelong uneager unanswered glance, hoping for what? The surprise gift of a smile? Nothing. The woman shook her head and said it. "Nothing." The door slammed behind her. Let it.

"I hate it here!" the girl yelled then. She picked up a stick and broke it and threw the pieces—one from each hand—at the laundry drying in the noon. Missed. Missed.

Then she turned on her bare, haughty heel and set off high-shouldered into the heat, quick but not far, not far enough—no road was *that* long—only as far as she dared. At the gate, a rusty chain swinging between two lichened posts, she stopped, then backed up the raw drive to make a run at the barrier, lofting, clearing it clean, her long hair wild in the sun. Triumphant, she looked back at the house where she caught at the dark window her granny's face in its perpetual eclipse of disappointment, old at fifty. She stepped back, but the girl saw her.

"You don't know me!" the girl shouted, chin high, and ran till her ribs ached.   5

As she rested in the rattling shade of the willows, the little dog found her. He could be counted on. He barked all the way, and squealed when she pulled the burr from his ear. They started back to the house for lunch. By then the mailman had long come and gone in the old ruts, leaving the one letter folded now to fit the woman's apron pocket.

If bad news darkened her granny's face, the girl ignored it. Didn't talk at all, another of her distancings, her defiances. So it was as they ate that the woman summarized, "Your daddy wants you to cash in the plane ticket and buy you something. School clothes. For here."

Pale, the girl stared, defenseless only an instant before blurting out, "You're lying."

The woman had to stretch across the table to leave her handprint on that blank cheek. She said, not caring if it stung or not, "He's been planning it since he sent you here."

"I could turn this whole house over, dump it! Leave you slobbering over that   10 stinking jealous dog in the dust!" The girl trembled with the vision, with the strength it gave her. It made her laugh. "Scatter the Holy Bible like confetti and ravel the crochet into miles of stupid string! I could! I will! I won't stay here!" But she didn't move, not until her tears rose to meet her color, and then to escape the shame of minding so much she fled. Just headed away, blind. It didn't matter, this time, how far she went.

The woman set her thoughts against fretting over their bickering, just went on unalarmed with chores, clearing off after the uneaten meal, bringing in the laundry, scattering corn for the chickens, ladling manure tea onto the porch flowers. She listened though. She always had been a listener. It gave her a cocked look. She forgot why she had gone into the girl's empty room, that ungirlish, tenuous lodging place with its bleak order, its ready suitcases never unpacked, the narrow bed, the contested radio on the windowsill. The woman drew the cracked shade down between the radio and the August sun. There wasn't anything else to do.

It was after six when she tied on her rough oxfords and walked down the drive and dropped the gate chain and headed back to the creosoted shed where she kept her tools. She took a hoe for snakes, a rake, shears to trim the grass where it grew, and seed in her pocket to scatter where it never had grown at all. She put the tools and her gloves and the bucket in the trunk of the old Chevy, its prime and rust like an Appaloosa's spots through the chalky white finish. She left the trunk open and the tool handles sticking out. She wasn't going far.

The heat of the day had broken, but the air was thick, sultry, weighted with honeysuckle in second bloom and the Nu-Grape scent of kudzu. The maple and poplar leaves turned over, quaking, silver. There wouldn't be any rain. She told the dog to stay, but he knew a trick. He stowed away when she turned her back, leaped right into the trunk with the tools, then gave himself away with exultant barks. Hearing him, her court jester, she stopped the car and welcomed him into the front seat beside her. Then they went on. Not a mile from her gate she turned onto the blue gravel of the cemetery lane, hauled the gearshift into reverse to whoa them, and got out to take the idle walk down to her buried hopes, bending all along to rout out a handful of weeds from between the markers of old acquaintance. She stood there and read, slow. The dog whined at her hem; she picked him up and rested her chin on his head, then he wriggled and whined to run free, contrary and restless as a child.

The crows called strong and bold MOM! MOM! A trick of the ear to hear it like that. She knew it was the crows, but still she looked around. No one called her that now. She was done with that. And what was it worth anyway? It all came to this: solitary weeding. The sinful fumble of flesh, the fear, the listening for a return that never came, the shamed waiting, the unanswered prayers, the perjury on the certificate— hadn't she lain there weary of the whole lie and it only beginning? and a voice telling her, "Here's your baby, here's your girl," and the swaddled package meaning no more to her than an extra anything, something store-bought, something she could take back for a refund.

15   "Tie her to the fence and give her a bale of hay," she had murmured, drugged, and they teased her, excused her for such a welcoming, blaming the anesthesia, but it went deeper than that; *she* knew, and the *baby* knew: there was no love in the begetting. That was the secret, unforgivable, that not another good thing could ever make up for, where all the bad had come from, like a visitation, a punishment. She knew that was why Sylvie had been wild, had gone to earth so early, and before dying had made this child in sudden wedlock, a child who would be just like her, would carry the hurting on into another generation. A matter of time. No use raising her hand. But she *had* raised her hand. Still wore on its palm the memory of the sting of the collision with the girl's cheek; had she broken her jaw? Her heart? Of course not. She said it aloud: "Takes more than that."

She went to work then, doing what she could with her old tools. She pecked the clay on Sylvie's grave, new-looking, unhealed after years. She tried again, scattering seeds from her pocket, every last possible one of them. Off in the west she could hear the pulpwood cutters sawing through another acre across the lake. Nearer, there was the racket of motorcycles laboring cross-country, insect-like, distracting.

She took her bucket to the well and hung it on the pump. She had half filled it when the bikers roared up, right down the blue gravel, straight at her. She let the bucket overflow, staring. On the back of one of the machines was the girl. Sylvie's girl! Her bare arms wrapped around the shirtless man riding between her thighs. They were first. The second biker rode alone. She studied their strangers' faces as they circled her. They were the enemy, all of them. Laughing. The girl was laughing too, laughing like her mama did. Out in the middle of nowhere the girl had found these two men, some moth-musk about her drawing them (too soon!) to what? She shouted it: "What in God's—" They roared off without answering her, and the bucket of water tipped over, spilling its stain blood-dark on the red dust.

The dog went wild barking, leaping after them, snapping at the tires, and there was no calling him down. The bikers made a wide circuit of the churchyard, then roared straight across the graves, leaping the ditch and landing upright on the road again, heading off toward the reservoir.

Furious, she ran to her car, past the barking dog, this time leaving him behind, driving after them, horn blowing nonstop, to get back what was not theirs. She drove after them knowing what they did not know, that all the roads beyond that point dead-ended. She surprised them, swinging the Impala across their path, cutting them off; let them hit it! They stopped. She got out, breathing hard, and said, when she could, "She's underage." Just that. And put out her claiming hand with an authority that made the girl's arms drop from the man's insolent waist and her legs tremble.

"I was just riding," the girl said, not looking up.   20

Behind them the sun was heading on toward down. The long shadows of the pines drifted back and forth in the same breeze that puffed the distant sails on the lake. Dead limbs creaked and clashed overhead like the antlers of locked and furious beasts.

"Sheeeut," the lone rider said. "I told you." He braced with his muddy boot and leaned out from his machine to spit. The man the girl had been riding with had the invading sort of eyes the woman had spent her lifetime bolting doors against. She met him now, face to face.

"Right there, missy," her granny said, pointing behind her to the car.

The girl slid off the motorcycle and stood halfway between her choices. She started slightly at the poosh! as he popped another top and chugged the beer in one uptilting of his head. His eyes never left the woman's. When he was through, he tossed the can high, flipping it end over end. Before it hit the ground he had his pistol out and, firing once, winged it into the lake.

"Freaking lucky shot," the other one grudged.   25

"I don't need luck," he said. He sighted down the barrel of the gun at the woman's head. "POW!" he yelled, and when she recoiled, he laughed. He swung around to the girl; he kept aiming the gun, here, there, high, low, all around. "Y'all settle it," he said, with a shrug.

The girl had to understand him then, had to know him, had to know better. But still she hesitated. He kept looking at her, then away.

"She's fifteen," her granny said. "You can go to jail."

"You can go to hell," he said.

30   "Probably will," her granny told him. "I'll save you a seat by the fire." She took the girl by the arm and drew her to the car; she backed up, swung around, and headed out the road toward the churchyard for her tools and dog. The whole way the girl said nothing, just hunched against the far door, staring hard-eyed out at the pines going past.

The woman finished watering the seed in, and collected her tools. As she worked, she muttered, "It's your own kin buried here, you might have the decency to glance this way one time . . ." The girl was finger-tweezing her eyebrows in the side mirror. She didn't look around as the dog and the woman got in. Her granny shifted hard, sending the tools clattering in the trunk.

When they came to the main road, there were the men. Watching for them. Waiting for them. They kicked their machines into life and followed, close, bumping them, slapping the old fenders, yelling. The girl gave a wild glance around at the one by her door and said, "Gran'ma?" and as he drew his pistol, "Gran'ma!" just as the gun nosed into the open window. She frantically cranked the glass up between her and the weapon, and her granny, seeing, spat, "Fool!" She never had been one to pray for peace or rain. She stamped the accelerator right to the floor.

The motorcycles caught up. Now she braked, hard, and swerved off the road into an alley between the pines, not even wide enough for the school bus, just a fire scrape that came out a quarter mile from her own house, if she could get that far. She slewed on the pine straw, then righted, tearing along the dark tunnel through the woods. She had for the time being bested them; they were left behind. She was winning. Then she hit the wallow where the tadpoles were already five weeks old. The Chevy plowed in and stalled. When she got it cranked again, they were stuck. The tires spattered mud three feet up the near trunks as she tried to spin them out, to rock them out. Useless. "Get out and run!" she cried, but the trees were too close on the passenger side. The girl couldn't open her door. She wasted precious time having to crawl out under the steering wheel. The woman waited but the dog ran on.

They struggled through the dusky woods, their pace slowed by the thick straw and vines. Overhead, in the last light, the martins were reeling free and sure after their prey.

35   "Why? Why?" the girl gasped, as they lunged down the old deer trail. Behind them they could hear shots, and glass breaking as the men came to the bogged car. The woman kept on running, swatting their way clear through the shoulder-high weeds. They could see the Greer cottage, and made for it. But it was ivied-over, padlocked, the woodpile dry-rotting under its tarp, the electric meterbox empty on the pole. No help there.

The dog, excited, trotted on, yelping, his lips white-flecked. He scented the lake and headed that way, urging them on with thirsty yips. On the clay shore, treeless, deserted, at the utter limit of land, they stood defenseless, listening to the men coming on, between them and home. The woman pressed her hands to her mouth, stifling her cough. She was exhausted. She couldn't think.

"We can get under!" the girl cried suddenly, and pointed toward the Greers' dock, gap-planked, its walkway grounded on the mud. They splashed out to it, wading in, the woman grabbing up the telltale, tattletale dog in her arms. They waded out to the far end and ducked under. There was room between the foam floats for them to crouch neck-deep.

The dog wouldn't hush, even then; never had yet, and there wasn't time to teach him. When the woman realized that, she did what she had to do. She grabbed him whimpering; held him; held him under till the struggle ceased and the bubbles rose silver from his fur. They crouched there then, the two of them, submerged to the shoulders, feet unsteady on the slimed lake bed. They listened. The sky went from rose to ocher to violet in the cracks over their heads. The motorcycles had stopped now. In the silence there was the glissando of locusts, the dry crunch of boots on the flinty beach, their low man-talk drifting as they prowled back and forth. One of them struck a match.

"—they in these woods we could burn 'em out."

The wind carried their voices away into the pines. Some few words eddied back. 40

"—lippy old smartass do a little work on her knees besides praying—"

Laughter. It echoed off the deserted house. They were getting closer.

One of them strode directly out to the dock, walked on the planks over their heads. They could look up and see his boot soles. He was the one with the gun. He slapped a mosquito on his bare back and cursed. The carp, roused by the troubling of the waters, came nosing around the dock, guzzling and snorting. The girl and her granny held still, so still. The man fired his pistol into the shadows, and a wounded fish thrashed, dying. The man knelt and reached for it, chuffing out his beery breath. He belched. He pawed the lake for the dead fish, cursing as it floated out of reach. He shot it again, firing at it till it sank and the gun was empty. Cursed that too. He stood then and unzipped and relieved himself of some of the beer. They had to listen to that. To know that about him. To endure that, unprotesting.

Back and forth on shore the other one ranged, restless. He lit another cigarette. He coughed. He called, "Hey! They got away, man, that's all. Don't get your shorts in a wad. Let's go."

"Yeah." He finished. He zipped. He stumped back across the planks and leaped 45 to shore, leaving the dock tilting amid widening ripples. Underneath, they waited.

The bike cranked. The other ratcheted, ratcheted, then coughed, caught, roared. They circled, cut deep ruts, slung gravel, and went. Their roaring died away and away. Crickets resumed and a near frog bic-bic-bicked.

Under the dock, they waited a little longer to be sure. Then they ducked below the water, scraped out from under the pontoon, and came up into free air, slogging toward shore. It had seemed warm enough in the water. Now they shivered. It was almost night. One streak of light still stood reflected on the darkening lake, drew itself thinner, narrowing into a final cancellation of day. A plane winked its way west.

The girl was trembling. She ran her hands down her arms and legs, shedding water like a garment. She sighed, almost a sob. The woman held the dog in her arms; she dropped to her knees upon the random stones and murmured, private, haggard, "Oh, honey," three times, maybe all three times for the dog, maybe once for each of them. The girl waited, watching. Her granny rocked the dog like a baby, like a dead child, rocked slower and slower and was still.

"I'm sorry," the girl said then, avoiding the dog's inert, empty eye.

50   "It was him or you," her granny said, finally, looking up. Looking her over. "Did they mess with you? With your britches? Did they?"

"No!" Then, quieter, "No, ma'am."

When the woman tried to stand up she staggered, lightheaded, clumsy with the freight of the dog. "No, ma'am," she echoed, fending off the girl's "Let me." And she said again, "It was him or you. I know that. I'm not going to rub your face in it." They saw each other as well as they could in that failing light, in any light.

The woman started toward home, saying, "Around here, we bear our own burdens." She led the way along the weedy shortcuts. The twilight bleached the dead limbs of the pines to bone. Insects sang in the thickets, silencing at their oncoming.

"We'll see about the car in the morning," the woman said. She bore her armful toward her own moth-ridden dusk-to-dawn security light with that country grace she had always had when the earth was reliably progressing underfoot. The girl walked close behind her, exactly where *she* walked, matching her pace, matching her stride, close enough to put her hand forth (if the need arose) and touch her granny's back where the faded voile was clinging damp, the merest gauze between their wounds.

QUESTIONS FOR DISCUSSION AND WRITING

1. How does the father's letter initiate the conflict in the story? How does Granny's decision to kill the dog mark the climax of the plot? How does the walk home suggest that the "squall" about "incidentals" has been resolved?

2. How does Granny describe her own behavior as a mother? What connection does she see between Sylvie and her daughter? How does she recognize the bikers as the "enemy"?

3. Why does the girl resist staying with the grandmother? How does the graveyard provide a larger setting for the story? How does the hiding place under the dock alter the girl's attitude toward her grandmother and her house?

4. Why does Hood begin the story from the girl's point of view and then shift to the grandmother's point of view? What is ironic about the girl's claim that her grandmother doesn't "know me"?

5. How many ways can you interpret the title of the story, "How Far She Went"? In what ways does the title refer to what the grandmother does? In what ways does it refer to what the girl learns?

Stories for Comparison

Flannery O'Connor's "A Good Man Is Hard to Find" (pages 967–979); Joyce Carol Oates's "Where Are You Going, Where Have You Been?" (pages 935–948).

54

....

ZORA NEALE HURSTON

Sweat

ZORA NEALE HURSTON (1903–1960) was born in Eatonville, Florida,
and educated at Howard University and Barnard College. After participating
in the Harlem Renaissance in the early 1920s, Hurston returned to Florida to
record the oral traditions of her native community. She published this folk
material in *Mules and Men* (1935) and recorded similar material in her major
novel, *Their Eyes Were Watching God* (1937), and her autobiography, *Dust
Tracks on a Road* (1939). Although she continued to publish folktales and
fiction throughout her life, her reputation languished, and she died penniless
in Florida. Her work was rediscovered by the women's movement, and she is
now regarded as a major American writer. "Sweat," reprinted from *Spunk:
The Selected Stories of Zora Neale Hurston* (1985), describes consequences
of *indecent* behavior.

IT WAS ELEVEN o'clock of a Spring night in Florida. It was Sunday. Any other
night, Delia Jones would have been in bed for two hours by this time. But she was
a washwoman, and Monday morning meant a great deal to her. So she collected the
soiled clothes on Saturday when she returned the clean things. Sunday night after
church, she sorted and put the white things to soak. It saved her almost a half-day's
start. A great hamper in the bedroom held the clothes that she brought home. It was
so much neater than a number of bundles lying around.

She squatted on the kitchen floor beside the great pile of clothes, sorting them into
small heaps according to color, and humming a song in a mournful key, but wondering
through it all where Sykes, her husband, had gone with her horse and buckboard.

Just then something long, round, limp and black fell upon her shoulders and
slithered to the floor beside her. A great terror took hold of her. It softened her knees
and dried her mouth so that it was a full minute before she could cry out or move.
Then she saw that it was the big bull whip her husband liked to carry when he drove.

She lifted her eyes to the door and saw him standing there bent over with laughter at her fright. She screamed at him.

"Sykes, what you throw dat whip on me like dat? You know it would skeer me— 5
looks just like a snake, an' you knows how skeered Ah is of snakes."

"Course Ah knowed it! That's how come Ah done it." He slapped his leg with his hand and almost rolled on the ground in his mirth. "If you such a big fool dat you got to have a fit over a earth worm or a string, Ah don't keer how bad Ah skeer you."

"You ain't got no business doing it. Gawd knows it's a sin. Some day Ah'm gointuh drop dead from some of yo' foolishness. 'Nother thing, where you been wid mah rig? Ah feeds dat pony. He ain't fuh you to be drivin' wid no bull whip."

"You sho' is one aggravatin' nigger woman!" he declared and stepped into the room. She resumed her work and did not answer him at once. "Ah done tole you time and again to keep them white folks' clothes outa dis house."

He picked up the whip and glared at her. Delia went on with her work. She went out into the yard and returned with a galvanized tub and set it on the washbench. She saw that Sykes had kicked all of the clothes together again, and now stood in her way truculently, his whole manner hoping, *praying,* for an argument. But she walked calmly around him and commenced to re-sort the things.

10 "Next time, Ah'm gointer kick 'em outdoors," he threatened as he struck a match along the leg of his corduroy breeches.

Delia never looked up from her work, and her thin, stooped shoulders sagged further.

"Ah ain't for no fuss t'night Sykes. Ah just come from taking sacrament at the church house."

He snorted scornfully. "Yeah, you just come from de church house on a Sunday night, but heah you is gone to work on them clothes. You ain't nothing but a hypocrite. One of them amen-corner Christians—sing, whoop, and shout, then come home and wash white folks' clothes on the Sabbath."

He stepped roughly upon the whitest pile of things, kicking them helter-skelter as he crossed the room. His wife gave a little scream of dismay, and quickly gathered them together again.

15 "Sykes, you quit grindin' dirt into these clothes! How can Ah git through by Sat'day if Ah don't start on Sunday?"

"Ah don't keer if you never git through. Anyhow, Ah done promised Gawd and a couple of other men, Ah ain't gointer have it in mah house. Don't gimme no lip neither, else Ah'll throw 'em out and put mah fist up side yo' head to boot."

Delia's habitual meekness seemed to slip from her shoulders like a blown scarf. She was on her feet; her poor little body, her bare knuckly hands bravely defying the strapping hulk before her.

"Looka heah, Sykes, you done gone too fur. Ah been married to you fur fifteen years, and Ah been takin' in washin' fur fifteen years. Sweat, sweat, sweat! Work and sweat, cry and sweat, pray and sweat!"

"What's that got to do with me?" he asked brutally.

20 "What's it got to do with you, Sykes? Mah tub of suds is filled yo' belly with vittles more times than yo' hands is filled it. Mah sweat is done paid for this house and Ah reckon Ah kin keep on sweatin' in it."

She seized the iron skillet from the stove and struck a defensive pose, which act surprised him greatly, coming from her. It cowed him and he did not strike her as he usually did.

"Naw you won't," she panted, "that ole snaggle-toothed black woman you run-nin' with ain't comin' heah to pile up on *mah* sweat and blood. You ain't paid for nothin' on this place, and Ah'm gointer stay right heah till Ah'm toted out foot foremost."

"Well, you better quit gittin' me riled up, else they'll be totin' you out sooner than you expect. Ah'm so tired of you Ah don't know whut to do. Gawd! How Ah hates skinny wimmen!"

A little awed by this new Delia, he sidled out of the door and slammed the back gate after him. He did not say where he had gone, but she knew too well. She knew very well that he would not return until nearly daybreak also. Her work over, she went on to bed but not to sleep at once. Things had come to a pretty pass!

She lay awake, gazing upon the debris that cluttered their matrimonial trail. Not an image left standing along the way. Anything like flowers had long ago been drowned in the salty stream that had been pressed from her heart. Her tears, her sweat, her blood. She had brought love to the union and he had brought a longing af-ter the flesh. Two months after the wedding, he had given her the first brutal beating. She had the memory of his numerous trips to Orlando with all of his wages when he had returned to her penniless, even before the first year had passed. She was young and soft then, but now she thought of her knotty, muscled limbs, her harsh knuckly hands, and drew herself up into an unhappy little ball in the middle of the big feather bed. Too late now to hope for love, even if it were not Bertha it would be someone else. This case differed from the others only in that she was bolder than the others. Too late for everything except her little home. She had built it for her old days, and planted one by one the trees and flowers there. It was lovely to her, lovely.

Somehow, before sleep came, she found herself saying aloud: "Oh well, what-ever goes over the Devil's back, is got to come under his belly. Sometime or ruther, Sykes, like everybody else, is gointer reap his sowing." After that she was able to build a spiritual earthworks against her husband. His shells could no longer reach her. Amen. She went to sleep and slept until he announced his presence in bed by kicking her feet and rudely snatching the covers away.

"Gimme some kivah heah, an' git yo' damn foots over on yo' own side! Ah oughter mash you in yo' mouf fuh drawing dat skillet on me."

Delia went clear to the rail without answering him. A triumphant indifference to all that he was or did.

2

The week was as full of work for Delia as all other weeks, and Saturday found her behind her little pony, collecting and delivering clothes.

It was a hot, hot day near the end of July. The village men on Joe Clarke's porch even chewed cane listlessly. They did not hurl the cane-knots as usual. They let them dribble over the edge of the porch. Even conversation had collapsed under the heat.

"Heah come Delia Jones," Jim Merchant said, as the shaggy pony came 'round the bend of the road toward them. The rusty buckboard was heaped with baskets of crisp, clean laundry.

"Yep," Joe Lindsay agreed. "Hot or col', rain or shine, jes'ez reg'lar ez de weeks roll roun' Delia carries 'em an' fetches 'em on Sat'day."

"She better if she wanter eat," said Moss. "Syke Jones ain't wuth de shot an' powder hit would tek tuh kill 'em. Not to *huh* he ain't."

"He sho' ain't," Walter Thomas chimed in. "It's too bad, too, cause she wuz a right pretty li'l trick when he got huh. Ah'd uh mah'ied huh mahself if he hadnter beat me to it."

35   Delia nodded briefly at the men as she drove past.

"Too much knockin' will ruin *any* 'oman. He done beat huh 'nough tuh kill three women, let 'lone change they looks," said Elijah Moseley. "How Syke kin stommuck dat big black greasy Mogul he's layin' roun' wid, gits me. Ah swear dat eight-rock couldn't kiss a sardine can Ah done thowed out de back do' 'way las' yeah."

"Aw, she's fat, thass how come. He's allus been crazy 'bout fat women," put in Merchant. "He'd a' been tied up wid one long time ago if he could a' found one tuh have him. Did Ah tell yuh 'bout him come sidlin' roun' *mah* wife—bringin' her a basket uh peecans outa his yard fuh a present? Yessir, mah wife! She tol' him tuh take 'em right straight back home, 'cause Delia works so hard ovah dat washtub she reckon everything on de place taste lak sweat an' soapsuds. Ah jus' wisht Ah'd a' caught 'im 'roun' dere! Ah'd a' made his hips ketch on fiah down dat shell road."

"Ah know he done it, too. Ah sees 'im grinnin' at every 'oman dat passes," Walter Thomas said. "But even so, he useter eat some mighty big hunks uh humble pie tuh git dat li'l 'oman he got. She wuz ez pritty ez a speckled pup! Dat wuz fifteen years ago. He useter be so skeered uh losin' huh, she could make him do some parts of a husband's duty. Dey never wuz de same in de mind."

"There oughter be a law about him," said Lindsay. "He ain't fit tuh carry guts tuh a bear."

40   Clarke spoke for the first time. "Tain't no law on earth dat kin make a man be decent if it ain't in 'im. There's plenty men dat takes a wife lak dey do a joint uh sugar-cane. It's round, juicy an' sweet when dey gits it. But dey squeeze an' grind, squeeze an' grind an' wring tell dey wring every drop uh pleasure dat's in 'em out. When dey's satisfied dat dey is wrung dry, dey treats 'em jes' lak dey do a cane-chew. Dey thows 'em away. Dey knows whut dey is doin' while dey is at it, an' hates theirselves fuh it but they keeps on hangin' after huh tell she's empty. Den dey hates huh fuh bein' a cane-chew an' in de way."

"We oughter take Syke an' dat stray 'oman uh his'n down in Lake Howell swamp an' lay on de rawhide till they cain't say Lawd a' mussy. He allus wuz uh ovahbearin niggah, but since dat white 'oman from up north done teached 'im how to run a automobile, he done got too beggety to live—an' we oughter kill 'im," Old Man Anderson advised.

A grunt of approval went around the porch. But the heat was melting their civic virtue and Elijah Moseley began to bait Joe Clarke.

"Come on, Joe, git a melon outa dere an' slice it up for yo' customers. We'se all sufferin' wid de heat. De bear's done got me!"

"Thass right, Joe, a watermelon is jes' whut Ah needs tuh cure de eppizudicks," Walter Thomas joined forces with Moseley. "Come on dere, Joe. We all is steady customers an' you ain't set us up in a long time. Ah chooses dat long, bowlegged Floridy favorite."

"A god, an' be dough. You all gimme twenty cents and slice away," Clarke re- 45 torted. "Ah needs a col' slice m'self. Heah, everybody chip in. Ah'll lend y'all mah meat knife."

The money was all quickly subscribed and the huge melon brought forth. At that moment, Sykes and Bertha arrived. A determined silence fell on the porch and the melon was put away again.

Merchant snapped down the blade of his jackknife and moved toward the store door.

"Come on in, Joe, an' gimme a slab uh sow belly an' uh pound uh coffee—almost fuhgot 'twas Sat'day. Got to git on home." Most of the men left also.

Just then Delia drove past on her way home, as Sykes was ordering magnificently for Bertha. It pleased him for Delia to see.

"Git whutsoever yo' heart desires, Honey. Wait a minute, Joe. Give huh two 50 bottles uh strawberry soda-water, uh quart parched ground-peas, an' a block uh chewin' gum."

With all this they left the store, with Sykes reminding Bertha that this was his town and she could have it if she wanted it.

The men returned soon after they left, and held their watermelon feast.

"Where did Syke Jones git da 'oman from nohow?" Lindsay asked.

"Ovah Apopka. Guess dey musta been cleanin' out de town when she lef'. She don't look lak a thing but a hunk uh liver wid hair on it."

"Well, she sho' kin squall," Dave Carter contributed. "When she gits ready tuh 55 laff, she jes' opens huh mouf an' latches it back tuh de las' notch. No ole granpa alligator down in Lake Bell ain't got nothin' on huh."

3

Bertha had been in town three months now. Sykes was still paying her room-rent at Della Lewis'—the only house in town that would have taken her in. Sykes took her frequently to Winter Park to "stomps." He still assured her that he was the swellest man in the state.

"Sho' you kin have dat li'l ole house soon's Ah git dat 'oman outa dere. Everything b'longs tuh me an' you sho' kin have it. Ah sho' 'bominates uh skinny 'oman. Lawdy, you sho' is got one portly shape on you! You kin git *anything* you wants. Dis is *mah* town an' you sho' kin have it."

Delia's work-worn knees crawled over the earth in Gethsemane and up the rocks of Calvary many, many times during these months. She avoided the villagers and meeting places in her efforts to be blind and deaf. But Bertha nullified this to a degree, by coming to Delia's house to call Sykes out to her at the gate.

Delia and Sykes fought all the time now with no peaceful interludes. They slept and ate in silence. Two or three times Delia had attempted a timid friendliness, but she was repulsed each time. It was plain that the breaches must remain agape.

60   The sun had burned July to August. The heat streamed down like a million hot arrows, smiting all things living upon the earth. Grass withered, leaves browned, snakes went blind in shedding and men and dogs went mad. Dog days!

Delia came home one day and found Sykes there before her. She wondered, but started to go on into the house without speaking, even though he was standing in the kitchen door and she must either stoop under his arm or ask him to move. He made no room for her. She noticed a soap box beside the steps, but paid no particular attention to it, knowing that he must have brought it there. As she was stooping to pass under his outstretched arm, he suddenly pushed her backward, laughingly.

"Look in de box dere Delia, Ah done brung yuh somethin'!"

She nearly fell upon the box in her stumbling, and when she saw what it held, she all but fainted outright.

"Syke! Syke, mah Gawd! You take dat rattlesnake 'way from heah! You *gottuh.* Oh, Jesus, have mussy!"

65   "Ah ain't got tuh do nuthin' uh de kin'—fact is Ah ain't got tuh do nothin' but die. Tain't no use uh you puttin' on airs makin' out lak you skeered uh dat snake—he's gointer stay right heah tell he die. He wouldn't bite me cause Ah knows how tuh handle 'im. Nohow he wouldn't risk breakin' out his fangs 'gin *yo* skinny laigs."

"Naw, now Syke, don't keep dat thing 'round tryin' tuh skeer me tuh death. You knows Ah'm even feared uh earth worms. Thass de biggest snake Ah evah did see. Kill 'im Syke, please."

"Doan ast me tuh do nothin' fuh yuh. Goin' 'round tryin' tuh be so damn asterperious. Naw, Ah ain't gonna kill it. Ah think uh damn sight mo' uh him dan you! Dat's a nice snake an' anybody doan lak 'im kin jes' hit de grit."

The village soon heard that Sykes had the snake, and came to see and ask questions.

"How de hen-fire did you ketch dat six-foot rattler, Syke?" Thomas asked.

70   "He's full uh frogs so he cain't hardly move, thass how Ah eased up on 'm. But Ah'm a snake charmer an' knows how tuh handle 'em. Shux, dat ain't nothin'. Ah could ketch one eve'y day if Ah so wanted tuh."

"Whut he needs is a heavy hick'ry club leaned real heavy on his head. Dat's de bes' way tuh charm a rattlesnake."

"Naw, Walt, y'all jes' don't understand dese diamon' backs lak Ah do," said Sykes in a superior tone of voice.

The village agreed with Walter, but the snake stayed on. His box remained by the kitchen door with its screen wire covering. Two or three days later it had digested its meal of frogs and literally came to life. It rattled at every movement in the kitchen or the yard. One day as Delia came down the kitchen steps she saw his chalky-white fangs curved like scimitars hung in the wire meshes. This time she did not run away with averted eyes as usual. She stood for a long time in the doorway in a red fury that grew bloodier for every second that she regarded the creature that was her torment.

That night she broached the subject as soon as Sykes sat down to the table.

75   "Syke, Ah wants you tuh take dat snake 'way fum heah. You done starved me an' Ah put up widcher, you done beat me an Ah took dat, but you done kilt all mah insides bringin' dat varmint heah."

Sykes poured out a saucer full of coffee and drank it deliberately before he answered her.

"A whole lot Ah keer 'bout how you feels inside uh out. Dat snake ain't goin' no damn wheah till Ah gits ready fuh 'im tuh go. So fur as beatin' is concerned, yuh ain't took near all dat you gointer take ef yuh stay 'round *me*."

Delia pushed back her plate and got up from the table. "Ah hates you, Sykes," she said calmly. "Ah hates you tuh de same degree dat Ah useter love yuh. Ah done took an' took till mah belly is full up tuh mah neck. Dat's de reason Ah got mah letter fum de church an' moved mah membership tuh Woodbridge—so Ah don't haftuh take no sacrament wid yuh. Ah don't wantuh see yuh 'round me atall. Lay 'round wid dat 'oman all yuh wants tuh, but gwan 'way fum me an' mah house. Ah hates yuh lak uh suck-egg dog."

Sykes almost let the huge wad of corn bread and collard greens he was chewing fall out of his mouth in amazement. He had a hard time whipping himself up to the proper fury to try to answer Delia.

"Well, Ah'm glad you does hate me. Ah'm sho' tiahed uh you hangin' ontuh me. 80 Ah don't want yuh. Look at yuh stringey ole neck! Yo' rawbony laigs an' arms is enough tuh cut uh man tuh death. You looks jes' lak de devvul's doll-baby tuh *me*. You cain't hate me no worse dan Ah hates you. Ah been hatin' you fuh years."

"Yo' ole black hide don't look lak nothin' tuh me, but uh passle uh wrinkled up rubber, wid yo' big ole yeahs flappin' on each side lak uh paih uh buzzard wings. Don't think Ah'm gointuh be run 'way fum mah house neither. Ah'm goin' tuh de white folks 'bout *you,* mah young man, de very nex' time you lay yo' han's on me. Mah cup is done run ovah." Delia said this with no signs of fear and Sykes departed from the house, threatening her, but made not the slightest move to carry out any of them.

That night he did not return at all, and the next day being Sunday, Delia was glad she did not have to quarrel before she hitched up her pony and drove the four miles to Woodbridge.

She stayed to the night service—"love feast"—which was very warm and full of spirit. In the emotional winds her domestic trials were borne far and wide so that she sang as she drove homeward,

> *Jurden water, black an' col*
> *Chills de body, not de soul*
> *An' Ah wantah cross Jurden in uh calm time.*

She came from the barn to the kitchen door and stopped.

"Whut's de mattah, ol' Satan, you ain't kickin' up yo' racket?" She addressed the snake's box. Complete silence. She went on into the house with a new hope in its birth struggles. Perhaps her threat to go to the white folks had frightened Sykes! Perhaps he was sorry! Fifteen years of misery and suppression had brought Delia to the place where she would hope *anything* that looked towards a way over or through her wall of inhibitions.

She felt in the match-safe behind the stove at once for a match. There was only 85 one there.

"Dat niggah wouldn't fetch nothin' heah tuh save his rotten neck, but he kin run thew whut Ah brings quick enough. Now he done toted off nigh on tuh haff uh box uh matches. He done had dat 'oman heah in mah house, too."

Nobody but a woman could tell how she knew this even before she struck the match. But she did and it put her into a new fury.

Presently she brought in the tubs to put the white things to soak. This time she decided she need not bring the hamper out of the bedroom; she would go in there and do the sorting. She picked up the pot-bellied lamp and went in. The room was small and the hamper stood hard by the foot of the white iron bed. She could sit and reach through the bedposts—resting as she worked.

"Ah wantah cross Jurden in uh calm time." She was singing again. The mood of the "love feast" had returned. She threw back the lid of the basket almost gaily. Then, moved by both horror and terror, she sprang back toward the door. *There lay the snake in the basket!* He moved sluggishly at first, but even as she turned round and round, jumped up and down in an insanity of fear, he began to stir vigorously. She saw him pouring his awful beauty from the basket upon the bed, then she seized the lamp and ran as fast as she could to the kitchen. The wind from the open door blew out the light and the darkness added to her terror. She sped to the darkness of the yard, slamming the door after her before she thought to set down the lamp. She did not feel safe even on the ground, so she climbed up in the hay barn.

90   There for an hour or more she lay sprawled upon the hay a gibbering wreck.

Finally she grew quiet, and after that came coherent thought. With this stalked through her a cold, bloody rage. Hours of this. A period of introspection, a space of retrospection, then a mixture of both. Out of this an awful calm.

"Well, Ah done de bes' Ah could. If things ain't right, Gawd knows tain't mah fault."

She went to sleep—a twitch sleep—and woke up to a faint gray sky. There was a loud hollow sound below. She peered out. Sykes was at the wood-pile, demolishing a wire-covered box.

He hurried to the kitchen door, but hung outside there some minutes before he entered, and stood some minutes more inside before he closed it after him.

95   The gray in the sky was spreading. Delia descended without fear now, and crouched beneath the low bedroom window. The drawn shade shut out the dawn, shut in the night. But the thin walls held back no sound.

"Dat ol' scratch is woke up now!" She mused at the tremendous whirr inside, which every woodsman knows, is one of the sound illusions. The rattler is a ventriloquist. His whirr sounds to the right, to the left, straight ahead, behind, close under foot—everywhere but where it is. Woe to him who guesses wrong unless he is prepared to hold up his end of the argument! Sometimes he strikes without rattling at all.

Inside, Sykes heard nothing until he knocked a pot lid off the stove while trying to reach the match-safe in the dark. He had emptied his pockets at Bertha's.

The snake seemed to wake up under the stove and Sykes made a quick leap into the bedroom. In spite of the gin he had had, his head was clearing now.

"Mah Gawd!" he chattered, "ef Ah could on'y strack uh light!"

The rattling ceased for a moment as he stood paralyzed. He waited. It seemed 100 that the snake waited also.

"Oh, fuh de light! Ah thought he'd be too sick"—Sykes was muttering to himself when the whirr began again, closer, right underfoot this time. Long before this, Sykes' ability to think had been flattened down to primitive instinct and he leaped—onto the bed.

Outside Delia heard a cry that might have come from a maddened chimpanzee, a stricken gorilla. All the terror, all the horror, all the rage that man possibly could express, without a recognizable human sound.

A tremendous stir inside there, another series of animal screams, the intermittent whirr of the reptile. The shade torn violently down from the window, letting in the red dawn, a huge brown hand seizing the window stick, great dull blows upon the wooden floor punctuating the gibberish of sound long after the rattle of the snake had abruptly subsided. All this Delia could see and hear from her place beneath the window, and it made her ill. She crept over to the four-o'clocks and stretched herself on the cool earth to recover.

She lay there. "Delia, Delia!" She could hear Sykes calling in a most despairing tone as one who expected no answer. The sun crept on up, and he called. Delia could not move—her legs had gone flabby. She never moved, he called, and the sun kept rising.

"Mah Gawd!" She heard him moan, "Mah Gawd fum Heben!" She heard him 105 stumbling about and got up from her flower-bed. The sun was growing warm. As she approached the door she heard him call out hopefully, "Delia, is dat you Ah heah?"

She saw him on his hands and knees as soon as she reached the door. He crept an inch or two toward her—all that he was able, and she saw his horribly swollen neck and his one open eye shining with hope. A surge of pity too strong to support bore her away from that eye that must, could not, fail to see the tubs. He would see the lamp. Orlando with its doctors was too far. She could scarcely reach the chinaberry tree, where she waited in the growing heat while inside she knew the cold river was creeping up and up to extinguish that eye which must know by now that she knew.

QUESTIONS FOR DISCUSSION AND WRITING

1. How does Hurston use Sykes's joke with the bullwhip to set up the story's conclusion? How does she use the men on the porch to interpret the conflicts in this story?

2. How does Sykes characterize Delia and Bertha? How does Delia describe her own behavior? How do the men on the porch, especially Clarke, assess Sykes's relationship with Delia?

3. How does Hurston use dialect to establish the historical and cultural setting of the story? How do Delia's job and Sykes's interest in cars clarify the racial setting for the story?

4. Who is the narrator in this story? How does the narrator distinguish herself from Delia, Sykes, and the men on the porch? How does the narrator use the men on the porch to enhance her point of view?

5. In what ways does the title of this story establish its theme? How does Delia's comment, "Sykes, like everybody else, is gointer reap his sowing," provide a moral for this story?

Stories for Comparison

Ernest Gaines's "The Sky Is Gray" (pages 533–554); Alice Walker's "To Hell with Dying" (pages 1159–1163).

55

SHIRLEY JACKSON

The Lottery

SHIRLEY JACKSON (1919–1965) was born in San Francisco and was educated at the University of Rochester and Syracuse University. In 1940, she married author and critic Stanley Edgar Hyman and settled in North Bennington, Vermont, where Hyman was on the faculty of Bennington College. Jackson published her first novel, *The Road Through the Wall,* in 1948, the same year she published her controversial first story "The Lottery" in *The New Yorker.* Jackson continued to publish novels that dealt with bizarre, gothic, and mythic elements such as *Hangsaman* (1951), *The Haunting of Hill House* (1959), and *We Have Always Lived in the Castle* (1962). But she could also write easily and with humor about family life, as in *Life Among the Savages* (1953), and produce fascinating stories for children, such as *9 Magic Wishes* (1963). Despite a productive writing career in which many of her novels and stories were adapted for stage and screen, Jackson's most famous story remains her first. "The Lottery," reprinted from *The Lottery; or, The Adventures of James Harris,* presents a community's annual reenactment of a mysterious ritual.

The morning of June 27th was clear and sunny, with the fresh warmth of a full-summer day; the flowers were blossoming profusely and the grass was richly

green. The people of the village began to gather in the square, between the post office and the bank, around ten o'clock; in some towns there were so many people that
the lottery took two days and had to be started on June 26th, but in this village, where
there were only about three hundred people, the whole lottery took less than two
hours, so it could begin at ten o'clock in the morning and still be through in time to
allow the villagers to get home for noon dinner.

The children assembled first, of course. School was recently over for the summer, and the feeling of liberty sat uneasily on most of them; they tended to gather together quietly for a while before they broke into boisterous play, and their talk was
still of the classroom and the teacher, of books and reprimands. Bobby Martin had
already stuffed his pockets full of stones, and the other boys soon followed his example, selecting the smoothest and roundest stones; Bobby and Harry Jones and
Dickie Delacroix—the villagers pronounced this name "Dellacroy"—eventually
made a great pile of stones in one corner of the square and guarded it against the
raids of the other boys. The girls stood aside, talking among themselves, looking
over their shoulders at the boys, and the very small children rolled in the dust or
clung to the hands of their older brothers or sisters.

Soon the men began to gather, surveying their own children, speaking of planting and rain, tractors and taxes. They stood together, away from the pile of stones in
the corner, and their jokes were quiet and they smiled rather than laughed. The
women, wearing faded house dresses and sweaters, came shortly after their menfolk.
They greeted one another and exchanged bits of gossip as they went to join their husbands. Soon the women, standing by their husbands, began to call to their children,
and the children came reluctantly, having to be called four or five times. Bobby Martin ducked under his mother's grasping hand and ran, laughing, back to the pile of
stones. His father spoke up sharply, and Bobby came quickly and took his place between his father and his oldest brother.

The lottery was conducted—as were the square dances, the teenage club, the
Halloween program—by Mr. Summers, who had time and energy to devote to civic
activities. He was a round-faced, jovial man and he ran the coal business, and people were sorry for him, because he had no children and his wife was a scold. When
he arrived in the square, carrying the black wooden box, there was a murmur of conversation among the villagers, and he waved and called, "Little late today, folks."
The postmaster, Mr. Graves, followed him, carrying a three-legged stool, and the
stool was put in the center of the square and Mr. Summers set the black box down
on it. The villagers kept their distance, leaving a space between themselves and the
stool, and when Mr. Summers said, "Some of you fellows want to give me a hand?"
there was a hesitation before two men, Mr. Martin and his oldest son, Baxter, came
forward to hold the box steady on the stool while Mr. Summers stirred up the papers
inside it.

The original paraphernalia for the lottery had been lost long ago, and the black
box now resting on the stool had been put into use even before Old Man Warner, the
oldest man in town, was born. Mr. Summers spoke frequently to the villagers about
making a new box, but no one liked to upset even as much tradition as was represented by the black box. There was a story that the present box had been made with

some pieces of the box that had preceded it, the one that had been constructed when the first people settled down to make a village here. Every year, after the lottery, Mr. Summers began talking again about a new box, but every year the subject was allowed to fade off without anything's being done. The black box grew shabbier each year; by now it was no longer completely black but splintered badly along one side to show the original wood color, and in some places faded or stained.

Mr. Martin and his oldest son, Baxter, held the black box securely on the stool until Mr. Summers had stirred the papers thoroughly with his hand. Because so much of the ritual had been forgotten or discarded, Mr. Summers had been successful in having slips of paper substituted for the chips of wood that had been used for generations. Chips of wood, Mr. Summers had argued, had been all very well when the village was tiny, but now that the population was more than three hundred and likely to keep on growing, it was necessary to use something that would fit more easily into the black box. The night before the lottery, Mr. Summers and Mr. Graves made up the slips of paper and put them in the box, and it was then taken to the safe of Mr. Summers's coal company and locked up until Mr. Summers was ready to take it to the square next morning. The rest of the year, the box was put away, sometimes one place, sometimes another; it had spent one year in Mr. Graves's barn and another year underfoot in the post office, and sometimes it was set on a shelf in the Martin grocery and left there.

There was a great deal of fussing to be done before Mr. Summers declared the lottery open. There were the lists to make up—of heads of families, heads of households in each family, members of each household in each family. There was the proper swearing-in of Mr. Summers by the postmaster, as the official of the lottery; at one time, some people remembered, there had been a recital of some sort, performed by the official of the lottery, a perfunctory, tuneless chant that had been rattled off duly each year; some people believed that the official of the lottery used to stand just so when he said or sang it, others believed that he was supposed to walk among the people, but years and years ago this part of the ritual had been allowed to lapse. There had been, also, a ritual salute, which the official of the lottery had had to use in addressing each person who came up to draw from the box, but this also had changed with time, until now it was felt necessary only for the official to speak to each person approaching. Mr. Summers was very good at all this; in his clean white shirt and blue jeans, with one hand resting carelessly on the black box, he seemed very proper and important as he talked interminably to Mr. Graves and the Martins.

Just as Mr. Summers finally left off talking and turned to the assembled villagers, Mrs. Hutchinson came hurriedly along the path to the square, her sweater thrown over her shoulders, and slid into place in the back of the crowd. "Clean forgot what day it was," she said to Mrs. Delacroix, who stood next to her, and they both laughed softly. "Thought my old man was out back stacking wood," Mrs. Hutchinson went on, "and then I looked out the window and the kids was gone, and then I remembered it was the twenty-seventh and came a-running." She dried her hands on her apron, and Mrs. Delacroix said, "You're in time, though. They're still talking away up there."

Mrs. Hutchinson craned her neck to see through the crowd and found her husband and children standing near the front. She tapped Mrs. Delacroix on the arm as a farewell and began to make her way through the crowd. The people separated good-humoredly to let her through; two or three people said, in voices just loud enough to be heard across the crowd, "Here comes your Missus, Hutchinson," and "Bill, she made it after all." Mrs. Hutchinson reached her husband, and Mr. Summers, who had been waiting, said cheerfully, "Thought we were going to have to get on without you, Tessie." Mrs. Hutchinson said, grinning, "Wouldn't have me leave m'dishes in the sink, now, would you, Joe?" and soft laughter ran through the crowd as the people stirred back into position after Mrs. Hutchinson's arrival.

"Well, now," Mr. Summers said soberly, "guess we better get started, get this 10 over with, so's we can go back to work. Anybody ain't here?"

"Dunbar," several people said. "Dunbar, Dunbar."

Mr. Summers consulted his list. "Clyde Dunbar," he said. "That's right. He's broke his leg, hasn't he? Who's drawing for him?"

"Me, I guess," a woman said, and Mr. Summers turned to look at her. "Wife draws for her husband," Mr. Summers said. "Don't you have a grown boy to do it for you, Janey?" Although Mr. Summers and everyone else in the village knew the answer perfectly well, it was the business of the official of the lottery to ask such questions formally. Mr. Summers waited with an expression of polite interest while Mrs. Dunbar answered.

"Horace's not but sixteen yet," Mrs. Dunbar said regretfully. "Guess I gotta fill in for the old man this year."

"Right," Mr. Summers said. He made a note on the list he was holding. Then he 15 asked, "Watson boy drawing this year?"

A tall boy in the crowd raised his hand. "Here," he said. "I'm drawing for m'mother and me." He blinked his eyes nervously and ducked his head as several voices in the crowd said things like "Good fellow, Jack," and "Glad to see your mother's got a man to do it."

"Well," Mr. Summers said, "guess that's everyone. Old Man Warner make it?"

"Here," a voice said, and Mr. Summers nodded.

A sudden hush fell on the crowd as Mr. Summers cleared his throat and looked at the list. "All ready?" he called. "Now, I'll read the names—heads of families first—and the men come up and take a paper out of the box. Keep the paper folded in your hand without looking at it until everyone has had a turn. Everything clear?"

The people had done it so many times that they only half-listened to the direc- 20 tions; most of them were quiet, wetting their lips, not looking around. Then Mr. Summers raised one hand high and said, "Adams." A man disengaged himself from the crowd and came forward. "Hi, Steve," Mr. Summers said, and Mr. Adams said, "Hi, Joe." They grinned at one another humorlessly and nervously. Then Mr. Adams reached into the black box and took out a folded paper. He held it firmly by one corner as he turned and went hastily back to his place in the crowd, where he stood a little apart from his family, not looking down at his hand.

"Allen," Mr. Summers said. "Anderson. . . . Bentham."

"Seems like there's no time at all between lotteries any more," Mrs. Delacroix said to Mrs. Graves in the back row. "Seems like we got through with the last one only last week."

"Time sure goes fast," Mrs. Graves said.

"Clark. . . . Delacroix."

25   "There goes my old man," Mrs. Delacroix said. She held her breath while her husband went forward.

"Dunbar," Mr. Summers said, and Mrs. Dunbar went steadily to the box while one of the women said, "Go on, Janey," and another said, "There she goes."

"We're next," Mrs. Graves said. She watched while Mr. Graves came around from the side of the box, greeted Mr. Summers gravely, and selected a slip of paper from the box. By now, all through the crowd there were men holding the small folded papers in their large hands, turning them over and over nervously. Mrs. Dunbar and her two sons stood together, Mrs. Dunbar holding the slip of paper.

"Harburt. . . . Hutchinson."

"Get up there, Bill," Mrs. Hutchinson said, and the people near her laughed.

30   "Jones."

"They do say," Mr. Adams said to Old Man Warner, who stood next to him, "that over in the north village they're talking of giving up the lottery."

Old Man Warner snorted. "Pack of crazy fools," he said. "Listening to the young folks, nothing's good enough for *them.* Next thing you know, they'll be wanting to go back to living in caves, nobody work any more, live *that* way for a while. Used to be a saying about 'Lottery in June, corn be heavy soon.' First thing you know, we'd all be eating stewed chickweed and acorns. There's *always* been a lottery," he added petulantly. "Bad enough to see young Joe Summers up there joking with everybody."

"Some places have already quit lotteries," Mrs. Adams said.

"Nothing but trouble in *that,*" Old Man Warner said stoutly. "Pack of young fools."

35   "Martin." And Bobby Martin watched his father go forward. "Overdyke. . . . Percy."

"I wish they'd hurry," Mrs. Dunbar said to her older son. "I wish they'd hurry."

"They're almost through," her son said.

"You get ready to run tell Dad," Mrs. Dunbar said.

Mr. Summers called his own name and then stepped forward precisely and selected a slip from the box. Then he called, "Warner."

40   "Seventy-seventh year I been in the lottery," Old Man Warner said as he went through the crowd. "Seventy-seventh time."

"Watson." The tall boy came awkwardly through the crowd. Someone said, "Don't be nervous, Jack," and Mr. Summers said, "Take your time, son."

"Zanini."

After that, there was a long pause, a breathless pause, until Mr. Summers, holding his slip of paper in the air, said, "All right, fellows." For a minute, no one moved, and then all the slips of paper were opened. Suddenly, all the women began to speak at once, saying, "Who is it?," "Who's got it?," "Is it the Dunbars?," "Is it the Watsons?" Then the voices began to say, "It's Hutchinson. It's Bill," "Bill Hutchinson's got it."

"Go tell your father," Mrs. Dunbar said to her older son.

People began to look around to see the Hutchinsons. Bill Hutchinson was stand-ing quiet, staring down at the paper in his hand. Suddenly, Tessie Hutchinson shouted to Mr. Summers, "You didn't give him time enough to take any paper he wanted. I saw you. It wasn't fair!"

"Be a good sport, Tessie," Mrs. Delacroix called, and Mrs. Graves said, "All of us took the same chance."

"Shut up, Tessie," Bill Hutchinson said.

"Well, everyone," Mr. Summers said, "that was done pretty fast, and now we've got to be hurrying a little more to get done in time." He consulted his next list. "Bill," he said, "you draw for the Hutchinson family. You got any other households in the Hutchinsons?"

"There's Don and Eva," Mrs. Hutchinson yelled. "Make *them* take their chance!"

"Daughters draw with their husbands' families, Tessie," Mr. Summers said gently. "You know that as well as anyone else."

"It wasn't *fair,*" Tessie said.

"I guess not, Joe," Bill Hutchinson said regretfully. "My daughter draws with her husband's family, that's only fair. And I've got no other family except the kids."

"Then, as far as drawing for families is concerned, it's you," Mr. Summers said in explanation, "and as far as drawing for households is concerned, that's you, too. Right?"

"Right," Bill Hutchinson said.

"How many kids, Bill?" Mr. Summers asked formally.

"Three," Bill Hutchinson said. "There's Bill, Jr., and Nancy, and little Dave. And Tessie and me."

"All right, then," Mr. Summers said. "Harry, you got their tickets back?"

Mr. Graves nodded and held up the slips of paper. "Put them in the box, then," Mr. Summers directed. "Take Bill's and put it in."

"I think we ought to start over," Mrs. Hutchinson said, as quietly as she could. "I tell you it wasn't *fair.* You didn't give him time enough to choose. *Every*body saw that."

Mr. Graves had selected the five slips and put them in the box, and he dropped all the papers but those onto the ground, where the breeze caught them and lifted them off.

"Listen, everybody," Mrs. Hutchinson was saying to the people around her.

"Ready, Bill?" Mr. Summers asked, and Bill Hutchinson, with one quick glance around at his wife and children, nodded.

"Remember," Mr. Summers said, "take the slips and keep them folded until each person has taken one. Harry, you help little Dave." Mr. Graves took the hand of the little boy, who came willingly with him up to the box. "Take a paper out of the box, Davy," Mr. Summers said. Davy put his hand into the box and laughed. "Take just *one* paper," Mr. Summers said. "Harry, you hold it for him." Mr. Graves took the child's hand and removed the folded paper from the tight fist and held it while little Dave stood next to him and looked up at him wonderingly.

"Nancy next," Mr. Summers said. Nancy was twelve, and her school friends breathed heavily as she went forward, switching her skirt, and took a slip daintily from the box. "Bill, Jr.," Mr. Summers said, and Billy, his face red and his feet over-large, nearly knocked the box over as he got a paper out. "Tessie," Mr. Summers said. She hesitated for a minute, looking around defiantly, and then set her lips and went up to the box. She snatched a paper out and held it behind her.

65   "Bill," Mr. Summers said, and Bill Hutchinson reached into the box and felt around, bringing his hand out at last with the slip of paper in it.

The crowd was quiet. A girl whispered, "I hope it's not Nancy," and the sound of the whisper reached the edges of the crowd.

"It's not the way it used to be," Old Man Warner said clearly. "People ain't the way they used to be."

"All right," Mr. Summers said. "Open the papers. Harry, you open little Dave's."

Mr. Graves opened the slip of paper and there was a general sigh through the crowd as he held it up and everyone could see that it was blank. Nancy and Bill, Jr., opened theirs at the same time, and both beamed and laughed, turning around to the crowd and holding their slips of paper above their heads.

70   "Tessie," Mr. Summers said. There was a pause, and then Mr. Summers looked at Bill Hutchinson, and Bill unfolded his paper and showed it. It was blank.

"It's Tessie," Mr. Summers said, and his voice was hushed. "Show us her paper, Bill."

Bill Hutchinson went over to his wife and forced the slip of paper out of her hand. It had a black spot on it, the black spot Mr. Summers had made the night before with the heavy pencil in the coal-company office. Bill Hutchinson held it up, and there was a stir in the crowd.

"All right, folks," Mr. Summers said. "Let's finish quickly."

Although the villagers had forgotten the ritual and lost the original black box, they still remembered to use stones. The pile of stones the boys had made earlier was ready; there were stones on the ground with the blowing scraps of paper that had come out of the box. Mrs. Delacroix selected a stone so large she had to pick it up with both hands and turned to Mrs. Dunbar. "Come on," she said. "Hurry up."

75   Mrs. Dunbar had small stones in both hands, and she said, gasping for breath, "I can't run at all. You'll have to go ahead and I'll catch up with you."

The children had stones already, and someone gave little Davy Hutchinson a few pebbles.

Tessie Hutchinson was in the center of a cleared space by now, and she held her hands out desperately as the villagers moved in on her. "It isn't fair," she said. A stone hit her on the side of the head.

Old Man Warner was saying, "Come on, come on, everyone." Steve Adams was in the front of the crowd of villagers, with Mrs. Graves beside him.

"It ain't fair, it isn't right," Mrs. Hutchinson screamed, and then they were upon her.

QUESTIONS FOR DISCUSSION AND WRITING

1. What are the first signs that something sinister lurks beneath the surface of this story? How does the end of the story alter our perception of the events of the day?

2. How does our first view of Tessie help to establish her character? To what extent is her final protest justified? How do the other characters portray themselves by their attitudes toward the ritual?

3. Why is Jackson purposely vague about where this story takes place? What do the characters in this particular community say about the way the lottery is practiced in nearby communities?

4. How does the objective point of view of the story help contribute to its festive tone? How is that tone reversed at the conclusion of the story?

5. Compare and contrast the lottery with other social or religious rituals. Why do communities honor the traditions of such rituals? How do they feel about individuals who rebel against them?

Stories for Comparison

Arthur C. Clarke's "The Star" (pages 383–388); Ursula K. Le Guin's "The Ones Who Walk Away from Omelas" (pages 144–150).

56

HENRY JAMES

The Real Thing

HENRY JAMES (1843–1916) was born in New York City but spent much of his childhood and adult life as a citizen of the world. He was educated privately by tutors in America and Europe until entering Harvard Law School at nineteen. But James quickly turned his attention to literature, publishing essays, reviews, and stories that confirmed his perception of himself as an attuned but detached spectator of life. After 1866, concluding that America was hostile toward creative talent, he spent most of the remainder of his life in Europe. In 1875, he published his first collection of short stories, *A Passionate Pilgrim,* and saw his first noteworthy novel, *Roderick Hudson,* serialized

in *The Atlantic Monthly,* the magazine edited by his friend William Dean
Howells. Thereafter James produced an astonishing amount of fiction, including classic novels such as *The American* (1877), *Daisy Miller* (1879), *The
Portrait of a Lady* (1881), *The Turn of the Screw* (1898), *The Wings of the
Dove* (1902), *The Ambassadors* (1903), and *The Golden Bowl* (1904). James
was preoccupied with the physical and psychological conditions that contribute to intellectual and aesthetic sensibility. "The Real Thing," reprinted
from the 26-volume New York edition of *The Novels and Tales of Henry
James* (1907–1917), tells of an artist's difficulties in using real people as
models for his work.

I

When the porter's wife, who used to answer the house-bell, announced "A gentleman and a lady, sir" I had, as I often had in those days—the wish being father to the thought—an immediate vision of sitters. Sitters my visitors in this case
proved to be; but not in the sense I should have preferred. There was nothing at first
however to indicate that they mightn't have come for a portrait. The gentleman, a
man of fifty, very high and very straight, with a moustache slightly grizzled and a
dark grey walking-coat admirably fitted, both of which I noted professionally—I
don't mean as a barber or yet as a tailor—would have struck me as a celebrity if
celebrities often were striking. It was a truth of which I had for some time been conscious that a figure with a good deal of frontage was, as one might say, almost never
a public institution. A glance at the lady helped to remind me of this paradoxical law:
she also looked too distinguished to be a "personality." Moreover one would scarcely
come across two variations together.

Neither of the pair immediately spoke—they only prolonged the preliminary
gaze suggesting that each wished to give the other a chance. They were visibly shy;
they stood there letting me take them in—which, as I afterwards perceived, was the
most practical thing they could have done. In this way their embarrassment served
their cause. I had seen people painfully reluctant to mention that they desired anything so gross as to be represented on canvas; but the scruples of my new friends appeared almost insurmountable. Yet the gentleman might have said "I should like a
portrait of my wife," and the lady might have said "I should like a portrait of my husband." Perhaps they weren't husband and wife—this naturally would make the matter more delicate. Perhaps they wished to be done together—in which case they
ought to have brought a third person to break the news.

"We come from Mr. Rivet," the lady finally said with a dim smile that had the
effect of a moist sponge passed over a "sunk" piece of painting, as well as of a vague
allusion to vanished beauty. She was as tall and straight, in her degree, as her companion, and with ten years less to carry. She looked as sad as a woman could look
whose face was not charged with expression; that is her tinted oval mask showed
waste as an exposed surface shows friction. The hand of time had played over her
freely, but to an effect of elimination. She was slim and stiff, and so well-dressed, in
dark blue cloth, with lappets and pockets and buttons, that it was clear she employed

the same tailor as her husband. The couple had an indefinable air of prosperous thrift—they evidently got a good deal of luxury for their money. If I was to be one of their luxuries it would behove me to consider my terms.

"Ah Claude Rivet recommended me?" I echoed; and I added that it was very kind of him, though I could reflect that, as he only painted landscape, this wasn't a sacrifice.

The lady looked very hard at the gentleman, and the gentleman looked round the ₅ room. Then staring at the floor a moment and stroking his moustache, he rested his pleasant eyes on me with the remark: "He said you were the right one."

"I try to be, when people want to sit."

"Yes, we should like to," said the lady anxiously.

"Do you mean together?"

My visitors exchanged a glance. "If you could do anything with *me* I suppose it would be double," the gentleman stammered.

"Oh yes, there's naturally a higher charge for two figures than for one."   ₁₀

"We should like to make it pay," the husband confessed.

"That's very good of you," I returned, appreciating so unwonted a sympathy—for I supposed he meant pay the artist.

A sense of strangeness seemed to dawn on the lady.

"We mean for the illustrations—Mr. Rivet said you might put one in."

"Put in—an illustration?" I was equally confused.   ₁₅

"Sketch her off, you know," said the gentleman, colouring.

It was only then that I understood the service Claude Rivet had rendered me; he had told them how I worked in black-and-white, for magazines, for storybooks, for sketches of contemporary life, and consequently had copious employment for models. These things were true, but it was not less true—I may confess it now; whether because the aspiration was to lead to everything or to nothing I leave the reader to guess—that I couldn't get the honours, to say nothing of the emoluments, of a great painter of portraits out of my head. My "illustrations" were my pot-boilers; I looked to a different branch of art—far and away the most interesting it had always seemed to me—to perpetuate my fame. There was no shame in looking to it also to make my fortune; but that fortune was by so much further from being made from the moment my visitors wished to be "done" for nothing. I was disappointed; for in the pictorial sense I had immediately *seen* them. I had seized their type—I had already settled what I would do with it. Something that wouldn't absolutely have pleased them, I afterwards reflected.

"Ah you're—you're—a—?" I began as soon as I had mastered my surprise. I couldn't bring out the dingy word "models": it seemed so little to fit the case.

"We haven't had much practice," said the lady.

"We've got to *do* something, and we've thought that an artist in your line might ₂₀ perhaps make something of us," her husband threw off. He further mentioned that they didn't know many artists and that they had gone first, on the off-chance—he painted views of course, but sometimes put in figures; perhaps I remembered—to Mr. Rivet, whom they had met a few years before at a place in Norfolk where he was sketching.

"We used to sketch a little ourselves," the lady hinted.

"It's very awkward, but we absolutely *must* do something," her husband went on.

"Of course we're not so *very* young," she admitted with a wan smile.

With the remark that I might as well know something more about them the husband had handed me a card extracted from a neat new pocket-book—their appurtenances were all of the freshest—and inscribed with the words "Major Monarch." Impressive as these words were they didn't carry my knowledge much further; but my visitor presently added: "I've left the army and we've had the misfortune to lose our money. In fact our means are dreadfully small."

25   "It's awfully trying—a regular strain," said Mrs. Monarch.

They evidently wished to be discreet—to take care not to swagger because they were gentlefolk. I felt them willing to recognize this as something of a drawback, at the same time that I guessed at an underlying sense—their consolation in adversity—that they *had* their points. They certainly had; but these advantages struck me as preponderantly social; such for instance as would help to make a drawing-room look well. However, a drawing-room was always, or ought to be, a picture.

In consequence of his wife's allusion to their age Major Monarch observed: "Naturally it's more for the figure that we thought of going in. We can still hold ourselves up." On the instant I saw that the figure was indeed their strong point. His "naturally" didn't sound vain, but it lighted up the question. "*She* has the best one," he continued, nodding at his wife with a pleasant after-dinner absence of circumlocution. I could only reply, as if we were in fact sitting over our wine, that this didn't prevent his own from being very good; which led him in turn to make answer: "We thought that if you ever had to do people like us we might be something like it. *She* particularly—for a lady in a book, you know."

I was so amused by them that, to get more of it, I did my best to take their point of view; and though it was an embarrassment to find myself appraising physically, as if they were animals on hire or useful blacks, a pair whom I should have expected to meet only in one of the relations in which criticism is tacit, I looked at Mrs. Monarch judicially enough to be able to exclaim after a moment with conviction: "Oh yes, a lady in a book!" She was singularly like a bad illustration.

"We'll stand up, if you like," said the Major; and he raised himself before me with a really grand air.

30   I could take his measure at a glance—he was six feet two and a perfect gentleman. It would have paid any club in process of formation and in want of a stamp to engage him at a salary to stand in the principal window. What struck me at once was that in coming to me they had rather missed their vocation; they could surely have been turned to better account for advertising purposes. I couldn't of course see the thing in detail, but I could see them make somebody's fortune—I don't mean their own. There was something in them for a waistcoat-maker, an hotel-keeper or a soap-vendor. I could imagine "We always use it" pinned on their bosoms with the greatest effect; I had a vision of the brilliancy with which they would launch a table d'hôte.

Mrs. Monarch sat still, not from pride but from shyness, and presently her husband said to her: "Get up, my dear, and show how smart you are." She obeyed, but she had no need to get up to show it. She walked to the end of the studio and then came back blushing, her fluttered eyes on the partner of her appeal. I was reminded of an incident I had accidentally had a glimpse of in Paris being with a friend there, a dramatist about to produce a play, when an actress came to him to ask to be entrusted with a part. She went through her paces before him, walked up and down as Mrs. Monarch was doing. Mrs. Monarch did it quite as well, but I abstained from applauding. It was very odd to see such people apply for such poor pay. She looked as if she had ten thousand a year. Her husband had used the word that described her: she was in the London current jargon essentially and typically "smart." Her figure was, in the same order of ideas, conspicuously and irreproachably "good." For a woman of her age her waist was surprisingly small; her elbow moreover had the orthodox crook. She held her head at the conventional angle, but why did she come to *me?* She ought to have tried on jackets at a big shop. I feared my visitors were not only destitute but "artistic"—which would be a great complication. When she sat down again I thanked her, observing that what a draughtsman most valued in his model was the faculty of keeping quiet.

"Oh *she* can keep quiet," said Major Monarch. Then he added jocosely: "I've always kept her quiet."

"I'm not a nasty fidget, am I?" It was going to wring tears from me, I felt, the way she hid her head, ostrich-like, in the other broad bosom.

The owner of this expanse addressed his answer to me. "Perhaps it isn't out of place to mention—because we ought to be quite business-like, oughtn't we?—that when I married her she was known as the Beautiful Statue."

"Oh dear!" said Mrs. Monarch ruefully.   35

"Of course I should want a certain amount of expression," I rejoined.

"Of *course!*"—and I had never heard such unanimity.

"And then I suppose you know that you'll get awfully tired."

"Oh we *never* get tired!" they eagerly cried.

"Have you had any kind of practice?"   40

They hesitated—they looked at each other. "We've been photographed— *immensely,*" said Mrs. Monarch.

"She means the fellows have asked us themselves," added the Major.

"I see—because you're so good-looking."

"I don't know what they thought, but they were always after us."

"We always got our photographs for nothing," smiled Mrs. Monarch.   45

"We might have brought some, my dear," her husband remarked.

"I'm not sure we have any left. We've given quantities away," she explained to me.

"With our autographs and that sort of thing," said the Major.

"Are they to be got in the shops?" I enquired as a harmless pleasantry.

"Oh yes, *hers*—they used to be."   50

"Not now," said Mrs. Monarch with her eyes on the floor.

2

I could fancy the "sort of thing" they put on the presentation copies of their photographs, and I was sure they wrote a beautiful hand. It was odd how quickly I was sure of everything that concerned them. If they were now so poor as to have to earn shillings and pence they could never have had much of a margin. Their good looks had been their capital, and they had good-humouredly made the most of the career that this resource marked out for them. It was in their faces, the blankness, the deep intellectual repose of the twenty years of country-house visiting that had given them pleasant intonations. I could see the sunny drawing-rooms, sprinkled with periodicals she didn't read, in which Mrs. Monarch had continuously sat; I could see the wet shrubberies in which she had walked, equipped to admiration for either exercise. I could see the rich covers the Major had helped to shoot and the wonderful garments in which, late at night, he repaired to the smoking-room to talk about them. I could imagine their leggings and waterproofs, their knowing tweeds and rugs, their rolls of sticks and cases of tackle and neat umbrellas; and I could evoke the exact appearance of their servants and the compact variety of their luggage on the platforms of country stations.

They gave small tips, but they were liked; they didn't do anything themselves, but they were welcome. They looked so well everywhere; they gratified the general relish for stature, complexion and "form." They knew it without fatuity or vulgarity, and they respected themselves in consequence. They weren't superficial; they were thorough and kept themselves up—it had been their line. People with such a taste for activity had to have some line. I could feel how even in a dull house they could have been counted on for the joy of life. At present something had happened—it didn't matter what, their little income had grown less, it had grown least—and they had to do something for pocket-money. Their friends could like them, I made out, without liking to support them. There was something about them that represented credit—their clothes, their manners, their type; but if credit is a large empty pocket in which an occasional chink reverberates, the chink at least must be audible. What they wanted of me was to help to make it so. Fortunately they had no children—I soon divined that. They would also perhaps wish our relations to be kept secret: this was why it was "for the figure"—the reproduction of the face would betray them.

I liked them—I felt, quite as their friends must have done—they were so simple; and I had no objection to them if they would suit. But somehow with all their perfections I didn't easily believe in them. After all they were amateurs, and the ruling passion of my life was the detestation of the amateur. Combined with this was another perversity—an innate preference for the represented subject over the real one: the defect of the real one was so apt to be a lack of representation. I like things that appeared; then one was sure. Whether they *were* or not was a subordinate and almost always a profitless question. There were other considerations, the first of which was that I already had two or three recruits in use, notably a young person with big feet, in alpaca, from Kilburn, who for a couple of years had come to me regularly for my illustrations and with whom I was still—perhaps ignobly—satisfied. I frankly explained to my visitors how the case stood, but they had taken more precautions than I supposed. They had reasoned out their opportunity, for Claude Rivet had told them of the projected *édition de luxe* of one of the writers of our day—the rarest of the novelists—who, long neglected by the multitudinous vulgar and dearly prized by the attentive (need I mention Philip Vincent?) had had the happy fortune of seeing, late in life, the dawn and then the full light of a higher criticism; an estimate in which on the part of the public there was something really of expiation. The edition preparing, planned by a publisher of taste, was practically an act of high reparation; the wood-cuts with which it was to be enriched were the homage of English art to one of the most independent representatives of English letters. Major and Mrs. Monarch confessed to me they had hoped I might be able to work *them* into my branch of the enterprise. They knew I was to do the first of the books, "Rutland Ramsay," but I had to make clear to them that my participation in the rest of the affair—this first book was to be a test—must depend on the satisfaction I should give. If this should be limited my employers would drop me with scarce common forms. It was therefore a crisis for me, and naturally I was making special preparations, looking about for new people, should they be necessary, and securing the best types. I admitted however that I should like to settle down to two or three good models who would do for everything.

"Should we have often to—a—put on special clothes?" Mrs. Monarch timidly demanded.

"Dear yes—that's half the business."

"And should we be expected to supply our own costumes?"

"Oh no; I've got a lot of things. A painter's models put on—or put off—anything he likes."

"And you mean—a—the same?"

"The same?"

Mrs. Monarch looked at her husband again.

"Oh she was just wondering," he explained, "if the costumes are in *general* use." I had to confess that they were, and I mentioned further that some of them—I had a lot of genuine greasy last-century things—had served their time, a hundred years ago, on living world-stained men and women; on figures not perhaps so far removed, in that vanished world, from *their* type, the Monarchs', *quoi!* of a breeched and bewigged age. "We'll put on anything that *fits*," said the Major.

"Oh I arrange that—they fit in the pictures."

"I'm afraid I should do better for the modern books. I'd come as you like," said Mrs. Monarch.

"She has got a lot of clothes at home: they might do for contemporary life," her husband continued.

"Oh I can fancy scenes in which you'd be quite natural." And indeed I could see the slipshod rearrangements of stale properties—the stories I tried to produce pictures for without the exasperation of reading them—whose sandy tracts the good lady might help to people. But I had to return to the fact that for this sort of work—the daily mechanical grind—I was already equipped: the people I was working with were fully adequate.

"We only thought we might be more like *some* characters," said Mrs. Monarch mildly, getting up.

Her husband also rose; he stood looking at me with a dim wistfulness that was touching in so fine a man.

"Wouldn't it be rather a pull sometimes to have—a—to have—?" He hung fire; he wanted me to help him by phrasing what he meant. But I couldn't—I didn't know.

So he brought it out awkwardly: "The *real* thing; a gentleman, you know, or a lady." I was quite ready to give a general assent—I admitted that there was a great deal in that. This encouraged Major Monarch to say, following up his appeal with an un-acted gulp: "It's awfully hard—we've tried everything." The gulp was communicative; it proved to be too much for his wife. Before I knew Mrs. Monarch had dropped again upon a divan and burst into tears. Her husband sat down beside her, holding one of her hands; whereupon she quickly dried her eyes with the other, while I felt embarrassed as she looked up at me. "There isn't a confounded job I haven't applied for—waited for—prayed for. You can fancy we'd be pretty bad first. Secretaryships and that sort of thing? You might as well ask for a peerage. I'd be *anything*—I'm strong; a messenger or a coalheaver. I'd put on a gold-laced cap and open carriage-doors in front of the haberdasher's; I'd hang about a station to carry portmanteaux; I'd be a postman. But they won't *look* at you; there are thousands as good as yourself already on the ground. *Gentlemen,* poor beggars, who've drunk their wine, who've kept their hunters!"

70   I was as reassuring as I knew how to be, and my visitors were presently on their feet again while, for the experiment, we agreed on an hour. We were discussing it when the door opened and Miss Churm came in with a wet umbrella. Miss Churm had to take the omnibus to Maida Vale and then walk half a mile. She looked a trifle blowsy and slightly splashed. I scarcely ever saw her come in without thinking fresh how odd it was that, being so little in herself, she should yet be so much in others. She was a meagre little Miss Churm, but was such an ample heroine of romance. She was only a freckled cockney, but she could represent everything, from a fine lady to a shepherdess; she had the faculty as she might have had a fine voice or long hair. She couldn't spell and she loved beer, but she had two or three "points," and practice, and a knack, and mother-wit, and a whimsical sensibility, and a love of the theatre, and seven sisters, and not an ounce of respect, especially for the *h.* The first thing my visitors saw was that her umbrella was wet, and in their spotless perfection they visibly winced at it. The rain had come on since their arrival.

"I'm all in a soak; there *was* a mess of people in the 'bus. I wish you lived near a stytion," said Miss Churm. I requested her to get ready as quickly as possible, and she passed into the room in which she always changed her dress. But before going out she asked me what she was to get into this time.

"It's the Russian princess, don't you know?" I answered; "The one with the 'golden eyes,' in black velvet, for the long thing in the *Cheapside.*"

"Golden eyes? I *say!*" cried Miss Churm, while my companions watched her with intensity as she withdrew. She always arranged herself, when she was late, before I could turn around; and I kept my visitors a little on purpose, so that they might get an idea, from seeing her, what would be expected of themselves. I mentioned that she was quite my notion of an excellent model—she was really very clever.

"Do you think she looks like a Russian princess?" Major Monarch asked with lurking alarm.

75   "When I make her, yes."

"Oh if you have to *make* her—!" he reasoned, not without point.

"That's the most you can ask. There are so many who are not makeable."

"Well now, *here's* a lady"—and with a persuasive smile he passed his arm into his wife's—"who's already made!"

"Oh I'm not a Russian princess," Mrs. Monarch protested a little coldly. I could see she had known some and didn't like them. There at once was a complication of a kind I never had to fear with Miss Churm.

This young lady came back in black velvet—the gown was rather rusty and very low on her lean shoulders—and with a Japanese fan in her red hands. I reminded her that in the scene I was doing she had to look over some one's head. "I forget whose it is; but it doesn't matter. Just look over a head."

"I'd rather look over a stove," said Miss Churm; and she took her station near the fire. She fell into position, settled herself into a tall attitude, gave a certain backward inclination to her head and a certain forward droop to her fan, and looked, at least to my prejudiced sense, distinguished and charming, foreign and dangerous. We left her looking so while I went downstairs with Major and Mrs. Monarch.

"I believe I could come about as near it as that," said Mrs. Monarch.

"Oh, you think she's shabby, but you must allow for the alchemy of art."

However, they went off with an evident increase of comfort founded on their demonstrable advantage in being the real thing. I could fancy them shuddering over Miss Churm. She was very droll about them when I went back, for I told her what they wanted.

"Well, if *she* can sit I'll tyke to bookkeeping," said my model.

"She's very ladylike," I replied as an innocent form of aggravation.

"So much the worse for *you.* That means she can't turn round."

"She'll do for the fashionable novels."

"Oh yes, she'll *do* for them!" my model humorously declared.

"Ain't they bad enough without her?" I had often sociably denounced them to Miss Churm.

3

It was for the elucidation of a mystery in one of these works that I first tried Mrs. Monarch. Her husband came with her, to be useful if necessary—it was sufficiently clear that as a general thing he would prefer to come with her. At first I wondered if this were for "propriety's" sake—if he were going to be jealous and meddling. The idea was too tiresome, and if it had been confirmed it would speedily have brought our acquaintance to a close. But I soon saw there was nothing in it and that if he accompanied Mrs. Monarch it was—in addition to the chance of being wanted—simply because he had nothing else to do. When they were separate his occupation was gone and they never *had* been separate. I judged rightly that in their awkward situation their close union was their main comfort and that this union had no weak spot. It was a real marriage, an encouragement to the hesitating, a nut for pessimists to crack. Their address was humble—I remember afterwards thinking it had been the only thing about them that was really professional—and I could fancy the lamentable lodgings in which the Major would have been left alone. He could sit there more or less grimly with his wife—he couldn't sit there anyhow without her.

He had too much tact to try and make himself agreeable when he couldn't be useful; so when I was too absorbed in my work to talk he simply sat and waited. But I liked to hear him talk—it made my work, when not interrupting it, less mechanical, less special. To listen to him was to combine the excitement of going out with the economy of staying at home. There was only one hindrance—that I seemed not to know any of the people this brilliant couple had known. I think he wondered extremely, during the term of our intercourse, whom the deuce I *did* know. He hadn't a stray sixpence of an idea to fumble for, so we didn't spin it very fine; we confined ourselves to questions of leather and even of liquor—saddlers and breeches-makers and how to get excellent claret cheap—and matters like "good trains" and the habits of small game. His lore on these last subjects was astonishing—he managed to interweave the station-master with the ornithologist. When he couldn't talk about greater things he could talk cheerfully about smaller, and since I couldn't accompany him into reminiscences of the fashionable world he could lower the conversation without a visible effort to my level.

So earnest a desire to please was touching in a man who could so easily have knocked one down. He looked after the fire and had an opinion on the draught of the stove without my asking him, and I could see that he thought many of my arrangements not half knowing. I remember telling him that if I were only rich I'd offer him a salary to come and teach me how to live. Sometimes he gave a random sigh of which the essence might have been: "Give me even such a bare old barrack as *this,* and I'd do something with it!" When I wanted to use him he came alone; which was an illustration of the superior courage of women. His wife could bear her solitary second floor, and she was in general more discreet; showing by various small reserves that she was alive to the propriety of keeping our relations markedly professional—not letting them slide into sociability. She wished it to remain clear that she and the Major were employed, not cultivated, and if she approved of me as a superior, who could be kept in his place, she never thought me quite good enough for an equal.

She sat with great intensity, giving the whole of her mind to it, and was capable of remaining for an hour almost as motionless as before a photographer's lens. I could see she had been photographed often, but somehow the very habit that made her good for that purpose unfitted her for mine. At first I was extremely pleased with her ladylike air, and it was a satisfaction, on coming to follow her lines, to see how good they were and how far they could lead the pencil. But after a little skirmishing I began to find her too insurmountably stiff; do what I would with it my drawing looked like a photograph or a copy of a photograph. Her figure had no variety of expression—she herself had no sense of variety. You may say that this was my business and was only a question of placing her. Yet I placed her in every conceivable position and she managed to obliterate their differences. She was always a lady certainly, and into the bargain was always the same lady. She was the real thing, but always the same thing. There were moments when I rather writhed under the serenity of her confidence that she *was* the real thing. All her dealings with me and all her husband's were an implication that this was lucky for *me.* Meanwhile I found myself trying to invent types that approached her own, instead of making her own transform itself—in the clever way that was not impossible for instance to poor Miss Churm. Arrange as I would and take the precautions I would, she always came out, in my pictures, too tall—landing me in the dilemma of having represented a fascinating woman as seven feet high, which (out of respect perhaps to my own very much scantier inches) was far from my idea of such personage.

The case was worse with the Major—nothing I could do would keep *him* down, so that he became useful only for the representation of brawny giants. I adored variety and range, I cherished human accidents, the illustrative note; I wanted to characterise closely, and the thing in the world I most hated was the danger of being ridden by a type. I had quarrelled with some of my friends about it; I had parted company with them for maintaining that one *had* to be, and that if the type was beautiful—witness Raphael and Leonardo—the servitude was only a gain. I was neither Leonardo nor Raphael—I might only be a presumptuous young modern searcher; but I held that everything was to be sacrificed sooner than character. When they claimed that the obsessional form could easily *be* character I retorted, perhaps superficially, "Whose?" It couldn't be everybody's—it might end in being nobody's.

After I had drawn Mrs. Monarch a dozen times I felt surer even than before that the value of such a model as Miss Churm resided precisely in the fact that she had no positive stamp, combined of course with the other fact that what she did have was a curious and inexplicable talent for imitation. Her usual appearance was like a curtain which she could draw up at request for a capital performance. This performance was simply suggestive; but it was a word to the wise—it was vivid and pretty. Sometimes even I thought it, though she was plain herself, too insipidly pretty; I made it a reproach to her that the figures drawn from her were monotonously (*bêtement,* as we used to say) graceful. Nothing made her more angry: it was so much her pride to feel she could sit for characters that had nothing in common with each other. She would accuse me at such moments of taking away her "reputytion."

It suffered a certain shrinkage, this queer quantity, from the repeated visits of my new friends. Miss Churm was greatly in demand, never in want of employment, so I had no scruple in putting her off occasionally, to try them more at my ease. It was certainly amusing at first to do the real thing—it was amusing to do Major Monarch's trousers. They *were* the real thing, even if he did come out colossal. It was amusing to do his wife's back hair—it was so mathematically neat—and the particular "smart" tension of her tight stays. She lent herself especially to positions in which the face was somewhat averted or blurred; she abounded in ladylike back views and *profils perdus.* When she stood erect she took naturally one of the attitudes in which court-painters represent queens and princesses; so that I found myself wondering whether, to draw out this accomplishment, I couldn't get the editor of the *Cheapside* to publish a really royal romance, "A Tale of Buckingham Palace." Sometimes however the real thing and the make-believe came into contact; by which I mean that Miss Churm, keeping an appointment or coming to make one on days when I had much work in hand, encountered her invidious rivals. The encounter was not on their part, for they noticed her no more than if she had been the housemaid; not from intentional loftiness, but simply because as yet, professionally, they didn't know how to fraternise, as I could imagine they would have liked—or at least that the Major would. They couldn't talk about the omnibus—they always walked; and they didn't know what else to try—she wasn't interested in good trains or cheap claret. Besides, they must have felt—in the air—that she was amused at them, secretly derisive of their ever knowing how. She wasn't a person to conceal the limits of her faith if she had had a chance to show them. On the other hand Mrs. Monarch didn't think her tidy; for why else did she take pains to say to me—it was going out of the way, for Mrs. Monarch—that she didn't like dirty women?

One day when my young lady happened to be present with my other sitters— she even dropped in, when it was convenient, for a chat—I asked her to be so good as to lend a hand in getting tea, a service with which she was familiar and which was one of a class that, living as I did in a small way, with slender domestic resources, I often appealed to my models to render. They liked to lay hands on my property, to break the sitting, and sometimes the china—it made them feel Bohemian. The next time I saw Miss Churm after this incident she surprised me greatly by making a scene about it—she accused me of having wished to humiliate her. She hadn't resented the outrage at the time, but had seemed obliging and amused, enjoying the comedy of asking Mrs. Monarch, who sat vague and silent, whether she would have cream and sugar, and putting an exaggerated simper into the question. She had tried intonations—as if she too wished to pass for the real thing—till I was afraid my other visitors would take offence.

Oh they were determined not to do this, and their touching patience was the measure of their great need. They would sit by the hour, uncomplaining, till I was ready to use them; they would come back on the chance of being wanted and would walk away cheerfully if it failed. I used to go to the door with them to see in what magnificent order they retreated. I tried to find other employment for them—I introduced them to several artists. But they didn't "take," for reasons I could appreciate, and I became rather anxiously aware that after such disappointments they fell back upon me with a heavier weight. They did me the honor to think me most *their* form. They weren't romantic enough for the painters, and in those days there were few serious workers in black-and-white. Besides, they had an eye to the great job I had mentioned to them—they had secretly set their hearts on supplying the right essence for my pictorial vindication of our fine novelist. They knew that for this undertaking I should want no costume-effects, none of the frippery of past ages—that it was a case in which everything would be contemporary and satirical and presumably genteel. If I could work them into it their future would be assured, for the labour would of course be long and the occupation steady.

100   One day Mrs. Monarch came without her husband—she explained his absence by his having had to go to the City. While she sat there in her usual relaxed majesty there came at the door a knock which I immediately recognised as the subdued appeal of a model out of work. It was followed by the entrance of a young man whom I at once saw to be a foreigner and who proved in fact an Italian acquainted with no English word but my name, which he uttered in a way that made it seem to include all others. I hadn't then visited his country, nor was I proficient in his tongue; but as he was not so meanly constituted—what Italian is?—as to depend only on that member for expression he conveyed to me, in familiar but graceful mimicry, that he was in search of exactly the employment in which the lady before me was engaged. I was

not struck with him at first, and while I continued to draw I dropped few signs of interest or encouragement. He stood his ground however—not importunately, but with a dumb dog-like fidelity in his eyes that amounted to innocent impudence, the manner of a devoted servant—he might have been in the house for years—unjustly suspected. Suddenly it struck me that this very attitude and expression made a picture; whereupon I told him to sit down and wait till I should be free. There was another picture in the way he obeyed me, and I observed as I worked that there were others still in the way he looked wonderingly, with his head thrown back, about the high studio. He might have been crossing himself in Saint Peter's. Before I finished I said to myself "The fellow's a bankrupt orangemonger, but a treasure."

When Mrs. Monarch withdrew he passed across the room like a flash to open the door for her, standing there with the rapt pure gaze of the young Dante spellbound by the young Beatrice. As I never insisted, in such situations, on the blankness of the British domestic, I reflected that he had the making of a servant—and I needed one, but couldn't pay him to be only that—as well as of a model; in short I resolved to adopt my bright adventurer if he would agree to officiate in the double capacity. He jumped at my offer, and in the event my rashness—for I had really known nothing about him—wasn't brought home to me. He proved a sympathetic though a desultory ministrant, and had in a wonderful degree the *sentiment de la pose.* It was uncultivated, instinctive, a part of the happy instinct that had guided him to my door and helped him to spell out my name on the card nailed to it. He had had no other introduction to me than a guess, from the shape of my high north window, seen outside, that my place was a studio and that as a studio it would contain an artist. He had wandered to England in search of fortune, like other itinerants, and had embarked, with a partner and a small green hand-cart, on the sale of penny ices. The ices had melted away and the partner had dissolved in their train. My young man wore tight yellow trousers with reddish stripes and his name was Oronte. He was sallow but fair, and when I put him into some old clothes of my own he looked like an Englishman. He was as good as Miss Churm, who could look, when requested, like an Italian.

4

I thought Mrs. Monarch's face slightly convulsed when, on her coming back with her husband, she found Oronte installed. It was strange to have to recognise in a scrap of a lazzarone a competitor to her magnificent Major. It was she who scented danger first, for the Major was anecdotically unconscious. But Oronte gave us tea, with a hundred eager confusions—he had never been concerned in so queer a process— and I think she thought better of me for having at last an "establishment." They saw a couple of drawings that I had made of the establishment, and Mrs. Monarch hinted that it never would have struck her he had sat for them. "Now the drawings you make from *us,* they look exactly like us," she reminded me, smiling in triumph; and I recognized that this was indeed just their defect. When I drew the Monarchs I couldn't anyhow get away from them—get into the character I wanted to represent; and I hadn't the least desire my model should be discoverable in my picture. Miss Churm never was, and Mrs. Monarch thought I hid her, very properly, because she was vulgar; whereas if she was lost it was only as the dead who go to heaven are lost—in the gain of an angel the more.

By this time I had got a certain start with "Rutland Ramsay," the first novel in the great projected series; that is I had produced a dozen drawings, several with the help of the Major and his wife, and I had sent them in for approval. My understanding with the publishers, as I have already hinted, had been that I was to be left to do my work, in this particular case, as I liked, with the whole book committed to me; but my connexion with the rest of the series was only contingent. There were moments when, frankly, it *was* a comfort to have the real thing under one's hand; for there were characters in "Rutland Ramsay" that were very much like it. There were people presumably as erect as the Major and women of as good a fashion as Mrs. Monarch. There was a great deal of country-house life—treated, it is true, in a fine fanciful ironical generalised way—and there was a considerable implication of knickerbockers and kilts. There were certain things I had to settle at the outset; such things for instance as the exact appearance of the hero and the particular bloom and figure of the heroine. The author of course gave me a lead, but there was a margin for interpretation. I took the Monarchs into my confidence, I told them frankly what I was about, I mentioned my embarrassments and alternatives. "Oh take *him!*" Mrs. Monarch murmured sweetly, looking at her husband; and "What could you want better than my wife?" the Major enquired with the comfortable candour that now prevailed between us.

I wasn't obliged to answer these remarks—I was only obliged to place my sitters. I wasn't easy in mind, and I postponed a little timidly perhaps the solving of my question. The book was a large canvas, the other figures were numerous, and I worked off at first some of the episodes in which the hero and the heroine were not concerned. When once I had set *them* up I should have to stick to them—I couldn't make my young man seven feet high in one place and five feet nine in another. I inclined on the whole to the latter measurement, though the Major more than once reminded me that *he* looked about as young as any one. It was indeed quite possible to arrange him, for the figure, so that it would have been difficult to detect his age. After the spontaneous Oronte had been with me a month, and after I had given him to understand several times over that his native exuberance would presently constitute an insurmountable barrier to our further intercourse, I waked to a sense of his heroic capacity. He was only five feet seven, but the remaining inches were latent. I tried him almost secretly at first for I was really rather afraid of the judgment my other models would pass on such a choice. If they regarded Miss Churm as little better than a snare what would they think of the representation by a person so little the real thing as an Italian street-vendor of a protagonist formed by a public school?

105   If I went a little in fear of them it wasn't because they bullied me, because they had got an oppressive foothold, but because in their really pathetic decorum and mysteriously permanent newness they counted on me so intensely. I was therefore very glad when Jack Hawley came home: he was always of such good counsel. He painted badly himself, but there was no one like him for putting his finger on the place. He had been absent from England for a year; he had been somewhere—I don't

remember where—to get a fresh eye. I was in a good deal of dread of any such organ, but we were old friends; he had been away for months and a sense of emptiness
was creeping into my life. I hadn't dodged a missile for a year.

He came back with a fresh eye, but with the same old black velvet blouse, and
the first evening he spent in my studio we smoked cigarettes till the small hours. He
had done no work himself, he had only got the eye; so the field was clear for the production of my little things. He wanted to see what I had produced for the *Cheapside,*
but he was disappointed in the exhibition. That at least seemed the meaning of two
or three comprehensive groans which, as he lounged on my big divan, his leg folded
under him, looking at my latest drawings, issued from his lips with the smoke of the
cigarette.

"What's the matter with you?" I asked.

"What's the matter with *you?*"

"Nothing save that I'm mystified."

"You are indeed. You're quite off the hinge. What's the meaning of this new fad?"   110
And he tossed me, with visible irreverence, a drawing in which I happened to have depicted both my elegant models. I asked if he didn't think it good, and he replied that
it struck him as execrable, given the sort of thing I had always represented myself to
him as wishing to arrive at; but I let that pass—I was so anxious to see exactly what
he meant. The two figures in the picture looked colossal, but I supposed this was *not*
what he meant, inasmuch as, for aught he knew to the contrary, I might have been trying for some such effect. I maintained that I was working exactly in the same way as
when he last had done me the honour to tell me I might do something some day. "Well,
there's a screw loose somewhere," he answered; "wait a bit and I'll discover it." I depended upon him to do so: where else was the fresh eye? But he produced at last nothing more luminous than "I don't know—I don't like your types." This was lame for a
critic who had never consented to discuss with me anything but the question of execution, the direction of strokes and the mystery of values.

"In the drawings you've been looking at I think my types are very handsome."

"Oh they won't do!"

"I've been working with new models."

"I see you have. *They* won't do."

"Are you very sure of that?"   115

"Absolutely—they're stupid."

"You mean *I* am—for I ought to get round that."

"You *can't*—with such people. Who are they?"

I told him, so far as was necessary, and he concluded heartlessly:

"Ce sont des gens qu'il faut mettre à la porte."   120

"You've never seen them; they're awfully good"—I flew to their defence.

"Not seen them? Why all this recent work of yours drops to pieces with them.
It's all I want to see of them."

"No one else has said anything against it—the *Cheapside* people are pleased."

"Every one else is an ass, and the *Cheapside* people the biggest asses of all.
Come, don't pretend at this time of day to have pretty illusions about the public, especially about publishers and editors. It's not for *such* animals you work—it's for

those who know, *coloro che sanno;* so keep straight for *me* if you can't keep straight for yourself. There was a certain sort of thing you used to try for—and a very good thing it was. But this twaddle isn't *in* it." When I talked with Hawley later about "Rutland Ramsay" and its possible successors he declared that I must get back into my boat again or I should go to the bottom. His voice in short was the voice of warning.

125   I noted the warning, but I didn't turn my friends out of doors. They bored me a good deal; but the very fact that they bored me admonished me not to sacrifice them—if there was anything to be done with them—simply to irritation. As I look back at this phase they seem to me to have pervaded my life not a little. I have a vision of them as most of the time in my studio, seated against the wall on an old velvet bench to be out of the way, and resembling the while a pair of patient courtiers in a royal ante-chamber. I'm convinced that during the coldest weeks of the winter they held their ground because it saved them fire. Their newness was losing its gloss, and it was impossible not to feel them objects of charity. Whenever Miss Churm arrived they went away, and after I was fairly launched in "Rutland Ramsay" Miss Churm arrived pretty often. They managed to express to me tacitly that they supposed I wanted her for the low life of the book, and I let them suppose it, since they had attempted to study the work—it was lying about the studio—without discovering that it dealt only with the highest circles. They had dipped into the most brilliant of our novelists without deciphering many passages. I still took an hour from them, now and again, in spite of Jack Hawley's warning: it would be time enough to dismiss them, if dismissal should be necessary, when the rigour of the season was over. Hawley had made their acquaintance—he had met them at my fireside—and thought them a ridiculous pair. Learning that he was a painter they tried to approach him, to show him too that they were the real thing; but he looked at them, across the big room, as if they were miles away: they were a compendium of everything he most objected to in the social system of his country. Such people as that, all convention and patent-leather, with ejaculations that stopped conversation, had no business in a studio. A studio was a place to learn to see, and how could you see through a pair of feather-beds?

The main inconvenience I suffered at their hands was that at first I was shy of letting it break upon them that my artful little servant had begun to sit to me for "Rutland Ramsay." They knew I had been odd enough—they were prepared by this time to allow oddity to artists—to pick a foreign vagabond out of the streets when I might have had a person with whiskers and credentials; but it was some time before they learned how high I rated his accomplishments. They found him in an attitude more than once, but they never doubted I was doing him as an organ-grinder. There were several things they never guessed, and one of them was that for a striking scene in the novel, in which a footman briefly figured, it occurred to me to make use of Major Monarch as the menial. I kept putting this off, I didn't like to ask him to don the livery—besides the difficulty of finding a livery to fit him. At last, one day late in the winter, when I was at work on the despised Oronte, who caught one's idea on the wing, and was in the glow of feeling myself go very straight, they came in, the Major and his wife, with their society laugh about nothing (there was less and less to laugh at); came on like country-callers—they always reminded me of that—who have walked across the park after church and are presently persuaded to stay to luncheon. Luncheon was over, but they could stay to tea—I knew they wanted it. The fit was on me, however, and I couldn't let my ardour cool and my work wait, with the fading daylight, while my model prepared it. So I asked Mrs. Monarch if she would mind laying it out—a request which for an instant brought all the blood to her face. Her eyes were on her husband's for a second, and some mute telegraphy passed between them. Their folly was over the next instant; his cheerful shrewdness put an end to it. So far from pitying their wounded pride, I must add, I was moved to give it as complete a lesson as I could. They bustled about together and got out the cups and saucers and made the kettle boil. I know they felt as if they were waiting on my servant, and when the tea was prepared I said: "He'll have a cup, please—he's tired." Mrs. Monarch brought him one where he stood, and he took it from her, as if he had been a gentleman at a party squeezing a crush-hat with an elbow.

Then it came over me that she had made a great effort for me—made it with a kind of nobleness—and that I owed her a compensation. Each time I saw her after this I wondered what the compensation could be. I couldn't go on doing the wrong thing to oblige them. Oh it *was* the wrong thing, the stamp of the work for which they sat—Hawley was not the only person to say it now. I sent in a large number of the drawings I had made for "Rutland Ramsay," and I received a warning that was more to the point than Hawley's. The artistic adviser of the house for which I was working was of opinion that many of my illustrations were not what had been looked for. Most of these illustrations were the subjects in which the Monarchs had figured. Without going into the question of what *had* been looked for, I had to face the fact that at this rate I shouldn't get the other books to do. I hurled myself in despair on Miss Churm—I put her through all her paces. I not only adopted Oronte publicly as my hero, but one morning when the Major looked in to see if I didn't require him to finish a *Cheapside* figure for which he had begun to sit the week before, I told him I had changed my mind—I'd do the drawing from my man. At this my visitor turned pale and stood looking at me. "Is *he* your idea of an English gentleman?" he asked.

I was disappointed, I was nervous, I wanted to get on with my work; so I replied with irritation: "Oh my dear Major—I can't be ruined for *you!*"

It was a horrid speech, but he stood another moment—after which, without a word, he quitted the studio. I drew a long breath, for I said to myself that I shouldn't see him again. I hadn't told him definitely that I was in danger of having my work rejected, but I was vexed at his not having felt the catastrophe in the air, read with me the moral of our fruitless collaboration, the lesson that in the deceptive atmosphere of art even the highest respectability may fail of being plastic.

I didn't owe my friends money, but I did see them again. They reappeared together three days later, and, given all the other facts, there was something tragic in that one. It was a clear proof they could find nothing else in life to do. They had threshed the matter out in a dismal conference—they had digested the bad news that they were not in for the series. If they weren't useful to me even for the *Cheapside* their function seemed difficult to determine, and I could only judge at first that they had come, forgivingly, decorously, to take a last leave. This made me rejoice in secret that I had little leisure for a scene; for I had placed both my other models in position together and I was pegging away at a drawing from which I hoped to derive glory. It had been suggested by the passage in which Rutland Ramsay, drawing up a chair to Artemisia's piano-stool, says extraordinary things to her while she ostensibly fingers out a difficult piece of music. I had done Miss Churm at the piano before—it was an attitude in which she knew how to take on an absolutely poetic grace. I wished the two figures to "compose" together with intensity, and my little Italian had entered perfectly into my conception. The pair were vividly before me, the piano had been pulled out; it was a charming show of blended youth and murmured love, which I had only to catch and keep. My visitors stood and looked at it, and I was friendly to them over my shoulder.

They made no response, but I was used to silent company and went on with my work, only a little disconcerted—even though exhilarated by the sense that *this* was at least the ideal thing—at not having got rid of them after all. Presently I heard Mrs. Monarch's sweet voice beside or rather above me: "I wish her hair were a little better done." I looked up and she was staring with a strange fixedness at Miss Churm, whose back was turned to her. "Do you mind my just touching it?" she went on—a question which made me spring up for an instant as with the instinctive fear that she might do the young lady a harm. But she quieted me with a glance I shall never forget—I confess I should like to have been able to paint *that*—and went for a moment to my model. She spoke to her softly, laying a hand on her shoulder and bending over her; and as the girl, understanding, gratefully assented, she disposed her rough curls, with a few quick passes, in such a way as to make Miss Churm's head twice as charming. It was one of the most heroic personal services I've ever seen rendered. Then Mrs. Monarch turned away with a low sigh and, looking about her as if for something to do, stooped to the floor with a noble humility and picked up a dirty rag that had dropped out of my paint-box.

The Major meanwhile had also been looking for something to do, and, wandering to the other end of the studio, saw before him my breakfast-things neglected, unremoved. "I say, can't I be useful *here?*" he called out to me with an irrepressible quaver. I assented with a laugh that I fear was awkward, and for the next ten minutes, while I worked, I heard the light clatter of china and the tinkle of spoons and glass. Mrs. Monarch assisted her husband—they washed up my crockery, they put it away. They wandered off into my little scullery, and I afterwards found that they had cleaned my knives and that my slender stock of plate had an unprecedented surface. When it came over me, the latent eloquence of what they were doing, I confess that my drawing was blurred for a moment—the picture swam. They had accepted their failure, but they couldn't accept their fate. They had bowed their heads in bewilderment to the perverse and cruel law in virtue of which the real thing could be so much less precious than the unreal; but they didn't want to starve. If my servants were my models; then my models might be my servants. They would reverse the parts—the others would sit for the ladies and gentlemen and *they* would do the work. They would still be in the studio—it was an intense dumb appeal to me not to turn them out. "Take us on," they wanted to say—"we'll do *anything*."

My pencil dropped from my hand; my sitting was spoiled and I got rid of my sitters, who were also evidently rather mystified and awestruck. Then, alone with the

Major and his wife I had a most uncomfortable moment. He put their prayer into a single sentence: "I say, you know—just let *us* do for you, can't you?" I couldn't—it was dreadful to see them emptying my slops; but I pretended I could, to oblige them, for about a week. Then I gave them a sum of money to go away, and I never saw them again. I obtained the remaining books, but my friend Hawley repeats that Major and Mrs. Monarch did me a permanent harm, got me into false ways. If it be true I'm content to have paid the price—for the memory.

QUESTIONS FOR DISCUSSION AND WRITING

1. How do the first two parts of the story establish the possibilities and limitations of "experimenting" with the real thing? How do the "warnings" in Part 4 help the narrator decide to end the experiment?

2. How does the narrator characterize the Monarchs? Why is it important that the narrator remarks that "it was odd how quickly I was sure of everything that concerns them"? By contrast, how does the narrator characterize Miss Churm and Oronte?

3. What does the narrator mean by saying "a studio was a place to learn to see"? What prevents him from seeing the Monarchs in his studio? Why might they be more accurately "seen" by photographers?

4. From the beginning, the first-person narrator admits his preference for "the represented subject over the real one." Why then does he continue to use the Monarchs as models? Why does he treasure their memory even though they may have harmed his painting?

5. What does this story reveal about the "alchemy of art"? What part does the artist have in making the real thing seem *real?*

Stories for Comparison

Ann Beattie's "The Working Girl (pages 285–290); Julio Cortázar's "We Love Glenda So Much" (pages 448–453).

57

···

S A R A H   O R N E   J E W E T T

A White Heron

SARAH ORNE JEWETT (1849–1909) was born in South Berwick, Maine,
the daughter of a country doctor. Although she attended Berwick Academy,
Jewett's real education came from reading and accompanying her father as he
called on sick people in the remote countryside. Prompted in part by the example of Harriet Beecher Stowe's novel about Maine, *The Pearl of Orr's Island* (1862), Jewett began writing sketches and stories about her native region. At the age of nineteen, she published her first story, "Mr. Bruce," in *The
Atlantic Monthly.* Her editor, William Dean Howells, encouraged her to publish *Deephaven,* a collection of her stories, in 1877. Her friendship with Anne
Fields, her publisher's wife, brought her frequently to Boston and resulted in
extensive European travel. However, she always returned to her native town,
where she wrote books such as the biography of her father, *A Country Doctor*
(1884), novels such as *A Marsh Island* (1886), and numerous short stories,
the best of which were collected in volumes such as *A White Heron* (1886)
and *The Country of the Pointed Firs* (1896). "A White Heron," the title story
from her 1886 collection, tells of a young girl's choice between the treasures
she can buy with money and the treasures she is given by nature.

I

The woods were already filled with shadows one June evening, just before eight
o'clock, though a bright sunset still glimmered faintly among the trunks of the
trees. A little girl was driving home her cow, a plodding, dilatory, provoking creature
in her behavior, but a valued companion for all that. They were going away from the
western light, and striking deep into the dark woods, but their feet were familiar with
the path, and it was no matter whether their eyes could see it or not.

There was hardly a night the summer through when the old cow could be found
waiting at the pasture bars; on the contrary, it was her greatest pleasure to hide herself away among the high huckleberry bushes, and though she wore a loud bell she
had made the discovery that if one stood perfectly still it would not ring. So Sylvia
had to hunt for her until she found her, and call Co'! Co'! with never an answering
Moo, until her childish patience was quite spent. If the creature had not given good

milk and plenty of it, the case would have seemed very different to her owners. Besides, Sylvia had all the time there was, and very little use to make of it. Sometimes in pleasant weather it was a consolation to look upon the cow's pranks as an intelligent attempt to play hide and seek, and as the child had no playmates she lent herself to this amusement with a good deal of zest. Though this chase had been so long that the wary animal herself had given an unusual signal of her whereabouts, Sylvia had only laughed when she came upon Mistress Moolly at the swamp-side, and urged her affectionately homeward with a twig of birch leaves. The old cow was not inclined to wander farther, she even turned in the right direction for once as they left the pasture, and stepped along the road at a good pace. She was quite ready to be milked now, and seldom stopped to browse. Sylvia wondered what her grandmother would say because they were so late. It was a great while since she had left home at half past five o'clock, but everybody knew the difficulty of making this errand a short one. Mrs. Tilley had chased the horned torment too many summer evenings herself to blame any one else for lingering, and was only thankful as she waited that she had Sylvia, nowadays, to give such valuable assistance. The good woman suspected that Sylvia loitered occasionally on her own account; there never was such a child for straying about out-of-doors since the world was made! Everybody said that it was a good change for a little maid who had tried to grow for eight years in a crowded manufacturing town, but, as for Sylvia herself, it seemed as if she never had been alive at all before she came to live at the farm. She thought often with wistful compassion of a wretched dry geranium that belonged to a town neighbor.

"'Afraid of folks,'" old Mrs. Tilley said to herself, with a smile, after she had made the unlikely choice of Sylvia from her daughter's houseful of children, and was returning to the farm. "'Afraid of folks,' they said! I guess she won't be troubled no great with 'em up to the old place!" When they reached the door of the lonely house and stopped to unlock it, and the cat came to purr loudly, and rub against them, a deserted pussy, indeed, but fat with young robins, Sylvia whispered that this was a beautiful place to live in, and she never should wish to go home.

The companions followed the shady wood-road, the cow taking slow steps, and the child very fast ones. The cow stopped long at the brook to drink, as if the pasture were not half a swamp, and Sylvia stood still and waited, letting her bare feet cool themselves in the shoal water, while the great twilight moths struck softly against her. She waded on through the brook as the cow moved away, and listened to the thrushes with a heart that beat fast with pleasure. There was a stirring in the great boughs overhead. They were full of little birds and beasts that seemed to be wide-awake, and going about their world, or else saying good-night to each other in sleepy twitters. Sylvia herself felt sleepy as she walked along. However, it was not much farther to the house, and the air was soft and sweet. She was not often in the woods so late as this, and it made her feel as if she were a part of the gray shadows and the moving leaves. She was just thinking how long it seemed since she first came to the farm a year ago, and wondering if everything went on in the noisy town just the same as when she was there; the thought of the great red-faced boy who used to chase and frighten her made her hurry along the path to escape from the shadow of the trees.

5   Suddenly this little woods-girl is horror-stricken to hear a clear whistle not very far away. Not a bird's whistle, which would have a sort of friendliness, but a boy's whistle, determined, and somewhat aggressive. Sylvia left the cow to whatever sad fate might await her, and stepped discreetly aside into the bushes, but she was just too late. The enemy had discovered her, and called out in a very cheerful and persuasive tone, "Halloa, little girl, how far is it to the road?" and trembling Sylvia answered almost inaudibly, "A good ways."

She did not dare to look boldly at the tall young man, who carried a gun over his shoulder, but she came out of her bush and again followed the cow, while he walked alongside.

"I have been hunting for some birds," the stranger said kindly, "and I have lost my way, and need a friend very much. Don't be afraid," he added gallantly. "Speak up and tell me what your name is, and whether you think I can spend the night at your house, and go out gunning early in the morning."

Sylvia was more alarmed than before. Would not her grandmother consider her much to blame? But who could have foreseen such an accident as this? It did not appear to be her fault, and she hung her head as if the stem of it were broken, but managed to answer, "Sylvy," with much effort when her companion again asked her name.

Mrs. Tilley was standing in the doorway when the trio came into view. The cow gave a loud moo by way of explanation.

10   "Yes, you'd better speak up for yourself, you old trial! Where'd she tucked herself away this time, Sylvy?" Sylvia kept an awed silence; she knew by instinct that her grandmother did not comprehend the gravity of the situation. She must be mistaking the stranger for one of the farmer-lads of the region.

The young man stood his gun beside the door, and dropped a heavy game-bag beside it; then he bade Mrs. Tilley good-evening, and repeated his wayfarer's story, and asked if he could have a night's lodging.

"Put me anywhere you like," he said. "I must be off early in the morning, before day; but I am very hungry, indeed. You can give me some milk at any rate, that's plain."

"Dear sakes, yes," responded the hostess, whose long slumbering hospitality seemed to be easily awakened. "You might fare better if you went out on the main road a mile or so, but you're welcome to what we've got. I'll milk right off, and you make yourself at home. You can sleep on husks or feathers," she proffered graciously. "I raised them all myself. There's good pasturing for geese just below here towards the ma'sh. Now step round and set a plate for the gentleman, Sylvy!" And Sylvia promptly stepped. She was glad to have something to do, and she was hungry herself.

It was a surprise to find so clean and comfortable a dwelling in this New England wilderness. The young man had known the horrors of its most primitive housekeeping, and the dreary squalor of that level of society which does not rebel at the companionship of hens. This was the best thrift of an old-fashioned farmstead, though on such a small scale that it seemed like a hermitage. He listened eagerly to the old woman's quaint talk, he watched Sylvia's pale face and shining gray eyes with ever growing enthusiasm, and insisted that this was the best supper he had eaten for a month; then, afterward, the new-made friends sat down in the doorway together while the moon came up.

Soon it would be berry-time, and Sylvia was a great help at picking. The cow was a good milker, though a plaguy thing to keep track of, the hostess gossiped frankly, adding presently that she had buried four children, so that Sylvia's mother, and a son (who might be dead) in California were all the children she had left. "Dan, my boy, was a great hand to go gunning," she explained sadly. "I never wanted for pa'tridges or gray squer'ls while he was to home. He's been a great wand'rer, I expect, and he's no hand to write letters. There, I don't blame him, I'd ha' seen the world myself if it had been so I could."

"Sylvia takes after him," the grandmother continued affectionately, after a minute's pause. "There ain't a foot o'ground she don't know her way over, and the wild creature's counts her one o'themselves. Squer'ls she'll tame to come an' feed right out o' her hands, and all sorts o'birds. Last winter she got the jay-birds to bangeing here, and I believe she'd 'a' scanted herself of her own meals to have plenty to throw out amongst 'em, if I hadn't kep' watch. Anything but crows, I tell her, I'm willin' to help support—though Dan he went an' tamed one o' them that did seem to have reason same as folks. It was round here a good spell after he went away. Dan an' his father they didn't hitch—but he never held up his head ag'in after Dan had dared him an' gone off."

The guest did not notice this hint of family sorrows in his eager interest in something else.

"So Sylvy knows all about birds, does she?" he exclaimed, as he looked round at the little girl who sat, very demure but increasingly sleepy, in the moonlight. "I am making a collection of birds myself. I have been at it ever since I was a boy." (Mrs. Tilley smiled.) "There are two or three very rare ones I have been hunting for these five years. I mean to get them on my own ground if they can be found."

"Do you cage 'em up?" asked Mrs. Tilley doubtfully, in response to this enthusiastic announcement.

"Oh, no, they're stuffed and preserved, dozens and dozens of them," said the ornithologist, "and I have shot or snared every one myself. I caught a glimpse of a white heron three miles from here on Saturday, and I have followed it in this direction. They have never been found in this district at all. The little white heron, it is," and he turned again to look at Sylvia with the hope of discovering that the rare bird was one of her acquaintances.

But Sylvia was watching a hop-toad in the narrow footpath.

"You would know the heron if you saw it," the stranger continued eagerly. "A queer tall white bird with soft feathers and long thin legs. And it would have a nest perhaps in the top of a high tree, made of sticks, something like a hawk's nest."

Sylvia's heart gave a wild beat; she knew that strange white bird, and had once stolen softly near where it stood in some bright green swamp grass, away over at the other side of the woods. There was an open place where the sunshine always seemed strangely yellow and hot, where tall, nodding rushes grew, and her grandmother had warned her that she might sink in the soft black mud underneath and never be heard of more. Not far beyond were the salt marshes and beyond those was the sea, the sea which Sylvia wondered and dreamed about, but never had looked upon, though its great voice could often be heard above the noise of the woods on stormy nights.

"I can't think of anything I should like so much as to find that heron's nest," the handsome stranger was saying. "I would give ten dollars to anybody who could show it to me," he added desperately, "and I mean to spend my whole vacation hunting for it if need be. Perhaps it was only migrating, or had been chased out of its own region by some bird of prey."

25   Mrs. Tilley gave amazed attention to all this, but Sylvia still watched the toad, not divining, as she might have done at some calmer time, that the creature wished to get to its hole under the doorstep, and was much hindered by the unusual spectators at that hour of the evening. No amount of thought, that night, could decide how many wished-for treasures the ten dollars, so lightly spoken of, would buy.

The next day the young sportsman hovered about the woods, and Sylvia kept him company, having lost her first fear of the friendly lad, who proved to be most kind and sympathetic. He told her many things about the birds and what they knew and where they lived and what they did with themselves. And he gave her a jack-knife, which she thought as great a treasure as if she were a desert-islander. All day long he did not once make her troubled or afraid except when he brought down some unsuspecting singing creature from its bough. Sylvia would have liked him vastly better without his gun; she could not understand why he killed the very birds he seemed to like so much. But as the day waned, Sylvia still watched the young man with loving admiration. She had never seen anybody so charming and delightful; the woman's heart, asleep in the child, was vaguely thrilled by a dream of love. Some premonition of that great power stirred and swayed these young foresters who traversed the solemn woodlands with soft-footed silent care. They stopped to listen to a bird's song; they pressed forward again eagerly, parting the branches—speaking to each other rarely and in whispers; the young man going first and Sylvia following, fascinated, a few steps behind, with her gray eyes dark with excitement.

She grieved because the longed-for white heron was elusive, but she did not lead the guest, she only followed, and there was no such thing as speaking first. The sound of her own unquestioned voice would have terrified her—it was hard enough to answer yes or no when there was need of that. At last evening began to fall, and they drove the cow home together, and Sylvia smiled with pleasure when they came to the place where she heard the whistle and was afraid only the night before.

2

Half a mile from home, at the farther edge of the woods, where the land was highest, a great pine-tree stood, the last of its generation. Whether it was left for a boundary mark, or for what reason, no one could say; the woodchoppers who had felled its mates were dead and gone long ago, and a whole forest of sturdy trees, pines and oaks and maples, had grown again. But the stately head of this old pine towered above them all and made a landmark for sea and shore miles and miles away. Sylvia knew it well. She had always believed that whoever climbed to the top of it could see the ocean; and the little girl had often laid her hand on the great rough trunk and looked up wistfully at those dark boughs that the wind always stirred, no matter how hot and still the air might be below. Now she thought of the tree with a new excitement, for why, if one climbed it at break of day, could not one see all the world, and easily discover whence the white heron flew, and mark the place, and find the hidden nest?

What a spirit of adventure, what wild ambition! What fancied triumph and delight and glory for the later morning when she could make known the secret! It was almost too real and too great for the childish heart to bear.

All night the door of the little house stood open, and the whippoorwills came and sang upon the very step. The young sportsman and his old hostess were sound asleep, but Sylvia's great design kept her broad awake and watching. She forgot to think of sleep. The short summer night seemed as long as the winter darkness, and at last when the whippoorwills ceased, and she was afraid the morning would after all come too soon, she stole out of the house and followed the pasture path through the woods, hastening toward the open ground beyond, listening with a sense of comfort and companionship to the drowsy twitter of a half-awakened bird, whose perch she had jarred in passing. Alas, if the great wave of human interest which flooded for the first time this dull little life should sweep away the satisfactions of an existence heart to heart with nature and the dumb life of the forest! 30

There was the huge tree asleep yet in the paling moonlight, and small and hopeful Sylvia began with utmost bravery to mount to the top of it, with tingling, eager blood coursing the channels of her whole frame, with her bare feet and fingers, that pinched and held like bird's claws to the monstrous ladder reaching up, up, almost to the sky itself. First she must mount the white oak tree that grew alongside, where she was almost lost among the dark branches and the green leaves heavy and wet with dew; a bird fluttered off its nest, and a red squirrel ran to and fro and scolded pettishly at the harmless house-breaker. Sylvia felt her way easily. She had often climbed there, and knew that higher still one of the oak's upper branches chafed against the pine trunk, just where its lower boughs were set close together. There, when she made the dangerous pass from one tree to the other, the great enterprise would really begin.

She crept out along the swaying oak limb at last, and took the daring step across into the old pine-tree. The way was harder than she thought; she must reach far and hold fast, the sharp dry twigs caught and held her and scratched her like angry talons, the pitch made her thin little fingers clumsy and stiff as she went round and round the tree's great stem, higher and higher upward. The sparrows and robins in the woods below were beginning to wake and twitter to the dawn, yet it seemed much lighter there aloft in the pine-tree, and the child knew that she must hurry if her project were to be of any use.

The tree seemed to lengthen itself out as she went up, and to reach farther and farther upward. It was like a great main-mast to the voyaging earth; it must truly have been amazed that morning through all its ponderous frame as it felt this determined spark of human spirit creeping and climbing from higher branch to branch. Who knows how steadily the least twigs held themselves to advantage this light, weak creature on her way! The old pine must have loved his new dependent. More than all the hawks, and bats, and moths, and even the sweet-voiced thrushes, was the brave, beating heart of the solitary gray-eyed child. And the tree stood still and held away the winds that June morning while the dawn grew bright in the east.

Sylvia's face was like a pale star, if one had seen it from the ground, when the last thorny bough was past, and she stood trembling and tired but wholly triumphant, high in the tree-top. Yes, there was the sea with the dawning sun making a golden dazzle over it, and toward that glorious east flew two hawks with slow-moving pinions. How low they looked in the air from that height when before one had only seen them far up, and dark against the blue sky. Their gray feathers were as soft as moths; they seemed only a little way from the tree, and Sylvia felt as if she too could go flying away among the clouds. Westward, the woodlands and farms reached miles and miles into the distance; here and there were church steeples, and white villages; truly it was a vast and awesome world.

35   The birds sang louder and louder. At last the sun came up bewilderingly bright. Sylvia could see the white sails of ships out at sea, and the clouds that were purple and rose-colored and yellow at first began to fade away. Where was the white heron's nest in the sea of green branches, and was this wonderful sight and pageant of the world the only reward for having climbed to such a giddy height? Now look down again, Sylvia, where the green marsh is set among the shining birches and dark hemlocks; there where you saw the white heron once you will see him again; look, look! a white spot of him like a single floating feather comes up from the dead hemlock and grows larger, and rises, and comes close at last, and goes by the landmark pine with a steady sweep of wing and outstretched slender neck and crested head. And wait! wait! do not move a foot or a finger, little girl, do not send an arrow of light and consciousness from your two eager eyes, for the heron has perched on a pine bough not far beyond yours, and cries back to his mate on the nest, and plumes his feathers for the new day!

The child gives a long sigh a minute later when a company of shouting cat-birds comes also to the tree, and vexed by their fluttering and lawlessness the solemn heron goes away. She knows his secret now, the wild, light, slender bird that floats and wavers, and goes back like an arrow presently to his home in the green world beneath. Then Sylvia, well satisfied, makes her perilous way down again, not daring to look far below the branch she stands on, ready to cry sometimes because her fingers ache and her lamed feet slip. Wondering over and over again what the stranger would say to her, and what he would think when she told him how to find his way straight to the heron's nest.

"Sylvy, Sylvy!" called the busy old grandmother again and again, but nobody answered, and the small husk bed was empty, and Sylvia had disappeared.

The guest waked from a dream, and remembering his day's pleasure hurried to dress himself that it might sooner begin. He was sure from the way the shy little girl looked once or twice yesterday that she had at least seen the white heron, and now she must really be persuaded to tell. Here she comes now, paler than ever, and her worn old frock is torn and tattered, and smeared with pine pitch. The grandmother and the sportsman stand in the door together and question her, and the splendid moment has come to speak of the dead hemlock-tree by the green marsh.

But Sylvia does not speak after all, though the old grandmother fretfully rebukes her, and the young man's kind appealing eyes are looking straight in her own. He can make them rich with money; he has promised it, and they are poor now. He is so well worth making happy, and he waits to hear the story she can tell.

No, she must keep silence! What is it that suddenly forbids her and makes her dumb? Has she been nine years growing, and now, when the great world for the first time puts out a hand to her, must she thrust it aside for a bird's sake? The murmur of the pine's green branches is in her ears, she remembers how the white heron came flying through the golden air and how they watched the sea and the morning together, and Sylvia cannot speak, she cannot tell the heron's secret and give its life away.

Dear loyalty, that suffered a sharp pang as the guest went away disappointed later in the day, that could have served and followed him and loved him as a dog loves! Many a night Sylvia heard the echo of his whistle haunting the pasture path as she came home with the loitering cow. She forgot even her sorrow at the sharp report of his gun and the piteous sight of thrushes and sparrows dropping silent to the ground, their songs hushed and their pretty feathers stained and wet with blood. Were the birds better friends than their hunter might have been—who can tell? Whatever treasures were lost to her, wood-lands and summer-time, remember! Bring your gifts and graces and tell your secrets to this lonely country child!

QUESTIONS FOR DISCUSSION AND WRITING

1. What is the major conflict Sylvia must resolve in the story? What motive prompts her to climb the pine tree? What decision does she make once she has made the climb?

2. How do Sylvia's mother and grandmother describe her? How does Sylvia characterize herself? Why is she attracted to the young man with the gun?

3. How does the rural setting for this story help shape Sylvia's attitudes and values? For example, why does she feel that "she never had been alive at all before she came to live on the farm"?

4. Although most of the story is told from Sylvia's point of view, the author shifts perspective several times. What kind of information does Jewett convey from these other perspectives?

5. In what sense does the last paragraph state the theme of the story? How would the omission of this paragraph change the story? Explain your answer.

Stories for Comparison

Ellen Gilchrist's "Among the Mourners" (pages 92–99); Alice Munro's "Wild Swans" (pages 927–935).

58

···

CHARLES   JOHNSON

The Sorcerer's Apprentice

CHARLES JOHNSON was born in 1948 in Evanston, Illinois, and educated
at Southern Illinois University and the State University of New York at Stony
Brook. He worked as a cartoonist and reporter for the *Chicago Tribune* and
as a member of the art staff at *St. Louis Proud* before accepting a position as
professor of English at the University of Washington, Seattle. Under the tute-
lage of the late author John Gardner, Johnson published his first novel, *Faith
and the Good Thing* (1974), a humorous folktale of a Southern black girl's
trip to Chicago. Johnson's second novel, *Oxherding Tale* (1982), a modern,
comic, philosophical slave narrative, tells of a young herdsman's search for
his rebellious ox. Johnson has also written for two collections of drawings,
Black Humor (1970) and *Half-Past Nation Time* (1972); written numerous
scripts for PBS, most notably "Charlie's Pad" (1970) and "Booker" (1983);
and published a collection of short stories, *The Sorcerer's Apprentice* (1986).
His third novel, *Middle Passage* (1990), won the National Book Award for
fiction. In "The Sorcerer's Apprentice," the title story from that collection, a
young boy attempts to understand the sorcerer's real lesson.

There was a time, long ago, when many sorcerers lived in South Carolina, men
not long from slavery who remembered the white magic of the Ekpe Cults and
the Cameroons, and by far the greatest of these wizards was a blacksmith named
Rubin Bailey. Believing he was old, and would soon die, the Sorcerer decided to pass
his learning along to an apprentice. From a family near Abbeville he selected a boy,
Allan, whose father, Richard Jackson, Rubin once healed after an accident, and for
this Allan loved the Sorcerer, especially the effects of his craft, which comforted the
sick, held back evil, and blighted the enemies of newly freed slaves with locusts and
bad health. "My house," Richard told the wizard, "has been honored." His son swore
to serve his teacher faithfully, then those who looked to the Sorcerer, in all ways.
With his father's blessing, the boy moved his belongings into the Sorcerer's home, a
houseboat covered with strips of scrap-metal, on the river.

But Rubin Bailey's first teachings seemed to Allan to be no teachings at all.
"Bring in fresh water," Rubin told his apprentice. "Scrape barnacles off the boat." He

never spoke of sorcery. Around the boy he tied his blacksmith's apron, and guided his hands in hammering out the horseshoes Rubin sold in town, but not once in the first month did Rubin pass along the recipes for magic. Patiently, Allan performed these duties in perfect submission to the Sorcerer, for it seemed rude to express displeasure to a man he wished to emulate, but his heart knocked for the higher knowledge, the techniques that would, he hoped, work miracles.

At last, as they finished a meal of boiled pork and collards one evening, he complained bitterly: "You haven't told me anything yet!" Allan regretted this outburst immediately, and lowered his head. "Have I done wrong?"

For a moment the Sorcerer was silent. He spiced his coffee with rum, dipped in his bread, chewed slowly, then looked up, steadily, at the boy. "You are the best of students. And you wish to do good, but you can't be too faithful, or too eager, or the good becomes evil."

"Now I don't understand," Allan said. "By themselves the tricks aren't good *or* 5 evil, and if you plan to do good, then the results must be good."

Rubin exhaled, finished his coffee, then shoved his plate toward the boy. "Clean the dishes," he said. Then, more gently: "What I know has worked I will teach. There is no certainty these things can work for you, or even for me, a second time. White magic comes and goes. I'm teaching you a trade, Allan. You will never starve. This is because after fifty years, I still can't foresee if an incantation will be magic or foolishness."

These were not, of course, the answers Allan longed to hear. He said, "Yes, sir," and quietly cleared away their dishes. If he had replied aloud to Rubin, as he did silently while toweling dry their silverware later that night, he would have told the Sorcerer, "You are the greatest magician in the world because you have studied magic and the long-dead masters of magic, and I believe, even if you do not, that the secret of doing good is a good heart and having a hundred spells at your disposal, so I will study everything—the words and timbre and tone of your voice as you conjure, and listen to those you have heard. Then I, too, will have magic and can do good." He washed his underwear in the moonlight, as is fitting for a fledgling magician, tossed his dishpan water into the river, and, after hanging his washpail on a hook behind Rubin's front door, undressed, and fell asleep with these thoughts: To do good is a very great thing, the only thing, but a magician must be able to conjure at a moment's notice. Surely it is all a question of know-how.

So it was that after a few months the Sorcerer's apprentice learned well and quickly when Rubin Bailey finally began to teach. In Allan's growth was the greatest joy. Each spell he showed proudly to his father and Richard's friends when he traveled home once a year. Unbeknownst to the Sorcerer, he held simple exhibits for their entertainment—harmless prestidigitation like throwing his voice or levitating logs stacked by the toolshed. However pleased Richard might have been, he gave no sign. Allan's father never joked or laughed too loudly. He was the sort of man who held his feelings in, and people took this for strength. Allan's mother, Beatrice, a tall, thick-waisted woman, had told him (for Richard would not) how when she was carrying Allan, they rode a haywagon to a scrub-ball in Abbeville on Freedom Day. Richard fell beneath the wagon. A wheel smashed his thumb open to the bone.

"Somebody better go for Rubin Bailey," was all Richard said, and he stared like it might be a stranger's hand. And Allan remembered Richard toiling so long in the sun he couldn't eat some evenings unless he first emptied his stomach by forcing himself to vomit. His father squirreled away money in their mattresses, saving for seven years to buy the land they worked. When he had $600—half what they needed—he grew afraid of theft, so Beatrice took their money to one of the banks in town. She stood in line behind a northern-looking Negro who said his name was Grady Armstrong. "I work for the bank across the street," he told Beatrice. "You wouldn't be interested in part-time work, would you? We need a woman to clean, someone reliable, but she has to keep her savings with us." Didn't they need the money? Beatrice would ask Allan, later, when Richard left them alone at night. Wouldn't the extra work help her husband? She followed Grady Armstrong, whose easy, loose-hinged walk led them to the second bank across the street. "Have you ever deposited money before?" asked Grady. "No," she said. Taking her envelope, he said, "Then I'll do it for you." On the boardwalk, Beatrice waited. And waited. After five minutes, she opened the door, found no Grady Armstrong, and flew screaming the fifteen miles back to the fields and Richard, who listened and chewed his lip, but said nothing. He leaned, Allan remembered, in the farmhouse door, smoking his cigars and watching only Lord knew what in the darkness—exactly as he stood the following year, when Beatrice, after swallowing rat poison, passed on.

Allan supposed it was risky to feel if you had grown up, like Richard, in a world of nightriders. There was too much to lose. Any attachment ended in separation, grief. If once you let yourself care, the crying might never stop. So he assumed his father was pleased with his apprenticeship to Rubin, though hearing him say this would have meant the world to Allan. He did not mind that somehow the Sorcerer's personality seemed to permeate each spell like sweat staining fresh wood, because this, too, seemed to be the way of things. The magic was Rubin Bailey's, but when pressed, the Sorcerer confessed that the spells had been in circulation for centuries. They were a web of history and culture, like the king-sized quilts you saw as curiosities at country fairs, sewn by every woman in Abbeville, each having finished only a section, a single flower perhaps, so no man, strictly speaking, could own a mystic spell. "But when you kill a bird by pointing," crabbed Rubin from his rocking chair, "you don't *haveta* wave your left hand in the air and pinch your forefinger and thumb together like I do."

10   "Did I do that?" asked Allan.

Rubin hawked and spit over the side of the houseboat. "Every time."

"I just wanted to get it right." Looking at his hand, he felt ashamed—he was, after all, right-handed—then shoved it deep into his breeches. "The way you do it is so beautiful."

"I know." Rubin laughed. He reached into his coat, brought out his pipe, and looked for matches. Allan stepped inside, and the Sorcerer shouted behind him, "You shouldn't do it because my own teacher, who wore out fifteen flying carpets in his lifetime, told me it was wrong."

"Wrong?" The boy returned. He held a match close to the bowl of Rubin's pipe, cupping the flame. "Then why do you do it?"

"It works best for me that way, Allan. I have arthritis." He slanted his eyes left 15
at his pupil. "Do you?"

The years passed, and Allan improved, even showing a certain flair, a style all
his own that pleased Rubin, who praised the boy for his native talent, which did not
come from knowledge and, it struck Allan, was wholly unreliable. When Esther
Peters, a seamstress, broke her hip, it was not Rubin who the old woman called, but
young Allan, who sat stiffly on a fiddle-back chair by her pallet, the fingers of his left
hand spread over the bony ledge of her brow and rheumy eyes, whispering the rune
that lifted her pain after Esther stopped asking, "Does he know what he doing,
Rubin? This ain't how you did when I caught my hand in that cotton gin." Afterwards, as they walked the dark footpath leading back to the river, Rubin in front, the
Sorcerer shared a fifth with the boy and paid him a terrifying compliment: "That was
the best I've seen anybody do the spell for exorcism." He stroked his pupil's head.
"God took *holt* of you back there—I don't see how you can do it that good again."
The smile at the corners of Allan's mouth weighed a ton. He handed back Rubin's
bottle, and said, "Me neither." The Sorcerer's flattery, if this was flattery, suspi-
ciously resembled Halloween candy with hemlock inside. Allan could not speak to
Rubin the rest of that night.

In the old days of sorcery, it often happened that pupils came to mistrust most
their finest creations, those frighteningly effortless works that flew mysteriously
from their lips when they weren't looking, and left the apprentice feeling, despite his
pride, as baffled as his audience and afraid for his future—this was most true when
the compliments compared a fledgling wizard to other magicians, as if the apprentice had achieved nothing new, or on his own. This is how Allan felt. The charm that
cured Esther had whipped through him like wind through a reedpipe, or—more exactly, like music struggling to break free, liberate its volume and immensity from the
confines of wood and brass. It made him feel unessential, anonymous, like a tool in
which the spell sang itself, briefly borrowing his throat, then tossed him, Allan, aside
when the miracle ended. To be so used was thrilling, but it gave the boy many bad
nights. He lay half on his bed, half off. While Rubin slept, he yanked on his breeches
and slipped outside. The river trembled with moonlight. Not far away, in a rowboat,
a young man unbuttoned his lover. Allan heard their laughter and fought down the
loneliness of a life devoted to discipline and sorcery. So many sacrifices. So many
hours spent hunched over yellow, worm-holed scrolls. He pitched small pebbles into
the water, and thought, If a conjurer cannot conjure at will, he is worthless. He must
have knowledge, an armory of techniques, a thousand strategies, if he is to unfailingly do good. Toward this end the apprentice applied himself, often despising the
spontaneity of his first achievement. He watched Rubin Bailey closely until on his
fifth year on the river he had stayed by the Sorcerer too long and there was no more
to learn.

"That can't be," said Allan. He was twenty-five, a full sorcerer himself by most
standards, very handsome, more like his father now, at the height of his technical
powers, with many honors and much brilliant thaumaturgy behind him, though none
half as satisfying as his first exorcism rune for Esther Peters. He had, generally, the
respect of everyone in Abbeville. And, it must be said, they waited eagerly for word

of his first solo demonstration. This tortured Allan. He paced around the table, where Rubin sat repairing a fishing line. His belongings, rolled in a blanket, lay by the door. He pleaded, "There must be *one* more strategy."

"One more maybe," agreed the Sorcerer. "But what you need to know, you'll learn."

20   "Without you?" Allan shuddered. He saw himself, in a flash of probable futures, failing Rubin. Dishonoring Richard. Ridiculed by everyone. "How *can* I learn without you?"

"You just do like you did that evening when you helped Esther Peters. . . ."

That wasn't me, thought Allan. I was younger. I don't know how, but everything worked then. You were behind me. I've tried. I've tried the rainmaking charm over and over. It *doesn't rain!* They're only words!

The old Sorcerer stood up and embraced Allan quickly, for he did not like sloppy good-byes or lingering glances or the silly things people said when they had to get across a room and out the door. "You go home and wait for your first caller. You'll do fine."

Allan followed his bare feet away from the houseboat, his head lowered and a light pain in his chest, a sort of flutter like a pigeon beating its wings over his heart— an old pain that first began when he suspected that pansophical knowledge counted for nothing. The apprentice said the spell for fair weather. Fifteen minutes later a light rain fell. He traipsed through mud into Abbeville, shoved his bag under an empty table in a tavern, and sat dripping in the shadows until he dried. A fat man pounded an off-key piano. Boot heels stamped the floor beneath Allan, who ordered tequila. He sucked lemon slices and drained off shot glasses. Gradually, liquor backwashed in his throat and the ache disappeared and his body felt transparent. Yet still he wondered: Was sorcery a gift given to a few, like poetry? Did the Lord come, lift you up, then drop you forever? If so, then he was finished, bottomed out, bellied up before he even began. He had not been born among the Allmuseri Tribe in Africa, like Rubin, if this was necessary for magic. He had not come to New Orleans in a slave clipper, or been sold at the Cabildo, if this was necessary. He had only, it seemed, a vast and painfully acquired yet hollow repertoire of tricks, and this meant he could be a parlor magician, which paid well enough, but he would never do good. If he could not help, what then? He knew no other trade. He had no other dignity. He had no other means to transform the world and no other influence upon men. His seventh tequila untasted, Allan squeezed the bridge of his nose with two fingers, rummaging through his mind for Rubin's phrase for the transmogrification of liquids into vapor. The demons of drunkenness (Saphathoral) and slow-thinking (Ruax) tangled his thoughts, but finally the words floated topside. Softly, he spoke the phrase, stunned at its beauty—at the Sorcerer's beauty, really—mumbling it under his breath so no one might hear, then opened his eyes on the soaking, square face of a man who wore a blue homespun shirt and butternut trousers, but had not been there an instant before: his father. Maybe he'd said the phrase for telekinesis. "Allan, I've been looking all over. How are you?"

25   "Like you see." His gaze dropped from his father to the full shot glass and he despaired.

"Are you sure you're all right? Your eyelids are puffy."

"I'm okay." He lifted the shot glass and made its contents vanish naturally. "I've had my last lesson."

"I know—I went looking for you on the river, and Rubin said you'd come home. Since I knew better, I came to Abbeville. There's a girl at the house wants to see you—Lizzie Harris. She was there when you sawed Deacon Wills in half." Richard picked up his son's bag. "She wants you to help her to—"

Allan shook his head violently. "Lizzie should see Rubin."

"She has." He reached for Allan's hat and placed it on his son's head. "He sent 30 her to you. She's been waiting for hours."

Much rain fell upon Allan and his father, who walked as if his feet hurt, as they left town, but mainly it fell on Allan. His father's confidence in him was painful, his chatter about his son's promising future like the chronicle of someone else's life. This was the night that was bound to come. And now, he thought as they neared the tiny, hip-roofed farmhouse, swimming in fog, I shall fall from humiliation to impotency, from impotency to failure, from failure to death. He leaned weakly against the porch rail. His father scrambled ahead of him, though he was a big man built for endurance and not for speed, and stepped back to open the door for Allan. The Sorcerer's apprentice, stepping inside, decided quietly, definitely, without hope that if this solo flight failed, he would work upon himself the one spell Rubin had described but dared not demonstrate. If he could not help this girl Lizzie—and he feared he could not—he would go back to the river and bring forth demons—horrors that broke a man in half, ate his soul, then dragged him below the ground, where, Allan decided, those who could not do well the work of a magician belonged.

"Allan's here," his father said to someone in the sitting room. "My son is a Conjure Doctor, you know."

"I seen him," said a girl's voice. "Looks like he knows everything there is to know about magic."

The house, full of heirlooms, had changed little since Allan's last year with Rubin. The furniture was darkened by use. All the mirrors in his mother's bedroom were still covered by cloth. His father left week-old dishes on the hob, footswept his cigars under the bare, loose floorboards, and paint on the front porch had begun to peel in large strips. There in the sitting room, Lizzie Harris sat on Beatrice's old flat-bottomed roundabout. She was twice as big as Allan remembered her. Her loose dress and breast exposed as she fed her baby made, he supposed, the difference. Allan looked away while Lizzie drew her dress up, then reached into her bead purse for a shinplaster—Civil War currency—which she handed to him. "This is all you have?" He returned her money, pulled a milk stool beside her, and said, "Please, sit down." His hands were trembling. He needed to hold something to hide the shaking. Allan squeezed both his knees. "Now," he said, "what's wrong with the child?"

"Pearl don't eat," said Lizzie. "She hasn't touched food in two days, and the 35 medicine Dr. Britton gave her makes her spit. It's a simple thing," the girl assured him. "Make her eat."

He lifted the baby off Lizzie's lap, pulling the covering from her face. That she was beautiful made his hands shake even more. She kept her fists balled at her cheeks. Her eyes were light, bread-colored, but latticed by blood vessels. Allan said to his father, without facing him, "I think I need boiled Hound's Tongue and Sage. They're in my bag. Bring me the water from the herbs in a bowl." He hoisted the baby higher on his right arm and, holding the spoon of cold cereal in his left hand, praying silently, began a litany of every spell he knew to disperse suffering and the afflictions of the spirit. From his memory, where techniques lay stacked like crates in a storage bin, Allan unleashed a salvo of incantations. His father, standing nearby with a discolored spoon and the bowl, held his breath so long Allan could hear flies gently beating against the lamp glass of the lantern. Allan, using the spoon like a horseshoe, slipped the potion between her lips. "Eat, Pearl," the apprentice whispered. "Eat and live." Pearl spit up on his shirt. Allan closed his eyes and repeated slowly every syllable of every word of every spell in his possession. And ever he pushed the spoon of cereal against the child's teeth, ever she pushed it away, gagging, swinging her head, and wailing so Allan had to shout each word above her voice. He oozed sweat now. Wind changing direction outside shifted the pressure inside the room so suddenly that Allan's stomach turned violently—it was as if the farmhouse, snatched up a thousand feet, now hung in space. Pearl spit first clear fluids. Then blood. The apprentice attacked this mystery with a dazzling array of devices, analyzed it, looked at her with the critical, wrinkled brow of a philosopher, and mimed the Sorcerer so perfectly it seemed that Rubin, not Allan, worked magic in the room. But he was not Rubin Bailey. And the child suddenly stopped its struggle and relaxed in the apprentice's arms.

Lizzie yelped. "Why ain't Pearl crying?" He began repeating, futilely, his spells for the fifth time. Lizzie snatched his arm with such strength her fingers left blue spots on his skin. "That's enough!" she said. "You give her to me!"

"There's another way," Allan said, "another charm I've seen." But Lizzie Harris had reached the door. She threw a brusque "Good-bye" behind her to Richard and nothing to Allan. He knew they were back on the ground when Lizzie disappeared outside. Within the hour she would be at Rubin's houseboat. In two hours she would be at Esther Peters's home, broadcasting his failure.

"Allan," said Richard, stunned. "It didn't work."

40   "It's never worked." Allan put away the bowl, looked around the farmhouse for his bag, then a pail, and kissed his father's rough cheek. Startled, Richard pulled back sharply, as if he had stumbled sideways against the kiln. "I'm sorry," said Allan. It was not an easy thing to touch a man who so guarded, and for good reason, his emotions. "I'm not much of a Sorcerer, or blacksmith, or anything else."

"You're not going out this late, are you?" His father struggled, and Allan felt guilty for further confusing him with feeling. "Allan. . . ."

His voice trailed off.

"There's one last spell I have to do." Allan touched his arm lightly, once, then drew back his hand. "Don't follow me, okay?"

On his way to the river Allan gathered the roots and stalks and stones he required to dredge up the demon kings. The sky was clear, the air dense, and the Devil was in it if he fouled even this conjuration. For now he was sure that white magic did not reside in ratioicination, education, or will. Skill was of no service. His talent was for pa(o)stiche. He could imitate but never truly heal; impress but never conjure beauty; ape the good but never again give rise to a genuine spell. For that God or Creation, or the universe—it had several names—had to seize you, *use* you, as the Sorcerer said, because it needed a womb, shake you down, speak through you until the pain pearled into a beautiful spell that snapped the world back together. It had abandoned Allan, this possession. It had taken him, in a way, like a lover, planted one pitiful seed, and said, "Bye now." This absence, this emptiness, this sterility he felt deep at his center. Beyond all doubt, he owed the universe far more than it owed him. To give was right; to ask wrong. From birth he was indebted to so many, like his father, and for so much. But you could not repay the universe, or anyone, or build a career as a Conjure Doctor on a single, brilliant spell. Talent, Allan saw, was a curse. To have served once—was this enough? Better perhaps never to have served at all than to go on, foolishly, in the wreckage of former grace, glossing over his frigidity with cheap fireworks, window dressing, a trashy display of pyrotechnics, gimmicks designed to distract others from seeing that the magician onstage was dead.

Now the Sorcerer's apprentice placed his stones and herbs into the pail, which 45 he filled with river water; then he built a fire behind a rock. Rags of fog floated over the waste-clogged riverbank as Allan drew a horseshoe in chalk. He sat cross-legged in wet grass that smelled faintly of oil and fish, faced east, and cursed at the top of his voice. "I conjure and I invoke thee, O Magoa, strong king of the East. I order thee to obey me, to send thy servants Onoskelis and Tepheus."

Two froglike shapes stitched from the fumes of Allan's potion began to take form above the pail.

Next he invoked the demon king of the North, who brought Ornia, a beautiful, blue-skinned lamia from the river bottom. Her touch, Allan knew, was death. She wore a black gown, a necklace of dead spiders, and entered through the opening of the enchanted horseshoe. The South sent Rabdos, a griffinlike hound, all teeth and hair, that hurtled toward the apprentice from the woods; and from the West issued Bazazath, and most terrible of all—a collage of horns, cloven feet, and goatish eyes so wild Allan wrenched away his head. Upriver, he saw kerosene lamplight moving from the direction of town. A faraway voice called, "Allan? Allan? Allan, is that you? Allan, are you out there?" His father. The one he had truly harmed. Allan frowned and faced those he had summoned.

"Apprentice," rumbled Bazazath, "*student,* you risk your life by opening hell."

"I am only that, a student," said Allan, "the one who studies beauty, who wishes to give it back, but who cannot serve what he loves."

"You are wretched, indeed," said Bazazath, and he glanced back at the others. 50 "Isn't he wretched?"

They said, as one, "Worse."

Allan did not understand. He felt Richard's presence hard by, heard him call from the mystic circle's edge, which no man or devil could break. "How am I worse?"

"Because," said the demon of the West, "to love the good, the beautiful is right, but to labor on and will the work when you are obviously *beneath* this service is to parody them, twist them beyond recognition, to lay hold of what was once beautiful and make it a monstrosity. It becomes black magic. Sorcery is relative, student—dialectical, if you like expensive speech. And this, exactly, is what you have done with the teachings of Rubin Bailey."

"No," blurted Allan.

55   The demon of the West smiled. "Yes."

"Then," Allan asked, "you must destroy me?" It was less a question than a request.

"That is why we are here." Bazazath opened his arms. "You must step closer."

He had not known before the real criminality of his deeds. How dreadful that love could disfigure the thing loved. Allan's eyes bent up toward Richard. It was too late for apologies. Too late for promises to improve. He had failed everyone, particularly his father, whose face now collapsed into tears, then hoarse weeping like some great animal with a broken spine. In a moment he would drop to both knees. Don't want me, thought Allan. Don't love me as I am. Could he do nothing right? His work caused irreparable harm—and his death, trivial as it was in his own eyes, that, too, would cause suffering. Why must his choices be so hard? If he returned home, his days would be a dreary marking time for magic, which might never come again, living to one side of what he had loved, and loved still, for fear of creating evil—this was surely the worst curse of all, waiting for grace, but in suicide he would drag his father's last treasure, dirtied as it was, into hell behind him.

"It grows late," said Bazazath. "Have you decided?"

60   The apprentice nodded, yes.

He scrubbed away part of the chalk circle with the ball of his foot, then stepped toward his father. The demons waited—two might still be had this night for the price of one. But Allan felt within his chest the first spring of resignation, a giving way of both the hunger to heal and the anxiety to avoid evil. Was this surrender the one thing the Sorcerer could not teach? His pupil did not know. Nor did he truly know, now that he was no longer a Sorcerer's apprentice with a bright future, how to comfort his father. Awkwardly, Allan lifted Richard's wrist with his right hand, for he was right-handed, then squeezed, tightly, the old man's thick, ruined fingers. For a second his father twitched back in an old slave reflex, the safety catch still on, then fell heavily toward his son. The demons looked on indifferently, then glanced at each other. After a moment, they left, seeking better game.

QUESTIONS FOR DISCUSSION AND WRITING

1. Why is Allan disappointed in his training? What does he learn from his failure to help Lizzie Harris? What prevents him from surrendering himself to the devils he summons?

2. How do the characterizations of Allan's mother and father help us understand his character and motives? How effective is Rubin as a sorcerer and a teacher?

3. How is this version of the rural South different from the usual stereotypes of the region? Given the time and place, why is it so important to Richard that his son become a sorcerer?

4. What kind of point of view is suggested by the first words of the story—"there was a time, long ago"?

5. What is the final and most difficult lesson Allan must learn? How does this lesson connect to his earlier discovery that he is the tool of another's force?

Stories for Comparison

James Baldwin's "Sonny's Blues" (pages 215–238); Zora Neale Hurston's "Sweat" (pages 671–680).

59

....

J A M E S   J O Y C E

Araby

JAMES JOYCE (1882–1941) was born in Dublin, Ireland, and was given a strict Jesuit education at schools such as Belvedere College in Dublin. During his last year at Belvedere, Joyce began to reject his Catholic faith, choosing instead to study modern languages at University College, Dublin. Joyce's literary hero was playwright Henrik Ibsen, whose plays embodied a theme that intrigued Joyce: the cost of individual rebellion in the face of community conformity. So that he could read and write about Ibsen's plays, Joyce taught himself Norwegian. In 1902, Joyce left home, religion, and country to spend the rest of his life as an exile in Europe. He lived briefly in Paris, Trieste, and Zurich, teaching school and writing stories about the various forms of intellectual paralysis he perceived in his homeland. Joyce published these stories, *Dubliners,* in 1914 and then, in 1916, produced a semi-autobiographical account of his own development as a writer, *A Portrait of the Artist as a Young Man.* In 1920 Joyce moved back to Paris, where he found support and sympathy for the literary innovations in his masterpiece, *Ulysses* (1922). Complex and uncompromising in its language, the book created such a public controversy that it was banned in America until a high court cleared the way for its publication in 1933. Ignored and often misunderstood, Joyce spent the remaining years of his life working on his final experimental epic, *Finnegans Wake* (1939). "Araby" and "The Dead" are both reprinted from *Dubliners.* The first story tells of a young boy's disappointment and the second of an older man's disillusionment.

N orth Richmond Street, being blind, was a quiet street except at the hour when the Christian Brothers' School set the boys free. An uninhabited house of two storeys stood at the blind end, detached from its neighbours in a square ground. The other houses of the street, conscious of decent lives within them, gazed at one another with brown imperturbable faces.

The former tenant of our house, a priest, had died in the back drawing-room. Air, musty from having been long enclosed, hung in all the rooms, and the waste room behind the kitchen was littered with old useless papers. Among these I found a few paper-covered books, the pages of which were curled and damp: *The Abbot,* by Walter Scott, *The Devout Communicant* and *The Memoirs of Vidocq.* I liked the last best because its leaves were yellow. The wild garden behind the house contained a central apple-tree and a few straggling bushes under one of which I found the late tenant's rusty bicycle-pump. He had been a very charitable priest; in his will he had left all his money to institutions and the furniture of his house to his sister.

When the short days of winter came dusk fell before we had well eaten our dinners. When we met in the street the houses had grown sombre. The space of sky above us was the colour of ever-changing violet and towards it the lamps of the street lifted their feeble lanterns. The cold air stung us and we played till our bodies glowed. Our shouts echoed in the silent street. The career of our play brought us through the dark muddy lanes behind the houses where we ran the gauntlet of the rough tribes from the cottages, to the back doors of the dark dripping gardens where odours arose from the ashpits, to the dark odorous stables where a coachman smoothed and combed the horse or shook music from the buckled harness. When we returned to the street light from the kitchen windows had filled the areas. If my uncle was seen turning the corner we hid in the shadow until we had seen him safely housed. Or if Mangan's sister came out on the doorstep to call her brother in to his tea we watched her from our shadow peer up and down the street. We waited to see whether she would remain or go in and, if she remained, we left our shadow and walked up to Mangan's steps resignedly. She was waiting for us, her figure defined by the light from the half-opened door. Her brother always teased her before he obeyed and I stood by the railings looking at her. Her dress swung as she moved her body and the soft rope of her hair tossed from side to side.

Every morning I lay on the floor in the front parlour watching her door. The blind was pulled down to within an inch of the sash so that I could not be seen. When she came out on the doorstep my heart leaped. I ran to the hall, seized my books and followed her. I kept her brown figure always in my eye, and, when we came near the point at which our ways diverged, I quickened my pace and passed her. This happened morning after morning. I had never spoken to her, except for a few casual words, and yet her name was like a summons to all my foolish blood.

5   Her image accompanied me even in places the most hostile to romance. On Saturday evenings when my aunt went marketing I had to go to carry some of the parcels. We walked through the flaring streets, jostled by drunken men and bargaining women, amid the curses of labourers, the shrill litanies of shop-boys who stood on guard by the barrels of pigs' cheeks, the nasal chanting of street-singers, who sang a *come-all-you* about O'Donovan Rossa, or a ballad about the troubles in our

native land. These noises converged in a single sensation of life for me: I imagined that I bore my chalice safely through a throng of foes. Her name sprang to my lips at moments in strange prayers and praises which I myself did not understand. My eyes were often full of tears (I could not tell why) and at times a flood from my heart seemed to pour itself out into my bosom. I thought little of the future. I did not know whether I would ever speak to her or not or, if I spoke to her, how I could tell her of my confused adoration. But my body was like a harp and her words and gestures were like fingers running upon the wires.

One evening I went into the back drawing-room in which the priest had died. It was a dark rainy evening and there was no sound in the house. Through one of the broken panes I heard the rain impinge upon the earth, the fine incessant needles of water playing in the sodden beds. Some distant lamp or lighted window gleamed below me. I was thankful that I could see so little. All my senses seemed to desire to veil themselves and, feeling that I was about to slip from them, I pressed the palms of my hands together until they trembled, murmuring: *"O love! O love!"* many times.

At last she spoke to me. When she addressed the first words to me I was so confused that I did not know what to answer. She asked me was I going to *Araby*. I forgot whether I answered yes or no. It would be a splendid bazaar, she said she would love to go.

"And why can't you?" I asked.

While she spoke she turned a silver bracelet round and round her wrist. She could not go, she said, because there would be a retreat that week in her convent. Her brother and two other boys were fighting for their caps and I was alone at the railings. She held one of the spikes, bowing her head towards me. The light from the lamp opposite our door caught the white curve of her neck, lit up her hair that rested there and, falling, lit up the hand upon the railing. It fell over one side of her dress and caught the white border of a petticoat, just visible as she stood at ease.

"It's well for you," she said.   10

"If I go," I said, "I will bring you something."

What innumerable follies laid waste my waking and sleeping thoughts after that evening! I wished to annihilate the tedious intervening days. I chafed against the work of school. At night in my bedroom and by day in the classroom her image came between me and the page I strove to read. The syllables of the word *Araby* were called to me through the silence in which my soul luxuriated and cast an Eastern enchantment over me. I asked for leave to go to the bazaar on Saturday night. My aunt was surprised and hoped it was not some Freemason affair. I answered few questions in class. I watched my master's face pass from amiability to sternness; he hoped I was not beginning to idle. I could not call my wandering thoughts together. I had hardly any patience with the serious work of life which, now that it stood between me and my desire, seemed to me child's play, ugly monotonous child's play.

On Saturday morning I reminded my uncle that I wished to go to the bazaar in the evening. He was fussing at the hallstand, looking for the hat-brush, and answered curtly:

"Yes, boy, I know."

15   As he was in the hall I could not go into the front parlour and lie at the window. I left the house in bad humour and walked slowly towards the school. The air was pitilessly raw and already my heart misgave me.

When I came home to dinner my uncle had not yet been home. Still it was early. I sat staring at the clock for some time and, when its ticking began to irritate me, I left the room. I mounted the staircase and gained the upper part of the house. The high cold empty gloomy rooms liberated me and I went from room to room singing. From the front window I saw my companions playing below in the street. Their cries reached me weakened and indistinct and, leaning my forehead against the cool glass, I looked over at the dark house where she lived. I may have stood there for an hour, seeing nothing but the brown-clad figure cast by my imagination, touched discreetly by the lamplight at the curved neck, at the hand upon the railing and at the border below the dress.

When I came downstairs again I found Mrs. Mercer sitting at the fire. She was an old garrulous woman, a pawnbroker's widow, who collected used stamps for some pious purpose. I had to endure the gossip of the tea-table. The meal was pro- longed beyond an hour and still my uncle did not come. Mrs. Mercer stood up to go: she was sorry she couldn't wait any longer, but it was after eight o'clock and she did not like to be out late, as the night air was bad for her. When she had gone I began to walk up and down the room, clenching my fists. My aunt said:

"I'm afraid you may put off your bazaar for this night of Our Lord."

At nine o'clock I heard my uncle's latchkey in the halldoor. I heard him talking to himself and heard the hallstand rocking when it had received the weight of his overcoat. I could interpret these signs. When he was midway through his dinner I asked him to give me the money to go to the bazaar. He had forgotten.

20   "The people are in bed and after their first sleep now," he said.

I did not smile. My aunt said to him energetically:

"Can't you give him the money and let him go? You've kept him late enough as it is."

My uncle said he was very sorry he had forgotten. He said he believed in the old saying: "All work and no play makes Jack a dull boy." He asked me where I was go- ing and, when I had told him a second time he asked me did I know *The Arab's Farewell to his Steed.* When I left the kitchen he was about to recite the opening lines of the piece to my aunt.

I held a florin tightly in my hand as I strode down Buckingham Street towards the station. The sight of the streets thronged with buyers and glaring with gas re- called to me the purpose of my journey. I took my seat in a third-class carriage of a deserted train. After an intolerable delay the train moved out of the station slowly. It crept onward among ruinous houses and over the twinkling river. At Westland Row Station a crowd of people pressed to the carriage doors; but the porters moved them back, saying that it was a special train for the bazaar. I remained alone in the bare carriage. In a few minutes the train drew up beside an improvised wooden platform. I passed out on to the road and saw by the lighted dial of a clock that it was ten min- utes to ten. In front of me was a large building which displayed the magical name.

I could not find any sixpenny entrance and, fearing that the bazaar would be 25 closed, I passed in quickly through a turnstile, handing a shilling to a weary-looking man. I found myself in a big hall girdled at half its height by a gallery. Nearly all the stalls were closed and the greater part of the hall was in darkness. I recognised a silence like that which pervades a church after a service. I walked into the centre of the bazaar timidly. A few people were gathered about the stalls which were still open. Before a curtain, over which the words *Café Chantant* were written in coloured lamps, two men were counting money on a salver. I listened to the fall of the coins.

Remembering with difficulty why I had come I went over to one of the stalls and examined porcelain vases and flowered tea-sets. At the door of the stall a young lady was talking and laughing with two young gentlemen. I remarked their English accents and listened vaguely to their conversation.

"Oh, I never said such a thing!"

"Oh, but you did!"

"Oh, but I didn't!"

"Didn't she say that?"

"Yes. I heard her." 30

"Oh, there's a . . . fib!"

Observing me the young lady came over and asked me did I wish to buy anything. The tone of her voice was not encouraging; she seemed to have spoken to me out of a sense of duty. I looked humbly at the great jars that stood like eastern guards at either side of the dark entrance to the stall and murmured:

"No, thank you."

The young lady changed the position of one of the vases and went back to the 35 two young men. They began to talk of the same subject. Once or twice the young lady glanced at me over her shoulder.

I lingered before her stall, though I knew my stay was useless, to make my interest in her wares seem the more real. Then I turned away slowly and walked down the middle of the bazaar. I allowed the two pennies to fall against the sixpence in my pocket. I heard a voice call from one end of the gallery that the light was out. The upper part of the hall was now completely dark.

Gazing up into the darkness I saw myself as a creature driven and derided by vanity; and my eyes burned with anguish and anger.

QUESTIONS FOR DISCUSSION AND WRITING

1. What does the narrator hope to accomplish by going to the bazaar? How does his uncle momentarily complicate his purpose? What prevents the boy from accomplishing his purpose once he arrives at the bazaar?

2. How does the narrator use external details to characterize Mangan's sister? What qualities or ideas does she seem to represent? For example, what does he mean by "I imagined that I bore my chalice safely through a throng of foes"?

3. In what ways does the setting of North Richmond Street help establish the tone of the story? How does the narrator perceive the priest's house, the market, and the bazaar?

4. To what extent does the narrator understand the motives for his actions? What change in his point of view does he acknowledge in the last paragraph of the story?

5. How does the story reveal the connection between the boy's sexual awakening and his yearning for idealized romance?

Stories for Comparison

Carson McCullers's "Sucker" (pages 824–831); W. D. Wetherell's "The Bass, the River, and Sheila Mant" (pages 1181–1186).

60

JAMES   JOYCE

The Dead

Lily, the caretaker's daughter, was literally run off her feet. Hardly had she brought one gentleman into the little pantry behind the office on the ground floor and helped him off with his overcoat than the wheezy hall-door bell clanged again and she had to scamper along the bare hallway to let in another guest. It was well for her she had not to attend to the ladies also. But Miss Kate and Miss Julia had thought of that and had converted the bathroom upstairs into a ladies' dressing-room. Miss Kate and Miss Julia were there, gossiping and laughing and fussing, walking after each other to the head of the stairs, peering down over the banisters and calling down to Lily to ask her who had come.

It was always a great affair, the Misses Morkan's annual dance. Everybody who knew them came to it, members of the family, old friends of the family, the members of Julia's choir, any of Kate's pupils that were grown up enough and even some of Mary Jane's pupils too. Never once had it fallen flat. For years and years it had gone off in splendid style as long as anyone could remember; ever since Kate and Julia, after the death of their brother Pat, had left the house in Stoney Batter and taken Mary Jane, their only niece, to live with them in the dark gaunt house on Usher's

Island, the upper part of which they had rented from Mr. Fulham, the cornfactor on the ground floor. That was a good thirty years ago if it was a day. Mary Jane, who was then a little girl in short clothes, was now the main prop of the household for she had the organ in Haddington Road. She had been through the Academy and gave a pupils' concert every year in the upper room of the Antient Concert Rooms. Many of her pupils belonged to better-class families on the Kingstown and Dalkey line. Old as they were, her aunts also did their share. Julia, though she was quite grey, was still the leading soprano in Adam and Eve's, and Kate, being too feeble to go about much, gave music lessons to beginners on the old square piano in the back room. Lily, the caretaker's daughter, did housemaid's work for them. Though their life was modest they believed in eating well; the best of everything: diamond-bone sirloins, three-shilling tea, and the best bottled stout. But Lily seldom made a mistake in the orders so that she got on well with her three mistresses. They were fussy, that was all. But the only thing they would not stand was back answers.

Of course they had good reason to be fussy on such a night. And then it was long after ten o'clock and yet there was no sign of Gabriel and his wife. Besides they were dreadfully afraid that Freddy Malins might turn up screwed. They would not wish for worlds that any of Mary Jane's pupils should see him under the influence; and when he was like that it was sometimes very hard to manage him. Freddy Malins always came late but they wondered what could be keeping Gabriel: and that was what brought them every two minutes to the banisters to ask Lily had Gabriel or Freddy come.

—O, Mr. Conroy, said Lily to Gabriel when she opened the door for him, Miss Kate and Miss Julia thought you were never coming. Good-night, Mrs. Conroy.

—I'll engage they did, said Gabriel, but they forgot that my wife here takes ₅ three mortal hours to dress herself.

He stood on the mat, scraping the snow from his goloshes, while Lily led his wife to the foot of the stairs and called out:

—Miss Kate, here's Mrs. Conroy.

Kate and Julia came toddling down the dark stairs at once. Both of them kissed Gabriel's wife, said she must be perished alive and asked was Gabriel with her.

—Here I am as right as the mail, Aunt Kate! Go on up. I'll follow, called out Gabriel from the dark.

He continued scraping his feet vigorously while the three women went upstairs, ₁₀ laughing, to the ladies' dressing-room. A light fringe of snow lay like a cape on the shoulders of his overcoat and like toecaps on the toes of his goloshes; and, as the buttons of his overcoat slipped with a squeaking noise through the snow-stiffened frieze, a cold fragrant air from out-of-doors escaped from crevices and folds.

—It is snowing again, Mr. Conroy? asked Lily.

She had preceded him into the pantry to help him off with his overcoat. Gabriel smiled at the three syllables she had given his surname and glanced at her. She was a slim, growing girl, pale in complexion and with hay-coloured hair. The gas in the pantry made her look still paler. Gabriel had known her when she was a child and used to sit on the lowest step nursing a rag doll.

—Yes, Lily, he answered, and I think we're in for a night of it.

He looked up at the pantry ceiling, which was shaking with the stamping and shuffling of feet on the floor above, listened for a moment to the piano and then glanced at the girl, who was folding his overcoat carefully at the end of a shelf.

15 —Tell me, Lily, he said in a friendly tone, do you still go to school?

—O no, sir, she answered. I'm done schooling this year and more.

—O, then, said Gabriel gaily. I suppose we'll be going to your wedding one of these fine days with your young man, eh?

The girl glanced back at him over her shoulder and said with great bitterness:

—The men that is now is only all palaver and what they can get out of you.

20 Gabriel coloured as if he felt he had made a mistake and, without looking at her, kicked off his goloshes and flicked actively with his muffler at his patent-leather shoes.

He was a stout tallish young man. The high colour of his cheeks pushed upwards even to his forehead where it scattered itself in a few formless patches of pale red; and on his hairless face there scintillated restlessly the polished lenses and the bright gilt rims of the glasses which screened his delicate and restless eyes. His glossy black hair was parted in the middle and brushed in a long curve behind his ears where it curled slightly beneath the groove left by his hat.

When he had flicked lustre into his shoes he stood up and pulled his waistcoat down more tightly on his plump body. Then he took a coin rapidly from his pocket.

—O Lily, he said, thrusting it into her hands, it's Christmastime, isn't it? Just . . . here's a little. . . .

He walked rapidly towards the door.

25 —O no, sir! cried the girl, following him. Really sir, I wouldn't take it.

—Christmas-time! Christmas-time! said Gabriel, almost trotting to the stairs and waving his hand to her in deprecation.

The girl, seeing that he had gained the stairs, called out after him:

—Well, thank you, sir.

He waited outside the drawing-room door until the waltz should finish, listening to the skirts that swept against it and to the shuffling of feet. He was still discomposed by the girl's bitter and sudden retort. It had cast a gloom over him which he tried to dispel by arranging his cuffs and the bows of his tie. Then he took from his waistcoat pocket a little paper and glanced at the headings he had made for his speech. He was undecided about the lines from Robert Browning for he feared they would be above the heads of his hearers. Some quotation that they could recognise from Shakespeare or from the Melodies would be better. The indelicate clacking of the men's heels and the shuffling of their soles reminded him that their grade of culture differed from his. He would only make himself ridiculous by quoting poetry to them which they could not understand. They would think that he was airing his superior education. He would fail with them just as he had failed with the girl in the pantry. He had taken up a wrong tone. His whole speech was a mistake from first to last, an utter failure.

30 Just then his aunts and his wife came out of the ladies' dressing-room. His aunts were two small plainly dressed old women. Aunt Julia was an inch or so the taller. Her hair, drawn low over the tops of her ears, was grey; and grey also, with

darker shadows, was her large flaccid face. Though she was stout in build and stood erect her slow eyes and parted lips gave her the appearance of a woman who did not know where she was or where she was going. Aunt Kate was more vivacious. Her face, healthier than her sister's, was all puckers and creases, like a shrivelled red apple, and her hair, braided in the same old-fashioned way, had not lost its ripe nut colour.

They both kissed Gabriel frankly. He was their favorite nephew, the son of their dead elder sister, Ellen, who had married T. J. Conroy of the Port and Docks.

—Gretta tells me you're not going to take a cab back to Monkstown to-night, Gabriel, said Aunt Kate.

—No, said Gabriel, turning to his wife, we had quite enough of that last year, hadn't we? Don't you remember, Aunt Kate, what a cold Gretta got out of it? Cab windows rattling all the way, and the east wind blowing in after we passed Merrion. Very jolly it was. Gretta caught a dreadful cold.

Aunt Kate frowned severely and nodded her head at every word.

—Quite right, Gabriel, quite right, she said. You can't be too careful.   35

—But as for Gretta there, said Gabriel, she'd walk home in the snow if she were let.

Mrs. Conroy laughed.

—Don't mind him, Aunt Kate, she said. He's really an awful bother, what with green shades for Tom's eyes at night and making him do the dumb-bells, and forcing Eva to eat the stirabout. The poor child! And she simply hates the sight of it! . . . O, but you'll never guess what he makes me wear now!

She broke out into a peal of laughter and glanced at her husband, whose admiring and happy eyes had been wandering from her dress to her face and hair. The two aunts laughed heartily too, for Gabriel's solicitude was a standing joke with them.

—Goloshes! said Mrs. Conroy. That's the latest. Whenever it's wet underfoot I 40 must put on my goloshes. To-night even he wanted me to put them on, but I wouldn't. The next thing he'll buy me will be a diving suit.

Gabriel laughed nervously and patted his tie reassuringly while Aunt Kate nearly doubled herself, so heartily did she enjoy the joke. The smile soon faded from Aunt Julia's face and her mirthless eyes were directed towards her nephew's face. After a pause she asked:

—And what are goloshes, Gabriel?

—Goloshes, Julia! exclaimed her sister. Goodness me, don't you know what goloshes are? You wear them over your . . . over your boots, Gretta, isn't it?

—Yes, said Mrs. Conroy. Guttapercha things. We both have a pair now. Gabriel says everyone wears them on the continent.

—O, on the continent, murmured Aunt Julia, nodding her head slowly.   45

Gabriel knitted his brows and said, as if he were slightly angered:

—It's nothing very wonderful but Gretta thinks it very funny because she says the word reminds her of Christy Minstrels.

—But tell me, Gabriel, said Aunt Kate, with brisk tact. Of course, you've seen about the room. Gretta was saying . . .

—O, the room is all right, replied Gabriel. I've taken one in the Gresham.

50 —To be sure, said Aunt Kate, by far the best thing to do. And the children, Gretta, you're not anxious about them?

—O, for one night, said Mrs. Conroy. Besides, Bessie will look after them.

—To be sure, said Aunt Kate again. What a comfort it is to have a girl like that, one you can depend on! There's that Lily, I'm sure I don't know what has come over her lately. She's not the girl she was at all.

Gabriel was about to ask his aunt some questions on this point but she broke off suddenly to gaze after her sister who had wandered down the stairs and was craning her neck over the banisters.

—Now, I ask you, she said, almost testily, where is Julia going? Julia! Julia! Where are you going?

55 Julia, who had gone halfway down one flight, came back and announced blandly:

—Here's Freddy.

At the same moment a clapping of hands and a final flourish of the pianist told that the waltz had ended. The drawing-room door was opened from within and some couples came out. Aunt Kate drew Gabriel aside hurriedly and whispered into his ear:

—Slip down, Gabriel, like a good fellow and see if he's all right, and don't let him up if he's screwed. I'm sure he's screwed. I'm sure he is.

Gabriel went to the stairs and listened over the banisters. He could hear two persons talking in the pantry. Then he recognised Freddy Malins' laugh. He went down the stairs noisily.

60 —It's such a relief, said Aunt Kate to Mrs. Conroy, that Gabriel is here. I always feel easier in my mind when he's here. . . . Julia, there's Miss Daly and Miss Power will take some refreshment. Thanks for your beautiful waltz, Miss Daly. It made lovely time.

A tall wizen-faced man, with a stiff grizzled moustache and swarthy skin, who was passing out with his partner said:

—And may we have some refreshment, too, Miss Morkan?

—Julia, said Aunt Kate summarily, and here's Mr. Browne and Miss Furlong. Take them in, Julia, with Miss Daly and Miss Power.

—I'm the man for the ladies, said Mr. Browne, pursing his lips until his moustache bristled and smiling in all his wrinkles. You know, Miss Morkan, the reason they are so fond of me is—

65 He did not finish his sentence, but, seeing that Aunt Kate was out of earshot, at once led the three young ladies into the back room. The middle of the room was occupied by two square tables placed end to end, and on these Aunt Julia and the caretaker were straightening and smoothing a large cloth. On the sideboard were arrayed dishes and plates, and glasses and bundles of knives and forks and spoons. The top of the closed square piano served also as a sideboard for viands and sweets. At a smaller sideboard in one corner two young men were standing, drinking hop-bitters.

Mr. Browne led his charges thither and invited them all, in jest, to some ladies' punch, hot, strong and sweet. As they said they never took anything strong he opened three bottles of lemonade for them. Then he asked one of the young men to move aside, and, taking hold of the decanter, filled out for himself a goodly measure of whisky. The young man eyed him respectfully while he took a trial sip.

—God help me, he said, smiling, it's the doctor's orders.

His wizened face broke into a broader smile, and the three young ladies laughed in musical echo to his pleasantry, swaying their bodies to and fro, with nervous jerks of their shoulders. The boldest said:

—O, now, Mr. Browne, I'm sure the doctor never ordered anything of the kind.   70

Mr. Browne took another sip of his whisky and said, with sidling mimicry:

—Well, you see, I'm like the famous Mrs. Cassidy, who is reported to have said: *Now, Mary Grimes, if I don't take it, make me take it, for I feel I want it.*

His hot face had leaned forward a little too confidentially and he had assumed a very low Dublin accent so that the young ladies, with one instinct, received his speech in silence. Miss Furlong, who was one of Mary Jane's pupils, asked Miss Daly what was the name of the pretty waltz she had played; and Mr. Browne, seeing that he was ignored, turned promptly to the two young men who were more appreciative.

A red-faced young woman, dressed in pansy, came into the room, excitedly clapping her hands and crying:

—Quadrilles! Quadrilles!

Close on her heels came Aunt Kate, crying: 75

—Two gentlemen and three ladies, Mary Jane!

—O, here's Mr. Bergin and Mr. Kerrigan, said Mary Jane. Mr. Kerrigan, will you take Miss Power? Miss Furlong, may I get you a partner, Mr. Bergin. O, that'll just do now.

—Three ladies, Mary Jane, said Aunt Kate.

The two young gentlemen asked the ladies if they might have the pleasure, and Mary Jane turned to Miss Daly.

—O, Miss Daly, you're really awfully good, after playing for the last two   80
dances, but really we're so short of ladies to-night.

—I don't mind in the least, Miss Morkan.

—But I've a nice partner for you, Mr. Bartell D'Arcy, the tenor. I'll get him to sing later on. All Dublin is raving about him.

—Lovely voice, lovely voice! said Aunt Kate.

As the piano had twice begun the prelude to the first figure Mary Jane led her recruits quickly from the room. They had hardly gone when Aunt Julia wandered slowly into the room, looking behind her at something.

—What is the matter, Julia? asked Aunt Kate anxiously. Who is it?   85

Julia, who was carrying in a column of table-napkins turned to her sister and said, simply, as if the question had surprised her:

—It's only Freddy, Kate, and Gabriel with him.

In fact right behind her Gabriel could be seen piloting Freddy Malins across the landing. The latter, a young man of forty, was of Gabriel's size and build, with very round shoulders. His face was fleshy and pallid, touched with colour only at the thick hanging lobes of his ears and at the wide wings of his nose. He had coarse features, a blunt nose, a convex and receding brow, tumid and protruded lips. His heavy-lidded eyes and the disorder of his scanty hair made him look sleepy. He was laughing heartily in a high key at a story which he had been telling Gabriel on the stairs and at the same time rubbing the knuckles of his left fist backwards and forwards into his left eye.

—Good-evening, Freddy, said Aunt Julia.

90   Freddy Malins bade the Misses Morkan good-evening in what seemed an off-hand fashion by reason of the habitual catch in his voice and then, seeing that Mr. Browne was grinning at him from the sideboard, crossed the room on rather shaky legs and began to repeat in an undertone the story he had just told to Gabriel.

—He's not so bad, is he? said Aunt Kate to Gabriel.

Gabriel's brows were dark but he raised them quickly and answered:

—O no, hardly noticeable.

—Now, isn't he a terrible fellow! she said. And his poor mother made him take the pledge on New Year's Eve. But come on, Gabriel, into the drawing-room.

95   Before leaving the room with Gabriel she signalled to Mr. Browne by frowning and shaking her forefinger in warning to and fro. Mr. Browne nodded in answer and, when she had gone, said to Freddy Malins:

—Now, then, Teddy, I'm going to fill you out a good glass of lemonade just to buck you up.

Freddy Malins, who was nearing the climax of his story, waved the offer aside impatiently but Mr. Browne, having first called Freddy Malins' attention to a disarray in his dress, filled out and handed him a full glass of lemonade. Freddy Malins' left hand accepted the glass mechanically, his right hand being engaged in the mechanical readjustment of his dress. Mr. Browne, whose face was once more wrinkling with mirth, poured out for himself a glass of whisky while Freddy Malins exploded, before he had well reached the climax of his story, in a kink of high-pitched bronchitic laughter and, setting down his untasted and overflowing glass, began to rub the knuckles of his left fist backwards and forwards into his left eye, repeating words of his last phrase as well as his fit of laughter would allow him.

Gabriel could not listen while Mary Jane was playing her Academy piece, full of runs and difficult passages, to the hushed drawing-room. He liked music but the piece she was playing had no melody for him and he doubted whether it had any melody for the other listeners, though they begged Mary Jane to play something. Four young men, who had come from the refreshment-room to stand in the doorway at the sound of the piano, had gone away quietly in couples after a few minutes. The only persons who seemed to follow the music were Mary Jane herself, her hands racing along the key-board or lifted from it at the pauses like those of a priestess in momentary imprecation, and Aunt Kate standing at her elbow to turn the page.

Gabriel's eyes, irritated by the floor, which glittered with beeswax under the heavy chandelier, wandered to the wall above the piano. A picture of the balcony scene in *Romeo and Juliet* hung there and beside it was a picture of the two murdered princes in the Tower which Aunt Julia had worked in red, blue and brown wools when she was a girl. Probably in the school they had gone to as girls that kind of work had been taught, for one year his mother had worked for him as a birthday present a waistcoat of purple tabinet, with little foxes' heads upon it, lined with brown satin and having round mulberry buttons. It was strange that his mother had had no musical talent though Aunt Kate used to call her the brains carrier of the Morkan family. Both she and Julia had always seemed a little proud of their serious and matronly sister. Her photograph stood before the pierglass. She held an open book on her knees and was pointing out something in it to Constantine who, dressed in a man-o'-war suit, lay at her feet. It was she who had chosen the names for her sons for she was very sensible of the dignity of family life. Thanks to her, Constantine was now senior curate in Balbriggan and, thanks to her, Gabriel himself had taken his degree in the Royal University. A shadow passed over his face as he remembered her sullen opposition to his marriage. Some slighting phrases she had used still rankled in his memory; she had once spoken of Gretta as being country cute and that was not true of Gretta at all. It was Gretta who had nursed her during all her last long illness in their house at Monkstown.

He knew that Mary Jane must be near the end of her piece for she was playing again the opening melody with runs of scales after every bar and while he waited for the end the resentment died down in his heart. The piece ended with a trill of octaves in the treble and a final deep octave in the bass. Great applause greeted Mary Jane as, blushing and rolling up her music nervously, she escaped from the room. The most vigorous clapping came from the four young men in the doorway who had gone away to the refreshment-room at the beginning of the piece but had come back when the piano had stopped.

Lancers were arranged. Gabriel found himself partnered with Miss Ivors. She was a frank-mannered talkative young lady, with a freckled face and prominent brown eyes. She did not wear a low-cut bodice and the large brooch which was fixed in the front of her collar bore on it an Irish device.

When they had taken their places she said abruptly:

—I have a crow to pluck with you.

—With me? said Gabriel.

She nodded her head gravely.

—What is it? asked Gabriel, smiling at her solemn manner.

—Who is G. C.? answered Miss Ivors, turning her eyes upon him.

Gabriel coloured and was about to knit his brows, as if he did not understand, when she said bluntly:

—O, innocent Amy! I have found out that you write for *The Daily Express.* Now, aren't you ashamed of yourself?

—Why should I be ashamed of myself? asked Gabriel, blinking his eyes and trying to smile.

—Well, I'm ashamed of you, said Miss Ivors frankly. To say you'd write for a rag like that. I didn't think you were a West Briton.

A look of perplexity appeared on Gabriel's face. It was true that he wrote a literary column every Wednesday in *The Daily Express,* for which he was paid fifteen shillings. But that did not make him a West Briton surely. The books he received for review were almost more welcome than the paltry cheque. He loved to feel the covers and turn over the pages of newly printed books. Nearly every day when his teaching in the college was ended he used to wander down the quays to the second-hall booksellers, to Hickey's on Bachelor's Walk, to Webb's or Massey's on Aston's Quay, or to O'Clohissey's in the by-street. He did not know how to meet her charge. He wanted to say that literature was above politics. But they were friends of many years' standing and their careers had been parallel, first at the University and then as teachers: he could not risk a grandiose phrase with her. He continued blinking his eyes and trying to smile and murmured lamely that he saw nothing political in writing reviews of books.

When their turn to cross had come he was still perplexed and inattentive. Miss Ivors promptly took his hand in a warm grasp and said in a soft friendly voice:

—Of course, I was only joking. Come, we cross now.

115   When they were together again she spoke of the University question, and Gabriel felt more at ease. A friend of hers had shown her his review of Browning's poems. That was how she had found out the secret: but she liked the review immensely. Then she said suddenly:

—O, Mr. Conroy, will you come for an excursion to the Aran Isles this summer? We're going to stay there a whole month. It will be splendid out in the Atlantic. You ought to come. Mr. Clancy is coming, and Mr. Kilkelly and Kathleen Kearney. It would be splendid for Gretta too if she'd come. She's from Connacht, isn't she?

—Her people are, said Gabriel shortly.

—But you will come, won't you? said Miss Ivors, laying her warm hand eagerly on his arm.

—The fact is, said Gabriel, I have already arranged to go—

120   —Go where? asked Miss Ivors.

—Well, you know, every year I go for a cycling tour with some fellows and so—

—But where? asked Miss Ivors.

—Well, we usually go to France or Belgium or perhaps Germany, said Gabriel awkwardly.

—And why do you go to France and Belgium, said Miss Ivors, instead of visiting your own land?

125   —Well, said Gabriel, it's partly to keep in touch with the languages and partly for a change.

—And haven't you your own language to keep in touch with—Irish? asked Miss Ivors.

—Well, said Gabriel, if it comes to that, you know, Irish is not my language.

Their neighbours had turned to listen to the cross-examination. Gabriel glanced right and left nervously and tried to keep his good humour under the ordeal which was making a blush invade his forehead.

—And haven't you your own land to visit, continued Miss Ivors, that you know nothing of, your own people, and your own country?

130   —O, to tell you the truth, retorted Gabriel suddenly, I'm sick of my own country, sick of it!

—Why? asked Miss Ivors.

Gabriel did not answer for his retort had heated him.

—Why? repeated Miss Ivors.

They had to go visiting together and, as he had not answered her, Miss Ivors said warmly:

—Of course, you've no answer.   135

Gabriel tried to cover his agitation by taking part in the dance with great energy. He avoided her eyes for he had seen a sour expression on her face. But when they met in the long chain he was surprised to feel his hand firmly pressed. She looked at him from under her brows for a moment quizzically until he smiled. Then, just as the chain was about to start again, she stood on tiptoe and whispered into his ear:

—West Briton!

When the lancers were over Gabriel went away to a remote corner of the room where Freddy Malin's mother was sitting. She was a stout feeble old woman with white hair. Her voice had a catch in it like her son's and she stuttered slightly. She had been told that Freddy had come and that he was nearly all right. Gabriel asked her whether she had had a good crossing. She lived with her married daughter in Glasgow and came to Dublin on a visit once a year. She answered placidly that she had had a beautiful crossing and that the captain had been most attentive to her. She spoke also of the beautiful house her daughter kept in Glasgow, and of all the nice friends they had there. While her tongue rambled on Gabriel tried to banish from his mind all memory of the unpleasant incident with Miss Ivors. Of course the girl or woman, or whatever she was, was an enthusiast but there was a time for all things. Perhaps he ought not to have answered her like that. But she had no right to call him a West Briton before people, even in joke. She had tried to make him ridiculous before people, heckling him and staring at him with her rabbit's eyes.

He saw his wife making her way towards him through the waltzing couples. When she reached him she said into his ear:

—Gabriel, Aunt Kate wants to know won't you carve the goose as usual. Miss   140
Daly will carve the ham and I'll do the pudding.

—All right, said Gabriel.

—She's sending in the younger ones first as soon as this waltz is over so that we'll have the table to ourselves.

—Were you dancing? asked Gabriel.

—Of course I was. Didn't you see me? What words had you with Molly Ivors?

—No words. Why? Did she say so?   145

—Something like that. I'm trying to get that Mr. D'Arcy to sing. He's full of conceit, I think.

—There were no words, said Gabriel moodily, only she wanted me to go for a trip to the west of Ireland and I said I wouldn't.

His wife clasped her hands excitedly and gave a little jump.

—O, do go, Gabriel, she cried. I'd love to see Galway again.

—You can go if you like, said Gabriel coldly.   150

She looked at him for a moment, then turned to Mrs. Malins and said:

—There's a nice husband for you, Mrs. Malins.

While she was threading her way back across the room Mrs. Malins, without adverting to the interruption, went on to tell Gabriel what beautiful places there were in Scotland and beautiful scenery. Her son-in-law brought them every year to the lakes and they used to go fishing. Her son-in-law was a splendid fisher. One day he caught a fish, a beautiful big big fish, and the man in the hotel boiled it for their dinner.

Gabriel hardly heard what she said. Now that supper was coming near he began to think again about his speech and about the quotation. When he saw Freddy Malins coming across the room to visit his mother Gabriel left the chair free for him and retired into the embrasure of the window. The room had already cleared and from the back room came the clatter of plates and knives. Those who still remained in the drawing-room seemed tired of dancing and were conversing quietly in little groups. Gabriel's warm trembling fingers tapped the cold pane of the window. How cool it must be outside! How pleasant it would be to walk out alone, first along by the river and then through the park! The snow would be lying on the branches of the trees and forming a bright cap on the top of the Wellington Monument. How much more pleasant it would be there than at the supper-table!

155   He ran over the headings of his speech: Irish hospitality, sad memories, the Three Graces, Paris, the quotation from Browning. He repeated to himself a phrase he had written in his review: *One feels that one is listening to a thought-tormented music.* Miss Ivors had praised the review. Was she sincere? Had she really any life of her own behind all her propagandism? There had never been any ill-feeling between them until that night. It unnerved him to think that she would be at the supper-table, looking up at him while he spoke with her critical quizzing eyes. Perhaps she would not be sorry to see him fail in his speech. An idea came into his mind and gave him courage. He would say, alluding to Aunt Kate and Aunt Julia: *Ladies and Gentlemen, the generation which is now on the wane among us may have had its faults but for my part I think it had certain qualities of hospitality, of humor, of humanity, which the new and very serious and hypereducated generation that is growing up around us seems to me to lack.* Very good: that was one for Miss Ivors. What did he care that his aunts were only two ignorant old women?

A murmur in the room attracted his attention. Mr. Browne was advancing from the door, gallantly escorting Aunt Julia, who leaned upon his arm, smiling and hanging her head. An irregular musketry of applause escorted her also as far as the piano and then, as Mary Jane seated herself on the stool, and Aunt Julia, no longer smiling, half turned so as to pitch her voice fairly into the room, gradually ceased. Gabriel recognized the prelude. It was that of an old song of Aunt Julia's—*Arrayed for the Bridal.* Her voice, strong and clear in tone, attacked with great spirit the runs which embellish the air and though she sang very rapidly she did not miss even the smallest of the grace notes. To follow the voice, without looking at the singer's face, was to feel and share the excitement of swift and secure flight. Gabriel applauded loudly with all the others at the close of the song and loud applause was borne in from the invisible supper-table. It sounded so genuine that a little colour struggled into Aunt Julia's face as she bent to replace in the music-stand the old leather-bound song-book that had her initials on the cover. Freddy Malins, who had listened with his head perched sideways to hear her better, was still applauding when everyone else had ceased and talking animatedly to his mother who nodded her head gravely and slowly in acquiescence. At last, when he could clap no more, he stood up suddenly and hurried across the room to Aunt Julia whose hand he seized and held in both his hands, shaking it when words failed him or the catch in his voice proved too much for him.

—I was just telling my mother, he said, I never heard you sing so well, never. No, I never heard your voice so good as it is to-night. Now! Would you believe that now? That's the truth. Upon my word and honour that's the truth. I never heard your voice sound so fresh and so . . . so clear and fresh, never.

Aunt Julia smiled broadly and murmured something about compliments as she released her hand from his grasp. Mr. Browne extended his open hand towards her and said to those who were near in the manner of a showman introducing a prodigy to an audience:

—Miss Julia Morkan, my latest discovery!

He was laughing very heartily at this himself when Freddy Malins turned to him   160 and said:

—Well, Browne, if you're serious you might make a worse discovery. All I can say is I never heard her sing half so well as I am coming here. And that's the honest truth.

—Neither did I, said Mr. Browne. I think her voice has greatly improved.

Aunt Julia shrugged her shoulders and said with meek pride:

—Thirty years ago I hadn't a bad voice as voices go.

—I often told Julia, said Aunt Kate emphatically, that she was simply thrown   165 away in that choir. But she never would be said by me.

She turned as if to appeal to the good sense of the others against a refractory child while Aunt Julia gazed in front of her, a vague smile of reminiscence playing on her face.

—No, continued Aunt Kate, she wouldn't be said or led by anyone, slaving there in that choir night and day, night and day. Six o'clock on Christmas morning! And all for what?

—Well, isn't it for the honour of God, Aunt Kate? asked Mary Jane, twisting round on the piano-stool and smiling.

Aunt Kate turned fiercely on her niece and said:

—I know all about the honour of God, Mary Jane, but I think it's not at all hon-   170 ourable for the pope to turn out the women out of the choirs that have slaved there all their lives and put little whipper-snappers of boys over their heads. I suppose it is for the good of the Church if the pope does it. But it's not just, Mary Jane, and it's not right.

She had worked herself into a passion and would have continued in defence of her sister for it was a sore subject with her but Mary Jane, seeing that all the dancers had come back, intervened pacifically:

—Now, Aunt Kate, you're giving scandal to Mr. Browne who is of the other persuasion.

Aunt Kate turned to Mr. Browne, who was grinning at this allusion to his religion, and said hastily:

—O, I don't question the pope's being right. I'm only a stupid old woman and I wouldn't presume to do such a thing. But there's such a thing as common every-day politeness and gratitude. And if I were in Julia's place I'd tell that Father Healy straight up to his face . . .

175　　—And besides, Aunt Kate, said Mary Jane, we really are all hungry and when we are hungry we are all very quarrelsome.

—And when we are thirsty we are also quarrelsome, added Mr. Browne.

—So that we had better go to supper, said Mary Jane, and finish the discussion afterwards.

On the landing outside the drawing-room Gabriel found his wife and Mary Jane trying to persuade Miss Ivors to stay for supper. But Miss Ivors, who had put on her hat and was buttoning her cloak, would not stay. She did not feel in the least hungry and she had already overstayed her time.

—But only for ten minutes, Molly, said Mrs. Conroy. That won't delay you.

180　　—To take a pick itself, said Mary Jane, after all your dancing.

—I really couldn't, said Miss Ivors.

—I am afraid you didn't enjoy yourself at all, said Mary Jane hopelessly.

—Ever so much, I assure you, said Miss Ivors, but you really must let me run off now.

—But how can you get home? asked Mrs. Conroy.

185　　—O, it's only two steps up the quay.

Gabriel hesitated a moment and said:

—If you will allow me, Miss Ivors, I'll see you home if you really are obliged to go.

But Miss Ivors broke away from them.

—I won't hear of it, she cried. For goodness sake go in to your suppers and don't mind me. I'm quite well able to take care of myself.

190　　—Well, you're the comical girl, Molly, said Mrs. Conroy frankly.

—*Beannacht libh,* cried Miss Ivors, with a laugh, as she ran down the staircase.

Mary Jane gazed after her, a moody puzzled expression on her face, while Mrs. Conroy leaned over the banisters to listen for the hall-door. Gabriel asked himself was he the cause of her abrupt departure. But she did not seem to be in ill humour: she had gone away laughing. He stared blankly down the staircase.

At that moment Aunt Kate came toddling out of the supper-room, almost wringing her hands in despair.

—Where is Gabriel? she cried. Where on earth is Gabriel? There's everyone waiting in there, stage to let, and nobody to carve the goose!

195　　—Here I am, Aunt Kate! cried Gabriel, with sudden animation, ready to carve a flock of geese, if necessary.

A fat brown goose lay at one end of the table and at the other end, on a bed of creased paper strewn with sprigs of parsley, lay a great ham, stripped of its outer skin and peppered over with crust crumbs, a neat paper frill round its shin and beside this was a round of spiced beef. Between these rival ends ran parallel lines of side-dishes: two little minsters of jelly, red and yellow; a shallow dish full of blocks of blancmange and red jam, a large green leaf-shaped dish with a stalk-shaped handle, on which lay bunches of purple raisins and peeled almonds, a companion dish on which lay a solid rectangle of Smyrna figs, a dish of custard topped with grated nutmeg, a small bowl full of chocolates and sweets wrapped in gold and silver papers and a glass vase in which stood some tall celery stalks. In the centre of the table there stood, as sentries to a fruit-stand which upheld a pyramid of oranges and American apples, two squat old-fashioned decanters of cut glass, one containing port and the other dark sherry. On the closed square piano a pudding in a huge yellow dish lay in waiting and behind it were three squads of bottles of stout and ale and minerals, drawn up according to the colours of their uniforms, the first two black, with brown and red labels, the third and smallest squad white, with transverse green sashes.

Gabriel took his seat boldly at the head of the table and, having looked to the edge of the carver, plunged his fork firmly into the goose. He felt quite at ease now for he was an expert carver and liked nothing better than to find himself at the head of a well-laden table.

—Miss Furlong, what shall I send you? he asked. A wing or a slice of the breast?

—Just a small slice of the breast.

—Miss Higgins, what for you?   200

—O, anything at all, Mr. Conroy.

While Gabriel and Miss Daly exchanged plates of goose and plates of ham and spiced beef Lily went from guest to guest with a dish of hot floury potatoes wrapped in a white napkin. This was Mary Jane's idea and she had also suggested apple sauce for the goose but Aunt Kate had said that plain roast goose without apple sauce had always been good enough for her and she hoped she might never eat worse. Mary Jane waited on her pupils and saw that they got the best slices and Aunt Kate and Aunt Julia opened and carried across from the piano bottles of stout and ale for the gentlemen and bottles of minerals for the ladies. There was a great deal of confusion and laughter and noise, the noise of orders and counter-orders, of knives and forks, of corks and glass-stoppers. Gabriel began to carve second helpings as soon as he had finished the first round without serving himself. Everyone protested loudly so that he compromised by taking a long draught of stout for he had found the carving hot work. Mary Jane settled down quietly to her supper but Aunt Kate and Aunt Julia were still toddling round the table, walking on each other's heels, getting in each other's way and giving each other unheeded orders. Mr. Browne begged of them to sit down and eat their suppers and so did Gabriel but they said there was time enough so that, at last, Freddy Malins stood up and, capturing Aunt Kate, plumped her down on her chair amid general laughter.

When everyone had been well served Gabriel said, smiling:

—Now, if anyone wants a little more of what vulgar people call stuffing let him or her speak.

A chorus of voices invited him to begin his own supper and Lily came forward   205
with three potatoes which she had reserved for him.

—Very well, said Gabriel amiably, as he took another preparatory draught, kindly forget my existence, ladies and gentlemen, for a few minutes.

He set to his supper and took no part in the conversation with which the table covered Lily's removal of the plates. The subject of talk was the opera company which was then at the Theatre Royal. Mr. Bartell D'Arcy, the tenor, a dark-complexioned young man with a smart moustache, praised very highly the leading contralto of the company but Miss Furlong thought she had a rather vulgar style of production. Freddy Malins said there was a negro chieftain singing in the second part of the Gaiety pantomime who had one of the finest tenor voices he had ever heard.

—Have you heard him? he asked Mr. Bartell D'Arcy across the table.

—No, answered Mr. Bartell D'Arcy carelessly.

210 —Because, Freddy Malins explained, now I'd be curious to hear your opinion of him. I think he has a grand voice.

—It takes Teddy to find out the really good things, said Mr. Browne familiarly to the table.

—And why couldn't he have a voice too? asked Freddy Malins sharply. Is it because he's only a black?

Nobody answered this question and Mary Jane led the table back to the legitimate opera. One of her pupils had given her a pass for *Mignon.* Of course it was very fine, she said, but it made her think of poor Georgina Burns. Mr. Browne could go back farther still, to the old Italian companies that used to come to Dublin—Tietjens, Ilma de Murzka, Campanini, the great Trebelli, Giuglini, Ravelli, Aramburo. Those were the days, he said, when there was something like singing to be heard in Dublin. He told too of how the top gallery of the old Royal used to be packed night after night, of how one night an Italian tenor had sung five encores to *Let Me Like a Soldier Fall,* introducing a high C every time, and of how the gallery boys would sometimes in their enthusiasm unyoke the horses from the carriage of some great *prima donna* and pull her themselves through the streets to her hotel. Why did they never play the grand old operas now, he asked, *Dinorah, Lucrezia Borgia?* Because they could not get the voices to sing them: that was why.

—O, well, said Mr. Bartell D'Arcy, I presume there are as good singers to-day as there were then.

215 —Where are they? asked Mr. Browne defiantly.

—In London, Paris, Milan, said Mr. Bartell D'Arcy warmly. I suppose Caruso, for example, is quite as good, if not better than any of the men you have mentioned.

—Maybe so, said Mr. Browne. But I may tell you I doubt it strongly.

—O, I'd give anything to hear Caruso sing, said Mary Jane.

—For me, said Aunt Kate, who had been picking a bone, there was only one tenor. To please me, I mean. But I suppose none of you ever heard of him.

220 —Who was he, Miss Morkan? asked Mr. Bartell D'Arcy politely.

—His name, said Aunt Kate, was Parkinson. I heard him when he was in his prime and I think he had then the purest tenor voice that was ever put into a man's throat.

—Strange, said Mr. Bartell D'Arcy. I never even heard of him.

—Yes, yes, Miss Morkan is right, said Mr. Browne. I remember hearing of old Parkinson but he's too far back for me.

—A beautiful pure sweet mellow English tenor, said Aunt Kate with enthusiasm.

225 Gabriel having finished, the huge pudding was transferred to the table. The clatter of forks and spoons began again. Gabriel's wife served out spoonfuls of the pudding and passed the plates down the table. Midway down they were held up by Mary Jane, who replenished them with raspberry or orange jelly or with blancmange and

jam. The pudding was of Aunt Julia's making and she received praises for it from all quarters. She herself said that it was not quite brown enough.

—Well, I hope, Miss Morkan, said Mr. Browne, that I'm brown enough for you because, you know, I'm all brown.

All the gentlemen, except Gabriel, ate some of the pudding out of compliment to Aunt Julia. As Gabriel never ate sweets the celery had been left for him. Freddy Malins also took a stalk of celery and ate it with his pudding. He had been told that celery was a capital thing for the blood and he was just then under doctor's care. Mrs. Malins, who had been silent all through the supper, said that her son was going down to Mount Melleray in a week or so. The table then spoke of Mount Melleray, how bracing the air was down there, how hospitable the monks were and how they never asked for a penny-piece from their guests.

—And you do mean to say, asked Mr. Browne incredulously, that a chap can go down there and put up there as if it were a hotel and live on the fat of the land and then come away without paying a farthing?

—O, most people give some donation to the monastery when they leave, said Mary Jane.

—I wish we had an institution like that in our Church, said Mr. Browne candidly. 230

He was astonished to hear that the monks never spoke, got up at two in the morning and slept in their coffins. He asked what they did it for.

—That's the rule of the order, said Aunt Kate firmly.

—Yes, but why? asked Mr. Browne.

Aunt Kate repeated that it was the rule, that was all. Mr. Browne still seemed not to understand. Freddy Malins explained to him as best he could, that the monks were trying to make up for the sins committed by all the sinners in the outside world. The explanation was not very clear for Mr. Browne grinned and said:

—I like that idea very much but wouldn't a comfortable spring bed do them as 235
well as a coffin?

—The coffin, said Mary Jane, is to remind them of their last end.

As the subject had grown lugubrious it was buried in a silence of the table during which Mrs. Malins could be heard saying to her neighbour in an indistinct undertone:

—They are very good men, the monks, very pious men.

The raisins and almonds and figs and apples and oranges and chocolates and sweets were now passed about the table and Aunt Julia invited all the guests to have either port or sherry. At first Mr. Bartell D'Arcy refused to take either but one of his neighbours nudged him and whispered something to him upon which he allowed his glass to be filled. Gradually as the last glasses were being filled the conversation ceased. A pause followed, broken only by the noise of the wine and by unsettlings of chairs. The Misses Morkan, all three, looked down at the tablecloth. Someone coughed once or twice and then a few gentlemen patted the table gently as a signal for silence. The silence came and Gabriel pushed back his chair and stood up.

The patting at once grew louder in encouragement and then ceased altogether. 240
Gabriel leaned his ten trembling fingers on the tablecloth and smiled nervously at the company. Meeting a row of upturned faces he raised his eyes to the chandelier. The

piano was playing a waltz tune and he could hear the skirts sweeping against the drawing-room door. People, perhaps, were standing in the snow on the quay outside, gazing up at the lighted windows and listening to the waltz music. The air was pure there. In the distance lay the park where the trees were weighted with snow. The Wellington Monument wore a gleaming cap of snow that flashed westward over the white field of Fifteen Acres.

He began:

—Ladies and Gentlemen.

—It has fallen to my lot this evening, as in years past, to perform a very pleasing task but a task for which I am afraid my poor powers as a speaker are all too inadequate.

—No, no! said Mr. Browne.

245 —But, however that may be, I can only ask you to-night to take the will for the deed and to lend me your attention for a few moments while I endeavour to express to you in words what my feelings are on this occasion.

—Ladies and Gentlemen. It is not the first time that we have gathered together under this hospitable roof, around this hospitable board. It is not the first time that we have been the recipients—or perhaps, I had better say, the victims—of the hospitality of certain good ladies.

He made a circle in the air with his arm and paused. Everyone laughed or smiled at Aunt Kate and Aunt Julia and Mary Jane who all turned crimson with pleasure. Gabriel went on more boldly:

—I feel more strongly with every recurring year that our country has no tradition which does it so much honour and which it should guard so jealously as that of its hospitality. It is a tradition that is unique as far as my experience goes (and I have visited not a few places abroad) among the modern nations. Some would say, perhaps, that with us it is rather a failing than anything to be boasted of. But granted even that, it is, to my mind, a princely failing, and one that I trust will long be cultivated among us. Of one thing, at least, I am sure. As long as this one roof shelters the good ladies aforesaid—and I wish from my heart it may do so for many and many a long year to come—the tradition of genuine warm-hearted courteous Irish hospitality, which our forefathers have handed down to us and which we in turn must hand down to our descendants, is still alive among us.

A hearty murmur of assent ran round the table. It shot through Gabriel's mind that Miss Ivors was not there and that she had gone away discourteously: and he said with confidence in himself:

250 —Ladies and Gentlemen.

—A new generation is growing up in our midst, a generation actuated by new ideas and new principles. It is serious and enthusiastic for these new ideas and its enthusiasm, even when it is misdirected, is, I believe, in the main sincere. But we are living in a sceptical and, if I may use the phrase, a thought-tormented age: and sometimes I fear that this new generation, educated or hypereducated as it is, will lack those qualities of humanity, of hospitality, of kindly humour which belonged to an older day. Listening tonight to the names of all those great singers of the past it seemed to me, I must confess, that we were living in a less spacious age. Those days might, without exaggeration, be called spacious days: and if they are gone beyond recall let us hope, at least, that in gatherings such as this we shall still speak of them with pride and affection, still cherish in our hearts the memory of those dead and gone great ones whose fame the world will not willingly let die.

—Hear, hear! said Mr. Browne loudly.

—But yet, continued Gabriel, his voice falling into a softer inflection, there are always in gatherings such as this sadder thoughts that will recur to our minds: thoughts of the past, of youth, of changes, of absent faces that we miss here tonight. Our path through life is strewn with many such sad memories: and were we to brood upon them always we could not find the heart to go on bravely with our work among the living. We have all of us living duties and living affections which claim, and rightly claim, our strenuous endeavours.

—Therefore, I will not linger on the past. I will not let any gloomy moralising intrude upon us here to-night. Here we are gathered together for a brief moment from the bustle and rush of our everyday routine. We are met here as friends, in the spirit of good-fellowship, as colleagues, also to a certain extent, in the true spirit of *camaraderie,* and as the guests of—what shall I call them?—the Three Graces of the Dublin musical world.

The table burst into applause and laughter at this sally. Aunt Julia vainly asked 255 each of her neighbours in turn to tell her what Gabriel had said.

—He says we are the Three Graces, Aunt Julia, said Mary Jane.

Aunt Julia did not understand but she looked up, smiling, at Gabriel, who continued in the same vein:

—Ladies and Gentlemen.

—I will not attempt to play to-night the part that Paris played on another occasion. I will not attempt to choose between them. The task would be an invidious one and one beyond my poor powers. For when I view them in turn, whether it be our chief hostess herself, whose good heart, whose too good heart, has become a byword with all who know her, or her sister, who seems to be gifted with perennial youth and whose singing must have been a surprise and a revelation to us all to-night, or, last but not least, when I consider our youngest hostess, talented, cheerful, hard-working and the best of nieces, I confess, Ladies and Gentlemen, that I do not know to which of them I should award the prize.

Gabriel glanced down at his aunts and, seeing the large smile on Aunt Julia's 260 face and the tears which had risen to Aunt Kate's eyes, hastened to his close. He raised his glass of port gallantly, while every member of the company fingered a glass expectantly, and said loudly:

—Let us toast them all three together. Let us drink to their health, wealth, long life, happiness and prosperity and may they long continue to hold the proud and self-won position which they hold in their profession and the position of honour and affection which they hold in our hearts.

All the guests stood up, glass in hand, and, turning towards the three seated ladies, sang in unison, with Mr. Browne as leader:

> For they are jolly gay fellows,
> For they are jolly gay fellows,
> For they are jolly gay fellows,
> Which nobody can deny.

Aunt Kate was making frank use of her handkerchief and even Aunt Julia seemed moved. Freddy Malins beat time with his pudding-fork and the singers turned towards one another, as if in melodious conference, while they sang, with emphasis:

> Unless he tells a lie,
> Unless he tells a lie.

Then, turning once more towards their hostesses, they sang:

> For they are jolly gay fellows,
> For they are jolly gay fellows,
> For they are jolly gay fellows,
> Which nobody can deny.

265   The acclamation which followed was taken up beyond the door of the supper-room by many of the other guests and renewed time after time, Freddy Malins acting as officer with his fork on high.

The piercing morning air came into the hall where they were standing so that Aunt Kate said:

—Close the door, somebody. Mrs. Malins will get her death of cold.

—Browne is out there, Aunt Kate, said Mary Jane.

—Browne is everywhere, said Aunt Kate, lowering her voice.

270   Mary Jane laughed at her tone.

—Really, she said archly, he is very attentive.

—He has been laid on here like the gas, said Aunt Kate in the same tone, all during the Christmas.

She laughed herself this time good-humouredly and then added quickly:

—But tell him to come in, Mary Jane, and close the door. I hope to goodness he didn't hear me.

275   At that moment the hall-door was opened and Mr. Browne came in from the doorstep, laughing as if his heart would break. He was dressed in a long green overcoat with mock astrakhan cuffs and collar and wore on his head an oval fur cap. He pointed down the snow-covered quay from where the sound of shrill prolonged whistling was borne in.

—Teddy will have all the cabs in Dublin out, he said.

Gabriel advanced from the little pantry behind the office, struggling into his overcoat and, looking round the hall, said:

—Gretta not down yet?

—She's getting on her things, Gabriel, said Aunt Kate.

—Who's playing up there? asked Gabriel.   280

—Nobody. They're all gone.

—O no, Aunt Kate, said Mary Jane. Bartell D'Arcy and Miss O'Callaghan aren't gone yet.

—Somebody is strumming at the piano, anyhow, said Gabriel.

Mary Jane glanced at Gabriel and Mr. Browne and said with a shiver:

—It makes me feel cold to look at you two gentlemen muffled up like that. I   285 wouldn't like to face your journey home at this hour.

—I'd like nothing better this minute, said Mr. Browne stoutly, than a rattling fine walk in the country or a fast drive with a good spanking goer between the shafts.

—We used to have a very good horse and trap at home, said Aunt Julia sadly.

—The never-to-be-forgotten Johnny, said Mary Jane, laughing.

Aunt Kate and Gabriel laughed too.

—Why, what was wonderful about Johnny? asked Mr. Browne.   290

—The late lamented Patrick Morkan, our grandfather, that is, explained Gabriel, commonly known in his later years as the old gentleman, with a glue-boiler.

—O, now, Gabriel, said Aunt Kate, laughing, he had a starch mill.

—Well, glue or starch, said Gabriel, the old gentleman had a horse by the name of Johnny. And Johnny used to work in the old gentleman's mill, walking round and round in order to drive the mill. That was all very well; but now comes the tragic part about Johnny. One fine day the old gentleman thought he'd like to drive out with the quality to a military review in the park.

—The Lord have mercy on his soul, said Aunt Kate compassionately.

—Amen, said Gabriel. So the old gentleman, as I said, harnessed Johnny and   295 put on his very best tall hat and his very best stock collar and drove out in grand style from his ancestral mansion somewhere near Back Lane, I think.

Everyone laughed, even Mrs. Malins, at Gabriel's manner and Aunt Kate said:

—O now, Gabriel, he didn't live in Back Lane, really. Only the mill was there.

—Out from the mansion of his forefathers, continued Gabriel, he drove with Johnny. And everything went on beautifully until Johnny came in sight of King Billy's statue: and whether he fell in love with the horse King Billy sits on or whether he thought he was back again in the mill, anyhow he began to walk round the statue.

Gabriel paced in a circle round the hall in his goloshes amid the laughter of the others.

—Round and round he went, said Gabriel, and the old gentleman, who was a   300 very pompous old gentleman, was highly indignant. *Go on, sir! What do you mean, sir? Johnny! Johnny! Most extraordinary conduct! Can't understand the horse!*

The peals of laughter which followed Gabriel's imitation of the incident were interrupted by a resounding knock at the hall-door. Mary Jane ran to open it and let in Freddy Malins. Freddy Malins, with his hat well back on his head and his shoulders humped with cold, was puffing and steaming after his exertions.

—I could only get one cab, he said.

—O, we'll find another along the quay, said Gabriel.

—Yes, said Aunt Kate. Better not keep Mrs. Malins standing in the draught.

305   Mrs. Malins was helped down the front steps by her son and Mr. Browne and, after many manœuvres, hoisted into the cab. Freddy Malins clambered in after her and spent a long time settling her on the seat, Mr. Browne helped him with advice. At last she was settled comfortably and Freddy Malins invited Mr. Browne into the cab. There was a good deal of confused talk, and then Mr. Browne got into the cab. The cabman settled his rug over his knees, and bent down for the address. The confusion grew greater and the cabman was directed differently by Freddy Malins and Mr. Browne, each of whom had his head out through a window of the cab. The difficulty was to know where to drop Mr. Browne along the route and Aunt Kate, Aunt Julia and Mary Jane helped the discussion from the doorstep with cross-directions and contradictions and abundance of laughter. As for Freddy Malins he was speechless with laughter. He popped his head in and out of the window every moment, to the great danger of his hat, and told his mother how the discussion was progressing till at last Mr. Browne shouted to the bewildered cabman above the din of everybody's laughter:

—Do you know Trinity College?

—Yes, sir, said the cabman.

—Well, drive bang up against Trinity College gates, said Mr. Browne, and then we'll tell you where to go. You understand now?

—Yes, sir, said the cabman.

310   —Make like a bird for Trinity College.

—Right, sir, cried the cabman.

The horse was whipped up and the cab rattled off along the quay amid a chorus of laughter and adieus.

Gabriel had not gone to the door with the others. He was in a dark part of the hall gazing up the staircase. A woman was standing near the top of the first flight, in the shadow also. He could not see her face but he could see the terracotta and salmonpink panels of her skirt which the shadow made appear black and white. It was his wife. She was leaning on the banisters, listening to something. Gabriel was surprised at her stillness and strained his ear to listen also. But he could hear little save the noise of laughter and dispute on the front steps, a few chords struck on the piano and a few notes of a man's voice singing.

He stood still in the gloom of the hall, trying to catch the air that the voice was singing and gazing up at his wife. There was grace and mystery in her attitude as if she were a symbol of something. He asked himself what is a woman standing on the stairs in the shadow, listening to distant music, a symbol of. If he were a painter he would paint her in that attitude. Her blue felt hat would show off the bronze of her hair against the darkness and the dark panels of her skirt would show off the light ones. *Distant Music* he would call the picture if he were a painter.

315   The hall-door was closed; and Aunt Kate, Aunt Julia and Mary Jane came down the hall, still laughing.

—Well, isn't Freddy terrible? said Mary Jane. He's really terrible.

Gabriel said nothing but pointed up the stairs towards where his wife was standing. Now that the hall-door was closed the voice and the piano could be heard more clearly. Gabriel held up his hand for them to be silent. The song seemed to be in the old Irish tonality and the singer seemed uncertain both of his words and of his voice. The voice, made plaintive by distance and by the singer's hoarseness, faintly illuminated the cadence of the air with words expressing grief:

> O, the rain falls on my heavy locks
> And the dew wets my skin,
> My babe lies cold . . .

—O, exclaimed Mary Jane. It's Bartell D'Arcy singing and he wouldn't sing all the night. O, I'll get him to sing a song before he goes.

—O do, Mary Jane, said Aunt Kate.

Mary Jane brushed past the others and ran to the staircase but before she reached 320
it the singing stopped and the piano was closed abruptly.

—O, what a pity! she cried. Is he coming down, Gretta?

Gabriel heard his wife answer yes and saw her come down towards them. A few steps behind her were Mr. Bartell D'Arcy and Miss O'Callaghan.

—O, Mr. D'Arcy, cried Mary Jane, it's downright mean of you to break off like that when we were all in raptures listening to you.

—I have been at him all the evening, said Miss O'Callaghan, and Mrs. Conroy too and he told us he had a dreadful cold and couldn't sing.

—O, Mr. D'Arcy, said Aunt Kate, now that was a great fib to tell.   325

—Can't you see that I'm as hoarse as a crow? said Mr. D'Arcy roughly.

He went into the pantry hastily and put on his overcoat. The others, taken aback by his rude speech, could find nothing to say. Aunt Kate wrinkled her brows and made signs to the others to drop the subject. Mr. D'Arcy stood swathing his neck carefully and frowning.

—It's the weather, said Aunt Julia, after a pause.

—Yes, everybody has colds, said Aunt Kate readily, everybody.

—They say, said Mary Jane, we haven't had snow like it for thirty years; and I 330
read this morning in the newspapers that the snow is general all over Ireland.

—I love the look of snow, said Aunt Julia sadly.

—So do I, said Miss O'Callaghan. I think Christmas is never really Christmas unless we have the snow on the ground.

—But poor Mr. D'Arcy doesn't like the snow, said Aunt Kate, smiling.

Mr. D'Arcy came from the pantry, fully swathed and buttoned, and in a repentant tone told them the history of his cold. Everyone gave him advice and said it was a great pity and urged him to be very careful of his throat in the night air. Gabriel watched his wife who did not join in the conversation. She was standing right under the dusty fanlight and the flame of the gas lit up the rich bronze of her hair which he had seen her drying at the fire few days before. She was in the same attitude and seemed unaware of the talk about her. At last she turned towards them and Gabriel saw that there was colour on her cheeks and that her eyes were shining. A sudden tide of joy went leaping out of his heart.

335   —Mr. D'Arcy, she said, what is the name of that song you were singing?

—It's called *The Lass of Aughrim,* said Mr. D'Arcy, but I couldn't remember it properly. Why? Do you know it?

—*The Lass of Aughrim,* she repeated. I couldn't think of the name.

—It's a very nice air, said Mary Jane. I'm sorry you were not in voice to-night.

—Now, Mary Jane, said Aunt Kate, don't annoy Mr. D'Arcy. I won't have him annoyed.

340   Seeing that all were ready to start she shepherded them to the door where good-night was said:

—Well, good-night, Aunt Kate, and thanks for the pleasant evening.

—Good-night, Gabriel. Good-night, Gretta!

—Good-night, Aunt Kate, and thanks ever so much. Good-night, Aunt Julia.

—O, good-night, Gretta, I didn't see you.

345   —Good-night, Mr. D'Arcy. Good-night, Miss O'Callaghan.

—Good-night, Miss Morkan.

—Good-night, again.

—Good-night, all. Safe home.

—Good-night. Good-night.

350   The morning was still dark. A dull yellow light brooded over the houses and the river; and the sky seemed to be descending. It was slushy underfoot; and only streaks and patches of snow lay on the roofs, on the parapets of the quay and on the area railings. The lamps were still burning redly in the murky air and, across the river, the palace of the Four Courts stood out menacingly against the heavy sky.

She was walking on before him with Mr. Bartell D'Arcy, her shoes in a brown parcel tucked under one arm and her hands holding her skirt up from the slush. She had no longer any grace of attitude but Gabriel's eyes were still bright with happiness. The blood went bounding along his veins; and the thoughts went rioting through his brain, proud, joyful, tender, valorous.

She was walking on before him so lightly and so erect that he longed to run after her noiselessly, catch her by the shoulders and say something foolish and affectionate into her ear. She seemed to him so frail that he longed to defend her against something and then to be alone with her. Moments of their secret life together burst like stars upon his memory. A heliotrope envelope was lying beside his breakfast-cup and he was caressing it with his hand. Birds were twittering in the ivy and the sunny web of the curtain was shimmering along the floor: he could not eat for happiness. They were standing on the crowded platform and he was placing a ticket inside the warm palm of her glove. He was standing with her in the cold, looking in through a grated window at a man making bottles in a roaring furnace. It was very cold. Her face, fragrant in the cold air, was quite close to his; and suddenly she called out to the man at the furnace:

—Is the fire hot, sir?

But the man could not hear her with the noise of the furnace. It was just as well. He might have answered rudely.

A wave of yet more tender joy escaped from his heart and went coursing in 355 warm flood along his arteries. Like the tender fires of stars moments of their life together, that no one knew of or would ever know of, broke upon and illumined his memory. He longed to recall to her those moments, to make her forget the years of their dull existence together and remember only their moments of ecstasy. For the years, he felt, had not quenched his soul or hers. Their children, his writing, her household cares had not quenched all their souls' tender fire. In one letter that he had written to her then he had said: *Why is it that words like these seem to me so dull and cold? Is it because there is no word tender enough to be your name?*

Like distant music these words that he had written years before were borne towards him from the past. He longed to be alone with her. When the others had gone away, when he and she were in their room in the hotel, then they would be alone together. He would call her softly:

—Gretta!

Perhaps she would not hear at once: she would be undressing. Then something in his voice would strike her. She would turn and look at him.

At the corner of Winetavern Street they met a cab. He was glad of its rattling noise as it saved him from conversation. She was looking out of the window and seemed tired. The others spoke only a few words, pointing out some building or street. The horse galloped along wearily under the murky morning sky, dragging his old rattling box after his heels, and Gabriel was again in a cab with her, galloping to catch the boat, galloping to their honeymoon.

As the cab drove across O'Connel Bridge Miss O'Callaghan said: 360

—They say you never cross O'Connel Bridge without seeing a white horse.

—I see a white man this time, said Gabriel.

—Where? asked Mr. Bartell D'Arcy.

Gabriel pointed to the statue, on which lay patches of snow. Then he nodded familiarly to it and waved his hand.

—Good-night, Dan, he said gaily. 365

When the cab drew up before the hotel Gabriel jumped out and, in spite of Mr. Bartell D'Arcy's protest, paid the driver. He gave the man a shilling over his fare. The man saluted and said:

—A prosperous New Year to you, sir.

—The same to you, said Gabriel cordially.

She leaned for a moment on his arm in getting out of the cab and while standing at the curbstone, bidding the others good-night. She leaned lightly on his arm, as lightly as when she had danced with him a few hours before. He had felt proud and happy then, happy that she was his, proud of her grace and wifely carriage. But now, after the kindling again of so many memories, the first touch of her body, musical and strange and perfumed, sent through him a keen pang of lust. Under cover of her silence he pressed her arm closely to his side; and, as they stood at the hotel door, he felt that they had escaped from their lives and duties, escaped from home and friends and run away together with wild and radiant hearts to a new adventure.

An old man was dozing in a great hooded chair in the hall. He lit a candle in the 370 office and went before them to the stairs. They followed him in silence, their feet falling in soft thuds on the thickly carpeted stairs. She mounted the stairs behind the porter, her head bowed in the ascent, her frail shoulders curved as with a burden, her skirt girt tightly about her. He could have flung his arms about her hips and held her still for his arms were trembling with desire to seize her and only the stress of his nails against the palms of his hands held the wild impulse of his body in check. The porter halted on the stairs to settle his guttering candle. They halted too on the steps below him. In the silence Gabriel could hear the falling of the molten wax into the tray and the thumping of his own heart against his ribs.

The porter led them along a corridor and opened a door. Then he set his unstable candle down on a toilet-table and asked at what hour they were to be called in the morning.

—Eight, said Gabriel.

The porter pointed to the tap of the electric-light and began a muttered apology but Gabriel cut him short.

—We don't want any light. We have light enough from the street. And I say, he added, pointing to the candle, you might remove that handsome article, like a good man.

375   The porter took up his candle again, but slowly for he was surprised by such a novel idea. Then he mumbled good-night and went out. Gabriel shot the lock to.

A ghostly light from the street lamp lay in a long shaft from one window to the door. Gabriel threw his overcoat and hat on a couch and crossed the room towards the window. He looked down into the street in order that his emotion might calm a little. Then he turned and leaned against a chest of drawers with his back to the light. She had taken off her hat and cloak and was standing before a large swinging mirror, unhooking her waist. Gabriel paused for a few moments, watching her, and then said:

—Gretta!

She turned away from the mirror slowly and walked along the shaft of light towards him. Her face looked so serious and weary that the words would not pass Gabriel's lips. No, it was not the moment yet.

—You looked tired, he said.

380   —I am a little, she answered.

—You don't feel ill or weak?

—No, tired: that's all.

She went on to the window and stood there, looking out. Gabriel waited again and then, fearing that diffidence was about to conquer him, he said abruptly:

—By the way, Gretta!

385   —What is it?

—You know that poor fellow Malins? he said quickly.

—Yes. What about him?

—Well, poor fellow, he's a decent sort of chap after all, continued Gabriel in a false voice. He gave me back that sovereign I lent him and I didn't expect it really. It's a pity he wouldn't keep away from that Browne, because he's not a bad fellow at heart.

He was trembling now with annoyance. Why did she seem so abstracted? He did not know how he could begin. Was she annoyed, too, about something? If she would only turn to him or come to him of her own accord! To take her as she was would be brutal. No, he must see some ardour in her eyes first. He longed to be master of her strange mood.

—When did you lend him the pound? she asked, after a pause. 390

Gabriel strove to restrain himself from breaking out into brutal language about the sottish Malins and his pound. He longed to cry to her from his soul, to crush her body against his, to overmaster her. But he said:

—O, at Christmas, when he opened that little Christmas-card shop in Henry Street.

He was in such a fever of rage and desire that he did not hear her come from the window. She stood before him for an instant, looking at him strangely. Then, suddenly raising herself on tiptoe and resting her hands lightly on his shoulders, she kissed him.

—You are a very generous person, Gabriel, she said.

Gabriel, trembling with delight at her sudden kiss and at the quaintness of her 395 phrase, put his hands on her hair and began smoothing it back, scarcely touching it with his fingers. The washing had made it fine and brilliant. His heart was brimming over with happiness. Just when he was wishing for it she had come to him of her own accord. Perhaps her thoughts had been running with his. Perhaps she had felt the impetuous desire that was in him and then the yielding mood had come upon her. Now that she had fallen to him so easily he wondered why he had been so diffident.

He stood, holding her head between his hands. Then, slipping one arm swiftly about her body and drawing her towards him, he said softly:

—Gretta dear, what are you thinking about?

She did not answer nor yield wholly to his arm. He said again, softly: 400

—Tell me what it is, Gretta. I think I know what is the matter. Do I know?

She did not answer at once. Then she said in an outburst of tears:

—O, I am thinking about that song, *The Lass of Aughrim.*

She broke loose from him and ran to the bed and, throwing her arms across the bed-rail, hid her face. Gabriel stood stock-still for a moment in astonishment and then followed her. As he passed in the way of the cheval-glass he caught sight of himself in full length, his broad, well-filled shirt-front, the face whose expression always puzzled him when he saw it in a mirror and his glimmering gilt-rimmed eye-glasses. He halted a few paces from her and said:

—What about the song? Why does that make you cry?

She raised her head from her arms and dried her eyes with the back of her hand like a child. A kinder note than he had intended went into his voice.

—Why, Gretta? he asked. 405

—I am thinking about a person long ago who used to sing that song.

—And who was the person long ago? asked Gabriel, smiling.

—It was a person I used to know in Galway when I was living with my grandmother, she said.

The smile passed away from Gabriel's face. A dull anger began to gather again at the back of his mind and the dull fires of his lust began to glow angrily in his veins.

—Someone you were in love with? he asked ironically. 410

—It was a young boy I used to know, she answered, named Michael Furey. He used to sing that song. *The Lass of Aughrim.* He was very delicate.

Gabriel was silent. He did not wish her to think that he was interested in this delicate boy.

—I can see him so plainly, she said after a moment. Such eyes as he had: big dark eyes! And such an expression in them—an expression!

—O then, you were in love with him? said Gabriel.

415   —I used to go out walking with him, she said, when I was in Galway.

A thought flew across Gabriel's mind.

—Perhaps that was why you wanted to go to Galway with that Ivors girl? he said coldly.

She looked at him and asked in surprise:

—What for?

420   Her eyes made Gabriel feel awkward. He shrugged his shoulders and said:

—How do I know? To see him perhaps.

She looked away from him along the shaft of light towards the window in silence.

—He is dead, she said at length. He died when he was only seventeen. Isn't it a terrible thing to die so young as that?

—What was he? asked Gabriel, still ironically.

425   —He was in the gasworks, she said.

Gabriel felt humiliated by the failure of his irony and by the evocation of this figure from the dead, a boy in the gasworks. While he had been full of memories of their secret life together, full of tenderness and joy and desire, she had been comparing him in her mind with another. A shameful consciousness of his own person assailed him. He saw himself as a ludicrous figure, acting as a pennyboy for his aunts, a nervous well-meaning sentimentalist, orating to vulgarians and idealising his own clownish lusts, the pitiable fatuous fellow he had caught a glimpse of in the mirror. Instinctively he turned his back more to the light lest she might see the shame that burned upon his forehead.

He tried to keep up his tone of cold interrogation but his voice when he spoke was humble and indifferent.

—I suppose you were in love with this Michael Furey, Gretta, he said.

—I was great with him at that time, she said.

430   Her voice was veiled and sad. Gabriel, feeling now how vain it would be to try to lead her whither he had purposed, caressed one of her hands and said, also sadly:

—And what did he die of so young, Gretta? Consumption, was it?

—I think he died for me, she answered.

A vague terror seized Gabriel at this answer as if, at that hour when he had hoped to triumph, some impalpable and vindictive being was coming against him, gathering forces against him in its vague world. But he shook himself free of it with an effort of reason and continued to caress her hand. He did not question her again for he felt that she would tell him of herself. Her hand was warm and moist: it did not respond to his touch but he continued to caress it just as he had caressed her first letter to him that spring morning.

—It was in the winter, she said, about the beginning of the winter when I was going to leave my grandmother's and come up here to the convent. And he was ill at the time in his lodgings in Galway and wouldn't be let out and his people in Oughterard were written to. He was in decline, they said, or something like that. I never knew rightly.

She paused for a moment and sighed.   435

—Poor fellow, she said. He was very fond of me and he was such a gentle boy. We used to go out together, walking, you know, Gabriel, like the way they do in the country. He was going to study singing only for his health. He had a very good voice, poor Michael Furey.

—Well; and then? asked Gabriel.

—And then when it came to the time for me to leave Galway and come up to the convent he was much worse and I wouldn't be let see him so I wrote a letter saying I was going up to Dublin and would be back in the summer and hoping he would be better then.

She paused for a moment to get her voice under control and then went on:

—Then the night before I left I was in my grandmother's house in Nun's Island,   440 packing up, and I heard gravel thrown up against the window. The window was so wet I couldn't see so I ran downstairs as I was and slipped out the back into the garden and there was the poor fellow at the end of the garden, shivering.

—And did you not tell him to go back? asked Gabriel.

—I implored of him to go home at once and told him he would get his death in the rain. But he said he did not want to live. I can see his eyes as well! He was standing at the end of the wall where there was a tree.

—And did he go home? asked Gabriel.

—Yes, he went home. And when I was only a week in the convent he died and he was buried in Oughterard where his people came from. O, the day I heard that, that he was dead!

She stopped, choking with sobs, and overcome by emotion, flung herself face   445 downward on the bed, sobbing in the quilt. Gabriel held her hand for a moment longer, irresolutely, and then, shy of intruding on her grief, let it fall gently and walked quietly to the window.

She was fast asleep.

Gabriel, leaning on his elbow, looked for a few moments unresentfully on her tangled hair and half-open mouth, listening to her deep-drawn breath. So she had had that romance in her life: a man had died for her sake. It hardly pained him now to think how poor a part he, her husband, had played in her life. He watched her while she slept as though he and she had never lived together as man and wife. His curious eyes rested long upon her face and on her hair: and, as he thought of what she must have been then, in that time of her first girlish beauty, a strange friendly pity for her entered his soul. He did not like to say even to himself that her face was no longer beautiful but he knew that it was no longer the face for which Michael Furey had braved death.

Perhaps she had not told him all the story. His eyes moved to the chair over which she had thrown some of her clothes. A petticoat string dangled to the floor. One boot stood upright, its limp upper fallen down: the fellow of it lay upon its side.

He wondered at his riot of emotions of an hour before. From what had it proceeded? From his aunt's supper, from his own foolish speech, from the wine and dancing, the merrymaking when saying good-night in the hall, the pleasure of the walk along the river in the snow. Poor Aunt Julia! She, too, would soon be a shade with the shade of Patrick Morkan and his horse. He had caught that haggard look upon her face for a moment when she was singing *Arrayed for the Bridal.* Soon, perhaps, he would be sitting in that same drawing-room, dressed in black, his silk hat on his knees. The blinds would be drawn down and Aunt Kate would be sitting beside him, crying and blowing her nose and telling him how Julia had died. He would cast about in his mind for some words that might console her, and would find only lame and useless ones. Yes, yes: that would happen very soon.

The air of the room chilled his shoulders. He stretched himself cautiously along under the sheets and lay down beside his wife. One by one they were all becoming shades. Better pass boldly into that other world, in the full glory of some passion, than fade and wither dismally with age. He thought of how she who lay beside him had locked in her heart for so many years that image of her lover's eyes when he had told her that he did not wish to live.

450   Generous tears filled Gabriel's eyes. He had never felt like that himself towards any woman but he knew that such a feeling must be love. The tears gathered more thickly in his eyes and in the partial darkness he imagined he saw the form of a young man standing under a dripping tree. Other forms were near. His soul had approached that region where dwell the vast hosts of the dead. He was conscious of, but could not apprehend, their wayward and flickering existence. His own identity was fading out into a grey impalpable world: the solid world itself which these dead had one time reared and lived in was dissolving and dwindling.

A few light taps upon the pane made him turn to the window. It had begun to snow again. He watched sleepily the flakes, silver and dark, falling obliquely against the lamplight. The time had come for him to set out on his journey westward. Yes, the newspapers were right: snow was general all over Ireland. It was falling on every part of the dark central plain, on the treeless hills, falling softly upon the Bog of Allen and, farther westward, softly falling into the dark mutinous Shannon waves. It was falling, too, upon every part of the lonely churchyard on the hill where Michael Furey lay buried. It lay thickly drifted on the crooked crosses and headstones, on the spears of the little gate, on the barren thorns. His soul swooned slowly as he heard the snow falling faintly through the universe and faintly falling, like the descent of their last end, upon all the living and the dead.

QUESTIONS FOR DISCUSSION AND WRITING

1. How does the opening scene prepare for Gabriel's entrance? What minor conflicts does he encounter throughout the evening? How do those conflicts reach a climax in the hotel room?

2. How do the various people at the party characterize Gabriel? What does he think of himself? How does he see himself in the mirror at the hotel room?

3. Why does Joyce spend so much time describing the conversation and activities at the annual dance? How does this setting compare with the setting in the garden at Galway, where Michael Furey comes to see Gretta?

4. How does Gabriel's point of view toward himself change during the course of the evening? What does he learn about himself once he hears the story of Michael Furey?

5. What events during the evening—especially Gabriel's speech and D'Arcy's song—establish the contrast between the romantic past and "living duties and affections"? How do Gabriel's final observations about the falling snow reveal his new awareness?

Stories for Comparison

Ethan Canin's "We Are Nighttime Travelers" (pages 339–350); Bobbie Ann Mason's "Shiloh" (pages 872–883).

61

F R A N Z   K A F K A

In the Penal Colony

FRANZ KAFKA (1883–1924) was born in Prague, Czechoslovakia, and educated at Karl Ferdinand University, where he earned a doctorate in jurisprudence. Rather than work as an attorney, he accepted a position as a civil service lawyer investigating workers' insurance claims. During the day, Kafka tried to fit into the mundane life of a civil servant, and at night, he wrote his dreamlike stories and novels about alienation, exile, fear, and failure. During his lifetime, Kafka published two short novels, *The Metamorphosis* (1915) and *In the Penal Colony* (1919), and two collections of stories, *The Country Doctor* (1919) and *The Hunger Artist* (1924). In 1924, Kafka died of tuberculosis in Berlin, leaving instructions with his literary executor, Max Brod, to destroy his published work and all his remaining manuscripts. Because he did not share Kafka's evaluation of this work, Brod disregarded his friend's request. In the next three years, Brod published three novels that brought Kafka posthumous fame as one of our century's great writers: *The Trial* (1925), *The Castle* (1926), and *Amerika* (1927). In the subsequent years his stories have been collected in *The Great Wall of China* (1933), *A Franz Kafka Miscellany* (1940), and *The Complete Stories* (1976). "In the Penal Colony," reprinted from *In the Penal Colony* (1948), dramatizes a terrifying method of inflicting punishment.

I t's a remarkable piece of apparatus," said the officer to the explorer and surveyed with a certain air of admiration the apparatus which was after all quite familiar to him. The explorer seemed to have accepted merely out of politeness the Commandant's invitation to witness the execution of a soldier condemned to death for disobedience and insulting behavior to a superior. Nor did the colony itself betray much interest in this execution. At least, in the small sandy valley, a deep hollow surrounded on all sides by naked crags, there was no one present save the officer, the explorer, the condemned man, who was a stupid-looking wide-mouthed creature with bewildered hair and face, and the soldier who held the heavy chain controlling the small chains locked on the prisoner's ankles, wrists and neck, chains which were themselves attached to each other by communicating links. In any case, the condemned man looked so like a submissive dog that one might have thought he could be left to run free on the surrounding hills and would only need to be whistled for when the execution was due to begin.

The explorer did not much care about the apparatus and walked up and down behind the prisoner with almost visible indifference while the officer made the last adjustments, now creeping beneath the structure, which was bedded deep in the earth, now climbing a ladder to inspect its upper parts. These were tasks that might well have been left to a mechanic, but the officer performed them with great zeal, whether because he was a devoted admirer of the apparatus or because of other reasons the work could be entrusted to no one else. "Ready now!" he called at last and climbed down from the ladder. He looked uncommonly limp, breathed with his mouth wide open and had tucked two fine ladies' handkerchiefs under the collar of his uniform. "These uniforms are too heavy for the tropics, surely," said the explorer, instead of making some inquiry about the apparatus, as the officer had expected. "Of course," said the officer, washing his oily and greasy hands in a bucket of water that stood ready, "but they mean home to us; we don't want to forget about home. Now just have a look at this machine," he added at once, simultaneously drying his hands on a towel and indicating the apparatus. "Up till now a few things still had to be set by hand, but from this moment it works all by itself." The explorer nodded and followed him. The officer, anxious to secure himself against all contingencies, said: "Things sometimes go wrong, of course; I hope that nothing goes wrong today, but we have to allow for the possibility. The machinery should go on working continuously for twelve hours. But if anything does go wrong it will only be some small matter that can be set right at once."

"Won't you take a seat?" he asked finally, drawing a cane chair out from among a heap of them and offering it to the explorer, who could not refuse it. He was now sitting at the edge of a pit, into which he glanced for a fleeting moment. It was not very deep. On one side of the pit the excavated soil had been piled up in a rampart, on the other side of it stood the apparatus. "I don't know," said the officer, "if the Commandant has already explained this apparatus to you." The explorer waved one hand vaguely; the officer asked for nothing better, since now he could explain the apparatus himself. "This apparatus," he said, taking hold of a crank handle and leaning against it, "was invented by our former Commandant. I assisted at the very earliest experiments and had a share in all the work until its completion. But the credit of inventing it belongs to him alone. Have you ever heard of our former Commandant? No? Well, it isn't saying too much if I tell you that the organization of the whole penal colony is his work. We who were his friends knew even before he died that the organization of the colony was so perfect that his successor, even with a thousand new schemes in his head, would find it impossible to alter anything, at least for many years to come. And our prophecy has come true; the new Commandant has had to acknowledge its truth. A pity you never met the old Commandant!—But," the officer interrupted himself, "I am rambling on, and here stands his apparatus before us. It consists, as you see, of three parts. In the course of time each of these parts has acquired a kind of popular nickname. The lower one is called the 'Bed,' the upper one the 'Designer,' and this one here in the middle that moves up and down is called the 'Harrow.'" "The Harrow?" asked the explorer. He had not been listening very attentively, the glare of the sun in the shadeless valley was altogether too strong, it was difficult to collect one's thoughts. All the more did he admire the officer, who in spite of his tight-fitting full-dress uniform coat, amply befrogged and weighed down by epaulettes, was pursuing his subject with such enthusiasm and, besides talking, was still tightening a screw here and there with a spanner. As for the soldier, he seemed to be in much the same condition as the explorer. He had wound the prisoner's chain round both his wrists, propped himself on his rifle, let his head hang and was paying no attention to anything. That did not surprise the explorer, for the officer was speaking French, and certainly neither the soldier nor the prisoner understood a word of French. It was all the more remarkable, therefore, that the prisoner was none the less making an effort to follow the officer's explanations. With a kind of drowsy persistence he directed his gaze wherever the officer pointed a finger, and at the interruption of the explorer's question he, too, as well as the officer, looked round.

"Yes, the Harrow," said the officer, "a good name for it. The needles are set in like the teeth of a harrow and the whole thing works something like a harrow, although its action is limited to one place and contrived with much more artistic skill. Anyhow, you'll soon understand it. On the Bed here the condemned man is laid—I'm going to describe the apparatus first before I set it in motion. Then you'll be able to follow the proceedings better. Besides, one of the cog wheels in the Designer is badly worn; it creaks a lot when it's working; you can hardly hear yourself speak; spare parts, unfortunately, are difficult to get here.—Well, here is the Bed, as I told you. It is completely covered with a layer of cotton wool; you'll find out why later. On this cotton wool the condemned man is laid, face down, quite naked, of course; here are straps for the hands, here for the feet, and here for the neck, to bind him fast. Here at the head of the bed, where the man, as I said, first lays down his face, is this little gag of felt, which can be easily regulated to go straight into his mouth. It is meant to keep him from screaming and biting his tongue. Of course the man is forced to take the felt into his mouth, for otherwise his neck would be broken by the strap." "Is that cotton wool?" asked the explorer, bending forward. "Yes, certainly," said the officer, with a smile, "feel it for yourself." He took the explorer's hand and guided it over the bed. "It's specially prepared cotton wool, that's why it looks so different; I'll tell you presently what it's for." The explorer already felt a dawning interest in the apparatus; he sheltered his eyes from the sun with one hand and gazed up at the structure. It was a huge affair. The Bed and the Designer were of the same size and looked like two dark wooden chests. The Designer hung about two meters above the Bed; each of them was bound at the corners with four rods of brass that almost flashed out rays in the sunlight. Between the chests shuttled the Harrow on a ribbon of steel.

5   The officer had scarcely noticed the explorer's previous indifference, but he was now well aware of his dawning interest; so he stopped explaining in order to leave a space of time for quiet observation. The condemned man imitated the explorer; since he could not use a hand to shelter his eyes he gazed upwards without shade.

"Well, the man lies down," said the explorer, leaning back in his chair and crossing his legs.

"Yes," said the officer, pushing his cap back a little and passing one hand over his heated face, "now listen! Both the Bed and the Designer have an electric battery each; the Bed needs one for itself, the Designer for the Harrow. As soon as the man is strapped down, the Bed is set in motion. It quivers in minute, very rapid vibrations, both from side to side and up and down. You will have seen similar apparatus in hospitals; but in our Bed the movements are all precisely calculated; you see, they have to correspond very exactly to the movements of the Harrow. And the Harrow is the instrument for the actual execution of the sentence."

"And how does the sentence run?" asked the explorer.

"You don't know that either?" said the officer in amazement, and bit his lips. "Forgive me if my explanations seem rather incoherent. I do beg your pardon. You see, the Commandant always used to do the explaining; but the new Commandant shirks this duty; yet that such an important visitor"—the explorer tried to deprecate the honor with both hands, the officer, however, insisted—"that such an important visitor should not even be told about the kind of sentence we pass is a new development, which—" He was just on the point of using strong language but checked himself and said only: "I was not informed, it is not my fault. In any case, I am certainly the best person to explain our procedure, since I have here"—he patted his breast pocket—"the relevant drawings made by our former Commandant."

10   "The Commandant's own drawings?" asked the explorer. "Did he combine everything in himself, then? Was he soldier, judge, mechanic, chemist and draughtsman?"

"Indeed he was," said the officer, nodding assent, with a remote, glassy look. Then he inspected his hands critically; they did not seem clean enough to him for touching the drawings; so he went over to the bucket and washed them again. Then he drew out a small leather wallet and said: "Our sentence does not sound severe. Whatever commandment the prisoner has disobeyed is written upon his body by the Harrow. This prisoner, for instance"—the officer indicated the man—"will have written on his body: HONOR THY SUPERIORS!"

The explorer glanced at the man; he stood, as the officer pointed him out, with bent head, apparently listening with all his ears in an effort to catch what was being said. Yet the movement of his blubber lips, closely pressed together, showed clearly that he could not understand a word. Many questions were troubling the explorer, but at the sight of the prisoner he asked only: "Does he know his sentence?" "No," said the officer, eager to go on with his exposition, but the explorer interrupted him: "He doesn't know the sentence that has been passed on him?" "No," said the officer again, pausing a moment as if to let the explorer elaborate his question, and then said: "There would be no point in telling him. He'll learn it on his body." The explorer intended to make no answer, but he felt the prisoner's gaze turned on him; it seemed to ask if he approved such ongoings. So he bent forward again, having already leaned back in his chair, and put another question: "But surely he knows that he has been sentenced?" "Nor that either," said the officer, smiling at the explorer as if expecting him to make further surprising remarks. "No," said the explorer, wiping his forehead, "then he can't know either whether his defense was effective?" "He has had no chance of putting up a defense," said the officer, turning his eyes away as if speaking to himself and so sparing the explorer the shame of hearing self-evident matters explained. "But he must have had some chance of defending himself," said the explorer, and rose from his seat.

The officer realized that he was in danger of having his exposition of the apparatus held up for a long time; so he went up to the explorer, took him by the arm, waved a hand towards the condemned man, who was standing very straight now that he had so obviously become the center of attention—the soldier had also given the chain a jerk—and said: "This is how the matter stands. I have been appointed judge in this penal colony. Despite my youth. For I was the former Commandant's assistant in all penal matters and know more about the apparatus than anyone. My guiding principle is this: Guilt is never to be doubted. Other courts cannot follow that principle, for they consist of several opinions and have higher courts to scrutinize them. That is not the case here, or at least, it was not the case in the former Commandant's time. The new man has certainly shown some inclination to interfere with my judgments, but so far I have succeeded in fending him off and will go on succeeding. You wanted to have the case explained; it is quite simple, like all of them. A captain reported to me this morning that this man, who had been assigned to him as a servant and sleeps before his door, had been asleep on duty. It is his duty, you see, to get up every time the hour strikes and salute the captain's door. Not an exacting duty, and very necessary, since he has to be a sentry as well as a servant, and must be alert in both functions. Last night the captain wanted to see if the man was doing his duty. He opened the door as the clock struck two and there was his man curled up asleep. He took his riding whip and lashed him across the face. Instead of getting up and begging pardon, the man caught hold of his master's legs, shook him and cried: 'Throw that whip away or I'll eat you alive.'—That's the evidence. The captain came to me an hour ago, I wrote down his statement and appended the sentence to it. Then I had the man put in chains. That was all quite simple. If I had first called the man before me and interrogated him, things would have got into a confused tangle. He would have told lies, and had I exposed these lies he would have backed them up with more lies, and so on and so forth. As it is, I've got him and I won't let him go.—Is that quite clear now? But we're wasting time, the execution should be beginning and I haven't finished explaining the apparatus yet." He pressed the explorer back into his chair, went up again to the apparatus and began: "As you see, the shape of the Harrow corresponds to the human form; here is the harrow for the torso, here are the harrows for the legs. For the head there is only this one small spike. Is that quite clear?" He bent amiably forward towards the explorer, eager to provide the most comprehensive explanations.

The explorer considered the Harrow with a frown. The explanation of the judicial procedure had not satisfied him. He had to remind himself that this was in any case a penal colony where extraordinary measures were needed and that military discipline must be enforced to the last. He also felt that some hope might be set on the new Commandant, who was apparently of a mind to bring in, although gradually, a new kind of procedure which the officer's narrow mind was incapable of understanding. This train of thought prompted his next question: "Will the Commandant attend the execution?" "It is not certain," said the officer, wincing at the direct question, and his friendly expression darkened. "That is just why we have to lose no time. Much as I dislike it, I shall have to cut my explanations short. But of course tomorrow, when the apparatus has been cleaned—its one drawback is that it gets so messy—I can recapitulate all the details. For the present, then, only the essentials.— When the man lies down on the Bed and it begins to vibrate, the Harrow is lowered onto his body. It regulates itself automatically so that the needles barely touch his skin; once contact is made the steel ribbon stiffens immediately into a rigid band. And then the performance begins. An ignorant onlooker would see no difference between one punishment and another. The Harrow appears to do its work with uniform regularity. As it quivers, its points pierce the skin of the body which is itself quivering from the vibration of the Bed. So that the actual progress of the sentence can be watched, the Harrow is made of glass. Getting the needles fixed in the glass was a technical problem, but after many experiments we overcame the difficulty. No trouble was too great for us to take, you see. And now anyone can look through the glass and watch the inscription taking form on the body. Wouldn't you care to come a little nearer and have a look at the needles?"

15   The explorer got up slowly, walked across and bent over the Harrow. "You see," said the officer, "there are two kinds of needles arranged in multiple patterns. Each long needle has a short one beside it. The long needle does the writing, and the short needle sprays a jet of water to wash away the blood and keep the inscription clear. Blood and water together are then conducted here through small runnels into this main runnel and down a waste pipe into the pit." With his finger the officer traced the exact course taken by the blood and water. To make the picture as vivid as possible he held both hands below the outlet of the waste pipe as if to catch the outflow, and when he did this the explorer drew back his head and feeling behind him with one hand sought to return to his chair. To his horror he found that the condemned man too had obeyed the officer's invitation to examine the Harrow at close quarters and had followed him. He had pulled forward the sleepy soldier with the chain and was bending over the glass. One could see that his uncertain eyes were trying to

perceive what the two gentlemen had been looking at, but since he had not understood the explanation he could not make head or tail of it. He was peering this way and that way. He kept running his eyes along the glass. The explorer wanted to drive him away, since what he was doing was probably culpable. But the officer firmly restrained the explorer with one hand and with the other took a clod of earth from the rampart and threw it at the soldier. He opened his eyes with a jerk, saw what the condemned man had dared to do, let his rifle fall, dug his heels into the ground, dragged his prisoner back so that the stumbled and fell immediately, and then stood looking down at him, watching him struggling and rattling in his chains. "Set him on his feet!" yelled the officer, for he noticed that the explorer's attention was being too much distracted by the prisoner. In fact he was even leaning right across the Harrow, without taking any notice of it, intent only on finding out what was happening to the prisoner. "Be careful with him!" cried the officer again. He ran round the apparatus, himself caught the condemned man under the shoulders and with the soldier's help got him up on his feet, which kept slithering from under him.

"Now I know all about it," said the explorer as the officer came back to him. "All except the most important thing," he answered, seizing the explorer's arm and pointing upwards: "In the Designer are all the cogwheels that control the movements of the Harrow, and this machinery is regulated according to the inscription demanded by the sentence. I am still using the guiding plans drawn by the former Commandant. Here they are"—he extracted some sheets from the leather wallet—"but I'm sorry I can't let you handle them, they are my most precious possessions. Just take a seat and I'll hold them in front of you like this, then you'll be able to see everything quite well." He spread out the first sheet of paper. The explorer would have liked to say something appreciative, but all he could see was a labyrinth of lines crossing and re-crossing each other, which covered the paper so thickly that it was difficult to discern the blank spaces between them. "Read it," said the officer. "I can't," said the explorer. "Yet it's clear enough," said the officer. "It's very ingenious," said the explorer evasively, "but I can't make it out." "Yes," said the officer with a laugh, putting the paper away again, "it's no calligraphy for school children. It needs to be studied closely. I'm quite sure that in the end you would understand it too. Of course the script can't be a simple one; it's not supposed to kill a man straight off, but only after an interval of, on an average, twelve hours; the turning point is reckoned to come at the sixth hour. So there have to be lots and lots of flourishes around the actual script; the script itself runs round the body only in a narrow girdle; the rest of the body is reserved for the embellishments. Can you appreciate now the work accomplished by the Harrow and the whole apparatus?—Just watch it!" He ran up the ladder, turned a wheel, called down: "Look out, keep to one side!" and everything started working. If the wheel had not creaked, it would have been marvelous. The officer, as if surprised by the noise of the wheel, shook his fist at it, then spread out his arms in excuse to the explorer and climbed down rapidly to peer at the working of the machine from below. Something perceptible to no one save himself was still not in order; he clambered up again, did something with both hands in the interior of the Designer, then slid down one of the rods, instead of using the ladder, so as to get down quicker, and with the full force of his lungs, to make himself heard at all in the noise, yelled in the explorer's ear: "Can you follow it? The Harrow is beginning to write; when it finishes the first draft of the inscription on the man's back, the layer of cotton wool begins to roll and slowly turns the body over, to give the Harrow fresh space for writing. Meanwhile the raw part that has been written on lies on the cotton wool, which is specially prepared to staunch the bleeding and so makes all ready for a new deepening of the script. Then these teeth at the edge of the Harrow, as the body turns further round, tear the cotton wool away from the wounds, throw it into the pit, and there is more work for the Harrow. So it keeps on writing deeper and deeper for the whole twelve hours. The first six hours the condemned man stays alive almost as before, he suffers only pain. After two hours the felt gag is taken away, for he has no longer strength to scream. Here, into this electrically heated basin at the head of the bed, some warm rice pap is poured, from which the man, if he feels like it, can take as much as his tongue can lap. Not one of them ever misses the chance. I can remember none, and my experience is extensive. Only about the sixth hour does the man lose all desire to eat. I usually kneel down here at that moment and observe what happens. The man rarely swallows his last mouthful, he only rolls it round his mouth and spits it out into the pit. I have to duck just then or he would spit it in my face. But how quiet he grows at just about the sixth hour! Enlightenment comes to the most dull-witted. It begins around the eyes. From there it radiates. A moment that might tempt one to get under the Harrow oneself. Nothing more happens than that the man begins to understand the inscription, he purses his mouth as if he were listening. You have seen how difficult it is to decipher the script with one's eyes; but our man deciphers it with his wounds. To be sure, that is a hard task; he needs six hours to accomplish it. By that time the Harrow has pierced him quite through and casts him into the pit, where he pitches down upon the blood and water and the cotton wool. Then the judgment has been fulfilled, and we, the soldier and I, bury him."

The explorer had inclined his ear to the officer and with his hands in his jacket pockets watched the machine at work. The condemned man watched it too, but uncomprehendingly. He bent forward a little and was intent on the moving needles when the soldier, at a sign from the officer, slashed through his shirt and trousers from behind with a knife, so that they fell off; he tried to catch at his falling clothes to cover his nakedness, but the soldier lifted him into the air and shook the last remnants from him. The officer stopped the machine, and in the sudden silence the condemned man was laid under the Harrow. The chains were loosened and the straps fastened on instead; in the first moment that seemed almost a relief to the prisoner. And now the Harrow was adjusted a little lower, since he was a thin man. When the needle points touched him a shudder ran over his skin; while the soldier was busy strapping his right hand, he flung out his left hand blindly; but it happened to be in the direction towards where the explorer was standing. The officer kept watching the explorer sideways, as if seeking to read from his face the impression made on him by the execution, which had been at least cursorily explained to him.

The wrist strap broke; probably the soldier had drawn it too tight. The officer had to intervene, the soldier held up the broken piece of strap to show him. So the officer went over to him and said, his face still turned towards the explorer: "This is a very complex machine, it can't be helped that things are breaking or giving way here and there; but one must not thereby allow oneself to be diverted in one's general judgment. In any case, this strap is easily made good; I shall simply use a chain; the delicacy of the vibrations for the right arm will of course be a little impaired." And while he fastened the chains, he added: "The resources for maintaining the machine are now very much reduced. Under the former Commandant I had free access to a sum of money set aside entirely for this purpose. There was a store, too, in which spare parts were kept for repairs of all kinds. I confess I have been almost prodigal with them, I mean in the past, not now as the new Commandant pretends, always looking for an excuse to attack our old way of doing things. Now he has taken charge of the machine money himself, and if I send for a new strap they ask for the broken old strap as evidence, and the new strap takes ten days to appear and then is of shoddy material and not much good. But how I am supposed to work the machine without a strap, that's something nobody bothers about."

The explorer thought to himself: It's always a ticklish matter to intervene decisively in other people's affairs. He was neither a member of the penal colony nor a citizen of the state to which it belonged. Were he to denounce this execution or actually try to stop it, they could say to him: You are a foreigner, mind your own business. He could make no answer to that, unless he were to add that he was amazed at himself in this connection, for he traveled only as an observer, with no intention at all of altering other people's methods of administering justice. Yet here he found himself strongly tempted. The injustice of the procedure and the inhumanity of the execution were undeniable. No one could suppose that he had any selfish interest in the matter, for the condemned man was a complete stranger, not a fellow countryman or even at all sympathetic to him. The explorer himself had recommendations from high quarters, had been received here with great courtesy, and the very fact that he had been invited to attend the execution seemed to suggest that his views would be welcome. And this was all the more likely since the Commandant, as he had heard only too plainly, was no upholder of the procedure and maintained an attitude almost of hostility to the officer.

At that moment the explorer heard the officer cry out in rage. He had just, with considerable difficulty, forced the felt gag into the condemned man's mouth when the man in an irresistible access of nausea shut his eyes and vomited. Hastily the officer snatched him away from the gag and tried to hold his head over the pit; but it was too late, the vomit was running all over the machine. "It's all the fault of that Commandant!" cried the officer, senselessly shaking the brass rods in front, "the machine is befouled like a pigsty." With trembling hands he indicated to the explorer what had happened. "Have I not tried for hours at a time to get the Commandant to understand that the prisoner must fast for a whole day before the execution. But our new, mild doctrine thinks otherwise. The Commandant's ladies stuff the man with sugar candy before he's led off. He has lived on stinking fish his whole life long and now he has to eat sugar candy! But it could still be possible, I should have nothing to say against it, but why won't they get me a new felt gag, which I have been begging for the last three months. How should a man not feel sick when he takes a felt gag into his mouth which more than a hundred men have already slobbered and gnawed in their dying moments?"

The condemned man had laid his head down and looked peaceful, the soldier was busy trying to clean the machine with the prisoner's shirt. The officer advanced towards the explorer, who in some vague presentiment fell back a pace, but the officer seized him by the hand, and drew him to one side. "I should like to exchange a few words with you in confidence," he said, "may I?" "Of course," said the explorer, and listened with downcast eyes.

"This procedure and method of execution, which you are now having the opportunity to admire, has at the moment no longer any open adherents in our colony. I am its sole advocate, and at the same time the sole advocate of the old Commandant's tradition. I can no longer reckon on any further extension of the method, it takes all my energy to maintain it as it is. During the old Commandant's lifetime the colony was full of his adherents; his strength of conviction I still have in some measure, but not an atom of his power; consequently the adherents have skulked out of sight, there are still many of them but none of them will admit it. If you were to go into the teahouse today, on execution day, and listen to what is being said, you would perhaps hear only ambiguous remarks. These would all be made by adherents, but under the present Commandant and his present doctrines they are of no use to me. And now I ask you: because of this Commandant and the women who influence him, is such a piece of work, the work of a lifetime"—he pointed to the machine—"to perish? Ought one to let that happen? Even if one has only come as a stranger to our island for a few days? But there's no time to lose, an attack of some kind is impending on my function as judge; conferences are already being held in the Commandant's office from which I am excluded; even your coming here today seems to me a significant move; they are cowards and use you as a screen, you, a stranger.— How different an execution was in the old days! A whole day before the ceremony the valley was packed with people; they all came only to look on; early in the morning the Commandant appeared with his ladies; fanfares roused the whole camp; I reported that everything was in readiness; the assembled company—no high official dared to absent himself—arranged itself round the machine; this pile of cane chairs is a miserable survival from that epoch. The machine was freshly cleaned and glittering, I got new spare parts for almost every execution. Before hundreds of spectators—all of them standing on tiptoe as far as the heights there—the condemned man was laid under the Harrow by the Commandant himself. What is left today for a common soldier to do was then my task, the task of the presiding judge, and was an honor for me. And then the execution began! No discordant noise spoilt the working of the machine. Many did not care to watch it but lay with closed eyes in the sand; they all knew: Now Justice is being done. In the silence one heard nothing but the condemned man's sighs, half muffled by the felt gag. Nowadays the machine can no longer wring from anyone a sigh louder than the felt gag can stifle; but in those days the writing needles let drop an acid fluid, which we're no longer permitted to use. Well, and then came the sixth hour! It was impossible to grant all the requests to be allowed to watch it from near by. The Commandant in his wisdom ordained that the children should have the preference; I, of course, because of my office had the privilege of always being at hand; often enough I would be squatting there with a small child in either arm. How we all absorbed the look of transfiguration on the face of the sufferer, how we bathed our cheeks in the radiance of that justice, achieved at last and fading so quickly! What times these were, my comrade!" The officer had obviously forgotten whom he was addressing; he had embraced the explorer and laid his head on his shoulder. The explorer was deeply embarrassed, impatiently he stared over the officer's head. The soldier had finished his cleaning job and was now pouring rice pap from a pot into the basin. As soon as the condemned man, who seemed to have recovered entirely, noticed this action he began to reach for the rice with his tongue. The soldier kept pushing him away, since the rice pap was certainly meant for a later hour, yet it was just as unfitting that the soldier himself should thrust his dirty hands into the basin and eat out of it before the other's avid face.

The officer quickly pulled himself together. "I didn't want to upset you," he said, "I know it is impossible to make those days credible now. Anyhow, the machine is still working and it is still effective in itself. It is effective in itself even though it stands alone in this valley. And the corpse still falls at the last into the pit with an incomprehensibly gentle wafting motion, even although there are no hundreds of people swarming round like flies as formerly. In those days we had to put a strong fence round the pit, it has long since been torn down."

The explorer wanted to withdraw his face from the officer and looked round him at random. The officer thought he was surveying the valley's desolation; so he seized him by the hands, turned him round to meet his eyes, and asked: "Do you realize the shame of it?"

But the explorer said nothing. The officer left him alone for a little; with legs apart, hands on hips, he stood very still, gazing at the ground. Then he smiled encouragingly at the explorer and said: "I was quite near you yesterday when the Commandant gave you the invitation. I heard him giving it. I know the Commandant. I divined at once what he was after. Although he is powerful enough to take measures against me, he doesn't dare to do it yet, he certainly means to use your verdict against me, the verdict of an illustrious foreigner. He has calculated it carefully: this is your second day on the island, you did not know the old Commandant and his ways, you are conditioned by European ways of thought, perhaps you object on principle to capital punishment in general and to such mechanical instruments of death in particular, besides you will see that the execution has no support from the public, a shabby ceremony—carried out with a machine already somewhat old and worn—now, taking all that into consideration, would it not be likely (so thinks the Commandant) that you might disapprove of my methods? And if you disapprove, you wouldn't conceal the fact (I'm still speaking from the Commandant's point of view), for you are a man to feel confidence in your own well-tried conclusions. True, you have seen and learned to appreciate the peculiarities of many peoples, and so you would not be likely to take a strong line against our proceedings, as you might do in your own country. But the Commandant has no need of that. A casual, even an unguarded remark will be enough. It doesn't even need to represent what you really think, so long as it can be used speciously to serve his purpose. He will try to prompt you with sly questions, of that I am certain. And his ladies will sit around you and prick up their ears; you might be saying something like this: 'In our country we have a different criminal procedure,' or 'In our country the prisoner is interrogated before

he is sentenced,' or 'We haven't used torture since the Middle Ages.' All these statements are as true as they seem natural to you, harmless remarks that pass no judgment on my methods. But how would the Commandant react to them? I can see him,
our good Commandant, pushing his chair away immediately and rushing on to the
balcony, I can see his ladies streaming out after him, I can hear his voice—the ladies
call it a voice of thunder—well, and this is what he says: 'A famous Western investigator, sent out to study criminal procedure in all the countries of the world, has just
said that our old tradition of administering justice is inhumane. Such a verdict from
such a personality makes it impossible for me to countenance these methods any
longer. Therefore from this very day I ordain . . .' and so on. You may want to inter-
pose that you never said any such thing, that you never called my methods inhumane,
on the contrary your profound experience leads you to believe they are most humane
and most in consonance with human dignity, and you admire the machine greatly—
but it will be too late; you won't even get onto the balcony, crowded as it will be with
ladies; you may try to draw attention to yourself; you may want to scream out; but a
lady's hand will close your lips—and I and the work of the old Commandant will be
done for."

The explorer had to suppress a smile; so easy, then, was the task he had felt to
be so difficult. He said evasively: "You overestimate my influence; the Commandant
has read my letters of recommendation, he knows that I am no expert in criminal
procedure. If I were to give an opinion, it would be as a private individual, an opinion no more influential than that of any ordinary person, and in any case much less
influential than that of the Commandant, who, I am given to understand, has very extensive powers in this penal colony. If his attitude to your procedure is as definitely
hostile as you believe, then I fear the end of your tradition is at hand, even without
any humble assistance from me."

Had it dawned on the officer at last? No, he still did not understand. He shook
his head emphatically, glanced briefly round at the condemned man and the soldier,
who both flinched away from the rice, came close up to the explorer and without
looking at his face but fixing his eye on some spot on his coat said in a lower voice
than before: "You don't know the Commandant; you feel yourself—forgive the
expression—a kind of outsider so far as all of us are concerned; yet, believe me, your
influence cannot be rated too highly. I was simply delighted when I heard that you
were to attend the execution all by yourself. The Commandant arranged it to aim a
blow at me, but I shall turn it to my advantage. Without being distracted by lying
whispers and contemptuous glances—which could not have been avoided had a
crowd of people attended the execution—you have heard my explanations, seen the
machine and are now in course of watching the execution. You have doubtless already formed your own judgment; if you still have some small uncertainties the sight
of the execution will resolve them. And now I make this request to you: help me
against the Commandant!"

The explorer would not let him go on. "How could I do that," he cried, "it's quite
impossible. I can neither help nor hinder you."

"Yes, you can," the officer said. The explorer saw with a certain apprehension
that the officer had clenched his fists. "Yes, you can," repeated the officer, still more .

insistently. "I have a plan that is bound to succeed. You believe your influence is insufficient. I know that it is sufficient. But even granted that you are right, is it not necessary, for the sake of preserving this tradition, to try even what might prove insufficient? Listen to my plan, then. The first thing necessary for you to carry it out is to be as reticent as possible today regarding your verdict on these proceedings. Unless you are asked a direct question you must say nothing at all; but what you do say must be brief and general; let it be remarked that you would prefer not to discuss the matter, that you are out of patience with it, that if you are to let yourself go you would use strong language. I don't ask you to tell any lies; by no means; you should only give curt answers, such as: 'Yes, I saw the execution,' or 'Yes, I had it explained to me.' Just that, nothing more. There are grounds enough for any impatience you betray, although not such as will occur to the Commandant. Of course, he will mistake your meaning and interpret it to please himself. That's what my plan depends on. Tomorrow in the Commandant's office there is to be a large conference of all the high administrative officials, the Commandant presiding. Of course the Commandant is the kind of man to have turned these conferences into public spectacles. He has had a gallery built that is always packed with spectators. I am compelled to take part in the conferences, but they make me sick with disgust. Now, whatever happens, you will certainly be invited to this conference; if you behave today as I suggest the invitation will become an urgent request. But if for some mysterious reason you're not invited, you'll have to ask for an invitation; there's no doubt of your getting it then. So tomorrow you're sitting in the Commandant's box with the ladies. He keeps looking up to make sure you're there. After various trivial and ridiculous matters, brought in merely to impress the audience—mostly harbor works, nothing but harbor works!—our judicial procedure comes up for discussion too. If the Commandant doesn't introduce it, or not soon enough, I'll see that it's mentioned. I'll stand up and report that today's execution has taken place. Quite briefly, only a statement. Such a statement is not usual, but I shall make it. The Commandant thanks me, as always, with an amiable smile, and then he can't restrain himself, he seizes the excellent opportunity. 'It has just been reported,' he will say, or words to that effect, 'that an execution has taken place. I should like merely to add that this execution was witnessed by the famous explorer who has, as you all know, honored our colony so greatly by his visit to us. His presence at today's session of our conference also contributes to the importance of this occasion. Should we not now ask the famous explorer to give us his verdict on our traditional mode of execution and the procedure that leads up to it?' Of course there is loud applause, general agreement, I am more insistent than anyone. The Commandant bows to you and says: 'Then in the name of the assembled company, I put the question to you.' And now you advance to the front of the box. Lay your hands where everyone can see them, or the ladies will catch them and press your fingers.—And then at last you can speak out. I don't know how I'm going to endure the tension of waiting for that moment. Don't put any restraint on yourself when you make your speech, publish the truth aloud, lean over the front of the box, shout, yes indeed, shout your verdict, your unshakable conviction, at the Commandant. Yet perhaps you wouldn't care to do that, it's not in keeping with your character, in your country perhaps people do these things differently, well, that's all right too, that will be quite as effective, don't even stand up, just say a few words, even in a whisper, so that only the officials beneath you will hear them, that will be quite enough, you don't even need to mention the lack of public support for the execution, the creaking wheel, the broken strap, the filthy gag of felt, no, I'll take all that upon me, and, believe me, if my indictment doesn't drive him out of the conference hall, it will force him to his knees to make the acknowledgment: Old Commandant, I humble myself before you.—That is my plan; will you help me to carry it out? But of course you are willing, what is more, you must." And the officer seized the explorer by both arms and gazed, breathing heavily, into his face. He had shouted the last sentence so loudly that even the soldier and the condemned man were startled into attending; they had not understood a word but they stopped eating and looked over at the explorer, chewing their previous mouthfuls.

30   From the very beginning the explorer had no doubt about what answer he must give; in his lifetime he had experienced too much to have an uncertainty here; he was fundamentally honorable and unafraid. And yet now, facing the soldier and the condemned man, he did hesitate, for as long as it took to draw one breath. At last, however, he said, as he had to: "No." The officer blinked several times but did not turn his eyes away. "Would you like me to explain?" asked the explorer. The officer nodded wordlessly. "I do not approve of your procedure," said the explorer then, "even before you took me into your confidence—of course I shall never in any circumstances betray your confidence—I was already wondering whether it would be my duty to intervene and whether my intervention would have the slightest chance of success. I realized to whom I ought to turn: to the Commandant, of course. You have made that fact even clearer, but without having strengthened my resolution; on the contrary, your sincere conviction has touched me, even though it cannot influence my judgment."

The officer remained mute, turned to the machine, caught hold of a brass rod, and then, leaning back a little, gazed at the Designer as if to assure himself that all was in order. The soldier and the condemned man seemed to have come to some understanding; the condemned man was making signs to the soldier, difficult though his movements were because of the tight straps; the soldier was bending down to him; the condemned man whispered something and the soldier nodded.

The explorer followed the officer and said: "You don't know yet what I mean to do. I shall tell the Commandant what I think of the procedure, certainly, but not at a public conference, only in private; nor shall I stay here long enough to attend any conference; I am going away early tomorrow morning, or at least embarking on my ship."

It did not look as if the officer had been listening. "So you did not find the procedure convincing," he said to himself and smiled, as an old man smiles at childish nonsense and yet pursues his own meditations behind the smile.

"Then the time has come," he said at last, and suddenly looked at the explorer with bright eyes that held some challenge, some appeal for co-operation. "The time for what?" asked the explorer uneasily, but got no answer.

35   "You are free," said the officer to the condemned man in the native tongue. The man did not believe it at first. "Yes, you are set free," said the officer. For the first time the condemned man's face woke to real animation. Was it true? Was it only a

caprice of the officer's, that might change again? Had the foreign explorer begged him off? What was it? One could read these questions on his face. But not for long. Whatever it might be, he wanted to be really free if he might, and he began to struggle so far as the Harrow permitted him.

"You'll burst my straps," cried the officer, "lie still! We'll soon loosen them." And signing the soldier to help him, he set about doing so. The condemned man laughed wordlessly to himself, now he turned his face left towards the officer, now right towards the soldier, nor did he forget the explorer.

"Draw him out," ordered the officer. Because of the Harrow this had to be done with some care. The condemned man had already torn himself a little in the back through his impatience.

From now on, however, the officer paid hardly any attention to him. He went up to the explorer, pulled out the small leather wallet again, turned over the papers in it, found the one he wanted and showed it to the explorer. "Read it," he said. "I can't," said the explorer, "I told you before that I can't make out these scripts." "Try taking a close look at it," said the officer and came quite near to the explorer so that they might read it together. But when even that proved useless, he outlined the script with his little finger, holding it high above the paper as if the surface dared not be sullied by touch, in order to help the explorer to follow the script in that way. The explorer did make an effort, meaning to please the officer in this respect at least, but he was quite unable to follow. Now the officer began to spell it, letter by letter, and then read out the words. "'BE JUST!' is what is written there," he said, "surely you can read it now." The explorer bent so close to the paper that the officer feared he might touch it and drew it farther away; the explorer made no remark, yet it was clear that he still could not decipher it. "'BE JUST!' is what is written there," said the officer once more. "Maybe," said the explorer, "I am prepared to believe you." "Well, then," said the officer, at least partly satisfied, and climbed up the ladder with the paper; very carefully he laid it inside the Designer and seemed to be changing the disposition of all the cogwheels; it was a troublesome piece of work and must have involved wheels that were extremely small, for sometimes the officer's head vanished altogether from sight inside the Designer, so precisely did he have to regulate the machinery.

The explorer, down below, watched the labor uninterruptedly, his neck grew stiff and his eyes smarted from the glare of sunshine over the sky. The soldier and the condemned man were now busy together. The man's shirt and trousers, which were already lying in the pit, were fished out by the point of the soldier's bayonet. The shirt was abominably dirty and its owner washed it in the bucket of water. When he put on the shirt and trousers both he and the soldier could not help guffawing, for the garments were of course slit up behind. Perhaps the condemned man felt it incumbent on him to amuse the soldier, he turned round and round in his slashed garments before the soldier, who squatted on the ground beating his knees with mirth. All the same, they presently controlled their mirth out of respect for the gentlemen.

When the officer had at length finished his task aloft, he surveyed the machinery in all its details once more, with a smile, but this time shut the lid of the Designer, which had stayed open till now, climbed down, looked into the pit and then at the condemned man, noting with satisfaction that the clothing had been taken out, then went over to wash his hands in the water bucket, perceived too late that it was disgustingly dirty, was unhappy because he could not wash his hands, in the end thrust them into the sand—this alternative did not please him, but he had to put up with it—then stood upright and began to unbutton his uniform jacket. As he did this, the two ladies' handkerchiefs he had tucked under his collar fell into his hands. "Here are your handkerchiefs," he said, and threw them to the condemned man. And to the explorer he said in explanation: "A gift from the ladies."

In spite of the obvious haste with which he was discarding first his uniform jacket and then all his clothing, he handled each garment with loving care, he even ran his fingers caressingly over the silver lace on the jacket and shook a tassel into place. This loving care was certainly out of keeping with the fact that as soon as he had a garment off he flung it at once with a kind of unwilling jerk into the pit. The last thing left to him was his short sword with the sword belt. He drew it out of the scabbard, broke it, then gathered all together, the bits of the sword, the scabbard and the belt, and flung them so violently down that they clattered into the pit.

Now he stood naked there. The explorer bit his lips and said nothing. He knew very well what was going to happen, but he had no right to obstruct the officer in anything. If the judicial procedure which the officer cherished were really so near its end—possibly as a result of his own intervention, as to which he felt himself pledged—then the officer was doing the right thing; in his place the explorer would not have acted otherwise.

The soldier and the condemned man did not understand at first what was happening, at first they were not even looking on. The condemned man was gleeful at having got the handkerchiefs back, but he was not allowed to enjoy them for long, since the soldier snatched them with a sudden, unexpected grab. Now the condemned man in turn was trying to twitch them from under the belt where the soldier had tucked them, but the soldier was on his guard. So they were wrestling, half in jest. Only when the officer stood quite naked was their attention caught. The condemned man especially seemed struck with the notion that some great change was impending. What had happened to him was now going to happen to the officer. Perhaps even to the very end. Apparently the foreign explorer had given the order for it. So this was revenge. Although he himself had not suffered to the end, he was to be revenged to the end. A broad, silent grin now appeared on his face and stayed there all the rest of the time.

The officer, however, had turned to the machine. It had been clear enough previously that he understood the machine well, but now it was almost staggering to see how he managed it and how it obeyed him. His hand had only to approach the Harrow for it to rise and sink several times till it was adjusted to the right position for receiving him; he touched only the edge of the Bed and already it was vibrating; the felt gag came to meet his mouth, one could see that the officer was really reluctant to take it but he shrank from it only a moment, soon he submitted and received it. Everything was ready, only the straps hung down at the sides, yet they were obviously unnecessary, the officer did not need to be fastened down. Then the condemned man noticed the loose straps, in his opinion the execution was incomplete unless the straps were buckled, he gestured eagerly to the soldier and they ran together to strap the officer down. The latter had already stretched out one foot to push the lever that started the Designer; he saw the two men coming up; so he drew his foot back and let himself be buckled in. But now he could not reach the lever; neither the soldier nor the condemned man would be able to find it, and the explorer was determined not to lift a finger. It was not necessary; as soon as the straps were fastened the machine began to work; the Bed vibrated, the needles flickered above the skin, the Harrow rose and fell. The explorer had been staring at it quite a while before he remembered that a wheel in the Designer should have been creaking; but everything was quiet, not even the slightest hum could be heard.

Because it was working so silently the machine simply escaped one's attention. 45 The explorer observed the soldier and the condemned man. The latter was the more animated of the two, everything in the machine interested him, now he was bending down and now stretching up on tiptoe, his forefinger was extended all the time pointing out details to the soldier. This annoyed the explorer. He was resolved to stay till the end, but he could not bear the sight of these two. "Go back home," he said. The soldier would have been willing enough, but the condemned man took the order as a punishment. With clasped hands he implored to be allowed to stay, and when the explorer shook his head and would not relent, he even went down on his knees. The explorer saw that it was no use merely giving orders, he was on the point of going over and driving them away. At that moment he heard a noise above him in the Designer. He looked up. Was that cogwheel going to make trouble after all? But it was something quite different. Slowly the lid of the Designer rose up and then clicked wide open. The teeth of a cogwheel showed themselves and rose higher, soon the whole wheel was visible, it was as if some enormous force were squeezing the Designer so that there was no longer room for the wheel, the wheel moved up till it came to the very edge of the Designer, fell down, rolled along the sand a little on its rim and then lay flat. But a second wheel was already rising after it, followed by many others, large and small and indistinguishably minute, the same thing happened to all of them, at every moment one imagined the Designer must now really be empty, but another complex of numerous wheels was already rising into sight, falling down, trundling along the sand and lying flat. This phenomenon made the condemned man completely forget the explorer's command, the cogwheels fascinated him, he was always trying to catch one and at the same time urging the soldier to help, but always drew back his hand in alarm, for another wheel always came hopping along which, at least on its first advance, scared him off.

The explorer, on the other hand, felt greatly troubled; the machine was obviously going to pieces; its silent working was a delusion; he had a feeling that he must now stand by the officer, since the officer was no longer able to look after himself. But while the tumbling cogwheels absorbed his whole attention he had forgotten to keep an eye on the rest of the machine; now that the last cogwheel had left the Designer, however, he bent over the Harrow and had a new and still more unpleasant surprise. The Harrow was not writing, it was only jabbing, and the bed was not turning the body over but only bringing it up quivering against the needles. The explorer wanted to do something, if possible, to bring the whole machine to a standstill, for this was no exquisite torture such as the officer desired, this was plain murder. He stretched out his hands. But at that moment the Harrow rose with the body spitted on it and moved to the side, as it usually did only when the twelfth hour had come. Blood was flowing in a hundred streams, not mingled with water, the water jets too had failed to function. And now the last action failed to fulfill itself, the body did not drop off the long needles, streaming with blood it went on hanging over the pit without falling into it. The Harrow tried to move back to its old position, but as if it had itself noticed that it had not yet got rid of its burden it stuck after all where it was, over the pit. "Come and help!" cried the explorer to the other two, and himself seized the officer's feet. He wanted to push against the feet while the others seized the head from the opposite side and so the officer might be slowly eased off the needles. But the other two could not make up their minds to come; the condemned man actually turned away; the explorer had to go over to them and force them into position at the officer's head. And here, almost against his will, he had to look at the face of the corpse. It was as it had been in life; no sign was visible of the promised redemption; what the others had found in the machine the officer had not found; the lips were firmly pressed together, the eyes were open, with the same expression as in life, the look was calm and convinced, through the forehead went the point of the great iron spike.

As the explorer, with the soldier and the condemned man behind him, reached the first houses of the colony, the soldier pointed to one of them and said: "This is the teahouse."

In the ground floor of the house was a deep, low, cavernous space, its walls and ceiling blackened with smoke. It was open to the road all along its length. Although this teahouse was very little different from the other houses of the colony, which were all very dilapidated, even up to the Commandant's palatial headquarters, it made on the explorer the impression of a historic tradition of some kind, and he felt the power of past days. He went near to it, followed by his companions, right up between the empty tables which stood in the street before it, and breathed the cool, heavy air that came from the interior. "The old man's buried here," said the soldier, "the priest wouldn't let him lie in the churchyard. Nobody knew where to bury him for a while, but in the end they buried him here. The officer never told you about that, for sure, because of course that's what he was most ashamed of. He even tried several times to dig the old man up by night, but he was always chased away." "Where is the grave?" asked the explorer, who found it impossible to believe the soldier. At once both of them, the soldier and the condemned man, ran before him pointing with outstretched hands in the direction where the grave should be. They led the explorer right up to the back wall, where guests were sitting at a few tables. They were apparently dock laborers, strong men with short, glistening, full black beards. None had a jacket, their shirts were torn, they were poor, humble creatures. As the explorer drew near, some of them got up, pressed close to the wall, and stared at him. "It's a foreigner," ran the whisper around him, "he wants to see the grave." They pushed one of the tables aside, and under it there was really a gravestone. It was a simple stone, low enough to be covered by a table. There was an inscription on it in very small letters, the explorer had to kneel down to read it. This was what it said: "Here rests the old Commandant. His adherents, who now must be nameless, have dug this grave and set up this stone. There is a prophecy that after a certain number of years the Commandant will rise again and lead his adherents from this house to recover the colony. Have faith and wait!" When the explorer had read this and risen to his feet he saw all the bystanders around him smiling, as if they too had read the inscription, had found it ridiculous and were expecting him to agree with them. The explorer ignored this, distributed a few coins among them, waiting till the table was pushed over the grave again, quitted the teahouse and made for the harbor.

The soldier and the condemned man had found some acquaintances in the teahouse, who detained them. But they must have soon shaken them off, for the explorer was only halfway down the long flight of steps leading to the boats when they came rushing after him. Probably they wanted to force him at the last minute to take them with him. While he was bargaining below with a ferryman to row him to the steamer, the two of them came headlong down the steps, in silence, for they did not dare to shout. But by the time they reached the foot of the steps the explorer was already in the boat, and the ferryman was just casting off from the shore. They could have jumped into the boat, but the explorer lifted a heavy knotted rope from the floor boards, threatened them with it and so kept them from attempting the leap.

QUESTIONS FOR DISCUSSION AND WRITING

1. How does the officer's explanation of the apparatus establish the conflicts in the story? When does the turning point occur in the story? How do the explorer's actions in the teahouse provide an ironic conclusion to the story?

2. What is the officer's motivation in the story? How does he contrast the policies of the old and new Commandants? In what ways does the explorer finally exchange roles with the officer?

3. How does the story reveal that all the characters are aliens in this setting? Why does the apparatus seem more important than the characters?

4. How does the flatly objective point of view intrigue and horrify the reader? How is this point of view explained by the explorer's admission that "he traveled only as an observer"?

5. What are the religious implications in the story concerning guilt, revelation through suffering, atonement, and redemption? What thematic point is made when the apparatus malfunctions and murders the officer?

Stories for Comparison

Joseph Conrad's "Heart of Darkness" (pages 388–447); Leslie Marmon Silko's "Storyteller" (pages 1058–1070).

62

....

JAMAICA KINCAID

Girl

JAMAICA KINCAID was born in 1949 in St. John's, Antigua, and educated
at Franconia College in New Hampshire. She began contributing stories to
Rolling Stone, The Paris Review, and *The New Yorker.* Her first collection of
stories, *At the Bottom of the River* (1983), won the Morton Dauwen Zabel
Award of the American Academy and Institute of Arts and Letters. Her two
novels, *Annie John* (1985) and *Lucy* (1990), focus on the struggles of young
girls to understand their heritage. She has also published a collection of essays about the West Indies, *A Small Place* (1988). In "Girl," reprinted from
At the Bottom of the River, a mother describes the appropriate behavior for a
young woman.

Wash the white clothes on Monday and put them on the stone heap; wash the
color clothes on Tuesday and put them on the clothesline to dry; don't walk
barehead in the hot sun; cook pumpkin fritters in very hot sweet oil; soak your little
cloths right after you take them off; when buying cotton to make yourself a nice
blouse, be sure that it doesn't have gum on it, because that way it won't hold up well
after a wash; soak salt fish overnight before you cook it; is it true that you sing benna
in Sunday school?; always eat your food in such a way that it won't turn someone
else's stomach; on Sundays try to walk like a lady and not like the slut you are so
bent on becoming; don't sing benna in Sunday school; you mustn't speak to wharf-
rat boys, not even to give directions; don't eat fruits on the street—flies will follow
you; *but I don't sing benna on Sundays at all and never in Sunday school;* this is how
to sew on a button; this is how to make a buttonhole for the button you have just
sewed on; this is how to hem a dress when you see the hem coming down and so to
prevent yourself from looking like the slut I know you are so bent on becoming; this
is how you iron your father's khaki shirt so that it doesn't have a crease; this is how
you iron your father's khaki pants so that they don't have a crease; this is how you
grow okra—far from the house, because okra tree harbors red ants; when you are
growing dasheen, make sure it gets plenty of water or else it makes your throat itch
when you are eating it; this is how you sweep a corner; this is how you sweep a
whole house; this is how you sweep a yard; this is how you smile to someone you

don't like too much; this is how you smile to someone you don't like at all; this is how you smile to someone you like completely; this is how you set a table for tea; this is how you set a table for dinner; this is how you set a table for dinner with an important guest; this is how you set a table for lunch; this is how you set a table for breakfast; this is how you behave in the presence of men who don't know you very well, and this way they won't recognize immediately the slut I have warned you against becoming; be sure to wash every day, even if it is with your own spit; don't squat down to play marbles—you are not a boy, you know; don't pick people's flowers—you might catch something; don't throw stones at blackbirds, because it might not be a blackbird at all; this is how to make a bread pudding; this is how to make doukona; this is how to make pepper pot; this is how to make a good medicine for a cold; this is how to make a good medicine to throw away a child before it even becomes a child; this is how to catch a fish; this is how to throw back a fish you don't like, and that way something bad won't fall on you; this is how to bully a man; this is how a man bullies you; this is how to love a man, and if this doesn't work there are other ways, and if they don't work don't feel too bad about giving up; this is how to spit up in the air if you feel like it, and this is how to move quick so that it doesn't fall on you; this is how to make ends meet; always squeeze bread to make sure it's fresh; *but what if the baker won't let me feel the bread?;* you mean to say that after all you are really going to be the kind of woman who the baker won't let near the bread?

QUESTIONS FOR DISCUSSION AND WRITING

1. In what way does this list of instructions constitute a plot? What is the conflict that the speaker is trying to resolve? How does the speaker's last question clarify that conflict?

2. In what way do these instructions characterize a "lady"? What sort of behavior is assumed by the repeated use of the word *slut?*

3. What details in this "story" suggest that the setting is the West Indies? For example, what are *benna* and *doukona?*

4. Who is the narrator of this story? How do her instructions—presented in one continuous sentence—reveal her character? How do the phrases in italics establish a different point of view within this sentence?

5. In what sense is this narrative an extended definition of the title—i.e., what a proper *girl* should be? As you assess these instructions, which ones seem important and which ones seem trivial? In what ways do the "girl's" objections reveal the archetypal tension between mothers and daughters?

Stories for Comparison:

Sandra Cisneros's "One Holy Night" (pages 377–382); Alice Munro's "Wild Swans" (pages 927–935).

63

D. H. LAWRENCE

Odour of Chrysanthemums

DAVID HERBERT LAWRENCE (1885–1930) was born in Eastwood, a coal mining town in the industrial midlands of England, and studied for two years at Nottingham University, where he obtained his teaching certificate. From 1909 to 1912, he worked as a schoolteacher at Croydon in south London, began writing romantic love poetry, and published three novels, *The White Peacock* (1911), *The Trespasser* (1912), and *Sons and Lovers* (1913). The last novel, largely autobiographical, was extremely successful, thus enabling Lawrence to give up his teaching position and to turn his full attention to writing. It was during this period that he met his wife, Frieda von Richthofen Weekley, the daughter of a Prussian nobleman. Although his marriage initiated one of Lawrence's most creative periods—*The Rainbow* (1915) and *Women in Love* (1920)—it also produced personal and political problems, many of the latter caused by Frieda's suspected ties to Germany during World War I. The Lawrences left England in 1919, traveling to Italy, Ceylon, Australia, Tahiti, Mexico, and finally New Mexico, where they settled on a primitive ranch near Taos. Lawrence's fiction during this period includes *Aaron's Rod* (1922), *Kangaroo* (1923), and *The Plumed Serpent* (1926), and concludes with his most controversial novel, *Lady Chatterley's Lover* (1928). Lawrence returned to England briefly before moving to Vence on the French Riviera, where he died of tuberculosis. His ashes were eventually returned to Taos. "Odour of Chrysanthemums," reprinted from the second volume of *The Complete Stories of D. H. Lawrence* (1934), dramatizes a woman's response to family tragedy. "The Rocking-Horse Winner," reprinted from the third volume of *The Complete Stories,* tells of a young boy's attempt to win his mother's love.

I

The small locomotive engine, Number 4, came clanking, stumbling down from Selston with seven full wagons. It appeared round the corner with loud threats of speed, but the colt that it startled from among the gorse, which still flickered indistinctly in the raw afternoon, out-distanced it at a canter. A woman, walking up the railway line to Underwood, drew back into the hedge, held her basket aside, and watched the footplate of the engine advancing. The trucks thumped heavily past, one by one, with slow inevitable movement, as she stood insignificantly trapped between the jolting black wagons and the hedge; then they curved away towards the coppice where the withered oak leaves dropped noiselessly, while the birds, pulling at the scarlet hips beside the track, made off into the dusk that had already crept into the spinney. In the open, the smoke from the engine sank and cleaved to the rough grass. The fields were dreary and forsaken, and in the marshy strip that led to the whimsey, a reedy pit-pond, the fowls had already abandoned their run among the alders, to roost in the tarred fowl-house. The pit-bank loomed up beyond the pond, flames like red sores licking its ashy sides, in the afternoon's stagnant light. Just beyond rose the tapering chimneys and the clumsy black headstocks of Brinsley Colliery. The two wheels were spinning fast up against the sky, and the winding engine rapped out its little spasms. The miners were being turned up.

The engine whistled as it came into the wide bay of railway lines beside the colliery, where rows of trucks stood in harbour.

Miners, single, trailing and in groups, passed like shadows diverging home. At the edge of the ribbed level of sidings squat a low cottage, three steps down from the cinder track. A large bony vine clutched at the house, as if to claw down the tiled roof. Round the bricked yard grew a few wintry primroses. Beyond, the long garden sloped down to a bush-covered brook course. There were some twiggy apple trees, winter-crack trees, and ragged cabbages. Beside the path hung dishevelled pink chrysanthemums, like pink cloths hung on bushes. A woman came stooping out of the felt-covered fowl-house, half-way down the garden. She closed and padlocked the door, then drew herself erect, having brushed some bits from her white apron.

She was a tall woman of imperious mien, handsome, with definite black eyebrows. Her smooth black hair was parted exactly. For a few moments she stood steadily watching the miners as they passed along the railway: then she turned towards the brook course. Her face was calm and set, her mouth was closed with disillusionment. After a moment she called:

"John!" There was no answer. She waited, and then said distinctly: 5

"Where are you?"

"Here!" replied a child's sulky voice from among the bushes. The woman looked piercingly through the dusk.

"Are you at that brook?" she asked sternly.

For answer the child showed himself before the raspberry-canes that rose like whips. He was a small, sturdy boy of five. He stood quite still, defiantly.

"Oh!" said the mother, conciliated. "I thought you were down at that wet 10 brook—and you remember what I told you————"

The boy did not move or answer.

"Come, come on in," she said more gently, "it's getting dark. There's your grandfather's engine coming down the line!"

The lad advanced slowly, with resentful, taciturn movement. He was dressed in trousers and waistcoat of cloth that was too thick and hard for the size of the garments. They were evidently cut down from a man's clothes.

As they went slowly towards the house he tore at the ragged wisps of chrysanthemums and dropped the petals in handfuls among the path.

15   "Don't do that—it does look nasty," said his mother. He refrained, and she, suddenly pitiful, broke off a twig with three or four wan flowers and held them against her face. When mother and son reached the yard her hand hesitated, and instead of laying the flower aside, she pushed it in her apron-band. The mother and son stood at the foot of the three steps looking across the bay of lines at the passing home of the miners. The trundle of the small train was imminent. Suddenly the engine loomed past the house and came to a stop opposite the gate.

The engine-driver, a short man with round grey beard, leaned out of the cab high above the woman.

"Have you got a cup of tea?" he said in a cheery, hearty fashion.

It was her father. She went in, saying she would mash. Directly, she returned.

"I didn't come to see you on Sunday," began the little grey-bearded man.

20   "I didn't expect you," said his daughter.

The engine-driver winced; then, reassuming his cheery, airy manner, he said:

"Oh, have you heard then? Well, and what do you think————?"

"I think it is soon enough," she replied.

At her brief censure the little man made an impatient gesture, and said coaxingly, yet with dangerous coldness:

25   "Well, what's a man to do? It's no sort of life for a man of my years, to sit at my own hearth like a stranger. And if I'm going to marry again it may as well be soon as late—what does it matter to anybody?"

The woman did not reply, but turned and went into the house. The man in the engine-cab stood assertive, till she returned with a cup of tea and a piece of bread and butter on a plate. She went up the steps and stood near the footplate of the hissing engine.

"You needn't 'a'brought me bread an' butter," said her father. "But a cup of tea"—he sipped appreciatively—"it's very nice." He sipped for a moment or two, then: "I hear as Walter's got another bout on," he said.

"When hasn't he?" said the woman bitterly.

"I heerd tell of him in the 'Lord Nelson' braggin' as he was going to spend that b———— afore he went: half a sovereign that was."

30   "When?" asked the woman.

"A' Sat'day night—I know that's true."

"Very likely," she laughed bitterly. "He gives me twenty-three shillings."

"Aye, it's a nice thing, when a man can do nothing with his money but make a beast of himself!" said the grey-whiskered man. The woman turned her head away. Her father swallowed the last of his tea and handed her the cup.

"Aye," he sighed, wiping his mouth. "It's a settler, it is————"

35   He put his hand on the lever. The little engine strained and groaned, and the train rumbled towards the crossing. The woman again looked across the metals. Darkness was settling over the spaces of the railway and trucks: the miners, in grey sombre groups, were still passing home. The winding engine pulsed hurriedly, with brief pauses. Elizabeth Bates looked at the dreary flow of men, then she went indoors. Her husband did not come.

The kitchen was small and full of firelight; red coals piled glowing up the chimney mouth. All the life of the room seemed in the white, warm hearth and the steel fender reflecting the red fire. The cloth was laid for tea; cups glinted in the shadows. At the back, where the lowest stairs protruded into the room, the boy sat struggling with a knife and a piece of white wood. He was almost hidden in the shadow. It was half-past four. They had but to await the father's coming to begin tea. As the mother watched her son's sullen little struggle with the wood, she saw herself in his silence and pertinacity; she saw the father in her child's indifference to all but himself. She seemed to be occupied by her husband. He had probably gone past his home, slunk past his own door, to drink before he came in, while his dinner spoiled and wasted in waiting. She glanced at the clock, then took the potatoes to strain them in the yard. The garden and fields beyond the brook were closed in uncertain darkness. When she rose with the saucepan, leaving the drain steaming into the night behind her, she saw the yellow lamps were lit along the high road that went up the hill away beyond the space of the railway lines and the field.

Then again she watched the men trooping home, fewer now and fewer.

Indoors the fire was sinking and the room was dark red. The woman put her saucepan on the hob, and set a batter-pudding near the mouth of the oven. Then she stood unmoving. Directly, gratefully, came quick young steps to the door. Someone hung on the latch a moment, then a little girl entered and began pulling off her outdoor things, dragging a mass of curls, just ripening from gold to brown, over her eyes with her hat.

Her mother chid her for coming late from school, and said she would have to keep her at home the dark winter days.

"Why, mother, it's hardly a bit dark yet. The lamp's not lighted, and my father's not home." 40

"No, he isn't. But it's a quarter to five! Did you see anything of him?"

The child became serious. She looked at her mother with large, wistful blue eyes.

"No, mother, I've never seen him. Why? Has he come up an' gone past, to Old Brinsley? He hasn't, mother, 'cos I never saw him."

"He'd watch that," said the mother bitterly, "he'd take care as you didn't see him. But you may depend upon it, he's seated in the 'Prince o' Wales.' He wouldn't be this late."

The girl looked at her mother piteously. 45

"Let's have our teas, mother, should we?" said she.

The mother called John to table. She opened the door once more and looked out across the darkness of the lines. All was deserted: she could not hear the winding-engines.

"Perhaps," she said to herself, "he's stopped to get some ripping done."

They sat down to tea. John, at the end of the table near the door, was almost lost in the darkness. Their faces were hidden from each other. The girl crouched against the fender slowly moving a thick piece of bread before the fire. The lad, his face a dusky mark on the shadow, sat watching her who was transfigured in the red glow.

"I do think it's beautiful to look in the fire," said the child. 50

"Do you?" said her mother. "Why?"

"It's so red, and full of little caves—and it feels so nice, and you can fair smell it."

"It'll want mending directly," replied her mother, "and then if your father comes he'll carry on and say there never is a fire when a man comes home sweating from the pit. A public-house is always warm enough."

There was silence till the boy said complainingly: "Make haste, our Annie."

55   "Well, I am doing! I can't make the fire do it no faster, can I?"

"She keeps wafflin' it about so's to make 'er slow," grumbled the boy.

"Don't have such an evil imagination, child," replied the mother.

Soon the room was busy in the darkness with the crisp sound of crunching. The mother ate very little. She drank her tea determinedly, and sat thinking. When she rose her anger was evident in the stern unbending of her head. She looked at the pudding in the fender, and broke out:

"It is a scandalous thing as a man can't even come home to his dinner! If it's crozzled up to a cinder I don't see why I should care. Past his very door he goes to get to a public-house, and here I sit with his dinner waiting for him————"

60   She went out. As she dropped piece after piece of coal on the red fire, the shadows fell on the walls, till the room was almost in total darkness.

"I canna see," grumbled the invisible John. In spite of herself, the mother laughed.

"You know the way to your mouth," she said. She set the dust-pan outside the door. When she came again like a shadow on the hearth, the lad repeated, complaining sulkily:

"I canna see."

"Good gracious!" cried the mother irritably, "you're as bad as your father if it's a bit dusk!"

65   Nevertheless, she took a paper spill from a sheaf on the mantelpiece and proceeded to light the lamp that hung from the ceiling in the middle of the room. As she reached up, her figure displayed itself just rounding with maternity.

"Oh, mother————!" exclaimed the girl.

"What?" said the woman, suspended in the act of putting the lamp-glass over the flame. The copper reflector shone handsomely on her, as she stood with uplifted arm, turning to face her daughter.

"You've got a flower in your apron!" said the child, in a little rapture at this unusual event.

"Goodness me!" exclaimed the woman, relieved. "One would think the house was afire." She replaced the glass and waited a moment before turning up the wick. A pale shadow was seen floating vaguely on the floor.

70   "Let me smell!" said the child, still rapturously, coming forward and putting her face to her mother's waist.

"Go along, silly!" said the mother, turning up the lamp. The light revealed their suspense so that the woman felt it almost unbearable. Annie was still bending at her waist. Irritably, the mother took the flowers out from her apron-band.

"Oh, mother—don't take them out!" Annie cried, catching her hand and trying to replace the sprig.

"Such nonsense!" said the mother, turning away. The child put the pale chrysanthemums to her lips, murmuring:

"Don't they smell beautiful!"

Her mother gave a short laugh.   75

"No," she said, "not to me. It was chrysanthemums when I married him, and chrysanthemums when you were born, and the first time they ever brought him home drunk, he'd got brown chrysanthemums in his button-hole."

She looked at the children. Their eyes and their parted lips were wondering. The mother sat rocking in silence for some time. Then she looked at the clock.

"Twenty minutes to six!" In a tone of fine bitter carelessness she continued: "Eh, he'll not come now till they bring him. There he'll stick! But he needn't come rolling in here in his pit-dirt, for *I* won't wash him. He can lie on the floor————Eh, what a fool I've been, what a fool! And this is what I came here for, to this dirty hole, rats and all, for him to slink past his very door. Twice last week—he's begun now————"

She silenced herself, and rose to clear the table.

While for an hour or more the children played, subduedly intent, fertile of imag-   80
ination, united in fear of the mother's wrath, and in dread of their father's home-coming, Mrs. Bates sat in her rocking-chair making a 'singlet' of thick cream-coloured flannel, which gave a dull wounded sound as she tore off the grey edge. She worked at her sewing with energy, listening to the children, and her anger wearied itself, lay down to rest, opening its eyes from time to time and steadily watching, its ears raised to listen. Sometimes even her anger quailed and shrank, and the mother suspended her sewing, tracing the footsteps that thudded along the sleepers outside; she would lift her head sharply to bid the children "hush," but she recovered herself in time, and the footsteps went past the gate, and the children were not flung out of their play-world.

But at last Annie sighed, and gave in. She glanced at her wagon of slippers, and loathed the game. She turned plaintively to her mother.

"Mother!"—but she was inarticulate.

John crept out like a frog from under the sofa. His mother glanced up.

"Yes," she said, "just look at those shirt-sleeves!"

The boy held them out to survey them, saying nothing. Then somebody called   85
in a hoarse voice away down the line, and suspense bristled in the room, till two people had gone by outside, talking.

"It is time for bed," said the mother.

"My father hasn't come," wailed Annie plaintively. But her mother was primed with courage.

"Never mind. They'll bring him when he does come—like a log." She meant there would be no scene. "And he may sleep on the floor till he wakes himself. I know he'll not go to work to-morrow after this!"

The children had their hands and faces wiped with a flannel. They were very quiet. When they had put on their nightdresses, they said their prayers, the boy mumbling. The mother looked down at them, at the brown silken bush of intertwining curls in the nape of the girl's neck, at the little black head of the lad, and her heart burst with anger at their father, who caused all three such distress. The children hid their faces in her skirts for comfort.

90   When Mrs. Bates came down, the room was strangely empty, with a tension of expectancy. She took up her sewing and stitched for some time without raising her head. Meantime her anger was tinged with fear.

2

The clock struck eight and she rose suddenly, dropping her sewing on her chair. She went to the stair-foot door, opened it, listening. Then she went out, locking the door behind her.

Something scuffled in the yard, and she started, though she knew it was only the rats with which the place was over-run. The night was very dark. In the great bay of railway lines, bulked with trucks, there was no trace of light, only away back she could see a few yellow lamps at the pit-top, and the red smear of the burning pit-bank on the night. She hurried along the edge of the track, then, crossing the converging lines, came to the stile by the white gates, whence she emerged on the road. Then the fear which had led her shrank. People were walking up to New Brinsley; she saw the lights in the houses; twenty yards farther on were the broad windows of the "Prince of Wales," very warm and bright, and the loud voices of men could be heard distinctly. What a fool she had been to imagine that anything had happened to him! He was merely drinking over there at the "Prince of Wales." She faltered. She had never yet been to fetch him, and she never would go. So she continued her walk towards the long straggling line of houses, standing back on the highway. She entered a passage between the dwellings.

"Mr. Rigley?—Yes! Did you want him? No, he's not in at this minute."

The raw-boned woman leaned forward from her dark scullery and peered at the other, upon whom fell a dim light through the blind of the kitchen window.

95   "Is it Mrs. Bates?" she asked in a tone tinged with respect.

"Yes. I wondered if your Master was at home. Mine hasn't come yet."

"'Asn't 'e! Oh, Jack's been 'ome an' 'ad 'is dinner an' gone out. 'E's just gone for 'alf an hour afore bed-time. Did you call at the 'Prince of Wales'?"

"No————"

"No, you didn't like————! It's not very nice." The other woman was indulgent. There was an awkward pause. "Jack never said nothink about—about your Master," she said.

100   "No!—I expect he's stuck in there!"

Elizabeth Bates said this bitterly, and with recklessness. She knew that the woman across the yard was standing at her door listening, but she did not care. As she turned:

"Stop a minute! I'll just go an' ask Jack if 'e knows anythink," said Mrs. Rigley.

"Oh no—I wouldn't like to put————!"

"Yes, I will, if you'll just step inside an' see as th' childer doesn't come downstairs and set theirselves afire."

105   Elizabeth Bates, murmuring a remonstrance, stepped inside. The other woman apologised for the state of the room.

The kitchen needed apology. There were little frocks and trousers and childish undergarments on the squab and on the floor, and a litter of playthings everywhere.

On the black American cloth of the table were pieces of bread and cake, crusts, slops, and a teapot with cold tea.

"Eh, ours is just as bad," said Elizabeth Bates, looking at the woman, not at the house. Mrs. Rigley put a shawl over her head and hurried out, saying:

"I shanna be a minute."

The other sat, noting with faint disapproval the general untidiness of the room. Then she fell to counting the shoes of various sizes scattered over the floor. There were twelve. She sighed and said to herself: "No wonder!"—glancing at the litter. There came the scratching of two pairs of feet on the yard, and the Rigleys entered. Elizabeth Bates rose. Rigley was a big man, with very large bones. His head looked particularly bony. Across his temple was a blue scar, caused by a wound got in the pit, a wound in which the coal-dust remained blue like tattooing.

"'Asna 'e come whoam yit?" asked the man, without any form of greeting, but with deference and sympathy. "I couldna say wheer he is—'e's non ower theer!"—he jerked his head to signify the "Prince of Wales." 110

"'E's 'appen gone up to th' 'Yew'," said Mrs. Rigley.

There was another pause. Rigley had evidently something to get off his mind:

"Ah left 'im finishin' a stint," he began. "Loose-all 'ad bin gone about ten minutes when we com'n away, an' I shouted: 'Are ter comin', Walt?' an' 'e said: 'Go on, Ah shanna be but a'ef a minnit,' so we com'n ter th' bottom, me an' Bowers, thinkin' as 'e wor just behint, an' 'ud come up i' th' next bantle————"

He stood perplexed, as if answering a charge of deserting his mate. Elizabeth Bates, now again certain of disaster, hastened to reassure him:

"I expect 'e's gone up to the' 'Yew Tree,' as you say. It's not the first time. I've fretted myself into a fever before now. He'll come home when they carry him." 115

"Ay, isn't it too bad!" deplored the other woman.

"I'll just step up to Dick's an' see if 'e *is* theer," offered the man, afraid of appearing alarmed, afraid of taking liberties.

"Oh, I wouldn't think of bothering you that far," said Elizabeth Bates, with emphasis, but he knew she was glad of his offer.

As they stumbled up the entry, Elizabeth Bates heard Rigley's wife run across the yard and open her neighbour's door. At this, suddenly all the blood in her body seemed to switch away from her heart.

"Mind!" warned Rigley. "Ah've said many a time as Ah'd fill up them ruts in this entry, sumb'dy 'll be breakin' their legs yit." 120

She recovered herself and walked quickly along with the miner.

"I don't like leaving the children in bed, and nobody in the house," she said.

"No, you dunna!" he replied courteously. They were soon at the gate of the cottage.

"Well, I shanna be many minnits. Dunna you be frettin' now, 'e'll be all right," said the butty.

"Thank you very much, Mr. Rigley," she replied. 125

"You're welcome!" he stammered, moving away. "I shanna be many minnits."

The house was quiet. Elizabeth Bates took off her hat and shawl, and rolled back the rug. When she had finished, she sat down. It was a few minutes past nine. She was startled by the rapid chuff of the winding-engine at the pit, and the sharp whirr of the brakes on the rope as it descended. Again she felt the painful sweep of her blood, and she put her hand to her side, saying aloud: "Good gracious!—it's only the nine o'clock deputy going down," rebuking herself.

She sat still, listening. Half an hour of this, and she was wearied out.

"What am I working myself up like this for?" she said pitiably to herself, "I s'll only be doing myself some damage."

130   She took out her sewing again.

At a quarter to ten there were footsteps. One person! She watched for the door to open. It was an elderly woman, in a black bonnet and a black woollen shawl—his mother. She was about sixty years old, pale, with blue eyes, and her face all wrinkled and lamentable. She shut the door and turned to her daughter-in-law peevishly.

"Eh, Lizzie, whatever shall we do, whatever shall we do!" she cried.

Elizabeth drew back a little, sharply.

"What is it, mother?" she said.

135   The elder woman seated herself on the sofa.

"I don't know, child, I can't tell you!"—she shook her head slowly. Elizabeth sat watching her, anxious and vexed.

"I don't know," replied the grandmother, sighing very deeply. "There's no end to my troubles, there isn't. The things I've gone through, I'm sure it's enough————!" She wept without wiping her eyes, the tears running.

"But, mother," interrupted Elizabeth, "what do you mean? What is it?"

The grandmother slowly wiped her eyes. The fountains of her tears were stopped by Elizabeth's directness. She wiped her eyes slowly.

140   "Poor child! Eh, you poor thing!" she moaned. "I don't know what we're going to do, I don't—and you as you are—it's a thing, it is indeed!"

Elizabeth waited.

"Is he dead?" she asked, and at the words her heart swung violently, though she felt a slight flush of shame at the ultimate extravagance of the question. Her words sufficiently frightened the old lady, almost brought her to herself.

"Don't say so, Elizabeth! We'll hope it's not as bad as that; no, may the Lord spare us that, Elizabeth. Jack Rigley came just as I was sittin' down to a glass afore going to bed, an' 'e said: ''Appen you'll go down th' line, Mrs. Bates. Walt's had an accident. 'Appen you'll go an' sit wi' 'er till we can get him home.' I hadn't time to ask him a word afore he was gone. An' I put my bonnet on an' come straight down, Lizzie. I thought to myself: 'Eh, that poor blessed child, if anybody should come an' tell her of a sudden, there's no knowin' what'll 'appen to 'er.' You mustn't let it upset you, Lizzie—or you know what to expect. How long is it, six months—or is it five, Lizzie? Ay!"—the old woman shook her head—"time slips on, it slips on! Ay!"

Elizabeth's thoughts were busy elsewhere. If he was killed—would she be able to manage on the little pension and what she could earn?—she counted up rapidly. If he was hurt—they wouldn't take him to the hospital—how tiresome he would be to nurse!—but perhaps she'd be able to get him away from the drink and his hateful ways. She would—while he was ill. The tears offered to come to her eyes at the picture. But what sentimental luxury was this she was beginning? She turned to consider the children. At any rate she was absolutely necessary for them. They were her business.

"Ay!" repeated the old woman, "it seems but a week or two since he brought me his first wages. Ay—he was a good lad, Elizabeth, he was, in his way. I don't know why he got to be such a trouble, I don't. He was a happy lad at home, only full of spirits. But there's no mistake he's been a handful of trouble, he has! I hope the Lord'll spare him to mend his ways. I hope so, I hope so. You've had a sight o' trouble with him, Elizabeth, you have indeed. But he was a jolly enough lad wi' me, he was, I can assure you. I don't know how it is. . . ."

The old woman continued to muse aloud, a monotonous irritating sound, while Elizabeth thought concentratedly, startled once, when she heard the winding-engine chuff quickly, and the brakes skirr with a shriek. Then she heard the engine more slowly, and the brakes made no sound. The old woman did not notice. Elizabeth waited in suspense. The mother-in-law talked, with lapses into silence.

"But he wasn't your son, Lizzie, an' it makes a difference. Whatever he was, I remember him when he was little, an' I learned to understand him and to make allowances. You've got to make allowances for them————"

It was half-past ten, and the old woman was saying: "But it's trouble from beginning to end; you're never too old for trouble, never too old for that————" when the gate banged back, and there were heavy feet on the steps.

"I'll go, Lizzie, let me go," cried the old woman, rising. But Elizabeth was at the door. It was a man in pit-clothes.

"They're bringin' 'im, Missis," he said. Elizabeth's heart halted a moment. Then it surged on again, almost suffocating her.

"Is he—is it bad?" she asked.

The man turned away, looking at the darkness:

"The doctor says 'e'd been dead hours. 'E saw 'im i' th' lamp-cabin."

The old woman, who stood just behind Elizabeth, dropped into a chair, and folded her hands, crying: "Oh, my boy, my boy!"

"Hush!" said Elizabeth, with a sharp twitch of a frown. "Be still, mother, don't waken th' children: I wouldn't have them down for anything!"

The old woman moaned softly, rocking herself. The man was drawing away. Elizabeth took a step forward.

"How was it?" she asked.

"Well, I couldn't say for sure," the man replied, very ill at ease. "'E wor finishin' a stint an' th' butties 'ad gone, an' a lot o' stuff come down atop 'n 'im."

"And crushed him?" cried the widow, with a shudder.

"No," said the man, "it fell at th' back of 'im. 'E wor under th' face, an' it niver touched 'im. It shut 'im in. It seems 'e wor smothered."

Elizabeth shrank back. She heard the old woman behind her cry:

"What?—what did 'e say it was?"

The man replied, more loudly: "'E wor smothered!"

Then the old woman wailed aloud, and this relieved Elizabeth.

"Oh, mother," she said, putting her hand on the old woman, "don't waken th' children, don't waken th' children."

She wept a little, unknowing, while the old mother rocked herself and moaned. Elizabeth remembered that they were bringing him home, and she must be ready. "They'll lay him in the parlour," she said to herself, standing a moment pale and perplexed.

Then she lighted a candle and went into the tiny room. The air was cold and damp, but she could not make a fire, there was no fireplace. She set down the candle and looked round. The candlelight glittered on the lustre-glasses, on the two vases that held some of the pink chrysanthemums, and on the dark mahogany. There was a cold, deathly smell of chrysanthemums in the room. Elizabeth stood looking at the flowers. She turned away, and calculated whether there would be room to lay him on the floor, between the couch and the chiffonier. She pushed the chairs aside. There would be room to lay him down and to step round him. Then she fetched the old red tablecloth, and another old cloth, spreading them down to save her bit of carpet. She shivered on leaving the parlour; so, from the dresser drawer she took a clean shirt and put it at the fire to air. All the time her mother-in-law was rocking herself in the chair and moaning.

"You'll have to move from there, mother," said Elizabeth. "They'll be bringing him in. Come in the rocker."

The old mother rose mechanically, and seated herself by the fire, continuing to lament. Elizabeth went into the pantry for another candle, and there, in the little penthouse under the naked tiles, she heard them coming. She stood still in the pantry doorway, listening. She heard them pass the end of the house, and come awkwardly down the three steps, a jumble of shuffling footsteps and muttering voices. The old woman was silent. The men were in the yard.

170   Then Elizabeth heard Matthews, the manager of the pit, say: "You go in first, Jim. Mind!"

The door came open, and the two women saw a collier backing into the room, holding one end of a stretcher, on which they could see the nailed pit-boots of the dead man. The two carriers halted, the man at the head stooping to the lintel of the door.

"Wheer will you have him?" asked the manager, a short, white-bearded man.

Elizabeth roused herself and came from the pantry carrying the unlighted candle.

"In the parlour," she said.

175   "In there, Jim!" pointed the manager, and the carriers backed round into the tiny room. The coat with which they had covered the body fell off as they awkwardly turned through the two doorways, and the women saw their man, naked to the waist, lying stripped for work. The old woman began to moan in a low voice of horror.

"Lay th' stretcher at th' side," snapped the manager, "an' put 'im on th' cloths. Mind now, mind! Look you now————!"

One of the men had knocked off a vase of chrysanthemums. He stared awkwardly, then they set down the stretcher. Elizabeth did not look at her husband. As soon as she could get in the room, she went and picked up the broken vase and the flowers.

"Wait a minute!" she said.

The three men waited in silence while she mopped up the water with a duster.

"Eh, what a job, what a job, to be sure!" the manager was saying, rubbing his brow with trouble and perplexity. "Never knew such a thing in my life, never! He'd no business to ha' been left. I never knew such a thing in my life! Fell over him clean as a whistle, an' shut him in. Not four foot of space, there wasn't—yet it scarce bruised him."

He looked down at the dead man, lying prone, half naked, all grimed with coal-dust.

"''Sphyxiated,' the doctor said. It *is* the most terrible job I've ever known. Seems as if it was done o' purpose. Clean over him, an' shut 'im in, like a mouse-trap"—he made a sharp, descending gesture with his hand.

The colliers standing by jerked aside their heads in hopeless comment.

The horror of the thing bristled upon them all.

Then they heard the girl's voice upstairs calling shrilly: "Mother, mother—who is it? Mother, who is it?"

Elizabeth hurried to the foot of the stairs and opened the door:

"Go to sleep!" she commanded sharply. "What are you shouting about? Go to sleep at once—there's nothing————"

Then she began to mount the stairs. They could hear her on the boards, and on the plaster floor of the little bedroom. They could hear her distinctly:

"What's the matter now?—what's the matter with you, silly thing?"—her voice was much agitated, with an unreal gentleness.

"I thought it was some men come," said the plaintive voice of the child. "Has he come?"

"Yes, they've brought him. There's nothing to make a fuss about. Go to sleep now, like a good child."

They could hear her voice in the bedroom, they waited whilst she covered the children under the bedclothes.

"Is he drunk?" asked the girl, timidly, faintly.

"No! No—he's not! He—he's asleep."

"Is he asleep downstairs?"

"Yes—and don't make a noise."

There was silence for a moment, then the men heard the frightened child again: "What's that noise?"

"It's nothing, I tell you, what are you bothering for?"

The noise was the grandmother moaning. She was oblivious of everything, sitting on her chair rocking and moaning. The manager put his hand on her arm and bade her "Sh—sh!!"

The old woman opened her eyes and looked at him. She was shocked by this interruption, and seemed to wonder.

"What time is it?" the plaintive thin voice of the child, sinking back unhappily into sleep, asked this last question.

"Ten o'clock," answered the mother more softly. Then she must have bent down and kissed the children.

Matthews beckoned to the men to come away. They put on their caps and took up the stretcher. Stepping over the body, they tiptoed out of the house. None of them spoke till they were far from the wakeful children.

205   When Elizabeth came down she found her mother alone on the parlour floor, leaning over the dead man, the tears dropping on him.

"We must lay him out," the wife said. She put on the kettle, then returning knelt at the feet, and began to unfasten the knotted leather laces. The room was clammy and dim with only one candle, so that she had to bend her face almost to the floor. At last she got off the heavy boots and put them away.

"You must help me now," she whispered to the old woman. Together they stripped the man.

When they arose, saw him lying in the naïve dignity of death, the women stood arrested in fear and respect. For a few moments they remained still, looking down, the old mother whimpering. Elizabeth felt countermanded. She saw him, how utterly inviolable he lay in himself. She had nothing to do with him. She could not accept it. Stooping, she laid her hand on him, in claim. He was still warm, for the mine was hot where he had died. His mother had his face between her hands, and was murmuring incoherently. The old tears fell in succession as drops from wet leaves; the mother was not weeping, merely her tears flowed. Elizabeth embraced the body of her husband, with cheek and lips. She seemed to be listening, inquiring, trying to get some connection. But she could not. She was driven away. He was impregnable.

She rose, went into the kitchen, where she poured warm water into a bowl, brought soap and flannel and a soft towel.

210   "I must wash him," she said.

Then the old mother rose stiffly, and watched Elizabeth as she carefully washed his face, carefully brushing the big blond moustache from his mouth with the flannel. She was afraid with a bottomless fear, so she ministered to him. The old woman, jealous, said:

"Let me wipe him!"—and she kneeled on the other side drying slowly as Elizabeth washed, her big black bonnet sometimes brushing the dark head of her daughter-in-law. They worked thus in silence for a long time. They never forgot it was death, and the touch of the man's dead body gave them strange emotions, different in each of the women; a great dread possessed them both, the mother felt the lie was given to her womb, she was denied; the wife felt the utter isolation of the human soul, the child within her was a weight apart from her.

At last it was finished. He was a man of handsome body, and his face showed no traces of drink. He was blond, full-fleshed, with fine limbs. But he was dead.

"Bless him," whispered his mother, looking always at his face, and speaking out of sheer terror. "Dear lad—bless him!" She spoke in a faint, sibilant ecstasy of fear and mother love.

215   Elizabeth sank down again to the floor, and put her face against his neck, and trembled and shuddered. But she had to draw away again. He was dead, and her living flesh had no place against his. A great dread and weariness held her: she was so unavailing. Her life was gone like this.

"White as milk he is, clear as a twelve-month baby, bless him, the darling!" the old mother murmured to herself. "Not a mark on him, clear and clean and white, beautiful as ever a child was made," she murmured with pride. Elizabeth kept her face hidden.

"He went peaceful, Lizzie—peaceful as sleep. Isn't he beautiful, the lamb? Ay—he must ha' made his peace, Lizzie. 'Appen he made it all right, Lizzie, shut in there. He'd have time. He wouldn't look like this if he hadn't made his peace. The lamb, the dear lamb. Eh, but he had a hearty laugh. I loved to hear it. He had the heartiest laugh, Lizzie, as a lad————"

Elizabeth looked up. The man's mouth was fallen back, slightly open under the cover of the moustache. The eyes, half shut, did not show glazed in the obscurity. Life with its smoky burning gone from him, had left him apart and utterly alien to her. And she knew what a stranger he was to her. In her womb was ice of fear, because of this separate stranger with whom she had been living as one flesh. Was this what it all meant—utter, intact separateness, obscured by heat of living? In dread she turned her face away. The fact was too deadly. There had been nothing between them, and yet they had come together, exchanging their nakedness repeatedly. Each time he had taken her, they had been two isolated beings, far apart as now. He was no more responsible than she. The child was like ice in her womb. For as she looked at the dead man, her mind, cold and detached, said clearly: "Who am I? What have I been doing? I have been fighting a husband who did not exist. *He* existed all the time. What wrong have I done? What was that I have been living with? There lies the reality, this man." And her soul died in her for fear: she knew she had never seen him, he had never seen her, they had met in the dark and had fought in the dark, not knowing whom they met nor whom they fought. And now she saw, and turned silent in seeing. For she had been wrong. She had said he was something he was not; she had felt familiar with him. Whereas he was apart all the while, living as she never lived, feeling as she never felt.

In fear and shame she looked at his naked body, that she had known falsely. And he was the father of her children. Her soul was torn from her body and stood apart. She looked at his naked body and was ashamed, as if she had denied it. After all, it was itself. It seemed awful to her. She looked at his face, and she turned her own face to the wall. For his look was other than hers, his way was not her way. She had denied him what he was—she saw it now. She had refused him as himself. And this had been her life, and his life. She was grateful to death, which restored the truth. And she knew she was not dead.

And all the while her heart was bursting with grief and pity for him. What had [220] he suffered? What stretch of horror for this helpless man! She was rigid with agony. She had not been able to help him. He had been cruelly injured, this naked man, this other being, and she could make no reparation. There were the children—but the children belonged to life. This dead man had nothing to do with them. He and she were only channels through which life had flowed to issue in the children. She was a mother—but how awful she knew it now to have been a wife. And he, dead now, how awful he must have felt it to be a husband. She felt that in the next world he would be a stranger to her. If they met there, in the beyond, they would only be ashamed of what had been before. The children had come, for some mysterious reason, out of both of them. But the children did not unite them. Now he was dead, she knew how eternally he was apart from her, how eternally he had nothing more to do with her. She saw this episode of her life closed. They had denied each other in life. Now he had withdrawn. An anguish came over her. It was finished then: it had become hopeless between them long before he died. Yet he had been her husband. But how little!

"Have you got his shirt, 'Lizabeth?"

Elizabeth turned without answering, though she strove to weep and behave as her mother-in-law expected. But she could not, she was silenced. She went into the kitchen and returned with the garment.

"It is aired," she said, grasping the cotton shirt here and there to try. She was almost ashamed to handle him; what right had she or anyone to lay hands on him; but her touch was humble on his body. It was hard work to clothe him. He was so heavy and inert. A terrible dread gripped her all the while: that he could be so heavy and utterly inert, unresponsive, apart. The horror of the distance between them was almost too much for her—it was so infinite a gap she must look across.

At last it was finished. They covered him with a sheet and left him lying, with his face bound. And she fastened the door of the little parlour, lest the children should see what was lying there. Then, with peace sunk heavy on her heart, she went about making tidy the kitchen. She knew she submitted to life, which was her immediate master. But from death, her ultimate master, she winced with fear and shame.

QUESTIONS FOR DISCUSSION AND WRITING

1. How does Lawrence establish the sense of time passing in the story? How does this element enhance the climax in the plot?

2. How does Lawrence reveal Elizabeth's character in her external actions with other characters—her father, daughter, son, and neighbors? In what sense do these external actions reveal her inner nature?

3. How do the connotative words in the first three paragraphs establish both the setting and tone for this story?

4. How do Lawrence's references to the main character as *Mother* and then *Elizabeth* mark a shift in the point of view in the story?

5. How does Elizabeth make chrysanthemums a unifying symbol in the story? In light of the scene with the corpse, how would you interpret the last two sentences of the story?

Stories for Comparison

Bobbie Ann Mason's "Shiloh" (pages 872–883); John Updike's "Separating" (pages 1142–1150).

64

D. H. LAWRENCE

The Rocking-Horse Winner

There was a woman who was beautiful, who started with all the advantages, yet she had no luck. She married for love, and the love turned to dust. She had bonny children, yet she felt they had been thrust upon her, and she could not love them. They looked at her coldly, as if they were finding fault with her. And hurriedly she felt she must cover up some fault in herself. Yet what it was that she must cover up she never knew. Nevertheless, when her children were present, she always felt the centre of her heart go hard. This troubled her, and in her manner she was all the more gentle and anxious for her children, as if she loved them very much. Only she herself knew that at the centre of her heart was a hard little place that could not feel love, no, not for anybody. Everybody else said of her: "She is such a good mother. She adores her children." Only she herself, and her children themselves, knew it was not so. They read it in each other's eyes.

There were a boy and two little girls. They lived in a pleasant house, with a garden, and they had discreet servants, and felt themselves superior to anyone in the neighbourhood.

Although they lived in style, they felt always an anxiety in the house. There was never enough money. The mother had a small income, and the father had a small income, but not nearly enough for the social position which they had to keep up. The father went into town to some office. But though he had good prospects, these prospects never materialised. There was always the grinding sense of the shortage of money, though the style was always kept up.

At last the mother said: "I will see if *I* can't make something." But she did not know where to begin. She racked her brains, and tried this thing and the other, but could not find anything successful. The failure made deep lines come into her face. Her children were growing up, they would have to go to school. There must be more money, there must be more money. The father, who was always very handsome and expensive in his tastes, seemed as if he never *would* be able to do anything worth doing. And the mother, who had a great belief in herself, did not succeed any better, and her tastes were just as expensive.

And so the house came to be haunted by the unspoken phrase: *There must be more money! There must be more money!* The children could hear it all the time, though nobody said it aloud. They heard it at Christmas, when the expensive and splendid toys filled the nursery. Behind the shining modern rocking-horse, behind the smart doll's house, a voice would start whispering: "There *must* be more money! There *must* be more money!" And the children would stop playing, to listen for a moment. They would look into each other's eyes, to see if they had all heard. And each one saw in the eyes of the other two that they too had heard. "There *must* be more money! There *must* be more money!"

It came whispering from the springs of the still-swaying rocking-horse, and even the horse, bending his wooden, champing head, heard it. The big doll, sitting so pink and smirking in her new pram, could hear it quite plainly, and seemed to be smirking all the more self-consciously because of it. The foolish puppy, too, that took the place of the teddy-bear, he was looking so extraordinarily foolish for no other reason but that he heard the secret whisper all over the house: "There *must* be more money!"

Yet nobody ever said it aloud. The whisper was everywhere, and therefore no one spoke it. Just as no one ever says: "We are breathing!" in spite of the fact that breath is coming and going all the time.

"Mother," said the boy Paul one day, "why don't we keep a car of our own? Why do we always use uncle's, or else a taxi?"

"Because we're the poor members of the family," said the mother.

10   "But why *are* we, mother?"

"Well—I suppose," she said slowly and bitterly, "it's because your father has no luck."

The boy was silent for some time.

"Is luck money, mother?" he asked, rather timidly.

"No, Paul. Not quite. It's what causes you to have money."

15   "Oh!" said Paul vaguely. "I thought when Uncle Oscar said *filthy lucker,* it meant money."

"*Filthy lucre* does mean money," said the mother. "But it's lucre, not luck."

"Oh!" said the boy. "Then what *is* luck, mother?"

"It's what causes you to have money. If you're lucky you have money. That's why it's better to be born lucky than rich. If you're rich, you may lose your money. But if you're lucky, you will always get more money."

"Oh! Will you? And is father not lucky?"

20   "Very unlucky, I should say," she said bitterly.

The boy watched her with unsure eyes.

"Why?" he asked.

"I don't know. Nobody ever knows why one person is lucky and another unlucky."

"Don't they? Nobody at all? Does *nobody* know?"

25   "Perhaps God. But He never tells."

"He ought to, then. And aren't you lucky either, mother?"

"I can't be, if I married an unlucky husband."

"But by yourself, aren't you?"

"I used to think I was, before I married. Now I think I am very unlucky indeed."

"Why?"   30

"Well—never mind! Perhaps I'm not really," she said.

The child looked at her to see if she meant it. But he saw, by the lines of her mouth, that she was only trying to hide something from him.

"Well, anyhow," he said stoutly, "I'm a lucky person."

"Why?" said his mother, with a sudden laugh.

He stared at her. He didn't even know why he had said it.   35

"God told me," he asserted, brazening it out.

"I hope He did, dear!" she said, again with a laugh, but rather bitter.

"He did, mother!"

"Excellent!" said the mother, using one of her husband's exclamations.

The boy saw she did not believe him; or rather, that she paid no attention to his   40
assertion. This angered him somewhat, and made him want to compel her attention.

He went off by himself, vaguely, in a childish way, seeking for the clue to "luck." Absorbed, taking no heed of other people, he went about with a sort of stealth, seeking inwardly for luck. He wanted luck, he wanted it, he wanted it. When the two girls were playing dolls in the nursery, he would sit on his big rocking-horse, charging madly into space, with a frenzy that made the little girls peer at him uneasily. Wildly the horse careered, the waving dark hair of the boy tossed, his eyes had a strange glare in them. The little girls dared not speak to him.

When he had ridden to the end of his mad little journey, he climbed down and stood in front of his rocking-horse, staring fixedly into its lowered face. Its red mouth was slightly open, its big eye was wide and glassy-bright.

"Now!" he would silently command the snorting steed. "Now, take me to where there is luck! Now take me!"

And he would slash the horse on the neck with the little whip he had asked Uncle Oscar for. He *knew* the horse could take him to where there was luck, if only he forced it. So he would mount again and start on his furious ride, hoping at last to get there. He knew he could get there.

"You'll break your horse, Paul!" said the nurse.   45

"He's always riding like that! I wish he'd leave off!" said his elder sister Joan.

But he only glared down on them in silence. Nurse gave him up. She could make nothing of him. Anyhow, he was growing beyond her.

One day his mother and his Uncle Oscar came in when he was on one of his furious rides. He did not speak to them.

"Hallo, you young jockey! Riding a winner?" said his uncle.

"Aren't you growing too big for a rocking-horse? You're not a very little boy any   50
longer, you know," said his mother.

But Paul only gave a blue glare from his big, rather close-set eyes. He would speak to nobody when he was in full tilt. His mother watched him with an anxious expression on her face.

At last he suddenly stopped forcing his horse into the mechanical gallop and slid down.

"Well, I got there!" he announced fiercely, his blue eyes still flaring, and his sturdy long legs straddling apart.

"Where did you get to?" asked his mother.

55 "Where I wanted to go," he flared back at her.

"That's right, son!" said Uncle Oscar. "Don't you stop till you get there. What's the horse's name?"

"He doesn't have a name," said the boy.

"Gets on without all right?" asked the uncle.

"Well, he has different names. He was called Sansovino last week."

60 "Sansovino, eh? Won the Ascot. How did you know this name?"

"He always talks about horse-races with Bassett," said Joan.

The uncle was delighted to find that his small nephew was posted with all the racing news. Bassett, the young gardener, who had been wounded in the left foot in the war and had got his present job through Oscar Cresswell, whose batman he had been, was a perfect blade of the "turf." He lived in the racing events, and the small boy lived with him.

Oscar Cresswell got it all from Bassett.

"Master Paul comes and asks me, so I can't do more than tell him, sir," said Bassett, his face terribly serious, as if he were speaking of religious matters.

65 "And does he ever put anything on a horse he fancies?"

"Well—I don't want to give him away—he's a young sport, a fine sport, sir. Would you mind asking him yourself? He sort of takes a pleasure in it, and perhaps he'd feel I was giving him away, sir, if you don't mind."

Bassett was serious as a church.

The uncle went back to his nephew and took him off for a ride in the car.

"Say, Paul, old man, do you ever put anything on a horse?" the uncle asked.

70 The boy watched the handsome man closely.

"Why, do you think I oughtn't to?" he parried.

"Not a bit of it! I thought perhaps you might give me a tip for the Lincoln."

The car sped on into the country, going down to Uncle Oscar's place in Hampshire.

"Honour bright?" said the nephew.

75 "Honour bright, son!" said the uncle.

"Well, then, Daffodil."

"Daffodil! I doubt it, sonny. What about Mirza?"

"I only know the winner," said the boy. "That's Daffodil."

"Daffodil, eh?"

80 There was a pause. Daffodil was an obscure horse comparatively.

"Uncle!"

"Yes, son?"

"You won't let it go any further, will you? I promised Bassett."

"Bassett be damned, old man! What's he got to do with it?"

85 "We're partners. We've been partners from the first. Uncle, he lent me my first five shillings, which I lost. I promised him, honour bright, it was only between me and him; only you gave me that ten-shilling note I started winning with, so I thought you were lucky. You won't let it go any further, will you?"

The boy gazed at his uncle from those big, hot, blue eyes, set rather close together. The uncle stirred and laughed uneasily.

"Right you are, son! I'll keep your tip private. Daffodil, eh? How much are you putting on him?"

"All except twenty pounds," said the boy. "I keep that in reserve."

The uncle thought it a good joke.

"You keep twenty pounds in reserve, do you, you young romancer? What are 90 you betting, then?"

"I'm betting three hundred," said the boy gravely. "But it's between you and me, Uncle Oscar! Honour bright?"

The uncle burst into a roar of laughter.

"It's between you and me all right, you young Nat Gould," he said, laughing. "But where's your three hundred?"

"Bassett keeps it for me. We're partners."

"You are, are you! And what is Bassett putting on Daffodil?"   95

"He won't go quite as high as I do, I expect. Perhaps he'll go a hundred and fifty."

"What, pennies?" laughed the uncle.

"Pounds," said the child, with a surprised look at his uncle. "Bassett keeps a bigger reserve than I do."

Between wonder and amusement Uncle Oscar was silent. He pursued the matter no further, but he determined to take his nephew with him to the Lincoln races.

"Now, son," he said, "I'm putting twenty on Mirza, and I'll put five on for you 100 on any horse you fancy. What's your pick?"

"Daffodil, uncle."

"No, not the fiver on Daffodil!"

"I should if it was my own fiver," said the child.

"Good! Good! Right you are! A fiver for me and a fiver for you on Daffodil."

The child had never been to a race-meeting before, and his eyes were blue fire. 105 He pursed his mouth tight and watched. A Frenchman just in front had put his money on Lancelot. Wild with excitement, he flayed his arms up and down, yelling "*Lancelot! Lancelot!*" in his French accent.

Daffodil came in first, Lancelot second, Mirza third. The child, flushed and with eyes blazing, was curiously serene. His uncle brought him four five-pound notes, four to one.

"What am I to do with these?" he cried, waving them before the boy's eyes.

"I suppose we'll talk to Bassett," said the boy. "I expect I have fifteen hundred now; and twenty in reserve; and this twenty."

His uncle studied him for some moments.

"Look here, son!" he said. "You're not serious about Bassett and that fifteen 110 hundred, are you?"

"Yes, I am. But it's between you and me, uncle. Honour bright?"

"Honour bright all right, son! But I must talk to Bassett."

"If you'd like to be a partner, uncle, with Bassett and me, we could all be partners. Only, you'd have to promise, honour bright, uncle, not to let it go beyond us three. Bassett and I are lucky, and you must be lucky, because it was your ten shillings I started winning with. . . ."

Uncle Oscar took both Bassett and Paul into Richmond Park for an afternoon, and there they talked.

115 "It's like this, you see, sir," Bassett said. "Master Paul would get me talking about racing events, spinning yarns, you know, sir. And he was always keen on knowing if I'd made or if I'd lost. It's about a year since, now, that I put five shillings on Blush of Dawn for him; and we lost. Then the luck turned, with that ten shillings he had from you: that we put on Singhalese. And since that time, it's been pretty steady, all things considering. What do you say, Master Paul?"

"We're all right when we're sure," said Paul. "It's when we're not quite sure that we go down."

"Oh, but we're careful then," said Bassett.

"But when are you *sure?*" smiled Uncle Oscar.

"It's Master Paul, sir," said Bassett in a secret, religious voice. "It's as if he had it from heaven. Like Daffodil, now, for the Lincoln. That was as sure as eggs."

120 "Did you put anything on Daffodil?" asked Oscar Cresswell.

"Yes, sir. I made my bet."

"And my nephew?"

Bassett was obstinately silent, looking at Paul.

"I made twelve hundred, didn't I, Bassett? I told uncle I was putting three hundred on Daffodil."

125 "That's right," said Bassett, nodding.

"But where's the money?" asked the uncle.

"I keep it safe locked up, sir. Master Paul he can have it any minute he likes to ask for it."

"What, fifteen hundred pounds?"

"And twenty! And *forty,* that is, with the twenty he made on the course."

130 "It's amazing!" said the uncle.

"If Master Paul offers you to be partners, sir, I would, if I were you: if you'll excuse me," said Bassett.

Oscar Cresswell thought about it.

"I'll see the money," he said.

They drove home again, and, sure enough, Bassett came round to the garden-house with fifteen hundred pounds in notes. The twenty pounds reserve was left with Joe Glee, in the Turf Commission deposit.

135 "You see, it's all right, uncle, when I'm *sure!* Then we go strong, for all we're worth. Don't we, Bassett?"

"We do that, Master Paul."

"And when are you sure?" said the uncle, laughing.

"Oh, well, sometimes I'm *absolutely* sure, like about Daffodil," said the boy; "and sometimes I have an idea; and sometimes I haven't even an idea, have I, Bassett? Then we're careful, because we mostly go down."

"You do, do you! And when you're sure, like about Daffodil, what makes you sure, sonny?"

"Oh, well, I don't know," said the boy uneasily. "I'm sure, you know, uncle; that's all."

"It's as if he had it from heaven, sir," Bassett reiterated.

"I should say so!" said the uncle.

But he became a partner. And when the Leger was coming on Paul was "sure" about Lively Spark, which was a quite inconsiderable horse. The boy insisted on putting a thousand on the horse, Bassett went for five hundred, and Oscar Cresswell two hundred. Lively Spark came in first, and the betting had been ten to one against him. Paul had made ten thousand.

"You see," he said, "I was absolutely sure of him."

Even Oscar Cresswell had cleared two thousand.   145

"Look here, son," he said, "this sort of thing makes me nervous."

"It needn't, uncle! Perhaps I shan't be sure again for a long time."

"But what are you going to do with your money?" asked the uncle.

"Of course," said the boy, "I started it for mother. She said she had no luck, because father is unlucky, so I thought if *I* was lucky, it might stop whispering."

"What might stop whispering?"   150

"Our house. I *hate* our house for whispering."

"What does it whisper?"

"Why—why"—the boy fidgeted—"why, I don't know. But it's always short of money, you know, uncle."

"I know it, son, I know it."

"You know people send mother writs, don't you, uncle?"   155

"I'm afraid I do," said the uncle.

"And then the house whispers, like people laughing at you behind your back. It's awful, that is! I thought if I was lucky———"

"You might stop it," added the uncle.

The boy watched him with big blue eyes, that had an uncanny cold fire in them, and he said never a word.

"Well, then!" said the uncle. "What are we doing?"   160

"I shouldn't like mother to know I was lucky," said the boy.

"Why not, son?"

"She'd stop me."

"I don't think she would."

"Oh!"—and the boy writhed in an odd way—"I *don't* want her to know, uncle." 165

"All right, son! We'll manage it without her knowing."

They managed it very easily. Paul, at the other's suggestion, handed over five thousand pounds to his uncle, who deposited it with the family lawyer, who was then to inform Paul's mother that a relative had put five thousand pounds into his hands, which sum was to be paid out a thousand pounds at a time, on the mother's birthday, for the next five years.

"So she'll have a birthday present of a thousand pounds for five successive years," said Uncle Oscar. "I hope it won't make it all the harder for her later."

Paul's mother had her birthday in November. The house had been "whispering" worse than ever lately, and, even in spite of his luck, Paul could not bear up against it. He was very anxious to see the effect of the birthday letter, telling his mother about the thousand pounds.

170   When there were no visitors, Paul now took his meals with his parents, as he was beyond the nursery control. His mother went into town nearly every day. She had discovered that she had an odd knack of sketching furs and dress materials, so she worked secretly in the studio of a friend who was the chief "artist" for the leading drapers. She drew the figures of ladies in furs and ladies in silk and sequins for the newspaper advertisements. This young woman artist earned several thousand pounds a year, but Paul's mother only made several hundred, and she was again dissatisfied. She so wanted to be first in something, and she did not succeed, even in making sketches for drapery advertisements.

She was down to breakfast on the morning of her birthday. Paul watched her face as she read her letters. He knew the lawyer's letter. As his mother read it, her face hardened and became more expressionless. Then a cold, determined look came on her mouth. She hid the letter under the pile of others, and said not a word about it.

"Didn't you have anything nice in the post for your birthday, mother?" said Paul.

"Quite moderately nice," she said, her voice cold and absent.

She went away to town without saying more.

175   But in the afternoon Uncle Oscar appeared. He said Paul's mother had had a long interview with the lawyer, asking if the whole five thousand could not be advanced at once, as she was in debt.

"What do you think, uncle?" said the boy.

"I leave it to you, son."

"Oh, let her have it, then! We can get some more with the other," said the boy.

"A bird in the hand is worth two in the bush, laddie!" said Uncle Oscar.

180   "But I'm sure to *know* for the Grand National; or the Lincolnshire; or else the Derby. I'm sure to know for *one* of them," said Paul.

So Uncle Oscar signed the agreement, and Paul's mother touched the whole five thousand. Then something very curious happened. The voices in the house suddenly went mad, like a chorus of frogs on a spring evening. There were certain new furnishings, and Paul had a tutor. He was *really* going to Eton, his father's school, in the following autumn. There were flowers in the winter, and a blossoming of the luxury Paul's mother had been used to. And yet the voices in the house, behind the sprays of mimosa and almond blossom, and from under the piles of iridescent cushions, simply trilled and screamed in a sort of ecstacy: "There *must* be more money! Oh-h-h; there *must* be more money. Oh, now, now-w! Now-w-w—there *must* be more money!—more than ever! More than ever!"

It frightened Paul terribly. He studied away at his Latin and Greek with his tutor. But his intense hours were spent with Bassett. The Grand National had gone by: he had not "known," and had lost a hundred pounds. Summer was at hand. He was in agony for the Lincoln. But even for the Lincoln he didn't "know," and he lost fifty pounds. He became wild-eyed and strange, as if something were going to explode in him.

"Let it alone, son! Don't you bother about it!" urged Uncle Oscar. But it was as if the boy couldn't really hear what his uncle was saying.

"I've got to know for the Derby! I've got to know for the Derby!" the child reiterated, his big blue eyes blazing with a sort of madness.

His mother noticed how overwrought he was.   185

"You'd better go to the seaside. Wouldn't you like to go now to the seaside, instead of waiting? I think you'd better," she said, looking down at him anxiously, her heart curiously heavy because of him.

But the child lifted his uncanny blue eyes.

"I couldn't possibly go before the Derby, mother!" he said. "I couldn't possibly!"

"Why not?" she said, her voice becoming heavy when she was opposed. "Why not? You can still go from the seaside to see the Derby with your Uncle Oscar, if that's what you wish. No need for you to wait here. Besides, I think you care too much about these races. It's a bad sign. My family has been a gambling family, and you won't know till you grow up how much damage it has done. But it has done damage. I shall have to send Bassett away, and ask Uncle Oscar not to talk racing to you, unless you promise to be reasonable about it: go away to the seaside and forget it. You're all nerves!"

"I'll do what you like, mother, so long as you don't send me away till after the   190
Derby," the boy said.

"Send you away from where? Just from this house?"

"Yes," he said, gazing at her.

"Why, you curious child, what makes you care about this house so much, suddenly? I never knew you loved it."

He gazed at her without speaking. He had a secret within a secret, something he had not divulged, even to Bassett or to his Uncle Oscar.

But his mother, after standing undecided and a little bit sullen for some mo-   195
ments, said:

"Very well, then! Don't go to the seaside till after the Derby, if you don't wish it. But promise me you won't let your nerves go to pieces. Promise you won't think so much about horse-racing and *events,* as you call them!"

"Oh no," said the boy casually. "I won't think much about them, mother. You needn't worry. I wouldn't worry, mother, if I were you."

"If you were me and I were you," said his mother, "I wonder what we *should* do!"

"But you know you needn't worry, mother, don't you?" the boy repeated.

"I should be awfully glad to know it," she said wearily.   200

"Oh, well, you *can,* you know. I mean, you *ought* to know you needn't worry," he insisted.

"Ought I? Then I'll see about it," she said.

Paul's secret of secrets was his wooden horse, that which had no name. Since he was emancipated from a nurse and a nursery-governess, he had had his rocking-horse removed to his own bedroom at the top of the house.

"Surely you're too big for a rocking-horse!" his mother had remonstrated.

205   "Well, you see, mother, till I can have a *real* horse, I like to have *some* sort of animal about," had been his quaint answer.

"Do you feel he keeps you company?" she laughed.

"Oh yes! He's very good, he always keeps me company, when I'm there," said Paul.

So the horse, rather shabby, stood in an arrested prance in the boy's bedroom.

The Derby was drawing near, and the boy grew more and more tense. He hardly heard what was spoken to him, he was very frail, and his eyes were really uncanny. His mother had sudden strange seizures of uneasiness about him. Sometimes, for half an hour, she would feel a sudden anxiety about him that was almost anguish. She wanted to rush to him at once, and know he was safe.

210   Two nights before the Derby, she was at a big party in town, when one of her rushes of anxiety about her boy, her first-born, gripped her heart till she could hardly speak. She fought with the feeling, might and main, for she believed in common sense. But it was too strong. She had to leave the dance and go downstairs to telephone to the country. The children's nursery-governess was terribly surprised and startled at being rung up in the night.

"Are the children all right, Miss Wilmot?"

"Oh yes, they are quite all right."

"Master Paul? Is he all right?"

"He went to bed as right as a trivet. Shall I run up and look at him?"

215   "No," said Paul's mother reluctantly. "No! Don't trouble. It's all right. Don't sit up. We shall be home fairly soon." She did not want her son's privacy intruded upon.

"Very good," said the governess.

It was about one o'clock when Paul's mother and father drove up to their house. All was still. Paul's mother went to her room and slipped off her white fur cloak. She had told her maid not to wait up for her. She heard her husband downstairs, mixing a whisky and soda.

And then, because of the strange anxiety at her heart, she stole upstairs to her son's room. Noiselessly she went along the upper corridor. Was there a faint noise? What was it?

She stood, with arrested muscles, outside his door, listening. There was a strange, heavy, and yet not loud noise. Her heart stood still. It was a soundless noise, yet rushing and powerful. Something huge, in violent, hushed motion. What was it? What in God's name was it? She ought to know. She felt that she knew the noise. She knew what it was.

220   Yet she could not place it. She couldn't say what it was. And on and on it went, like a madness.

Softly, frozen with anxiety and fear, she turned the doorhandle.

The room was dark. Yet in the space near the window, she heard and saw something plunging to and fro. She gazed in fear and amazement.

Then suddenly she switched on the light, and saw her son, in his green pyjamas, madly surging on the rocking-horse. The blaze of light suddenly lit him up, as he urged the wooden horse, and lit her up, as she stood, blonde, in her dress of pale green and crystal, in the doorway.

"Paul!" she cried. "Whatever are you doing?"

"It's Malabar!" he screamed in a powerful, strange voice. "It's Malabar!" 225

His eyes blazed at her for one strange and senseless second, as he ceased urging his wooden horse. Then he fell with a crash to the ground, and she, all her tormented motherhood flooding upon her, rushed to gather him up.

But he was unconscious, and unconscious he remained, with some brain-fever. He talked and tossed, and his mother sat stonily by his side.

"Malabar! It's Malabar! Bassett, Bassett, I *know!* It's Malabar!"

So the child cried, trying to get up and urge the rocking-horse that gave him his inspiration.

"What does he mean by Malabar?" asked the heart-frozen mother. 230

"I don't know," said the father stonily.

"What does he mean by Malabar?" she asked her brother Oscar.

"It's one of the horses running for the Derby," was the answer.

And, in spite of himself, Oscar Cresswell spoke to Bassett, and himself put a thousand on Malabar: at fourteen to one.

The third day of the illness was critical: they were waiting for a change. The 235 boy, with his rather long, curly hair, was tossing ceaselessly on the pillow. He neither slept nor regained consciousness, and his eyes were like blue stones. His mother sat, feeling her heart had gone, turned actually into a stone.

In the evening, Oscar Cresswell did not come, but Bassett sent a message, saying could he come up for one moment, just one moment? Paul's mother was very angry at the intrusion, but on second thoughts she agreed. The boy was the same. Perhaps Bassett might bring him to consciousness.

The gardener, a shortish fellow with a little brown moustache and sharp little brown eyes, tiptoed into the room, touched his imaginary cap to Paul's mother, and stole to the bedside, staring with glittering, smallish eyes at the tossing, dying child.

"Master Paul!" he whispered. "Master Paul! Malabar came in first all right, a clean win. I did as you told me. You've made over seventy thousand pounds, you have; you've got over eighty thousand. Malabar came in all right, Master Paul."

"Malabar! Malabar! Did I say Malabar, mother? Did I say Malabar? Do you think I'm lucky, mother? I knew Malabar, didn't I? Over eighty thousand pounds! I call that lucky, don't you, mother? Over eighty thousand pounds? I knew, didn't I know I knew? Malabar came in all right. If I ride my horse till I'm sure, then I tell you, Bassett, you can go as high as you like. Did you go for all you were worth, Bassett?"

"I went a thousand on it, Master Paul." 240

"I never told you, mother, that if I can ride my horse, and *get there,* then I'm absolutely sure—oh, absolutely! Mother, did I ever tell you? I *am* lucky!"

"No, you never did," said his mother.

But the boy died in the night.

And even as he lay dead, his mother heard her brother's voice saying to her: "My God, Hester, you're eighty-odd thousand to the good, and a poor devil of a son to the bad. But, poor devil, poor devil, he's best gone out of a life where he rides his rocking-horse to find a winner."

QUESTIONS FOR DISCUSSION AND WRITING

1. How does the opening paragraph establish the context for the action of the story? How does Paul's birthday gift to his mother bring the story to its climax? How do Uncle Oscar's final words resolve the conflicts in the plot?

2. How does Lawrence characterize Paul's mother and father? How does Paul characterize himself? What qualities does Uncle Oscar possess that prompt Paul to include him as a partner?

3. In what sense is the house haunted? How does it provide the setting necessary for Paul's knowledge? Where does Paul's rocking horse take him?

4. What would have been the effect of allowing Paul to tell his own story? Compare and contrast the mother's and Uncle Oscar's point of view toward Paul.

5. What does this story reveal about luck? What does Paul actually hope to win?

Stories for Comparison

William Faulkner's "Barn Burning" (pages 491–504); John Updike's "A & P" (pages 1136–1141).

65

....

DORIS LESSING

A Woman on a Roof

DORIS LESSING was born in 1919 in Kermanshah, Persia, and was raised on a remote tobacco farm in southern Rhodesia. She attended a Catholic convent in Salisbury for a few years, but dropped out because of eye trouble and returned to her family's farm to complete her education through independent reading. In 1937, Lessing returned to Salisbury, where she worked as a part-time secretary and became involved in radical politics. By the time she left Africa for England in 1949, she had been married and divorced twice. In 1950, Lessing published her first novel, *The Grass Is Singing,* about the psychological and social causes of violence in South Africa. Her other early works also drew on her African experience: *Martha's Quest* (1952), *Five* (1953), and *A Proper Marriage* (1954). In 1956, Lessing returned to

Rhodesia to write *Going Home* (1957) but was prohibited from entering South Africa because of her liberal racial views. In 1962, she published *The Golden Notebook,* a novel that combined her interest in social commentary and psychological analysis. Lessing's later novels have moved increasingly away from realism toward fantasy as she has worked out certain psychological theories in *Briefing for a Descent into Hell* (1971) or explored the realm of science fiction in *Canopus in Argos: Archives* (1981). Her recent work includes *The Diaries of Jane Somers* (1984), *The Good Terrorist* (1985), and *Love, Again* (1996). "A Woman on a Roof," reprinted from *A Man and Two Women* (1963), reports the attempts of three workers to come to terms with their fantasies about a woman sunbather.

It was during the week of hot sun, that June.

Three men were at work on the roof, where the leads got so hot they had the idea of throwing water on to cool them. But the water steamed, then sizzled; and they made jokes about getting an egg from some woman in the flats under them, to poach it for their dinner. By two it was not possible to touch the guttering they were replacing, and they speculated about what workmen did in regularly hot countries. Perhaps they should borrow kitchen gloves with the egg? They were all a bit dizzy, not used to the heat; and they shed their coats and stood side by side squeezing themselves into a foot-wide patch of shade against a chimney, careful to keep their feet in the thick socks and boots out of the sun. There was a fine view across several acres of roofs. Not far off a man sat in a deck chair reading the newspaper. Then they saw her, between chimneys, about fifty yards away. She lay face down on a brown blanket. They could see the top part of her: black hair, a flushed solid back, arms spread out.

"She's stark naked," said Stanley, sounding annoyed.

Harry, the oldest, a man of about forty-five, said: "Looks like it."

Young Tom, seventeen, said nothing, but he was excited and grinning.

Stanley said: "Someone'll report her if she doesn't watch out."

"She thinks no one can see," said Tom, craning his head all ways to see more.

At this point the woman, still lying prone, brought her two hands up behind her shoulders with the ends of her scarf in them, tied it behind her back, and sat up. She wore a red scarf tied around her breasts and brief red bikini pants. This being the first day of the sun she was white, flushing red. She sat smoking, and did not look up when Stanley let out a wolf whistle. Harry said: "Small things amuse small minds," leading the way back to their part of the roof, but it was scorching. Harry said: "Wait, I'm going to rig up some shade," and disappeared down the skylight into the building. Now that he'd gone, Stanley and Tom went to the farthest point they could to peer at the woman. She had moved, and all they could see were two pink legs stretched on the blanket. They whistled and shouted but the legs did not move. Harry came back with a blanket and shouted: "Come on, then." He sounded irritated with them. They clambered back to him and he said to Stanley: "What about your missus?" Stanley was newly married, about three months. Stanley said, jeering: "What about my missus?"—preserving his independence. Tom said nothing, but his mind was full of the nearly naked woman. Harry slung the blanket, which he had borrowed from a friendly woman downstairs, from the stem of a television aerial to a row of chimney-pots. This shade fell across the piece of gutter they had to replace. But the shade kept moving, they had to adjust the blanket, and not much progress was made. At last some of the heat left the roof, and they worked fast, making up for lost time. First Stanley, then Tom, made a trip to the end of the roof to see the woman. "She's on her back," Stanley said, adding a jest which made Tom snicker, and the older man smiled tolerantly. Tom's report was that she hadn't moved, but it was a lie. He wanted to keep what he had seen to himself: he had caught her in the act of rolling down the little red pants over her hips, till they were no more than a small triangle. She was on her back, fully visible, glistening with oil.

Next morning, as soon as they came up, they went to look. She was already there, face down, arms spread out, naked except for the little red pants. She had turned brown in the night. Yesterday she was a scarlet-and-white woman, today she was a brown woman. Stanley let out a whistle. She lifted her head, startled, as if she'd been asleep, and looked straight over at them. The sun was in her eyes, she blinked and stared, then she dropped her head again. At this gesture of indifference, they all three, Stanley, Tom and old Harry, let out whistles and yells. Harry was doing it in parody of the younger men, making fun of them, but he was also angry. They were all angry because of her utter indifference to the three men watching her.

10   "Bitch," said Stanley.

"She should ask us over," said Tom, snickering.

Harry recovered himself and reminded Stanley: "If she's married, her old man wouldn't like that."

"Christ," said Stanley virtuously, "if my wife lay about like that, for everyone to see, I'd soon stop her."

Harry said, smiling: "How do you know, perhaps she's sunning herself at this very moment?"

15   "Not a chance, not on our roof." The safety of his wife put Stanley into a good humor, and they went to work. But today it was hotter than yesterday; and several times one or the other suggested they should tell Matthew, the foreman, and ask to leave the roof until the heat wave was over. But they didn't. There was work to be done in the basement of the big block of flats, but up here they felt free, on a different level from ordinary humanity shut in the streets or the buildings. A lot more people came out on to the roofs that day, for an hour at midday. Some married couples sat side by side in deck chairs, the women's legs stockingless and scarlet, the men in vests with reddening shoulders.

The woman stayed on her blanket, turning herself over and over. She ignored them, no matter what they did. When Harry went off to fetch more screws, Stanley said: "Come on." Her roof belonged to a different system of roofs, separated from theirs at one point by about twenty feet. It meant a scrambling climb from one level to another, edging along parapets, clinging to chimneys, while their big boots slipped and slithered, but at last they stood on a small square projecting roof looking straight down at her, close. She sat smoking, reading a book. Tom thought she looked like a poster, or a magazine cover, with the blue sky behind her and her legs stretched out.

Behind her a great crane at work on a new building in Oxford Street swung its black arm across roofs in a great arc. Tom imagined himself at work on the crane, adjusting the arm to swing over and pick her up and swing her back across the sky to drop her near him.

They whistled. She looked up at them, cool and remote, then went on reading. Again, they were furious. Or, rather, Stanley was. His sun-heated face was screwed into a rage as he whistled again and again, trying to make her look up. Young Tom stopped whistling. He stood beside Stanley, excited, grinning; but he felt as if he were saying to the woman: Don't associate me with *him,* for his grin was apologetic. Last night he had thought of the unknown woman before he slept, and she had been tender with him. This tenderness he was remembering as he shifted his feet by the jeering, whistling Stanley, and watched the indifferent, healthy brown woman a few feet off, with the gap that plunged to the street between them. Tom thought it was romantic, it was like being high on two hilltops. But there was a shout from Harry, and they clambered back. Stanley's face was hard, really angry. The boy kept looking at him and wondered why he hated the woman so much, for by now he loved her.

They played their little games with the blanket, trying to trap shade to work under; but again it was not until nearly four that they could work seriously, and they were exhausted, all three of them. They were grumbling about the weather by now. Stanley was in a thoroughly bad humor. When they made their routine trip to see the woman before they packed up for the day, she was apparently asleep, face down, her back all naked save for the scarlet triangle on her buttocks. "I've got a good mind to report her to the police," said Stanley, and Harry said: "What's eating you? What harm's she doing?"

"I tell you, if she was my wife!"

"But she isn't is she?" Tom knew that Harry, like himself, was uneasy at Stanley's 20 reaction. He was normally a sharp young man, quick at his work, making a lot of jokes, good company.

"Perhaps it will be cooler tomorrow," said Harry.

But it wasn't; it was hotter, if anything, and the weather forecast said the good weather would last. As soon as they were on the roof, Harry went over to see if the woman was there, and Tom knew it was to prevent Stanley going, to put off his bad humor. Harry had grownup children, a boy the same age as Tom, and the youth trusted and looked up to him.

Harry came back and said: "She's not there."

"I bet her old man put his foot down," said Stanley, and Harry and Tom caught each other's eyes and smiled behind the young married man's back.

Harry suggested they should get permission to work in the basement, and they 25 did, that day. But before packing up Stanley said: "Let's have a breath of fresh air." Again Harry and Tom smiled at each other as they followed Stanley up to the roof, Tom in the devout conviction that he was there to protect the woman from Stanley. It was about five-thirty, and a calm, full sunlight lay over the roofs. The great crane still swung its black arm from Oxford Street to above their heads. She was not there. Then there was a flutter of white from behind a parapet, and she stood up, in a belted, white dressing-gown. She had been there all day, probably, but on a different patch of roof, to hide from them. Stanley did not whistle; he said nothing, but watched the woman bend to collect papers, books, cigarettes, then fold the blanket over her arm. Tom was thinking: If they weren't here, I'd go over and say . . . what? But he knew from his nightly dreams of her that she was kind and friendly. Perhaps she would ask him down to her flat? Perhaps . . . He stood watching her disappear down the skylight. As she went, Stanley let out a shrill derisive yell; she started, and it seemed as if she nearly fell. She clutched to save herself, they could hear things falling. She looked straight at them, angry. Harry said, facetiously: "Better be careful on those slippery ladders, love." Tom knew he said it to save her from Stanley, but she could not know it. She vanished, frowning. Tom was full of a secret delight, because he knew her anger was for the others, not for him.

"Roll on some rain," said Stanley, bitter, looking at the blue evening sky.

Next day was cloudless, and they decided to finish the work in the basement. They felt excluded, shut in the grey cement basement fitting pipes, from the holiday atmosphere of London in a heat wave. At lunchtime they came up for some air, but while the married couples, and the men in shirt-sleeves or vests, were there, she was not there, either on her usual patch of roof or where she had been yesterday. They all, even Harry, clambered about, between chimney-pots, over parapets, the hot leads stinging their fingers. There was not a sign of her. They took off their shirts and vests and exposed their chests, feeling their feet sweaty and hot. They did not mention the woman. But Tom felt alone again. Last night she had him into her flat: it was big and had fitted white carpets and a bed with a padded white leather head-board. She wore a black filmy negligée and her kindness to Tom thickened his throat as he remembered it. He felt she had betrayed him by not being there.

And again after work they climbed up, but still there was nothing to be seen of her. Stanley kept repeating that if it was as hot as this tomorrow he wasn't going to work and that's all there was to it. But they were all there next day. By ten the temperature was in the middle seventies, and it was eighty long before noon. Harry went to the foreman to say it was impossible to work on the leads in that heat; but the foreman said there was nothing else he could put them on, and they'd have to. At midday they stood, silent, watching the skylight on her roof open, and then she slowly emerged in her white gown, holding a bundle of blanket. She looked at them, gravely, then went to the part of the roof where she was hidden from them. Tom was pleased. He felt she was more his when the other men couldn't see her. They had taken off their shirts and vests, but now they put them back again, for they felt the sun bruising their flesh. "She must have the hide of a rhino," said Stanley, tugging at guttering and swearing. They stopped work, and sat in the shade, moving around behind chimney stacks. A woman came to water a yellow window box opposite them. She was middle-aged, wearing a flowered summer dress. Stanley said to her: "We need a drink more than them." She smiled and said: "Better drop down to the pub quick, it'll be closing in a minute." They exchanged pleasantries, and she left them with a smile and a wave.

"Not like Lady Godiva," said Stanley. "She can give us a bit of a chat and a smile."

"You didn't whistle at *her*," said Tom, reproving.

"Listen to him," said Stanley, "you didn't whistle, then?"

But the boy felt as if he hadn't whistled, as if only Harry and Stanley had. He was making plans, when it was time to knock off work, to get left behind and somehow make his way over to the woman. The weather report said the hot spell was due to break, so he had to move quickly. But there was no chance of being left. The other two decided to knock off work at four, because they were exhausted. As they went down, Tom quickly climbed a parapet and hoisted himself higher by pulling his weight up a chimney. He caught a glimpse of her lying on her back, her knees up, eyes closed, a brown woman lolling in the sun. He slipped and clattered down, as Stanley looked for information: "She's gone down," he said. He felt as if he had protected her from Stanley, and that she must be grateful to him. He could feel the bond between the woman and himself.

Next day, they stood around on the landing below the roof, reluctant to climb up into the heat. The woman who had lent Harry the blanket came out and offered them a cup of tea. They accepted gratefully, and sat around Mrs. Pritchett's kitchen an hour or so, chatting. She was married to an airline pilot. A smart blonde, of about thirty, she had an eye for the handsome sharp-faced Stanley; and the two teased each other while Harry sat in a corner, watching, indulgent, though his expression reminded Stanley that he was married. And young Tom felt envious of Stanley's ease in badinage; felt, too, that Stanley's getting off with Mrs. Pritchett left his romance with the woman on the roof safe and intact.

"I thought they said the heat wave'd break," said Stanley, sullen, as the time approached when they really would have to climb up into the sunlight.

"You don't like it, then?" asked Mrs. Pritchett.   35

"All right for some," said Stanley. "Nothing to do but lie about as if it was a beach up there. Do you ever go up?"

"Went up once," said Mrs. Pritchett. "But it's a dirty place up there, and it's too hot."

"Quite right too," said Stanley.

Then they went up, leaving the cool neat little flat and the friendly Mrs. Pritchett.

As soon as they were up they saw her. The three men looked at her, resentful at   40 her ease in this punishing sun. Then Harry said, because of the expression on Stanley's face: "Come on, we've got to pretend to work, at least."

They had to wrench another length of guttering that ran beside a parapet out of its bed, so that they could replace it. Stanley took it in his two hands, tugged, swore, stood up. "Fuck it," he said, and sat down under a chimney. He lit a cigarette. "Fuck them," he said. "What do they think we are, lizards? I've got blisters all over my hands." Then he jumped up and climbed over the roofs and stood with his back to them. He put his fingers either side of his mouth and let out a shrill whistle. Tom and Harry squatted, not looking at each other, watching him. They could just see the woman's head, the beginnings of her brown shoulders. Stanley whistled again. Then he began stamping with his feet, and whistled and yelled and screamed at the woman, his face getting scarlet. He seemed quite mad, as he stamped and whistled, while the woman did not move, she did not move a muscle.

"Barmy," said Tom.

"Yes," said Harry, disapproving.

Suddenly the older man came to a decision. It was, Tom knew, to save some sort of scandal or real trouble over the woman. Harry stood up and began packing tools into a length of oily cloth. "Stanley," he said, commanding. At first Stanley took no notice, but Harry said: "Stanley, we're packing it in, I'll tell Matthew."

45   Stanley came back, cheeks mottled, eyes glaring.

"Can't go on like this," said Harry. "It'll break in a day or so. I'm going to tell Matthew we've got sunstroke, and if he doesn't like, it's too bad." Even Harry sounded aggrieved, Tom noted. The small, competent man, the family man with his grey hair, who was never at a loss, sounded really off balance. "Come on," he said, angry. He fitted himself into the open square in the roof, and went down, watching his feet on the ladder. Then Stanley went, with not a glance at the woman. Then Tom, who, his throat beating with excitement, silently promised her on a backward glance: Wait for me, wait, I'm coming.

On the pavement Stanley said: "I'm going home." He looked white now, so perhaps he really did have sunstroke. Harry went off to find the foreman, who was at work on the plumbing of some flats down the street. Tom slipped back, not into the building they had been working on, but the building on whose roof the woman lay. He went straight up, no one stopping him. The skylight stood open, with an iron ladder leading up. He emerged on to the roof a couple of yards from her. She sat up, pushing back her black hair with both hands. The scarf across her breasts bound them tight, and brown flesh bulged around it. Her legs were brown and smooth. She stared at him in silence. The boy stood grinning, foolish, claiming the tenderness he expected from her.

"What do you want?" she asked.

"I . . . I came to . . . make your acquaintance," he stammered, grinning, pleading with her.

50   They looked at each other, the slight, scarlet-faced excited boy, and the serious, nearly naked woman. Then, without a word, she lay down on her brown blanket, ignoring him.

"You like the sun, do you?" he enquired of her glistening back.

Not a word. He felt panic, thinking of how she had held him in her arms, stroked his hair, brought him where he sat, lordly, in her bed, a glass of some exhilarating liquor he had never tasted in life. He felt that if he knelt down, stroked her shoulders, her hair, she would turn and clasp him in her arms.

He said: "The sun's all right for you, isn't it?"

She raised her head, set her chin on two small fists. "Go away," she said. He did not move. "Listen," she said, in a slow reasonable voice, where anger was kept in check, though with difficulty; looking at him, her face weary with anger, "if you get a kick out of seeing women in bikinis, why don't you take a sixpenny bus ride to the Lido? You'd see dozens of them, without all this mountaineering."

55   She hadn't understood him. He felt her unfairness pale him. He stammered: "But I like you, I've been watching you and . . ."

"Thanks," she said, and dropped her face again, turned away from him.

She lay there. He stood there. She said nothing. She had simply shut him out. He stood, saying nothing at all, for some minutes. He thought: She'll have to say something if I stay. But the minutes went past, with no sign of them in her, except in the tension of her back, her thighs, her arms—the tension of waiting for him to go.

He looked up at the sky, where the sun seemed to spin in heat; and over the roofs where he and his mates had been earlier. He could see the heat quivering where they had worked. And they expect us to work in these conditions! he thought, filled with righteous indignation. The woman hadn't moved. A bit of hot wind blew her black hair softly; it shone, and was iridescent. He remembered how he had stroked it last night.

Resentment of her at last moved him off and away down the ladder, through the building, into the street. He got drunk then, in hatred of her.

Next day when he woke the sky was grey. He looked at the wet grey and 60 thought, vicious: Well, that's fixed you, hasn't it now? That's fixed you good and proper.

The three men were at work early on the cool leads, surrounded by damp drizzling roofs where no one came to sun themselves, black roofs, slimy with rain. Because it was cool now, they would finish the job that day, if they hurried.

QUESTIONS FOR DISCUSSION AND WRITING

1. How does the conflict between the three workers and the woman change during six days of good weather? How does Stanley's yell bring this conflict to a crisis? How does the rain resolve the conflict?

2. How does each man characterize himself by his attitude toward the woman on the roof? For example, why does Stanley approve of the woman who waters the window box? Why does Tom think he is different from the others? Why does Harry ask his foreman if they can work somewhere else?

3. Is this a story about setting or a story about character? For example, how does the sun affect the workers' ability to do their job? Why do the workers resent the woman's leisure in the sun?

4. Although the point of view is omniscient, the story is told from the workers' point of view. What evidence in the story suggests that the woman is changing her point of view toward the men who are watching her?

5. What does the woman symbolize for each man? How does the gap in the roof enrich the significance of each of these symbols? What does Tom discover about the woman and himself when he is able to gain access to her roof?

Stories for Comparison

Witi Ihimaera's "His First Ball" (pages 107–116); Russell Banks's "Sarah Cole: A Type of Love Story" (pages 245–261).

66

J A C K   L O N D O N

To Build a Fire

JACK LONDON (1876–1916) was born in San Francisco and attended Oak-land High School and the University of California, Berkeley. London's formal education was intermittent and brief. At fourteen, he bought a sloop and became an oyster pirate, raiding the oyster beds in San Francisco Bay. At seventeen, he joined a sealing expedition that took him to Japan and Siberia. When London returned, he tramped throughout the United States, joining Coxey's Army of unemployed workers in its march on Washington and becoming a member of the Socialist Labor Party. In 1897, at the age of twenty-one, London joined the gold rush to the Klondike. Although he was unsuccessful as a miner, London decided to write about his experiences in the Yukon—publishing his first short story, "To the Man on the Trail," in *Overland Monthly* in 1899. He published his first collection of stories, *Son of the Wolf,* in 1900 and his first novel, *The Call of the Wild,* in 1903. The latter became an instant best-seller, making London the highest-paid writer of his time. During the remaining years of his life, he produced almost fifty volumes of prose. As a journalist, London covered the Russian-Japanese War, the San Francisco earthquake, and the Mexican Revolution. His later works include *The Sea Wolf* (1904), *White Fang* (1906), *The Iron Heel* (1908), and *Martin Eden* (1909). The last book, largely autobiographical, chronicles London's literary success, disenchantment with socialism, and thoughts about suicide. "To Build a Fire," reprinted from *Lost Face* (1910), tells the story of one man's struggle for survival in an indifferent universe.

D ay had broken cold and grey, exceedingly cold and grey, when the man turned aside from the main Yukon trail and climbed the high earth-bank, where a dim and little-travelled trail led eastward through the fat spruce timberland. It was a steep bank, and he paused for breath at the top, excusing the act to himself by looking at his watch. It was nine o'clock. There was no sun nor hint of sun, though there was not a cloud in the sky. It was a clear day, and yet there seemed an intangible pall over the face of things, a subtle gloom that made the day dark, and that was due to the absence of sun. This fact did not worry the man. He was used to the lack of sun. It had been days since he had seen the sun, and he knew that a few more days must pass before that cheerful orb, due south, would just peep above the skyline and dip immediately from view.

The man flung a look back along the way he had come. The Yukon lay a mile wide and hidden under three feet of ice. On top of this ice were as many feet of snow. It was all pure white, rolling in gentle undulations where the ice jams of the freeze-up had formed. North and south, as far as his eye could see, it was unbroken white, save for a dark hairline that curved and twisted from around the spruce-covered island to the south, and that curved and twisted away into the north, where it disappeared behind another spruce-covered island. This dark hairline was the trail—the main trail—that led south five hundred miles to the Chilcoot Pass, Dyea, and salt water; and that led north seventy miles to Dawson, and still on to the north a thousand miles to Nulato, and finally to St. Michael, on Bering Sea, a thousand miles and half a thousand more.

But all this—the mysterious, far-reaching hairline trail, the absence of sun from the sky, the tremendous cold, and the strangeness and weirdness of it all—made no impression on the man. It was not because he was long used to it. He was a newcomer in the land, a *chechaquo,* and this was his first winter. The trouble with him was that he was without imagination. He was quick and alert in the things of life, but only in the things, and not in the significances. Fifty degrees below zero meant eighty-odd degrees of frost. Such fact impressed him as being cold and uncomfortable, and that was all. It did not lead him to meditate upon his frailty as a creature of temperature, and upon man's frailty in general, able only to live within certain narrow limits of heat and cold; and from there on it did not lead him to the conjectural field of immortality and man's place in the universe. Fifty degrees below zero stood for a bite of frost that hurt and that must be guarded against by the use of mittens, ear flaps, warm moccasins, and thick socks. Fifty degrees below zero. That there should be anything more to it than that was a thought that never entered his head.

As he turned to go on, he spat speculatively. There was a sharp explosive crackle that startled him. He spat again. And again, in the air, before it could fall to the snow, the spittle crackled. He knew that at fifty below spittle crackled on the snow, but this spittle had crackled in the air. Undoubtedly it was colder than fifty below—how much colder he did not know. But the temperature did not matter. He was bound for the old claim on the left fork of Henderson Creek, where the boys were already. They had come over across the divide from the Indian Creek country, while he had come the roundabout way to take a look at the possibilities of getting out logs in the spring from the islands in the Yukon. He would be in to camp by six o'clock; a bit after dark, it was true, but the boys would be there, a fire would be going, and a hot supper would be ready. As for lunch, he pressed his hand against the protruding bundle under his jacket. It was also under his shirt, wrapped up in a handkerchief and lying against the naked skin. It was the only way to keep the biscuits from freezing. He smiled agreeably to himself as he thought of those biscuits, each cut open and sopped in bacon grease, and each enclosing a generous slice of fried bacon.

He plunged in among the big spruce trees. The trail was faint. A foot of snow 5 had fallen since the last sled had passed over, and he was glad he was without a sled, travelling light. In fact, he carried nothing but the lunch wrapped in the handkerchief.

He was surprised, however, at the cold. It certainly was cold, he concluded, as he rubbed his numb nose and cheekbones with his mittened hand. He was a warm-whiskered man, but the hair on his face did not protect the high cheekbones and the eager nose that thrust itself aggressively into the frosty air.

At the man's heels trotted a dog, a big native husky, the proper wolf-dog, grey-coated and without any visible or temperamental difference from its brother, the wild wolf. The animal was depressed by the tremendous cold. It knew that it was no time for travelling. Its instinct told it a truer tale than was told to the man by the man's judgment. In reality, it was not merely colder than fifty below zero; it was colder than sixty below, than seventy below. It was seventy-five below zero. Since the freezing point is thirty-two above zero, it meant that one hundred and seven degrees of frost obtained. The dog did not know anything about thermometers. Possibly in its brain there was no sharp consciousness of a condition of very cold such as was in the man's brain. But the brute had its instinct. It experienced a vague but menacing apprehension that subdued it and made it slink along at the man's heels, and that made it question eagerly every unwonted movement of the man as if expecting him to go into camp and to seek shelter somewhere and build a fire. The dog had learned fire, and it wanted fire, or else to burrow under the snow and cuddle its warmth away from the air.

The frozen moisture of its breathing had settled on its fur in a fine powder of frost, and especially were its jowls, muzzle, and eyelashes whitened by its crystalled breath. The man's red beard and moustache were likewise frosted, but more solidly, the deposit taking the form of ice and increasing with every warm, moist breath he exhaled. Also, the man was chewing tobacco, and the muzzle of ice held his lips so rigidly that he was unable to clear his chin when he expelled the juice. The result was that a crystal beard of the colour and solidity of amber was increasing its length on his chin. If he fell down it would shatter itself, like glass, into brittle fragments. But he did not mind the appendage. It was the penalty all tobacco chewers paid in that country, and he had been out before in two cold snaps. They had not been so cold as this, he knew, but by the spirit thermometer at Sixty Mile he knew they had been registered at fifty below and at fifty-five.

He held on through the level stretch of woods for several miles, crossed a wide flat of nigger heads, and dropped down a bank to the frozen bed of a small stream. This was Henderson Creek, and he knew he was ten miles from the forks. He looked at his watch. It was ten o'clock. He was making four miles an hour, and he calculated that he would arrive at the forks at half-past twelve. He decided to celebrate that event by eating his lunch there.

The dog dropped in again at his heels, with a tail drooping discouragement, as the man swung along the creek bed. The furrow of the old sled trail was plainly visible, but a dozen inches of snow covered up the marks of the last runners. In a month no man had come up or down that silent creek. The man held steadily on. He was not much given to thinking, and just then particularly he had nothing to think about save that he would eat lunch at the forks and that at six o'clock he would be in camp with the boys. There was nobody to talk to; and, had there been, speech would have been impossible because of the ice muzzle on his mouth. So he continued monotonously to chew tobacco and to increase the length of his amber beard.

Once in a while the thought reiterated itself that it was very cold and that he had never experienced such cold. As he walked along he rubbed his cheekbones and nose with the back of his mittened hand. He did this automatically, now and again changing hands. But, rub as he would, the instant he stopped his cheekbones went numb, and the following instant the end of his nose went numb. He was sure to frost his cheeks; he knew that, and experienced a pang of regret that he had not devised a nose strap of the sort Bud wore in cold snaps. Such a strap passed across the cheeks, as well, and saved them. But it didn't matter much, after all. What were frosted cheeks? A bit painful, that was all; they were never serious.

Empty as the man's mind was of thoughts, he was keenly observant, and he noticed the changes in the creeks, the curves and bends and timber jams, and always he sharply noted where he placed his feet. Once, coming round a bend, he shied abruptly, like a startled horse, curved away from the place where he had been walking, and retreated several paces back along the trail. The creek he knew was frozen clear to the bottom—no creek could contain water in that arctic winter—but he knew also that there were springs that bubbled out from the hillsides and ran along under the snow and on top of the ice of the creek. He knew that the coldest snaps never froze these springs, and he knew likewise their danger. They were traps. They hid pools of water under the snow that might be three inches deep, or three feet. Sometimes a skin of ice half an inch thick covered them, and in turn was covered by snow. Sometimes there were alternate layers of water and ice skin, so that when one broke through he kept on breaking through for a while, sometimes wetting himself to the waist.

That was why he had shied in such a panic. He had felt the give under his feet and heard the crackle of a snow-hidden ice skin. And to get his feet wet in such a temperature meant trouble and danger. At the very least it meant delay, for he would be forced to stop and build a fire, and under its protection to bare his feet while he dried his socks and moccasins. He stood and studied the creek bed and its banks, and decided that the flow of water came from the right. He reflected awhile, rubbing his nose and cheeks, then skirted to the left, stepping gingerly and testing the footing for each step. Once clear of the danger, he took a fresh chew of tobacco and swung along at his four-mile gait.

In the course of the next two hours he came upon several similar traps. Usually the snow above the hidden pools had a sunken, candied appearance that advertised the danger. Once again, however, he had a close call; and once, suspecting danger, he compelled the dog to go on in front. The dog did not want to go. It hung back until the man shoved it forward, and then it went quickly across the white, unbroken surface. Suddenly it broke through, floundered to one side, and got away to firmer footing. It had wet its forefeet and legs, and almost immediately the water that clung to it turned to ice. It made quick efforts to lick the ice off its legs, then dropped down in the snow and began to bite out the ice that had formed between the toes. This was a matter of instinct. To permit the ice to remain would mean sore feet. It did not know this. It merely obeyed the mysterious prompting that arose from the deep crypts of its being. But the man knew, having achieved a judgment on the subject, and he removed the mitten from his right hand and helped to tear out the ice particles. He did not expose his fingers more than a minute, and was astonished at the swift numbness that smote them. It certainly was cold. He pulled on the mitten hastily, and beat the hand savagely across his chest.

At twelve o'clock the day was at its brightest. Yet the sun was too far south on its winter journey to clear the horizon. The bulge of the earth intervened between it and Henderson Creek, where the man walked under a clear sky at noon and cast no shadow. At half-past twelve, to the minute, he arrived at the forks of the creek. He was pleased at the speed he had made. If he kept it up, he would certainly be with the boys by six. He unbuttoned his jacket and shirt and drew forth his lunch. The action consumed no more than a quarter of a minute, yet in that brief moment the numbness laid hold of the exposed fingers. He did not put the mitten on, but, instead, struck the fingers a dozen sharp smashes against his leg. Then he sat down on a snow-covered log to eat. The sting that followed upon the striking of his fingers against his leg ceased so quickly that he was startled. He had had no chance to take a bit of biscuit. He struck the fingers repeatedly and returned them to the mitten, baring the other hand for the purpose of eating. He tried to take a mouthful, but the ice muzzle prevented. He had forgotten to build a fire and thaw out. He chuckled at his foolishness, and as he chuckled he noted the numbness creeping into the exposed fingers. Also, he noted that the stinging which had first come to his toes when he sat down was already passing away. He wondered whether the toes were warm or numb. He moved them inside the moccasins and decided that they were numb.

15   He pulled the mitten on hurriedly and stood up. He was a bit frightened. He stamped up and down until the stinging returned into the feet. It certainly was cold, was his thought. That man from Sulphur Creek had spoken the truth when telling how cold it sometimes got in the country. And he had laughed at him at the time! That showed one must not be too sure of things. There was no mistake about it, it *was* cold. He strode up and down, stamping his feet and threshing his arms, until reassured by the returning warmth. Then he got out matches and proceeded to make a fire. From the undergrowth, where high water of the previous spring had lodged a supply of seasoned twigs, he got his firewood. Working carefully from a small beginning, he soon had a roaring fire, over which he thawed the ice from his face and in the protection of which he ate his biscuits. For the moment the cold of space was outwitted. The dog took satisfaction in the fire, stretching out close enough for warmth and far enough away to escape being singed.

When the man had finished, he filled his pipe and took his comfortable time over a smoke. Then he pulled on his mittens, settled the ear-flaps of his cap firmly about his ears, and took the creek trail up the left fork. The dog was disappointed and yearned back towards the fire. This man did not know cold. Possibly all the generations of his ancestry had been ignorant of cold, of real cold, of cold one hundred and seven degrees below freezing point. But the dog knew; all its ancestry knew, and it had inherited the knowledge. And it knew that it was not good to walk abroad in such fearful cold. It was the time to lie snug in a hole in the snow and wait for a curtain of cloud to be drawn across the face of outer space whence this cold came. On the other hand, there was no keen intimacy between the dog and the man. The one was the toil slave of the other, and the only caresses it had ever received were the caresses of the whip lash and of harsh and menacing throat sounds that threatened the whip lash. So the dog made no effort to communicate its apprehension to the man. It was not concerned in the welfare of the man; it was for its own sake that it yearned back towards the fire. But the man whistled, and spoke to it with the sound of whip lashes, and the dog swung in at the man's heels and followed after.

The man took a chew of tobacco and proceeded to start a new amber beard. Also, his moist breath quickly powdered with white his moustache, eyebrows, and lashes. There did not seem to be so many springs on the left fork of the Henderson, and for half an hour the man saw no signs of any. And then it happened. At a place where there were no signs, where the soft, unbroken snow seemed to advertise solidity beneath, the man broke through. It was not deep. He wet himself half-way to the knees before he floundered out to the firm crust.

He was angry, and cursed his luck aloud. He had hoped to get into camp with the boys at six o'clock, and this would delay him an hour, for he would have to build a fire and dry out his footgear. This was imperative at that low temperature—he knew that much; and he turned aside to the bank, which he climbed. On top, tangled in the underbrush about the trunks of several small spruce trees, was a high-water deposit of dry firewood—sticks and twigs, principally, but also larger portions of seasoned branches and fine, dry, last year's grasses. He threw down several large pieces on top of the snow. This served for a foundation and prevented the young flame from drowning itself in the snow it otherwise would melt. The flame he got by touching a match to a small shred of birch bark that he took from his pocket. This burned even more readily than paper. Placing it on the foundation, he fed the young flame with wisps of dry grass and with the tiniest dry twigs.

He worked slowly and carefully, keenly aware of his danger. Gradually, as the flame grew stronger, he increased the size of the twigs with which he fed it. He squatted in the snow pulling the twigs out from their entanglement in the brush and feeding directly to the flame. He knew there must be no failure. When it is seventy-five below zero, a man must not fail in his first attempt to build a fire—that is, if his feet are wet. If his feet are dry, and he fails, he can run along the trail for half a mile and restore his circulation. But the circulation of wet and freezing feet cannot be restored by running when it is seventy-five below. No matter how fast he runs, the wet feet will freeze the harder.

All this the man knew. The old-timer on Sulphur Creek had told him about it the previous fall, and now he was appreciating the advice. Already all sensation had gone out of his feet. To build the fire he had been forced to remove his mittens, and the fingers had quickly gone numb. His pace of four miles an hour had kept his heart pumping blood to the surface of his body and to all the extremities. But the instant he stopped, the action of the pump eased down. The cold of space smote the unprotected tip of the planet, and he, being on that unprotected tip, received the full force of the blow. The blood of his body recoiled before it. The blood was alive, like the dog, and like the dog it wanted to hide away and cover itself up from the fearful cold. So long as he walked four miles an hour, he pumped that blood, willy-nilly, to the surface; but now it ebbed away and sank down into the recesses of his body. The extremities were the first to feel its absence. His wet feet froze faster, and his exposed fingers numbed the faster, though they had not yet begun to freeze. Nose and cheeks were already freezing, while the skin of all his body chilled as it lost its blood.

But he was safe. Toes and nose and cheeks would be only touched by the frost, for the fire was beginning to burn with strength. He was feeding it with twigs the size of his finger. In another minute he would be able to feed it with branches the size of his wrist, and then he could remove his wet footgear, and, while it dried, he could keep his naked feet warm by the fire, rubbing them at first, of course, with snow. The fire was a success. He was safe. He remembered the advice of the old-timer on Sulphur Creek, and smiled. The old-timer had been very serious in laying down the law that no man must travel alone in the Klondike after fifty below. Well, here he was; he had had the accident; he was alone; and he had saved himself. Those old-timers were rather womanish, some of them, he thought. All a man had to do was to keep his head, and he was all right. Any man who was a man could travel alone. But it was surprising, the rapidity with which his cheeks and nose were freezing. And he had not thought his fingers could go lifeless in so short a time. Lifeless they were, for he could scarcely make them move together to grip a twig, and they seemed remote from his body and from him. When he touched a twig, he had to look and see whether or not he had hold of it. The wires were pretty well down between him and his finger ends.

All of which counted for little. There was the fire, snapping and crackling and promising life with every dancing flame. He started to untie his moccasins. They were coated with ice; the thick German socks were like sheaths of iron halfway to the knees; and the moccasin strings were like rods of steel all twisted and knotted as by some conflagration. For a moment he tugged with his numb fingers, then, realizing the folly of it, he drew his sheath knife.

But before he could cut the strings, it happened. It was his own fault, or, rather, his mistake. He should not have built the fire under the spruce tree. He should have built it in the open. But it had been easier to pull the twigs from the brush and drop them directly on the fire. Now the tree under which he had done this carried a weight of snow on its boughs. No wind had blown for weeks, and each bough was fully freighted. Each time he had pulled a twig he had communicated a slight agitation to the tree—an imperceptible agitation, so far as he was concerned, but an agitation sufficient to bring about the disaster. High up in the tree one bough capsized its load of snow. This fell on the boughs beneath, capsizing them. This process continued, spreading out and involving the whole tree. It grew like an avalanche, and it descended without warning upon the man and the fire, and the fire was blotted out! Where it had burned was a mantle of fresh and disordered snow.

The man was shocked. It was as though he had just heard his own sentence of death. For a moment he sat and stared at the spot where the fire had been. Then he grew very calm. Perhaps the old-timer on Sulphur Creek was right. If he had only had a trail mate he would have been in no danger now. The trail mate could have built the fire. Well, it was up to him to build the fire over again, and this second time there must be no failure. Even if he succeeded, he would most likely lose some toes. His feet must be badly frozen by now, and there would be some time before the second fire was ready.

Such were his thoughts, but he did not sit and think them. He was busy all the time they were passing through his mind. He had made a new foundation for a fire, this time in the open, where no treacherous tree could blot it out. Next he gathered dry grasses and tiny twigs from the high-water flotsam. He could not bring his fingers together to pull them out, but he was able to gather them by the handful. In this way he got many rotten twigs and bits of green moss that were undesirable, but it was the best he could do. He worked methodically, even collecting an armful of the larger branches to be used later when the fire gathered strength. And all the while the dog sat and watched him, a certain yearning wistfulness in its eyes, it looked upon him as the fire provider, and the fire was slow in coming.

When all was ready, the man reached in his pocket for a second piece of birch bark. He knew the bark was there, and, though he could not feel it with his fingers, he could hear its crisp rustling as he fumbled for it. Try as he would, he could not clutch hold of it. And all the time, in his consciousness, was the knowledge that each instant his feet were freezing. This thought tended to put him in a panic, but he fought against it and kept calm. He pulled on his mittens with his teeth, and threshed his arms back and forth, beating his hands with all his might against his sides. He did this sitting down, and he stood up to do it; and all the while the dog sat in the snow, its wolf brush of a tail curled around warmly over its forefeet, its sharp wolf ears pricked forward intently as it watched the man. And the man, as he beat and threshed with his arms and hands, felt a great surge of envy as he regarded the creature that was warm and secure in its natural covering.

After a time he was aware of the first faraway signals of sensation in his beaten fingers. The faint tingling grew stronger till it evolved into a stinging ache that was excruciating, but which the man hailed with satisfaction. He stripped the mitten from his right hand and fetched forth the birch bark. The exposed fingers were quickly going numb again. Next he brought out his bunch of sulphur matches. But the tremendous cold had already driven the life out of his fingers. In his effort to separate one match from the others, the whole bunch fell in the snow. He tried to pick it out of the snow, but failed. The dead fingers could neither touch nor clutch. He was very careful. He drove the thought of his freezing feet, and nose, and cheeks, out of his mind, devoting his whole soul to the matches. He watched, using the sense of vision in place of that of touch, and when he saw his fingers on each side the bunch, he closed them—that is, he willed to close them, for the wires were down, and the fingers did not obey. He pulled the mitten on the right hand, and beat it fiercely against the knee. Then with both mittened hands, he scooped the bunch of matches, along with much snow, into his lap. Yet he was no better off.

After some manipulation he managed to get the bunch between the heels of his mittened hands. In this fashion he carried it to his mouth. The ice crackled and snapped when by a violent effort he opened his mouth. He drew the lower jaw in, curled the upper lip out of the way, and scraped the bunch with his upper teeth in order to separate a match. He succeeded in getting one, which he dropped on his lap. He was no better off. He could not pick it up. Then he devised a way. He picked it

up in his teeth and scratched it on his leg. Twenty times he scratched before he succeeded in lighting it. As it flamed he held it with his teeth to the birth bark. But the
burning brimstone went up his nostrils and into his lungs, causing him to cough spas-
modically. The match fell into the snow and went out.

The old-timer on Sulphur Creek was right, he thought in the moment of controlled despair that ensued: after fifty below, a man should travel with a partner. He
beat his hands, but failed in exciting any sensation. Suddenly he bared both hands,
removing the mittens with his teeth. He caught the whole bunch between the heels
of his hands. His arm muscles not being frozen enabled him to press the hand heels
tightly against the matches. Then he scratched the bunch along his leg. It flared into
flame, seventy sulphur matches at once! There was no wind to blow them out. He
kept his head to one side to escape the strangling fumes, and held the blazing bunch
to the birch bark. As he so held it, he became aware of sensation in his hand. His
flesh was burning. He could smell it. Deep down below the surface he could feel it.
The sensation developed into pain that grew acute. And still he endured it, holding
the flame of the matches clumsily to the bark that would not light readily because his
own burning hands were in the way, absorbing most of the flame.

30   At last, when he could endure no more, he jerked his hands apart. The blazing
matches fell sizzling into the snow, but the birch bark was alight. He began laying
dry grasses and tiniest twigs on the flame. He could not pick and choose, for he had
to lift the fuel between the heels of his hands. Small pieces of rotten wood and green
moss clung to the twigs, and he bit them off as well as he could with his teeth. He
cherished the flame carefully and awkwardly. It meant life, and it must not perish.
The withdrawal of blood from the surface of his body now made him begin to shiver,
and he grew more awkward. A large piece of green moss fell squarely on the little
fire. He tried to poke it out with his fingers, but his shivering frame made him poke
too far, and he disrupted the nucleus of the little fire, the burning grasses and tiny
twigs separating and scattering. He tried to poke them together again, but in spite of
the tenseness of the effort, his shivering got away with him, and the twigs were hopelessly scattered. Each twig gushed a puff of smoke and went out. The fire provider
had failed. As he looked apathetically about him, his eyes chanced on the dog, sitting across the ruins of the fire from him, in the snow, making restless, hunching
movements, slightly lifting one forefoot and then the other, shifting its weight back
and forth on them with wistful eagerness.

The sight of the dog put a wild idea into his head. He remembered the tale
of the man, caught in a blizzard, who killed a steer and crawled inside the carcass, and so was saved. He would kill the dog and bury his hands in the warm
body until the numbness went out of them. Then he could build another fire. He
spoke to the dog, calling it to him; but in his voice was a strange note of fear
that frightened the animal, who had never known the man to speak in such a
way before. Something was the matter, and its suspicious nature sensed danger—
it knew not what danger, but somewhere, somehow, in its brain arose an apprehension of the man. It flattened its ears down at the sound of the man's voice,
and its restless, hunching movements and the liftings and shiftings of its forefeet
became more pronounced; but it would not come to the man. He got on his

hands and knees and crawled toward the dog. This unusual posture again excited suspicion, and the animal sidled mincingly away.

The man sat up in the snow for a moment and struggled for calmness. Then he pulled on his mittens, by means of his teeth, and got upon his feet. He glanced down at first in order to assure himself that he was really standing up, for the absence of sensation in his feet left him unrelated to the earth. His erect position in itself started to drive the webs of suspicion from the dog's mind; and when he spoke peremptorily, with the sound of whip lashes in his voice, the dog rendered its customary allegiance and came to him. As it came within reaching distance, the man lost his control. His arms flashed out to the dog, and he experienced genuine surprise when he discovered that his hands could not clutch, that there was neither bend nor feeling in the fingers. He had forgotten for the moment that they were frozen and that they were freezing more and more. All this happened quickly, and before the animal could get away, he encircled its body with his arms. He sat down in the snow, and in his fashion held the dog, while it snarled and whined and struggled.

But it was all he could do, hold its body encircled in his arms and sit there. He realized he could not kill the dog. There was no way to do it. With his helpless hands he could neither draw nor hold his sheath knife nor throttle the animal. He released it, and it plunged wildly away, with tail between its legs, and still snarling. It halted forty feet away and surveyed him curiously, with ears pricked forward.

The man looked down at his hands in order to locate them, and found them hanging on the ends of his arms. It struck him as curious that one should have to use his eyes in order to find out where his hands were. He began threshing his arms back and forth, beating the mittened hands against his sides. He did this for five minutes, violently, and his heart pumped enough blood up to the surface to put a stop to his shivering. But no sensation was aroused in the hands. He had an impression that they hung like weights on the ends of his arms, but when he tried to run the impression down, he could not find it.

A certain fear of death, dull and oppressive, came to him. This fear quickly became poignant as he realized that it was no longer a mere matter of freezing his fingers and toes, or of losing his hands and feet, but that it was a matter of life and death with the chances against him. This threw him into a panic, and he turned and ran up the creek bed along the old, dim trail. The dog joined in behind him and kept up with him. He ran blindly, without intention, in fear such as he had never known in his life. Slowly, as he ploughed and floundered through the snow, he began to see things again—the banks of the creek, the old timber jams, the leafless aspens, and the sky. The running made him feel better. He did not shiver. Maybe, if he ran on, his feet would thaw out; and, anyway, if he ran far enough, he would reach camp and the boys. Without doubt he would lose some fingers and toes and some of his face; but the boys would take care of him, and save the rest of him when he got there. And at the same time there was another thought in his mind that said he would never get to the camp and the boys; that it was too many miles away, that the freezing had too great a start on him, and that he would soon be stiff and dead. This thought he kept in the background and refused to consider. Sometimes it pushed itself forward and demanded to be heard, but he thrust it back and strove to think of other things.

It struck him as curious that he could run at all on feet so frozen that he could not feel them when they struck the earth and took the weight of his body. He seemed to himself to skim along above the surface, and to have no connection with the earth. Somewhere he had once seen a winged Mercury, and he wondered if Mercury felt as he felt when skimming over the earth.

His theory of running until he reached camp and the boys had one flaw in it: he lacked the endurance. Several times he stumbled, and finally he tottered, crumpled up, and fell. When he tried to rise, he failed. He must sit and rest, he decided, and next time he would merely walk and keep on going. As he sat and regained his breath, he noted that he was feeling quite warm and comfortable. He was not shivering, and it even seemed that a warm glow had come to his chest and trunk. And yet, when he touched his nose or cheeks, there was no sensation. Running would not thaw them out. Nor would it thaw out his hands and feet. Then the thought came to him that the frozen portions of his body must be extending. He tried to keep this thought down, to forget it, to think of something else; he was aware of the panicky feeling that it caused, and he was afraid of the panic. But the thought asserted itself, and persisted, until it produced a vision of his body totally frozen. This was too much, and he made another wild run along the trail. Once he slowed down to a walk, but the thought of the freezing extending itself made him run again.

And all the time the dog ran with him, at his heels. When he fell down a second time, it curled its tail over its forefeet and sat in front of him, facing him, curiously eager and intent. The warmth and security of the animal angered him, and he cursed it till it flattened down its ears appeasingly. This time the shivering came more quickly upon the man. He was losing in his battle with the frost. It was creeping into his body from all sides. The thought of it drove him on, but he ran no more than a hundred feet, when he staggered and pitched headlong. It was his last panic. When he had recovered his breath and control, he sat up and entertained in his mind the conception of meeting death with dignity. However, the conception did not come to him in such terms. His idea of it was that he had been making a fool of himself, running around like a chicken with its head cut off—such was the simile that occurred to him. Well, he was bound to freeze anyway, and he might as well take it decently. With this new-found peace of mind came the first glimmerings of drowsiness. A good idea, he thought, to sleep off to death. It was like taking an anaesthetic. Freezing was not so bad as people thought. There were lots worse ways to die.

He pictured the boys finding his body next day. Suddenly he found himself with them, coming along the trail looking for himself. And, still with them, he came around a turn in the trail and found himself lying in the snow. He did not belong with himself any more, for even then he was out of himself, standing with the boys and looking at himself in the snow. It certainly was cold, was his thought. When he got back to the States he could tell the folks what real cold was. He drifted on from this to a vision of the old-timer on Sulphur Creek. He could see him quite clearly, warm and comfortable, and smoking a pipe.

40   "You were right, old hoss; you were right," the man mumbled to the old-timer of Sulphur Creek.

Then the man drowsed off into what seemed to him the most comfortable and satisfying sleep he had ever known. The dog sat facing him and waiting. The brief day drew to a close in a long, slow twilight. There were no signs of a fire to be made, and, besides, never in the dog's experience had it known a man to sit like that in the snow and make no fire. As the twilight drew on, its eager yearning for the fire mastered it, and with a great lifting and shifting of forefeet, it whined softly, then flattened its ears down in anticipation of being chidden by the man. But the man remained silent. Later the dog whined loudly. And still later it crept close to the man and caught the scent of death. This made the animal bristle and back away. A little longer it delayed, howling under the stars that leaped and danced and shone brightly in the cold sky. Then it turned and trotted up the trail in the direction of the camp it knew, where were the other food providers and fire providers.

QUESTIONS FOR DISCUSSION AND WRITING

1. What external and internal conflicts does the man face on his journey? How does each of the three fires he attempts to build bring those conflicts to a climax?

2. What is significant about London's characterization of the nameless protagonist as a man "without imagination"? How does the protagonist characterize himself? How does he compare himself to the "old-timer"?

3. In what sense is the setting a trap? What specific traps is the man able to avoid? What prevents him from avoiding all the traps?

4. How does the man's point of view toward his own judgment change during the course of his journey? What is the dog's point of view toward the man and his decisions?

5. How do London's statements about man's place in the universe establish the theme of this story? How does the story advance this theme by illustrating the relationship of caution, courage, and foolishness?

Stories for Comparison

Stephen Crane's "The Open Boat" (pages 453–471); Ernest Hemingway's "Big Two-Hearted River" (pages 650–664).

67

....

C A R S O N   M c C U L L E R S

Sucker

CARSON McCULLERS (1917–1967) was born in Columbus, Georgia. After graduating from high school, she worked briefly as a reporter for the *Columbus Enquirer* before going to New York to study at the Juilliard School of Music. In New York, McCullers changed her mind and enrolled in writing courses at Columbia University and New York University. In 1940, at the age of twenty-three, she published her first novel, *The Heart Is a Lonely Hunter,* a book that attracted wide critical attention as the newest example of Southern gothic fiction. After her second novel, *Reflections in a Golden Eye* (1941), McCullers began contributing stories to magazines such as *Vogue, The New Yorker,* and *Mademoiselle.* Her third novel, *The Member of the Wedding* (1946), was later adapted for a play and a film, the stage version winning both the New York Critics Circle and Donaldson awards. As a young adult, McCullers suffered a series of strokes, and by the age of thirty-one her entire left side was paralyzed. Although writing became an ordeal, she continued to compose and dictate her work, such as the novel *Clock Without Hands* (1961), until she died of a brain hemorrhage at the age of fifty. Her short stories are collected in *The Ballad of the Sad Café* (1951), *The Mortgaged Heart* (1971), and *Collected Stories* (1973). In "Sucker," reprinted from *The Mortgaged Heart,* a young boy tries to explain what prompted him to betray his younger "brother."

I T WAS ALWAYS like I had a room to myself. Sucker slept in my bed with me but that didn't interfere with anything. The room was mine and I used it as I wanted to. Once I remember sawing a trap door in the floor. Last year when I was a sophomore in high school I tacked on my wall some pictures of girls from magazines and one of them was just in her underwear. My mother never bothered me because she had the younger kids to look after. And Sucker thought anything I did was always swell.

Whenever I would bring any of my friends back to my room all I had to do was just glance once at Sucker and he would get up from whatever he was busy with and maybe half smile at me, and leave without saying a word. He never brought kids back there. He's twelve, four years younger than I am, and he always knew without me even telling him that I didn't want kids that age meddling with my things.

Half the time I used to forget that Sucker isn't my brother. He's my first cousin but practically ever since I remember he's been in our family. You see his folks were killed in a wreck when he was a baby. To me and my kid sisters he was like our brother.

Sucker used to always remember and believe every word I said. That's how he got his nick-name. Once a couple of years ago I told him that if he'd jump off our garage with an umbrella it would act as a parachute and he wouldn't fall hard. He did it and busted his knee. That's just one instance. And the funny thing was that no matter how many times he got fooled he would still believe me. Not that he was dumb in other ways—it was just the way he acted with me. He would look at everything I did and quietly take it in.

There is one thing I have learned, but it makes me feel guilty and is hard to fig- 5
ure out. If a person admires you a lot you despise him and don't care—and it is the person who doesn't notice you that you are apt to admire. This is not easy to realize. Maybelle Watts, this senior at school, acted like she was the Queen of Sheba and even humiliated me. Yet at this same time I would have done anything in the world to get her attentions. All I could think about day and night was Maybelle until I was nearly crazy. When Sucker was a little kid and on up until the time he was twelve I guess I treated him as bad as Maybelle did me.

Now that Sucker has changed so much it is a little hard to remember him as he used to be. I never imagined anything would suddenly happen that would make us both very different. I never knew that in order to get what has happened straight in my mind I would want to think back on him as he used to be and compare and try to get things settled. If I could have seen ahead maybe I would have acted different.

I never noticed him much or thought about him and when you consider how long we have had the same room together it is funny the few things I remember. He used to talk to himself a lot when he'd think he was alone—all about him fighting gangsters and being on ranches and that sort of kids' stuff. He'd get in the bathroom and stay as long as an hour and sometimes his voice would go up high and excited and you could hear him all over the house. Usually, though, he was very quiet. He didn't have many boys in the neighborhood to buddy with and his face had the look of a kid who is watching a game and waiting to be asked to play. He didn't mind wearing the sweaters and coats that I outgrew, even if the sleeves did flop down too big and make his wrists look as thin and white as a little girl's. That is how I remember him—getting a little bigger every year but still being the same. That was Sucker up until a few months ago when all this trouble began.

Maybelle was somehow mixed up in what happened so I guess I ought to start with her. Until I knew her I hadn't given much time to girls. Last fall she sat next to me in General Science class and that was when I first began to notice her. Her hair is the brightest yellow I ever saw and occasionally she will wear it set into curls with some sort of gluey stuff. Her fingernails are pointed and manicured and painted a shiny red. All during class I used to watch Maybelle, nearly all the time except when I thought she was going to look my way or when the teacher called on me. I couldn't keep my eyes off her hands, for one thing. They are very little and white except for that red stuff, and when she would turn the pages of her book she always licked her thumb and held out her little finger and turned very slowly. It is impossible to describe Maybelle. All the boys are crazy about her but she didn't even notice me. For one thing she's almost two years older than I am. Between periods I used to try and pass very close to her in the halls but she would hardly ever smile at me. All I could do was sit and look at her in class—and sometimes it was like the whole room could hear my heart beating and I wanted to holler or light out and run for Hell.

At night, in bed, I would imagine about Maybelle. Often this would keep me from sleeping until as late as one or two o'clock. Sometimes Sucker would wake up and ask me why I couldn't get settled and I'd tell him to hush his mouth. I suppose I was mean to him lots of times. I guess I wanted to ignore somebody like Maybelle did me. You could always tell by Sucker's face when his feelings were hurt. I don't remember all the ugly remarks I must have made because even when I was saying them my mind was on Maybelle.

10   That went on for nearly three months and then somehow she began to change. In the halls she would speak to me and every morning she copied my homework. At lunch time once I danced with her in the gym. One afternoon I got up nerve and went around to her house with a carton of cigarettes. I knew she smoked in the girls' basement and sometimes outside of school—and I didn't want to take her candy because I think that's been run into the ground. She was very nice and it seemed to me everything was going to change.

It was that night when this trouble really started. I had come into my room late and Sucker was already asleep. I felt too happy and keyed up to get in a comfortable position and I was awake thinking about Maybelle a long time. Then I dreamed about her and it seemed I kissed her. It was a surprise to wake up and see the dark. I lay still and a little while passed before I could come to and understand where I was. The house was quiet and it was a very dark night.

Sucker's voice was a shock to me. "Pete? . . ."

I didn't answer anything or even move.

"You do like me as much as if I was your own brother, don't you, Pete?"

15   I couldn't get over the surprise of everything and it was like this was the real dream instead of the other.

"You have liked me all the time like I was your own brother, haven't you?"

"Sure," I said.

Then I got up for a few minutes. It was cold and I was glad to come back to bed. Sucker hung on to my back. He felt little and warm and I could feel his warm breathing on my shoulder.

"No matter what you did I always knew you liked me."

20   I was wide awake and my mind seemed mixed up in a strange way. There was this happiness about Maybelle and all that—but at the same time something about Sucker and his voice when he said these things made me take notice. Anyway I guess you understand people better when you are happy than when something is worrying you. It was like I had never really thought about Sucker until then. I felt I had always been mean to him. One night a few weeks before I had heard him crying in the dark. He said he had lost a boy's beebee gun and was scared to let anybody know. He

wanted me to tell him what to do. I was sleepy and tried to make him hush and when he wouldn't I kicked at him. That was just one of the things I remembered. It seemed to me he had always been a lonesome kid. I felt bad.

There is something about a dark cold night that makes you feel close to someone you're sleeping with. When you talk together it is like you are the only people awake in the town.

"You're a swell kid, Sucker," I said.

It seemed to me suddenly that I did like him more than anybody else I knew—more than any other boy, more than my sisters, more in a certain way even than Maybelle. I felt good all over and it was like when they play sad music in the movies. I wanted to show Sucker how much I really thought of him and make up for the way I had always treated him.

We talked for a good while that night. His voice was fast and it was like he had been saving up these things to tell me for a long time. He mentioned that he was going to try to build a canoe and that the kids down the block wouldn't let him in on their football team and I don't know what all. I talked some too and it was a good feeling to think of him taking in everything I said so seriously. I even spoke of Maybelle a little, only I made out like it was her who had been running after me all this time. He asked questions about high school and so forth. His voice was excited and he kept on talking fast like he could never get the words out in time. When I went to sleep he was still talking and I could still feel his breathing on my shoulder, warm and close.

During the next couple of weeks I saw a lot of Maybelle. She acted as though 25 she really cared for me a little. Half the time I felt so good I hardly knew what to do with myself.

But I didn't forget about Sucker. There were a lot of old things in my bureau drawer I'd been saving—boxing gloves and Tom Swift books and second rate fishing tackle. All this I turned over to him. We had some more talks together and it was really like I was knowing him for the first time. When there was a long cut on his cheek I knew he had been monkeying around with this new first razor set of mine, but I didn't say anything. His face seemed different now. He used to look timid and sort of like he was afraid of a whack over the head. That expression was gone. His face, with those wide-open eyes and his ears sticking out and his mouth never quite shut, had the look of a person who is surprised and expecting something swell.

Once I started to point him out to Maybelle and tell her he was my kid brother. It was an afternoon when a murder mystery was on at the movie. I had earned a dollar working for my Dad and I gave Sucker a quarter to go and get candy and so forth. With the rest I took Maybelle. We were sitting near the back and I saw Sucker come in. He began to stare at the screen the minute he stepped past the ticket man and he stumbled down the aisle without noticing where he was going. I started to punch Maybelle but couldn't quite make up my mind. Sucker looked a little silly—walking like a drunk with his eyes glued to the movie. He was wiping his reading glasses on his shirt tail and his knickers flopped down. He went on until he got to the first few rows where the kids usually sit. I never did punch Maybelle. But I got to thinking it was good to have both of them at the movie with the money I earned.

I guess things went on like this for about a month or six weeks. I felt so good I couldn't settle down to study or put my mind on anything. I wanted to be friendly with everybody. There were times when I just had to talk to some person. And usually that would be Sucker. He felt as good as I did. Once he said: "Pete, I am gladder that you are like my brother than anything else in the world."

Then something happened between Maybelle and me. I never have figured out just what it was. Girls like her are hard to understand. She began to act different toward me. At first I wouldn't let myself believe this and tried to think it was just my imagination. She didn't act glad to see me anymore. Often she went out riding with this fellow on the football team who owns this yellow roadster. The car was the color of her hair and after school she would ride off with him, laughing and looking into his face. I couldn't think of anything to do about it and she was on my mind all day and night. When I did get a chance to go out with her she was snippy and didn't seem to notice me. This made me feel like something was the matter—I would worry about my shoes clopping too loud on the floor or the fly of my pants, or the bumps on my chin. Sometimes when Maybelle was around, a devil would get into me and I'd hold my face stiff and call grown men by their last names without the Mister and say rough things. In the night I would wonder what made me do all this until I was too tired for sleep.

30   At first I was so worried I just forgot about Sucker. Then later he began to get on my nerves. He was always hanging around until I would get back from high school, always looking like he had something to say to me or wanted me to tell him. He made me a magazine rack in his Manual Training class and one week he saved his lunch money and bought me three packs of cigarettes. He couldn't seem to take it in that I had things on my mind and didn't want to fool with him. Every afternoon it would be the same—him in my room with this waiting expression on his face. Then I wouldn't say anything or I'd maybe answer him rough-like and he would finally go on out.

I can't divide that time up and say this happened one day and that the next. For one thing I was so mixed up the weeks just slid along into each other and I felt like Hell and didn't care. Nothing definite was said or done. Maybelle still rode around with this fellow in his yellow roadster and sometimes she would smile at me and sometimes not. Every afternoon I went from one place to another where I thought she would be. Either she would act almost nice and I would begin thinking how nice things would finally clear up and she would care for me—or else she'd behave so that if she hadn't been a girl I'd have wanted to grab her by that white little neck and choke her. The more ashamed I felt for making a fool of myself the more I ran after her.

Sucker kept getting on my nerves more and more. He would look at me as though he sort of blamed me for something, but at the same time knew that it wouldn't last long. He was growing fast and for some reason began to stutter when he talked. Sometimes he had nightmares or would throw up his breakfast. Mom got him a bottle of cod liver oil.

Then the finish came between Maybelle and me. I met her going to the drug store and asked for a date. When she said no I remarked something sarcastic. She told me she was sick and tired of my being around and that she had never cared a rap about me. She said all that. I just stood there and didn't answer anything. I walked home very slowly.

For several afternoons I stayed in my room by myself. I didn't want to go anywhere or talk to anyone. When Sucker would come in and look at me sort of funny I'd yell at him to get out. I didn't want to think of Maybelle and I sat at my desk reading *Popular Mechanics* or whittling at a toothbrush rack I was making. It seemed to me I was putting that girl out of my mind pretty well.

But you can't help what happens to you at night. That is what made things how they are now.

You see a few nights after Maybelle said those words to me I dreamed about her again. It was like that first time and I was squeezing Sucker's arm so tight I woke him up. He reached for my hand.

"Pete, what's the matter with you?"

All of a sudden I felt so mad my throat choked—at myself and the dream and Maybelle and Sucker and every single person I knew. I remembered all the times Maybelle had humiliated me and everything bad that had ever happened. It seemed to me for a second that nobody would ever like me but a sap like Sucker.

"Why is it we aren't buddies like we were before? Why—?"

"Shut your damn trap!" I threw off the cover and got up and turned on the light. He sat in the middle of the bed, his eyes blinking and scared.

There was something in me and I couldn't help myself. I don't think anybody ever gets that mad but once. Words came without me knowing what they would be. It was only afterward that I could remember each thing I said and see it all in a clear way.

"Why aren't we buddies? Because you're the dumbest slob I ever saw! Nobody cares anything about you! And just because I felt sorry for you sometimes and tried to act decent don't think I give a damn about a dumb-bunny like you!"

If I'd talked loud or hit him it wouldn't have been so bad. But my voice was slow and like I was very calm. Sucker's mouth was part way open and he looked as though he'd knocked his funny bone. His face was white and sweat came out on his forehead. He wiped it away with the back of his hand and for a minute his arm stayed raised that way as though he was holding something away from him.

"Don't you know a single thing? Haven't you ever been around at all? Why don't you get a girl friend instead of me? What kind of a sissy do you want to grow up to be anyway?"

I didn't know what was coming next. I couldn't help myself or think.

Sucker didn't move. He had on one of my pajama jackets and his neck stuck out skinny and small. His hair was damp on his forehead.

"Why do you always hang around me? Don't you know when you're not wanted?"

Afterward I could remember the change in Sucker's face. Slowly that blank look went away and he closed his mouth. His eyes got narrow and his fists shut. There had never been such a look on him before. It was like every second he was getting older. There was a hard look to his eyes you don't see usually in a kid. A drop of sweat rolled down his chin and he didn't notice. He just sat there with those eyes on me and he didn't speak and his face was hard and didn't move.

"No you don't know when you're not wanted. You're too dumb. Just like your name—a dumb Sucker."

50   It was like something had busted inside me. I turned off the light and sat down in the chair by the window. My legs were shaking and I was so tired I could have bawled. The room was cold and dark. I sat there for a long time and smoked a squashed cigarette I had saved. Outside the yard was black and quiet. After a while I heard Sucker lie down.

I wasn't mad any more, only tired. It seemed awful to me that I had talked like that to a kid only twelve. I couldn't take it all in. I told myself I would go over to him and try to make it up. But I just sat there in the cold until a long time had passed. I planned how I could straighten it out in the morning. Then, trying not to squeak the springs, I got back in bed.

Sucker was gone when I woke up the next day. And later when I wanted to apologize as I had planned he looked at me in this new hard way so that I couldn't say a word.

All of that was two or three months ago. Since then Sucker has grown faster than any boy I ever saw. He's almost as tall as I am and his bones have gotten heavier and bigger. He won't wear any of my old clothes any more and has bought his first pair of long pants—with some leather suspenders to hold them up. Those are just the changes that are easy to see and put into words.

Our room isn't mine at all any more. He's gotten up this gang of kids and they have a club. When they aren't digging trenches in some vacant lot and fighting they are always in my room. On the door there is some foolishness written in Mercurochrome saying "Woe to the Outsider who Enters" and signed with crossed bones and their secret initials. They have rigged up a radio and every afternoon it blares out music. Once as I was coming in I heard a boy telling something in a loud voice about what he saw in the back of his big brother's automobile. I could guess what I didn't hear. *That's what her and my brother do. It's the truth—parked in the car.* For a minute Sucker looked surprised and his face was almost like it used to be. Then he got hard and tough again. "Sure, dumbbell. We know all that." They didn't notice me. Sucker began telling them how in two years he was planning to be a trapper in Alaska.

55   But most of the time Sucker stays by himself. It is worse when we are alone together in the room. He sprawls across the bed in those long corduroy pants with the suspenders and just stares at me with that hard, half-sneering look. I fiddle around my desk and can't get settled because of those eyes of his. And the thing is I just have to study because I've gotten three bad cards this term already. If I flunk English I can't graduate next year. I don't want to be a bum and I just have to get my mind on it. I don't care a flip for Maybelle or any particular girl any more and it's only this thing between Sucker and me that is the trouble now. We never speak except when we have to before the family. I don't even want to call him Sucker any more and unless I forget I call him by his real name, Richard. At night I can't study with him in the room and I have to hang around the drug store, smoking and doing nothing, with the fellows who loaf there.

More than anything I want to be easy in my mind again. And I miss the way Sucker and I were for a while in a funny, sad way that before this I never would have believed. But everything is so different that there seems to be nothing I can do to get it right. I've sometimes thought if we could have it out in a big fight that would help. But I can't fight him because he's four years younger. And another thing—sometimes this look in his eyes makes me almost believe that if Sucker could he would kill me.

QUESTIONS FOR DISCUSSION AND WRITING

1. How does McCullers use phrases such as "a few months ago when all this trouble began" to foreshadow the action in the story? How does Pete's abusive language serve as the climax of the story? How does he respond to Richard's changed behavior at the end of his narrative?

2. How does McCullers keep Pete a sympathetic character even after he does regrettable things? How does Pete explain the changes in Maybelle's character? How does Pete's theory of admiration explain how he, Maybelle, and Richard act toward one another?

3. How does the private world of the room serve as a useful setting for the story? How does the meaning of the room change for Pete by the end of the story?

4. In what sense is Pete a reliable narrator? Why does he feel guilty and confused about the events he narrates? How do the narrator's behavior and use of language reveal his immaturity?

5. How does the title of the story reveal its major theme? In what ways does the title refer to Pete and Maybelle as well as Richard? How does the story account for human cruelty among usually decent people?

Stories for Comparison

Alice Adams's "Truth or Consequences" (pages 164–174); Isaac Bashevis Singer's "Gimpel the Fool" (pages 1070–1080).

68

···

D E N N I S   M c F A R L A N D

Nothing to Ask For

DENNIS McFARLAND was born in 1950 in Mobile, Alabama, and was educated at Brooklyn College and Goddard College. He has taught at Stanford
University, where he served as a Wallace E. Stegner Fellow, and at Emerson
College in Boston, Massachusetts. He has published his short stories in magazines such as *Sequoia, Mademoiselle, Vogue,* and *The New Yorker.* His
novel, *The Music Room* (1990), describes how a privileged family, rich in talent and promise, is overwhelmed by alcoholism. "Nothing to Ask For,"
reprinted from *The New Yorker,* documents how two friends—one gay, one
straight—confront the devastating effects of AIDS.

Inside Mack's apartment, a concentrator—a medical machine that looks like an
elaborate stereo speaker on casters—sits behind an orange swivel chair, making
its rhythmic, percussive noise like ocean waves, taking in normal filthy air, humidi-
fying it, and filtering out everything but the oxygen, which it sends through clear
plastic tubing to Mack's nostrils. He sits on the couch, as usual, channel grazing, the
remote-control button under his thumb, and he appears to be scrutinizing the short
segments of what he sees on the TV screen with Zen-like patience. He has planted
one foot on the bevelled edge of the long oak coffee table, and he dangles one leg—
thinner at the thigh than my wrist—over the other. In the sharp valley of his lap,
Eberhardt, his old long-haired dachshund, lies sleeping. The table is covered with
two dozen medicine bottles, though Mack has now taken himself off all drugs except
cough syrup and something for heartburn. Also, stacks of books and pamphlets—
though he has lost the ability to read—on how to heal yourself, on Buddhism, on
Hinduism, on dying. In one pamphlet there's a long list that includes most human
ailments, the personality traits and character flaws that cause these ailments, and the
affirmations that need to be said in order to overcome them. According to this well-
intentioned misguidedness, most disease is caused by self-hatred, or rejection of reality, and almost anything can be cured by learning to love yourself—which is accomplished by saying, aloud and often, "I love myself." Next to these books are
pamphlets and Xeroxed articles describing more unorthodox remedies—herbal
brews, ultrasound, lemon juice, urine, even penicillin. And, in a ceramic dish next to

these, a small, waxy envelope that contains "ash"—a very fine, gray-white, spiritu-
ally enhancing powder materialized out of thin air by Swami Lahiri Baba.

As I change the plastic liner inside Mack's trash can, into which he throws his
millions of Kleenex, I block his view of the TV screen—which he endures serenely,
his head perfectly still, eyes unaverted. "Do you remember old Dorothy Hughes?"
he asks me. "What do you suppose ever happened to her?"

"I don't know," I say. "I saw her years ago on the nude beach at San Gregorio.
With some black guy who was down by the surf doing cartwheels. She pretended she
didn't know me."

"I don't blame her," says Mack, making bug-eyes. "I wouldn't like to be seen
with any grownup who does cartwheels, would you?"

"No," I say.   5

Then he asks, "Was everybody we knew back then crazy?"

What Mack means by "back then" is our college days, in Santa Cruz, when we
judged almost everything in terms of how freshly it rejected the status quo: the famous professor who began his twentieth-century-philosophy class by tossing pink
rubber dildos in through the classroom window; Antonioni and Luis Buñuel
screened each weekend in the dormitory basement; the artichokes in the student
garden, left on their stalks and allowed to open and become what they truly were—
enormous, purple-hearted flowers. There were no paving-stone quadrangles or venerable colonnades—our campus was the redwood forest, the buildings nestled
among the trees, invisible one from the other—and when we emerged from the
woods at the end of the school day, what we saw was nothing more or less than the
sun setting over the Pacific. We lived with thirteen other students, in a rented Vic-
torian mansion on West Cliff Drive, and at night the yellow beacon from the nearby
lighthouse invaded our attic windows; we drifted to sleep listening to the barking
of seals. On weekends we had serious softball games in the vacant field next to the
house—us against a team of tattooed, long-haired townies—and afterward, keyed
up, tired and sweating, Mack and I walked the north shore to a place where we
could watch the waves pound into the rocks and send up sun-ignited columns of
water twenty-five and thirty feet tall. Though most of what we initiated "back then"
now seems to have been faddish and wrongheaded, our friendship was exceptionally sane and has endured for twenty years. It endured the melodramatic confusion
of Dorothy Hughes, our beautiful short-stop—I loved her, but she loved Mack. It
endured the subsequent revelation that Mack was gay—any tension on that count
managed by him with remarks about what a homely bastard I was. It endured his
fury and frustration over my low-bottom alcoholism, and my sometimes raging (and
*en*raging) process of getting clean and sober. And it has endured the onlooking
fisheyes of his long string of lovers and my two wives. Neither of us had a bio-
logical brother—that could account for something—but at recent moments when I
have felt most frightened, now that Mack is so ill, I've thought that we persisted
simply because we couldn't let go of the sense of *thoroughness* our friendship gave
us; we constantly reported to each other on our separate lives, as if we knew that
by doing so we were getting more from life than we would ever have been entitled
to individually.

In answer to his question—was everybody crazy back then—I say, "Yes, I think so."

He laughs, then coughs. When he coughs these days—which is often—he goes on coughing until a viscous, bloody fluid comes up, which he catches in a Kleenex and tosses into the trash can. Earlier, his doctors could drain his lungs with a needle through his back—last time they collected an entire litre from one lung—but now that Mack has developed the cancer, there are tumors that break up the fluid into many small isolated pockets, too many to drain. Radiation or chemotherapy would kill him; he's too weak even for a flu shot. Later today, he will go to the hospital for another bronchoscopy; they want to see if there's anything they can do to help him, though they have already told him there isn't. His medical care comes in the form of visiting nurses, physical therapists, and a curious duo at the hospital: one doctor who is young, affectionate, and incompetent but who comforts and consoles, hugs and holds hands; another—old, rude, brash, and expert—who says things like "You might as well face it. You're going to die. Get your papers in order." In fact, they've given Mack two weeks to two months, and it has now been ten weeks.

10   "Oh, my God," cries Lester, Mack's lover, opening the screen door, entering the room, and looking around. "I don't recognize this hovel. And what's that wonderful smell?"

This morning, while Lester was out, I vacuumed and generally straightened up. Their apartment is on the ground floor of a building like all the buildings in this Southern California neighborhood—a two-story motel-like structure of white stucco and steel railings. Outside the door are an X-rated hibiscus (blood red, with its jutting, yellow powder-tipped stamen), a plastic macaw on a swing, two enormous yuccas; inside, carpet, and plainness. The wonderful smell is the turkey I'm roasting; Mack can't eat anything before the bronchoscopy, but I figure it will be here for them when they return from the hospital, and they can eat off it for the rest of the week.

Lester, a South Carolina boy in his late twenties, is sick, too—twice he has nearly died of pneumonia—but he's in a healthy period now. He's tall, thin, and bearded, a devotee of the writings of Shirley MacLaine—an unlikely guru, if you ask me, but my wife, Marilyn, tells me I'm too judgmental. Probably she is right.

The dog, Eberhardt, has woken up and waddles sleepily over to where Lester stands. Lester extends his arm toward Mack, two envelopes in his hand, and after a moment's pause Mack reaches for them. It's partly this typical hesitation of Mack's—a slowing of the mind, actually—that makes him appear serene, contemplative these days. Occasionally, he really does get confused, which terrifies him. But I can't help thinking that something in there has sharpened as well—maybe a kind of simplification. Now he stares at the top envelope for a full minute, as Lester and I watch him. This is something we do: we watch him. "Oh-h-h," he says, at last. "A letter from my mother."

"And one from Lucy, too," says Lester. "Isn't that nice?"

15   "I guess," says Mack. Then: "Well, yes. It is."

"You want me to open them?" I ask.

"Would you?" he says, handing them to me. "Read 'em to me, too."

They are only cards, with short notes inside, both from Des Moines. Mack's mother says it just makes her *sick* that he's sick, wants to know if there's anything he needs. Lucy, the sister, is gushy, misremembers a few things from the past, says she's writing instead of calling because she knows she will cry if she tries to talk. Lucy, who refused to let Mack enter her house at Christmastime one year—actually left him on the stoop in sub-zero cold—until he removed the gold earring from his ear. Mack's mother, who waited until after the funeral last year to let Mack know that his father had died; Mack's obvious illness at the funeral would have been an embarrassment.

But they've come around, Mack has told me in the face of my anger.

I said better late than never.

And Mack, all forgiveness, all humility, said that's exactly right: much better.

"Mrs. Mears is having a craft sale today," Lester says. Mrs. Mears, an elderly neighbor, lives out back in a cottage with her husband. "You guys want to go?"

Eberhardt, hearing "go," begins leaping at Lester's shins, but when we look at Mack, his eyelids are at half-mast—he's half asleep.

We watch him for a moment, and I say, "Maybe in a little while, Lester."

Lester sits on the edge of his bed reading the newspaper, which lies flat on the spread in front of him. He has his own TV in his room, and a VCR. On the dresser, movies whose cases show men in studded black leather jockstraps, with gloves to match—dungeon masters of startling handsomeness. On the floor, a stack of gay magazines. Somewhere on the cover of each of these magazines the word "macho" appears; and inside some of them, in the personal ads, men, meaning to attract others, refer to themselves as pigs. "Don't putz," Lester says to me as I straighten some things on top of the dresser. "Enough already."

I wonder where he picked up "putz"—surely not in South Carolina. I say, "You need to get somebody in. To help. You need to arrange it now. What if you were suddenly to get sick again?"

"I know," he says. "He's gotten to be quite a handful, hasn't he? Is he still asleep?"

"Yes," I answer. "Yes and yes."

The phone rings and Lester reaches for it. As soon as he begins to speak I can tell, from his tone, that it's my four-year-old on the line. After a moment, Lester says, "Kit," smiling, and hands me the phone, then returns to his newspaper.

I sit on the other side of the bed, and after I say hello, Kit says, "We need some milk."

"O.K.," I say. "Milk. What are you up to this morning?"

"Being angry mostly," she says.

"Oh?" I say. "Why?"

"Mommy and I are not getting along very well."

"That's too bad," I say. "I hope you won't stay angry for long."

"We won't," she says. "We're going to make up in a minute."

"Good," I say.

"When are you coming home?"

20
25
30
35

"In a little while."

40   "After my nap?"

"Yes," I say. "Right after your nap."

"Is Mack very sick?"

She already knows the answer, of course. "Yes," I say.

"Is he going to die?"

45   This one, too. "Most likely," I say. "He's that sick."

"Bye," she says suddenly—her sense of closure always takes me by surprise—and I say, "Don't stay angry for long, O.K.?"

"You already said that," she says, rightly, and I wait for a moment, half expecting Marilyn to come onto the line; ordinarily she would, and hearing her voice right now would do me good. After another moment, though, there's the click.

Marilyn is back in school, earning a Ph.D. in religious studies. I teach sixth grade, and because I'm faculty adviser for the little magazine the sixth graders put out each year, I stay late many afternoons. Marilyn wanted me home this Saturday morning. "You're at work all week," she said, "and then you're over there on Saturday. Is that fair?"

I told her I didn't know—which was the honest truth. Then, in a possibly dramatic way, I told her that fairness was not my favorite subject these days, given that my best friend was dying.

50   We were in our kitchen, and through the window I could see Kit playing with a neighbor's cat in the back yard. Marilyn turned on the hot water in the kitchen sink and stood still while the steam rose into her face. "It's become a question of where you belong," she said at last. "I think you're too involved."

For this I had no answer, except to say, "I agree"—which wasn't really an answer, since I had no intention of staying home, or becoming less involved, or changing anything.

Now Lester and I can hear Mack's scraping cough in the next room. We are silent until he stops. "By the way," Lester says at last, taking the telephone receiver out of my hand, "have you noticed that he *listens* now?"

"I know," I say. "He told me he'd finally entered his listening period."

"Yeah," says Lester, "as if it's the natural progression. You blab your whole life away, ignoring other people, and then right before you die you start to listen."

55   The slight bitterness in Lester's tone makes me feel shaky inside. It's true that Mack was always a better talker than a listener, but I suddenly feel that I'm walking a thin wire, and that anything like collusion would throw me off balance. All I know for sure is that I don't want to hear any more. Maybe Lester reads this in my face, because what he says next sounds like an explanation: he tells me that his poor old backwoods mother was nearly deaf when he was growing up, that she relied almost entirely on reading lips. "All she had to do when she wanted to turn me off," he says, "was to just turn her back on me. Simple," he says, making a little circle with his finger. "No more Lester."

"That's terrible," I say.

"I was a terrible coward," he says. "Can you imagine Kit letting you get away with something like that? She'd bite your kneecaps."

"Still," I say, "that's terrible."

Lester shrugs his shoulders, and after another moment I say, "I'm going to the Kmart. Mack needs a padded toilet seat. You want anything?"

"Yeah," he says. "But they don't sell it at Kmart."   60

"What is it?" I ask.

"It's a *joke,* Dan, for Chrissake," he says. "Honestly, I think you've completely lost your sense of humor."

When I think about this, it seems true.

"Are you coming back?" he asks.

"Right back," I answer. "If you think of it, baste the turkey."   65

"How could I not think of it?" he says, sniffing the air.

In the living room, Mack is lying with his eyes open now, staring blankly at the TV. At the moment, a shop-at-home show is on, but he changes channels, and an announcer says, "When we return, we'll talk about tree pruning," and Mack changes the channel again. He looks at me, nods thoughtfully, and says, "Tree pruning. Interesting. It's just like the way they put a limit on your credit card, so you don't spend too much."

"I don't understand," I say.

"Oh, you know," he says. "Pruning the trees. Didn't the man just say something about pruning trees?" He sits up and adjusts the plastic tube in one nostril.

"Yes," I say.   70

"Well, it's like the credit cards. The limit they put on the credit cards is . . ." He stops talking and looks straight into my eyes, frightened. "It doesn't make any sense, does it?" he says. "Jesus Christ. I'm not making sense."

Way out east on University, there is a video arcade every half mile or so. Adult peepshows. Also a McDonald's, and the rest. Taverns—the kind that are open at eight in the morning—with clever names: Tobacco Rhoda's, the Cruz Inn. Bodegas that smell of cat piss and are really fronts for numbers games. Huge discount stores. Lester, who is an expert in these matters, has told me that all these places feed on addicts. "What do you think—those peepshows stay in business on the strength of the occasional customer? No way. It's a steady clientele of people in there every day, for hours at a time, dropping in quarters. That whole strip of road is *made* for addicts. And all the strips like it. That's what America's all about, you know. You got your alcoholics in the bars. Your food addicts sucking it up at Jack-in-the-Box—you ever go in one of those places and count the fat people? You got your sex addicts in the peepshows. Your shopping addicts at the Kmart. Your gamblers running numbers in the bodegas and your junkies in the alley-ways. We're all nothing but a bunch of addicts. The whole fucking addicted country."

In the arcades, says Lester, the videos show myriad combinations and arrangements of men and women, men and men, women and women. Some show older men being serviced by eager, selfless young women who seem to live for one thing only, who can't get enough. Some of these women have put their hair into pigtails and shaved themselves—they're supposed to look like children. Inside the peepshow booths there's semen on the floor. And in the old days, there were glory holes cut into the wooden walls between some of the booths, so, if it pleased you, you could communicate with your neighbor. Not anymore. Mack and Lester tell me that some things have changed. The holes have been boarded up. In the public men's rooms you no longer read, scribbled in the stalls, "All faggots should die." You read, "All faggots should die of AIDS." Mack rails against the moratorium on fetal-tissue research, the most promising avenue for a cure. "If it was Legionnaires dying, we wouldn't have any moratorium," he says. And he often talks about Africa, where governments impede efforts to teach villagers about condoms: a social worker, attempting to explain their use, isn't allowed to remove the condoms from their foil packets; in another country, with a slightly more liberal government, a field nurse stretches a condom over his hand, to show how it works, and later villagers are found wearing the condoms like mittens, thinking this will protect them from disease. Lester laughs at these stories but shakes his head. In our own country, something called "family values" has emerged with clarity. "*Whose* family?" Mack wants to know, holding out his hands palms upward. "I mean we *all* come from families, don't we? The dizziest queen comes from a family. The axe-murderer. Even Dan *Quayle* comes from a family of some kind."

But Mack and Lester are dying, Mack first. As I steer my pickup into the parking lot at the Kmart, I almost clip the front fender of a big, deep-throated Chevy that's leaving. I have startled the driver, a young Chicano boy with four kids in the back seat, and he flips me the bird—aggressively, his arm out the window—but I feel protected today by my sense of purpose: I have come to buy a padded toilet seat for my friend.

75   When he was younger, Mack wanted to be a cultural anthropologist, but he was slow to break in after we were out of graduate school—never landed anything more than a low-paying position assisting someone else, nothing more than a student's job, really. Eventually, he began driving a tour bus in San Diego, which not only provided a steady income but suited him so well that in time he was managing the line and began to refer to the position not as his job but as his calling. He said that San Diego was like a pretty blond boy without too many brains. He knew just how to play up its cultural assets while allowing its beauty to speak for itself. He said he liked being "at the controls." But he had to quit work over a year ago, and now his hands have become so shaky that he can no longer even manage a pen and paper.

When I get back to the apartment from my trip to the Kmart, Mack asks me to take down a letter for him to an old high-school buddy back in Des Moines, a country-and-Western singer who has sent him a couple of her latest recordings. *"Whenever I met a new doctor or nurse,"* he dictates, *"I always asked them whether they believed in miracles."*

Mack sits up a bit straighter and rearranges the pillows behind his back on the couch. "What did I just say?" he asks me.

"'I always asked them whether they believed in miracles.'"

"Yes," he says, and continues. *"And if they said no, I told them I wanted to see someone else. I didn't want them treating me. Back then, I was hoping for a miracle, which seemed reasonable.* Do you think this is too detailed?" he asks me.

"No," I say. "I think it's fine."

"I don't want to depress her."

"Go on," I say.

"*But now I have lung cancer,*" he continues. "*So now I need not one but two miracles. That doesn't seem as possible somehow.* Wait. Did you write 'possible' yet?"

"No," I say. "'That doesn't seem as . . .'"

"Reasonable," he says. "Didn't I say 'reasonable' before?"

"Yes," I say. "'That doesn't seem as reasonable somehow.'"

"Yes," he says. "How does that sound?"

"It sounds fine, Mack. It's not for publication, you know."

"It's not?" he says, feigning astonishment. "I thought it was: 'Letters of an AIDS Victim.'" He says this in a spooky voice and makes his bug-eyes. Since his head is a perfect skull, the whole effect really is a little spooky.

"What else?" I say.

"*Thank you for your nice letter,*" he continues, "*and for the tapes.*" He begins coughing—a horrible, rasping seizure. Mack has told me that he has lost all fear; he said he realized this a few weeks ago, on the skyride at the zoo. But when the coughing sets in, when it seems that it may never stop, I think I see terror in his eyes: he begins tapping his breastbone with the fingers of one hand, as if he's trying to wake up his lungs, prod them to do their appointed work. Finally he does stop, and he sits for a moment in silence, in thought. Then he dictates: "*It makes me very happy that you are so successful.*"

At Mrs. Mears' craft sale, in the alley behind her cottage, she has set up several card tables: Scores of plastic dolls with hand-knitted dresses, shoes, and hats. Handmade doll furniture. Christmas ornaments. A whole box of knitted bonnets and scarves for dolls. Also, some baked goods. Now, while Lester holds Eberhardt, Mrs. Mears, wearing a large straw hat and sunglasses, outfits the dachshund in one of the bonnets and scarves. "There now," she says. "Have you ever seen anything so *precious?* I'm going to get my camera."

Mack sits in a folding chair by one of the tables; next to him sits Mr. Mears, also in a folding chair. The two men look very much alike, though Mr. Mears is not nearly as emaciated as Mack. And of course Mr. Mears is eighty-seven. Mack, on the calendar, is not quite forty. I notice that Mack's shoelaces are untied, and I kneel to tie them. "The thing about reincarnation," he's saying to Mr. Mears, "is that you can't remember anything and you don't recognize anybody."

"Consciously," says Lester, butting in. "*Sub*consciously you do."

"Subconsciously," says Mack. "What's the point? I'm not the least bit interested."

Mr. Mears removes his houndstooth-check cap and scratches his bald, freckled head. "I'm not, either," he says with great resignation.

As Mrs. Mears returns with the camera, she says, "Put him over there, in Mack's lap."

"It doesn't matter whether you're interested or not," says Lester, dropping Eberhardt into Mack's lap.

"Give me good old-fashioned Heaven and Hell," says Mr. Mears.

100   "I should think you would've had enough of that already," says Lester.

Mr. Mears gives Lester a suspicious look, then gazes down at his own knees. "Then give me nothing," he says finally.

I stand up and step aside just in time for Mrs. Mears to snap the picture. "Did you ever *see* anything?" she says, all sunshades and yellow teeth, but as she heads back toward the cottage door, her face is immediately serious. She takes me by the arm and pulls me along, reaching for something from one of the tables—a doll's bed, white with a red strawberry painted on the headboard. "For your little girl," she says aloud. Then she whispers, "You better get him out of the sun, don't you think? He doesn't look so good."

But when I turn again, I see that Lester is already helping Mack out of his chair. "Here—let me," says Mrs. Mears, reaching an arm toward them, and she escorts Mack up the narrow, shaded sidewalk, back toward the apartment building. Lester moves alongside me and says, "Dan, do you think you could give Mack his bath this afternoon? I'd like to take Eberhardt for a walk."

"Of course," I say, quickly.

105   But a while later—after I have drawn the bath, after I've taken a large beach towel out of the linen closet, refolded it into a thick square, and put it into the water to serve as a cushion for Mack to sit on in the tub; when I'm holding the towel under, against some resistance, waiting for the bubbles to stop surfacing, and there's something horrible about it, like drowning a small animal—I think Lester has tricked me into this task of bathing Mack, and the saliva in my mouth suddenly seems to taste of Scotch, which I have not actually tasted in nine years.

There is no time to consider any of this, however, for in a moment Mack enters the bathroom, trailing his tubes behind him, and says, "Are you ready for my Auschwitz look?"

"I've seen it before," I say.

And it's true. I have, a few times, helping him with his shirt and pants after Lester has bathed him and gotten him into his underwear. But that doesn't feel like preparation. The sight of him naked is like a powerful, scary drug: you forget between trips, remember only when you start to come on to it again. I help him off with his clothes now and guide him into the tub and gently onto the underwater towel. "That's nice," he says, and I begin soaping the hollows of his shoulders, the hard washboard of his back. This is not human skin as we know it but something already dead—so dry, dense, and pleasantly brown as to appear manufactured. I soap the cage of his chest, his stomach—the hard, depressed abdomen of a greyhound—the steep vaults of his armpits, his legs, his feet. Oddly, his hands and feet appear almost normal, even a bit swollen. At last I give him the slippery bar of soap. "Your turn," I say.

"My poor cock," he says as he begins to wash himself.

110   When he's done, I rinse him all over with the hand spray attached to the faucet. I lather the feathery white wisps of his hair—we have to remove the plastic oxygen tubes for this—then rinse again. "You know," he says, "I know it's irrational, but I feel kind of turned off to sex."

The apparent understatement of this almost takes my breath away. "There are more important things," I say.

"Oh, I know," he says. "I just hope Lester's not too unhappy." Then, after a moment, he says, "You know, Dan, it's only logical that they've all given up on me. And I've accepted it mostly. But I still have days when I think I should at least be given a chance."

"You can ask them for anything you want, Mack," I say.

"I know," he says. "That's the problem—there's nothing to ask for."

"Mack," I say. "I think I understand what you meant this morning about the tree   115
pruning and the credit cards."

"You do?"

"Well, I think your mind just shifted into metaphor. Because I can see that pruning trees is like imposing a limit—just like the limit on the credit cards."

Mack is silent, pondering this. "Maybe," he says at last, hesitantly—a moment of disappointment for us both.

I get him out and hooked up to the oxygen again, dry him off, and begin dressing him. Somehow I get the oxygen tubes trapped between his legs and the elastic waistband of his sweatpants—no big deal, but I suddenly feel panicky—and I have to take them off his face again to set them to rights. After he's safely back on the living-room couch and I've returned to the bathroom, I hear him: low, painful-sounding groans. "Are you all right?" I call from the hallway.

"Oh, yes," he says, "I'm just moaning. It's one of the few pleasures I have left."   120

The bathtub is coated with a crust of dead skin, which I wash away with the sprayer. Then I find a screwdriver and go to work on the toilet seat. After I get the old one off, I need to scrub around the area where the plastic screws were. I've sprinkled Ajax all around the rim of the bowl and found the scrub brush when Lester appears at the bathroom door, back with Eberhardt from their walk. "Oh, Dan, really," he says. "You go too far. Down on your knees now, scrubbing our toilet."

"Lester, leave me alone," I say.

"Well, it's true," he says. "You really do."

"Maybe I'm working out my survivor's guilt," I say, "if you don't mind."

"You mean because your best buddy's dying and you're not?"   125

"Yes," I say. "It's very common."

He parks one hip on the edge of the sink. And after a moment he says this: "Danny boy, if you feel guilty about surviving . . . that's not irreversible, you know. I could fix that."

We are both stunned. He looks at me. In another moment, there are tears in his eyes. He quickly closes the bathroom door, moves to the tub and turns on the water, sits on the side, and bursts into sobs. "I'm sorry," he says. "I'm so sorry."

"Forget it," I say.

He begins to compose himself almost at once. "This is what Jane Alexander did   130
when she played Eleanor Roosevelt," he says. "Do you remember? When she needed to cry she'd go in the bathroom and turn on the water, so nobody could hear her. Remember?"

In the pickup, on the way to the hospital, Lester—in the middle, between Mack and me—says, "Maybe after they're down there you could doze off, but on the *way* down, they want you awake." He's explaining the bronchoscopy to me—the insertion of the tube down the windpipe—with which he is personally familiar: "They reach certain points on the way down where they have to ask you to swallow."

"*He's* not having the test, is he?" Mack says, looking confused.

"No, of course not," says Lester.

"Didn't you just say to him that he had to swallow?"

135   "I meant *anyone,* Mack," says Lester.

"Oh," says Mack. "Oh, yeah."

"The general 'you,'" Lester says to me. "He keeps forgetting little things like that."

Mack shakes his head, then points at his temple with one finger. "My mind," he says.

Mack is on tank oxygen now, which comes with a small caddy. I push the caddy, behind him, and Lester assists him along the short walk from the curb to the hospital's front door and the elevators. Nine years ago, it was Mack who drove *me* to a different wing of this same hospital—against my drunken, slobbery will—to dry out. And as I watch him struggle up the low inclined ramp toward the glass-and-steel doors, I recall the single irrefutable thing he said to me in the car on the way. "You stink," he said. "You've puked and probably pissed your pants and you *stink,*" he said—my loyal, articulate, and best friend, saving my life, and causing me to cry like a baby.

140   Inside the clinic upstairs, the nurse, a sour young blond woman in a sky-blue uniform who looks terribly overworked, says to Mack, "You know better than to be late."

We are five minutes late to the second. Mack looks at her incredulously. He stands with one hand on the handle of the oxygen-tank caddy. He straightens up, perfectly erect—the indignant, shockingly skeletal posture of a man fasting to the death for some holy principle. He gives the nurse the bug-eyes, and says, "And you know better than to keep me waiting every time I come over here for some goddam procedure. But get over yourself: shit happens."

He turns and winks at me.

Though I've offered to return for them afterward, Lester has insisted on taking a taxi, so I will leave them here and drive back home, where again I'll try—successfully, this time—to explain to my wife how all this feels to me, and where, a few minutes later, I'll stand outside the door to my daughter's room, comforted by the music of her small high voice as she consoles her dolls.

Now the nurse gets Mack into a wheelchair and leaves us in the middle of the reception area; then, from the proper position at her desk, she calls Mack's name, and says he may proceed to the laboratory.

145   "Dan," Mack says, stretching his spotted, broomstick arms toward me. "Old pal. Do you remember the Christmas we drove out to Des Moines on the motorcycle?"

We did go to Des Moines together, one very snowy Christmas—but of course we didn't go on any motorcycle, not in December.

"We had fun," I say and put my arms around him, awkwardly, since he is sitting.

"Help me up," he whispers—confidentially—and I begin to lift him.

QUESTIONS FOR DISCUSSION AND WRITING

1. How do the following scenes provide the structure for the plot—Mack's rejection by his family, the narrator's quarrel with his wife, the narrator's encounter with Lester in the bathroom, and Mack's confrontation with the nurse?

2. What ways does the narrator characterize Mack so that he appears more than simply a victim? How does the narrator reveal his character through his attitude toward friendship?

3. How do the University of California, Santa Cruz; Mack's apartment; the strip east on University; and the hospital form the literal and symbolic settings for the story?

4. Why does McFarland choose a straight rather than gay narrator for this story? What are the advantages of selecting a narrator who does not appear to analyze his feelings?

5. In what sense is Lester's assessment of the various addictions on the strip a fair assessment of American life? How does Mack interpret the phrase "family values"?

Stories for Comparison

Katherine Anne Porter's "The Jilting of Granny Weatherall" (pages 1017–1024); Leo Tolstoy's "The Death of Ivan Ilych" (pages 1096–1135).

69

·····

NAGIB MAHFOUZ

The Happy Man

NAGIB MAHFOUZ was born in 1911 in Cairo, Egypt, and was educated at the University of Cairo. He has worked as a civil servant in various Egyptian government agencies for most of his career. His writing first became known to American readers with the translation of *Midaq Alley* (1947) and his critically acclaimed Cairo Trilogy (1956–1957). In 1967, Mahfouz published *Children of Gebelawi,* an allegorical narrative about humanity's quest for religion. Its allusions to the three monotheistic religions prompted Islamic fundamentalists to ban the book. Mahfouz's work focuses on the crisis of identity and conscience suffered in periods of social and political turmoil; sixteen of his novels have been adapted for films in Egypt. In 1988, he won the Nobel Prize for Literature. In "The Happy Man," reprinted from *God's World: An Anthology of Short Stories* (1973), a journalist is mystified by his sudden feelings of happiness.

H e woke up in the morning and discovered that he was happy. "What's this?" he asked himself. He could not think of any word which described his state of mind more accurately and precisely than "happy." This was distinctly peculiar when compared with the state he was usually in when he woke up. He would be half-asleep from staying so late at the newspaper office. He would face life with a sense of strain and contemplation. Then he would get up, whetting his determination to face up to all inconveniences and withstand all difficulties.

Today he felt happy, full of happiness as a matter of fact. There was no arguing about it. The symptoms were quite clear and their vigour and obviousness were such as to impose themselves on his senses and mind all at once. Yes, indeed; he was happy. If this was not happiness, then what was? He felt that his limbs were well proportioned and functioning perfectly. They were working in superb harmony with each other and with the world around him. Inside him, he felt a boundless power, an imperishable energy, an ability to achieve anything with confidence, precision, and obvious success. His heart was overflowing with love for people, animals and things, and with an all-engulfing sense of optimism and joy. It was as if he were no longer troubled or bothered by fear, anxiety, sickness, death, argument, or the question of earning a living. Even more important than that, and something he could not analyze, it was a feeling which penetrated to every cell of his body and soul, it played a tune full of delight, pleasure, serenity and peace, and hummed in its incredible melodies the whispering sound of the world which is denied to the unhappy.

He felt drunk with ecstasy and savoured it slowly with a feeling of surprise. He asked himself where it had come from and how; the past provided no explanation and the future could not justify it. Where did it come from, then, and how?! How long would it last? Would it stay with him till breakfast? Would it give him enough time to get to the newspaper office? Just a minute though, he thought . . . it won't last because it can't. If it did, man would be turned into an angel or something even higher. So he told himself that he should devote his attention to savouring it, living with it, and storing up its nectar before it became a mere memory with no way of proving it or even being sure that it had ever existed.

He ate his breakfast with a relish, and this time nothing distracted his attention while he was eating. He gave 'Uncle' Bashir who was waiting on him such a beaming smile that the poor man felt rather alarmed and taken aback. Usually he would only look in his direction to give orders or ask questions; although, on most occasions, he treated him fairly well.

5   "Tell me, 'Uncle' Bashir," he asked the servant, "am I a happy man?"

The poor man was startled. He realized why his servant was confused; for the first time ever he was talking to him as a colleague or friend. He encouraged his servant to forget about his worries and asked him with unusual insistence to answer his question.

"Through God's grace and favour, you are happy," the servant replied.

"You mean, I should be happy. Anyone with my job, living in my house, and enjoying my health, should be happy. That's what you want to say. But do you think I'm really happy?"

The servant replied, "You work too hard, Sir," after yet more insistence, "it's more than any man can stand. . . ."

He hesitated, but his master gestured to him to continue with what he had to say.   10

"You get angry a lot," he said, "and have fierce arguments with your neighbors. . . ."

He interrupted him by laughing loudly. "What about you," he asked, "don't you have any worries?"

"Of course, no man can be free of worry."

"You mean that complete happiness is an impossible quest?"

"That applies to life in general. . . ."   15

How could he have dreamed up this incredible happiness? He or any other human being? It was a strange, unique happiness, as though it were a private secret he had been given. In the meeting hall of the newspaper building, he spotted his main rival in this world sitting down thumbing through a magazine. The man heard his footsteps, but did not look up from the magazine. He had undoubtedly noticed him in some way and was therefore pretending to ignore him so as to keep his own peace of mind. At some circulation meetings, they would argue so violently with each other that sparks began to fly and they would exchange bitter words. One stage more, and they would come to blows. A week ago, his rival had won in the union elections and he had lost. He had felt pierced by a sharp, poisoned arrow, and the world had darkened before his eyes. Now here he was approaching his rival's seat; the sight of him sitting there did not make him excited, nor did the memories of their dispute spoil his composure. He approached him with a pure and carefree heart, feeling drunk with his incredible happiness; his face showed an expression full of tolerance and forgiveness. It was as though he were approaching some other man towards whom he had never had any feelings of enmity, or perhaps he might be renewing a friendship again. "Good morning!" he said without feeling any compunction.

The man looked up in amazement. He was silent for a few moments until he recovered, and then returned the greeting curtly. It was as though he did not believe his eyes and ears.

He sat down alongside the man. "Marvellous weather today. . . ." he said.

"Okay. . . ." the other replied guardedly.

"Weather to fill your heart with happiness."   20

His rival looked at him closely and cautiously. "I'm glad that you're so happy. . . ." he muttered.

"Inconceivably happy. . . ." he replied with a laugh.

"I hope," the man continued in a rather hesitant tone of voice, "that I shan't spoil your happiness at the meeting of the administrative council. . . ."

"Not at all. My views are well known, but I don't mind if the members adopt your point of view. That won't spoil my happiness!"

25   "You've changed a great deal overnight," the man said with a smile.

"The fact is that I'm happy, inconceivably happy."

The man examined his face carefully. "I bet your dear son has changed his mind about staying in Canada?!" he asked.

"Never, never, my friend," he replied, laughing loudly. "He is still sticking to his decision. . . ."

"But that was the principal reason for your being so sad. . . ."

30   "Quite true. I've often begged him to come back out of pity for me in my loneliness and to serve his country. But he told me that he's going to open an engineering office with a Canadian partner; in fact, he's invited me to join him in it. Let him live where he'll be happy. I'm quite happy here—as you can see, inconceivably happy. . . ."

The man still looked a little doubtful. "Quite extraordinarily brave!" he said.

"I don't know what it is, but I'm happy in the full meaning of the word."

Yes indeed, this was full happiness; full, firm, weighty, and vital. As deep as absolute power, widespread as the wind, fierce as fire, bewitching as scent, transcending nature. It could not possibly last.

The other man warmed to his display of affection. "The truth is," he said, "that I always picture you as someone with a fierce and violent temperament which causes him a good deal of trouble and leads him to trouble other people too."

35   "Really?"

"You don't know how to make a truce, you've no concept of intermediate solutions. You work with your nerves, with the marrow in your bones. You fight bitterly as though any problem is a matter of life and death!"

"Yes, that's true."

He accepted the criticism without any difficulty and with an open heart. His wave expanded into a boundless ocean of happiness. He struggled to control an innocent, happy laugh which the other man interpreted in a way far removed from its pure motives. "So then," he asked, "you think it's necessary to be able to take a balanced view of events, do you?"

"Of course. I remember, by way of example, the argument we had the day before yesterday about racism. We both had the same views on the subject; it's something worth being zealous about, even to the point of anger. But what kind of anger? An intellectual anger, abstract to a certain extent; not the type which shatters your nerves, ruins your digestion, and gives you palpitations. Not so?"

40   "That's obvious; I quite understand. . . ."

He struggled to control a second laugh and succeeded. His heart refused to renounce one drop of its joy. Racism, Vietnam, Palestine, . . . no problem could assail that fortress of happiness which was encircling his heart. When he remembered a problem, his heart guffawed. He was happy. It was a tyrannical happiness, despising all misery and laughing at any hardship; it wanted to laugh, dance, sing, and distribute its spirit of laughter, dancing and singing among the various problems of the world.

He could not bear to stay in his office at the newspaper; he felt no desire to work at all. He hated the very idea of thinking about his daily business, and completely failed to bring his mind down from its stronghold in the kingdom of happiness. How could he possibly write about a trolley bus falling into the Nile when he was so intoxicated by this frightening happiness? Yes, it really was frightening. How could it be anything else, when there was no reason for it at all, when it was so strong that it made him exhausted and paralyzed his will; apart from the fact that it had been with him for half a day without letting up in the slightest degree?!

He left the pages of paper blank and started walking backwards and forwards across the room, laughing and cracking his fingers. . . .

He felt slightly worried; it did not penetrate deep enough to spoil his happiness, but paused on the surface of his mind like an abstract idea. It occurred to him that he might recall the tragedies of his life so that he could test their effect on his happiness. Perhaps they would be able to bring back some idea of balance or security, at least until his happiness began to flag a little. For example, he remembered his wife's death in all its various aspects and details. What had happened? The event appeared to him as a series of movements without any meaning or effect, as though it had happened to some other woman, the wife of another man, in some distant historical age. In fact, it had a contagious effect which prompted a smile, and then even provoked laughter. He could not stop himself laughing, and there he was guffawing, ha . . . ha . . . ha!

The same thing happened when he remembered the first letter his son had sent him saying that he wanted to emigrate to Canada. The sound of his guffaws as he paraded the bloody tragedies of the world before him would have attracted the attention of the newspaper workers and passers-by in the street, had it not been for the thickness of the walls. He could do nothing to dislodge his happiness. Memories of unhappy times hit him like waves being thrown on to a sandy beach under the golden rays of the sun.

He excused himself from attending the administrative council and left the newspaper office without writing a word. After lunch, he lay down on his bed as usual but could not sleep. In fact, sleep seemed an impossibility to him. Nothing gave him any indication that it was coming, even slowly. He was in a place alight and gleaming, resounding with sleeplessness and joy. He had to calm down and relax, to quieten his senses and limbs, but how could he do it? He gave up trying to sleep, and got up. He began to hum as he was walking around his house. If this keeps up, he told himself, I won't be able to sleep, just as I can't work or feel sad. It was almost time for him to go to the club, but he did not feel like meeting any friends. What was the point of exchanging views on public affairs and private worries?! What would they think if they found him laughing at every major problem? What would they say? How would they picture things? How would they explain it? No, he did not need anyone, nor did he want to spend the evening talking. He should be by himself, and go for a long walk to get rid of some of his excess vitality and think about his situation. What had happened to him? How was it that this incredible happiness had overwhelmed him? How long would he have to carry it on his shoulders? Would it keep depriving him of work, friends, sleep and peace of mind?! Should he resign himself to it? Should he abandon himself to the flood to play with him as the whim took it? Or should he look for a way out for himself through thought, action, or advice?

When he was called into the examination room in the clinic of his friend, the specialist in internal medicine, he felt a little alarmed. The doctor looked at him with a smile. "You don't look like someone who's complaining about being ill," he said.

"I haven't come to see you because I'm ill," he told the doctor in a hesitant tone of voice, "but because I'm happy!"

The doctor looked piercingly at him with a questioning air.

50   "Yes," he repeated to underline what he had said, "because I'm happy!"

There was a period of silence. On one side, there was anxiety, and on the other, questioning and amazement.

"It's an incredible feeling which can't be defined in any other way, but it's very serious. . . ."

The doctor laughed. "I wish your illness was contagious," he said, prodding him jokingly.

"Don't treat it as a joke. It's very serious, as I told you. I'll describe it to you. . . ."

55   He told him all about his happiness from the time he had woken up in the morning till he had felt compelled to visit him.

"Haven't you been taking drugs, alcohol, or tranquillizers?"

"Absolutely nothing like that."

"Have you had some success in an important sphere of your life; work . . . love . . . money?"

"Nothing like that either. I've twice as much to worry about as I have to make me feel glad. . . ."

60   "Perhaps if you were patient for a while. . . ."

"I've been patient all day. I'm afraid I'll be spending the night wandering around. . . ."

The doctor gave him a precise, careful, and comprehensive examination and then shrugged his shoulders in despair. "You're a picture of health," he said.

"And so?"

"I could advise you to take a sleeping pill, but it would be better if you consulted a nerve specialist. . . ."

65   The examination was repeated in the nerve specialist's clinic with the self-same precision, care, and comprehensiveness. "Your nerves are sound," the doctor told him, "they're in enviable condition!"

"Haven't you got a plausible explanation for my condition?" he asked hopefully.

"Consult a gland specialist!" the doctor replied, shaking his head.

The examination was conducted for a third time in the gland specialist's clinic with the same precision, care and comprehensiveness. "I congratulate you!" the doctor told him. "Your glands are in good condition!"

He laughed. He apologized for laughing, laughing as he did so. Laughter was his way of expressing his alarm and despair.

He left the clinic with the feeling that he was alone; alone in the hands of his ₇₀ tyrannical happiness with no helper, no guide and no friend. Suddenly, he remembered the doctor's sign he sometimes saw from the window of his office in the newspaper building. It was true that he had no confidence in psychiatrists even though he had read about the significance of psychoanalysis. Apart from that, he knew that their tentacles were very long and they kept their patients tied in a sort of long association. He laughed as he remembered the method of cure through free association and the problems which it eventually uncovers. He was laughing as his feet carried him towards the psychiatrist's clinic, and imagined the doctor listening to his incredible complaints about feeling happy, when he was used to hearing people complain about hysteria, schizophrenia, anxiety, and so on.

"The truth is, Doctor, that I've come to see you because I'm happy!"

He looked at the doctor to see what effect his statement had had on him, but noticed that he was keeping his composure. He felt ridiculous. "I'm inconceivably happy. . . ." he said in a tone of confidence.

He began to tell the doctor his story, but the latter stopped him with a gesture of his hand. "An overwhelming, incredible, debilitating happiness?" he asked quietly.

He stared at him in amazement and was on the point of saying something, but the doctor spoke first. "A happiness which has made you stop working," he asked, "abandon your friends, and detest going to sleep . . . ?"

"You're a miracle!" he shouted. ₇₅

"Every time you get involved in some misfortune," the psychiatrist continued quietly, "you dissolve into laughter . . . ?"

"Sir . . . are you familiar with the invisible?"

"No!" he said with a smile, "nothing like that. But I get a similar case in my clinic at least once a week!"

"Is it an epidemic?" he asked.

"I didn't say that, and I wouldn't claim that it's been possible to analyze one ₈₀ case into its primary elements as yet."

"But is it a disease?"

"All the cases are still under treatment."

"But are you satisfied without any doubt that they aren't natural cases . . . ?"

"That's a necessary assumption for the job; there's only. . . ."

"Have you noticed any of them to be deranged in. . . ." he asked anxiously, ₈₅ pointing to his head.

"Absolutely not," the doctor replied convincingly. "I assure you that they're all intelligent in every sense of the word. . . ."

The doctor thought for a moment. "We should have two sessions a week, I think?" he said.

"Very well. . . ." he replied in resignation.

"There's no sense in getting alarmed or feeling sad. . . ."

Alarmed, sad? He smiled, and his smile kept on getting broader. A laugh ₉₀ slipped out, and before long, he was dissolving into laughter. He was determined to control himself, but his resistance collapsed completely. He started guffawing loudly. . . .

QUESTIONS FOR DISCUSSION AND WRITING

1. What are the major conflicts in this story about a man who seems to have no more conflicts in his life? Why are these conflicts left unresolved at the end of the story? In what sense does this story have a "happy ending"?

2. How does the protagonist's encounter with other people help us contrast his present self with his previous character? How does his laughter suggest different things about him throughout the story?

3. Why are we given so little sense of a particular time or place in the story? What is the implicit evidence that the story may be set in a developing nation? Does such evidence alter our interpretation of the story?

4. What are the advantages of the limited third-person point of view in this story? How might this nameless character change his story if he told it in the first person?

5. How does the catalog of nouns in the second paragraph give us a sense of "happiness"? How do the terms *tyrannical, frightening,* and *debilitating* suggest the paradoxical themes of this story?

Stories for Comparison

Kurt Vonnegut, Jr.'s "Harrison Bergeron" (pages 138–144); John Cheever's "The Swimmer" (pages 368–376).

70

....

B E R N A R D   M A L A M U D

The Magic Barrel

BERNARD MALAMUD (1914–1986) was born in Brooklyn, New York, and educated at the City College of New York and Columbia University. During the 1940s, he worked as a clerk for the Bureau of the Census and as an evening high school teacher in New York City. From 1949 until 1961, Malamud taught writing at Oregon State University, where he began publishing his short stories and novels. His work from this period includes three novels—*The Natural* (1952), *The Assistant* (1957), and *A New Life*

(1961)—and a collection of short stories, *The Magic Barrel* (1958), which won the National Book Award. In 1961, Malamud accepted a teaching position at Bennington College, Vermont. He continued to produce major novels such as *The Fixer* (1966), which was awarded a Pulitzer Prize, *The Tenants* (1971), and *Dublin's Lives* (1979). His later short stories, published first in magazines such as *Partisan Review, Harper's Bazaar,* and *The New Yorker,* have been collected in *Idiots First* (1963), *Pictures of Fidelman* (1969), *Rembrandt's Hat* (1973), and, most recently, *The Stories of Bernard Malamud* (1983). "The Magic Barrel," the title story from Malamud's most famous collection, tells of a young rabbinical student's attempt to find love through a marriage broker.

N ot long ago there lived in uptown New York, in a small, almost meager room, though crowded with books, Leo Finkle, a rabbinical student in the Yeshivah University. Finkle, after six years of study, was to be ordained in June and had been advised by an acquaintance that he might find it easier to win himself a congregation if he were married. Since he had no present prospects of marriage, after two tormented days of turning it over in his mind, he called in Pinye Salzman, a marriage broker whose two-line advertisement he had read in the *Forward*.

The matchmaker appeared one night out of the dark fourth-floor hallway of the graystone rooming house where Finkle lived, grasping a black, strapped portfolio that had been worn thin with use. Salzman, who had been long in the business, was of slight but dignified build, wearing an old hat, and an overcoat too short and tight for him. He smelled frankly of fish, which he loved to eat, and although he was missing a few teeth, his presence was not displeasing, because of an amiable manner curiously contrasted with mournful eyes. His voice, his lips, his wisp of beard, his bony fingers were animated, but give him a moment of repose and his mild blue eyes revealed a depth of sadness, a characteristic that put Leo a little at ease although the situation, for him, was inherently tense.

He at once informed Salzman why he had asked him to come, explaining that his home was in Cleveland, and that but for his parents, who had married comparatively late in life, he was alone in the world. He had for six years devoted himself almost entirely to his studies, as a result of which, understandably, he had found himself without time for a social life and the company of young women. Therefore he thought it the better part of trial and error—of embarrassing fumbling—to call in an experienced person to advise him on these matters. He remarked in passing that the function of the marriage broker was ancient and honorable, highly approved in the Jewish community, because it made practical the necessary without hindering joy. Moreover, his own parents had been brought together by a matchmaker. They had made, if not a financially profitable marriage— since neither had possessed any worldly goods to speak of—at least a successful one in the sense of their everlasting devotion to each other. Salzman listened in embarrassed surprise, sensing a sort of apology. Later, however, he experienced a glow of pride in his work, an emotion that had left him years ago, and he heartily approved of Finkle.

The two went to their business. Leo had led Salzman to the only clear place in the room, a table near a window that overlooked the lamp-lit city. He seated himself at the matchmaker's side but facing him, attempting by an act of will to suppress the unpleasant tickle in his throat. Salzman eagerly unstrapped his portfolio and removed a loose rubber band from a thin packet of much-handled cards. As he flipped through them, a gesture and sound that physically hurt Leo, the student pretended not to see and gazed steadfastly out the window. Although it was still February, winter was on its last legs, signs of which he had for the first time in years begun to notice. He now observed the round white moon, moving high in the sky through a cloud menagerie, and watched with half-open mouth as it penetrated a huge hen, and dropped out of her like an egg laying itself. Salzman, though pretending through eyeglasses he had just slipped on, to be engaged in scanning the writing on the cards, stole occasional glances at the young man's distinguished face, noting with pleasure the long, severe scholar's nose, brown eyes heavy with learning, sensitive yet ascetic lips, and a certain, almost hollow quality of the dark cheeks. He gazed around at shelves upon shelves of books and let out a soft, contented sigh.

5   When Leo's eyes fell upon the cards, he counted six spread out in Salzman's hand.

"So few?" he asked in disappointment.

"You wouldn't believe me how much cards I got in my office," Salzman replied. "The drawers are already filled to the top, so I keep them now in a barrel, but is every girl good for a new rabbi?"

Leo blushed at this, regretting all he had revealed of himself in a curriculum vitae he had sent to Salzman. He had thought it best to acquaint him with his strict standards and specifications, but in having done so, felt he had told the marriage broker more than was absolutely necessary.

He hesitantly inquired, "Do you keep photographs of your clients on file?"

10   "First comes family, amount of dowry, also what kind promises," Salzman replied, unbuttoning his tight coat and settling himself in the chair. "After comes pictures, rabbi."

"Call me Mr. Finkle. I'm not yet a rabbi."

Salzman said he would, but instead called him doctor, which he changed to rabbi when Leo was not listening too attentively.

Salzman adjusted his horn-rimmed spectacles, gently cleared his throat and read in an eager voice the contents of the top card:

"Sophie P. Twenty-four years. Widow one year. No children. Educated high school and two years college. Father promises eight thousand dollars. Has wonderful wholesale business. Also real estate. On the mother's side comes teachers, also one actor. Well known on Second Avenue."

15   Leo gazed up in surprise. "Did you say a widow?"

"A widow don't mean spoiled, rabbi. She lived with her husband maybe four months. He was a sick boy she made a mistake to marry him."

"Marrying a widow has never entered my mind."

"This is because you have no experience. A widow, especially if she is young and healthy like this girl, is a wonderful person to marry. She will be thankful to you the rest of her life. Believe me, if I was looking now for a bride, I would marry a widow."

Leo reflected, then shook his head.

Salzman hunched his shoulders in an almost imperceptible gesture of disappointment. He placed the card down on the wooden table and began to read another:

"Lily H. High school teacher. Regular. Not a substitute. Has savings and new
Dodge car. Lived in Paris one year. Father is successful dentist thirty-five years. Interested in professional man. Well Americanized family. Wonderful opportunity."

"I knew her personally," said Salzman. "I wish you could see this girl. She is a
doll. Also very intelligent. All day you could talk to her about books and theater and
what not. She also knows current events."

"I don't believe you mentioned her age?"

"Her age?" Salzman said, raising his brows. "Her age is thirty-two years."

Leo said after a while, "I'm afraid that seems a little too old."

Salzman let out a laugh. "So how old are you, rabbi?"

"Twenty-seven."

"So what is the difference, tell me, between twenty-seven and thirty-two?
My own wife is seven years older than me. So what did I suffer?—Nothing. If
Rothschild's daughter wants to marry you, would you say on account her age, no?"

"Yes," Leo said dryly.

Salzman shook off the no in the yes. "Five years don't mean a thing. I give you
my word that when you will live with her for one week, you will forget her age.
What does it mean five years—that she lived more and knows more than somebody
who is younger? On this girl, God bless you, years are not wasted. Each one that it
comes makes better the bargain."

"What subject does she teach in high school?"

"Languages. If you heard the way she speaks French, you will think it is music.
I am in the business twenty-five years, and I recommend her with my whole heart.
Believe me, I know what I'm talking, rabbi."

"What's on the next card?" Leo said abruptly.

Salzman reluctantly turned up the third card:

"Ruth K. Nineteen years. Honor student. Father offers thirteen thousand cash to
the right bridegroom. He is a medical doctor. Stomach specialist with marvelous
practice. Brother in law owns own garment business. Particular people."

Salzman looked as if he had read his trump card.

"Did you say nineteen?" Leo said with interest.

"On the dot."

"Is she attractive?" He blushed. "Pretty?"

Salzman kissed his finger tips. "A little doll. On this I give you my word. Let me
call the father tonight and you will see what means pretty."

But Leo was troubled. "You're sure she's that young?"

"This I am positive. The father will show you the birth certificate."

"Are you positive there isn't something wrong with her?" Leo insisted.

"Who says there is wrong?"

"I don't understand why an American girl her age should go to a marriage broker."

A smile spread over Salzman's face.

"So for the same reason you went, she comes."

Leo flushed. "I am pressed for time."

Salzman, realizing he had been tactless, quickly explained. "The father came, not her. He wants she should have the best, so he looks around himself. When we will locate the right boy he will introduce him and encourage. This makes a better marriage than if a young girl without experience takes for herself. I don't have to tell you this."

50   "But don't you think this young girl believes in love?" Leo spoke uneasily.

Salzman was about to guffaw but caught himself and said soberly, "Love comes with the right person, not before."

Leo parted dry lips but did not speak. Noticing that Salzman had snatched a glance at the next card, he cleverly asked, "How is her health?"

"Perfect," Salzman said, breathing with difficulty. "Of course, she is a little lame on her right foot from an auto accident that it happened to her when she was twelve years, but nobody notices on account she is so brilliant and also beautiful."

Leo got up heavily and went to the window. He felt curiously bitter and upbraided himself for having called in the marriage broker. Finally, he shook his head.

55   "Why not?" Salzman persisted, the pitch of his voice rising.

"Because I detest stomach specialists."

"So what do you care what is his business? After you marry her do you need him? Who says he must come every Friday night in your house?"

Ashamed of the way the talk was going, Leo dismissed Salzman, who went home with heavy, melancholy eyes.

Though he had felt only relief at the marriage broker's departure, Leo was in low spirits the next day. He explained it as arising from Salzman's failure to produce a suitable bride for him. He did not care for his type of clientele. But when Leo found himself hesitating whether to seek out another matchmaker, one more polished than Pinye, he wondered if it could be—his protestations to the contrary, and although he honored his father and mother—that he did not, in essence, care for the matchmaking institution? This thought he quickly put out of mind yet found himself still upset. All day he ran around in the woods—missed an important appointment, forgot to give out his laundry, walked out of a Broadway cafeteria without paying and had to run back with the ticket in his hand; had even not recognized his landlady in the street when she passed with a friend and courteously called out, "A good evening to you, Doctor Finkle." By nightfall, however, he had regained sufficient calm to sink his nose into a book and there found peace from his thoughts.

60   Almost at once there came a knock on the door. Before Leo could say enter, Salzman, commercial cupid, was standing in the room. His face was gray and meager, his expression hungry, and he looked as if he would expire on his feet. Yet the marriage broker managed, by some trick of the muscles, to display a broad smile.

"So good evening. I am invited?"

Leo nodded, disturbed to see him again, yet unwilling to ask the man to leave.

Beaming still, Salzman laid his portfolio on the table. "Rabbi, I got for you tonight good news."

"I've asked you not to call me rabbi. I'm still a student."

65   "Your worries are finished. I have for you a first-class bride."

"Leave me in peace concerning this project." Leo pretended lack of interest.

"The world will dance at your wedding."

"Please, Mr. Salzman, no more."

"But first must come back my strength," Salzman said weakly. He fumbled with the portfolio straps and took out of the leather case an oily paper bag, from which he extracted a hard, seeded roll and a small, smoked white fish. With a quick motion of his hand he stripped the fish out of its skin and began ravenously to chew. "All day in a rush," he muttered.

Leo watched him eat.   70

"A sliced tomato you have maybe?" Salzman hesitantly inquired.

"No."

The marriage broker shut his eyes and ate. When he had finished he carefully cleaned up the crumbs and rolled up the remains of the fish, in the paper bag. His spectacled eyes roamed the room until he discovered, amid some piles of books, a one-burner gas stove. Lifting his hat he humbly asked, "A glass tea you got, rabbi?"

Conscience-stricken, Leo rose and brewed the tea. He served it with a chunk of lemon and two cubes of lump sugar, delighting Salzman.

After he had drunk his tea, Salzman's strength and good spirits were restored.   75

"So tell me, rabbi," he said amiably, "you considered some more the three clients I mentioned yesterday?"

"There was no need to consider."

"Why not?"

"None of them suits me."

"What then suits you?"   80

Leo let it pass because he could only give a confused answer.

Without waiting for a reply, Salzman asked, "You remember this girl I talked to you—the high school teacher?"

"Age thirty-two?"

But, surprisingly, Salzman's face lit in a smile. "Age twenty-nine."

Leo shot him a look. "Reduced from thirty-two?"   85

"A mistake," Salzman avowed. "I talked today with the dentist. He took me to his safety deposit box and showed me the birth certificate. She was twenty-nine years last August. They made her a party in the mountains where she went for her vacation. When her father spoke to me the first time I forgot to write the age and I told you thirty-two, but now I remember this was a different client, a widow."

"The same one you told me about? I thought she was twenty-four?"

"A different. Am I responsible that the world is filled with widows?"

"No, but I'm not interested in them, nor for that matter, in school teachers."

Salzman pulled his clasped hands to his breast. Looking at the ceiling he de- 90 voutly exclaimed, "Yiddishe kinder, what can I say to somebody that he is not interested in high school teachers? So what then you are interested?"

Leo flushed but controlled himself.

"In what else will you be interested," Salzman went on, "if you not interested in this fine girl that she speaks four languages and has personally in the bank ten thousand dollars? Also her father guarantees further twelve thousand. Also she has a new car, wonderful clothes, talks on all subjects, and she will give you a first-class home and children. How near do we come in our life to paradise?"

"If she's so wonderful, why wasn't she married ten years ago?"

"Why?" Salzman with a heavy laugh. "—Why? Because she is *partikiler.* This is why. She wants the *best.*"

95   Leo was silent, amused at how he had entangled himself. But Salzman had aroused his interest in Lily H., and he began seriously to consider calling on her. When the marriage broker observed how intently Leo's mind was at work on the facts he had supplied, he felt certain they would soon come to an agreement.

Late Saturday afternoon, conscious of Salzman, Leo Finkle walked with Lily Hirschorn along Riverside Drive. He walked briskly and erectly, wearing with distinction the black fedora he had that morning taken with trepidation out of the dusty hat box on his closet shelf, and the heavy black Saturday coat he had thoroughly whisked clean. Leo also owned a walking stick, a present from a distant relative, but quickly put temptation aside and did not use it. Lily, petite and not unpretty, had on something signifying the approach of spring. She was au courant, animatedly, with all sorts of subjects, and he weighed her words and found her surprisingly sound— score another for Salzman, whom he uneasily sensed to be somewhere around, hiding perhaps high in a tree along the street, flashing the lady signals with a pocket mirror; or perhaps a cloven-hoofed Pan, piping nuptial ditties as he danced his invisible way before them, strewing wild buds on the walk and purple grapes in their path, symbolizing fruit of a union, though there was of course still none.

Lily startled Leo by remarking, "I was thinking of Mr. Salzman, a curious figure, wouldn't you say?"

Not certain what to answer, he nodded.

She bravely went on, blushing, "I for one am grateful for his introducing us. Aren't you?"

100   He courteously replied, "I am."

"I mean," she said with a little laugh—and it was all in good taste, or at least gave the effect of being not in bad—"do you mind that we came together so?"

He was not displeased with her honesty, recognizing that she meant to set the relationship aright, and understanding that it took a certain amount of experience in life, and courage, to want to do it quite that way. One had to have some sort of past to make that kind of beginning.

He said that he did not mind. Salzman's function was traditional and honorable—valuable for what it might achieve, which, he pointed out, was frequently nothing.

Lily agreed with a sigh. They walked on for a while and she said after a long silence, again with a nervous laugh, "Would you mind if I asked you something a little bit personal? Frankly, I find the subject fascinating." Although Leo shrugged, she went on half embarrassedly, "How was it that you came to your calling? I mean was it a sudden passionate inspiration?"

105   Leo, after a time, slowly replied, "I was always interested in the Law."

"You saw revealed in it the presence of the Highest?"

He nodded and changed the subject. "I understand that you spent a little time in Paris, Miss Hirschorn?"

"Oh, did Mr. Salzman tell you, Rabbi Finkle?" Leo winced but she went on, "It was ages ago and almost forgotten. I remember I had to return for my sister's wedding."

And Lily would not be put off. "When," she asked in a trembly voice, "did you become enamoured of God?"

He stared at her. Then it came to him that she was talking not about Leo Finkle, but of a total stranger, some mystical figure, perhaps even passionate prophet that Salzman had dreamed up for her—no relation to the living or dead. Leo trembled with rage and weakness. The trickster had obviously sold her a bill of goods, just as he had him, who'd expected to become acquainted with a young lady of twenty-nine, only to behold, the moment he laid eyes upon her strained and anxious face, a woman past thirty-five and aging rapidly. Only his self control had kept him this long in her presence.

"I am not," he said gravely, "a talented religious person," and in seeking words to go on, found himself possessed by shame and fear. "I think," he said in a strained manner, "that I came to God not because I loved Him, but because I did not."

This confession he spoke harshly because its unexpectedness shook him.

Lily wilted. Leo saw a profusion of loaves of bread go flying like ducks high over his head, not unlike the winged loaves by which he had counted himself to sleep last night. Mercifully, then, it snowed, which he would not put past Salzman's machinations.

He was infuriated with the marriage broker and swore he would throw him out of the room the minute he reappeared. But Salzman did not come that night, and when Leo's anger had subsided, an unaccountable despair grew in its place. At first he thought this was caused by his disappointment in Lily, but before long it became evident that he had involved himself with Salzman without a true knowledge of his own intent. He gradually realized—with an emptiness that seized him with six hands—that he had called in the broker to find him a bride because he was incapable of doing it himself. This terrifying insight he had derived as a result of his meeting and conversation with Lily Hirschorn. Her probing questions had somehow irritated him into revealing—to himself more than her—the true nature of his relationship to God, and from that it had come upon him, with shocking force, that apart from his parents, he had never loved anyone. Or perhaps it went the other way, that he did not love God so well as he might, because he had not loved man. It seemed to Leo that his whole life stood starkly revealed and he saw himself for the first time as he truly was—unloved and loveless. This bitter but somehow not fully unexpected revelation brought him to a point of panic, controlled only by extraordinary effort. He covered his face with his hands and cried.

The week that followed was the worst of his life. He did not eat and lost weight. His beard darkened and grew ragged. He stopped attending seminars and almost never opened a book. He seriously considered leaving the Yeshivah, although he was deeply troubled at the thought of the loss of all his years of study—saw them like pages torn from a book, strewn over the city—and at the devastating effect of this decision upon his parents. But he had lived without knowledge of himself, and never in the Five Books and all the Commentaries—mea culpa—had the truth been revealed to him. He did not know where to turn, and in all this desolating loneliness there was no *to whom,* although he often thought of Lily but not once could bring himself to go downstairs and make the call. He became touchy and irritable, especially with his landlady, who asked him all manner of personal questions; on the other hand, sensing his own disagreeableness, he waylaid her on the stairs and apologized abjectly, until mortified, she ran from him. Out of this, however, he drew the consolation that he was a Jew and that a Jew suffered. But gradually, as the long and terrible week drew to a close, he regained his composure and some idea of purpose in life: to go on as planned. Although he was imperfect, the ideal was not. As for his quest of a bride, the thought of continuing afflicted him with anxiety and heartburn, yet perhaps with this new knowledge of himself he would be more successful than in the past. Perhaps love would now come to him and a bride to that love. And for this sanctified seeking who needed a Salzman?

The marriage broker, a skeleton with haunted eyes, returned that very night. He looked, withal, the picture of frustrated expectancy—as if he had steadfastly waited the week at Miss Lily Hirschorn's side for a telephone call that never came.

Casually coughing, Salzman came immediately to the point: "So how did you like her?"

Leo's anger rose and he could not refrain from chiding the matchmaker: "Why did you lie to me, Salzman?"

Salzman's pale face went dead white, the world had snowed on him.

120   "Did you not state that she was twenty-nine?" Leo insisted.

"I give you my word—"

"She was thirty-five, if a day. *At least* thirty-five."

"Of this don't be too sure. Her father told me—"

"Never mind. The worst of it was that you lied to her."

125   "How did I lie to her, tell me?"

"You told her things about me that weren't true. You made me out to be more, consequently less than I am. She had in mind a totally different person, a sort of semimystical Wonder Rabbi."

"All I said, you was a religious man."

"I can imagine."

Salzman sighed. "This is my weakness that I have," he confessed. "My wife says to me I shouldn't be a salesman, but when I have two fine people that they would be wonderful to be married, I am so happy that I talk too much." He smiled wanly. "This is why Salzman is a poor man."

130   Leo's anger left him. "Well, Salzman, I'm afraid that's all."

The marriage broker fastened hungry eyes on him.

"You don't want any more a bride?"

"I do," said Leo, "but I have decided to seek her in a different way. I am no longer interested in an arranged marriage. To be frank, I now admit the necessity of premarital love. That is, I want to be in love with the one I marry."

"Love?" said Salzman, astounded. After a moment he remarked, "For us, our love is our life, not for the ladies. In the ghetto they—"

"I know, I know," said Leo. "I've thought of it often. Love, I have said to my-self, should be a by-product of living and worship rather than its own end. Yet for myself I find it necessary to establish the level of my need and fulfill it."

Salzman shrugged but answered, "Listen, rabbi, if you want love, this I can find for you also. I have such beautiful clients that you will love them the minute your eyes will see them."

Leo smiled unhappily. "I'm afraid you don't understand."

But Salzman hastily unstrapped his portfolio and withdrew a manila packet from it.

"Pictures," he said, quickly laying the envelope on the table.

Leo called after him to take the pictures away, but as if on the wings of the wind, Salzman had disappeared.

March came. Leo had returned to his regular routine. Although he felt not quite himself yet—lacked energy—he was making plans for a more active social life. Of course it would cost something, but he was an expert in cutting corners; and when there were no corners left he would make circles rounder. All the while Salzman's pictures had laid on the table, gathering dust. Occasionally as Leo sat studying, or enjoying a cup of tea, his eyes fell on the manila envelope, but he never opened it.

The days went by and no social life to speak of developed with a member of the opposite sex—it was difficult, given the circumstances of his situation. One morning Leo toiled up the stairs to his room and stared out the window at the city. Although the day was bright his view of it was dark. For some time he watched the people in the street below hurrying along and then turned with a heavy heart to his little room. On the table was the packet. With a sudden relentless gesture he tore it open. For a half-hour he stood by the table in a state of excitement, examining the photographs of the ladies Salzman had included. Finally, with a deep sigh he put them down. There were six, of varying degrees of attractiveness, but look at them long enough and they all became Lily Hirschorn: all past their prime, all starved behind bright smiles, not a true personality in the lot. Life, despite their frantic yoohooings, had passed them by; they were pictures in a brief case that stank of fish. After a while, however, as Leo attempted to return the photographs into the envelope, he found in it another, a snapshot of the type taken by a machine for a quarter. He gazed at it a moment and let out a cry.

Her face deeply moved him. Why, he could at first not say. It gave him the im-pression of youth—spring flowers, yet age—a sense of having been used to the bone, wasted; this came from the eyes, which were hauntingly familiar, yet absolutely strange. He had a vivid impression that he had met her before, but try as he might he could not place her although he could almost recall her name, as if he had read it in her own handwriting. No, this couldn't be; he would have remembered her. It was not, he affirmed, that she had an extraordinary beauty—no, though her face was at-tractive enough; it was that *something* about her moved him. Feature for feature, even some of the ladies of the photographs could do better; but she leaped forth to his heart—had *lived,* or wanted to—more than just wanted, perhaps regretted how she had lived—had somehow deeply suffered: it could be seen in the depths of those reluctant eyes, and from the way the light enclosed and shone from her, and within her, opening realms of possibility: this was her own. Her he desired. His head ached and eyes narrowed with the intensity of his gazing, then as if an obscure fog had blown up in the mind, he experienced fear of her and was aware that he had received an impression, somehow, of evil. He shuddered, saying softly, it is thus with us all. Leo brewed some tea in a small pot and sat sipping it without sugar, to calm himself. But before he had finished drinking, again with excitement he examined the face and found it good: good for Leo Finkle. Only such a one could understand him and help him seek whatever he was seeking. She might, perhaps, love him. How she had happened to be among the discards in Salzman's barrel he could never guess, but he knew he must urgently go find her.

Leo rushed downstairs, grabbed up the Bronx telephone book, and searched for Salzman's home address. He was not listed, nor was his office. Neither was he in the Manhattan book. But Leo remembered having written down the address on a slip of paper after he had read Salzman's advertisement in the "personals" column of the *Forward.* He ran up to his room and tore through his papers, without luck. It was exasperating. Just when he needed the matchmaker he was nowhere to be found. Fortunately Leo remembered to look in his wallet. There on a card he found his name written and a Bronx address. No phone number was listed, the reason—Leo now recalled—he had originally communicated with Salzman by letter. He got on his coat, put a hat on over his skull cap and hurried to the subway station. All the way to the far end of the Bronx he sat on the edge of his seat. He was more than once tempted to take out the picture and see if the girl's face was as he remembered it, but he refrained, allowing the snapshot to remain in his inside coat pocket, content to have her so close. When the train pulled into the station he was waiting at the door and bolted out. He quickly located the street Salzman had advertised.

145   The building he sought was less than a block from the subway, but it was not an office building, nor even a loft, nor a store in which one could rent office space. It was a very old tenement house. Leo found Salzman's name in pencil on a soiled tag under the bell and climbed three dark flights to his apartment. When he knocked, the door was opened by a thin, asthmatic, gray-haired woman, in felt slippers.

"Yes?" she said, expecting nothing. She listened without listening. He could have sworn he had seen her, too, before but knew it was an illusion.

"Salzman—does he live here? Pinye Salzman," he said, "the matchmaker?"

She stared at him a long minute. "Of course."

He felt embarrassed. "Is he in?"

150   "No." Her mouth, though left open, offered nothing more.

"The matter is urgent. Can you tell me where his office is?"

"In the air." She pointed upward.

"You mean he has no office?" Leo asked.

"In his socks."

155   He peered into the apartment. It was sunless and dingy, one large room divided by a half-open curtain, beyond which he could see a sagging metal bed. The near side of the room was crowded with rickety chairs, old bureaus, a three-legged table,

racks of cooking utensils, and all the apparatus of a kitchen. But there was no sign of Salzman or his magic barrel, probably also a figment of the imagination. An odor of frying fish made Leo weak to the knees.

"Where is he?" he insisted. "I've got to see your husband."

At length she answered, "So who knows where he is? Every time he thinks a new thought he runs to a different place. Go home, he will find you."

"Tell him Leo Finkle."

She gave no sign she had heard.

He walked downstairs, depressed.

But Salzman, breathless, stood waiting at his door.

Leo was astounded and overjoyed. "How did you get here before me?"

"I rushed."

"Come inside."

They entered. Leo fixed tea, and a sardine sandwich for Salzman. As they were drinking he reached behind him for the packet of pictures and handed them to the marriage broker.

Salzman put down his glass and said expectantly, "You found somebody you like?"

"Not among these."

The marriage broker turned away.

"Here is the one I want." Leo held forth the snapshot.

Salzman slipped on his glasses and took the picture into his trembling hand. He turned ghastly and let out a groan.

"What's the matter?" cried Leo.

"Excuse me. Was an accident this picture. She isn't for you."

Salzman frantically shoved the manila packet into his portfolio. He thrust the snapshot into his pocket and fled down the stairs.

Leo, after momentary paralysis, gave chase and cornered the marriage broker in the vestibule. The landlady made hysterical outcries but neither of them listened.

"Give me back the picture, Salzman."

"No." The pain in his eyes was terrible.

"Tell me who she is then."

"This I can't tell you. Excuse me."

He made to depart, but Leo, forgetting himself, seized the matchmaker by his tight coat and shook him frenziedly.

"Please," sighed Salzman. "*Please.*"

Leo ashamedly let him go. "Tell me who she is," he begged. "It's very important for me to know."

"She is not for you. She is a wild one—wild, without shame. This is not a bride for a rabbi."

"What do you mean wild?"

"Like an animal. Like a dog. For her to be poor was a sin. This is why to me she is dead now."

"In God's name, what do you mean?"

"Her I can't introduce to you," Salzman cried.

"Why are you so excited?"

"Why, he asks," Salzman said, bursting into tears. "This is my baby, my Stella, she should burn in hell."

Leo hurried up to bed and hid under the covers. Under the covers he thought his life through. Although he soon fell asleep he could not sleep her out of his mind. He woke, beating his breast. Though he prayed to be rid of her, his prayers went unanswered. Through days of torment he endlessly struggled not to love her; fearing success, he escaped it. He then concluded to convert her to goodness, himself to God. The idea alternately nauseated and exalted him.

190   He perhaps did not know that he had come to a final decision until he encountered Salzman in a Broadway cafeteria. He was sitting alone at a rear table, sucking the bony remains of a fish. The marriage broker appeared haggard, and transparent to the point of vanishing.

Salzman looked up at first without recognizing him. Leo had grown a pointed beard and his eyes were weighted with wisdom.

"Salzman," he said, "love has at last come to my heart."

"Who can love from a picture?" mocked the marriage broker.

"It is not impossible."

195   "If you can love her, then you can love anybody. Let me show you some new clients that they just sent me their photographs. One is a little doll."

"Just her I want," Leo murmured.

"Don't be a fool, doctor. Don't bother with her."

"Put me in touch with her, Salzman," Leo said humbly. "Perhaps I can be of service."

Salzman had stopped eating and Leo understood with emotion that it was now arranged.

200   Leaving the cafeteria, he was, however, afflicted by a tormenting suspicion that Salzman had planned it all to happen this way.

Leo was informed by letter that she would meet him on a certain corner, and she was there one spring night, waiting under a street lamp. He appeared, carrying a small bouquet of violets and rosebuds. Stella stood by the lamp post, smoking. She wore white with red shoes, which fitted his expectations, although in a troubled moment he had imagined the dress red, and only the shoes white. She waited uneasily and shyly. From afar he saw that her eyes—clearly her father's—were filled with desperate innocence. He pictured, in her, his own redemption. Violins and lit candles revolved in the sky. Leo ran forward with flowers outthrust.

Around the corner, Salzman, leaning against a wall, chanted prayers for the dead.

QUESTIONS FOR DISCUSSION AND WRITING

1. What is the basic conflict that motivates Leo to seek out the services of a marriage broker? How does his meeting with Lily bring that conflict to a climax? In what way is his meeting with Stella designed to resolve that conflict?

2. How does Salzman characterize himself by the way he describes the three possible prospects? How does Leo reveal his own character by his reaction to these descriptions?

3. Why does Leo believe in the tradition of the marriage broker? Why is it appropriate that Salzman's office is "in the air"? How do Salzman's magical comings and goings suggest that there is something of the trickster about him?

4. What does Leo learn about himself during his conversation with Lily? What does he suspect about Salzman after their conversation regarding Stella?

5. What does this story suggest about the nature of love, suffering, and happiness? Why is Leo attracted to Stella's picture? What is ambiguous about her appearance when he meets her? Why is Salzman nearby chanting the prayers for the dead?

Stories for Comparison

Nathaniel Hawthorne's "Rappaccini's Daughter" (pages 619–640); Isaac Bashevis Singer's "Gimpel the Fool" (pages 1070–1080).

71

PAULE MARSHALL

To Da-duh, In Memoriam

". . . Oh Nana! all of you is not involved in this evil business Death,
Nor all of us in life."
—From "At My Grandmother's Grave," by Lebert Bethune

PAULE MARSHALL was born in 1929 in Brooklyn, New York, to parents who had recently emigrated from Barbados. After completing her education at Brooklyn College and Hunter College, Marshall worked as a librarian for the New York Public Library and as a staff writer for a small black magazine, *Our World,* traveling on assignment to South America and the West Indies. Her first novel, *Brown Girl, Brownstones* (1959), is a semi-autobiographical account of the coming of age of a young black woman. Her second substantial work, *Soul Clap Hands and Sing* (1961), is a collection of novellas that deal with the common experience of blacks in "Brooklyn," "Barbados," "British Guiana," and "Brazil." Her other works, *The Chosen Place, The Timeless People* (1969), *Praisesong for the Widow* (1983), *Reena and Other*

Stories (1983), and *Daughters* (1991), present black women as major actors in the social, political, and cultural issues of their country. "To Da-duh, In Memoriam," reprinted from *Reena and Other Stories,* contrasts the experiences of an old woman who has lived in the natural beauty of Barbados with those of her granddaughter, who has grown up in the urban splendor of New York City.

I did not see her at first I remember. For not only was it dark inside the crowded disembarkation shed in spite of the daylight flooding in from outside, but standing there waiting for her with my mother and sister I was still somewhat blinded from the sheen of tropical sunlight on the water of the bay which we had just crossed in the landing boat, leaving behind us the ship that had brought us from New York lying in the offing. Besides, being only nine years of age at the time and knowing nothing of islands I was busy attending to the alien sights and sounds of Barbados, the unfamiliar smells.

I did not see her, but I was alerted to her approach by my mother's hand which suddenly tightened around mine, and looking up I traced her gaze through the gloom in the shed until I finally made out the small, purposeful, painfully erect figure of the old woman headed our way.

Her face was drowned in the shadow of an ugly rolled-brim brown felt hat, but the details of her slight body and of the struggle taking place within it were clear enough—an intense, unrelenting struggle between her back which was beginning to bend ever so slightly under the weight of her eighty-odd years and the rest of her which sought to deny those years and hold that back straight, keep it in line. Moving swiftly toward us (so swiftly it seemed she did not intend stopping when she reached us but would sweep past us out the doorway which opened onto the sea and like Christ walk upon the water!), she was caught between the sunlight at her end of the building and the darkness inside—and for a moment she appeared to contain them both: the light in the long severe old-fashioned white dress she wore which brought the sense of a past that was still alive into our bustling present and in the snatch of white at her eye; the darkness in her black high-top shoes and in her face which was visible now that she was closer.

It was as stark and fleshless as a death mask, that face. The maggots might have already done their work, leaving only the framework of bone beneath the ruined skin and deep wells at the temple and jaw. But her eyes were alive, unnervingly so for one so old, with a sharp light that flicked out of the dim clouded depths like a lizard's tongue to snap up all in her view. Those eyes betrayed a child's curiosity about the world, and I wondered vaguely seeing them, and seeing the way the bodice of her ancient dress had collapsed in on her flat chest (what had happened to her breasts?), whether she might not be some kind of child at the same time that she was a woman, with fourteen children, my mother included, to prove it. Perhaps she was both, both child and woman, darkness and light, past and present, life and death—all the opposites contained and reconciled in her.

"My Da-duh," my mother said formally and stepped forward. The name sounded like thunder fading softly in the distance.

"Child," Da-duh said, and her tone, her quick scrutiny of my mother, the brief embrace in which they appeared to shy from each other rather than touch, wiped out the fifteen years my mother had been away and restored the old relationship. My mother, who was such a formidable figure in my eyes, had suddenly with a word been reduced to my status.

"Yes, God is good," Da-duh said with a nod that was like a tic. "He has spared me to see my child again."

We were led forward then, apologetically because not only did Da-duh prefer boys but she also liked her grandchildren to be "white," that is, fair-skinned; and we had, I was to discover, a number of cousins, the outside children of white estate managers and the like, who qualified. We, though, were as black as she.

My sister being the oldest was presented first. "This one takes after the father," my mother said and waited to be reproved.

Frowning, Da-duh tilted my sister's face toward the light. But her frown soon gave way to a grudging smile, for my sister with her large mild eyes and little broad winged nose, with our father's high-cheeked Barbadian cast to her face, was pretty.

"She's goin' be lucky," Da-duh said and patted her once on the cheek. "Any girl child that takes after the father does be lucky."

She turned then to me. But oddly enough she did not touch me. Instead leaning close, she peered hard at me, and then quickly drew back. I thought I saw her hand start up as though to shield her eyes. It was almost as if she saw not only me, a thin truculent child who it was said took after no one but myself, but something in me which for some reason she found disturbing, even threatening. We looked silently at each other for a long time there in the noisy shed, our gaze locked. She was the first to look away.

"But Adry," she said to my mother and her laugh was cracked, thin, apprehensive. "Where did you get this one here with this fierce look?"

"We don't know where she came out of, my Da-duh," my mother said, laughing also. Even I smiled to myself. After all I had won the encounter. Da-duh had recognized my small strength—and this was all I ever asked of the adults in my life then.

"Come, soul," Da-duh said and took my hand. "You must be one of those New York terrors you hear so much about."

She led us, me at her side and my sister and mother behind, out of the shed into the sunlight that was like a bright driving summer rain and over to a group of people clustered beside a decrepit lorry. They were our relatives, most of them from St. Andrews although Da-duh herself lived in St. Thomas, the women wearing bright print dresses, the colors vivid against their darkness, the men rusty black suits that encased them like straitjackets. Da-duh, holding fast to my hand, became my anchor as they circled round us like a nervous sea, exclaiming, touching us with their calloused hands, embracing us shyly. They laughed in awed bursts: "But look Adry got big-big children!"/ "And see the nice things they wearing, wrist watch and all!"/ "I tell you, Adry has done all right for sheself in New York. . . ."

Da-duh, ashamed at their wonder, embarrassed for them, admonished them the while. "But oh Christ," she said, "why you all got to get on like you never saw people from 'Away' before? You would think New York is the only place in the world to hear wunna. That's why I don't like to go anyplace with you St. Andrews people, you know. You all ain't been colonized."

We were in the back of the lorry finally, packed in among the barrels of ham, flour, cornmeal and rice and the trunks of clothes that my mother had brought as gifts. We made our way slowly through Bridgetown's clogged streets, part of a funereal procession of cars and open-sided buses, bicycles and donkey carts. The dim little limestone shops and offices along the way marched with us, at the same mournful pace, toward the same grave ceremony—as did the people, the women balancing huge baskets on top their heads as if they were no more than hats they wore to shade them from the sun. Looking over the edge of the lorry I watched as their feet slurred the dust. I listened, and their voices, raw and loud and dissonant in the heat, seemed to be grappling with each other high overhead.

Da-duh sat on a trunk in our midst, a monarch amid her court. She still held my hand, but it was different now. I had suddenly become her anchor, for I felt her fear of the lorry with its asthmatic motor (a fear and distrust, I later learned, she held of all machines) beating like a pulse in her rough palm.

20   As soon as we left Bridgetown behind though, she relaxed, and while the others around us talked she gazed at the canes standing tall on either side of the winding marl road. "C'dear," she said softly to herself after a time. "The canes this side are pretty enough."

They were too much for me. I thought of them as giant weeds that had overrun the island, leaving scarcely any room for the small tottering houses of sunbleached pine we passed or the people, dark streaks as our lorry hurtled by. I suddenly feared that we were journeying, unaware that we were, toward some dangerous place where the canes, grown as high and thick as a forest, would close in on us and run us through with their stiletto blades. I longed then for the familiar: for the street in Brooklyn where I lived, for my father who had refused to accompany us ("Blowing out good money on foolishness," he had said of the trip), for a game of tag with my friends under the chestnut tree outside our aging brownstone house.

"Yes, but wait till you see St. Thomas canes," Da-duh was saying to me. "They's canes father, bo," she gave a proud arrogant nod. "Tomorrow, God willing, I goin' take you out in the ground and show them to you."

True to her word Da-duh took me with her the following day out into the ground. It was a fairly large plot adjoining her weathered board and shingle house and consisting of a small orchard, a good-sized canepiece and behind the canes, where the land sloped abruptly down, a gully. She had purchased it with Panama money sent her by her eldest son, my uncle Joseph, who had died working on the canal. We entered the ground along a trail no wider than her body and as devious and complex as her reasons for showing me her land. Da-duh strode briskly ahead, her slight form filled out this morning by the layers of sacking petticoats she wore under her working dress to protect her against the damp. A fresh white cloth, elaborately arranged around her head, added to her height, and lent her a vain, almost roguish air.

Her pace slowed once we reached the orchard, and glancing back at me occasionally over her shoulder, she pointed out the various trees.

"This is a breadfruit," she said. "That one yonder is a papaw. Here's a guava. 25 This is a mango. I know you don't have anything like these in New York. Here's a sugar apple." (The fruit looked more like artichokes than apples to me.) "This one bears limes. . . ." She went on for some time, intoning the names of the trees as though they were those of her gods. Finally, turning to me, she said, "I know you don't have anything this nice where you come from." Then, as I hesitated: "I said I know you don't have anything this nice where you come from. . . ."

"No," I said and my world did seem suddenly lacking.

Da-duh nodded and passed on. The orchard ended and we were on the narrow cart road that led through the canepiece, the canes clashing like swords above my cowering head. Again she turned and her thin muscular arms spread wide, her dim gaze embracing the small field of canes, she said—and her voice almost broke under the weight of her pride, "Tell me, have you got anything like these in that place where you were born?"

"No."

"I din' think so. I bet you don't even know that these canes here and the sugar you eat is one and the same thing. That they does throw the canes into some damn machine at the factory and squeeze out all the little life in them to make sugar for you all so in New York to eat. I bet you don't know that."

"I've got two cavities and I'm not allowed to eat a lot of sugar."   30

But Da-duh didn't hear me. She had turned with an inexplicably angry motion and was making her way rapidly out of the canes and down the slope at the edge of the field which led to the gully below. Following her apprehensively down the incline amid a stand of banana plants whose leaves flapped like elephants' ears in the wind, I found myself in the middle of a small tropical wood— a place dense and damp and gloomy and tremulous with the fitful play of light and shadow as the leaves high above moved against the sun that was almost hidden from view. It was a violent place, the tangled foliage fighting each other for a chance at the sunlight, the branches of the trees locked in what seemed an immemorial struggle, one both necessary and inevitable. But despite the violence, it was pleasant, almost peaceful in the gully, and beneath the thick undergrowth the earth smelled like spring.

This time Da-duh didn't even bother to ask her usual question, but simply turned and waited for me to speak.

"No," I said, my head bowed. "We don't have anything like this in New York."

"Ah," she cried, her triumph complete. "I din' think so. Why, I've heard that's a place where you can walk till you near drop and never see a tree."

"We've got a chestnut tree in front of our house," I said.   35

"Does it bear?" She waited. "I ask you, does it bear?"

"Not anymore," I muttered. "It used to, but not anymore."

She gave the nod that was like a nervous twitch. "You see," she said. "Nothing can bear there." Then, secure behind her scorn, she added, "But tell me, what's this snow like that you hear so much about?"

Looking up, I studied her closely, sensing my chance, and then I told her, describing at length and with as much drama as I could summon not only what snow in the city was like, but what it would be like here, in her perennial summer kingdom.

40   ". . . And you see all these trees you got here," I said. "Well, they'd be bare. No leaves, no fruit, nothing. They'd be covered in snow. You see your canes. They'd be buried under tons of snow. The snow would be higher than your head, higher than your house, and you wouldn't be able to come down into this here gully because it would be snowed under. . . ."

She searched my face for the lie, still scornful but intrigued. "What a thing, huh?" she said finally, whispering it softly to herself.

"And when it snows you couldn't dress like you are now," I said. "Oh no, you'd freeze to death. You'd have to wear a hat and gloves and galoshes and ear muffs so your ears wouldn't freeze and drop off, and a heavy coat. I've got a Shirley Temple coat with fur on the collar. I can dance. You wanna see?"

Before she could answer I began, with a dance called the Truck which was popular back then in the 1930s. My right forefinger waving, I trucked around the nearby trees and around Da-duh's awed and rigid form. After the Truck I did the Suzy-Q, my lean hips swishing, my sneakers sidling zigzag over the ground. "I can sing," I said and did so, starting with "I'm Gonna Sit Right Down and Write Myself a Letter," then without pausing, "Tea for Two," and ending with "I Found a Million Dollar Baby in a Five and Ten Cent Store."

For long moments afterwards Da-duh stared at me as if I were a creature from Mars, an emissary from some world she did not know but which intrigued her and whose power she both felt and feared. Yet something about my performance must have pleased her, because bending down she slowly lifted her long skirt and then, one by one, the layers of petticoats until she came to a drawstring purse dangling at the end of a long strip of cloth tied round her waist. Opening the purse she handed me a penny. "Here," she said half-smiling against her will. "Take this to buy yourself a sweet at the shop up the road. There's nothing to be done with you, soul."

45   From then on, whenever I wasn't taken to visit relatives, I accompanied Da-duh out into the ground, and alone with her amid the canes or down in the gully I told her about New York. It always began with some slighting remark on her part: "I know they don't have anything this nice where you come from," or "Tell me, I hear those foolish people in New York does do such and such. . . ." But as I answered, recreating my towering world of steel and concrete and machines for her, building the city out of words, I would feel her give way. I came to know the signs of her surrender: the total stillness that would come over her little hard dry form, the probing gaze that like a surgeon's knife sought to cut through my skull to get at the images there, to see if I were lying; above all, her fear, a fear nameless and profound, the same one I had felt beating in the palm of her hand that day in the lorry.

Over the weeks I told her about refrigerators, radios, gas stoves, elevators, trolley cars, wringer washing machines, movies, airplanes, the cyclone at Coney Island, subways, toasters, electric lights: "At night, see, all you have to do is flip this little switch on the wall and all the lights in the house go on. Just like that. Like magic. It's like turning on the sun at night."

"But tell me," she said to me once with a faint mocking smile, "do the white people have all these things too or it's only the people looking like us?"

I laughed. "What d'ya mean," I said. "The white people have even better." Then: "I beat up a white girl in my class last term."

"Beating up white people!" Her tone was incredulous.

"How you mean!" I said, using an expression of hers. "She called me a name."   50

For some reason Da-duh could not quite get over this and repeated in the same hushed, shocked voice, "Beating up white people now! Oh, the lord, the world's changing up so I can scarce recognize it anymore."

One morning toward the end of our stay, Da-duh led me into a part of the gully that we had never visited before, an area darker and more thickly overgrown than the rest, almost impenetrable. There in a small clearing amid the dense bush, she stopped before an incredibly tall royal palm which rose cleanly out of the ground, and drawing the eye up with it, soared high above the trees around it into the sky. It appeared to be touching the blue dome of sky, to be flaunting its dark crown of fronds right in the blinding white face of the late morning sun.

Da-duh watched me a long time before she spoke, and then she said very quietly, "All right, now, tell me if you've got anything this tall in that place you're from."

I almost wished, seeing her face, that I could have said no. "Yes," I said. "We've got buildings hundred of times this tall in New York. There's one called the Empire State Building that's the tallest in the world. My class visited it last year and I went all the way to the top. It's got over a hundred floors. I can't describe how tall it is. Wait a minute. What's the name of that hill I went to visit the other day, where they have the police station?"

"You mean Bissex?"   55

"Yes, Bissex. Well, the Empire State Building is way taller than that."

"You're lying now!" she shouted, trembling with rage. Her hand lifted to strike me.

"No, I'm not," I said. "It really is, if you don't believe me I'll send you a picture postcard of it soon as I get back home so you can see for yourself. But it's way taller than Bissex."

All the fight went out of her at that. The hand poised to strike me fell limp to her side, and as she stared at me, seeing not me but the building that was taller than the highest hill she knew, the small stubborn light in her eyes (it was the same amber as the flame in the kerosene lamp she lit at dusk) began to fail. Finally, with a vague gesture that even in the midst of her defeat still tried to dismiss me and my world, she turned and started back through the gully, walking slowly, her steps groping and uncertain, as if she were suddenly no longer sure of the way, while I followed triumphant yet strangely saddened behind.

The next morning I found her dressed for our morning walk but stretched out on   60 the Berbice chair in the tiny drawing room where she sometimes napped during the afternoon heat, her face turned to the window beside her. She appeared thinner and suddenly indescribably old.

"My Da-duh," I said.

"Yes, nuh," she said. Her voice was listless and the face she slowly turned my way was, now that I think back on it, like a Benin mask, the features drawn and almost distorted by an ancient abstract sorrow.

"Don't you feel well?" I asked.

"Girl, I don't know."

65   "My Da-duh, I goin' boil you some bush tea," my aunt, Da-duh's youngest child, who lived with her, called from the shed roof kitchen.

"Who tell you I need bush tea?" she cried, her voice assuming for a moment its old authority. "You can't even rest nowadays without some malicious person looking for you to be dead. Come girl," she motioned me to a place beside her on the old-fashioned lounge chair, "give us a tune."

I sang for her until breakfast at eleven, all my brash irreverent Tin Pan Alley songs, and then just before noon we went out into the ground. But it was a short, dispirited walk. Da-duh didn't even notice that the mangoes were beginning to ripen and would have to be picked before the village boys got to them. And when she paused occasionally and looked out across the canes or up at her trees it wasn't as if she were seeing them but something else. Some huge, monolithic shape had imposed itself, it seemed, between her and the land, obstructing her vision. Returning to the house she slept the entire afternoon on the Berbice chair.

She remained like this until we left, languishing away the mornings on the chair at the window gazing out at the land as if it were already doomed; then, at noon, taking the brief stroll with me through the ground during which she seldom spoke, and afterwards returning home to sleep till almost dusk sometimes.

On the day of our departure she put on the austere, ankle-length white dress, the black shoes and brown felt hat (her town clothes she called them), but she did not go with us to town. She saw us off on the road outside her house and in the midst of my mother's tearful protracted farewell, she leaned down and whispered in my ear, "Girl, you're not to forget now to send me the picture of that building, you hear."

70   By the time I mailed her the large colored picture postcard of the Empire State Building she was dead. She died during the famous '37 strike which began shortly after we left. On the day of her death England sent planes flying low over the island in a show of force—so low, according to my aunt's letter, that the downdraft from them shook the ripened mangoes from the trees in Da-duh's orchard. Frightened, everyone in the village fled into the canes. Except Da-duh. She remained in the house at the window so my aunt said, watching as the planes came swooping and screaming like monstrous birds down over the village, over her house, rattling her trees and flattening the young canes in her field. It must have seemed to her lying there that they did not intend pulling out of their dive, but like the hard-back beetles which hurled themselves with suicidal force against the walls of the house at night, those menacing silver shapes would hurl themselves in an ecstasy of self-immolation onto the land, destroying it utterly.

When the planes finally left and the villagers returned they found her dead on the Berbice chair at the window.

She died and I lived, but always, to this day even, within the shadow of her death. For a brief period after I was grown I went to live alone, like one doing penance, in a loft above a noisy factory in downtown New York and there painted seas of sugar-cane and huge swirling Van Gogh suns and palm trees striding like brightly-plumed Tutsi warriors across a tropical landscape, while the thunderous tread of the machines downstairs jarred the floor beneath my easel, mocking my efforts.

QUESTIONS FOR DISCUSSION AND WRITING

1. How does the meeting at the airport establish the tension between the narrator and Da-duh? Why does Da-duh refuse to go to town when the narrator's family leaves? Why does the narrator describe her paintings and the thunderous machines at the end of the story?

2. What is significant about the narrator's first view of Da-duh? In what ways do Da-duh's tours of the ground and questions about New York City exhibit her qualities as woman and child? What do the narrator's "performances" reveal about her character?

3. How does Da-duh describe her world? How does the narrator describe New York City? How does the narrator's description of the Empire State Building affect Da-duh's attitude toward her "ground"?

4. How does the narrator's first sentence suggest her difficulties in interpreting the events in the story? Now that she has grown up, why does she describe her life as doing "penance"?

5. How does Da-duh's reaction to the English airplanes establish her attitude toward change? How does the title of the story suggest what the narrator has learned about herself and her grandmother?

Stories for Comparison

Katherine Mansfield's "Her First Ball" (pages 102–106); Sarah Orne Jewett's "A White Heron" (pages 706–714).

72

....

BOBBIE ANN MASON

Shiloh

BOBBIE ANN MASON was born in 1940 in Mayfield, Kentucky, and educated at the University of Kentucky, the State University of New York at
Binghamton, and the University of Connecticut. In the 1960s Mason worked
as a writer for various fan magazines, including *Movie Stars, Movie Life,* and
T.V. Star Parade. After several years of writing about such teen idols as
Fabian and Annette Funicello, Mason decided to return to graduate school to
study literature, writing her doctoral dissertation on Nabokov. After graduate
school, she immersed herself in popular culture once again by reading children's books such as the Nancy Drew series. In 1972 Mason accepted a
teaching position at Mansfield State College in Pennsylvania. In 1974 she
published her first book, *Nabokov's Garden: A Study of Ada,* and in 1975 her
second, *The Girl Sleuth: A Feminist Guide to the Bobbsey Twins, Nancy
Drew and Their Sisters.* Mason has contributed most of her short stories to
The New Yorker. Her recent work includes three novels, *In Country* (1985),
Spence and Lila (1988) and, *Feather Crowns* (1993), and a collection of stories, *Love Life: Stories* (1989). "Shiloh," reprinted from *Shiloh and Other
Stories* (1982), describes the marriage of a disabled truck driver and his wife.

Leroy Moffitt's wife, Norma Jean, is working on her pectorals. She lifts three-
pound dumbbells to warm up, then progresses to a twenty-pound barbell. Standing with her legs apart, she reminds Leroy of Wonder Woman.

"I'd give anything if I could just get these muscles to where they're real hard,"
says Norma Jean. "Feel this arm. It's not as hard as the other one."

"That's 'cause you're right-handed," says Leroy, dodging as she swings the barbell in an arc.

"Do you think so?"

5   "Sure."

Leroy is a truckdriver. He injured his leg in a highway accident four months ago,
and his physical therapy, which involves weights and a pulley, prompted Norma Jean
to try building herself up. Now she is attending a body-building class. Leroy has been
collecting temporary disability since his tractor-trailer jackknifed in Missouri, badly
twisting his left leg in its socket. He has a steel pin in his hip. He will probably not be

able to drive his rig again. It sits in the backyard, like a gigantic bird that has flown home to roost. Leroy has been home in Kentucky for three months, and his leg is almost healed, but the accident frightened him and he does not want to drive any more long hauls. He is not sure what to do next. In the meantime, he makes things from craft kits. He started by building a miniature log cabin from notched Popsicle sticks. He varnished it and placed it on the TV set, where it remains. It reminds him of a rustic Nativity scene. Then he tried string art (sailing ships on black velvet), a macramé owl kit, a snap-together B-17 Flying Fortress, and a lamp made out of a model truck, with a light fixture screwed in the top of the cab. At first the kits were diversions, something to kill time, but now he is thinking about building a full-scale log house from a kit. It would be considerably cheaper than building a regular house, and besides, Leroy has grown to appreciate how things are put together. He has begun to realize that in all the years he was on the road he never took time to examine anything. He was always flying past scenery.

"They won't let you build a log cabin in any of the new subdivisions," Norma Jean tells him.

"They will if I tell them it's for you," he says, teasing her. Ever since they were married, he has promised Norma Jean he would build her a new home one day. They have always rented, and the house they live in is small and nondescript. It does not even feel like a home, Leroy realizes now.

Norma Jean works at the Rexall drugstore, and she has acquired an amazing amount of information about cosmetics. When she explains to Leroy the three stages of complexion care, involving creams, toners, and moisturizers, he thinks happily of other petroleum products—axle grease, diesel fuel. This is a connection between him and Norma Jean. Since he has been home, he has felt unusually tender about his wife and guilty over his long absences. But he can't tell what she feels about him. Norma Jean has never complained about his traveling; she has never made hurt remarks, like calling his truck a "widow-maker." He is reasonably certain she has been faithful to him, but he wishes she would celebrate his permanent homecoming more happily. Norma Jean is often startled to find Leroy at home, and he thinks she seems a little disappointed about it. Perhaps he reminds her too much of the early days of their marriage, before he went on the road. They had a child who died as an infant, years ago. They never speak about their memories of Randy, which have almost faded, but now that Leroy is home all the time, they sometimes feel awkward around each other, and Leroy wonders if one of them should mention the child. He has the feeling that they are waking up out of a dream together—that they must create a new marriage, start afresh. They are lucky they are still married. Leroy has read that for most people losing a child destroys the marriage—or else he heard this on *Donahue*. He can't always remember where he learns things anymore.

At Christmas, Leroy bought an electric organ for Norma Jean. She used to play 10 the piano when she was in high school. "It don't leave you," she told him once. "It's like riding a bicycle."

The new instrument had so many keys and buttons that she was bewildered by it at first. She touched the keys tentatively, pushed some buttons, then pecked out "Chopsticks." It came out in an amplified fox-trot rhythm, with marimba sounds.

"It's an orchestra!" she cried.

The organ had a pecan-look finish and eighteen preset chords, with optional flute, violin, trumpet, clarinet, and banjo accompaniments. Norma Jean mastered the organ almost immediately. At first she played Christmas songs. Then she bought *The Sixties Songbook* and learned every tune in it, adding variations to each with the rows of brightly colored buttons.

"I didn't like these old songs back then," she said. "But I have this crazy feeling I missed something."

15   "You didn't miss a thing," said Leroy.

Leroy likes to lie on the couch and smoke a joint and listen to Norma Jean play "Can't Take My Eyes Off You" and "I'll Be Back." He is back again. After fifteen years on the road, he is finally settling down with the woman he loves. She is still pretty. Her skin is flawless. Her frosted curls resemble pencil trimmings.

Now that Leroy has come home to stay, he notices how much the town has changed. Subdivisions are spreading across western Kentucky like an oil slick. The sign at the edge of town says "Pop: 11,500"—only seven hundred more than it said twenty years before. Leroy can't figure out who is living in all the new houses. The farmers who used to gather around the courthouse square on Saturday afternoons to play checkers and spit tobacco juice have gone. It has been years since Leroy has thought about the farmers, and they have disappeared without his noticing.

Leroy meets a kid named Stevie Hamilton in the parking lot at the new shopping center. While they pretend to be strangers meeting over a stalled car, Stevie tosses an ounce of marijuana under the front seat of Leroy's car. Stevie is wearing orange jogging shoes and a T-shirt that says CHATTAHOOCHEE SUPER-RAT. His father is a prominent doctor who lives in one of the expensive subdivisions in a new white-columned brick house that looks like a funeral parlor. In the phone book under his name there is a separate number, with the listing "Teenagers."

"Where do you get this stuff?" asks Leroy. "From your pappy?"

20   "That's for me to know and you to find out," Stevie says. He is slit-eyed and skinny.

"What else you got?"

"What you interested in?"

"Nothing special. Just wondered."

Leroy used to take speed on the road. Now he has to go slowly. He needs to be mellow. He leans back against the car and says, "I'm aiming to build me a log house, soon as I get time. My wife, though, I don't think she likes the idea."

25   "Well, let me know when you want me again," Stevie says. He has a cigarette in his cupped palm, as though sheltering it from the wind. He takes a long drag, then stomps it on the asphalt and slouches away.

Stevie's father was two years ahead of Leroy in high school. Leroy is thirty-four. He married Norma Jean when they were both eighteen, and their child Randy was born a few months later, but he died at the age of four months and three days. He would be about Stevie's age now. Norma Jean and Leroy were at the drive-in, watching a double feature (*Dr. Strangelove* and *Lover Come Back),* and the baby was sleeping in the back seat. When the first movie ended, the baby was dead. It was the sudden infant death syndrome. Leroy remembers handing Randy to a nurse at the emergency room, as though he were offering her a large doll as a present. A dead baby feels like a sack of flour. "It just happens sometimes," said the doctor, in what Leroy always recalls as a nonchalant tone. Leroy can hardly remember the child anymore, but he still sees vividly a scene from *Dr. Strangelove* in which the President of the United States was talking in a folksy voice on the hot line to the Soviet premier about the bomber accidentally headed toward Russia. He was in the War Room, and the world map was lit up. Leroy remembers Norma Jean standing catatonically beside him in the hospital and himself thinking: Who is this strange girl? He had forgotten who she was. Now scientists are saying that crib death is caused by a virus. Nobody knows anything, Leroy thinks. The answers are always changing.

When Leroy gets home from the shopping center, Norma Jean's mother, Mabel Beasley, is there. Until this year, Leroy has not realized how much time she spends with Norma Jean. When she visits, she inspects the closets and then the plants, informing Norma Jean when a plant is droopy or yellow. Mabel calls the plants "flowers," although there are never any blooms. She always notices if Norma Jean's laundry is piling up. Mabel is a short, overweight woman whose tight, brown-dyed curls look more like a wig than the actual wig she sometimes wears. Today she has brought Norma Jean an off-white dust ruffle she made for the bed; Mabel works in a custom-upholstery shop.

"This is the tenth one I made this year," Mabel says. "I got started and couldn't stop."

"It's real pretty," says Norma Jean.

"Now we can hide things under the bed," says Leroy, who gets along with his mother-in-law primarily by joking with her. Mabel has never really forgiven him for disgracing her by getting Norma Jean pregnant. When the baby died, she said that fate was mocking her.

"What's that thing?" Mabel says to Leroy in a loud voice, pointing to a tangle of yarn on a piece of canvas.

Leroy holds it up for Mabel to see. "It's my needlepoint," he explains. "This is a *Star Trek* pillow cover."

"That's what a woman would do," says Mabel. "Great day in the morning!"

"All the big football players on TV do it," he says.

"Why, Leroy, you're always trying to fool me. I don't believe you for one minute. You don't know what to do with yourself—that's the whole trouble. Sewing!"

"I'm aiming to build us a log house," says Leroy. "Soon as my plans come."

"Like *heck* you are," says Norma Jean. She takes Leroy's needlepoint and shoves it into a drawer. "You have to find a job first. Nobody can afford to build now anyway."

Mabel straightens her girdle and says, "I still think before you get tied down y'all ought to take a little run to Shiloh."

"One of these days, Mama," Norma Jean says impatiently.

40   Mabel is talking about Shiloh, Tennessee. For the past few years, she has been urging Leroy and Norma Jean to visit the Civil War battleground there. Mabel went there on her honeymoon—the only real trip she ever took. Her husband died of a perforated ulcer when Norma Jean was ten, but Mabel, who was accepted into the United Daughters of the Confederacy in 1975, is still preoccupied with going back to Shiloh.

"I've been to kingdom come and back in that truck out yonder," Leroy says to Mabel, "but we never yet set foot in that battleground. Ain't that something? How did I miss it?"

"It's not even that far," Mabel says.

After Mabel leaves, Norma Jean reads to Leroy from a list she has made. "Things you could do," she announces. "You could get a job as a guard at Union Carbide, where they'd let you set on a stool. You could get on at the lumberyard. You could do a little carpenter work, if you want to build so bad. You could—"

"I can't do something where I'd have to stand up all day."

45   "You ought to try standing up all day behind a cosmetics counter. It's amazing that I have strong feet, coming from two parents that never had strong feet at all." At the moment Norma Jean is holding on to the kitchen counter, raising her knees one at a time as she talks. She is wearing two-pound ankle weights.

"Don't worry," says Leroy. "I'll do something."

"You could truck calves to slaughter for somebody. You wouldn't have to drive any big old truck for that."

"I'm going to build you this house," says Leroy. "I want to make you a real home."

"I don't want to live in any log cabin."

50   "It's not a cabin. It's a house."

"I don't care. It looks like a cabin."

"You and me together could lift those logs. It's just like lifting weights."

Norma Jean doesn't answer. Under her breath, she is counting. Now she is marching through the kitchen. She is doing goose steps.

Before his accident, when Leroy came home he used to stay in the house with Norma Jean, watching TV in bed and playing cards. She would cook fried chicken, picnic ham, chocolate pie—all his favorites. Now he is home alone much of the time. In the mornings, Norma Jean disappears, leaving a cooling place in the bed. She eats a cereal called Body Buddies, and she leaves the bowl on the table, with the soggy tan balls floating in a milk puddle. He sees things about Norma Jean that he never realized before. When she chops onions, she stares off into a corner, as if she can't bear to look. She puts on her house slippers almost precisely at nine o'clock every evening and nudges her jogging shoes under the couch. She saves bread heels for the birds. Leroy watches the birds at the feeder. He notices the peculiar way goldfinches fly past the window. They close their wings, then fall, then spread their wings to catch and lift themselves. He wonders if they close their eyes when they fall. Norma Jean closes her eyes when they are in bed. She wants the lights turned out. Even then, he is sure she closes her eyes.

He goes for long drives around town. He tends to drive a car rather carelessly.   55
Power steering and an automatic shift make a car feel so small and inconsequential
that his body is hardly involved in the driving process. His injured leg stretches out
comfortably. Once or twice he has almost hit something, but even the prospect of an
accident seems minor in a car. He cruises the new subdivisions, feeling like a criminal rehearsing for a robbery. Norma Jean is probably right about a log house being
inappropriate here in the new subdivisions. All the houses look grand and complicated. They depress him.

One day when Leroy comes home from a drive he finds Norma Jean in tears.
She is in the kitchen making a potato and mushroom-soup casserole, with grated-
cheese topping. She is crying because her mother caught her smoking.

"I didn't hear her coming. I was standing here puffing away pretty as you
please," Norma Jean says, wiping her eyes.

"I knew it would happen sooner or later," says Leroy, putting his arm around her.

"She don't know the meaning of the word 'knock,'" says Norma Jean. "It's a
wonder she hadn't caught me years ago."

"Think of it this way," Leroy says. "What if she caught me with a joint?"   60

"You better not let her!" Norma Jean shrieks. "I'm warning you, Leroy Moffitt!"

"I'm just kidding. Here, play me a tune. That'll help you relax."

Norma Jean puts the casserole in the oven and sets the timer. Then she plays a
ragtime tune, with horns and banjo, as Leroy lights up a joint and lies on the couch,
laughing to himself about Mabel's catching him at it. He thinks of Stevie Hamilton—
a doctor's son pushing grass. Everything is funny. The whole town seems crazy and
small. He is reminded of Virgil Mathis, a boastful policeman Leroy used to shoot pool
with. Virgil recently led a drug bust in a back room at a bowling alley, where he seized
ten thousand dollars' worth of marijuana. The newspaper had a picture of him holding up the bags of grass and grinning widely. Right now, Leroy can imagine Virgil
breaking down the door and arresting him with a lungful of smoke. Virgil would probably have been alerted to the scene because of all the racket Norma Jean is making.
Now she sounds like a hard-rock band. Norma Jean is terrific. When she switches to
a Latin-rhythm version of "Sunshine Superman," Leroy hums along. Norma Jean's
foot goes up and down, up and down.

"Well, what do you think?" Leroy says, when Norma Jean pauses to search
through her music.

"What do I think about what?"   65

His mind had gone blank. Then he says, "I'll sell my rig and build us a house."
That wasn't what he wanted to say. He wanted to know what she thought—what she
really thought—about them.

"Don't start in on that again," says Norma Jean. She begins playing "Who'll Be
the Next in Line?"

Leroy used to tell hitchhikers his whole life story—about his travels, his home-
town, the baby. He would end with a question: "Well, what do you think?" It was just
a rhetorical question. In time, he had the feeling that he'd been telling the same story
over and over to the same hitchhikers. He quit talking to hitchhikers when he realized
how his voice sounded—whining and self-pitying, like some teenage-tragedy song.

Now Leroy has the sudden impulse to tell Norma Jean about himself, as if he had just met her. They have known each other so long they have forgotten a lot about each other. They could become reacquainted. But when the oven timer goes off and she runs to the kitchen, he forgets why he wants to do this.

The next day, Mabel drops by. It is Saturday and Norma Jean is cleaning. Leroy is studying the plans of his log house, which have finally come in the mail. He has them spread out on the table—big sheets of stiff blue paper, with diagrams and numbers printed in white. While Norma Jean runs the vacuum, Mabel drinks coffee. She sets her coffee cup on a blueprint.

70   "I'm just waiting for time to pass," she says to Leroy, drumming her fingers on the table.

As soon as Norma Jean switches off the vacuum, Mabel says in a loud voice, "Did you hear about the datsun dog that killed the baby?"

Norma Jean says, "The word is 'dachshund.'"

"They put the dog on trial. It chewed the baby's legs off. The mother was in the next room all the time." She raises her voice. "They thought it was neglect."

Norma Jean is holding her ears. Leroy manages to open the refrigerator and get some Diet Pepsi to offer Mabel. Mabel still has some coffee and she waves away the Pepsi.

75   "Datsuns are like that," Mabel says. "They're jealous dogs. They'll tear a place to pieces if you don't keep an eye on them."

"You better watch out what you're saying, Mabel," says Leroy.

"Well, facts is facts."

Leroy looks out the window at his rig. It is like a huge piece of furniture gathering dust in the backyard. Pretty soon it will be an antique. He hears the vacuum cleaner. Norma Jean seems to be cleaning the living room rug again.

Later, she says to Leroy, "She just said that about the baby because she caught me smoking. She's trying to pay me back."

80   "What are you talking about?" Leroy says, nervously shuffling blueprints.

"You know good and well," Norma Jean says. She is sitting in a kitchen chair with her feet up and her arms wrapped around her knees. She looks small and helpless. She says, "The very idea, her bringing up a subject like that! Saying it was neglect."

"She didn't mean that," Leroy says.

"She might not have *thought* she meant it. She always says things like that. You don't know how she goes on."

"But she didn't really mean it. She was just talking."

85   Leroy opens a king-sized bottle of beer and pours it into two glasses, dividing it carefully. He hands a glass to Norma Jean and she takes it from him mechanically. For a long time, they sit by the kitchen window watching the birds at the feeder.

Something is happening. Norma Jean is going to night school. She has graduated from her six-week body-building course and now she is taking an adult-education course in composition at Paducah Community College. She spends her evenings outlining paragraphs.

"First you have a topic sentence," she explains to Leroy. "Then you divide it up. Your secondary topic has to be connected to your primary topic."

To Leroy, this sounds intimidating. "I never was any good in English," he says. "It makes a lot of sense."

"What are you doing this for, anyhow?"   90

She shrugs. "It's something to do." She stands up and lifts her dumbbells a few times.

"Driving a rig, nobody cared about my English."

"I'm not criticizing your English."

Norma Jean used to say, "If I lose ten minutes' sleep, I just drag all day." Now she stays up late, writing compositions. She got a B on her first paper—a how-to-theme on soup-based casseroles. Recently Norma Jean has been cooking unusual foods—tacos, lasagna, Bombay chicken. She doesn't play the organ anymore, though her second paper was called "Why Music Is Important to Me." She sits at the kitchen table, concentrating on her outlines, while Leroy plays with his log house plans, practicing with a set of Lincoln Logs. The thought of getting a truck-load of notched, numbered logs scares him, and he wants to be prepared. As he and Norma Jean work together at the kitchen table, Leroy has the hopeful thought that they are sharing something, but he knows he is a fool to think this. Norma Jean is miles away. He knows he is going to lose her. Like Mabel, he is just waiting for time to pass.

One day, Mabel is there before Norma Jean gets home from work, and Leroy   95 finds himself confiding in her. Mabel, he realizes, must know Norma Jean better than he does.

"I don't know what's got into that girl," Mabel says. "She used to go to bed with the chickens. Now you say she's up all hours. Plus her a-smoking. I like to died."

"I want to make her this beautiful home," Leroy says, indicating the Lincoln Logs. "I don't think she even wants it. Maybe she was happier with me gone."

"She don't know what to make of you, coming home like this."

"Is that it?"

Mabel takes the roof off his Lincoln Log cabin. "You couldn't get *me* in a log   100 cabin," she says. "I was raised in one. It's no picnic, let me tell you."

"They're different now," says Leroy.

"I tell you what," Mabel says, smiling oddly at Leroy.

"What?"

"Take her on down to Shiloh. Y'all need to get out together, stir a little. Her brain's all balled up over them books."

Leroy can see traces of Norma Jean's features in her mother's face. Mabel's   105 worn face has the texture of crinkled cotton, but suddenly she looks pretty. It occurs to Leroy that Mabel has been hinting all along that she wants them to take her with them to Shiloh.

"Let's all go to Shiloh," he says. "You and me and her. Come Sunday."

Mabel throws up her hand in protest. "Oh, no, not me. Young folks want to be by theirselves."

When Norma Jean comes in with groceries, Leroy says excitedly, "Your mama here's been dying to go to Shiloh for thirty-five years. It's about time we went, don't you think?"

"I'm not going to butt in on anybody's second honeymoon," Mabel says.

110   "Who's going on a honeymoon, for Christ's sake?" Norma Jean says loudly.

"I never raised no daughter of mine to talk that-a-way," Mabel says.

"You ain't seen nothing yet," says Norma Jean. She starts putting away boxes and cans, slamming cabinet doors.

"There's a log cabin at Shiloh," Mabel says. "It was there during the battle. There's bullet holes in it."

"When are you going to *shut up* about Shiloh, Mama?" asks Norma Jean.

115   "I always thought Shiloh was the prettiest place, so full of history," Mabel goes on. "I just hoped y'all could see it once before I die, so you could tell me about it." Later, she whispers to Leroy, "You do what I said. A little change is what she needs."

"Your name means 'the king,'" Norma Jean says to Leroy that evening. He is trying to get her to go to Shiloh, and she is reading a book about another century.

"Well, I reckon I ought to be right proud."

"I guess so."

"Am I still king around here?"

120   Norma Jean flexes her biceps and feels them for hardness. "I'm not fooling around with anybody, if that's what you mean," she says.

"Would you tell me if you were?"

"I don't know."

"What does *your* name mean?"

"It was Marilyn Monroe's real name."

125   "No kidding!"

"Norma comes from the Normans. They were invaders," she says. She closes her book and looks hard at Leroy. "I'll go to Shiloh with you if you'll stop staring at me."

On Sunday, Norma Jean packs a picnic and they go to Shiloh. To Leroy's relief, Mabel says she does not want to come with them. Norma Jean drives, and Leroy, sitting beside her, feels like some boring hitchhiker she has picked up. He tries some conversation, but she answers him in monosyllables. At Shiloh, she drives aimlessly through the park, past bluffs and trails and steep ravines. Shiloh is an immense place, and Leroy cannot see it as a battleground. It is not what he expected. He thought it would look like a golf course. Monuments are everywhere, showing through the thick clusters of trees. Norma Jean passes the log cabin Mabel mentioned. It is surrounded by tourists looking for bullet holes.

"That's not the kind of log house I've got in mind," says Leroy apologetically.

"I know *that.*"

130   "This is a pretty place. Your mama was right."

"It's O.K.," says Norma Jean. "Well, we've seen it. I hope she's satisfied."

They burst out laughing together.

At the park museum, a movie on Shiloh is shown every half hour, but they decide that they don't want to see it. They buy a souvenir Confederate flag for Mabel, and then they find a picnic spot near the cemetery. Norma Jean has brought a picnic cooler, with pimiento sandwiches, soft drinks, and Yodels. Leroy eats a sandwich and then smokes a joint, hiding it behind the picnic cooler. Norma Jean has quit smoking altogether. She is picking cake crumbs from the cellophane wrapper, like a fussy bird.

Leroy says, "So the boys in gray ended up in Corinth. The Union soldiers zapped 'em finally. April 7, 1862."

They both know that he doesn't know any history. He is just talking about some 135 of the historical plaques they have read. He feels awkward, like a boy on a date with an older girl. They are still just making conversation.

"Corinth is where Mama eloped to," says Norma Jean.

They sit in silence and stare at the cemetery for the Union dead and, beyond, at a tall cluster of trees. Campers are parked nearby, bumper to bumper, and small children in bright clothing are cavorting and squealing. Norma Jean wads up the cake wrapper and squeezes it tightly in her hand. Without looking at Leroy, she says, "I want to leave you."

Leroy takes a bottle of Coke out of the cooler and flips off the cap. He holds the bottle poised near his mouth but cannot remember to take a drink. Finally he says, "No, you don't."

"Yes, I do."

"I won't let you."   140

"You can't stop me."

"Don't do me that way."

Leroy knows Norma Jean will have her own way. "Didn't I promise to be home from now on?" he says.

"In some ways, a woman prefers a man who wanders," says Norma Jean. "That sounds crazy, I know."

"You're not crazy."   145

Leroy remembers to drink from his Coke. Then he says, "Yes, you *are* crazy. You and me could start all over again. Right back at the beginning."

"We *have* started all over again," says Norma Jean. "And this is how it turned out."

"What did I do wrong?"

"Nothing."

"Is this one of those women's lib things?" Leroy asks.   150

"Don't be funny."

The cemetery, a green slope dotted with white markers, looks like a subdivision site. Leroy is trying to comprehend that his marriage is breaking up, but for some reason he is wondering about white slabs in a graveyard.

"Everything was fine till Mama caught me smoking," says Norma Jean, standing up. "That's set something off."

"What are you talking about?"

"She won't leave me alone—*you* won't leave me alone." Norma Jean seems to 155 be crying, but she is looking away from him. "I feel eighteen again. I can't face that all over again." She starts walking away. "No, it *wasn't* fine. I don't know what I'm saying. Forget it."

Leroy takes a lungful of smoke and closes his eyes as Norma Jean's words sink in. He tries to focus on the fact that thirty-five hundred soldiers died on the grounds around him. He can only think of that war as a board game with plastic soldiers. Leroy almost smiles, as he compares the Confederates' daring attack on the Union camps and Virgil Mathis's raid on the bowling alley. General Grant, drunk and furious, shoved the Southerners back to Corinth, where Mabel and Jet Beasley were married years later, when Mabel was still thin and good-looking. The next day, Mabel and Jet visited the battleground, and then Norma Jean was born, and then she married Leroy and they had a baby, which they lost, and now Leroy and Norma Jean are here at the same battleground. Leroy knows he is leaving out a lot. He is leaving out the insides of history. History was always just names and dates to him. It occurs to him that building a house out of logs is similarly empty—too simple. And the real inner workings of a marriage, like most of history, have escaped him. Now he sees that building a log house is the dumbest idea he could have had. It was clumsy of him to think Norma Jean would want a log house. It was a crazy idea. He'll have to think of something else, quickly. He will wad the blueprints into tight balls and fling them into the lake. Then he'll get moving again. He opens his eyes. Norma Jean has moved away and is walking through the cemetery, following a serpentine brick path.

Leroy gets up to follow his wife, but his good leg is asleep and his bad leg still hurts him. Norma Jean is far away, walking rapidly toward the bluff by the river, and he tries to hobble toward her. Some children run past him, screaming noisily. Norma Jean has reached the bluff, and she is looking out over the Tennessee River. Now she turns toward Leroy and waves her arms. Is she beckoning to him? She seems to be doing an exercise for her chest muscles. The sky is unusually pale—the color of the dust ruffle Mabel made for their bed.

QUESTIONS FOR DISCUSSION AND WRITING

1. How does Leroy's accident produce new conflicts in his marriage? What old conflicts have he and Norma Jean failed to resolve? How does the trip to Shiloh clarify these conflicts?

2. How do Leroy's diversions with craft kits establish his character? How do Norma Jean's body building, organ playing, and night school establish her character? What effect does Mabel have on her children?

3. Now that he is no longer on the road, what details does Leroy notice about his home and community? What does he hope to accomplish by building a log cabin? Why is the Shiloh battleground—and, in particular, the log cabin filled with bullet holes—an appropriate setting for the conclusion of the story?

4. In what sense is this story, told from Leroy's point of view, similar to the stories he used to tell hitchhikers in his rig? What specific evidence prompts him to suggest that something is happening to his marriage?

5. What does Leroy learn about "the insides of history" at Shiloh? How does this lesson pertain to Leroy and Norma Jean's life? What have they "swept under" the dust ruffle made for their bed?

Stories for Comparison

James Joyce's "The Dead" (pages 728–756); John Steinbeck's "The Chrysanthemums" (pages 1081–1089).

73

....

H E R M A N   M E L V I L L E

Bartleby the Scrivener
A Story of Wall-Street

HERMAN MELVILLE (1819–1891) was born in New York City, the son of a merchant who went bankrupt in 1830. Two years later his father died, and Melville was forced to withdraw from school, working briefly as a farm laborer, a bank messenger, a clerk in his brother's store, and after two additional years of education, an elementary schoolteacher. In 1839, Melville escaped the boredom of the schoolroom for life at sea, traveling to Liverpool as a merchant seaman. On his return, Melville tried to find employment writing documents for lawyers. But in 1841 he gave up his ambition to be a legal scrivener and shipped out to the South Pacific, where during the next four years he jumped ship, lived among the cannibals, took part in a mutiny, worked as a harpooner, and found his way home on the American naval frigate *United States*. Melville began writing about his adventures in novels such as *Typee* (1846), *Omoo* (1847), and *Redburn* (1849). These early books established Melville's reputation as a popular adventure writer—as "the man who lived among the cannibals"—but that reputation soon declined when he began publishing more philosophical books such as *Mardi* (1849) and his masterpiece, *Moby-Dick* (1851). Although his work continued to receive enthusiastic criticism from fellow writers such as Nathaniel Hawthorne, Melville's later novels—including *Pierre* (1852) and *The Confidence-Man* (1857)—were commercial failures. He drifted from one job to another, finally acquiring the position of collector of customs at New York harbor. During this period, Melville wrote a long poetic account of a pilgrimage to the Holy Land, *Clarel* (1876), which was virtually ignored by the critics.

Believing his work was a public failure, Melville became bitter and eventually died in obscurity. In the 1920s, Melville's reputation was restored and another masterpiece, *Billy Budd* (1924), was discovered in his literary effects. "Bartleby the Scrivener: A Story of Wall-Street," reprinted from *Piazza Tales* (1856), recounts a good and earnest man's attempt to understand another man's "passive resistance."

I am a rather elderly man. The nature of my avocations, for the last thirty years, has brought me into more than ordinary contact with what would seem an interesting and somewhat singular set of men, of whom, as yet, nothing, that I know of, has ever been written—I mean, the law-copyists, or scriveners. I have known very many of them, professionally and privately, and, if I pleased, could relate divers histories, at which good-natured gentlemen might smile, and sentimental souls might weep. But I waive the biographies of all other scriveners, for a few passages in the life of Bartleby, who was a scrivener, the strangest I ever saw, or heard of. While, of other law-copyists, I might write the complete life, of Bartleby nothing of that sort can be done. I believe that no materials exist for a full and satisfactory biography of this man. It is an irreparable loss to literature. Bartleby was one of those beings of whom nothing is ascertainable, except from the original sources, and, in his case, those are very small. What my own astonished eyes saw of Bartleby, *that* is all I know of him, except, indeed, one vague report, which will appear in the sequel.

Ere introducing the scrivener, as he first appeared to me, it is fit I make some mention of myself, my employees, my business, my chambers, and general surroundings; because some such description is indispensable to an adequate understanding of the chief character about to be presented. Imprimis: I am a man who, from his youth upwards, has been filled with a profound conviction that the easiest way of life is the best. Hence, though I belong to a profession proverbially energetic and nervous, even to turbulence, at times, yet nothing of that sort have I ever suffered to invade my peace. I am one of those unambitious lawyers who never addresses a jury, or in any way draws down public applause; but, in the cool tranquillity of a snug retreat, do a snug business among rich men's bonds, and mortgages, and title-deeds. All who know me, consider me an eminently *safe* man. The late John Jacob Astor, a personage little given to poetic enthusiasm, had no hesitation in pronouncing my first grand point to be prudence; my next, method. I do not speak it in vanity, but simply record the fact, that I was not unemployed in my profession by the late John Jacob Astor; a name which, I admit, I love to repeat; for it hath a rounded and orbicular sound to it, and rings like unto bullion. I will freely add, that I was not insensible to the late John Jacob Astor's good opinion.

Some time prior to the period at which this little history begins, my avocations had been largely increased. The good old office, now extinct in the State of New York, of a Master in Chancery, had been conferred upon me. It was not a very arduous office, but very pleasantly remunerative. I seldom lose my temper; much more seldom indulge in dangerous indignation at wrongs and outrages; but, I must be permitted to be rash here, and declare that I consider the sudden and violent abrogation of the office of Master in Chancery, by the new Constitution, as a—premature act; inasmuch as I had counted upon a life-lease of the profits, whereas I only received those of a few short years. But this is by the way.

My chambers were up stairs, at No.———Wall Street. At one end, they looked upon the white wall of the interior of a spacious sky-light shaft, penetrating the building from top to bottom.

This view might have been considered rather tame than otherwise, deficient in what landscape painters call "life." But, if so, the view from the other end of my chambers offered, at least, a contrast, if nothing more. In that direction, my windows commanded an unobstructed view of a lofty brick wall, black by age and everlasting shade; which wall required no spyglass to bring out its lurking beauties, but, for the benefit of all near-sighted spectators, was pushed up to within ten feet of my window panes. Owing to the great height of the surrounding buildings, and my chambers being on the second floor, the interval between this wall and mine not a little resembled a huge square cistern.

At the period just preceding the advent of Bartleby, I had two persons as copyists in my employment, and a promising lad as an office-boy. First, Turkey; second, Nippers; third, Ginger Nut. These may seem names, the like of which are not usually found in the Directory. In truth, they were nicknames, mutually conferred upon each other by my three clerks, and were deemed expressive of their respective persons or characters. Turkey was a short, pursy Englishman, of about my own age— that is, somewhere not far from sixty. In the morning, one might say, his face was of a fine florid hue, but after twelve o'clock, meridian—his dinner hour—it blazed like a grate full of Christmas coals; and continued blazing—but, as it were, with a gradual wane—till six o'clock P.M., or thereabouts; after which, I saw no more of the proprietor of the face, which, gaining its meridian with the sun, seemed to set with it, to rise, culminate, and decline the following day, with the like regularity and undiminished glory. There are many singular coincidences I have known in the course of my life, not the least among which was the fact, that, exactly when Turkey displayed his fullest beams from his red and radiant countenance, just then, too, at that critical moment, began the daily period when I considered his business capacities as seriously disturbed for the remainder of the twenty-four hours. Not that he was absolutely idle, or averse to business, then; far from it. The difficulty was, he was apt to be altogether too energetic. There was a strange, inflamed, flurried, flighty recklessness of activity about him. He would be incautious in dipping his pen into his inkstand. All his blots upon my documents were dropped there after twelve o'clock meridian. Indeed, not only would he be reckless, and sadly given to making blots in the afternoon, but, some days, he went further, and was rather noisy. At such times, too, his face flamed with augmented blazonry, as if cannel coal had been heaped on anthracite. He made an unpleasant racket with his chair; spilled his sand-box; in mending his pens, impatiently split them all to pieces, and threw them on the floor in a sudden passion; stood up, and leaned over his table, boxing his papers about in a most indecorous manner, very sad to behold in an elderly man like him. Nevertheless, as he was in many ways a most valuable person to me, and all the time before twelve o'clock meridian, was the quickest, steadiest creature, too, accomplishing a great deal of work in a style not easily to be matched—for these reasons, I was willing to overlook his eccentricities, though, indeed, occasionally, I remonstrated with him. I did this very gently, however, because, though the civilest, nay, the blandest and most reverential of men in the morning, yet, in the afternoon, he was disposed, upon provocation, to be slightly rash with his tongue—in fact, insolent. Now, valuing his morning services as I did, and resolved not to lose them—yet, at the same time, made uncomfortable by his inflamed ways after twelve o'clock—and being a man of peace, unwilling by my admonitions to call forth unseemly retorts from him, I took upon me, one Saturday noon (he was always worse on Saturdays) to hint to him, very kindly, that, perhaps, now that he was growing old, it might be well to abridge his labors; in short, he need not come to my chambers after twelve o'clock, but, dinner over, had best go home to his lodgings, and rest himself till tea-time. But no; he insisted upon his afternoon devotions. His countenance became intolerably fervid, as he oratorically assured me—gesticulating with a long ruler at the other end of the room—that if his services in the morning were useful, how indispensable, then, in the afternoon?

"With submission, sir," said Turkey, on this occasion, "I consider myself your right-hand man. In the morning I but marshal and deploy my columns; but in the afternoon I put myself at their head, and gallantly charge the foe, thus"—and he made a violent thrust with the ruler.

"But the blots, Turkey," intimated I.

"True; but, with submission, sir, behold these hairs! I am getting old. Surely, sir, a blot or two of a warm afternoon is not to be severely urged against gray hairs. Old age—even if it blot the page—is honorable. With submission, sir, we *both* are getting old."

This appeal to my fellow-feeling was hardly to be resisted. At all events, I saw that go he would not. So, I made up my mind to let him stay, resolving, nevertheless, to see to it that, during the afternoon, he had to do with my less important papers.

Nippers, the second on my list, was a whiskered, sallow, and upon the whole, rather piratical-looking young man, of about five and twenty. I always deemed him the victim of two evil powers—ambition and indigestion. The ambition was evinced by a certain impatience of the duties of a mere copyist, an unwarrantable usurpation of strictly professional affairs, such as the original drawing up of legal documents. The indigestion seemed betokened in an occasional nervous testiness and grinning irritability, causing the teeth to audibly grind together over mistakes committed in copying; unnecessary maledictions, hissed, rather than spoken, in the heat of business; and especially by a continual discontent with the height of the table where he worked. Though of a very ingenious, mechanical turn, Nippers could never get this table to suit him. He put chips under it, blocks of various sorts, bits of pasteboard, and at last went so far as to attempt an exquisite adjustment, by final pieces of folded blotting-paper. But no invention would answer. If, for the sake of easing his back, he brought the table lid at a sharp angle well up towards his chin, and wrote there like a man using the steep roof of a Dutch house for his desk, then he declared that it stopped the circulation in his arms. If now he lowered the table to his waistbands, and stooped over it in writing, then there was a sore aching in his back. In short, the truth of the matter was, Nippers knew not what he wanted. Or, if he wanted anything, it was to be rid of a scrivener's table altogether. Among the manifestations of his diseased ambition was a fondness he had for receiving visits from certain ambiguous-looking fellows in seedy coats, whom he called his clients. Indeed, I was aware that not only was he, at times, considerable of a ward-politician, but he occasionally did a little business at the Justices' courts, and was not unknown on the steps of the Tombs. I have good reason to believe, however, that one individual who called upon him at my chambers, and who, with a grand air, he insisted was his client, was no other than a dun, and the alleged title-deed, a bill. But, with all his failings, and the annoyances he caused me, Nippers, like his compatriot Turkey, was a very useful man to me; wrote a neat, swift hand; and, when he chose, was not deficient in a gentlemanly sort of deportment. Added to this, he always dressed in a gentlemanly sort of way; and so, incidentally, reflected credit upon my chambers. Whereas, with respect to Turkey, I had much ado to keep him from being a reproach to me. His clothes were apt to look oily, and smell of eating-houses. He wore his pantaloons very loose and baggy in summer. His coats were execrable; his hat not to be handled. But while the hat was a thing of indifference to me, inasmuch as his natural civility and deference, as a dependent Englishman, always led him to doff it the moment he entered the room, yet his coat was another matter. Concerning his coats, I reasoned with him; but with no effect. The truth was, I suppose, that a man with so small an income could not afford to sport such a lustrous face and a lustrous coat at one and the same time. As Nippers once observed, Turkey's money went chiefly for red ink. One winter day, I presented Turkey with a highly respectable-looking coat of my own—a padded gray coat, of a most comfortable warmth, and which buttoned straight up from the knee to the neck. I thought Turkey would appreciate the favor, and abate his rashness and obstreperousness of afternoons. But no; I verily believe that buttoning himself up in so downy and blanket-like a coat had a pernicious effect upon him—upon the same principle that too much oats are bad for horses. In fact, precisely as a rash, restive horse is said to feel his oats, so Turkey felt his coat. It made him insolent. He was a man whom prosperity harmed.

Though, concerning the self-indulgent habits of Turkey, I had my own private surmises, yet, touching Nippers, I was well persuaded that, whatever might be his faults in other respects, he was, at least, a temperate young man. But, indeed, nature herself seemed to have been his vintner, and, at his birth, charged him so thoroughly with an irritable, brandy-like disposition, that all subsequent potations were needless. When I consider how, amid the stillness of my chambers, Nippers would sometimes impatiently rise from his seat, and stooping over his table, spread his arms wide apart, seize the whole desk, and move it, and jerk it, with a grim, grinding motion on the floor, as if the table were a perverse voluntary agent and vexing him, I plainly perceive that, for Nippers, brandy-and-water were altogether superfluous.

It was fortunate for me that, owing to its peculiar cause—indigestion—the irritability and consequent nervousness of Nippers were mainly observable in the morning, while in the afternoon he was comparatively mild. So that, Turkey's paroxysms only coming on about twelve o'clock, I never had to do with their eccentricities at one time. Their fits relieved each other, like guards. When Nippers's was on,

Turkey's was off; and *vice versa.* This was a good natural arrangement, under the circumstances.

Ginger Nut, the third on my list, was a lad, some twelve years old. His father was a car-man, ambitious of seeing his son on the bench instead of a cart, before he died. So he sent him to my office, as student at law, errand-boy, cleaner and sweeper, at the rate of one dollar a week. He had a little desk to himself; but he did not use it much. Upon inspection, the drawer exhibited a great array of shells of various sorts of nuts. Indeed, to this quick-witted youth, the whole noble science of the law was contained in a nutshell. Not the least among the employments of Ginger Nut, as well as one which he discharged with the most alacrity, was his duty as cake and apple purveyor for Turkey and Nippers. Copying law-papers being proverbially a dry, husky sort of business, my two scriveners were fain to moisten their mouths very often with Spitzenbergs, to be had at the numerous stalls nigh the Custom House and Post Office. Also, they sent Ginger Nut very frequently for that peculiar cake— small, flat, round, and very spicy—after which he had been named by them. Of a cold morning, when business was but dull, Turkey would gobble up scores of these cakes, as if they were mere wafers—indeed, they sell them at the rate of six or eight for a penny—the scrape of his pen blending with the crunching of the crisp particles in his mouth. Rashest of all the fiery afternoon blunders and flurried rashnesses of Turkey, was his once moistening a ginger-cake between his lips, and clapping it on to a mortgage, for a seal. I came within an ace of dismissing him then. But he mollified me by making an oriental bow, and saying—

15   "With submission, sir, it was generous of me to find you in stationery on my own account."

Now my original business—that of a conveyancer and title hunter, and drawer-up of recondite documents of all sorts—was considerably increased by receiving the master's office. There was now great work for scriveners. Not only must I push the clerks already with me, but I must have additional help.

In answer to my advertisement, a motionless young man one morning stood upon my office threshold, the door being open, for it was summer. I can see that figure now—pallidly neat, pitiably respectable, incurably forlorn! It was Bartleby.

After a few words touching his qualifications, I engaged him, glad to have among my corps of copyists a man of so singularly sedate an aspect, which I thought might operate beneficially upon the flighty temper of Turkey, and the fiery one of Nippers.

I should have stated before that ground glass folding-doors divided my premises into two parts, one of which was occupied by my scriveners, the other by myself. According to my humor, I threw open these doors, or closed them. I resolved to assign Bartleby a corner by the folding-doors, but on my side of them, so as to have this quiet man within easy call, in case any trifling thing was to be done. I placed his desk close up to a small side-window in that part of the room, a window which originally had afforded a lateral view of certain grimy backyards and bricks, but which, owing to subsequent erections, commanded at present no view at all, though it gave some light. Within three feet of the panes was a wall, and the light came down from far above, between two lofty buildings, as from a very small opening in a dome. Still further to a satisfactory arrangement, I procured a high green folding screen, which might entirely isolate Bartleby from my sight, though not remove him from my voice. And thus, in a manner, privacy and society were conjoined.

At first, Bartleby did an extraordinary quantity of writing. As if long famishing 20 for something to copy, he seemed to gorge himself on my documents. There was no pause for digestion. He ran a day and night line, copying by sun-light and by candle-light. I should have been quite delighted with his application, had he been cheerfully industrious. But he wrote on silently, palely, mechanically.

It is, of course, an indispensable part of a scrivener's business to verify the accuracy of his copy, word by word. Where there are two or more scriveners in an office, they assist each other in this examination, one reading from the copy, the other holding the original. It is a very dull, wearisome, and lethargic affair. I can readily imagine that, to some sanguine temperaments, it would be altogether intolerable. For example, I cannot credit that the mettlesome poet, Byron, would have contentedly sat down with Bartleby to examine a law document of, say five hundred pages, closely written in a crimpy hand.

Now and then, in the haste of business, it had been my habit to assist in comparing some brief document myself, calling Turkey or Nippers for this purpose. One object I had, in placing Bartleby so handy to me behind the screen, was to avail myself of his services on such trivial occasions. It was on the third day, I think, of his being with me, and before any necessity had arisen for having his own writing examined, that, being much hurried to complete a small affair I had in hand, I abruptly called to Bartleby. In my haste and natural expectancy of instant compliance, I sat with my head bent over the original on my desk, and my right hand sideways, and somewhat nervously extended with the copy, so that, immediately upon emerging from his retreat, Bartleby might snatch it and proceed to business without the least delay.

In this very attitude did I sit when I called to him, rapidly stating what it was I wanted him to do—namely, to examine a small paper with me. Imagine my surprise, nay, my consternation, when, without moving from his privacy, Bartleby, in a singularly mild, firm voice, replied, "I would prefer not to."

I sat awhile in perfect silence, rallying my stunned faculties. Immediately it occurred to me that my ears had deceived me, or Bartleby had entirely misunderstood my meaning. I repeated my request in the clearest tone I could assume; but in quite as clear a one came the previous reply, "I would prefer not to."

"Prefer not to," echoed I, rising in high excitement, and crossing the room with 25 a stride. "What do you mean? Are you moon-struck? I want you to help me compare this sheet here—take it," and I thrust it towards him.

"I would prefer not to," said he.

I looked at him steadfastly. His face was leanly composed; his gray eye dimly calm. Not a wrinkle of agitation rippled him. Had there been the least uneasiness, anger, impatience, or impertinence in his manner; in other words, had there been any thing ordinarily human about him, doubtless I should have violently dismissed him from the premises. But as it was, I should have as soon thought of turning my pale plaster-of-paris bust of Cicero out of doors. I stood gazing at him awhile, as he went on with his own writing, and then reseated myself at my desk. This is very strange, thought I. What had one best do? But my business hurried me. I concluded to forget the matter for the present, reserving it for my future leisure. So calling Nippers from the other room, the paper was speedily examined.

A few days after this, Bartleby concluded four lengthy documents, being quadruplicates of a week's testimony taken before me in my High Court of Chancery. It became necessary to examine them. It was an important suit, and great accuracy was imperative. Having all things arranged, I called Turkey, Nippers, and Ginger Nut from the next room, meaning to place the four copies in the hands of my four clerks, while I should read from the original. Accordingly, Turkey, Nippers, and Ginger Nut had taken their seats in a row, each with his document in his hand, when I called to Bartleby to join this interesting group.

"Bartleby! quick, I am waiting."

30   I heard a slow scrape of his chair legs on the uncarpeted floor, and soon he appeared standing at the entrance of his hermitage.

"What is wanted?" said he, mildly.

"The copies, the copies," said I, hurriedly. "We are going to examine them. There—" and I held towards him the fourth quadruplicate.

"I would prefer not to," he said, and gently disappeared behind the screen.

For a few moments I was turned into a pillar of salt, standing at the head of my seated column of clerks. Recovering myself, I advanced towards the screen, and demanded the reason for such extraordinary conduct.

35   "*Why* do you refuse?"

"I would prefer not to."

With any other man I should have flown outright into a dreadful passion, scorned all further words, and thrust him ignominiously from my presence. But there was something about Bartleby that not only strangely disarmed me, but in a wonderful manner, touched and disconcerted me. I began to reason with him.

"These are your own copies we are about to examine. It is labor saving to you, because one examination will answer for your four papers. It is common usage. Every copyist is bound to help examine his copy. Is it not so? Will you not speak? Answer!"

"I prefer not to," he replied in a flutelike tone. It seemed to me that, while I had been addressing him, he carefully revolved every statement that I made; fully comprehended the meaning; could not gainsay the irresistable conclusion; but, at the same time, some paramount consideration prevailed with him to reply as he did.

40   "You are decided, then, not to comply with my request—a request made according to common usage and common sense?"

He briefly gave me to understand, that on that point my judgment was sound. Yes: his decision was irreversible.

It is not seldom the case that, when a man is browbeaten in some unprecedented and violently unreasonable way, he begins to stagger in his own plainest faith. He begins, as it were, vaguely to surmise that, wonderful as it may be, all the justice and all the reason is on the other side. Accordingly, if any disinterested persons are present, he turns to them for some reinforcement of his own faltering mind.

"Turkey," said I, "what do you think of this? Am I not right?"

"With submission, sir," said Turkey, in his blandest tone, "I think that you are."

"Nippers," said I, "what do *you* think of it?"   45

"I think I should kick him out of the office."

(The reader, of nice perceptions, will here perceive that, it being morning, Turkey's answer is couched in polite and tranquil terms, but Nippers replies in ill-tempered ones. Or, to repeat a previous sentence, Nippers's ugly mood was on duty, and Turkey's off.)

"Ginger Nut," said I, willing to enlist the smallest suffrage in my behalf, "what do *you* think of it?"

"I think, sir, he's a little *luny*," replied Ginger Nut, with a grin.

"You hear what they say," said I, turning towards the screen, "come forth and do   50 your duty."

But he vouchsafed no reply. I pondered a moment in sore perplexity. But once more business hurried me. I determined again to postpone the consideration of this dilemma to my future leisure. With a little trouble we made out to examine the papers without Bartleby, though at every page or two Turkey deferentially dropped his opinion, that this proceeding was quite out of the common; while Nippers, twitching in his chair with a dyspeptic nervousness, ground out, between his set teeth, occasional hissing maledictions against the stubborn oaf behind the screen. And for his (Nippers's) part, this was the first and the last time he would do another man's business without pay.

Meanwhile Bartleby sat in his hermitage, oblivious to everything but his own peculiar business there.

Some days passed, the scrivener being employed upon another lengthy work. His late remarkable conduct led me to regard his ways narrowly. I observed that he never went to dinner; indeed, that he never went anywhere. As yet I had never, of my personal knowledge, known him to be outside of my office. He was a perpetual sentry in the corner. At about eleven o'clock though, in the morning, I noticed that Ginger Nut would advance toward the opening in Bartleby's screen, as if silently beckoned thither by a gesture invisible to me where I sat. The boy would then leave the office, jingling a few pence, and reappear with a handful of ginger-nuts, which he delivered in the hermitage, receiving two of the cakes for his trouble.

He lives, then, on ginger-nuts, thought I; never eats a dinner, properly speaking; he must be a vegetarian, then; but no; he never eats even vegetables; he eats nothing but ginger-nuts. My mind then ran on in reveries concerning the probable effects upon the human constitution of living entirely on ginger-nuts. Ginger-nuts are so called, because they contain ginger as one of their peculiar constituents, and the final flavoring one. Now, what was ginger? A hot, spicy thing. Was Bartleby hot and spicy? Not at all. Ginger, then, had no effect upon Bartleby. Probably he preferred it should have none.

Nothing so aggravates an earnest person as a passive resistance. If the individ-   55 ual so resisted be of a not inhumane temper, and the resisting one perfectly harmless in his passivity, then, in the better moods of the former, he will endeavor charitably to construe to his imagination what proves impossible to be solved by his judgment.

Even so, for the most part, I regarded Bartleby and his ways. Poor fellow! thought I, he means no mischief; it is plain he intends no insolence; his aspect sufficiently evinces that his eccentricities are involuntary. He is useful to me. I can get along with him. If I turn him away, the chances are he will fall in with some less-indulgent employer, and then he will be rudely treated, and perhaps driven forth miserably to starve. Yes. Here I can cheaply purchase a delicious self-approval. To befriend Bartleby; to humor him in his strange willfulness, will cost me little or nothing, while I lay up in my soul what will eventually prove a sweet morsel for my conscience. But this mood was not invariable with me. The passiveness of Bartleby sometimes irritated me. I felt strangely goaded on to encounter him in new opposition—to elicit some angry spark from him answerable to my own. But, indeed, I might as well have essayed to strike fire with my knuckles against a bit of Windsor soap. But one afternoon the evil impulse in me mastered me, and the following little scene ensued:

"Bartleby," said I, "when those papers are all copied, I will compare them with you."

"I would prefer not to."

"How? Surely you do not mean to persist in that mulish vagary?"

No answer.

60   I threw open the folding-doors near by, and, turning upon Turkey and Nippers, exclaimed:

"Bartleby a second time says, he won't examine his papers. What do you think of it, Turkey?"

It was afternoon, be it remembered. Turkey sat glowing like a brass boiler; his bald head steaming; his hands reeling among his blotted papers.

"Think of it?" roared Turkey; "I think I'll just step behind his screen, and black his eyes for him!"

So saying, Turkey rose to his feet and threw his arms into a pugilistic position. He was hurrying away to make good his promise, when I detained him, alarmed at the effect of incautiously rousing Turkey's combativeness after dinner.

65   "Sit down, Turkey," said I, "and hear what Nippers has to say. What do you think of it, Nippers? Would I not be justified in immediately dismissing Bartleby?"

"Excuse me, that is for you to decide, sir. I think his conduct quite unusual, and, indeed, unjust, as regards Turkey and myself. But it may only be a passing whim."

"Ah," exclaimed I, "you have strangely changed your mind, then—you speak very gently of him now."

"All beer," cried Turkey: "gentleness is effects of beer—Nippers and I dined together to-day. You see how gentle *I* am, sir. Shall I go and black his eyes?"

"You refer to Bartleby, I suppose. No, not to-day, Turkey," I replied; "pray, put up your fists."

70   I closed the doors, and again advanced towards Bartleby. I felt additional incentives tempting me to my fate. I burned to be rebelled against again. I remembered that Bartleby never left the office.

"Bartleby," said I, "Ginger Nut is away; just step around to the Post Office, won't you? (it was but a three minutes' walk), and see if there is anything for me."

"I would prefer not to."

"You *will* not?"

"I *prefer* not."

I staggered to my desk, and sat there in a deep study. My blind inveteracy re- 75
turned. Was there any other thing in which I could procure myself to be ignominiously repulsed by this lean, penniless wight?—my hired clerk? What added thing is
there, perfectly reasonable, that he will be sure to refuse to do? "Bartleby!"

No answer.

"Bartleby," in a louder tone.

No answer.

"Bartleby," I roared.

Like a very ghost, agreeably to the laws of magical invocation, at the third sum- 80
mons, he appeared at the entrance of his hermitage.

"Go to the next room, and tell Nippers to come to me."

"I prefer not to," he respectfully and slowly said and mildly disappeared.

"Very good, Bartleby," said I, in a quiet sort of serenely-severe, self-possessed
tone, intimating the unalterable purpose of some terrible retribution very close at
hand. At the moment I half intended something of the kind. But upon the whole, as
it was drawing towards my dinner-hour, I thought it best to put on my hat and walk
home for the day, suffering much from perplexity and distress of mind.

Shall I acknowledge it? The conclusion of this whole business was, that it soon
became a fixed fact of my chambers, that a pale young scrivener, by the name of
Bartleby, had a desk there; that he copied for me at the usual rate of four cents a folio (one hundred words); but he was permanently exempt from examining the work
done by him, that duty being transferred to Turkey and Nippers, out of compliment,
doubtless, to their superior acuteness; moreover, said Bartleby was never, on any account, to be dispatched on the most trivial errand of any sort; and that even if entreated to take upon him such a matter, it was generally understood that he would
"prefer not to"—in other words, he would refuse point blank.

As days passed on, I became considerably reconciled to Bartleby; his steadi- 85
ness, his freedom from all dissipation, his incessant industry (except when he chose
to throw himself into a standing revery behind his screen), his great stillness, his un-
alterableness of demeanor under all circumstances, made him a valuable acquisition.
One prime thing was this—*he was always there*—first thing in the morning, continually through the day, and the last at night. I had a singular confidence in his honesty. I felt my most precious papers perfectly safe in his hands. Sometimes, to be
sure, I could not, for the very soul of me, avoid falling into sudden spasmodic passions with him. For it was exceedingly difficult to bear in mind all the time those
strange peculiarities, privileges, and unheard of exemptions, forming the tacit stipu-
lations on Bartleby's part under which he remained in my office. Now and then, in
the eagerness of dispatching pressing business, I would inadvertently summon
Bartleby, in a short, rapid tone, to put his finger, say, on the incipient tie of a bit of
red tape with which I was about compressing some papers. Of course, from behind
the screen the usual answer, "I prefer not to," was sure to come; and then, how could
a human creature, with the common infirmities of our nature, refrain from bitterly

exclaiming upon such perverseness—such unreasonableness. However, every added repulse of this sort which I received only tended to lessen the probability of my repeating the inadvertence.

Here it must be said, that according to the custom of most legal gentlemen occupying chambers in densely-populated law buildings, there were several keys to my door. One was kept by a woman residing in the attic, which person weekly scrubbed and daily swept and dusted my apartments. Another was kept by Turkey for convenience sake. The third I sometimes carried in my own pocket. The fourth I knew not who had.

Now, one Sunday morning I happened to go to Trinity Church, to hear a celebrated preacher, and finding myself rather early on the ground I thought I would walk around to my chambers for a while. Luckily I had my key with me; but upon applying it to the lock, I found it resisted by something inserted from inside. Quite surprised, I called out; when to my consternation a key was turned from within; and thrusting his lean visage at me, and holding the door ajar, the apparition of Bartleby appeared, in his shirt sleeves, and otherwise in a strangely tattered *déshabillé,* saying quietly that he was sorry, but he was deeply engaged just then, and—preferred not admitting me at present. In a brief word or two, he moreover added, that perhaps I had better walk around the block two or three times, and by that time he would probably have concluded his affairs.

Now, the utterly unsurmised appearance of Bartleby, tenanting my law-chambers on a Sunday morning, with his cadaverously gentlemanly *nonchalance,* yet withal firm and self-possessed, had such a strange effect upon me, that incontinently I slunk away from my own door, and did as desired. But not without sundry twinges of impotent rebellion against the mild effrontery of this unaccountable scrivener. Indeed, it was his wonderful mildness chiefly, which not only disarmed me, but unmanned me as it were. For I consider that one, for the time, is somehow unmanned when he tranquilly permits his hired clerk to dictate to him, and order him away from his own premises. Furthermore, I was full of uneasiness as to what Bartleby could possibly be doing in my office in his shirt sleeves, and in an otherwise dismantled condition of a Sunday morning. Was anything amiss going on? Nay, that was out of the question. It was not to be thought of for a moment that Bartleby was an immoral person. But what could he be doing there?—copying? Nay again, whatever might be his eccentricities, Bartleby was an eminently decorous person. He would be the last man to sit down to his desk in any state approaching to nudity. Besides, it was Sunday; and there was something about Bartleby that forbade the supposition that he would by any secular occupation violate the proprieties of the day.

Nevertheless, my mind was not pacified; and full of a restless curiosity, at last I returned to the door. Without hindrance, I inserted my key, opened it, and entered. Bartleby was not to be seen. I looked round anxiously, peeped behind his screen; but it was very plain that he was gone. Upon more closely examining the place, I surmised that for an indefinite period Bartleby must have eaten, dressed, and slept in my office, and that, too, without plate, mirror, or bed. The cushioned seat of a rickety old sofa in one corner bore the faint impress of a lean, reclining form. Rolled away under his desk, I found a blanket; under the empty grate, a blacking box and brush; on a chair, a tin basin, with soap and a ragged towel; in a newspaper a few crumbs of ginger-nuts and a morsel of cheese. Yes, thought, I, it is evident enough that Bartleby has been making his home here, keeping bachelor's hall all by himself. Immediately then the thought came sweeping across me, what miserable friendlessness and loneliness are here revealed! His poverty is great; but his solitude, how horrible! Think of it. Of a Sunday, Wall Street is deserted as Petra; and every night of every day it is an emptiness. This building, too, which of week-days hums with industry and life, at nightfall echoes with sheer vacancy, and all through Sunday is forlorn. And here Bartleby makes his home; sole spectator of a solitude which he has seen all populous—a sort of innocent and transformed Marius brooding among the ruins of Carthage!

For the first time in my life a feeling of over-powering stinging melancholy 90 seized me. Before, I had never experienced aught but a not unpleasing sadness. The bond of a common humanity now drew me irresistibly to gloom. A fraternal melancholy! for both I and Bartleby were sons of Adam. I remembered the bright silks and sparkling faces I had seen that day, in gala trim, swan-like sailing down the Mississippi of Broadway; and I contrasted them with the pallid copyist, and thought to myself, Ah, happiness courts the light, so we deem the world is gay; but misery hides aloof, so we deem that misery there is none. These sad fancyings—chimeras, doubtless, of a sick and silly brain—led on to other and more special thoughts, concerning the eccentricities of Bartleby. Presentiments of strange discoveries hovered round me. The scrivener's pale form appeared to me laid out, among uncaring strangers, in its shivering winding sheet.

Suddenly, I was attracted by Bartleby's closed desk, the key in open sight left in the lock.

I mean no mischief, seek the gratification of no heartless curiosity, thought I; besides, the desk is mine, and its contents, too, so I will make bold to look within. Everything was methodically arranged, the papers smoothly placed. The pigeon holes were deep, and removing the files of documents, I groped into their recesses. Presently I felt something there, and dragged it out. It was an old bandana handkerchief, heavy and knotted. I opened it, and saw it was a savings bank.

I now recalled all the quiet mysteries which I had noted in the man. I remembered that he never spoke but to answer; that, though at intervals he had considerable time to himself, yet I had never seen him reading—no, not even a newspaper; that for long periods he would stand looking out, at his pale window behind the screen, upon the dead brick wall; I was quite sure he never visited any refectory or eating house; while his pale face clearly indicated that he never drank beer like Turkey, or tea and coffee even, like other men; that he never went anywhere in particular that I could learn; never went out for a walk, unless, indeed, that was the case at present; that he had declined telling who he was, or whence he came, or whether he had any relatives in the world; that though so thin and pale, he never complained of ill health. And more than all, I remembered a certain unconscious air of pallid— how shall I call it?—of pallid haughtiness, say, or rather an austere reserve about him, which had positively awed me into tame compliance with his eccentricities, when I had feared to ask him to do the slightest incidental thing for me, even though I might know, from his long-continued motionlessness, that behind his screen he must be standing in one of those dead-wall reveries of his.

Revolving all these things, and coupling them with the recently discovered fact, that he made my office his constant abiding place and home, and not forgetful of his morbid moodiness; revolving all these things, a prudential feeling began to steal over me. My first emotions had been those of pure melancholy and sincerest pity; but just in proportion as the forlornness of Bartleby grew and grew to my imagination, did that same melancholy merge into fear, that pity into repulsion. So true it is, and so terrible, too, that up to a certain point the thought or sight of misery enlists our best affections; but, in certain special cases, beyond that point it does not go. They err who would assert that invariably this is owing to the inherent selfishness of the human heart. It rather proceeds from a certain hopelessness of remedying excessive and organic ill. To a sensitive being, pity is not seldom pain. And when at last it is perceived that such pity cannot lead to effectual succor, common sense bids the soul be rid of it. What I saw that morning persuaded me that the scrivener was the victim of innate and incurable disorder. I might give alms to his body; but his body did not pain him; it was his soul that suffered, and his soul I could not reach.

95   I did not accomplish the purpose of going to Trinity Church that morning. Somehow, the things I had seen disqualified me for the time from churchgoing. I walked homeward, thinking what I would do with Bartleby. Finally, I resolved upon this—I would put certain calm questions to him the next morning, touching his history, etc., and if he declined to answer them openly and unreservedly (and I supposed he would prefer not), then to give him a twenty dollar bill over and above whatever I might owe him, and tell him his services were no longer required; but that if in any other way I could assist him, I would be happy to do so, especially if he desired to return to his native place, wherever that might be, I would willingly help to defray the expenses. Moreover, if after reaching home, he found himself at any time in want of aid, a letter from him would be sure of a reply.

The next morning came.

"Bartleby," said I, gently calling to him behind his screen.

No reply.

"Bartleby," said I, in a still gentler tone, "come here; I am not going to ask you to do anything you would prefer not to do—I simply wish to speak to you."

100   Upon this he noiselessly slid into view.

"Will you tell me, Bartleby, where you were born?"

"I would prefer not to."

"Will you tell me *anything* about yourself?"

"I would prefer not to."

105   "But what reasonable objection can you have to speak to me? I feel friendly towards you."

He did not look at me while I spoke, but kept his glance fixed upon my bust of Cicero, which, as I then sat, was directly behind me, some six inches above my head.

"What is your answer, Bartleby," said I, after waiting a considerable time for a reply, during which his countenance remained immovable, only there was the faintest conceivable tremor of the white attenuated mouth.

"At present I prefer to give no answer," he said, and retired into his hermitage.

It was rather weak in me I confess, but his manner, on this occasion, nettled me. Not only did there seem to lurk in it a certain calm disdain, but his perverseness seemed ungrateful, considering the undeniable good usage and indulgence he had received from me.

Again I sat ruminating what I should do. Mortified as I was at his behavior, and resolved as I had been to dismiss him when I entered my office, nevertheless I strangely felt something superstitious knocking at my heart, and forbidding me to carry out my purpose, and denouncing me for a villain if I dared to breathe one bitter word against this forlornest of mankind. At last, familiarly drawing my chair behind his screen, I sat down and said: "Bartleby, never mind, then, about revealing your history; but let me entreat you, as a friend, to comply as far as may be with the usages of this office. Say now, you will help me to examine papers to-morrow or next day; in short, say now, that in a day or two you will begin to be a little reasonable:— say so, Bartleby." 110

"At present I would prefer not to be a little reasonable," was his mildly cadaverous reply.

Just then the folding-doors opened, and Nippers approached. He seemed suffering from an unusually bad night's rest, induced by severer indigestion than common. He overheard those final words of Bartleby.

"*Prefer not*, eh?" gritted Nippers—"I'd *prefer* him, if I were you, sir," addressing me—"I'd *prefer* him; I'd give him preferences, the stubborn mule! What is it, sir, pray, that he *prefers* not to do now?"

Bartleby moved not a limb.

"Mr. Nippers," said I, "I'd prefer that you would withdraw at present." 115

Somehow, of late, I had got into the way of involuntarily using this word "prefer" upon all sorts of not exactly suitable occasions. And I trembled to think that my contact with the scrivener had already and seriously affected me in a mental way. And what further and deeper aberration might it not yet produce? This apprehension had not been without efficacy in determining me to summary measures.

As Nippers, looking very sour and sulky, was departing, Turkey blandly and deferentially approached.

"With submission, sir," said he, "yesterday I was thinking about Bartleby here, and I think that if he would but prefer to take a quart of good ale every day, it would do much towards mending him, and enabling him to assist in examining his papers."

"So you have got the word, too," said I, slightly excited.

"With submission, what word, sir?" asked Turkey, respectfully crowding himself into the contracted space behind the screen, and by so doing, making me jostle the scrivener. "What word, sir?" 120

"I would prefer to be left alone here," said Bartleby, as if offended at being mobbed in his privacy.

"*That's* the word, Turkey," said I—"*that's* it."

"Oh, *prefer?* oh yes—queer word. I never use it myself. But, sir, as I was saying, if he would but prefer—"

"Turkey," interrupted I, "you will please withdraw."

125   "Oh certainly, sir, if you prefer that I should."

As he opened the folding-door to retire, Nippers at his desk caught a glimpse of me, and asked whether I would prefer to have a certain paper copied on blue paper or white. He did not in the least roguishly accent the word prefer. It was plain that it involuntarily rolled from his tongue. I thought to myself, surely I must get rid of a demented man, who already has in some degree turned the tongues, if not the heads of myself and clerks. But I thought it prudent not to break the dismission at once.

The next day I noticed that Bartleby did nothing but stand at his window in his dead-wall revery. Upon asking him why he did not write, he said that he had decided upon doing no more writing.

"Why, how now? What next?" exclaimed I, "do no more writing?"

"No more."

130   "And what is the reason?"

"Do you not see the reason for yourself?" he indifferently replied.

I looked steadfastly at him, and perceived that his eyes looked dull and glazed. Instantly it occurred to me, that his unexampled diligence in copying by his dim window for the first few weeks of his stay with me might have temporarily impaired his vision.

I was touched. I said something in condolence with him. I hinted that of course he did wisely in abstaining from writing for a while; and urged him to embrace that opportunity of taking wholesome exercise in the open air. This, however, he did not do. A few days after this, my other clerks being absent, and being in a great hurry to dispatch certain letters by the mail, I thought that, having nothing else earthly to do, Bartleby would surely be less inflexible than usual, and carry these letters to the post-office. But he blankly declined. So, much to my inconvenience, I went myself.

Still added days went by. Whether Bartleby's eyes improved or not, I could not say. To all appearance I thought they did. But when I asked him if they did, he vouchsafed no answer. At all events, he would do no copying. At last, in reply to my urgings, he informed me that he had permanently given up copying.

135   "What!" exclaimed I; "suppose your eyes should get entirely well—better than ever before—would you not copy then?"

"I have given up copying," he answered, and slid aside.

He remained as ever, a fixture in my chamber. Nay—if that were possible—he became still more of a fixture than before. What was to be done? He would do nothing in the office; why should he stay there? In plain fact, he had now become a millstone to me, not only useless as a necklace, but afflictive to bear. Yet I was sorry for him. I speak less than truth when I say that, on his own account, he occasioned me uneasiness. If he would but have named a single relative or friend, I would instantly have written, and urged their taking the poor fellow away to some convenient retreat. But he seemed alone, absolutely alone in the universe. A bit of wreck in the mid Atlantic. At length, necessities connected with my business tyrannized over all other considerations. Decently as I could, I told Bartleby that in six days time he must un-conditionally leave the office. I warned him to take measures, in the interval, for procuring some other abode. I offered to assist him in his endeavor, if he himself would but take the first step towards a removal. "And when you finally quit me, Bartleby," added I, "I shall see that you go not away entirely unprovided. Six days from this hour, remember."

At the expiration of that period, I peeped behind the screen, and lo! Bartleby was there.

I buttoned up my coat, balanced myself; advanced slowly towards him, touched his shoulder, and said, "The time has come; you must quit this place; I am sorry for you; here is money; but you must go."

"I would prefer not," he replied, with his back still towards me.   140

"You *must.*"

He remained silent.

Now I had an unbounded confidence in this man's common honesty. He had fre-quently restored to me sixpences and shillings carelessly dropped upon the floor, for I am apt to be very reckless in such shirt-button affairs. The proceeding, then, which followed will not be deemed extraordinary.

"Bartleby," said I, "I owe you twelve dollars on account; here are thirty-two; the odd twenty are yours—Will you take it?" and I handed the bills towards him.

But he made no motion.   145

"I will leave them here, then," putting them under a weight on the table. Then taking my hat and cane and going to the door, I tranquilly turned and added—"After you have removed your things from these offices, Bartleby, you will of course lock the door—since every one is now gone for the day but you— and if you please, slip your key underneath the mat, so that I may have it in the morning. I shall not see you again; so good-by to you. If, hereafter, in your new place of abode, I can be of any service to you, do not fail to advise me by letter. Good-by, Bartleby, and fare you well."

But he answered not a word; like the last column of some ruined temple, he re-mained standing mute and solitary in the middle of the otherwise deserted room.

As I walked home in a pensive mood, my vanity got the better of my pity. I could not but highly plume myself on my masterly management in getting rid of Bartleby. Masterly I call it, and such it must appear to any dispassionate thinker. The beauty of my procedure seemed to consist in its perfect quietness. There was no vul-gar bullying, no bravado of any sort, no choleric hectoring, and striding to and fro across the apartment, jerking out vehement commands for Bartleby to bundle him-self off with his beggarly traps. Nothing of the kind. Without loudly bidding Bartleby depart—as an inferior genius might have done—I *assumed* the ground that depart he must; and upon that assumption built all I had to say. The more I thought over my procedure, the more I was charmed with it. Nevertheless, next morning, upon awak-ening, I had my doubts—I had somehow slept off the fumes of vanity. One of the coolest and wisest hours a man has, is just after he awakes in the morning. My pro-cedure seemed as sagacious as ever—but only in theory. How it would prove in practice—there was the rub. It was truly a beautiful thought to have assumed

Bartleby's departure; but, after all, that assumption was simply my own, and none of Bartleby's. The great point was, not whether I had assumed that he would quit me, but whether he would prefer so to do. He was more a man of preferences than assumptions.

After breakfast, I walked down town, arguing the probabilities *pro* and *con*. One moment I thought it would prove a miserable failure, and Bartleby would be found all alive at my office as usual; the next moment it seemed certain that I should find his chair empty. And so I kept veering about. At the corner of Broadway and Canal Street, I saw quite an excited group of people standing in earnest conversation.

150   "I'll take odds he doesn't," said a voice as I passed.

"Doesn't go?—done!" said I; "put up your money."

I was instinctively putting my hand in my pocket to produce my own, when I remembered that this was an election day. The words I had overheard bore no reference to Bartleby, but to the success or non-success of some candidate for the mayoralty. In my intent frame of mind, I had, as it were, imagined that all Broadway shared in my excitement, and were debating the same question with me. I passed on, very thankful that the uproar of the street screened my momentary absent-mindedness.

As I had intended, I was earlier than usual at my office door. I stood listening for a moment. All was still. He must be gone. I tried the knob. The door was locked. Yes, my procedure had worked to a charm; he indeed must be vanished. Yet a certain melancholy mixed with this: I was almost sorry for my brilliant success. I was fumbling under the door mat for the key, which Bartleby was to have left there for me, when accidentally my knee knocked against a panel, producing a summoning sound, and in response a voice came to me from within—"Not yet; I am occupied."

It was Bartleby.

155   I was thunderstruck. For an instant I stood like the man who, pipe in mouth, was killed one cloudless afternoon long ago in Virginia, by summer lightning; at his own warm open window he was killed, and remained leaning out there upon the dreamy afternoon, till some one touched him, when he fell.

"Not gone!" I murmured at last. But again obeying that wondrous ascendancy which the inscrutable scrivener had over me, and from which ascendancy, for all my chafing, I could not completely escape, I slowly went down stairs and out into the street, and while walking round the block, considered what I should next do in this unheard-of perplexity. Turn the man out by an actual thrusting I could not; to drive him away by calling him hard names would not do; calling in the police was an unpleasant idea; and yet, permit him to enjoy his cadaverous triumph over me—this, too, I could not think of. What was to be done? or, if nothing could be done, was there anything further that I could *assume* in the matter? Yes, as before I had prospectively assumed that Bartleby would depart, so now I might retrospectively assume that departed he was. In the legitimate carrying out of this assumption, I might enter my office in a great hurry, and pretending not to see Bartleby at all, walk straight against him as if he were air. Such a proceeding would in a singular degree have the appearance of a home-thrust. It was hardly possible that Bartleby could withstand such an application of the doctrine of assumptions. But upon second thoughts the success of the plan seemed rather dubious. I resolved to argue the matter over with him again.

"Bartleby," said I, entering the office, with a quietly severe expression, "I am seriously displeased. I am pained, Bartleby. I had thought better of you. I had imagined you of such a gentlemanly organization, that in any delicate dilemma a slight hint would suffice—in short, an assumption. But it appears I am deceived. Why," I added, unaffectedly starting, "you have not even touched that money yet," pointing to it, just where I had left it the evening previous.

He answered nothing.

"Will you, or will you not, quit me?" I now demanded in a sudden passion, advancing close to him.

"I would prefer *not* to quit you," he replied, gently emphasizing the *not*.   160

"What earthly right have you to stay here? Do you pay any rent? Do you pay my taxes? Or is this property yours?"

He answered nothing.

"Are you ready to go on and write now? Are your eyes recovered? Could you copy a small paper for me this morning? or help examine a few lines? or step round to the post-office? In a word, will you do anything at all, to give a coloring to your refusal to depart the premises?"

He silently retired into his hermitage.

I was now in such a state of nervous resentment that I thought it but prudent to   165 check myself at present from further demonstrations. Bartleby and I were alone. I remembered the tragedy of the unfortunate Adams and the still more unfortunate Colt in the solitary office of the latter; and how poor Colt, being dreadfully incensed by Adams, and imprudently permitting himself to get wildly excited, was at unawares hurried into his fatal act—an act which certainly no man could possibly deplore more than the actor himself. Often it had occurred to me in my ponderings upon the subject, that had that altercation taken place in the public street, or at a private residence, it would not have terminated as it did. It was the circumstance of being alone in a solitary office, up stairs, of a building entirely unhallowed by humanizing domestic associations—an uncarpeted office, doubtless, of a dusty, haggard sort of appearance—this it must have been, which greatly helped to enhance the irritable desperation of the hapless Colt.

But when this old Adam of resentment rose in me and tempted me concerning Bartleby, I grappled him and threw him. How? Why, simply by recalling the divine injunction: "A new commandment give I unto you, that ye love one another." Yes, this it was that saved me. Aside from higher considerations, charity often operates as a vastly wise and prudent principle—a great safeguard to its possessor. Men have committed murder for jealousy's sake, and anger's sake, and hatred's sake, and selfishness' sake, and spiritual pride's sake; but no man that ever I heard of, ever committed a diabolical murder for sweet charity's sake. Mere self-interest, then, if no better motive can be enlisted, should, especially with high-tempered men, prompt all beings to charity and philanthropy. At any rate, upon the occasion in question, I strove to drown my exasperated feelings towards the scrivener by benevolently construing his conduct. Poor fellow, poor fellow! thought I, he don't mean anything; and besides, he has seen hard times, and ought to be indulged.

I endeavored, also, immediately to occupy myself, and at the same time to comfort my despondency. I tried to fancy, that in the course of the morning, at such time as might prove agreeable to him, Bartleby, of his own free accord, would emerge from his hermitage and take up some decided line of march in the direction of the door. But no. Half-past twelve o'clock came; Turkey began to glow in the face, overturn his inkstand, and become generally obstreperous; Nippers abated down into quietude and courtesy; Ginger Nut munched his noon apple; and Bartleby remained standing at his window in one of his profoundest dead-wall reveries. Will it be credited? Ought I to acknowledge it? That afternoon I left the office without saying one further word to him.

Some days now passed, during which, at leisure intervals I looked a little into "Edwards on the Will," and "Priestly on Necessity." Under the circumstances, those books induced a salutary feeling. Gradually I slid into the persuasion that these troubles of mine, touching the scrivener, had been all predestinated from eternity, and Bartleby was billeted upon me for some mysterious purpose of an all-wise Providence, which it was not for a mere mortal like me to fathom. Yes, Bartleby, stay there behind your screen, thought I; I shall persecute you no more; you are harmless and noiseless as any of these old chairs; in short, I never feel so private as when I know you are here. At last I see it, I feel it; I penetrate to the predestinated purpose of my life. I am content. Others may have loftier parts to enact; but my mission in this world, Bartleby, is to furnish you with office-room for such period as you may see fit to remain.

I believe that this wise and blessed frame of mind would have continued with me, had it not been for the unsolicited and uncharitable remarks obtruded upon me by my professional friends who visited the rooms. But thus it often is, that the constant friction of illiberal minds wears out at last the best resolves of the more generous. Though to be sure, when I reflected upon it, it was not strange that people entering my office should be struck by the peculiar aspect of the unaccountable Bartleby, and so be tempted to throw out some sinister observations concerning him. Sometimes an attorney, having business with me, and calling at my office, and finding no one but the scrivener there, would undertake to obtain some sort of precise information from him touching my whereabouts; but without heeding his idle talk, Bartleby would remain standing immovable in the middle of the room. So after contemplating him in that position for a time, the attorney would depart, no wiser than he came.

170   Also, when a reference was going on, and the room full of lawyers and witnesses, and business driving fast, some deeply-occupied legal gentleman present, seeing Bartleby wholly unemployed, would request him to run round to his (the legal gentleman's) office and fetch some papers for him. Thereupon, Bartleby would tranquilly decline, and yet remain idle as before. Then the lawyer would give a great stare, and turn to me. And what could I say? At last I was made aware that all through the circle of my professional acquaintance, a whisper of wonder was running round, having reference to the strange creature I kept at my office. This worried me very

much. And as the idea came upon me of his possibly turning out a long-lived man, and keep occupying my chambers, and denying my authority; and perplexing my visitors; and scandalizing my professional reputation; and casting a general gloom over the premises; keeping soul and body together to the last upon his savings (for doubtless he spent but half a dime a day), and in the end perhaps outlive me, and claim possession of my office by right of his perpetual occupancy: as all these dark anticipations crowded upon me more and more, and my friends continually intruded their relentless remarks upon the apparition in my room; a great change was wrought in me. I resolved to gather all my faculties together, and forever rid me of this intolerable incubus.

Ere revolving any complicated project, however, adapted to this end, I first simply suggested to Bartleby the propriety of his permanent departure. In a calm and serious tone, I commended the idea to his careful and mature consideration. But, having taken three days to meditate upon it, he apprised me, that his original determination remained the same; in short, that he still preferred to abide with me.

What shall I do? I now said to myself, buttoning up my coat to the last button. What shall I do? what ought I to do? what does conscience say I *should* do with this man, or, rather, ghost? Rid myself of him, I must; go, he shall. But how? You will not thrust him, the poor, pale, passive mortal—you will not thrust such a helpless creature out of your door? you will not dishonor yourself by such cruelty? No, I will not, I cannot do that. Rather would I let him live and die here, and then mason up his remains in the wall. What, then, will you do? For all your coaxing, he will not budge. Bribes he leaves under your own paper-weight on your table; in short, it is quite plain that he prefers to cling to you.

Then something severe, something unusual must be done. What! surely you will not have him collared by a constable, and commit his innocent pallor to the common jail? And upon what ground could you procure such a thing to be done?—a vagrant, is he? What! he a vagrant, a wanderer, who refuses to budge? It is because he will *not* be a vagrant, then, that you seek to count him *as* a vagrant. That is too absurd. No visible means of support: there I have him. Wrong again: for indubitably he *does* support himself, and that is the only unanswerable proof that any man can show of his possessing the means so to do. No more, then. Since he will not quit me, I must quit him. I will change my offices; I will move elsewhere, and give him fair notice, that if I find him on my new premises I will then proceed against him as a common trespasser.

Acting accordingly, next day I thus addressed him: "I find these chambers too far from the City Hall; the air is unwholesome. In a word, I propose to remove my offices next week, and shall no longer require your services. I tell you this now, in order that you may seek another place."

He made no reply; and nothing more was said.   175

On the appointed day I engaged carts and men, proceeded to my chambers, and, having but little furniture, everything was removed in a few hours. Throughout, the scrivener remained standing behind the screen, which I directed to be removed the last thing. It was withdrawn; and, being folded up like a huge folio, left him the motionless occupant of a naked room. I stood in the entry watching him a moment, while something from within me upbraided me.

I re-entered, with my hand in my pocket—and—and my heart in my mouth.

"Good-by, Bartleby; I am going—good-by, and God some way bless you; and take that," slipping something in his hand. But it dropped upon the floor, and then—strange to say—I tore myself from him whom I had so longed to be rid of.

Established in my new quarters, for a day or two I kept the door locked, and started at every footfall in the passages. When I returned to my rooms, after any little absence, I would pause at the threshold for an instant, and attentively listen, ere applying my key. But these fears were needless. Bartleby never came nigh me.

180   I thought all was going well, when a perturbed-looking stranger visited me, inquiring whether I was the person who had recently occupied rooms at No.————— Wall Street.

Full of forebodings, I replied that I was.

"Then, sir," said the stranger, who proved a lawyer, "you are responsible for the man you left there. He refuses to do any copying; he refuses to do anything; he says he prefers not to; and he refuses to quit the premises."

"I am very sorry, sir," said I, with assumed tranquillity, but an inward tremor, "but, really, the man you allude to is nothing to me—he is no relation or apprentice of mine, that you should hold me responsible for him."

"In mercy's name, who is he?"

185   "I certainly cannot inform you. I know nothing about him. Formerly I employed him as a copyist; but he has done nothing for me now for some time past."

"I shall settle him, then—good morning, sir."

Several days passed, and I heard nothing more; and, though I often felt a charitable prompting to call at the place and see poor Bartleby, yet a certain squeamishness, of I know not what, withheld me.

All is over with him, by this time, thought I, at last, when, through another week, no further intelligence reached me. But, coming to my room the day after, I found several persons waiting at my door in a high state of nervous excitement.

"That's the man—here he comes," cried the foremost one, whom I recognized as the lawyer who had previously called upon me alone.

190   "You must take him away, sir, at once," cried a portly person among them, advancing upon me, and whom I knew to be the landlord of No.————— Wall Street. "These gentlemen, my tenants, cannot stand it any longer; Mr. B—," pointing to the lawyer, "has turned him out of his room, and he now persists in haunting the building generally, sitting upon the banisters of the stairs by day, and sleeping in the entry by night. Everybody is concerned; clients are leaving the offices; some fears are entertained of a mob; something you must do, and that without delay."

Aghast at this torrent, I fell back before it, and would fain have locked myself in my new quarters. In vain I persisted that Bartleby was nothing to me—no more than to any one else. In vain—I was the last person known to have anything to do with him, and they held me to the terrible account. Fearful, then, of being exposed in the papers (as one person present obscurely threatened), I considered the matter, and, at length, said, that if the lawyer would give me a confidential interview with the scrivener, in his (the lawyer's) own room, I would, that afternoon, strive my best to rid them of the nuisance they complained of.

Going up stairs to my old haunt, there was Bartleby silently sitting upon the banister at the landing.

"What are you doing here, Bartleby?" said I.

"Sitting upon the banister," he mildly replied.

I motioned him into the lawyer's room, who then left us.   195

"Bartleby," said I, "are you aware that you are the cause of great tribulation to me, by persisting in occupying the entry after being dismissed from the office?"

No answer.

"Now one of two things must take place. Either you must do something, or something must be done to you. Now what sort of business would you like to engage in? Would you like to re-engage in copying for some one?"

"No; I would prefer not to make any change."

"Would you like a clerkship in a dry-goods store?"   200

"There is too much confinement about that. No, I would not like a clerkship; but I am not particular."

"Too much confinement," I cried, "why you keep yourself confined all the time!"

"I would prefer not to take a clerkship," he rejoined, as if to settle that little item at once.

"How would a bar-tender's business suit you? There is no trying of the eyesight in that."

"I would not like it at all; though, as I said before, I am not particular."   205

His unwonted wordiness inspirited me. I returned to the charge.

"Well, then, would you like to travel through the country collecting bills for the merchants? That would improve your health."

"No, I would prefer to be doing something else."

"How, then, would going as a companion to Europe, to entertain some young gentleman with your conversation—how would that suit you?"

"Not at all. It does not strike me that there is anything definite about that. I like   210
to be stationary. But I am not particular."

"Stationary you shall be, then," I cried, now losing all patience, and, for the first time in all my exasperating connection with him, fairly flying into a passion. "If you do not go away from these premises before night, I shall feel bound—indeed, I *am* bound—to—to—to quit the premises myself!" I rather absurdly concluded, knowing not with what possible threat to try to frighten his immobility into compliance. Despairing of all further efforts, I was precipitately leaving him, when a final thought occurred to me—one which had not been wholly unindulged before.

"Bartleby," said I, in the kindest tone I could assume under such exciting circumstances, "will you go home with me now—not to my office, but my dwelling—and remain there till we can conclude upon some convenient arrangement for you at our leisure? Come, let us start now, right away."

"No: at present I would prefer not to make any change at all."

I answered nothing; but, effectually dodging every one by the suddenness and rapidity of my flight, rushed from the building, ran up Wall Street towards Broadway, and, jumping into the first omnibus, was soon removed from pursuit. As soon as tranquillity returned, I distinctly perceived that I had now done all that I possibly could, both in respect to the demands of the landlord and his tenants, and with regard to my own desire and sense of duty, to benefit Bartleby, and shield him from rude persecution. I now strove to be entirely care-free and quiescent; and my conscience justified me in the attempt; though, indeed, it was not so successful as I could have wished. So fearful was I of being again hunted out by the incensed landlord and his exasperated tenants, that, surrendering my business to Nippers, for a few days, I drove about the upper part of the town and through the suburbs, in my rockaway; crossed over to Jersey City and Hoboken, and paid fugitive visits to Manhattanville and Astoria. In fact, I almost lived in my rockaway for the time.

215   When again I entered my office, lo, a note from the landlord lay upon the desk. I opened it with trembling hands. It informed me that the writer had sent to the police, and had Bartleby removed to the Tombs as a vagrant. Moreover, since I knew more about him than any one else, he wished me to appear at that place, and make a suitable statement of the facts. These tidings had a conflicting effect upon me. At first I was indignant; but, at last, almost approved. The landlord's energetic, summary disposition, had led him to adopt a procedure which I do not think I would have decided upon myself; and yet, as a last resort, under such peculiar circumstances, it seemed the only plan.

As I afterwards learned, the poor scrivener, when told that he must be conducted to the Tombs, offered not the slightest obstacle, but, in his pale, unmoving way, silently acquiesced.

Some of the compassionate and curious bystanders joined the party; and headed by one of the constables arm in arm with Bartleby, the silent procession filed its way through all the noise, and heat, and joy of the roaring thoroughfares at noon.

The same day I received the note, I went to the Tombs, or, to speak more properly, the Halls of Justice. Seeking the right officer, I stated the purpose of my call, and was informed that the individual I described was, indeed, within. I then assured the functionary that Bartleby was a perfectly honest man, and greatly to be compassionated, however unaccountably eccentric. I narrated all I knew, and closed by suggesting the idea of letting him remain in as indulgent confinement as possible, till something less harsh might be done—though, indeed, I hardly knew what. At all events, if nothing else could be decided upon, the alms-house must receive him. I then begged to have an interview.

Being under no disgraceful charge, and quite serene and harmless in all his ways, they had permitted him freely to wander about the prison, and, especially, in the inclosed grass-platted yards thereof. And so I found him there, standing all alone in the quietest of the yards, his face towards a high wall, while all around, from the narrow slits of the jail windows, I thought I saw peering out upon him the eyes of murderers and thieves.

220   "Bartleby!"

"I know you," he said, without looking round—"and I want nothing to say to you."

"It was not I that brought you here, Bartleby," said I, keenly pained at his implied suspicion. "And to you, this should not be so vile a place. Nothing reproachful attaches to you by being here. And see, it is not so sad a place as one might think. Look, there is the sky, and here is the grass."

"I know where I am," he replied, but would say nothing more, and so I left him.

As I entered the corridor again, a broad meat-like man, in an apron, accosted me, and, jerking his thumb over his shoulder, said—"Is that your friend?"

"Yes." 225

"Does he want to starve? If he does, let him live on the prison fare, that's all."

"Who are you?" asked I, not knowing what to make of such an unofficially speaking person in such a place.

"I am the grub-man. Such gentlemen as have friends here, hire me to provide them with something good to eat."

"Is this so?" said I, turning to the turnkey.

He said it was. 230

"Well, then," said I, slipping some silver into the grub-man's hands (for so they called him), "I want you to give particular attention to my friend there; let him have the best dinner you can get. And you must be as polite to him as possible."

"Introduce me, will you?" said the grub-man, looking at me with an expression which seemed to say he was all impatience for an opportunity to give a specimen of his breeding.

Thinking it would prove of benefit to the scrivener, I acquiesced; and, asking the grub-man his name, went up with him to Bartleby.

"Bartleby, this is a friend; you will find him very useful to you."

"Your sarvant, sir, your sarvant," said the grub-man, making a low saluta- 235 tion behind his apron. "Hope you find it pleasant here, sir; nice grounds—cool apartments—hope you'll stay with us sometime—try to make it agreeable. What will you have for dinner to-day?"

"I prefer not to dine to-day," said Bartleby, turning away. "It would disagree with me; I am unused to dinners." So saying, he slowly moved to the other side of the inclosure, and took up a position fronting the dead-wall.

"How's this?" said the grub-man, addressing me with a stare of astonishment. "He's odd, ain't he?"

"I think he is a little deranged," said I, sadly.

"Deranged? deranged is it? Well, now, upon my word, I thought that friend of yourn was a gentleman forger; they are always pale and genteel-like, them forgers. I can't help pity 'em—can't help it, sir. Did you know Monroe Edwards?" he added, touchingly, and paused. Then, laying his hand piteously on my shoulder, sighed, "he died of consumption at Sing-Sing. So you weren't acquainted with Monroe?"

"No, I was never socially acquainted with any forgers. But I cannot stop longer. 240 Look to my friend yonder. You will not lose by it. I will see you again."

Some few days after this, I again obtained admission to the Tombs, and went through the corridors in quest of Bartleby; but without finding him.

"I saw him coming from his cell not long ago," said a turnkey, "may be he's gone to loiter in the yards."

So I went in that direction.

"Are you looking for the silent man?" said another turnkey, passing me. "Yonder he lies—sleeping in the yard there. 'Tis not twenty minutes since I saw him lie down."

245   The yard was entirely quiet. It was not accessible to the common prisoners. The surrounding walls of amazing thickness, kept off all sounds behind them. The Egyptian character of the masonry weighed upon me with its gloom. But a soft imprisoned turf grew under foot. The heart of the eternal pyramids, it seemed, wherein, by some strange magic, through the clefts, grass-seed, dropped by birds, had sprung.

Strangely huddled at the base of the wall, his knees drawn up, and lying on his side, his head touching the cold stones, I saw the wasted Bartleby. But nothing stirred. I paused; then went close up to him; stooped over, and saw that his dim eyes were open; otherwise he seemed profoundly sleeping. Something prompted me to touch him. I felt his hand, when a tingling shiver ran up my arm and down my spine to my feet.

The round face of the grub-man peered upon me now. "His dinner is ready. Won't he dine to-day, either? Or does he live without dining?"

"Lives without dining," said I, and closed the eyes.

"Eh!—He's asleep, ain't he?"

250   "With kings and counselors," murmured I.

There would seem little need for proceeding further in this history. Imagination will readily supply the meagre recital of poor Bartleby's interment. But, ere parting with the reader, let me say, that if this little narrative has sufficiently interested him, to awaken curiosity as to who Bartleby was, and what manner of life he led prior to the present narrator's making his acquaintance, I can only reply, that in such curiosity I fully share, but am wholly unable to gratify it. Yet here I hardly know whether I should divulge one little item of rumor, which came to my ear a few months after the scrivener's decease. Upon what basis it rested, I could never ascertain; and hence, how true it is I cannot now tell. But, inasmuch as this vague report has not been without a certain suggestive interest to me, however said, it may prove the same with some others; and so I will briefly mention it. The report was this: that Bartleby had been a subordinate clerk in the Dead Letter Office at Washington, from which he had been suddenly removed by a change in the administration. When I think over this rumor, hardly can I express the emotions which seize me. Dead letters! does it not sound like dead men? Conceive a man by nature and misfortune prone to a pallid hopelessness, can any business seem more fitted to heighten it than that of continually handling these dead letters, and assorting them for the flames? For by the cart-load they are annually burned. Some times from out the folded paper the pale clerk takes a ring—the finger it was meant for, perhaps, moulders in the grave; a bank-note sent in swiftest charity—he whom it would relieve, nor eats nor hungers any more; pardon for those who died despairing; hope for those who died unhoping; good tidings for those who died stifled by unrelieved calamities. On errands of life, these letters speed to death.

Ah, Bartleby! Ah, humanity!

QUESTIONS FOR DISCUSSION AND WRITING

1. What are the stages in Bartleby's gradual withdrawal from human contact? What kind of conflicts does Bartleby's presence create for the narrator and his friends? How does the rumor of Bartleby's previous employment at the Dead Letter Office suggest a resolution for the story?

2. How does the narrator characterize his three employees—Turkey, Nippers, and Ginger Nut? What does he know about the external aspects of Bartleby's character? What does he fail to understand about the internal aspects of Bartleby's character?

3. How does the narrator describe the setting for his story? How does this atmosphere gradually change as a result of Bartleby's presence? How does the subtitle, "A Story of Wall-Street," characterize this atmosphere?

4. How does the narrator's admission that he is an "eminently safe" man help establish his point of view toward the events of the story? In what ways does his point of view change as a result of his association with Bartleby?

5. How does this story define the words *pity, charity, responsibility?* What is the "common bond" the narrator feels toward Bartleby? Why does he abandon him? What is the meaning of his last words, "Ah, Bartleby! Ah, humanity!"?

Stories for Comparison

Joseph Conrad's "Heart of Darkness" (pages 388–447); Philip Roth's "Defender of the Faith" (pages 1036–1057).

74

Y U K I O   M I S H I M A

Patriotism

YUKIO MISHIMA (1925–1970), the pen name of Kimitake Hiraoka, was born in Tokyo, Japan, to a family of Samurai nobility, a tradition that combined spiritual dedication and the martial arts. As a young man, Mishima was convinced that he would die for the Emperor during World War II, but he failed the army physical. His rejection caused him great personal dishonor, and he dedicated himself to building up his frail physique. At the end of the war, Mishima studied law at Tokyo University and worked briefly as a civil servant in the Finance Ministry. In 1949, Mishima published his first novel, *Confessions of a Mask,* a chronicle of his life from early childhood through the war. The success of this book allowed Mishima to pursue his writing full time, composing an astonishing number of poems, stories, and plays. He rejected the Western influences on postwar Japan, preferring the classic traditions of Japanese literature, as evidenced in his modernized versions of the Noh plays. The best-known English translations of his work include *The Temple of the Golden Pavilion* (1959), *The Sailor Who Fell from Grace with the Sea* (1965), and his masterful tetralogy, *The Sea of Fertility* (1975). In 1968, Mishima founded a private army, the Shield Society, with the intent of returning Japan to the Samurai tradition. In 1970, Mishima and four of his followers captured the headquarters of Japan's Eastern Ground Self-Defense Forces. When his demands went unheeded, he committed suicide according to the ritual of *seppuku,* a ceremony reserved for the Samurai warrior. "Patriotism," reprinted from *Death in Midsummer and Other Stories* (1966), realistically portrays a domestic version of this ancient ritual.

I

On the twenty-eighth of February, 1936 (on the third day, that is, of the February 26 Incident), Lieutenant Shinji Takeyama of the Konoe Transport Battalion—profoundly disturbed by the knowledge that his closest colleagues had been with the mutineers from the beginning, and indignant at the imminent prospect of Imperial troops attacking Imperial troops—took his officer's sword and ceremonially disemboweled himself in the eight-mat room of his private residence in the sixth block of Aoba-chō, in Yotsuya Ward. His wife, Reiko, followed him, stabbing herself to death. The lieutenant's farewell note consisted of one sentence: "Long live the Imperial Forces." His wife's, after apologies for her unfilial conduct in thus preceding her parents to the grave, concluded: "The day which, for a soldier's wife, had to come, has come. . . ." The last moments of this heroic and dedicated couple were such as to make the gods themselves weep. The lieutenant's age, it should be noted, was thirty-one, his wife's twenty-three; and it was not half a year since the celebration of their marriage.

2

Those who saw the bride and bridegroom in the commemorative photograph—perhaps no less than those actually present at the lieutenant's wedding—had exclaimed in wonder at the bearing of this handsome couple. The lieutenant, majestic in military uniform, stood protectively beside his bride, his right hand resting upon his sword, his officer's cap held at his left side. His expression was severe, and his dark brows and wide-gazing eyes well conveyed the clear integrity of youth. For the beauty of the bride in her white over-robe no comparisons were adequate. In the eyes, round beneath soft brows, in the slender, finely shaped nose, and in the full lips, there was both sensuousness and refinement. One hand, emerging shyly from a sleeve of the over-robe, held a fan, and the tips of the fingers, clustering delicately, were like the bud of a moonflower.

After the suicide, people would take out this photograph and examine it, and sadly reflect that too often there was a curse on these seemingly flawless unions. Perhaps it was no more than imagination, but looking at the picture after the tragedy it almost seemed as if the two young people before the gold-lacquered screen were gazing, each with equal clarity, at the deaths which lay before them.

Thanks to the good offices of their go-between, Lieutenant General Ozeki, they had been able to set themselves up in a new home at Aoba-chō in Yotsuya. "New home" is perhaps misleading. It was an old three-room rented house backing onto a small garden. As neither the six- nor the four-and-a-half-mat room downstairs was favored by the sun, they used the upstairs eight-mat room as both bedroom and guest room. There was no maid, so Reiko was left alone to guard the house in her husband's absence.

The honeymoon trip was dispensed with on the grounds that these were times of national emergency. The two of them had spent the first night of their marriage at this house. Before going to bed, Shinji, sitting erect on the floor with his sword laid before him, had bestowed upon his wife a soldierly lecture. A woman who had become the wife of a soldier should know and resolutely accept that her husband's death might come at any moment. It could be tomorrow. It could be the day after. But, no matter when it came—he asked—was she steadfast in her resolve to accept it? Reiko rose to her feet, pulled open a drawer of the cabinet, and took out what was the most prized of her new possessions, the dagger her mother had given her. Returning to her place, she laid the dagger without a word on the mat before her, just as her husband had laid his sword. A silent understanding was achieved at once, and the lieutenant never again sought to test his wife's resolve.

In the first few months of her marriage Reiko's beauty grew daily more radiant, shining serene like the moon after rain.

As both were possessed of young, vigorous bodies, their relationship was passionate. Nor was this merely a matter of the night. On more than one occasion, returning home straight from maneuvers, and begrudging even the time it took to remove his mud-splashed uniform, the lieutenant had pushed his wife to the floor almost as soon as he had entered the house. Reiko was equally ardent in her response. For a little more or a little less than a month, from the first night of their marriage Reiko knew happiness, and the lieutenant, seeing this, was happy too.

Reiko's body was white and pure, and her swelling breasts conveyed a firm and chaste refusal; but, upon consent, those breasts were lavish with their intimate, welcoming warmth. Even in bed these two were frighteningly and awesomely serious. In the very midst of wild, intoxicating passion, their hearts were sober and serious.

By day the lieutenant would think of his wife in the brief rest periods between training; and all day long, at home, Reiko would recall the image of her husband. Even when apart, however, they had only to look at the wedding photograph for their happiness to be once more confirmed. Reiko felt not the slightest surprise that a man who had been a complete stranger until a few months ago should now have become the sun about which her whole world revolved.

10   All these things had a moral basis, and were in accordance with the Education Rescript's injunction that "husband and wife should be harmonious." Not once did Reiko contradict her husband, nor did the lieutenant ever find reason to scold his wife. On the god shelf below the stairway, alongside the tablet from the Great Ise Shrine, were set photographs of their Imperial Majesties, and regularly every morning, before leaving for duty, the lieutenant would stand with his wife at this hallowed place and together they would bow their heads low. The offering water was renewed each morning, and the sacred sprig of *sasaki* was always green and fresh. Their lives were lived beneath the solemn protection of the gods and were filled with an intense happiness which set every fiber in their bodies trembling.

3

Although Lord Privy Seal Saitō's house was in their neighborhood, neither of them heard any noise of gunfire on the morning of February 26. It was a bugle, sounding muster in the dim, snowy dawn, when the ten-minute tragedy had already ended, which first disrupted the lieutenant's slumbers. Leaping at once from his bed, and without speaking a word, the lieutenant donned his uniform, buckled on the sword held ready for him by his wife, and hurried swiftly out into the snow-covered streets of the still darkened morning. He did not return until the evening of the twenty-eight.

Later, from the radio news, Reiko learned the full extent of this sudden eruption of violence. Her life throughout the subsequent two days was lived alone, in complete tranquility and behind locked doors.

In the lieutenant's face, as he hurried silently out into the snowy morning, Reiko had read the determination to die. If her husband did not return, her own decision was made: she too would die. Quietly she attended to the disposition of her personal possessions. She chose her sets of visiting kimonos as keepsakes for friends of her schooldays, and she wrote a name and address on the stiff paper wrapping in which each was folded. Constantly admonished by her husband never to think of the morrow, Reiko had not even kept a diary and was now denied the pleasure of assiduously rereading her record of the happiness of the past few months and consigning each page to the fire as she did so. Ranged across the top of the radio were a small china dog, a rabbit, a squirrel, a bear, a fox. There were also a small vase and a water pitcher. These comprised Reiko's one and only collection. But it would hardly do, she imagined, to give such things as keepsakes. Nor again would it be quite proper to ask specifically for them to be included in the coffin. It seemed to Reiko, as these thoughts passed through her mind, that the expressions on the small animals' faces grew even more lost and forlorn.

Reiko took the squirrel in her hand and looked at it. And then, her thoughts turning to a realm far beyond these childlike affections, she gazed up into the distance at the great sunlike principle which her husband embodied. She was ready, and happy, to be hurtled along to her destruction in that gleaming sun chariot—but now, for these few moments of solitude, she allowed herself to luxuriate in this innocent attachment to trifles. The time when she had genuinely loved these things, however, was long past. Now she merely loved the memory of having once loved them, and their place in her heart had been filled by more intense passions, by a more frenzied happiness. . . . For Reiko had never, even to herself, thought of those soaring joys of the flesh as a mere pleasure. The February cold, and the icy touch of the china squirrel, had numbed Reiko's slender fingers; yet, even so, in her lower limbs, beneath the ordered repetition of the pattern which crossed the skirt of her trim *meisen* kimono, she could feel now, as she thought of the lieutenant's powerful arms reaching out toward her, a hot moistness of the flesh which defied the snows.

She was not in the least afraid of the death hovering in her mind. Waiting alone 15 at home, Reiko firmly believed that everything her husband was feeling or thinking now, his anguish and distress, was leading her—just as surely as the power in his flesh—to a welcome death. She felt as if her body could melt away with ease and be transformed to the merest fraction of her husband's thought.

Listening to the frequent announcements on the radio, she heard the names of several of her husband's colleagues mentioned among those of the insurgents. This was news of death. She followed the developments closely, wondering anxiously, as the situation became daily more irrevocable, why no Imperial ordinance was sent down, and watching what had at first been taken as a movement to restore the nation's honor come gradually to be branded with the infamous name of mutiny. There was no communication from the regiment. At any moment, it seemed, fighting might commence in the city streets, where the remains of the snow still lay.

Toward sundown on the twenty-eighth Reiko was startled by a furious pounding on the front door. She hurried downstairs. As she pulled with fumbling fingers at the bolt, the shape dimly outlined beyond the frosted-glass panel made no sound, but she knew it was her husband. Reiko had never known the bolt on the sliding door to be so stiff. Still it resisted. The door just would not open.

In a moment, almost before she knew she had succeeded, the lieutenant was standing before her on the cement floor inside the porch, muffled in a khaki greatcoat, his top boots heavy with slush from the street. Closing the door behind him, he returned the bolt once more to its socket. With what significance, Reiko did not understand.

"Welcome home."

Reiko bowed deeply, but her husband made no response. As he had already un- 20 fastened his sword and was about to remove his greatcoat, Reiko moved around behind to assist. The coat, which was cold and damp and had lost the odor of horse dung it normally exuded when exposed to the sun, weighed heavily upon her arm. Draping it across a hanger, and cradling the sword and leather belt in her sleeves, she waited while her husband removed his top boots and then followed behind him into the "living room." This was the six-mat room downstairs.

Seen in the clear light from the lamp, her husband's face, covered with a heavy growth of bristle, was almost unrecognizably wasted and thin. The cheeks were hollow, their luster and resilience gone. In his normal good spirits he would have changed into old clothes as soon as he was home and have pressed her to get supper at once, but now he sat before the table still in his uniform, his head drooping dejectedly. Reiko refrained from asking whether she should prepare the supper.

After an interval the lieutenant spoke.

"I knew nothing. They hadn't asked me to join. Perhaps out of consideration, because I was newly married. Kanō, and Homma too, Yamaguchi."

Reiko recalled momentarily the faces of high-spirited young officers, friends of her husband, who had come to the house occasionally as guests.

25   "There may be an Imperial ordinance sent down tomorrow. They'll be posted as rebels, I imagine. I shall be in command of a unit with orders to attack them. . . . I can't do it. It's impossible to do a thing like that."

He spoke again.

"They've taken me off guard duty, and I have permission to return home for one night. Tomorrow morning, without question, I must leave to join the attack. I can't do it, Reiko."

Reiko sat erect with lowered eyes. She understood clearly that her husband had spoken of his death. The lieutenant was resolved. Each word, being rooted in death, emerged sharply and with powerful significance against this dark, unmovable background. Although the lieutenant was speaking of his dilemma, already there was no room in his mind for vacillation.

However, there was a clarity, like the clarity of a stream fed from melting snows, in the silence which rested between them. Sitting in his own home after the long two-day ordeal, and looking across at the face of his beautiful wife, the lieutenant was for the first time experiencing true peace of mind. For he had at once known, though she said nothing, that his wife divined the resolve which lay beneath his words.

30   "Well, then . . ." The lieutenant's eyes opened wide. Despite his exhaustion they were strong and clear, and now for the first time they looked straight into the eyes of his wife. "Tonight I shall cut my stomach."

Reiko did not flinch.

Her round eyes showed tension, as taut as the clang of a bell.

"I am ready," she said. "I ask permission to accompany you."

The lieutenant felt almost mesmerized by the strength in those eyes. His words flowed swiftly and easily, like the utterances of a man in delirium, and it was beyond his understanding how permission in a matter of such weight could be expressed so casually.

35   "Good. We'll go together. But I want you as a witness, first, for my own suicide. Agreed?"

When this was said a sudden release of abundant happiness welled up in both their hearts. Reiko was deeply affected by the greatness of her husband's trust in her. It was vital for the lieutenant, whatever else might happen, that there should be no irregularity in his death. For that reason there had to be a witness. The fact that he had chosen his wife for this was the first mark of his trust. The second, and even greater mark, was that though he had pledged that they should die together he did not intend to kill his wife first—he had deferred her death to a time when he would no longer be there to verify it. If the lieutenant had been a suspicious husband, he would doubtless, as in the usual suicide pact, have chosen to kill his wife first.

When Reiko said, "I ask permission to accompany you," the lieutenant felt these words to be the final fruit of the education which he had himself given his wife, starting on the first night of their marriage, and which had schooled her, when the moment came, to say what had to be said without a shadow of hesitation. This flattered the lieutenant's opinion of himself as a self-reliant man. He was not so romantic or conceited as to imagine that the words were spoken spontaneously, out of love for her husband.

With happiness welling almost too abundantly in their hearts, they could not help smiling at each other. Reiko felt as if she had returned to her wedding night.

Before her eyes was neither pain nor death. She seemed to see only a free and limitless expanse opening out into vast distances.

"The water is hot. Will you take your bath now?"   40

"Ah yes, of course."

"And supper . . . ?"

The words were delivered in such level, domestic tones that the lieutenant came near to thinking, for the fraction of a second, that everything had been a hallucination.

"I don't think we'll need supper. But perhaps you could warm some sake?"

"As you wish."   45

As Reiko rose and took a *tanzen* gown from the cabinet for after the bath, she purposely directed her husband's attention to the open drawer. The lieutenant rose, crossed to the cabinet, and looked inside. From the ordered array of paper wrappings he read, one by one, the addresses of the keepsakes. There was no grief in the lieutenant's response to this demonstration of heroic resolve. His heart was filled with tenderness. Like a husband who is proudly shown the childish purchases of a young wife, the lieutenant, overwhelmed by affection, lovingly embraced his wife from behind and implanted a kiss upon her neck.

Reiko felt the roughness of the lieutenant's unshaven skin against her neck. This sensation, more than being just a thing of this world, was for Reiko almost the world itself, but now—with the feeling that it was soon to be lost forever—it had freshness beyond all her experience. Each moment had its own vital strength, and the senses in every corner of her body were reawakened. Accepting her husband's caresses from behind, Reiko raised herself on the tips of her toes, letting the vitality seep through her entire body.

"First the bath, and then, after some sake . . . lay out the bedding upstairs, will you?"

The lieutenant whispered the words into his wife's ear. Reiko silently nodded.

Flinging off his uniform, the lieutenant went to the bath. To faint background   50
noises of slopping water Reiko tended the charcoal brazier in the living room and began the preparations for warming the sake.

Taking the *tanzen,* a sash, and some underclothes, she went to the bathroom to ask how the water was. In the midst of a coiling cloud of steam the lieutenant was sitting cross-legged on the floor, shaving, and she could dimly discern the rippling movements of the muscles on his damp, powerful back as they responded to the movement of his arms.

There was nothing to suggest a time of any special significance. Reiko, going busily about her tasks, was preparing side dishes from odds and ends in stock. Her hands did not tremble. If anything, she managed even more efficiently and smoothly than usually. From time to time, it is true, there was a strange throbbing deep within her breast. Like distant lightning, it had a moment of sharp intensity and then vanished without trace. Apart from that, nothing was in any way out of the ordinary.

The lieutenant, shaving in the bathroom, felt his warmed body miraculously healed at last of the desperate tiredness of the days of indecision and filled—in spite of the death which lay ahead—with pleasurable anticipation. The sound of his wife going about her work came to him faintly. A healthy physical craving, submerged for two days, re-asserted itself.

The lieutenant was confident there had been no impurity in that joy they had experienced when resolving upon death. They had both sensed at that moment—though not, of course, in any clear and conscious way—that those permissible pleasures which they shared in private were once more beneath the protection of Righteousness and Divine Power, and of a complete and unassailable morality. On looking into each other's eyes and discovering there an honorable death, they had felt themselves safe once more behind steel walls which none could destroy, encased in an impenetrable armor of Beauty and Truth. Thus, so far from seeing any inconsistency or conflict between the urges of his flesh and the sincerity of his patriotism, the lieutenant was even able to regard the two as parts of the same thing.

55   Thrusting his face close to the dark, cracked, misted wall mirror, the lieutenant shaved himself with great care. This would be his death face. There must be no unsightly blemishes. The clean-shaven face gleamed once more with a youthful luster, seeming to brighten the darkness of the mirror. There was a certain elegance, he even felt, in the association of death with this radiantly healthy face.

Just as it looked now, this would become his death face! Already, in fact, it had half departed from the lieutenant's personal possession and had become the bust above a dead soldier's memorial. As an experiment he closed his eyes tight. Everything was wrapped in blackness, and he was no longer a living, seeing creature.

Returning from the bath, the traces of the shave glowing faintly blue beneath his smooth cheeks, he seated himself beside the now well-kindled charcoal brazier. Busy though Reiko was, he noticed, she had found time lightly to touch up her face. Her cheeks were gay and her lips moist. There was no shadow of sadness to be seen. Truly, the lieutenant felt, as he saw this mark of his young wife's passionate nature, he had chosen the wife he ought to have chosen.

As soon as the lieutenant had drained his sake cup he offered it to Reiko. Reiko had never before tasted sake, but she accepted without hesitation and sipped timidly.

"Come here," the lieutenant said.

60   Reiko moved to her husband's side and was embraced as she leaned backward across his lap. Her breast was in violent commotion, as if sadness, joy, and the potent sake were mingling and reacting within her. The lieutenant looked down into his wife's face. It was the last face he would see in this world, the last face he would see of his wife. The lieutenant scrutinized the face minutely, with the eyes of a traveler bidding farewell to splendid vistas which he will never revisit. It was a face he could not tire of looking at—the features regular yet not cold, the lips lightly closed with a soft strength. The lieutenant kissed those lips, unthinkingly. And suddenly, though

there was not the slightest distortion of the face into the unsightliness of sobbing, he noticed that tears were welling slowly from beneath the long lashes of the closed eyes and brimming over into a glistening stream.

When, a little later, the lieutenant urged that they should move to the upstairs bedroom, his wife replied that she would follow after taking a bath. Climbing the stairs alone to the bedroom, where the air was already warmed by the gas heater, the lieutenant lay down on the bedding with arms outstretched and legs apart. Even the time at which he lay waiting for his wife to join him was no later and no earlier than usual.

He folded his hands beneath his head and gazed at the dark boards of the ceiling in the dimness beyond the range of the standard lamp. Was it death he was now waiting for? Or a wild ecstasy of the senses? The two seemed to overlap, almost as if the object of this bodily desire was death itself. But, however that might be, it was certain that never before had the lieutenant tasted such total freedom.

There was the sound of a car outside the window. He could hear the screech of its tires skidding in the snow piled at the side of the street. The sound of its horn re-echoed from near-by walls. . . . Listening to these noises he had the feeling that this house rose like a solitary island in the ocean of a society going as restlessly about its business as ever. All around, vastly and untidily, stretched the country for which he grieved. He was to give his life for it. But would that great country, with which he was prepared to remonstrate to the extent of destroying himself, take the slightest heed of his death? He did not know; and it did not matter. He was a battlefield without glory, a battlefield where none could display deeds of valor: it was the front line of the spirit.

Reiko's footsteps sounded on the stairway. The steep stairs in this old house creaked badly. There were fond memories in that creaking, and many a time, while waiting in bed, the lieutenant had listened to its welcome sound. At the thought that he would hear it no more he listened with intense concentration, striving for every corner of every moment of this precious time to be filled with the sound of those soft footfalls on the creaking stairway. The moments seemed transformed to jewels, sparkling with inner light.

Reiko wore a Nagoya sash about the waist of her *yukata,* but as the lieutenant reached toward it, its redness sobered by the dimness of the light, Reiko's hand moved to his assistance and the sash fell away, slithering swiftly to the floor. As she stood before him, still in her *yukata,* the lieutenant inserted his hands through the side slits beneath each sleeve, intending to embrace her as she was; but at the touch of his finger tips upon the warm naked flesh, and as the armpits closed gently about his hands, his whole body was suddenly aflame.

In a few moments the two lay naked before the glowing gas heater.

Neither spoke the thought, but their hearts, their bodies, and their pounding breasts blazed with the knowledge that this was the very last time. It was as if the words "The Last Time" were spelled out, in invisible brushstrokes, across every inch of their bodies.

The lieutenant drew his wife close and kissed her vehemently. As their tongues explored each other's mouths, reaching out into the smooth, moist interior, they felt as if the still-unknown agonies of death had tempered their senses to the keenness of red-hot steel. The agonies they could not yet feel, the distant pains of death, had refined their awareness of pleasure.

"This is the last time I shall see your body," said the lieutenant. "Let me look at it closely." And, tilting the shade on the lampstand to one side, he directed the rays along the full length of Reiko's outstretched form.

70   Reiko lay still with her eyes closed. The light from the low lamp clearly revealed the majestic sweep of her white flesh. The lieutenant, not without a touch of egocentricity, rejoiced that he would never see this beauty crumble in death.

At his leisure, the lieutenant allowed the unforgettable spectacle to engrave itself upon his mind. With one hand he fondled the hair, with the other he softly stroked the magnificent face, implanting kisses here and there where his eyes lingered. The quiet coldness of the high, tapering forehead, the closed eyes with their long lashes beneath faintly etched brows, the set of the finely shaped nose, the gleam of teeth glimpsed between full, regular lips, the soft cheeks and the small, wise chin . . . these things conjured up in the lieutenant's mind the vision of a truly radiant death face, and again and again he pressed his lips tight against the white throat—where Reiko's own hand was soon to strike—and the throat reddened faintly beneath his kisses. Returning to the mouth he laid his lips against it with the gentlest of pressures, and moved them rhythmically over Reiko's with the light rolling motion of a small boat. If he closed his eyes, the world became a rocking cradle.

Wherever the lieutenant's eyes moved his lips faithfully followed. The high, swelling breasts, surmounted by nipples like the buds of a wild cherry, hardened as the lieutenant's lips closed about them. The arms flowed smoothly downward from each side of the breast, tapering toward the wrists, yet losing nothing of their roundness or symmetry, and at their tips were those delicate fingers which had held the fan at the wedding ceremony. One by one, as the lieutenant kissed them, the fingers withdrew behind their neighbor as if in shame. . . . The natural hollow curving between the bosom and the stomach carried in its lines a suggestion not only of softness but of resilient strength, and while it gave forewarning of the rich curves spreading outward from here to the hips it had, in itself, an appearance only of restraint and proper discipline. The whiteness and richness of the stomach and hips was like milk brimming in a great bowl, and the sharply shadowed dip of the navel could have been the fresh impress of a raindrop, fallen there that very moment. Where the shadows gathered more thickly, hair clustered, gentle and sensitive, and as the agitation mounted in the now no longer passive body there hung over this region a scent like the smoldering of fragrant blossoms, growing steadily more pervasive.

At length, in a tremulous voice, Reiko spoke.

"Show me. . . . Let me look too, for the last time."

75   Never before had he heard from his wife's lips so strong and unequivocal a request. It was as if something which her modesty had wished to keep hidden to the end had suddenly burst its bonds of constraint. The lieutenant obediently lay back and surrendered himself to his wife. Lithely she raised her white, trembling body, and—burning with an innocent desire to return to her husband what he had done for

her—placed two white fingers on the lieutenant's eyes, which gazed fixedly up at her, and gently stroked them shut.

Suddenly overwhelmed by tenderness, her cheeks flushed by a dizzying uprush of emotion, Reiko threw her arms about the lieutenant's close-cropped head. The bristly hairs rubbed painfully against her breast, the prominent nose was cold as it dug into her flesh and his breath was hot. Relaxing her embrace, she gazed down at her husband's masculine face. The severe brows, the closed eyes, the splendid bridge of the nose, the shapely lips drawn firmly together . . . the blue, clean-shaven cheeks reflecting the light and gleaming smoothly. Reiko kissed each of these. She kissed the broad nape of the neck, the strong, erect shoulders, the powerful chest with its twin circles like shields and its russet nipples. In the armpits, deeply shadowed by the ample flesh of the shoulders and chest, a sweet and melancholy odor emanated from the growth of hair, and in the sweetness of this odor was contained, somehow, the essence of young death. The lieutenant's naked skin glowed like a field of barley, and everywhere the muscles showed in sharp relief, converging on the lower abdomen about the small, unassuming navel. Gazing at the youthful, firm stomach, modestly covered by a vigorous growth of hair, Reiko thought of it as it was soon to be, cruelly cut by the sword, and she laid her head upon it, sobbing in pity, and bathed it with kisses.

At the touch of his wife's tears upon his stomach the lieutenant felt ready to endure with courage the cruelest agonies of his suicide.

What ecstasies they experienced after these tender exchanges may well be imagined. The lieutenant raised himself and enfolded his wife in a powerful embrace, her body now limp with exhaustion after her grief and tears. Passionately they held their faces close, rubbing cheek against cheek. Reiko's body was trembling. Their breasts, moist with sweat, were tightly joined, and every inch of the young and beautiful bodies had become so much one with the other that it seemed impossible there should ever again be a separation. Reiko cried out. From the heights they plunged into the abyss, and from the abyss they took wing and soared once more to dizzying heights. The lieutenant panted like the regimental standard-bearer on a rout march. . . . As one cycle ended, almost immediately a new wave of passion would be generated, and together—with no trace of fatigue—they would climb again in a single breathless movement to the very summit.

4

When the lieutenant at last turned away, it was not from weariness. For one thing, he was anxious not to undermine the considerable strength he would need in carrying out his suicide. For another, he would have been sorry to mar the sweetness of these last memories by overindulgence.

Since the lieutenant had clearly desisted, Reiko too, with her usual compliance, 80 followed his example. The two lay naked on their backs, with fingers interlaced, staring fixedly at the dark ceiling. The room was warm from the heater, and even when the sweat had ceased to pour from their bodies they felt no cold. Outside, in the hushed night, the sounds of passing traffic had ceased. Even the noise of the trains and streetcars around Yotsuya station did not penetrate this far. After echoing through the region bounded by the moat, they were lost in the heavily wooded park fronting the broad driveway before Akasaka Palace. It was hard to believe in the tension gripping this whole quarter, where the two factions of the bitterly divided Imperial Army now confronted each other, poised for battle.

Savoring the warmth glowing within themselves, they lay still and recalled the ecstasies they had just known. Each moment of the experience was relived. They remembered the taste of kisses which had never wearied, the touch of naked flesh, episode after episode of dizzying bliss. But already, from the dark boards of the ceiling, the face of death was peering down. These joys had been final, and their bodies would never know them again. Not that joy of this intensity—and the same thought had occurred to them both—was ever likely to be re-experienced, even if they should live on to old age.

The feel of their fingers intertwined—this too would soon be lost. Even the wood-grain patterns they now gazed at on the dark ceiling boards would be taken from them. They could feel death edging in, nearer and nearer. There could be no hesitation now. They must have the courage to reach out to death themselves, and to seize it.

"Well, let's make our preparations," said the lieutenant. The note of determination in the words was unmistakable, but at the same time Reiko had never heard her husband's voice so warm and tender.

After they had risen, a variety of tasks awaited them.

85   The lieutenant, who had never once before helped with the bedding, now cheerfully slid back the door of the closet, lifted the mattress across the room by himself, and stowed it away inside.

Reiko turned off the gas heater and put away the lamp standard. During the lieutenant's absence she had arranged this room carefully, sweeping and dusting it to a fresh cleanness, and now—if one overlooked the rosewood table drawn into one corner—the eight-mat room gave all the appearance of a reception room ready to welcome an important guest.

"We've seen some drinking here, haven't we? With Kanō and Homma and Noguchi . . ."

"Yes, they were great drinkers, all of them."

"We'll be meeting them before long, in the other world. They'll tease us, I imagine, when they find I've brought you with me.

90   Descending the stairs, the lieutenant turned to look back into this calm, clean room, now brightly illuminated by the ceiling lamp. There floated across his mind the faces of the young officers who had drunk there, and laughed, and innocently bragged. He had never dreamed then that he would one day cut open his stomach in this room.

In the two rooms downstairs husband and wife busied themselves smoothly and serenely with their respective preparations. The lieutenant went to the toilet, and then to the bathroom to wash. Meanwhile Reiko folded away her husband's padded robe, placed his uniform tunic, his trousers, and a newly cut bleached loincloth in the bathroom, and set out sheets of paper on the living room table for the farewell notes. Then she removed the lid from the writing box and began rubbing ink from the ink tablet. She had already decided upon the wording of her own note.

Reiko's fingers pressed hard upon the cold gilt letters of the ink tablet, and the water in the shallow well at once darkened, as if a black cloud had spread across it. She stopped thinking that this repeated action, the pressure from her fingers, this rise and fall of faint sound, was all and solely for death. It was a routine domestic task, a simple paring away of time until death should finally stand before her. But somehow, in the increasingly smooth motion of the tablet rubbing on the stone, and in the scent from the thickening ink, there was unspeakable darkness.

Neat in his uniform, which he now wore next to his skin, the lieutenant emerged from the bathroom. Without a word he seated himself at the table, bolt upright, took a brush in his hand, and stared undecidedly at the paper before him.

Reiko took a white silk kimono with her and entered the bathroom. When she reappeared in the living room, clad in the white kimono and with her face lightly made up, the farewell note lay completed on the table beneath the lamp. The thick black brushstrokes said simply:

"Long Live the Imperial Forces—Army Lieutenant Takeyama Shinji." 95

While Reiko sat opposite him writing her own note, the lieutenant gazed in silence, intensely serious, at the controlled movement of his wife's pale fingers as they manipulated the brush.

With their respective notes in their hands—the lieutenant's sword strapped to his side, Reiko's small dagger thrust into the sash of her white kimono—the two of them stood before the god shelf and silently prayed. Then they put out all the downstairs lights. As he mounted the stairs the lieutenant turned his head and gazed back at the striking, white-clad figure of his wife, climbing behind him, with lowered eyes, from the darkness beneath.

The farewell notes were laid side by side in the alcove of the upstairs room. They wondered whether they ought not to remove the hanging scroll, but since it had been written by their go-between, Lieutenant General Ozeki, and consisted, moreover, of two Chinese characters signifying "Sincerity," they left it where it was. Even if it were to become stained with splashes of blood, they felt that the lieutenant general would understand.

The lieutenant, sitting erect with his back to the alcove, laid his sword on the floor before him.

Reiko sat facing him, a mat's width away. With the rest of her so severely white 100 the touch of rouge on her lips seemed remarkably seductive.

Across the dividing mat they gazed intently into each other's eyes. The lieutenant's sword lay before his knees. Seeing it, Reiko recalled their first night and was overwhelmed with sadness. The lieutenant spoke, in a hoarse voice:

"As I have no second to help me I shall cut deep. It may look unpleasant, but please do not panic. Death of any sort is a fearful thing to watch. You must not be discouraged by what you see. Is that all right?"

"Yes."

Reiko nodded deeply.

105   Looking at the slender white figure of his wife the lieutenant experienced a bizarre excitement. What he was about to perform was an act in his public capacity as a soldier, something he had never previously shown his wife. It called for a resolution equal to the courage to enter battle; it was a death of no less degree and quality than death in the front line. It was his conduct on the battlefield that he was now to display.

Momentarily the thought led the lieutenant to a strange fantasy. A lonely death on the battlefield, a death beneath the eyes of his beautiful wife . . . in the sensation that he was now to die in these two dimensions, realizing an impossible union of them both, there was sweetness beyond words. This must be the very pinnacle of good fortune, he thought. To have every moment of his death observed by those beautiful eyes—it was like being borne to death on a gentle, fragrant breeze. There was some special favor here. He did not understand precisely what it was, but it was a domain unknown to others: a dispensation granted to no one else had been permitted to himself. In the radiant, bride-like figure of his white-robed wife the lieutenant seemed to see a vision of all those things he had loved and for which he was to lay down his life—the Imperial Household, the Nation, the Army Flag. All these, no less than the wife who sat before him, were presences observing him closely with clear and never-faltering eyes.

Reiko too was gazing intently at her husband, so soon to die, and she thought that never in this world had she seen anything so beautiful. The lieutenant always looked well in uniform, but now, as he contemplated death with severe brows and firmly closed lips, he revealed what was perhaps masculine beauty at its most superb.

"It's time to go," the lieutenant said at last.

Reiko bent her body low to the mat in a deep bow. She could not raise her face. She did not wish to spoil her make-up with tears, but the tears could not be held back.

110   When at length she looked up she saw hazily through the tears that her husband had wound a white bandage around the blade of his now unsheathed sword, leaving five or six inches of naked steel showing at the point.

Resting the sword in its cloth wrapping on the mat before him, the lieutenant rose from his knees, resettled himself cross-legged, and unfastened the hooks of his uniform collar. His eyes no longer saw his wife. Slowly, one by one, he undid the flat brass buttons. The dusky brown chest was revealed, and then the stomach. He unclasped his belt and undid the buttons of his trousers. The pure whiteness of the thickly coiled loincloth showed itself. The lieutenant pushed the cloth down with both hands, further to ease his stomach, and then reached for the white-bandaged blade of his sword. With his left hand he massaged his abdomen, glancing downward as he did so.

To reassure himself on the sharpness of his sword's cutting edge the lieutenant folded back the left trouser flap, exposing a little of his thigh, and lightly drew the blade across the skin. Blood welled up in the wound at once, and several streaks of red trickled downward, glistening in the strong light.

It was the first time Reiko had ever seen her husband's blood, and she felt a violent throbbing in her chest. She looked at her husband's face. The lieutenant was looking at the blood with calm appraisal. For a moment—though thinking at the same time that it was hollow comfort—Reiko experienced a sense of relief.

The lieutenant's eyes fixed his wife with an intense, hawk-like stare. Moving the sword around to his front, he raised himself slightly on his hips and let the upper half of his body lean over the sword point. That he was mustering his whole strength was apparent from the angry tension of the uniform at his shoulders. The lieutenant aimed to strike deep into the left of his stomach. His sharp cry pierced the silence of the room.

Despite the effort he had himself put into the blow, the lieutenant had the impression that someone else had struck the side of his stomach agonizingly with a thick rod of iron. For a second or so his head reeled and he had no idea what had happened. The five or six inches of naked point had vanished completely into his flesh, and the white bandage, gripped in his clenched fist, pressed directly against his stomach.

He returned to consciousness. The blade had certainly pierced the wall of the stomach, he thought. His breathing was difficult, his chest thumped violently, and in some far deep region, which he could hardly believe was a part of himself, a fearful and excruciating pain came welling up as if the ground had split open to disgorge a boiling stream of molten rock. The pain came suddenly nearer, with terrifying speed. The lieutenant bit his lower lip and stifled an instinctive moan.

Was this *seppuku?*—he was thinking. It was a sensation of utter chaos, as if the sky had fallen on his head and the world was reeling drunkenly. His will power and courage, which had seemed so robust before he made the incision, had now dwindled to something like a single hairlike thread of steel, and he was assailed by the uneasy feeling that he must advance along this thread, clinging to it with desperation. His clenched fist had grown moist. Looking down, he saw that both his hand and the cloth about the blade were drenched in blood. His loincloth too was dyed a deep red. It struck him as incredible that, amidst this terrible agony, things which could be seen could still be seen, and existing things existed still.

The moment the lieutenant thrust the sword into his left side and she saw the deathly pallor fall across his face, like an abruptly lowered curtain, Reiko had to struggle to prevent herself from rushing to his side. That was the duty her husband had laid upon her. Opposite her, a mat's space away, she could clearly see her husband biting his lip to stifle the pain. The pain was there, with absolute certainty, before her eyes. And Reiko had no means of rescuing him from it.

The sweat glistened on her husband's forehead. The lieutenant closed his eyes, and then opened them again, as if experimenting. The eyes had lost their luster, and seemed innocent and empty like the eyes of a small animal.

The agony before Reiko's eyes burned as strong as the summer sun, utterly remote from the grief which seemed to be tearing herself apart within. The pain grew steadily in stature, stretching upward. Reiko felt that her husband had already become a man in a separate world, a man whose whole being had been resolved into pain, a prisoner in a cage of pain where no hand could reach out to him. But Reiko felt no pain at all. Her grief was not pain. As she thought about this, Reiko began to feel as if someone had raised a cruel wall of glass high between herself and her husband.

Ever since her marriage her husband's existence had been her own existence, and every breath of his had been a breath drawn by herself. But now, while her husband's existence in pain was a vivid reality, Reiko could find in this grief of hers no certain proof at all of her own existence.

With only his right hand on the sword the lieutenant began to cut sideways across his stomach. But as the blade became entangled with the entrails it was pushed constantly outward by their soft resilience; and the lieutenant realized that it would be necessary, as he cut, to use both hands to keep the point pressed deep into his stomach. He pulled the blade across. It did not cut as easily as he had expected. He directed the strength of his whole body into his right hand and pulled again. There was a cut of three or four inches.

The pain spread slowly outward from the inner depths until the whole stomach reverberated. It was like the wild clanging of a bell. Or like a thousand bells which jangled simultaneously at every breath he breathed and every throb of his pulse, rocking his whole being. The lieutenant could no longer stop himself from moaning. But by now the blade had cut its way through to below the navel, and when he noticed this he felt a sense of satisfaction, and a renewal of courage.

The volume of blood had steadily increased, and now it spurted from the wound as if propelled by the beat of the pulse. The mat before the lieutenant was drenched red with splattered blood, and more blood overflowed onto it from pools which gathered in the folds of the lieutenant's khaki trousers. A spot, like a bird, came flying across to Reiko and settled on the lap of her white silk kimono.

125   By the time the lieutenant had at last drawn the sword across the right side of his stomach, the blade was already cutting shallow and had revealed its naked tip, slippery with blood and grease. But, suddenly stricken by a fit of vomiting, the lieutenant cried out hoarsely. The vomiting made the fierce pain fiercer still, and the stomach, which had thus far remained firm and compact, now abruptly heaved, opening wide its wound, and the entrails burst through, as if the wound too were vomiting. Seemingly ignorant of their master's suffering, the entrails gave an impression of robust health and almost disagreeable vitality as they slipped smoothly out and spilled over into the crotch. The lieutenant's head dropped, his shoulders heaved, his eyes opened to narrow slits, and a thin trickle of saliva dribbled from his mouth. The gold markings on his epaulettes caught the light and glinted.

Blood was scattered everywhere. The lieutenant was soaked in it to his knees, and he sat now in a crumpled and listless posture, one hand on the floor. A raw smell filled the room. The lieutenant, his head drooping, retched repeatedly, and the movement showed vividly in his shoulders. The blade of the sword, now pushed back by the entrails and exposed to its tip, was still in the lieutenant's right hand.

It would be difficult to imagine a more heroic sight than that of the lieutenant at this moment, as he mustered his strength and flung back his head. The movement was performed with sudden violence, and the back of his head struck with a sharp crack against the alcove pillar. Reiko had been sitting until now with her face lowered, gazing in fascination at the tide of blood advancing toward her knees, but the sound took her by surprise and she looked up.

The lieutenant's face was not the face of a living man. The eyes were hollow, the skin parched, the once so lustrous cheeks and lips the color of dried mud. The right hand alone was moving. Laboriously gripping the sword, it hovered shakily in the air like the hand of a marionette and strove to direct the point at the base of the lieutenant's throat. Reiko watched her husband make this last, most heart-rending, futile exertion. Glistening with blood and grease, the point was thrust at the throat again and again. And each time it missed its aim. The strength to guide it was no longer there. The straying point struck the collar and the collar badges. Although its hooks had been unfastened, the stiff military collar had closed together again and was protecting the throat.

Reiko could bear the sight no longer. She tried to go to her husband's help, but she could not stand. She moved through the blood on her knees, and her white skirts grew deep red. Moving to the rear of her husband, she helped no more than by loosening the collar. The quivering blade at last contacted the naked flesh of the throat. At that moment Reiko's impression was that she herself had propelled her husband forward; but that was not the case. It was a movement planned by the lieutenant himself, his last exertion of strength. Abruptly he threw his body at the blade, and the blade pierced his neck, emerging at the nape. There was a tremendous spurt of blood and the lieutenant lay still, cold blue-tinged steel protruding from his neck at the back.

5

Slowly, her socks slippery with blood, Reiko descended the stairway. The upstairs 130 room was now completely still.

Switching on the ground-floor lights, she checked the gas jet and the main gas plug and poured water over the smoldering, half-buried charcoal in the brazier. She stood before the upright mirror in the four-and-a-half-mat room and held up her skirts. The bloodstains made it seem as if a bold, vivid pattern was printed across the lower half of her white kimono. When she sat down before the mirror, she was conscious of the dampness and coldness of her husband's blood in the region of her thighs, and she shivered. Then, for a long while, she lingered over her toilet preparations. She applied the rouge generously to her cheeks, and her lips too she painted heavily. This was no longer make-up to please her husband. It was make-up for the world which she would leave behind, and there was a touch of the magnificent and the spectacular in her brushwork. When she rose, the mat before the mirror was wet with blood. Reiko was not concerned about this.

Returning from the toilet, Reiko stood finally on the cement floor of the porchway. When her husband had bolted the door here last night it had been in preparation for death. For a while she stood immersed in the consideration of a simple problem. Should she now leave the bolt drawn? If she were to lock the door, it could be that the neighbors might not notice their suicide for several days. Reiko did not relish the thought of their two corpses putrefying before discovery. After all, it seemed, it would be best to leave it open. . . . She released the bolt, and also drew open the frosted-glass door a fraction. . . . At once a chill wind blew in. There was no sign of anyone in the midnight streets, and stars glittered ice-cold through the trees in the large house opposite.

Leaving the door as it was, Reiko mounted the stairs. She had walked here and there for some time and her socks were no longer slippery. About halfway up, her nostrils were already assailed by a peculiar smell.

The lieutenant was lying on his face in a sea of blood. The point protruding from his neck seemed to have grown even more prominent than before. Reiko walked heedlessly across the blood. Sitting beside the lieutenant's corpse, she stared intently at the face, which lay on one cheek on the mat. The eyes were opened wide, as if the lieutenant's attention had been attracted by something. She raised the head, folding it in her sleeve, wiped the blood from the lips, and bestowed a last kiss.

135   Then she rose and took from the closet a new white blanket and a waist cord. To prevent any derangement of her skirts, she wrapped the blanket about her waist and bound it there firmly with the cord.

Reiko sat herself on a spot about one foot distant from the lieutenant's body. Drawing the dagger from her sash, she examined its dully gleaming blade intently, and held it to her tongue. The taste of the polished steel was slightly sweet.

Reiko did not linger. When she thought how the pain which had previously opened such a gulf between herself and her dying husband was now to become a part of her own experience, she saw before her only the joy of herself entering a realm her husband had already made his own. In her husband's agonized face there had been something inexplicable which she was seeing for the first time. Now she would solve the riddle. Reiko sensed that at last she too would be able to taste the true bitterness and sweetness of that great moral principle in which her husband believed. What had until now been tasted only faintly through her husband's example she was about to savor directly with her own tongue.

Reiko rested the point of the blade against the base of her throat. She thrust hard. The wound was only shallow. Her head blazed, and her hands shook uncontrollably. She gave the blade a strong pull sideways. A warm substance flooded into her mouth, and everything before her reddened, in a vision of spouting blood. She gathered her strength and plunged the point of the blade deep into her throat.

QUESTIONS FOR DISCUSSION AND WRITING

1. What questions does Mishima raise by summarizing the "facts" of the story in the first paragraph? How does Shinji's "soldierly lecture" on his wedding night help answer some of those questions? How does Reiko's little dagger foreshadow how she will respond to the potential crisis Shinji has explained?

2. How do Shinji's and Reiko's suicide notes help to establish their characters? What other aspects of their character do they reveal in their last night of lovemaking?

3. Why is the couple's home an appropriate place for their joint suicide? What effect will their deaths have on the outside world? Why does Shinji still insist that his act was "on the front line of the spirit"?

4. The first two parts of the story are told from an objective point of view. The rest of the story, though still omniscient, is told from Reiko's point of view. How do her attitude and emotions influence her role as "witness"?

5. What kind of "patriotism" is exhibited by this "heroic and dedicated couple"? Does Mishima show us that their act is beautiful and meaningful, not merely a gory ritual? Explain your answer.

Stories for Comparison

Nadine Gordimer's "Town and Country Lovers" (pages 594–606); Joyce Carol Oates's "The Lady with the Pet Dog" (pages 63–76).

75

....

ALICE MUNRO

Wild Swans

ALICE MUNRO was born in 1931 in Wingham, Ontario, attended the University of Western Ontario, and moved to Victoria, British Columbia, where she founded a bookstore with her husband, James Munro. In the 1950s she began publishing stories based on the experiences and traditions of the farmers and townspeople of southwestern Ontario. These stories were collected in *Dance of the Happy Shades* (1968), which won the Governor General's Literary Award, the highest award for Canadian writers. Munro's novel *Lives of Girls and Women* (1971) won the Canadian Booksellers Award. Since 1972, Munro has lived with her second husband in the small town of Clinton, Ontario. Her recent short-story collections—*Something I've Been Meaning to Tell You* (1974), *Who Do You Think You Are?* (1978), *The Progress of Love* (1986), *The Moons of Jupiter* (1991), and *Open Secret Stories* (1994)— characterize the problems of women with high aspirations trapped by the values and customs of Canadian provincialism. In 1979, Munro published *The Beggar Maid,* which also won the Governor General's Literary Award. This novel, much like her first, uses two central characters to establish the continuity among several groups of tales. In "Wild Swans," reprinted from *The Beggar Maid,* a young girl dares to "enter on a preposterous adventure."

Flo said to watch for White Slavers. She said this was how they operated: an old woman, a motherly or grandmotherly sort, made friends while riding beside you on a bus or train. She offered you candy, which was drugged. Pretty soon you began to droop and mumble, were in no condition to speak for yourself. Oh, help, the woman said, my daughter (granddaughter) is sick, please somebody help me get her off so that she can recover in the fresh air. Up stepped a polite gentleman, pretending to be a stranger, offering assistance. Together, at the next stop, they hustled you off the train or bus, and that was the last the ordinary world ever saw of you. They kept you a prisoner in the White Slave place (to which you had been transported drugged and bound so you wouldn't even know where you were), until such time as you were thoroughly degraded and in despair, your insides torn up by drunken men and invested with vile disease, your mind destroyed by drugs, your hair and teeth fallen out. It took about three years, for you to get to this state. You wouldn't want to go home, then, maybe couldn't remember home, or find your way if you did. So they let you out on the streets.

Flo took ten dollars and put it in a little cloth bag which she sewed to the strap of Rose's slip. Another thing likely to happen was that Rose would get her purse stolen.

Watch out, Flo said as well, for people dressed up as ministers. They were the worst. That disguise was commonly adopted by White Slavers, as well as those after your money.

Rose said she didn't see how she could tell which ones were disguised.

5   Flo had worked in Toronto once. She had worked as a waitress in a coffee shop in Union Station. That was how she knew all she knew. She never saw sunlight, in those days, except on her days off. But she saw plenty else. She saw a man cut another man's stomach with a knife, just pull out his shirt and do a tidy cut, as if it was a watermelon not a stomach. The stomach's owner just sat looking down surprised, with no time to protest. Flo implied that that was nothing, in Toronto. She saw two bad women (that was what Flo called whores, running the two words together, like badminton) get into a fight, and a man laughed at them, other men stopped and laughed and egged them on, and they had their fists full of each other's hair. At last the police came and took them away, still howling and yelping.

She saw a child die of a fit, too. Its face was black as ink.

"Well I'm not scared," said Rose provokingly. "There's the police, anyway."

"Oh, them! They'd be the first ones to diddle you!"

She did not believe anything Flo said on the subject of sex. Consider the undertaker.

10   A little bald man, very neatly dressed, would come into the store sometimes and speak to Flo with a placating expression.

"I only wanted a bag of candy. And maybe a few packages of gum. And one or two chocolate bars. Could you go to the trouble of wrapping them?"

Flo in her mock-deferential tone would assure him that she could. She wrapped them in heavy-duty white paper, so they were something like presents. He took his time with the selection, humming and chatting, then dawdled for a while. He might ask how Flo was feeling. And how Rose was, if she was there.

"You look pale. Young girls need fresh air." To Flo he would say, "You work too hard. You've worked hard all your life."

"No rest for the wicked," Flo would say agreeably.

15   When he went out she hurried to the window. There it was—the old black hearse with its purple curtains.

"He'll be after them today!" Flo would say as the hearse rolled away at a gentle pace, almost a funeral pace. The little man had been an undertaker, but he was retired now. The hearse was retired too. His sons had taken over the undertaking and bought a new one. He drove the old hearse all over the country, looking for women. So Flo said. Rose could not believe it. Flo said he gave them the gum and the candy. Rose said he probably ate them himself. Flo said he had been seen, he had been heard. In mild weather he drove with the windows down, singing, to himself or to somebody out of sight in the back.

> Her brow is like the snowdrift
> Her throat is like the swan

Flo imitated him singing. Gently overtaking some woman walking on a back road, or resting at a country crossroads. All compliments and courtesy and chocolate bars, offering a ride. Of course every woman who reported being asked said she had turned him down. He never pestered anybody, drove politely on. He called in at houses, and if the husband was home he seemed to like just as well as anything to sit and chat. Wives said that was all he ever did anyway but Flo did not believe it.

"Some women are taken in," she said. "A number." She liked to speculate on what the hearse was like inside. Plush. Plush on the walls and the roof and the floor. Soft purple, the color of the curtains, the color of dark lilacs.

All nonsense, Rose thought. Who could believe it, of a man that age?

Rose was going to Toronto on the train for the first time by herself. She had been once before, but that was with Flo, long before her father died. They took along their own sandwiches and bought milk from the vendor on the train. It was sour. Sour chocolate milk. Rose kept taking tiny sips, unwilling to admit that something so much desired could fail her. Flo sniffed it, then hunted up and down the train until she found the old man in his red jacket, with no teeth and the tray hanging around his neck. She invited him to sample the chocolate milk. She invited people nearby to smell it. He let her have some ginger ale for nothing. It was slightly warm.

"I let him know," Flo said looking around after he had left. "You have to let them [20] know."

A woman agreed with her but most people looked out the window. Rose drank the warm ginger ale. Either that, or the scene with the vendor, or the conversation Flo and the agreeing woman now got into about where they came from, why they were going to Toronto, and Rose's morning constipation which was why she was lacking color, or the small amount of chocolate milk she had got inside her, caused her to throw up in the train toilet. All day long she was afraid people in Toronto could smell vomit on her coat.

This time Flo started the trip off by saying, "Keep an eye on her, she's never been away from home before!" to the conductor, then looking around and laughing, to show that was jokingly meant. Then she had to get off. It seemed the conductor had no more need for jokes than Rose had, and no intention of keeping an eye on anybody. He never spoke to Rose except to ask for her ticket. She had a window seat, and was soon extraordinarily happy. She felt Flo receding, West Hanratty flying away from her, her own wearying self discarded as easily as everything else. She loved the towns less and less known. A woman was standing at her back door in her nightgown, not caring if everybody on the train saw her. They were traveling south, out of the snow belt, into an earlier spring, a tenderer sort of landscape. People could grow peach trees in their backyards.

Rose collected in her mind the things she had to look for in Toronto. First, things for Flo. Special stockings for her varicose veins. A special kind of cement for sticking handles on pots. And a full set of dominoes.

For herself Rose wanted to buy hair-remover to put on her arms and legs, and if possible an arrangement of inflatable cushions, supposed to reduce your hips and thighs. She thought they probably had hair-remover in the drugstore in Hanratty, but the woman in there was a friend of Flo's and told everything. She told Flo who bought hair dye and slimming medicine and French safes. As for the cushion business, you could send away for it but there was sure to be a comment at the Post Office, and Flo knew people there as well. She also planned to buy some bangles, and an angora sweater. She had great hopes of silver bangles and powder-blue angora. She thought they could transform her, make her calm and slender and take the frizz out of her hair, dry her underarms and turn her complexion to pearl.

25   The money for these things, as well as the money for the trip, came from a prize Rose had won, for writing an essay called "Art and Science in the World of Tomorrow." To her surprise, Flo asked if she could read it, and while she was reading it, she remarked that they must have thought they had to give Rose the prize for swallowing the dictionary. Then she said shyly, "It's very interesting."

She would have to spend the night at Cela McKinney's. Cela McKinney was her father's cousin. She had married a hotel manager and thought she had gone up in the world. But the hotel manager came home one day and sat down on the dining room floor between two chairs and said, "I am never going to leave this house again." Nothing unusual had happened, he had just decided not to go out of the house again, and he didn't, until he died. That had made Cela McKinney odd and nervous. She locked her doors at eight o'clock. She was also very stingy. Supper was usually oatmeal porridge, with raisins. Her house was dark and narrow and smelled like a bank.

The train was filling up. At Brantford a man asked if she would mind if he sat down beside her.

"It's cooler out than you'd think," he said. He offered her part of his newspaper. She said no thanks.

Then lest he think her rude she said it really was cooler. She went on looking out the window at the spring morning. There was no snow left, down here. The trees and bushes seemed to have a paler bark than they did at home. Even the sunlight looked different. It was as different from home, here, as the coast of the Mediterranean would be, or the valleys of California.

30   "Filthy windows, you'd think they'd take more care," the man said. "Do you travel much by train?"

She said no.

Water was lying in the fields. He nodded at it and said there was a lot this year.

"Heavy snows."

She noticed his saying *snows,* a poetic-sounding word. Anyone at home would have said *snow.*

"I had an unusual experience the other day. I was driving out in the country. In 35 fact I was on my way to see one of my parishioners, a lady with a heart condition—"

She looked quickly at his collar. He was wearing an ordinary shirt and tie and a dark blue suit.

"Oh, yes," he said. "I'm a United Church minister. But I don't always wear my uniform. I wear it for preaching in. I'm off duty today."

"Well as I said I was driving through the country and I saw some Canada geese down on a pond, and I took another look, and there were some swans down with them. A whole great flock of swans. What a lovely sight they were. They would be on their spring migration, I expect, heading up north. What a spectacle. I never saw anything like it."

Rose was unable to think appreciatively of the wild swans because she was afraid he was going to lead the conversation from them to Nature in general and then to God, the way a minister would feel obliged to do. But he did not, he stopped with the swans.

"A very fine sight. You would have enjoyed them."   40

He was between fifty and sixty years old, Rose thought. He was short, and energetic-looking, with a square ruddy face and bright waves of gray hair combed straight up from his forehead. When she realized he was not going to mention God she felt she ought to show her gratitude.

She said they must have been lovely.

"It wasn't even a regular pond, it was only some water lying in a field. It was just luck the water was lying there and they came down and I came driving by at the right time. Just luck. They come in at the east end of Lake Erie, I think. But I never was lucky enough to see them before."

She turned by degrees to the window, and he returned to his paper. She remained slightly smiling, so as not to seem rude, not to seem to be rejecting conversation altogether. The morning really was cool, and she had taken down her coat off the hook where she put it when she first got on the train, she had spread it over herself, like a lap robe. She had set her purse on the floor when the minister sat down, to give him room. He took the sections of the paper apart, shaking and rustling them in a leisurely, rather showy, way. He seemed to her the sort of person who does everything in a showy way. A ministerial way. He brushed aside the sections he didn't want at the moment. A corner of newspaper touched her leg, just at the edge of her coat.

She thought for some time that it was the paper. Then she said to herself, what 45 if it is a hand? That was the kind of thing she could imagine. She would sometimes look at men's hands, at the fuzz on their forearms, their concentrating profiles. She would think about everything they could do. Even the stupid ones. For instance the driver-salesman who brought the bread to Flo's store. The ripeness and confidence of manner, the settled mixture of ease and alertness with which he handled the bread truck. A fold of mature belly over the belt did not displease her. Another time she had her eye on the French teacher at school. Not a Frenchman at all, really, his name was McLaren, but Rose thought teaching French had rubbed off on him, made him look like one. Quick and sallow; sharp shoulders; hooked nose and sad eyes. She saw him lapping and coiling his way through slow pleasures, a perfect autocrat of indulgences. She had a considerable longing to be somebody's object. Pounded, pleasured, reduced, exhausted.

But what if it was a hand? What if it really was a hand? She shifted slightly, moved as much as she could toward the window. Her imagination seemed to have created this reality, a reality she was not prepared for at all. She found it alarming. She was concentrating on that leg, that bit of skin with the stocking over it. She could not bring herself to look. Was there a pressure, or was there not? She shifted again. Her legs had been, and remained, tightly closed. It was. It was a hand. It was a hand's pressure.

Please don't. That was what she tried to say. She shaped the words in her mind, tried them out, then couldn't get them past her lips. Why was that? The embarrassment, was it, the fear that people might hear? People were all around them, the seats were full.

It was not only that.

She did manage to look at him, not raising her head but turning it cautiously. He had tilted his seat back and closed his eyes. There was his dark blue suit sleeve, disappearing under the newspaper. He had arranged the paper so that it overlapped Rose's coat. His hand was underneath, simply resting, as if flung out in sleep.

50   Now, Rose could have shifted the newspaper and removed her coat. If he was not asleep, he would have been obliged to draw back his hand. If he was asleep, if he did not draw it back, she could have whispered, *Excuse me,* and set his hand firmly on his own knee. This solution, so obvious and foolproof, did not occur to her. And she would have to wonder, why not? The minister's hand was not, or not yet, at all welcome to her. It made her feel uncomfortable, resentful, slightly disgusted, trapped and wary. But she could not take charge of it, to reject it. She could not insist that it was there, when he seemed to be insisting that it was not. How could she declare him responsible, when he lay there so harmless and trusting, resting himself before his busy day, with such a pleased and healthy face? A man older than her father would be, if he were living, a man used to deference, an appreciator of Nature, delighter in wild swans. If she did say *Please don't* she was sure he would ignore her, as if overlooking some silliness or impoliteness on her part. She knew that as soon as she said it she would hope he had not heard.

But there was more to it than that. Curiosity. More constant, more imperious, than any lust. A lust in itself, that will make you draw back and wait, wait too long, risk almost anything, just to see what will happen. *To see what will happen.*

The hand began, over the next several miles, the most delicate, the most timid, pressures and investigations. Not asleep. Or if he was, his hand wasn't. She did feel disgust. She felt a faint, wandering nausea. She thought of flesh: lumps of flesh, pink snouts, fat tongues, blunt fingers, all on their way trotting and creeping and lolling and rubbing, looking for their comfort. She thought of cats in heat rubbing themselves along the top of board fences, yowling with their miserable complaint. It was pitiful, infantile, this itching and shoving and squeezing. Spongy tissues, inflamed membranes, tormented nerve-ends, shameful smells; humiliation.

All that was starting. His hand, that she wouldn't ever have wanted to hold, that she wouldn't have squeezed back, his stubborn patient hand was able, after all, to get the ferns to rustle and the streams to flow, to waken a sly luxuriance.

Nevertheless, she would rather not. She would still rather not. Please remove this, she said out the window. Stop it, please, she said to the stumps and barns. The hand moved up her leg past the top of her stocking to her bare skin, had moved higher, under her suspender, reached her underpants and the lower part of her belly. Her legs were still crossed, pinched together. While her legs stayed crossed she could lay claim to innocence, she had not admitted anything. She could still believe that she would stop this in a minute. Nothing was going to happen, nothing more. Her legs were never going to open.

But they were. They were. As the train crossed the Niagra Escarpment above 55 Dundas, as they looked down at the preglacial valley, the silver-wooded rubble of little hills, as they came sliding down to the shores of Lake Ontario, she would make this slow, and silent, and definite, declaration, perhaps disappointing as much as satisfying the hand's owner. He would not lift his eyelids, his face would not alter, his fingers would not hesitate, but would go powerfully and discreetly to work. Invasion, and welcome, and sunlight flashing far and wide on the lake water; miles of bare orchards stirring round Burlington.

This was disgrace, this was beggary. But what harm in that, we say to ourselves at such moments, what harm in anything, the worse the better, as we ride the cold wave of greed, of greedy assent. A stranger's hand, or root vegetables or humble kitchen tools that people tell jokes about; the world is tumbling with innocent-seeming objects ready to declare themselves, slippery and obliging. She was careful of her breathing. She could not believe this. Victim and accomplice she was borne past Glassco's Jams and Marmalades, past the big pulsating pipes of oil refineries. They glided into suburbs where bedsheets, and towels used to wipe up intimate stains, flapped leeringly on the clotheslines, where even the children seemed to be frolicking lewdly in the schoolyards, and the very truckdrivers stopped at the railway crossings must be thrusting their thumbs gleefully into curled hands. Such cunning antics now, such popular visions. The gates and towers of the Exhibition Grounds came into view, the painted domes and pillars floated marvelously against her eyelids' rosy sky. Then flew apart in celebration. You could have had such a flock of birds, wild swans, even, wakened under one big dome together, exploding from it, taking to the sky.

She bit the edge of her tongue. Very soon the conductor passed through the train, to stir the travelers, warn them back to life.

In the darkness under the station the United Church minister, refreshed, opened his eyes and got his paper folded together, then asked if she would like some help with her coat. His gallantry was self-satisfied, dismissive. No, said Rose, with a sore tongue. He hurried out of the train ahead of her. She did not see him in the station. She never saw him again in her life. But he remained on call, so to speak, for years and years, ready to slip into place at a critical moment, without even any regard, later on, for husband or lovers. What recommended him? She could never understand it. His simplicity, his arrogance, his perversely appealing lack of handsomeness, even of ordinary grown-up masculinity?

When he stood up she saw that he was shorter even than she had thought, that his face was pink and shiny, that there was something crude and pushy and childish about him.

Was he a minister, really, or was that only what he said? Flo had mentioned people who were not ministers, dressed up as if they were. Not real ministers dressed as if they were not. Or, stranger still, men who were not real ministers pretending to be real but dressed as if they were not. But that she had come as close as she had, to what could happen, was an unwelcome thing. Rose walked through Union Station feeling the little bag with the ten dollars rubbing at her, knew she would feel it all day long, rubbing its reminder against her skin.

60   She couldn't stop getting Flo's messages, even with that. She remembered, because she was in Union Station, that there was a girl named Mavis working here, in the Gift Shop, when Flo was working in the coffee shop. Mavis had warts on her eyelids that looked like they were going to turn into sties but they didn't, they went away. Maybe she had them removed, Flo didn't ask. She was very good-looking, without them. There was a movie star in those days she looked a lot like. The movie star's name was Frances Farmer.

Frances Farmer. Rose had never heard of her.

That was the name. And Mavis went and bought herself a big hat that dipped over one eye and a dress entirely made of lace. She went off for the weekend to Georgian Bay, to a resort up there. She booked herself in under the name of Florence Farmer. To give everybody the idea she was really the other one, Frances Farmer, but calling herself Florence because she was on holiday and didn't want to be recognized. She had a little cigarette holder that was black and mother-of-pearl. She could have been arrested, Flo said. For the *nerve*.

Rose almost went over to the Gift Shop, to see if Mavis was still there and if she could recognize her. She thought it would be an especially fine thing, to manage a transformation like that. To dare it; to get away with it, to enter on preposterous adventures in your own, but newly named, skin.

QUESTIONS FOR DISCUSSION AND WRITING

1. How do Flo's warnings foreshadow the conflicts in the story? How does Mavis's story serve as a denouement for the whole story?

2. How does Flo know what she knows? How are Flo and Rose characterized by the purchases Rose will make in Toronto? Why is Rose unable to defend herself against the self-described minister's attentions?

3. What details suggest the claustrophobic world of West Hanratty? How do Rose's expectations about a "tenderer sort of landscape" reveal what she really seeks on this trip?

4. How does the third-person narrator depict Rose's conflicting emotions? What evidence suggests that the narrator is sympathetic toward Rose and unsympathetic toward Flo?

5. How is the theme of the story implied by the title? How can Rose be both "victim" and "accomplice" in her "preposterous adventure"? In what sense is Rose "transformed" by this experience?

Stories for Comparison

Alice Adams's "Truth or Consequences" (pages 164–173); Sandra Cisneros's "One Holy Night" (pages 377–382).

76

JOYCE   CAROL   OATES

Where Are You Going, Where Have You Been?

JOYCE CAROL OATES was born in 1938 in Lockport, New York, and educated at Syracuse University and the University of Wisconsin. Even as an undergraduate, Oates was a prolific writer, winning the 1959 *Mademoiselle* college fiction award for her short story "In the Old World." While she was a graduate student, Oates published stories in magazines such as *Cosmopolitan, Prairie Schooner,* and *The Literary Review.* She accepted her first teaching assignment at the University of Detroit and then moved to the University of Windsor in Ontario, where she taught and wrote for twelve years. Since 1978, she has been a member of the faculty at Princeton University. By any standards, Oates's literary productivity has been astonishing. By 1982, she had published almost forty books, including over a dozen novels and about one hundred short stories. She has also written several volumes of literary criticism, such as *New Heaven, New Earth: The Visionary Experience in Literature* (1974), a study of Henry James, Virginia Woolf, D. H. Lawrence, Franz Kafka, and Flannery O'Connor, authors who, like Oates, try to fuse the materialistic and symbolic worlds. Oates's best-known novels include *A Garden of Earthly Delights* (1967), *Them* (1969)—which won the National Book Award—*Wonderland* (1971), *Do with Me What You Will* (1973), *Childwold* (1976), *Angel of Light* (1981), *A Bloodsmoor Romance* (1982), *You Must Remember This* (1987), and *Black Water* (1992). Her short stories have been published in a wide range of magazines and collected in volumes such as *By the North Gate* (1963), *The Wheel of Love* (1970), *Marriages and Infidelities* (1972), *Nightside* (1977), *A Sentimental Education* (1980), *Last Days* (1984) and *Will You Always Love Me?*

(1996). "Where Are You Going, Where Have You Been?," reprinted from *The Wheel of Love,* describes a girl's terrifying encounter with a demonic figure from a drive-in restaurant.

Her name was Connie. She was fifteen and she had a quick nervous giggling habit of craning her neck to glance into mirrors or checking other people's faces to make sure her own was all right. Her mother, who noticed everything and knew everything and who hadn't much reason any longer to look at her own face, always scolded Connie about it. "Stop gawking at yourself, who are you? You think you're so pretty?" she would say. Connie would raise her eyebrows at these familiar complaints and look right through her mother, into a shadowy vision of herself as she was right at that moment: she knew she was pretty and that was everything. Her mother had been pretty once too, if you could believe those old snapshots in the album, but now her looks were gone and that was why she was always after Connie.

"Why don't you keep your room clean like your sister? How've you got your hair fixed—what the hell stinks? Hair spray? You don't see your sister using that junk."

Her sister June was twenty-four and still lived at home. She was a secretary in the high school Connie attended, and if that wasn't bad enough—with her in the same building—she was so plain and chunky and steady that Connie had to hear her praised all the time by her mother and her mother's sisters. June did this, June did that, she saved money and helped clean the house and cooked and Connie couldn't do a thing, her mind was all filled with trashy daydreams. Their father was away at work most of the time and when he came home he wanted supper and he read the newspaper at supper and after supper he went to bed. He didn't bother talking much to them, but around his bent head Connie's mother kept picking at her until Connie wished her mother were dead and she herself were dead and it were all over. "She makes me want to throw up sometimes," she complained to her friends. She had a high, breathless, amused voice which made everything she said sound a little forced, whether it was sincere or not.

There was one good thing: June went places with girlfriends of hers, girls who were just as plain and steady as she, and so when Connie wanted to do that her mother had no objections. The father of Connie's best girlfriend drove the girls the three miles to town and left them off at a shopping plaza, so that they could walk through the stores or go to a movie, and when he came to pick them up again at eleven he never bothered to ask what they had done.

5   They must have been familiar sights, walking around that shopping plaza in their shorts and flat ballerina slippers that always scuffed the sidewalk, with charm bracelets jingling on their thin wrists; they would lean together to whisper and laugh secretly if someone passed by who amused or interested them. Connie had long dark blond hair that drew anyone's eye to it, and she wore part of it pulled up on her head and puffed out and the rest of it she let fall down her back. She wore a pullover jersey blouse that looked one way when she was at home and another way when she was away from home. Everything about her had two sides to it, one for home and

one for anywhere that was not home: her walk that could be childlike and bobbing, or languid enough to make anyone think she was hearing music in her head, her mouth which was pale and smirking most of the time, but bright and pink on these evenings out, her laugh which was cynical and drawling at home—"Ha, ha, very funny"—but high-pitched and nervous anywhere else, like the jingling of the charms on her bracelet.

Sometimes they did go shopping or to a movie. But sometimes they went across the highway, ducking fast across the busy road, to a drive-in restaurant where older kids hung out. The restaurant was shaped like a big bottle, though squatter than a real bottle, and on its cap was a revolving figure of a grinning boy who held a hamburger aloft. One night in midsummer they ran across, breathless with daring, and right away someone leaned out a car window and invited them over, but it was just a boy from high school they didn't like. It made them feel good to be able to ignore him. They went up through the maze of parked and cruising cars to the bright-lit, fly-infested restaurant, their faces pleased and expectant as if they were entering a sacred building that loomed out of the night to give them what haven and what blessing they yearned for. They sat at the counter and crossed their legs at the ankles, their thin shoulders rigid with excitement, and listened to the music that made everything so good: the music was always in the background like music at a church service, it was something to depend upon.

A boy named Eddie came in to talk with them. He sat backward on his stool, turning himself jerkily around in semicircles and then stopping and turning again, and after a while he asked Connie if she would like something to eat. She said she did and so she tapped her friend's arm on her way out—her friend pulled her face up into a brave droll look—and Connie said she would meet her at eleven, across the way. "I just hate to leave her like that," Connie said earnestly, but the boy said that she wouldn't be alone for long. So they went out to his car and on the way Connie couldn't help but let her eyes wander over the windshields and faces all around her, her face gleaming with a joy that had nothing to do with Eddie or even this place; it might have been the music. She drew her shoulders up and sucked in her breath with the pure pleasure of being alive, and just at that moment she happened to glance at a face just a few feet from hers. It was a boy with shaggy black hair, in a convertible jalopy painted gold. He stared at her and then his lips widened into a grin. Connie slit her eyes at him and turned away, but she couldn't help glancing back and there he was still watching her. He wagged a finger and laughed and said, "Gonna get you, baby," and Connie turned away again without Eddie noticing anything.

She spent three hours with him, at the restaurant where they ate hamburgers and drank Cokes in wax cups that were always sweating, and then down an alley a mile or so away, and when he left her off at five to eleven only the movie house was still open at the plaza. Her girlfriend was there, talking with a boy. When Connie came up the two girls smiled at each other and Connie said, "How was the movie?" and the girl said, "*You* should know." They rode off with the girl's father, sleepy and pleased, and Connie couldn't help but look at the darkened shopping plaza with its big empty parking lot and its signs that were faded and ghostly now, and over at the drive-in restaurant where cars were still circling tirelessly. She couldn't hear the music at this distance.

Next morning June asked her how the movie was and Connie said, "So-so."

10   She and that girl and occasionally another girl went out several times a week that way, and the rest of the time Connie spent around the house—it was summer vacation—getting in her mother's way and thinking, dreaming, about the boys she met. But all the boys fell back and dissolved into a single face that was not even a face, but an idea, a feeling, mixed up with the urgent insistent pounding of the music and the humid night air of July. Connie's mother kept dragging her back to the daylight by finding things for her to do or saying, suddenly, "What's this about the Pettinger girl?"

And Connie would say nervously, "Oh, her. That dope." She always drew thick clear lines between herself and such girls, and her mother was simple and kindly enough to believe her. Her mother was so simple, Connie thought, that it was maybe cruel to fool her so much. Her mother went scuffling around the house in old bedroom slippers and complained over the telephone to one sister about the other, then the other called up and the two of them complained about the third one. If June's name was mentioned her mother's tone was approving, and if Connie's name was mentioned it was disapproving. This did not really mean she disliked Connie and actually Connie thought that her mother preferred her to June because she was prettier, but the two of them kept up a pretense of exasperation, a sense that they were tugging and struggling over something of little value to either of them. Sometimes, over coffee, they were almost friends, but something would come up—some vexation that was like a fly buzzing suddenly around their heads—and their faces went hard with contempt.

One Sunday Connie got up at eleven—none of them bothered with church—and washed her hair so that it could dry all day long, in the sun. Her parents and sister were going to a barbecue at an aunt's house and Connie said no, she wasn't interested, rolling her eyes to let her mother know just what she thought of it. "Stay home alone then," her mother said sharply. Connie sat out back in a lawn chair and watched them drive away, her father quiet and bald, hunched around so that he could back the car out, her mother with a look that was still angry and not at all softened through the windshield, and in the back seat poor old June all dressed up as if she didn't know what a barbecue was, with all the running yelling kids and the flies. Connie sat with her eyes closed in the sun, dreaming and dazed with the warmth about her as if this were a kind of love, the caresses of love, and her mind slipped over onto thoughts of the boy she had been with the night before and how nice he had been, how sweet it always was, not the way someone like June would suppose but sweet, gentle, the way it was in movies and promised in songs; and when she opened her eyes she hardly knew where she was, the back yard ran off into weeds and a fence line of trees and behind it the sky was perfectly blue and still. The asbestos "ranch house" that was now three years old startled her—it looked small. She shook her head as if to get awake.

It was too hot. She went inside the house and turned on the radio to drown out the quiet. She sat on the edge of her bed, barefoot, and listened for an hour and a half to a program called XYZ Sunday Jamboree, record after record of hard, fast, shrieking songs she sang along with, interspersed by exclamations from "Bobby King":

"An' look here you girls at Napoleon's—Son and Charley want you to pay real close attention to this song coming up!"

And Connie paid close attention herself, bathed in a glow of slow-pulsed joy that seemed to rise mysteriously out of the music itself and lay languidly about the airless little room, breathed in and breathed out with each gentle rise and fall of her chest.

After a while she heard a car coming up the drive. She sat up at once, startled, 15 because it couldn't be her father so soon. The gravel kept crunching all the way in from the road—the driveway was long—and Connie ran to the window. It was a car she didn't know. It was an open jalopy, painted a bright gold that caught the sunlight opaquely. Her heart began to pound and her fingers snatched at her hair, checking it, and she whispered "Christ, Christ," wondering how bad she looked. The car came to a stop at the side door and the horn sounded four short taps as if this were a signal Connie knew.

She went into the kitchen and approached the door slowly, then hung out the screen door, her bare toes curling down off the step. There were two boys in the car and now she recognized the driver: he had shaggy, shabby black hair that looked crazy as a wig and he was grinning at her.

"I ain't late, am I?" he said.

"Who the hell do you think you are?" Connie said.

"Toldja I'd be out, didn't I?"

"I don't even know who you are."   20

She spoke sullenly, careful to show no interest or pleasure, and he spoke in a fast bright monotone. Connie looked past him to the other boy, taking her time. He had fair brown hair, with a lock that fell onto his forehead. His sideburns gave him a fierce, embarrassed look, but so far he hadn't even bothered to glance at her. Both boys wore sunglasses. The driver's glasses were metallic and mirrored everything in miniature.

"You wanta come for a ride?" he said.

Connie smirked and let her hair fall loose over one shoulder.

"Don'tcha like my car? New paint job," he said. "Hey."

"What?"   25

"You're cute."

She pretended to fidget, chasing flies away from the door.

"Don'tcha believe me, or what?" he said.

"Look, I don't even know who you are," Connie said in disgust.

"Hey, Ellie's got a radio, see. Mine's broken down." He lifted his friend's arm 30 and showed her the little transistor the boy was holding, and now Connie began to hear the music. It was the same program that was playing inside the house.

"Bobby King?" she said.

"I listen to him all the time. I think he's great."

"He's kind of great," Connie said reluctantly.

"Listen, that guy's *great*. He knows where the action is."

Connie blushed a little, because the glasses made it impossible for her to see just 35 what this boy was looking at. She couldn't decide if she liked him or if he was just a jerk, and so she dawdled in the doorway and wouldn't come down or go back inside. She said, "What's all that stuff painted on your car?"

"Can'tcha read it?" He opened the door very carefully, as if he was afraid it might fall off. He slid out just as carefully, planting his feet firmly on the ground, the tiny metallic world in his glasses slowing down like gelatine hardening and in the midst of it Connie's bright green blouse. "This here is my name, to begin with," he said. ARNOLD FRIEND was written in tarlike black letters on the side, with a drawing of a round grinning face that reminded Connie of a pumpkin, except it wore sunglasses. "I wanta introduce myself, I'm Arnold Friend and that's my real name and I'm gonna be your friend, honey, and inside the car's Ellie Oscar, he's kinda shy." Ellie brought his transistor radio up to his shoulder and balanced it there. "Now these numbers are a secret code, honey," Arnold Friend explained. He read off the numbers 33, 19, 17 and raised his eyebrows at her to see what she thought of that, but she didn't think much of it. The left rear fender had been smashed and around it was written, on the gleaming gold background: DONE BY CRAZY WOMAN DRIVER. Connie had to laugh at that. Arnold Friend was pleased at her laughter and looked up at her. "Around the other side's a lot more—you wanta come and see them?"

"No."

"Why not?"

"Why should I?"

40   "Don'tcha wanta see what's on the car? Don'tcha wanta go for a ride?"

"I don't know."

"Why not?"

"I got things to do."

"Like what?"

45   "Things."

He laughed as if she had said something funny. He slapped his thighs. He was standing in a strange way, leaning back against the car as if he were balancing himself. He wasn't tall, only an inch or so taller than she would be if she came down to him. Connie liked the way he was dressed, which was the way all of them dressed; tight faded jeans stuffed into black, scuffed boots, a belt that pulled his waist in and showed how lean he was, and a white pullover shirt that was a little soiled and showed the hard small muscles of his arms and shoulders. He looked as if he probably did hard work, lifting and carrying things. Even his neck looked muscular. And his face was a familiar face, somehow: the jaw and chin and cheeks slightly darkened, because he hadn't shaved for a day or two, and the nose long and hawklike, sniffing as if she were a treat he was going to gobble up and it was all a joke.

"Connie, you ain't telling the truth. This is your day set aside for a ride with me and you know it," he said, still laughing. The way he straightened and recovered from his fit of laughing showed that it had been all fake.

"How do you know what my name is?" she said suspiciously.

"It's Connie."

50   "Maybe and maybe not."

"I know my Connie," he said, wagging his finger. Now she remembered him even better, back at the restaurant, and her cheeks warmed at the thought of how she sucked in her breath just at the moment she passed him—how she must have looked at him. And he had remembered her. "Ellie and I come out here especially for you," he said. "Ellie can sit in back. How about it?"

"Where?"

"Where what?"

"Where're we going?"

He looked at her. He took off the sunglasses and she saw how pale the skin 55 around his eyes was, like holes that were not in shadow but instead in light. His eyes were like chips of broken glass that catch the light in an amiable way. He smiled. It was as if the idea of going for a ride somewhere, to some place, was a new idea to him.

"Just for a ride, Connie sweetheart."

"I never said my name was Connie," she said.

"But I know what it is. I know your name and all about you, lots of things," Arnold Friend said. He had not moved yet but stood still leaning back against the side of his jalopy. "I took a special interest in you, such a pretty girl, and found out all about you—like I know your parents and sister are gone somewhere and I know where and how long they're going to be gone, and I know who you were with last night, and your best girlfriend's name is Betty. Right?"

He spoke in a simple lilting voice, exactly as if he were reciting the words to a song. His smile assured her that everything was fine. In the car Ellie turned up the volume on his radio and did not bother to look around at them.

"Ellie can sit in the back seat," Arnold Friend said. He indicated his friend with 60 a casual jerk of his chin, as if Ellie did not count and she should not bother with him.

"How'd you find out all that stuff?" Connie said.

"Listen: Betty Schultz and Tony Fitch and Jimmy Pettinger and Nancy Pettinger," he said, in a chant. "Raymond Stanley and Bob Hutter—"

"Do you know all those kids?"

"I know everybody."

"Look, you're kidding. You're not from around here."   65

"Sure."

"But—how come we never saw you before?"

"Sure you saw me before," he said. He looked down at his boots, as if he were a little offended. "You just don't remember."

"I guess I'd remember you," Connie said.

"Yeah?" He looked up at this, beaming. He was pleased. He began to mark time 70 with the music from Ellie's radio, tapping his fists lightly together. Connie looked away from his smile to the car, which was painted so bright it almost hurt her eyes to look at it. She looked at that name, ARNOLD FRIEND. And up at the front fender was an expression that was familiar—MAN THE FLYING SAUCERS. It was an expression kids had used the year before, but didn't use this year. She looked at it for a while as if the words meant something to her that she did not yet know.

"What're you thinking about? Huh?" Arnold Friend demanded. "Not worried about your hair blowing around in the car, are you?"

"No."

"Think I maybe can't drive good?"

"How do I know?"

75   "You're a hard girl to handle. How come?" he said. "Don't you know I'm your friend? Didn't you see me put my sign in the air when you walked by?"

"What sign?"

"My sign." And he drew an X in the air, leaning out toward her. They were maybe ten feet apart. After his hand fell back to his side the X was still in the air, almost visible. Connie let the screen door close and stood perfectly still inside it, listening to the music from her radio and the boy's blend together. She stared at Arnold Friend. He stood there so stiffly relaxed, pretending to be relaxed, with one hand idly on the door handle as if he were keeping himself up that way and had no intention of ever moving again. She recognized most things about him, the tight jeans that showed his thighs and buttocks and the greasy leather boots and the tight shirt, and even that slippery friendly smile of his, that sleepy dreamy smile that all the boys used to get across ideas they didn't want to put into words. She recognized all this and also the singsong way he talked, slightly mocking, kidding, but serious and a little melancholy, and she recognized the way he tapped one fist against the other in homage of the perpetual music behind him. But all these things did not come together.

She said suddenly, "Hey, how old are you?"

His smile faded. She could see then that he wasn't a kid, he was much older—thirty, maybe more. At this knowledge her heart began to pound faster.

80   "That's a crazy thing to ask. Can'tcha see I'm your own age?"

"Like hell you are."

"Or maybe a coupla years older. I'm eighteen."

"Eighteen?" she said doubtfully.

He grinned to reassure her and lines appeared at the corners of his mouth. His teeth were big and white. He grinned so broadly his eyes became slits and she saw how thick the lashes were, thick and black as if painted with a black tarlike material. Then he seemed to become embarrassed, abruptly, and looked over his shoulder at Ellie. "*Him,* he's crazy," he said. "Ain't he a riot, he's a nut, a real character." Ellie was still listening to the music. His sunglasses told nothing about what he was thinking. He wore a bright orange shirt unbuttoned halfway to show his chest, which was a pale, bluish chest and not muscular like Arnold Friend's. His shirt collar was turned up all around and the very tips of the collar pointed out past his chin as if they were protecting him. He was pressing the transistor radio up against his ear and sat there in a kind of daze, right in the sun.

85   "He's kinda strange," Connie said.

"Hey, she says you're kinda strange! Kinda strange!" Arnold Friend cried. He pounded on the car to get Ellie's attention. Ellie turned for the first time and Connie saw with shock that he wasn't a kid either—he had a fair, hairless face, cheeks reddened slightly as if the veins grew too close to the surface of his skin, the face of a forty-year-old baby. Connie felt a wave of dizziness rise in her at this sight and she stared at him as if waiting for something to change the shock of the moment, make it all right again. Ellie's lips kept shaping words, mumbling along with the words blasting in his ear.

"Maybe you two better go away," Connie said faintly.

"What? How come?" Arnold Friend cried. "We come out here to take you for a ride. It's Sunday." He had the voice of the man on the radio now. It was the same voice, Connie thought. "Don'tcha know it's Sunday all day and honey, no matter who you were with last night today you're with Arnold Friend and don't you forget it!—Maybe you better step out here," he said, and this last was in a different voice. It was a little flatter, as if the heat was finally getting to him.

"No. I got things to do."

"Hey."   90

"You two better leave."

"We ain't leaving until you come with us."

"Like hell I am—"

"Connie, don't fool around with me. I mean, I mean, don't fool *around,*" he said, shaking his head. He laughed incredulously. He placed his sunglasses on top of his head, carefully, as if he were indeed wearing a wig, and brought the stems down behind his ears. Connie stared at him, another wave of dizziness and fear rising in her so that for a moment he wasn't even in focus but was just a blur, standing there against his gold car, and she had the idea that he had driven up the driveway all right but had come from nowhere before that and belonged nowhere and that everything about him and even about the music that was so familiar to her was only half real.

"If my father comes and sees you—"   95

"He ain't coming. He's at a barbecue."

"How do you know that?"

"Aunt Tillie's. Right now they're—uh—they're drinking. Sitting around," he said vaguely, squinting as if he were staring all the way to town and over to Aunt Tillie's back yard. Then the vision seemed to get clear and he nodded energetically. "Yeah. Sitting around. There's your sister in a blue dress, huh? And high heels, the poor sad bitch—nothing like you, sweetheart! And your mother's helping some fat woman with the corn, they're cleaning the corn—husking the corn—"

"What fat woman?" Connie cried.

"How do I know what fat woman, I don't know every goddam fat woman in the   100 world!" Arnold laughed.

"Oh, that's Mrs. Hornby . . . Who invited her?" Connie said. She felt a little light-headed. Her breath was coming quickly.

"She's too fat. I don't like them fat. I like them the way you are, honey," he said, smiling sleepily at her. They stared at each other for a while, through the screen door. He said softly, "Now what you're going to do is this: you're going to come out that door. You're going to sit up front with me and Ellie's going to sit in the back, the hell with Ellie, right? This isn't Ellie's date. You're my date. I'm your lover, honey."

"What? You're crazy—"

"Yes, I'm your lover. You don't know what that is, but you will," he said. "I know that too. I know all about you. But look: it's real nice and you couldn't ask for nobody better than me, or more polite. I always keep my word. I'll tell you how it is, I'm always nice at first, the first time. I'll hold you so tight you won't think you have to try to get away or pretend anything because you'll know you can't.

And I'll come inside you where it's all secret and you'll give in to me and you'll love me—"

105   "Shut up! You're crazy!" Connie said. She backed away from the door. She put her hands against her ears as if she'd heard something terrible, something not meant for her. "People don't talk like that, you're crazy," she muttered. Her heart was almost too big now for her chest and its pumping made sweat break out all over her. She looked out to see Arnold Friend pause and then take a step toward the porch lurching. He almost fell. But, like a clever drunken man, he managed to catch his balance. He wobbled in his high boots and grabbed hold of one of the porch posts.

"Honey?" he said. "You still listening?"

"Get the hell out of here!"

"Be nice, honey. Listen."

"I'm going to call the police—"

110   He wobbled again and out of the side of his mouth came a fast spat curse, an aside not meant for her to hear. But even this "Christ!" sounded forced. Then he began to smile again. She watched this smile come, awkward as if he were smiling from inside a mask. His whole face was a mask, she thought wildly, tanned down onto his throat but then running out as if he had plastered makeup on his face but had forgotten about his throat.

"Honey—? Listen, here's how it is. I always tell the truth and I promise you this: I ain't coming in that house after you."

"You better not! I'm going to call the police if you—if you don't—"

"Honey," he said, talking right through her voice, "honey, I'm not coming in there but you are coming out here. You know why?"

She was panting. The kitchen looked like a place she had never seen before, some room she had run inside but which wasn't good enough, wasn't going to help her. The kitchen window had never had a curtain, after three years, and there were dishes in the sink for her to do—probably—and if you ran your hand across the table you'd probably feel something sticky there.

115   "You listening, honey? Hey?"

"—going to call the police—"

"Soon as you touch the phone I don't need to keep my promise and can come inside. You won't want that."

She rushed forward and tried to lock the door. Her fingers were shaking. "But why lock it," Arnold Friend said gently, talking right into her face. "It's just a screen door. It's just nothing." One of his boots was at a strange angle, as if his foot wasn't in it. It pointed out to the left, bent at the ankle. "I mean, anybody can break through a screen door and glass and wood and iron or anything else if he needs to, anybody at all and specially Arnold Friend. If the place got lit up with a fire honey you'd come runnin' out into my arms, right into my arms an' safe at home—like you knew I was your lover and'd stopped fooling around. I don't mind a nice shy girl but I don't like no fooling around." Part of those words were spoken with a slight rhythmic lilt, and Connie somehow recognized them—the echo of a song from last year, about a girl rushing into her boyfriend's arms and coming home again—

Connie stood barefoot on the linoleum floor, staring at him. "What do you want?" she whispered.

"I want you," he said.

"What?"

"Seen you that night and thought, that's the one, yes sir. I never needed to look any more."

"But my father's coming back. He's coming to get me. I had to wash my hair first—" She spoke in a dry, rapid voice, hardly raising it for him to hear.

"No, your Daddy is not coming and yes, you had to wash your hair and you washed it for me. It's nice and shining and all for me, I thank you, sweetheart," he said, with a mock bow, but again he almost lost his balance. He had to bend and adjust his boots. Evidently his feet did not go all the way down; the boots must have been stuffed with something so that he would seem taller. Connie stared out at him and behind him Ellie in the car, who seemed to be looking off toward Connie's right into nothing. This Ellie said, pulling the words out of the air one after another as if he were just discovering them, "You want me to pull out the phone?"

"Shut your mouth and keep it shut," Arnold Friend said, his face red from bending over or maybe from embarrassment because Connie had seen his boots. "This ain't none of your business."

"What—what are you doing? What do you want?" Connie said. "If I call the police they'll get you, they'll arrest you—"

"Promise was not to come in unless you touch that phone, and I'll keep that promise," he said. He resumed his erect position and tried to force his shoulders back. He sounded like a hero in a movie, declaring something important. He spoke too loudly and it was as if he were speaking to someone behind Connie. "I ain't made plans for coming in that house where I don't belong but just for you to come out to me, the way you should. Don't you know who I am?"

"You're crazy," she whispered. She backed away from the door but did not want to go into another part of the house, as if this would give him permission to come through the door. "What do you . . . You're crazy, you . . ."

"Huh? What're you saying, honey?"

Her eyes darted everywhere in the kitchen. She could not remember what it was, this room.

"This is how it is, honey; you come out and we'll drive away, have a nice ride. But if you don't come out we're gonna wait till your people come home and then they're all going to get it."

"You want that telephone pulled out?" Ellie said. He held the radio away from his ear and grimaced, as if without the radio the air was too much for him.

"I toldja shut up, Ellie," Arnold Friend said, "you're deaf, get a hearing aid, right? Fix yourself up. This little girl's no trouble and's gonna be nice to me, so Ellie keep to yourself, this ain't your date—right? Don't hem in on me. Don't hog. Don't crush. Don't bird dog. Don't trail me," he said in a rapid meaningless voice, as if he were running through all the expressions he'd learned but was no longer sure which one of them was in style, then rushing on to new ones, making them up with his eyes closed, "Don't crawl under my fence, don't squeeze in my chipmunk hole, don't sniff my glue, suck my popsicle, keep your own greasy fingers on yourself!" He shaded his eyes and peered in at Connie, who was backed against the kitchen table. "Don't mind him honey he's just a creep. He's a dope. Right? I'm the boy for you and like I said you come out here nice like a lady and give me your hand, and nobody else gets hurt, I mean, your nice old bald-headed daddy and your mummy and your sister in her high heels. Because listen: why bring them in this?"

"Leave me alone," Connie whispered.

135   "Hey, you know that old woman down the road, the one with the chickens and stuff—you know her?"

"She's dead!"

"Dead? What? You know her?" Arnold Friend said.

"She's dead—"

"Don't you like her?"

140   "She dead—she's—she isn't here any more—"

"But don't you like her, I mean, you got something against her? Some grudge or something?" Then his voice dipped as if he were conscious of a rudeness. He touched the sunglasses perched on top of his head as if to make sure they were still there. "Now you be a good girl."

"What are you going to do?"

"Just two things, or maybe three," Arnold Friend said. "But I promise it won't last long and you'll like me the way you get to like people you're close to. You will. It's all over for you here, so come on out. You don't want your people in any trouble, do you?"

She turned and bumped against a chair or something, hurting her leg, but she ran into the back room and picked up the telephone. Something roared in her ear, a tiny roaring, and she was so sick with fear that she could do nothing but listen to it—the telephone was clammy and very heavy and her fingers groped down to the dial but were too weak to touch it. She began to scream into the phone, into the roaring. She cried out, she cried for her mother, she felt her breath start jerking back and forth in her lungs as if it were something Arnold Friend were stabbing her with again and again with no tenderness. A noisy sorrowful wailing rose all about her and she was locked inside it the way she was locked inside this house.

145   After a while she could hear again. She was sitting on the floor with her wet back against the wall.

Arnold Friend was saying from the door, "That's a good girl. Put the phone back."

She kicked the phone away from her.

"No, honey. Pick it up. Put it back right."

She picked it up and put it back. The dial tone stopped.

150   "That's a good girl. Now you come outside."

She was hollow with what had been fear, but what was now just an emptiness. All that screaming had blasted it out of her. She sat, one leg cramped under her, and deep inside her brain was something like a pinpoint of light that kept going and would not let her relax. She thought, I'm not going to see my mother again. She thought, I'm not going to sleep in my bed again. Her bright green blouse was all wet.

Arnold Friend said, in a gentle-loud voice that was like a stage voice, "The place where you came from ain't there any more, and where you had in mind to go is canceled out. This place you are now—inside your daddy's house—is nothing but a cardboard box I can knock down any time. You know that and always did know it. You hear me?"

She thought, I have got to think. I have to know what to do.

"We'll go out to a nice field, out in the country here where it smells so nice and it's sunny," Arnold Friend said. "I'll have my arms tight around you so you won't need to try to get away and I'll show you what love is like, what it does. The hell with this house! It looks solid all right," he said. He ran a fingernail down the screen and the noise did not make Connie shiver, as it would have the day before. "Now put your hand on your heart, honey. Feel that? That feels solid too, but we know better, be nice to me, be sweet like you can because what else is there for a girl like you but to be sweet and pretty and give in?—and get away before her people come back?"

She felt her pounding heart. Her hand seemed to enclose it. She thought for the 155 first time in her life that it was nothing that was hers, that belonged to her, but just a pounding, living thing inside this body that wasn't really hers either.

"You don't want them to get hurt," Arnold Friend went on. "Now get up, honey. Get up all by yourself."

She stood.

"Now turn this way. That's right. Come over here to me—Ellie, put that away, didn't I tell you? You dope. You miserable creepy dope," Arnold Friend said. His words were not angry but only part of an incantation. The incantation was kindly. "Now come out through the kitchen to me honey, and let's see a smile, try it, you're a brave sweet little girl and now they're eating corn and hot dogs cooked to bursting over an outdoor fire, and they don't know one thing about you and never did and honey you're better than them because not a one of them would have done this for you."

Connie felt the linoleum under her feet; it was cool. She brushed her hair back out of her eyes. Arnold Friend let go of the post tentatively and opened his arms for her, his elbows pointing in toward each other and his wrists limp, to show that this was an embarrassed embrace and a little mocking, he didn't want to make her self-conscious.

She put out her hand against the screen. She watched herself push the door 160 slowly open as if she were safe back somewhere in the other doorway, watching this body and this head of long hair moving out into the sunlight where Arnold Friend waited.

"My sweet little blue-eyed girl," he said, in a half-sung sigh that had nothing to do with her brown eyes but was taken up just the same by the vast sunlit reaches of the land behind him and on all sides of him, so much land that Connie had never seen before and did not recognize except to know that she was going to it.

QUESTIONS FOR DISCUSSION AND WRITING

1. How do Connie's trashy daydreams lead inevitably to her meeting with a person such as Arnold Friend? What "promise" does Arnold make to Connie? How does Connie's attempt to call for help bring the plot to its climax?

2. How does the opening paragraph of the story establish Connie's character? How does Arnold's car embody his personality? How does Connie's perception of Arnold change once she realizes that he is not a teenager?

3. Why is the drive-in restaurant an appropriate place for Connie's first encounter with Arnold? How does the screen door of Connie's house suggest the precariousness of her situation?

4. How does Connie's recognition that "everything about her had two sides to it" clarify her point of view toward Arnold? How does the author use the music on Ellie's radio to underscore Connie's increasing sense of terror?

5. How does the title of the story comment on its theme? What prompts Connie to go with Arnold to the land that she "had never seen before"?

Stories for Comparison

Elizabeth Bowen's "The Demon Lover" (pages 281–304); Mary Hood's "How Far She Went" (pages 664–670).

77

....

E D N A   O ' B R I E N

A Scandalous Woman

EDNA O'BRIEN was born in 1936 in Tuamgraney, County Clare, Ireland, and was educated at the Pharmaceutical College of Ireland. Her first novel, *The Country Girls* (1960), began a trilogy of novels, including *The Lonely Girl* (1962) and *Girls in Their Married Bliss* (1964), that described the tragicomic adventures of young Irish women. Many of O'Brien's short stories have been published as collections, including *A Scandalous Woman and Other Stories* (1974), *A Frantic Woman* (1984), and *An Edna O'Brien Reader* (1994). She has also written works of nonfiction, including *Vanishing Ireland* (1986); children's books, such as *Tales for the Telling: Irish Folk and Fairy Stories* (1986); and numerous plays for the stage, screen, and television, including *The Gathering* (1974). In "A Scandalous Woman," the title story of that collection, a woman recalls her role as accomplice in her friend's scandal.

Everyone in our village was unique and one or two of the girls were beautiful. There were others before and after but it was with Eily I was connected. Sometimes one finds oneself in the swim, one is wanted, one is favored, one is privy, and then it happens, the destiny, and then it is over and one sits back and knows alas that it is someone else's turn.

Hers was the face of a madonna. She had brown hair, a great crop of it, fair skin, and eyes that were as big and as soft and as transparent as ripe gooseberries. She was always a little out of breath and gasped when one approached, then embraced and said "darling." That was when we met in secret.

In front of her parents and others she was somewhat stubborn and withdrawn and there was a story that when young she always lived under the table to escape her father's thrashings. For one Advent she thought of being a nun but that fizzled out and her chief interests became clothes and needlework. She helped on the farm and used not to be let out much in the summer because of all the extra work. She loved the main road with the cars and the bicycles and the buses and had no interest at all in the sidecar that her parents used for conveyance. She would work like a horse to get to the main road before dark to see the passers-by. She was swift as a colt. My father never stopped praising this quality in her and put it down to muscle. It was well known that Eily and her family hid their shoes in a hedge near the road so that they would have clean footwear when they went to Mass, or to market, or later on, in Eily's case, to the dress dance.

The dress dance in aid of the new mosaic altar marked her debut. She wore a georgette dress and court shoes threaded with silver and gold. The dress had come from America long before but had been restyled by Eily, and during the week before the dance she was never to be seen without a bunch of pins in her mouth as she tried out some different mode. Peter the Master, one of the local tyrants, stood inside the door with two or three of his cronies, both to count the money and to survey the couples and comment on their clumsiness or on their dancing "technique." When Eily arrived in her tweed coat and said "Evening, gentlemen," no one passed any remark, but the moment she slipped off the coat and the transparency of the georgette, plus her naked shoulders, were revealed, Peter the Master spat into the palm of his hand and said didn't she strip a fine woman.

The locals were mesmerized. She was not off the floor once, and the more she 5 danced the more fetching she became, and was saying "ooh" and "aah" as her partners spun her round and round. Eventually one of the ladies in charge of the supper had to take her into the supper room and fan her with a bit of cardboard. First I was let to look in the window, admiring the couples and the hanging streamers and the very handsome men in the orchestra with their sideburns and striped suits. Then, in the supper room where I had stolen to, Eily confided to me that something out of this world had taken place. Almost immediately after that she was brought home by her sister Nuala.

Eily and Nuala always quarreled—issues such as who would milk, or who would separate the milk, or who would draw water from the well, or who would churn, or who would bake bread. Usually Eily got the lighter tasks because of her breathlessness and her accomplishments with the needle. She was wonderful at knitting and could copy any stitch just from seeing it in a magazine or in a knitting pattern. I used to go over there to play and though they were older than me they used to beg me to come, bribing me with empty spools or scraps of cloth for my dolls. Sometimes we played hide and seek, sometimes we played families and gave ourselves posh names and posh jobs, and we used to paint each other with the dye from plants or blue bags and treat each other's faces as if they were palettes and then laugh and marvel at the blues and indigos and pretend to be natives and do hula hula and eat dock leaves. Once Nuala made me cry by saying I was adopted and that my mother was not my real mother at all. Eily had to pacify me by spitting on dock leaves and putting them all over my face as a mask.

Nuala was happiest when someone was upset and almost always she trumped for playing hospital. She was doctor and Eily was nurse. Nuala liked to operate with a big black carving knife, and long before she commenced she gloated over the method and over what tumors she was going to remove. She used to say that there would be nothing but a shell left by the time she had finished, and that one wouldn't be able to have babies or women's complaints ever. She had names for the female parts—Susies for the breasts, Florrie for the stomach, and Matilda for lower down. She would sharpen and resharpen the knife on the steps and order Eily to get the hot water and the soap, to sterilize the utensils, and to have to hand a big winding sheet.

Eily also had to don an apron, a white apron, that formerly she had worn at cookery classes. The kettle always took an age to boil on the open hearth, and very often Nuala threw sugar on it to encourage the flame. The two doors would be wide open, a bucket to one and a stone to the other, Nuala would be sharpening the knife and humming "Waltzing Matilda," the birds would almost always be singing or chirruping, the dogs would be outside on their hindquarters, snapping at flies, and I would be lying on the kitchen table terrified and in a state of undress. Now and then, when I caught Eily's eye, she would raise hers to heaven as much as to say "you poor little mite," but she never contradicted Nuala or disobeyed orders.

Nuala would don her mask. It was a bright-red papier-mâché mask that had been in the house from the time when some mummers came on the Day of the Wren, got bitten by the dog, and lost some of their regalia, including the mask and a legging. Before she commenced she let out a few dry, knowing coughs, exactly imitating the doctor's dry, knowing coughs. I shall never stop remembering those last few seconds, as she snapped the elastic band around the back of her head and said to Eily, "All set, Nurse?"

10   For some reason I always looked upwards and backwards and therefore could see the dresser upside down, and the contents of it. There was a whole row of jugs, mostly white jugs with sepia designs of corn, or cattle, or a couple toiling in the fields. The jugs hung on hooks at the edge of the dresser and behind them were the plates with ripe pears painted in the center of each plate. But most beautiful of all were the little dessert dishes of carnival glass, with their orange tints and their scalloped edges. I used to say good-by to them, and then it would be time to close eyes before the ordeal.

She never called it an operation, just an "op," the same as the doctor did. I would feel the point of the knife like the point of a compass going around my scarcely formed breasts. My bodice would not be removed, just lifted up. She would comment on what she saw and say "interesting" or "quite" or "oh dearie me" as the case may be, and then when she got at the stomach she would always say "tut tut tut" and "What nasty business have we got here." She would list the unwholesome things I had been eating, such as sherbet or rainbow toffees, hit the stomach with the flat of the knife, and order two spoons of turpentine and three spoons of castor oil before commencing. These potions had then to be downed. Meanwhile Eily, as the considerate nurse, would be mopping the doctor's brow and handing extra implements such as sugar tongs, spoon, or fork. The spoon was to flatten the tongue and make the patient say "aah." Scabs or cuts would be regarded as nasty devils, and elastic marks a sign of debauchery. I would also have to make a general confession. I used to lie there praying that their mother would come home unexpectedly. It was always a Tuesday, the day their mother went to the market to sell things, to buy commodities, and to draw her husband's pension. I used to wait for a sound from the dogs. They were vicious dogs and bit everyone except their owners, and on my arrival there I used to have to yell for Eily to come out and escort me past them.

All in all it was a woeful event, but still I went each Tuesday on the way home from school, and by the time their mother returned all would be over and I would be sitting demurely by the fire, waiting to be offered a shop biscuit, which of course at first I made a great pretense of refusing.

Eily always conveyed me down the first field as far as the white gate, and though the dogs snarled and showed their teeth, they never tried biting once I was leaving. One evening, though it was nearly milking time, she came further. I thought it was to gather a few hazelnuts, because there was a little tree between our boundary and theirs that was laden with them. You had only to shake the tree for the nuts to come tumbling down, and you had only to sit on the nearby wobbly wall, take one of the loose stones, and crack away to your heart's content. They were just ripe, and they tasted young and clean and helped as well to get all fur off the backs of the teeth. So we sat on the wall, but Eily did not reach up and draw a branch and therefore a shower of nuts down. Instead she asked me what I thought of Romeo. He was a new bank clerk, a Protestant, and to me a right toff in his plus fours with his white sports bicycle. The bicycle had a dynamo attached so that he was never without lights. He rode the bicycle with his body hunched forward, so that as she mentioned him I could see his snout and his lock of falling hair coming towards me on the road. He also distinguished himself by riding the bicycle into shops or hallways. In fact he was scarcely ever off it. It seems he had danced with her the night she wore the green georgette and next day left a note in the hedge where she and her family kept their shoes. She said it was the grace of God that she had gone there first thing that morning, otherwise the note might have come into someone else's hand. He had made an assignation for the following Sunday, and she did not know how she was going to get out of her house and under what excuse. At least Nuala was gone, to Technical School where she was learning to be a domestic-economy instructress, and my sisters had returned to the convent, so that we were able to hatch it without the bother of them eavesdropping on us. I said yes, that I would be her accomplice, without knowing what I was letting myself in for.

On the Sunday I told my parents that I was going with Eily to visit a cousin of theirs in the hospital, and she in turn told her parents that we were visiting a cousin of mine. We met at the white gate and both of us were peppering. She had an old black dirndl skirt which she slipped out of, and underneath was her cerise dress with the slits at the side. It was a most compromising garment. She wore a brooch at the bosom. Her mother's brooch, a plain flat gold pin with a little star in the center that shone feverishly. She took out her little gold flapjack and proceeded to dab powder on. The puff was dry so she removed the little muslin cover and made me hold it delicately while she dipped into the powder proper. It was ocher stuff and completely wrecked her complexion. Then she applied lipstick, wet her kiss curl, and made me kneel down in the field and promise never ever to split.

15   We went towards the hospital, but instead of going up that dark cedar-lined avenue, we crossed over a field, nearly drowning ourselves in the swamp, and stooping so as not to be sighted. I said we were like soldiers in a war and should have worn green or brown as camouflage. Her bright bottom, bobbing up and down, could easily have been spotted by anyone going along the road.

When we got to the thick of the woods Romeo was there. He looked very indifferent, his face forward, his head almost as low as the handlebars of the bicycle, and he surveyed us carefully as we approached. Then he let out a couple of whistles to let her know how welcome she was. She stood beside him and I faced them, and we all remarked what a fine evening it was. I could hardly believe my eyes when I saw his hand go round her waist, and then her dress, crumpled as it was, being raised up from the back, and though the two of them stood perfectly still, they were both looking at each other intently and making signs with their lips. Her dress was above the back of her knees. Eily began to get very flushed and he studied her face most carefully, asking if it was nice, nice. I was told by him to run along: "Run along, Junior" was what he said. I went and adhered to the bark of a tree, eyes closed, fists closed, and every bit of me in a clinch. Not long after, Eily hollered, and on the way home and walking very smartly she and I discussed growing pains and she said there were no such things but that it was all rheumatism.

So it continued Sunday after Sunday, with one holy day, Ascension Thursday, thrown in. We got wizard in our excuses—once it was to practice with the school choir, another time it was to teach the younger children how to receive Holy Communion, and once—this was our riskiest ploy—it was to get gooseberries from an old crank called Miss MacNamara. That proved to be dangerous because both our mothers were hoping for some, either for eating or stewing, and we had to say that Miss MacNamara was not home, whereupon they said weren't the bushes there anyhow with the gooseberries hanging off. For a moment I imagined that I had actually been there, in the little choked garden, with the bantam hens and the small moldy bushes weighed down with the big hairy gooseberries that were soft to the touch and that burst when you bit into them.

We used to pray on the way home, say prayers and ejaculations, and very often when we leant against the grass bank while she donned her old skirt and her old canvas shoes we said one or another of the mysteries of the Rosary. She had new shoes that were clogs really and that her mother had not seen. They were olive green and she had bought them from a Gypsy woman in return for a tablecloth of her mother's that she had stolen. It was a special cloth that had been sent all the way from Australia by a nun. She was a thief as well. One day all these sins would have to be reckoned with. I used to shudder at night when I went over the number of commandments we were both breaking, but I grieved more on her behalf, because she was breaking the worst one of all in those embraces and transactions with him. She never discussed him except to say that his middle name was Jack.

During those weeks my mother used to say I was pale and why wasn't I eating and why did I gargle so often with salt and water. These were forms of atonement to God. Even seeing Eily on Tuesdays was no longer the source of delight that it used to be. I was wracked. I used to say "Is this a dagger which I see before me?" and memorized all the queer people around who had visions and suffered from delusions. The same would be our cruel cup. She flared up. Marry, did I or did I not love her? Of course I loved her and would hang for her but she was asking me to do the two hardest things on earth—to disobey God and my own mother. Often she took huff and swore that she would get someone else—usually Una, my greatest rival—to play gooseberry for her and be her dogsbody in her whole secret life. But then she would make up and be waiting for me on the road as I came from school, and we would climb in over the wall that led to their fields, and we would link and discuss the possible excuse for the following Sunday. Once she suggested wearing the green georgette, and even I, who also lacked restraint in matters of dress, thought it would draw untoward attention to her, since it was a dance dress and since, as Peter the Master said, "She looked stripped in it." I said Mrs. Bolan would smell a rat. Mrs. Bolan was one of the many women who were always prowling and turning up at graveyards or in the slate quarry to see if there were courting couples. She always said she was looking for stray turkeys or turkey eggs, but in fact she had no fowl and was known to tell tales. As a result of her, one temporary schoolteacher had had to leave the neighborhood, do a flit in the night, without even having time to get her shoes back from the cobbler's. But Eily said that we would never be found out, that the god Cupid was on our side, and while I was with her I believed it.

I had a surprise a few evenings later. Eily was lying in wait for me on the way 20 home from school. She peeped up over the wall, said "yoo hoo," and then darted down again. I climbed over. She was wearing nothing under her dress since it was such a scorching day. We walked for a bit, then we flopped down against a cock of hay—the last one in the field, as the twenty-three other cocks had been brought in the day before. It looked a bit silly and was there only because of an accident—the mare had bolted and broken away from the hay cart and nearly strangled the driver, who was himself an idiot and whose chin was permanently smeared with spittle. She said to close my eyes, open my hand, and see what God would give me.

There are moments in life when the pleasure is more than one can bear, and one descends willy-nilly into a wild tunnel of flounder and vertigo. It happens on swing boats and chaireoplanes, it happens maybe at waterfalls, it is said to happen to some when they fall in love, but it happened to me that day, propped against the cock of hay, the sun shining, a breeze commencing, the clouds like cruisers in the heavens on their way to some distant port. I closed my eyes, and then the cold thing hit the palm of my hand, fitting it exactly, and my fingers came over it to further the hold on it and to guess what it was. I did not dare say in case I should be wrong. It was of course a little bottle, with a screw-on cap and a label adhering to one side, but it was too much to hope that it would be my favorite perfume, the one called Mischief. She was urging me to guess. I feared that it might be an empty bottle, though such a gift would not be wholly unwelcome since the remains of the smell always lingered, or that it might be a cheaper perfume, a less mysterious one named after a carnation or a poppy, a perfume that did not send shivers of joy down my throat and through my swallow to my very heart.

At last I opened my eyes, and there it was, my most prized thing, in a little dark-blue bottle with a silverish label and a little rubber stopper, and inside the precious stuff itself. I unscrewed the cap, lifted off the little rubber top, and a drop was assigned to the flat of my finger and then conveyed to a particular spot in the hollow behind the left ear. She did exactly the same and we kissed each other and breathed in the rapturous smell. The smell of hay intervened, so we ran to where there was no hay and kissed again. That moment had an air of mystery and sanctity about it, what with the surprise and our speechlessness, and a realization somewhere in the back of my mind that we were engaged in rotten business indeed, and that our larking days were over.

If things went well my mother had a saying that it was all too good to be true. It proved prophetic the following Saturday, because as my hair was being washed at the kitchen table Eily arrived and sat at the end of the table and kept snapping her fingers in my direction. When I looked up from my expanse of suds I saw that she was on the verge of tears and was blotchy all over. My mother almost scalded me, because in welcoming Eily she had forgotten to add the cold water to the pot of boiling water, and I screamed and leapt about the kitchen shouting hellfire and purgatory.

Afterwards Eily and I went around to the front of the house and sat on the step, where she told me that all was U.P. She had gone to him, as was her wont, under the bridge where he did a spot of fishing each Friday, and he told her to make herself scarce. She refused, whereupon he moved downstream, and the moment she followed he waded into the water. He kept telling her to beat it, beat it.

25   She sat on the little milk stool, where he in fact had been sitting, and then he did a terrible thing—he cast his rod in her direction and almost removed one of her eyes with the nasty hook. She burst into tears and I began to plait her hair for comfort's sake. She swore that she would throw herself in the selfsame river before the night was out, then said it was only a lover's quarrel, then said that he would have to see her, and finally announced that her heart was utterly broken in smithereens.

I had the little bottle of perfume in my pocket, and I held it up to the light to show how sparing I had been with it, but she was interested in nothing, only the ways and means of recovering him, or then again of taking her own life. Apart from drowning, she considered hanging, or the intake of a bottle of Jeyes Fluid or a few grains of the strychnine that her father had for foxes.

Her father was a very gruff man who never spoke to the family except to order his meals and to tell the girls to mind their books. He himself had never gone to school but had great acumen in the buying and selling of cattle and sheep, and put that down to the fact that he had met the scholars. He was an old man with an atrocious temper, and once on a fair day had ripped the clothing off an auctioneer who tried to diddle him over the price of an aladdin lamp.

My mother came to sit with us, and this alarmed me since my mother never took the time to sit, either indoors or outdoors. She began to talk to Eily about knitting, about a new tweedex wool, asking if she secured some would Eily help her knit a three-quarter-length jacket. Eily had knitted lots of things for us, including the dress I was wearing—a salmon pink, with scalloped edges and a border of white angora decorating those edges. At that very second, as I had the angora to my face tickling it, my mother said to Eily that once she had gone to a fortuneteller, had removed her wedding ring as a decoy, and when the fortuneteller asked was she married she had replied no. Then the fortuneteller said, "How come you have four children?" My mother said they were uncanny, those ladies, with their Gypsy blood and their clairvoyant powers. I guessed exactly what Eily was thinking. Could we find a fortuneteller or a witch who could predict her future?

There was a witch twenty miles away who ran a public house and who was notorious, but who only took people on a whim. When my mother ran off to see if the racket in the henhouse was because of a fox, I said to Eily that instead of consulting a witch we ought first to resort to other things, such as novenas, putting wedding cake under our pillows, or gathering bottles of dew in the early morning and putting them in a certain fort to make a wish. Anyhow how could we get to a village twenty miles away, unless it was on foot or by bicycle, and neither of us had a machine. Nevertheless, the following Sunday we were to be found setting off with a bottle of tea, a little puncture kit, and eight shillings, which was all the money we managed to scrape together.

We were not long started when Eily complained of feeling weak, and suddenly the bicycle was wobbling all over the road and she came a cropper as she tried to slow it down by heading for a grass bank. Her brakes were nonexistent, as indeed were mine. They were borrowed bicycles. I had to use the same method to dismount, and the two of us, with our front wheels wedged into the bank and our handlebars askew, caused a passing motorist to call out that we were a right pair of Mohawks and a danger to the county council.

I gave her a sup of tea and forced on her one of the eggs which we had stolen from various nests and which were intended as a bribe for our witch. Along with the eggs we had a little fletch of home-cured bacon. She cracked it on the handlebars, and with much persuasion from me swallowed it whole, saying it was worse than castor oil. It being Sunday, she recalled other Sundays and where she would be at that exact moment, and she prayed to St. Anthony to please bring him back. We had heard that he went to Limerick most weekends now, and there was a rumor that he was going out with a bacon-curer's daughter and that they were getting engaged.

The woman who opened the side door of the pub said that the witch did not live there any longer. She was very cross and had eyebrows that met, and these as well as the hairs in her head were a yellowish-gray. She told us to leave her threshold at once, and how dare we intrude upon her Sunday leisure. She closed the door in our faces. I said to Eily, "That's her." And just as we were screwing up our courage to knock again, she reopened the door and said who in the name of Jacob had sent us. I said we'd come a long way, miles and miles, I showed the eggs and the bacon in its dusting of saltpeter, and she said she was extremely busy, seeing as it was her birthday and that sons and daughters and cousins were coming for a high tea. She opened and closed the door numerous times, and through it all we stood our ground until finally we were brought in, but it was my fortune she wanted to tell.

The kitchen was tiny and stuffy, and the same linoleum was on the floor as on the little wobbling table. There was a sort of wooden armchair for her, a bench for visitors, and a stove that was smoking. Two rhubarb tarts were cooling on top, and that plus a card were the only indications of a birthday celebration. A small man, her husband, excused himself and wedged sideways through another door.

I pleaded with her to take Eily rather than me, and after much dithering and even going out to the garden to empty tea leaves, she said that maybe she would but that we were pests, the pair of us. I was sent to join her husband in the little pantry and was nearly smothered from the puffing of his pipe. There was also a strong smell of flour, and no furniture except a sewing machine with a half-finished garment, a shift, wedged in under the needle. He talked in a whisper, said that the Mau Mau would come to Ireland and that St. Columbus would rise from his grave to make it once again the island of saints and scholars. I was certain that I would suffocate.

35   But it was worth it. Eily was jubilant. Things could not have been better. The witch had not only seen his initial, J, but seen it twice in a concoction that she had done with the whites of one of the eggs and some gruel. Yes, things had been bad, very bad, there had been grievous misunderstandings, but all was to be changed, and leaning across the table she said to Eily, "Ah sure, you'll end your days with him."

Cycling home was a joy. We spun downhill, saying to hell with safety, to hell with brakes, saluting strangers, admiring all the little cottages and the outhouses and the milk tanks and the whining mongrels, and had no nerves passing the haunted house. In fact we would have liked to see an apparition on that most buoyant of days. When we got to the crossroads that led to our own village, Eily had a strong presentiment, as indeed had I, that he would be there waiting for us, contrite, in a hair shirt, on bended knees. But he was not. There was the usual crowd of lads playing pitch and toss. A couple of the younger ones tried to impede us by standing in front of the bikes, and Eily blushed red. She was a favorite with everyone that summer, and she had a different dress for every day of the week. She was called a fashion plate. We said good night and knew that it did not matter, that though he had not been waiting for us, before long he and Eily would be united. She resolved to be patient and be a little haughty and not seek him out.

Three weeks later, on a Saturday night, my mother was soaking her feet in a mixture of warm water and washing soda when a rap came on the scullery window. We both trembled. There was a madman who had taken up residence in a boghole and we were certain that it must be him. "Call your father," she said. My father had gone to bed in a huff because she had given him a boiled egg instead of a fry for his tea. I didn't want to leave her alone and unattended so I yelled up to my father, and at the same time a second assault was delivered on the windowpane. I heard the words "sir, sir."

It was Eily's father, since he was the only person who called my father sir. When we opened the door to him the first thing I saw was the slash hook in his hand and then the condition of his hair, which was upstanding and wild. He said, "I'll hang, draw, and quarter him," and my mother said, "Come in, Mr. Hogan," not knowing who this graphic fate was intended for. He said he had found his daughter in the limekiln with the bank clerk, in the most satanic position, with her belly showing.

My first thought was one of delight at their reunion, and then I felt piqued that Eily hadn't told me but had chosen instead to meet him at night in that disused kiln that reeked of damp. Better the woods, I thought, and the call of the cuckoo, and myself keeping some kind of watch, though invariably glued to the bark of a tree.

He said he had come to fetch a lantern so that he could follow them, as they had scattered in different directions, and he did not know which of them to kill first. My father, whose good humor was restored by this sudden and unexpected intrusion, said to hold on for a moment, to step inside and they would consider a plan of campaign. Mr. Hogan left his cap on the step, a thing he always did, and my mother begged him to bring it in since the new pup ate every article of clothing it could find. Only that very morning my mother had looked out on the field and thought she saw flakes of snow, but in fact it was her line of washing, chewed to pieces. He refused to bring in his cap, which to me was a perfect example of how stubborn he was and how awkward things were going to be. At once my father ordered my mother to make tea, and though he was still gruff, there was between them now an understanding, because of the worse tragedy that loomed. 40

My mother seemed the most perturbed, made a hopeless cup of tea, cut the bread in agricultural hunks, and did everything wrong, as if she herself had just been found out in some base transaction. After the men had gone out on their search party she got me to go down on my knees to pray with her, and I found it hard to pray because I was already thinking of the flogging I would get for being implicated. She cross-examined me. Did I know anything about it? Had Eily ever met him before? Why had she made herself so much style, especially that slit skirt?

I said no to everything. These noes were much too hastily delivered, and it was only that my mother was so busy cogitating and surmising that kept her from suspecting something for sure. Kneeling there, I saw them trace every movement of ours, get bits of information from this one and that one—the so-called cousins, the woman who had promised us the gooseberries, and Mrs. Bolan. I knew we had no hope.

Eily! Her most precious thing was gone, her jewel. The inside of one was like a little watch, and once the jewel or jewels were gone the outside was nothing but a sham. I saw her die in the cold limekiln, and then again in a sickroom, and then stretched out on an operating table the very way that I used to be. She had joined that small sodality of scandalous women who had conceived children without securing fathers, and who were damned in body and soul. Had they convened they would have been a band of seven or eight and might have sent up an unholy wail to their maker and their seducers. The one thing I could not endure was the thought of her stomach protuberant, and a baby coming out and saying "ba ba." Had I had the chance to see her I would have suggested that we run away with Gypsies.

Poor Eily, from then on she was kept under lock and key and allowed out only to Mass, and then so concealed was she, with a mantilla over her face, that she was not even able to make a lip sign to me. Never did she look so beautiful as on those subsequent Sundays in chapel, her hair and her face veiled, her eyes like smoking tragedies peering through. I once sat directly in front of her, and when we stood up for the first Gospel I stared up into her face—and got such a dig in the ribs from my mother that I toppled over.

45   A mission commenced the following week, and a strange priest with a beautiful accent and a strong sense of rhetoric delivered the sermons each evening. It was better than a theater—the chapel in a state of hush, scores of candles like running stairways, all lit, extra flowers on the altar, a medley of smells, the white linen, and the place so packed that we youngsters had to sit on the altar steps and so got to see everything clearer, including the priest's Adam's apple as it bobbed up and down. Always I could sight Eily, hemmed in by her mother and some other old woman, pale and impassive, and I was certain that she was about to die.

On the evening that the sermon centered on the sixth commandment, we youngsters were kept outside until Benediction time. We spent the time wandering through the stalls, looking at the tiers of rosary beads that were as dazzling as necklaces, all hanging side by side and quivering in the breeze, all colors and of different stones; then of course the bright scapulars, and all kinds of little medals and beautiful crucifixes that were bigger than the girth of one's hand, and even some that had a little cavity within where a relic was contained; and also beautiful prayer books and missals, some with gold edging and little holders made of filigree.

When we trooped in for the Benediction Eily slipped me a holy picture. It said "Remembrance is all I ask, but if Remembrance should prove a task, Forget me." I was musing on it and swallowing back my tears at the very moment that she began to retch and was hefted out by four of the men. They bore her aloft as if she was a corpse or a litter. I said to my mother that most likely Eily would die and my mother said if only such a solution could occur. My mother already knew.

The next evening Eily was in our house, in the front room, and though I was not admitted I listened at the door, and ran off only when there was a scream or a blow or a thud. She was being questioned about each and every event and about the bank clerk and what exactly were her associations with him. She said no over and over again and at moments was quite defiant and, as they said, an "upstart." One minute they were asking her kindly, another minute they were heckling, another minute her father swore that it was to the lunatic asylum that she would be sent, and then at once her mother was condemning her for not having milked for two weeks.

They were contrariness itself. How could she have milked when she was locked in the room off the kitchen where they stowed the oats and which was teeming with mice? I knew for a fact that her meals—a hunk of bread and a mug of weak tea—were handed in to her twice a day and that she had nothing else to do, only cry, and think, and sit herself upon the oats and run her fingers through it, and probably have to keep making noises to frighten off the mice. When they were examining her my mother was the most reasonable but also the most exacting. My mother would ask such things as "Where did you meet? How long were you together? Were others present?" Eily denied ever having met him and was spry enough to say, "What do you take me for, Mrs. Brady, a hussy?" But that must have incurred some sort of a belt from her father, because I heard my mother say that there was no need to resort to savagery. I almost swooned when on the glass panel of our hall door I saw a shadow, then knuckles, and through the glass the appearance of a brown habit such as the missioner wore.

He saw Eily alone, and we all waited in the kitchen, the men supping tea, my mother segmenting a grapefruit to offer to the priest. It seemed odd fare to give him in the evening, but she was used to entertaining priests only at breakfast time, when one came every five or ten years to say Mass in the house in order to rebless it and put pay to the handiwork of the devil. When he was leaving, the missioner shook hands with each of us and then patted my hair. Watching his sallow face and his rimless spectacles, and drinking in his beautiful speaking voice, I thought that if I were Eily I would prefer him to the bank clerk and would do anything to get to be in his company.

I had one second with Eily, while they all trooped out to open the gate for the priest and to wave him off. She said for God's sake not to split on her. Then she was taken upstairs by my mother, and when they re-emerged Eily was wearing one of my mother's mackintoshes, a Mrs. Miniver hat, and a pair of old sunglasses. It was a form of disguise since they were setting out on a journey. Eily's father wanted to put a halter round her but my mother said it wasn't the Middle Ages. I was enjoined to wash cups and saucers, to empty the ashtray, and to plump the cushions again, but once they were gone I was unable to move because of a dreadful pain that gripped the lower part of my back and stomach, and I was convinced that I too was having a baby and that if I were to move or part my legs some terrible thing would come ushering out.

The following morning Eily's father went to the bank, where he broke two glass panels, sent coins flying about the place, assaulted the bank manager, and tried to saw off part of the bank clerk's anatomy. Two customers, the butcher and the undertaker, had to intervene, and the lady clerk who was in the cloakroom managed to get to the telephone to call the barracks. When the Sergeant came on the scene, Eily's father was being held down, his hands tied with a skipping rope, but he was still trying to aim a kick at the blackguard who had ruined his daughter. Very quickly the Sergeant got the gist of things. It was agreed that Jack—that was the bank clerk's name—would come to their house that evening. Though the whole occasion was to be fraught with misfortune, my mother, upon hearing of it, said that some sort of buffet would have to be considered.

It proved to be an arduous day. The oats had to be shoveled out of the room, and the women were left to do it since my father was busy seeing the solicitor and the priest, and Eily's father remained in the town drinking and boasting about what he wouldn't have done to the bugger if only the Sergeant hadn't come on the scene.

Eily was silence itself. She didn't even smile at me when I brought the basket of groceries that her mother had sent me to fetch. Her mother kept referring to the fact that they would never provide bricks and mortar for the new house now. For years she and her husband had been skimping and saving, intending to build a house two fields nearer the road. It was to be identical to their own house, that is to say a cement two-story house, but with the addition of a lavatory and a tiny hall inside the front door, so that, as she said, if company came they could be vetted there instead of plunging straight into the kitchen. She was a backward woman and probably because of living in the fields she had no friends and had never stepped inside anyone else's door. She always washed out of doors at the rain barrel and never called her husband anything but mister. Unpacking the groceries, she said that it was a pity to waste them on him, and the only indulgence she permitted herself was to smell these things, especially the packet of raspberry-and-custard biscuits. There was blackcurrant jam, a Scirbona Swiss roll, a tin of herrings in tomato sauce, a loaf, and a large tin of fruit cocktail.

55   Eily kept whitening and rewhitening her buckskin shoes. No sooner were they out on the window than she would bring them in and whiten them again. The women were in the room putting the oats into sacks. They didn't have much to say. My mother used always to laugh because when they met Mrs. Hogan used to say "Any newses?" and look up at her with that wild stare, opening her mouth to show the big gaps between her front teeth. Now the "newses" had at last come to her own door, and though she must have minded dreadfully she seemed vexed more than ashamed, as if it was inconvenience rather than disgrace that had hit her. But from that day on she almost stopped calling Eily by her pet name, which was Babbie.

I said to Eily that if she liked we could make toffee, because making toffee always amused her. She pretended not to hear. Even to her mother she refused to speak, and when asked a question she bared her teeth like one of the dogs. She even wanted one of the dogs, Spot, to bite me, and led him to me by the ear, but he was more interested in a sheep's head that I had brought from the town.

It was an arduous day, what with carting out the oats in cans and buckets and repouring it into sacks, moving a table and tea chests in there, finding suitable covers for them, laying the table properly, getting rid of all the cobwebs in the corners, sweeping up the soot that had fallen down the chimney, and even running up a little curtain. Eily had to hem it and as she sat outside the back door I could see her face and her expression and she looked very stubborn and not nearly so amiable as before.

My mother provided a roast chicken, some pickles, and freshly boiled beets. She skinned the hot beets with her hands and said, "Ah you've made your bed now," but Eily gave no evidence of having heard. She simply washed her face in the aluminum basin, combed her hair severely back, put on her whitened shoes, and then turned around to make sure that the seams of her stockings were straight.

Her father came home drunk, and he looked like a younger man trotting up the fields in his oatmeal-colored socks. He'd lost his shoes. When he saw the sitting room that had up to then been the oats room, he took off his hat and exclaimed, "Am I in my own house at all, mister?"

My father arrived full of important news, which he kept saying he would dis- 60 cuss later. We waited in a ring, seated around the fire, and the odd words said were said only by the men and then without any point. They discussed a beast that had had some ailment.

The dogs were the first to let us know. We all jumped up and looked through the window. The bank clerk was coming on foot, and my mother said to look at that swagger, and wasn't it the swagger of a hobo. Eily ran to look in the mirror that was fixed to the window ledge. For some extraordinary reason my father went out to meet him and straightaway produced a packet of cigarettes. The two of them came in smoking, and he was shown to the sitting room, which was directly inside the door to the left. There were no drinks on offer since the women decided that the men might only get obstreperous. Eily's father kept pointing to the glories of the room, and lifted up a bit of cretonne to make sure that it was a tea chest underneath and not a piece of pricey mahogany. My father said, "Well, Mr. Jacksie, you'll have to do your duty by her and make an honest woman of her." Eily was standing by the window looking out at the oncoming dark. The bank clerk said, "Why so?" and whistled in a way that I had heard him whistle in the past. He did not seem put out. I was afraid that on impulse he might rush over and put his hands somewhere on Eily's person. Eily's father mortified us all by saying she had a porker in her, and the bank clerk said so had many a lass, whereupon he got a slap across the face and was told to sit down and behave himself.

From that moment on he must have realized he was lost. On all other occasions I had seen him wear a khaki jacket and plus fours, but that evening he wore a brown suit that gave him a certain air of reliability and dullness. He didn't say a word to Eily, or even look in her direction as she sat on a little stool staring out the window and biting on the little lavalier that she wore around her neck. My father said he had been pup enough and the only thing to do was to own up to it and marry her. The bank clerk put forward three objections—one that he had no house, two that he had no money, and three that he was not considering marrying.

During the supper Eily's mother refused to sit down, and stayed in the kitchen nursing the big tin of fruit cocktail and having feeble jabs at it with the old iron tin-opener. She talked aloud to herself about the folks "hither" in the room and what a sorry pass things had come to. As usual my mother ate only the pope's nose and saved the men the breasts of chicken. Matters changed every other second. They were polite to him, remembering his status as a bank clerk, then they were asking him what kind of crops grew in his part of the country, and then again they would refer to him as if he was not there, saying "The pup likes his bit of meat." He was told that he would marry her on the Wednesday week, that he was being transferred from the bank, that he would go with his new wife and take rooms in a midland town.

He just shrugged and I was thinking that he would probably vanish on the morrow but I didn't know that they had alerted everyone and that when he did in fact try to leave at dawn the following morning, three strong men impeded him and brought him up the mountain for a drive in their lorry. For a week after he was indisposed and it is said that his black eyes were as big as bubble gum. It left a permanent hole in his lower cheek, as if a little pebble of flesh had been tweezed out of him.

65   Anyhow they discussed the practicalities of the wedding while they ate their fruit cocktail. It was served in the little carnival dishes and I thought of the numerous operations that Nuala had done, and how if it was left to Eily and me things would not be nearly so crucial. I did not want her to have to marry him and I almost blurted that out. But the plans were going ahead, he was being told that it would cost him ten pounds, that it would be in the sacristy of the Catholic church, since he was a Protestant, and that there were to be no guests except those present and Eily's former teacher, a Miss Melody. Even her sister Nuala was not going to be told until after the event. They kept asking him was that clear, and he kept saying "Oh yeh" as if it were a simple matter of whether he would have more fruit cocktail or not. The number of cherries were few and far between and for some reason had a faint mauve hue to them. I got one and my mother passed me hers. Eily ate well but listlessly, as if she weren't there at all. Towards the end my father sang "Master McGrath," a song about a greyhound, and Mr. Hogan told the ghost story about seeing the headless liveried man at a crossroads when he was a boy.

Going down the field, Eily was told to walk on ahead with her intended, probably so that she could discuss her trousseau or any last-minute things. The stars were never so bright or so numerous and the moonlight cast as white a glow as if it were morning and the world was veiled with frost. Eily and he walked in utter silence. At last she looked up at him and said something, and all he did was to draw away from her, and there was such a distance between them as a cart or a car could pass through. She edged a little to the right to get nearer, and as she did he moved further away so that eventually she was on the edge of a path and he was right in by the hedge hitting the bushes with a bit of a stick he had picked up. We followed behind, the grownups discussing whether or not it would rain the next day but no doubt wondering what Eily had endeavored to say to him.

They met twice more before the wedding, once in the sitting room of the hotel, when the traveling solicitor drew up the papers guaranteeing her a dowry of two hundred pounds, and once in the city when he was sent with her to the jeweler's to buy a wedding ring. It was the same city as where he had been seeing the bacon-curer's daughter and Eily said that in the jeweler's he expressed the wish that she would drop dead.

At the wedding breakfast itself there were only sighs and tears, and the teacher as was her wont stood in front of the fire and, mindless of the mixed company, hitched up her dress behind, the better to warm the cheeks of her bottom. In his giving-away speech my father said they had only to make the best of it. Eily sniveled, her mother wept and wept and said, "Oh Babbie, Babbie," and the groom said, "Once bitten twice shy."

The reception was in their new lodgings, and my mother said that she thought it was bad form the way the landlady included herself in the proceedings. My mother also said that their household utensils were pathetic, two forks, two knives, two spoons, an old kettle, an egg saucepan, a primus, and as she said not even a nice enamel bin for the bread but a rusted biscuit tin.

When they came to leave Eily tried to dart into the back of the car, tried it more than once, just like an animal trying to get back to its den.

On returning home, my mother let me put on her lipstick, and praised me untowardly for being such a good, such a pure little girl, and never did I feel so guilty because of the leading part I had played in Eily's romance. The only thing that my mother had eaten at the wedding was a jelly made with milk. We tried it the following Sunday, a raspberry-flavored jelly made with equal quantities of milk and water and then whisked. It was like a beautiful pink tongue dotted with spittle, and it tasted slippery.

I had not been found out, had received no punishment, and life was getting back to normal again. I gargled with salt and water, on Sundays longed for visitors that never came, and on Monday mornings had all my books newly covered so that the teacher would praise me. Ever since the scandal she was enjoining us to go home in pairs, to speak Irish, and not to walk with any sense of provocation. Yet she herself stood by the fire grate, and after having hitched up her dress petted her own thighs. When she lost her temper, she threw chalk or implements at us and used very bad language.

It was a wonderful year for lilac, and the window sills were full of it, first the big moist bunches with the lovely cool green leaves, and then a wilting display, and following that the seeds in pools all over the sills and the purple itself much sadder and more dolorous than when first plucked off the trees.

When I daydreamed, which was often, it hinged on Eily. Did she have a friend, did her husband love her, was she homesick, and above all was her body swelling up? She wrote to her mother every second week. Her mother used to come with her apron on and the letter in one of those pockets, and sit on the back step and hesitate before reading it. She never came in, being too shy, but she would sit there while my mother fetched her a cup of raspberry cordial. We all had a sweet tooth. The letters told next to nothing, only such things as that their chimney had caught fire, or a boy herding goats found an old coin in a field, or could her mother root out some old clothes from a trunk and send them to her as she hadn't got a stitch. "Tis style enough she has," her mother would say bitterly, and then advise that it was better to cut my hair and not have me go around in ringlets, because as she said, "Fine feathers make fine birds." Now and then she would cry and then feed the birds the crumbs of the biscuit or shortbread that my mother had given her. She liked the birds and in secret in her own yard made little perches for them, and if you please hung bits of colored rags and the shaving mirror for them to amuse themselves by.

My mother had made a quilt for Eily, and I believe that was the only wedding present she received. They parceled it together. It was a red flannel quilt, lined with white, and had a herringbone stitch around the edge. It was not like the big soft quilt that once occupied the entire window of the draper's, a pink satin onto which one's body could sink, then levitate.

One day her mother looked right at me and said, "Has she passed any more worms?" I had passed a big tapeworm and that was a talking point for a week or so after the furor of the wedding had died down. Then she gave me a half a crown. It was some way of thanking me for being a friend of Eily's.

When her son was born the family received a wire. He was given the name of Jack, the same as his father, and I thought how the witch had been right when she had seen the initial twice, but how we had misconstrued it and took it to be glad tidings.

Eily began to grow odd, began talking to herself, and then her lovely hair began to fall out in clumps. I would hear her mother tell my mother these things. The news came in snatches, first from a family who had gone up there to buy grazing, and then from a private nurse who had to give Eily pills and potions. Eily's own letters were disconnected, and she asked about dead people or people she'd hardly known. Her mother meant to go by bus one day and stay overnight, but she postponed it until her arthritis got too bad and she was not able to go out at all.

Four years later, at Christmastime, Eily, her husband, and their three children paid a visit home, and she kept eyeing everything, and told people to please stop staring at her, and then she went round the house and looked under the beds for some spy whom she believed to be there. She was dressed in brown and had brown fur-backed gloves. Her husband was very suave, had let his hair grow long, and during the tea kept pressing his knee against mine and asking me which did I like best, sweet or savory. The only moment of levity was when the three children, clothes and all, got into a pig trough and began to bask in it. Eily laughed her head off as they were being hosed down by her mother. Then they had to be put into the settle bed, alongside the sacks of flour and the brooms and the bric-a-brac, while their clothes were first washed and then put on a little wooden horse to dry before the fire. They were laughing but their teeth chattered. Eily didn't remember me very clearly and kept asking me if I was the eldest or the middle girl in the family. We heard later that her husband had got promoted and was running a little shop on the side and had young girls working as his assistants.

80   Walking up a street in a city with my own mother, under not very happy circumstances, we saw this wild creature coming towards us talking and debating to herself. Her hair was gray and frizzled, her costume was streelish, and she looked at us, and then peered, as if she were going to pounce on us, and then she started to laugh at us, or rather to sneer, and she stalked away and pounced on some other persons.

My mother said, "I think that was Eily," and warned me not to look back—I was pregnant at the time and in no way elated by it. We both walked on in terror and then ducked into the porchway of a shop, so that we could follow her with our eyes without ourselves being seen.

She was being avoided by all sorts of people, and by now she was shouting something and brandishing her fist and struggling to get heard. I shook, as indeed the child within me was induced to shake, and for one moment I wanted to go down that street to her but my mother held me back and said that she was dangerous, and that in my condition I must not go. I did not need much in the way of persuading.

She moved on and by now several people were laughing and looking after her and I was unable to move and all the gladness of our summer day, and a little bottle of Mischief, pressed itself into the palm of my hand again, and I saw her lithe and beautiful as she once was, and in the street a great flood of light pillared itself about a little cock of hay that was dancing deliriously around.

I did go in search of her years later—I hankered to meet and to talk. My husband waited up at the cross, and I went down the narrow steep road with my son, who was thrilled to be approaching a shop.

Eily was inside the counter, her head bent over a pile of bills that she was attaching to a skewer. She looked up and smiled. The same face but much coarser. Her hair was permed, and a newly pared pencil protruded from it. She was pleased to see me and at once reached out and handed my son a fistful of rainbow toffees.

It was the very same as if we'd parted only a little while ago. She didn't shake hands or make any special fuss, she simply said, "Talk of an angel," because she had been thinking of me that very morning. Her children were helping—one was weighing sugar, the little girl was funneling castor oil into four-ounce bottles, and her eldest son was up on a ladder fixing a flex to a ceiling light. He said my name, said it with surprise, as soon as she introduced me, but she told him to whist. For her own children she had no time because they were already grown, but for my son she was full of welcome and kept saying he was a cute little fellow. She weighed him on the big meal scales and then let him scoop the grain with a little trowel and let it slide down the length of his arm, which made him gurgle.

People kept coming in and out and she went on talking to me while still serving them. She was complete mistress of her surroundings and said what a pity that her husband was away, off on the lorry doing the door-to-door orders. He had given up banking, found the business more profitable. She winked each time she hit the cash register, letting me see what an expert she was. Whenever there was a lull I thought of saying something, but my son's pranks commandeered the occasion. She was very keen to offer me something and ripped the glass paper off a two-pound box of chocolates and lay them before me, slantwise, propped against a can of something. They were eminently inviting and when I refused she made some reference to the figure.

"You were always too generous," I said, sounding like my mother or some stiff relation.

"Go on," she said, and biffed me.

It seemed the right moment to broach it, but how?

"How are you?" I said. She said that as I could see she was topping, getting on a bit, and the children were great sorts, and the next time I came I'd have to give her notice so that we could have a singsong. I didn't say that my husband was up at the road and by now would be looking at his watch and saying "damn" and maybe would have got out to polish or do some cosseting to the vintage motorcar that he loved so.

I said again and again it was lamentable. "Remember the old days, Eily?"

"Not much," she said.

"The good old days," I said.

95   "They're all much of a muchness," she said. She was in no mood to discuss the past.

"Bad," I said.

"No, busy," she said.

My first thought was they must have drugged the feelings out of her, they must have given her some strange notions when she was mad, and along with removing her cares they had taken her spirit away. There are times when the thing we are seeing changes before our very eyes, and if it is a landscape we praise nature, and if it is celestial we invoke God, but if it is a loved one who defects, we excuse ourselves and say we have to be somewhere and are already late for our next appointment. We do not stay to put pennies over the half-dead eyes.

She kissed me and put a little holy water on my forehead, delving it in deeply, as if I were dough. They waved to us, and my son could not return those waves, encumbered as he was with the various presents that both the children and Eily had showered on him. It was beginning to spot with rain, and what with that and the holy water and the red rowan tree bright and instinct with life, I thought that ours was indeed a land of shame, a land of murder, and a land of strange sacrificial women.

QUESTIONS FOR DISCUSSION AND WRITING

1. In what ways does "playing" doctor foreshadow the events of the story? What is significant about the scene in which Eily gives the narrator a bottle of "Mischief"? How does the final scene in Eily's shop serve as the story's denouement?

2. How do Eily's clothes and hair help to characterize her throughout the story? What details are used to characterize the minor characters in the story—Nuala, the bank clerk, the narrator's mother, Eily's father, the priest?

3. In what specific ways does the story reveal the stunting effects of the culture on its women? How does the community eliminate any possibility of escape from this cultural tyranny?

4. How does the narrator interpret her growth from childhood to young adulthood? How does she feel about her roles as Eily's *accomplice* and as a *mother?*

5. How does the narrator illustrate the validity of the assertions in the opening paragraph? How does the story confirm the point in the last sentence that Ireland is a land of "strange sacrificial women"?

Stories for Comparison

Fiona Barr's "The Wall-Reader" (pages 262–267); Anton Chekhov's "The Lady with the Dog" (pages 51–62).

78

FLANNERY O'CONNOR

A Good Man Is Hard to Find

FLANNERY O'CONNOR (1925–1964) was born in Savannah, Georgia, and educated at Georgia State College for Women and the University of Iowa. After completing her graduate work at the University of Iowa Writer's Workshop in 1947, she lived for two years in New York City. However, O'Connor returned to her mother's farm near Milledgeville, Georgia, when she discovered that she had contracted lupus erythematosus, the systemic disease that had killed her father and of which she herself was to die. For the last fourteen years of her life, she lived a quiet, productive life on the farm—raising peacocks, painting, and writing the extraordinary stories and novels that won her worldwide acclaim. Her novels, *Wise Blood* (1952)—adapted to film in 1980—and *The Violent Bear It Away* (1960), both deal with fanatical preachers: one is an urban minister of the "Church of God without Christ"; the other is a rural prophet struggling to save his grandson from his atheist nephew. Both novels reveal O'Connor's preoccupation with the gothic distortions of contemporary religion as well as the profound Roman Catholic faith that is at the bottom of all her work. Her thirty-one carefully crafted stories, combining grotesque comedy and violent tragedy, appear in *A Good Man Is Hard to Find* (1955), *Everything That Rises Must Converge* (1965), and *The Complete Stories* (1971), which won the National Book Award. A selection of her letters, edited by Sally Fitzgerald, was published under the title *The Habit of Being* (1979). "A Good Man Is Hard to Find" describes the tragic fate that befalls a family on its trip to Florida. "Revelation" dramatizes the ironic discoveries a woman makes about the order of things.

The grandmother didn't want to go to Florida. She wanted to visit some of her connections in east Tennessee and she was seizing at every chance to change Bailey's mind. Bailey was the son she lived with, her only boy. He was sitting on the edge of his chair at the table, bent over the orange sports section of the *Journal.* "Now look here, Bailey," she said, "see here, read this," and she stood with one hand on her thin hip and the other rattling the newspaper at his bald head. "Here this fellow that calls himself The Misfit is aloose from the Federal Pen and headed toward Florida and you read here what it says he did to these people. Just you read it. I wouldn't take my children in any direction with a criminal like that aloose in it. I couldn't answer to my conscience if I did."

Bailey didn't look up from his reading so she wheeled around then and faced the children's mother, a young woman in slacks, whose face was as broad and innocent as a cabbage and was tied around with a green head-kerchief that had two points on the top like a rabbit's ears. She was sitting on the sofa, feeding the baby his apricots out of a jar. "The children have been to Florida before," the old lady said. "You all ought to take them somewhere else for a change so they would see different parts of the world and be broad. They never have been to east Tennessee."

The children's mother didn't seem to hear her but the eight-year-old boy, John Wesley, a stocky child with glasses, said, "If you don't want to go to Florida, why dontcha stay at home?" He and the little girl, June Star, were reading the funny papers on the floor.

"She wouldn't stay at home to be queen for a day," June Star said without raising her yellow head.

5   "Yes and what would you do if this fellow, The Misfit, caught you?" the grandmother asked.

"I'd smack his face," John Wesley said.

"She wouldn't stay at home for a million bucks," June Star said. "Afraid she'd miss something. She has to go everywhere we go."

"All right, Miss," the grandmother said. "Just remember that the next time you want me to curl your hair."

June Star said her hair was naturally curly.

10   The next morning the grandmother was the first one in the car, ready to go. She had her big black valise that looked like the head of a hippopotamus in one corner, and underneath it she was hiding a basket with Pitty Sing, the cat, in it. She didn't intend for the cat to be left alone in the house for three days because he would miss her too much and she was afraid he might brush against one of the gas burners and accidentally asphyxiate himself. Her son, Bailey, didn't like to arrive at a motel with a cat.

She sat in the middle of the back seat with John Wesley and June Star on either side of her. Bailey and the children's mother and the baby sat in front and they left Atlanta at eight forty-five with the mileage on the car at 55890. The grandmother wrote this down because she thought it would be interesting to say how many miles they had been when they got back. It took them twenty minutes to reach the outskirts of the city.

The old lady settled herself comfortably, removing her white cotton gloves and putting them up with her purse on the shelf in front of the back window. The children's mother still had on slacks and still had her head tied up in a green kerchief, but the grandmother had on a navy blue straw sailor hat with a bunch of white violets on the brim and a navy blue dress with a small white dot in the print. Her collars and cuffs were white organdy trimmed with lace and at her neckline she had pinned a purple spray of cloth violets containing a sachet. In case of an accident, anyone seeing her dead on the highway would know at once that she was a lady.

She said she thought it was going to be a good day for driving, neither too hot nor too cold, and she cautioned Bailey that the speed limit was fifty-five miles an hour and that the patrolmen hid themselves behind billboards and small clumps of trees and sped out after you before you had a chance to slow down. She pointed out interesting details of the scenery: Stone Mountain; the blue granite that in some places came up to both sides of the highway; the brilliant red clay banks slightly streaked with purple; and the various crops that made rows of green lace-work on the ground. The trees were full of silver-white sunlight and the meanest of them sparkled. The children were reading comic magazines and their mother had gone back to sleep.

"Let's go through Georgia fast so we won't have to look at it much," John Wesley said.

"If I were a little boy," said the grandmother, "I wouldn't talk about my native 15 state that way. Tennessee has the mountains and Georgia has the hills."

"Tennessee is just a hillbilly dumping ground," John Wesley said, "and Georgia is a lousy state, too."

"You said it," June Star said.

"In my time," said the grandmother, folding her thin veined fingers, "children were more respectful of their native states and their parents and everything else. People did right then. Oh look at the cute little pickaninny!" she said and pointed to a Negro child standing in the door of a shack. "Wouldn't that make a picture, now?" she asked and they all turned and looked at the little Negro out of the back window. He waved.

"He didn't have any britches on," June Star said.

"He probably didn't have any," the grandmother explained. "Little niggers in the 20 country don't have things like we do. If I could paint, I'd paint that picture," she said.

The children exchanged comic books.

The grandmother offered to hold the baby and the children's mother passed him over the front seat to her. She set him on her knee and bounced him and told him about the things they were passing. She rolled her eyes and screwed up her mouth and stuck her leathery thin face into his smooth bland one. Occasionally he gave her a faraway smile. They passed a large cotton field with five or six graves fenced in the middle of it, like a small island. "Look at the graveyard!" the grandmother said, pointing it out. "That was the old family burying ground. That belonged to the plantation."

"Where's the plantation?" John Wesley asked.

"Gone With the Wind," said the grandmother. "Ha. Ha."

When the children finished all the comic books they had brought, they opened 25 the lunch and ate it. The grandmother ate a peanut butter sandwich and an olive and would not let the children throw the box and the paper napkins out the window. When there was nothing else to do they played a game by choosing a cloud and making the other two guess what shape it suggested. John Wesley took one the shape of a cow and June Star guessed a cow and John Wesley said, no, an automobile, and June Star said he didn't play fair, and they began to slap each other over the grandmother.

The grandmother said she would tell them a story if they would keep quiet. When she told a story, she rolled her eyes and waved her head and was very dramatic. She said once when she was a maiden lady she had been courted by a Mr. Edgar Atkins Teagarden from Jasper, Georgia. She said he was a very good-looking man and a gentleman and that he brought her a watermelon every Saturday afternoon with his initials cut in it, E. A. T. Well, one Saturday, she said, Mr. Teagarden brought the watermelon and there was nobody at home and he left it on the front porch and returned in his buggy to Jasper, but she never got the watermelon, she said, because a nigger boy ate it when he saw the initials, E. A. T! This story tickled John Wesley's funny bone and he giggled and giggled but June Star didn't think it was any good. She said she wouldn't marry a man that just brought her a watermelon on Saturday. The grandmother said she would have done well to marry Mr. Teagarden because he was a gentleman and had bought Coca-Cola stock when it first came out and that he had died only a few years ago, a very wealthy man.

They stopped at The Tower for barbecued sandwiches. The Tower was a part stucco and part wood filling station and dance hall set in a clearing outside of Timothy. A fat man named Red Sammy Butts ran it and there were signs stuck here and there on the building and for miles up and down the highway saying, TRY RED SAMMY'S FAMOUS BARBECUE. NONE LIKE FAMOUS RED SAMMY'S! RED SAM! THE FAT BOY WITH THE HAPPY LAUGH! A VETERAN! RED SAMMY'S YOUR MAN!

Red Sammy was lying on the bare ground outside The Tower with his head under a truck while a gray monkey about a foot high, chained to a small chinaberry tree, chattered nearby. The monkey sprang back into the tree and got on the highest limb as soon as he saw the children jump out of the car and run toward him.

Inside, The Tower was a long dark room with a counter at one end and tables at the other and dancing space in the middle. They sat down at a board table next to the nickelodeon and Red Sam's wife, a tall burnt-brown woman with hair and eyes lighter than her skin, came and took their order. The children's mother put a dime in the machine and played "The Tennessee Waltz," and the grandmother said that tune always made her want to dance. She asked Bailey if he would like to dance but he only glared at her. He didn't have a naturally sunny disposition like she did and trips made him nervous. The grandmother's brown eyes were very bright. She swayed her head from side to side and pretended she was dancing in her chair. June Star said play something she could tap to so the children's mother put in another dime and played a fast number and June Star stepped out onto the dance floor and did her tap routine.

30   "Ain't she cute?" Red Sam's wife said, leaning over the counter. "Would you like to come be my little girl?"

"No I certainly wouldn't," June Star said. "I wouldn't live in a broken-down place like this for a million bucks!" and she ran back to the table.

"Ain't she cute?" the woman repeated, stretching her mouth politely.

"Aren't you ashamed?" hissed the grandmother.

Red Sam came in and told his wife to quit lounging on the counter and hurry up with these people's order. His khaki trousers reached just to his hip bones and his stomach hung over them like a sack of meal swaying under his shirt. He came over and sat down at a table nearby and let out a combination sigh and yodel. "You can't win," he said. "You can't win," and he wiped his sweating red face off with a gray handkerchief. "These days you don't know who to trust," he said. "Ain't that the truth?"

"People are certainly not nice like they used to be," said the grandmother.   35

"Two fellers come in here last week," Red Sammy said, "driving a Chrysler. It was a old beat-up car but it was a good one and these boys looked all right to me. Said they worked at the mill and you know I let them fellers charge the gas they bought? Now why did I do that?"

"Because you're a good man!" the grandmother said at once.

"Yes'm, I suppose so," Red Sam said as if he were struck with this answer.

His wife brought the orders, carrying the five plates all at once without a tray, two in each hand and one balanced on her arm. "It isn't a soul in this green world of God's that you can trust," she said. "And I don't count nobody out of that, not nobody," she repeated, looking at Red Sammy.

"Did you read about that criminal, The Misfit, that's escaped?" asked the   40
grandmother.

"I wouldn't be a bit surprised if he didn't attack this place right here," said the woman. "If he hears about it being here, I wouldn't be none surprised to see him. If he hears it's two cent in the cash register, I wouldn't be a tall surprised if he . . ."

"That'll do," Red Sam said. "Go bring these people their Co'-Colas," and the woman went off to get the rest of the order.

"A good man is hard to find," Red Sammy said. "Everything is getting terrible. I remember the day you could go off and leave your screen door unlatched. Not no more."

He and the grandmother discussed better times. The old lady said that in her opinion Europe was entirely to blame for the way things were now. She said the way Europe acted you would think we were made of money and Red Sam said it was no use talking about it, she was exactly right. The children ran outside into the white sunlight and looked at the monkey in the lacy chinaberry tree. He was busy catching fleas on himself and biting each one carefully between his teeth as if it were a delicacy.

They drove off again into the hot afternoon. The grandmother took cat naps and   45
woke up every few minutes with her own snoring. Outside of Toombsboro she woke up and recalled an old plantation that she had visited in this neighborhood once when she was a young lady. She said the house had six white columns across the front and that there was an avenue of oaks leading up to it and two little wooden trellis arbors on either side in front where you sat down with your suitor after a stroll in the garden. She recalled exactly which road to turn off to get to it. She knew that Bailey would not be willing to lose any time looking at an old house, but the more she talked about it, the more she wanted to see it once again and find out if the little twin arbors were still standing. "There was a secret panel in this house," she said craftily, not telling the truth but wishing that she were, "and the story went that all the family silver was hidden in it when Sherman came through but it was never found . . ."

"Hey!" John Wesley said. "Let's go see it! We'll find it! We'll poke all the wood-work and find it! Who lives there? Where do you turn off at? Hey Pop, can't we turn off there?"

"We never have seen a house with a secret panel!" June Star shrieked. "Let's go to the house with the secret panel! Hey Pop, can't we go see the house with the se-cret panel!"

"It's not far from here, I know," the grandmother said. "It wouldn't take over twenty minutes."

Bailey was looking straight ahead. His jaw was as rigid as a horseshoe. "No," he said.

50   The children began to yell and scream that they wanted to see the house with the secret panel. John Wesley kicked the back of the front seat and June Star hung over her mother's shoulder and whined desperately into her ear that they never had any fun even on their vacation, that they could never do what THEY wanted to do. The baby began to scream and John Wesley kicked the back of the seat so hard that his father could feel the blows in his kidney.

"All right!" he shouted and drew the car to a stop at the side of the road. "Will you all shut up? Will you all just shut up for one second? If you don't shut up, we won't go anywhere."

"It would be very educational for them," the grandmother murmured.

"All right," Bailey said, "but get this: this is the only time we're going to stop for anything like this. This is the one and only time."

"The dirt road that you have to turn down is about a mile back," the grandmother directed. "I marked it when we passed."

55   "A dirt road," Bailey groaned.

After they had turned around and were headed toward the dirt road, the grand-mother recalled other points about the house, the beautiful glass over the front door-way and the candle-lamp in the hall. John Wesley said that the secret panel was prob-ably in the fireplace.

"You can't go inside this house," Bailey said. "You don't know who lives there."

"While you all talk to the people in front, I'll run around behind and get in a window," John Wesley suggested.

"We'll all stay in the car," his mother said.

60   They turned onto the dirt road and the car raced roughly along in a swirl of pink dust. The grandmother recalled the times when there were no paved roads and thirty miles was a day's journey. The dirt road was hilly and there were sudden washes in it and sharp curves on dangerous embankments. All at once they would be on a hill, looking down over the blue tops of trees for miles around, then the next minute, they would be in a red depression with the dust-coated trees looking down on them.

"This place had better turn up in a minute," Bailey said, "or I'm going to turn around."

The road looked as if no one had traveled on it in months.

"It's not much farther," the grandmother said and just as she said it, a horrible thought came to her. The thought was so embarrassing that she turned red in the face and her eyes dilated and her feet jumped up, upsetting her valise in the corner. The instant the valise moved, the newspaper top she had over the basket under it rose with a snarl and Pitty Sing, the cat, sprang onto Bailey's shoulder.

The children were thrown to the floor and their mother, clutching the baby, was thrown out the door onto the ground; the old lady was thrown into the front seat. The car turned over once and landed right-side-up in a gulch off the side of the road. Bailey remained in the driver's seat with the cat—gray-striped with a broad white face and an orange nose—clinging to his neck like a caterpillar.

As soon as the children saw they could move their arms and legs, they scram- 65 bled out of the car, shouting, "We've had an ACCIDENT!" The grandmother was curled up under the dashboard, hoping she was injured so that Bailey's wrath would not come down on her all at once. The horrible thought she had had before the accident was that the house she had remembered so vividly was not in Georgia but in Tennessee.

Bailey removed the cat from his neck with both hands and flung it out the window against the side of a pine tree. Then he got out of the car and started looking for the children's mother. She was sitting against the side of the red gutted ditch, holding the screaming baby, but she only had a cut down her face and a broken shoulder. "We've had an ACCIDENT!" the children screamed in a frenzy of delight.

"But nobody's killed," June Star said with disappointment as the grandmother limped out of the car, her hat still pinned to her head but the broken front brim standing up at a jaunty angle and the violet spray hanging off the side. They all sat down in the ditch, except the children, to recover from the shock. They were all shaking.

"Maybe a car will come along," said the children's mother hoarsely.

"I believe I have injured an organ," said the grandmother, pressing her side, but no one answered her. Bailey's teeth were clattering. He had on a yellow sport shirt with bright blue parrots designed in it and his face was as yellow as the shirt. The grandmother decided that she would not mention that the house was in Tennessee.

The road was about ten feet above and they could see only the tops of the trees 70 on the other side of it. Behind the ditch they were sitting in there were more woods, tall and dark and deep. In a few minutes they saw a car some distance away on top of a hill, coming slowly as if the occupants were watching them. The grandmother stood up and waved both arms dramatically to attract their attention. The car continued to come on slowly, disappeared around a bend and appeared again, moving even slower, on top of the hill they had gone over. It was a big black battered hearse-like automobile. There were three men in it.

It came to a stop just over them and for some minutes, the driver looked down with a steady expressionless gaze to where they were sitting, and didn't speak. Then he turned his head and muttered something to the other two and they got out. One was a fat boy in black trousers and a red sweat shirt with a silver stallion embossed on the front of it. He moved around on the right side of them and stood staring, his mouth partly open in a kind of loose grin. The other had on khaki pants and a blue striped coat and a gray hat pulled down very low, hiding most of his face. He came around slowly on the left side. Neither spoke.

The driver got out of the car and stood by the side of it, looking down at them. He was an older man than the other two. His hair was just beginning to gray and he wore silver-rimmed spectacles that gave him a scholarly look. He had a long creased face and didn't have on any shirt or undershirt. He had on blue jeans that were too tight for him and was holding a black hat and a gun. The two boys also had guns.

"We've had an ACCIDENT!" the children screamed.

The grandmother had the peculiar feeling that the bespectacled man was someone she knew. His face was as familiar to her as if she had known him all her life but she could not recall who he was. He moved away from the car and began to come down the embankment, placing his feet carefully so that he wouldn't slip. He had on tan and white shoes and no socks, and his ankles were red and thin. "Good afternoon," he said. "I see you all had you a little spill."

75   "We turned over twice!" said the grandmother.

"Oncet," he corrected. "We seen it happen. Try their car and see will it run, Hiram," he said quietly to the boy with the gray hat.

"What you got that gun for?" John Wesley asked. "Whatcha gonna do with that gun?"

"Lady," the man said to the children's mother, "would you mind calling them children to sit down by you? Children make me nervous. I want all you all to sit down right together there where you're at."

"What are you telling US what to do for?" June Star asked.

80   Behind them the line of woods gaped like a dark open mouth. "Come here," said their mother.

"Look here now," Bailey began suddenly, "we're in a predicament! We're in . . ."

The grandmother shrieked. She scrambled to her feet and stood staring. "You're The Misfit!" she said. "I recognized you at once!"

"Yes'm," the man said, smiling slightly as if he were pleased in spite of himself to be known, "but it would have been better for all of you, lady, if you hadn't of reckernized me."

Bailey turned his head sharply and said something to his mother that shocked even the children. The old lady began to cry and The Misfit reddened.

85   "Lady," he said, "don't you get upset. Sometimes a man says things he don't mean. I don't reckon he meant to talk to you thataway."

"You wouldn't shoot a lady, would you?" the grandmother said and removed a clean handkerchief from her cuff and began to slap at her eyes with it.

The Misfit pointed the toe of his shoe into the ground and made a little hole and then covered it up again. "I would hate to have to," he said.

"Listen," the grandmother almost screamed, "I know you're a good man. You don't look a bit like you have common blood. I know you must come from nice people!"

"Yes mam," he said, "finest people in the world." When he smiled he showed a row of strong white teeth. "God never made a finer woman than my mother and my daddy's heart was pure gold," he said. The boy with the red sweat shirt had come around behind them and was standing with his gun at his hip. The Misfit squatted down on the ground. "Watch them children, Bobby Lee," he said. "You know they make me nervous." He looked at the six of them huddled together in front of him and he seemed to be embarrassed as if he couldn't think of anything to say. "Ain't a cloud in the sky," he remarked, looking up at it. "Don't see no sun but don't see no cloud neither."

"Yes, it's a beautiful day," said the grandmother. "Listen," she said, "you shouldn't   90 call yourself The Misfit because I know you're a good man at heart. I can just look at you and tell."

"Hush!" Bailey yelled. "Hush! Everybody shut up and let me handle this!" He was squatting in the position of a runner about to sprint forward but he didn't move.

"I pre-chate that, lady," The Misfit said and drew a little circle in the ground with the butt of his gun.

"It'll take a half a hour to fix this here car," Hiram called, looking over the raised hood of it.

"Well, first you and Bobby Lee get him and that little boy to step over yonder with you," The Misfit said, pointing to Bailey and John Wesley. "The boys want to ast you something," he said to Bailey. "Would you mind stepping back in them woods there with them?"

"Listen," Bailey began, "we're in a terrible predicament! Nobody realizes what   95 this is," his voice cracked. His eyes were as blue and intense as the parrots in his shirt and he remained perfectly still.

The grandmother reached up to adjust her hat brim as if she were going to the woods with him but it came off in her hand. She stood staring at it and after a second she let it fall on the ground. Hiram pulled Bailey up by the arms as if he were assisting an old man. John Wesley caught hold of his father's hand and Bobby Lee followed. They went off toward the woods and just as they reached the dark edge, Bailey turned and supporting himself against a gray naked pine trunk, he shouted, "I'll be back in a minute, Mamma, wait on me!"

"Come back this instant!" his mother shrilled but they all disappeared into the woods.

"Bailey Boy!" the grandmother called in a tragic voice but she found she was looking at The Misfit squatting on the ground in front of her. "I just know you're a good man," she said desperately. "You're not a bit common!"

"Nome, I ain't a good man," The Misfit said after a second as if he had considered her statement carefully, "but I ain't the worst in the world neither. My daddy said I was a different breed of dog from my brothers and sisters. 'You know,' Daddy said, 'it's some that can live their whole life out without asking about it and it's others has to know why it is, and this boy is one of the latters. He's going to be into everything!'" He put on his black hat and looked up suddenly and then away deep into the woods as if he were embarrassed again. "I'm sorry I don't have on a shirt before you ladies," he said, hunching his shoulders slightly. "We buried our clothes that we had on when we escaped and we're just making do until we can get better. We borrowed these from some folks we met," he explained.

"That's perfectly all right," the grandmother said. "Maybe Bailey has an extra   100 shirt in his suitcase."

"I'll look and see terrectly," The Misfit said.

"Where are they taking him?" the children's mother screamed.

"Daddy was a card himself," The Misfit said. "You couldn't put anything over on him. He never got in trouble with the Authorities though. Just had the knack of handling them."

"You could be honest too if you'd only try," said the grandmother. "Think how wonderful it would be to settle down and live a comfortable life and not have to think about somebody chasing you all the time."

105   The Misfit kept scratching in the ground with the butt of his gun as if he were thinking about it. "Yes'm, somebody is always after you," he murmured.

The grandmother noticed how thin his shoulder blades were just behind his hat because she was standing up looking down at him. "Do you ever pray?" she asked.

He shook his head. All she saw was the black hat wiggle between his shoulder blades. "Nome," he said.

There was a pistol shot from the woods, followed closely by another. Then silence. The old lady's head jerked around. She could hear the wind move through the tree tops like a long satisfied insuck of breath. "Bailey Boy!" she called.

"I was a gospel singer for a while," The Misfit said. "I been most everything. Been in the arm service, both land and sea, at home and abroad, been twice married, been an undertaker, been with the railroads, plowed Mother Earth, been in a tornado, seen a man burnt alive oncet," and looked up at the children's mother and the little girl who were sitting close together, their faces white and their eyes glassy; "I even seen a woman flogged," he said.

110   "Pray, pray," the grandmother began, "pray, pray . . ."

"I never was a bad boy that I remember of," The Misfit said in an almost dreamy voice, "but somewheres along the line I done something wrong and got sent to the penitentiary. I was buried alive," and he looked up and held her attention to him by a steady stare.

"That's when you should have started to pray," she said. "What did you do to get sent to the penitentiary that first time?"

"Turn to the right, it was a wall," The Misfit said, looking up again at the cloudless sky. "Turn to the left, it was a wall. Look up it was a ceiling, look down it was a floor. I forgot what I done, lady. I set there and set there, trying to remember what it was I done and I ain't recalled it to this day. Oncet in a while, I would think it was coming to me, but it never come."

"Maybe they put you in by mistake," the old lady said vaguely.

115   "Nome," he said. "It wasn't no mistake. They had the papers on me."

"You must have stolen something," she said.

The Misfit sneered slightly. "Nobody had nothing I wanted," he said. "It was a head-doctor at the penitentiary said what I had done was kill my daddy but I know that for a lie. My daddy died in nineteen ought nineteen of the epidemic flu and I never had a thing to do with it. He was buried in the Mount Hopewell Baptist churchyard and you can go there and see for yourself."

"If you would pray," the old lady said, "Jesus would help you."

"That's right," The Misfit said.

120   "Well then, why don't you pray?" she asked trembling with delight suddenly.

"I don't want no hep," he said. "I'm doing all right by myself."

Bobby Lee and Hiram came ambling back from the woods. Bobby Lee was dragging a yellow shirt with bright blue parrots in it.

"Throw me that shirt, Bobby Lee," The Misfit said. The shirt came flying at him and landed on his shoulder and he put it on. The grandmother couldn't name what the shirt reminded her of. "No, lady," The Misfit said while he was buttoning it up, "I found out the crime don't matter. You can do one thing or you can do another, kill a man or take a tire off his car, because sooner or later you're going to forget what it was you done and just be punished for it."

The children's mother had begun to make heaving noises as if she couldn't get her breath. "Lady," he asked, "would you and that little girl like to step off yonder with Bobby Lee and Hiram and join your husband?"

"Yes, thank you," the mother said faintly. Her left arm dangled helplessly and 125 she was holding the baby, who had gone to sleep, in the other. "Hep that lady up, Hiram," The Misfit said as she struggled to climb out of the ditch, "and Bobby Lee, you hold onto that little girl's hand."

"I don't want to hold hands with him," June Star said. "He reminds me of a pig."

The fat boy blushed and laughed and caught her by the arm and pulled her off into the woods after Hiram and her mother.

Alone with The Misfit, the grandmother found that she had lost her voice. There was not a cloud in the sky nor any sun. There was nothing around her but woods. She wanted to tell him that he must pray. She opened and closed her mouth several times before anything came out. Finally she found herself saying, "Jesus, Jesus," meaning, Jesus will help you, but the way she was saying it, it sounded as if she might be cursing.

"Yes'm," The Misfit said as if he agreed. "Jesus thrown everything off balance. It was the same case with Him as with me except He hadn't committed any crime and they could prove I had committed one because they had the papers on me. Of course," he said, "they never shown me my papers. That's why I sign myself now. I said long ago, you get you a signature and sign everything you do and keep a copy of it. Then you'll know what you done and you can hold up the crime to the punishment and see do they match and in the end you'll have something to prove you ain't been treated right. I call myself The Misfit," he said, "because I can't make what all I done wrong fit what all I gone through in punishment."

There was a piercing scream from the woods, followed closely by a pistol re- 130 port. "Does it seem right to you, lady, that one is punished a heap and another ain't punished at all?"

"Jesus!" the old lady cried. "You've got good blood! I know you wouldn't shoot a lady! I know you come from nice people! Pray! Jesus, you ought not to shoot a lady. I'll give you all the money I've got!"

"Lady," The Misfit said, looking beyond her far into the woods, "there never was a body that give the undertaker a tip."

There were two more pistol reports and the grandmother raised her head like a parched old turkey hen crying for water and called, "Bailey Boy, Bailey Boy!" as if her heart would break.

"Jesus was the only One that ever raised the dead," The Misfit continued, "and He shouldn't have done it. He thrown everything off balance. If He did what He said, then it's nothing for you to do but throw away everything and follow him, and if He didn't, then it's nothing for you to do but enjoy the few minutes you got left the best way you can—by killing somebody or burning down his house or doing some other meanness to him. No pleasure but meanness," he said and his voice had become almost a snarl.

135   "Maybe He didn't raise the dead," the old lady mumbled, not knowing what she was saying and feeling so dizzy that she sank down in the ditch with her legs twisted under her.

"I wasn't there so I can't say He didn't," The Misfit said. "I wisht I had of been there," he said, hitting the ground with his fist. "It ain't right I wasn't there because if I had of been there I would of known. Listen lady," he said in a high voice, "if I had of been there I would of known and I wouldn't be like I am now." His voice seemed about to crack and the grandmother's head cleared for an instant. She saw the man's face twisted close to her own as if he were going to cry and she murmured, "Why you're one of my babies. You're one of my own children!" She reached out and touched him on the shoulder. The Misfit sprang back as if a snake had bitten him and shot her three times through the chest. Then he put his gun down on the ground and took off his glasses and began to clean them.

Hiram and Bobby Lee returned from the woods and stood over the ditch, looking down at the grandmother who half sat and half lay in a puddle of blood with her legs crossed under her like a child's and her face smiling up at the cloudless sky.

Without his glasses, The Misfit's eyes were red-rimmed and pale and defenseless-looking. "Take her off and throw her where you thrown the others," he said, picking up the cat that was rubbing itself against his leg.

"She was a talker, wasn't she?" Bobby Lee said, sliding down the ditch with a yodel.

140   "She would have been a good woman," The Misfit said, "if it had been somebody there to shoot her every minute of her life."

"Some fun!" Bobby Lee said.

"Shut up, Bobby Lee," The Misfit said. "It's no real pleasure in life."

QUESTIONS FOR DISCUSSION AND WRITING

1. How does the grandmother's early apprehension about the trip to Florida foreshadow the major crisis in the story? Explain why the grandmother's recognition of The Misfit triggers that crisis. How do The Misfit's final comments on the grandmother bring the crisis to its denouement?

2. How does the grandmother's relationship to her family characterize her personality? What function does the character of Red Sam serve in the story? How does The Misfit's description of his life justify his name?

3. How do the grandmother's memories of other places and times lead her to the wrong place at the wrong time? In what ways do the characters' positive comments on the weather contrast with the horrible events that take place?

4. How does June Star's assertion that the grandmother is "afraid she'd miss something" help establish the grandmother's point of view in the early part of the story? Once she realizes the intentions of The Misfit, how does her point of view change?

5. How do The Misfit's final words illustrate his attitude toward the events of the afternoon? Explain how the title comments on the theme of the story. How does The Misfit define crime and punishment, goodness and evil? What does he mean when he says that Jesus "thrown everything off balance"?

Stories for Comparison

Joyce Carol Oates's "Where Are You Going, Where Have You Been?" (pages 935–947); Doris Lessing's "A Woman on a Roof" (pages 804–811).

79

FLANNERY O'CONNOR

Revelation

The doctor's waiting room, which was very small, was almost full when the Turpins entered and Mrs. Turpin, who was very large, made it look even smaller by her presence. She stood looming at the head of the magazine table set in the center of it, a living demonstration that the room was inadequate and ridiculous. Her little bright black eyes took in all the patients as she sized up the seating situation. There was one vacant chair and a place on the sofa occupied by a blond child in a dirty blue romper who should have been told to move over and make room for the lady. He was five or six, but Mrs. Turpin saw at once that no one was going to tell him to move over. He was slumped down in the seat, his arms idle at his sides and his eyes idle in his head; his nose ran unchecked.

Mrs. Turpin put a firm hand on Claud's shoulder and said in a voice that included anyone who wanted to listen, "Claud, you sit in that chair there," and gave him a push down into the vacant one. Claud was florid and bald and sturdy, somewhat shorter than Mrs. Turpin, but he sat down as if he were accustomed to doing what she told him to.

Mrs. Turpin remained standing. The only man in the room besides Claud was a lean stringy old fellow with a rusty hand spread out on each knee, whose eyes were closed as if he were asleep or dead or pretending to be so as not to get up and offer her his seat. Her gaze settled agreeably on a well-dressed grey-haired lady whose eyes met hers and whose expression said: if that child belonged to me, he would have some manners and move over—there's plenty of room there for you and him too.

Claud looked up with a sigh and made as if to rise.

5   "Sit down," Mrs. Turpin said. "You know you're not supposed to stand on that leg. He has an ulcer on his leg," she explained.

Claud lifted his foot onto the magazine table and rolled his trouser leg up to reveal a purple swelling on a plump marble-white calf.

"My!" the pleasant lady said. "How did you do that?"

"A cow kicked him," Mrs. Turpin said.

"Goodness!" said the lady.

10   Claud rolled his trouser leg down.

"Maybe the little boy would move over," the lady suggested, but the child did not stir.

"Somebody will be leaving in a minute," Mrs. Turpin said. She could not understand why a doctor—with as much money as they made charging five dollars a day to just stick their head in the hospital door and look at you—couldn't afford a decent-sized waiting room. This one was hardly bigger than a garage. The table was cluttered with limp-looking magazines and at one end of it there was a big green glass ash tray full of cigaret butts and cotton wads with little blood spots on them. If she had had anything to do with the running of the place, that would have been emptied every so often. There were no chairs against the wall at the head of the room. It had a rectangular-shaped panel in it that permitted a view of the office where the nurse came and went and the secretary listened to the radio. A plastic fern in a gold pot sat in the opening and trailed its fronds down almost to the floor. The radio was softly playing gospel music.

Just then the inner door opened and a nurse with the highest stack of yellow hair Mrs. Turpin had ever seen put her face in the crack and called for the next patient. The woman sitting beside Claud grasped the two arms of her chair and hoisted herself up; she pulled her dress free from her legs and lumbered through the door where the nurse disappeared.

Mrs. Turpin eased into the vacant chair, which held her tight as a corset. "I wish I could reduce," she said, and rolled her eyes and gave a comic sigh.

15   "Oh, *you* aren't fat," the stylish lady said.

"Ooooo I am too," Mrs. Turpin said. "Claud he eats all he wants to and never weighs over one hundred and seventy-five pounds, but me I just look at something good to eat and I gain some weight," and her stomach and shoulders shook with laughter. "You can eat all you want to, can't you, Claud?" she asked, turning to him.

Claud only grinned.

"Well, as long as you have such a good disposition," the stylish lady said, "I don't think it makes a bit of difference what size you are. You just can't beat a good disposition."

Next to her was a fat girl of eighteen or nineteen, scowling into a thick blue book which Mrs. Turpin saw was entitled *Human Development*. The girl raised her head' and directed her scowl at Mrs. Turpin as if she did not like her looks. She appeared annoyed that anyone should speak while she tried to read. The poor girl's face was blue with acne and Mrs. Turpin thought how pitiful it was to have a face like that at that age. She gave the girl a friendly smile but the girl only scowled the harder. Mrs. Turpin herself was fat but she had always had good skin, and, though she was forty-seven years old, there was not a wrinkle in her face except around her eyes from laughing too much.

Next to the ugly girl was the child, still in exactly the same position, and next to 20 him was a thin leathery old woman in a cotton print dress. She and Claud had three sacks of chicken feed in their pump house that was in the same print. She had seen from the first that the child belonged with the old woman. She could tell by the way they sat—kind of vacant and white-trashy, as if they would sit there until Doomsday if nobody called and told them to get up. And at right angles but next to the well-dressed pleasant lady was a lank-faced woman who was certainly the child's mother. She had on a yellow sweat shirt and wine-colored slacks, both gritty-looking, and the rims of her lips were stained with snuff. Her dirty yellow hair was tied behind with a little piece of red paper ribbon. Worse than niggers any day, Mrs. Turpin thought.

The gospel hymn playing was, "When I looked up and He looked down," and Mrs. Turpin, who knew it, supplied the last line mentally, "And wona these days I know I'll we-eara crown."

Without appearing to, Mrs. Turpin always noticed people's feet. The well-dressed lady had on red and grey suede shoes to match her dress. Mrs. Turpin had on her good black patent leather pumps. The ugly girl had on Girl Scout shoes and heavy socks. The old woman had on tennis shoes and the white-trashy mother had on what appeared to be bedroom slippers, black straw with gold braid threaded through them—exactly what you would have expected her to have on.

Sometimes at night when she couldn't go to sleep. Mrs. Turpin would occupy herself with the question of who she would have chosen to be if she couldn't have been herself. If Jesus had said to her before he made her, "There's only two places available for you. You can either be a nigger or white-trash," what would she have said? "Please, Jesus, please," she would have said, "just let me wait until there's another place available," and he would have said, "No, you have to go right now and I have only those two places so make up your mind." She would have wiggled and squirmed and begged and pleaded but it would have been no use and finally she would have said, "All right, make me a nigger then—but that don't mean a trashy one." And he would have made her a neat clean respectable Negro-woman, herself but black.

Next to the child's mother was a red-headed youngish woman, reading one of the magazines and working a piece of chewing gum, hell for leather, as Claud would say. Mrs. Turpin could not see the woman's feet. She was not white-trash, just common. Sometimes Mrs. Turpin occupied herself at night naming the classes of people. On the bottom of the heap were most colored people, not the kind she would have been if she had been one, but most of them; then next to them—not above, just away from—were the white-trash; then above them were the home-owners, and above them the home-and-land owners, to which she and Claud belonged. Above she and

Claud were people with a lot of money and much bigger houses and much more land. But here the complexity of it would begin to bear in on her, for some of the people with a lot of money were common and ought to be below she and Claud and some of the people who had good blood had lost their money and had to rent and then there were colored people who owned their homes and land as well. There was a colored dentist in town who had two red Lincolns and a swimming pool and a farm with registered white-face cattle on it. Usually by the time she had fallen asleep all the classes of people were moiling and roiling around in her head, and she would dream they were all crammed in together in a box car, being ridden off to be put in a gas oven.

25 "That's a beautiful clock," she said and nodded to her right. It was a big wall clock, the face encased in a brass sunburst.

"Yes, it's very pretty," the stylish lady said agreeably. "And right on the dot too," she added, glancing at her watch.

The ugly girl beside her cast an eye upward at the clock, smirked, then looked directly at Mrs. Turpin and smirked again. Then she returned her eyes to her book. She was obviously the lady's daughter because, although they didn't look anything alike as to disposition, they both had the same shape of face and the same blue eyes. On the lady they sparkled pleasantly but in the girl's seared face they appeared alternately to smolder and to blaze.

What if Jesus had said, "All right, you can be white-trash or a nigger or ugly"!

Mrs. Turpin felt an awful pity for the girl, though she thought it was one thing to be ugly and another to act ugly.

30 The woman with the snuff-stained lips turned around in her chair and looked up at the clock. Then she turned back and appeared to look a little to the side of Mrs. Turpin. There was a cast in one of her eyes. "You want to know wher you can get you one of themther clocks?" she asked in a loud voice.

"No, I already have a nice clock," Mrs. Turpin said. Once somebody like her got a leg in the conversation, she would be all over it.

"You can get you one with green stamps," the woman said. "That's most likely wher he got hisn. Save you up enough, you can get you most anythang. I got me some joo'ry."

Ought to have got you a wash rag and some soap, Mrs. Turpin thought.

"I get contour sheets with mine," the pleasant lady said.

35 The daughter slammed her book shut. She looked straight in front of her, directly through Mrs. Turpin and on through the yellow curtain and the plate glass window which made the wall behind her. The girl's eyes seemed lit all of a sudden with a peculiar light, an unnatural light like night road signs give. Mrs. Turpin turned her head to see if there was anything going on outside that she should see, but she could not see anything. Figures passing cast only a pale shadow through the curtain. There was no reason the girl should single her out for her ugly looks.

"Miss Finley," the nurse said, cracking the door. The gum-chewing woman got up and passed in front of her and Claud and went into the office. She had on red high-heeled shoes.

Directly across the table, the ugly girl's eyes were fixed on Mrs. Turpin as if she had some very special reason for disliking her.

"This is wonderful weather, isn't it?" the girl's mother said.

"It's good weather for cotton if you can get the niggers to pick it," Mrs. Turpin said, "but niggers don't want to pick cotton any more. You can't get the white folks to pick it and now you can't get the niggers—because they got to be right up there with the white folks."

"They gonna *try* anyways," the white-trash woman said, leaning forward.   40

"Do you have one of those cotton-picking machines?" the pleasant lady asked.

"No," Mrs. Turpin said, "they leave half the cotton in the field. We don't have much cotton anyway. If you want to make it farming now, you have to have a little of everything. We got a couple of acres of cotton and a few hogs and chickens and just enough white-face that Claud can look after them himself."

"One thang I don't want," the white-trash woman said, wiping her mouth with the back of her hands. "Hogs. Nasty stinking things, a-gruntin and a-rootin all over the place."

Mrs. Turpin gave her the merest edge of her attention. "Our hogs are not dirty and they don't stink," she said. "They're cleaner than some children I've seen. Their feet never touch the ground. We have a pig parlor—that's where you raise them on concrete," she explained to the pleasant lady, "and Claud scoots them down with the hose every afternoon and washes off the floor." Cleaner by far than that child right there, she thought. Poor nasty little thing. He had not moved except to put the thumb of his dirty hand into his mouth.

The woman turned her face away from Mrs. Turpin. "I know I wouldn't scoot   45 down no hog with no hose," she said to the wall.

You wouldn't have no hog to scoot down, Mrs. Turpin said to herself.

"A-gruntin and a-rootin and a-groanin," the woman muttered.

"We got a little of everything," Mrs. Turpin said to the pleasant lady. "It's no use in having more than you can handle yourself with help like it is. We found enough niggers to pick our cotton this year but Claud he has to go after them and take them home again in the evening. They can't walk that half a mile. No they can't. I tell you," she said and laughed merrily, "I sure am tired of buttering up niggers, but you got to love em if you want em to work for you. When they come in the morning, I run out and I say, 'Hi yawl this morning?' and when Claud drives them off to the field I just wave to beat the band and they just wave back." And she waved her hand rapidly to illustrate.

"Like you read out of the same book," the lady said, showing she understood perfectly.

"Child, yes," Mrs. Turpin said. "And when they come in from the field, I run out   50 with a bucket of icewater. That's the way it's going to be from now on," she said. "You may as well face it."

"One thang I know," the white-trash woman said. "Two things I ain't going to do: love no niggers or scoot down no hog with no hose." And she let out a bark of contempt.

The look that Mrs. Turpin and the pleasant lady exchanged indicated they both understood that you had to *have* certain things before you could *know* certain things. But every time Mrs. Turpin exchanged a look with the lady, she was aware that the ugly girl's peculiar eyes were still on her, and she had trouble bringing her attention back to the conversation.

"When you got something," she said, "you got to look after it." And when you ain't got a thing but breath and britches, she added to herself, you can afford to come to town every morning and just sit on the Court House coping and spit.

A grotesque revolving shadow passed across the curtain behind her and was thrown palely on the opposite wall. Then a bicycle clattered down against the outside of the building. The door opened and a colored boy glided in with a tray from the drug store. It had two large red and white paper cups on it with tops on them. He was a tall, very black boy in discolored white pants and a green nylon shirt. He was chewing gum slowly, as if to music. He set the tray down in the office opening next to the fern and stuck his head through to look for the secretary. She was not in there. He rested his arms on the ledge and waited, his narrow bottom stuck out, swaying slowly to the left and right. He raised a hand over his head and scratched the base of his skull.

55   "You see that button there, boy?" Mrs. Turpin said. "You can punch that and she'll come. She's probably in the back somewhere."

"Is thas right?" the boy said agreeably, as if he had never seen the button before. He leaned to the right and put his finger on it. "She sometime out," he said and twisted around to face his audience, his elbows behind him on the counter. The nurse appeared and he twisted back again. She handed him a dollar and he rooted in his pocket and made the change and counted it out to her. She gave him fifteen cents for a tip and he went out with the empty tray. The heavy door swung to slowly and closed at length with the sound of suction. For a moment no one spoke.

"They ought to send all them niggers back to Africa," the white-trash woman said. "That's wher they come from in the first place."

"Oh, I couldn't do without my good colored friends," the pleasant lady said.

"There's a heap of things worse than a nigger," Mrs. Turpin agreed. "It's all kinds of them just like it's all kinds of us."

60   "Yes, and it takes all kinds to make the world go round," the lady said in her musical voice.

As she said it, the raw-complexioned girl snapped her teeth together. Her lower lip turned downwards and inside out, revealing the pale pink inside of her mouth. After a second it rolled back up. It was the ugliest face Mrs. Turpin had ever seen anyone make and for a moment she was certain that the girl had made it at her. She was looking at her as if she had known and disliked her all her life—all of Mrs. Turpin's life, it seemed too, not just all the girl's life. Why, girl, I don't even know you, Mrs. Turpin said silently.

She forced her attention back to the discussion. "It wouldn't be practical to send them back to Africa," she said. "They wouldn't want to go. They got it too good here."

"Wouldn't be what they wanted—if I had anythang to do with it," the woman said.

"It wouldn't be a way in the world you could get all the niggers back over there," Mrs. Turpin said. "They'd be hiding out and lying down and turning sick on you and wailing and hollering and raring and pitching. It wouldn't be a way in the world to get them over there."

"They got over here," the trashy woman said. "Get back like they got over."   65

"It wasn't so many of them then," Mrs. Turpin explained.

The woman looked at Mrs. Turpin as if here was an idiot indeed but Mrs. Turpin was not bothered by the look, considering where it came from.

"Nooo," she said, "they're going to stay here where they can go to New York and marry white folks and improve their color. That's what they all want to do, every one of them, improve their color."

"You know what comes of that, don't you?" Claud asked.

"No, Claud, what?" Mrs. Turpin said.   70

Claud's eyes twinkled. "White-faced niggers," he said with never a smile.

Everybody in the office laughed except the white-trash and the ugly girl. The girl gripped the book in her lap with white fingers. The trashy woman looked around her from face to face as if she thought they were all idiots. The old woman in the feed sack dress continued to gaze expressionless across the floor at the high-top shoes of the man opposite her, the one who had been pretending to be asleep when the Turpins came in. He was laughing heartily, his hands still spread out on his knees. The child had fallen to the side and was lying now almost face down in the old woman's lap.

While they recovered from their laughter, the nasal chorus on the radio kept the room from silence.

> *"You go to blank blank*
> *And I'll go to mine*
> *But we'll all blank along*
> *To-geth-ther,*
> *And all along the blank*
> *We'll hep each other out*
> *Smile-ling in any kind of*
> *Weath-ther!"*

Mrs. Turpin didn't catch every word but she caught enough to agree with the spirit of the song and it turned her thoughts sober. To help anybody out that needed it was her philosophy of life. She never spared herself when she found somebody in need, whether they were white or black, trash or decent. And of all she had to be thankful for, she was most thankful that this was so. If Jesus had said, "You can be high society and have all the money you want and be thin and svelte-like, but you can't be a good woman with it," she would have had to say, "Well don't make me that then. Make me a good woman and it don't matter what else, how fat or how ugly or how poor!" Her heart rose. He had not made her a nigger or white-trash or ugly!

He had made her herself and given her a little of everything. Jesus, thank you! she said. Thank you thank you thank you! Whenever she counted her blessings she felt as buoyant as if she weighed one hundred and twenty-five pounds instead of one hundred and eighty.

75   "What's wrong with your little boy?" the pleasant lady asked the white-trashy woman.

"He has a ulcer," the woman said proudly. "He ain't give me a minute's peace since he was born. Him and her are just alike," she said, nodding at the old woman, who was running her leathery fingers through the child's pale hair. "Look like I can't get nothing down them two but Co'Cola and candy."

That's all you try to get down em, Mrs. Turpin said to herself. Too lazy to light the fire. There was nothing you could tell her about people like them that she didn't know already. And it was not just that they didn't have anything. Because if you gave them everything, in two weeks it would all be broken or filthy or they would have chopped it up for lightwood. She knew all this from her own experience. Help them you must, but help them you couldn't.

All at once the ugly girl turned her lips inside out again. Her eyes were fixed like two drills on Mrs. Turpin. This time there was no mistaking that there was something urgent behind them.

Girl, Mrs. Turpin exclaimed silently, I haven't done a thing to you! The girl might be confusing her with somebody else. There was no need to sit by and let herself be intimidated. "You must be in college," she said boldly, looking directly at the girl. "I see you reading a book there."

80   The girl continued to stare and pointedly did not answer.

Her mother blushed at this rudeness. "The lady asked you a question, Mary Grace," she said under her breath.

"I have ears," Mary Grace said.

The poor mother blushed again. "Mary Grace goes to Wellesley College," she explained. She twisted one of the buttons on her dress. "In Massachusetts," she added with a grimace. "And in the summer she just keeps right on studying. Just reads all the time, a real book worm. She's done real well at Wellesley; she's taking English and Math and History and Psychology and Social Studies," she rattled on, "and I think it's too much. I think she ought to get out and have fun."

The girl looked as if she would like to hurl them all through the plate glass window.

85   "Way up north," Mrs. Turpin murmured and thought, well, it hasn't done much for her manners.

"I'd almost rather to have him sick," the white-trash woman said, wrenching the attention back to herself. "He's so mean when he ain't. Look like some children just take natural to meanness. It's some gets bad when they get sick but he was the opposite. Took sick and turned good. He don't give me no trouble now. It's me waitin to see the doctor," she said.

If I was going to send anybody back to Africa, Mrs. Turpin thought, it would be your kind, woman. "Yes, indeed," she said aloud, but looking up at the ceiling, "it's a heap of things worse than a nigger." And dirtier than a hog, she added to herself.

"I think people with bad dispositions are more to be pitied than anyone on earth," the pleasant lady said in a voice that was decidedly thin.

"I thank the Lord he has blessed me with a good one," Mrs. Turpin said. "The day has never dawned that I couldn't find something to laugh at."

"Not since she married me anyways," Claud said with a comical straight face.   90

Everybody laughed except the girl and the white-trash.

Mrs. Turpin's stomach shook. "He's such a caution," she said, "that I can't help but laugh at him."

The girl made a loud ugly noise through her teeth.

Her mother's mouth grew thin and tight. "I think the worst thing in the world," she said, "is an ungrateful person. To have everything and not appreciate it. I know a girl," she said, "who has parents who would give her anything, a little brother who loves her dearly, who is getting a good education, who wears the best clothes, but who can never say a kind word to anyone, who never smiles, who just criticizes and complains all day long."

"Is she too old to paddle?" Claud asked.   95

The girl's face was almost purple.

"Yes," the lady said, "I'm afraid there's nothing to do but leave her to her folly. Some day she'll wake up and it'll be too late."

"It never hurt anyone to smile," Mrs. Turpin said. "It just makes you feel better all over."

"Of course," the lady said sadly, "but there are just some people you can't tell anything to. They can't take criticism."

"If it's one thing I am," Mrs. Turpin said with feeling, "it's grateful. When I   100 think who all I could have been besides myself and what all I got, a little of everything, and a good disposition besides, I just feel like shouting, 'Thank you, Jesus, for making everything the way it is!' It could have been different!" For one thing, somebody else could have got Claud. At the thought of this, she was flooded with gratitude and a terrible pang of joy ran through her. "Oh thank you, Jesus, Jesus, thank you!" she cried aloud.

The book struck her directly over her left eye. It struck almost at the same instant that she realized the girl was about to hurl it. Before she could utter a sound, the raw face came crashing across the table toward her, howling. The girl's fingers sank like clamps into the soft flesh of her neck. She heard the mother cry out and Claud shout, "Whoa!" There was an instant when she was certain that she was about to be in an earthquake.

All at once her vision narrowed and she saw everything as if it were happening in a small room far away, or as if she were looking at it through the wrong end of a telescope. Claud's face crumpled and fell out of sight. The nurse ran in, then out, then in again. Then the gangling figure of the doctor rushed out of the inner door. Magazines flew this way and that as the table turned over. The girl fell with a thud and Mrs. Turpin's vision suddenly reversed itself and she saw everything large instead of small. The eyes of the white-trashy woman were staring hugely at the floor. There the girl, held down on one side by the nurse and on the other by her mother, was wrenching and turning in their grasp. The doctor was kneeling astride her, trying to hold her arm down. He managed after a second to sink a long needle into it.

Mrs. Turpin felt entirely hollow except for her heart which swung from side to side as if it were agitated in a great empty drum of flesh.

"Somebody that's not busy call for the ambulance," the doctor said in the off-hand voice young doctors adopt for terrible occasions.

105   Mrs. Turpin could not have moved a finger. The old man who had been sitting next to her skipped numbly into the office and made the call, for the secretary still seemed to be gone.

"Claud!" Mrs. Turpin called.

He was not in his chair. She knew she must jump up and find him but she felt like some one trying to catch a train in a dream, when everything moves in slow motion and the faster you try to run the slower you go.

"Here I am," a suffocated voice, very unlike Claud's, said.

He was doubled up in the corner on the floor, pale as paper, holding his leg. She wanted to get up and go to him but she could not move. Instead, her gaze was drawn slowly downward to the churning face on the floor, which she could see over the doctor's shoulder.

110   The girl's eyes stopped rolling and focused on her. They seemed a much lighter blue than before, as if a door that had been tightly closed behind them was now open to admit light and air.

Mrs. Turpin's head cleared and her power of motion returned. She leaned forward until she was looking directly into the fierce brilliant eyes. There was no doubt in her mind that the girl did know her, knew her in some intense and personal way, beyond time and place and condition. "What you got to say to me?" she asked hoarsely and held her breath, waiting, as for a revelation.

The girl raised her head. Her gaze locked with Mrs. Turpin's. "Go back to hell where you came from, you old wart hog," she whispered. Her voice was low but clear. Her eyes burned for a moment as if she saw with pleasure that her message had struck its target.

Mrs. Turpin sank back in her chair.

After a moment the girl's eyes closed and she turned her head wearily to the side.

115   The doctor rose and handed the nurse the empty syringe. He leaned over and put both hands for a moment on the mother's shoulders, which were shaking. She was sitting on the floor, her lips pressed together, holding Mary Grace's hand in her lap. The girl's fingers were gripped like a baby's around her thumb. "Go on to the hospital," he said. "I'll call and make the arrangements."

"Now let's see that neck," he said in a jovial voice to Mrs. Turpin. He began to inspect her neck with his first two fingers. Two little moon-shaped lines like pink fish bones were indented over her windpipe. There was the beginning of an angry red swelling above her eye. His fingers passed over this also.

"Lea' me be," she said thickly and shook him off. "See about Claud. She kicked him."

"I'll see about him in a minute," he said and felt her pulse. He was a thin grey-haired man, given to pleasantries. "Go home and have yourself a vacation the rest of the day," he said and patted her on the shoulder.

Quit your pattin me, Mrs. Turpin growled to herself.

"And put an ice pack over that eye," he said. Then he went and squatted down [120] beside Claud and looked at his leg. After a moment he pulled him up and Claud limped after him into the office.

Until the ambulance came, the only sounds in the room were the tremulous moans of the girl's mother, who continued to sit on the floor. The white-trash woman did not take her eyes off the girl. Mrs. Turpin looked straight ahead at nothing. Presently the ambulance drew up, a long dark shadow, behind the curtain. The attendants came in and set the stretcher down beside the girl and lifted her expertly onto it and carried her out. The nurse helped the mother gather up her things. The shadow of the ambulance moved silently away and the nurse came back in the office.

"That ther girl is going to be a lunatic, ain't she?" the white-trash woman asked the nurse, but the nurse kept on to the back and never answered her.

"Yes, she's going to be a lunatic," the white-trash woman said to the rest of them.

"Po' critter," the old woman murmured. The child's face was still in her lap. His eyes looked idly out over her knees. He had not moved during the disturbance except to draw one leg up under him.

"I thank Gawd," the white-trash woman said fervently, "I ain't a lunatic." [125]

Claud came limping out and the Turpins went home.

As their pick-up truck turned into their own dirt road and made the crest of the hill, Mrs. Turpin gripped the window ledge and looked out suspiciously. The land sloped gracefully down through a field dotted with lavender weeds and at the start of the rise their small yellow frame house, with its little flower beds spread out around it like a fancy apron, sat primly in its accustomed place between two giant hickory trees. She would not have been startled to see a burnt wound between two blackened chimneys.

Neither of them felt like eating so they put on their house clothes and lowered the shade in the bedroom and lay down, Claud with his leg on a pillow and herself with a damp washcloth over her eye. The instant she was flat on her back, the image of a razor-backed hog with warts on its face and horns coming out behind its ears snorted into her head. She moaned, a low quiet moan.

"I am not," she said tearfully, "a wart hog. From hell." But the denial had no force. The girl's eyes and her words, even the tone of her voice, low but clear, directed only to her, brooked no repudiation. She had been singled out for the message, though there was trash in the room to whom it might justly have been applied. The full force of this fact struck her only now. There was a woman there who was neglecting her own child but she had been overlooked. The message had been given to Ruby Turpin, a respectable, hard-working, church-going woman. The tears dried. Her eyes began to burn instead with wrath.

She rose on her elbow and the washcloth fell into her hand. Claud was lying on [130] his back, snoring. She wanted to tell him what the girl had said. At the same time, she did not wish to put the image of herself as a wart hog from hell into his mind.

"Hey, Claud," she muttered and pushed his shoulder.

Claud opened one pale baby blue eye.

She looked into it warily. He did not think about anything. He just went his way.

"Wha, whasit?" he said and closed the eye again.

135   "Nothing," she said. "Does your leg pain you?"

"Hurts like hell," Claud said.

"It'll quit terreckly," she said and lay back down. In a moment Claud was snoring again. For the rest of the afternoon they lay there. Claud slept. She scowled at the ceiling. Occasionally she raised her fist and made a small stabbing motion over her chest as if she was defending her innocence to invisible guests who were like the comforters of Job, reasonable-seeming but wrong.

About five-thirty Claud stirred. "Got to go after those niggers," he sighed, not moving.

She was looking straight up as if there were unintelligible handwriting on the ceiling. The protuberance over her eye had turned a greenish-blue. "Listen here," she said.

140   "What?"

"Kiss me."

Claud leaned over and kissed her loudly on the mouth. He pinched her side and their hands interlocked. Her expression of ferocious concentration did not change. Claud got up, groaning and growling, and limped off. She continued to study the ceiling.

She did not get up until she heard the pick-up truck coming back with the Negroes. Then she rose and thrust her feet in her brown oxfords, which she did not bother to lace, and stumped out onto the back porch and got her red plastic bucket. She emptied a tray of ice cubes into it and filled it half full of water and went out into the back yard. Every afternoon after Claud brought the hands in, one of the boys helped him put out hay and the rest waited in the back of the truck until he was ready to take them home. The truck was parked in the shade under one of the hickory trees.

"Hi yawl this evening?" Mrs. Turpin asked grimly, appearing with the bucket and the dipper. There were three women and a boy in the truck.

145   "Us doin nicely," the oldest woman said. "Hi you doin?" and her gaze stuck immediately on the dark lump on Mrs. Turpin's forehead. "You done fell down, ain't you?" she asked in a solicitous voice. The old woman was dark and almost toothless. She had on an old felt had of Claud's set back on her head. The other two women were younger and lighter and they both had new bright green sun hats. One of them had hers on her head; the other had taken hers off and the boy was grinning beneath it.

Mrs. Turpin set the bucket down on the floor of the truck. "Yawl hep yourselves," she said. She looked around to make sure Claud had gone. "No. I didn't fall down," she said, folding her arms. "It was something worse than that."

"Ain't nothing bad happen to you!" the old woman said. She said it as if they all knew that Mrs. Turpin was protected in some special way by Divine Providence. "You just had you a little fall."

"We were in town at the doctor's office for where the cow kicked Mr. Turpin," Mrs. Turpin said in a flat tone that indicated they could leave off their foolishness.

"And there was this girl there. A big fat girl with her face all broke out. I could look at that girl and tell she was peculiar but I couldn't tell how. And me and her mama were just talking and going along and all of a sudden WHAM! She throws this big book she was reading at me and . . ."

"Naw!" the old woman cried out.

"And then she jumps over the table and commences to choke me."   150

"Naw!" they all exclaimed, "naw!"

"Hi come she do that?" the old woman asked. "What ail her?"

Mrs. Turpin only glared in front of her.

"Somethin ail her," the old woman said.

"They carried her off in an ambulance," Mrs. Turpin continued, "but before she   155
went she was rolling on the floor and they were trying to hold her down to give her a shot and she said something to me." She paused. "You know what she said to me?"

"What she say?" they asked.

"She said," Mrs. Turpin began, and stopped, her face very dark and heavy. The sun was getting whiter and whiter, blanching the sky overhead so that the leaves of the hickory tree were black in the face of it. She could not bring forth the words. "Something real ugly," she muttered.

"She sho shouldn't said nothin ugly to you," the old woman said. "You so sweet. You the sweetest lady I know."

"She pretty too," the one with the hat on said.

"And stout," the other one said. "I never knowed no sweeter white lady."   160

"That's the truth befo' Jesus," the old woman said. "Amen! You des as sweet and pretty as you can be."

Mrs. Turpin knew just exactly how much Negro flattery was worth and it added to her rage. "She said," she began again and finished this time with a fierce rush of breath, "that I was an old wart hog from hell."

There was an astounded silence.

"Where she at?" the youngest woman cried in a piercing voice.

"Lemme see her. I'll kill her!"   165

"I'll kill her with you!" the other one cried.

"She b'long in the sylum," the old woman said emphatically. "You the sweetest white lady I know."

"She pretty too," the other two said. "Stout as she can be and sweet. Jesus satisfied with her!"

"Deed he is," the old woman declared.

Idiots! Mrs. Turpin growled to herself. You could never say anything intelligent   170
to a nigger. You could talk at them but not with them. "Yawl ain't drunk your water," she said shortly. "Leave the bucket in the truck when you're finished with it. I got more to do than just stand around and pass the time of day," and she moved off and into the house.

She stood for a moment in the middle of the kitchen. The dark protuberance over her eye looked like a miniature tornado cloud which might any moment sweep across the horizon of her brow. Her lower lip protruded dangerously. She squared her massive shoulders. Then she marched into the front of the house and out the side door and started down the road to the pig parlor. She had the look of a woman going single-handed, weaponless, into battle.

The sun was a deep yellow now like a harvest moon and was riding westward very fast over the far tree line as if it meant to reach the hogs before she did. The road was rutted and she kicked several good-sized stones out of her path as she strode along. The pig parlor was on a little knoll at the end of a lane that ran off from the side of the barn. It was a square of concrete as large as a small room, with a board fence about four feet high around it. The concrete floor sloped slightly so that the hog wash could drain off into a trench where it was carried to the field for fertilizer. Claud was standing on the outside, on the edge of the concrete, hanging onto the top board, hosing down the floor inside. The hose was connected to the faucet of a water trough nearby.

Mrs. Turpin climbed up beside him and glowered down at the hogs inside. There were seven long-snouted bristly shoats in it—tan with liver-colored spots—and an old sow a few weeks off from farrowing. She was lying on her side grunting. The shoats were running about shaking themselves like idiot children, their little slit pig eyes searching the floor for anything left. She had read that pigs were the most intelligent animal. She doubted it. They were supposed to be smarter than dogs. There had even been a pig astronaut. He had performed his assignment perfectly but died of a heart attack afterwards because they left him in his electric suit, sitting upright throughout his examination when naturally a hog should be on all fours.

A-gruntin and a-rootin and a-groanin.

175 "Gimme that hose," she said, yanking it away from Claud. "Go on and carry them niggers home and then get off that leg."

"You look like you might have swallowed a mad dog," Claud observed, but he got down and limped off. He paid no attention to her humors.

Until he was out of earshot, Mrs. Turpin stood on the side of the pen, holding the hose and pointing the stream of water at the hind quarters of any shoat that looked as if it might try to lie down. When he had had time to get over the hill, she turned her head slightly and her wrathful eyes scanned the path. He was nowhere in sight. She turned back again and seemed to gather herself up. Her shoulders rose and she drew in her breath.

"What do you send me a message like that for?" she said in a low fierce voice, barely above a whisper but with the force of a shout in its concentrated fury. "How am I a hog and me both? How am I saved and from hell too?" Her free fist was knotted and with the other she gripped the hose, blindly pointing the stream of water in and out of the eye of the old sow whose outraged squeal she did not hear.

The pig parlor commanded a view of the back pasture where their twenty beef cows were gathered around the hay-bales Claud and the boy had put out. The freshly cut pasture sloped down to the highway. Across it was their cotton field and beyond that a dark green dusty wood which they owned as well. The sun was behind the wood, very red, looking over the paling of trees like a farmer inspecting his own hogs.

180 "Why me?" she rumbled. "It's no trash around here, black or white, that I haven't given to. And break my back to the bone every day working. And do for the church."

She appeared to be the right size woman to command the arena before her. "How am I a hog?" she demanded. "Exactly how am I like them?" and she jabbed the stream of water at the shoats. "There was plenty of trash there. It didn't have to be me."

"If you like trash better, go get yourself some trash then," she railed. "You could have made me trash. Or a nigger. If trash is what you wanted why didn't you make me trash?" She shook her fist with the hose in it and a watery snake appeared momentarily in the air. "I could quit working and take it easy and be filthy," she growled. "Lounge about the sidewalks all day drinking root beer. Dip snuff and spit in every puddle and have it all over my face. I could be nasty.

"Or you could have made me a nigger. It's too late for me to be a nigger," she said with deep sarcasm, "but I could act like one. Lay down in the middle of the road and stop traffic. Roll on the ground."

In the deepening light everything was taking on a mysterious hue. The pasture was growing a peculiar glassy green and the streak of highway had turned lavender. She braced herself for a final assault and this time her voice rolled out over the pasture. "Go on," she yelled, "call me a hog! Call me a hog again. From hell. Call me a wart hog from hell. Put that bottom rail on top. There'll still be a top and bottom!"

A garbled echo returned to her. 185

A final surge of fury shook her and she roared, "Who do you think you are?"

The color of everything, field and crimson sky, burned for a moment with a transparent intensity. The question carried over the pasture and across the highway and the cotton field and returned to her clearly like an answer from beyond the wood.

She opened her mouth but no sound came out of it.

A tiny truck, Claud's, appeared on the highway, heading rapidly out of sight. Its gears scraped thinly. It looked like a child's toy. At any moment a bigger truck might smash into it and scatter Claud's and the niggers' brains all over the road.

Mrs. Turpin stood there, her gaze fixed on the highway, all her muscles rigid, 190 until in five or six minutes the truck reappeared, returning. She waited until it had had time to turn into their own road. Then like a monumental statue coming to life, she bent her head slowly and gazed, as if through the very heart of mystery, down into the pig parlor at the hogs. They had settled all in one corner around the old sow who was grunting softly. A red glow suffused them. They appeared to pant with a secret life.

Until the sun slipped finally behind the tree line, Mrs. Turpin remained there with her gaze bent to them as if she were absorbing some abysmal life-giving knowledge. At last she lifted her head. There was only a purple streak in the sky, cutting through a field of crimson and leading, like an extension of the highway, into the descending dusk. She raised her hands from the side of the pen in a gesture hieratic and profound. A visionary light settled in her eyes. She saw the streak as a vast swinging bridge extending upward from the earth through a field of living fire. Upon it a vast horde of souls were rumbling toward heaven. There were whole companies of white-trash, clean for the first time in their lives, and bands of black niggers in white robes, and battalions of freaks and lunatics shouting and clapping and leaping like frogs. And bringing up the end of the procession was a tribe of people whom she recognized at once as those who, like herself and Claud, had always had a little of everything and the God-given wit to use it right. She leaned forward to observe them closer. They were marching behind the others with great dignity, accountable as they had always been for good order and common sense and respectable behavior. They alone were on key. Yet she could see by their shocked and altered faces that even their virtues were being burned away. She lowered her hands and gripped the rail of the hog pen, her eyes small but fixed unblinkingly on what lay ahead. In a moment the vision faded but she remained where she was, immobile.

At length she got down and turned off the faucet and made her slow way on the darkening path to the house. In the woods around her the invisible cricket choruses had struck up, but what she heard were the voices of the souls climbing upward into the starry field and shouting hallelujah.

QUESTIONS FOR DISCUSSION AND WRITING

1. How do the various revelations mark the development of the story? How does Mrs. Turpin's conflict with people evolve into her final conflict with God?

2. How does Mrs. Turpin characterize herself? What clues does O'Connor provide that explain why Mary Grace accuses Mrs. Turpin of being a "wart hog from hell"? What does the story reveal finally about Mrs. Turpin's good disposition?

3. How does Mrs. Turpin impose her sense of social order on the group in the waiting room? In what ways is the pig parlor like the waiting room?

4. How do Mrs. Turpin's internal and external dialogues complement each other? How accurately does Mrs. Turpin report the events in the waiting room to the farmhands?

5. On what perception does Mrs. Turpin base her belief in order and goodness? How does her "revelation" alter this perception?

Stories for Comparison

Mary Wilkins Freeman's "The Revolt of 'Mother'" (pages 520–532); Leo Tolstoy's "The Death of Ivan Ilych" (pages 1096–1135).

80

....

F R A N K   O ' C O N N O R

Guests of the Nation

FRANK O'CONNOR (1903–1966), the pen name for Michael John
O'Donovan was born in Cork, Ireland. Although he briefly attended the
Christian Brothers School in Cork, his family's poverty forced him to forgo
any formal education. While still in his teens, O'Connor joined the Irish Re-
publican Army (IRA) and fought in the civil war from 1922 to 1923. Arrested and imprisoned, O'Connor continued his self-education while serving
as the prison librarian until he was released in 1923. O'Connor was hired by
the Irish Carnegie United Kingdom Trust to organize rural libraries, an activity that put him in contact with the leaders of the Irish Literature Revival,
most notably William Butler Yeats and others associated with the Abbey Theatre Company in Dublin. In the 1930s he began publishing his short stories in
American magazines such as *The New Yorker, Holiday,* and *Esquire.* His
stories, which attempt to record the oral quality of the Irish people and which
appear in more than twenty volumes, are most accessible in *Collected Stories*
(1981). O'Connor also wrote novels, including *Dutch Interior* (1940); travel
literature, *Irish Miles* (1947); literary criticism, *The Lonely Voice* (1963); and
two volumes of an autobiography, *An Only Child* (1961) and *My Father's
Son* (1969). "Guests of the Nation," reprinted from *Collected Stories,*
recounts the experiences of several Irishmen who must choose between
loyalty to their guests and duty to their nation.

I

At dusk the big Englishman, Belcher, would shift his long legs out of the ashes
and say "Well, chums, what about it?" and Noble or me would say "All right,
chum" (for we had picked up some of their curious expressions), and the little Englishman, Hawkins, would light the lamp and bring out the cards. Sometimes
Jeremiah Donovan would come up and supervise the game and get excited over
Hawkins's cards, which he always played badly, and shout at him as if he was one
of our own, "Ah, you divil, you, why didn't you play the tray?"

But ordinarily Jeremiah was a sober and contented poor devil like the big
Englishman, Belcher, and was looked up to only because he was a fair hand at

documents, though he was slow enough even with them. He wore a small cloth hat and big gaiters over his long pants, and you seldom saw him with his hands out of his pockets. He reddened when you talked to him, tilting from toe to heel and back, and looking down all the time at his big farmer's feet. Noble and me used to make fun of his broad accent, because we were from the town.

I couldn't at the time see the point of me and Noble guarding Belcher and Hawkins at all, for it was my belief that you could have planted that pair down any-where from this to Claregalway and they'd have taken root there like a native weed. I never in my short experience seen two men to take to the country as they did.

They were handed on to us by the Second Battalion when the search for them became too hot, and Noble and myself, being young, took over with a natural feel-ing of responsibility, but Hawkins made us look like fools when he showed that he knew the country better than we did.

5   "You're the bloke they calls Bonaparte," he says to me. "Mary Brigid O'Connell told me to ask you what you done with the pair of her brother's socks you borrowed."

For it seemed, as they explained it, that the Second used to have little evenings, and some of the girls of the neighborhood turned in, and, seeing they were such de-cent chaps, our fellows couldn't leave the two Englishmen out of them. Hawkins learned to dance "The Walls of Limerick," "The Siege of Ennis," and "The Waves of Tory" as well as any of them, though, naturally, we couldn't return the compliment, because our lads at that time did not dance foreign dances on principle.

So whatever privileges Belcher and Hawkins had with the Second they just nat-urally took with us, and after the first day or two we gave up all pretense of keeping a close eye on them. Not that they could have got far, for they had accents you could cut with a knife and wore khaki tunics and overcoats with civilian pants and boots. But it's my belief that they never had any idea of escaping and were quite content to be where they were.

It was a treat to see how Belcher got off with the old woman of the house where we were staying. She was a great warrant to scold, and cranky even with us, but before ever she had a chance of giving our guests, as I may call them, a lick of her tongue, Belcher had made her his friend for life. She was breaking sticks, and Belcher, who hadn't been more than ten minutes in the house, jumped up from his seat and went over to her.

"Allow me, madam," he says, smiling his queer little smile, "please allow me"; and he takes the bloody hatchet. She was struck too paralytic to speak, and after that, Belcher would be at her heels, carrying a bucket, a basket, or a load of turf, as the case might be. As Noble said, he got into looking before she leapt, and hot water, or any little thing she wanted, Belcher would have it ready for her. For such a huge man (and though I am five foot ten myself I had to look up at him) he had an uncommon shortness—or should I say lack?—of speech. It took us some time to get used to him, walking in and out, like a ghost, without a word. Especially because Hawkins talked enough for a platoon, it was strange to hear big Belcher with his toes in the ashes come out with a solitary "Excuse me, chum," or "That's right, chum." His one and only passion was cards, and I will say for him that he was a good cardplayer. He could have fleeced myself and Noble, but whatever we lost to him Hawkins lost to us, and Hawkins played with the money Belcher gave him.

Hawkins lost to us because he had too much old gab, and we probably lost to [10] Belcher for the same reason. Hawkins and Noble would spit at one another about religion into the early hours of the morning, and Hawkins worried the soul out of Noble, whose brother was a priest, with a string of questions that would puzzle a cardinal. To make it worse, even in treating of holy subjects, Hawkins had a deplorable tongue. I never in all my career met a man who could mix such a variety of cursing and bad language into an argument. He was a terrible man, and a fright to argue. He never did a stroke of work, and when he had no one else to talk to, he got stuck in the old woman.

He met his match in her, for one day when he tried to get her to complain profanely of the drought, she gave him a great come-down by blaming it entirely on Jupiter Pluvius (a deity neither Hawkins nor I had ever heard of, though Noble said that among the pagans it was believed that he had something to do with the rain). Another day he was swearing at the capitalists for starting the German war when the old lady laid down her iron, puckered up her little crab's mouth, and said: "Mr. Hawkins, you can say what you like about the war, and think you'll deceive me because I'm only a simple poor country-woman, but I know what started the war. It was the Italian Count that stole the heathen divinity out of the temple in Japan. Believe me, Mr. Hawkins, nothing but sorrow and want can follow the people that disturb the hidden powers."

A queer old girl, all right.

2

We had our tea one evening, and Hawkins lit the lamp and we all sat into cards. Jeremiah Donovan came in too, and sat down and watched us for a while, and it suddenly struck me that he had no great love for the two Englishmen. It came as a great surprise to me, because I hadn't noticed anything about him before.

Late in the evening a really terrible argument blew up between Hawkins and Noble, about capitalists and priests and love of your country.

"The capitalists," says Hawkins with an angry gulp, "pays the priests to tell you [15] about the next world so as you won't notice what the bastards are up to in this."

"Nonsense, man!" says Noble, losing his temper. "Before ever a capitalist was thought of, people believed in the next world."

Hawkins stood up as though he was preaching a sermon.

"Oh, they did, did they?" he says with a sneer. "They believed all the things you believe, isn't that what you mean? And you believe that God created Adam, and Adam created Shem, and Shem created Jehoshaphat. You believe all that silly old fairytale about Eve and Eden and the apple. Well, listen to me, chum. If you're entitled to hold a silly belief like that, I'm entitled to hold my silly belief—which is that the first thing your God created was a bleeding capitalist, with morality and Rolls-Royce complete. Am I right, chum?" he says to Belcher.

"You're right, chum," says Belcher with his amused smile, and got up from the table to stretch his long legs into the fire and stroke his moustache. So, seeing that Jeremiah Donovan was going, and that there was no knowing when the argument about religion would be over, I went out with him. We strolled down to the village together, and then he stopped and started blushing and mumbling and saying I ought to be behind, keeping guard on the prisoners. I didn't like the tone he took with me, and anyway I was bored with life in the cottage, so I replied by asking him what the hell we wanted guarding them at all for. I told him I'd talked it over with Noble, and that we'd both rather be out with a fighting column.

20   "What use are those fellows to us?" says I.

He looked at me in surprise and said: "I thought you knew we were keeping them as hostages."

"Hostages?" I said.

"The enemy have prisoners belonging to us," he says, "and now they're talking of shooting them. If they shoot our prisoners, we'll shoot theirs."

"Shoot them?" I said.

25   "What else did you think we were keeping them for?" he says.

"Wasn't it very unforeseen of you not to warn Noble and myself of that in the beginning?" I said.

"How was it?" says he. "You might have known it."

"We couldn't know it, Jeremiah Donovan," says I. "How could we when they were on our hands so long?"

"The enemy have our prisoners as long and longer," says he.

30   "That's not the same thing at all," says I.

"What difference is there?" says he.

I couldn't tell him, because I knew he wouldn't understand. If it was only an old dog that was going to the vet's, you'd try and not get too fond of him, but Jeremiah Donovan wasn't a man that would ever be in danger of that.

"And when is this thing going to be decided?" says I.

"We might hear tonight," he says. "Or tomorrow or the next day at latest. So if it's only hanging round here that's a trouble to you, you'll be free soon enough."

35   It wasn't the hanging round that was a trouble to me at all by this time. I had worse things to worry about. When I got back to the cottage the argument was still on. Hawkins was holding forth in his best style, maintaining that there was no next world, and Noble was maintaining that there was; but I could see that Hawkins had had the best of it.

"Do you know what, chum?" he was saying with a saucy smile. "I think you're just as big a bleeding unbeliever as I am. You say you believe in the next world, and you know just as much about the next world as I do, which is sweet damn-all. What's heaven? You don't know. Where's heaven? You don't know. You know sweet damn-all! I ask you again, do they wear wings?"

"Very well, then," says Noble, "they do. Is that enough for you? They do wear wings."

"Where do they get them, then? Who makes them? Have they a factory for wings? Have they a sort of store where you hands in your chit and takes your bleeding wings?"

"You're an impossible man to argue with," says Noble. "Now, listen to me—" And they were off again.

40   It was long after midnight when we locked up and went to bed. As I blew out the candle I told Noble what Jeremiah Donovan was after telling me. Noble took it

very quietly. When we'd been in bed about an hour he asked me did I think we ought to tell the Englishmen. I didn't think we should, because it was more than likely that the English wouldn't shoot our men, and even if they did, the brigade officers, who were always up and down with the Second Battalion and knew the Englishmen well, wouldn't be likely to want them plugged. "I think so too," says Noble. "It would be great cruelty to put the wind up them now."

"It was very unforeseen of Jeremiah Donovan anyhow," says I.

It was next morning that we found it so hard to face Belcher and Hawkins. We went about the house all day scarcely saying a word. Belcher didn't seem to notice; he was stretched into the ashes as usual, with his usual look of waiting in quietness for something unforeseen to happen, but Hawkins noticed and put it down to Noble's being beaten in the argument of the night before.

"Why can't you take a discussion in the proper spirit?" he says severely. "You and your Adam and Eve! I'm a Communist, that's what I am. Communist or anarchist, it all comes to much the same thing." And for hours he went round the house, muttering when the fit took him. "Adam and Eve! Adam and Eve! Nothing better to do with their time than picking bleeding apples!"

3

I don't know how we got through that day, but I was very glad when it was over, the tea things were cleared away, and Belcher said in his peaceful way: "Well, chums, what about it?" We sat round the table and Hawkins took out the cards, and just then I heard Jeremiah Donovan's footsteps on the path and a dark presentiment crossed my mind. I rose from the table and caught him before he reached the door.

"What do you want?" I asked.   45

"I want those two soldier friends of yours," he says, getting red.

"Is that the way, Jeremiah Donovan?" I asked.

"That's the way. There were four of our lads shot this morning, one of them a boy of sixteen."

"That's bad," I said.

At that moment Noble followed me out, and the three of us walked down the   50
path together, talking in whispers. Feeney, the local intelligence officer, was standing by the gate.

"What are you going to do about it?" I asked Jeremiah Donovan.

"I want you and Noble to get them out; tell them they're being shifted again; that'll be the quietest way."

"Leave me out of that," says Noble under his breath.

Jeremiah Donovan looks at him hard.

"All right," he says. "You and Feeney get a few tools from the shed and dig a   55
hole by the far end of the bog. Bonaparte and myself will be after you. Don't let anyone see you with the tools. I wouldn't like it to go beyond ourselves."

We saw Feeney and Noble go round to the shed and went in ourselves. I left Jeremiah Donovan to do the explanations. He told them that he had orders to send them back to the Second Battalion. Hawkins let out a mouthful of curses, and you could see that though Belcher didn't say anything, he was a bit upset too. The old woman was for having them stay in spite of us, and she didn't stop advising them until Jeremiah Donovan lost his temper and turned on her. He had a nasty temper, I noticed. It was pitch-dark in the cottage by this time, but no one thought of lighting the lamp, and in the darkness the two Englishmen fetched their topcoats and said good-bye to the old woman.

"Just as a man makes a home of a bleeding place, some bastard at headquarters thinks you're too cushy and shunts you off," says Hawkins, shaking her hand.

"A thousand thanks, madam," says Belcher. "A thousand thanks for everything"—as though he'd made it up.

We went round to the back of the house and down towards the bog. It was only then that Jeremiah Donovan told them. He was shaking with excitement.

"There were four of our fellows shot in Cork this morning and now you're to be shot as a reprisal."

"What are you talking about?" snaps Hawkins. "It's bad enough being mucked about as we are without having to put up with your funny jokes."

"It isn't a joke," says Donovan. "I'm sorry, Hawkins, but it's true," and begins on the usual rigamarole about duty and how unpleasant it is.

I never noticed that people who talk a lot about duty find it much of a trouble to them.

"Oh, cut it out!" says Hawkins.

"Ask Bonaparte," says Donovan, seeing that Hawkins isn't taking him seriously. "Isn't it true, Bonaparte?"

"It is," I say, and Hawkins stops.

"Ah, for Christ's sake, chum."

"I mean it, chum," I say.

"You don't sound as if you meant it."

"If he doesn't mean it, I do," says Donovan, working himself up.

"What have you against me, Jeremiah Donovan?"

"I never said I had anything against you. But why did your people take out four of our prisoners and shoot them in cold blood?"

He took Hawkins by the arm and dragged him on, but it was impossible to make him understand that we were in earnest. I had the Smith and Wesson in my pocket and I kept fingering it and wondering what I'd do if they put up a fight for it or ran, and wishing to God they'd do one or the other. I knew if they did run for it, that I'd never fire on them. Hawkins wanted to know was Noble in it, and when we said yes, he asked why Noble wanted to plug him. Why did any of us want to plug him? What had he done to us? Weren't we all chums? Didn't we understand him and didn't he understand us? Did we imagine for an instant that he'd shoot us for all the so-and-so officers in the so-and-so British Army?

By this time we'd reached the bog, and I was so sick I couldn't even answer him. We walked along the edge of it in the darkness, and every now and then Hawkins would call a halt and begin all over again, as if he was wound up, about our being chums, and I knew that nothing but the sight of the grave would convince him that we had to do it. And all the time I was hoping that something would happen; that they'd run for it or that Noble would take over the responsibility from me. I had the feeling that it was worse on Noble than on me.

4

At last we saw the lantern in the distance and made towards it. Noble was carrying 75 it, and Feeney was standing somewhere in the darkness behind him, and the picture of them so still and silent in the bogland brought it home to me that we were in earnest, and banished the last bit of hope I had.

Belcher, on recognizing Noble, said: "Hallo, chum," in his quiet way, but Hawkins flew at him at once, and the argument began all over again, only this time Noble had nothing to say for himself and stood with his head down, holding the lantern between his legs.

It was Jeremiah Donovan who did the answering. For the twentieth time, as though it was haunting his mind, Hawkins asked if anybody thought he'd shoot Noble.

"Yes, you would," says Jeremiah Donovan.

"No, I wouldn't, damn you!"

"You would, because you'd know you'd be shot for not doing it." 80

"I wouldn't, not if I was to be shot twenty times over. I wouldn't shoot a pal. And Belcher wouldn't—isn't that right, Belcher?"

"That's right, chum," Belcher said, but more by way of answering the question than of joining in the argument. Belcher sounded as though whatever unforeseen thing he'd always been waiting for had come at last.

"Anyway, who says Noble would be shot if I wasn't? What do you think I'd do if I was in his place, out in the middle of a blasted bog?"

"What would you do?" asks Donovan.

"I'd go with him wherever he was going, of course. Share my last bob with him 85 and stick by him through thick and thin. No one can ever say of me that I let down a pal."

"We had enough of this," says Jeremiah Donovan, cocking his revolver. "Is there any message you want to send?"

"No, there isn't."

"Do you want to say your prayers?"

Hawkins came out with a cold-blooded remark that even shocked me and turned on Noble again.

"Listen to me, Noble," he says. "You and me are chums. You can't come over to 90 my side, so I'll come over to your side. That show you I mean what I say? Give me a rifle and I'll go along with you and the other lads."

Nobody answered him. We knew that was no way out.

"Hear what I'm saying?" he says. "I'm through with it. I'm a deserter or anything else you like. I don't believe in your stuff, but it's no worse than mine. That satisfy you?"

Noble raised his head, but Donovan began to speak and he lowered it again without replying.

"For the last time, have you any messages to send?" says Donovan in a cold, excited sort of voice.

95   "Shut up, Donovan! You don't understand me, but these lads do. They're not the sort to make a pal and kill a pal. They're not the tools of any capitalist."

I alone of the crowd saw Donovan raise his Webley to the back of Hawkins's neck, and as he did so I shut my eyes and tried to pray. Hawkins had begun to say something else when Donovan fired, and as I opened my eyes at the bang, I saw Hawkins stagger at the knees and lie out flat at Noble's feet, slowly and as quiet as a kid falling asleep, with the lantern-light on his lean legs and bright farmer's boots. We all stood very still, watching him settle out in the last agony.

Then Belcher took out a handkerchief and began to tie it about his own eyes (in our excitement we'd forgotten to do the same for Hawkins), and, seeing it wasn't big enough, turned and asked for the loan of mine. I gave it to him and he knotted the two together and pointed with his foot at Hawkins.

"He's not quite dead," he says. "Better give him another."

Sure enough, Hawkins's left knee is beginning to rise. I bend down and put my gun to his head; then, recollecting myself, I get up again. Belcher understands what's in my mind.

100   "Give him his first," he says. "I don't mind. Poor bastard, we don't know what's happening to him now."

I knelt and fired. By this time I didn't seem to know what I was doing. Belcher, who was fumbling a bit awkwardly with the handkerchiefs, came out with a laugh as he heard the shot. It was the first time I heard him laugh and it sent a shudder down my back; it sounded so unnatural.

"Poor bugger!" he said quietly. "And last night he was so curious about it all. It's very queer, chums, I always think. Now he knows as much about it as they'll ever let him know, and last night he was all in the dark."

Donovan helped him to tie the handkerchiefs about his eyes. "Thanks, chum," he said. Donovan asked if there were any messages he wanted sent.

"No, chum," he says. "Not for me. If any of you would like to write to Hawkins's mother, you'll find a letter from her in his pocket. He and his mother were great chums. But my missus left me eight years ago. Went away with another fellow and took the kid with her. I like the feeling of a home, as you may have noticed, but I couldn't start again after that."

105   It was an extraordinary thing, but in those few minutes Belcher said more than in all the weeks before. It was just as if the sound of the shot had started a flood of talk in him and he could go on the whole night like that, quite happily, talking about himself. We stood round like fools now that he couldn't see us any longer. Donovan looked at Noble, and Noble shook his head. Then Donovan raised his Webley, and at that moment Belcher gives his queer laugh again. He may have thought we were talking about him, or perhaps he noticed the same thing I'd noticed and couldn't understand it.

"Excuse me, chums," he says. "I feel I'm talking the hell of a lot, and so silly, about my being so handy about a house and things like that. But this thing came on me suddenly. You'll forgive me, I'm sure."

"You don't want to say a prayer?" asked Donovan.

"No, chum," he says. "I don't think it would help. I'm ready, and you boys want to get it over."

"You understand that we're only doing our duty?" says Donovan.

Belcher's head was raised like a blind man's, so that you could only see his chin and the tip of his nose in the lantern-light.

"I never could make out what duty was myself," he said. "I think you're all good lads, if that's what you mean. I'm not complaining."

Noble, just as if he couldn't bear any more of it, raised his fist at Donovan, and in a flash Donovan raised his gun and fired. The big man went over like a sack of meal, and this time there was no need of a second shot.

I don't remember much about the burying, but that it was worse than all the rest because we had to carry them to the grave. It was all made lonely with nothing but a patch of lantern-light between ourselves and the dark, and birds hooting and screeching all round, disturbed by the guns. Noble went through Hawkins's belongings to find the letter from his mother, and then joined his hands together. He did the same with Belcher. Then, when we'd filled in the grave, we separated from Jeremiah Donovan and Feeney and took our tools back to the shed. All the way we didn't speak a word. The kitchen was dark and cold as we'd left it, and the old woman was sitting over the hearth, saying her beads. We walked past her into the room, and Noble struck a match to light the lamp. She rose quietly and came to the doorway with all her cantankerousness gone.

"What did ye do with them?" she asked in a whisper, and Noble started so that the match went out in his hand.

"What's that?" he asked without turning round.

"I heard ye," she said.

"What did you hear?" asked Noble.

"I heard ye. Do ye think I didn't hear ye, putting the spade back in the houseen?"

Noble struck another match and this time the lamp lit for him.

"Was that what ye did to them?" she asked.

Then, by God, in the very doorway, she fell on her knees and began praying, and after looking at her for a minute or two Noble did the same by the fireplace. I pushed my way out past her and left them at it. I stood at the door, watching the stars and listening to the shrieking of the birds dying out over the bogs. It is so strange what you feel at times like that you can't describe it. Noble says he saw everything ten times the size, as though there were nothing in the whole world but that little patch of bog with the two Englishmen stiffening into it, but with me it was as if the patch of bog where the Englishmen were was a million miles away, and even Noble and the old woman, mumbling behind me, and the birds and the bloody stars were all far away, and I was somehow very small and very lost and lonely like a child astray in the snow. And anything that happened to me afterwards, I never felt the same about again.

QUESTIONS FOR DISCUSSION AND WRITING

1. How does the card game help establish the existing relationships in the story? How does Jeremiah Donovan's revelation change those relationships and bring the story to its climax?

2. How does the narrator describe the difference between Hawkins and Belcher? How does he characterize the difference between himself and Donovan? What function does the old woman's character have in the development of the story?

3. The setting for this story is the Anglo–Irish war, in which the Irish fought for independence in 1919–1921. How do the men's arguments about religion and politics help explain the conflicts that started the war between the English and the Irish? How does the word *chum* serve as a counterpoint to these arguments?

4. What is the narrator's point of view toward his duty as guard? How does his point of view change once he realizes that he will have to kill his hostages? What do his final words reveal about what he has learned?

5. How does the title of the story establish its theme? In what sense are Hawkins and Belcher "guests"? To what extent does duty to "nation" justify their murder?

Stories for Comparison

Albert Camus's "The Guest" (pages 329–338); Philip Roth's "Defender of the Faith" (pages 1036–1057).

81

··

T I L L I E   O L S E N

I Stand Here Ironing

TILLIE OLSEN was born in 1913 in Omaha, Nebraska. After graduating from high school, she worked in industry and as a typist-transcriber. In the 1930s, Olsen became active in the labor movement, trying to organize a union among the meat packers in Kansas City, and wrote *Yonnondio: From the Thirties,* a novel that chronicles the struggles of a working-class family. The novel was lost before it could be published, but it was later reclaimed and acknowledged as one of the best works of fiction to emerge from the Depression. In 1936, she married Jack Olsen, a printer, and gave up writing for the next fifteen years to raise four children. In the early 1950s, Olsen returned to writing, and her stories attracted a small but enthusiastic group of readers. In 1961, her novella *Tell Me a Riddle* won the O. Henry Award. On the basis of this newly established reputation, Olsen was asked to serve as writer-in-residence at Amherst College, Stanford University, the

Massachusetts Institute of Technology, and the University of California at San Diego. During this period, she published the long-lost *Yonnondio* (1974), two works of nonfiction, *Rebecca Harding Davis: Life in the Iron Mills* (1972) and *Silences* (1978), and an anthology, *Mother to Daughter, Daughter to Mother* (1984). The latter is a series of meditations on the problems faced by women writers. "I Stand Here Ironing," reprinted from *Tell Me a Riddle* (1961), is a mother's attempt to explain the circumstances that shaped her daughter's character.

I stand here ironing, and what you asked me moves tormented back and forth with the iron.

"I wish you would manage the time to come in and talk with me about your daughter. I'm sure you can help me understand her. She's a youngster who needs help and whom I'm deeply interested in helping."

"Who needs help." . . . Even if I came, what good would it do? You think because I am her mother I have a key, or that in some way you could use me as a key? She has lived for nineteen years. There is all that life that has happened outside of me, beyond me.

And when is there time to remember, to sift, to weigh, to estimate, to total? I will start and there will be an interruption and I will have to gather it all together again. Or I will become engulfed with all I did or did not do, with what should have been and what cannot be helped.

She was a beautiful baby. The first and only one of our five that was beautiful at ⁵ birth. You do not guess how new and uneasy her tenancy in her now-loveliness. You did not know her all those years she was thought homely, or see her poring over her baby pictures, making me tell her over and over how beautiful she had been—and would be, I would tell her—and was now, to the seeing eye. But the seeing eyes were few or nonexistent. Including mine.

I nursed her. They feel that's important nowadays. I nursed all the children, but with her, with all the fierce rigidity of first motherhood, I did like the books then said. Though her cries battered me to trembling and my breasts ached with swollenness, I waited till the clock decreed.

Why do I put that first? I do not even know if it matters, or if it explains anything.

She was a beautiful baby. She blew shining bubbles of sound. She loved motion, loved light, loved color and music and textures. She would lie on the floor in her blue overalls patting the surface so hard in ecstasy her hands and feet would blur. She was a miracle to me, but when she was eight months old I had to leave her daytimes with the woman downstairs to whom she was no miracle at all, for I worked or looked for work and for Emily's father, who "could no longer endure" (he wrote in his good-bye note) "sharing want with us."

I was nineteen. It was the pre-relief, pre-WPA world of the depression. I would start running as soon as I got off the streetcar, running up the stairs, the place smelling sour, and awake or asleep to startle awake, when she saw me she would break into a clogged weeping that could not be comforted, a weeping I can hear yet.

10   After a while I found a job hashing at night so I could be with her days, and it was better. But it came to where I had to bring her to his family and leave her.

It took a long time to raise the money for her fare back. Then she got chicken pox and I had to wait longer. When she finally came, I hardly knew her, walking quick and nervous like her father, looking like her father, thin, and dressed in a shoddy red that yellowed her skin and glared at the pockmarks. All the baby loveliness gone.

She was two. Old enough for nursery school they said, and I did not know then what I know now—the fatigue of the long day, and the lacerations of group life in the kinds of nurseries that are only parking places for children.

Except that it would have made no difference if I had known. It was the only place there was. It was the only way we could be together, the only way I could hold a job.

And even without knowing, I knew. I knew the teacher that was evil because all these years it has curdled into my memory, the little boy hunched in the corner, her rasp, "why aren't you outside, because Alvin hits you? that's no reason, go out, scaredy." I knew Emily hated it even if she did not clutch and implore "don't go Mommy" like the other children, mornings.

15   She always had a reason why we should stay home. Momma, you look sick. Momma, I feel sick. Momma, the teachers aren't there today, they're sick. Momma, we can't go, there was a fire there last night. Momma, it's a holiday today, no school, they told me.

But never a direct protest, never rebellion. I think of our others in their three-, four-year-oldness—the explosions, the tempers, the denunciations, the demands—and I feel suddenly ill. I put the iron down. What in me demanded that goodness in her? And what was the cost, the cost to her of such goodness?

The old man living in the back once said in his gentle way: "You should smile at Emily more when you look at her." What *was* in my face when I looked at her? I loved her. There were all the acts of love.

It was only with the others I remembered what he said, and it was the face of joy, and not of care or tightness or worry I turned to them—too late for Emily. She does not smile easily, let alone almost always as her brothers and sisters do. Her face is closed and sombre, but when she wants, how fluid. You must have seen it in her pantomimes, you spoke of her rare gift for comedy on the stage that rouses a laughter out of the audience so dear they applaud and applaud and do not want to let her go.

Where does it come from, that comedy? There was none of it in her when she came back to me that second time, after I had had to send her away again. She had a new daddy now to learn to love, and I think perhaps it was a better time.

20   Except when we left her alone nights, telling ourselves she was old enough.

"Can't you go some other time, Mommy, like tomorrow?" she would ask. "Will it be just a little while you'll be gone? Do you promise?"

The time we came back, the front door open, the clock on the floor in the hall. She rigid awake. "It wasn't just a little while. I didn't cry. Three times I called you, just three times, and then I ran downstairs to open the door so you could come faster. The clock talked loud. I threw it away, it scared me what it talked."

She said the clock talked loud again that night I went to the hospital to have Susan. She was delirious with the fever that comes before red measles, but she was fully conscious all the week I was gone and the week after we were home when she could not come near the new baby or me.

She did not get well. She stayed skeleton thin, not wanting to eat, and night after night she had nightmares. She would call for me, and I would rouse from exhaustion to sleepily call back: "You're all right, darling, go to sleep, it's just a dream," and if she still called, in a sterner voice, "now go to sleep, Emily, there's nothing to hurt you." Twice, only twice, when I had to get up for Susan anyhow, I went in to sit with her.

Now when it is too late (as if she could let me hold and comfort her like I do the   25 others) I get up and go to her at once at her moan or restless stirring. "Are you awake, Emily? Can I get you something?" And the answer is always the same: "No, I'm all right, go back to sleep, Mother."

They persuaded me at the clinic to send her away to a convalescent home in the country where "she can have the kind of food and care you can't manage for her, and you'll be free to concentrate on the new baby." They still send children to that place. I see pictures on the society page of sleek young women planning affairs to raise money for it, or dancing at the affairs, or decorating Easter eggs or filling Christmas stockings for the children.

They never have a picture of the children so I do not know if the girls still wear those gigantic red bows and the ravaged looks on the every other Sunday when parents can come to visit "unless otherwise notified"—as we were notified the first six weeks.

Oh it is a handsome place, green lawns and tall trees and fluted flower beds. High up on the balconies of each cottage the children stand, the girls in their red bows and white dresses, the boys in white suits and giant red ties. The parents stand below shrieking up to be heard and the children shriek down to be heard, and between them the invisible wall "Not To Be Contaminated by Parental Germs or Physical Affection."

There was a tiny girl who always stood hand in hand with Emily. Her parents never came. One visit she was gone. "They moved her to Rose Cottage," Emily shouted in explanation. "They don't like you to love anybody here."

She wrote once a week, the labored writing of a seven-year-old. "I am fine. How   30 is the baby. If I write my letter nicely I will have a star. Love." There never was a star. We wrote every other day, letters she could never hold or keep but only hear read—once. "We simply do not have room for children to keep any personal possessions," they patiently explained when we pieced one Sunday's shrieking together to plead how much it would mean to Emily, who loved so to keep things, to be allowed to keep her letters and cards.

Each visit she looked frailer. "She isn't eating," they told us.

(They had runny eggs for breakfast or mush with lumps, Emily said later. I'd hold it in my mouth and not swallow. Nothing ever tasted good, just when they had chicken.)

It took us eight months to get her released home, and only the fact that she gained back so little of her seven lost pounds convinced the social worker.

I used to try to hold and love her after she came back, but her body would stay stiff, and after a while she'd push away. She ate little. Food sickened her, and I think much of life too. Oh she had physical lightness and brightness, twinkling by on skates, bouncing like a ball up and down up and down over the jump rope, skimming over the hill; but these were momentary.

35   She fretted about her appearance, thin and dark and foreign-looking at a time when every little girl was supposed to look or thought she should look a chubby blonde replica of Shirley Temple. The doorbell sometimes rang for her, but no one seemed to come and play in the house or be a best friend. Maybe because we moved so much.

There was a boy she loved painfully through two school semesters. Months later she told me how she had taken pennies from my purse to buy him candy. "Licorice was his favorite and I brought him some every day, but he still liked Jennifer better'n me. Why, Mommy?" The kind of question for which there is no answer.

School was a worry to her. She was not glib in a world where glibness and quickness were easily confused with ability to learn. To her overworked and exasperated teachers she was an overconscientious "slow learner" who kept trying to catch up and was absent entirely too often.

I let her be absent, though sometimes the illness was imaginary. How different from my now-strictness about attendance with the others. I wasn't working. We had a new baby, I was home anyhow. Sometimes, after Susan grew old enough, I would keep her home from school, too, to have them all together.

Mostly Emily had asthma, and her breathing, harsh and labored, would fill the house with a curiously tranquil sound. I would bring the two old dresser mirrors and her boxes of collections to her bed. She would select beads and single earrings, bottle tops and shells, dried flowers and pebbles, old postcards and scraps, all sorts of oddments; then she and Susan would play Kingdom, setting up landscapes and furniture, peopling them with action.

40   Those were the only times of peaceful companionship between her and Susan. I have edged away from it, that poisonous feeling between them, that terrible balancing of hurts and needs I had to do between the two, and did so badly, those earlier years.

Oh there are conflicts between the others too, each one human, needing, demanding, hurting, taking—but only between Emily and Susan, no, Emily toward Susan that corroding resentment. It seems so obvious on the surface, yet it is not obvious. Susan, the second child, Susan, golden- and curly-haired and chubby, quick and articulate and assured, everything in appearance and manner Emily was not; Susan, not able to resist Emily's precious things, losing or sometimes clumsily breaking them; Susan telling jokes and riddles to company for applause while Emily sat silent (to say to me later: that was *my* riddle, Mother, I told it to Susan); Susan, who for all the five years' difference in age was just a year behind Emily in developing physically.

I am glad for that slow physical development that widened the difference between her and her contemporaries, though she suffered over it. She was too vulnerable for that terrible world of youthful competition, of preening and parading, of constant measuring of yourself against every other, of envy, "If I had that copper hair," "If I had that skin. . . ." She tormented herself enough about not looking like the others, there was enough of the unsureness, the having to be conscious of words before you speak, the constant caring—what are they thinking of me? without having it all magnified by the merciless physical drives.

Ronnie is calling. He is wet and I change him. It is rare there is such a cry now. That time of motherhood is almost behind me when the ear is not one's own but must always be racked and listening for the child cry, the child call. We sit for a while and I hold him, looking out over the city spread in charcoal with its soft aisles of light. "*Shoogily,*" he breathes and curls closer. I carry him back to bed, asleep. *Shoogily.* A funny word, a family word, inherited from Emily, invented by her to say: *comfort.*

In this and other ways she leaves her seal, I say aloud. And startle at my saying it. What do I mean? What did I start to gather together, to try and make coherent? I was at the terrible, growing years. War years. I do not remember them well. I was working, there were four smaller ones now, there was not time for her. She had to help be a mother, and housekeeper, and shopper. She had to set her seal. Mornings of crisis and near hysteria trying to get lunches packed, hair combed, coats and shoes found, everyone to school or Child Care on time, the baby ready for transportation. And always the paper scribbled on by a smaller one, the book looked at by Susan then mislaid, the homework not done. Running out to that huge school where she was one, she was lost, she was a drop; suffering over the unpreparedness, stammering and unsure in her classes.

There was so little time left at night after the kids were bedded down. She would   45
struggle over books, always eating (it was in those years she developed her enormous appetite that is legendary in our family) and I would be ironing, or preparing food for the next day, or writing V-mail to Bill, or tending the baby. Sometimes, to make me laugh, or out of her despair, she would imitate happenings or types at school.

I think I said once: "Why don't you do something like this in the school amateur show?" One morning she phoned me at work, hardly understandable through the weeping: "Mother, I did it. I won, I won; they gave me first prize; they clapped and clapped and wouldn't let me go."

Now suddenly she was Somebody, and as imprisoned in her difference as she had been in anonymity.

She began to be asked to perform at other high schools, even in colleges, then at city and statewide affairs. The first one we went to, I only recognized her that first moment when thin, shy, she almost drowned herself into the curtains. Then: Was this Emily? The control, the command, the convulsing and deadly clowning, the spell, then the roaring, stamping audience, unwilling to let this rare and precious laughter out of their lives.

Afterwards: You ought to do something about her with a gift like that—but without money or knowing how, what does one do? We have left it all to her, and the gift has as often eddied inside, clogged and clotted, as been used and growing.

50   She is coming. She runs up the stairs two at a time with her light graceful step, and I know she is happy tonight. Whatever it was that occasioned your call did not happen today.

"Aren't you ever going to finish the ironing, Mother? Whistler painted his mother in a rocker. I'd have to paint mine standing over an ironing board." This is one of her communicative nights and she tells me everything and nothing as she fixes herself a plate of food out of the icebox.

She is so lovely. Why did you want me to come in at all? Why were you concerned? She will find her way.

She starts up the stairs to bed. "Don't get me up with the rest in the morning." "But I thought you were having midterms." "Oh, those," she comes back in, kisses me, and says quite lightly, "in a couple of years when we'll all be atom-dead they won't matter a bit."

She has said it before. She *believes* it. But because I have been dredging the past, and all that compounds a human being is so heavy and meaningful in me, I cannot endure it tonight.

55   I will never total it all. I will never come in to say: She was a child seldom smiled at. Her father left me before she was a year old. I had to work her first six years when there was work, or I sent her home and to his relatives. There were years she had care she hated. She was dark and thin and foreign-looking in a world where the prestige went to blondeness and curly hair and dimples, she was slow where glibness was prized. She was a child of anxious, not proud, love. We were poor and could not afford for her the soil of easy growth. I was a young mother, I was a distracted mother. There were the other children pushing up, demanding. Her younger sister seemed all that she was not. There were years she did not want me to touch her. She kept too much in herself, her life was such she had to keep too much in herself. My wisdom came too late. She has much to her and probably little will come of it. She is a child of her age, of depression, of war, of fear.

Let her be. So all that is in her will not bloom—but in how many does it? There is still enough left to live by. Only help her to know—help make it so there is cause for her to know—that she is more than this dress on the ironing board, helpless before the iron.

QUESTIONS FOR DISCUSSION AND WRITING

1. How does the opening question about Emily establish the basic conflicts in the story? Why does Emily's mother think it is impossible to answer the question? In what sense do her concluding remarks provide a satisfactory resolution to the conflict?

2. How does the mother's account of Emily's childhood help characterize her daughter? How does the mother's description of her first child help define her

own character? How have circumstances helped shape a different character for Susan and the other children?

3. Why is the ironing board an appropriate setting for the telling of this story? How is poverty an important condition of setting in Emily's story? How does Emily respond to the various places she must live—the nursery, the convalescent home, the school, and home?

4. How does the mother's inability to account for "all that life that has happened outside me, beyond me" explain her point of view toward the story of her daughter? To what extent does the summary paragraph retell her story? Why won't she be able to "total it all"?

5. What has Emily's mother learned as a result of her daughter's experience? Has her wisdom come "too late"? Explain your answer.

Stories for Comparison

William Faulkner's "Barn Burning" (pages 491–504); Ann Beattie's "The Working Girl" (pages 285–290).

82

....

E D G A R   A L L A N   P O E

The Cask of Amontillado

EDGAR ALLAN POE (1809–1849) was born in Boston, Massachusetts, the son of traveling actors. Before he was three, his father deserted the family, his mother died, and he was adopted by John Allan of Richmond, Virginia, who saw to Poe's education in England, at the University of Virginia, and finally at West Point. Poe's drinking and gambling constantly strained his relationship with his foster father and eventually resulted in his dismissal from the Academy. He then moved to Baltimore to live with his aunt and to devote himself to a literary career. In 1832, he published five of his stories in the *Saturday Courier,* and in 1833 he won first prize in a short-story contest sponsored by a Baltimore newspaper. Encouraged by this success, he returned to Richmond in 1835 to edit *The Southern Literary Messenger,* in which he published highly influential literary criticism. In 1836, he married Virginia Clemm, his cousin, then not quite fourteen. Although Poe's work for the *Messenger* helped make it a leading critical magazine, his salary was so low that he resigned and moved to New York to look for work. His addiction to drink and drugs was a constant source of difficulty for him, contributing to his poverty, poor health, and early death. Nevertheless, in the next ten years he was able to publish his classic novel *The Narrative of Arthur Gordon Pym* (1838), famous poems, *The Raven and Other Poems* (1845), and stories in two notable forms: tales of gothic terror and tales of deduction or ratiocination (the precursor of the modern detective story). "The Cask of Amontillado," first published in *Godey's Lady's Book* (November 1846), is the dramatic retelling of the murder of a man unaware of his own fate.

T he thousand injuries of Fortunato I had borne as I best could, but when he ventured upon insult I vowed revenge. You, who so well know the nature of my soul, will not suppose, however, that I gave utterance to a threat. *At length* I would be avenged; this was a point definitely settled—but the very definitiveness with which it was resolved precluded the idea of risk. I must not only punish but punish with impunity. A wrong is unredressed when retribution overtakes its redresser. It is equally unredressed when the avenger fails to make himself felt as such to him who has done the wrong.

It must be understood that neither by word nor deed had I given Fortunato cause to doubt my good will. I continued, as was my wont, to smile in his face, and he did not perceive that my smile *now* was at the thought of his immolation.

He had a weak point—this Fortunato—although in other regards he was a man to be respected and even feared. He prided himself on his connoisseurship in wine. Few Italians have the true virtuoso spirit. For the most part their enthusiasm is adopted to suit the time and opportunity, to practice imposture upon the British and Austrian millionaires. In painting and gemmary, Fortunato, like his countrymen, was quack, but in the matter of old wines he was sincere. In this respect I did not differ from him materially;—I was skillful in the Italian vintages myself, and bought largely whenever I could.

It was about dusk, one evening during the supreme madness of the carnival season, that I encountered my friend. He accosted me with excessive warmth, for he had been drinking much. The man wore motley. He had on a tight-fitting parti-striped dress, and his head was surmounted by the conical cap and bells. I was so pleased to see him that I thought I should never have done wringing his hand.

5   I said to him—"My dear Fortunato, you are luckily met. How remarkably well you are looking to-day. But I have received a pipe of what passes for Amontillado, and I have my doubts."

"How?" said he. "Amontillado? A pipe? Impossible! And in the middle of the carnival!"

"I have my doubts," I replied; "and I was silly enough to pay the full Amontillado price without consulting you in the matter. You were not to be found, and I was fearful of losing a bargain."

10   "Amontillado!"

"I have my doubts."

"Amontillado!"

"And I must satisfy them."

"Amontillado!"

"As you are engaged, I am on my way to Luchresi. If any one has a critical turn, it is he. He will tell me————"

"Luchresi cannot tell Amontillado from Sherry."

"And yet some fools will have it that his taste is a match for your own."   15

"Come, let us go."

"Whither?"

"To your vaults."

"My friend, no; I will not impose upon your good nature. I perceive you have an engagement. Luchresi————"

"I have no engagement;—come."   20

"My friend, no. It is not the engagement, but the severe cold with which I perceive you are afflicted. The vaults are insufferably damp. They are encrusted with nitre."

"Let us go, nevertheless. The cold is merely nothing. Amontillado! You have been imposed upon. And as for Luchresi, he cannot distinguish Sherry from Amontillado."

Thus speaking, Fortunato possessed himself of my arm; and putting on a mask of black silk and drawing a *roquelaire* closely about my person, I suffered him to hurry me to my palazzo.

There were no attendants at home; they had absconded to make merry in honor of the time. I had told them that I should not return until the morning, and had given them explicit orders not to stir from the house. These orders were sufficient, I well knew, to insure their immediate disappearance, one and all, as soon as my back was turned.

I took from their sconces two flambeaux, and giving one to Fortunato, bowed   25
him through several suites of rooms to the archway that led into the vaults. I passed down a long and winding staircase, requesting him to be cautious as he followed. We came at length to the foot of the descent, and stood together on the damp ground of the catacombs of the Montresors.

The gait of my friend was unsteady, and the bells upon his cap jingled as he strode.

"The pipe?" said he.

"It is farther on," said I; "but observe the white web-work which gleams from these cavern walls."

He turned towards me, and looked into my eyes with two filmy orbs that distilled the rheum of intoxication.

"Nitre?" he asked at length.   30

"Nitre," I replied. "How long have you had that cough?"

"Ugh! ugh! ugh!—ugh! ugh! ugh!—ugh! ugh! ugh! ugh! ugh! ugh!—ugh! ugh! ugh!"

My poor friend found it impossible to reply for many minutes.

"It is nothing," he said, at last.

"Come," I said, with decision, "we will go back; your health is precious. You are   35
rich, respected, admired, beloved; you are happy, as once I was. You are a man to be

missed. For me it is no matter. We will go back; you will be ill, and I cannot be responsible. Besides, there is Luchresi————"

"Enough," he said; "the cough is a mere nothing; it will not kill me. I shall not die of a cough."

"True—true," I replied; "and, indeed, I had no intention of alarming you unnecessarily—but you should use all proper caution. A draft of this Medoc will defend us from the damps."

Here I knocked off the neck of a bottle which I drew from a long row of its fellows that lay upon the mold.

"Drink," I said, presenting him the wine.

40　He raised it to his lips with a leer. He paused and nodded to me familiarly, while his bells jingled.

"I drink," he said, "to the buried that repose around us."

"And I to your long life."

He again took my arm, and we proceeded.

"These vaults," he said, "are extensive."

45　"The Montresors," I replied, "were a great and numerous family."

"I forget your arms."

"A huge human foot d'or, in a field azure; the foot crushes a serpent rampant whose fangs are imbedded in the heel."

"And the motto?"

"Nemo me impune lacessit."

50　"Good!" he said.

The wine sparkled in his eyes and the bells jingled. My own fancy grew warm with the Medoc. We had passed through long walls of piled skeletons, with casks and puncheons intermingling, into the inmost recesses of the catacombs. I paused again, and this time I made bold to seize Fortunato by an arm above the elbow.

"The nitre!" I said; "see, it increases. It hangs like moss upon the vaults. We are below the river's bed. The drops of moisture trickle among the bones. Come, we will go back ere it is too late. Your cough————"

"It is nothing," he said; "let us go on. But first, another draft of the Medoc."

I broke and reached him a flagon of De Grâve. He emptied it at a breath. His eyes flashed with a fierce light. He laughed and threw the bottle upward with a gesticulation I did not understand.

55　I looked at him in surprise. He repeated the movement—a grotesque one.

"You do not comprehend?" he said.

"Not I," I replied.

"Then you are not of the brotherhood."

"How?"

60　"You are not of the masons."

"Yes, yes," I said; "yes, yes."

"You? Impossible! A mason?"

"A mason," I replied.

"A sign," he said, "a sign."

65　"It is this," I answered, producing from beneath the folds of my *roquelaire* a trowel.

"You jest," he exclaimed, recoiling a few paces. "But let us proceed to the Amontillado."

"Be it so," I said, replacing the tool beneath the cloak and again offering him my arm. He leaned upon it heavily. We continued our route in search of the Amontillado. We passed through a range of low arches, descended, passed on, and descending again, arrived at a deep crypt, in which the foulness of the air caused our flambeaux rather to glow than flame.

At the most remote end of the crypt there appeared another less spacious. Its walls had been lined with human remains, piled to the vault overhead, in the fashion of the great catacombs of Paris. Three sides of this interior crypt were still ornamented in this manner. From the fourth the bones had been thrown down, and lay promiscuously upon the earth, forming at one point a mound of some size. Within the wall thus exposed by the displacing of the bones, we perceived a still interior crypt or recess, in depth about four feet, in width three, in height six or seven. It seemed to have been constructed for no especial use within itself, but formed merely the interval between two of the colossal supports of the roof of the catacombs, and was backed by one of their circumscribing walls of solid granite.

It was in vain that Fortunato, uplifting his dull torch, endeavored to pry into the depth of the recess. Its termination the feeble light did not enable us to see.

"Proceed," I said; "herein is the Amontillado. As for Luchresi———"   70

"He is an ignoramus," interrupted my friend, as he stepped unsteadily forward, while I followed immediately at his heels. In an instant he had reached the extremity of the niche, and finding his progress arrested by the rock, stood stupidly bewildered. A moment more and I had fettered him to the granite. In its surface were two iron staples, distant from each other about two feet, horizontally. From one of these depended a short chain, from the other a padlock. Throwing the links about his waist, it was but the work of a few seconds to secure it. He was too much astounded to resist. Withdrawing the key I stepped back from the recess.

"Pass your hand," I said, "over the wall; you cannot help feeling the nitre. Indeed it is *very* damp. Once more let me *implore* you to return. No? Then I must positively leave you. But I must first render you all the little attentions in my power."

"The Amontillado!" ejaculated my friend, not yet recovered from his astonishment.

"True," I replied; "the Amontillado."

As I said these words I busied myself among the pile of bones of which I have   75
before spoken. Throwing them aside, I soon uncovered a quantity of building stone and mortar. With these materials and with the aid of my trowel, I began vigorously to wall up the entrance of the niche.

I had scarcely laid the first tier of the masonry when I discovered that the intoxication of Fortunato had in a great measure worn off. The earliest indication I had of this was a low moaning cry from the depth of the recess. It was *not* the cry of a drunken man. There was then a long and obstinate silence. I laid the second tier, and the third, and the fourth; and then I heard the furious vibrations of the chain. The noise lasted for several minutes, during which, that I might hearken to it with the more satisfaction, I ceased my labors and sat down upon the bones. When at last the clanking subsided, I resumed the trowel, and finished without interruption the fifth, the sixth, and the seventh tier. The wall was now nearly upon a level with my breast. I again paused, and holding the flambeaux over the masonwork, threw a few feeble rays upon the figure within.

A succession of loud and shrill screams, bursting suddenly from the throat of the chained form, seemed to thrust me violently back. For a brief moment I hesitated, I trembled. Unsheathing my rapier, I began to grope with it about the recess; but the thought of an instant reassured me. I placed my hand upon the solid fabric of the catacombs, and felt satisfied. I reapproached the wall. I replied to the yells of him who clamored. I reechoed, I aided, I surpassed them in volume and in strength. I did this, and the clamorer grew still.

It was now midnight, and my task was drawing to a close. I had completed the eighth, the ninth and the tenth tier. I had finished a portion of the last and the eleventh; there remained but a single stone to be fitted and plastered in. I struggled with its weight; I placed it partially in its destined position. But now there came from out the niche a low laugh that erected the hairs upon my head. It was succeeded by a sad voice, which I had difficulty in recognizing as that of the noble Fortunato. The voice said—

"Ha! ha! ha!—he! he! he!—a very good joke, indeed—an excellent jest. We will have many a rich laugh about it at the palazzo—he! he! he!—over our wine—he! he! he!"

80   "The Amontillado!" I said.

"He! he! he!—he! he! he!—yes, the Amontillado. But is it not getting late? Will not they be awaiting us at the palazzo, the Lady Fortunato and the rest? Let us be gone."

"Yes," I said, "let us be gone."

"For the love of God, Montresor!"

"Yes," I said, "for the love of God!"

85   But to these words I hearkened in vain for a reply. I grew impatient. I called aloud—

"Fortunato!"

No answer. I called again—

"Fortunato!"

No answer still. I thrust a torch through the remaining aperture and let it fall within. There came forth in return only a jingling of the bells. My heart grew sick; it was the dampness of the catacombs that made it so. I hastened to make an end of my labor. I forced the last stone into its position; I plastered it up. Against the new masonry I reerected the old rampart of bones. For the half of a century no mortal has disturbed them. *In pace requiescat!*

QUESTIONS FOR DISCUSSION AND WRITING

1. How does Montresor's opening paragraph explain the conflict in the story and foreshadow its resolution? How does Montresor's apparent concern for Fortunato's health enhance the suspense of the inevitable climax?

2. How do Montresor's name, attire, coat of arms, and family motto—"No one provokes me with impunity"—help to establish his character? Explain how Fortunato's name, costume, and love of wine help define his character. How does Montresor use his knowledge of Fortunato's character to manipulate him?

3. How does "the supreme madness of the carnival season" provide an appropriate environment for Montresor to initiate his plot? How do the catacombs provide the appropriate setting for Montresor's revenge?

4. What does Montresor assume his "reader" knows about "the nature of [his] soul"? What do Montresor's own screams reveal about his point of view toward his revenge? Why has he waited a half-century to tell this story?

5. How does the opening paragraph define the conditions for satisfactory revenge? In what ways does Montresor's scheme fulfill those conditions? How might the final *"In pace requiescat"* ("May he rest in peace") apply to the narrator as well as his victim?

Stories for Comparison:

Chinua Achebe's "Vengeful Creditor" (pages 153–163); Nathaniel Hawthorne's "Rappaccini's Daughter" (pages 619–640).

83

K A T H E R I N E   A N N E   P O R T E R

The Jilting of Granny Weatherall

KATHERINE ANNE PORTER (1890–1980) was born in Indian Creek, Texas, and was educated at a Catholic convent and a series of private schools in Texas and Louisiana. She married at the age of sixteen, but left her husband five years later to pursue a career in journalism, working on newspapers in Chicago, San Antonio, and Denver. Surviving a near-fatal attack of influenza in 1919, she worked as a ghost writer in Greenwich Village, where she became acquainted with Mexican artists. In 1920, she went to Mexico to study art and became involved in revolutionary political movements. It was during this period that she began publishing short stories in various national magazines. In 1930, she collected those stories in *Flowering Judas.* The success of this volume enabled her to take a boat from Vera

Cruz, Mexico, to Bremerhaven, Germany, a cruise that became the basis of her best-selling novel, *Ship of Fools* (1962). After several years abroad and a second marriage, Porter returned to the United States in 1937 and soon thereafter published three novellas in *Pale Horse, Pale Rider* (1939). During her third marriage, to a professor at Louisiana State University, she wrote the stories that were collected in *The Leaning Tower* (1944). In the 1950s, Porter was a lecturer at Stanford, the University of Michigan, and other universities while she worked on *Ship of Fools*. In the 1960s, Porter published her *Collected Stories* (1965), which won both the Pulitzer Prize and the National Book Award. Her later books are *Collected Essays* (1970) and an account of her participation in the protest over the Sacco-Vanzetti trial in the 1920s, *The Never Ending Wrong* (1977). "The Jilting of Granny Weatherall," reprinted from *Flowering Judas,* describes an old woman's deathbed memories.

S he flicked her wrist neatly out of Doctor Harry's pudgy careful fingers and pulled the sheet up to her chin. The brat ought to be in knee breeches. Doctoring around the country with spectacles on his nose! "Get along now, take your schoolbooks and go. There's nothing wrong with me."

Doctor Harry spread a warm paw like a cushion on her forehead where the forked green vein danced and made her eyelids twitch. "Now, now, be a good girl, and we'll have you up in no time."

"That's no way to speak to a woman nearly eighty years old just because she's down. I'd have you respect your elders, young man."

"Well, Missy, excuse me." Doctor Harry patted her cheek. "But I've got to warn you, haven't I? You're a marvel, but you must be careful or you're going to be good and sorry."

5   "Don't tell me what I'm going to be. I'm on my feet now, morally speaking. It's Cornelia. I had to go to bed to get rid of her."

Her bones felt loose, and floated around in her skin, and Doctor Harry floated like a balloon around the foot of the bed. He floated and pulled down his waistcoat and swung his glasses on a cord. "Well, stay where you are, it certainly can't hurt you."

"Get along and doctor your sick," said Granny Weatherall. "Leave a well woman alone. I'll call for you when I want you. . . . Where were you forty years ago when I pulled through milk-leg and double pneumonia? You weren't even born. Don't let Cornelia lead you on," she shouted, because Doctor Harry appeared to float up to the ceiling and out. "I pay my own bills, and I don't throw my money away on nonsense!"

She meant to wave good-by, but it was too much trouble. Her eyes closed of themselves, it was like a dark curtain drawn around the bed. The pillow rose and floated under her, pleasant as a hammock in a light wind. She listened to the leaves rustling outside the window. No, somebody was swishing newspapers: no, Cornelia and Doctor Harry were whispering together. She leaped broad awake, thinking they whispered in her ear.

"She was never like this, *never* like this!" "Well, what can we expect?" "Yes, eighty years old. . . ."

Well, and what if she was? She still had ears. It was like Cornelia to whisper 10 around doors. She always kept things secret in such a public way. She was always being tactful and kind. Cornelia was dutiful; that was the trouble with her. Dutiful and good: "So good and dutiful," said Granny, "that I'd like to spank her." She saw herself spanking Cornelia and making a fine job of it.

"What'd you say, Mother?"

Granny felt her face tying up in hard knots.

"Can't a body think, I'd like to know?"

"I thought you might want something."

"I do. I want a lot of things. First off, go away and don't whisper."   15

She lay and drowsed, hoping in her sleep that the children would keep out and let her rest a minute. It had been a long day. Not that she was tired. It was always pleasant to snatch a minute now and then. There is always so much to be done, let me see: tomorrow.

Tomorrow was far away and there was nothing to trouble about. Things were finished somehow when the time came; thank God there was always a little margin over for peace: then a person could spread out the plan of life and tuck in the edges orderly. It was good to have everything clean and folded away, with the hair brushes and tonic bottles sitting straight on the white embroidered linen: the day started without fuss and the pantry shelves laid out with rows of jelly glasses and brown jugs and white stone-china jars with blue whirligigs and words painted on them: coffee, tea, sugar, ginger, cinnamon, allspice: and the bronze clock with the lion on top nicely dusted off. The dust that lion could collect in twenty-four hours! The box in the attic with all those letters tied up, well she'd have to go through that tomorrow. All those letters—George's letters and John's letters and her letters to them both—lying around for the children to find afterwards made her uneasy. Yes, that would be tomorrow's business. No use to let them know how silly she had been once.

While she was rummaging around she found death in her mind and it felt clammy and unfamiliar. She had spent so much time preparing for death there was no need for bringing it up again. Let it take care of itself now. When she was sixty she had felt very old, finished, and went around making farewell trips to see her children and grandchildren, with a secret in her mind: This is the very last of your mother, children! Then she made her will and came down with a long fever. That was all just a notion like a lot of other things, but it was lucky too, for she had once and for all got over the idea of dying for a long time. Now she couldn't be worried. She hoped she had better sense now. Her father had lived to be one hundred and two years old and had drunk a noggin of strong hot toddy on his last birthday. He told the reporters it was his daily habit, and he owed his long life to that. He had made quite a scandal and was very pleased about it. She believed she'd just plague Cornelia a little.

"Cornelia! Cornelia!" No footsteps, but a sudden hand on her cheek. "Bless you, where have you been?"

"Here, mother."   20

"Well, Cornelia, I want a noggin of hot toddy."

"Are you cold, darling?"

"I'm chilly, Cornelia. Lying in bed stops the circulation. I must have told you that a thousand times."

Well, she could just hear Cornelia telling her husband that Mother was getting childish and they'd have to humor her. The thing that most annoyed her was that Cornelia thought she was deaf, dumb, and blind. Little hasty glances and tiny gestures tossed around her and over her head saying, "Don't cross her, let her have her way, she's eighty years old," and she sitting there as if she lived in a thin glass cage. Sometimes Granny almost made up her mind to pack up and move back to her own house where nobody could remind her every minute that she was old. Wait, wait, Cornelia, till your own children whisper behind your back!

25   In her day she had kept a better house and had got more work done. She wasn't too old yet for Lydia to be driving eighty miles for advice when one of the children jumped the track, and Jimmy still dropped in and talked things over: "Now, Mammy, you've a good business head, I want to know what you think of this? . . ." Old Cornelia couldn't change the furniture around without asking. Little things, little things! They had been so sweet when they were little. Granny wished the old days were back again with the children young and everything to be done over. It had been a hard pull, but not too much for her. When she thought of all the food she had cooked, and all the clothes she had cut and sewed, and all the gardens she had made—well, the children showed it. There they were, made out of her, and they couldn't get away from that. Sometimes she wanted to see John again and point to them and say, Well, I didn't do so badly, did I? But that would have to wait. That was for tomorrow. She used to think of him as a man, but now all the children were older than their father, and he would be a child beside her if she saw him now. It seemed strange and there was something wrong in the idea. Why, he couldn't possibly recognize her. She had fenced in a hundred acres once, digging the post holes herself and clamping the wires with just a negro boy to help. That changed a woman. John would be looking for a young woman with the peaked Spanish comb in her hair and the painted fan. Digging post holes changed a woman. Riding country roads in the winter when women had their babies was another thing: sitting up nights with sick horses and sick negroes and sick children and hardly ever losing one. John, I hardly ever lost one of them! John would see that in a minute, that would be something he could understand, she wouldn't have to explain anything!

It made her feel like rolling up her sleeves and putting the whole place to rights again. No matter if Cornelia was determined to be everywhere at once, there were a great many things left undone on this place. She would start tomorrow and do them. It was good to be strong enough for everything, even if all you made melted and changed and slipped under your hands, so that by the time you finished you almost forgot what you were working for. What was it I set out to do? she asked herself intently, but she could not remember. A fog rose over the valley, she saw it marching across the creek swallowing the trees and moving up the hill like an army of ghosts. Soon it would be at the near edge of the orchard, and then it was time to go in and light the lamps. Come in, children, don't stay out in the night air.

Lighting the lamps had been beautiful. The children huddled up to her and breathed like little calves waiting at the bars in the twilight. Their eyes followed the match and watched the flame rise and settle in a blue curve, then they moved away from her. The lamp was lit, they didn't have to be scared and hang on to mother any more. Never, never, never more. God, for all my life I thank Thee. Without Thee, my God, I could never have done it. Hail, Mary, full of grace.

I want you to pick all the fruit this year and see that nothing is wasted. There's always someone who can use it. Don't let good things rot for want of using. You waste life when you waste good food. Don't let things get lost. It's bitter to lose things. Now, don't let me get to thinking, not when I am tired and taking a little nap before supper. . . .

The pillow rose about her shoulders and pressed against her heart and the memory was being squeezed out of it: oh, push down the pillow, somebody: it would smother her if she tried to hold it. Such a fresh breeze blowing and such a green day with no threats in it. But he had not come, just the same. What does a woman do when she has put on the white veil and set out the white cake for a man and he doesn't come? She tried to remember. No, I swear he never harmed me but in that. He never harmed me but in that . . . and what if he did? There was the day, the day, but a whirl of dark smoke rose and covered it, crept up and over into the bright field where everything was planted so carefully in orderly rows. That was hell, she knew hell when she saw it. For sixty years she had prayed against remembering him and against losing her soul in the deep pit of hell, and now the two things were mingled in one and the thought of him was a smoky cloud from hell that moved and crept in her head when she had just got rid of Doctor Harry and was trying to rest a minute. Wounded vanity, Ellen, said a sharp voice in the top of her mind. Don't let your wounded vanity get the upper hand of you. Plenty of girls get jilted. You were jilted, weren't you? Then stand up to it. Her eyelids wavered and let in streamers of blue-gray light like tissue paper over her eyes. She must get up and pull the shades down or she'd never sleep. She was in bed again and the shades were not down. How could that happen? Better turn over, hide from the light, sleeping in the light gave you nightmares. "Mother, how do you feel now?" and a stinging wetness on her forehead. But I don't like having my face washed in cold water!

Hapsy? George? Lydia? Jimmy? No, Cornelia, and her features were swollen   30
and full of little puddles. "They're coming, darling, they'll all be here soon." Go wash your face, child, you look funny.

Instead of obeying, Cornelia knelt down and put her head on the pillow. She seemed to be talking but there was no sound. "Well, are you tongue-tied? Whose birthday is it? Are you going to give a party?"

Cornelia's mouth moved urgently in strange shapes. "Don't do that, you bother me, daughter."

"Oh, no, Mother. Oh, no. . . ."

Nonsense. It was strange about children. They disputed your every word. "No what, Cornelia?"

"Here's Doctor Harry."   35

"I won't see that boy again. He just left five minutes ago."

"That was this morning, Mother. It's night now. Here's the nurse."

"This is Doctor Harry, Mrs. Weatherall. I never saw you look so young and happy!"

"Ah, I'll never be young again—but I'd be happy if they'd let me lie in peace and get rested."

40   She thought she spoke up loudly, but no one answered. A warm weight on her forehead, a warm bracelet on her wrist, and a breeze went on whispering, trying to tell her something. A shuffle of leaves in the everlasting hand of God. He blew on them and they danced and rattled. "Mother, don't mind, we're going to give you a little hypodermic." "Look here, daughter, how do ants get in this bed? I saw sugar ants yesterday." Did you send for Hapsy too?

It was Hapsy she really wanted. She had to go a long way back through a great many rooms to find Hapsy standing with a baby on her arm. She seemed to herself to be Hapsy also, and the baby on Hapsy's arm was Hapsy and himself and herself, all at once, and there was no surprise in the meeting. Then Hapsy melted from within and turned flimsy as gray gauze and the baby was a gauzy shadow, and Hapsy came up close and said, "I thought you'd never come," and looked at her very searchingly and said, "You haven't changed a bit!" They leaned forward to kiss, when Cornelia began whispering from a long way off, "Oh, is there anything you want to tell me? Is there anything I can do for you?"

Yes, she had changed her mind after sixty years and she would like to see George. I want you to find George. Find him and be sure to tell him I forgot him. I want him to know I had my husband just the same and my children and my house like any other woman. A good house too and a good husband that I loved and fine children out of him. Better than I hoped for even. Tell him I was given back everything he took away and more. Oh, no, oh, God, no, there was something else besides the house and the man and the children. Oh, surely they were not all? What was it? Something not given back. . . . Her breath crowded down under her ribs and grew into a monstrous frightening shape with cutting edges; it bored up into her head, and the agony was unbelievable: Yes, John, get the doctor now, no more talk, my time has come.

When this one was born it should be the last. The last. It should have been born first, for it was the one she had truly wanted. Everything came in good time. Nothing left out, left over. She was strong, in three days she would be as well as ever. Better. A woman needed milk in her to have her full health.

"Mother, do you hear me?"

45   "I've been telling you—"

"Mother, Father Connolly's here."

"I went to Holy Communion only last week. Tell him I'm not so sinful as all that."

"Father just wants to speak to you."

He could speak as much as he pleased. It was like him to drop in and inquire about her soul as if it were a teething baby, and then stay on for a cup of tea and a round of cards and gossip. He always had a funny story of some sort, usually about an Irishman who made his little mistakes and confessed them, and the point lay in some absurd thing he would blurt out in the confessional showing his struggles between native piety and original sin. Granny felt easy about her soul. Cornelia, where are your manners? Give Father Connolly a chair. She had her secret comfortable understanding with a few favorite saints who cleared a straight road to God for her. All as surely signed and sealed as the papers for the new Forty Acres. Forever . . . heirs and assigns forever. Since the day the wedding cake was not cut, but thrown out and wasted. The whole bottom dropped out of the world, and there she was blind and sweating with nothing under her feet and the walls falling away. His hand had caught her under the breast, she had not fallen, there was the freshly polished floor with the green rug on it, just as before. He had cursed like a sailor's parrot and said, "I'll kill him for you." Don't lay a hand on him, for my sake leave something to God. "Now, Ellen, you must believe what I tell you. . . ."

So there was nothing, nothing to worry about any more, except sometimes in 50 the night one of the children screamed in a nightmare, and they both hustled out shaking and hunting for the matches and calling, "There, wait a minute, here we are!" John, get the doctor now, Hapsy's time has come. But there was Hapsy standing by the bed in a white cap. "Cornelia, tell Hapsy to take off her cap. I can't see her plain."

Her eyes opened very wide and the room stood out like a picture she had seen somewhere. Dark colors with the shadows rising towards the ceiling in long angles. The tall black dresser gleamed with nothing on it but John's picture, enlarged from a little one, with John's eyes very black when they should have been blue. You never saw him, so how do you know how he looked? But the man insisted the copy was perfect, it was very rich and handsome. For a picture, yes, but it's not my husband. The table by the bed had a linen cover and a candle and a crucifix. The light was blue from Cornelia's silk lampshades. No sort of light at all, just frippery. You had to live forty years with kerosene lamps to appreciate honest electricity. She felt very strong and she saw Doctor Harry with a rosy nimbus around him.

"You look like a saint, Doctor Harry, and I vow that's as near as you'll ever come to it."

"She's saying something."

"I heard you, Cornelia. What's all this carrying-on?"

"Father Connolly's saying—"   55

Cornelia's voice staggered and bumped like a cart in a bad road. It rounded corners and turned back again and arrived nowhere. Granny stepped up in the cart very lightly and reached for the reins, but a man sat beside her and she knew him by his hands, driving the cart. She did not look in his face, for she knew without seeing, but looked instead down the road where the trees leaned over and bowed to each other and a thousand birds were singing a Mass. She felt like singing too, but she put her hand in the bosom of her dress and pulled out a rosary, and Father Connolly murmured Latin in a very solemn voice and tickled her feet. My God, will you stop that nonsense? I'm a married woman. What if he did run away and leave me to face the priest by myself? I found another a whole world better. I wouldn't have exchanged my husband for anybody except St. Michael himself, and you may tell him that for me with a thank you in the bargain.

Light flashed on her closed eyelids, and a deep roaring shook her. Cornelia, is that lightning? I hear thunder. There's going to be a storm. Close all the windows. Call the children in. . . . "Mother, here we are, all of us." "Is that you, Hapsy?" "Oh no, I'm Lydia. We drove as fast as we could." Their faces drifted above her, drifted away. The rosary fell out of her hands and Lydia put it back. Jimmy tried to help, their hands fumbled together, and Granny closed two fingers around Jimmy's thumb. Beads wouldn't do, it must be something alive. She was so amazed her thoughts ran round and round. So, my dear Lord, this is my death and I wasn't even thinking about it. My children have come to see me die. But I can't, it's not time. Oh, I always hated surprises. I wanted to give Cornelia the amethyst set—Cornelia, you're to have the amethyst set, but Hapsy's to wear it when she wants, and, Doctor Harry, do shut up. Nobody sent for you. Oh, my dear Lord, do wait a minute. I meant to do something about the Forty Acres, Jimmy doesn't need it and Lydia will later on, with that worthless husband of hers. I meant to finish the altar cloth and send six bottles of wine to Sister Borgia for her dyspepsia. I want to send six bottles of wine to Sister Borgia, Father Connolly, now don't let me forget.

Cornelia's voice made short turns and tilted over and crashed. "Oh, Mother, oh, Mother, oh, Mother. . . ."

"I'm not going, Cornelia. I'm taken by surprise. I can't go."

60   You'll see Hapsy again. What about her? "I thought you'd never come." Granny made a long journey outward, looking for Hapsy. What if I don't find her? What then? Her heart sank down and down, there was no bottom to death, she couldn't come to the end of it. The blue light from Cornelia's lampshade drew into a tiny point in the center of her brain, it flickered and winked like an eye, quietly it fluttered and dwindled. Granny lay curled down within herself, amazed and watchful, staring at the point of light that was herself; her body was now only a deeper mass of shadow in an endless darkness and this darkness would curl around the light and swallow it up. God, give a sign!

For the second time there was no sign. Again no bridegroom and the priest in the house. She could not remember any other sorrow because this grief wiped them all away. Oh, no, there's nothing more cruel than this—I'll never forgive it. She stretched herself with a deep breath and blew out the light.

QUESTIONS FOR DISCUSSION AND WRITING

1. How does Granny's opening conversation with Doctor Harry establish the situation to be dramatized in the story? How do Granny's memories prepare her for her death?

2. How does Granny's last name, "Weatherall," describe her character? How does Granny characterize her husband and children? What does she want to tell George?

3. How does Granny's concern for order help portray the environment she wanted to create for her life? In particular, how does Granny describe the bedroom where she is dying?

4. How do the comments of the doctor, the priest, and Cornelia help establish the restricted focus of Granny's point of view? In what manner does Granny's preoccupation with the "point of light" toward the end of the story heighten the difference between her point of view and the points of view of those who are attending her?

5. How does Granny compare the experience of being jilted with the experience of death? What will she "never forgive"?

Stories for Comparison

Leo Tolstoy's "The Death of Ivan Ilych" (pages 1096–1135); Alice Walker's "To Hell with Dying" (pages 1159–1163).

84

....

THOMAS   PYNCHON

Entropy

Boris has just given me a summary of his views.
He is a weather prophet. The weather will continue bad, he says.
There will be more calamities, more death, more despair.
Not the slightest indication of a change anywhere. . . . We must get into step,
a lockstep toward the prison of death. There is no escape.
The weather will not change.

—Tropic of Cancer

THOMAS PYNCHON was born in 1937 in Glen Cove, Long Island, New York, and was educated at Cornell University. After working briefly at Boeing Aircraft, Seattle, as a technical writer, Pynchon traveled to Mexico to finish his first novel, *V* (1963). Since that time the most noteworthy biographical fact about Pynchon has been his anonymity. He never claimed the William Faulkner First Novel Award for *V* and refused the National Book Award for *Gravity's Rainbow* (1973), preferring to avoid publicity and to live in seclusion. Pynchon's other work includes two novels, *The Crying of Lot 49* (1966) and *Vineland* (1990), and a collection of short stories, *Slow Learner* (1984). "Entropy," reprinted from *Slow Learner,* explores the changes in an "open" and a "closed" information system.

D ownstairs, Meatball Mulligan's lease-breaking party was moving into its 40th hour. On the kitchen floor, amid a litter of empty champagne fifths, were Sandor Rojas and three friends, playing spit in the ocean and staying awake on Heidseck and benzedrine pills. In the living room Duke, Vincent, Krinkles and Paco sat crouched over a 15-inch speaker which had been bolted into the top of a wastepaper basket, listening to 27 watts' worth of *The Heroes' Gate at Kiev*. They all wore hornrimmed sunglasses and rapt expressions, and smoked funny-looking cigarettes which contained not, as you might expect, tobacco, but an adulterated form of *cannabis sativa*. This group was the Duke di Angelis quartet. They recorded for a local label called Tambú and had to their credit one 10″ LP entitled *Songs of Outer Space*. From time to time one of them would flick the ashes from his cigarette into the speaker cone to watch them dance around. Meatball himself was sleeping over by the window, holding an empty magnum to his chest as if it were a teddy bear. Several government girls, who worked for people like the State Department and NSA, had passed out on couches, chairs and in one case the bathroom sink.

This was in early February of '57 and back then there were a lot of American expatriates around Washington, D.C., who would talk, every time they met you, about how someday they were going to go over to Europe for real but right now it seemed they were working for the government. Everyone saw a fine irony in this. They would stage, for instance, polyglot parties where the newcomer was sort of ignored if he couldn't carry on simultaneous conversations in three or four languages. They would haunt Armenian delicatessens for weeks at a stretch and invite you over for bulghour and lamb in tiny kitchens whose walls were covered with bullfight posters. They would have affairs with sultry girls from Andalucía or the Midi who studied economics at Georgetown. Their Dôme was a collegiate Rathskeller out on Wisconsin Avenue called the Old Heidelberg and they had to settle for cherry blossoms instead of lime trees when spring came, but in its lethargic way their life provided, as they said, kicks.

At the moment, Meatball's party seemed to be gathering its second wind. Outside there was rain. Rain splatted against the tar paper on the roof and was fractured into a fine spray off the noses, eyebrows and lips of wooden gargoyles under the eaves, and ran like drool down the windowpanes. The day before, it had snowed and the day before that there had been winds of gale force and before that the sun had made the city glitter bright as April, though the calendar read early February. It is a curious season in Washington, this false spring. Somewhere in it are Lincoln's Birthday and the Chinese New Year, and a forlornness in the streets because cherry blossoms are weeks away still and, as Sarah Vaughan has put it, spring will be a little late this year. Generally crowds like the one which would gather in the Old Heidelberg on weekday afternoons to drink Würtzburger and to sing Lili Marlene (not to mention The Sweetheart of Sigma Chi) are inevitably and incorrigibly Romantic. And as every good Romantic knows, the soul (*spiritus, ruach, pneuma*) is nothing, substantially, but air; it is only natural that warpings in the atmosphere should be recapitulated in those who breathe it. So that over and above the public components— holidays, tourist attractions—there are private meanderings, linked to the climate as if this spell were a *stretto* passage in the year's fugue: haphazard weather, aimless loves, unpredicted commitments: months one can easily spend *in* fugue, because oddly enough, later on, winds, rains, passions of February and March are never remembered in that city, it is as if they had never been.

The last bass notes of *The Heroes' Gate* boomed up through the floor and woke Callisto from an uneasy sleep. The first thing he became aware of was a small bird he had been holding gently between his hands, against his body. He turned his head sidewise on the pillow to smile down at it, at its blue hunched-down head and sick, lidded eyes, wondering how many more nights he would have to give it warmth before it was well again. He had been holding the bird like that for three days: it was the only way he knew to restore its health. Next to him the girl stirred and whimpered, her arm thrown across her face. Mingled with the sounds of the rain came the first tentative, querulous morning voices of the other birds, hidden in philodendrons and small fan palms: patches of scarlet, yellow and blue laced through this Rousseau-like fantasy, this hothouse jungle it had taken him seven years to weave together. Hermetically sealed, it was a tiny enclave of regularity in the city's chaos, alien to the vagaries of the weather, of national politics, of any civil disorder. Through trial-and-error Callisto had perfected its ecological balance, with the help of the girl its artistic harmony, so that the swayings of its plant life, the stirrings of its birds and human inhabitants were all as integral as the rhythms of a perfectly-executed mobile. He and the girl could no longer, of course, be omitted from that sanctuary; they had become necessary to its unity. What they needed from outside was delivered. They did not go out.

"Is he all right," she whispered. She lay like a tawny question mark facing him, 5 her eyes suddenly huge and dark and blinking slowly. Callisto ran a finger beneath the feathers at the base of the bird's neck; caressed it gently. "He's going to be well, I think. See: he hears his friends beginning to wake up." The girl had heard the rain and the birds even before she was fully awake. Her name was Aubade: she was part French and part Annamese, and she lived on her own curious and lonely planet, where the clouds and the odor of poincianas, the bitterness of wine and the accidental fingers at the small of her back or feathery against her breasts came to her reduced inevitably to the terms of sound: of music which emerged at intervals from a howling darkness of discordancy. "Aubade," he said, "go see." Obedient, she arose; padded to the window, pulled aside the drapes and after a moment said: "It is 37. Still 37." Callisto frowned. "Since Tuesday, then," he said. "No change." Henry Adams, three generations before his own, had stared aghast at Power; Callisto found himself now in much the same state over Thermodynamics, the inner life of that power, realizing like his predecessor that the Virgin and the dynamo stand as much for love as for power; that the two are indeed identical; and that love therefore not only makes the world go round but also makes the boccie ball spin, the nebula precess. It was this latter or sidereal element which disturbed him. The cosmologists had predicted an eventual heat-death for the universe (something like Limbo: form and motion abolished, heat-energy identical at every point in it); the meteorologists, day-to-day, staved it off by contradicting with a reassuring array of varied temperatures.

But for three days now, despite the changeful weather, the mercury had stayed at 37 degrees Fahrenheit. Leery at omens of apocalypse, Callisto shifted beneath the covers. His fingers pressed the bird more firmly, as if needing some pulsing or suffering assurance of an early break in the temperature.

It was that last cymbal crash that did it. Meatball was hurled wincing into consciousness as the synchronized wagging of heads over the wastebasket stopped. The final hiss remained for an instant in the room, then melted into the whisper of rain outside. "Aarrgghh," announced Meatball in the silence, looking at the empty magnum. Krinkles, in slow motion, turned, smiled and held out a cigarette. "Tea time, man," he said. "No, no," said Meatball. "How many times I got to tell you guys. Not at my place. You ought to know, Washington is lousy with Feds." Krinkles looked wistful. "Jeez, Meatball," he said, "you don't want to do nothing no more." "Hair of dog," said Meatball. "Only hope. Any juice left?" He began to crawl toward the kitchen. "No champagne, I don't think," Duke said. "Case of tequila behind the icebox." They put on an Earl Bostic side. Meatball paused at the kitchen door, glowering at Sandor Rojas. "Lemons," he said after some thought. He crawled to the refrigerator and got out three lemons and some cubes, found the tequila and set about restoring order to his nervous system. He drew blood once cutting the lemons and had to use two hands squeezing them and his foot to crack the ice tray but after about ten minutes he found himself, through some miracle, beaming down into a monster tequila sour. "That looks yummy," Sandor Rojas said. "How about you make me one." Meatball blinked at him. *"Kitchi lofass a shegitbe,"* he replied automatically, and wandered away into the bathroom. "I say," he called out a moment later to no one in particular. "I say, there seems to be a girl or something sleeping in the sink." He took her by the shoulders and shook. "Wha," she said. "You don't look too comfortable," Meatball said. "Well," she agreed. She stumbled to the shower, turned on the cold water and sat down crosslegged in the spray. "That's better," she smiled.

"Meatball," Sandor Rojas yelled from the kitchen. "Somebody is trying to come in the window. A burglar, I think. A second-story man." "What are you worrying about," Meatball said. "We're on the third floor." He loped back into the kitchen. A shaggy woebegone figure stood out on the fire escape, raking his fingernails down the windowpane. Meatball opened the window. "Saul," he said.

"Sort of wet out," Saul said. He climbed in, dripping. "You heard, I guess."

10   "Miriam left you," Meatball said, "or something, is all I heard."

There was a sudden flurry of knocking at the front door. "Do come in," Sandor Rojas called. The door opened and there were three coeds from George Washington, all of whom were majoring in philosophy. They were each holding a gallon of Chianti. Sandor leaped up and dashed into the living room. "We heard there was a party," one blonde said. "Young blood," Sandor shouted. He was an ex-Hungarian freedom fighter who had easily the worst chronic case of what certain critics of the middle class have called Don Giovannism in the District of Columbia. *Purche porti la gonnella, voi sapete quel che fa.* Like Pavlov's dog: a contralto voice or a whiff of Arpège and Sandor would begin to salivate. Meatball regarded the trio blearily as they filed into the kitchen; he shrugged. "Put the wine in the icebox," he said "and good morning."

Aubade's neck made a golden bow as she bent over the sheets of foolscap, scribbling away in the green murk of the room. "As a young man at Princeton," Callisto was dictating, nestling the bird against the gray hairs of his chest, "Callisto had learned a mnemonic device for remembering the Laws of Thermodynamics: you can't win, things are going to get worse before they get better, who says they're going to get better. At the age of 54, confronted with Gibbs' notion of the universe, he suddenly realized that undergraduate cant had been oracle, after all. That spindly maze of equations became, for him, a vision of ultimate, cosmic heat-death. He had known all along, of course, that nothing but a theoretical engine or system ever runs at 100% efficiency; and about the theorem of Clausius, which states that the entropy of an isolated system always continually increases. It was not, however, until Gibbs and Boltzmann brought to this principle the methods of statistical mechanics that the horrible significance of it all dawned on him: only then did he realize that the isolated system—galaxy, engine, human being, culture, whatever—must evolve spontaneously toward the Condition of the More Probable. He was forced, therefore, in the sad dying fall of middle age, to a radical reëvaluation of everything he had learned up to then; all the cities and seasons and casual passions of his days had now to be looked at in a new and elusive light. He did not know if he was equal to the task. He was aware of the dangers of the reductive fallacy and, he hoped, strong enough not to drift into the graceful decadence of an enervated fatalism. His had always been a vigorous, Italian sort of pessimism: like Machiavelli, he allowed the forces of *virtù* and *fortuna* to be about 50/50; but the equations now introduced a random factor which pushed the odds to some unutterable and indeterminate ratio which he found himself afraid to calculate." Around him loomed vague hothouse shapes; the pitifully small heart fluttered against his own. Counterpointed against his words the girl heard the chatter of birds and fitful car honkings scattered along the wet morning and Earl Bostic's alto rising in occasional wild peaks through the floor. The architectonic purity of her world was constantly threatened by such hints of anarchy: gaps and excrescences and skew lines, and a shifting or tilting of planes to which she had continually to readjust lest the whole structure shiver into a disarray of discrete and meaningless signals. Callisto had described the process once as a kind of "feedback": she crawled into dreams each night with a sense of exhaustion, and a desperate resolve never to relax that vigilance. Even in the brief periods when Callisto made love to her, soaring above the bowing of taut nerves in haphazard double-stops would be the one singing string of her determination.

"Nevertheless," continued Callisto, "he found in entropy or the measure of disorganization for a closed system an adequate metaphor to apply to certain phenomena in his own world. He saw, for example, the younger generation responding to Madison Avenue with the same spleen his own had once reserved for Wall Street: and in American 'consumerism' discovered a similar tendency from the least to the most probable, from differentiation to sameness, from ordered individuality to a kind of chaos. He found himself, in short, restating Gibbs' prediction in social terms, and envisioned a heat-death for his culture in which ideas, like heat-energy, would no longer be transferred, since each point in it would ultimately have the same quantity of energy; and intellectual motion would, accordingly, cease." He glanced up suddenly. "Check it now," he said. Again she rose and peered out at the thermometer. "37," she said. "The rain has stopped." He bent his head quickly and held his lips against a quivering wing. "Then it will change soon," he said, trying to keep his voice firm.

Sitting on the stove Saul was like any big rag doll that a kid has been taking out some incomprehensible rage on. "What happened," Meatball said. "If you feel like talking, I mean."

"Of course I feel like talking," Saul said. "One thing I did, I slugged her."

"Discipline must be maintained."

"Ha, ha. I wish you'd been there. Oh Meatball, it was a lovely fight. She ended up throwing a *Handbook of Chemistry and Physics* at me, only it missed and went through the window, and when the glass broke I reckon something in her broke too. She stormed out of the house crying, out in the rain. No raincoat or anything."

"She'll be back."

"No."

"Well." Soon Meatball said: "It was something earth-shattering, no doubt. Like who is better, Sal Mineo or Ricky Nelson."

"What it was about," Saul said, "was communication theory. Which of course makes it very hilarious."

"I don't know anything about communication theory."

"Neither does my wife. Come right down to it, who does? That's the joke."

When Meatball saw the kind of smile Saul had on his face he said: "Maybe you would like tequila or something."

"No. I mean, I'm sorry. It's a field you can go off the deep end in, is all. You get where you're watching all the time for security cops: behind bushes, around corners. MUFFET is top secret."

"Wha."

"Multi-unit factorial field electronic tabulator."

"You were fighting about that."

"Miriam has been reading science fiction again. That and *Scientific American.* It seems she is, as we say, bugged at this idea of computers acting like people. I made the mistake of saying you can just as well turn that around, and talk about human behavior like a program fed into an IBM machine."

"Why not," Meatball said.

"Indeed, why not. In fact it is sort of crucial to communication, not to mention information theory. Only when I said that she hit the roof. Up went the balloon. And I can't figure out *why.* If anybody should know why, I should. I refuse to believe the government is wasting taxpayers' money on me, when it has so many bigger and better things to waste it on."

Meatball made a moue. "Maybe she thought you were acting like a cold, dehumanized amoral scientist type."

"My god," Saul flung up an arm. "Dehumanized. How much more human can I get? I worry, Meatball, I do. There are Europeans wandering around North Africa these days with their tongues torn out of their heads because those tongues have spoken the wrong words. Only the Europeans thought they were the right words."

"Language barrier," Meatball suggested.

Saul jumped down off the stove. "That," he said, angry, "is a good candidate for 35 sick joke of the year. No, ace, it is *not* a barrier. If it is anything it's a kind of leak-age. Tell a girl: 'I love you.' No trouble with two-thirds of that, it's a closed circuit. Just you and she. But that nasty four-letter word in the middle, *that's* the one you have to look out for. Ambiguity. Redundance. Irrelevance, even. Leakage. All this is noise. Noise screws up your signal, makes for disorganization in the circuit."

Meatball shuffled around. "Well, now, Saul," he muttered, "you're sort of, I don't know, expecting a lot from people. I mean, you know. What it is is, most of the things we say, I guess, are mostly noise."

"Ha! Half of what you just said, for example."

"Well, you do it too."

"I know." Saul smiled grimly. "It's a bitch, ain't it."

"I bet that's what keeps divorce lawyers in business. Whoops." 40

"Oh I'm not sensitive. Besides," frowning, "you're right. You find I think that most 'successful' marriages—Miriam and me, up to last night—are sort of founded on compromises. You never run at top efficiency, usually all you have is a minimum basis for a workable thing. I believe the phrase is Togetherness."

"Aarrgghh."

"Exactly. You find that one a bit noisy, don't you. But the noise content is dif-ferent for each of us because you're a bachelor and I'm not. Or wasn't. The hell with it."

"Well sure," Meatball said, trying to be helpful, "you were using different words. By 'human being' you meant something that you can look at like it was a computer. It helps you think better on the job or something. But Miriam meant some-thing entirely—"

"The hell with it." 45

Meatball fell silent. "I'll take that drink," Saul said after a while.

The card game had been abandoned and Sandor's friends were slowly getting wasted on tequila. On the living room couch, one of the coeds and Krinkles were en-gaged in amorous conversation. "No," Krinkles was saying, "no, I can't put Dave *down*. In fact I give Dave a lot of credit, man. Especially considering his accident and all." The girl's smile faded. "How terrible," she said. "What accident?" "Hadn't you heard?" Krinkles said. "When Dave was in the army, just a private E-2, they sent him down to Oak Ridge on special duty. Something to do with the Manhattan Proj-ect. He was handling hot stuff one day and got an overdose of radiation. So now he's got to wear lead gloves all the time." She shook her head sympathetically. "What an awful break for a piano-player."

Meatball had abandoned Saul to a bottle of tequila and was about to go to sleep in a closet when the front door flew open and the place was invaded by five enlisted personnel of the U.S. Navy, all in varying stages of abomination. "This is the place," shouted a fat, pimply seaman apprentice who had lost his white hat. "This here is the hoorhouse that chief was telling us about." A stringy-looking 3rd class boatswain's mate pushed him aside and cased the living room. "You're right, Slab," he said. "But it don't look like much, even for Stateside. I seen better tail in Naples, Italy." "How much, hey," boomed a large seaman with adenoids, who was holding a Mason jar full of white lightning. "Oh, my god," said Meatball.

Outside the temperature remained constant at 37 degrees Fahrenheit. In the hothouse Aubade stood absently caressing the branches of a young mimosa, hearing a motif of sap-rising, the rough and unresolved anticipatory theme of those fragile pink blossoms which, it is said, insure fertility. That music rose in a tangled tracery: arabesques of order competing fugally with the improvised discords of the party downstairs, which peaked sometimes in cusps and ogees of noise. That precious signal-to-noise ratio, whose delicate balance required every calorie of her strength, seesawed inside the small tenuous skull as she watched Callisto, sheltering the bird. Callisto was trying to confront any idea of the heat-death now, as he nuzzled the feathery lump in his hands. He sought correspondences. Sade, of course. And Temple Drake, gaunt and hopeless in her little park in Paris, at the end of *Sanctuary*. Final equilibrium. *Nightwood*. And the tango. Any tango, but more than any perhaps the sad sick dance in Stravinsky's *L'Histoire du Soldat*. He thought back: what had tango music been for them after the war, what meanings had he missed in all the stately coupled automatons in the *cafés-dansants,* or in the metronomes which had ticked behind the eyes of his own partners? Not even the clean constant winds of Switzerland could cure the *grippe espagnole:* Stravinsky had had it, they all had had it. And how many musicians were left after Passchendaele, after the Marne? It came down in this case to seven: violin, double-bass. Clarinet, bassoon. Cornet, trombone. Tympani. Almost as if any tiny troupe of saltimbanques had set about conveying the same information as a full pit-orchestra. There was hardly a full complement left in Europe. Yet with violin and tympani Stravinsky had managed to communicate in that tango the same exhaustion, the same airlessness one saw in the slicked-down youths who were trying to imitate Vernon Castle, and in their mistresses, who simply did not care. *Ma maîtresse.* Celeste. Returning to Nice after the second war he had found that café replaced by a perfume shop which catered to American tourists. And no secret vestige of her in the cobblestones or in the old pension next door; no perfume to match her breath heavy with the sweet Spanish wine she always drank. And so instead he had purchased a Henry Miller novel and left for Paris, and read the book on the train so that when he arrived he had been given at least a little forewarning. And saw that Celeste and the others and even Temple Drake were not all that had changed. "Aubade," he said, "my head aches." The sound of his voice generated in the girl an answering scrap of melody. Her movement toward the kitchen, the towel, the cold water, and his eyes following her formed a weird and intricate canon; as she placed the compress on his forehead his sigh of gratitude seemed to signal a new subject, another series of modulations.

50   "No," Meatball was still saying, "no, I'm afraid not. This is not a house of ill repute. I'm sorry, really I am." Slab was adamant. "But the chief said," he kept repeating. The seaman offered to swap the moonshine for a good piece. Meatball looked around frantically, as if seeking assistance. In the middle of the room, the Duke di Angelis quartet were engaged in a historic moment. Vincent was seated and the others standing: they were going through the motions of a group having a session, only without instruments. "I say," Meatball said. Duke moved his head a few

times, smiled faintly, lit a cigarette, and eventually caught sight of Meatball. "Quiet, man," he whispered. Vincent began to fling his arms around, his fists clenched; then, abruptly, was still, then repeated the performance. This went on for a few minutes while Meatball sipped his drink moodily. The navy had withdrawn to the kitchen. Finally at some invisible signal the group stopped tapping their feet and Duke grinned and said, "At least we ended together."

Meatball glared at him. "I say," he said. "I have this new conception, man," Duke said. "You remember your namesake. You remember Gerry."

"No," said Meatball. "I'll remember April, if that's any help."

"As a matter of fact," Duke said, "it was Love for Sale. Which shows how much you know. The point is, it was Mulligan, Chet Baker and that crew, way back then, out yonder. You dig?"

"Baritone sax," Meatball said. "Something about a baritone sax."

"But no piano, man. No guitar. Or accordion. You know what that means."   55

"Not exactly," Meatball said.

"Well first let me just say, that I am no Mingus, no John Lewis. Theory was never my strong point. I mean things like reading were always difficult for me and all—"

"I know," Meatball said drily. "You got your card taken away because you changed key on Happy Birthday at a Kiwanis Club picnic."

"Rotarian. But it occurred to me, in one of these flashes of insight, that if that first quartet of Mulligan's had no piano, it could only mean one thing."

"No chords," said Paco, the baby-faced bass.   60

"What he is trying to say," Duke said, "is no root chords. Nothing to listen to while you blow a horizontal line. What one does in such a case is, one *thinks* the roots."

A horrified awareness was dawning on Meatball. "And the next logical extension," he said.

"Is to think everything," Duke announced with simple dignity. "Roots, line, everything."

Meatball looked at Duke, awed. "But," he said.

"Well," Duke said modestly, "there are a few bugs to work out."   65

"But," Meatball said.

"Just listen," Duke said. "You'll catch on." And off they went again into orbit, presumably somewhere around the asteroid belt. After a while Krinkles made an embouchure and started moving his fingers and Duke clapped his hand to his forehead. "Oaf!" he roared. "The new head we're using, you remember, I wrote last night?" "Sure," Krinkles said, "the new head. I come in on the bridge. All your heads I come in then." "Right," Duke said. "So why—" "Wha," said Krinkles, "16 bars, I wait, I come in—" "16?" Duke said. "No. No, Krinkles. Eight you waited. You want me to sing it? A cigarette that bears a lipstick's traces, an airline ticket to romantic places." Krinkles scratched his head. "These Foolish Things, you mean." "Yes," Duke said, "yes, Krinkles. Bravo." "Not I'll Remember April," Krinkles said. *"Minghe morte,"* said Duke. "I *figured* we were playing it a little slow," Krinkles said. Meatball chuckled. "Back to the old drawing board," he said. "No, man," Duke said, "back to the airless void." And they took off again, only it seemed Paco was playing in G sharp while the rest were in E flat, so they had to start all over.

In the kitchen two of the girls from George Washington and the sailors were singing Let's All Go Down and Piss on the Forrestal. There was a two-handed, bilingual *morra* game on over by the icebox. Saul had filled several paper bags with water and was sitting on the fire escape, dropping them on passersby in the street. A fat government girl in a Bennington sweatshirt, recently engaged to an ensign attached to the Forrestal, came charging into the kitchen, head lowered, and butted Slab in the stomach. Figuring this was as good an excuse for a fight as any, Slab's buddies piled in. The *morra* players were nose-to-nose, screaming *trois, sette* at the tops of their lungs. From the shower the girl Meatball had taken out of the sink announced that she was drowning. She had apparently sat on the drain and the water was now up to her neck. The noise in Meatball's apartment had reached a sustained, ungodly crescendo.

Meatball stood and watched, scratching his stomach lazily. The way he figured, there were only about two ways he could cope: (a) lock himself in the closet and maybe eventually they would all go away, or (b) try to calm everybody down, one by one. (a) was certainly the more attractive alternative. But then he started thinking about that closet. It was dark and stuffy and he would be alone. He did not feature being alone. And then this crew off the good ship Lollipop or whatever it was might take it upon themselves to kick down the closet door, for a lark. And if that happened he would be, at the very least, embarrassed. The other way was more a pain in the neck, but probably better in the long run.

70   So he decided to try and keep his lease-breaking party from deteriorating into total chaos: he gave wine to the sailors and separated the *morra* players; he introduced the fat government girl to Sandor Rojas, who would keep her out of trouble; he helped the girl in the shower to dry off and get into bed; he had another talk with Saul; he called a repairman for the refrigerator, which someone had discovered was on the blink. This is what he did until nightfall, when most of the revellers had passed out and the party trembled on the threshold of its third day.

Upstairs Callisto, helpless in the past, did not feel the faint rhythm inside the bird begin to slacken and fail. Aubade was by the window, wandering the ashes of her own lovely world; the temperature held steady, the sky had become a uniform darkening gray. Then something from downstairs—a girl's scream, an overturned chair, a glass dropped on the floor, he would never know what exactly—pierced that private time-warp and he became aware of the faltering, the constriction of muscles, the tiny tossings of the bird's head; and his own pulse began to pound more fiercely, as if trying to compensate. "Aubade," he called weakly, "he's dying." The girl, flowing and rapt, crossed the hothouse to gaze down at Callisto's hands. The two remained like that, poised, for one minute, and two, while the heartbeat ticked a graceful diminuendo down at last into stillness. Callisto raised his head slowly. "I held him," he protested, impotent with the wonder of it, "to give him the warmth of my body. Almost as if I were communicating life to him, or a sense of life. What has happened? Has the transfer of heat ceased to work? Is there no more . . ." He did not finish.

"I was just at the window," she said. He sank back, terrified. She stood a moment more, irresolute; she had sensed his obsession long ago, realized somehow that that constant 37 was now decisive. Suddenly then, as if seeing the single and unavoidable conclusion to all this she moved swiftly to the window before Callisto could speak; tore away the drapes and smashed out the glass with two exquisite hands which came away bleeding and glistening with splinters; and turned to face the man on the bed and wait with him until the moment of equilibrium was reached, when 37 degrees Fahrenheit should prevail both outside and inside, and forever, and the hovering, curious dominant of their separate lives should resolve into a tonic of darkness and the final absence of all motion.

QUESTIONS FOR DISCUSSION AND WRITING

1. How does Pynchon intertwine events in the two apartments to form a unified story? What decision serves as the climax to Meatball's story? What act serves as the climax of Callisto's story? Do the two strands of the story reach similar or contrasting conclusions?

2. How do Meatball and Callisto resemble each other in terms of their situations and philosophies? How does Pynchon use the large cast of minor characters at the party to illustrate the themes of his story? For example, how does he use Saul's argument with Miriam to illustrate the problem of "entropy"?

3. How do the two apartments, the two worlds in the story, contrast with one another? Why is it significant that these two worlds coexist in Washington, D.C.?

4. What tone is established by the particular narrative voice in this story? How is that tone affected by Callisto's dictating his narrative to Aubade?

5. What do the opening quotation from a Henry Miller novel and the unchanging temperature of 37 degrees suggest about the main theme of the story? What do the bird's death and the broken window suggest about the inevitable fate of Callisto's world? What seems to be the inevitable fate of Meatball's world?

Stories for Comparison

John Barth's "Lost in the Funhouse" (pages 268–284); Pamela Zoline's "The Heat Death of the Universe" (pages 1207–1218).

85

....

PHILIP ROTH

Defender of the Faith

PHILIP ROTH was born in 1933 in Newark, New Jersey, and educated at
Rutgers, Bucknell, and the University of Chicago. As a graduate student, he
worked as an instructor in the University of Chicago's humanities program
and began publishing stories in magazines such as *Paris Review, The New
Yorker,* and *Harper's.* In 1959, he collected five of his stories and a novella in
Goodbye, Columbus, a volume that won the National Book Award. The success of his first book encouraged Roth to give up graduate study and teaching
to pursue a full-time career as a writer. In 1962, he published his first full-
length novel, *Letting Go,* followed by *When She Was Good* (1967) and his
controversial best-seller *Portnoy's Complaint* (1969). Roth often indulges his
strong satiric impulse, as in *Our Gang (Starring Tricky and His Friends)*
(1971), *The Breast* (1972), and *The Great American Novel* (1973). But he is
also interested in the personal and cultural dilemmas of the Jewish American
writer, as is evident in his critical self-appraisal *Reading Myself and Others*
(1975) and in his semi-autobiographical novels *The Professor of Desire*
(1977), *The Ghost Writer* (1979), *Zuckerman Unbound* (1981), and *The
Anatomy Lesson* (1983). His most recent novels include *The Counterlife*
(1986), *Deception* (1990), and *Sabbath's Theatre* (1995). Roth continues to
be a prolific writer of short fiction, but many of his stories remain uncol-
lected. "Defender of the Faith," reprinted from *Goodbye, Columbus,* tells of
an Army sergeant's dilemma defending the values of both his religion and his
profession.

In May of 1945, only a few weeks after the fighting had ended in Europe, I was
rotated back to the States, where I spent the remainder of the war with a training
company at Camp Crowder, Missouri. Along with the rest of the Ninth Army, I had
been racing across Germany so swiftly during the late winter and spring that when I
boarded the plane, I couldn't believe its destination lay to the west. My mind might
inform me otherwise, but there was an inertia of the spirit that told me we were flying to a new front, where we would disembark and continue our push eastward—
eastward until we'd circled the globe, marching through villages along whose twisting, cobbled streets crowds of the enemy would watch us take possession of what,

up till then, they'd considered their own. I had changed enough in two years not to mind the trembling of old people, the crying of the very young, the uncertainty and fear in the eyes of the once arrogant. I had been fortunate enough to develop an infantryman's heart, which, like his feet, at first aches and swells but finally grows horny enough for him to travel the weirdest paths without feeling a thing.

Captain Paul Barrett was my C.O. in Camp Crowder. The day I reported for duty, he came out of his office to shake my hand. He was short, gruff, and fiery, and—indoors or out—he wore his polished helmet liner pulled down to his little eyes. In Europe, he had received a battlefield commission and a serious chest wound, and he'd been returned to the States only a few months before. He spoke easily to me, and at the evening formation he introduced me to the troops. "Gentlemen," he said. "Sergeant Thurston, as you know, is no longer with this company. Your new first sergeant is Sergeant Nathan Marx, here. He is a veteran of the European theater, and consequently will expect to find a company of soldiers here, and not a company of *boys*."

I sat up late in the orderly room that evening, trying half-heartedly to solve the riddle of duty rosters, personnel forms, and morning reports. The Charge of Quarters slept with his mouth open on a mattress on the floor. A trainee stood reading the next day's duty roster, which was posted on the bulletin board just inside the screen door. It was a warm evening, and I could hear radios playing dance music over in the barracks. The trainee, who had been staring at me whenever he thought I wouldn't notice, finally took a step in my direction.

"Hey, Sarge—we having a G.I. party tomorrow night?" he asked. A G.I. party is a barracks cleaning.

"You usually have them on Friday nights?" I asked him.   5

"Yes," he said, and then he added, mysteriously, "that's the whole thing."

"Then you'll have a G.I. party."

He turned away, and I heard him mumbling. His shoulders were moving and I wondered if he was crying.

"What's your name, soldier?" I asked.

He turned, not crying at all. Instead, his green-speckled eyes, long and narrow,   10 flashed like fish in the sun. He walked over to me and sat on the edge of my desk. He reached out a hand. "Sheldon," he said.

"Stand on your feet, Sheldon."

Getting off the desk, he said, "Sheldon Grossbart." He smiled at the familiarity into which he'd led me.

"You against cleaning the barracks Friday night, Grossbart?" I said. "Maybe we shouldn't have G.I. parties. Maybe we should get a maid." My tone startled me. I felt I sounded like every top sergeant I had ever known.

"No, Sergeant." He grew serious, but with a seriousness that seemed to be only the stifling of a smile. "It's just—G.I. parties on Friday night, of all nights."

He slipped up onto the corner of the desk again—not quite sitting, but not quite   15 standing, either. He looked at me with those speckled eyes flashing, and then made a gesture with his hand. It was very slight—no more than a movement back and forth of the wrist—and yet it managed to exclude from our affairs everything else in the orderly room, to make the two of us the center of the world. It seemed, in fact, to exclude everything even about the two of us except our hearts.

"Sergeant Thurston was one thing," he whispered, glancing at the sleeping C.Q., "but we thought that with you here things might be a little different."

"We?"

"The Jewish personnel."

"Why?" I asked, harshly. "What's on your mind?" Whether I was still angry at the "Sheldon" business, or now at something else, I hadn't time to tell, but clearly I was angry.

20 "We thought you—Marx, you know, like Karl Marx. The Marx Brothers. Those guys are all—M-a-r-x. Isn't that how *you* spell it, Sergeant?"

"M-a-r-x."

"Fishbein said—" He stopped. "What I mean to say, Sergeant—" His face and neck were red, and his mouth moved but no words came out. In a moment, he raised himself to attention, gazing down at me. It was as though he had suddenly decided he could expect no more sympathy from me than from Thurston, the reason being that I was of Thurston's faith, and not his. The young man had managed to confuse himself as to what my faith really was, but I felt no desire to straighten him out. Very simply, I didn't like him.

When I did nothing but return his gaze, he spoke, in an altered tone. "You see, Sergeant," he explained to me, "Friday nights, Jews are supposed to go to services."

"Did Sergeant Thurston tell you you couldn't go to them when there was a G.I. party?"

25 "No."

"Did he say you had to stay and scrub the floors?"

"No, Sergeant."

"Did the Captain say you had to stay and scrub the floors?"

"That isn't it, Sergeant. It's the other guys in the barracks." He leaned toward me. "They think we're goofing off. But we're not. That's when Jews go to services, Friday night. We have to."

30 "Then go."

"But the other guys make accusations. They have no right."

"That's not the Army's problem, Grossbart. It's a personal problem you'll have to work out yourself."

"But it's *unfair.*"

I got up to leave. "There's nothing I can do about it," I said.

35 Grossbart stiffened and stood in front of me. "But this is a matter of *religion,* sir."

"Sergeant," I said.

"I mean, 'Sergeant,'" he said, almost snarling.

"Look, go see the chaplain. You want to see Captain Barrett, I'll arrange an appointment."

"No, no. I don't want to make trouble, Sergeant. That's the first thing they throw up to you. I just want my rights!"

40 "Damn it, Grossbart, stop whining. You have your rights. You can stay and scrub floors or you can go to shul—"

The smile swam in again. Spittle gleamed at the corners of his mouth. "You mean church, Sergeant."

"I mean shul, Grossbart!"

I walked past him and went outside. Near me, I heard the scrunching of the guard's boots on gravel. Beyond the lighted windows of the barracks, young men in T shirts and fatigue pants were sitting on their bunks, polishing their rifles. Suddenly there was a light rustling behind me. I turned and saw Grossbart's dark frame fleeing back to the barracks, racing to tell his Jewish friends that they were right—that, like Karl and Harpo, I was one of them.

The next morning, while chatting with Captain Barrett, I recounted the incident of the previous evening. Somehow, in the telling, it must have seemed to the Captain that I was not so much explaining Grossbart's position as defending it. "Marx, I'd fight side by side with a nigger if the fella proved to me he was a man. I pride myself," he said, looking out the window, "that I've got an open mind. Consequently, Sergeant, nobody gets special treatment here, for the good *or* the bad. All a man's got to do is prove himself. A man fires well on the range, I give him a weekend pass. He scores high in P.T., he gets a weekend pass. He *earns* it." He turned from the window and pointed a finger at me. "You're a Jewish fella, am I right, Marx?"

"Yes, sir."

45

"And I admire you. I admire you because of the ribbons on your chest. I judge a man by what he shows me on the field of battle, Sergeant. It's what he's got *here,*" he said, and then, though I expected he would point to his chest, he jerked a thumb toward the buttons straining to hold his blouse across his belly. "Guts," he said.

"O.K., sir. I only wanted to pass on to you how the men felt."

"Mr. Marx, you're going to be old before your time if you worry about how the men feel. Leave that stuff to the chaplain—that's his business, not yours. Let's us train these fellas to shoot straight. If the Jewish personnel feels the other men are accusing them of goldbricking—well, I just don't know. Seems awful funny that suddenly the Lord is calling so loud in Private Grossman's ear he's just got to run to church."

"Synagogue," I said.

"Synagogue is right, Sergeant. I'll write that down for handy reference. Thank 50 you for stopping by."

That evening, a few minutes before the company gathered outside the orderly room for the chow formation, I called the C.Q., Corporal Robert LaHill, in to see me. LaHill was a dark, burly fellow whose hair curled out of his clothes wherever it could. He had a glaze in his eyes that made one think of caves and dinosaurs. "LaHill," I said, "when you take the formation, remind the men that they're free to attend church services *whenever* they are held, provided they report to the orderly room before they leave the area."

LaHill scratched his wrist, but gave no indication that he'd heard or understood.

"LaHill," I said, "*church.* You remember? Church, priest, Mass, confession."

He curled one lip into a kind of smile; I took it for a signal that for a second he had flickered back up into the human race.

55   "Jewish personnel who want to attend services this evening are to fall out in front of the orderly room at 1900," I said. Then, as an afterthought, I added, "By order of Captain Barrett."

A little while later, as the day's last light—softer than any I had seen that year—began to drop over Camp Crowder, I heard LaHill's thick, inflectionless voice outside my window: "Give me your ears, troopers. Toppie says for me to tell you that at 1900 hours all Jewish personnel is to fall out in front, here, if they want to attend the Jewish Mass."

At seven o'clock, I looked out the orderly-room window and saw three soldiers in starched khakis standing on the dusty quadrangle. They looked at their watches and fidgeted while they whispered back and forth. It was getting dimmer, and, alone on the otherwise deserted field, they looked tiny. When I opened the door, I heard the noise of the G.I. party coming from the surrounding barracks—bunks being pushed to the walls, faucets pounding water into buckets, brooms whisking at the wooden floors, cleaning the dirt away for Saturday's inspection. Big puffs of cloth moved round and round on the windowpanes. I walked outside, and the moment my foot hit the ground I thought I heard Grossbart call to the others, "'Ten-*hut!*" Or maybe, when they all three jumped to attention, I imagined I heard the command.

Grossbart stepped forward, "Thank you, sir," he said.

"'Sergeant,' Grossbart," I reminded him. "You call officers 'sir.' I'm not an officer. You've been in the Army three weeks—you know that."

60   He turned his palms out at his sides to indicate that, in truth, he and I lived beyond convention. "Thank you anyway," he said.

"Yes," a tall boy behind him said. "Thanks a lot."

And the third boy whispered, "Thank you," but his mouth barely fluttered, so that he did not alter by more than a lip's movement his posture of attention.

"For what?" I asked.

Grossbart snorted happily. "For the announcement. The Corporal's announcement. It helped. It made it—"

65   "Fancier." The tall boy finished Grossbart's sentence.

Grossbart smiled. "He means formal, sir. Public," he said to me. "Now it won't seem as though we're just taking off—goldbricking because the work has begun."

"It was by order of Captain Barrett," I said.

"Aaah, but you pull a little weight," Grossbart said. "So we thank you." Then he turned to his companions. "Sergeant Marx, I want you to meet Larry Fishbein."

The tall boy stepped forward and extended his hand. I shook it. "You from New York?" he asked.

70   "Yes."

"Me, too." He had a cadaverous face that collapsed inward from his cheekbone to his jaw, and when he smiled—as he did at the news of our communal attachment—revealed a mouthful of bad teeth. He was blinking his eyes a good deal, as though he were fighting back tears. "What borough?" he asked.

I turned to Grossbart. "It's five after seven. What time are services?"

"Shul," he said, smiling, "is in ten minutes. I want you to meet Mickey Halpern. This is Nathan Marx, our sergeant."

The third boy hopped forward. "Private Michael Halpern." He saluted.

"Salute officers, Halpern," I said. The boy dropped his hand, and, on its way 75 down, in his nervousness, checked to see if his shirt pockets were buttoned.

"Shall I march them over, sir?" Grossbart asked. "Or are you coming along?"

From behind Grossbart, Fishbein piped up. "Afterward, they're having refreshments. A ladies auxiliary from St. Louis, the rabbi told us last week."

"The chaplain," Halpern whispered.

"You're welcome to come along," Grossbart said.

To avoid his plea, I looked away, and saw, in the windows of the barracks, a 80 cloud of faces staring out at the four of us. "Hurry along, Grossbart," I said.

"O.K., then," he said. He turned to the others. "Double time, *march!*"

They started off, but ten feet away Grossbart spun around and, running backward, called to me, "Good *shabbus,* sir!" And then the three of them were swallowed into the alien Missouri dusk.

Even after they had disappeared over the parade ground, whose green was now a deep blue, I could hear Grossbart singing the double-time cadence, and as it grew dimmer and dimmer, it suddenly touched a deep memory—as did the slant of the light—and I was remembering the shrill sounds of a Bronx playground where, years ago, beside the Grand Concourse, I had played on long spring evenings such as this. It was a pleasant memory for a young man so far from peace and home, and it brought so many recollections with it that I began to grow exceedingly tender about myself. In fact, I indulged myself in a reverie so strong that I felt as though a hand were reaching down inside me. It had to reach so very far to touch me! It had to reach past those days in the forests of Belgium, and past the dying I'd refused to weep over; past the nights in German farmhouses whose books we'd burned to warm us; past endless stretches when I had shut off all softness I might feel for my fellows, and had managed even to deny myself the posture of a conqueror—the swagger that I, as a Jew, might well have worn as my boots whacked against the rubble of Wesel, Münster, and Braunschweig.

But now one night noise, one rumor of home and time past, and memory plunged down through all I had anesthetized, and came to what I suddenly remembered was myself. So it was not altogether curious that, in search of more of me, I found myself following Grossbart's tracks to Chapel No. 3, where the Jewish services were being held.

I took a seat in the last row, which was empty. Two rows in front of me sat 85 Grossbart, Fishbein, and Halpern, holding little white Dixie cups. Each row of seats was raised higher than the one in front of it, and I could see clearly what was going on. Fishbein was pouring the contents of his cup into Grossbart's, and Grossbart looked mirthful as the liquid made a purple arc between Fishbein's hand and his. In the glaring yellow light, I saw the chaplain standing on the platform at the front; he was chanting the first line of the responsive reading. Grossbart's prayer book remained closed on his lap; he was swishing the cup around. Only Halpern responded to the chant by praying. The fingers of his right hand were spread wide across the cover of his open book. His cap was pulled down low onto his brow, which made it round, like a yarmulke. From time to time, Grossbart wet his lips at the cup's edge;

Fishbein, his long yellow face a dying light bulb, looked from here to there, craning forward to catch sight of the faces down the row, then of those in front of him, then behind. He saw me, and his eyelids beat a tattoo. His elbow slid into Grossbart's side, his neck inclined toward his friend, he whispered something, and then, when the congregation next responded to the chant, Grossbart's voice was among the others. Fishbein looked into his book now, too; his lips, however, didn't move.

Finally, it was time to drink the wine. The chaplain smiled down at them as Grossbart swigged his in one long gulp, Halpern sipped, meditating, and Fishbein faked devotion with an empty cup. "As I look down amongst the congregation"—the chaplain grinned at the word—"this night, I see many new faces, and I want to welcome you to Friday-night services here at Camp Crowder. I am Major Leo Ben Ezra, your chaplain." Though an American, the chaplain spoke deliberately—syllable by syllable, almost—as though to communicate, above all, with the lip readers in his audience. "I have only a few words to say before we adjourn to the refreshment room, where the kind ladies of the Temple Sinai, St. Louis, Missouri, have a nice setting for you."

Applause and whistling broke out. After another momentary grin, the chaplain raised his hands, palms out, his eyes flicking upward a moment, as if to remind the troops where they were and Who Else might be in attendance. In the sudden silence that followed, I thought I heard Grossbart cackle, "Let the goyim clean the floors!" Were those the words? I wasn't sure, but Fishbein, grinning, nudged Halpern. Halpern looked dumbly at him, then went back to his prayer book, which had been occupying him all through the rabbi's talk. One hand tugged at the black kinky hair that stuck out under his cap. His lips moved.

The rabbi continued. "It is about the food that I want to speak to you for a moment. I know, I know, I know," he intoned, wearily, "how in the mouths of most of you the *trafe* food tastes like ashes. I know how you gag, some of you, and how your parents suffer to think of their children eating foods unclean and offensive to the palate. What can I tell you? I can only say, close your eyes and swallow as best you can. Eat what you must to live, and throw away the rest. I wish I could help more. For those of you who find this impossible, may I ask that you try and try, but then come to see me in private. If your revulsion is so great, we will have to seek aid from those higher up."

A round of chatter rose and subsided. Then everyone sang "Ain Kelohainu"; after all those years, I discovered I still knew the words. Then, suddenly, the service over, Grossbart was upon me. "Higher up? He means the General?"

90   "Hey, Shelly," Fishbein said, "he means God." He smacked his face and looked at Halpern. "How high can you go!"

"Sh-h-h!" Grossbart said. "What do you think Sergeant?"

"I don't know," I said. "You better ask the chaplain."

"I'm going to. I'm making an appointment to see him in private. So is Mickey." Halpern shook his head. "No, no, Sheldon—"

95   "You have rights, Mickey." Grossbart said. "They can't push us around."

"It's O.K.," said Halpern. "It bothers my mother, not me."

Grossbart looked at me. "Yesterday he threw up. From the hash. It was all ham and God knows what else."

"I have a cold—that was why," Halpern said. He pushed his yarmulke back into a cap.

"What about you, Fishbein?" I asked. "You kosher, too?"

He flushed. "A little. But I'll let it ride. I have a very strong stomach, and I don't 100 eat a lot anyway." I continued to look at him, and he held up his wrist to reinforce what he'd just said; his watch strap was tightened to the last hole, and he pointed that out to me.

"But services are important to you?" I asked him.

He looked at Grossbart. "Sure, sir."

"'Sergeant.'"

"Not so much at home," said Grossbart, stepping between us, "but away from home it gives one a sense of his Jewishness."

"We have to stick together," Fishbein said.   105

I started to walk toward the door; Halpern stepped back to make way for me.

"That's what happened to Germany," Grossbart was saying, loud enough for me to hear. "They didn't stick together. They let themselves get pushed around."

I turned. "Look, Grossbart. This is the Army, not summer camp."

He smiled. "So?"

Halpern tried to sneak off, but Grossbart held his arm.   110

"Grossbart, how old are you?" I asked.

"Nineteen."

"And you?" I said to Fishbein.

"The same. The same month, even."

"And what about him?" I pointed to Halpern, who had by now made it safely to 115 the door.

"Eighteen," Grossbart whispered. "But like he can't tie his shoes or brush his teeth himself. I feel sorry for him."

"I feel sorry for all of us, Grossbart," I said, "but just act like a man. Just don't overdo it."

"Overdo what, sir?"

"The 'sir' business, for one thing. Don't overdo that," I said.

I left him standing there. I passed by Halpern, but he did not look at me. Then I 120 was outside, but, behind, I heard Grossbart call, "Hey, Mickey, my *leben,* come on back. Refreshments!"

"*Leben!*" My grandmother's word for me!

One morning a week later, while I was working at my desk, Captain Barrett shouted for me to come into his office. When I entered, he had his helmet liner squashed down so far on his head that I couldn't even see his eyes. He was on the phone, and when he spoke to me, he cupped one hand over the mouthpiece. "Who the hell is Grossbart?"

"Third platoon, Captain," I said. "A trainee."

"What's all this stink about food? His mother called a goddam congressman about the food." He uncovered the mouthpiece and slid his helmet up until I could see his bottom eyelashes. "Yes, sir," he said into the phone. "Yes, sir. I'm still here, sir. I'm asking Marx, here, right now—"

125 He covered the mouthpiece again and turned his head back toward me. "Lightfoot Harry's on the phone," he said, between his teeth. "This congressman calls General Lyman, who calls Colonel Sousa, who calls the Major, who calls me. They're just dying to stick this thing on me. Whatsa matter?" He shook the phone at me. "I don't feed the troops? What is this?"

"Sir, Grossbart is strange—" Barrett greeted that with a mockingly indulgent smile. I altered my approach. "Captain, he's a very orthodox Jew, and so he's only allowed to eat certain foods."

"He throws up, the congressman said. Every time he eats something, his mother says, he throws up!"

"He's accustomed to observing the dietary laws, Captain."

"So why's his old lady have to call the White House?"

130 "Jewish parents, sir—they're apt to be more protective than you expect. I mean, Jews have a very close family life. A boy goes away from home, sometimes the mother is liable to get very upset. Probably the boy mentioned something in a letter, and his mother misinterpreted."

"I'd like to punch him one right in the mouth," the Captain said. "There's a war on, and he wants a silver platter!"

"I don't think the boy's to blame, sir. I'm sure we can straighten it out by just asking him. Jewish parents worry—"

"*All* parents worry, for Christ's sake. But they don't get on their high horse and start pulling strings—"

I interrupted, my voice higher, tighter than before. "The home life, Captain, is very important—but you're right, it may sometimes get out of hand. It's a very wonderful thing, Captain, but because it's so close, this kind of thing . . ."

135 He didn't listen any longer to my attempt to present both myself and Lightfoot Harry with an explanation for the letter. He turned back to the phone. "Sir?" he said. "Sir—Marx, here, tells me Jews have a tendency to be pushy. He says he thinks we can settle it right here in the company . . . Yes, sir . . . I *will* call back, sir, soon as I can." He hung up. "Where are the men, Sergeant?"

"On the range."

With a whack on the top of his helmet, he crushed it down over his eyes again, and charged out of his chair. "We're going for a ride," he said.

The Captain drove, and I sat beside him. It was a hot spring day, and under my newly starched fatigues I felt as though my armpits were melting down into my sides and chest. The roads were dry, and by the time we reached the firing range, my teeth felt gritty with dust, though my mouth had been shut the whole trip. The Captain slammed the brakes on and told me to get the hell out and find Grossbart.

I found him on his belly, firing wildly at the five-hundred-feet target. Waiting their turns behind him were Halpern and Fishbein. Fishbein, wearing a pair of steel-rimmed G.I. glasses I hadn't seen on him before, had the appearance of an old peddler who would gladly have sold you his rifle and the cartridges that were slung all over him. I stood back by the ammo boxes, waiting for Grossbart to finish spraying the distant target. Fishbein straggled back to stand near me.

"Hello, Sergeant Marx," he said.   140

"How are you?" I mumbled.

"Fine, thank you. Sheldon's really a good shot."

"I didn't notice."

"I'm not so good, but I think I'm getting the hang of it now. Sergeant, I don't mean to, you know, ask what I shouldn't—" The boy stopped. He was trying to speak intimately, but the noise of the shooting forced him to shout at me.

"What is it?" I asked. Down the range, I saw Captain Barrett standing up in the   145 jeep, scanning the line for me and Grossbart.

"My parents keep asking and asking where we're going," Fishbein said. "Everybody says the Pacific. I don't care, but my parents—If I could relieve their minds, I think I could concentrate more on my shooting."

"I don't know where, Fishbein. Try to concentrate anyway."

"Sheldon says you might be able to find out."

"I don't know a thing, Fishbein. You just take it easy, and don't let Sheldon—"

"*I'm* taking it easy, Sergeant. It's at home—"   150

Grossbart had finished on the line, and was dusting his fatigues with one hand. I called to him. "Grossbart, the Captain wants to see you."

He came toward us. His eyes blazed and twinkled. "Hi!"

"Don't point that rifle!" I said.

"I wouldn't shoot you, Sarge." He gave me a smile as wide as a pumpkin, and turned the barrel aside.

"Damn you, Grossbart, this is no joke! Follow me."   155

I walked ahead of him, and had the awful suspicion that, behind me, Grossbart was *marching,* his rifle on his shoulder as though he were a one-man detachment. At the jeep, he gave the Captain a rifle salute. "Private Sheldon Grossbart, sir."

"At ease, Grossman." The Captain sat down, slid over the empty seat, and, crooking a finger, invited Grossbart closer.

"Bart, sir. Sheldon Gross*bart.* It's a common error." Grossbart nodded at me: *I* understood, he indicated. I looked away just as the mess truck pulled up to the range, disgorging a half-dozen K.P.s with rolled-up sleeves. The mess sergeant screamed at them while they set up the chow line equipment.

"Grossbart, your mama wrote some congressman that we don't feed you right. Do you know that?" the Captain said.

"It was my father, sir. He wrote to Representative Franconi that my religion for-   160 bids me to eat certain foods."

"What religion is that, Grossbart?"

"Jewish."

"'Jewish, *sir,*'" I said to Grossbart.

"Excuse me, sir, Jewish, sir."

"What have you been living on?" the Captain asked. "You've been in the Army   165 a month already. You don't look to me like you're falling to pieces."

"I eat because I have to, sir. But Sergeant Marx will testify to the fact that I don't eat one mouthful more than I need to in order to survive."

"Is that so, Marx?" Barrett asked.

"I've never seen Grossbart eat, sir," I said.

"But you heard the rabbi," Grossbart said. "He told us what to do, and I listened."

170   The Captain looked at me. "Well, Marx?"

"I still don't know what he eats and doesn't eat, sir."

Grossbart raised his arms to plead with me, and it looked for a moment as though he were going to hand me his weapon to hold. "But, Sergeant—"

"Look, Grossbart, just answer the Captain's questions," I said sharply.

Barrett smiled at me, and I resented it. "All right, Grossbart," he said. "What is it you want? The little piece of paper? You want out?"

175   "No, sir. Only to be allowed to live as a Jew. And for the others, too."

"What others?"

"Fishbein, sir, and Halpern."

"They don't like the way we serve, either?"

"Halpern throws up, sir. I've seen it."

180   "I thought *you* throw up."

"Just once, sir. I didn't know the sausage was sausage."

"We'll give menus, Grossbart. We'll show training films about the food, so you can identify when we're trying to poison you."

Grossbart did not answer. The men had been organized into two long chow lines. At the tail end of one, I spotted Fishbein—or, rather, his glasses spotted me. They winked sunlight back at me. Halpern stood next to him, patting the inside of his collar with a khaki handkerchief. They moved with the line as it began to edge up toward the food. The mess sergeant was still screaming at the K.P.s. For a moment, I was actually terrified by the thought that somehow the mess sergeant was going to become involved in Grossbart's problem.

"Marx," the Captain said, "you're a Jewish fella—am I right?"

185   I played straight man. "Yes, sir."

"How long you been in the Army? Tell this boy."

"Three years and two months."

"A year in combat, Grossbart. Twelve goddam months in combat all through Europe. I admire this man." The Captain snapped a wrist against my chest. "Do you hear him peeping about the food? Do you? I want an answer, Grossbart. Yes or no."

"No, sir."

190   "And why not? He's a Jewish fella."

"Some things are more important to some Jews than other things to other Jews."

Barrett blew up. "Look, Grossbart. Marx, here, is a good man—a goddam hero. When you were in high school, Sergeant Marx was killing Germans. Who does more for the Jews—you, by throwing up over a lousy piece of sausage, a piece of first-cut meat, or Marx, by killing those Nazi bastards? If I was a Jew, Grossbart, I'd kiss this man's feet. He's a goddam hero, and *he* eats what we give him. Why do you have to cause trouble is what I want to know! What is it you're buckin' for—a discharge?"

"No, sir."

"I'm talking to a wall! Sergeant, get him out of my way." Barrett swung himself back into the driver's seat. "I'm going to see the chaplain." The engine roared, the jeep spun around in a whirl of dust, and the Captain was headed back to camp.

For a moment, Grossbart and I stood side by side, watching the jeep. Then he 195 looked at me and said, "I don't want to start trouble. That's the first thing they toss up to us."

When he spoke, I saw that his teeth were white and straight, and the sight of them suddenly made me understand that Grossbart actually did have parents—that once upon a time someone had taken little Sheldon to the dentist. He was their son. Despite all the talk about his parents, it was hard to believe in Grossbart as a child, an heir—as related by blood to anyone, mother, father, or, above all, to me. This re- alization led me to another.

"What does your father do, Grossbart?" I asked as we started to walk back to- ward the chow line.

"He's a tailor."

"An American?"

"Now, yes. A son in the Army," he said, jokingly. 200

"And your mother?" I asked.

He winked. "A *ballabusta.* She practically sleeps with a dustcloth in her hand."

"She's also an immigrant?"

"All she talks is Yiddish, still."

"And your father, too?" 205

"A little English, 'Clean,' 'Press,' 'Take the pants in.' That's the extent of it. But they're good to me."

"Then, Grossbart—" I reached out and stopped him. He turned toward me, and when our eyes met, his seemed to jump back, to shiver in their sockets. "Grossbart— you were the one who wrote that letter, weren't you?"

It took only a second or two for his eyes to flash happy again. "Yes." He walked on, and I kept pace. "It's what my father *would* have written if he had known how. It was his name, though. *He* signed it. He even mailed it. I sent it home. For the New York postmark."

I was astonished, and he saw it. With complete seriousness, he thrust his right arm in front of me. "Blood is blood, Sergeant," he said, pinching the blue vein in his wrist.

"What the hell *are* you trying to do, Grossbart?" I asked. "I've seen you eat. Do 210 you know that? I told the Captain I don't know what you eat, but I've seen you eat like a hound at chow."

"We work hard, Sergeant. We're in training. For a furnace to work, you've got to feed it coal."

"Why did you say in the letter that you threw up all the time?"

"I was really talking about Mickey there. I was talking *for* him. He would never write, Sergeant, though I pleaded with him. He'll waste away to nothing if I don't help. Sergeant, I used my name—my father's name—but it's Mickey, and Fishbein, too, I'm watching out for."

"You're a regular Messiah, aren't you?"

215   We were at the chow line now.

"That's a good one, Sergeant," he said, smiling. "But who knows? Who can tell? Maybe you're the Messiah—a little bit. What Mickey says is the Messiah is a collective idea. He went to Yeshiva, Mickey, for a while. He says *together* we're the Messiah. Me a little bit, you a little bit. You should hear that kid talk, Sergeant, when he gets going."

"Me a little bit, you a little bit," I said. "You'd like to believe that, wouldn't you, Grossbart? That would make everything so clean for you."

"It doesn't seem too bad a thing to believe, Sergeant. It only means we should all *give* a little, is all."

I walked off to eat my rations with the other noncoms.

220   Two days later, a letter addressed to Captain Barrett passed over my desk. It had come through the chain of command—from the office of Congressman Franconi, where it had been received, to General Lyman, to Colonel Sousa, to Major Lamont, now to Captain Barrett. I read it over twice. It was dated May 14, the day Barrett had spoken with Grossbart on the rifle range.

Dear Congressman:

First let me thank you for your interest in behalf of my son, Private Sheldon Grossbart. Fortunately, I was able to speak with Sheldon on the phone the other night, and I think I've been able to solve our problem. He is, as I mentioned in my last letter, a very religious boy, and it was only with the greatest difficulty that I could persuade him that the religious thing to do—what God Himself would want Sheldon to do—would be to suffer the pangs of religious remorse for the good of his country and all mankind. It took some doing, Congressman, but finally he saw the light. In fact, what he said (and I wrote down the words on a scratch pad so as never to forget), what he said was "I guess you're right, Dad. So many millions of my fellow-Jews gave up their lives to the enemy, the least I can do is live for a while minus a bit of my heritage so as to help end this struggle and regain for all the children of God dignity and humanity." That, Congressman, would make any father proud.

By the way, Sheldon wanted me to know—and to pass on to you—the name of a soldier who helped him reach this decision: SERGEANT NATHAN MARX. Sergeant Marx is a combat veteran who is Sheldon's first sergeant. This man has helped Sheldon over some of the first hurdles he's had to face in the Army, and is in part responsible for Sheldon's changing his mind about the dietary laws. I know Sheldon would appreciate any recognition Marx could receive.

Thank you and good luck. I look forward to seeing your name on the next election ballot.

Respectfully,
Samuel E. Grossbart

Attached to the Grossbart communiqué was another, addressed to General Marshall Lyman, the post commander, and signed by Representative Charles E.

Franconi, of the House of Representatives. The communiqué informed General Lyman that Sergeant Nathan Marx was a credit to the U.S. Army and the Jewish people.

What was Grossbart's motive in recanting? Did he feel he'd gone too far? 225 Was the letter a strategic retreat—a crafty attempt to strengthen what he considered our alliance? Or had he actually changed his mind, via an imaginary dialogue between Grossbart *père* and Grossbart *fils?* I was puzzled, but only for a few days—that is, only until I realized that, whatever his reasons, he had actually decided to disappear from my life; he was going to allow himself to become just another trainee. I saw him at inspection, but he never winked; at chow formations, but he never flashed me a sign. On Sunday, with the other trainees, he would sit around watching the noncoms' softball team, for which I pitched, but not once did he speak an unnecessary word to me. Fishbein and Halpern retreated, too—at Grossbart's command, I was sure. Apparently he had seen that wisdom lay in turning back before he plunged over into the ugliness of privilege undeserved. Our separation allowed me to forgive him our past encounters, and finally, to admire him for his good sense.

Meanwhile, free of Grossbart, I grew used to my job and my administrative tasks. I stepped on a scale one day, and discovered I had truly become a noncombatant; I had gained seven pounds. I found patience to get past the first three pages of a book. I thought about the future more and more, and wrote letters to girls I'd known before the war. I even got a few answers. I sent away to Columbia for a Law School catalogue. I continued to follow the war in the Pacific, but it was not my war. I thought I could see the end, and sometimes, at night, I dreamed that I was walking on the streets of Manhattan—Broadway, Third Avenue, 116th Street, where I had lived the three years I attended Columbia. I curled myself around these dreams and I began to be happy.

And then, one Sunday, when everybody was away and I was alone in the orderly room reading a month-old copy of the *Sporting News,* Grossbart reappeared.

"You a baseball fan, Sergeant?"

I looked up. "How are you?"

"Fine," Grossbart said. "They're making a soldier out of me."   230

"How are Fishbein and Halpern?"

"Coming along," he said. "We've got no training this afternoon. They're at the movies."

"How come you're not with them?"

"I wanted to come over and say hello."

He smiled—a shy, regular-guy smile, as though he and I well knew that our 235 friendship drew its sustenance from unexpected visits, remembered birthdays, and borrowed lawnmowers. At first it offended me, and then the feeling was swallowed by the general uneasiness I felt at the thought that everyone on the post was locked away in a dark movie theater and I was here alone with Grossbart. I folded up my paper.

"Sergeant," he said, "I'd like to ask a favor. It is a favor, and I'm making no bones about it."

He stopped, allowing me to refuse him a hearing—which, of course, forced me into a courtesy I did not intend. "Go ahead."

"Well, actually, it's two favors."

I said nothing.

"The first one's about these rumors. Everybody says we're going to the Pacific."

"As I told your friend Fishbein, I don't know," I said. "You'll just have to wait to find out. Like everybody else."

"You think there's a chance of any of us going East?"

"Germany?" I said. "Maybe."

"I meant New York."

"I don't think so, Grossbart. Offhand."

"Thanks for the information, Sergeant," he said.

"It's not information, Grossbart. Just what I surmise."

"It certainly would be good to be near home. My parents—you know." He took a step toward the door and then turned back. "Oh, the other thing. May I ask the other?"

"What is it?"

"The other thing is—I've got relatives in St. Louis, and they say they'll give me a whole Passover dinner if I can get down there. God, Sergeant, that'd mean an awful lot to me."

I stood up. "No passes during basic, Grossbart."

"But we're off from now till Monday morning, Sergeant. I could leave the post and no one would even know."

"I'd know. You'd know."

"But that's all. Just the two of us. Last night, I called my aunt, and you should have heard her. 'Come—come,' she said. 'I got gefilte fish, *chrain*—the works!' Just a day, Sergeant. I'd take the blame if anything happened."

"The Captain isn't here to sign a pass."

"You could sign."

"Look, Grossbart—"

"Sergeant, for two months, practically, I've been eating *trafe* till I want to die."

"I thought you'd made up your mind to live with it. To be minus a little bit of heritage."

He pointed a finger at me. "You!" he said. "That wasn't for you to read."

"I read it. So what?"

"The letter was addressed to a congressman."

"Grossbart, don't feed me any baloney. You *wanted* me to read it."

"Why are you persecuting me, Sergeant?"

"Are you kidding!"

"I've run into this before," he said, "but never from my own!"

"Get out of here, Grossbart! Get the hell out of my sight!"

He did not move. "Ashamed, that's what you are," he said. "So you take it out on the rest of us. They say Hitler himself was half a Jew. Hearing you, I wouldn't doubt it."

"What are you trying to do with me, Grossbart?" I asked him. "What are you after? You want me to give you special privileges, to change the food, to find out about your orders, to give you weekend passes."

"You even talk like a goy!" Grossbart shook his fist. "Is this just a weekend pass   270
I'm asking for? Is a Seder sacred, or not?"

Seder! It suddenly occurred to me that Passover had been celebrated weeks before. I said so.

"That's right," he replied. "Who says no? A month ago—and I was in the field eating hash! And now all I ask is a simple favor. A Jewish boy I thought would understand. My aunt's willing to go out of her way—to make a Seder a month later . . ." He turned to go, mumbling.

"Come back here!" I called. He stopped and looked at me. "Grossbart, why can't you be like the rest? Why do you have to stick out like a sore thumb?"

"Because I'm a Jew, Sergeant. I *am* different. Better, maybe not. But different."

"This is a war, Grossbart. For the time being *be* the same."   275

"I refuse."

"What?"

"I refuse. I can't stop being me, that's all there is to it." Tears came to his eyes. "It's a hard thing to be a Jew. But now I understand what Mickey says—it's a harder thing to stay one." He raised a hand sadly toward me. "Look at *you*."

"Stop crying!"

"Stop this, stop that, stop the other thing! *You* stop, Sergeant. Stop closing your   280
heart to your own!" And, wiping his face with his sleeve, he ran out the door. "The least we can do for one another—the least . . ."

An hour later, looking out of the window, I saw Grossbart headed across the field. He wore a pair of starched khakis and carried a little leather ditty bag. I went out into the heat of the day. It was quiet; not a soul was in sight except, over by the mess hall, four K.P.'s sitting around a pan, sloped forward from their waists, gabbing and peeling potatoes in the sun.

"Grossbart!" I called.

He looked toward me and continued walking.

"Grossbart, get over here!"

He turned and came across the field. Finally, he stood before me.   285

"Where are you going?" I asked.

"St. Louis. I don't care."

"You'll get caught without a pass."

"So I'll get caught without a pass."

"You'll go to the stockade."   290

"I'm *in* the stockade." He made an about-face and headed off.

I let him go only a step or two. "Come back here," I said, and he followed me into the office, where I typed out a pass and signed the Captain's name, and my own initials after it.

He took the pass and then, a moment later, reached out and grabbed my hand. "Sergeant, you don't know how much this means to me."

"O.K.," I said. "Don't get in any trouble."

"I wish I could show you how much this means to me."

"Don't do me any favors. Don't write any more congressmen for citations."

He smiled. "You're right. I won't. But let me do something."

"Bring me a piece of that gefilte fish. Just get out of here."

"I will!" he said. "With a slice of carrot and a little horseradish. I won't forget."

"All right. Just show your pass at the gate. And don't tell *anybody*."

"I won't. It's a month late, but a good Yom Tov to you."

"Good Yom Tov, Grossbart," I said.

"You're a good Jew, Sergeant. You like to think you have a hard heart, but underneath you're a fine, decent man. I mean that."

Those last three words touched me more than any words from Grossbart's mouth had the right to. "All right, Grossbart," I said. "Now call me 'sir,' and get the hell out of here."

He ran out the door and was gone. I felt very pleased with myself; it was a great relief to stop fighting Grossbart, and it had cost me nothing. Barrett would never find out, and if he did, I could manage to invent some excuse. For a while, I sat at my desk, comfortable in my decision. Then the screen door flew back and Grossbart burst in again. "Sergeant!" he said. Behind him I saw Fishbein and Halpern, both in starched khakis, both carrying ditty bags like Grossbart's.

"Sergeant, I caught Mickey and Larry coming out of the movies. I almost missed them."

"Grossbart—did I say to tell no one?" I said.

"But my aunt said I could bring friends. That I should, in fact."

"*I'm* the Sergeant, Grossbart—not your aunt!"

Grossbart looked at me in disbelief. He pulled Halpern up by his sleeve. "Mickey, tell the Sergeant what this would mean to you."

Halpern looked at me and, shrugging, said, "A lot."

Fishbein stepped forward without prompting. "This would mean a great deal to me and my parents, Sergeant Marx."

"No!" I shouted.

Grossbart was shaking his head. "Sergeant, I could see you denying me, but how can you deny Mickey, a Yeshiva boy—that's beyond me."

"I'm not denying Mickey anything," I said. "You just pushed a little too hard, Grossbart. *You* denied him."

"I'll give him my pass, then," Grossbart said. "I'll give him my aunt's address and a little note. At least let him go."

In a second, he had crammed the pass into Halpern's pants pocket. Halpern looked at me, and so did Fishbein. Grossbart was at the door, pushing it open. "Mickey, bring me a piece of gefilte fish, at least," he said, and then he was outside again.

The three of us looked at one another, and then I said, "Halpern, hand that pass over."

He took it from his pocket and gave it to me. Fishbein had now moved to the doorway, where he lingered. He stood there for a moment with his mouth slightly open, and then he pointed to himself. "And me?" he asked.

His utter ridiculousness exhausted me. I slumped down in my seat and felt 320
pulses knocking at the back of my eyes. "Fishbein," I said, "you understand I'm not
trying to deny you anything, don't you? If it was my Army, I'd serve gefilte fish in
the mess hall. I'd sell *kugel* in the PX, honest to God."

Halpern smiled.

"You understand, don't you, Halpern?"

"Yes, Sergeant."

"And you, Fishbein? I don't want enemies. I'm just like you—I want to serve
my time and go home. I miss the same things you miss."

"Then, Sergeant," Fishbein said, "why don't you come, too?"   325

"Where?"

"To St. Louis. To Shelly's aunt. We'll have a regular Seder. Play hide-the-
matzoh." He gave me a broad, black-toothed smile.

I saw Grossbart again, on the other side of the screen.

"Psst!" He waved a piece of paper. "Mickey, here's the address. Tell her I
couldn't get away."

Halpern did not move. He looked at me, and I saw the shrug moving up his arms 330
into his shoulders again. I took the cover off my typewriter and made out passes for
him and Fishbein. "Go," I said. "The three of you."

I thought Halpern was going to kiss my hand.

That afternoon, in a bar in Joplin, I drank beer and listened with half an ear to
the Cardinal game. I tried to look squarely at what I'd become involved in, and began to wonder if perhaps the struggle with Grossbart wasn't as much my fault as
his. What was I that I had to *muster* generous feelings? Who was I to have been
feeling so grudging, so tight-hearted? After all, I wasn't being asked to move the
world. Had I a right, then, or a reason, to clamp down on Grossbart, when that
meant clamping down on Halpern, too? And Fishbein—that ugly, agreeable soul?
Out of the many recollections of my childhood that had tumbled over me these past
days I heard my grandmother's voice: "What are you making a *tsimmes?*" It was
what she would ask my mother when, say, I cut myself while doing something I
shouldn't have done, and her daughter was busy bawling me out. I needed a hug
and a kiss, and my mother would moralize. But my grandmother knew—mercy
overrides justice. I should have known it, too. Who was Nathan Marx to be such a
penny pincher with kindness? Surely, I thought, the Messiah himself—if He
should ever come—won't niggle over nickels and dimes. God willing, he'll hug
and kiss.

The next day, while I was playing softball over on the parade ground, I
decided to ask Bob Wright, who was noncom in charge of Classification and
Assignment, where he thought our trainees would be sent when their cycle
ended, in two weeks. I asked casually, between innings, and he said, "They're
pushing them all into the Pacific. Shulman cut the orders on your boys the
other day."

The news shocked me, as though I were the father of Halpern, Fishbein, and
Grossbart.

335   That night, I was just sliding into sleep when someone tapped on my door. "Who is it?" I asked.

"Sheldon."

He opened the door and came in. For a moment, I felt his presence without being able to see him. "How was it?" I asked.

He popped into sight in the near-darkness before me. "Great, Sergeant." Then he was sitting on the edge of the bed. I sat up.

"How about you?" he asked. "Have a nice weekend?"

340   "Yes."

"The others went to sleep." He took a deep, paternal breath. We sat silent for a while, and a homey feeling invaded my ugly little cubicle; the door was locked, the cat was out, the children were safely in bed.

"Sergeant, can I tell you something? Personal?"

I did not answer, and he seemed to know why. "Not about me. About Mickey. Sergeant, I never felt for anybody like I feel for him. Last night I heard Mickey in the bed next to me. He was crying so, it could have broken your heart. Real sobs."

"I'm sorry to hear that."

345   "I had to talk to him to stop him. He held my hand, Sergeant—he wouldn't let it go. He was almost hysterical. He kept saying if he only knew where we were going. Even if he knew it *was* the Pacific, that would be better than nothing. Just to know."

Long ago, someone had taught Grossbart the sad rule that only lies can get the truth. Not that I couldn't believe in the fact of Halpern's crying; his eyes *always* seemed red-rimmed. But, fact or not, it became a lie when Grossbart uttered it. He was entirely strategic. But then—it came with the force of indictment—so was I! There are strategies of aggression, but there are strategies of retreat as well. And so, recognizing that I myself had not been without craft and guile, I told him what I knew. "It is the Pacific."

He let out a small gasp, which was not a lie. "I'll tell him. I wish it was otherwise."

"So do I."

He jumped on my words. "You mean you think you could do something? A change, maybe?"

350   "No, I couldn't do a thing."

"Don't you know anybody over at C. and A.?"

"Grossbart, there's nothing I can do," I said. "If your orders are for the Pacific, then it's the Pacific."

"But Mickey—"

"Mickey, you, me—everybody, Grossbart. There's nothing to be done. Maybe the war'll end before you go. Pray for a miracle."

355   "But—"

"Good night, Grossbart." I settled back, and was relieved to feel the springs unbend as Grossbart rose to leave. I could see him clearly now; his jaw had dropped, and he looked like a dazed prizefighter. I noticed for the first time a little paper bag in his hand.

"Grossbart." I smiled. "My gift?"

"Oh, yes, Sergeant. Here—from all of us." He handed me the bag. "It's egg roll."

"Egg roll?" I accepted the bag and felt a damp grease spot on the bottom. I opened it, sure that Grossbart was joking.

"We thought you'd probably like it. You know—Chinese egg roll. We thought you'd probably have a taste for—" 360

"Your aunt served egg roll?"

"She wasn't home."

"Grossbart, she invited you. You told me she invited you and your friends."

"I know," he said. "I just reread the letter. *Next* week."

I got out of bed and walked to the window. "Grossbart," I said. But I was not calling to him. 365

"What?"

"What are you, Grossbart? Honest to God, what are you?"

I think it was the first time I'd asked him a question for which he didn't have an immediate answer.

"How can you do this to people?" I went on.

"Sergeant, the day away did us all a world of good. Fishbein, you should see him, he *loves* Chinese food." 370

"But the Seder," I said.

"We took second best, Sergeant."

Rage came charging at me. I didn't sidestep. "Grossbart, you're a liar!" I said. "You're a schemer and a crook. You've got no respect for anything. Nothing at all. Not for me, the truth—not even for poor Halpern. You use us all—"

"Sergeant, Sergeant, I feel for Mickey. Honest to God, I do. I *love* Mickey. I try—"

"You try! You feel!" I lurched toward him and grabbed his shirt front. I shook him furiously. "Grossbart, get out! Get out and stay the hell away from me. Because if I see you, I'll make your life miserable. *You understand that?*" 375

"Yes."

I let him free, and when he walked from the room, I wanted to spit on the floor where he had stood. I couldn't stop the fury. It engulfed me, owned me, till it seemed I could only rid myself of it with tears or an act of violence. I snatched from the bed the bag Grossbart had given me and, with all my strength, threw it out the window. And the next morning, as the men policed the area around the barracks, I heard a great cry go up from one of the trainees, who had been anticipating only his morning handful of cigarette butts and candy wrappers. "Egg roll!" he shouted. "Holy Christ, Chinese goddam egg roll!"

A week later, when I read the orders that had come down from C. and A., I couldn't believe my eyes. Every single trainee was to be shipped to Camp Stoneman, California, and from there to the Pacific—every trainee but one. Private Sheldon Grossbart. He was to be sent to Fort Monmouth, New Jersey. I read the mimeographed sheet several times. Dee, Farrell, Fishbein, Fuselli, Fylypowycz, Glinicki, Gromke, Gucwa, Halpern, Hardy, Helebrandt, right down to Anton Zygadlo—all were to be headed West before the month was out. All except Grossbart. He had pulled a string, and I wasn't it.

I lifted the phone and called C. and A.

380 The voice on the other end said smartly, "Corporal Shulman, sir."

"Let me speak to Sergeant Wright."

"Who is this calling, sir?"

"Sergeant Marx."

And, to my surprise, the voice said, "*Oh!*" Then, "Just a minute, Sergeant."

385 Shulman's "*Oh!*" stayed with me while I waited for Wright to come to the phone. Why "*Oh!*"? Who was Shulman? And then, so simply, I knew I'd discovered the string that Grossbart had pulled. In fact, I could hear Grossbart the day he'd discovered Shulman in the PX, or in the bowling alley, or maybe even at services. "Glad to meet you. Where you from? Bronx? Me, too. Do you know So-and-So? And So-and-So? Me, too! You work at C. and A.? Really? Hey, how's chances of getting East? Could you do something? Change something? Swindle, cheat, lie? We gotta help each other, you know. If the Jews in Germany . . ."

Bob Wright answered the phone. "How are you, Nate? How's the pitching arm?"

"Good. Bob, I wonder if you could do me a favor." I heard clearly my own words, and they so reminded me of Grossbart that I dropped more easily than I could have imagined into what I had planned. "This may sound crazy, Bob, but I got a kid here on orders to Monmouth who wants them changed. He had a brother killed in Europe, and he's hot to go to the Pacific. Says he'd feel like a coward if he wound up Stateside. I don't know, Bob—can anything be done? Put somebody else in the Monmouth slot?"

"Who?" he asked cagily.

"Anybody. First guy in the alphabet. I don't care. The kid just asked if something could be done."

390 "What's his name?"

"Grossbart, Sheldon."

Wright didn't answer.

"Yeah," I said. "He's a Jewish kid, so he thought I could help him out. You know."

"I guess I can do something," he finally said. "The Major hasn't been around for weeks. Temporary duty to the golf course. I'll try, Nate, that's all I can say."

395 "I'd appreciate it, Bob. See you Sunday." And I hung up, perspiring.

The following day, the corrected orders appeared: Fishbein, Fuselli, Fylypowycz, Glinicki, Gromke, Grossbart, Gucwa, Halpern, Hardy . . . Lucky Private Harley Alton was to go to Fort Monmouth, New Jersey, where, for some reason or other, they wanted an enlisted man with infantry training.

After chow that night, I stopped back at the orderly room to straighten out the guard-duty roster. Grossbart was waiting for me. He spoke first.

"You son of a bitch!"

I sat down at my desk, and while he glared at me, I began to make the necessary alterations in the duty roster.

400 "What do you have against me?" he cried. "Against my family? Would it kill you for me to be near my father, God knows how many months he has left to him?"

"Why so?"

"His heart," Grossbart said. "He hasn't had enough troubles in a lifetime, you've got to add to them. I curse the day I ever met you, Marx! Shulman told me what happened over there. There's no limit to your anti-Semitism, is there? The damage you've done here isn't enough. You have to make a special phone call! You really want me dead!"

I made the last notations in the duty roster and got up to leave. "Good night, Grossbart."

"You owe me an explanation!" He stood in my path.

"Sheldon, you're the one who owes explanations."   405

He scowled. "To *you?*"

"To me, I think so—yes. Mostly to Fishbein and Halpern."

"That's right, twist things around. I owe nobody nothing. I've done all I could for them. Now I think I've got the right to watch out for myself."

"For each other we have to learn to watch out, Sheldon. You told me yourself."

"You call this watching out for me—what you did?"   410

"No. For all of us."

I pushed him aside and started for the door. I heard his furious breathing behind me, and it sounded like steam rushing from an engine of terrible strength.

"*You'll* be all right," I said from the door. And, I thought, so would Fishbein and Halpern be all right, even in the Pacific, if only Grossbart continued to see—in the obsequiousness of the one, the soft spirituality of the other—some profit for himself.

I stood outside the orderly room, and I heard Grossbart weeping behind me. Over in the barracks, in the lighted windows, I could see the boys in their T shirts sitting on their bunks talking about their orders, as they'd been doing for the past two days. With a kind of quiet nervousness, they polished shoes, shined belt buckles, squared away underwear, trying as best they could to accept their fate. Behind me, Grossbart swallowed hard, accepting his. And then, resisting with all my will an impulse to turn and seek pardon for my vindictiveness, I accepted my own.

QUESTIONS FOR DISCUSSION AND WRITING

1. How many different conflicts does Sheldon Grossbart create in attempting to claim his rights? Explain how Grossbart's trip to St. Louis brings these conflicts to a crisis. How does Marx resolve the trouble Grossbart causes?

2. How does Marx characterize the three Jewish recruits to Captain Barrett? How does Captain Barrett describe Marx to the three recruits? What specific features of Grossbart's character does Marx find most exasperating?

3. What details in the story best reveal the value of army life as Marx sees it? What past life has he "anesthetized" in order to pursue his life in the army? How does Grossbart's attempt to evoke that other life give him a momentary advantage in his attempt to manipulate Marx?

4. How does Marx's first-person narration help characterize the dilemmas that Grossbart forces him to face? How do Marx's actions and judgments alter his initial description of his "infantryman's heart"? To what extent does his final decision reestablish that point of view?

5. Why does Grossbart's defense of his faith seem "entirely strategic"? How many different "faiths" is Marx asked to defend in this story? Is he able to defend them all? Explain your answer.

Stories for Comparison

Albert Camus's "The Guest" (pages 329–338); Frank O'Connor's "Guests of the Nation" (pages 995–1003).

86

....

LESLIE MARMON SILKO

Storyteller

LESLIE MARMON SILKO, a Laguna Pueblo Indian, was born in 1948 in New Mexico and educated at the University of New Mexico. After teaching at various colleges, she became a professor of English at the University of Arizona. Silko's first novel, *Ceremony* (1977), is regarded as one of the most important books in modern Native American literature. Her second novel, *Almanac of the Dead* (1991), deals with the reclamation of the New World by its indigenous people. She has also published a collection of poems, *Laguna Woman: Poems* (1994); a collection of folktales, stories, and familiar narratives, *Storyteller* (1981); and a series of essays on Native American life today, *Yellow Woman and the Beauty of the Spirit* (1996). In "Storyteller," the title story of that collection, a young girl's curiosity enables her to interpret her grandfather's story.

Every day the sun came up a little lower on the horizon, moving more slowly until one day she got excited and started calling the jailer. She realized she had been sitting there for many hours, yet the sun had not moved from the center of the sky. The color of the sky had not been good lately; it had been pale blue, almost white, even when there were no clouds. She told herself it wasn't a good sign for the sky to be indistinguishable from the river ice, frozen solid and white against the earth. The tundra rose up behind the river but all the boundaries between the river and hills and sky were lost in the density of the pale ice.

She yelled again, this time some English words which came randomly into her mouth, probably swear words she'd heard from the oil drilling crews last winter. The jailer was an Eskimo, but he would not speak Yupik to her. She had watched people in other cells, when they spoke to him in Yupik he ignored them until they spoke English.

He came and stared at her. She didn't know if he understood what she was telling him until he glanced behind her at the small high window. He looked at the sun, and turned and walked away. She could hear the buckles on his heavy snow-mobile boots jingle as he walked to the front of the building.

It was like the other buildings that white people, the Gussucks, brought with them: BIA and school buildings, portable buildings that arrived sliced in halves, on barges coming up the river. Squares of metal panelling bulged out with the layers of insulation stuffed inside. She had asked once what it was and someone told her it was to keep out the cold. She had not laughed then, but she did now. She walked over to the small double-pane window and she laughed out loud. They thought they could keep out the cold with stringy yellow wadding. Look at the sun. It wasn't moving; it was frozen, caught in the middle of the sky. Look at the sky, solid as the river with ice which had trapped the sun. It had not moved for a long time; in a few more hours it would be weak, and heavy frost would begin to appear on the edges and spread across the face of the sun like a mask. Its light was pale yellow, worn thin by the winter.

She could see people walking down the snow-packed roads, their breath steam- 5
ing out from their parka hoods, faces hidden and protected by deep ruffs of fur. There were no cars or snowmobiles that day; the cold had silenced their machines. The metal froze; it split and shattered. Oil hardened and moving parts jammed solidly. She had seen it happen to their big yellow machines and the giant drill last winter when they came to drill their test holes. The cold stopped them, and they were helpless against it.

Her village was many miles upriver from this town, but in her mind she could see it clearly. Their house was not near the village houses. It stood alone on the bank upriver from the village. Snow had drifted to the eaves of the roof on the north side, but on the west side, by the door, the path was almost clear. She had nailed scraps of red tin over the logs last summer. She had done it for the bright red color, not for added warmth the way the village people had done. This final winter had been coming even then; there had been signs of its approach for many years.

She went because she was curious about the big school where the Government sent all the other girls and boys. She had not played much with the village children while she was growing up because they were afraid of the old man, and they ran when her grandmother came. She went because she was tired of being alone with the old woman whose body had been stiffening for as long as the girl could remember. Her knees and knuckles were swollen grotesquely, and the pain had squeezed the brown skin of her face tight against the bones; it left her eyes hard like river stone.

The girl asked once what it was that did this to her body, and the old woman had raised up from sewing a sealskin boot, and stared at her.

"The joints," the old woman said in a low voice, whispering like wind across the roof, "the joints are swollen with anger."

Sometimes she did not answer and only stared at the girl. Each year she spoke less and less, but the old man talked more—all night sometimes, not to anyone but himself; in a soft deliberate voice, he told stories, moving his smooth brown hands above the blankets. He had not fished or hunted with the other men for many years, although he was not crippled or sick. He stayed in his bed, smelling like dry fish and urine, telling stories all winter; and when warm weather came, he went to his place on the river bank. He sat with a long willow stick, poking at the smoldering moss he burned against the insects while he continued with the stories.

10   The trouble was that she had not recognized the warnings in time. She did not see what the Gussuck school would do to her until she walked into the dormitory and realized that the old man had not been lying about the place. She thought he had been trying to scare her as he used to when she was very small and her grandmother was outside cutting up fish. She hadn't believed what he told her about the school because she knew he wanted to keep her there in the log house with him. She knew what he wanted.

The dormitory matron pulled down her underpants and whipped her with a leather belt because she refused to speak English.

"Those backwards village people," the matron said, because she was an Eskimo who had worked for the BIA a long time, "they kept this one until she was too big to learn." The other girls whispered in English. They knew how to work the showers, and they washed and curled their hair at night. They ate Gussuck food. She lay on her bed and imagined what her grandmother might be sewing, and what the old man was eating in his bed. When summer came, they sent her home.

The way her grandmother had hugged her before she left for school had been a warning too, because the old woman had not hugged or touched her for many years. Not like the old man, whose hands were always hunting, like ravens circling lazily in the sky, ready to touch her. She was not surprised when the priest and the old man met her at the landing strip, to say that the old lady was gone. The priest asked her where she would like to stay. He referred to the old man as her grandfather, but she did not bother to correct him. She had already been thinking about it; if she went with the priest, he would send her away to a school. But the old man was different. She knew he wouldn't send her back to school. She knew he wanted to keep her.

He told her one time, that she would get too old for him faster than he got too old for her; but again she had not believed him because sometimes he lied. He had lied about what he would do with her if she came into his bed. But as the years passed, she realized what he said was true. She was restless and strong. She had no patience with the old man who had never changed his slow smooth motions under the blankets.

15   The old man was in his bed for the winter; he did not leave it except to use the slop bucket in the corner. He was dozing with his mouth open slightly; his lips

quivered and sometimes they moved like he was telling a story even while he dreamed. She pulled on the sealskin boots, the mukluks with the bright red flannel linings her grandmother had sewn for her, and she tied the braided red yarn tassels around her ankles over the gray wool pants. She zipped the wolfskin parka. Her grandmother had worn it for many years, but the old man said that before she died, she instructed him to bury her in an old black sweater, and to give the parka to the girl. The wolf pelts were creamy colored and silver, almost white in some places, and when the old lady had walked across the tundra in the winter, she was invisible in the snow.

She walked toward the village, breaking her own path through the deep snow. A team of sled dogs tied outside a house at the edge of the village leaped against their chains to bark at her. She kept walking, watching the dusky sky for the first evening stars. It was warm and the dogs were alert. When it got cold again, the dogs would lie curled and still, too drowsy from the cold to bark or pull at the chains. She laughed loudly because it made them howl and snarl. Once the old man had seen her tease the dogs and he shook his head. "So that's the kind of woman you are," he said, "in the wintertime the two of us are no different from those dogs. We wait in the cold for someone to bring us a few dry fish."

She laughed out loud again, and kept walking. She was thinking about the Gussuck oil drillers. They were strange; they watched her when she walked near their machines. She wondered what they looked like underneath their quilted goosedown trousers; she wanted to know how they moved. They would be something different from the old man.

The old man screamed at her. He shook her shoulders so violently that her head bumped against the log wall. "I smelled it!" he yelled, "as soon as I woke up! I am sure of it now. You can't fool me!" His thin legs were shaking inside the baggy wool trousers; he stumbled over her boots in his bare feet. His toenails were long and yellow like bird claws; she had seen a gray crane last summer fighting another in the shallow water on the edge of the river. She laughed out loud and pulled her shoulder out of his grip. He stood in front of her. He was breathing hard and shaking; he looked weak. He would probably die next winter.

"I'm warning you," he said, "I'm warning you." He crawled back into his bunk then, and reached under the old soiled feather pillow for a piece of dry fish. He lay back on the pillow, staring at the ceiling and chewed dry strips of salmon. "I don't know what the old woman told you," he said, "but there will be trouble." He looked over to see if she was listening. His face suddenly relaxed into a smile, his dark slanty eyes were lost in wrinkles of brown skin. "I could tell you, but you are too good for warnings now. I can smell what you did all night with the Gussucks."

She did not understand why they came there, because the village was small and so far upriver that even some Eskimos who had been away to school did not want to come back. They stayed downriver in the town. They said the village was too quiet. They were used to the town where the boarding school was located, with electric lights and running water. After all those years away at school, they had forgotten how to set nets in the river and where to hunt seals in the fall. When she asked the old man why the Gussucks bothered to come to the village, his narrow eyes got bright with excitement.

"They only come when there is something to steal. The fur animals are too difficult for them to get now, and the seals and fish are hard to find. Now they come for oil deep in the earth. But this is the last time for them." His breathing was wheezy and fast; his hands gestured at the sky. "It is approaching. As it comes, ice will push across the sky." His eyes were open wide and he stared at the low ceiling rafters for hours without blinking. She remembered all this clearly because he began the story that day, the story he told from that time on. It began with a giant bear which he described muscle by muscle, from the curve of the ivory claws to the whorls of hair at the top of the massive skull. And for eight days he did not sleep, but talked continuously of the giant bear whose color was pale blue glacier ice.

The snow was dirty and worn down in a path to the door. On either side of the path, the snow was higher than her head. In front of the door there were jagged yellow stains melted into the snow where men had urinated. She stopped in the entry way and kicked the snow off her boots. The room was dim; a kerosene lantern by the cash register was burning low. The long wooden shelves were jammed with cans of beans and potted meats. On the bottom shelf a jar of mayonnaise was broken open, leaking oily white clots on the floor. There was no one in the room except the yellowish dog sleeping in the front of the long glass display case. A reflection made it appear to be lying on the knives and ammunition inside the case. Gussucks kept dogs inside their houses with them; they did not seem to mind the odors which seeped out of the dogs. "They tell us we are dirty for the food we eat—raw fish and fermented meat. But we do not live with dogs," the old man once said. She heard voices in the back room, and the sound of bottles set down hard on tables.

They were always confident. The first year they waited for the ice to break up on the river, and then they brought their big yellow machines up river on barges. They planned to drill their test holes during the summer to avoid the freezing. But the imprints and graves of their machines were still there, on the edge of the tundra above the river, where the summer mud had swallowed them before they ever left sight of the river. The village people had gathered to watch the white men, and to laugh as they drove the giant machines, one by one, off the steel ramp into the bogs; as if sheer numbers of vehicles would somehow make the tundra solid. But the old man said they behaved like desperate people, and they would come back again. When the tundra was frozen solid, they returned.

Village women did not even look through the door to the back room. The priest had warned them. The storeman was watching her because he didn't let Eskimos or Indians sit down at the tables in the back room. But she knew he couldn't throw her out if one of his Gussuck customers invited her to sit with him. She walked across the room. They stared at her, but she had the feeling she was walking for someone else, not herself, so their eyes did not matter. The red-haired man pulled out a chair and motioned for her to sit down. She looked back at the storeman while the red-haired man poured her a glass of red sweet wine. She wanted to laugh at the storeman the way she laughed at the dogs, straining against the chains, howling at her.

The red-haired man kept talking to the other Gussucks sitting around the table, [25] but he slid one hand off the top of the table to her thigh. She looked over at the storeman to see if he was still watching her. She laughed out loud at him and the red-haired man stopped talking and turned to her. He asked if she wanted to go. She nodded and stood up.

Someone in the village had been telling him things about her, he said as they walked down the road to his trailer. She understood that much of what he was saying, but the rest she did not hear. The whine of the big generators at the construction camp sucked away the sound of his words. But English was of no concern to her anymore, and neither was anything the Christians in the village might say about her or the old man. She smiled at the effect of the subzero air on the electric lights around the trailers; they did not shine. They left only flat yellow holes in the darkness.

It took him a long time to get ready, even after she had undressed for him. She waited in the bed with the blankets pulled close, watching him. He adjusted the thermostat and lit candles in the room, turning out the electric lights. He searched through a stack of record albums until he found the right one. She was not sure about the last thing he did: he taped something on the wall behind the bed where he could see it while he lay on top of her. He was shriveled and white from the cold; he pushed against her body for warmth. He guided her hands to his thighs; he was shivering.

She had returned a last time because she wanted to know what it was he stuck on the wall above the bed. After he finished each time, he reached up and pulled it loose, folding it carefully so that she could not see it. But this time she was ready; she waited for his fast breathing and sudden collapse on top of her. She slid out from under him and stood up beside the bed. She looked at the picture while she got dressed. He did not raise his face from the pillow, and she thought she heard teeth rattling together as she left the room.

She heard the old man move when she came in. After the Gussuck's trailer, the log house felt cool. It smelled like dry fish and cured meat. The room was dark except for the blinking yellow flame in the mica window of the oil stove. She squatted in front of the stove and watched the flames for a long time before she walked to the bed where her grandmother had slept. The bed was covered with a mound of rags and fur scraps the old woman had saved. She reached into the mound until she felt something cold and solid wrapped in a wool blanket. She pushed her fingers around it until she felt smooth stone. Long ago, before the Gussucks came, they had burned whale oil in the big stone lamp which made light and heat as well. The old woman had saved everything they would need when the time came.

In the morning, the old man pulled a piece of dry caribou meat from under the [30] blankets and offered it to her. While she was gone, men from the village had brought a bundle of dry meat. She chewed it slowly, thinking about the way they still came from the village to take care of the old man and his stories. But she had a story now, about the red-haired Gussuck. The old man knew what she was thinking, and his smile made his face seem more round than it was.

"Well," he said, "what was it?"

"A woman with a big dog on top of her."

He laughed softly to himself and walked over to the water barrel. He dipped the tin cup into the water.

"It doesn't surprise me," he said.

35　　"Grandma," she said, "there was something red in the grass that morning. I remember." She had not asked about her parents before. The old woman stopped splitting the fish bellies open for the willow drying racks. Her jaw muscles pulled so tightly against her skull, the girl thought the old woman would not be able to speak.

"They bought a tin can full of it from the storeman. Late at night. He told them it was alcohol safe to drink. They traded a rifle for it." The old woman's voice sounded like each word stole strength from her. "It made no difference about the rifle. That year the Gussuck boats had come, firing big guns at the walrus and seals. There was nothing left to hunt after that anyway. So," the old lady said, in a low soft voice the girl had not heard for a long time, "I didn't say anything to them when they left that night."

"Right over there," she said, pointing at the fallen poles, half buried in the river sand and tall grass, "in the summer shelter. The sun was high half the night then. Early in the morning when it was still low, the policeman came around. I told the interpreter to tell him that the storeman had poisoned them." She made outlines in the air in front of her, showing how their bodies lay twisted on the sand; telling the story was like laboring to walk through deep snow; sweat shone in the white hair around her forehead. "I told the priest too, after he came. I told him the storeman lied." She turned away from the girl. She held her mouth even tighter, set solidly, not in sorrow or anger, but against the pain, which was all that remained. "I never believed," she said, "not much anyway. I wasn't surprised when the priest did nothing."

The wind came off the river and folded the tall grass into itself like river waves. She could feel the silence the story left, and she wanted to have the old woman go on.

"I heard sounds that night, grandma. Sounds like someone was singing. It was light outside. I could see something red on the ground." The old woman did not answer her; she moved to the tub full of fish on the ground beside the workbench. She stabbed her knife into the belly of a whitefish and lifted it onto the bench. "The Gussuck storeman left the village right after that," the old woman said as she pulled the entrails from the fish, "otherwise, I could tell you more." The old woman's voice flowed with the wind blowing off the river; they never spoke of it again.

40　　When the willows got their leaves and the grass grew tall along the river banks and around the sloughs, she walked early in the morning. While the sun was still low on the horizon, she listened to the wind off the river; its sound was like the voice that day long ago. In the distance, she could hear the engines of the machinery the oil drillers had left the winter before, but she did not go near the village or the store. The sun never left the sky and the summer became the same long day, with only the winds to fan the sun into brightness or allow it to slip into twilight.

She sat beside the old man at his place on the river bank. She poked the smoky fire for him, and felt herself growing wide and thin in the sun as if she had been split from belly to throat and strung on the willow pole in preparation for the winter to come. The old man did not speak anymore. When men from the village brought him fresh fish he hid them deep in the river grass where it was cool. After he went inside, she split the fish open and spread them to dry on the willow frame the way the old woman had done. Inside, he dozed and talked to himself. He had talked all winter, softly and incessantly, about the giant polar bear stalking a lone hunter across Bering Sea ice. After all the months the old man had been telling the story, the bear was within a hundred feet of the man; but the ice fog had closed in on them now and the man could only smell the sharp ammonia odor of the bear, and hear the edge of the snow crust crack under the giant paws.

One night she listened to the old man tell the story all night in his sleep, describing each crystal of ice and the slightly different sounds they made under each paw; first the left and then the right paw, then the hind feet. Her grandmother was there suddenly, a shadow around the stove. She spoke in her low wind voice and the girl was afraid to sit up to hear more clearly. Maybe what she said had been to the old man because he stopped telling the story and began to snore softly the way he had long ago when the old woman had scolded him for telling his stories while others in the house were trying to sleep. But the last words she heard clearly: "It will take a long time, but the story must be told. There must not be any lies." She pulled the blankets up around her chin, slowly, so that her movements would not be seen. She thought her grandmother was talking about the old man's bear story; she did not know about the other story then.

She left the old man wheezing and snoring in his bed. She walked through river grass glistening with frost; the bright green summer color was already fading. She watched the sun move across the sky, already lower on the horizon, already moving away from the village. She stopped by the fallen poles of the summer shelter where her parents had died. Frost glittered on the river sand too; in a few more weeks there would be snow. The predawn light would be the color of an old woman. An old woman sky full of snow. There had been something red lying on the ground the morning they died. She looked for it again, pushing aside the grass with her foot. She knelt in the sand and looked under the fallen structure for some trace of it. When she found it, she would know what the old woman had never told her. She squatted down close to the gray poles and leaned her back against them. The wind made her shiver.

The summer rain had washed the mud from between the logs; the sod blocks stacked as high as her belly next to the log walls had lost their square-cut shape and had grown into soft mounds of tundra moss and stiff-bladed grass bending with clusters of seed bristles. She looked at the northwest, in the direction of the Bering Sea. The cold would come down from there to find narrow slits in the mud, rainwater holes in the outer layer of sod which protected the log house. The dark green tundra stretched away flat and continuous. Somewhere the sea and the land met; she knew by their dark green colors there were no boundaries between them. That was how the cold would come: when the boundaries were gone the polar ice would range across the land into the sky. She watched the horizon for a long time. She would stand in that place on the north side of the house and she would keep watch on the northwest horizon, and eventually she would see it come. She would watch for its approach in the stars, and hear it come with the wind. These preparations were unfamiliar, but gradually she recognized them as she did her own footprints in the snow.

45   She emptied the slop jar beside his bed twice a day and kept the barrel full of water melted from river ice. He did not recognize her anymore, and when he spoke to her, he called her by her grandmother's name and talked about people and events from long ago, before he went back to telling the story. The giant bear was creeping across the new snow on its belly, close enough now that the man could hear the rasp of its breathing. On and on in a soft singing voice, the old man caressed the story, repeating the words again and again like gentle strokes.

The sky was gray like a river crane's egg; its density curved into the thin crust of frost already covering the land. She looked at the bright red color of the tin against the ground and the sky and she told the village men to bring the pieces for the old man and her. To drill the test holes in the tundra, the Gussucks had used hundreds of barrels of fuel. The village people split open the empty barrels that were abandoned on the river bank, and pounded the red tin into flat sheets. The village people were using the strips of tin to mend walls and roofs for winter. But she nailed it on the log walls for its color. When she finished, she walked away with the hammer in her hand, not turning around until she was far away, on the ridge above the river banks, and then she looked back. She felt a chill when she saw how the sky and the land were already losing their boundaries, already becoming lost in each other. But the red tin penetrated the thick white color of earth and sky; it defined the boundaries like a wound revealing the ribs and heart of a great caribou about to bolt and be lost to the hunter forever. That night the wind howled and when she scratched a hole through the heavy frost on the inside of the window, she could see nothing but the impenetrable white; whether it was blowing snow or snow that had drifted as high as the house, she did not know.

It had come down suddenly, and she stood with her back to the wind looking at the river, its smoky water clotted with ice. The wind had blown the snow over the frozen river, hiding thin blue streaks where fast water ran under ice translucent and fragile as memory. But she could see shadows of boundaries, outlines of paths which were slender branches of solidity reaching out from the earth. She spent days walking on the river, watching the colors of ice that would safely hold her, kicking the heel of her boot into the snow crust, listening for a solid sound. When she could feel the paths through the soles of her feet, she went to the middle of the river where the fast gray water churned under a thin pane of ice. She looked back. On the river bank in the distance she could see the red tin nailed to the log house, something not swallowed up by the heavy white belly of the sky or caught in the folds of the frozen earth. It was time.

The wolverine fur around the hood of her parka was white with the frost from her breathing. The warmth inside the store melted it, and she felt tiny drops of water on her face. The storeman came in from the back room. She unzipped the parka and stood by the oil stove. She didn't look at him, but stared instead at the yellowish dog, covered with scabs of matted hair, sleeping in front of the stove. She thought of the Gussuck's picture, taped on the wall above the bed and she laughed out loud. The sound of her laughter was piercing; the yellow dog jumped to its feet and the hair bristled down its back. The storeman was watching her. She wanted to laugh again because he didn't know about the ice. He did not know that it was prowling the earth, or that it had already pushed its way into the sky to seize the sun. She sat down in the chair by the stove and shook her long hair loose. He was like a dog tied up all winter, watching while the others got fed. He remembered how she had gone with the oil drillers, and his blue eyes moved like flies crawling over her body. He held his thin pale lips like he wanted to spit on her. He hated the people because they had something of value, the old man said, something which the Gussucks could never have. They thought they could take it, suck it out of the earth or cut it from the mountains; but they were fools.

There was a matted hunk of dog hair on the floor by her foot. She thought of the yellow insulation coming unstuffed: their defense against the freezing going to pieces as it advanced on them. The ice was crouching on the northwest horizon like the old man's bear. She laughed out loud again. The sun would be down now; it was time.

The first time he spoke to her, she did not hear what he said, so she did not answer or even look up at him. He spoke to her again but his words were only noises coming from his pale mouth, trembling now as his anger began to unravel. He jerked her up and the chair fell over behind her. His arms were shaking and she could feel his hands tense up, pulling the edges of the parka tighter. He raised his fist to hit her, his thin body quivering with rage; but the fist collapsed with the desire he had for the valuable things, which, the old man had rightly said, was the only reason they came. She could hear his heart pounding as he held her close and arched his hips against her, groaning and breathing in spasms. She twisted away from him and ducked under his arms.

She ran with a mitten over her mouth, breathing through the fur to protect her lungs from the freezing air. She could hear him running behind her, his heavy breathing, the occasional sound of metal jingling against metal. But he ran without his parka or mittens, breathing the frozen air; its fire squeezed the lungs against the ribs and it was enough that he could not catch her near his store. On the river bank he realized how far he was from his stove, and the wads of yellow stuffing that held off the cold. But the girl was not able to run very fast through the deep drifts at the edge of the river. The twilight was luminous and he could still see clearly for a long distance; he knew he could catch her so he kept running.

When she neared the middle of the river she looked over her shoulder. He was not following her tracks; he went straight across the ice, running the shortest distance to reach her. He was close then; his face was twisted and scarlet from the exertion and the cold. There was satisfaction in his eyes; he was sure he could outrun her.

She was familiar with the river, down to the instant ice flexed into hairline fractures, and the cracking bone-sliver sounds gathered momentum with the opening ice until the churning gray water was set free. She stopped and turned to the sound of the river and the rattle of swirling ice fragments where he fell through. She pulled off a mitten and zipped the parka to her throat. She was conscious then of her own rapid breathing.

She moved slowly, kicking the ice ahead with the heel of her boot, feeling for sinews of ice to hold her. She looked ahead and all around herself; in the twilight, the dense white sky had merged into the flat snow-covered tundra. In the frantic running she had lost her place on the river. She stood still. The east bank of the river was lost in the sky; the boundaries had been swallowed by the freezing white. But then, in the distance, she saw something red, and suddenly it was as she had remembered it all those years.

55   She sat on her bed and while she waited, she listened to the old man. The hunter had found a small jagged knoll on the ice. He pulled his beaver fur cap off his head; the fur inside it steamed with his body heat and sweat. He left it upside down on the ice for the great bear to stalk, and he waited downwind on top of the ice knoll; he was holding the jade knife.

She thought she could see the end of his story in the way he wheezed out the words; but still he reached into his cache of dry fish and dribbled water into his mouth from the tin cup. All night she listened to him describe each breath the man took, each motion of the bear's head as it tried to catch the sound of the man's breathing, and tested the wind for his scent.

The state trooper asked her questions, and the woman who cleaned house for the priest translated them into Yupik. They wanted to know what happened to the store-man, the Gussuck who had been seen running after her down the road onto the river late last evening. He had not come back, and the Gussuck boss in Anchorage was concerned about him. She did not answer for a long time because the old man suddenly sat up in his bed and began to talk excitedly, looking at all of them—the trooper in his dark glasses and the housekeeper in her corduroy parka. He kept saying, "The story! The story! Eh-ya! The great bear! The hunter!"

They asked her again, what happened to the man from the Northern Commercial store. "He lied to them. He told them it was safe to drink. But I will not lie." She stood up and put on the gray wolfskin parka. "I killed him," she said, "but I don't lie."

The attorney came back again, and the jailer slid open the steel doors and opened the cell to let him in. He motioned for the jailer to stay to translate for him. She laughed when she saw how the jailer would be forced by this Gussuck to speak Yupik to her. She liked the Gussuck attorney for that, and for the thinning hair on his head. He was very tall, and she like to think about the exposure of his head to the freezing; she wondered if he would feel the ice descending from the sky before the others did. He wanted to know why she told the state trooper she had killed the store-man. Some village children had seen it happen, he said, and it was an accident. "That's all you have to say to the judge: it was an accident." He kept repeating it over and over again to her, slowly in a loud but gentle voice: "It was an accident. He was running after you and he fell through the ice. That's all you have to say in court. That's all. And they will let you go home. Back to your village." The jailer translated the words sullenly, staring down at the floor. She shook her head. "I will not change the story, not even to escape this place and go home. I intended that he die. The story must be told as it is." The attorney exhaled loudly; his eyes looked tired. "Tell her that she could not have killed him that way. He was a white man. He ran after her without a parka or mittens. She could not have planned that." He paused and turned toward the cell door. "Tell her I will do all I can for her. I will explain to the judge that her mind is confused." She laughed out loud when the jailer translated what the attorney said. The Gussucks did not understand the story; they could not see the way it must be told, year after year as the old man had done, without lapse or silence.

She looked out the window at the frozen white sky. The sun had finally broken 60 loose from the ice but it moved like a wounded caribou running on strength which only dying animals find, leaping and running on bullet-shattered lungs. Its light was weak and pale; it pushed dimly through the clouds. She turned and faced the Gussuck attorney.

"It began a long time ago," she intoned steadily, "in the summertime. Early in the morning, I remember, something red in the tall river grass. . . ."

The day after the old man died, men from the village came. She was sitting on the edge of her bed, across from the woman the trooper hired to watch her. They came into the room slowly and listened to her. At the foot of her bed they left a king salmon that had been slit open wide and dried last summer. But she did not pause or hesitate; she went on with the story, and she never stopped, not even when the woman got up to close the door behind the village men.

The old man would not change the story even when he knew the end was approaching. Lies could not stop what was coming. He thrashed around on the bed, pulling the blankets loose, knocking bundles of dried fish and meat on the floor. The hunter had been on the ice for many hours. The freezing winds on the ice knoll had numbed his hands in the mittens, and the cold had exhausted him. He felt a single muscle tremor in his hand that he could not stop, and the jade knife fell; it shattered on the ice, and the blue glacier bear turned slowly to face him.

QUESTIONS FOR DISCUSSION AND WRITING

1. How does the color red serve as a structuring device in this story? How does the plot of the old man's story about the ice-blue bear parallel the story as a whole? Why does Silko begin her story with the protagonist's recognition that the sun is frozen in the sky?

2. What do we understand about the protagonist as a result of her frequent observations about the disappearance of all boundaries in her world? What does her laughter reveal about her character?

3. What are the fundamental differences between the Yupik and Gussuck cultures? What are the differences between the grandfather's cabin and the oil-driller's trailer? How do the two cultures' attitudes toward dogs reveal their differences?

4. How do we know the narrator's sympathies are with the Yupiks even though she seems to maintain an objective point of view about the facts? Why does the protagonist insist on her guilt in the "murder" of the storekeeper? How does the lawyer reinterpret her story?

5. What does the "story" reveal about the importance of *storytellers* and *stories* to a culture? What sort of cultural narrative would the Gussucks tell to explain their behavior in the Yupik world?

Stories for Comparison

Margaret Atwood's "Dancing Girls" (pages 204–214); Louise Erdrich's "The Red Convertible" (pages 483–490).

87

....

ISAAC BASHEVIS SINGER

Gimpel the Fool

ISAAC BASHEVIS SINGER (1904–1991) was born in Radzymin, Poland, and educated at Tachkemoni Rabbinical Seminary in Warsaw. After working for over a decade as translator and editor for the Polish press, he emigrated to the United States in 1935 and worked for the *Jewish Daily Forward* in New York City, where he began publishing his stories and sketches in Yiddish. Before he felt sufficiently fluent in English, Singer had to rely on other people to translate his writing. In 1950, he published his first novel in America, *The Family Moskat*, but his discovery by American readers was probably initiated in 1953 by Saul Bellow's magnificent translation of "Gimpel the Fool" for *Partisan Review*. Most of Singer's works draw upon his experiences in the Yiddish-speaking Jewish ghettos of Poland and are preoccupied with the problems of sin and the character of the religious life. His novels include *The Magician of Lublin* (1960), *The Slave* (1962), *The Manor* (1968), *Enemies: A Love Story* (1972), and *Shosha* (1978). He is also the author of an award-winning children's book, *A Day of Pleasure* (1970), and an autobiography, *In My Father's Court* (1966). Singer's many stories are collected in volumes such as *The Spinoza of Market Street and Other Stories* (1961), *A Friend of Kafka's* (1970), and *A Crown of Feathers* (1973), which won the National Book Award. His *Collected Stories* (1981) won the Pulitzer Prize. In 1978, Singer was awarded the Nobel Prize for Literature. "Gimpel the Fool," reprinted from *A Treasury of Yiddish Stories* (1953), tells of a man who was thought a fool because of his belief that "everything is possible."

I

I am Gimpel the fool. I don't think myself a fool. On the contrary. But that's what folks call me. They gave me the name while I was still in school. I had seven names in all: imbecile, donkey, flax-head, dope, glump, ninny, and fool. The last name stuck. What did my foolishness consist of? I was easy to take in. They said, "Gimpel, you know the rabbi's wife has been brought to childbed?" So I skipped school. Well, it turned out to be a lie. How was I supposed to know? She hadn't had a big belly. But I never looked at her belly. Was that really so foolish? The gang laughed and hee-hawed, stomped and danced and chanted a good-night prayer. And instead of the raisins they give when a woman's lying in, they stuffed my hand full of goat turds. I was no weakling. If I slapped someone he'd see all the way to Cracow. But I'm really not a slugger by nature. I think to myself: Let it pass. So they take advantage of me.

I was coming home from school and heard a dog barking. I'm not afraid of dogs, but of course I never want to start up with them. One of them may be mad, and if he bites there's not a Tartar in the world who can help you. So I made tracks. Then I looked around and saw the whole market place wild with laughter. It was no dog at all but Wolf-Leib the Thief. How was I supposed to know it was he? It sounded like a howling bitch.

When the pranksters and leg-pullers found that I was easy to fool, every one of them tried his luck with me. "Gimpel, the Czar is coming to Frampol; Gimpel, the moon fell down in Turbeen; Gimpel, little Hodel Furpiece found a treasure behind the bathhouse." And I like a golem believed everyone. In the first place, everything is possible, as it is written in the Wisdom of the Fathers, I've forgotten just how. Second, I had to believe when the whole town came down on me! If I ever dared to say, "Ah, you're kidding!" There was trouble. People got angry. "What do you mean! You want to call everyone a liar?" What was I to do? I believed them, and I hope at least that did them some good.

I was an orphan. My grandfather who brought me up was already bent toward the grave. So they turned me over to a baker, and what a time they gave me there! Every woman or girl who came to bake a batch of noodles had to fool me at least once. "Gimpel, there's a fair in heaven; Gimpel, the rabbi gave birth to a calf in the seventh month; Gimpel, a cow flew over the roof and laid brass eggs." A student from the yeshiva came once to buy a roll, and he said, "You, Gimpel, while you stand here scraping with your baker's shovel the Messiah has come. The dead have arisen." "What do you mean?" I said. "I heard no one blowing the ram's horn!" He said, "Are you deaf?" And all began to cry, "We heard it, we heard!" Then in came Rietze the Candle-dipper and called out in her hoarse voice, "Gimpel, your father and mother have stood up from the grave. They're looking for you."

5   To tell the truth, I knew very well that nothing of the sort had happened, but all the same, as folks were talking, I threw on my wool vest and went out. Maybe something had happened. What did I stand to lose by looking? Well, what a cat music went up! And then I took a vow to believe nothing more. But that was no go either. They confused me so that I didn't know the big end from the small.

I went to the rabbi to get some advice. He said, "It is written, better to be a fool all your days than for one hour to be evil. You are not a fool. They are the fools. For he who causes his neighbor to feel shame loses Paradise himself." Nevertheless the rabbi's daughter took me in. As I left the rabbinical court she said, "Have you kissed the wall yet?" I said, "No; what for?" She answered, "It's the law; you've got to do it after every visit." Well, there didn't seem to be any harm in it. And she burst out laughing. It was a fine trick. She put one over on me, all right.

I wanted to go off to another town, but then everyone got busy matchmaking, and they were after me so they nearly tore my coat tails off. They talked at me and talked until I got water on the ear. She was no chaste maiden, but they told me she was virgin pure. She had a limp, and they said it was deliberate, from coyness. She had a bastard, and they told me the child was her little brother. I cried, "You're wasting your time. I'll never marry that whore." But they said indignantly, "What a way to talk! Aren't you ashamed of yourself? We can take you to the rabbi and have you fined for giving her a bad name." I saw then that I wouldn't escape them so easily and I thought: They're set on making me their butt. But when you're married the husband's the master, and if that's all right with her it's agreeable to me too. Besides, you can't pass through life unscathed, nor expect to.

I went to her clay house, which was built on the sand, and the whole gang hollering and chorusing, came after me. They acted like bear-baiters. When we came to the well they stopped all the same. They were afraid to start anything with Elka. Her mouth would open as if it were on a hinge, and she had a fierce tongue. I entered the house. Lines were strung from wall to wall and clothes were drying. Barefoot she stood by the tub, doing the wash. She was dressed in a worn hand-me-down gown of plush. She had her hair put up in braids and pinned across her head. It took my breath away, almost, the reek of it all.

Evidently she knew who I was. She took a look at me and said, "Look who's here! He's come, the drip. Grab a seat."

10   I told her all; I denied nothing. "Tell me the truth," I said, "are you really a virgin; and is that mischievous Yechiel actually your little brother? Don't be deceitful with me, for I'm an orphan."

"I'm an orphan myself," she answered, "and whoever tries to twist you up, may the end of his nose take a twist. But don't let them think they can take advantage of me. I want a dowry of fifty guilders, and let them take up a collection besides. Otherwise they can kiss my you-know-what." She was very plainspoken. I said, "It's the bride and not the groom who gives a dowry." Then she said, "Don't bargain with me. Either a flat 'yes' or a flat 'no'—Go back where you came from."

I thought: No bread will ever be baked from *this* dough. But ours is not a poor town. They consented to everything and proceeded with the wedding. It so happened that there was a dysentery epidemic at the time. The ceremony was held at the cemetery gates, near the little corpse-washing hut. The fellows got drunk. While the marriage contract was being drawn up I heard the most pious high rabbi ask, "Is the bride a widow or a divorced woman?" And the sexton's wife answered for her, "Both a widow and divorced." It was a black moment for me. But what was I to do, run away from under the marriage canopy?

There was singing and dancing. An old granny danced opposite me, hugging a braided white *chalah*. The master of revels made a "God 'a mercy" in memory of the bride's parents. The schoolboys threw burrs, as on Tishe b'Av fast day. There were a lot of gifts after the sermon: a noodle board, a kneading trough, a bucket, brooms, ladles, household articles galore. Then I took a look and saw two strapping young men carrying a crib. "What do we need this for?" I asked. So they said, "Don't rack your brains about it. It's all right, it'll come in handy." I realized I was going to be rooked. Take it another way though, what did I stand to lose? I reflected: I'll see what comes of it. A whole town can't go altogether crazy.

2

At night I came where my wife lay, but she wouldn't let me in. "Say, look here, is this what they married us for?" I said. And she said, "My monthly has come." "But yesterday they took you to the ritual bath, and that's afterward, isn't it supposed to be?" "Today isn't yesterday," said she, "and yesterday's not today. You can beat it if you don't like it." In short, I waited.

Not four months later she was in childbed. The townsfolk hid their laughter with   15
their knuckles. But what could I do? She suffered intolerable pains and clawed at the walls. "Gimpel," she cried, "I'm going. Forgive me!" The house filled with women. They were boiling pans of water. The screams rose to the welkin.

The thing to do was to go to the House of Prayer to repeat Psalms, and that was what I did.

The townsfolk liked that, all right. I stood in a corner saying Psalms and prayers, and they shook their heads at me. "Pray, pray!" they told me. "Prayer never made any woman pregnant." One of the congregation put a straw to my mouth and said, "Hay for the cows." There was something to that too, by God!

She gave birth to a boy. Friday at the synagogue the sexton stood up before the Ark, pounded on the reading table, and announced, "The wealthy Reb Gimpel invites the congregation to a feast in honor of the birth of a son." The whole House of Prayer rang with laughter. My face was flaming. But there was nothing I could do. After all, I *was* the one responsible for the circumcision honors and rituals.

Half the town came running. You couldn't wedge another soul in. Women brought peppered chick-peas, and there was a keg of beer from the tavern. I ate and drank as much as anyone, and they all congratulated me. Then there was a circumcision, and I named the boy after my father, may he rest in peace. When all were gone and I was left with my wife alone, she thrust her head through the bed-curtain and called me to her.

"Gimpel," said she, "why are you silent? Has your ship gone and sunk?"   20

"What shall I say?" I answered. "A fine thing you've done to me! If my mother had known of it she'd have died a second time."

She said, "Are you crazy, or what?"

"How can you make such a fool," I said, "of one who should be the lord and master?"

"What's the matter with you?" she said. "What have you taken it into your head to imagine?"

25 I saw that I must speak bluntly and openly. "Do you think this is the way to use an orphan?" I said. "You have borne a bastard."

She answered, "Drive this foolishness out of your head. The child is yours."

"How can he be mine?" I argued. "He was born seventeen weeks after the wedding."

She told me then that he was premature. I said, "Isn't he a little too premature?" She said, she had had a grandmother who carried just as short a time and she resembled this grandmother of hers as one drop of water does another. She swore to it with such oaths that you would have believed a peasant at the fair if he had used them. To tell the plain truth, I didn't believe her; but when I talked it over next day with the schoolmaster he told me that the very same thing had happened to Adam and Eve. Two they went up to bed, and four they descended.

"There isn't a woman in the world who is not the granddaughter of Eve," he said.

30 That was how it was; they argued me dumb. But then, who really knows how such things are?

I began to forget my sorrow. I loved the child madly, and he loved me too. As soon as he saw me he'd wave his little hands and want me to pick him up, and when he was colicky I was the only one who could pacify him. I bought him a little bone teething ring and a little gilded cap. He was forever catching the evil eye from someone, and then I had to run to get one of those abracadabras for him that would get him out of it. I worked like an ox. You know how expenses go up when there's an infant in the house. I don't want to lie about it; I didn't dislike Elka either, for that matter. She swore at me and cursed, and I couldn't get enough of her. What strength she had! One of her looks could rob you of the power of speech. And her orations! Pitch and sulphur, that's what they were full of, and yet somehow also full of charm. I adored her every word. She gave me bloody wounds though.

In the evening I brought her a white loaf as well as a dark one, and also poppy-seed rolls I baked myself. I thieved because of her and swiped everything I could lay hands on: macaroons, raisins, almonds, cakes. I hope I may be forgiven for stealing from the Saturday pots the women left to warm in the baker's oven. I would take out scraps of meat, a chunk of pudding, a chicken leg or head, a piece of tripe, whatever I could nip quickly. She ate and became fat and handsome.

I had to sleep away from home all during the week, at the bakery. On Friday nights when I got home she always made an excuse of some sort. Either she had heartburn, or a stitch in the side, or hiccups, or headaches. You know what women's excuses are. I had a bitter time of it. It was rough. To add to it, this little brother of hers, the bastard, was growing bigger. He'd put lumps on me, and when I wanted to hit back she'd open her mouth and curse so powerfully I saw a green haze floating before my eyes. Ten times a day she threatened to divorce me. Another man in my place would have taken French leave and disappeared. But I'm the type that bears it and says nothing. What's one to do? Shoulders are from God, and burdens too.

One night there was a calamity in the bakery; the oven burst, and we almost had a fire. There was nothing to do but go home, so I went home. Let me, I thought, also taste the joy of sleeping in bed in mid-week. I didn't want to wake the sleeping mite and tiptoed into the house. Coming in, it seemed to me that I heard not the snoring of one but, as it were, a double snore, one a thin enough snore and the other like the snoring of a slaughtered ox. Oh, I didn't like that! I didn't like it at all. I went up to the bed, and things suddenly turned black. Next to Elka lay a man's form. Another in my place would have made an uproar, and enough noise to rouse the whole town, but the thought occurred to me that I might wake the child. A little thing like that— why frighten a little swallow, I thought. All right then, I went back to the bakery and stretched out on a sack of flour and till morning I never shut an eye. I shivered as if I had had malaria. "Enough of being a donkey," I said to myself. "Gimpel isn't going to be a sucker all his life. There's a limit even to the foolishness of a fool like Gimpel."

In the morning I went to the rabbi to get advice, and it made a great commotion 35 in the town. They sent the beadle for Elka right away. She came, carrying the child. And what do you think she did? She denied it, denied everything, bone and stone! "He's out of his head," she said. "I know nothing of dreams or divinations." They yelled at her, warned her, hammered on the table, but she stuck to her guns: it was a false accusation, she said.

The butchers and the horse-traders took her part. One of the lads from the slaughterhouse came by and said to me, "We've got our eye on you, you're a marked man." Meanwhile the child started to bear down and soiled itself. In the rabbinical court there was an Ark of the Covenant, and they couldn't allow that, so they sent Elka away.

I said to the rabbi, "What shall I do?"

"You must divorce her at once," said he.

"And what if she refuses?" I asked.

He said, "You must serve the divorce. That's all you'll have to do."   40

I said, "Well, all right, Rabbi. Let me think about it."

"There's nothing to think about," said he. "You mustn't remain under the same roof with her."

"And if I want to see the child?" I asked.

"Let her go, the harlot," said he, "and her brood of bastards with her."

The verdict he gave was that I mustn't even cross her threshold—never again, 45 as long as I should live.

During the day it didn't bother me so much. I thought: It was bound to happen, the abscess had to burst. But at night when I stretched out upon the sacks I felt it all very bitterly. A longing took me, for her and for the child. I wanted to be angry, but that's my misfortune exactly, I don't have it in me to be really angry. In the first place—this was how my thoughts went—there's bound to be a slip sometimes. You can't live without errors. Probably that lad who was with her led her on and gave her presents and what not, and women are often long on hair and short on sense, and so he got around her. And then since she denies it so, maybe I was only seeing things? Hallucinations do happen. You see a figure or a mannikin or something, but when you come up closer it's nothing, there's not a thing there. And if that's so, I'm doing her an injustice. And when I got so far in my thoughts I started to weep. I sobbed so that I wet the flour where I lay. In the morning I went to the rabbi and told him that I had made a mistake. The rabbi wrote on with his quill, and he said that if that were so he would have to reconsider the whole case. Until he had finished I wasn't to go near my wife, but I might send her bread and money by messenger.

3

Nine months passed before all the rabbis could come to an agreement. Letters went back and forth. I hadn't realized that there could be so much erudition about a matter like this.

Meanwhile Elka gave birth to still another child, a girl this time. On the Sabbath I went to the synagogue and invoked a blessing on her. They called me up to the Torah, and I named the child for my mother-in-law—may she rest in peace. The louts and loudmouths of the town who came into the bakery gave me a going over. All Frampol refreshed its spirits because of my trouble and grief. However, I resolved that I would always believe what I was told. What's the good of *not* believing? Today it's your wife you don't believe; tomorrow it's God Himself you won't take stock in.

By an apprentice who was her neighbor I sent her daily a corn or a wheat loaf, or a piece of pastry, rolls or bagels, or, when I got the chance, a slab of pudding, a slice of honeycake, or wedding strudel—whatever came my way. The apprentice was a good-hearted lad, and more than once he added something on his own. He had formerly annoyed me a lot, plucking my nose and digging me in the ribs, but when he started to be a visitor to my house he became kind and friendly. "Hey, you, Gimpel," he said to me, "you have a very decent little wife and two fine kids. You don't deserve them."

50   "But the things people say about her," I said.

"Well, they have long tongues," he said, "and nothing to do with them but babble. Ignore it as you ignore the cold of last winter."

One day the rabbi sent for me and said, "Are you certain, Gimpel, that you were wrong about your wife?"

I said, "I'm certain."

"Why, but look here! You yourself saw it."

55   "It must have been a shadow," I said.

"The shadow of what?"

"Just one of the beams, I think."

"You can go home then. You owe thanks to the Yanover rabbi. He found an obscure reference in Maimonides that favored you."

I seized the rabbi's hand and kissed it.

60   I wanted to run home immediately. It's no small thing to be separated for so long a time from wife and child. Then I reflected: I'd better go back to work now, and go

home in the evening. I said nothing to anyone, although as far as my heart was concerned it was like one of the Holy Days. The women teased and twitted me as they did every day, but my thought was: Go on, with your loose talk. The truth is out, like the oil upon the water. Maimonides says it's right, and therefore it is right!

At night, when I had covered the dough to let it rise, I took my share of bread and a little sack of flour and started homeward. The moon was full and the stars were glistening, something to terrify the soul. I hurried onward, and before me darted a long shadow. It was winter, and a fresh snow had fallen. I had a mind to sing, but it was growing late and I didn't want to wake the householders. Then I felt like whistling, but I remembered that you don't whistle at night because it brings the demons out. So I was silent and walked as fast as I could.

Dogs in the Christian yards barked at me when I passed, but I thought: Bark your teeth out! What are you but mere dogs? Whereas I am a man, the husband of a fine wife, the father of promising children.

As I approached the house my heart started to pound as though it were the heart of a criminal. I felt no fear, but my heart went thump! thump! Well, no drawing back. I quietly lifted the latch and went in. Elka was asleep. I looked at the infant's cradle. The shutter was closed, but the moon forced its way through the cracks. I saw the newborn child's face and loved it as soon as I saw it—immediately—each tiny bone.

Then I came nearer to the bed. And what did I see but the apprentice lying there beside Elka. The moon went out all at once. It was utterly black, and I trembled. My teeth chattered. The bread fell from my hands, and my wife waked and said, "Who is that, ah?"

I muttered, "It's me."   65

"Gimpel?" she asked. "How come you're here? I thought it was forbidden."

"The rabbi said," I answered and shook as with a fever.

"Listen to me, Gimpel," she said, "go out to the shed and see if the goat's all right. It seems she's been sick." I have forgotten to say that we had a goat. When I heard she was unwell I went into the yard. The nanny goat was a good little creature. I had a nearly human feeling for her.

With hesitant steps I went up to the shed and opened the door. The goat stood there on her four feet. I felt her everywhere, drew her by the horns, examined her udders, and found nothing wrong. She had probably eaten too much bark. "Good night, little goat," I said. "Keep well." And the little beast answered with a "Maa" as though to thank me for the good will.

I went back. The apprentice had vanished.   70

"Where," I asked, "is the lad?"

"What lad?" my wife answered.

"What do you mean?" I said. "The apprentice. You were sleeping with him."

"The things I have dreamed this night and the night before," she said, "may they come true and lay you low, body and soul! An evil spirit has taken root in you and dazzles your sight." She screamed out, "You hateful creature! You moon calf! You spook! You uncouth man! Get out, or I'll scream all Frampol out of bed!"

Before I could move, her brother sprang out from behind the oven and struck   75
me a blow on the back of the head. I thought he had broken my neck. I felt that

something about me was deeply wrong, and I said, "Don't make a scandal. All that's needed now is that people should accuse me of raising spooks and *dybbuks*." For that was what she had meant. "No one will touch bread of my baking."

In short, I somehow calmed her.

"Well," she said, "that's enough. Lie down, and be shattered by wheels."

Next morning I called the apprentice aside. "Listen here, brother!" I said. And so on and so forth. "What do you say?" He stared at me as though I had dropped from the roof or something.

"I swear," he said, "you'd better go to an herb doctor or some healer. I'm afraid you have a screw loose, but I'll hush it up for you." And that's how the thing stood.

80   To make a long story short, I lived twenty years with my wife. She bore me six children, four daughters and two sons. All kinds of things happened, but I neither saw nor heard. I believed, and that's all. The rabbi recently said to me, "Belief in itself is beneficial. It is written that a good man lives by his faith."

Suddenly my wife took sick. It began with a trifle, a little growth upon the breast. But she evidently was not destined to live long; she had no years. I spent a fortune on her. I have forgotten to say that by this time I had a bakery of my own and in Frampol was considered to be something of a rich man. Daily the healer came, and every witch doctor in the neighborhood was brought. They decided to use leeches, and after that to try cupping. They even called a doctor from Lublin, but it was too late. Before she died she called me to her bed and said, "Forgive me, Gimpel."

I said, "What is there to forgive? You have been a good and faithful wife."

"Woe, Gimpel!" she said. "It was ugly how I deceived you all these years. I want to go clean to my Maker, and so I have to tell you that the children are not yours."

If I had been clouted on the head with a piece of wood it couldn't have bewildered me more.

85   "Whose are they?" I asked.

"I don't know," she said. "There were a lot . . . but they're not yours." And as she spoke she tossed her head to the side, her eyes turned glassy, and it was all up with Elka. On her whitened lips there remained a smile.

I imagined that, dead as she was, she was saying, "I deceived Gimpel. That was the meaning of my brief life."

4

One night, when the period of mourning was done, as I lay dreaming on the flour sacks, there came the Spirit of Evil himself and said to me, "Gimpel, why do you sleep?"

I said, "What should I be doing? Eating *kreplach?*"

90   "The whole world deceives you," he said, "and you ought to deceive the world in your turn."

"How can I deceive the world?" I asked him.

He answered, "You might accumulate a bucket of urine every day and at night pour it into the dough. Let the sages of Frampol eat filth."

"What about the judgment in the world to come?" I said.

"There is no world to come," he said. "They've sold you a bill of goods and talked you into believing you carried a cat in your belly. What nonsense!"

"Well then," I said, "and is there a God?"   95

He answered, "There is no God either."

"What," I said, "*is* there, then?"

"A thick mire."

He stood before my eyes with a goatish beard and horn, long-toothed, and with a tail. Hearing such words, I wanted to snatch him by the tail, but I tumbled from the flour sacks and nearly broke a rib. Then it happened that I had to answer the call of nature, and, passing, I saw the risen dough, which seemed to say to me, "Do it!" In brief, I let myself be persuaded.

At dawn the apprentice came. We kneaded the bread, scattered caraway seeds   100 on it, and set it to bake. Then the apprentice went away, and I was left sitting in the little trench by the oven, on a pile of rags. Well, Gimpel, I thought, you've revenged yourself on them for all the shame they've put on you. Outside the frost glittered, but it was warm beside the oven. The flames heated my face. I bent my head and fell into a doze.

I saw in a dream, at once, Elka in her shroud. She called to me, "What have you done, Gimpel?"

I said to her, "It's all your fault," and started to cry.

"You fool!" she said. "You fool! Because I was false is everything false too? I never deceived anyone but myself. I'm paying for it all, Gimpel. They spare you nothing here."

I looked at her face. It was black; I was startled and waked, and remained sitting dumb. I sensed that everything hung in the balance. A false step now and I'd lose Eternal Life. But God gave me His help. I seized the long shovel and took out the loaves, carried them into the yard, and started to dig a hole in the frozen earth.

My apprentice came back as I was doing it. "What are you doing, boss?" he   105 said, and grew pale as a corpse.

"I know what I'm doing," I said, and I buried it all before his very eyes.

Then I went home, took my hoard from its hiding place, and divided it among the children. "I saw your mother tonight," I said. "She's turning black, poor thing."

They were so astounded they couldn't speak a word.

"Be well," I said, "and forget that such a one as Gimpel ever existed." I put on my short coat, a pair of boots, took the bag that held my prayer shawl in one hand, my stock in the other, and kissed the *mezzuzah*. When people saw me in the street they were greatly surprised.

"Where are you going?" they said.   110

I answered, "Into the world." And so I departed from Frampol.

I wandered over the land, and good people did not neglect me. After many years I became old and white; I heard a great deal, many lies and falsehoods, but the longer I lived the more I understood that there were really no lies. Whatever doesn't really happen is dreamed at night. It happens to one if it doesn't happen to another, tomorrow if not today, or a century hence if not next year. What difference can it make? Often I heard tales of which I said, "Now this is a thing that cannot happen." But before a year had elapsed I heard that it actually had come to pass somewhere.

Going from place to place, eating at strange tables, it often happens that I spin yarns—improbable things that could never have happened—about devils, magicians, windmills, and the like. The children run after me, calling, "Grandfather, tell us a story." Sometimes they ask for particular stories, and I try to please them. A fat young boy once said to me, "Grandfather, it's the same story you told us before." The little rogue, he was right.

So it is with dreams too. It is many years since I left Frampol, but as soon as I shut my eyes I am there again. And whom do you think I see? Elka. She is standing by the washtub, as at our first encounter, but her face is shining and her eyes are as radiant as the eyes of a saint, and she speaks outlandish words to me, strange things. When I wake I have forgotten it all. But while the dream lasts I am comforted. She answers all my queries, and what comes out is that all is right. I weep and implore, "Let me be with you." And she consoles me and tells me to be patient. The time is nearer than it is far. Sometimes she strokes and kisses me and weeps upon my face. When I awaken I feel her lips and taste the salt of her tears.

115   No doubt the world is entirely an imaginary world, but it is only once removed from the true world. At the door of the hovel where I lie, there stands the plank on which the dead are taken away. The gravedigger Jew has his spade ready. The grave waits and the worms are hungry; the shrouds are prepared—I carry them in my beggar's sack. Another *shnorrer* is waiting to inherit my bed of straw. When the time comes I will go joyfully. Whatever may be there, it will be real, without complication, without ridicule, without deception. God be praised: there even Gimpel cannot be deceived.

QUESTIONS FOR DISCUSSION AND WRITING

1. How do Gimpel's first two sentences establish the conflict in his story? Why does Gimpel finally decide to resist the devil's temptation? How does Gimpel's last dream of Elka bring the story to an appropriate conclusion?

2. How does Gimpel's belief that "everything is possible" help perpetuate his neighbors' perception of him as a fool? In what way does Gimpel's marriage to Elka portray the ancient stereotype of the husband as cuckold? How does Gimpel's treatment of Elka and her children suggest that he may be wise rather than foolish?

3. How does the small village of Frampol contribute to the social and psychological forces that form Gimpel? Why does he decide to leave Frampol? How is he treated outside his native setting?

4. Why does Gimpel's explanation of his own point of view help us see him as something more than a fool? How do his trips to the rabbi help confirm his belief in his own point of view?

5. What does Gimpel's experience suggest about the relationship of wisdom and ignorance, faith and doubt? How does Gimpel's discovery "that there were really no lies" help him come to terms with his life in this world and prepare him for the world hereafter?

Stories for Comparison

Sherwood Anderson's "I'm a Fool" (pages 195–203); John Updike's "A & P" (pages 1136–1141).

88

JOHN STEINBECK

The Chrysanthemums

JOHN STEINBECK (1902–1968) was born in Salinas, California, and intermittently attended Stanford University, leaving in 1925 to work his way to New York on a cattle boat to pursue a writing career. He was unable to find sufficient employment, so he returned to California and worked throughout the Depression at various jobs: fruit picker, surveyor, chemical-laboratory assistant, and caretaker for a large estate on Lake Tahoe. Steinbeck's first novels, such as *Cup of Gold* (1929) and *To a God Unknown* (1933), attracted little attention. But with the publication of *Tortilla Flat* (1935), *In Dubious Battle* (1936), and *The Grapes of Wrath* (1939), his classic account of the Joad family's journey from Oklahoma to California, Steinbeck established himself as one of America's major literary talents. During World War II, he served as a journalist in Italy and Russia, continuing to publish noteworthy fiction such as *Cannery Row* (1945) and *The Wayward Bus* (1947), as well as several works of nonfiction such as *Bombs Away* (1942) and *Russian Journal* (1948). After the war, Steinbeck published two major novels, *East of Eden* (1952), a national best-seller, and *Winter of Our Discontent* (1961). In 1962, Steinbeck was awarded the Nobel Prize for Literature. The same year marked the publication of *Travels with Charley: In Search of America,* a journal of his tour across America in a camper with his pet poodle. Steinbeck's best-known short stories appear in *The Long Valley* (1938). "The Chrysanthemums," reprinted from that collection, describes a woman's momentary attraction to a freer, more fulfilling life.

The high grey-flannel fog of winter closed off the Salinas Valley from the sky and from all the rest of the world. On every side it sat like a lid on the mountains and made of the great valley a closed pot. On the broad, level land floor the gang plows bit deep and left the black earth shining like metal where the shares had cut. On the foothill ranches across the Salinas River, the yellow stubble fields seemed to be bathed in pale cold sunshine, but there was no sunshine in the valley now in December. The thick willow scrub along the river flamed with sharp and positive yellow leaves.

It was a time of quiet and of waiting. The air was cold and tender. A light wind blew up from the southwest so that the farmers were mildly hopeful of a good rain before long; but fog and rain do not go together.

Across the river, on Henry Allen's foothill ranch there was little work to be done, for the hay was cut and stored and the orchards were plowed up to receive the rain deeply when it should come. The cattle on the higher slopes were becoming shaggy and rough-coated.

Elisa Allen, working in her flower garden, looked down across the yard and saw Henry, her husband, talking to two men in business suits. The three of them stood by the tractor shed, each man with one foot on the side of the little Fordson. They smoked cigarettes and studied the machine as they talked.

5   Elisa watched them for a moment and then went back to her work. She was thirty-five. Her face was lean and strong and her eyes were as clear as water. Her figure looked blocked and heavy in her gardening costume, a man's black hat pulled low down over her eyes, clod-hopper shoes, a figured print dress almost completely covered by a big corduroy apron with four big pockets to hold the snips, the trowel and scratcher, the seeds and the knife she worked with. She wore heavy leather gloves to protect her hands while she worked.

She was cutting down the old year's chrysanthemum stalks with a pair of short and powerful scissors. She looked down toward the men by the tractor shed now and then. Her face was eager and mature and handsome; even her work with the scissors was over-eager, over-powerful. The chrysanthemum stems seemed too small and easy for her energy.

She brushed a cloud of hair out of her eyes with the back of her glove, and left a smudge of earth on her cheek in doing it. Behind her stood the neat white farm house with red geraniums close-banked around it as high as the windows. It was a hard-swept looking little house with hard-polished windows, and a clean mud-mat on the front steps.

Elisa cast another glance toward the tractor shed. The strangers were getting into their Ford coupe. She took off a glove and put her strong fingers down into the forest of new green chrysanthemum sprouts that were growing around the old roots. She spread the leaves and looked down among the close-growing stems. No aphids were there, no sowbugs or snails or cutworms. Her terrier fingers destroyed such pests before they could get started.

Elisa started at the sound of her husband's voice. He had come near quietly, and he leaned over the wire fence that protected her flower garden from cattle and dogs and chickens.

"At it again," he said. "You've got a strong new crop coming."   10

Elisa straightened her back and pulled on the gardening glove again. "Yes. They'll be strong this coming year." In her tone and on her face there was a little smugness.

"You've got a gift with things," Henry observed. "Some of those yellow chrysanthemums you had this year were ten inches across. I wish you'd work out in the orchard and raise some apples that big."

Her eyes sharpened. "Maybe I could do it, too. I've a gift with things, all right. My mother had it. She could stick anything in the ground and make it grow. She said it was having planters' hands that knew how to do it."

"Well, it sure works with flowers," he said.

"Henry, who were those men you were talking to?"   15

"Why, sure, that's what I came to tell you. They were from the Western Meat Company. I sold those thirty head of three-year-old steers. Got nearly my own price, too."

"Good," she said. "Good for you."

"And I thought," he continued, "I thought how it's Saturday afternoon, and we might go into Salinas for dinner at a restaurant, and then to a picture show—to celebrate, you see."

"Good," she repeated. "Oh, yes. That will be good."

Henry put on his joking tone. "There's fights tonight. How'd you like to go to   20
the fights?"

"Oh, no," she said breathlessly. "No, I wouldn't like fights."

"Just fooling, Elisa. We'll go to a movie. Let's see. It's two now. I'm going to take Scotty and bring down those steers from the hill. It'll take us maybe two hours. We'll go in town about five and have dinner at the Cominos Hotel. Like that?"

"Of course I'll like it. It's good to eat away from home."

"All right, then. I'll go get up a couple of horses."

She said, "I'll have plenty of time to transplant some of these sets, I guess."   25

She heard her husband calling Scotty down by the barn. And a little later she saw the two men ride up the pale yellow hillside in search of the steers.

There was a little square sandy bed kept for rooting the chrysanthemums. With her trowel she turned the soil over and over, and smoothed it and patted it firm. Then she dug ten parallel trenches to receive the sets. Back at the chrysanthemum bed she pulled out the little crisp shoots, trimmed off the leaves of each one with her scissors and laid it on a small orderly pile.

A squeak of wheels and plod of hoofs came from the road. Elisa looked up. The country road ran along the dense bank of willows and cottonwoods that bordered the river, and up this road came a curious vehicle, curiously drawn. It was an old spring-wagon, with a round canvas top on it like the corner of a prairie schooner. It was drawn by an old bay horse and a little grey-and-white burro. A big stubble-bearded man sat between the cover flaps and drove the crawling team. Underneath the wagon, between the hind wheels, a lean and rangy mongrel dog walked sedately. Words were painted on the canvas, in clumsy, crooked letters. "Pots, pans, knives, sisors, lawn mores, Fixed." Two rows of articles, and

the triumphantly definitive "Fixed" below. The black paint had run down in little sharp points beneath each letter.

Elisa, squatting on the ground, watched to see the crazy, loose-jointed wagon
pass by. But it didn't pass. It turned into the farm road in front of her house, crooked
old wheels skirling and squeaking. The rangy dog darted from between the wheels
and ran ahead. Instantly the two ranch shepherds flew out at him. Then all three
stopped, and with stiff and quivering tails, with taut straight legs, with ambassadorial
dignity, they slowly circled, sniffing daintily. The caravan pulled up to Elisa's wire
fence and stopped. Now the newcomer dog, feeling out-numbered, lowered his tail
and retired under the wagon with raised hackles and bared teeth.

30   The man on the wagon seat called out, "That's a bad dog in a fight when he gets
started."

Elisa laughed. "I see he is. How soon does he generally get started?"

The man caught up her laughter and echoed it heartily. "Sometimes not for
weeks and weeks," he said. He climbed stiffly down, over the wheel. The horse and
the donkey drooped like unwatered flowers.

Elisa saw that he was a very big man. Although his hair and beard were greying, he did not look old. His worn black suit was wrinkled and spotted with grease.
The laughter had disappeared from his face and eyes the moment his laughing voice
ceased. His eyes were dark, and they were full of the brooding that gets in the eyes
of teamsters and of sailors. The calloused hands he rested on the wire fence were
cracked, and every crack was a black line. He took off his battered hat.

"I'm off my general road, ma'am," he said. "Does this dirt road cut over across
the river to the Los Angeles highway?"

35   Elisa stood up and shoved the thick scissors in her apron pocket. "Well, yes, it
does, but it winds around and then fords the river. I don't think your team could pull
through the sand."

He replied with some asperity, "It might surprise you what them beasts can pull
through."

"When they get started?" she asked.

He smiled for a second. "Yes. When they get started."

"Well," said Elisa, "I think you'll save time if you go back to the Salinas road
and pick up the highway there."

40   He drew a big finger down the chicken wire and made it sing. "I ain't in any
hurry, ma'am. I go from Seattle to San Diego and back every year. Takes all my time.
About six months each way. I aim to follow nice weather."

Elisa took off her gloves and stuffed them in the apron pocket with the scissors.
She touched the under edge of her man's hat, searching for fugitive hairs. "That
sounds like a nice kind of a way to live," she said.

He leaned confidentially over the fence. "Maybe you noticed the writing on
my wagon. I mend pots and sharpen knives and scissors. You got any of them
things to do?"

"Oh, no," she said, quickly. "Nothing like that." Her eyes hardened with
resistance.

"Scissors is the worst thing," he explained. "Most people just ruin scissors trying to sharpen 'em, but I know how. I got a special tool. It's a little bobbit kind of thing, and patented. But it sure does the trick."

"No. My scissors are all sharp."   45

"All right, then. Take a pot," he continued earnestly, "a bent pot, or a pot with a hole. I can make it like new so you don't have to buy no new ones. That's a saving for you."

"No," she said shortly. "I tell you I have nothing like that for you to do."

His face fell to an exaggerated sadness. His voice took on a whining undertone. "I ain't had a thing to do today. Maybe I won't have no supper tonight. You see I'm off my regular road. I know folks on the highway clear from Seattle to San Diego. They save their things for me to sharpen up because they know I do it so good and save them money."

"I'm sorry," Elisa said irritably. "I haven't anything for you to do."

His eyes left her face and fell to searching the ground. They roamed about until 50
they came to the chrysanthemum bed where she had been working. "What's them plants, ma'am?"

The irritation and resistance melted from Elisa's face. "Oh, those are chrysanthemums, giant whites and yellows. I raise them every year, bigger than anybody around here."

"Kind of a long-stemmed flower? Looks like a quick puff of colored smoke?" he asked.

"That's it. What a nice way to describe them."

"They smell kind of nasty till you get used to them," he said.

"It's a good bitter smell," she retorted, "not nasty at all."   55

He changed his tone quickly. "I like the smell myself."

"I had ten-inch blooms this year," she said.

The man leaned farther over the fence. "Look. I know a lady down the road a piece, has got the nicest garden you ever seen. Got nearly every kind of flower but no chrysanthemums. Last time I was mending a copper-bottom washtub for her (that's a hard job but I do it good), she said to me, 'If you ever run acrost some nice chrysanthemums I wish you'd try to get me a few seeds.' That's what she told me."

Elisa's eyes grew alert and eager. "She couldn't have known much about chrysanthemums. You *can* raise them from seed, but it's much easier to root the little sprouts you see there."

"Oh," he said. "I s'pose I can't take none to her, then."   60

"Why yes you can," Elisa cried. "I can put some in damp sand, and you can carry them right along with you. They'll take root in the pot if you keep them damp. And then she can transplant them."

"She'd sure like to have some, ma'am. You say they're nice ones?"

"Beautiful," she said. "Oh, beautiful." Her eyes shone. She tore off the battered hat and shook out her dark pretty hair. "I'll put them in a flower pot, and you can take them right with you. Come into the yard."

While the man came through the picket gate Elisa ran excitedly along the geranium-bordered path to the back of the house. And she returned carrying a big red flower pot. The gloves were forgotten now. She kneeled on the ground by the starting bed and dug up the sandy soil with her fingers and scooped it into the bright new flower pot. Then she picked up the little pile of shoots she had prepared. With her strong fingers she pressed them into the sand and tamped around them with her knuckles. The man stood over her. "I'll tell you what to do," she said. "You remember so you can tell the lady."

65   "Yes, I'll try to remember."

"Well, look. These will take root in about a month. Then she must set them out, about a foot apart in good rich earth like this, see?" She lifted a handful of dark soil for him to look at. "They'll grow fast and tall. Now remember this: In July tell her to cut them down, about eight inches from the ground."

"Before they bloom?" he asked.

"Yes, before they bloom." Her face was tight with eagerness. "They'll grow right up again. About the last of September the buds will start."

She stopped and seemed perplexed. "It's the budding that takes the most care," she said hesitantly. "I don't know how to tell you." She looked deep into his eyes, searchingly. Her mouth opened a little, and she seemed to be listening. "I'll try to tell you," she said. "Did you ever hear of planting hands?"

70   "Can't say I have, ma'am."

"Well, I can only tell you what it feels like. It's when you're picking off the buds you don't want. Everything goes right down into your fingertips. You watch your fingers work. They do it themselves. You can feel how it is. They pick and pick the buds. They never make a mistake. They're with the plant. Do you see? Your fingers and the plant. You can feel that, right up your arm. They know. They never make a mistake. You can feel it. When you're like that you can't do anything wrong. Do you see that? Can you understand that?"

She was kneeling on the ground looking up at him. Her breast swelled passionately.

The man's eyes narrowed. He looked away self-consciously. "Maybe I know," he said. "Sometimes in the night in the wagon there—"

Elisa's voice grew husky. She broke in on him, "I've never lived as you do, but I know what you mean. When the night is dark—why, the stars are sharp-pointed, and there's quiet. Why, you rise up and up! Every pointed star gets driven into your body. It's like that. Hot and sharp and—lovely."

75   Kneeling there, her hand went out toward his leg in the greasy black trousers. Her hesitant fingers almost touched the cloth. Then her hand dropped to the ground. She crouched low like a fawning dog.

He said, "It's nice, just like you say. Only when you don't have no dinner, it ain't."

She stood up then, very straight, and her face was ashamed. She held the flower pot out to him and placed it gently in his arms. "Here. Put it in your wagon, on the seat, where you can watch it. Maybe I can find something for you to do."

At the back of the house she dug in the can pile and found two old and battered aluminum saucepans. She carried them back and gave them to him. "Here, maybe you can fix these."

His manner changed. He became professional. "Good as new I can fix them." At the back of his wagon he set a little anvil, and out of an oily tool box dug a small machine hammer. Elisa came through the gate to watch him while he pounded out the dents in the kettles. His mouth grew sure and knowing. At a difficult part of the work he sucked his upper-lip.

"You sleep right in the wagon?" Elisa asked.   80

"Right in the wagon, ma'am. Rain or shine I'm dry as a cow in there."

"It must be nice," she said. "It must be very nice. I wish women could do such things."

"It ain't the right kind of a life for a woman."

Her upper lip raised a little, showing her teeth. "How do you know? How can you tell?" she said.

"I don't know, ma'am," he protested. "Of course I don't know. Now here's your   85 kettles, done. You don't have to buy no new ones."

"How much?"

"Oh, fifty cents'll do. I keep my prices down and my work good. That's why I have all them satisfied customers up and down the highway."

Elisa brought him a fifty-cent piece from the house and dropped it in his hand. "You might be surprised to have a rival some time. I can sharpen scissors, too. And I can beat the dents out of little pots. I could show you what a woman might do."

He put his hammer back in the oily box and shoved the little anvil out of sight. "It would be a lonely life for a woman, ma'am, and a scarey life, too, with animals creeping under the wagon all night." He climbed over the singletree, steadying himself with a hand on the burro's white rump. He settled himself in the seat, picked up the lines. "Thank you kindly, ma'am," he said. "I'll do like you told me; I'll go back and catch the Salinas road."

"Mind," she called, "if you're long in getting there, keep the sand damp."   90

"Sand, ma'am? . . . Sand? Oh, sure. You mean around the chrysanthemums. Sure I will." He clucked his tongue. The beasts leaned luxuriously into their collars. The mongrel dog took his place between the back wheels. The wagon turned and crawled out the entrance road and back the way it had come, along the river.

Elisa stood in front of her wire fence watching the slow progress of the caravan. Her shoulders were straight, her head thrown back, her eyes half-closed, so that the scene came vaguely into them. Her lips moved silently, forming the words "Good-bye—good-bye." Then she whispered, "That's a bright direction. There's a glowing there." The sound of her whisper startled her. She shook herself free and looked about to see whether anyone had been listening. Only the dogs had heard. They lifted their heads toward her from their sleeping in the dust, and then stretched out their chins and settled asleep again. Elisa turned and ran hurriedly into the house.

In the kitchen she reached behind the stove and felt the water tank. It was full of hot water from the noonday cooking. In the bathroom she tore off her soiled clothes and flung them into the corner. And then she scrubbed herself with a little block of pumice, legs and thighs, loins and chest and arms, until her skin was scratched and red. When she had dried herself she stood in front of a mirror in her bedroom and looked at her body. She tightened her stomach and threw out her chest. She turned and looked over her shoulder at her back.

After a while she began to dress, slowly. She put on her newest underclothing and her nicest stockings and the dress which was the symbol of her prettiness. She worked carefully on her hair, penciled her eyebrows and rouged her lips.

95   Before she was finished she heard the little thunder of hoofs and the shouts of Henry and his helper as they drove the red steers into the corral. She heard the gate bang shut and set herself for Henry's arrival.

His step sounded on the porch. He entered the house calling, "Elisa, where are you?"

"In my room, dressing. I'm not ready. There's hot water for your bath. Hurry up. It's getting late."

When she heard him splashing in the tub, Elisa laid his dark suit on the bed, and shirt and socks and tie beside it. She stood his polished shoes on the floor beside the bed. Then she went to the porch and sat primly and stiffly down. She looked toward the river road where the willow-line was still yellow with frosted leaves so that under the high grey fog they seemed a thin band of sunshine. This was the only color in the grey afternoon. She sat unmoving for a long time. Her eyes blinked rarely.

Henry came banging out of the door, shoving his tie inside his vest as he came. Elisa stiffened and her face grew tight. Henry stopped short and looked at her. "Why—why, Elisa. You look so nice!"

100   "Nice? You think I look nice? What do you mean by 'nice'?"

Henry blundered on. "I don't know. I mean you look different, strong and happy."

"I am strong? Yes, strong. What do you mean 'strong'?"

He looked bewildered. "You're playing some kind of a game," he said helplessly. "It's a kind of play. You look strong enough to break a calf over your knee, happy enough to eat it like a watermelon."

For a second she lost her rigidity. "Henry! Don't talk like that. You didn't know what you said." She grew complete again. "I'm strong," she boasted. "I never knew before how strong."

105   Henry looked down toward the tractor shed, and when he brought his eyes back to her, they were his own again. "I'll get out the car. You can put on your coat while I'm starting."

Elisa went into the house. She heard him drive to the gate and idle down his motor, and then she took a long time to put on her hat. She pulled it here and pressed it there. When Henry turned the motor off she slipped into her coat and went out.

The little roadster bounced along on the dirt road by the river, raising the birds and driving the rabbits into the brush. Two cranes flapped heavily over the willow-line and dropped into the river-bed.

Far ahead on the road Elisa saw a dark speck. She knew.

She tried not to look as they passed it, but her eyes would not obey. She whispered to herself sadly, "He might have thrown them off the road. That wouldn't have been much trouble, not very much. But he kept the pot," she explained. "He had to keep the pot. That's why he couldn't get them off the road."

The roadster turned a bend and she saw the caravan ahead. She swung full around toward her husband so she could not see the little covered wagon and the mismatched team as the car passed them. [110]

In a moment it was over. The thing was done. She did not look back.

She said loudly, to be heard above the motor, "It will be good, tonight, a good dinner."

"Now you're changed again," Henry complained. He took one hand from the wheel and patted her knee. "I ought to take you in to dinner oftener. It would be good for both of us. We get so heavy out on the ranch."

"Henry," she asked, "could we have wine at dinner?"

"Sure we could. Say! That will be fine." [115]

She was silent for a while; then she said, "Henry, at those prize fights, do the men hurt each other very much?"

"Sometimes a little, not often. Why?"

"Well, I've read how they break noses, and blood runs down their chests. I've read how the fighting gloves get heavy and soggy with blood."

He looked around at her. "What's the matter, Elisa? I didn't know you read things like that." He brought the car to a stop, then turned to the right over the Salinas River bridge.

"Do any women ever go to the fights?" she asked. [120]

"Oh, sure, some. What's the matter, Elisa? Do you want to go? I don't think you'd like it, but I'll take you if you really want to go."

She relaxed limply in the seat. "Oh, no. No. I don't want to go. I'm sure I don't." Her face was turned away from him. "It will be enough if we can have wine. It will be plenty." She turned up her coat collar so he could not see that she was crying weakly—like an old woman.

QUESTIONS FOR DISCUSSION AND WRITING

1. How does Elisa's meeting with the tinker produce the conflict in the story? How does that conflict reach its climax when Elisa and Henry pass the tinker on the way to town? To what extent does Elisa's statement, "It will be enough if we can have wine. It will be plenty," resolve that conflict?

2. How does Steinbeck's description of Elisa's attire and "gift" help establish her character? What hidden qualities in her character are revealed in her conversation with the tinker? What two character transformations does Henry notice in his wife toward the end of the story?

3. How does Steinbeck's initial description of the Salinas Valley as a "closed pot" help establish the mood of the story? How does Elisa's speculation about the tinker's travels reveal her dissatisfaction with her life?

4. In what ways does Elisa's observation of her husband and the two men from behind the wire fence of her flower garden establish her point of view in this story?
How does her observation of herself in the mirror after her bath suggest a change
in her point of view?

5. What do the chrysanthemums symbolize at the beginning of the story, at the time
when Elisa gives them to the tinker, and at the end when she suspects he has discarded them? How do the tinker's description of the flower as a "quick puff of
colored smoke" and Elisa's description of it as having a "good bitter smell" suggest ways to interpret its symbolic significance?

Stories for Comparison

D. H. Lawrence's "Odour of Chrysanthemums" (pages 778–792); Bobbie Ann
Mason's "Shiloh" (pages 872–882).

89

JAMES   THURBER

The Greatest Man in the World

JAMES THURBER (1894–1961) was born in Columbus, Ohio, and attended
Ohio State University. Accidentally blinded in one eye as a child, Thurber was
rejected for military service in World War I, but he worked briefly for the State
Department in Paris as a code clerk. After the war, he returned home to write
for the *Columbus Dispatch* and to compose and direct musical comedies for a
theatrical group at Ohio State University. In 1924, he traveled to Paris as a correspondent for the *Chicago Tribune* and the next year to New York to work for
the *New York Evening Post.* In 1927, Thurber joined the staff of *The New
Yorker* and remained there as a writer and editor until 1935, when he resigned
to work on his own writing. But he continued to contribute stories, prose
sketches, and drawings to the magazine until his death. His recollections of
The New Yorker are contained in his book *The Years with Ross* (1959). In
1929, Thurber published his first book, *Is Sex Necessary?,* in collaboration
with E. B. White. In the 1930s, he published his *New Yorker* writings and
drawings in volumes such as *The Owl in the Attic and Other Perplexities*
(1931), *The Seal in the Bedroom and Other Predicaments* (1932), *The Middle-
Aged Man on the Flying Trapeze* (1935), and *Let Your Mind Alone!* (1937).

In 1940, Thurber collaborated with Elliott Nugent on the successful Broadway play *The Male Animal.* Despite his failing eyesight, Thurber continued writing humor and satire until his death. Other books of his include *Fables for Our Time and Famous Poems Illustrated* (1940), *The Beast in Me and Other Animals* (1948), *Thurber Country* (1953), and *Lanterns and Lances* (1961). In "The Greatest Man in the World," reprinted from *The Middle-Aged Man on the Flying Trapeze,* a garage mechanic's "heroics" create a national crisis.

L ooking back on it now, from the vantage point of 1940, one can only marvel that it hadn't happened long before it did. The United States of America had been, ever since Kitty Hawk, blindly constructing the elaborate petard by which, sooner or later, it must be hoist. It was inevitable that some day there would come roaring out of the skies a national hero of insufficient intelligence, background, and character successfully to endure the mounting orgies of glory prepared for aviators who stayed up a long time or flew a great distance. Both Lindbergh and Byrd, fortunately for national decorum and international amity, had been gentlemen; so had our other famous aviators. They wore their laurels gracefully, withstood the awful weather of publicity, married excellent women, usually of fine family, and quietly retired to private life and the enjoyment of their varying fortunes. No untoward incidents, on a worldwide scale, marred the perfection of their conduct on the perilous heights of fame. The exception to the rule was, however, bound to occur and it did, in July, 1937, when Jack ("Pal") Smurch, erstwhile mechanic's helper in a small garage in Westfield, Iowa, flew a second-hand, single-motored Bresthaven Dragon-Fly III monoplane all the way around the world, without stopping.

Never before in the history of aviation had such a flight as Smurch's ever been dreamed of. No one had even taken seriously the weird floating auxiliary gas tanks, invention of the mad New Hampshire professor of astronomy, Dr. Charles Lewis Gresham, upon which Smurch placed full reliance. When the garage worker, a slightly built, surly, unprepossessing young man of twenty-two, appeared at Roosevelt Field early in July, 1937, slowly chewing a great quid of scrap tobacco, and announced "Nobody ain't seen no flyin' yet," the newspapers touched briefly and satirically upon his projected twenty-five-thousand-mile flight. Aëronautical and automotive experts dismissed the idea curtly, implying that it was a hoax, a publicity stunt. The rusty, battered, second-hand plane wouldn't go. The Gresham auxiliary tanks wouldn't work. It was simply a cheap joke.

Smurch, however, after calling on a girl in Brooklyn who worked in the flap-folding department of a large paper-box factory, a girl whom he later described as his "sweet patootie," climbed nonchalantly into his ridiculous plane at dawn of the memorable seventh of July, 1937, spit a curve of tobacco juice into the still air, and took off, carrying with him only a gallon of bootleg gin and six pounds of salami.

When the garage boy thundered out over the ocean the papers were forced to record, in all seriousness, that a mad, unknown young man—his name was variously misspelled—had actually set out upon a preposterous attempt to span the world in a rickety, one-engined contraption, trusting to the long-distance refuelling device of a crazy schoolmaster. When, nine days later, without having stopped once, the tiny plane appeared above San Francisco Bay, headed for New York, spluttering and choking, to be sure, but still magnificently and miraculously aloft, the headlines, which long since had crowded everything else off the front page—even the shooting of the Governor of Illinois by the Vileti gang—swelled to unprecedented size, and the news stories began to run to twenty-five and thirty columns. It was noticeable, however, that the accounts of the epoch-making flight touched rather lightly upon the aviator himself. This was not because facts about the hero as a man were too meagre, but because they were too complete.

5   Reporters, who had been rushed out to Iowa when Smurch's plane was first sighted over the little French coast town of Serly-le-Mer, to dig up the story of the great man's life, had promptly discovered that the story of his life could not be printed. His mother, a sullen short-order cook in a shack restaurant on the edge of a tourists' camping ground near Westfield, met all inquiries as to her son with an angry "Ah, the hell with him; I hope he drowns." His father appeared to be in jail somewhere for stealing spotlights and laprobes from tourists' automobiles; his young brother, a weak-minded lad, had but recently escaped from the Preston, Iowa, Reformatory and was already wanted in several Western towns for the theft of money-order blanks from post offices. These alarming discoveries were still piling up at the very time that Pal Smurch, the greatest hero of the twentieth century, blear-eyed, dead for sleep, half-starved, was piloting his crazy junk-heap high above the region in which the lamentable story of his private life was being unearthed, headed for New York and a greater glory than any man of his time had ever known.

The necessity for printing some account in the papers of the young man's career and personality had led to a remarkable predicament. It was of course impossible to reveal the facts, for a tremendous popular feeling in favor of the young hero had sprung up, like a grass fire, when he was halfway across Europe on his flight around the globe. He was, therefore, described as a modest chap, taciturn, blond, popular with his friends, popular with girls. The only available snapshot of Smurch, taken at the wheel of a phony automobile in a cheap photo studio at an amusement park, was touched up so that the little vulgarian looked quite handsome. His twisted leer was smoothed into a pleasant smile. The truth was, in this way, kept from the youth's ecstatic compatriots; they did not dream that the Smurch family was despised and feared by its neighbors in the obscure Iowa town, nor that the hero himself, because of numerous unsavory exploits, had come to be regarded in Westfield as a nuisance and a menace. He had, the reporters discovered, once knifed the principal of his high school—not mortally, to be sure, but he had knifed him; and on another occasion, surprised in the act of stealing an altarcloth from a church, he had bashed the sacristan over the head with a pot of Easter lilies; for each of these offences he had served a sentence in the reformatory.

Inwardly, the authorities, both in New York and in Washington, prayed that an understanding Providence might, however awful such a thing seemed, bring disaster to the rusty, battered plane and its illustrious pilot, whose unheard-of flight had aroused the civilized world to hosannas of hysterical praise. The authorities were convinced that the character of the renowned aviator was such that the limelight of adulation was bound to reveal him, to all the world, as a congenital hooligan mentally and morally unequipped to cope with his own prodigious fame. "I trust," said the Secretary of State, at one of many secret Cabinet meetings called to consider the national dilemma, "I trust that his mother's prayer will be answered," by which he referred to Mrs. Emma Smurch's wish that her son might be drowned. It was, however, too late for that—Smurch had leaped the Atlantic and then the Pacific as if they were millponds. At three minutes after two o'clock on the afternoon of July 17, 1937, the garage boy brought his idiotic plane into Roosevelt Field for a perfect three-point landing.

It had, of course, been out of the question to arrange a modest little reception for the greatest flier in the history of the world. He was received at Roosevelt Field with such elaborate and pretentious ceremonies as rocked the world. Fortunately, however, the worn and spent hero promptly swooned, had to be removed bodily from his plane, and was spirited from the field without having opened his mouth once. Thus he did not jeopardize the dignity of this first reception, a reception illumined by the presence of the Secretaries of War and the Navy, Mayor Michael J. Moriarity of New York, the Premier of Canada, Governors Fanniman, Groves, McFeely, and Critchfield, and a brilliant array of European diplomats. Smurch did not, in fact, come to in time to take part in the gigantic hullabaloo arranged at City Hall for the next day. He was rushed to a secluded nursing home and confined in bed. It was nine days before he was able to get up, or to be more exact, before he was permitted to get up. Meanwhile the greatest minds in the country, in solemn assembly, had arranged a secret conference of city, state, and government officials, which Smurch was to attend for the purpose of being instructed in the ethics and behavior of heroism.

On the day that the little mechanic was finally allowed to get up and dress and, for the first time in two weeks, took a great chew of tobacco, he was permitted to receive the newspapermen—this by way of testing him out. Smurch did not wait for questions. "Youse guys," he said—and the *Times* man winced—"youse guys can tell the cock-eyed world dat I put it over on Lindbergh, see? Yeh—an' made an ass o' them two frogs." The "two frogs" was a reference to a pair of gallant French fliers who, in attempting a flight only halfway round the world, had, two weeks before, unhappily been lost at sea. The *Times* man was bold enough, at this point, to sketch out for Smurch the accepted formula for interviews in cases of this kind; he explained that there should be no arrogant statements belittling the achievements of other heroes, particularly heroes of foreign nations. "Ah, the hell with that," said Smurch. "I did it, see? I did it, an' I'm talkin' about it." And he did talk about it.

None of this extraordinary interview was, of course, printed. On the contrary, 10 the newspapers, already under the disciplined direction of a secret directorate created for the occasion and composed of statesmen and editors, gave out to a panting and restless world that "Jacky," as he had been arbitrarily nicknamed, would consent to say only that he was very happy and that anyone could have done what he did.

"My achievement has been, I fear, slightly exaggerated," the *Times* man's article had him protest, with a modest smile. These newspaper stories were kept from the hero, a restriction which did not serve to abate the rising malevolence of his temper. The situation was, indeed, extremely grave, for Pal Smurch was, as he kept insisting, "rarin' to go." He could not much longer be kept from a nation clamorous to lionize him. It was the most desperate crisis the United States of America had faced since the sinking of the *Lusitania*.

On the afternoon of the twenty-seventh of July, Smurch was spirited away to a conference-room in which were gathered mayors, governors, government officials, behaviorist psychologists, and editors. He gave them each a limp, moist paw and a brief unlovely grin. "Hah ya?" he said. When Smurch was seated, the Mayor of New York arose and, with obvious pessimism, attempted to explain what he must say and how he must act when presented to the world, ending his talk with a high tribute to the hero's courage and integrity. The Mayor was followed by Governor Fanniman of New York, who, after a touching declaration of faith, introduced Cameron Spottiswood, Second Secretary of the American Embassy in Paris, the gentleman selected to coach Smurch in the amenities of public ceremonies. Sitting in a chair, with a soiled yellow tie in his hand and his shirt open at the throat, unshaved, smoking a rolled cigarette, Jack Smurch listened with a leer on his lips. "I get ya, I get ya," he cut in, nastily. "Ya want me to ack like a softy, huh? Ya want me to ack like that —— —— baby-face Lindbergh, huh? Well, nuts to that, see?" Everyone took in his breath sharply; it was a sigh and a hiss. "Mr. Lindbergh," began a United States Senator, purple with rage, "and Mr. Byrd—" Smurch, who was paring his nails with a jackknife, cut in again. "Byrd!" he exclaimed. "Aw fa God's sake, *dat* big—" Somebody shut off his blasphemies with a sharp word. A newcomer had entered the room. Everyone stood up, except Smurch, who, still busy with his nails, did not even glance up. "Mr. Smurch," said someone, sternly, "the President of the United States!" It had been thought that the presence of the Chief Executive might have a chastening effect upon the young hero, and the former had been, thanks to the remarkable coöperation of the press, secretly brought to the obscure conference-room.

A great, painful silence fell. Smurch looked up, waved a hand at the President. "How ya comin'?" he asked, and began rolling a fresh cigarette. The silence deepened. Someone coughed in a strained way. "Geez, it's hot, ain't it?" said Smurch. He loosened two more shirt buttons, revealing a hairy chest and the tattooed word "Sadie" enclosed in a stencilled heart. The great and important men in the room, faced by the most serious crisis in recent American history, exchanged worried frowns. Nobody seemed to know how to proceed. "Come awn, come awn," said Smurch. "Let's get the hell out of here! When do I start cuttin' in on de parties, huh? And what's they goin' to be *in* it?" He rubbed a thumb and forefinger together meaningly. "Money!" exclaimed a state senator, shocked, pale. "Yeh, money," said Pal, flipping his cigarette out of a window. "An' big money." He began rolling a fresh cigarette. "Big money," he repeated, frowning over the rice paper. He tilted back in his chair, and leered at each gentleman, separately, the leer of an animal that knows its power, the leer of a leopard loose in a bird-and-dog shop. "Aw fa God's sake, let's get some place where it's cooler," he said. "I been cooped up plenty for three weeks!"

Smurch stood up and walked over to an open window, where he stood staring down into the street, nine floors below. The faint shouting of newsboys floated up to him. He made out his name. "Hot dog!" he cried, grinning, ecstatic. He leaned out over the sill. "You tell 'em, babies!" he shouted down. "Hot diggity dog!" In the tense little knot of men standing behind him, a quick, mad impulse flared up. An unspoken word of appeal, of command, seemed to ring through the room. Yet it was deadly silent. Charles K. L. Brand, secretary to the Mayor of New York City, happened to be standing nearest Smurch; he looked inquiringly at the President of the United States. The President, pale, grim, nodded shortly. Brand, a tall, powerfully built man, once a tackle at Rutgers, stepped forward, seized the greatest man in the world by his left shoulder and the seat of his pants, and pushed him out the window.

"My God, he's fallen out the window!" cried a quick-witted editor.

"Get me out of here!" cried the President. Several men sprang to his side and he   15 was hurriedly escorted out of a door toward a side-entrance of the building. The editor of the Associated Press took charge, being used to such things. Crisply he ordered certain men to leave, others to stay; quickly he outlined a story which all the papers were to agree on, sent two men to the street to handle that end of the tragedy, commanded a Senator to sob and two Congressmen to go to pieces nervously. In a word, he skillfully set the stage for the gigantic task that was to follow, the task of breaking to a grief-stricken world the sad story of the untimely, accidental death of its most illustrious and spectacular figure.

The funeral was, as you know, the most elaborate, the finest, the solemnest, and the saddest ever held in the United States of America. The monument in Arlington Cemetery, with its clean white shaft of marble and the simple device of a tiny plane carved on its base, is a place for pilgrims, in deep reverence, to visit. The nations of the world paid lofty tributes to little Jacky Smurch, America's greatest hero. At a given hour there were two minutes of silence throughout the nation. Even the inhabitants of the small, bewildered town of Westfield, Iowa, observed this touching ceremony; agents of the Department of Justice saw to that. One of them was especially assigned to stand grimly in the doorway of a little shack restaurant on the edge of the tourists' camping ground just outside the town. There, under his stern scrutiny, Mrs. Emma Smurch bowed her head above two hamburger steaks sizzling on her grill—bowed her head and turned away, so that the Secret Service man could not see the twisted, strangely familiar, leer on her lips.

QUESTIONS FOR DISCUSSION AND WRITING

1. How does Pal Smurch's stunt create a "most desperate crisis"? How does the "accident" resolve that crisis? Why does Thurber conclude his story with a return visit to Smurch's mother?

2. How does Thurber use the examples of Lindbergh and Byrd to establish the qualifications for a hero? What does Smurch's language reveal about his class, character, and motivations? What does Smurch mean by the word *softy?*

3. How does Thurber's description of politicians, newspaper reporters, and hero worshippers clarify the setting for this story? Why do the reporters refuse to report their discoveries about Smurch's life or their interview with him?

4. How does the narrator's use of superlatives help establish the story's satiric tone? What assumptions does he make about the merit of popular culture and its heroes?

5. What does this story reveal about the "hero making" process in American culture? Who do we admire, and why do we admire them? How do public stunts, rituals, and media "reporting" contribute to the selection and interpretation of such heroes?

Stories for Comparison

T. Coraghessan Boyle's "Heart of a Champion" (pages 305–310); Julio Cortázar's "We Love Glenda So Much" (pages 448–452).

90

....

LEO   TOLSTOY

The Death of Ivan Ilych

LEO TOLSTOY (1828–1910) was born into the Russian nobility at Yasnaya Polyana, his family's estate south of Moscow, and was privately tutored through his restless and reckless youth. After a brief stay at Kazan University, he joined the Russian army and began writing sketches of military life during the Crimean War (1835–1856), as well as three autobiographical novels, *Childhood* (1852), *Boyhood* (1854), and *Youth* (1857). Tolstoy left the army in 1856 and traveled in Europe before returning to his family estate to start a progressive school for children. In 1862, he married, published a novel, *The Cossacks,* and began work on his epic of the Napoleonic wars, *War and Peace,* which was finally published in 1869. Tolstoy spent the next eight years completing his second masterpiece, *Anna Karenina* (1876), the story of a woman who is destroyed by her passions and society's hypocrisy. About 1889, Tolstoy underwent a religious conversion and dedicated his life to propagating his own version of radical Christianity. He published his new views in volumes of nonfiction such as *What Men Live By* (1881), *My Confession* (1882), *What I Believe* (1884), and *The Kingdom of God Is Within You* (1893). Tolstoy's fiction during this period, *The Death of Ivan Ilych* (1886), *The Kreutzer Sonata* (1890), and *Resurrection* (1899), is powerful as literature, if on a much smaller scale than his two great works. Troubled by his spiritual turmoil, Tolstoy left his home and family to seek exile in a monastery. But he never reached his destination, dying in the waiting room of a railway station. *The Death of Ivan Ilych* records the tragic life of a man who discovers too late that he did not live as he ought to have lived.

I

During an interval in the Melvinski trial in the large building of the Law Courts the members and public prosecutor met in Ivan Egorovich Shebek's private room, where the conversation turned on the celebrated Krasovski case. Fedor Vasilievich warmly maintained that it was not subject to their jurisdiction, Ivan Egorovich maintained the contrary, while Peter Ivanovich, not having entered into the discussion at the start, took no part in it but looked through the *Gazette* which had just been handed in.

"Gentlemen," he said, "Ivan Ilych has died!"

"You don't say so!"

"Here, read it yourself," replied Peter Ivanovich, handing Fedor Vasilievich the paper still damp from the press. Surrounded by a black border were the words "Praskovya Fedorovna Golovina, with profound sorrow, informs relatives and friends of the demise of her beloved husband Ivan Ilych Golovin, Member of the Court of Justice, which occurred on February the 4th of this year 1882. The funeral will take place on Friday at one o'clock in the afternoon."

Ivan Ilych had been a colleague of the gentlemen present and was liked by 5 them all. He had been ill for some weeks with an illness said to be incurable. His post had been kept open for him, but there had been conjectures that in case of his death Alexeev might receive his appointment, and that either Vinnikov or Shtabel would succeed Alexeev. So on receiving the news of Ivan Ilych's death the first thought of each of the gentlemen in that private room was of the changes and promotions it might occasion among themselves or their acquaintances.

"I shall be sure to get Shtabel's place or Vinnikov's," thought Fedor Vasilievich. "I was promised that long ago, and the promotion means an extra eight hundred rubles a year for me besides the allowance."

"Now I must apply for my brother-in-law's transfer from Kaluga," thought Peter Ivanovich. "My wife will be very glad, and then she won't be able to say that I never do anything for her relations."

"I thought he would never leave his bed again," said Peter Ivanovich aloud. "It's very sad."

"But what really was the matter with him?"

"The doctors couldn't say—at least they could, but each of them said something 10 different. When last I saw him I thought he was getting better."

"And I haven't been to see him since the holidays. I always meant to go."

"Had he any property?"

"I think his wife had a little—but something quite trifling."

"We shall have to go see her, but they live so terribly far away."

15   "Far away from you, you mean. Everything's far away from your place."

"You see, he never can forgive my living on the other side of the river," said Peter Ivanovich, smiling at Shebek. Then, still talking of the distances between different parts of the city, they returned to the Court.

Besides considerations as to the possible transfers and promotions likely to result from Ivan Ilych's death, the mere fact of the death of a near acquaintance aroused, as usual, in all who heard of it the complacent feeling that "it is he who is dead and not I."

Each one thought or felt, "Well, he's dead but I'm alive!" But the more intimate of Ivan Ilych's acquaintances, his so-called friends, could not help thinking also that they would now have to fulfill the very tiresome demands of propriety by attending the funeral service and paying a visit of condolence to the widow.

Fedor Vasilievich and Peter Ivanovich had been his nearest acquaintances. Peter Ivanovich had studied law with Ivan Ilych and had considered himself to be under obligations to him.

20   Having told his wife at dinner-time of Ivan Ilych's death, and of his conjecture that it might be possible to get her brother transferred to their circuit, Peter Ivanovich sacrificed his usual nap, put on his evening clothes, and drove to Ivan Ilych's house.

At the entrance stood a carriage and two cabs. Leaning against the wall in the hall downstairs near the cloak-stand was a coffin-lid covered with cloth of gold, ornamented with gold cord and tassels, that had been polished up with metal powder. Two ladies in black were taking off their fur cloaks. Peter Ivanovich recognized one of them as Ivan Ilych's sister, but the other was a stranger to him. His colleague Schwartz was just coming downstairs, but on seeing Peter Ivanovich enter he stopped and winked at him, as if to say: "Ivan Ilych has made a mess of things—not like you and me."

Schwartz's face with his Piccadilly whiskers, and his slim figure in evening dress, had as usual an air of elegant solemnity which contrasted with the playfulness of his character and had a special piquancy here, or so it seemed to Peter Ivanovich.

Peter Ivanovich allowed the ladies to precede him and slowly followed them upstairs. Schwartz did not come down but remained where he was, and Peter Ivanovich understood that he wanted to arrange where they should play bridge that evening. The ladies went upstairs to the widow's room, and Schwartz with seriously compressed lips but a playful look in his eyes, indicated by a twist of his eye-brows the room to the right where the body lay.

Peter Ivanovich, like everyone else on such occasions, entered feeling uncertain what he would have to do. All he knew was that at such times it is always safe to cross oneself. But he was not quite sure whether one should make obeisances while doing so. He therefore adopted a middle course. On entering the room he began crossing himself and made a slight movement resembling a bow. At the same time, as far as the motion of his head and arm allowed, he surveyed the room. Two young men—apparently nephews, one of whom was a high school pupil—were leaving the room, crossing themselves as they did so. An old woman was standing motionless, and a lady with strangely arched eyebrows was saying something to her in a whisper. A vigorous, resolute Church Reader, in a frock-coat, was reading something in a loud voice with an expression that precluded any contradiction. The butler's assistant, Gerasim, stepping lightly in front of Peter Ivanovich, was strewing something on the floor. Noticing this, Peter Ivanovich was immediately aware of a faint odour of a decomposing body.

The last time he had called on Ivan Ilych, Peter Ivanovich had seen Gerasim in the study. Ivan Ilych had been particularly fond of him and he was performing the duty of a sick nurse. 25

Peter Ivanovich continued to make the sign of the cross slightly inclining his head in an intermediate direction between the coffin, the Reader, and the icons on the table in a corner of the room. Afterwards, when it seemed to him that this movement of his arm in crossing himself had gone on too long, he stopped and began to look at the corpse.

The dead man lay, as dead men always lie, in a specially heavy way, his rigid limbs sunk in the soft cushions of the coffin, with the head forever bowed on the pillow. His yellow waxen brow with bald patches over his sunken temples was thrust up in the way peculiar to the dead, the protruding nose seeming to press on the upper lip. He was much changed and had grown even thinner since Peter Ivanovich had last seen him, but, as is always the case with the dead, his face was handsomer and above all more dignified than when he was alive. The expression on the face said that what was necessary had been accomplished, and accomplished rightly. Besides this there was in that expression a reproach and a warning to the living. This warning seemed to Peter Ivanovich out of place, or at least not applicable to him. He felt a certain discomfort and so he hurriedly crossed himself once more and turned and went out of the door—too hurriedly and too regardless of propriety, as he himself was aware.

Schwartz was waiting for him in the adjoining room with legs spread wide apart and both hands toying with his top-hat behind his back. The mere sight of that playful, well-groomed, and elegant figure refreshed Peter Ivanovich. He felt that Schwartz was above all these happenings and would not surrender to any depressing influences. His very look said that this incident of a church service for Ivan Ilych could not be a sufficient reason for infringing the order of the session—in other words, that it would certainly not prevent his unwrapping a new pack of cards and shuffling them that evening while a footman placed four fresh candles on the table: in fact, there was no reason for supposing that this incident would hinder their spending the evening agreeably. Indeed he said this in a whisper as Peter Ivanovich passed him, proposing that they should meet for a game at Fedor Vasilievich's. But apparently Peter Ivanovich was not destined to play bridge that evening. Praskovya Fedorovna (a short, fat woman who despite all efforts to the contrary had continued to broaden steadily from her shoulders downwards and who had the same extraordinarily arched eyebrows as the lady who had been standing by the coffin), dressed all in black, her head covered with lace, came out of her own room with some other ladies, conducted them to the room where the dead body lay, and said: "The service will begin immediately. Please go in."

Schwartz, making an indefinite bow, stood still, evidently neither accepting nor declining this invitation. Praskovya Fedorovna, recognizing Peter Ivanovich, sighed, went close up to him, took his hand, and said: "I know you were a true friend to Ivan Ilych . . ." and looked at him awaiting some suitable response. And Peter Ivanovich knew that, just as it had been the right thing to cross himself in that room, so what he had to do here was to press her hand, sigh, and say, "Believe me . . ." So he did all this and as he did it felt that the desired result had been achieved: that both he and she were touched.

30   "Come with me. I want to speak to you before it begins," said the widow. "Give me your arm."

Peter Ivanovich gave her his arm and they went to the inner room, passing Schwartz who winked at Peter Ivanovich compassionately.

"That does for our bridge! Don't object if we find another player. Perhaps you can cut in when you do escape," said his playful look.

Peter Ivanovich sighed still more deeply and despondently, and Praskovya Fedorovna pressed his arm gratefully. When they reached the drawing-room, uphol-stered in pink cretonne and lighted by a dim lamp, they sat down at the table—she on a sofa and Peter Ivanovich on a low pouffe, the springs of which yielded spas-modically under his weight. Praskovya Fedorovna had been on the point of warning him to take another seat, but felt that such a warning was out of keeping with her present condition and so changed her mind. As he sat down on the pouffe Peter Ivanovich recalled how Ivan Ilych had arranged this room and had consulted him re-garding this pink cretonne with green leaves. The whole room was full of furniture and knick-knacks, and on her way to the sofa the lace of the widow's black shawl caught on the carved edge of the table. Peter Ivanovich rose to detach it, and the springs on the pouffe, relieved of his weight, rose also and gave him a push. The widow began detaching her shawl herself, and Peter Ivanovich again sat down, sup-pressing the rebellious springs of the pouffe under him. But the widow had not quite freed herself and Peter Ivanovich got up again, and again the pouffe rebelled and even creaked. When this was all over she took out a clean cambric handkerchief and began to weep. The episode with the shawl and the struggle with the pouffe had cooled Peter Ivanovich's emotions and he sat there with a sullen look on his face. This awkward situation was interrupted by Sokolov, Ivan Ilych's butler, who came to report that the plot in the cemetery that Praskovya Fedorovna had chosen would cost two hundred rubles. She stopped weeping and, looking at Peter Ivanovich with the air of a victim, remarked in French that it was very hard for her. Peter Ivanovich made a silent gesture signifying his full conviction that it must indeed be so.

"Please smoke," she said in a magnanimous yet crushed voice, and turned to dis-cuss with Sokolov the price of the plot for the grave.

35   Peter Ivanovich while lighting his cigarette heard her inquiring very circum-stantially into the price of different plots in the cemetery and finally decide which she would take. When that was done she gave instructions about engaging the choir. Sokolov then left the room.

"I look after everything myself," she told Peter Ivanovich, shifting the albums that lay on the table; and noticing that the table was endangered by his cigarette-ash, she immediately passed him an ashtray, saying as she did so: "I consider it an affectation to say that my grief prevents my attending to practical affairs. On the contrary, if anything can—I won't say console me, but—distract me, it is seeing to everything concerning him." She again took out her handkerchief as if preparing to cry, but suddenly, as if mastering her feeling, she shook herself and began to speak calmly. "But there is something I want to talk to you about."

Peter Ivanovich bowed, keeping control of the springs of the pouffe, which immediately began quivering under him.

"He suffered terribly the last few days."

"Did he?" said Peter Ivanovich.

"Oh, terribly! He screamed unceasingly, not for minutes but for hours. For the last three days he screamed incessantly. It was unendurable. I cannot understand how I bore it; you could hear him three rooms off. Oh, what I have suffered!"

"Is it possible that he was conscious all that time?" asked Peter Ivanovich.

"Yes," she whispered. "To the last moment. He took leave of us a quarter of an hour before he died, and asked us to take Volodya away."

The thought of the sufferings of this man he had known so intimately, first as a merry little boy, then as a school-mate, and later as a grown-up colleague, suddenly struck Peter Ivanovich with horror, despite an unpleasant consciousness of his own and this woman's dissimulation. He again saw that brow, and that nose pressing down on the lip, and felt afraid for himself.

"Three days of frightful suffering and then death! Why, that might suddenly, at any time, happen to me," he thought, and for a moment felt terrified. But—he did not himself know how—the customary reflection at once occurred to him that this had happened to Ivan Ilych and not to him, and that it should not and could not happen to him, and that to think that it could would be yielding to depression which he ought not to do, as Schwartz's expression plainly showed. After which reflection Peter Ivanovich felt reassured, and began to ask with interest about the details of Ivan Ilych's death, as though death was an accident natural to Ivan Ilych but certainly not to himself.

After many details of the really dreadful physical sufferings Ivan Ilych had endured (which details he learnt only from the effect those sufferings had produced on Praskovya Fedorovna's nerves) the widow apparently found it necessary to get to business.

"Oh, Peter Ivanovich, how hard it is! How terribly, terribly hard!" and she again began to weep.

Peter Ivanovich sighed and waited for her to finish blowing her nose. When she had done so he said, "Believe me . . ." and she again began talking and brought out what was evidently her chief concern with him—namely, to question him as to how she could obtain a grant of money from the government on the occasion of her husband's death. She made it appear that she was asking Peter Ivanovich's advice about her pension, but he soon saw that she already knew about that to the minutest detail, more even than he did himself. She knew how much could be got out of the government in consequence of her husband's death, but wanted to find out whether she could not possibly extract something more. Peter Ivanovich tried to think of some means of doing so, but after reflecting for a while and, out of propriety, condemning the government for its niggardliness, he said he thought that nothing more could be got. Then she sighed and evidently began to devise means of getting rid of her visitor. Noticing this, he put out his cigarette, rose, pressed her hand, and went out into the anteroom.

In the dining-room where the clock stood that Ivan Ilych had liked so much and had bought at an antique shop, Peter Ivanovich met a priest and a few acquaintances who had come to attend the service, and he recognized Ivan Ilych's daughter, a handsome young woman. She was in black and her slim figure appeared slimmer than ever. She had a gloomy, determined, almost angry expression, and bowed to Peter Ivanovich as though he were in some way to blame. Behind her, with the same offended look, stood a wealthy young man, an examining magistrate, whom Peter Ivanovich also knew and who was her fiancé, as he had heard. He bowed mournfully to them and was about to pass into the death-chamber, when from under the stairs appeared the figure of Ivan Ilych's schoolboy son, who was extremely like his father. He seemed a little Ivan Ilych, such as Peter Ivanovich remembered when they studied law together. His tear-stained eyes had in them the look that is seen in the eyes of boys of thirteen or fourteen who are not pure-minded. When he saw Peter Ivanovich he scowled morosely and shame-facedly. Peter Ivanovich nodded to him and entered the death-chamber. The service began: candles, groans, incense, tears, and sobs. Peter Ivanovich stood looking gloomily down at his feet. He did not look once at the dead man, did not yield to any depressing influence, and was one of the first to leave the room. There was no one in the anteroom, but Gerasim darted out of the dead man's room, rummaged with his strong hands among the fur coats to find Peter Ivanovich's and helped him on with it.

"Well, friend Gerasim," said Peter Ivanovich, so as to say something. "It's a sad affair, isn't it?"

50   "It's God's will. We shall all come to it some day," said Gerasim, displaying his teeth—the even, white teeth of a healthy peasant—and, like a man in the thick of urgent work, he briskly opened the front door, called the coachman, helped Peter Ivanovich into the sledge, and sprang back to the porch as if in readiness for what he had to do next.

Peter Ivanovich found the fresh air particularly pleasant after the smell of incense, the dead body, and carbolic acid.

"Where to, sir?" asked the coachman.

"It's not too late even now. . . . I'll call around on Fedor Vasilievich."

He accordingly drove there and found them just finishing the first rubber, so that it was quite convenient for him to cut in.

2

55   Ivan Ilych's life had been most simple and most ordinary and therefore most terrible.

He had been a member of the Court of Justice, and died at the age of forty-five. His father had been an official who after serving in various ministries and departments of Petersburg had made the sort of career which brings men to positions from which by reason of their long service they cannot be dismissed, though they are obviously unfit to hold any responsible position, and for whom therefore posts are specially created, which though fictitious carry salaries of from six to ten thousand rubles that are not fictitious, and in receipt of which they live on to a great age.

Such was the Privy Councillor and superfluous member of various superfluous institutions, Ilya Epimovich Golovin.

He had three sons, of whom Ivan Ilych was the second. The eldest son was following in his father's footsteps only in another department, and was already approaching that stage in the service at which a similar sinecure would be reached. The third son was a failure. He had ruined his prospects in a number of positions and was now serving in the railway department. His father and brothers, and still more their wives, not merely disliked meeting him, but avoided remembering his existence unless compelled to do so. His sister had married Baron Greff, a Petersburg official of her father's type. Ivan Ilych was *le phénix de la famille* as people said. He was neither as cold and formal as his elder brother nor as wild as the younger, but was a happy mean between them—an intelligent, polished, lively and agreeable man. He had studied with his younger brother at the School of Law, but the latter had failed to complete the course and was expelled when he was in the fifth class. Ivan Ilych finished the course well. Even when he was at the School of Law he was just what he remained for the rest of his life: a capable, cheerful, good-natured, and social man, though strict in the fulfilment of what he considered to be his duty: and he considered his duty to be what was so considered by those in authority. Neither as a boy nor as a man was he a toady, but from early youth was by nature attracted to people of high station as a fly is drawn to the light, assimilating their ways and views of life and establishing friendly relations with them. All the enthusiasms of childhood and youth passed without leaving much trace on him; he succumbed to sensuality, to vanity, and latterly among the highest classes to liberalism, but always within limits which his instinct unfailingly indicated to him as correct.

At school he had done things which had formerly seemed to him very horrid and made him feel disgusted with himself when he did them; but when later on he saw that such actions were done by people of good position and that they did not regard them as wrong, he was able not exactly to regard them as right, but to forget about them entirely or not be at all troubled at remembering them.

Having graduated from the School of Law and qualified for the tenth rank of 60 civil service, and having received money from his father for his equipment, Ivan Ilych ordered himself clothes at Scharmer's, the fashionable tailor, hung a medallion inscribed *respice finem* on his watch-chain, took leave of his professor and the prince who was patron of the school, had a farewell dinner with his comrades at Donon's first-class restaurant, and with his new and fashionable portmanteau, linen, clothes, shaving and other toilet appliances, and a travelling rug, all purchased at the best shops, he set off for one of the provinces where, through his father's influence, he had been attached to the Governor as an official for special service.

In the province Ivan Ilych soon arranged as easy and agreeable a position for himself as he had had at the School of Law. He performed his official tasks, made his career, and at the same time amused himself pleasantly and decorously. Occasionally he paid official visits to country districts, where he behaved with dignity both to his superiors and inferiors, and performed the duties entrusted to him, which related chiefly to the sectarians, with an exactness and incorruptible honesty of which he could not but feel proud.

In official matters, despite his youth and taste for frivolous gaiety, he was exceedingly reserved, punctilious, and even severe; but in society he was often amusing and witty, and always good-natured, correct in his manner, and *bon enfant,* as the governor and his wife—with whom he was like one of the family—used to say of him.

In the provinces he had an affair with a lady who made advances to the elegant young lawyer, and there was also a milliner; and there were carousals with aides-de-camp who visited the district, and after-supper visits to a certain outlying street of doubtful reputation; and there was too some obsequiousness to his chief and even to his chief's wife, but all this was done with such a tone of good breeding that no hard names could be applied to it. It all came under the heading of the French saying: *"Il faut que jeunesse se passe."* It was all done with clean hands, in clean linen, with French phrases, and above all among people of the best society and consequently with the approval of people of rank.

So Ivan Ilych served for five years and then came a change in his official life. The new and reformed judicial institutions were introduced, and new men were needed. Ivan Ilych became such a new man. He was offered the post of Examining Magistrate, and he accepted it though the post was in another province and obliged him to give up the connexions he had formed and to make new ones. His friends met to give him a send-off; they had a group-photograph taken and presented him with a silver cigarette-case, and he set off to his new post.

65   As examining magistrate Ivan Ilych was just as *comme il faut* and decorous a man, inspiring general respect and capable of separating his official duties from his private life, as he had been when acting as an official on special service. His duties now as examining magistrate were far more interesting and attractive than before. In his former position it had been pleasant to wear an undress uniform made by Scharmer, and to pass through the crowd of petitioners and officials who were timorously awaiting an audience with the governor, and who envied him as with free and easy gait he went straight into his chief's private room to have a cup of tea and a cigarette with him. But not many people had then been directly dependent on him—only police officials and the sectarians when he went on speciical missions—and he liked to treat them politely, almost as comrades, as if he were letting them feel that he who had the power to crush them was treating them in this simple, friendly way. There were then but few such people. But now, as an examining magistrate, Ivan Ilych felt that everyone without exception, even the most important and self-satisfied, was in his power, and that he need only write a few words on a sheet of paper with a certain heading, and this or that important, self-satisfied person would be brought before him in the role of an accused person or a witness, and if he did not choose to allow him to sit down, would have to stand before him and answer his questions. Ivan Ilych never abused his power; he tried on the contrary to soften its expression, but the consciousness of it and of the possibility of softening its effect, supplied the chief interest and attraction of his office. In his work itself, especially in his examinations, he very soon acquired a method of eliminating all considerations irrelevant to the legal aspect of

the case, and reducing even the most complicated case to a form in which it would be presented on paper only in its externals, completely excluding his personal opinion of the matter, while above all observing every prescribed formality. The work was new and Ivan Ilych was one of the first men to apply the new Code of 1864.

On taking up the post of examining magistrate in a new town, he made new ac-quaintances and connexions, placed himself on a new footing, and assumed a some-what different tone. He took up an attitude of rather dignified aloofness towards the provincial authorities, but picked out the best circle of legal gentlemen and wealthy gentry living in the town and assumed a tone of slight dissatisfaction with the gov-ernment, of moderate liberalism, and of enlightened citizenship. At the same time, without at all altering the elegance of his toilet, he ceased shaving his chin and al-lowed his beard to grow as it pleased.

Ivan Ilych settled down very pleasantly in this new town. The society there, which inclined towards opposition to the Governor, was friendly, his salary was larger, and he began to play *vint,* which he found added not a little to the pleasure of life, for he had a capacity for cards, played good-humouredly, and calculated rapidly and astutely, so that he usually won.

After living there for two years he met his future wife, Praskovya Fedorovna Mikhel, who was the most attractive, clever, and brilliant girl of the set in which he moved, and among other amusements and relaxations from his labours as examining magistrate, Ivan Ilych established light and playful relations with her.

While he had been an official on special service he had been accustomed to dance, but now as an examining magistrate it was exceptional for him to do so. If he danced now, he did it as if to show that though he served under the reformed order of things, and had reached the fifth official rank, yet when it came to dancing he could do it better than most people. So at the end of an evening he sometimes danced with Praskovya Fedorovna, and it was chiefly during these dances that he captivated her. She fell in love with him. Ivan Ilych had at first no definite intention of marry-ing, but when the girl fell in love with him he said to himself: "Really, why shouldn't I marry?"

Praskovya Fedorovna came of a good family, was not bad looking and had some little property. Ivan Ilych might have aspired to a more brilliant match, but even this was good. He had his salary, and she, he hoped, would have an equal income. She was well connected, and was a sweet, pretty, and thoroughly correct young woman. To say that Ivan Ilych married because he fell in love with Praskovya Fedorovna and found that she sympathized with his views of life would be as incorrect as to say that he married because his social circle approved of the match. He was swayed by both these considerations: the marriage gave him personal satisfaction, and at the same time it was considered the right thing by the most highly placed of his associates.

So Ivan Ilych got married.

The preparations for marriage and the beginning of married life, with its conju-gal caresses, the new furniture, new crockery, and new linen, were very pleasant un-til his wife became pregnant—so that Ivan Ilych had begun to think that marriage would not impair the easy, agreeable, gay and always decorous character of his life, approved of by society and regarded by himself as natural, but would even improve it. But from the first months of his wife's pregnancy, something new, unpleasant, depressing, and unseemly, and from which there was no way of escape, unexpectedly showed itself.

His wife, without any reason—*de gaieté de coeur* as Ivan Ilych expressed it to himself—began to disturb the pleasure and propriety of their life. She began to be jealous without any cause, expected him to devote his whole attention to her, found fault with everything, and made coarse and ill-mannered scenes.

At first Ivan Ilych hoped to escape from the unpleasantness of this state of affairs by the same easy and decorous relation to life that had served him heretofore: he tried to ignore his wife's disagreeable moods, continued to live in his usual easy and pleasant way, invited friends to his house for a game of cards, and also tried going out to his club or spending his evenings with friends. But one day his wife began upbraiding him so vigorously, using such coarse words, and continued to abuse him every time he did not fulfil her demands, so resolutely and with such evident determination not to give way till he submitted—that is, till he stayed at home and was bored just as she was—that he became alarmed. He now realized that matrimony—at any rate with Praskovya Fedorovna—was not always conducive to the pleasures and amenities of life but on the contrary often infringed both comfort and propriety, and that he must therefore entrench himself against such infringement. And Ivan Ilych began to seek for means of doing so. His official duties were the one thing that imposed upon Praskovya Fedorovna, and by means of his official work and the duties attached to it he began struggling with his wife to secure his own independence.

75   With the birth of their child, the attempts to feed it and the various failures in doing so, and with the real and imaginary illnesses of mother and child, in which Ivan Ilych's sympathy was demanded but about which he understood nothing, the need of securing for himself an existence outside his family life became still more imperative.

As his wife grew more irritable and exacting and Ivan Ilych transferred the centre of gravity of his life more and more to his official work, so did he grow to like his work better and became more ambitious than before.

Very soon, within a year of his wedding, Ivan Ilych had realized that marriage, though it may add some comforts to life, is in fact a very intricate and difficult affair towards which in order to perform one's duty, that is, to lead a decorous life approved of by society, one must adopt a definite attitude just as towards one's official duties.

And Ivan Ilych evolved such an attitude towards married life. He only required of it those conveniences—dinner at home, housewife, and bed—which it could give him, and above all that propriety of external forms required by public opinion. For the rest he looked for light-hearted pleasure and propriety, and was very thankful when he found them, but if he met with antagonism and querulousness he at once retired into his separate fenced-off world of official duties, where he found satisfaction.

Ivan Ilych was esteemed a good official, and after three years was made Assistant Public Prosecutor. His new duties, their importance, the possibility of indicting and imprisoning anyone he chose, the publicity his speeches received, and the success he had in all these things, made his work still more attractive.

More children came. His wife became more and more querulous and ill- tempered, but the attitude Ivan Ilych had adopted towards his home life rendered him almost impervious to her grumbling.

After seven years' service in that town he was transferred to another province as Public Prosecutor. They moved, but were short of money and his wife did not like the place they moved to. Though the salary was higher the cost of living was greater, besides which two of their children died and family life became still more unpleasant for him.

Praskovya Fedorovna blamed her husband for every inconvenience they encountered in their new home. Most of the conversations between husband and wife, especially as to the children's education, led to topics which recalled former disputes, and those disputes were apt to flare up again at any moment. There remained only those rare periods of amorousness which still came to them at times but did not last long. These were islets at which they anchored for a while and then again set out upon that ocean of veiled hostility which showed itself in their aloofness from one another. This aloofness might have grieved Ivan Ilych had he considered that it ought not to exist, but he now regarded the position as normal, and even made it the goal at which he aimed in family life. His aim was to free himself more and more from those unpleasantnesses and to give them a semblance of harmlessness and propriety. He attained this by spending less and less time with his family, and when obliged to be at home he tried to safeguard his position by the presence of outsiders. The chief thing, however, was that he had his official duties. The whole interest of his life now centered in the official world and that interest absorbed him. The consciousness of his power, being able to ruin anybody he wished to ruin, the importance, even the external dignity of his entry into court, or meetings with his subordinates, his success with superiors and inferiors, and above all his masterly handling of cases, of which he was conscious—all this gave him pleasure and filled his life, together with chats with his colleagues, dinners, and bridge. So that on the whole Ivan Ilych's life continued to flow as he considered it should do—pleasantly and properly.

So things continued for another seven years. His eldest daughter was already sixteen, another child had died, and only one son was left, a schoolboy and a subject of dissension. Ivan Ilych wanted to put him in the School of Law, but to spite him Praskovya Fedorovna entered him at the High School. The daughter had been educated at home and had turned out well: the boy did not learn badly either.

3

So Ivan Ilych lived for seventeen years after his marriage. He was already a Public Prosecutor of long standing, and had declined several proposed transfers while awaiting a more desirable post, when an unanticipated and unpleasant occurrence quite upset the peaceful course of his life. He was expecting to be offered the post of presiding judge in a University town, but Happe somehow came to the front and obtained the appointment instead. Ivan Ilych became irritable, reproached Happe, and quarrelled both with him and with his immediate superiors—who became colder to him and again passed him over when other appointments were made.

85   This was in 1880, the hardest year of Ivan Ilych's life. It was then that it became evident on the one hand that his salary was insufficient for them to live on, and on the other that he had been forgotten, and not only this, but that what was for him the greatest and most cruel injustice appeared to others a quite ordinary occurrence. Even his father did not consider it his duty to help him. Ivan Ilych felt himself abandoned by everyone, and that they regarded his position with a salary of 3,500 rubles as quite normal and even fortunate. He alone knew that with the consciousness of the injustices done him, with his wife's incessant nagging, and with the debts he had contracted by living beyond his means, his position was far from normal.

In order to save money that summer he obtained leave of absence and went with his wife to live in the country at her brother's place.

In the country, without his work, he experienced *ennui* for the first time in his life, and not only *ennui* but intolerable depression, and he decided that it was impossible to go on living like that, and that it was necessary to take energetic measures.

Having passed a sleepless night pacing up and down the veranda, he decided to go to Petersburg and bestir himself, in order to punish those who had failed to appreciate him and to get transferred to another ministry.

Next day, despite many protests from his wife and her brother, he started for Petersburg with the sole object of obtaining a post with a salary of five thousand rubles a year. He was no longer bent on any particular department, or tendency, or kind of activity. All he now wanted was an appointment to another post with a salary of five thousand rubles, either in the administration, in the banks, with the railways, in one of the Empress Marya's Institutions, or even in the customs—but it had to carry with it a salary of five thousand rubles and be in a ministry other than that in which they had failed to appreciate him.

90   And this quest of Ivan Ilych's was crowned with remarkable and unexpected success. At Kursk an acquaintance of his, F. I. Ilyin, got into the first-class carriage, sat down beside Ivan Ilych, and told him of a telegram just received by the Governor of Kursk announcing that a change was about to take place in the ministry: Peter Ivanovich was to be superseded by Ivan Semenovich.

The proposed change, apart from its significance for Russia, had a special significance for Ivan Ilych, because by bringing forward a new man, Peter Petrovich, and consequently his friend Zachar Ivanovich, it was highly favourable for Ivan Ilych, since Zachar Ivanovich was a friend and colleague of his.

In Moscow this news was confirmed, and on reaching Petersburg Ivan Ilych found Zachar Ivanovich and received a definite promise of an appointment in his former Department of Justice.

A week later he telegraphed to his wife: "Zachar in Miller's place. I shall receive appointment on presentation of report."

Thanks to this change of personnel, Ivan Ilych had unexpectedly obtained an appointment in his former ministry which placed him two stages above his former colleagues besides giving him five thousand rubles salary and three thousand five hundred rubles for expenses connected with his removal. All his ill humour towards his former enemies and the whole department vanished, and Ivan Ilych was completely happy.

He returned to the country more cheerful and contented than he had been for a 95
long time. Praskovya Fedorovna also cheered up and a truce was arranged between
them. Ivan Ilych told of how he had been feted by everybody in Petersburg, how all
those who had been his enemies were put to shame and now fawned on him, how envious they were of his appointment, and how much everybody in Petersburg had
liked him.

Praskovya Fedorovna listened to all this and appeared to believe it. She did not
contradict anything, but only made plans for her life in the town to which they were
going. Ivan Ilych saw with delight that these plans were his plans, that he and his
wife agreed, and that, after a stumble, his life was regaining its due and natural character of pleasant lightheartedness and decorum.

Ivan Ilych had come back for a short time only, for he had to take up his new
duties on the 10th of September. Moreover, he needed time to settle into the new
place, to move all his belongings from the province, and to buy and order many additional things: in a word, to make such arrangements as he had resolved on, which
were almost exactly what Praskovya Fedorovna too had decided on.

Now that everything had happened so fortunately, and that he and his wife were
at one in their aims and moreover saw so little of one another, they got on together
better than they had done since the first years of marriage. Ivan Ilych had thought of
taking his family away with him at once, but the insistence of his wife's brother and
her sister-in-law, who had suddenly become particularly amiable and friendly to him
and his family, induced him to depart alone.

So he departed, and the cheerful state of mind induced by his success and by the
harmony between his wife and himself, the one intensifying the other, did not leave
him. He found a delightful house, just the thing both he and his wife had dreamt of.
Spacious, lofty reception rooms in the old style, a convenient and dignified study,
rooms for his wife and daughter, a study for his son—it might have been specially
built for them. Ivan Ilych himself superintended the arrangement, chose the wall-
papers, supplemented the furniture (preferably with antiques which he considered
particularly *comme il faut*), and supervised the upholstering. Everything progressed
and progressed and approached the ideal he had set himself: even when things were
only half completed they exceeded his expectations. He saw what a refined and elegant character, free from vulgarity, it would all have when it was ready. On falling
asleep he pictured to himself how the reception-room would look. Looking at the yet
unfinished drawing-room he could see the fireplace, the screen, the what-not, the little chairs dotted here and there, the dishes and plates on the walls, and the bronzes,
as they would be when everything was in place. He was pleased by the thought of
how his wife and daughter, who shared his taste in this matter, would be impressed
by it. They were certainly not expecting as much. He had been particularly successful in finding, and buying cheaply, antiques which gave a particularly aristocratic
character to the whole place. But in his letters he intentionally understated everything in order to be able to surprise them. All this so absorbed him that his new
duties—though he liked his official work—interested him less than he had expected.
Sometimes he even had moments of absentmindedness during the Court Sessions,
and would consider whether he should have straight or curved cornices for his

curtains. He was so interested in it all that he often did things himself, rearranging the furniture, or rehanging the curtains. Once when mounting a step-ladder to show the upholsterer, who did not understand, how he wanted the hangings draped, he made a false step and slipped, but being a strong and agile man he clung on and only knocked his side against the knob of the window frame. The bruised place was painful but the pain soon passed, and he felt particularly bright and well just then. He wrote: "I feel fifteen years younger." He thought he would have everything ready by September, but it dragged on till mid-October. But the result was charming not only in his eyes but to everyone who saw it.

100   In reality it was just what is usually seen in the houses of people of moderate means who want to appear rich, and therefore succeed only in resembling others like themselves: there were damasks, dark wood, plants, rugs, and dull and polished bronzes—all the things people of a certain class have in order to resemble other people of that class. His house was so like the others that it would never have been noticed, but to him it all seemed to be quite exceptional. He was very happy when he met his family at the station and brought them to the newly furnished house all lit up, where a footman in a white tie opened the door into the hall decorated with plants, and when they went on into the drawing-room and the study uttering exclamations of delight. He conducted them everywhere, drank in their praises eagerly, and beamed with pleasure. At tea that evening, when Praskovya Federovna among other things asked him about his fall, he laughed, and showed them how he had gone flying and had frightened the upholsterer.

"It's a good thing I'm a bit of an athlete. Another man might have been killed, but I merely knocked myself, just here; it hurts when it's touched, but it's passing off already—it's only a bruise."

So they began living in their new home—in which, as always happens, when they got thoroughly settled in they found they were just one room short—and with the increased income, which as always was just a little (some five hundred rubles) too little, but it was all very nice.

Things went particularly well at first, before everything was finally arranged and while something had still to be done: this thing bought, that thing ordered, another thing moved, and something else adjusted. Though there were some disputes between husband and wife, they were both so well satisfied and had so much to do that it all passed off without any serious quarrels. When nothing was left to arrange it became rather dull and something seemed to be lacking, but they were then making acquaintances, forming habits, and life was growing fuller.

Ivan Ilych spent his mornings at the law court and came home to dinner, and at first he was generally in a good humour, though he occasionally became irritable just on account of his house. (Every spot on the tablecloth or the upholstery, and every broken window-blind string, irritated him. He had devoted so much trouble to arranging it all that every disturbance of it distressed him.) But on the whole his life ran its course as he believed life should do: easily, pleasantly, and decorously.

105   He got up at nine, drank his coffee, read the paper, and then put on his undress uniform and went to the law courts. There the harness in which he worked had already been stretched to fit him and he donned it without a hitch: petitioners, inquiries

at the chancery, the chancery itself, and the sittings public and administrative. In all this the thing was to exclude everything fresh and vital, which always disturbs the regular course of official business, and to admit only official relations with people, and then only on official grounds. A man would come, for instance, wanting some information. Ivan Ilych, as one in whose sphere the matter did not lie, would have nothing to do with him: but if the man had some business with him in his official capacity, something that could be expressed on officially stamped paper, he would do everything, positively everything he could within the limits of such relations, and in doing so would maintain the semblance of friendly human relations, that is, would observe the courtesies of life. As soon as the official relations ended, so did everything else. Ivan Ilych possessed this capacity to separate his real life from the official side of affairs and not mix the two, in the highest degree, and by long practice and natural aptitude had brought it to such a pitch that sometimes, in the manner of a virtuoso, he would even allow himself to let the human and official relations mingle. He let himself do this just because he felt that he could at any time he chose resume the strictly official attitude again and drop the human relation. And he did it all easily, pleasantly, correctly, and even artistically. In the intervals between the sessions he smoked, drank tea, chatted a little about politics, a little about general topics, a little about cards, but most of all about official appointments. Tired, but with the feelings of a virtuoso—one of the first violins who has played his part in an orchestra with precision—he would return home to find that his wife and daughter had been out paying calls, or had a visitor, and that his son had been to school, had done his homework with his tutor, and was duly learning what is taught at High Schools. Everything was as it should be. After dinner, if they had no visitors, Ivan Ilych sometimes read a book that was being much discussed at the time, and in the evening settled down to work, that is, read official papers, compared the depositions of witnesses, and noted paragraphs of the Code applying to them. This was neither dull nor amusing. It was dull when he might have been playing bridge, but if no bridge was available it was at any rate better than doing nothing or sitting with his wife. Ivan Ilych's chief pleasure was giving little dinners to which he invited men and women of good social position, and just as his drawing-room resembled all other drawing-rooms so did his enjoyable little parties resemble all other such parties.

Once they even gave a dance. Ivan Ilych enjoyed it and everything went off well, except that it led to a violent quarrel with his wife about the cakes and sweets. Praskovya Federovna had made her own plans, but Ivan Ilych insisted on getting everything from an expensive confectioner and ordered too many cakes, and the quarrel occurred because some of those cakes were left over and the confectioner's bill came to forty-five rubles. It was a great and disagreeable quarrel. Praskovya Federovna called him "a fool and an imbecile," and he clutched at his head and made angry allusions to divorce.

But the dance itself had been enjoyable. The best people were there, and Ivan Ilych had danced with Princess Trufonova, a sister of the distinguished founder of the Society "Bear my Burden."

The pleasures connected with his work were pleasures of ambition; his social pleasures were those of vanity; but Ivan Ilych's greatest pleasure was playing bridge.

He acknowledged that whatever disagreeable incident happened in his life, the pleasure that beamed like a ray of light above everything else was to sit down to bridge with good players, not noisy partners, and of course to four-handed bridge (with five players it was annoying to have to stand out, though one pretended not to mind), to play a clever and serious game (when the cards allowed it) and then to have supper and drink a glass of wine. After a game of bridge, especially if he had won a little (to win a large sum was unpleasant), Ivan Ilych went to bed in specially good humour.

So they lived. They formed a circle of acquaintances among the best people and were visited by people of importance and by young folk. In their views as to their acquaintances, husband, wife and daughter were entirely agreed, and tacitly and unanimously kept at arm's length and shook off the various shabby friends and relations who, with much show of affection, gushed into the drawing-room with its Japanese plates on the walls. Soon these shabby friends ceased to obtrude themselves and only the best people remained in the Golovins' set.

Young men made up to Lisa, and Petrishchev, an examining magistrate and Dmitri Ivanovich Petrishchev's son and sole heir, began to be so attentive to her that Ivan Ilych had already spoken to Praskovya Federovna about it, and considered whether they should not arrange a party for them or get up some private theatricals.

So they lived, and all went well, without change, and life flowed pleasantly.

4

They were all in good health. It could not be called ill health if Ivan Ilych sometimes said that he had a queer taste in his mouth and felt some discomfort in his left side.

But this discomfort increased and, though not exactly painful, grew into a sense of pressure in his side accompanied by ill humour. And his irritability became worse and worse and began to mar the agreeable, easy, and correct life that had established itself in the Golovin family. Quarrels between husband and wife became more and more frequent, and soon the ease and amenity disappeared and even the decorum was barely maintained. Scenes again became frequent, and very few of those islets remained on which husband and wife could meet without an explosion. Praskovya Federovna now had good reason to say that her husband's temper was trying. With characteristic exaggeration she said he had always had a dreadful temper, and that it had needed all her good nature to put up with it for twenty years. It was true that now the quarrels were started by him. His bursts of temper always came just before dinner, often just as he began to eat his soup. Sometimes he noticed that a plate or dish was chipped, or the food was not right, or his son put his elbow on the table, or his daughter's hair was not done as he liked it, and for all this he blamed Praskovya Federovna. At first she retorted and said disagreeable things to him, but once or twice he fell into such a rage at the beginning of dinner that she realized it was due to some physical derangement brought on by taking food, and so she restrained herself and did not answer, but only hurried to get the dinner over. She regarded this self-restraint as highly praiseworthy. Having come to the conclusion that her husband had a dreadful temper and made her life miserable, she began to feel sorry for herself, and the more she pitied herself the more she hated her husband. She began to wish he would die; yet she did not want him to die because then his salary would cease. And this irritated her against him still more. She considered herself dreadfully unhappy just because not even his death could save her, and though she concealed her exasperation, that hidden exasperation of hers increased his irritation also.

After one scene in which Ivan Ilych had been particularly unfair and after which he had said in explanation that he certainly was irritable but that it was due to his not being well, she said that if he was ill it should be attended to, and insisted on his going to see a celebrated doctor.

He went. Everything took place as he had expected and as it always does. There was the usual waiting and the important air assumed by the doctor, with which he was so familiar (resembling that which he himself assumed in court), and the sounding and listening, and the questions which called for answers that were foregone conclusions and were evidently unnecessary, and the look of importance which implied that "if only you put yourself in our hands we will arrange everything—we know indubitably how it has to be done, always in the same way for everybody alike." It was all just as it was in the law courts. The doctor put on just the same air towards him as he himself put on towards an accused person.

The doctor said that so-and-so indicated that there was so-and-so inside the patient, but if the investigation of so-and-so did not confirm this, then he must assume that and that. If he assumed that and that, then . . . and so on. To Ivan Ilych only one question was important: was his case serious or not? But the doctor ignored that inappropriate question. From his point of view it was not the one under consideration, the real question was to decide between a floating kidney, chronic catarrh, or appendicitis. It was not a question of Ivan Ilych's life or death, but one between a floating kidney and appendicitis. And that question the doctor solved brilliantly, as it seemed to Ivan Ilych, in favour of the appendix, with the reservation that should an examination of the urine give fresh indications the matter would be reconsidered. All this was just what Ivan Ilych had himself brilliantly accomplished a thousand times in dealing with men on trial. The doctor summed up just as brilliantly, looking over his spectacles triumphantly and even gaily at the accused. From the doctor's summing up Ivan Ilych concluded that things were bad, but that for the doctor, and perhaps for everybody else, it was a matter of indifference, though for him it was bad. And this conclusion struck him painfully, arousing in him a great feeling of pity for himself and of bitterness towards the doctor's indifference to a matter of such importance.

He said nothing of this, but rose, placed the doctor's fee on the table, and remarked with a sigh: "We sick people probably often put inappropriate questions. But tell me, in general, is this complaint dangerous, or not? . . ."

The doctor looked at him sternly over his spectacles with one eye, as if to say: "Prisoner, if you will not keep to the questions put to you, I shall be obliged to have you removed from the court."

"I have already told you what I consider necessary and proper. The analysis may show something more." And the doctor bowed.

Ivan Ilych went out slowly, seated himself disconsolately in his sledge, and drove home. All the way home he was going over what the doctor had said, trying to translate those complicated, obscure, scientific phrases into plain language and find in them an answer to the question: "Is my condition bad? Is it very bad? Or is there as yet nothing much wrong?" And it seemed to him that the meaning of what the doctor had said was that it was very bad. Everything in the streets seemed depressing. The cabmen, the houses, the passers-by, and the shops, were dismal. His ache, this dull gnawing ache that never ceased for a moment, seemed to have acquired a new and more serious significance from the doctor's dubious remarks. Ivan Ilych now watched it with a new and oppressive feeling.

He reached home and began to tell his wife about it. She listened, but in the middle of his account his daughter came in with her hat on, ready to go out with her mother. She sat down reluctantly to listen to this tedious story, but could not stand it long, and her mother too did not hear him to the end.

"Well, I am very glad," she said. "Mind now to take your medicine regularly. Give me the prescription and I'll send Gerasim to the chemist's." And she went to get ready to go out.

While she was in the room Ivan Ilych had hardly taken time to breathe, but he sighed deeply when she left it.

"Well," he thought, "perhaps it isn't so bad after all."

125   He began taking his medicine and following the doctor's directions, which had been altered after the examination of the urine. But then it happened that there was a contradiction between the indications drawn from the examination of the urine and the symptoms that showed themselves. It turned out that what was happening differed from what the doctor had told him, and that he had either forgotten, or blundered, or hidden something from him. He could not, however, be blamed for that, and Ivan Ilych still obeyed his orders implicitly and at first derived some comfort from doing so.

From the time of his visit to the doctor, Ivan Ilych's chief occupation was the exact fulfilment of the doctor's instructions regarding hygiene and the taking of medicine, and the observation of his pain and his excretions. His chief interests came to be people's ailments and people's health. When sickness, deaths, or recoveries were mentioned in his presence, especially when the illness resembled his own, he listened with agitation which he tried to hide, asked questions, and applied what he heard to his own case.

The pain did not grow less, but Ivan Ilych made efforts to force himself to think that he was better. And he could do this so long as nothing agitated him. But as soon as he had any unpleasantness with his wife, any lack of success in his official work, or held bad cards at bridge, he was at once acutely sensible of his disease. He had formerly borne such mischances, hoping soon to adjust what was wrong, to master it and attain success, or make a grand slam. But now every mischance upset him and plunged him into despair. He would say to himself: "There now, just as I was beginning to get better and the medicine had begun to take effect, comes this accursed misfortune, or unpleasantness . . ."And he was furious with the mishap, or with the people who were causing the unpleasantness and killing him, for he felt that this fury was killing him but could not restrain it. One would have thought that it should have been clear to him that this exasperation with circumstances and people aggravated his illness, and that he ought therefore to ignore unpleasant occurrences. But he drew the very opposite conclusion: he said that he needed peace, and he watched for everything that might disturb it and became irritable at the slightest infringement of it. His condition was rendered worse by the fact that he read medical books and consulted doctors. The progress of his disease was so gradual that he could deceive himself when comparing one day with another—the difference was so slight. But when he consulted the doctors it seemed to him that he was getting worse, and even very rapidly. Yet despite this he was continually consulting them.

That month he went to see another celebrity, who told him almost the same as the first had done but put his questions rather differently, and the interview with this celebrity only increased Ivan Ilych's doubts and fears. A friend of a friend of his, a very good doctor, diagnosed his illness again quite differently from the others, and though he predicted recovery, his questions and suppositions bewildered Ivan Ilych still more and increased his doubts. A homeopathist diagnosed the disease in yet another way, and prescribed medicine which Ivan Ilych took secretly for a week. But after a week, not feeling any improvement and having lost confidence both in the former doctor's treatment and in this one's, he became still more despondent. One day a lady acquaintance mentioned a cure effected by a wonder-working icon. Ivan Ilych caught himself listening attentively and beginning to believe that it had occurred. This incident alarmed him. "Has my mind really weakened to such an extent?" he asked himself. "Nonsense! It's all rubbish. I mustn't give way to nervous fears but having chosen a doctor must keep strictly to his treatment. That is what I will do. Now it's all settled. I won't think about it, but will follow the treatment seriously till summer, and then we shall see. From now there must be no more of this wavering!" This was easy to say but impossible to carry out. The pain in his side oppressed him and seemed to grow worse and more incessant, while the taste in his mouth grew stranger and stranger. It seemed to him that his breath had a disgusting smell, and he was conscious of a loss of appetite and strength. There was no deceiving himself: something terrible, new, and more important than anything before in his life, was taking place within him of which he alone was aware. Those about him did not understand or would not understand it, but thought everything in the world was going on as usual. That tormented Ivan Ilych more than anything. He saw that his household, especially his wife and daughter who were in a perfect whirl of visiting, did not understand anything of it and were annoyed that he was so depressed and so exacting, as if he were to blame for it. Though they tried to disguise it he saw that he was an obstacle in their path, and that his wife had adopted a definite line in regard to his illness and kept to it regardless of anything he said or did. Her attitude was this: "You know," she would say to her friends, "Ivan Ilych can't do as other people do, and keep to the treatment prescribed for him. One day he'll take his drops and keep strictly to his diet and go to bed in good time, but the next day unless I watch him he'll suddenly forget his medicine, eat sturgeon—which is forbidden—and sit up playing cards till one o'clock in the morning."

"Oh, come, when was that?" Ivan Ilych would ask in vexation. "Only once at Peter Ivanovich's."

"And yesterday with Shebek."

130

"Well, even if I hadn't stayed up, this pain would have kept me awake."

"Be that as it may you'll never get well like that, but will always make us wretched."

Praskovya Federovna's attitude to Ivan Ilych's illness, as she expressed it both to others and to him, was that it was his own fault and was another of the annoyances he caused her. Ivan Ilych felt that this opinion escaped her involuntarily—but that did not make it easier for him.

At the law courts too, Ivan Ilych noticed, or thought he noticed, a strange attitude towards himself. It sometimes seemed to him that people were watching him inquisitively as a man whose place might soon be vacant. Then again, his friends would suddenly begin to chaff him in a friendly way about his low spirits, as if the awful, horrible, and unheard-of thing that was going on within him, incessantly gnawing at him and irresistibly drawing him away, was a very agreeable subject for jests. Schwartz in particular irritated him by his jocularity, vivacity, and *savoir-faire,* which reminded him of what he himself had been ten years ago.

135   Friends came to make up a set and they sat down to cards. They dealt, bending the new cards to soften them, and he sorted the diamonds in his hand and found he had seven. His partner said "No trumps" and supported him with two diamonds. What more could be wished for? It ought to be jolly and lively. They would make a grand slam. But suddenly Ivan Ilych was conscious of that gnawing pain, that taste in his mouth, and it seemed ridiculous that in such circumstances he should be pleased to make a grand slam.

He looked at his partner Mikhail Mikhaylovich, who rapped the table with his strong hand and instead of snatching up the tricks pushed the cards courteously and indulgently towards Ivan Ilych that he might have the pleasure of gathering them up without the trouble of stretching out his hand for them. "Does he think I am too weak to stretch out my arm?" thought Ivan Ilych, and forgetting what he was doing he over-trumped his partner, missing the grand slam by three tricks. And what was most awful of all was that he saw how upset Mikhail Mikhaylovich was about it but did not himself care. And it was dreadful to realize why he did not care.

They all saw that he was suffering, and said: "We can stop if you are tired. Take a rest." Lie down? No, he was not at all tired, and he finished the rubber. All were gloomy and silent. Ivan Ilych felt that he diffused this gloom over them and could not dispel it. They had supper and went away, and Ivan Ilych was left alone with the consciousness that his life was poisoned and was poisoning the lives of others, and that this poison did not weaken but penetrated more and more deeply into his whole being.

With this consciousness, and with physical pain besides the terror, he must go to bed, often to lie awake the greater part of the night. Next morning he had to get up again, dress, go to the law courts, speak, and write; or if he did not go out, spend at home those twenty-four hours a day each of which was a torture. And he had to live thus all alone on the brink of an abyss, with no one who understood or pitied him.

5

So one month passed and then another. Just before the New Year his brother-in-law came to town and stayed at their house. Ivan Ilych was at the law courts and Praskovya Federovna had gone shopping. When Ivan Ilych came home and entered his study he found his brother-in-law there—a healthy, florid man—unpacking his portmanteau himself. He raised his head on hearing Ivan Ilych's footsteps and looked up at him for a moment without a word. That stare told Ivan Ilych everything. His brother-in-law opened his mouth to utter an exclamation of surprise but checked himself, and that action confirmed it all.

"I have changed, eh?"   140

"Yes, there is a change."

And after that, try as he would to get his brother-in-law to return to the subject of his looks, the latter would say nothing about it. Praskovya Federovna came home and her brother went out to her. Ivan Ilych locked the door and began to examine himself in the glass, first full face, then in profile. He took up a portrait of himself taken with his wife, and compared it with what he saw in the glass. The change in him was immense. Then he bared his arms to the elbow, looked at them, drew the sleeves down again, sat down on an ottoman, and grew blacker than night.

"No, no, this won't do!" he said to himself, and jumped up, went to the table, took up some law papers and began to read them, but could not continue. He unlocked the door and went into the reception-room. The door leading to the drawing-room was shut. He approached it on tiptoe and listened.

"No, you are exaggerating!" Praskovya Federovna was saying.

"Exaggerating! Don't you see it? Why, he's a dead man! Look at his eyes—   145
there's no light in them. But what is it that is wrong with him?"

"No one knows. Nikolaevich (that was another doctor) said something, but I don't know what. And Leshchetitsky (this was the celebrated specialist) said quite the contrary . . ."

Ivan Ilych walked away, went to his own room, lay down, and began musing: "The kidney, a floating kidney." He recalled all the doctors had told him of how it detached itself and swayed about. And by an effort of imagination he tried to catch that kidney and arrest it and support it. So little was needed for this, it seemed to him. "No, I'll go to see Peter Ivanovich again." (That was the friend whose friend was a doctor.) He rang, ordered the carriage, and got ready to go.

"Where are you going, Jean?" asked his wife, with a specially sad and exceptionally kind look.

This exceptionally kind look irritated him. He looked morosely at her.

"I must go to see Peter Ivanovich."   150

He went to see Peter Ivanovich, and together they went to see his friend, the doctor. He was in, and Ivan Ilych had a long talk with him.

Reviewing the anatomical and physiological details of what in the doctor's opinion was going on inside him, he understood it all.

There was something, a small thing, in the vermiform appendix. It might all come right. Only stimulate the energy of one organ and check the activity of another, then absorption would take place and everything would come right. He got home rather late for dinner, ate his dinner, and conversed cheerfully, but could not for a long time bring himself to go back to work in his room. At last, however, he went to his study and did what was necessary, but the consciousness that he had put something aside—an important, intimate matter which he would revert to when his work was done—never left him. When he had finished his work he remembered that this intimate matter was the thought of his vermiform appendix. But he did not give himself up to it, and went to the drawing-room for tea. There were callers there, including the examining magistrate who was a desirable match for his daughter, and they were conversing, playing the piano and singing. Ivan Ilych, as Praskovya Federovna remarked, spent that evening more cheerfully than usual, but he never for a moment forgot that he had postponed the important matter of the appendix. At eleven o'clock he said good-night and went to his bedroom. Since his illness he had slept alone in a small room next to his study. He undressed and took up a novel by Zola, but instead of reading it he fell into thought, and in his imagination that desired improvement in the vermiform appendix occurred. There was the absorption and evacuation and the reestablishment of normal activity. "Yes, that's it!" he said to himself. "One need only assist nature, that's all." He remembered his medicine, rose, took it, and lay down on his back watching for the beneficent action of the medicine and for it to lessen the pain. "I need only take it regularly and avoid all injurious influences. I am already feeling better, much better." He began touching his side: it was not painful to the touch. "There, I really don't feel it. It's much better already." He put out the light and turned on his side . . . "The appendix is getting better, absorption is occurring." Suddenly he felt the old, familiar, dull, gnawing pain, stubborn and serious. There was the same familiar loathsome taste in his mouth. His heart sank and he felt dazed. "My God! My God!" he muttered. "Again, again! And it will never cease." And suddenly the matter presented itself in a quite different aspect. "Vermiform appendix! Kidney!" he said to himself. "It's not a question of appendix or kidney, but of life and . . . death. Yes, life was there and now it is going, going and I cannot stop it. Yes. Why deceive myself? Isn't it obvious to everyone but me that I'm dying, and that it's only a question of weeks, days . . . it may happen this moment. There was light and now there is darkness. I was here and now I'm going there! Where?" A chill came over him, his breathing ceased, and he felt only the throbbing of his heart.

"When I am not, what will there be? There will be nothing. Then where shall I be when I am no more? Can this be dying? No, I don't want to!" He jumped up and tried to light the candle, felt for it with trembling hands, dropped candle and candlestick on the floor, and fell back on his pillow.

155   "What's the use? It makes no difference," he said to himself, staring with wide-open eyes into the darkness. "Death. Yes, death. And none of them know or wish to know it, and they have no pity for me. Now they are playing." (He heard through the door the distant sound of a song and its accompaniment.) "It's all the same to them, but they will die too! Fools! I first, and they later, but it will be the same for them. And now they are merry . . . the beasts!"

Anger choked him and he was agonizingly, unbearably miserable. "It is impossible that all men have been doomed to suffer this awful horror!" He raised himself.

"Something must be wrong. I must calm myself—must think it all over from the beginning." And he again began thinking. "Yes, the beginning of my illness: I knocked my side, but I was still quite well that day and the next. It hurt a little, then rather more. I saw the doctors, then followed despondency and anguish, more doctors, and I drew nearer to the abyss. My strength grew less and I kept coming nearer and nearer, and now I have wasted away and there is no light in my eyes. I think of the appendix—but this is death! I think of mending the appendix, and all the while here is death! Can it really be death?" Again terror seized him and he gasped for breath. He leant down and began feeling for the matches, pressing with his elbow on the stand beside the bed. It was in his way and hurt him, he grew furious with it, pressed on it still harder, and upset it. Breathless and in despair he fell on his back, expecting death to come immediately.

Meanwhile the visitors were leaving. Praskovya Federovna was seeing them off. She heard something fall and came in.

"What has happened?"

"Nothing. I knocked it over accidentally."   160

She went out and returned with a candle. He lay there panting heavily, like a man who has run a thousand yards, and stared upwards at her with a fixed look.

"What is it, Jean?"

"No . . . o . . . thing. I upset it." ("Why speak of it? She won't understand," he thought.)

And in truth she did not understand. She picked up the stand, lit his candle, and hurried away to see another visitor off. When she came back he still lay on his back looking upwards.

"What is it? Do you feel worse?"   165

"Yes."

She shook her head and sat down.

"Do you know, Jean, I think we must ask Leshchetitsky to come and see you here."

This meant calling in the famous specialist, regardless of expense. He smiled malignantly and said "No." She remained a little longer and then went up to him and kissed his forehead.

While she was kissing him he hated her from the bottom of his soul and with   170
difficulty refrained from pushing her away.

"Good-night. Please God you'll sleep."

"Yes."

6

Ivan Ilych saw that he was dying, and he was in continual despair.

In the depth of his heart he knew he was dying, but not only was he not accustomed to the thought, he simply did not and could not grasp it.

The syllogism he had learnt from Kiezewetter's Logic: "Caius is a man, men are   175
mortal, therefore Caius is mortal," had always seemed to him correct as applied to Caius, but certainly not as applied to himself. That Caius—man in the abstract—was mortal, was perfectly correct, but he was not Caius, not an abstract man, but a creature quite, quite separate from all others. He had been little Vanya, with a mamma and a papa; with Mitya and Volodya, and the toys, a coachman and a nurse, afterwards with Katenka and with all the joys, griefs, and delights of childhood, boyhood, and youth. What did Caius know of the smell of that striped leather ball Vanya had

been so fond of? Had Caius kissed his mother's hand like that, and did the silk of her dress rustle so for Caius? Had he rioted like that at school when the pastry was bad? Had Caius been in love like that? Could Caius preside at a session as he did? "Caius really was mortal, and it was right for him to die; but for me, little Vanya, Ivan Ilych, with all my thoughts and emotions, it's altogether a different matter. It cannot be that I ought to die. That would be too terrible."

Such was his feeling.

"If I had to die like Caius I should have known it was so. An inner voice would have told me so, but there was nothing of the sort in me and I and all my friends felt that our case was quite different from that of Caius. And now here it is!" he said to himself. "It can't be. It's impossible! But here it is. How is this? How is one to understand it?"

He could not understand it, and tried to drive this false, incorrect, morbid thought away and to replace it by other proper and healthy thoughts. But that thought and not the thought only but the reality itself, seemed to come and confront him.

And to replace that thought he called up a succession of others, hoping to find in them some support. He tried to get back into the former current of thoughts that had once screened the thought of death from him. But strange to say, all that had formerly shut off, hidden, and destroyed, his consciousness of death, no longer had that effect. Ivan Ilych now spent most of his time in attempting to re-establish that old current. He would say to himself: "I will take up my duties again—after all I used to live by them." And banishing all doubts he would go to the law courts, enter into conversation with his colleagues, and sit carelessly as was his wont, scanning the crowd with a thoughtful look and leaning both his emaciated arms on the arms of his oak chair; bending over as usual to a colleague and drawing his papers nearer he would interchange whispers with him, and then suddenly raising his eyes and sitting erect would pronounce certain words and open the proceedings. But suddenly in the midst of those proceedings the pain in his side, regardless of the stage the proceedings had reached, would begin its own gnawing work. Ivan Ilych would turn his attention to it and try to drive the thought of it away, but without success. *It* would come and stand before him and look at him, and he would be petrified and the light would die out of his eyes, and he would again begin asking himself whether *It* alone was true. And his colleagues and subordinates would see with surprise and distress that he, the brilliant and subtle judge, was becoming confused and making mistakes. He would shake himself, try to pull himself together, manage somehow to bring the sitting to a close, and return home with the sorrowful consciousness that his judicial labours could not as formerly hide from him what he wanted them to hide, and could not deliver him from *It*. And what was worst of all was that *It* drew his attention to itself not in order to make him take some action but only that he should look at *It*, look it straight in the face: look at it and without doing anything, suffer inexpressibly.

And to save himself from this condition Ivan Ilych looked for consolations—new screens—and new screens were found and for a while seemed to save him, but then they immediately fell to pieces or rather became transparent, as if *It* penetrated them and nothing could veil *It*.

In these latter days he would go into the drawing-room he had arranged—that drawing-room where he had fallen and for the sake of which (how bitterly ridiculous it seemed) he had sacrificed his life—for he knew that his illness originated with that knock. He would enter and see that something had scratched the polished table. He would look for the cause of this and find that it was the bronze ornamentation of an album, that had got bent. He would take up the expensive album which he had lovingly arranged, and feel vexed with his daughter and her friends for their untidiness—for the album was torn here and there and some of the photographs turned upside down. He would put it carefully in order and bend the ornamentation back into position. Then it would occur to him to place all those things in another corner of the room, near the plants. He could call the footman, but his daughter or wife would come to help him. They would not agree, and his wife would contradict him, and he would dispute and grow angry. But that was all right, for then he did not think about *It. It* was invisible.

But then, when he was moving something himself, his wife would say: "Let the servants do it. You will hurt yourself again." And suddenly *It* would flash through the screen and he would see it. It was just a flash, and he hoped it would disappear, but he would involuntarily pay attention to his side. "It sits there as before, gnawing just the same!" And he could no longer forget *It,* but could distinctly see it looking at him from behind the flowers. "What is it all for?"

"It really is so! I lost my life over that curtain as I might have done when storming a fort. Is that possible? How terrible and how stupid. It can't be true! It can't, but it is!"

He would go to his study, lie down, and again be alone with *It:* face to face with *It.* And nothing could be done with *It* except to look at it and shudder.

7

How it happened it is impossible to say because it came about step by step, unnoticed, but in the third month of Ivan Ilych's illness, his wife, his daughter, his son, his acquaintances, the doctors, the servants, and above all he himself, were aware that the whole interest he had for other people was whether he would soon vacate his place, and at last release the living from the discomfort caused by his presence and be himself released from his sufferings.

He slept less and less. He was given opium and hypodermic injections of morphine, but this did not relieve him. The dull depression he experienced in a somnolent condition at first gave him a little relief, but only as something new, afterwards it became as distressing as the pain itself or even more so.

Special foods were prepared for him by the doctors' orders, but all those foods became increasingly distasteful and disgusting to him.

For his excretions also special arrangements had to be made, and this was a torment to him every time—a torment from the uncleanliness, the unseemliness, and the smell, and from knowing that another person had to take part in it.

But just through this most unpleasant matter Ivan Ilych obtained comfort. Gerasim, the butler's young assistant, always came in to carry the things out. Gerasim was a clean, fresh peasant lad, grown stout on town food and always cheerful and bright. At first the sight of him, in his clean Russian peasant costume, engaged on that disgusting task embarrassed Ivan Ilych.

190   Once when he got up from the commode too weak to draw up his trousers, he dropped into a soft armchair and looked with horror at his bare, enfeebled thighs with the muscles so sharply marked on them.

Gerasim with a firm light tread, his heavy boots emitting a pleasant smell of tar and fresh winter air, came in wearing a clean Hessian apron, the sleeves of his print shirt tucked up over his strong bare young arms; and refraining from looking at his sick master out of consideration for his feelings, and restraining the joy of life that beamed from his face, went up to the commode.

"Gerasim!" said Ivan Ilych in a weak voice.

Gerasim started, evidently afraid he might have committed some blunder, and with a rapid movement turned his fresh, kind, simple young face which just showed the first downy signs of a beard.

"Yes, sir?"

195   "That must be very unpleasant for you. You must forgive me. I am helpless."

"Oh, why, sir," and Gerasim's eyes beamed and he showed his glistening white teeth, "what's a little trouble? It's a case of illness with you, sir."

And his deft strong hands did their accustomed task, and he went out of the room stepping lightly. Five minutes later he was lightly returned.

Ivan Ilych was still sitting in the same position in the armchair.

"Gerasim," he said when the latter had replaced the freshly-washed utensil. "Please come here and help me." Gerasim went up to him. "Lift me up. It is hard for me to get up, and I have sent Dmitri away."

200   Gerasim went up to him, grasped his master with his strong arms deftly but gently, in the same way that he stepped—lifted him, supported him with one hand, and with the other drew up his trousers and would have set him down again, but Ivan Ilych asked to be led to the sofa. Gerasim, without an effort and without apparent pressure, led him, almost lifting him, to the sofa and placed him on it.

"Thank you. How easily and well you do it all!"

Gerasim smiled again and turned to leave the room. But Ivan Ilych felt his presence such a comfort that he did not want to let him go.

"One thing more, please move up that chair. No, the other one—under my feet. It is easier for me when my feet are raised."

Gerasim brought the chair, set it down gently in place, and raised Ivan Ilych's legs on to it. It seemed to Ivan Ilych that he felt better while Gerasim was holding up his legs.

205   "It's better when my legs are higher," he said. "Place that cushion under them."

Gerasim did so. He again lifted the legs and placed them, and again Ivan Ilych felt better while Gerasim held his legs. When he set them down Ivan Ilych fancied he felt worse.

"Gerasim," he said. "Are you busy now?"

"Not at all, sir," said Gerasim, who had learnt from the townsfolk how to speak to gentlefolk.

"What have you still to do?"

210   "What have I to do? I've done everything except chopping the logs for tomorrow."

"Then hold my legs up a bit higher, can you?"

"Of course I can. Why not?" And Gerasim raised his master's legs higher and Ivan Ilych thought that in that position he did not feel any pain at all.

"And how about the logs?"

"Don't trouble about that, sir. There's plenty of time."

Ivan Ilych told Gerasim to sit down and hold his legs, and began to talk to him.   215 And strange to say it seemed to him that he felt better while Gerasim held his legs up.

After that Ivan Ilych would sometimes call Gerasim and get him to hold his legs on his shoulders, and he liked talking to him. Gerasim did it all easily, willingly, simply, and with a good nature that touched Ivan Ilych. Health, strength, and vitality in other people were offensive to him, but Gerasim's strength and vitality did not mortify but soothed him.

What tormented Ivan Ilych most was the deception, the lie, which for some reason they all accepted, that he was not dying but was simply ill, and that he only need keep quiet and undergo a treatment and then something very good would result. He however knew that do what they would nothing would come of it, only still more agonizing suffering and death. This deception tortured him—their not wishing to admit what they all knew and what he knew, but wanting to lie to him concerning his terrible condition, and wishing and forcing him to participate in that lie. Those lies—lies enacted over him on the eve of his death and destined to degrade this awful, solemn act to the level of their visitings, their curtains, their sturgeon for dinner—were a terrible agony for Ivan Ilych. And strangely enough, many times when they were going through their antics over him he had been within a hairbreadth of calling out to them: "Stop lying! You know and I know that I am dying. Then at least stop lying about it!" But he had never had the spirit to do it. The awful, terrible act of his dying was, he could see, reduced by those about him to the level of a casual, unpleasant, and almost indecorous incident (as if someone entered a drawing-room diffusing an unpleasant odour) and this was done by that very decorum which he had served all his life long. He saw that no one felt for him, because no one even wished to grasp his position. Only Gerasim recognized it and pitied him. And so Ivan Ilych felt at ease only with him. He felt comforted when Gerasim supported his legs (sometimes all night long) and refused to go to bed, saying: "Don't you worry, Ivan Ilych. I'll get sleep enough later on," or when he suddenly became familiar and exclaimed: "If you weren't sick it would be another matter, but as it is, why should I grudge a little trouble?" Gerasim alone did not lie; everything showed that he alone understood the facts of the case and did not consider it necessary to disguise them, but simply felt sorry for his emaciated and enfeebled master. Once when Ivan Ilych was sending him away he even said straight out: "We shall all of us die, so why should I grudge a little trouble?"—expressing the fact that he did not think his work burdensome, because he was doing it for a dying man and hoped someone would do the same for him when his time came.

Apart from this lying, or because of it, what most tormented Ivan Ilych was that no one pitied him as he wished to be pitied. At certain moments after prolonged suffering he wished most of all (though he would have been ashamed to confess it) for someone to pity him as a sick child is pitied. He longed to be petted and comforted. He knew he was an important functionary, that he had a beard turning grey, and that therefore what he longed for was impossible, but still he longed for it. And in Gerasim's attitude towards him there was something akin to what he wished for, and so that attitude comforted him. Ivan Ilych wanted to weep, wanted to be petted and cried over, and then his colleague Shebek would come, and instead of weeping and being petted, Ivan Ilych would assume a serious, and profound air, and by force of habit would express his opinion on a decision of the Court of Cassation and would stubbornly insist on that view. This falsity around him and within him did more than anything else to poison his last days.

8

It was morning. He knew it was morning because Gerasim had gone, and Peter the footman had come and put out the candles, drawn back one of the curtains, and begun quietly to tidy up. Whether it was morning or evening, Friday or Sunday, made no difference, it was all just the same: the gnawing, unmitigated, agonizing pain, never ceasing for an instant, the consciousness of life inexorably waning but not yet extinguished, the approach of that ever dreaded and hateful Death which was the only reality, and always the same falsity. What were days, weeks, hours, in such a case?

220   "Will you have some tea, sir?"

"He wants things to be regular, and wishes the gentlefolk to drink tea in the morning," thought Ivan Ilych, and only said "No."

"Wouldn't you like to move onto the sofa, sir?"

"He wants to tidy up the room, and I'm in the way. I am uncleanliness and disorder," he thought, and said only:

"No, leave me alone."

225   The man went on bustling about. Ivan Ilych stretched out his hand. Peter came up, ready to help.

"What is it, sir?"

"My watch."

Peter took the watch which was close at hand and gave it to his master.

"Half-past eight. Are they up?"

230   "No sir, except Vladimir Ivanich" (the son) "who has gone to school. Praskovya Fedorovna ordered me to wake her if you asked for her. Shall I do so?"

"No, there's no need to." "Perhaps I'd better have some tea," he thought, and added aloud: "Yes, bring me some tea."

Peter went to the door but Ivan Ilych dreaded being left alone. "How can I keep him here? Oh yes, my medicine." "Peter, give me my medicine." "Why not? Perhaps it may still do me some good." He took a spoonful and swallowed it. "No, it won't help. It's all tomfoolery, all deception," he decided as soon as he became aware of the familiar, sickly, hopeless taste. "No, I can't believe in it any longer. But the pain, why this pain? If it would only cease just for a moment!" And he moaned. Peter turned towards him. "It's all right. Go and fetch me some tea."

Peter went out. Left alone Ivan Ilych groaned not so much with pain, terrible though that was, as from mental anguish. Always and for ever the same, always these endless days and nights. If only it would come quicker! If only *what* would come quicker? Death, darkness? . . . No, no! Anything rather than death!

When Peter returned with the tea on a tray, Ivan Ilych stared at him for a time in perplexity, not realizing who and what he was. Peter was disconcerted by that look and his embarrassment brought Ivan Ilych to himself.

"Oh, tea! All right, put it down. Only help me to wash and put on a clean shirt."   235

And Ivan Ilych began to wash. With pauses for rest, he washed his hands and then his face, cleaned his teeth, brushed his hair, and looked in the glass. He was terrified by what he saw, especially by the limp way in which his hair clung to his pallid forehead.

While his shirt was being changed he knew he would be still more frightened at the sight of his body, so he avoided looking at it. Finally he was ready. He drew on a dressing-gown, wrapped himself in a plaid, and sat down in the armchair to take his tea. For a moment he felt refreshed, but as soon as he began to drink the tea he was again aware of the same taste, and the pain also returned. He finished it with an effort, and then lay down stretching out his legs, and dismissed Peter.

Always the same. Now a spark of hope flashes up, then a sea of despair rages, and always pain; always pain, always despair, and always the same. When alone he had a dreadful and distressing desire to call someone, but he knew beforehand that with others present it would be still worse. "Another dose of morphine—to lose consciousness. I will tell him, the doctor, that he must think of something else. It's impossible, impossible, to go on like this."

An hour and another pass like that. But now there is a ring at the door bell. Perhaps it's the doctor? It is. He comes in fresh, hearty, plump, and cheerful, with that look on his face that seems to say: "There now, you're in a panic about something, but we'll arrange it all for you directly!" The doctor knows this expression is out of place here, but he has put it on once for all and can't take it off—like a man who has put on a frock-coat in the morning to pay a round of calls.

The doctor rubs his hands vigorously and reassuringly.   240

"Brr! How cold it is! There's such a sharp frost; just let me warm myself!" he says, as if it were only a matter of waiting till he was warm, and then he would put everything right.

"Well now, how are you?"

Ivan Ilych feels that the doctor would like to say: "Well, how are your affairs?" but that even he feels that this would not do, and says instead: "What sort of a night have you had?"

Ivan Ilych looks at him as much as to say: "Are you really never ashamed of lying?" But the doctor does not wish to understand this question, and Ivan Ilych says: "Just as terrible as ever. The pain never leaves me and never subsides. If only something . . ."

"Yes, you sick people are always like that. . . . There, now I think I am warm   245 enough. Even Praskovya Fedorovna, who is so particular, could find no fault with my temperature. Well, now I can say good-morning," and the doctor presses his patient's hand.

Then, dropping his former playfulness, he begins with a most serious face to examine the patient, feeling his pulse and taking his temperature, and then begins the sounding and auscultation.

Ivan Ilych knows quite well and definitely that all this is nonsense and pure deception, but when the doctor, getting down on his knee, leans over him, putting his ear first higher then lower, and performs various gymnastic movements over him with a significant expression on his face, Ivan Ilych submits to it all as he used to submit to the speeches of the lawyers, though he knew very well that they were all lying and why they were lying.

The doctor, kneeling on the sofa, is still sounding him when Praskovya Fedorovna's silk dress rustles at the door and she is heard scolding Peter for not having let her know of the doctor's arrival.

She comes in, kisses her husband, and at once proceeds to prove that she has been up a long time already, and only owing to a misunderstanding failed to be there when the doctor arrived.

250   Ivan Ilych looks at her, scans her all over, sets against her the whiteness and plumpness and cleanness of her hands and neck, the gloss of her hair, and the sparkle of her vivacious eyes. He hates her with his whole soul. And the thrill of hatred he feels for her makes him suffer from her touch.

Her attitude towards him and his disease is still the same. Just as the doctor had adopted a certain relation to his patient which he could not abandon, so had she formed one towards him—that he was not doing something he ought to do and was himself to blame, and that she reproached him lovingly for this—and she could not now change that attitude.

"You see he doesn't listen to me and doesn't take his medicine at the proper time. And above all he lies in a position that is no doubt bad for him—with his legs up."

She described how he made Gerasim hold his legs up.

The doctor smiled with a contemptuous affability that said: "What's to be done? These sick people do have foolish fancies of that kind, but we must forgive them."

255   When the examination was over the doctor looked at his watch, and then Praskovya Fedorovna announced to Ivan Ilych that it was of course as he pleased, but she had sent to-day for a celebrated specialist who would examine him and have a consultation with Michael Danilovich (their regular doctor).

"Please don't raise any objections. I am doing this for my own sake," she said ironically, letting it be felt that she was doing it all for his sake and only said that to leave him no right to refuse. He remained silent, knitting his brows. He felt that he was so surrounded and involved in a mesh of falsity that it was hard to unravel anything.

Everything she did for him was entirely for her own sake, and she told him she was doing for herself what she actually was doing for herself, as if that was so incredible that he must understand the opposite.

At half-past eleven the celebrated specialist arrived. Again the sounding began and the significant conversations in his presence and in another room, about the kidneys and the appendix, and the questions and answers, with such an air of importance that again, instead of the real question of life and death which now alone confronted him, the question arose of the kidney and appendix which were not behaving as they ought to and would now be attacked by Michael Danilovich and the specialist and forced to amend their ways.

The celebrated specialist took leave of him with a serious though not hopeless look, and in reply to the timid question Ivan Ilych, with eyes glistening with fear and hope, put to him as to whether there was a chance of recovery, said that he could not vouch for it but there was a possibility. The look of hope with which Ivan Ilych watched the doctor out was so pathetic that Praskovya Fedorovna, seeing it, even wept as she left the room to hand the doctor his fee.

The gleam of hope kindled by the doctor's encouragement did not last long. The same room, the same pictures, curtains, wall-paper, medicine bottles, were all there, and the same aching suffering body, and Ivan Ilych began to moan. They gave him a subcutaneous injection and he sank into oblivion.

It was twilight when he came to. They brought him his dinner and he swallowed some beef tea with difficulty, and then everything was the same again and night was coming on.

After dinner, at seven o'clock, Praskovya Fedorovna came into the room in evening dress, her full bosom pushed up by her corset, and with traces of powder on her face. She had reminded him in the morning that they were going to the theatre. Sarah Bernhardt was visiting the town and they had a box, which he had insisted on their taking. Now he had forgotten about it and her toilet offended him, but he concealed his vexation when he remembered that he had himself insisted on their securing a box and going because it would be an instructive and aesthetic pleasure for the children.

Praskovya Fedorovna came in, self-satisfied but yet with a rather guilty air. She sat down and asked how he was but, as he saw, only for the sake of asking and not in order to learn about it, knowing that there was nothing to learn—and then went on to what she really wanted to say: that she would not on any account have gone but that the box had been taken and Helen and their daughter were going, as well as Petrishchev (the examining magistrate, their daughter's fiancé) and that it was out of the question to let them go alone; but that she would have much preferred to sit with him for a while; and he must be sure to follow the doctor's orders while she was away.

"Oh, and Fedor Petrovich" (the fiancé) "would like to come in. May he? And Lisa?"

"All right."

Their daughter came in in full evening dress, her fresh young flesh exposed (making a show of that very flesh which in his own case caused so much suffering), strong, healthy, evidently in love, and impatient with illness, suffering, and death, because they interfered with her happiness.

Fedor Petrovich came in too, in evening dress, his hair curled *á la Capoul,* a tight stiff collar round his long sinewy neck, an enormous white shirt-front and narrow black trousers tightly stretched over his strong thighs. He had one white glove tightly drawn on, and was holding his opera hat in his hand.

Following him the schoolboy crept in unnoticed, in a new uniform, poor little fellow, and wearing gloves. Terribly dark shadows showed under his eyes, the meaning of which Ivan Ilych knew well.

His son had always seemed pathetic to him, and now it was dreadful to see the boy's frightened look of pity. It seemed to Ivan Ilych that Vasya was the only one besides Gerasim who understood and pitied him.

270   They all sat down and again asked how he was. A silence followed. Lisa asked her mother about the opera-glasses, and there was an altercation between mother and daughter as to who had taken them and where they had been put. This occasioned some unpleasantness.

Fedor Petrovich inquired of Ivan Ilych whether he had ever seen Sarah Bernhardt. Ivan Ilych did not at first catch the question, but then replied: "No, have you seen her before?"

"Yes, in *Adrienne Lecouvreur*."

Praskovya Fedorovna mentioned some roles in which Sarah Bernhardt was particularly good. Her daughter disagreed. Conversation sprang up as to the elegance and realism of her acting—the sort of conversation that is always repeated and is always the same.

In the midst of the conversation Fedor Petrovich glanced at Ivan Ilych and became silent. The others also looked at him and grew silent. Ivan Ilych was staring with glittering eyes straight before him, evidently indignant with them. This had to be rectified, but it was impossible to do so. The silence had to be broken, but for a time no one dared to break it and they all became afraid that the conventional deception would suddenly become obvious and the truth become plain to all. Lisa was the first to pluck up courage and break that silence, but by trying to hide what everybody was feeling, she betrayed it.

275   "Well, if we are going it's time to start," she said, looking at her watch, a present from her father, and with a faint and significant smile at Fedor Petrovich relating to something known only to them. She got up with a rustle of her dress.

They all rose, said good-night, and went away.

When they had gone it seemed to Ivan Ilych that he felt better; the falsity had gone with them. But the pain remained—that same pain and that same fear that made everything monotonously alike, nothing harder and nothing easier. Everything was worse.

Again minute followed minute and hour followed hour. Everything remained the same and there was no cessation. And the inevitable end of it all became more and more terrible.

"Yes, send Gerasim here," he replied to a question Peter asked.

9

280   His wife returned late at night. She came in on tiptoe, but he heard her, opened his eyes, and made haste to close them again. She wished to send Gerasim away and to sit with him herself, but he opened his eyes and said: "No, go away."

"Are you in great pain?"

"Always the same."

"Take some opium."

He agreed and took some. She went away.

Till about three in the morning he was in a state of stupefied misery. It seemed to him that he and pain were being thrust into a narrow, deep black sack, but though they were pushed further and further in they could not be pushed to the bottom. And this, terrible enough in itself, was accompanied by suffering. He was frightened yet wanted to fall through the sack, he struggled but yet co-operated. And suddenly he broke through, fell, and regained consciousness. Gerasim was sitting at the foot of the bed dozing quietly and patiently, while he himself lay with his emaciated stockinged legs resting on Gerasim's shoulders; the same shaded candle was there and the same unceasing pain.

"Go away, Gerasim," he whispered.

"It's all right, sir. I'll stay a while."

"No. Go away."

He removed his legs from Gerasim's shoulders, turned sideways onto his arm, and felt sorry for himself. He only waited till Gerasim had gone into the next room and then restrained himself no longer but wept like a child. He wept on account of his helplessness, his terrible loneliness, the cruelty of man, the cruelty of God, and the absence of God.

"Why hast Thou done all this? Why hast Thou brought me here? Why, why dost Thou torment me so terribly?"

He did not expect an answer and yet wept because there was no answer and could be none. The pain again grew more acute, but he did not stir and did not call. He said to himself: "Go on! Strike me! But what is it for? What have I done to Thee? What is it for?"

Then he grew quiet and not only ceased weeping but even held his breath and became all attention. It was as though he were listening not to an audible voice but to the voice of his soul, to the current of thoughts arising within him.

"What is it you want?" was the clear conception capable of expression in words, that he heard.

"What do you want? What do you want?" he repeated to himself.

"What do I want? To live and not to suffer," he answered.

And again he listened with such concentrated attention that even his pain did not distract him.

"To live? How?" asked his inner voice.

"Why, to live as I used to—well and pleasantly."

"As you lived before, well and pleasantly?" the voice repeated.

And in imagination he began to recall the best moments of his pleasant life. But strange to say none of these best moments of his pleasant life now seemed at all what they had then seemed—none of them except the first recollections of childhood. There, in childhood, there had been something really pleasant with which it would be possible to live if it could return. But the child who had experienced that happiness existed no longer, it was like a reminiscence of somebody else.

As soon as the period began which had produced the present Ivan Ilych, all that had then seemed joys now melted before his sight and turned into something trivial and often nasty.

And the further he departed from childhood and the nearer he came to the present the more worthless and doubtful were the joys. This began with the School of Law. A little that was really good was still found there—there was light-heartedness, friendship, and hope. But in the upper classes there had already been fewer of such good moments. Then during the first years of his official career, when he was in the service of the Governor, some pleasant moments again occurred: They were the memories of love for a woman. Then all became confused and there was still less of what was good; later on again there was still less that was good, and the further he went the less there was. His marriage, a mere accident, then the disenchantment that followed it, his wife's bad breath and the sensuality and hypocrisy: then that deadly official life and those preoccupations about money, a year of it, and two, and ten, and twenty, and always the same thing. And the longer it lasted the more deadly it became. "It is as if I had been going downhill while I imagined I was going up. And that is really what it was. I was going up in public opinion, but to the same extent life was ebbing away from me. And now it is all done and there is only death."

"Then what does it mean? Why? It can't be that life is so senseless and horrible. But if it really has been so horrible and senseless, why must I die and die in agony? There is something wrong!"

"Maybe I did not live as I ought to have done," it suddenly occurred to him. "But how could that be, when I did everything properly?" he replied, and immediately dismissed from his mind this, the sole solution of all the riddles of life and death, as something quite impossible.

305 "Then what do you want now? To live? Live how? Live as you lived in the law courts when the usher proclaimed 'The judge is coming!'" "The judge is coming, the judge!" he repeated to himself. "Here he is, the judge. But I am not guilty!" he exclaimed angrily. "What is it for?" And he ceased crying, but turning his face to the wall continued to ponder on the same question: Why, and for what purpose, is there all this horror? But however much he pondered he found no answer. And whenever the thought occurred to him, as it often did, that it all resulted from his not having lived as he ought to have done, he at once recalled the correctness of his whole life and dismissed so strange an idea.

10

Another fortnight passed. Ivan Ilych now no longer left his sofa. He would not lie in bed but lay on the sofa, facing the wall nearly all the time. He suffered ever the same unceasing agonies and in his loneliness pondered always on the same insoluble question: "What is this? Can it be that it is Death?" And the inner voice answered: "Yes, it is Death."

"Why these sufferings?" And the voice answered, "For no reason—they just are so." Beyond and besides this there was nothing.

From the very beginning of his illness, ever since he had first been to see the doctor, Ivan Ilych's life had been divided between two contrary and alternating moods: now it was despair and the expectation of this uncomprehended and terrible death, and now hope and an intently interested observation of the functioning of his organs. Now before his eyes there was only a kidney or an intestine that temporarily evaded its duty, and now only that incomprehensible and dreadful death from which it was impossible to escape.

These two states of mind had alternated from the very beginning of his illness, but the further it progressed the more doubtful and fantastic became the conception of the kidney, and the more real the sense of impending death.

He had but to call to mind what he had been three months before and what he 310 was now, to call to mind with what regularity he had been going downhill, for every possibility of hope to be shattered.

Latterly during that loneliness in which he found himself as he lay facing the back of the sofa, a loneliness in the midst of a populous town and surrounded by numerous acquaintances and relations but that yet could not have been more complete anywhere—either at the bottom of the sea or under the earth—during that terrible loneliness Ivan Ilych had lived only in memories of the past. Pictures of his past rose before him one after another. They always began with what was nearest in time and then went back to what was more remote—to his childhood—and rested there. If he thought of the stewed prunes that had been offered him that day, his mind went back to the raw shrivelled French plums of his childhood, their peculiar flavour and the flow of saliva when he sucked their stones, and along with the memory of that taste came a whole series of memories of those days: his nurse, his brother, and their toys. "No, I mustn't think of that. . . . It is too painful," Ivan Ilych said to himself, and brought himself back to the present—to the bottom of the back of the sofa and the creases in its morocco. "Morocco is expensive, but it does not wear well: There had been a quarrel about it. It was a different kind of quarrel and a different kind of morocco that time when we tore father's portfolio and were punished, and mamma brought us some tarts. . . ." And again his thoughts dwelt on his childhood, and again it was painful and he tried to banish them and fix his mind on something else.

Then again together with that chain of memories another series passed through his mind—of how his illness had progressed and grown worse. There also the further back he looked the more life there had been. There had been more of what was good in life and more of life itself. The two merged together. "Just as the pain went on getting worse and worse so my life grew worse and worse," he thought. "There is one bright spot there at the back, at the beginning of life, and afterwards all becomes blacker and blacker and proceeds more and more rapidly—in inverse ratio to the square of the distance from death," thought Ivan Ilych. And the example of a stone falling downwards with increasing velocity entered his mind. Life, a series of increasing sufferings, flies, further and further towards its end—the most terrible suffering. "I am flying. . . ." He shuddered, shifted himself, and tried to resist, but was already aware that resistance was impossible, and again with eyes weary of gazing but unable to cease seeing what was before them, he stared at the back of the sofa and waited—awaiting the dreadful fall and shock and destruction.

"Resistance is impossible!" he said to himself. "If I could only understand what it is all for! But that too is impossible. An explanation would be possible if it could be said that I have not lived as I ought to. But it is impossible to say that," and he remembered all the legality, correctitude, and propriety of his life. "That at any rate can certainly not be admitted," he thought, and his lips smiled ironically as if someone could see that smile and be taken in by it. "There is no explanation! Agony, death. . . . What for?"

II

Another two weeks went by in this way and during that fortnight an event occurred that Ivan Ilych and his wife had desired. Petrishchev formally proposed. It happened in the evening. The next day Praskovya Fedorovna came into her husband's room considering how best to inform him of it, but that very night there had been a fresh change for the worse in his condition. She found him still lying on the sofa but in a different position. He lay on his back, groaning and staring fixedly straight in front of him.

315 She began to remind him of his medicines, but he turned his eyes towards her with such a look that she did not finish what she was saying; so great an animosity, to her in particular, did that look express.

"For Christ's sake, let me die in peace!" he said.

She would have gone away, but just then their daughter came in and went up to say good morning. He looked at her as he had done at his wife, and in reply to her inquiry about his health said dryly that he would soon free them all of himself. They were both silent and after sitting with him for a while went away.

"Is it our fault?" Lisa said to her mother. "It's as if we were to blame! I am sorry for papa, but why should we be tortured?"

The doctor came at his usual time. Ivan Ilych answered "Yes" and "No," never taking his angry eyes from him, and at last said: "You know you can do nothing for me, so leave me alone."

320 "We can ease your sufferings."

"You can't even do that. Let me be."

The doctor went into the drawing-room and told Praskovya Fedorovna that the case was very serious and that the only resource left was opium to allay her husband's sufferings, which must be terrible.

It was true, as the doctor said, that Ivan Ilych's physical sufferings were terrible, but worse than the physical sufferings were his mental sufferings which were his chief torture.

His mental sufferings were due to the fact that that night, as he looked at Gerasim's sleepy, good-natured face with its prominent cheek-bones, the question suddenly occurred to him: "What if my whole life has really been wrong?"

325 It occurred to him that what had appeared perfectly impossible before, namely that he had not spent his life as he could have done, might after all be true. It occurred to him that his scarcely perceptible attempts to struggle against what was considered good by the most highly placed people, those scarcely noticeable impulses which he had immediately suppressed, might have been the real thing, and all the rest false. And his professional duties and the whole arrangement of his life and of his family, and all his social and official interests, might all have been false. He tried

to defend all those things to himself and suddenly felt the weakness of what he was defending. There was nothing to defend.

"But if that is so," he said to himself, "and I am leaving this life with the consciousness that I have lost all that was given me and it is impossible to rectify it—what then?"

He lay on his back and began to pass his life in review in quite a new way. In the morning when he saw first his footman, then his wife, then his daughter, and then the doctor, their every word and movement confirmed to him the awful truth that had been revealed to him during the night. In them he saw himself—all that for which he had lived—and saw clearly that it was not real at all, but a terrible and huge deception which had hidden both life and death. This consciousness intensified his physical suffering tenfold. He groaned and tossed about, and pulled at his clothing which choked and stifled him. And he hated them on that account.

He was given a large dose of opium and became unconscious, but at noon his sufferings began again. He drove everybody away and tossed from side to side.

His wife came to him and said:

"Jean, my dear, do this for me. It can't do any harm and often helps. Healthy people often do it." 330

He opened his eyes wide.

"What? Take communion? Why? It's unnecessary! However. . . ."

She began to cry.

"Yes, do, my dear. I'll send for our priest. He is such a nice man."

"All right. Very well," he muttered. 335

When the priest came and heard his confession, Ivan Ilych was softened and seemed to feel a relief from his doubts and consequently from his sufferings, and for a moment there came a ray of hope. He again began to think of the vermiform appendix and the possibility of correcting it. He received the sacrament with tears in his eyes.

When they laid him down again afterwards he felt a moment's ease, and the hope that he might live awoke in him again. He began to think of the operation that had been suggested to him. "To live! I want to live!" he said to himself.

His wife came in to congratulate him after his communion, and when uttering the usual conventional words she added:

"You feel better, don't you?"

Without looking at her he said "Yes." 340

Her dress, her figure, the expression of her face, the tone of her voice, all revealed the same thing. "This is wrong, it is not as it should be. All you have lived for and still live for is falsehood and deception, hiding life and death from you." And as soon as he admitted that thought, his hatred and his agonizing physical suffering again sprang up, and with that suffering a consciousness of the unavoidable, approaching end. And to this was added a new sensation of grinding shooting pain and a feeling of suffocation.

The expression of his face when he uttered that "yes" was dreadful. Having uttered it, he looked her straight in the eyes, turned on his face with a rapidity extraordinary in his weak state and shouted:

"Go away! Go away and leave me alone!"

12

From that moment the screaming began that continued for three days, and was so terrible that one could not hear it through two closed doors without horror. At the moment he answered his wife he realized that he was lost, that there was no return, that the end had come, the very end, and his doubts were still unsolved and remained doubts.

345   "Oh! Oh! Oh!" he cried in various intonations. He had begun by screaming "I won't!" and continued screaming on the letter "o."

For three whole days, during which time did not exist for him, he struggled in that black sack into which he was being thrust by an invisible, resistless force. He struggled as a man condemned to death struggles in the hands of the executioner, knowing that he cannot save himself. And every moment he felt that despite all his efforts he was drawing nearer and nearer to what terrified him. He felt that his agony was due to his being thrust into that black hole and still more to his not being able to get right into it. He was hindered from getting into it by his conviction that his life had been a good one. That very justification of his life held him fast and prevented his moving forward, and it caused him most torment of all.

Suddenly some force struck him in the chest and side, making it still harder to breathe, and he fell through the hole and there at the bottom was a light. What had happened to him was like the sensation one sometimes experiences in a railway carriage when one thinks one is going backwards while one is really going forwards and suddenly becomes aware of the real direction.

"Yes, it was all not the right thing," he said to himself, "but that's no matter. It can be done. But what *is* the right thing?" he asked himself, and suddenly grew quiet.

This occurred at the end of the third day, two hours before his death. Just then his schoolboy son had crept softly in and gone up to the bedside. The dying man was still screaming desperately and waving his arms. His hand fell on the boy's head, and the boy caught it, pressed it to his lips, and began to cry.

350   At that very moment Ivan Ilych fell through and caught sight of the light, and it was revealed to him that though his life had not been what it should have been, this could still be rectified. He asked himself, "What *is* the right thing?" and grew still, listening. Then he felt that someone was kissing his hand. He opened his eyes, looked at his son, and felt sorry for him. His wife came up to him and he glanced at her. She was gazing at him open-mouthed, with undried tears on her nose and cheek and a despairing look on her face. He felt sorry for her too.

"Yes, I am making them wretched," he thought. "They are sorry, but it will be better for them when I die." He wished to say this but had not the strength to utter it. "Besides, why speak? I must act," he thought. With a look at his wife he indicated his son and said: "Take him away . . . sorry for him . . . sorry for you too. . . ." He tried to add, "forgive me," but said "forego" and waved his hand, knowing that He whose understanding mattered would understand.

And suddenly it grew clear to him that what had been oppressing him and would not leave him was all dropping away at once from two sides, from ten sides, and from all sides. He was sorry for them, he must act so as not to hurt them: release them and free himself from these sufferings. "How good and how simple!" he thought. "And the pain?" he asked himself. "What has become of it? Where are you, pain?"

He turned his attention to it.

"Yes, here it is. Well, what of it? Let the pain be."

"And death . . . where is it?"

He sought his former accustomed fear of death and did not find it. "Where is it? What death?" There was no fear because there was no death.

In place of death there was light.

"So that's what it is!" he suddenly exclaimed aloud. "What joy!"

To him all this happened in a single instant, and the meaning of that instant did not change. For those present his agony continued for another two hours. Something rattled in his throat, his emaciated body twitched, then the gasping and rattle became less and less frequent.

"It is finished!" said someone near him.

He heard these words and repeated them in his soul.

"Death is finished," he said to himself. "It is no more!"

He drew in a breath, stopped in the midst of a sigh, stretched out, and died.

QUESTIONS FOR DISCUSSION AND WRITING

1. How does the response of Ivan's associates to the news of his death introduce the conflicts that will be revealed in the story? How does Ivan's fall from the stepladder mark a turning point in his life? What conclusions does Ivan come to during his three days of screaming?

2. How does Ivan characterize himself through his decisions about his career, wife, children, and amusements? In what ways does his character change once he becomes ill? How does Gerasim reveal the limitations in Ivan and his family?

3. How does Ivan's preoccupation with his social and physical setting help explain the difficulty he has in coming to terms with his death? How does the bridge game symbolize the kind of life that Ivan and his friends value?

4. In what ways do Peter Ivanovich and Ivan Ilych share a similar point of view toward life? How does Ivan's ability to eliminate "all considerations irrelevant to the legal aspect of the case" reveal his attitude toward his clients? How does he react when his doctors exhibit a similar attitude toward him?

5. The first sentence of Part 2 seems at first to be a paradox: "Ivan Ilych's life had been most simple and most ordinary and therefore most terrible." In what ways does the rest of the story explain how a simple and ordinary life can be terrible? Does Ivan's perception of this truth come too late to redeem him? Explain your answer.

Stories for Comparison

John Cheever's "The Swimmer" (pages 368–376); Katherine Anne Porter's "The Jilting of Granny Weatherall" (pages 1017–1024).

91

<hr />

JOHN UPDIKE

A & P

JOHN UPDIKE was born in 1932 in Shillington, Pennsylvania, and educated at Harvard University. Upon graduation, he spent a year at Oxford studying at the Ruskin School of Drawing and Fine Arts. In 1955, he returned from England and joined the staff of *The New Yorker,* where he published his first stories, but two years later he left the magazine to pursue a full-time writing career. Updike's first book, *The Poorhouse Fair* (1959), was a moderate success, but his next novel, *Rabbit, Run* (1960), was acclaimed one of the best novels of the decade. His fascination with the leading character in this novel, Harry ("Rabbit") Angstrom, prompted Updike to write three sequels, *Rabbit Redux* (1971), *Rabbit Is Rich* (1981), and *Rabbit at Rest* (1990). The first of these was awarded both the National Book Award and the Pulitzer Prize. His other novels include *The Centaur* (1963), which won Updike's first National Book Award, *Couples* (1968), *A Month of Sundays* (1975), *The Coup* (1978), *The Witches of Eastwick* (1984), *Roger's Version* (1986), and *In the Beauty of the Lilies* (1996). Updike's poetry appeared in *The Carpentered Hen and Other Tame Creatures* (1958), *Telephone Poles and Other Poems* (1963), *Midpoint and Other Poems* (1969), and *Tossing and Turning* (1977). Updike's finely crafted short stories have been collected in *The Same Door* (1959), *Pigeon Feathers* (1962), *The Music School* (1966), *Museums and Women* (1972), *Too Far to Go* (1979), and *Trust Me* (1987). "A & P," reprinted from *Pigeon Feathers,* recounts a young boy's attempt to make a heroic stand. "Separating," reprinted from *Problems and Other Stories* (1981), documents a suburban couple's attempt to explain their disintegrating marriage to their children.

In walks these three girls in nothing but bathing suits. I'm in the third checkout slot, with my back to the door, so I don't see them until they're over by the bread. The one that caught my eye first was the one in the plaid green two-piece. She was a chunky kid, with a good tan and a sweet broad soft-looking can with those two crescents of white just under it, where the sun never seems to hit, at the top of the backs of her legs. I stood there with my hand on a box of HiHo crackers trying to remember if I rang it up or not. I ring it up again and the customer starts giving me hell. She's one of these cash-register-watchers, a witch about fifty with rouge on her cheekbones and no eyebrows, and I know it made her day to trip me up. She'd been watching cash registers for fifty years and probably never seen a mistake before.

By the time I got her feathers smoothed and her goodies into a bag—she gives me a little snort in passing, if she'd been born at the right time they would have burned her over in Salem—by the time I get her on her way the girls had circled around the bread and were coming back, without a pushcart, back my way along the counters, in the aisle between the checkouts and the Special bins. They didn't even have shoes on. There was this chunky one, with the two-piece—it was bright green and the seams on the bra were still sharp and her belly was still pretty pale so I guessed she just got it (the suit)—there was this one, with one of those chubby berry-faces, the lips all bunched together under her nose, this one, and a tall one, with black hair that hadn't quite frizzed right, and one of these sunburns right across under the eyes, and a chin that was too long—you know, the kind of girl other girls think is very "striking" and "attractive" but never quite makes it, as they very well know, which is why they like her so much—and then the third one, that wasn't quite so tall. She was the queen. She kind of led them, the other two peeking around and making their shoulders round. She didn't look around, not this queen, she just walked straight on slowly, on these long white prima-donna legs. She came down a little hard on her heels, as if she didn't walk in her bare feet that much, putting down her heels and then letting the weight move along to her toes as if she was testing the floor with every step, putting a little deliberate extra action into it. You never know for sure how girls' minds work (do you really think it's a mind in there or just a little buzz like a bee in a glass jar?) but you got the idea she had talked the other two into coming in here with her, and now she was showing them how to do it, walk slow and hold yourself straight.

She had on a kind of dirty-pink—beige maybe, I don't know—bathing suit with a little nubble all over it and, what got me, the straps were down. They were off her shoulders looped loose around the cool tops of her arms, and I guess as a result the suit had slipped a little on her, so all around the top of the cloth there was this shining rim. If it hadn't been there you wouldn't have known there could have been anything whiter than those shoulders. With the straps pushed off, there was nothing between the top of the suit and the top of her head except just *her,* this clean bare plane of the top of her chest down from the shoulder bones like a dented sheet of metal tilted in the light. I mean, it was more than pretty.

She had sort of oaky hair that the sun and salt had bleached, done up in a bun that was unravelling, and a kind of prim face. Walking into the A & P with your straps down, I suppose it's the only kind of face you *can* have. She held her head so high her neck, coming up out of those white shoulders, looked kind of stretched, but I didn't mind. The longer her neck was, the more of her there was.

She must have felt in the corner of her eye me and over my shoulder Stokesie ⁵ in the second slot watching, but she didn't tip. Not this queen. She kept her eyes moving across the racks, and stopped, and turned so slow it made my stomach rub the inside of my apron, and buzzed to the other two, who kind of huddled against her for relief, and then they all three of them went up the cat-and-dog-food-breakfast-cereal-macaroni-rice-raisins-seasonings-spreads-spaghetti-soft-drinks-crackers-and-cookies aisle. From the third slot I look straight up this aisle to the meat counter, and I watched them all the way. The fat one with the tan sort of fumbled with the cookies, but on second thought she put the package back. The sheep pushing their carts down the aisle—the girls were walking against the usual traffic (not that we have one-way signs or anything)—were pretty hilarious. You could see them, when Queenie's white shoulders dawned on them, kind of jerk, or hop, or hiccup, but their eyes snapped back to their own baskets and on they pushed. I bet you could set off dynamite in an A & P and the people would by and large keep reaching and checking oatmeal off their lists and muttering "Let me see, there was a third thing, began with A, asparagus, no, ah, yes, applesauce!" or whatever it is they do mutter. But there was no doubt, this jiggled them. A few houseslaves in pin curlers even looked around after pushing their carts past to make sure what they had seen was correct.

You know, it's one thing to have a girl in a bathing suit down on the beach, where what with the glare nobody can look at each other much anyway, and another thing in the cool of the A & P, under the fluorescent lights, against all those stacked packages, with her feet paddling along naked over our checkerboard green-and-cream rubber-tile floor.

"Oh Daddy," Stokesie said beside me. "I feel so faint."

"Darling," I said. "Hold me tight." Stokesie's married, with two babies chalked up on his fuselage already, but as far as I can tell that's the only difference. He's twenty-two, and I was nineteen this April.

"Is it done?" he asks, the responsible married man finding his voice. I forgot to say he thinks he's going to be manager some sunny day, maybe in 1990 when it's called the Great Alexandrov and Petrooshki Tea Company or something.

10   What he meant was, our town is five miles from a beach, with a big summer colony out on the Point, but we're right in the middle of town, and the women generally put on a shirt or shorts or something before they get out of the car into the street. And anyway these are usually women with six children and varicose veins mapping their legs and nobody, including them, could care less. As I say, we're right in the middle of town, and if you stand at our front doors you can see two banks and the Congregational church and the newspaper store and the three real-estate offices and about twenty-seven old freeloaders tearing up Central Street because the sewer broke again. It's not as if we're on the Cape, we're north of Boston and there's people in this town haven't seen the ocean for twenty years.

The girls had reached the meat counter and were asking McMahon something. He pointed, they pointed, and they shuffled out of sight behind a pyramid of Diet Delight peaches. All that was left for us to see was old McMahon patting his mouth and looking after them sizing up their joints. Poor kids, I began to feel sorry for them, they couldn't help it.

Now here comes the sad part of the story, at least my family says it's sad, but I don't think it's so sad myself. The store's pretty empty, it being Thursday afternoon, so there was nothing much to do except lean on the register and wait for the girls to show up again. The whole store was like a pinball machine and I didn't know which tunnel they'd come out of. After a while they came around out of the far aisle, around the light bulbs, records at discount of the Caribbean Six or Tony Martin Sings or some such gunk you wonder they waste the wax on, sixpacks of candy bars, and plastic toys done up in cellophane that fall apart when a kid looks at them anyway. Around they come, Queenie still leading the way, and holding a little gray jar in her hand. Slots Three through Seven are unmanned and I could see her wondering between Stokes and me, but Stokesie with his usual luck draws an old party in baggy gray pants who stumbles up with four giant cans of pineapple juice (what do these bums *do* with all that pineapple juice? I've often asked myself) so the girls come to me. Queenie puts down the jar and I take it into my fingers icy cold. Kingfish Fancy Herring Snacks in Pure Sour Cream: 49¢. Now her hands are empty, not a ring or a bracelet, bare as God made them, and I wonder where the money's coming from. Still with that prim look she lifts a folded dollar bill out of the hollow at the center of her nubbled pink top. The jar went heavy in my hand. Really, I thought that was so cute.

Then everybody's luck begins to run out. Lengel comes in from haggling with a truck full of cabbages on the lot and is about to scuttle into that door marked MANAGER behind which he hides all day when the girls touch his eye. Lengel's pretty dreary, teaches Sunday school and the rest, but he doesn't miss that much. He comes over and says, "Girls, this isn't the beach."

Queenie blushes, though maybe it's just a brush of sunburn I was noticing for the first time, now that she was so close. "My mother asked me to pick up a jar of herring snacks." Her voice kind of startled me, the way voices do when you see the people first, coming out so flat and dumb yet kind of tony, too, the way it ticked over "pick up" and "snacks." All of a sudden I slid right down her voice into her living room. Her father and the other men were standing around in ice-cream coats and bow ties and the women were in sandals picking up herring snacks on toothpicks off a big glass plate and they were all holding drinks the color of water with olives and sprigs of mint in them. When my parents have somebody over they get lemonade and if it's a real racy affair Schlitz in tall glasses with "They'll Do It Every Time" cartoons stencilled on.

"That's all right," Lengel said. "But this isn't the beach." His repeating this 15 struck me as funny, as if it had just occurred to him, and he had been thinking all these years the A & P was a great big dune and he was the head lifeguard. He didn't like my smiling—as I say he doesn't miss much—but he concentrates on giving the girls that sad Sunday-school-superintendent stare.

Queenie's blush is no sunburn now, and the plump one in plaid, that I liked better from the back—a really sweet can—pipes up, "We weren't doing any shopping. We just came in for one thing."

"That makes no difference," Lengel tells her, and I could see from the way his eyes went that he hadn't noticed she was wearing a two-piece before. "We want you decently dressed when you come in here."

"We *are* decent," Queenie says suddenly, her lower lip pushing, getting sore now that she remembers her place, a place from which the crowd that runs the A & P must look pretty crummy. Fancy Herring Snacks flashed in her very blue eyes.

"Girls, I don't want to argue with you. After this come in here with your shoulders covered. It's our policy." He turns his back. That's policy for you. Policy is what the kingpins want. What the others want is juvenile delinquency.

20   All this while, the customers had been showing up with their carts but, you know, sheep, seeing a scene, they had all bunched up on Stokesie, who shook open a paper bag as gently as peeling a peach, not wanting to miss a word. I could feel in the silence everybody getting nervous, most of all Lengel, who asks me, "Sammy, have you rung up their purchase?"

I thought and said "No" but it wasn't about that I was thinking. I go through the punches, 4, 9, GROC, TOT—it's more complicated than you think, and after you do it often enough, it begins to make a little song, that you hear words to, in my case "Hello (*bing*) there, you (*gung*) hap-py *pee*-pul (*splat*)!"—the *splat* being the drawer flying out. I uncrease the bill, tenderly as you may imagine, it just having come from between the two smoothest scoops of vanilla I had ever known were there, and pass a half and a penny into her narrow pink palm, and nestle the herrings in a bag and twist its neck and hand it over, all the time thinking.

The girls, and who'd blame them, are in a hurry to get out, so I say "I quit" to Lengel quick enough for them to hear, hoping they'll stop and watch me, their unsuspected hero. They keep right on going, into the electric eye; the door flies open and they flicker across the lot to their car, Queenie and Plaid and Big Tall Goony-Goony (not that as raw material she was so bad), leaving me with Lengel and a kink in his eyebrow.

"Did you say something, Sammy?"

"I said I quit."

25   "I thought you did."

"You didn't have to embarrass them."

"It was they who were embarrassing us."

I started to say something that came out "Fiddle-de-doo." It's a saying of my grandmother's, and I know she would have been pleased.

"I don't think you know what you're saying," Lengel said.

30   "I know you don't," I said. "But I do." I pull the bow at the back of my apron and start shrugging it off my shoulders. A couple customers that had been heading for my slot begin to knock against each other, like scared pigs in a chute.

Lengel sighs and begins to look very patient and old and gray. He's been a friend of my parents for years. "Sammy, you don't want to do this to your Mom and Dad," he tells me. It's true, I don't. But it seems to me that once you begin a gesture it's fatal not to go through with it. I fold the apron, "Sammy" stitched in red on the pocket, and put it on the counter, and drop the bow tie on top of it. The bow tie is theirs, if you've ever wondered. "You'll feel this for the rest of your life," Lengel says, and I know it's true, too, but remembering how he made the pretty girl blush makes me so scrunchy inside I punch the No Sale tab and the machine whirs "pee-pul" and the drawer splats out. One advantage to this scene taking place in summer, I can follow this up with a clean exit, there's no fumbling around getting your coat and galoshes, I just saunter into the electric eye in my white shirt that my mother ironed the night before, and the door heaves itself open, and outside the sunshine is skating around on the asphalt.

I look around for my girls, but they're gone, of course. There wasn't anybody but some young married screaming with her children about some candy they didn't get by the door of a powder-blue Falcon station wagon. Looking back in the big windows, over the bags of peat moss and aluminum lawn furniture stacked on the pavement, I could see Lengel in my place in the slot, checking the sheep through. His face was dark gray and his back stiff, as if he'd just had an injection of iron, and my stomach kind of fell as I felt how hard the world was going to be to me hereafter.

QUESTIONS FOR DISCUSSION AND WRITING

1. How does the appearance of three girls in bathing suits in the A & P create the initial conflict in this story? What other conflicts does Sammy's confrontation with Lengel produce? To what extent does Sammy's decision to quit provide a satisfactory resolution to those conflicts?

2. How does Sammy's characterization of the three girls help describe him? How does his name for the third girl, Queenie, justify his lengthy description of her? How does Queenie's purchase reveal the difference between her world and Sammy's world?

3. How does the title of the story call attention to its setting? What assumptions does Sammy make about his readers' familiarity with this setting? How does he compare his store to those nearer the beach?

4. What is the ironic difference between the narrator's view of himself and the reader's view of him? How do the comments of Stokesie and Lengel help qualify Sammy's first-person presentation of the events in the story?

5. What does the story reveal about the causes and effects of "heroic" action? Why has his experience led Sammy to conclude that the world was going to be hard to him "hereafter"?

Stories for Comparison

Carson McCullers's "Sucker" (pages 824–831); W. D. Wetherell's "The Bass, the River, and Sheila Mant" (pages 1181–1186).

92

JOHN   UPDIKE

Separating

The day was fair. Brilliant. All that June the weather had mocked the Maples' internal misery with solid sunlight—golden shafts and cascades of green in which their conversations had wormed unseeing, their sad murmuring selves the only stain in Nature. Usually by this time of the year they had acquired tans; but when they met their elder daughter's plane on her return from a year in England they were almost as pale as she, though Judith was too dazzled by the sunny opulent jumble of her native land to notice. They did not spoil her homecoming by telling her immediately. Wait a few days, let her recover from jet lag, had been one of their formulations, in that string of gray dialogues—over coffee, over cocktails, over Cointreau—that had shaped the strategy of their dissolution, while the earth performed its annual stunt of renewal unnoticed beyond their closed windows. Richard had thought to leave at Easter; Joan had insisted they wait until the four children were at last assembled, with all exams passed and ceremonies attended, and the bauble of summer to console them. So he had drudged away, in love, in dread, repairing screens, getting the mowers sharpened, rolling and patching their new tennis court.

The court, clay, had come through its first winter pitted and windswept bare of redcoat. Years ago, the Maples had observed how often, among their friends, divorce followed a dramatic home improvement, as if the marriage were making one last twitchy effort to live; their own worst crisis had come amid the plaster dust and exposed plumbing of a kitchen renovation. Yet, a summer ago, as canary-yellow bulldozers gaily churned a grassy, daisy-dotted knoll into a muddy plateau, and a crew of pigtailed young men raked and tamped clay into a plane, this transformation did not strike them as ominous, but festive in its impudence; their marriage could rend the earth for fun. The next spring, waking each day at dawn to a sliding sensation as if the bed were being tipped, Richard found the barren tennis court, its net and tapes still rolled in the barn, an environment congruous with his mood of purposeful desolation, and the crumbling of handfuls of clay into cracks and holes (dogs had frolicked on the court in a thaw; rivulets had evolved trenches) an activity suitably elemental and interminable. In his sealed heart he hoped the day would never come.

Now it was here. A Friday. Judith was reacclimated; all four children were assembled, before jobs and camps and visits again scattered them. Joan thought they should be told one by one. Richard was for making an announcement at the table. She said, "I think just making an announcement is a cop-out. They'll start quarrelling and playing to each other instead of focussing. They're each individuals, you know, not just some corporate obstacle to your freedom."

"O.K., O.K. I agree." Joan's plan was exact. That evening, they were giving Judith a belated welcome-home dinner, of lobster and champagne. Then, the party over, they, the two of them, who nineteen years before would push her in a baby carriage along Tenth Street to Washington Square, were to walk her out of the house, to the bridge across the salt creek, and tell her, swearing her to secrecy. Then Richard Jr., who was going directly from work to a rock concert in Boston, would be told, either late when he returned on the train or early Saturday morning before he went off to his job; he was seventeen and employed as one of a golf-course maintenance crew. Then the two younger children, John and Margaret, could, as the morning wore on, be informed.

"Mopped up, as it were," Richard said.   5

"Do you have any better plan? That leaves you the rest of Saturday to answer any questions, pack, and make your wonderful departure."

"No," he said, meaning he had no better plan, and agreed to hers, though it had an edge of false order, a plea for control in the semblance of its achievement, like Joan's long chore lists and financial accountings and, in the days when he first knew her, her too copious lecture notes. Her plan turned one hurdle for him into four—four knife-sharp walls, each with a sheer blind drop on the other side.

All spring he had been morbidly conscious of insides and outsides, of barriers and partitions. He and Joan stood as a thin barrier between the children and the truth. Each moment was a partition, with the past on one side and the future on the other, a future containing this unthinkable *now*. Beyond four knife-like walls a new life for him waited vaguely. His skull cupped a secret, a white face, a face both frightened and soothing, both strange and known, that he wanted to shield from tears, which he felt all about him, solid as the sunlight. So haunted, he had become obsessed with battening down the house against his absence, replacing screens and sash cords, hinges and latches—a Houdini making things snug before his escape.

The lock. He had still to replace a lock on one of the doors of the screened porch. The task, like most such, proved more difficult than he had imagined. The old lock, aluminum frozen by corrosion, had been deliberately rendered obsolete by manufacturers. Three hardware stores had nothing that even approximately matched the mortised hole its removal (surprisingly easy) left. Another hole had to be gouged, with bits too small and saws too big, and the old hole fitted with a block of wood—the chisels dull, the saw rusty, his fingers thick with lack of sleep. The sun poured down, beyond the porch, on a world of neglect. The bushes already needed pruning, the windward side of the house was shedding flakes of paint, rain would get in when he was gone, insects, rot, death. His family, all those he would lose, filtered through the edges of his awareness as he struggled with screw holes, splinters, opaque instructions, minutiae of metal.

10   Judith sat on the porch, a princess returned from exile. She regaled them with stories of fuel shortages, of bomb scares in the Underground, of Pakistani workmen loudly lusting after her as she walked past on her way to dance school. Joan came and went, in and out of the house, calmer than she should have been, praising his struggles with the lock as if this were one more and not the last of their chain of shared chores. The younger of his sons, John, now at fifteen suddenly, unwittingly handsome, for a few minutes held the rickety screen door while his father clumsily hammered and chiseled, each blow a kind of sob in Richard's ears. His younger daughter, having been at a slumber party, slept on the porch hammock through all the noise—heavy and pink, trusting and forsaken. Time, like the sunlight, continued relentlessly; the sunlight slowly slanted. Today was one of the longest days. The lock clicked, worked. He was through. He had a drink; he drank it on the porch, listening to his daughter. "It was so sweet," she was saying, "during the worst of it, how all the butcher's and bakery shops kept open by candlelight. They're all so plucky and cute. From the papers, things sounded so much worse here—people shooting people in gas lines, and everybody freezing."

Richard asked her, "Do you still want to live in England forever?" *Forever:* the concept, now a reality upon him, pressed and scratched at the back of his throat.

"No," Judith confessed, turning her oval face to him, its eyes still childishly far apart, but the lips set as over something succulent and satisfactory. "I was anxious to come home. I'm an American." She was a woman. They had raised her; he and Joan had endured together to raise her, alone of the four. The others had still some raising left in them. Yet it was the thought of telling Judith—the image of her, their first baby, walking between them arm in arm to the bridge—that broke him. The partition between himself and the tears broke. Richard sat down to the celebratory meal with the back of his throat aching; the champagne, the lobster seemed phases of sunshine; he saw them and tasted them through tears. He blinked, swallowed, croakily joked about hay fever. The tears would not stop leaking through; they came not through a hole that could be plugged but through a permeable spot in a membrane, steadily, purely, endlessly, fruitfully. They became, his tears, a shield for himself against these others—their faces, the fact of their assembly, a last time as innocents, at a table where he sat the last time as head. Tears dropped from his nose as he broke the lobster's back; salt flavored his champagne as he sipped it; the raw clench at the back of his throat was delicious. He could not help himself.

His children tried to ignore his tears. Judith, on his right, lit a cigarette, gazed upward in the direction of her too energetic, too sophisticated exhalation; on her other side, John earnestly bent his face to the extraction of the last morsels—legs, tail segments—from the scarlet corpse. Joan, at the opposite end of the table, glanced at him surprised, her reproach displaced by a quick grimace, of forgiveness, or of salute to his superior gift of strategy. Between them, Margaret, no longer called Bean, thirteen and large for her age, gazed from the other side of his pane of tears as if into a shopwindow at something she coveted—at her father, a crystalline heap of splinters and memories. It was not she, however, but John who, in the kitchen, as they cleared the plates and carapaces away, asked Joan the question: *"Why is Daddy crying?"*

Richard heard the question but not the murmured answer. Then he heard Bean cry, "Oh, no-oh!"—the faintly dramatized exclamation of one who had long expected it.

John returned to the table carrying a bowl of salad. He nodded tersely at his fa- 15 ther and his lips shaped the conspiratorial words "She told."

"Told what?" Richard asked aloud, insanely.

The boy sat down as if to rebuke his father's distraction with the example of his own good manners and said quietly, "The separation."

Joan and Margaret returned; the child, in Richard's twisted vision, seemed diminished in size, and relieved, relieved to have had the boogeyman at last proved real. He called out to her—the distances at the table had grown immense—"You knew, you always knew," but the clenching at the back of his throat prevented him from making sense of it. From afar he heard Joan talking, levelly, sensibly, reciting what they had prepared: it was a separation for the summer, an experiment. She and Daddy both agreed it would be good for them; they needed space and time to think; they liked each other but did not make each other happy enough, somehow.

Judith, imitating her mother's factual tone, but in her youth off-key, too cool, said, "I think it's silly. You should either live together or get divorced."

Richard's crying, like a wave that has crested and crashed, had become tu- 20 multuous; but it was overtopped by another tumult, for John, who had been so reserved, now grew larger and larger at the table. Perhaps his younger sister's being credited with knowing set him off. "Why didn't you *tell* us?" he asked, in a large round voice quite unlike his own. "You should have *told* us you weren't getting along."

Richard was startled into attempting to force words through his tears. "We *do* get along, that's the trouble, so it doesn't show even to us—" "That we do not love each other" was the rest of the sentence; he couldn't finish it.

Joan finished for him, in her style. "And we've always, *especially,* loved our children."

John was not mollified. "What do you care about *us?*" he boomed. "We're just little things you *had.*" His sisters' laughing forced a laugh from him, which he turned hard and parodistic: "Ha ha *ha.*" Richard and Joan realized simultaneously that the child was drunk, on Judith's homecoming champagne. Feeling bound to keep the center of the stage, John took a cigarette from Judith's pack, poked it into his mouth, let it hang from his lower lip, and squinted like a gangster.

"You're not little things we had," Richard called to him. "You're the whole point. But you're grown. Or almost."

The boy was lighting matches. Instead of holding them to his cigarette (for they 25 had never seen him smoke; being "good" had been his way of setting himself apart), he held them to his mother's face, closer and closer, for her to blow out. Then he lit the whole folder—a hiss and then a torch, held against his mother's face. Prismed by his tears, the flame filled Richard's vision; he didn't know how it was extinguished. He heard Margaret say, "Oh stop showing off," and saw John, in response, break the cigarette in two and put the halves entirely into his mouth and chew, sticking out his tongue to display the shreds to his sister.

Joan talked to him, reasoning—a fountain of reason, unintelligible. "Talked about it for years . . . our children must help us . . . Daddy and I both want . . ." As the boy listened, he carefully wadded a paper napkin into the leaves of his salad, fashioned a ball of paper and lettuce, and popped it into his mouth, looking around the table for the expected laughter. None came. Judith said, "Be mature," and dismissed a plume of smoke.

Richard got up from this stifling table and led the boy outside. Though the house was in twilight, the outdoors still brimmed with light, the long waste light of high summer. Both laughing, he supervised John's spitting out the lettuce and paper and tobacco into the pachysandra. He took him by the hand—a square gritty hand, but for its softness a man's. Yet, it held on. They ran together up into the field, past the tennis court. The raw banking left by the bulldozers was dotted with daisies. Past the court and a flat stretch where they used to play family baseball stood a soft green rise glorious in the sun, each weed and species of grass distinct as illumination on parchment. "I'm sorry, so sorry," Richard cried. "You were the only one who ever tried to help me with all the goddam jobs around this place."

Sobbing, safe within his tears and the champagne, John explained, "It's not just the separation, it's the whole crummy year, I *hate* that school, you can't make any friends, the history teacher's a scud."

They sat on the crest of the rise, shaking and warm from their tears but easier in their voices, and Richard tried to focus on the child's sad year—the weekdays long with homework, the weekends spent in his room with model airplanes, while his parents murmured down below, nursing their separation. How selfish, how blind, Richard thought; his eyes felt scoured. He told his son, "We'll think about getting you transferred. Life's too short to be miserable."

30   They had said what they could, but did not want the moment to heal, and talked on, about the school, about the tennis court, whether it would ever again be as good as it had been that first summer. They walked to inspect it and pressed a few more tapes more firmly down. A little stiltedly, perhaps trying to make too much of the moment, to prolong it. Richard led the boy to the spot in the field where the view was best, of the metallic blue river, the emerald marsh, the scattered islands velvet with shadow in the low light, the white bits of beach far away. "See," he said. "It goes on being beautiful. It'll be here tomorrow."

"I know," John answered, impatiently. The moment had closed.

Back in the house, the others had opened some white wine, the champagne being drunk, and still sat at the table, the three females, gossiping. Where Joan sat had become the head. She turned, showing him a tearless face, and asked, "All right?"

"We're fine," he said, resenting it, though relieved, that the party went on without him.

In bed she explained, "I couldn't cry I guess because I cried so much all spring. It really wasn't fair. It's your idea, and you make it look as though I was kicking you out."

35   "I'm sorry," he said. "I couldn't stop. I wanted to but couldn't't."

"You *didn't* want to. You loved it. You were having your way, making a general announcement."

"I love having it over," he admitted. "God, those kids were great. So brave and funny." John, returned to the house, had settled to a model airplane in his room, and kept shouting down to them, "I'm O.K. No sweat." "And the way," Richard went on, cozy in his relief, "they never questioned the reasons we gave. No thought of a third person. Not even Judith."

"That *was* touching," Joan said.

He gave her a hug. "You were great too. Thank you." Guiltily, he realized he did not feel separated.

"You still have Dickie to do," she told him. These words set before him a black 40 mountain in the darkness; its cold breath, its near weight affected his chest. Of the four children Dickie was most nearly his conscience. Joan did not need to add, "That's one piece of your dirty work I won't do for you."

"I know. I'll do it. You go to sleep."

Within minutes, her breathing slowed, became oblivious and deep. It was quarter to midnight. Dickie's train from the concert would come in at one-fourteen. Richard set the alarm for one. He had slept atrociously for weeks. But whenever he closed his lids some glimpse of the last hours scorched them—Judith exhaling toward the ceiling in a kind of aversion, Bean's mute staring, the sunstruck growth of the field where he and John had rested. The mountain before him moved closer, moved within him; he was huge, momentous. The ache at the back of his throat felt stale. His wife slept as if slain beside him. When, exasperated by his hot lids, his crowded heart, he rose from bed and dressed, she awoke enough to turn over. He told her then, "If I could undo it all, I would."

"Where would you begin?" she asked. There was no place. Giving him courage, she was always giving him courage. He put on shoes without socks in the dark. The children were breathing in their rooms, the downstairs was hollow. In their confusion they had left lights burning. He turned off all but one, the kitchen overhead. The car started. He had hoped it wouldn't. He met only moonlight on the road; it seemed a diaphanous companion, flickering in the leaves along the roadside, haunting his rearview mirror like a pursuer, melting under his headlights. The center of town, not quite deserted, was eerie at this hour. A young cop in uniform kept company with a gang of T-shirted kids on the steps of the bank. Across from the railroad station, several bars kept open. Customers, mostly young, passed in and out of the warm night, savoring summer's novelty. Voices shouted from cars as they passed; an immense conversation seemed in progress. Richard parked and in his weariness put his head on the passenger seat, out of the commotion and wheeling lights. It was as when, in the movies, an assassin grimly carries his mission through the jostle of a carnival— except the movies cannot show the precipitous, palpable slope you cling to within. You cannot climb back down; you can only fall. The synthetic fabric of the car seat, warmed by his cheek, confided to him an ancient, distant scent of vanilla.

A train whistle caused him to lift his head. It was on time; he had hoped it would be late. The slender drawgates descended. The bell of approach tingled

happily. The great metal body, horizontally fluted, rocked to a stop, and sleepy teenagers disembarked, his son among them. Dickie did not show surprise that his father was meeting him at this terrible hour. He sauntered to the car with two friends,
both taller than he. He said "Hi" to his father and took the passenger's seat with an
exhausted promptness that expressed gratitude. The friends got into the back, and
Richard was grateful; a few more minutes' postponement would be won by driving
them home.

45   He asked, "How was the concert?"

"Groovy," one boy said from the back seat.

"It bit," the other said.

"It was O.K.," Dickie said, moderate by nature, so reasonable that in his childhood the unreason of the world had given him headaches, stomach aches, nausea.
When the second friend had been dropped off at his dark house, the boy blurted,
"Dad, my eyes are killing me with hay fever! I'm out there cutting that mothering
grass all day!"

"Do we still have those drops?"

50   "They didn't do any good last summer."

"They might this." Richard swung a U-turn on the empty street. The drive
home took a few minutes. The mountain was here, in his throat. "Richard," he
said, and felt the boy, slumped and rubbing his eyes, go tense at his tone, "I
didn't come to meet you just to make your life easier. I came because your
mother and I have some news for you, and you're a hard man to get ahold of
these days. It's sad news."

"That's O.K." The reassurance came out soft, but quick, as if released from the
tip of a spring.

Richard had feared that his tears would return and choke him, but the boy's
manliness set an example, and his voice issued forth steady and dry. "It's sad news,
but it needn't be tragic news, at least for you. It should have no practical effect on
your life, though it's bound to have an emotional effect. You'll work at your job, and
go back to school in September. Your mother and I are really proud of what you're
making of your life; we don't want that to change at all."

"Yeah," the boy said lightly, on the intake of his breath, holding himself up.
They turned the corner; the church they went to loomed like a gutted fort. The home
of the woman Richard hoped to marry stood across the green. Her bedroom light
burned.

55   "Your mother and I," he said, "have decided to separate. For the summer. Nothing legal, no divorce yet. We want to see how it feels. For some years now, we
haven't been doing enough for each other, making each other as happy as we should
be. Have you sensed that?"

"No," the boy said. It was an honest, unemotional answer: true or false in a quiz.

Glad for the factual basis, Richard pursued, even garrulously, the details. His
apartment across town, his utter accessibility, the split vacation arrangements, the
advantages to the children, the added mobility and variety of the summer. Dickie listened, absorbing. "Do the others know?"

Richard described how they had been told.

"How did they take it?"

"The girls pretty calmly. John flipped out; he shouted and ate a cigarette and made a salad out of his napkin and told us how much he hated school."

His brother chuckled. "He did?"

"Yeah. The school issue was more upsetting for him than Mom and me. He seemed to feel better for having exploded."

"He did?" The repetition was the first sign that he was stunned.

"Yes. Dickie, I want to tell you something. This last hour, waiting for your train to get in, has been about the worst of my life. I hate this. *Hate* it. My father would have died before doing it to me." He felt immensely lighter, saying this. He had dumped the mountain on the boy. They were home. Moving swiftly as a shadow, Dickie was out of the car, through the bright kitchen. Richard called after him, "Want a glass of milk or anything?"

"No thanks."

"Want us to call the course tomorrow and say you're too sick to work?"

"No, that's all right." The answer was faint, delivered at the door to his room; Richard listened for the slam of a tantrum. The door closed normally. The sound was sickening.

Joan had sunk into that first deep trough of sleep and was slow to awake. Richard had to repeat, "I told him."

"What did he say?"

"Nothing much. Could you go say good night to him? Please."

She left their room, without putting on a bathrobe. He sluggishly changed back into his pajamas and walked down the hall. Dickie was already in bed, Joan was sitting beside him, and the boy's bedside clock radio was murmuring music. When she stood, an inexplicable light—the moon?—outlined her body through the nightie. Richard sat on the warm place she had indented on the child's narrow mattress. He asked him, "Do you want the radio on like that?"

"It always is."

"Doesn't it keep you awake? It would me."

"No."

"Are you sleepy?"

"Yeah."

"Good. Sure you want to get up and go to work? You've had a big night."

"I want to."

Away at school this winter he had learned for the first time that you can go short of sleep and live. As an infant he had slept with an immobile sweating intensity that had alarmed his babysitters. As the children aged, he became the first to go to bed, earlier for a time than his younger brother and sister. Even now, he would go slack in the middle of a television show, his sprawled legs hairy and brown. "O.K. Good boy. Dickie, listen. I love you so much, I never knew how much until now. No matter how this works out, I'll always be with you. Really."

Richard bent to kiss an averted face but his son, sinewy, turned and with wet cheeks embraced him and gave him a kiss, on the lips, passionate as a woman's. In his father's ear he moaned one word, the crucial, intelligent word: "*Why?*"

Why. It was a whistle of wind in a crack, a knife thrust, a window thrown open on emptiness. The white face was gone, the darkness was featureless. Richard had forgotten why.

QUESTIONS FOR DISCUSSION AND WRITING

1. What strategy do Joan and Richard design to tell their children about their separation? How does Richard's behavior at dinner sabotage that strategy? How does his son's final question sustain the unresolved conflicts in the story?

2. How does Richard's preoccupation with repair work suggest that he is "a Houdini making things snug before his escape"? How does Joan's refusal to do Richard's "dirty work" alter our perception of his character? What qualities of each parent seem to be embodied in each child?

3. In what sense does the external setting match the Maples' internal misery? What ironic relationship do the Maples observe between attempts at home improvement and divorce? How do the tennis court and the broken lock confirm this observation?

4. Although the story is told from Richard's point of view, he becomes less of a sympathetic character as the story progresses. What specific revelations cause us to reassess Richard's responsibility for the separation?

5. Why is it significant that in spite of all the stated reasons for the Maples' separation, Richard cannot answer his son's final question?

Stories for Comparison

Gail Godwin's "Dream Children" (pages 583–593); James Joyce's "The Dead" (pages 728–756).

93

ALICE WALKER

Everyday Use

ALICE WALKER was born in 1944 in Eatonton, Georgia, attended Spelman College, and graduated from Sarah Lawrence College. She then became active in the civil rights movement, helping to register voters in Georgia, teaching in the Head Start program in Mississippi, and working on the staff of the New York City welfare department. In 1968 Walker joined the faculty at Jackson State College to teach writing and black literature. In subsequent years she began her own writing career while working as a writer-in-residence at Wellesley College, the University of California, Berkeley, and Brandeis University. She has also been a scholar at the Bread Loaf Writers' Conference and a fellow at the Radcliffe Institute. Walker has contributed her stories, poems, and essays to magazines such as *Negro Digest, Harper's,* and *Black World* and serves as a contributing editor to *Freedomways* and *Ms.* She has written a children's biography, *Langston Hughes, American Poet* (1973), edited an important literary anthology, *I Love Myself When I'm Laughing . . . And Then Again When I'm Looking Mean and Impressive: A Zora Neale Hurston Reader* (1979), and compiled several collections of her essays, *In Search of Our Mothers' Gardens* (1983), *Living By the Word* (1988), and *The Same River Twice* (1986). These works reveal her interest in the themes of sexism and racism, themes she embodies in her three widely acclaimed novels: *The Third Life of Grange Copeland* (1970), *Meridian* (1976), and especially *The Color Purple* (1982), which received both the American Book Award and the Pulitzer Prize. Her recent novel, *Possessing the Secret of Joy* (1992), and stories *In Love and Trouble: Stories of Black Women* (1973) and *You Can't Keep a Good Woman Down* (1981), also examine the complex experiences of black women. "Everyday Use" focuses on a family reunion that produces a conflict between two definitions of the family's heritage. "To Hell with Dying" documents a family's attempt to conquer death through love.

I will wait for her in the yard that Maggie and I made so clean and wavy yesterday afternoon. A yard like this is more comfortable than most people know. It is not just a yard. It is like an extended living room. When the hard clay is swept clean as a floor and the fine sand around the edges lined with tiny, irregular grooves anyone can come and sit and look up into the elm tree and wait for the breezes that never come inside the house.

Maggie will be nervous until after her sister goes: she will stand hopelessly in corners homely and ashamed of the burn scars down her arms and legs, eyeing her sister with a mixture of envy and awe. She thinks her sister has held life always in the palm of one hand, that "no" is a word the world never learned to say to her.

You've no doubt seen those TV shows where the child who has "made it" is confronted, as a surprise, by her own mother and father, tottering in weakly from backstage. (A pleasant surprise, of course: What would they do if parent and child came on the show only to curse out and insult each other?) On TV mother and child embrace and smile into each other's faces. Sometimes the mother and father weep, the child wraps them in her arms and leans across the table to tell how she would not have made it without their help. I have seen these programs.

Sometimes I dream a dream in which Dee and I are suddenly brought together on a TV program of this sort. Out of a dark and soft-seated limousine I am ushered into a bright room filled with many people. There I meet a smiling, gray, sporty man like Johnny Carson who shakes my hand and tells me what a fine girl I have. Then we are on the stage and Dee is embracing me with tears in her eyes. She pins on my dress a large orchid, even though she has told me once that she thinks orchids are tacky flowers.

5   In real life I am a large, big-boned woman with rough, man-working hands. In the winter I wear flannel nightgowns to bed and overalls during the day. I can kill and clean a hog as mercilessly as a man. My fat keeps me hot in zero weather. I can work all day, breaking ice to get water for washing. I can eat pork liver cooked over the open fire minutes after it comes steaming from the hog. One winter I knocked a bull calf straight in the brain between the eyes with a sledge hammer and had the meat hung up to chill before nightfall. But of course all this does not show on television. I am the way my daughter would want me to be: a hundred pounds lighter, my skin like an uncooked barley pancake. My hair glistens in the hot bright lights. Johnny Carson has much to do to keep up with my quick and witty tongue.

But that is a mistake. I know even before I wake up. Who ever knew a Johnson with a quick tongue? Who can even imagine me looking a strange white man in the eye? It seems to me I have talked to them always with one foot raised in flight, with my head turned in whichever way is farthest from them. Dee, though. She would always look anyone in the eye. Hesitation was no part of her nature.

"How do I look, Mama?" Maggie says, showing just enough of her thin body enveloped in pink skirt and red blouse for me to know she's there, almost hidden by the door.

"Come out into the yard," I say.

Have you ever seen a lame animal, perhaps a dog run over by some careless person rich enough to own a car, sidle up to someone who is ignorant enough to be kind to him? That is the way my Maggie walks. She has been like this, chin on chest, eyes on ground, feet in shuffle, ever since the fire that burned the other house to the ground.

Dee is lighter than Maggie, with nicer hair and a fuller figure. She's a woman now, though sometimes I forget. How long ago was it that the other house burned? Ten, twelve years? Sometimes I can still hear the flames and feel Maggie's arm sticking to me, her hair smoking and her dress falling off her in little black papery flakes. Her eyes seemed stretched open, blazed open by the flames reflected in them. And Dee. I see her standing off under the sweet gum tree she used to dig gum out of; a look of concentration on her face as she watched the last dingy gray board of the house fall in toward the red-hot brick chimney. Why don't you do a dance around the ashes? I'd wanted to ask her. She had hated the house that much.

I used to think she hated Maggie, too. But that was before we raised the money, the church and me, to send her to Augusta to school. She used to read to us without pity; forcing words, lies, other folks' habits, whole lives upon us two, sitting trapped and ignorant underneath her voice. She washed us in a river of make-believe, burned us with a lot of knowledge we didn't necessarily need to know. Pressed us to her with the serious way she read, to shove us away at just the moment, like dimwits, we seemed about to understand.

Dee wanted nice things. A yellow organdy dress to wear to her graduation from high school; black pumps to match a green suit she'd made from an old suit somebody gave me. She was determined to stare down any disaster in her efforts. Her eyelids would not flicker for minutes at a time. Often I fought off the temptation to shake her. At sixteen she had a style of her own: and knew what style was.

I never had an education myself. After second grade the school was closed down. Don't ask me why: in 1927 colored asked fewer questions than they do now. Sometimes Maggie reads to me. She stumbles along good-naturedly but can't see well. She knows she is not bright. Like good looks and money, quickness passed her by. She will marry John Thomas (who has mossy teeth in an earnest face) and then I'll be free to sit here and I guess just sing church songs to myself. Although I never was a good singer. Never could carry a tune. I was always better at a man's job. I used to love to milk till I was hoofed in the side in '49. Cows are soothing and slow and don't bother you, unless you try to milk them the wrong way.

I have deliberately turned my back on the house. It is three rooms, just like the one that burned, except the roof is tin; they don't make shingle roofs any more. There are no real windows, just some holes cut in the sides, like the portholes in a ship, but not round and not square, with rawhide holding the shutters up on the outside. This house is in a pasture, too, like the other one. No doubt when Dee sees it she will want to tear it down. She wrote me once that no matter where we "choose" to live, she will manage to come see us. But she will never bring her friends. Maggie and I thought about this and Maggie asked me, "Mama, when did Dee ever *have* any friends?"

She had a few. Furtive boys in pink shirts hanging about on washday after school. Nervous girls who never laughed. Impressed with her they worshiped the well-turned phrase, the cute shape, the scalding humor that erupted like bubbles in lye. She read to them.

When she was courting Jimmy T she didn't have much time to pay to us, but turned all her faultfinding power on him. He *flew* to marry a cheap gal from a family of ignorant flashy people. She hardly had time to recompose herself.

When she comes I will meet—but there they are!

Maggie attempts to make a dash for the house, in her shuffling way, but I stay her with my hand. "Come back here," I say. And she stops and tries to dig a well in the sand with her toe.

It is hard to see them clearly through the strong sun. But even the first glimpse of leg out of the car tells me it is Dee. Her feet were always neat-looking, as if God himself had shaped them with a certain style. From the other side of the car comes a short, stocky man. Hair is all over his head a foot long and hanging from his chin like a kinky mule tail. I hear Maggie suck in her breath. "Uhnnnh," is what it sounds like. Like when you see the wriggling end of a snake just in front of your foot on the road. "Uhnnnh."

20   Dee next. A dress down to the ground, in this hot weather. A dress so loud it hurts my eyes. There are yellows and oranges enough to throw back the light of the sun. I feel my whole face warming from the heat waves it throws out. Earrings, too, gold and hanging down to her shoulders. Bracelets dangling and making noises when she moves her arm up to shake the folds of the dress out of her armpits. The dress is loose and flows, and as she walks closer, I like it. I hear Maggie go "Uhnnnh" again. It is her sister's hair. It stands straight up like the wool on a sheep. It is black as night and around the edges are two long pigtails that rope about like small lizards disappearing behind her ears.

"Wa-su-zo-Tean-o!" she says, coming on in that gliding way the dress makes her move. The short stocky fellow with the hair to his navel is all grinning and he follows up with "Asalamalakim, my mother and sister!" He moves to hug Maggie but she falls back, right up against the back of my chair. I feel her trembling there and when I look up I see the perspiration falling off her chin.

"Don't get up," says Dee. Since I am stout it takes something of a push. You can see me trying to move a second or two before I make it. She turns, showing white heels through her sandals, and goes back to the car. Out she peeks next with a Polaroid. She stoops down quickly and lines up picture after picture of me sitting there in front of the house with Maggie cowering behind me. She never takes a shot without making sure the house is included. When a cow comes nibbling around the edge of the yard she snaps it and me and Maggie *and* the house. Then she puts the Polaroid in the back seat of the car, and comes up and kisses me on the forehead.

Meanwhile Asalamalakim is going through the motions with Maggie's hand. Maggie's hand is as limp as a fish, and probably as cold, despite the sweat, and she keeps trying to pull it back. It looks like Asalamalakim wants to shake hands but wants to do it fancy. Or maybe he don't know how people shake hands. Anyhow, he soon gives up on Maggie.

"Well," I say. "Dee."

25   "No, Mama," she says. "Not 'Dee,' Wangero Leewanika Kemanjo!"

"What happened to 'Dee'?" I wanted to know.

"She's dead," Wangero said. "I couldn't bear it any longer being named after the people who oppress me."

"You know as well as me you was named after your aunt Dicie," I said. Dicie is my sister. She named Dee. We called her "Big Dee" after Dee was born.

"But who was *she* named after?" asked Wangero.

"I guess after Grandma Dee," I said.   30

"And who was she named after?" asked Wangero.

"Her mother," I said, and saw Wangero was getting tired. "That's about as far back as I can trace it," I said. Though, in fact, I probably could have carried it back beyond the Civil War through the branches.

"Well," said Asalamalakim, "there you are."

"Uhnnnh," I heard Maggie say.

"There I was not," I said, "before 'Dicie' cropped up in our family, so why   35
should I try to trace it that far back?"

He just stood there grinning, looking down on me like somebody inspecting a Model A car. Every once in a while he and Wangero sent eye signals over my head.

"How do you pronounce this name?" I asked.

"You don't have to call me by it if you don't want to," said Wangero.

"Why shouldn't I?" I asked. "If that's what you want us to call you, we'll call you."

"I know it might sound awkward at first," said Wangero.   40

"I'll get used to it," I said. "Ream it out again."

Well, soon we got the name out of the way. Asalamalakim had a name twice as long and three times as hard. After I tripped over it two or three times he told me just call him Hakim-a-barber. I wanted to ask him was he a barber, but I didn't really think he was, so I didn't ask.

"You must belong to those beef-cattle peoples down the road," I said. They said "Asalamalakim" when they met you, too, but they didn't shake hands. Always too busy: feeding the cattle, fixing the fences, putting up salt-lick shelters, throwing down hay. When the white folks poisoned some of the herd the men stayed up all night with rifles in their hands. I walked a mile and a half just to see the sight.

Hakim-a-barber said, "I accept some of their doctrines, but farming and raising cattle is not my style." (They didn't tell me, and I didn't ask, whether Wangero [Dee] had really gone and married him.)

We sat down to eat and right away he said he didn't eat collards and pork was   45
unclean. Wangero, though, went on through the chitlins and corn bread, the greens and everything else. She talked a blue streak over the sweet potatoes. Everything delighted her. Even the fact that we still used the benches her daddy made for the table when we couldn't afford to buy chairs.

"Oh, Mama!" she cried. Then turned to Hakim-a-barber. "I never knew how lovely these benches are. You can feel the rump prints," she said, running her hands underneath her and along the bench. Then she gave a sigh and her hand closed over Grandma Dee's butter dish. "That's it!" she said. "I knew there was something I wanted to ask you if I could have." She jumped up from the table and went over in the corner where the churn stood, the milk in its clabber by now. She looked at the churn and looked at it.

"This churn top is what I need," she said. "Didn't Uncle Buddy whittle it out of a tree you all used to have?"

"Yes," I said.

"Uh huh," she said happily. "And I want the dasher, too."

50   "Uncle Buddy whittle that, too?" asked the barber.

Dee (Wangero) looked up at me.

"Aunt Dee's first husband whittled the dash," said Maggie so low you almost couldn't hear her. "His name was Henry, but they called him Stash."

"Maggie's brain is like an elephant's," Wangero said, laughing. "I can use the churn top as a centerpiece for the alcove table," she said, sliding a plate over the churn, "and I'll think of something artistic to do with the dasher."

When she finished wrapping the dasher the handle stuck out. I took it for a moment in my hands. You didn't even have to look close to see where hands pushing the dasher up and down to make butter had left a kind of sink in the wood. In fact, there were a lot of small sinks; you could see where thumbs and fingers had sunk into the wood. It was beautiful light yellow wood, from a tree that grew in the yard where Big Dee and Stash had lived.

55   After dinner Dee (Wangero) went to the trunk at the foot of my bed and started rifling through it. Maggie hung back in the kitchen over the dishpan. Out came Wangero with two quilts. They had been pieced by Grandma Dee and then Big Dee and me had hung them on the quilt frames on the front porch and quilted them. One was in the Lone Star pattern. The other was Walk Around the Mountain. In both of them were scraps of dresses Grandma Dee had worn fifty and more years ago. Bits and pieces of Grandpa Jarrell's Paisley shirts. And one teeny faded blue piece, about the size of a penny matchbox, that was from Great Grandpa Ezra's uniform that he wore in the Civil War.

"Mama," Wangero said sweet as a bird. "Can I have these old quilts?"

I heard something fall in the kitchen, and a minute later the kitchen door slammed.

"Why don't you take one or two of the others?" I asked. "These old things was just done by me and Big Dee from some tops your grandma pieced before she died."

"No," said Wangero. "I don't want those. They are stitched around the borders by machine."

60   "That's made them last better," I said.

"That's not the point," said Wangero. "These are all pieces of dresses Grandma used to wear. She did all this stitching by hand. Imagine!" She held the quilts securely in her arms, stroking them.

"Some of the pieces, like those lavender ones, come from old clothes her mother handed down to her," I said, moving up to touch the quilts. Dee (Wangero) moved back just enough so that I couldn't reach the quilts. They already belonged to her.

"Imagine!" she breathed again, clutching them closely to her bosom.

"The truth is," I said, "I promised to give them quilts to Maggie, for when she marries John Thomas."

She gasped like a bee had stung her.   65

"Maggie can't appreciate these quilts!" she said. "She'd probably be backward enough to put them to everyday use."

"I reckon she would," I said. "God knows I been saving 'em for long enough with nobody using 'em. I hope she will!" I didn't want to bring up how I had offered Dee (Wangero) a quilt when she went away to college. Then she had told me they were old-fashioned, out of style.

"But they're *priceless!*" she was saying now, furiously; for she has a temper. "Maggie would put them on the bed and in five years they'd be in rags. Less than that!"

"She can always make some more," I said. "Maggie knows how to quilt."

Dee (Wangero) looked at me with hatred. "You just will not understand. The   70
point is these quilts, *these* quilts!"

"Well," I said, stumped. "What would *you* do with them?"

"Hang them," she said. As if that was the only thing you *could* do with quilts.

Maggie by now was standing in the door. I could almost hear the sound her feet made as they scraped over each other.

"She can have them, Mama," she said, like somebody used to never winning anything, or having anything reserved for her. "I can 'member Grandma Dee without the quilts."

I looked at her hard. She had filled her bottom lip with checkerberry snuff and it   75
gave her face a kind of dopey, hangdog look. It was Grandma Dee and Big Dee who taught her how to quilt herself. She stood there with her scarred hands hidden in the folds of her skirt. She looked at her sister with something like fear but she wasn't mad at her. This was Maggie's portion. This was the way she knew God to work.

When I looked at her like that something hit me in the top of my head and ran down to the soles of my feet. Just like when I'm in church and the spirit of God touches me and I get happy and shout. I did something I never had done before: hugged Maggie to me, then dragged her on into the room, snatched the quilts out of Miss Wangero's hands and dumped them into Maggie's lap. Maggie just sat there on my bed with her mouth open.

"Take one or two of the others," I said to Dee.

But she turned without a word and went out to Hakim-a-barber.

"You just don't understand," she said, as Maggie and I came out to the car.

"What don't I understand?" I wanted to know.   80

"Your heritage," she said. And then she turned to Maggie, kissed her, and said, "You ought to try to make something of yourself, too, Maggie. It's really a new day for us. But from the way you and Mama still live you'd never know it."

She put on some sunglasses that hid everything above the tip of her nose and her chin.

Maggie smiled; maybe at the sunglasses. But a real smile, not scared. After we watched the car dust settle I asked Maggie to bring me a dip of snuff. And then the two of us sat there just enjoying, until it was time to go in the house and go to bed.

QUESTIONS FOR DISCUSSION AND WRITING

1. How do the mother's observations about the family reunions presented on television introduce the conflicts in the story? Why does the mother's decision to give the quilts to Maggie mark the climax of the story? How do Wangero's comments about heritage and advancement bring the story to its ironic conclusion?

2. How does the mother's description of her working ability help to establish her character? How do Maggie's scars explain her apprehension about her sister's visit? In what way do Dee's attire, boyfriend, and new name comment on her mother's observation that Dee "knew what style was"?

3. How do the mother's opening and closing references to the yard evoke the setting of the story? Why does the mother suspect that Wangero will want to "tear down" the house? Why does Wangero photograph the house and pay so much attention to the benches, the churn, and the quilts?

4. What is the mother's point of view toward Maggie's accident and Wangero's education? How does she explain the cause of her dramatic decision at the end of the story?

5. How do the quilts symbolize the conflict of tradition and progress? For example, why did Wangero refuse the quilt when she went to college? Why does she now suggest that putting them to "everyday use" is backward? How would you compare the mother's comment that "Maggie knows how to quilt" with Wangero's comment that her sister should "make something" of herself?

Stories for Comparison

Paule Marshall's "To Da-duh, In Memoriam" (pages 863–871); Tillie Olsen's "I Stand Here Ironing" (pages 1004–1010).

94

ALICE WALKER

To Hell with Dying

T o hell with dying," my father would say. "These children want Mr. Sweet!"
Mr. Sweet was a diabetic and an alcoholic and a guitar player and lived down
the road from us on a neglected cotton farm. My older brothers and sisters got the
most benefit from Mr. Sweet, for when they were growing up he had quite a few
years ahead of him and so was capable of being called back from the brink of death
any number of times—whenever the voice of my father reached him as he lay ex-
piring. "To hell with dying, man," my father would say, pushing the wife away from
the bedside (in tears although she knew the death was not necessarily the last one unless Mr. Sweet really wanted it to be). "These children want Mr. Sweet!" And they
did want him, for at a signal from Father they would come crowding around the bed
and throw themselves on the covers, and whoever was the smallest at the time would
kiss him all over his wrinkled brown face and tickle him so that he would laugh all
down in his stomach, and his mustache, which was long and sort of straggly, would
shake like Spanish moss and was also that color.

Mr. Sweet had been ambitious as a boy, wanted to be a doctor or lawyer or
sailor, only to find that black men fare better if they are not. Since he could become
none of these things he turned to fishing as his only earnest career and playing the
guitar as his only claim to doing anything extraordinarily well. His son, the only one
that he and his wife, Miss Mary, had, was shiftless as the day is long and spent
money as if he were trying to see the bottom of the mint, which Mr. Sweet would
tell him was the clean brown palm of his hand. Miss Mary loved her "baby," however, and worked hard to get him the "li'l necessaries" of life, which turned out
mostly to be women.

Mr. Sweet was a tall, thinnish man with thick kinky hair going dead white. He
was dark brown, his eyes were squinty and sort of bluish, and he chewed Brown Mule
tobacco. He was constantly on the verge of being blind drunk, for he brewed his own
liquor and was not in the least a stingy sort of man, and was always very melancholy
and sad, though frequently when he was "feelin' good" he'd dance around the yard
with us, usually keeling over just as my mother came to see what the commotion was.

Toward all of us children he was very kind, and had the grace to be shy with us, 5
which is unusual in grown-ups. He had great respect for my mother for she never

held his drunkenness against him and would let us play with him even when he was about to fall in the fireplace from drink. Although Mr. Sweet would sometimes lose complete or nearly complete control of his head and neck so that he would loll in his chair, his mind remained strangely acute and his speech not too affected. His ability to be drunk and sober at the same time made him an ideal playmate, for he was as weak as we were and we could usually best him in wrestling, all the while keeping a fairly coherent conversation going.

We never felt anything of Mr. Sweet's age when we played with him. We loved his wrinkles and would draw some on our brows to be like him, and his white hair was my special treasure and he knew it and would never come to visit us just after he had had his hair cut off at the barbershop. Once he came to our house for something, probably to see my father about fertilizer for his crops because, although he never paid the slightest attention to his crops, he liked to know what things would be best to use on them if he ever did. Anyhow, he had not come with his hair since he had just had it shaved off at the barbershop. He wore a huge straw hat to keep off the sun and also to keep his head away from me. But as soon as I saw him I ran up and demanded that he take me up and kiss me with his funny beard which smelled so strongly of tobacco. Looking forward to burying my small fingers into his wooly hair I threw away his hat only to find he had done something to his hair, that it was no longer there! I let out a squall which made my mother think that Mr. Sweet had finally dropped me in the well or something and from that day I've been wary of men in hats. However, not long after, Mr. Sweet showed up with his hair grown out and just as white and kinky and impenetrable as it ever was.

Mr. Sweet used to call me his princess, and I believed it. He made me feel pretty at five and six, and simply outrageously devastating at the blazing age of eight and a half. When he came to our house with his guitar the whole family would stop whatever they were doing to sit around him and listen to him play. He liked to play "Sweet Georgia Brown," that was what he called me sometimes, and also he liked to play "Caldonia" and all sorts of sweet, sad, wonderful songs which he sometimes made up. It was from one of these songs that I heard that he had had to marry Miss Mary when he had in fact loved somebody else (now living in Chi-ca-go, or De-stroy, Michigan). He was not sure that Joe Lee, her "baby," was also his baby. Sometimes he would cry and that was an indication that he was about to die again. And so we would all get prepared, for we were sure to be called upon.

I was seven the first time I remember actually participating in one of Mr. Sweet's "revivals"—my parents told me I had participated before, I had been the one chosen to kiss him and tickle him long before I knew the rite of Mr. Sweet's rehabilitation. He had come to our house, it was a few years after his wife's death, and was very sad, and also, typically, very drunk. He sat on the floor next to me and my older brother, the rest of the children were grown up and lived elsewhere, and began to play his guitar and cry. I held his woolly head in my arms and wished I could have been old enough to have been the woman he loved so much and that I had not been lost years and years ago.

When he was leaving, my mother said to us that we'd better sleep light that night for we'd probably have to go over to Mr. Sweet's before daylight. And we did. For soon after we had gone to bed one of the neighbors knocked on our door and called my father and said that Mr. Sweet was sinking fast and if he wanted to get in a word before the crossover he'd better shake a leg and get over to Mr. Sweet's house. All the neighbors knew to come to our house if something was wrong with Mr. Sweet, but they did not know how we always managed to make him well, or at least stop him from dying, when he was so often near death. As soon as we heard the cry we got up, my brother and I and my mother and father, and put on our clothes. We hurried out of the house and down the road for we were always afraid that we might someday be too late and Mr. Sweet would get tired of dallying.

When we got to the house, a very poor shack really, we found the front room full of neighbors and relatives and someone met us at the door and said it was all very sad that old Mr. Sweet Little (for Little was his family name, although we mostly ignored it) was about to kick the bucket. My parents were advised not to take my brother and me into the "death room," seeing we were so young and all, but we were so much more accustomed to the death room than he that we ignored him and dashed in without giving his warnings a second thought. I was almost in tears, for these deaths upset me fearfully, and the thought of how much depended on me and my brother (who was such a ham most of the time) made me very nervous.

The doctor was bending over the bed and turned back to tell us for at least the tenth time in the history of my family that, alas, old Mr. Sweet Little was dying and that the children had best not see the face of implacable death (I didn't know what "implacable" was, but whatever it was, Mr. Sweet was not!). My father pushed him rather abruptly out of the way saying, as he always did and very loudly for he was saying it to Mr. Sweet, "To hell with dying, man, these children want Mr. Sweet"— which was my cue to throw myself upon the bed and kiss Mr. Sweet all around the whiskers and under the eyes and around the collar of his nightshirt where he smelled so strongly of all sorts of things, mostly liniment.

I was very good at bringing him around, for as soon as I saw that he was struggling to open his eyes I knew he was going to be all right, and so could finish my revival sure of success. As soon as his eyes were open he would begin to smile and that way I knew that I had surely won. Once, though, I got a tremendous scare, for he could not open his eyes and later I learned that he had had a stroke and that one side of his face was stiff and hard to get into motion. When he began to smile I could tickle him in earnest because I was sure that nothing would get in the way of his laughter, although once he began to cough so hard that he almost threw me off his stomach, but that was when I was very small, little more than a baby, and my bushy hair had gotten in his nose.

When we were sure he would listen to us we would ask him why he was in bed and when he was coming to see us again and could we play his guitar, which more than likely would be leaning against the bed. His eyes would get all misty and he would sometimes cry out loud, but we never let it embarrass us, for he knew that we loved him and that we sometimes cried too for no reason. My parents would leave the room to just the three of us; Mr. Sweet, by that time, would be propped up in bed with a number of pillows behind his head and with me sitting and lying on his shoulder and along his chest. Even when he had trouble breathing he would not ask me to get down. Looking into my eyes he would shake his white head and run a scratchy old finger all around my hairline, which was rather low down, nearly to my eyebrows, and made some people say I looked like a baby monkey.

My brother was very generous in all this, he let me do all the revivaling—he had done it for years before I was born and so was glad to be able to pass it on to someone new. What he would do while I talked to Mr. Sweet was pretend to play the guitar, in fact pretend that he was a young version of Mr. Sweet, and it always made Mr. Sweet glad to think that someone wanted to be like him—of course, we did not know this then, we played the thing by ear, and whatever he seemed to like, we did. We were desperately afraid that he was just going to take off one day and leave us.

15   It did not occur to us that we were doing anything special; we had not learned that death was final when it did come. We thought nothing of triumphing over it so many times, and in fact became a trifle contemptuous of people who let themselves be carried away. It did not occur to us that if our father had been dying we could not have stopped it, that Mr. Sweet was the only person over whom we had power.

When Mr. Sweet was in his eighties I was studying in the university many miles from home. I saw him whenever I went home, but he was never on the verge of dying that I could tell and I began to feel that my anxiety for his health and psychological well-being was unnecessary. By this time he not only had a mustache but a long flowing snow-white beard, which I loved and combed and braided for hours. He was very peaceful, fragile, gentle, and the only jarring note about him was his old steel guitar, which he still played in the old sad, sweet, down-home blues way.

On Mr. Sweet's ninetieth birthday I was finishing my doctorate in Massachusetts and had been making arrangements to go home for several weeks' rest. That morning I got a telegram telling me that Mr. Sweet was dying again and could I please drop everything and come home. Of course I could. My dissertation could wait and my teachers would understand when I explained to them when I got back. I ran to the phone, called the airport, and within four hours I was speeding along the dusty road to Mr. Sweet's.

The house was more dilapidated than when I was last there, barely a shack, but it was overgrown with yellow roses which my family had planted many years ago. The air was heavy and sweet and very peaceful. I felt strange walking through the gate and up the old rickety steps. But the strangeness left me as I caught sight of the long white beard I loved so well flowing down the thin body over the familiar quilt coverlet. Mr. Sweet!

His eyes were closed tight and his hands, crossed over his stomach, were thin and delicate, no longer scratchy. I remembered how always before I had run and jumped up on him just anywhere; now I knew he would not be able to support my weight. I looked around at my parents, and was surprised to see that my father and mother also looked old and frail. My father, his own hair very gray, leaned over the quietly sleeping old man, who, incidentally, smelled still of wine and tobacco, and said, as he'd done so many times, "To hell with dying, man! My daughter is home to see Mr. Sweet!" My brother had not been able to come as he was in the war in Asia. I bent down and gently stroked the closed eyes and gradually they began to open. The closed, wine-stained lips twitched a little, then parted in a warm, slightly embarrassed smile. Mr. Sweet could see me and he recognized me and his eyes looked very spry and twinkly for a moment. I put my head down on the pillow next to his and we just looked at each other for a long time. Then he began to trace my peculiar hairline with a thin, smooth finger. I closed my eyes when his finger halted above my ear (he used to rejoice at the dirt in my ears when I was little), his hand stayed cupped around my cheek. When I opened my eyes, sure that I had reached him in time, his were closed.

Even at twenty-four how could I believe that I had failed? that Mr. Sweet was 20 really gone? He had never gone before. But when I looked at my parents I saw that they were holding back tears. They had loved him dearly. He was like a piece of rare and delicate china which was always being saved from breaking and which finally fell. I looked long at the old face, the wrinkled forehead, the red lips, the hands that still reached out to me. Soon I felt my father pushing something cool into my hands. It was Mr. Sweet's guitar. He had asked them months before to give it to me; he had known that even if I came next time he would not be able to respond in the old way. He did not want me to feel that my trip had been for nothing.

The old guitar! I plucked the strings, hummed "Sweet Georgia Brown." The magic of Mr. Sweet lingered still in the cool steel box. Through the window I could catch the fragrant delicate scent of tender yellow roses. The man on the high old-fashioned bed with the quilt coverlet and the flowing white beard had been my first love.

QUESTIONS FOR DISCUSSION AND WRITING

1. How do the three presentations of the ritualistic revivals form the dramatic structure of the story? In what way does playing the guitar mark the success of the revival? How does playing the guitar provide an appropriate ending for the last attempt to revive Mr. Sweet?

2. How does Mr. Sweet's name suggest his character? What qualities does he possess that make everyone love him in spite of his weaknesses? How does the narrator respond to Mr. Sweet's description of her as a "princess"?

3. How do Mr. Sweet's dreams and disappointments help establish the setting of the story? How does his relationship with the narrator's family evoke a world of abundant life in spite of his failures?

4. At the beginning of the story, the narrator seems to be speaking collectively for all the children in her family. At what point in the story does the point of view shift from "we" to "I"? How do the narrator's growth and education affect her point of view in the last scene?

5. What does the ritual of revival suggest about the restorative powers of love? What other assumptions about death does the narrator form as a result of her experience with Mr. Sweet? Why is it significant that she does not understand the meaning of the word *implacable*?

Stories for Comparison

Charles Johnson's "The Sorcerer's Apprentice (pages 714–722); Eudora Welty's "A Worn Path" (pages 1174–1180).

95

EUDORA WELTY

Why I Live at the P.O.

EUDORA WELTY was born in 1909 in Jackson, Mississippi, and educated at Mississippi State College for Women, the University of Wisconsin, and, for a brief period, the School of Business at Columbia University. During the Depression, Welty returned to Mississippi to write for newspapers and radio stations and to photograph and interview local residents for the Works Progress Administration. Welty's photographs were exhibited in New York City in 1936. During the 1930s Welty also began to publish her short stories in magazines such as *The Southern Review, The New Yorker,* and *The Atlantic Monthly,* winning the 1941 O. Henry Award for "A Worn Path." Welty has continued to live in Jackson, where she has written an impressive body of fiction that evokes a strong sense of her "place." Her stories have been collected in *A Curtain of Green and Other Stories* (1941), *The Wide Net and Other Stories* (1943), *The Golden Apples* (1949), *The Bride of the Innisfallen and Other Stories* (1955), and *The Collected Stories of Eudora Welty* (1980). Welty is also the author of three longer works of fiction, *The Ponder Heart* (1954), *Losing Battles* (1970), and *The Optimist's Daughter* (1972), which was awarded the Pulitzer Prize. Welty's collection of essays and reviews, *The Eye of the Story,* appeared in 1977. In her most recent book, *One Writer's Beginnings* (1984), she discusses the origins of her craft. "Why I Live at the P.O." and "A Worn Path" are reprinted from *A Curtain of Green.* The first dramatizes the comic conflicts in an extended Southern family; the second documents an old woman's arduous journey to accomplish an important mission.

I was getting along fine with Mama, Papa-Daddy and Uncle Rondo until my sister Stella-Rondo just separated from her husband and came back home again. Mr. Whitaker! Of course I went with Mr. Whitaker first, when he first appeared here in China Grove, taking "Pose Yourself!" photos, and Stella-Rondo broke us up. Told him I was one-sided. Bigger on one side than the other, which is a deliberate, calculated falsehood: I'm the same. Stella-Rondo is exactly twelve months to the day younger than I am and for that reason she's spoiled.

She's always had anything in the world she wanted and then she'd throw it away. Papa-Daddy gave her this gorgeous Add-a-Pearl necklace when she was eight years old and she threw it away playing baseball when she was nine, with only two pearls.

So as soon as she got married and moved away from home the first thing she did was separate! From Mr. Whitaker! This photographer with the popeyes she said she trusted. Came home from one of those towns up in Illinois and to our complete surprise brought this child of two.

Mama said she like to made her drop dead for a second. "Here you had this marvelous blonde child and never so much as wrote your mother a word about it," says Mama. "I'm thoroughly ashamed of you." But of course she wasn't.

Stella-Rondo just calmly takes off this *hat,* I wish you could see it. She says,   5 "Why, Mama, Shirley-T.'s adopted, I can prove it."

"How?" says Mama, but all I says was, "H'm!" There I was over the hot stove, trying to stretch two chickens over five people and a completely unexpected child into the bargain, without one moment's notice.

"What do you mean—'H'm!'?" says Stella-Rondo, and Mama says, "I heard that, Sister."

I said that oh, I didn't mean a thing, only that whoever Shirley-T. was, she was the spit-image of Papa-Daddy if he'd cut off his beard, which of course he'd never do in the world. Papa-Daddy's Mama's papa and sulks.

Stella-Rondo got furious! She said, "Sister, I don't need to tell you you got a lot of nerve and always did have and I'll thank you to make no future reference to my adopted child whatsoever."

"Very well," I said. "Very well, very well. Of course I noticed at once she looks   10 like Mr. Whitaker's side too. That frown. She looks like a cross between Mr. Whitaker and Papa-Daddy."

"Well, all I can say is she isn't."

"She looks exactly like Shirley Temple to me," says Mama, but Shirley-T. just ran away from her.

So the first thing Stella-Rondo did at the table was turn Papa-Daddy against me.

"Papa-Daddy," she says. He was trying to cut up his meat. "Papa-Daddy!" I was taken completely by surprise. Papa-Daddy is about a million years old and's got this long-long beard. "Papa-Daddy, Sister says she fails to understand why you don't cut off your beard."

So Papa-Daddy l-a-y-s down his knife and fork! He's real rich. Mama says he   15 is, he says he isn't. So he says, "Have I heard correctly? You don't understand why I don't cut off my beard?"

"Why," I says, "Papa-Daddy, of course I understand, I did not say any such of a thing, the idea!"

He says, "Hussy!"

I says, "Papa-Daddy, you know I wouldn't any more want you to cut off your beard than the man in the moon. It was the farthest thing from my mind! Stella-Rondo sat there and made that up while she was eating breast of chicken."

But he says, "So the postmistress fails to understand why I don't cut off my beard. Which job I got you through my influence with the government. 'Bird's nest'—is that what you call it?"

20   Not that it isn't the next to smallest P.O. in the entire state of Mississippi.

I says, "Oh, Papa-Daddy," I says, "I didn't say any such of a thing, I never dreamed it was a bird's nest, I have always been grateful though this is the next to smallest P.O. in the state of Mississippi, and I do not enjoy being referred to as a hussy by my own grandfather."

But Stella-Rondo says, "Yes, you did say it too. Anybody in the world could of heard you, that had ears."

"Stop right there," says Mama, looking at *me.*

So I pulled my napkin straight back through the napkin ring and left the table.

25   As soon as I was out of the room Mama says, "Call her back, or she'll starve to death," but Papa-Daddy says, "This is the beard I started growing on the Coast when I was fifteen years old." He would of gone on till nightfall if Shirley-T. hadn't lost the Milky Way she ate in Cairo.

So Papa-Daddy says, "I am going out and lie in the hammock, and you can all sit here and remember my words: I'll never cut off my beard as long as I live, even one inch, and I don't appreciate it in you at all." Passed right by me in the hall and went straight out and got in the hammock.

It would be a holiday. It wasn't five minutes before Uncle Rondo suddenly appeared in the hall in one of Stella-Rondo's flesh-colored kimonos, all cut on the bias, like something Mr. Whitaker probably thought was gorgeous.

"Uncle Rondo!" I says. "I didn't know who that was! Where are you going?"

"Sister," he says, "get out of my way, I'm poisoned."

30   "If you're poisoned stay away from Papa-Daddy," I says. "Keep out of the hammock. Papa-Daddy will certainly beat you on the head if you come within forty miles of him. He thinks I deliberately said he ought to cut off his beard after he got me the P.O., and I've told him and told him and told him, and he acts like he just don't hear me. Papa-Daddy must of gone stone deaf."

"He picked a fine day to do it then," says Uncle Rondo, and before you could say "Jack Robinson" flew out in the yard.

What he'd really done, he'd drunk another bottle of that prescription. He does it every single Fourth of July as sure as shooting, and it's horribly expensive. Then he falls over in the hammock and snores. So he insisted on zigzagging right on out to the hammock, looking like a half-wit.

Papa-Daddy woke up with this horrible yell and right there without moving an inch he tried to turn Uncle Rondo against me. I heard every word he said. Oh, he told Uncle Rondo I didn't learn to read till I was eight years old and he didn't see how in the world I ever got the mail put up at the P.O., much less read it all, and he said if Uncle Rondo could only fathom the lengths he had gone to get me that job! And he said on the other hand he thought Stella-Rondo had a brilliant mind and deserved credit for getting out of town. All the time he was just lying there swinging as pretty as you please and looping out his beard, and poor Uncle Rondo was *pleading* with him to slow down the hammock, it was making him dizzy as a witch to watch it. But that's what Papa-Daddy likes about a hammock. So Uncle Rondo was too dizzy to get turned against me for the time being. He's Mama's only brother and is a good case of a one-track mind. Ask anybody. A certified pharmacist.

Just then I heard Stella-Rondo raising the upstairs window. While she was married she got this peculiar idea that it's cooler with the windows shut and locked. So she has to raise the window before she can make a soul hear her outdoors.

So she raises the window and says, *"Oh!"* You would have thought she was 35 mortally wounded.

Uncle Rondo and Papa-Daddy didn't even look up, but kept right on with what they were doing. I had to laugh.

I flew up the stairs and threw the door open! I says, "What in the wide world's the matter, Stella-Rondo? You mortally wounded?"

"No," she says, "I am not mortally wounded but I wish you would do me the favor of looking out that window there and telling me what you see."

So I shade my eyes and look out the window.

"I see the front yard," I says.   40

"Don't you see any human beings?" she says.

"I see Uncle Rondo trying to run Papa-Daddy out of the hammock," I says. "Nothing more. Naturally, it's so suffocating-hot in the house, with all the windows shut and locked, everybody who cares to stay in their right mind will have to go out and get in the hammock before the Fourth of July is over."

"Don't you notice anything different about Uncle Rondo?" asks Stella-Rondo.

"Why, no, except he's got on some terrible-looking flesh-colored contraption I wouldn't be found dead in, is all I can see," I says.

"Never mind, you won't be found dead in it, because it happens to be part of my 45 trousseau, and Mr. Whitaker took several dozen photographs of me in it," says Stella-Rondo. "What on earth could Uncle Rondo *mean* by wearing part of my trousseau out in the broad open daylight without saying so much as 'Kiss my foot,' *knowing* I only got home this morning after my separation and hung my negligee up on the bathroom door, just as nervous as I could be?"

"I'm sure I don't know, and what do you expect me to do about it?" I says. "Jump out the window?"

"No, I expect nothing of the kind. I simply declare that Uncle Rondo looks like a fool in it, that's all," she says. "It makes me sick to my stomach."

"Well, he looks as good as he can," I says. "As good as anybody in reason could." I stood up for Uncle Rondo, please remember. And I said to Stella-Rondo, "I think I would do well not to criticize so freely if I were you and came home with a two-year-old child I had never said a word about, and no explanation whatever about my separation."

"I asked you the instant I entered this house not to refer one more time to my adopted child, and you gave me your word of honor you would not," was all Stella-Rondo would say, and started pulling out every one of her eyebrows with some cheap Kress tweezers.

So I merely slammed the door behind me and went down and made some green- 50 tomato pickle. Somebody had to do it. Of course Mama had turned both the niggers loose; she always said no earthly power could hold one anyway on the Fourth of July, so she wouldn't even try. It turned out that Jaypan fell in the lake and came within a very narrow limit of drowning.

So Mama trots in. Lifts up the lid and says, "H'm! Not very good for your Uncle Rondo in his precarious condition, I must say. Or poor little adopted Shirley-T. Shame on you!"

That made me tired. I says, "Well, Stella-Rondo had better thank her lucky stars it was her instead of me came trotting in with that very peculiar-looking child. Now if it had been me that trotted in from Illinois and brought a peculiar-looking child of two, I shudder to think of the reception I'd of got, much less controlled the diet of an entire family."

"But you must remember, Sister, that you were never married to Mr. Whitaker in the first place and didn't go up to Illinois to live," says Mama, shaking a spoon in my face. "If you had I would of been just as overjoyed to see you and your little adopted girl as I was to see Stella-Rondo, when you wound up with your separation and came on back home."

"You would not," I says.

55 "Don't contradict me, I would," says Mama.

But I said she couldn't convince me though she talked till she was blue in the face. Then I said, "Besides, you know as well as I do that that child is not adopted."

"She most certainly is adopted," says Mama, stiff as a poker.

I says, "Why, Mama, Stella-Rondo had her just as sure as anything in this world, and just too stuck up to admit it."

"Why, Sister," said Mama. "Here I thought we were going to have a pleasant Fourth of July, and you start right out not believing a word your own baby sister tells you!"

60 "Just like Cousin Annie Flo. Went to her grave denying the facts of life," I remind Mama.

"I told you if you ever mentioned Annie Flo's name I'd slap your face," says Mama, and slaps my face.

"All right, you wait and see," I says.

"I," says Mama, "*I* prefer to take my children's word for anything when it's humanly possible." You ought to see Mama, she weighs two hundred pounds and has real tiny feet.

Just then something perfectly horrible occurred to me.

65 "Mama," I says, "can that child talk?" I simply had to whisper! "Mama, I wonder if that child can be—you know—in any way? Do you realize," I says, "that she hasn't spoken one single, solitary word to a human being up to this minute? This is the way she looks," I says, and I looked like this.

Well, Mama and I just stood there and stared at each other. It was horrible!

"I remember well that Joe Whitaker frequently drank like a fish," says Mama. "I believed to my soul he drank *chemicals*." And without another word she marches to the foot of the stairs and calls Stella-Rondo.

"Stella-Rondo? O-o-o-o-o! Stella-Rondo!"

"What?" says Stella-Rondo from upstairs. Not even the grace to get up off the bed.

70 "Can that child of yours talk?" asks Mama.

Stella-Rondo says, "Can she what?"

"Talk! Talk!" says Mama. "Burdyburdyburdyburdy!"

So Stella-Rondo yells back, "Who says she can't talk?"

"Sister says so," says Mama.

"You didn't have to tell me, I know whose word of honor don't mean a thing in   75
this house," says Stella-Rondo.

And in a minute the loudest Yankee voice I ever heard in my life yells out,
"OE'm Pop-OE the Sailor-r-r-r Ma-a-an!" and then somebody jumps up and down
in the upstairs hall. In another second the house would of fallen down.

"Not only talks, she can tap-dance!" calls Stella-Rondo. "Which is more than
some people I won't name can do."

"Why, the little precious darling thing!" Mama says, so surprised. "Just as smart
as she can be!" Starts talking baby talk right there. Then she turns on me. "Sister,
you ought to be thoroughly ashamed! Run upstairs this instant and apologize to
Stella-Rondo and Shirley-T."

"Apologize for what?" I says. "I merely wondered if the child was normal, that's
all. Now that she's proved she is, why, I have nothing further to say."

But Mama just turned on her heel and flew out, furious. She ran right upstairs   80
and hugged the baby. She believed it was adopted. Stella-Rondo hadn't done a thing
but turn her against me from upstairs while I stood there helpless over the hot stove.
So that made Mama, Papa-Daddy and the baby all on Stella-Rondo's side.

Next, Uncle Rondo.

I must say that Uncle Rondo has been marvelous to me at various times in the
past and I was completely unprepared to be made to jump out of my skin, the way it
turned out. Once Stella-Rondo did something perfectly horrible to him—broke a
chain letter from Flanders Field—and he took the radio back he had given her and
gave it to me. Stella-Rondo was furious! For six months we all had to call her Stella
instead of Stella-Rondo, or she wouldn't answer. I always thought Uncle Rondo had
all the brains of the entire family. Another time he sent me to Mammoth Cave, with
all expenses paid.

But this would be the day he was drinking that prescription, the Fourth of July.

So at supper Stella-Rondo speaks up and says she thinks Uncle Rondo ought to
try to eat a little something. So finally Uncle Rondo said he would try a little cold
biscuits and ketchup, but that was all. So *she* brought it to him.

"Do you think it wise to disport with ketchup in Stella-Rondo's flesh-colored   85
kimono?" I says. Trying to be considerate! If Stella-Rondo couldn't watch out for
her trousseau, somebody had to.

"Any objections?" asks Uncle Rondo, just about to pour out all the ketchup.

"Don't mind what she says, Uncle Rondo," says Stella-Rondo. "Sister has
been devoting this solid afternoon to sneering out my bedroom window at the
way you look."

"What's that?" says Uncle Rondo. Uncle Rondo has got the most terrible temper in the world. Anything is liable to make him tear the house down if it comes at
the wrong time.

So Stella-Rondo says, "Sister says, 'Uncle Rondo certainly does look like a fool
in that pink kimono!'"

Do you remember who it was really said that?   90

Uncle Rondo spills out all the ketchup and jumps out of his chair and tears off the kimono and throws it down on the dirty floor and puts his foot on it. It had to be sent all the way to Jackson to the cleaners and re-pleated.

"So that's your opinion of your Uncle Rondo, is it?" he says. "I look like a fool, do I? Well, that's the last straw. A whole day in this house with nothing to do, and then to hear you come out with a remark like that behind my back!"

"I didn't say any such of a thing, Uncle Rondo," I says, "and I'm not saying who did, either. Why, I think you look all right. Just try to take care of yourself and not talk and eat at the same time," I says. "I think you better go lie down."

"Lie down my foot," says Uncle Rondo. I ought to of known by that he was fixing to do something perfectly horrible.

95 So he didn't do anything that night in the precarious state he was in—just played Casino with Mama and Stella-Rondo and Shirley-T. and gave Shirley-T. a nickel with a head on both sides. It tickled her nearly to death, and she called him "Papa." But at 6:30 A.M. the next morning, he threw a whole five-cent package of some unsold one-inch firecrackers from the store as hard as he could into my bedroom and they every one went off. Not one bad one in the string. Anybody else, there'd be one that wouldn't go off.

Well, I'm just terribly susceptible to noise of any kind, the doctor has always told me I was the most sensitive person he had ever seen in his whole life, and I was simply prostrated. I couldn't eat! People tell me they heard it as far as the cemetery, and old Aunt Jep Patterson, that had been holding her own so good, thought it was Judgment Day and she was going to meet her whole family. It's usually so quiet here.

And I'll tell you it didn't take me any longer than a minute to make up my mind what to do. There I was with the whole entire house on Stella-Rondo's side and turned against me. If I have anything at all I have pride.

So I just decided I'd go straight down to the P.O. There's plenty of room there in the back, I says to myself.

Well! I made no bones about letting the family catch on to what I was up to. I didn't try to conceal it.

100 The first thing they knew, I marched in where they were all playing Old Maid and pulled the electric oscillating fan out by the plug, and everything got real hot. Next I snatched the pillow I'd done the needlepoint on right off the davenport from behind Papa-Daddy. He went "Ugh!" I beat Stella-Rondo up the stairs and finally found my charm bracelet in her bureau drawer under a picture of Nelson Eddy.

"So that's the way the land lies," says Uncle Rondo. There he was, piecing on the ham. "Well, Sister, I'll be glad to donate my army cot if you got any place to set it up, providing you'll leave right this minute and let me get some peace." Uncle Rondo was in France.

"Thank you kindly for the cot and 'peace' is hardly the word I would select if I had to resort to firecrackers at 6:30 A.M. in a young girl's bedroom," I says back to him. "And as to where I intend to go, you seem to forget my position as postmistress of China Grove, Mississippi," I says. "I've always got the P.O."

Well, that made them all sit up and take notice.

I went out front and started digging up some four-o'clocks to plant around the P.O.

"Ah-ah-ah!" says Mama, raising the window. "Those happen to be my four-o'clocks. Everything planted in that star is mine. I've never known you to make anything grow in your life."

"Very well," I says. "But I take the fern. Even you, Mama, can't stand there and deny that I'm the one watered that fern. And I happen to know where I can send in a box top and get a packet of one thousand mixed seeds, no two the same kind, free."

"Oh, where?" Mama wants to know.

But I says, "Too late. You 'tend to your house, and I'll 'tend to mine. You hear things like that all the time if you know how to listen to the radio. Perfectly marvelous offers. Get anything you want free."

So I hope to tell you I marched in and got that radio, and they could of all bit a nail in two, especially Stella-Rondo, that it used to belong to, and she well knew she couldn't get it back, I'd sue for it like a shot. And I very politely took the sewing-machine motor I helped pay the most on to give Mama for Christmas back in 1929, and a good big calendar, with the first-aid remedies on it. The thermometer and the Hawaiian ukulele certainly were rightfully mine, and I stood on the step-ladder and got all my watermelon-rind preserves and every fruit and vegetable I'd put up, every jar. Then I began to pull the tacks out of the bluebird wall vases on the archway to the dining room.

"Who told you you could have those, Miss Priss?" says Mama, fanning as hard as she could.

"I bought 'em and I'll keep track of 'em," I says. "I'll tack 'em up one on each side the post-office window, and you can see 'em when you come to ask me for your mail, if you're so dead to see 'em."

"Not I! I'll never darken the door to that post office again if I live to be a hundred," Mama says. "Ungrateful child! After all the money we spent on you at the Normal."

"Me either," says Stella-Rondo. "You can just let my mail lie there and *rot,* for all I care. I'll never come and relieve you of a single, solitary piece."

"I should worry," I says. "And who you think's going to sit down and write you all those big fat letters and postcards, by the way? Mr. Whitaker? Just because he was the only man ever dropped down in China Grove and you got him—unfairly—is he going to sit down and write you a lengthy correspondence after you come home giving no rhyme nor reason whatsoever for your separation and no explanation for the presence of that child? I may not have your brilliant mind, but I fail to see it."

So Mama says, "Sister, I've told you a thousand times that Stella-Rondo simply got homesick, and this child is far too big to be hers," and she says, "Now, why don't you all just sit down and play Casino?"

Then Shirley-T. sticks out her tongue at me in this perfectly horrible way. She has no more manners than the man in the moon. I told her she was going to cross her eyes like that some day and they'd stick.

"It's too late to stop me now," I says. "You should have tried that yesterday. I'm going to the P.O. and the only way you can possibly see me is to visit me there."

So Papa-Daddy says, "You'll never catch me setting foot in that post office, even if I should take a notion into my head to write a letter some place." He says, "I won't have you reachin' out of that little old window with a pair of shears and cuttin' off any beard of mine. I'm too smart for you!"

"We all are," says Stella-Rondo.

120   But I said, "If you're so smart, where's Mr. Whitaker?"

So then Uncle Rondo says, "I'll thank you from now on to stop reading all the orders I get on postcards and telling everybody in China Grove what you think is the matter with them," but I says, "I draw my own conclusions and will continue in the future to draw them." I says, "if people want to write their inmost secrets on penny postcards, there's nothing in the wide world you can do about it, Uncle Rondo."

"And if you think we'll ever *write* another postcard you're sadly mistaken," says Mama.

"Cutting off your nose to spite your face then," I says. "But if you're all determined to have no more to do with the U.S. mail, think of this: What will Stella-Rondo do now, if she wants to tell Mr. Whitaker to come after her?"

"Wah!" says Stella-Rondo. I knew she'd cry. She had a conniption fit right there in the kitchen.

125   "It will be interesting to see how long she holds out," I says. "And now—I am leaving."

"Good-bye," says Uncle Rondo.

"Oh, I declare," says Mama, "to think that a family of mine should quarrel on the Fourth of July, or the day after, over Stella-Rondo leaving old Mr. Whitaker and having the sweetest little adopted child! It looks like we'd all be glad!"

"Wah!" says Stella-Rondo, and has a fresh conniption fit.

"He left *her*——you mark my words," I says. "That's Mr. Whitaker. I know Mr. Whitaker. After all, I knew him first. I said from the beginning he'd up and leave her. I foretold every single thing that's happened."

130   "Where did he go?" asks Mama.

"Probably to the North Pole, if he knows what's good for him," I says.

But Stella-Rondo just bawled and wouldn't say another word. She flew to her room and slammed the door.

"Now look what you've gone and done, Sister," says Mama. "You go apologize."

"I haven't got time, I'm leaving," I says.

135   "Well, what are you waiting around for?" asks Uncle Rondo.

So I just picked up the kitchen clock and marched off, without saying "Kiss my foot" or anything, and never did tell Stella-Rondo good-bye.

There was a nigger girl going along on a little wagon right in front.

"Nigger girl," I says, "come help me haul these things down the hill, I'm going to live in the post office."

Took her nine trips in her express wagon. Uncle Rondo came out on the porch and threw her a nickel.

140   And that's the last I've laid eyes on any of my family or my family laid eyes on me for five solid days and nights. Stella-Rondo may be telling the most horrible tales in the world about Mr. Whitaker, but I haven't heard them. As I tell everybody, I draw my own conclusions.

But oh, I like it here. It's ideal, as I've been saying. You see, I've got everything cater-cornered, the way I like it. Hear the radio? All the war news. Radio, sewing machine, book ends, ironing board and that great big piano lamp—peace, that's what I like. Butterbean vines planted all along the front where the strings are.

Of course, there's not much mail. My family are naturally the main people in China Grove, and if they prefer to vanish from the face of the earth, for all the mail they get or the mail they write, why, I'm not going to open my mouth. Some of the folks here in town are taking up for me and some turned against me. I know which is which. There are always people who will quit buying stamps just to get on the right side of Papa-Daddy.

But here I am, and here I'll stay. I want the world to know I'm happy.

And if Stella-Rondo should come to me this minute, on bended knees, and *attempt* to explain the incidents of her life with Mr. Whitaker, I'd simply put my fingers in both my ears and refuse to listen.

QUESTIONS FOR DISCUSSION AND WRITING

1. How does the return of Stella-Rondo reestablish the conflicts in the family? How does the discussion of Uncle Rondo's attire bring these conflicts to a crisis?

2. What do we learn about the character of the narrator by the ways in which she describes Mr. Whitaker, Papa-Daddy, and Shirley-T.? How do her judgments justify Stella-Rondo's accusation that she is "one-sided"?

3. What aspects of the setting would have to be explained to someone not familiar with the American South in the 1940s? In what sense is the P.O. an "ideal" setting for the narrator at the end of the story?

4. Who seems to be the audience for the story? How do we know the narrator is unreliable?

5. What does this story reveal about the nature of family life? Why do the weaknesses and failures in this family seem funny rather than tragic or pathetic?

Stories for Comparison

Ellen Gilchrist's "Among the Mourners" (pages 92–101); Flannery O'Connor's "A Good Man Is Hard to Find" (pages 967–978).

96

EUDORA   WELTY

A Worn Path

It was December—a bright frozen day in the early morning. Far out in the country there was an old Negro woman with her head tied in a red rag, coming along a path through the pinewoods. Her name was Phoenix Jackson. She was very old and small and she walked slowly in the dark pine shadows, moving a little from side to side in her steps, with the balanced heaviness and lightness of a pendulum in a grandfather clock. She carried a thin, small cane made from an umbrella, and with this she kept tapping the frozen earth in front of her. This made a grave and persistent noise in the still air, that seemed meditative like the chirping of a solitary little bird.

She wore a dark striped dress reaching down to her shoe tops, and an equally long apron of bleached sugar sacks, with a full pocket: all neat and tidy, but every time she took a step she might have fallen over her shoelaces, which dragged from her unlaced shoes. She looked straight ahead. Her eyes were blue with age. Her skin had a pattern all its own of numberless branching wrinkles and as though a whole little tree stood in the middle of her forehead, but a golden color ran underneath, and the two knobs of her cheeks were illuminated by a yellow burning under the dark. Under the red rag her hair came down on her neck in the frailest of ringlets, still black, and with an odor like copper.

Now and then there was a quivering in the thicket. Old Phoenix said, "Out of my way, all you foxes, owls, beetles, jack rabbits, coons and wild animals! . . . Keep out from under these feet, little bob-whites. . . . Keep the big wild hogs out of my path. Don't let none of those come running my direction. I got a long way." Under her small black-freckled hand her cane, limber as a buggy whip, would switch at the brush as if to rouse up any hiding things.

On she went. The woods were deep and still. The sun made the pine needles almost too bright to look at, up where the wind rocked. The cones dropped as light as feathers. Down in the hollow was the mourning dove—it was not too late for him.

5   The path ran up a hill. "Seem like there is chains about my feet, time I get this far," she said, in the voice of argument old people keep to use with themselves. "Something always take a hold of me on this hill—pleads I should stay."

After she got to the top she turned and gave a full, severe look behind her where she had come. "Up through pines," she said at length. "Now down through oaks."

Her eyes opened their widest, and she started down gently. But before she got to the bottom of the hill a bush caught her dress.

Her fingers were busy and intent, but her skirts were full and long, so that before she could pull them free in one place they were caught in another. It was not possible to allow the dress to tear. "I in the thorny bush," she said. "Thorns, you doing your appointed work. Never want to let folks pass, no sir. Old eyes thought you was a pretty little *green* bush."

Finally, trembling all over, she stood free, and after a moment dared to stoop for her cane.

"Sun so high!" she cried, leaning back and looking, while the thick tears went   10
over her eyes. "The time getting all gone here."

At the foot of this hill was a place where a log was laid across the creek.

"Now comes the trial," said Phoenix.

Putting her right foot out, she mounted the log and shut her eyes. Lifting her skirt, leveling her cane fiercely before her, like a festival figure in some parade, she began to march across. Then she opened her eyes and she was safe on the other side.

"I wasn't as old as I thought," she said.

But she sat down to rest. She spread her skirts on the bank around her and folded   15
her hands over her knees. Up above her was a tree in a pearly cloud of mistletoe. She did not dare to close her eyes, and when a little boy brought her a plate with a slice of marble-cake on it she spoke to him. "That would be acceptable," she said. But when she went to take it there was just her own hand in the air.

So she left that tree, and had to go through a barbed-wire fence. There she had to creep and crawl, spreading her knees and stretching her fingers like a baby trying to climb the steps. But she talked loudly to herself: she could not let her dress be torn now, so late in the day, and she could not pay for having her arm or her leg sawed off if she got caught fast where she was.

At last she was safe through the fence and risen up out in the clearing. Big dead trees, like black men with one arm, were standing in the purple stalks of the withered cotton field. There sat a buzzard.

"Who you watching?"

In the furrow she made her way along.

"Glad this not the season for bulls," she said, looking sideways, "and the good   20
Lord made his snakes to curl up and sleep in the winter. A pleasure I don't see no two-headed snake coming around that tree, where it come once. It took a while to get by him, back in the summer."

She passed through the old cotton and went into a field of dead corn. It whispered and shook and was taller than her head. "Through the maze now," she said, for there was no path.

Then there was something tall, black, and skinny there, moving before her.

At first she took it for a man. It could have been a man dancing in the field. But she stood still and listened, and it did not make a sound. It was as silent as a ghost.

"Ghost," she said sharply, "who be you the ghost of? For I have heard of nary death close by."

25   But there was no answer—only the ragged dancing in the wind.

She shut her eyes, reached out her hand, and touched a sleeve. She found a coat and inside that an emptiness, cold as ice.

"You scarecrow," she said. Her face lighted. "I ought to be shut up for good," she said with laughter. "My senses is gone. I too old. I the oldest people I ever know. Dance, old scarecrow," she said, "while I dancing with you."

She kicked her foot over the furrow, and with mouth drawn down, shook her head once or twice in a little strutting way. Some husks blew down and whirled in streamers about her skirts.

Then she went on, parting her way from side to side with the cane, through the whispering field. At last she came to the end, to a wagon track where the silver grass blew between the red nuts. The quail were walking around like pullets, seeming all dainty and unseen.

30   "Walk pretty," she said. "This the easy place. This the easy going."

She followed the track, swaying through the quiet bare fields, through the little strings of trees silver in their dead leaves, past cabins silver from weather, with the doors and windows boarded shut, all like old women under a spell sitting there. "I walking in their sleep," she said, nodding her head vigorously.

In a ravine she went where a spring was silent flowing through a hollow log. Old Phoenix bent and drank. "Sweet-gum makes the water sweet," she said, and drank more. "Nobody know who made this well, for it was here when I was born."

The track crossed a swampy part where the moss hung as white as lace from every limb. "Sleep on, alligators, and blow your bubbles." Then the track went into the road.

Deep, deep the road went down between the high green-colored banks. Overhead the live-oaks met, and it was as dark as a cave.

35   A black dog with a lolling tongue came up out of the weeds by the ditch. She was meditating, and not ready, and when he came at her she only hit him a little with her cane. Over she went in the ditch, like a little puff of milkweed.

Down there, her senses drifted away. A dream visited her, and she reached her hand up, but nothing reached down and gave her a pull. So she lay there and presently went to talking. "Old woman," she said to herself, "that black dog come up out of the weeds to stall you off, and now there he sitting on his fine tail, smiling at you."

A white man finally came along and found her—a hunter, a young man, with his dog on a chain.

"Well, Granny!" he laughed. "What are you doing there?"

"Lying on my back like a June-bug waiting to be turned over, mister," she said, reaching up her hand.

40   He lifted her up, gave her a swing in the air, and set her down. "Anything broken, Granny?"

"No, sir, them old dead weeds is springy enough," said Phoenix, when she had got her breath. "I thank you for your trouble."

"Where do you live, Granny?" he asked, while the two dogs were growling at each other.

"Away back yonder, sir, behind the ridge. You can't even see it from here."

"On your way home?"

"No sir, I going to town."   45

"Why, that's too far! That's as far as I walk when I come out myself, and I get something for my trouble." He patted the stuffed bag he carried, and there hung down a little closed claw. It was one of the bob-whites, and its beak hooked bitterly to show it was dead. "Now you go home, Granny!"

"I bound to go to town, mister," said Phoenix. "The time come around."

He gave another laugh, filling the whole landscape. "I know you old colored people! Wouldn't miss going to town to see Santa Claus!"

But something held old Phoenix very still. The deep lines in her face went into a fierce and different radiation. Without warning, she had seen with her own eyes a flashing nickel fall out of the man's pocket onto the ground.

"How old are you, Granny?" he was saying.   50

"There is no telling, mister," she said, "no telling."

Then she gave a little cry and clapped her hands and said, "Git on away from here, dog! Look! Look at that dog!" She laughed as if in admiration. "He ain't scared of nobody. He a big black dog." She whispered, "Sic him!"

"Watch me get rid of that cur," said the man. "Sic him, Pete! Sic him!"

Phoenix heard the dogs fighting, and heard the man running and throwing sticks. She even heard a gunshot. But she was slowly bending forward by that time, further and further forward, the lids stretched down over her eyes, as if she were doing this in her sleep. Her chin was lowered almost to her knees. The yellow palm of her hand came out from the fold of her apron. Her fingers slid down and along the ground under the piece of money with the grace and care they would have in lifting an egg from under a setting hen. Then she slowly straightened up, she stood erect, and the nickel was in her apron pocket. A bird flew by. Her lips moved. "God watching me the whole time. I come to stealing."

The man came back, and his own dog panted about them. "Well, I scared him   55 off that time," he said, and then he laughed and lifted his gun and pointed it at Phoenix.

She stood straight and faced him.

"Doesn't the gun scare you?" he said, still pointing it.

"No, sir, I seen plenty go off closer by, in my day, and for less than what I done," she said, holding utterly still.

He smiled, and shouldered the gun. "Well, Granny," he said, "you must be a hundred years old, and scared of nothing. I'd give you a dime if I had any money with me. But you take my advice and stay home, and nothing will happen to you."

"I bound to go on my way, mister," said Phoenix. She inclined her head in the   60 red rag. Then they went in different directions, but she could hear the gun shooting again and again over the hill.

She walked on. The shadows hung from the oak trees to the road like curtains. Then she smelled wood-smoke, and smelled the river, and she saw a steeple and the cabins on their steep steps. Dozens of little black children whirled around her. There ahead was Natchez shining. Bells were ringing. She walked on.

In the paved city it was Christmas time. There were red and green electric lights strung and criss-crossed everywhere, and all turned on in the daytime. Old Phoenix would have been lost if she had not distrusted her eyesight and depended on her feet to know where to take her.

She paused quietly on the sidewalk where people were passing by. A lady came along in the crowd, carrying an armful of red-, green- and silver-wrapped presents; she gave off perfume like the red roses in hot summer, and Phoenix stopped her.

"Please, missy, will you lace up my shoe?" She held up her foot.

65   "What do you want, Grandma?"

"See my shoe," said Phoenix. "Do all right for out in the country, but wouldn't look right to go in a big building."

"Stand still then, Grandma," said the lady. She put her packages down on the sidewalk beside her and laced and tied both shoes tightly.

"Can't lace 'em with a cane," said Phoenix. "Thank you, missy. I doesn't mind asking a nice lady to tie up my shoe, when I gets out on the street."

Moving slowly and from side to side, she went into the big building, and into a tower of steps, where she walked up and around and around until her feet knew to stop.

70   She entered a door, and there she saw nailed up on the wall the document that had been stamped with the gold seal and framed in the gold frame, which matched the dream that was hung up in her head.

"Here I be," she said. There was a fixed and ceremonial stiffness over her body.

"A charity case, I suppose," said an attendant who sat at the desk before her.

But Phoenix only looked above her head. There was sweat on her face, the wrinkles in her skin shone like a bright net.

"Speak up, Grandma," the woman said. "What's your name? We must have your history, you know. Have you been here before? What seems to be the trouble with you?"

75   Old Phoenix only gave a twitch to her face as if a fly were bothering her.

"Are you deaf?" cried the attendant.

But then the nurse came in.

"Oh, that's just old Aunt Phoenix," she said. "She doesn't come for herself—she has a little grandson. She makes these trips just as regular as clockwork. She lives away back off the Old Natchez Trace." She bent down. "Well, Aunt Phoenix, why don't you just take a seat? We won't keep you standing after your long trip." She pointed.

The old woman sat down, bolt upright in the chair.

80   "Now, how is the boy?" asked the nurse.

Old Phoenix did not speak.

"I said, how is the boy?"

But Phoenix only waited and stared straight ahead, her face very solemn and withdrawn into rigidity.

"Is his throat any better?" asked the nurse. "Aunt Phoenix, don't you hear me? Is your grandson's throat any better since the last time you came for the medicine?"

With her hands on her knees, the old woman waited, silent, erect and motionless, just as if she were in armor.

"You mustn't take up our time this way, Aunt Phoenix," the nurse said. "Tell us quickly about your grandson, and get it over. He isn't dead, is he?"

At last there came a flicker and then a flame of comprehension across her face, and she spoke.

"My grandson. It was my memory had left me. There I sat and forgot why I made my long trip."

"Forgot?" The nurse frowned. "After you came so far?"

Then Phoenix was like an old woman begging a dignified forgiveness for waking up frightened in the night. "I never did go to school, I was too old at the Surrender," she said in a soft voice. "I'm an old woman without an education. It was my memory fail me. My little grandson, he is just the same, and I forgot it in the coming."

"Throat never heals, does it?" said the nurse, speaking in a loud, sure voice to old Phoenix. By now she had a card with something written on it, a little list. "Yes. Swallowed lye. When was it?—January—two-three years ago—"

Phoenix spoke unasked now. "No, missy, he not dead, he just the same. Every little while his throat begin to close up again, and he not able to swallow. He not get his breath. He not able to help himself. So the time come around, and I go on another trip for the soothing medicine."

"All right. The doctor said as long as you came to get it, you could have it," said the nurse. "But it's an obstinate case."

"My little grandson, he sit up there in the house all wrapped up, waiting by himself," Phoenix went on. "We is the only two left in the world. He suffer and it don't seem to put him back at all. He got a sweet look. He going to last. He wear a little patch quilt and peep out holding his mouth open like a little bird. I remembers so plain now. I not going to forget him again, no, the whole enduring time. I could tell him from all the others in creation."

"All right." The nurse was trying to hush her now. She brought her a bottle of medicine. "Charity," she said, making a check mark in a book.

Old Phoenix held the bottle close to her eyes, and then carefully put it into her pocket.

"I thank you," she said.

"It's Christmas time, Grandma," said the attendant. "Could I give you a few pennies out of my purse?"

"Five pennies is a nickel," said Phoenix stiffly.

"Here's a nickel," said the attendant.

Phoenix rose carefully and held out her hand. She received the nickel and then fished the other nickel out of her pocket and laid it beside the new one. She stared at her palm closely, with her head on one side.

Then she gave a tap with her cane on the floor.

"This is what come to me to do," she said. "I going to the store and buy my child a little windmill they sells, made out of paper. He going to find it hard to believe there such a thing in the world. I'll march myself back where he waiting, holding it straight up in his hand."

She lifted her free hand, gave a little nod, turned around, and walked out of the doctor's office. Then her slow step began on the stairs, going down.

QUESTIONS FOR DISCUSSION AND WRITING

1. What does Welty accomplish by withholding the purpose of Phoenix's journey until the end of the story? To what extent does the hunter's comment about "getting something for [his] trouble" foreshadow the climax of the story? Why does Phoenix's decision to buy a paper windmill bring the story to a satisfactory conclusion?

2. What specific details of Phoenix's external appearance and behavior help establish her character? In what ways does Phoenix's name provide a clue to her character? How do the attendant and nurse characterize themselves and Phoenix during their conversation about the grandson?

3. How does the title define the setting of the story? What landmarks on the path are familiar to Phoenix? What objects and events surprise her? How does her concern about tying her shoes signal her arrival in a new setting?

4. What effect does Welty create by using an objective rather than first-person point of view in this story? What does Phoenix's conversation with herself reveal about her attitude toward herself and her journey?

5. What does this story reveal about the trials, wisdom, and dignity of old age? To what extent does the hunter's allusion to Santa Claus or the nurse's notation of "charity" demean the achievement of Phoenix's journey?

Stories for Comparison

Ernest Gaines's "The Sky Is Gray" (pages 533–553); Dennis McFarland's "Nothing to Ask For" (pages 832–842).

97

W.   D.   W E T H E R E L L

The Bass, the River, and Sheila Mant

WALTER DAVID WETHERELL was born in 1948 in Mineola, New York, and educated at Hofstra University. After working at a variety of odd jobs—movie extra, tour guide, and free-lance journalist—he taught in the creative writing program at the University of Vermont. During this period Wetherell published short stories in magazines such as the *Virginia Quarterly Review, The Adventure,* and *New England Quarterly.* His other works include a novel, *Souvenirs* (1981), and a collection of essays, *Vermont River* (1984). Wetherell's story "The Man Who Loved Levittown" won the O. Henry Prize for the best short story of the year in 1983, and his collection of stories by the same title won the Heinz Literature Prize in 1985. His recent works include *Hyannis Boat and Other Stories* (1989), *Chekhov's Sister* (1990), *Upland Stream* (1991), *Wherever That Great Heart May Be* (1996), and *The Wisest Man in America* (1996). "The Bass, the River, and Sheila Mant," reprinted from *The Man Who Loved Levittown* (1985), recounts the comic twists in a romantic summer fantasy.

There was a summer in my life when the only creature that seemed lovelier to me than a largemouth bass was Sheila Mant. I was fourteen. The Mants had rented the cottage next to ours on the river; with their parties, their frantic games of softball, their constant comings and goings, they appeared to me denizens of a brilliant existence. "Too noisy by half," my mother quickly decided, but I would have given anything to be invited to one of their parties, and when my parents went to bed I would sneak through the woods to their hedge and stare enchanted at the candlelit swirl of white dresses and bright, paisley skirts.

Sheila was the middle daughter—at seventeen, all but out of reach. She would spend her days sunbathing on a float my Uncle Sierbert had moored in their cove, and before July was over I had learned all her moods. If she lay flat on the diving board with her hand trailing idly in the water, she was pensive, not to be disturbed. On her side, her head propped up by her arm, she was observant, considering those around her with a look that seemed queenly and severe. Sitting up, arms tucked around her long, suntanned legs, she was approachable, but barely, and it was only in those glorious moments when she stretched herself prior to entering the water that her various suitors found the courage to come near.

These were many. The Dartmouth heavyweight crew would scull by her house on their way upriver, and I think all eight of them must have been in love with her at various times during the summer; the coxswain would curse them through his megaphone, but without effect—there was always a pause in their pace when they passed Sheila's float. I suppose to these jaded twenty-year-olds she seemed the incarnation of innocence and youth, while to me she appeared unutterably suave, the epitome of sophistication. I was on the swim team at school, and to win her attention would do endless laps between my house and the Vermont shore, hoping she would notice the beauty of my flutter kick, the power of my crawl. Finishing, I would boost myself up onto our dock and glance casually over toward her, but she was never watching, and the miraculous day she was, I immediately climbed the diving board and did my best tuck and a half for her, and continued diving until she had left and the sun went down and my longing was like a madness and I couldn't stop.

It was late August by the time I got up the nerve to ask her out. The tortured will-I's, won't-I's, the agonized indecision over what to say, the false starts toward her house and embarrassed retreats—the details of these have been seared from my memory, and the only part I remember clearly is emerging from the woods toward dusk while they were playing softball on their lawn, as bashful and frightened as a unicorn.

5   Sheila was stationed halfway between first and second, well outside the infield. She didn't seem surprised to see me—as a matter of fact, she didn't seem to see me at all.

"If you're playing second base, you should move closer," I said.

She turned—I took the full brunt of her long red hair and well-spaced freckles.

"I'm playing outfield," she said. "I don't like the responsibility of having a base."

"Yeah, I can understand that," I said, though I couldn't. "There's a band in Dixford tomorrow night at nine. Want to go?"

10   One of her brothers sent the ball sailing over the leftfielder's head; she stood and watched it disappear toward the river.

"You have a car?" she said, without looking up.

I played my master stroke. "We'll go by canoe."

I spent all of the following day polishing it. I turned it upside down on our lawn and rubbed every inch with Brillo, hosing off the dirt, wiping it with chamois until it gleamed as bright as aluminum ever gleamed. About five, I slid it into the water, arranging cushions near the bow so Sheila could lean on them if she was in one of her pensive moods, propping up my father's transistor radio by the middle thwart so we could have music when we came back. Automatically, without thinking about it, I mounted my Mitchell reel on my Pfleuger spinning rod and stuck it in the stern.

I say automatically, because I never went anywhere that summer without a fishing rod. When I wasn't swimming laps to impress Sheila, I was back in our driveway practicing casts, and when I wasn't practicing casts, I was tying the line to

Tosca, our springer spaniel, to test the reel's drag, and when I wasn't doing any of those things, I was fishing the river for bass.

Too nervous to sit at home, I got in the canoe early and started paddling in a huge circle that would get me to Sheila's dock around eight. As automatically as I brought along my rod, I tied on a big Rapala plug, let it down into the water, let out some line and immediately forgot all about it.

It was already dark by the time I glided up to the Mants' dock. Even by day the river was quiet, most of the summer people preferring Sunapee or one of the other nearby lakes, and at night it was a solitude difficult to believe, a corridor of hidden life that ran between banks like a tunnel. Even the stars were part of it. They weren't as sharp anywhere else; they seemed to have chosen the river as a guide on their slow wheel toward morning, and in the course of the summer's fishing, I had learned all their names.

I was there ten minutes before Sheila appeared. I heard the slam of their screen door first, then saw her in the spotlight as she came slowly down the path. As beautiful as she was on the float, she was even lovelier now—her white dress went perfectly with her hair, and complemented her figure even more than her swimsuit.

It was her face that bothered me. It had on its delightful fullness a very dubious expression.

"Look," she said. "I can get Dad's car."

"It's faster this way," I lied. "Parking's tense up there. Hey, it's safe. I won't tip it or anything."

She let herself down reluctantly into the bow. I was glad she wasn't facing me. When her eyes were on me, I felt like diving in the river again from agony and joy.

I pried the canoe away from the dock and started paddling upstream. There was an extra paddle in the bow, but Sheila made no move to pick it up. She took her shoes off, and dangled her feet over the side.

Ten minutes went by.

"What kind of band?" she said.

"It's sort of like folk music. You'll like it."

"Eric Caswell's going to be there. He strokes number four."

"No kidding?" I said. I had no idea who she meant.

"What's that sound?" she said, pointing toward shore.

"Bass. That splashing sound?"

"Over there."

"Yeah, bass. They come into the shallows at night to chase frogs and moths and things. Big largemouths. *Micropetrus salmonides,*" I added, showing off.

"I think fishing's dumb," she said, making a face. "I mean, it's boring and all. Definitely dumb."

Now I have spent a great deal of time in the years since wondering why Sheila Mant should come down so hard on fishing. Was her father a fisherman? Her antipathy toward fishing nothing more than normal filial rebellion? Had she tried it once? A messy encounter with worms? It doesn't matter. What does, is that at that fragile moment in time I would have given anything not to appear dumb in Sheila's severe and unforgiving eyes.

She hadn't seen my equipment yet. What I *should* have done, of course, was push the canoe in closer to shore and carefully slide the rod into some branches where I could pick it up again in the morning. Failing that I could have surreptitiously dumped the whole outfit overboard, written off the forty or so dollars as love's tribute. What I actually *did* do was gently lean forward, and slowly, ever so slowly, push the rod back through my legs toward the stern where it would be less conspicuous.

35   It must have been just exactly what the bass was waiting for. Fish will trail a lure sometimes, trying to make up their mind whether or not to attack, and the slight pause in the plug's speed caused by my adjustment was tantalizing enough to overcome the bass's inhibitions. My rod, safely out of sight at last, bent double. The line, tightly coiled, peeled off the spool with the shrill, tearing zip of a high-speed drill.

Four things occurred to me at once. One, that it was a bass. Two, that it was a big bass. Three, that it was the biggest bass I had ever hooked. Four, that Sheila Mant must not know.

"What was that?" she said, turning half around.

"Uh, what was what?"

"That buzzing noise."

40   "Bats."

She shuddered, quickly drew her feet back into the canoe. Every instinct I had told me to pick up the rod and strike back at the bass, but there was no need to—it was already solidly hooked. Downstream, an awesome distance downstream, it jumped clear of the water, landing with a concussion heavy enough to ripple the entire river. For a moment, I thought it was gone, but then the rod was bending again, the tip dancing into the water. Slowly, not making any motion that might alert Sheila, I reached down to tighten the drag.

While all this was going on, Sheila had begun talking and it was a few minutes before I was able to catch up with her train of thought.

"I went to a party there. These fraternity men. Katherine says I could get in there if I wanted. I'm thinking more of UVM or Bennington. Somewhere I can ski."

The bass was slanting toward the rocks on the New Hampshire side by the ruins of Donaldson's boathouse. It had to be an old bass—a young one probably wouldn't have known the rocks were there. I brought the canoe back into the middle of the river, hoping to head it off.

45   "That's neat," I mumbled. "Skiing. Yeah, I can see that."

"Eric said I have the figure to model, but I thought I should get an education first. I mean, it might be a while before I get started and all. I was thinking of getting my hair styled, more swept back? I mean, Ann-Margret? Like hers, only shorter?"

She hesitated. "Are we going backward?"

We were. I had managed to keep the bass in the middle of the river away from the rocks, but it had plenty of room there, and for the first time a chance to exert its full strength. I quickly computed the weight necessary to draw a fully loaded canoe backwards—the thought of it made me feel faint.

"It's just the current," I said hoarsely. "No sweat or anything."

I dug in deeper with my paddle. Reassured, Sheila began talking about some- 50
thing else, but all my attention was taken up now with the fish. I could feel its desperation as the water grew shallower. I could sense the extra strain on the line, the
frantic way it cut back and forth in the water. I could visualize what it looked like—
the gape of its mouth, the flared gills and thick, vertical tail. The bass couldn't have
encountered many forces in its long life that it wasn't capable of handling, and the
unrelenting tug at its mouth must have been a source of great puzzlement and mounting panic.

Me, I had problems of my own. To get to Dixford, I had to paddle up a sluggish
stream that came into the river beneath a covered bridge. There was a shallow sand-
bar at the mouth of this stream—weeds on one side, rocks on the other. Without
doubt, this is where I would lose the fish.

"I have to be careful with my complexion. I tan, but in segments. I can't figure
out if it's even worth it. I shouldn't even do it probably. I saw Jackie Kennedy in
Boston and she wasn't tan at all."

Taking a deep breath, I paddled as hard as I could for the middle, deepest part
of the bar. I could have threaded the eye of a needle with the canoe, but the pull on
the stern threw me off and I overcompensated—the canoe veered left and scraped
bottom. I pushed the paddle down and shoved. A moment of hesitation . . . a moment
more. . . . The canoe shot clear into the deeper water of the stream. I immediately
looked down at the rod. It was bent in the same, tight arc—miraculously, the bass
was still on.

The moon was out now. It was low and full enough that its beam shone directly
on Sheila there ahead of me in the canoe, washing her in a creamy, luminous glow.
I could see the lithe, easy shape of her figure. I could see the way her hair curled
down off her shoulders, the proud, alert tilt of her head, and all these things were as
a tug on my heart. Not just Sheila, but the aura she carried about her of parties and
casual touchings and grace. Behind me, I could feel the strain of the bass, steadier
now, growing weaker, and this was another tug on my heart, not just the bass but the
beat of the river and the slant of the stars and the small of the night, until finally it
seemed I would be torn apart between longings, split in half. Twenty yards ahead of
us was the road, and once I pulled the canoe up on shore, the bass would be gone,
irretrievably gone. If instead I stood up, grabbed the rod and started pumping, I
would have it—as tired as the bass was, there was no chance it could get away.
I reached down for the rod, hesitated, looked up to where Sheila was stretching herself lazily toward the sky, her small breasts rising beneath the soft fabric of her dress,
and the tug was too much for me, and quicker than it takes to write down, I pulled a
penknife from my pocket and cut the line in half.

With a sick, nauseous feeling in my stomach, I saw the rod unbend.   55

"My legs are sore," Sheila whined. "Are we there yet?"

Through a superhuman effort of self-control, I was able to beach the canoe and
help Sheila off. The rest of the night is much foggier. We walked to the fair—there
was the smell of popcorn, the sound of guitars. I may have danced once or twice with
her, but all I really remember is her coming over to me once the music was done to
explain that she would be going home in Eric Caswell's Corvette.

"Okay," I mumbled.

For the first time that night she looked at me, really looked at me.

60   "You're a funny kid, you know that?"

Funny. Different. Dreamy. Odd. How many times was I to hear that in the years to come, all spoken with the same quizzical, half-accusatory tone Sheila used then. Poor Sheila! Before the month was over, the spell she cast over me was gone, but the memory of that lost bass haunted me all summer and haunts me still. There would be other Sheila Mants in my life, other fish, and though I came close once or twice, it was these secret, hidden tuggings in the night that claimed me, and I never made the same mistake again.

QUESTIONS FOR DISCUSSION AND WRITING

1. How does the title suggest the major conflicts in the story? Where is the climax in the story? How does the dance serve as an anticlimax?

2. What does Sheila Mant represent to the narrator? How do Sheila's conversation and actions on the date reveal her true character? In what sense is the narrator a "funny kid"?

3. What are the differences between the dreamy summer world of the narrator and the "too noisy by half" world of the Mants?

4. What are the advantages of having the adult tell the story rather than the fourteen-year-old?

5. What was the mistake that the narrator never repeated?

Stories for Comparison

Sherwood Anderson's "I'm a Fool" (pages 195–203); John Updike's "A & P" (pages 1136–1141).

98

EDITH WHARTON

Roman Fever

EDITH WHARTON (1862–1937) was born in New York City and educated by private tutors in her family's homes in Paris, New York City, and Newport, Rhode Island. She published her first poems anonymously in *The Atlantic Monthly* in 1880 and collected them into a small volume of verse that she arranged to have published privately. Her marriage in 1885 to Boston banker Edward Wharton gave her the leisure to pursue her writing. She began writing stories for the popular magazines and published her first collection, *The Greater Inclination,* in 1899. In a sense, her prolific writing was therapy for her troubled marriage, which finally ended in divorce in 1913. The publication of *The House of Mirth* (1905) established her reputation as a major talent and led to other masterpieces such as *Ethan Frome* (1911), *The Custom of the Country* (1913), *Summer* (1917), and *The Age of Innocence* (1920), for which she was awarded the Pulitzer Prize. After her divorce, Wharton lived most of her life in France. During World War I, she worked on behalf of Belgian orphans and wrote propaganda for the Allied cause, as in *Fighting France, From Dunkerque to Belfort* (1915) and *The Marne* (1918), a war novel. She was awarded the French Cross of the Legion of Honor for her efforts. In 1924, Wharton published four novelettes, *Old New York,* the second of which *(Old Maid)* won a Pulitzer Prize when it was adapted for the stage under the title *The Fifties* (1935). Her numerous short stories appear in volumes such as *Crucial Instances* (1901), *The Hermit and the Wild Woman* (1908), and *Tales of Men and Ghosts* (1910). "Roman Fever," reprinted from *The World Over* (1936), dramatizes the story of two women, each of whom has spent most of her life seeing the other "through the wrong end of her little telescope."

I

From the table at which they had been lunching two American ladies of ripe but well-cared-for middle age moved across the lofty terrace of the Roman restaurant and, leaning on its parapet, looked first at each other, and then down on the outspread glories of the Palatine and the Forum, with the same expression of vague but benevolent approval.

As they leaned there a girlish voice echoed up gaily from the stairs leading to the court below. "Well, come along, then," it cried, not to them but to an invisible companion, "and let's leave the young things to their knitting"; and a voice as fresh laughed back: "Oh, look here, Babs, not actually *knitting*—" "Well, I mean figuratively," rejoined the first. "After all, we haven't left our poor parents much else to do. . . ." and at that point the turn of the stairs engulfed the dialogue.

The two ladies looked at each other again, this time with a tingle of smiling embarassment, and the smaller and paler one shook her head and colored slightly.

"Barbara!" she murmured, sending an unheard rebuke after the mocking voice in the stairway.

5   The other lady, who was fuller, and higher in color, with a small determined nose supported by vigorous black eyebrows, gave a good-humored laugh. "That's what our daughters think of us!"

Her companion replied by a deprecating gesture. "Not of us individually. We must remember that. It's just the collective modern idea of Mothers. And you see—" Half-guiltily she drew from her handsomely mounted black handbag a twist of crimson silk run through by two fine knitting needles. "One never knows," she murmured. "The new system has certainly given us a good deal of time to kill; and sometimes I get tired just looking—even at this." Her gesture was now addressed to the stupendous scene at their feet.

The dark lady laughed again, and they both relapsed upon the view, contemplating it in silence, with a sort of diffused serenity which might have been borrowed from the spring effulgence of the Roman skies. The luncheon hour was long past, and the two had their end of the vast terrace to themselves. At its opposite extremity a few groups, detained by a lingering look at the outspread city, were gathering up guidebooks and fumbling for tips. The last of them scattered, and the two ladies were alone on the air-washed height.

"Well, I don't see why we shouldn't just stay here," said Mrs. Slade, the lady of the high color and energetic brows. Two derelict basket chairs stood near, and she pushed them into the angle of the parapet, and settled herself in one, her gaze upon the Palatine. "After all, it's still the most beautiful view in the world."

"It always will be, to me," assented her friend Mrs. Ansley, with so slight a stress on the "me" that Mrs. Slade, though she noticed it, wondered if it were not merely accidental, like the random underlinings of old-fashioned letter writers.

10   "Grace Ansley was always old-fashioned," she thought; and added aloud, with a retrospective smile: "It's a view we've both been familiar with for a good many years. When we first met here we were younger than our girls are now. You remember?"

"Oh, yes, I remember," murmured Mrs. Ansley, with the same undefinable stress. "There's that headwaiter wondering," she interpolated. She was evidently far less sure than her companion of herself and of her rights in the world.

"I'll cure him of wondering," said Mrs. Slade, stretching her hand toward a bag as discreetly opulent-looking as Mrs. Ansley's. Signing to the headwaiter, she explained that she and her friend were old lovers of Rome, and would like to spend the end of the afternoon looking down on the view—that is, if it did not disturb the service? The headwaiter, bowing over her gratuity, assured her that the ladies were most welcome, and would be still more so if they would condescend to remain for dinner. A full-moon night, they would remember. . . .

Mrs. Slade's black brows drew together, as though references to the moon were out of place and even unwelcome. But she smiled away her frown as the headwaiter retreated. "Well, why not? We might do worse. There's no knowing, I suppose, when the girls will be back. Do you even know back from *where?* I don't!"

Mrs. Ansley again colored slightly. "I think those young Italian aviators we met at the Embassy invited them to fly to Tarquinia for tea. I suppose they'll want to wait and fly back by moonlight."

"Moonlight—moonlight! What a part it still plays. Do you suppose they're as   15 sentimental as we were?"

"I've come to the conclusion that I don't in the least know what they are," said Mrs. Ansley. "And perhaps we didn't know much more about each other."

"No; perhaps we didn't."

Her friend gave her a shy glance. "I never should have supposed you were sentimental, Alida."

"Well, perhaps I wasn't." Mrs. Slade drew her lids together in retrospect; and for a few moments the two ladies, who had been intimate since childhood, reflected how little they knew each other. Each one, of course, had a label ready to attach to the other's name; Mrs. Delphin Slade, for instance, would have told herself, or anyone who asked her, that Mrs. Horace Ansley, twenty-five years ago, had been exquisitely lovely—no, you wouldn't believe it, would you? . . . though, of course, still charming, distinguished. . . . Well, as a girl she had been exquisite; far more beautiful than her daughter Barbara, though certainly Babs, according to the new standards at any rate, was more effective—had more *edge,* as they say. Funny where she got it, with those two nullities as parents. Yes; Horace Ansley was—well, just the duplicate of his wife. Museum specimens of old New York. Good-looking, irreproachable, exemplary. Mrs. Slade and Mrs. Ansley had lived opposite each other—actually as well as figuratively—for years. When the drawing-room curtains in No. 20 East 73rd Street were renewed, No. 23, across the way, was always aware of it. And of all the movings, buyings, travels, anniversaries, illnesses—the tame chronicle of an estimable pair. Little of it escaped Mrs. Slade. But she had grown bored with it by the time her husband made his big *coup* in Wall Street, and when they bought in upper Park Avenue had already begun to think: "I'd rather live opposite a speakeasy for a change; at least one might see it raided." The idea of seeing Grace raided was so amusing that (before the move) she launched it at a woman's lunch. It made a hit, and went the rounds—she sometimes wondered if it had crossed the street, and reached Mrs. Ansley. She hoped not, but didn't much mind. Those were the days when respectability was at a discount, and it did the irreproachable no harm to laugh at them a little.

A few years later, and not many months apart, both ladies lost their husbands.   20 There was an appropriate exchange of wreaths and condolences, and a brief renewal of intimacy in the half-shadow of their mourning; and now, after another interval, they had run across each other in Rome, at the same hotel, each of them the modest appendage of a salient daughter. The similarity of their lot had again drawn them together, lending itself to mild jokes, and the mutual confession that, if in old days it must have been tiring to "keep up" with daughters, it was now, at times, a little dull not to.

No doubt, Mrs. Slade reflected, she felt her unemployment more than poor Grace ever would. It was a big drop from being the wife of Delphin Slade to being his widow. She had always regarded herself (with a certain conjugal pride) as his equal in social gifts, as contributing her full share to the making of the exceptional couple they were: but the difference after his death was irremediable. As the wife of the famous corporation lawyer, always with an international case or two on hand, every day brought its exciting and unexpected obligation: the impromptu entertaining of eminent colleagues from abroad, the hurried dashes on legal business to London, Paris or Rome, where the entertaining was so handsomely reciprocated; the amusement of hearing in her wake: "What, that handsome woman with the good clothes and the eyes is Mrs. Slade—*the* Slade's wife? Really? Generally the wives of celebrities are such frumps."

Yes; being *the* Slade's widow was a dullish business after that. In living up to such a husband all her faculties had been engaged; now she had only her daughter to live up to, for the son who seemed to have inherited his father's gifts had died suddenly in boyhood. She had fought through that agony because her husband was there, to be helped and to help; now, after the father's death, the thought of the boy had become unbearable. There was nothing left but to mother her daughter; and dear Jenny was such a perfect daughter that she needed no excessive mothering. "Now with Babs Ansley I don't know that I *should* be so quiet," Mrs. Slade sometimes half-enviously reflected; but Jenny, who was younger than her brilliant friend, was that rare accident, an extremely pretty girl who somehow made youth and prettiness seem as safe as their absence. It was all perplexing—and to Mrs. Slade a little boring. She wished that Jenny would fall in love—with the wrong man, even; that she might have to be watched, out-maneuvered, rescued. And instead, it was Jenny who watched her mother, kept her out of drafts, made sure that she had taken her tonic. . . .

Mrs. Ansley was much less articulate than her friend, and her mental portrait of Mrs. Slade was slighter, and drawn with fainter touches. "Alida Slade's awfully brilliant; but not as brilliant as she thinks," would have summed it up; though she would have added, for the enlightenment of strangers, that Mrs. Slade had been an extremely dashing girl; much more so than her daughter, who was pretty, of course, and clever in a way, but had none of her mother's—well, "vividness," someone had once called it. Mrs. Ansley would take up current words like this, and cite them in quotation marks, as unheard-of audacities. No; Jenny was not like her mother. Sometimes Mrs. Ansley thought Alida Slade was disappointed; on the whole she had had a sad life. Full of failures and mistakes; Mrs. Ansley had always been rather sorry for her. . . .

So these two ladies visualized each other, each through the wrong end of her little telescope.

2

25 For a long time they continued to sit side by side without speaking. It seemed as though, to both, there was a relief in laying down their somewhat futile activities in

the presence of the vast Memento Mori which faced them. Mrs. Slade sat quite still, her eyes fixed on the golden slope of the Palace of the Caesars, and after a while Mrs. Ansley ceased to fidget with her bag, and she too sank into meditation. Like many intimate friends, the two ladies had never before had occasion to be silent together, and Mrs. Ansley was slightly embarrassed by what seemed, after so many years, a new stage in their intimacy, and one with which she did not yet know how to deal.

Suddenly the air was full of that deep clangor of bells which periodically covers Rome with a roof of silver. Mrs. Slade glanced at her wristwatch. "Five o'clock already," she said, as though surprised.

Mrs. Ansley suggested interrogatively: "There's bridge at the Embassy at five." For a long time Mrs. Slade did not answer. She appeared to be lost in contemplation, and Mrs. Ansley thought the remark had escaped her. But after a while she said, as if speaking out of a dream: "Bridge, did you say? Not unless you want to. . . . But I don't think I will, you know."

"Oh, no," Mrs. Ansley hastened to assure her. "I don't care to at all. It's so lovely here; and so full of old memories, as you say." She settled herself in her chair, and almost furtively drew forth her knitting. Mrs. Slade took sideway note of this activity, but her own beautifully cared-for hands remained motionless on her knee.

"I was just thinking," she said slowly, "what different things Rome stands for to each generation of travelers. To our grandmothers, Roman fever; to our mothers, sentimental dangers—how we used to be guarded!—to our daughters, no more dangers than the middle of Main Street. They don't know it—but how much they're missing!"

The long golden light was beginning to pale, and Mrs. Ansley lifted her knitting a little closer to her eyes. "Yes; how we were guarded!"

"I always used to think," Mrs. Slade continued, "that our mothers had a much more difficult job than our grandmothers. When Roman fever stalked the streets it must have been comparatively easy to gather in the girls at the danger hour; but when you and I were young, with such beauty calling us, and the spice of disobedience thrown in, and no worse risk than catching cold during the cool hour after sunset, the mothers used to be put to it to keep us in—didn't they?"

She turned again toward Mrs. Ansley, but the latter had reached a delicate point in her knitting. "One, two, three—slip two; yes, they must have been," she assented, without looking up.

Mrs. Slade's eyes rested on her with a deepened attention. "She can knit—in the face of *this!* How like her. . . ."

Mrs. Slade leaned back, brooding, her eyes ranging from the ruins which faced her to the long green hollow of the Forum, the fading glow of the church fronts beyond it, and the outlying immensity of the Colosseum. Suddenly she thought: "It's all very well to say that our girls have done away with sentiment and moonlight. But if Babs Ansley isn't out to catch that young aviator—the one who's a Marchese— then I don't know anything. And Jenny has no chance beside her. I know that too. I wonder if that's why Grace Ansley likes the two girls to go everywhere together? My poor Jenny as a foil—!" Mrs. Slade gave a hardly audible laugh, and at the sound Mrs. Ansley dropped her knitting.

35   "Yes—?"

"I—oh, nothing. I was only thinking how your Babs carries everything before her. That Campolieri boy is one of the best matches in Rome. Don't look so innocent, my dear—you know he is. And I was wondering, ever so respectfully, you understand . . . wondering how two such exemplary characters as you and Horace had managed to produce anything quite so dynamic." Mrs. Slade laughed again, with a touch of asperity.

Mrs. Ansley's hands lay inert across her needles. She looked straight out at the great accumulated wreckage of passion and splendor at her feet. But her small profile was almost expressionless. At length she said: "I think you overrate Babs, my dear."

Mrs. Slade's tone grew easier. "No; I don't. I appreciate her. And perhaps envy you. Oh, my girl's perfect; if I were a chronic invalid I'd—well, I think I'd rather be in Jenny's hands. There must be times . . . but there! I always wanted a brilliant daughter . . . and never quite understood why I got an angel instead."

Mrs. Ansley echoed her laugh in a faint murmur. "Babs is an angel too."

40   "Of course—of course! But she's got rainbow wings. Well, they're wandering by the sea with their young men; and here we sit . . . and it all brings back the past a little too acutely."

Mrs. Ansley had resumed her knitting. One might almost have imagined (if one had known her less well, Mrs. Slade reflected) that, for her also, too many memories rose from the lengthening shadows of those august rains. But no; she was simply absorbed in her work. What was there for her to worry about? She knew that Babs would almost certainly come back engaged to the extremely eligible Campolieri. "And she'll sell the New York house, and settle down near them in Rome, and never be in their way . . . she's much too tactful. But she'll have an excellent cook, and just the right people in for bridge and cocktails . . . and a perfectly peaceful old age among her grandchildren."

Mrs. Slade broke off this prophetic flight with a recoil of self-disgust. There was no one of whom she had less right to think unkindly than of Grace Ansley. Would she never cure herself of envying her? Perhaps she had begun too long ago.

She stood up and leaned against the parapet, filling her troubled eyes with the tranquilizing magic of the hour. But instead of tranquilizing her the sight seemed to increase her exasperation. Her gaze turned toward the Colosseum. Already its golden flank was drowned in purple shadow, and above it the sky curved crystal clear, without light or color. It was the moment when afternoon and evening hang balanced in mid-heaven.

Mrs. Slade turned back and laid her hand on her friend's arm. The gesture was so abrupt that Mrs. Ansley looked up, startled.

45   "The sun's set. You're not afraid, my dear?"

"Afraid—?"

"Of Roman fever or pneumonia? I remember how ill you were that winter. As a girl you had a very delicate throat, hadn't you?"

"Oh, we're all right up here. Down below, in the Forum, it does get deathly cold, all of a sudden . . . but not here."

"Ah, of course you know because you had to be so careful." Mrs. Slade turned back to the parapet. She thought: "I must make one more effort not to hate her." Aloud she said: "Whenever I look at the Forum from up here, I remember that story about a great-aunt of yours, wasn't she? A dreadfully wicked great-aunt?"

"Oh, yes; great-aunt Harriet. The one who was supposed to have sent her young 50 sister out to the Forum after sunset to gather a night-blooming flower for her album. All our great-aunts and grandmothers used to have albums of dried flowers."

Mrs. Slade nodded. "But she really sent her because they were in love with the same man—"

"Well, that was the family tradition. They said Aunt Harriet confessed it years afterwards. At any rate, the poor little sister caught the fever and died. Mother used to frighten us with the story when we were children."

"And you frightened *me* with it, that winter when you and I were here as girls. The winter I was engaged to Delphin."

Mrs. Ansley gave a faint laugh. "Oh, did I? Really frighten you? I don't believe you're easily frightened."

"Not often; but I was then. I was easily frightened because I was too happy. I 55 wonder if you know what that means?"

"I—yes . . ." Mrs. Ansley faltered.

"Well, I suppose that was why the story of your wicked aunt made such an impression on me. And I thought: 'There's no more Roman fever, but the Forum is deathly cold after sunset—especially after a hot day. And the Colosseum's even colder and damper.'"

"The Colosseum—?"

"Yes. It wasn't easy to get in, after the gates were locked for the night. Far from easy. Still, in those days it could be managed; it *was* managed, often. Lovers met there who couldn't meet elsewhere. You knew that?"

"I—I dare say. I don't remember."
 60
"You don't remember? You don't remember going to visit some ruins or other one evening, just after dark, and catching a bad chill? You were supposed to have gone to see the moon rise. People always said that expedition was what caused your illness."

"There was a moment's silence; then Mrs. Ansley rejoined: "Did they? It was all so long ago."

"Yes. And you got well again—so it didn't matter. But I suppose it struck your friends—the reason given for your illness, I mean—because everybody knew you were so prudent on account of your throat, and your mother took such care of you. . . . You *had* been out late sight-seeing, hadn't you, that night?"

"Perhaps I had. The most prudent girls aren't always prudent. What made you think of it now?"

Mrs. Slade seemed to have no answer ready. But after a moment she broke out: 65 "Because I simply can't bear it any longer—!"

Mrs. Ansley lifted her head quickly. Her eyes were wide and very pale. "Can't bear what?"

"Why—your not knowing that I've always known why you went."

"Why I went—?"

"Yes. You think I'm bluffing, don't you? Well, you went to meet the man I was engaged to—and I can repeat every word of the letter that took you there."

70 　 While Mrs. Slade spoke Mrs. Ansley had risen unsteadily to her feet. Her bag, her knitting and gloves, slid in a panic-stricken heap to the ground. She looked at Mrs. Slade as though she were looking at a ghost.

"No, no—don't," she faltered out.

"Why not? Listen, if you don't believe me. 'My one darling, things can't go on like this. I must see you alone. Come to the Colosseum immediately after dark tomorrow. There will be somebody to let you in. No one whom you need fear will suspect'—but perhaps you've forgotten what the letter said?"

Mrs. Ansley met the challenge with an unexpected composure. Steadying herself against the chair she looked at her friend, and replied: "No; I know it by heart too."

"And the signature? 'Only *your* D.S.' Was that it? I'm right, am I? That was the letter that took you out that evening after dark?"

75 　 Mrs. Ansley was still looking at her. It seemed to Mrs. Slade that a slow struggle was going on behind the voluntarily controlled mask of her small quiet face. "I shouldn't have thought she had herself so well in hand," Mrs. Slade reflected, almost resentfully. But at this moment Mrs. Ansley spoke. "I don't know how you knew. I burnt that letter at once."

"Yes; you would, naturally—you're so prudent!" The sneer was open now. "And if you burnt the letter you're wondering how on earth I know what was in it. That's it, isn't it?"

Mrs. Slade waited, but Mrs. Ansley did not speak.

"Well, my dear, I know what was in that letter because I wrote it!"

"You wrote it?"

80 　 "Yes."

The two women stood for a minute staring at each other in the last golden light. Then Mrs. Ansley dropped back into her chair. "Oh," she murmured, and covered her face with her hands.

Mrs. Slade waited nervously for another word or movement. None came, and at length she broke out: "I horrify you."

Mrs. Ansley's hands dropped to her knee. The face they uncovered was streaked with tears. "I wasn't thinking of you. I was thinking——it was the only letter I ever had from him!"

"And I wrote it. Yes; I wrote it! But I was the girl he was engaged to. Did you happen to remember that?"

85 　 Mrs. Ansley's head drooped again. "I'm not trying to excuse myself . . . I remembered. . . ."

"And still you went?"

"Still I went."

Mrs. Slade stood looking down on the small bowed figure at her side. The flame of her wrath had already sunk, and she wondered why she had ever thought there would be any satisfaction in inflicting so purposeless a wound on her friend. But she had to justify herself.

"You do understand? I'd found out—and I hated you, hated you. I knew you were in love with Delphin—and I was afraid; afraid of you, of your quiet ways, your sweetness . . . your . . . well, I wanted you out of the way, that's all. Just for a few weeks; just till I was sure of him. So in a blind fury I wrote that letter . . . I don't know why I'm telling you now."

"I suppose," said Mrs. Ansley slowly, "it's because you've gone on hating me."   90

"Perhaps. Or because I wanted to get the whole thing off my mind." She paused. "I'm glad you destroyed the letter. Of course I never thought you'd die."

Mrs. Ansley relapsed into silence, and Mrs. Slade, leaning over her, was conscious of a strange sense of isolation, of being cut off from the warm current of human communion. "You think me a monster!"

"I don't know. . . . It was the only letter I had, and you say he didn't write it?"

"Ah, how you care for him still!"

"I cared for that memory," said Mrs. Ansley.   95

Mrs. Slade continued to look down at her. She seemed physically reduced by the blow—as if, when she got up, the wind might scatter her like a puff of dust. Mrs. Slade's jealousy suddenly leapt up again at the sight. All these years the woman had been living on that letter. How she must have loved him, to treasure the mere memory of its ashes! The letter of the man her friend was engaged to. Wasn't it she who was the monster?

"You tried your best to get him away from me, didn't you? But you failed; and I kept him. That's all."

"Yes. That's all."

"I wish now I hadn't told you. I'd no idea you'd feel about it as you do; I thought you'd be amused. It all happened so long ago, as you say; and you must do me the justice to remember that I had no reason to think you'd ever taken it seriously. How could I, when you were married to Horace Ansley two months afterward? As soon as you could get out of bed your mother rushed you off to Florence and married you. People were rather surprised—they wondered at its being done so quickly; but I thought I knew. I had an idea you did it out of *pique*—to be able to say you'd got ahead of Delphin and me. Girls have such silly reasons for doing the most serious things. And your marrying so soon convinced me that you'd never really cared."

"Yes. I suppose it would," Mrs. Ansley assented.   100

The clear heaven overhead was emptied of all its gold. Dusk spread over it, abruptly darkening the Seven Hills. Here and there lights began to twinkle through the foliage at their feet. Steps were coming and going on the deserted terrace— waiters looking out of the doorway at the head of the stairs, then reappearing with trays and napkins and flasks of wine. Tables were moved, chairs straightened. A feeble string of electric lights flickered out. Some vases of faded flowers were carried away, and brought back replenished. A stout lady in a dust coat suddenly appeared, asking in broken Italian if anyone had seen the elastic band which held together her tattered Baedeker. She poked with her stick under the table at which she had lunched, the waiters assisting.

The corner where Mrs. Slade and Mrs. Ansley sat was still shadowy and deserted. For a long time neither of them spoke. At length Mrs. Slade began again: "I suppose I did it as a sort of joke—"

"A joke?"

"Well, girls are ferocious sometimes, you know. Girls in love especially. And I remember laughing to myself all that evening at the idea that you were waiting around there in the dark, dodging out of sight, listening for every sound, trying to get in—Of course I was upset when I heard you were so ill afterward."

105   Mrs. Ansley had not moved for a long time. But now she turned slowly toward her companion. "But I didn't wait. He'd arranged everything. He was there. We were let in at once," she said.

Mrs. Slade sprang up from her leaning position. "Delphin there? They let you in?—Ah, now you're lying!" she burst out with violence.

Mrs. Ansley's voice grew clearer, and full of surprise. "But of course he was there. Naturally he came—"

"Came? How did he know he'd find you there? You must be raving!"

Mrs. Ansley hesitated, as though reflecting. "But I answered the letter. I told him I'd be there. So he came."

110   Mrs. Slade flung her hands up to her face. "Oh, God—you answered! I never thought of your answering. . . ."

"It's odd you never thought of it, if you wrote the letter."

"Yes. I was blind with rage."

Mrs. Ansley rose, and drew her fur scarf about her. "It is cold here. We'd better go. . . . I'm sorry for you," she said, as she clasped the fur about her throat.

The unexpected words sent a pang through Mrs. Slade. "Yes; we'd better go." She gathered up her bag and cloak. "I don't know why you should be sorry for me," she muttered.

115   Mrs. Ansley stood looking away from her toward the dusky secret mass of the Colosseum. "Well—because I didn't have to wait that night."

Mrs. Slade gave an unquiet laugh. "Yes; I was beaten there. But I oughtn't to begrudge it to you, I suppose. At the end of all these years. After all, I had everything; I had him for twenty-five years. And you had nothing but that one letter that he didn't write."

Mrs. Ansley was again silent. At length she turned toward the door of the terrace. She took a step, and turned back, facing her companion.

"I had Barbara," she said, and began to move ahead of Mrs. Slade toward the stairway.

QUESTIONS FOR DISCUSSION AND WRITING

1. How does the departure of Jenny and Babs evoke their mothers' feelings of discontent? How does Mrs. Slade's confession about the letter bring the story to its climax? How does Mrs. Ansley's final confession provide the story with its denouement?

2. How does Mrs. Slade characterize herself, Jenny, Babs, and Mrs. Ansley in the first part of the story? Although "less articulate," how does Mrs. Ansley's initial characterization of Mrs. Slade provide early clues to her hidden wisdom? How do

the revelations in the second part of the story alter our perception of these two middle-aged women?

3. What has Rome represented to the grandmothers, mothers, and daughters in this story? What did Mrs. Ansley's wicked great-aunt contribute to the folklore of "Roman fever"? Why do the time (late afternoon) and the place (a terrace overlooking the Colosseum) provide an appropriate setting for this story?

4. Although Wharton's point of view in the story is objective, she devotes more of her attention to the "vivid" Mrs. Slade. How does this emphasis enhance the power of the paler Mrs. Ansley's revelation?

5. Why does the apparently stronger Mrs. Slade envy Mrs. Ansley? Why does the apparently slighter Mrs. Ansley pity Mrs. Slade? What does this story suggest about the ability of intimate friends to know and understand one another?

Stories for Comparison

Margaret Atwood's "Dancing Girls" (pages 204–214); Henry James's "The Real Thing" (pages 687–705).

99

RICHARD   WRIGHT

The Man Who Was Almost a Man

RICHARD WRIGHT (1908–1960) was born in Natchez, Mississippi, and spent most of his childhood traveling through the South as his mother looked for work as a cook or maid. The family soon dissolved, and Richard was forced into a series of orphanages and foster homes. After the ninth grade, he struck out on his own, living briefly in Memphis before traveling to Chicago, where he worked as a postal clerk. During the Depression, Wright became associated with writers and politicians of the radical left and began to publish poems in *Left Front*. He also wrote a series of short stories, *Uncle Tom's Children* (1938), which won first prize in a WPA competition. In 1937, Wright moved to New York, where he wrote for *New Masses* and *The Daily Worker.* But as he pointed out in a famous *Harper's* article, "I Tried to Be a Communist" (1944), Wright preferred to tell stories of individuals rather than preach propaganda to the masses. In 1940, he published his brutally realistic novel *Native Son,* establishing himself as America's foremost black writer. In 1945, he published his autobiography, *Black Boy.* After World War II, at the invitation of Gertrude Stein, Wright moved to Paris, where he found the racial atmosphere more conducive to his literary and political interests. His later novels, *The Outsider* (1953) and *The Long Dream* (1958), were mainly influenced by the philosophy of French existentialism. And his nonfiction, such as *Black Power* (1954), reveals his growing interest in the politics of Africa. "The Man Who Was Almost a Man," reprinted from *Eight Men* (1940), is an account of a young boy's attempt to prove his maturity.

Dave struck out across the fields, looking homeward through paling light. Whut's the use talkin wid em niggers in the field? Anyhow, his mother was putting supper on the table. Them niggers can't understan nothing. One of these days he was going to get a gun and practice shooting, then they couldn't talk to him as though he were a little boy. He slowed, looking at the ground. Shucks, Ah ain scareda them even ef they are biggern me! Aw, Ah know whut Ahma do. Ahm going by ol Joe's sto n git that Sears Roebuck catlog n look at them guns. Mebbe Ma will lemme buy one when she gits mah pay from ol man Hawkins. Ahma beg her t gimme some money. Ahm ol ernough to hava gun. Ahm seventeen. Almost a man. He strode, feeling his long loose-jointed limbs. Shucks, a man oughta have little gun aftah he done worked hard all day.

He came in sight of Joe's store. A yellow lantern glowed on the front porch. He mounted steps and went through the screen door, hearing it bang behind him. There was a strong smell of coal oil and mackerel fish. He felt very confident until he saw fat Joe walk in through the rear door, then his courage began to ooze.

"Howdy, Dave! Whutcha want?"

"How yuh, Mistah Joe? Aw, Ah don wanna buy nothing. Ah jus wanted t see ef yuhd lemme look at tha catlog erwhile."

5 "Sure! You wanna see it here?"

"Nawsuh. Ah wants t take it home wid me. Ah'll bring it back termorrow when Ah come in from the fiels."

"You plannin on buying something?"

"Yessuh."

"Your ma lettin you have your own money now?"

10 "Shucks. Mistah Joe, Ahm gittin t be a man like anybody else!"

Joe laughed and wiped his greasy white face with a red bandanna.

"What you plannin on buyin?"

Dave looked at the floor, scratched his head, scratched his thigh, and smiled. Then he looked up shyly.

"Ah'll tell yuh, Mistah Joe, ef yuh promise yuh won't tell."

15 "I promise."

"Waal, Ahma buy a gun."

"A gun? What you want with a gun?"

"Ah wanna keep it."

"You ain't nothing but a boy. You don't need a gun."

"Aw, lemme have the catlog, Mistah Joe. Ah'll bring it back."   20

Joe walked through the rear door. Dave was elated. He looked around at barrels of sugar and flour. He heard Joe coming back. He craned his neck to see if he were bringing the book. Yeah, he's got it. Gawddog, he's got it!

"Here, but be sure you bring it back. It's the only one I got."

"Sho, Mistah Joe."

"Say, if you wanna buy a gun, why don't you buy one from me? I gotta gun to sell."

"Will it shoot?"   25

"Sure it'll shoot."

"Whut kind is it?"

"Oh, it's kinda old . . . a left-hand Wheeler. A pistol. A big one."

"Is it got bullets in it?"

"It's loaded."   30

"Kin Ah see it?"

"Where's your money?"

"What yuh wan fer it?"

"I'll let you have it for two dollars."

"Just two dollahs? Shucks, Ah could buy tha when Ah git mah pay."   35

"I'll have it here when you want it."

"Awright, suh. Ah be in fer it."

He went through the door, hearing it slam again behind him. Ahma git some money from Ma n buy me a gun! Only two dollahs! He tucked the thick catalogue under his arm and hurried.

"Where yuh been, boy?" His mother held a steaming dish of black-eyed peas.

"Aw, Ma, Ah just stopped down the road t talk wid the boys."   40

"Yuh know bettah t keep suppah waiting."

He sat down, resting the catalogue on the edge of the table.

"Yuh git up from there and git to the well n wash yosef! Ah ain feedin no hogs in mah house!"

She grabbed his shoulder and pushed him. He stumbled out of the room, then came back to get the catalogue.

"Whut this?"   45

"Aw, Ma, it's jusa catlog."

"Who yuh git it from?"

"From Joe, down at the sto."

"Waal, thas good. We kin use it in the outhouse."

"Naw, Ma." He grabbed for it. "Gimme ma catlog, Ma."   50

She held onto it and glared at him.

"Quit hollerin at me! Whut's wrong wid yuh? Yuh crazy?"

"But Ma, please. It ain mine! It's Joe's! He tol me t bring it back t im termorrow."

She gave up the book. He stumbled down the back steps, hugging the thick book under his arm. When he had splashed water on his face and hands, he groped back to the kitchen and fumbled in a corner for the towel. He bumped into a chair; it clattered to the floor. The catalogue sprawled at his feet. When he had dried his eyes he snatched up the book and held it again under his arms. His mother stood watching him.

"Now, ef yuh gonna act a fool over that ol book, Ah'll take it n burn it up."

"Naw, Ma, please."

"Waal, set down n be still!"

He sat down and drew the oil lamp close. He thumbed page after page, unaware of the food his mother set on the table. His father came in. Then his small brother.

"Whutcha got there, Dave?" his father asked.

"Jusa catlog," he answered, not looking up.

"Yeah, here they is!" His eyes glowed at blue-and-black revolvers. He glanced up, feeling sudden guilt. His father was watching him. He eased the book under the table and rested it on his knees. After the blessing was asked, he ate. He scooped up peas and swallowed fat meat without chewing. Buttermilk helped to wash it down. He did not want to mention money before his father. He would do much better by cornering his mother when she was alone. He looked at his father uneasily out of the edge of his eye.

"Boy, how come yuh don quit foolin wid tha book n eat yo suppah?"

"Yessuh."

"How you n ol man Hawkins gitten erlong?"

"Suh?"

"Can't yuh hear? Why don yuh listen? Ah ast yu how wuz yuh n ol man Hawkins gittin erlong?"

"Oh, swell, Pa. Ah plows mo lan than anybody over there."

"Waal, yuh oughta keep you mind on whut yuh doin."

"Yessuh."

He poured his plate full of molasses and sopped it up slowly with a chunk of cornbread. When his father and brother had left the kitchen, he still sat and looked again at the guns in the catalogue, longing to muster courage enough to present his case to his mother. Lawd, ef Ah only had tha pretty one! He could almost feel the slickness of the weapon with his fingers. If he had a gun like that he would polish it and keep it shining so it would never rust. N Ah'd keep it loaded, by Gawd!

"Ma?" His voice was hesitant.

"Hunh?"

"Ol man Hawkins give yuh mah money yit?"

"Yeah, but ain no usa yuh thinking about throwin nona it erway. Ahm keepin tha money sos yuh kin have cloes t go to school this winter."

He rose and went to her side with the open catalogue in his palms. She was washing dishes, her head bent low over a pan. Shyly he raised the book. When he spoke, his voice was husky, faint.

"Ma, Gawd knows Ah wans one of these."

"One of whut?" she asked, not raising her eyes.

"One of these," he said again, not daring even to point. She glanced up at the page, then at him with wide eyes.

"Nigger, is yuh gone plumb crazy?"

"Aw, Ma—"   80

"Git outta here! Don yuh talk t me bout no gun! Yuh a fool!"

"Ma, Ah kin buy one fer two dollahs."

"Not ef Ah knows it, yuh ain!"

"But yuh promised me one—"

"Ah don care what Ah promised! Yuh ain nothing but a boy yit!"   85

"Ma ef yuh lemme buy one Ah'll *never* ast yuh fer nothing no mo."

"Ah tol yuh t git outta here! Yuh ain gonna toucha penny of tha money fer no gun! Thas how come Ah has Mistah Hawkins t pay yu wages t me, cause Ah knows yuh ain got no sense."

"But, Ma, we needa gun. Pa ain got no gun. We needa gun in the house. Yuh kin never tell whut might happen."

"Now don yuh try to maka fool outta me, boy! Ef we did hava gun, yuh wouldn't have it!"

He laid the catalogue down and slipped his arm around her waist.   90

"Aw, Ma, Ah done worked hard alla summer n ain ast yuh fer nothing, is Ah, now?"

"Thas whut yuh spose t do!"

"But Ma, Ah wans a gun. Yuh kin lemme have two dollahs outta mah money. Please, Ma. I kin give it to Pa . . . Please, Ma! Ah loves yuh, Ma."

When she spoke her voice came soft and low.

"What yu wan wida gun, Dave? Yuh don need no gun. Yuh'll git in trouble.   95
N ef yo pa jus thought Ah let yuh have money t buy a gun he'd hava fit."

"Ah'll hide it, Ma. It ain but two dollahs."

"Lawd, chil, whut's wrong wid yuh?"

"Ain nothin wrong, Ma. Ahm almos a man now. Ah wans a gun."

"Who gonna sell yuh a gun?"

"Ol Joe at the sto."   100

"N it don cos but two dollahs?"

"Thas all, Ma. Jus two dollahs. Please, Ma."

She was stacking the plates away; her hands moved slowly, reflectively. Dave kept an anxious silence. Finally, she turned to him.

"Ah'll let yuh git tha gun ef yuh promise me one thing."

"Whut's tha, Ma?"   105

"Yuh bring it straight back t me, yuh hear? It be fer Pa."

"Yessum! Lemme go now, Ma."

She stooped, turned slightly to one side, raised the hem of her dress, rolled down the top of her stocking, and came up with a slender wad of bills.

"Here," she said. "Lawd knows yuh don need no gun. But yer pa does. Yuh bring it right back t me, yuh hear? Ahma put it up. Now ef yuh don, Ahma have yuh pa lick yuh so hard yuh won fergit it."

"Yessum."   110

He took the money, ran down the steps, and across the yard.

"Dave! Yuuuuu Daaaaave!"

He heard, but he was not going to stop now. "Naw, Lawd!"

The first movement he made the following morning was to reach under his pillow for the gun. In the gray light of dawn he held it loosely, feeling a sense of power. Could kill a man with a gun like this. Kill anybody, black or white. And if he were holding his gun in his hand, nobody could run over him; they would have to respect him. It was a big gun, with a long barrel and a heavy handle. He raised and lowered it in his hand, marveling at its weight.

115   He had not come straight home with it as his mother had asked; instead he had stayed out in the fields, holding the weapon in his hand, aiming it now and then at some imaginary foe. But he had not fired it; he had been afraid that his father might hear. Also he was not sure he knew how to fire it.

To avoid surrendering the pistol he had not come into the house until he knew that they were all asleep. When his mother had tiptoed to his bedside late that night and demanded the gun, he had first played possum; then he had told her that the gun was hidden outdoors, that he would bring it to her in the morning. Now he lay turning it slowly in his hands. He broke it, took out the cartridges, felt them, and then put them back.

He slid out of bed, got a long strip of old flannel from a trunk, wrapped the gun in it, and tied it to his naked thigh while it was still loaded. He did not go in to breakfast. Even though it was not yet daylight, he started for Jim Hawkins' plantation. Just as the sun was rising he reached the barns where the mules and plows were kept.

"Hey! That you, Dave?"

He turned. Jim Hawkins stood eying him suspiciously.

120   "What're yuh doing here so early?"

"Ah didn't know Ah wuz gittin up so early, Mistah Hawkins. Ah was fixin t hitch up ol Jenny n take her t the fiels."

"Good. Since you're so early, how about plowing that stretch down by the woods?"

"Suits me, Mistah Hawkins."

"O.K. Go to it!"

125   He hitched Jenny to a plow and started across the fields. Hot dog! This was just what he wanted. If he could get down by the woods, he could shoot his gun and nobody would hear. He walked behind the plow, hearing the traces creaking, feeling the gun tied tight to his thigh.

When he reached the woods, he plowed two whole rows before he decided to take out the gun. Finally, he stopped, looked in all directions, then untied the gun and held it in his hand. He turned to the mule and smiled.

"Know whut this is, Jenny? Naw, yuh wouldn know! Yuhs jusa ol mule! Anyhow, this is a gun, n it kin shoot, by Gawd!"

He held the gun at arm's length. Whut t hell, Ahma shoot this thing! He looked at Jenny again.

"Lissen here, Jenny! When Ah pull this ol trigger, Ah don wan yuh to run n acka fool now?"

130   Jenny stood with head down, her short ears pricked straight. Dave walked off about twenty feet, held the gun far out from him at arm's length, and turned his head.

Hell, he told himself, Ah ain afraid. The gun felt loose in his fingers; he waved it wildly for a moment. Then he shut his eyes and tightened his forefinger. Bloom! A report half deafened him and he thought his right hand was torn from his arm. He heard Jenny whinnying and galloping over the field, and he found himself on his knees, squeezing his fingers hard between his legs. His hand was numb; he jammed it into his mouth, trying to warm it, trying to stop the pain. The gun lay at his feet. He did not quite know what had happened. He stood up and stared at the gun as though it were a living thing. He gritted his teeth and kicked the gun. Yuh almos broke mah arm! He turned to look for Jenny; she was far over the fields, tossing her head and kicking wildly.

"Hol on there, ol mule!"   135

When he caught up with her she stood trembling, walling her big white eyes at him. The plow was far away; the traces had broken. Then Dave stopped short, looking, not believing. Jenny was bleeding. Her left side was red and wet with blood. He went closer. Lawd, have mercy! Wondah did Ah shoot this mule? He grabbed for Jenny's mane. She flinched, snorted, whirled, tossing her head.

"Hol on now! Hol on."

Then he saw the hole in Jenny's side, right between the ribs. It was round, wet, red. A crimson stream streaked down the front leg, flowing fast. Good Gawd! Ah wuzn't shootin at tha mule. He felt panic. He knew he had to stop that blood, or Jenny would bleed to death. He had never seen so much blood in all his life. He chased the mule for half a mile, trying to catch her. Finally she stopped, breathing hard, stumpy tail half arched. He caught her mane and led her back to where the plow and gun lay. Then he stooped and grabbed handfuls of damp black earth and tried to plug the bullet hole. Jenny shuddered, whinnied, and broke from him.

"Hol on! Hol on now!"

He tried to plug it again, but blood came anyhow. His fingers were hot and sticky. He rubbed dirt into his palms, trying to dry them. Then again he attempted to plug the bullet hole, but Jenny shied away, kicking her heels high. He stood helpless. He had to do something. He ran at Jenny; she dodged him. He watched a red stream of blood flow down Jenny's leg and form a bright pool at her feet.

"Jenny . . . Jenny," he called weakly.   140

His lips trembled. She's bleeding t death! He looked in the direction of home, wanting to go back, wanting to get help. But he saw the pistol lying in the damp black clay. He had a queer feeling that if he only did something, this would not be; Jenny would not be there bleeding to death.

When he went to her this time, she did not move. She stood with sleepy, dreamy eyes; and when he touched her she gave a low-pitched whinny and knelt to the ground, her front knees slopping in blood.

"Jenny . . . Jenny . . ." he whispered.

For a long time she held her neck erect; then her head sank, slowly. Her ribs swelled with a mighty heave and she went over.

Dave's stomach felt empty, very empty. He picked up the gun and held it gingerly between his thumb and forefinger. He buried it at the foot of a tree. He took a stick and tried to cover the pool of blood with dirt—but what was the use? There was

Jenny lying with her mouth open and her eyes walled and glassy. He could not tell Jim Hawkins he had shot his mule. But he had to tell something. Yeah, Ah'll tell em Jenny started gittin wil n fell on the joint of the plow. . . . But that would hardly happen to a mule. He walked across the field slowly, head down.

It was sunset. Two of Jim Hawkins' men were over near the edge of the woods digging a hole in which to bury Jenny. Dave was surrounded by a knot of people, all of whom were looking down at the dead mule.

"I don't see how in the world it happened," said Jim Hawkins for the tenth time.

145   The crowd parted and Dave's mother, father, and small brother pushed into the center.

"Where Dave?" his mother called.

"There he is," said Jim Hawkins.

His mother grabbed him.

"Whut happened, Dave? Whut yuh done?"

150   "Nothin."

"C'mon, boy, talk," his father said.

Dave took a deep breath and told the story he knew nobody believed.

"Waal," he drawled. "Ah brung ol Jenny down here sos Ah could do mah plowin. Ah plowed bout two rows, just like yuh see." He stopped and pointed at the long rows of upturned earth. "Then somethin musta been wrong wid ol Jenny. She wouldn ack right a-tall. She started snortin n kickin her heels. Ah tried t hol her, but she pulled erway, rearin n goin in. Then when the point of the plow was stickin up in the air, she swung erroun n twisted herself back on it . . . She stuck herself n started t bleed. N fo Ah could do anything, she wuz dead."

"Did you ever hear of anything like that in all your life?" asked Jim Hawkins.

155   There were white and black standing in the crowd. They murmured. Dave's mother came close to him and looked hard into his face. "Tell the truth, Dave," she said.

"Looks like a bullet hole to me," said one man.

"Dave, whut yuh do wid tha gun?" his mother asked.

The crowd surged in, looking at him. He jammed his hands into his pockets, shook his head slowly from left to right, and backed away. His eyes were wide and painful.

"Did he hava gun?" asked Jim Hawkins.

160   "By Gawd, Ah tol yuh tha wuz a gun wound," said a man, slapping his thigh.

His father caught his shoulders and shook him till his teeth rattled.

"Tell whut happened, yuh rascal! Tell whut . . ."

Dave looked at Jenny's stiff legs and began to cry.

"Whu yuh do wid tha gun?" his mother asked.

165   "Whut wuz he doin wida gun?" his father asked.

"Come on and tell the truth," said Hawkins. "Ain't nobody going to hurt you . . ."

His mother crowded close to him.

"Did yuh shoot tha mule, Dave?"

Dave cried, seeing blurred white and black faces.

"Ahh ddinn gggo tt sshooot hher . . . Ah sswear tt Gawd Ahh ddin. . . . Ah wuz   170
a-tryin t ssee ef the gggun would sshoot—"

"Where yuh git the gun from?" his father asked.

"Ah got it from Joe, at the sto."

"Where yuh git the money?"

"Ma give it t me."

"He kept worryin me, Bob. Ah had t. Ah tol im t bring the gun right back   175
t me . . . It was fer yuh, the gun."

"But how yuh happen to shoot that mule?" asked Jim Hawkins.

"Ah wuzn shootin at the mule, Mistah Hawkins! The gun jumped when Ah
pulled the trigger . . . N fo Ah knowed anythin Jenny was there a-bleedin."

Somebody in the crowd laughed. Jim Hawkins walked close to Dave and looked
into his face.

"Well, looks like you have bought you a mule, Dave."

"Ah swear fo Gawd. Ah didn go t kill the mule, Mistah Hawkins!"   180

"But you killed her!"

All the crowd was laughing now. They stood up tiptoe and poked heads over one
another's shoulders.

"Well, boy, looks like yuh done bought a dead mule! Hahaha!"

"Ain tha ershame."

"Hohohohoho."   185

Dave stood, head down, twisting his feet in the dirt.

"Well, you needn't worry about it, Bob," said Jim Hawkins to Dave's father.
"Just let the boy keep on working and pay me two dollars a month."

"Whut yuh wan fer yo mule, Mistah Hawkins?"

Jim Hawkins screwed up his eyes.

"Fifty dollars."   190

"Whut yuh do wid tha gun?" Dave's father demanded.

Dave said nothing.

"Yuh wan me t take a tree n beat yuh till yuh talk!"

"Nawsuh!"

"Whut yuh do wid it?"   195

"Ah throwed it erway."

"Where?"

"Ah . . . Ah throwed it in the creek."

"Waal, c mon home. N firs thing in the mawnin git to tha creek n fin tha gun."

"Yessuh."   200

"Whut yuh pay fer it?"

"Two dollahs."

"Take tha gun n git yo money back n carry it t Mistah Hawkins, yuh hear?
N don fergit Ahma lam you black bottom good fer this! Now march yoself on
home, suh!"

Dave turned and walked slowly. He heard people laughing. Dave glared, his
eyes welling with tears. Hot anger bubbled in him. Then he swallowed and stumbled on.

205   That night Dave did not sleep. He was glad that he had gotten out of killing the mule so easily, but he was hurt. Something hot seemed to turn over inside him each time he remembered how they had laughed. He tossed on his bed, feeling his hard pillow. N Pa says he's gonna beat me . . . He remembered other beatings, and his back quivered. Naw, naw, Ah sho don wan im t beat me tha way no mo. Dam em all! Nobody ever gave him anything. All he did was work. They treat me like a mule, n then they beat me. He gritted his teeth. N Ma had t tell on me.

Well, if he had to, he would take old man Hawkins that two dollars. But that meant selling the gun. And he wanted to keep that gun. Fifty dollars for a dead mule.

He turned over, thinking how he had fired the gun. He had an itch to fire it again. Ef other men kin shoota gun, by Gawd, Ah kin! He was still, listening. Mebbe they all sleepin now. The house was still. He heard the soft breathing of his brother. Yes, now! He would go down and get that gun and see if he could fire it! He eased out of bed and slipped into overalls.

The moon was bright. He ran almost all the way to the edge of the woods. He stumbled over the ground, looking for the spot where he had buried the gun. Yeah, here it is. Like a hungry dog scratching for a bone, he pawed it up. He puffed his black cheeks and blew dirt from the trigger and barrel. He broke it and found four cartridges unshot. He looked around; the fields were filled with silence and moonlight. He clutched the gun stiff and hard in his fingers. But, as soon as he wanted to pull the trigger, he shut his eyes and turned his head. Naw, Ah can't shoot wid mah eyes closed n mah head turned. With effort he held his eyes open; then he squeezed. *Blooooom!* He was stiff, not breathing. The gun was still in his hands. Dammit, he'd done it! He fired again. *Blooooom!* He smiled. *Blooooom! Blooooom! Click, click.* There! It was empty. If anybody could shoot a gun, he could. He put the gun into his hip pocket and started across the field.

When he reached the top of a ridge he stood straight and proud in the moonlight, looking at Jim Hawkins' big white house, feeling the gun sagging in his pocket. Lawd, ef Ah had just one mo bullet Ah'd taka shot at tha house. Ah'd like t scare ol man Hawkins jusa little . . . Jusa enough t let im know Dave Saunders is a man.

210   To his left the road curved, running to the tracks of the Illinois Central. He jerked his head, listening. From far off came a faint *hoooof-hoooof; hoooof-hoooof* . . . He stood rigid. Two dollahs a mont. Les see now . . . Tha means it'll take bout two years. Shucks! Ah'll be dam!

He started down the road, toward the tracks. Yeah, here she comes! He stood beside the track and held himself stiffly. Here she comes, erroun the ben . . . C mon, yuh slow poke! C mon! He had his hand on his gun; something quivered in his stomach. Then the train thundered past, the gray and brown box cars rumbling and clinking. He gripped the gun tightly; then he jerked his hand out of his pocket. Ah betcha Bill wouldn't do it! Ah betcha . . . The cars slid past, steel grinding upon steel. Ahm ridin yuh ternight, so hep me Gawd! He was hot all over. He hesitated just a moment; then he grabbed, pulled atop of a car, and lay flat. He felt his pocket; the gun was still there. Ahead the long rails were glinting in the moonlight, stretching away, away to somewhere, somewhere where he could be a man . . .

QUESTIONS FOR DISCUSSION AND WRITING

1. How does Dave's desire to own a gun reveal the essential conflict in the story? How does his accidental shooting of Jenny the mule bring that conflict to a crisis? To what extent does Dave's decision to jump a freight provide a satisfactory solution to that conflict?

2. How do the other characters in the story—Mr. Joe, Jim Hawkins, and Dave's mother and father—see Dave? How does he see himself? What does the crowd's laughter reveal about the limits of Dave's self-perception?

3. What does Wright's description of the field, the store, and the house suggest about the nature of Dave's environment? How does the financial arrangement about the dead mule intensify Dave's hostility toward his environment? What kind of environment does Dave hope to find at the end of his train ride?

4. How does the shift from standard English to dialect enhance the reader's understanding of Dave's point of view? In particular, how does Wright use dialect to document Dave's anguished attempt to save Jenny and his angry response to his public humiliation?

5. What does the title suggest about the theme of the story? What are the conditions and responsibilities for manhood? Is Dave correct in assuming that he can achieve his manhood only in some other place? Explain your answer.

Stories for Comparison

James Baldwin's "Sonny's Blues" (pages 215–237); Ralph Ellison's "Battle Royal" (pages 472–482).

IOO

....

PAMELA ZOLINE

The Heat Death of the Universe

PAMELA ZOLINE was born in 1941 in Chicago and educated at the Slade School of Fine Arts in London. She currently works as a painter and environmental activist in Telluride, Colorado. Her first book, *Annika and the Wolves* (1985), is a fairy tale about children and wolves. Her first collection of short stories, *The Heat Death of the Universe and Other Stories* (1988), earned recognition as an "underground" classic. In "The Heat Death of the Universe," the title story from that collection, a housewife is overwhelmed by the chaos in her "system."

1. ONTOLOGY: That branch of metaphysics which concerns itself with the problems of the nature of existence or being.

2. Imagine a pale blue morning sky, almost green, with clouds only at the rims. The earth rolls and the sun appears to mount, mountains erode, fruits decay, the Foraminifera adds another chamber to its shell, babies' fingernails grow as does the hair of the dead in their graves, and in egg timers the sands fall and the eggs cook on.

3. Sarah Boyle thinks of her nose as too large, though several men have cherished it. The nose is generous and performs a well-calculated geometric curve, at the arch of which the skin is drawn very tight and a faint whiteness of bone can be seen showing through, it has much the same architectural tension and sense of mathematical calculation as the day after Thanksgiving breastbone on the carcass of turkey; her maiden name was Sloss, mixed German, English and Irish descent; in grade school she was very bad at playing softball and, besides being chosen last for the team, was always made to play center field, no one could ever hit to center field; she loves music best of all the arts, and of music, Bach, J.S.; she lives in California, though she grew up in Boston and Toledo.

4. BREAKFAST TIME AT THE BOYLES' HOUSE ON LA FLORIDA STREET, ALAMEDA, CALIFORNIA, THE CHILDREN DEMAND SUGAR FROSTED FLAKES.

    With some reluctance Sarah Boyle dishes out Sugar Frosted Flakes to her children, already hearing the decay set in upon the little milk-white teeth, the bony whine of the dentist's drill. The dentist is a short, gentle man with a moustache who sometimes reminds Sarah of an uncle who lives in Ohio. One bowl per child.

5. If one can imagine it considered as an abstract object, by members of a totally separate culture, one can see that the cereal box might seem a beautiful thing. The solid rectangle is neatly joined and classical in proportions, on it are squandered wealths of richest colors, virgin blues, crimsons, dense ochres, precious pigments once reserved for sacred paintings and as cosmetics for the blind faces of marble gods. Giant size. Net Weight 16 ounces, 250 grams. "They're tigeriffic!" says Tony the Tiger. The box blatts promises: Energy, Nature's Own Goodness, an endless pubescence. On its back is a mask of William Shakespeare to be cut out, folded, worn by thousands of tiny Shakespeares in Kansas City, Detroit, Tucson, San Diego, Tampa. He appears at once more kindly and somewhat more vacant than we are used to seeing him. Two or more of the children lay claim to the mask, but Sarah puts off that Solomon's decision until such time as the box is empty.

6. A notice in orange flourishes states that a Surprise Gift is to be found some-where in the package, nestled amongst the golden flakes. So far it has not been unearthed, and the children request more cereal than they wish to eat, great yellow heaps of it, to hurry the discovery. Even so, at the end of the meal, some layers of flakes remain in the box and the Gift must still be among them.

7. There is even a Special Offer of a secret membership, code and magic ring; these to be obtained by sending in the box top with 50¢.

8. Three offers on one cereal box. To Sarah Boyle this seems to be oversell. Per-haps something is terribly wrong with the cereal and it must be sold quickly, got off the shelves before the news breaks. Perhaps it causes a special, cruel Cancer in little children. As Sarah Boyle collects the bowls printed with bunnies and baseball statistics, still slopping half full of milk and wilted flakes, she imagines *in her mind's eye* the headlines, "Nation's Small Fry Stricken, Fate's Finger Sugar Coated, Lethal Sweetness Socks Tots."

9. Sarah Boyle is a vivacious and intelligent young wife and mother, educated at a fine Eastern college, proud of her growing family which keeps her busy and happy around the house.

10. BIRTHDAY.
   Today is the birthday of one of the children. There will be a party in the late afternoon.

11. CLEANING UP THE HOUSE. ONE.
   Cleaning up the kitchen. Sarah Boyle puts the bowls, plates, glasses and sil-verware into the sink. She scrubs at the stickiness on the yellow-marbled formica table with a blue synthetic sponge, a special blue which we shall see again. There are marks of children's hands in various sizes printed with sugar and grime on all the table's surfaces. The marks catch the light, they appear and disappear according to the position of the observing eye. The floor sweepings include a triangular half of toast spread with grape jelly, bobby pins, a green band-aid, flakes, a doll's eye, dust, dog's hair and a button.

12. Until we reach the statistically likely planet and begin to converse with whatever green-faced, teleporting denizens thereof—considering only this shrunk and communication-ravaged world—can we any more postulate a separate culture? Viewing the metastasis of Western Culture, it seems progressively less likely. Sarah Boyle imagines a whole world which has become like California, all topo-graphical imperfections sanded away with the sweet-smelling burr of the plas-tic surgeon's cosmetic polisher; a world populace dieting, leisured, similar in pink and mauve hair and rhinestone shades. A land Cunt Pink and Avocado Green, brassiered and girdled by monstrous complexities of Super Highways, a California endless and unceasing, embracing and transforming the entire globe, California, California!

13. INSERT ONE. ON ENTROPY.

ENTROPY: A quantity introduced in the first place to facilitate the calculations, and to give clear expressions to the results of thermodynamics. Changes
of entropy can be calculated only for a reversible process, and may then be defined as the ratio of the amount of heat taken up to the absolute temperature at
which the heat is absorbed. Entropy changes for actual irreversible processes
are calculated by postulating equivalent theoretical reversible changes. The entropy of a system is a measure of its degree of disorder. The total entropy of
any isolated system can never decrease in any change; it must either increase
(irreversible process) or remain constant (reversible process). The total entropy
of the Universe therefore is increasing, tending toward a maximum, corresponding to complete disorder of the particles in it (assuming that it may be
regarded as an isolated system). See *Heat Death of the Universe*.

14. CLEANING UP THE HOUSE. TWO.

Washing the baby's diapers. Sarah Boyle writes notes to herself all over the
house; a mazed wild script larded with arrows, diagrams, pictures; graffiti on
every available surface in a desperate/heroic attempt to index, record, bluff, invoke, order and placate. On the fluted and flowered white plastic lid of the diaper bin she has written in Blushing Pink Nitetime lipstick a phrase to ward off
fumey ammoniac despair: "The nitrogen cycle is the vital round of organic and
inorganic exchange on earth. The sweet breath of the Universe." On the wall by
the washing machine are Yin and Yang signs, mandalas and the words, "Many
young wives feel trapped. It is a contemporary sociological phenomenon which
may be explained in part by a gap between changing living patterns and the ac-
commodation of social services to these patterns." Over the stove she had written "Help, Help, Help, Help, Help."

15. Sometimes she numbers or letters the things in a room, writing the assigned
character on each object. There are 819 separate moveable objects in the living
room, counting books. Sometimes she labels objects with their names, or with
false names, thus on her bureau the hair brush is labeled HAIR BRUSH, the
cologne, COLOGNE, the hand cream, CAT. She is passionately fond of children's
dictionaries, encyclopedias, ABCs and all reference books, transfixed and comforted at their simulacra of a complete listing and ordering.

16. On the door of a bedroom are written two definitions from reference books,
"GOD: An object of worship"; "HOMEOSTASIS: Maintenance of constancy of internal environment."

17. Sarah Boyle washes the diapers, washes the linen, Oh Saint Veronica, changes
the sheets on the baby's crib. She begins to put away some of the toys, stepping
over and around the organizations of playthings which still seem inhabited.
There are various vehicles, and articles of medicine, domesticity and war; whole
zoos of stuffed animals, bruised and odorous with years of love; hundreds of
small figures, plastic animals, cowboys, cars, spacemen, with which the children
make sub and supra worlds in their play. One of Sarah's favorite toys is the

Baba, the wooden Russian doll which, opened, reveals a smaller but otherwise identical doll which opens to reveal, etc., a lesson in infinity at least to the number of seven dolls.

18. Sarah Boyle's mother has been dead for two years. Sarah Boyle thinks of music as the formal articulation of the passage of time, and of Bach as the most poignant rendering of this. Her eyes are sometimes the color of the aforementioned kitchen sponge. Her hair is natural spaniel brown; months ago on an hysterical day she dyed it red, so now it is two-toned with a stripe in the middle, like the painted walls of slum buildings or old schools.

19. INSERT TWO. HEAT DEATH OF THE UNIVERSE.
   The second law of thermodynamics can be interpreted to mean that the ENTROPY of a closed system tends toward a maximum and that its available ENERGY tends toward a minimum. It has been held that the Universe constitutes a thermodynamically closed system, and if this were true it would mean that a time must finally come when the Universe "unwinds" itself, no energy being available for use. This state is referred to as the "heat death of the Universe." It is by no means certain, however, that the Universe can be considered as a closed system in this sense.

20. Sarah Boyle pours out a Coke from the refrigerator and lights a cigarette. The coldness and sweetness of the thick brown liquid make her throat ache and her teeth sting briefly, sweet juice of my youth, her eyes glass with the carbonation, she thinks of the Heat Death of the Universe. A logarithmic of those late summer days, endless as the Irish serpent twisting through jeweled manuscripts forever, tail in mouth, the heat pressing, bloating, doing violence. The Los Angeles sky becomes so filled and bleached with detritus that it loses all color and silvers like a mirror, reflecting back the fricasseeing earth. Everything becoming warmer and warmer, each particle of matter becoming more agitated, more excited until the bonds shatter, the glues fail, the deodorants lose their seals. She imagines the whole of New York City melting like a Dali into a great chocolate mass, a great soup, the Great Soup of New York.

21. CLEANING UP THE HOUSE. THREE.
   Beds made. Vacuuming the hall, a carpet of faded flowers, vines and leaves which endlessly wind and twist into each other in a fevered and permanent ecstasy. Suddenly the vacuum blows instead of sucks, spewing marbles, dolls' eyes, dust, crackers. An old trick. "Oh my god," says Sarah. The baby yells on cue for attention/changing/food. Sarah kicks the vacuum cleaner and it retches and begins working again.

22. AT LUNCH ONLY ONE GLASS OF MILK IS SPILLED.
   At lunch only one glass of milk is spilled.

23. The plants need watering, Geranium, Hyacinth, Lavender, Avocado, Cyclamen. Feed the fish, happy fish with china castles and mermaids in the bowl. The turtle looks more and more unwell and is probably dying.

24. Sarah Boyle's blue eyes, how blue? Bluer far and of a different quality than the Nature metaphors which were both engine and fuel to so much of precedent literature. A fine, modern, acid, synthetic blue; the shiny cerulean of the skies on postcards sent from lush subtropics, the natives grinning ivory ambivalent grins in their dark faces; the promising, fat, unnatural blue of the heavy tranquillizer capsule; the cool, mean blue of that fake kitchen sponge; the deepest, most unbelievable azure of the tiled and mossless interiors of California swimming pools. The chemists in their kitchens cooked, cooled and distilled this blue from thousands of colorless and wonderfully constructed crystals, each one unique and nonpareil; and now that color hisses, bubbles, burns in Sarah's eyes.

25. INSERT THREE. ON LIGHT.

LIGHT: Name given to the agency by means of which a viewed object influences the observer's eyes. Consists of electromagnetic radiation within the wavelength range 4×10^{-5} cm. to 7×10^{-5} cm. approximately; variations in the wavelength produce different sensations in the eye, corresponding to different colors. See color vision.

26. LIGHT AND CLEANING THE LIVING ROOM.

All the objects (819) and surfaces in the living room are dusty, gray common dust as though this were the den of a giant, molting mouse. Suddenly quantities of waves or particles of very strong sunlight speed in through the window, and everything incandesces, multiple rainbows. Poised in what has become a solid cube of light, like an ancient insect trapped in amber, Sarah Boyle realizes that the dust is indeed the most beautiful stuff in the room, a manna for the eyes. Duchamp, that father of thought, has set with fixative some dust which fell on one of his sculptures, counting it as part of the work. "That way madness lies, says Sarah," says Sarah. The thought of ordering a household on Dada principles balloons again. All the rooms would fill up with objects, newspapers and magazines would compost, the potatoes in the rack, the canned green beans in the garbage can would take new heart and come to life again, reaching out green shoots toward the sun. The plants would grow wild and wind into a jungle around the house, splitting plaster, tearing shingles, the garden would enter in at the door. The goldfish would die, the birds would die, we'd have them stuffed; the dog would die from lack of care, and probably the children—all stuffed and sitting around the house, covered with dust.

27. INSERT FOUR. DADA.

DADA (Fr., hobby-horse) was a nihilistic precursor of Surrealism, invented in Zurich during World War I, a product of hysteria and shock lasting from about 1915 to 1922. It was deliberately anti-art and anti-sense, intended to outrage and scandalize, and its most characteristic production was the reproduction of the *Mona Lisa* decorated with a moustache and the obscene caption LHOOQ (read: *elle a chaud au cul*) "by" Duchamp. Other manifestations included Arp's collages of colored paper cut out at random and shuffled, ready-made objects such as the bottle drier and the bicycle wheel "signed" by Duchamp, Picabia's drawings of bits of machinery with incongruous titles, incoherent poetry, a lecture given by 38 lecturers in unison, and an exhibition in Cologne in 1920, held in an annex to a café lavatory, at which a chopper was provided for spectators to smash the exhibits with—which they did.

28. TIME PIECES AND OTHER MEASURING DEVICES.

In the Boyle house there are four clocks; three watches (one a Mickey Mouse watch which does not work); two calendars and two engagement books; three rulers; a yard stick; a measuring cup; a set of red plastic measuring spoons which includes a tablespoon, a teaspoon, a one-half teaspoon, one-fourth teaspoon and one-eighth teaspoon; an egg timer; an oral thermometer and a rectal thermometer; a Boy Scout compass; a barometer in the shape of a house, in and out of which an old woman and an old man chase each other forever without fulfilment; a bathroom scale; an infant scale; a tape measure which can be pulled out of a stuffed felt strawberry; a wall on which the children's heights are marked; a metronome.

29. Sarah Boyle finds a new line in her face after lunch while cleaning the bathroom. It is as yet hardly visible, running from the midpoint of her forehead to the bridge of her nose. By inward curling of her eyebrows she can etch it clearly as it will come to appear in the future. She marks another mark on the wall where she has drawn out a scoring area. Face Lines and Other Limitations of Mortality, the heading says. There are thirty-two marks, counting this latest one.

30. Sarah Boyle is a vivacious and witty young wife and mother, educated at a fine Eastern college, proud of her growing family which keeps her happy and busy around the house, involved in many hobbies and community activities, and only occasionally given to obsessions concerning Time/Entropy/Chaos and Death.

31. Sarah Boyle is never quite sure how many children she has.

32. Sarah thinks from time to time; Sarah is occasionally visited with this thought; at times this thought comes upon Sarah, that there are things to be hoped for, accomplishments to be desired beyond the mere reproductions, mirror reproduction of one's kind. The babies. Lying in bed at night sometimes the memory of the act of birth, always the hue and texture of red plush theater seats, washes up; the rending which always, at a certain intensity of pain, slipped into landscapes, the sweet breath of the sweating nurse. The wooden Russian doll has bright, perfectly round red spots on her cheeks, she splits in the center to reveal a doll smaller but in all other respects identical with round bright red spots on her cheeks, etc.

33. How fortunate for the species, Sarah muses or is mused, that children are as ingratiating as we know them. Otherwise they would soon be salted off for the leeches they are, and the race would extinguish itself in a fair sweet flowering, the last generations' massive achievement in the arts and pursuits of high civilization. The finest women would have their tubes tied off at the age of twelve, or perhaps refrain altogether from the Act of Love? All interests would be bent

to a refining and perfecting of each febrile sense, each fluid hour, with no more cowardly investment in immortality via the patchy and too often disappointing vegetables of one's own womb.

34. INSERT FIVE. LOVE.
LOVE: a typical sentiment involving fondness for, or attachment to, an object, the idea of which is emotionally colored whenever it arises in the mind, and capable, as Shand has pointed out, of evoking any one of a whole gamut of primary emotions, according to the situation in which the object is placed, or represented; often, and by psychoanalysts always, used in the sense of *sex-love* or even *lust* (q.v.).

35. Sarah Boyle has at times felt a unity with her body, at other times a complete separation. The mind/body duality considered. The time/space duality considered. The male/female duality considered. The matter/energy duality considered. Sometimes, at extremes, her Body seems to her an animal on a leash, taken for walks in the park by her Mind. The lamp posts of experience. Her arms are lightly freckled, and when she gets very tired the places under her eyes become violet.

36. Housework is never completed, the chaos always lurks ready to encroach on any area left unweeded, a jungle filled with dirty pans and the roaring of giant stuffed toy animals suddenly turned savage. Terrible glass eyes.

37. SHOPPING FOR THE BIRTHDAY CAKE.
Shopping in the supermarket with the baby in front of the cart and a larger child holding on. The light from the ice-cube-tray-shaped fluorescent lights is mixed blue and pink and brighter, colder, and cheaper than daylight. The doors swing open just as you reach out your hand for them, Tantalus, moving with a ghastly quiet swing. Hot dogs for the party. Potato chips, gum drops, a paper table cloth with birthday designs, hot dog buns, catsup, mustard, picalilli, balloons, instant coffee Continental style, dog food, frozen peas, ice cream, frozen lima beans, frozen broccoli in butter sauce, paper birthday hats, paper napkins in three colors, a box of Sugar Frosted Flakes with a Wolfgang Amadeus Mozart mask on the back, bread, pizza mix. The notes of a just graspable music filter through the giant store, for the most part bypassing the brain and acting directly on the liver, blood and lymph. The air is delicately scented with aluminum. Half and half cream, tea bags, bacon, sandwich meat, strawberry jam. Sarah is in front of the shelves of cleaning products now, and the baby is beginning to whine. Around her are whole libraries of objects, offering themselves. Some of that same old hysteria that had incarnadined her hair rises up again, and she does not refuse it. There is one moment when she can choose direction, like standing on a chalk drawn X, a hot cross bun, and she does not choose calm and measure. Sarah Boyle begins to pick out, methodically, deliberately and with a careful ecstasy, one of every cleaning product which the store sells. Window Cleaner, Glass Cleaner, Brass Polish, Silver Polish, Steel Wool, eighteen different brands of Detergent, Disinfectant, Toilet Cleanser, Water Softener, Fabric

Softener, Drain Cleanser, Spot Remover, Floor Wax, Furniture Wax, Car Wax, Carpet Shampoo, Dog Shampoo, Shampoo for people with dry, oily and normal hair, for people with dandruff, for people with gray hair. Tooth Paste, Tooth Powder, Denture Cleaner, Deodorants, Antiperspirants, Antiseptics, Soaps, Cleansers, Abrasives, Oven Cleansers, Makeup Removers. When the same products appear in different sizes Sarah takes one of each size. For some products she accumulates whole little families of containers: a giant Father bottle of shampoo, a Mother bottle, an Older Sister bottle just smaller than the Mother bottle, and a very tiny Baby Brother bottle. Sarah fills three shopping carts and has to have help wheeling them all down the aisles. At the check-out counter her laughter and hysteria keep threatening to overflow as the pale blonde clerk with no eyebrows like the *Mona Lisa* pretends normality and disinterest. The bill comes to $57.53 and Sarah has to write a check. Driving home, the baby strapped in the drive-a-cot and the paper bags bulging in the back seat, she cries.

38. BEFORE THE PARTY.

Mrs. David Boyle, mother-in-law of Sarah Boyle, is coming to the party of her grandchild. She brings a toy, a yellow wooden duck on a string, made in Austria; the duck quacks as it is pulled along the floor. Sarah is filling paper cups with gum drops and chocolates, and Mrs. David Boyle sits at the kitchen table and talks to her. She is talking about several things, she is talking about her garden which is flourishing except for a plague of rare black beetles, thought to have come from Hong Kong, which are undermining some of the most delicate growths at the roots, and feasting on the leaves of other plants. She is talking about a sale of household linens which she plans to attend on the following Tuesday. She is talking about her neighbor who has cancer and is wasting away. The neighbor is a Catholic woman who had never had a day's illness in her life until the cancer struck, and now she is, apparently, failing with dizzying speed. The doctor says her body's chaos, chaos, cells running wild all over, says Mrs. David Boyle. When I visited her she hardly *knew* me, can hardly *speak,* can't keep herself *clean,* says Mrs. David Boyle.

39. Sometimes Sarah can hardly remember how many cute, chubby little children she has.

40. When she used to stand out in center field far away from the other players, she used to make up songs and sing them to herself.

41. She thinks of the end of the world by ice.

42. She thinks of the end of the world by water.

43. She thinks of the end of the world by nuclear war.

44. There must be more than this, Sarah Boyle thinks, from time to time. What could one do to justify one's passage? Or less ambitiously, to change, even in the motion of the smallest mote, the course and circulation of the world? Sometimes Sarah's dreams are of heroic girth, a new symphony using laboratories of

machinery and all invented instruments, at once giant in scope and intelligible to all, to heal the bloody breach; a series of paintings which would transfigure and astonish and calm the frenzied art world in its panting race; a new novel that would refurbish language. Sometimes she considered the mystical, the streaky and random, and it seems that one change, no matter how small, would be enough. Turtles are supposed to live for many years. To carve a name, date and perhaps a word of hope upon a turtle's shell, then set him free to wend the world, surely this one act might cancel out absurdity?

45. Mrs. David Boyle has a faint moustache, like Duchamp's *Mona Lisa.*

46. THE BIRTHDAY PARTY.

Many children, dressed in pastels, sit around the long table. They are exhausted and overexcited from games fiercely played, some are flushed and wet, others unnaturally pale. This general agitation, and the paper party hats they wear, combine to make them appear a dinner party of debauched midgets. It is time for the cake. A huge chocolate cake in the shape of a rocket and launching pad and covered with blue and pink icing is carried in. In the hush the birthday child begins to cry. He stops crying, makes a wish and blows out the candles.

47. One child will not eat hot dogs, ice cream or cake, and asks for cereal. Sarah pours him out a bowl of Sugar Frosted Flakes, and a moment later he chokes. Sarah pounds him on the back and out spits a tiny green plastic snake with red glass eyes, the Surprise Gift. All the children want it.

48. AFTER THE PARTY THE CHILDREN ARE PUT TO BED.

Bath time. Observing the nakedness of children, pink and slippery as seals, squealing as seals, now the splashing, grunting and smacking of cherry flesh on raspberry flesh reverberate in the pearl tiled steamy cubicle. The nakedness of children is so much more absolute than that of the mature. No musky curling hair to indicate the target points, no knobbly clutch of plane and fat and curvature to ennoble this prince of beasts. All well-fed naked children appear edible, Sarah's teeth hum in her head with memory of bloody feastings, prehistory. Young humans appear too like the young of other species for smugness, and the comparison is not even in their favor, they are much the most peeled and unsupple of those young. Such pinkness, such utter nuded pinkness; the orifices neatly incised, rimmed with a slightly deeper rose, the incessant demands for breast time milks of many sorts.

49. INSERT SIX. WEINER ON ENTROPY.

In Gibbs' Universe order is least probable, chaos most probable. But while the Universe as a whole, if indeed there is a whole Universe, tends to run down, there are local enclaves whose direction seems opposed to that of the Universe at large and in which there is a limited and temporary tendency for organization to increase. Life finds its home in some of these enclaves.

50. Sarah Boyle imagines, in her mind's eye, cleaning and ordering the whole world, even the Universe. Filling the great spaces of Space with a marvelous

sweet smelling, deep cleansing foam. Deodorizing rank caves and volcanoes. Scrubbing rocks.

51. INSERT SEVEN. TURTLES.

Many different species of carnivorous Turtles live in the fresh waters of the tropical and temperate zones of various continents. Most Northerly of the European Turtles (extending as far as Holland and Lithuania) is the European Pond Turtle (*Emys orbicularis*). It is from 8 to 10 inches long and may live a hundred years.

52. CLEANING UP AFTER THE PARTY.

Sarah is cleaning up after the party. Gum drops and melted ice cream surge off paper plates, making holes in the paper tablecloth through the printed roses. A fly has died a splendid death in a pool of strawberry ice cream. Wet jelly beans stain all they touch, finally becoming themselves colorless, opaque white like flocks of tamed or sleeping maggots. Plastic favors mount half-eaten pieces of blue cake. Strewn about are thin strips of fortune papers from the Japanese poppers. Upon them are printed strangely assorted phrases selected by apparently unilingual Japanese. Crowds of delicate yellow people spending great chunks of their lives in producing these most ephemeral of objects, and inscribing thousands of fine papers with absurd and incomprehensible messages. "The very hairs of your head are all numbered," reads one. Most of the balloons have popped. Someone has planted a hot dog in the daffodil pot. A few of the helium balloons have escaped their owners and now ride the ceiling. Another fortune paper reads, "Emperor's horses meet death worse, numbers, numbers."

53. She is very tired, violet under the eyes, mauve beneath the eyes. Her uncle in Ohio used to get the same marks under his eyes. She goes to the kitchen to lay the table for tomorrow's breakfast, then she sees that in the turtle's bowl the turtle is floating, still, on the surface of the water. Sarah Boyle pokes at it with a pencil but it does not move. She stands for several minutes looking at the dead turtle on the surface of the water. She is crying again.

54. She begins to cry. She goes to the refrigerator and takes out a carton of eggs, white eggs, extra large. She throws them one by one onto the kitchen floor which is patterned with strawberries in squares. They break beautifully. There is a Secret Society of Dentists, all moustached, with Special Code and Magic Rings. She begins to cry. She takes up three bunny dishes and throws them against the refrigerator, they shatter, and then the floor is covered with shards, chunks of partial bunnies, an ear, an eye here, a paw; Stockton, California, Acton, California, Chico, California, Redding, California, Glen Ellen, California, Cadix, California, Angels Camps, California, Half Moon Bay. The total ENTROPY of the Universe therefore is increasing, tending toward a maximum, corresponding to complete disorder of the particles in it. She is crying, her mouth is open. She throws a jar of grape jelly and it smashes the window over the sink. Her eyes are blue. She begins to open her mouth. It has been held that the Universe constitutes a thermodynamically closed system, and if this were true it would mean

that a time must finally come when the Universe "unwinds" itself, no energy being available for use. This state is referred to as the "Heat Death of the Universe." Sarah Boyle begins to cry. She throws a jar of strawberry jam against the stove, enamel chips off and the stove begins to bleed. Bach had twenty children, how many children has Sarah Boyle? Her mouth is open. Her mouth is opening. She turns on the water and fills the sinks with detergent. She writes on the kitchen wall, "William Shakespeare has Cancer and lives in California." She writes, "Sugar Frosted Flakes are the Food of the Gods." The water foams up in the sink, overflowing, bubbling onto the strawberry floor. She is about to begin to cry. Her mouth is opening. She is crying. She cries. How can one ever tell whether there are one or many fish? She begins to break glasses and dishes, she throws cups and cooking pots and jars of food which shatter and break and spread over the kitchen. The sand keeps falling, very quietly, in the egg timer. The old man and woman in the barometer never catch each other. She picks up eggs and throws them into the air. She begins to cry. She opens her mouth. The eggs arch slowly through the kitchen, like a baseball, hit high against the spring sky, seen from far away. They go higher and higher in the stillness, hesitate at the zenith, then begin to fall away slowly, slowly, through the fine, clear air.

QUESTIONS FOR DISCUSSION AND WRITING

1. How do Sarah Boyle's preparation and celebration for her child's birthday party *seem* to provide a structure for the plot? How does Zoline's use of numbered and titled paragraphs outline the real "plot" of the story? How is Sarah's final breakdown foreshadowed throughout the story?

2. How does paragraph 30, especially the line about her obsessions, help characterize Sarah? What is the source of her "hysteria"? What do her numbering and indexing of the objects in her house and her decision to purchase the cleaning supplies reveal about her internal battle?

3. What are the implications of Sarah's recognition that the entire world is becoming California? How would "ordering" a household on Dada principles reverse our sense of the power of setting to shape our lives?

4. What is the effect of shifting the point of view throughout from Sarah and her inner battles to scientific discussions of physics and other natural phenomena? How would Sarah describe her emotional journey in this story if she told it in the first person?

5. What are the thematic connections between housework and entropy? How does the final scene illustrate the "heat death of the universe"?

Stories for Comparison

Charlotte Perkins Gilman's "The Yellow Wallpaper" (pages 117–128); Thomas Pynchon's "Entropy" (pages 1025–1035).

GLOSSARY OF CRITICAL TERMS

ALLEGORY A story in which the characters and their actions are equated with general truths about human conduct. The characters in an allegory often represent abstract concepts, such as faith, innocence, or evil. See *SYMBOL.*

ALLUSION A reference to a famous historical, fictional, or mythological person, place, or event outside the story. Allusions enrich a story by suggesting similarities to comparable circumstances in another time or place.

ANTAGONIST The character (or force) that is in direct conflict with the protagonist. An antagonist may be another person, the physical or social environment, or some aspect of the protagonist's personality. See *PROTAGONIST.*

ANTICLIMAX A ludicrous or trivial incident that occurs instead of an expected event of significance. Sometimes the anticlimax appears in the middle of the story as an intentional digression. More often it takes place after the story has reached its climax. See *CLIMAX.*

ARCHETYPE An image, plot pattern, or character type that recurs frequently in myth, religion, folklore, or literature. According to the psychologist Carl Jung, archetypal experiences such as birth and death form part of the "collective unconscious" that the mind inherits from its racial or cultural past.

AUTHORIAL STATEMENT An interpretation of the events in a story by the author or indirectly by one of the characters. See *THEME.*

CHARACTER A person in the story. Most stories contain one or more major characters and several minor characters.

DYNAMIC CHARACTER A person who undergoes significant development or change during the story.

FLAT CHARACTER A person with little depth or complexity who may be described in one or two phrases.

ROUND CHARACTER A person with a fully developed, complex (even contradictory) personality who defies simple analysis or description.

STATIC CHARACTER A person who remains essentially unchanged throughout the story.

CHARACTERIZATION The methods by which writers create, reveal, or develop their characters. Writers can focus on the *external reality* of the characters by describing their appearance, actions, or manner of speech. They can also portray the *inner reality* of their characters by revealing their thoughts and feelings.

CLIMAX The moment in the story when the major action reaches its turning point. The climax (also called the *crisis*) marks the end of the story's development and propels it toward conclusion. See *ANTICLIMAX.*

COMPLICATION That part of the plot in which the various conflicts that have been introduced in the exposition are developed in greater detail before they reach the climax.

CONFLICT The struggle that grows out of the collision of various forces within a story. Although such conflicts may be many, often clashing with one another on several levels, they usually occur in three patterns: (1) the conflict between one person and another, (2) the conflict between a person and that person's physical or social environment, (3) the conflict between a person and some aspect of his or her personality. See *ANTAGONIST; PROTAGONIST.*

CONNOTATION The suggested or implied meaning of a word, as contrasted with its literal meaning or *denotation.* These additional associations may be personal (the result of individual experience) or universal (the product of the collective human experience). See *DENOTATION.*

CRISIS See *CLIMAX.*

CRITICAL ANALYSIS The systematic division of a work of literature (in this case a short story) into its various parts (or elements) in order to achieve a better understanding of the whole.

DENOTATION The literal dictionary definition of a word, apart from any emotional or intellectual association or *connotation* it may evoke. See *CONNOTATION.*

DENOUEMENT A French word meaning the untangling of a knot. As applied to fiction, the term refers to the conclusion of a story where the various conflicts (knots) are resolved (untangled). The denouement may add a surprising twist to the story, but it does not usually add new information. See *RESOLUTION.*

DIALOGUE The direct speech of characters in a story, punctuated by quotation marks. Dialogue can be used to introduce or explain the conflict in a plot, to represent the qualities of various characters, or to reveal the point of view of the central character or narrator.

DRAMATIC IRONY See *IRONY.*

DYNAMIC CHARACTER See *CHARACTER.*

EPISODE A brief period of action, often complete in itself, that forms part of a larger narrative. A story may contain several related episodes that advance the plot toward the single scene or episode that marks the climax.

EXPOSITION The part of the story, near the beginning, that introduces ("exposes") the elements of setting, character, and conflict that exist prior to the major action of the story.

FABLE A brief narrative devised to illustrate a moral lesson. The chief characters in a fable are often animals who talk and act like human beings. The plots of many fables come from folklore or superstition and focus on unusual or supernatural events.

FLASHBACK An interruption in the flow of a story to introduce an earlier scene or episode. Various devices ranging from simple recollection to dream sequences can be used to present information from the past that helps explain or comment on the present situation in the narrative.

FLAT CHARACTER See *CHARACTER.*

FOIL A character who enhances and clarifies the features of the protagonist by providing a direct and distinctive contrast to the major character.

FORESHADOWING The introduction of clues early in the story to suggest or anticipate significant events that will develop later.

IMAGERY The use of words or figures of speech to create a mental picture. Imagery exploits all five senses to produce a single powerful impression or to create a cluster of impressions that conveys a dominant mood.

IRONY A term that suggests some sort of discrepancy between appearance and reality. Although irony is a broad term that can be applied to events both trivial and tragic, it depends on the ability of the reader to recognize contradictions and incongruities. Irony usually takes three forms:

1. VERBAL IRONY is speech in which what is said is directly opposite to what is meant. Verbal irony differs from sarcasm in that the tone of the speaker is lighter, even though the effect produced may be just as devastating.

2. DRAMATIC IRONY is a circumstance in which characters reveal their inability to understand their own situation. Dramatic irony is most effective when characters make fateful choices based on information that the reader realizes is incorrect.

3. SITUATIONAL IRONY is a situation that demonstrates an incongruity between what the reader expects or presumes to be appropriate and what actually occurs.

METAPHOR A figure of speech in which an imaginative comparison is made between two dissimilar things without the use of the word *like* or *as*.

MOTIVATION The character traits, environmental forces, desires, and goals that alone or in combination explain a character's pattern of behavior.

NARRATOR The person who tells the story. The narrator may be a character who is directly or indirectly involved in the action, or a detached observer who wants to explain what happened. See also *POINT OF VIEW*.

OBJECTIVE POINT OF VIEW See *POINT OF VIEW*.

OMNISCIENT POINT OF VIEW See *POINT OF VIEW*.

PACE The speed with which events are narrated. Some stories can be told quickly, with details omitted, time compressed, and events summarized. Others must be told slowly, with all details included, time extended, and events dramatized as scenes. The pace of a story will vary according to the nature of the events being recounted and their importance to the plot.

PARABLE A short narrative offered as an answer to a difficult moral question or to illustrate a moral truth. See *FABLE*.

PARADOX A rhetorical device making an assertion that on one level appears to be a contradiction but that on another level may be actually true.

PARODY A composition that imitates the distinctive features of a serious piece of writing for comic or satiric purposes. See *SATIRE*.

PLOT The essential structure of a story arranged according to a coherent sequence of events. The plot is usually divided into three major parts: (1) the *EXPOSITION*, where the existing conflicts are established; (2) the *COMPLICATION*, where new conflicts are introduced or old conflicts are increased in intensity until they reach a *CLIMAX* or *CRISIS*; and (3) the *DENOUEMENT*, where the conflicts are resolved.

POINT OF VIEW The vantage point or perspective from which the story is told. Point of view refers to both position (the narrator's proximity to the action in time and space) and person (the narrator's character and attitude). See also *NARRATOR*. There are four basic points of view:

1. THIRD-PERSON OMNISCIENT The narrator, usually assumed to be the author, tells the story. He or she can move at will through time, across space, and into the mind of each character to tell us anything we need to know to understand the story.

2. THIRD-PERSON LIMITED OMNISCIENT Although the author is still the narrator, he or she gives up total omniscience and limits the point of view to the experience and perception of one character in the story. Instead of knowing everything, the reader knows only what this one character knows or is able to learn.

3. FIRST-PERSON The author selects one of the characters in the narrative to tell the story. This character may be involved in the action or may view it from the position of an observer. This character may tell about events as they are happening or many years after they have taken place.

4. OBJECTIVE The author presents the external action of the story as if it were being filmed by a movie camera. The story is presented without any attempt to comment on or interpret the characters' private thoughts or feelings. All that the reader knows about the event must be inferred from the characters' public words and deeds.

PROTAGONIST The character who is engaged in the central conflict of the story, sometimes called the hero or heroine. See *ANTAGONIST; CHARACTER; CONFLICT; FOIL.*

REFLEXIVE FICTION Fiction in which the reader is reminded directly or indirectly that the story is artifice, the creation of a writer who is consciously shaping all the narrative elements, not reporting facts. The effect is to draw the reader into a consideration of the creative process as well as that which is created; it is an increasingly common approach in modern writing, especially in experimental fiction. See *VERISIMILITUDE.*

RESOLUTION The events that occur after the climax and bring the conflicts in the story to an appropriate conclusion. See *DENOUEMENT; PLOT.*

REVERSAL A sudden change or turnabout in the fortunes of the protagonist.

ROUND CHARACTER See *CHARACTER.*

SATIRE A work of literature that ridicules vice or folly in ideas, institutions, or individuals. Although a satiric work treats its subject with varying degrees of amusement and scorn, its ultimate purpose is to bring about improvement by calling attention— either directly or indirectly—to higher standards of human behavior. See PARODY.

SETTING The time, place, and social reality within which a story takes place. In a limited sense, setting refers to the physical landscape; in a broader sense, setting refers to the cultural landscape—the assumptions, rituals, and shared beliefs that shape the characters and their world.

STATIC CHARACTER See *CHARACTER.*

STEREOTYPE An oversimplified character who recurs so frequently in literary works that his or her behavior has become predictable.

STYLE A writer's distinctive manner of expression. Among the many features that characterize a writer's style are diction, sentence structure, and strategies for selecting, analyzing, and interpreting experience. See *TONE; VOICE.*

SYMBOL A person, act, or thing that has both literal significance and additional abstract meanings. Unlike an allegory, where such things are equated with one or two abstract ideas, a symbol usually refers to several complex ideas that may radiate contradictory or ambiguous meanings. See *ALLEGORY.*

THEME The central or unifying idea about human experience that grows out of all the other elements in the story. Occasionally the theme may be stated directly by the author or indirectly by one of the characters. More often the theme must be derived from an attempt to understand the complex interaction of forces within the narrative.

TONE The author's attitude toward the situations and characters in the story. By combining a variety of verbal strategies— diction, sentence structure, imagery, and symbolism—authors create a tone that establishes the mood, atmosphere, or emotional coloring of a story. See *STYLE, VOICE.*

VERISIMILITUDE The attempt to make fictional elements seem lifelike and real rather than creations of the writer. Until very recently, most fiction aimed at a sense of verisimilitude. See *REFLEXIVE FICTION.*

VOICE The personality of the author or narrator that is revealed through a distinctive and habitual mode of expression. See *STYLE; TONE.*

COPYRIGHTS AND ACKNOWLEDGMENTS

CHINUA ACHEBE "Vengeful Creditor" From GIRLS AT WAR AND OTHER STORIES by Chinua Achebe. Copyright © 1972. 1973 by Chinua Achebe. Used by permission of Doubleday, a division of Bantam Doubleday Dell Publishing Group, Inc. and Harold Ober Associates, Incorporated.

ALICE ADAMS "Truth or Consequences" From TO SEE YOU AGAIN by Alice Adams. Copyright © 1982 by Alice Adams. Reprinted by permission of Alfred A. Knopf, Inc.

ISABEL ALLENDE "Phantom Palace" Reprinted with permission of Scribner, a Division of Simon & Schuster from THE STORIES OF EVA LUNA by Isabel Allende, translated from the Spanish by Margaret Sayers Peden. Copyright © 1989 by Isabel Allende. English Translation Copyright © 1991 by Macmillan Publishing Company.

RUDOLFO A. ANAYA "B. Traven Is Alive and Well in Cuernavaca" From THE ANAYA READER. Copyright © 1995 by Rudolfo Anaya. Published by Warner Books. Originally published in Escolios, Vol. IV, #1-2, May-Nov. 1979. Reprinted by permission of Susan Bergholz Literary Services, New York. All rights reserved.

SHERWOOD ANDERSON "I'm a Fool" Reprinted by permission of Harold Ober Associates. Copyright © 1922 by The Dial Publishing Company. Copyright © renewed 1949 by Eleanor Copenhaver Anderson.

MARGARET ATWOOD "Dancing Girls" Reprinted with permission of Simon & Schuster from DANCING GIRLS AND OTHER STORIES by Margaret Atwood. Copyright © 1977, 1982 by O.W. Toad, Ltd. From DANCING GIRLS AND OTHER STORIES by Margaret Atwood. Used by permission of McClelland & Stewart, Inc., Toronto, The Canadian Publishers.

JAMES BALDWIN "Sonny Blues" was originally published in Partisan Review. Collected in GOING TO MEET THE MAN, © 1965 by James Baldwin. Copyright renewed. Published by Vintage Books. Reprinted by arrangement with the James Baldwin Estate.

TONI CADE BAMBARA "The Lesson" From GORILLA, MY LOVE by Toni Cade Bambara. Copyright © 1972 by Toni Cade Bambara. Reprinted by permission of Random House, Inc.

RUSSELL BANKS "Sarah Cole: A Type of Love Story" ALL PAGES from "SARAH COLE: A TYPE OF LOVE STORY" FROM SUCCESS STORIES by RUSSELL BANKS. Copyright © 1985 by Russell Banks. Reprinted by permission of Harper-Collins Publishers, Inc. This story originally appeared in The Missouri Review.

FIONA BARR "The Wall-Reader" Permission granted by Fiona Barr. Copyright 1985 © 1995.

JOHN BARTH "Lost in the Funhouse," copyright © 1967 by The Atlantic Monthly Company. From LOST IN THE FUNHOUSE by John Barth. Used by permission of Doubleday, a division of Bantam Doubleday Dell Publishing Group, Inc.

ANN BEATTIE "The Working Girl" From WHAT WAS MINE AND OTHER STORIES by Ann Beattie. Copyright © 1991 by Irony and Pity, Inc. Reprinted by permission of Random House, Inc.

JORGE LUIS BORGES "The Garden of Forking Paths" by Jorge Luis Borges, translated by Donald A. Yates, from LABYRINTHS. Copyright © 1962, 1964 by New Directions Publishing Corp. Reprinted by permission of New Directions Publishing Corp.

ELIZABETH BOWEN "The Demon Lover" From COLLECTED STORIES by Elizabeth Bowen. Copyright 1946 and renewed 1974 by Elizabeth Bowen. Reprinted by permission of Alfred A. Knopf. Inc.

T. CORAGHESSAN BOYLE "Heart of a Champion" by T. Coraghessan Boyle. Copyright © 1974 by T. Coraghessan Boyle. Reprinted by permission of Georges Borchardt, Inc. for the author.

LARRY BROWN "Kubuku Rides (This Is It)" From FACING THE MUSIC by Larry Brown. Copyright © 1988 by the author. Story first published in The Greensboro Review. Reprinted by permission of Algonquin Books of Chapel Hill, a division of Workman Publishing.

ITALO CALVINO "The Form of Space" From COSMICOMICS by Italo Calvino, translated by William Weaver, copyright © 1965 by Giulio Einaudi editore s.p.a., Torino, English translation by William Weaver, copyright© 1968 by Harcourt Brace & Company and Jonathan Cape Ltd., reprinted by permission of Harcourt Brace & Company. Copyright © 1968, Italo Calvino, first published in Le Cosmicomiche, reprinted with the permission of the Wylie Agency, Inc.

ALBERT CAMUS "The Guest" From EXILE AND THE KINGDOM by Albert Camus, trans., Justin O'Brien. Copyright © 1957, 1958 by Alfred A. Knopf, Inc. Reprinted by permission of the publisher.

ETHAN CANIN "We Are Nighttime Travelers" from EMPEROR OF THE AIR. Copyright © 1988 by Ethan Canin. Reprinted by permission of Houghton Mifflin Company. All rights reserved.

RAYMOND CARVER "A Small, Good Thing" From CATHEDRAL by Raymond Carver. Copyright © 1981, 1982, 1983 by Raymond Carver. Reprinted by permission of Alfred A. Knopf, Inc.

JOHN CHEEVER "The Swimmer" From THE STORIES OF JOHN CHEEVER by John Cheever. Copyright © 1965 by John Cheever. Reprinted by permission of Alfred A. Knopf, Inc.

SANDRA CISNEROS "One Holy Night" From WOMAN HOLLERING CREEK. Copyright © 1991 by Sandra Cisneros. Published by Vintage Books, division of Random House, Inc., and originally in hardcover by Random House, Inc. Reprinted by permission of Susan Bergholz Literary Services, New York. All rights reserved.

ARTHUR C. CLARKE "The Star" From THE NINE BILLION NAMES OF GOD, THE BEST SHORT STORIES OF ARTHUR C. CLARKE, copyright © 1967 and renewed 1995 by Arthur C. Clarke, reprinted by permission of Harcourt Brace & Company.

JULIO CORTÁZAR "We Love Glenda So Much" From WE LOVE GLENDA SO MUCH AND OTHER TALES by Julio Cortázar, trans., Gregory Rabassa. Translation Copyright © 1983 by Alfred A. Knopf, Inc. Reprinted by permission of the publisher.

RALPH ELLISON "Battle Royal" From INVISIBLE MAN by Ralph Ellison. Copyright © 1948 by Ralph Ellison. Reprinted by permission of Random House, Inc.

LOUISE ERDRICH "The Red Convertible" From LOVE MEDICINE by Louise Erdrich, revised edition. Copyright © 1984, 1993 by Louise Erdrich. Reprinted by permission of Henry Holt and Co., Inc.

WILLIAM FAULKNER "Barn Burning" From COLLECTED STORIES OF WILLIAM FAULKNER by William Faulkner. Copyright © 1930 and renewed 1958 by William Faulkner. Reprinted by permission of Random House, Inc.

WILILIAM FAULKNER "A Rose for Emily" From COLLECTED STORIES OF WILLIAM FAULKNER by William Faulkner. Copyright © 1950 by Random House, Inc. and renewed 1977 by Jill Faulkner Summers. Reprinted by permission of Random House, Inc.

F. SCOTT FITZGERALD "Babylon Revisited" Reprinted with permission of Scribner, a Division of Simon & Schuster, from THE SHORT STORIES OF F. SCOTT FITZGERALD, edited by Matthew J. Bruccoli. Copyright 1931 by The Curtis Publishing Company. Copyright renewed © 1959 by Frances Scott Fitzgerald Lanahan.

ERNEST J. GAINES "The Sky Is Gray," copyright © 1963 by Ernest J. Gaines, from BLOODLINE by Ernest J. Gaines. Used by permission of Doubleday, a division of Bantam Doubleday Dell Publishing Group, Inc.

WITI IHIMAERA "Dear Miss Mansfield" From DEAR MISS MANSFIELD, published by Penguin Books New Zealand.

GABRIEL GARCIA MARQUEZ "A Very Old Man with Enormous Wings" ALL PAGES from "A VERY OLD MAN WITH ENORMOUS WINGS" from LEAF STORM AND OTHER STORIES by GABRIEL GARCIA MARQUEZ and TRANSLATED BY GREGORY RABASSA. Copyright © 1971 by Gabriel Garcia Marquez. Reprinted by permission of HarperCollins Publishers, Inc.

WILLIAM GASS "In the Heart of the Heart of the Country" Reprinted by permission of International Creative Management, Inc. Copyright © 1968 by William Gass.

ELLEN GILCHRIST "Among the Mourners" From THE AGE OF MIRACLES by Ellen Gilchrist. Copyright © 1995 by Ellen Gilchrist. By permission of Little, Brown and Company.

ELLEN GILCHRIST "Traceleen, She's Still Talking" From VICTORY OVER JAPAN by Ellen Gilchrist. Copyright © 1983, 1984 by Ellen Gilchrist. By permission of Little, Brown and Company.

GAIL GODWIN "Dream Children" From DREAM CHILDREN by Gail Godwin. Copyright © 1976 by Gail Godwin. Reprinted by permission of Alfred A. Knopf, Inc.

NADINE GORDIMER "Town and Country Lovers, One," copyright © 1975 by Nadine Gordimer, "Town and Country Lovers, Two," copyright © 1975 by Nadine Gordimer, from SOLDIER'S EMBRACE by Nadine Gordimer. Used by permission of Viking Penguin, a division of Penguin Books USA Inc.

GRAHAM GREENE "The Destructors," copyright © 1955, 1983 by Graham Greene, from COLLECTED STORIES OF GRAHAM GREENE by Graham Greene. Used by permission of Viking Penguin, a division of Penguin Books USA Inc. From COLLECTED POEMS by Graham Greene. Published by Heinemann. Used by permission of David Higham Associates Ltd., London.

ERNEST HEMINGWAY "Big Two-Hearted River" Reprinted with permission of Scribner, a Division of Simon & Schuster, From THE COMPLETE SHORT STORIES OF ERNEST HEMINGWAY. Copyright 1925 Charles Scribner's Sons. Copyright renewed 1953 by Ernest Hemingway.

MARY HOOD "How Far She Went" From HOW FAR SHE WENT: STORIES BY MARY HOOD. Reprinted by permission of The University of Georgia Press. Copyright © 1984.

ZORA NEAL HURSTON "Sweat" AS TAKEN from THE COMPLETE STORIES by ZORA NEALE HURSTON. Introduction copyright © 1995 by Henry Louis Gates,

Jr. and Sieglinde Lemke. Compilation copyright © 1995 by Vivian Bowden, Lois J. Hurston Gaston, Clifford Hurston, Lucy Ann Hurston, Winifred Hurston Clark, Zora Mack Goins, Edgar Hurston, Sr., and Barbara Hurston Lewis. Afterword and Bibliography copyright © 1995 by Henry Louis Gates. Reprinted by permission of HarperCollins Publishers, Inc. "Sweat" was originally published in Fire, November 1926.

SHIRLEY JACKSON "The Lottery" From THE LOTTERY AND OTHER STORIES by Shirley Jackson. Copyright © 1948, 1949 by Shirley Jackson, and copyright renewed © 1976, 1977 by Lawrence Hyman, Barry Hyman, Mrs. Sarah Webster and Mrs. Joanne Schnurer.

CHARLES JOHNSON "The Sorcerer's Apprentice" Reprinted with the permission of Scribner, a Division of Simon & Schuster from THE SORCERER'S APPRENTICE by Charles Johnson. Copyright © 1983 by Charles Johnson.

FRANZ KAFKA "In the Penal Colony" From FRANZ KAFKA: THE COMPLETE STORIES by Nahum N. Glatzer, editor, translated by Willa and Edwin Muir. Copyright © 1946, 1947, 1948, 1949, 1954, 1958, 1971 by Schocken Books Inc. Reprinted by permission of Schocken Books, published by Pantheon Books, a division of Random House, Inc.

JAMAICA KINCAID "Girl" From AT THE BOTTOM OF THE RIVER by Jamaica Kincaid. Copyright © 1983 by Jamaica Kincaid.

D.H. LAWRENCE "Odour of Chrysanthemums," copyright 1933 by the Estate of D.H. Lawrence, renewed © 1961 by Angelo Ravagli and C.M. Weekley, Executors of the Estate of Frieda Lawrence. From COMPLETE STORIES OF D.H. LAWRENCE by D.H. Lawrence. Used by permission of Viking Penguin, a division of Penguin Books USA Inc.

D.H. LAWRENCE "The Rocking-Horse Winner" by D.H. Lawrence, copyright 1933 by the Estate of D.H. Lawrence, renewed © 1961 by Angelo Ravagli and C.M. Weekley, Executors of the Estate of Frieda Lawrence. From COMPLETE STORIES OF D.H. LAWRENCE by D.H. Lawrence. Used by permission of Viking Penguin, a division of Penguin Books USA Inc.

URSULA K. LEGUIN "The Ones Who Walk Away from Omelas" Copyright © 1973 by Ursula K. Le Guin; first appeared in New Dimensions 3; reprinted by permission of the author and the author's agent, Virginia Kidd.

DORIS LESSING "Woman on a Roof" From STORIES by Doris Lessing.Copyright © 1978 by Doris Lessing. Reprinted by permission of Alfred A. Knopf, Inc. Copyright: © 1963 Doris Lessing. Reproduced by kind permission of Jonathan Clowes Ltd., London, on behalf of Doris Lessing.

NAGIB MAHFUZ "The Happy Man" From GOD'S WORLD: AN ANTHOLOGY OF SHORT STORIES, trans. by Akef Abadir and Roger Allen. Copyright © 1973. Originally published by Bibliotheca Islamica, Box 14474, Minneapolis, MN.

BERNARD MALAMUD "The Magic Barrel" From THE MAGIC BARREL by Bernard Malamud. Copyright © 1958, 1986 by Bernard Malamud.

PAULE MARSHALL "To Da-Duh, In Memoriam" Reprinted, by permission, from Paule Marshall, "To Da-Duh, In Memoriam," Reena and Other Stories (New York: The Feminist Press at The City University of New York, 1983), pp. 95-106. © 1983 by Paule Marshall.

BOBBIE ANN MASON "SHILOH" from SHILOH AND OTHER STORIES by BOBBIE ANN MASON. Copyright © 1982 by Bobbie Ann Mason. Reprinted by permission of HarperCollins Publishers, Inc. "Shiloh" originally appeared in The New Yorker Magazine.

CARSON McCULLERS "Sucker" From THE MORTGAGED HEART by Carson McCullers. Copyright 1940, 1941, 1942, 1945, 1949, 1953, © 1956, 1959, 1963, 1967, 1971 by Floria V. Lasky, Executrix of the Estate of Carson McCullers. Reprinted by permission of Houghton Mifflin Co. All rights reserved.

DENNIS McFARLAND "NOTHING TO ASK FOR" by Dennis McFarland. First published in The New Yorker. Copyright © 1989 by Dennis McFarland. Reprinted by permission of Brandt & Brandt Literary Agents, Inc.

YUKIO MISHIMA "Patriotism" By Yukio Mishima, translated by Geoffrey W. Sargent, from DEATH IN MIDSUMMER. Copyright © 1966 by New Directions Publishing Corp. Reprinted by permission of New Directions Publishing Corp.

ALICE MUNRO "Wild Swans" From THE BEGGAR MAID by Alice Munro. Copyright © 1977, 1978 by Alice Munro. Reprinted by permission of Alfred A. Knopf, Inc. From WHO DO YOU THINK YOU ARE (Canadian title for THE BEGGAR MAID) by Alice Munro © 1978. Reprinted by permission of Macmillan Canada.

JOYCE CAROL OATES "The Lady with the Pet Dog" Copyright © 1972 by Joyce Carol Oates. Reprinted by permission of John Hawkins & Associates, Inc.

JOYCE CAROL OATES "Where Are You Going, Where Have You Been" Copyright © 1970 by Joyce Carol Oates. Reprinted by permission of John Hawkins & Associates, Inc.

EDNA O'BRIEN "A Scandalous Woman" Copyright © 1972, by Edna O'Brien, reprinted with the permission of The Wylie Agency, Inc.

FLANNERY O'CONNOR "A Good Man Is Hard to Find" From A GOOD MAN IS HARD TO FIND AND OTHER STORIES, copyright © 1953 by Flannery O'Connor and renewed 1981 by Regina O'Connor, reprinted by permission of Harcourt Brace & Company.

FLANNERY O'CONNOR "Revelation" From THE COMPLETE STORIES by Flannery O'Connor. Copyright © 1971 by the Estate of Mary Flannery O'Connor.

FRANK O'CONNOR "Guests of the Nation" From COLLECTED STORIES by Frank O'Connor. Copyright © 1981 by Harriet O'Donovan Sheehy, Executrix of the Estate of Frank O'Connor. Reprinted by permision of Alfred A. Knopf, Inc. Reprinted by arrangement with the Joan Daves Agency, c/o Writers House, Inc., as agent for the proprieter.

TILLIE OLSEN "I Stand Here Ironing," copyright © 1956, 1957, 1960, 1961 by Tillie Olsen, from TELL ME A RIDDLE by Tillie Olsen. Introduction by John Leonard. Used by permission of Delacorte Press/Seymour Lawrence, a division of Bantam Doubleday Dell Publishing Group, Inc.

KATHERINE ANN PORTER "The Jilting of Granny Weatherall" from FLOWERING JUDAS AND OTHER STORIES, copyright 1930 and renewed 1958 by Katherine Ann Porter, reprinted by permission of Harcourt Brace & Company.

THOMAS PYNCHON "Entropy" From SLOW LEARNER: EARLY STORIES by Thomas Pynchon. Copyright © 1984 by Thomas Pynchon. By permission of Little, Brown and Company.

PHILIP ROTH "Defender of the Faith" From GOODBYE, COLUMBUS. Copyright © 1959, renewed 1987 by Philip Roth. Reprinted by permission of Houghton Mifflin Co. All rights reserved.

LESLIE MARMON SILKO "The Storyteller" Copyright © 1981 by Leslie Marmon Silko. Reprinted from Storyteller by Leslie Marmon Silko, published by Seaver Books, New York, New York.

ISAAC BASHEVIS SINGER "Gimpel the Fool" by Isaac Bashevis Singer, translated by Saul Bellow, copyright 1953 by The Partisan Review, renewed © 1981 by Issac Bashevis Singer, from A TREASURY OF YIDDISH STORIES by Irving Howe and Eliezer Greenberg. Used by permission of Viking Penguin, a division of Penguin Books USA Inc.

JOHN STEINBECK "The Chrysanthemums," copyright 1937, renewed © 1965 by John Steinbeck, from THE LONG VALLEY by John Steinbeck. Used by permission of Viking Penguin, a division of Penguin Books USA Inc.

JAMES THURBER "The Greatest Man in the World" Copyright © 1935 James Thurber. Copyright © 1963 Rosemary A. Thurber. From The Middle-Aged Man on the Flying Trapeze, published by HarperCollins.

JOHN UPDIKE "A & P" From PIGEON FEATHERS AND OTHER STORIES by John Updike. Copyright © 1962 by John Updike. Reprinted by permission of Alfred A. Knopf, Inc. Originally appeared in "The New Yorker."

JOHN UPDIKE "Separating" From PROBLEMS AND OTHER STORIES by John Updike. Copyright © 1975 by John Updike. Reprinted by permission of Alfred A. Knopf, Inc.

KURT VONNEGUT "Harrison Bergeron" by Kurt Vonnegut, from WELCOME TO THE MONKEY HOUSE by Kurt Vonnegut, Jr. Copyright © 1961 by Kurt Vonnegut, Jr. Used by permission of Delacorte Press/Seymour Lawrence, a division of Bantam Doubleday Dell Publishing Group, Inc.

ALICE WALKER "Everyday Use" From IN LOVE & OTHER TROUBLES: STORIES OF BLACK WOMEN, copyright © 1973 by Alice Walker, reprinted by permission of Harcourt Brace & Company.

ALICE WALKER "To Hell With Dying" from IN LOVE & OTHER TROUBLES: STORIES OF BLACK WOMEN, copyright © 1967 and renewed 1995 by Alice Walker, reprinted by permission of Harcourt Brace & Company.

W.D. WETHERELL "The Bass, the River, and Sheila Mant" From THE MAN WHO LOVED LEVITTOWN, by W.D. Wetherell, © 1985. Reprinted by permission of the University of Pittsburgh Press.

EUDORA WELTY "Why I Live at the P.O." From A CURTAIN OF GREEN AND OTHER STORIES, copyright 1941 and renewed 1969 by Eudora Welty, reprinted by permission of Harcourt Brace & Company.

EUDORA WELTY "A Worn Path" From A CURTAIN OF GREEN AND OTHER STORIES, copyright © 1939 and renewed 1967 by Eudora Welty, reprinted by permission of Harcourt Brace & Company.

EDITH WHARTON "Roman Fever" Reprinted with the permission of Scribner, a Division of Simon & Schuster from ROMAN FEVER AND OTHER STORIES by Edith Wharton. Copyright © 1934 by Liberty Magazine, renewed 1962 by William R. Tyler.

RICHARD WRIGHT "THE MAN WHO WAS ALMOST A MAN" From EIGHT MEN by RICHARD WRIGHT. Copyright 1940 © 1961 by Richard Wright. Copyright renewed 1989 by Ellen Wright. Reprinted by permission of HarperCollins Publishers, Inc.

PAMELA ZOLINE "The Heat Death of the Universe" Copyright 1988 by Pamela Zoline. From the collection: The Heat Death of the Universe and Other Stories by Pamela Zoline. Reprinted by permission of the publisher, McPherson & Company (POB 1126, Kingston, New York 12402). All rights reserved.